I0788481

# RITES OF POSSESSION
## THE COMPLETE SERIES

EVA CHASE

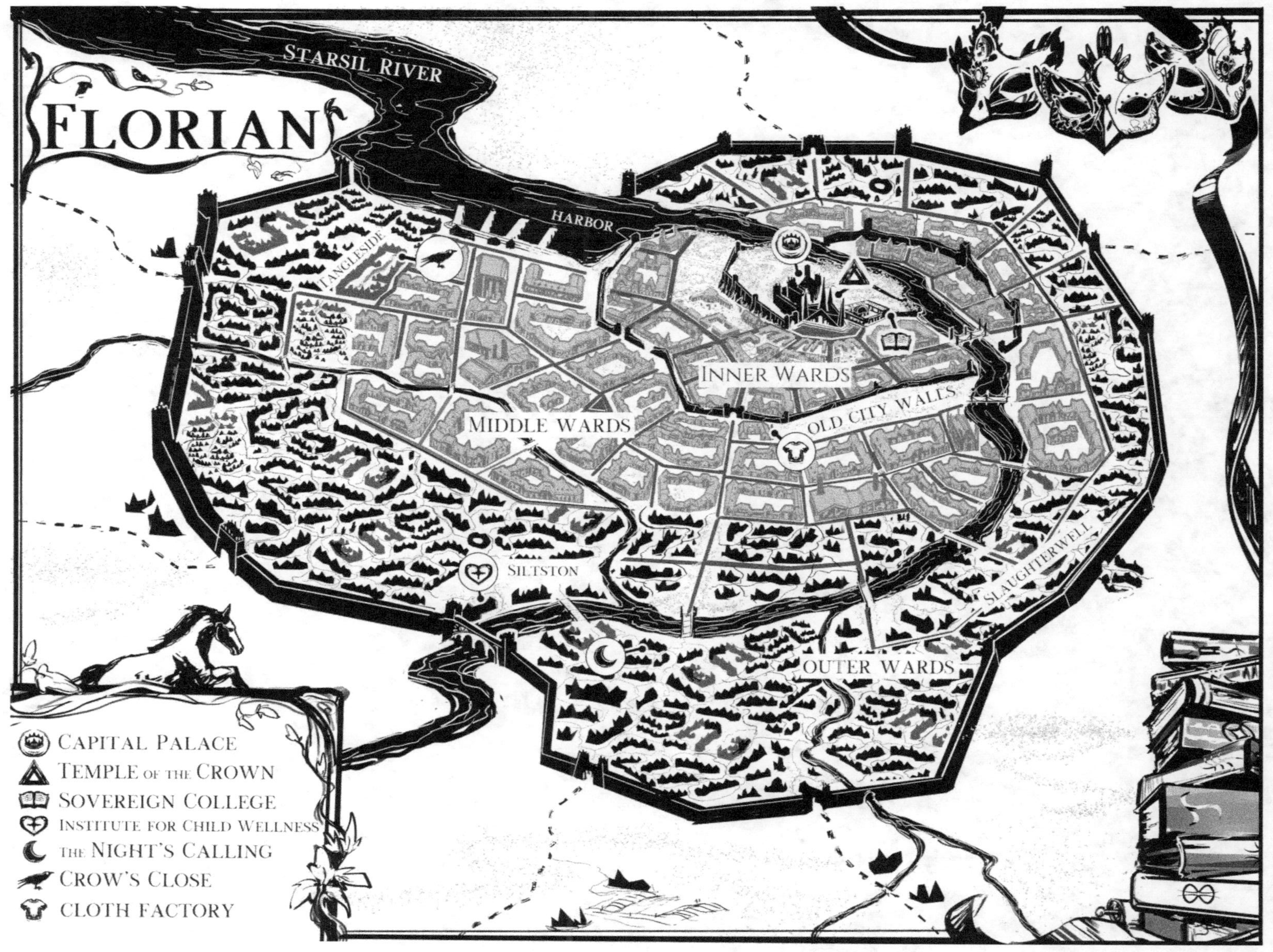

FLORIAN
STARSIL RIVER
HARBOR
TANGLESIDE
INNER WARDS
OLD CITY WALLS
MIDDLE WARDS
SLAUGHTERWELL
SILTSTON
OUTER WARDS
CAPITAL PALACE
TEMPLE OF THE CROWN
SOVEREIGN COLLEGE
INSTITUTE FOR CHILD WELLNESS
THE NIGHT'S CALLING
CROW'S CLOSE
CLOTH FACTORY

SILANA
BRYFEEN
GOTEA
VELDUNY
ICAR
SEAFELL CHANNEL
SUNBLOWN SEA
PIMA
NIKODI
EPPUN PROVINCE
COLIZ
TEMPLE TRANQUIL SKIES
SEDGE
STARSIL RIVER
TUPNO
THE PINCH
IBLIN
REGICA
ZULINA
FLORIAN
ABERNI PROVINCE
THE HAVEN
MAJOR PAWLEM'S FORT
MIPONE
COUNTRY BORDERS
PROVINCES
COUNTIES
ROYAL RESIDENCES
FORTS

# The Gods of the Abandoned Realms

**THE ALL-GIVER** (the Great God, the One) - overseer of all existence, creator of the godlen

## THE GODLEN OF THE SKY

**Estera** - wisdom, knowledge, and education

**Inganne** - creativity, play, childhood, and dreams

**Kosmel** - luck, trickery, and rebellion

## THE GODLEN OF THE EARTH

**Creaden** - royalty, leadership, justice, and construction

**Prospira** - fertility, wealth, harvest, and parenthood

**Sabrelle** - warfare, sports, and hunting

**THE GODLEN OF THE SEA**

**Ardone** - love, beauty, and bodily pleasures

**Elox** - health, medicine, and peace

**Jurnus** - communication, travel, and weather

# Thief of Silver and Souls

## Rites of Possession #1

# ONE

The scars on my back scrape the wagon's underside through my hooded tunic. I creep onward in my hunched pose, absorbing the prickle of pain.

It's a reminder of where I came from.

The heroes in fables and histories don't scuttle around beneath horse-drawn wagons in the shadows and dirt. They stride forward under the sun to carry out their virtuous deeds.

If the stories are true, you'd figure most of them stood ten feet tall and shone sunlight out of their exalted asses too.

But I'm not any kind of hero. I'm a monster with a broken soul.

I'd like to think that qualifies me to identify other sorts of monsters. Like the charm merchant who owns this wagon, whose soul I'm willing to bet is at least badly smudged.

He's parked off to the side of the ramshackle square on the fringes of the city, and a small crowd has already gathered to ogle his wares. With every false promise that rolls off his lying tongue, my grimace deepens.

The trinkets jingle as he holds up one and another. "Blessed by Elox himself! Keep this charm close, and you'll be free of illness for a year. This one, touched by Prospira's promise—plant it with your gardens for twice the yield."

Sure, and my spit turns shit into gold.

The arid breeze sends a tickle of dust into my nose. I stifle a sneeze and ease even closer to the swarm of legs just beyond the wagon.

The shadows and the dirt-brown fabric of my tunic make me all but invisible. Just in case, I tug the hood farther over my pale face and tuck back a few stray wisps of my reddish-blond hair.

A voice I recognize speaks up, sweet but thin. "Will the Elox-blessed charm help someone who's already sick? My son—he's been down with a fever."

I wince. It's Zuzanna—the housewife with the dotted curtains and Elox's sigil carved into every wall of her rickety house. Her appeals to the godlen of healing haven't brought any miracles yet. Her frail son is ill more often than he's not.

But she can't help grasping at any slim chance she gets.

The merchant answers in a tone slick as oil. "Oh, for one already ill, I have a stronger charm. It only costs a few bits more."

Murmurs ripple through the gathered onlookers. I can taste the tang of hope in the air—but it's all in vain.

Charms imbued with godlen-blessed magic exist, but not for the prices at which the merchant is hawking his fakes. The residents of this neighborhood could never afford the real thing.

I've crossed paths with legitimate relics a few times, and they give off a thrum of power that quivers right through the center of me. From the trinkets hanging from the display over my head, I sense only a brief tingle.

It's probably a dusting of conjured happiness that will satisfy the buyers for the first week or two.

A deeper prickle races into my skin whenever the merchant speaks. Most of the scam artists who prey on the city's poor have gifts of their own: a knack for encouraging trust, a talent for persuasion.

They can always find new customers. Hope is in awfully short supply on these streets. Plenty of people can't resist the gamble.

I blink, and an image of my father flits behind my eyelids. Years ago, setting a charm on the foot of the bed where Ma lay wasting away.

The sham didn't so much as quiet her whimpers.

This fraud's current targets can spare far fewer coins than Da was able to. But Zuzanna is already fishing in her purse.

She'll be skipping dinner for weeks.

My fingernails dig into my palms. I picture myself leaping out and condemning the fraud directly, but the weight of experience holds me in place.

It'd be nowhere near as simple as popping up to say, "Hello, I'm Ivy, your hunter of scams. This man is a crook!"

I have no proof I can present to the crowd that will conquer the hope the conman has stirred up. I learned long ago that the guards supplied by city's elite care more about keeping tax-paying merchants happy than protecting the needy.

And when I try to set things right head-on, there's too much chance of it going horribly wrong instead. It's safer for all of us if I stick to the shadows.

I can deal out justice my own way.

As the merchant accepts Zuzanna's payment, I palm my favorite knife. He drops the smaller coins into the change purse at his hip—and a larger piece of silver into the broader pouch at his back, bulging with the earnings from past sales.

He thinks his money is safer back there, out of reach of the people he can see. A smile curls my lips.

He's all but handed the loot to me. So kind of him.

The crooks who prey on the fringes of the capital have become warier as word of vanishing money has gotten around. But I never leave an obvious sign of exactly when or where I've done my work, and I've got a multitude of tricks up my sleeves.

I wait until the merchant turns to face the rest of the onlookers again. With his billowing trousers hiding my slight frame from view, I tip out of the shadows and flick the blade of my knife across the pouch's side.

As the merchant answers a man's question about strength-enhancing charms, I give the leather bag a gentle palpitation. Several thick coins, each enough to feed a family for a day, roll from the small hole into my hand.

While I slide my first plunder into a hidden inner pocket by my waist, the merchant swivels to pluck a charm off his display. I hold still, crouched beneath the wagon.

A flash of sapphire blue at the edge of the crowd catches my gaze, and my body goes totally rigid.

Heart thudding, I track the soldier's stroll toward the wagon. His glossy black boots and trim pants gleam in the late-afternoon sun.

The capital city's official police force, the Crown's Watch, doesn't patrol the outskirts of Florian often. They're more concerned with protecting the gentlefolk in the buffed stone houses closer to the royal palace.

But if this soldier notices me at work, he'll feel the need to intervene. And if the Watch gets their hands on me, they might realize there's a whole lot more than petty thievery they can charge me with.

One wrong movement will mean a trip straight to the gallows.

The shiny black boots come to a stop less than ten feet away. I grit my teeth, bracing myself to bolt.

Anyone else might pray to the godlen for luck or protection at a moment like this, but the last thing I'll ever want is their attention. Our lesser gods would be the first to punish me for what I am.

I can't even say I wouldn't deserve it.

The hiss of my mother's voice rises up in the back of my mind. *You brought a curse down on our house. It was all you, wasn't it?*

The scars on my back itch. I swallow thickly and shove the memory away.

Maybe I can never make up for the horrors I've committed. Maybe my soul is forfeit. But I need to live if I'm going to write a new story for myself.

I'm never going to be a hero, but when I meet my end, *I* want to be sure I was more than a villain. No matter what anyone else will see when that noose tightens around my neck.

The soldier's voice rings out, arrogant and bored. "No one here's giving you any trouble I hope, good merchant?"

"I've received an excellent welcome," the merchant replies smoothly.

The boots turn. The soldier ambles off, and I gradually let out my breath.

The conman goes on plying his wares. He *is* making good business, cajoling yet another customer into handing over their sparse earnings.

His success makes him confident—and careless. While he deals with a lonely spinster and then a struggling shopkeeper, I massage more coins out of his pouch. Taking the silver a few coins at a time ensures he doesn't register the lightening of the weight at his back.

The crowd thins. I slip a final bunch of silver into one of my pockets before feeding a few handfuls of pebbles into the merchant's pouch to replace what I've stolen.

If he gives the bag a pat, it'll feel suitably full.

May it take him until nightfall to realize that he's lost nearly all of his stash.

With another grim smile, I pull back. I have to slink well clear of the wagon before the merchant sets off.

I'm just drawing my body around when something spooks the horse.

At the gelding's squeal, my head jerks around. He rears, and a brief twinkle of light darts beneath his flailing forelegs.

It could be a trick of the eye—or it could be a daimon making mischief, as the wandering spirit-creatures so enjoy doing.

I don't have time to contemplate the possibilities, because as the horse's hooves hit the ground, he springs forward, dragging the wagon.

My stomach lurches. In a second, I'll be exposed.

An urge punches me from the inside out, as if an impatient hand has wrenched through me from gut to sternum. It thrusts toward the world outside, determined to fling forth the supernatural power coiled within my body and latch on to the fastest way to save my skin.

*No!*

I slam down on the impulse with all the self-control I've spent years honing and whip myself around. My back jars against the hard-packed dirt with a pang of my scars, but I'm already heaving upward.

My fingers and the toes of my boots snag on the nooks in the underside of the wagon. Every muscle strains as I cling to the shaky handholds I've caught.

My shortened right forefinger wavers in the air. A half-bit crime lord cut it off at the first knuckle years ago when I hadn't yet learned all the lessons of the streets, but I've never missed that fraction of a digit more.

The wagon jolts with the gelding's next yank. He hurtles forward with a frantic whinny, leaving the charms clattering on their shelves and the merchant cursing. Someone shouts advice from the crowd while a child bursts out laughing.

An ache spreads through my limbs with the effort to hold myself off the ground—and a sharper pain lances through my chest. I clamp my lips against a gasp of agony.

*Gods smite me, not again…*

The pain ignores my silent plea. It sears up to my shoulders and down to my pelvis, lashing this way and that like a bonfire in the wind.

Fuck, this is even worse than the last time.

I squeeze my eyes shut against the burn of unbidden tears and clutch at the wagon with every ounce of my will. If I can tolerate the agony for a few seconds… a few seconds more…

The wagon careens onward. The magic I refused to use rails at my body, punishing me for my defiance.

One of my feet slips and bounces off the dirt with a fresh burst of pain through my heel. I fling it back upward—

And the wheels on either side of me grind to a halt.

The biting fire of my magic's resentment gradually fades away while the merchant berates his gelding. The horse stomps his hooves before finally settling.

An ache lingers in my muscles, my fingers throbbing in their desperate hold. I count out several more thumps of my pulse before deciding it's safe to lower myself.

The conman's voice sweetens as he offers apologies to the prospective customers who've followed him down the road. While he beckons the curious over again, I release a shaky breath and scan my surroundings for a viable escape route.

There: a narrow lane between two of the shabby wooden buildings. I roll out on the opposite side of the wagon and dart away before my luck runs out.

When you've been living on the city's streets as long as I have, you can always find your way. The lane leads to an alley which ends at a rubbish heap which connects to another alley.

My heel twinges whenever I set the foot I banged down, but I manage to walk steadily and silently. The tight fabric of my hidden pockets squeezes my bounty close and keeps the coins from jingling.

The sooner I can unload my loot, the less chance someone who doesn't deserve it will make a try for it.

It won't go straight back into the hands of the people the merchant duped today. I have a cycle of rounds throughout the outer wards so that I'm distributing my spoils evenly.

I dodge a pool of piss at one corner and skirt a pile of poisoned rat corpses at another. A pungent stink seeps through the rest of the awful smells, welcoming me to my destination.

The neighborhood of Slaughterwell got its name from the slaughterhouses where the farmers bring their livestock, which stand just beyond the nearby city wall. Even at night, the reek never quite fades.

No one lives here unless they can't find a way to live anywhere else.

As I walk on, the power inside me nibbles at the edges of my awareness with a cajoling tone that reminds me of the fraud merchant.

If I let the magic out, it could wash away the stench. It could carry me straight to my destination without my taking another step.

*That might be true,* I retort. *But what will you ruin in the meantime?*

It doesn't have an answer to that.

Brief nips of pain quiver through my nerves, but nothing I can't tune out. The magic only really lashes out when I've refused a particularly good reason to use it.

The fits of agony only started a year ago… and they've become more frequent and intense by the month. I don't want to think too hard about what that might mean for my future.

Around me, the taller wooden buildings give way to smaller but equally lopsided shacks. Here and there, twists of stems and errant leaves poke from gaps where vegetation has merged with the frames.

Every neighborhood has a few eager gardeners who've sacrificed a bit of themselves in exchange for a gift of encouraging plants. Trading favors so they'll coax a sapling or a shrub into patching up a deteriorating building is often cheaper than buying the supplies and skills for a more traditional fix.

Half of these buildings would be heaps of debris if not for the intertwined plants holding them steady.

When I reach the row of houses I'm aiming for, I veer into the dingy back gardens. I'd rather no one can ever identify the person behind my anonymous donations.

At each home, I leave a small stack of coins on a window ledge. Here and there, I glance through the ragged curtains at the signs of life within.

At Marta's house with the drooping shingles and the tufts of thistledown protruding along the edge of the roof, I hear a familiar grunt. Beyond the bedroom window, the avid lover rocks with some new man. He ruts into her as she arches back against the sheets.

Her eager moan sets off an unwelcome pulse of heat between my legs. She sounds like she's having a much more thrilling time than any of my hasty roll-abouts have given me.

Of course, I haven't exactly had a broad selection of potential partners. It's been a couple of years since the last time I dared get that close to anyone.

I slink on to the next house, shedding the pinch of longing the private image brought. One by one, I leave coins for Bogusi the cook, Anielle the seamstress, and Oska the butcher's assistant.

These people have never properly met me, but I've spent years watching over them. Sharing their joys and sorrows in snippets of conversations overheard.

They're the closest thing I have to a family now—a very large family, even if they barely know I exist.

At the last house in the row, two little girls scamper around the patchy yard. I crouch by the refuse bin, the previous pinching sensation expanding to squeeze my heart.

The younger girl trips and tumbles across the gritty soil. At her yelp, I sway forward and then catch myself.

It isn't my place to jump in. I'm helping in my own way—the way that doesn't risk anyone getting more hurt than they already are.

The older girl has already dashed to her sister's side. "It's okay. Let's get a bit of water to wash the scrape."

I remain frozen until they vanish through the back door. Then I breeze by as stealthily as a spirit, leaving an extra coin in the stack on their window.

But as I pause at the crossroads, a hollow forms in the pit of my stomach. My hand lifts of its own accord to my left arm, where I keep the ivory ribbon tied just above my elbow.

Is anything I do now really enough?

I jerk my fingers to one of my still-full pockets, forcing a grin to chase away my unsettled emotions. I'm accomplishing more than nothing, anyway. I've seen the glimmers of happiness a few extra coins can spark.

I head across the street to the next row of houses. As I reach a low fence around a garden, a cry splits the air from farther up the road.

A rough, pained cry cut off an instant later with a gurgle.

My feet stall, my gut twisting. A shriek like that can't mean anything short of horrific.

But I don't get involved—not directly. If I try to step in…

I know how much horror *I* can bring about even when I want to do the right thing.

That thought—the thought that's held me back a thousand times before—crosses my mind, and my gaze snags on the trickle of liquid seeping over the dirt road from an alleyway. The fading sun lights it crimson.

Blood.

My feet move without consulting the rest of me. I sprint toward the alley even as both my head and my heart tangle up with indecision.

I'm not supposed to intervene. Not like this—not when my control might slip—

There has to be *something* I can do with just my hands and the skills I've learned. I know how to stop bleeding, how to bind a wound. I—

I throw myself into the alley and skid to a halt just before I smack into the body slumped there.

It's a woman, glossy chestnut hair scattered around her pale, blood-flecked face. Her dark cloak has fallen away from a violet silk dress that manages to shimmer even amid the grime of the alley. Gold glints at her wrist.

Someone like her doesn't belong *here*. She—

She's bleeding out from a gash where a knife's stabbed into the side of her neck.

Snapping out of my shock, I drop to my knees and press my fingers to the wound around the blade. Yanking the knife out will only make the blood flow faster.

Not that it's flowing at all slowly as it is.

The woman's eyelids flutter. She's still alive, however many fleeting seconds she has left. Her life is gushing away in a pulsing torrent beneath my useless hands.

My magic resonates through my limbs, prickling into my bones. My posture stiffens against it.

No. The power inside me can't save a life.

I know *that* better than I know anything in my whole damned existence.

The noblewoman's lips part, but nothing comes out except another sputter of blood. Gods above, she doesn't look any older than my twenty years.

My gaze locks with hers beneath her twitching eyelids. She stares back at me with desperate intensity.

I open my mouth to stammer some kind of apology, as if anything I can say would make up for the dire end she's about to meet… and the whole world spins.

My vision grays. A whirl of images floods my consciousness.

Stone towers. Crumpled papers. Piles of books on a table.

Spinning dresses in a rainbow of colors. A reflection preening in a mirror.

Four men. Four men standing around a desk, each of them so striking I don't know where to look first.

One impossibly tall and brawny, with hair the same dark red as the blood I've been trying to stanch.

Another warm and grinning wide as his tawny waves swoop over deep green eyes.

The third with a sharply bright gaze behind the polished mask that covers most of his bronze-brown face.

The last with a wry smirk curling his rosy lips beneath the fall of his sun-kissed hair.

All of them are gazing back at me, so avidly my nerves shiver as if a bolt of lightning has crackled through me.

The bolt blazes right through my skull, hazing my mind white and then black and then—

I drag in a hitch of breath as I come back to myself, gaping down at the woman in the silk dress.

Her eyes have hazed. Her body lies motionless, her skin waxen. Even her eyelids have frozen in place.

What under the gods' gaze just happened?

A shout travels from somewhere down the street. Footsteps pound toward me.

My pulse stutters. I glance over the noblewoman, but death emanates from every inch of her body.

She's gone. There's nothing I can do for her.

I can only make sure I don't follow the same path.

I shove to my feet and run.

# Two

E ven after I've left the noblewoman's gory corpse far behind me, my heart keeps beating too fast. I hunch down at the edge of one of the stone-lined culverts that wind from the Starsil River. My hands shake as I rub the blood off them.

I suck in the sour air and will my nerves to settle. It's over now.

It was none of my business anyway. I didn't even know her.

And it isn't as if I'm a stranger to death. I've witnessed it more times than I care to count.

I've dealt it out myself, wittingly or not.

But something about that moment when her gaze bored into mine leaves a lingering uneasiness that I can't totally shed.

So, I simply ignore it. I straighten up, give the soles of my leather boots a quick rinse as well, and check my tunic and breeches.

A few speckles of blood hit my sleeves, but they're barely discernable in the dirt-brown linen. There've been plenty of days I've gotten more soiled.

If anything, I got off easy.

I can't quite convince myself to laugh. It's as if I can feel the noblewoman still staring at me.

When I touch my pockets to confirm I haven't lost my remaining loot, a strange lump meets my fingers at my hip. I fish inside the pocket and pull out a delicate chain.

A bracelet.

The metal links glint gold in the dwindling sunlight. They hold a thin gold bar imprinted with a few abstract shapes that don't match any symbols I know and two small red gems on either side. Rubies, I'd wager.

I study the bracelet for a minute, my body tensed. I must have taken it off the noblewoman.

I don't *remember* pilfering her jewelry. Maybe my thieving instincts kicked in and my hand moved of its own accord during the brief spell when I blanked out?

If I hadn't taken the bracelet, whoever found her body probably would have. I can wait a few weeks to make sure there's no furor around her death and then see if I can hawk it without drawing unwanted attention.

But I'd rather not have it at all. In these neighborhoods, a piece this expensive makes a person an automatic target.

I was trying to *save* her, not steal from her.

At least, that's what I thought I was doing. No matter how much good I try to do...

My stomach lurches. I shove the bracelet back into my pocket.

It's a problem for another day. I have other tasks to finish.

Returning to my planned donation route doesn't seem like the wisest idea when I had a very good reason for fleeing. I consider my mental map of the city and decide I'll skip ahead to the edge of Slaughterwell. I can double back for the families I missed in a few days when I've got more bounty.

Having a clear plan boosts my spirits. I hop across the culvert and follow its curving path to more rows of drooping houses.

Here and there, I dodge the tiny dishes left out by doorways. Even though the people of Slaughterwell don't have much, many never fail to offer tidbits of fruit or dried meat to the local spirit-creatures.

I don't think anyone has ever witnessed a daimon partaking of the edible endowments. Common thought is that even if the invisible beings that flit through our lives in their chaotic ways never touch the stuff and it's only stray cats and dogs chowing down, they appreciate the generosity all the same. They might treat the households that made the gesture with more kindness in their rambling folly.

Maybe if the charms merchant had offered more respect, they'd have left his horse alone.

I have just enough coins left for my own generosity to make it to one of my favorite homes. The faint buzzing of bees tickles my ears before I reach the gnarled oak that juts up on the border between two small gardens.

As I set the last stack of silver on the back windowsill, a giggle tinkles from just beyond the rear door. I dart back to the shelter of the tree, a smile springing to my lips.

While the door creaks open, I scale the twisted branches. My fingers brush the soft leaves of the ivy that loops around them.

It was this vine that inspired my chosen name, years ago on an evening like this.

I sprawl out on the branch that's become my regular perch. From that vantage point, I have a view through the oak's leaves down into Ewalin's yard.

Ewalin and her mother, Frida, stroll over to the hutch that holds the beehive. As Ewalin lifts the lid, Frida hangs back with a teasing shake of her head. "I swear those creatures are twice as unnerving in the dark."

Ewalin laughs. "Doesn't stop you from wanting their honey in your tea, though, does it?"

As she reaches into the hutch, she hums under her breath. The stump of her little finger, cut off halfway down its length, gleams pale against her deep brown skin.

Unlike my severed finger, Ewalin gave up hers voluntarily. Every mortal gets one chance to ask for a gift of magical talent at twelve years old, when they dedicate themselves to a godlen. But such a gift requires a sacrifice in return.

I've heard Ewalin talk wryly about her dedication ceremony. She asked Prospira, the godlen of agriculture and abundance, for sway over animals, but she was too nervous to offer up much of herself. So she can't easily cajole horses or pigs or even chickens, but she does well with bees.

It's not a bad gift for half a finger. She can only manage one hive, but it produces enough honey to supplement the family's meager income.

Ewalin draws out her spoon holding a small lump of honey. She dips it straight into the mug her mother has cupped in her hands.

As she stirs, Frida smiles. "Ah, a few stings would be worth it for the sweetness."

Ewalin clicks her tongue. "They've never stung you. They're good little mites."

"They are. And so are you." Frida winks at her daughter. Then her voice drops low. "Did you hear about the ants that got into Soral's house?"

"Hmm, no. Did her 'whimsical' baking style finally catch up with her?"

As they fall into their usual pattern of neighborhood gossip, I rest my chin on my folded hands.

Most of the lingering uneasiness from my bloody encounter earlier fades away with the rhythm of their affectionately amused voices.

I first stumbled on the pair of them nearly eight years ago, when I'd only been on the streets for a few months and hadn't yet figured out how to be anything but an urchin. My twelve-year-old self perched in this tree and watched the two of them banter and share stories, and I imagined I might somehow drop into their lives and they'd take me in as one of the family.

That would be something, wouldn't it? To have a mother or a grandmother, or people like them, who laughed with me and whispered silly confidences?

Then Frida says, "Where's that son-in-law of mine gotten to this late?"

Ewalin raises her eyebrows. "You didn't know? Word went round that soldiers caught a riven sorcerer in one of the outer provinces. They brought him in to be executed tonight. Darek wanted to see it."

She gives a little shudder and taps her hand down her front in the gesture of the divinities: three fingers to the forehead, heart, and gut before fisting her hand over her sternum. "I'd rather not be near one of those fiends."

Frida's mouth tightens in sympathetic agreement. "It's a gruesome business all around. But it makes some people feel better seeing with their own eyes that the king is dealing with the menace."

My pulse has leapt to rattle in the base of my throat. An execution tonight? I managed to miss any mention of the arrested sorcerer before now.

In the startled scattering of my thoughts, a rush of dizziness sweeps through me. My gut tips over, and my chin bobs. My hands clamp around the branch instinctively to keep my balance.

With a shake of my head, I manage to clear it. I must still be thrown off by the dead woman to be so unsettled by the news.

Frida and Ewalin are meandering back toward the house now. Ewalin spots the glint of silver at the window.

"Oh, we've been visited by the Hand of Kosmel!" She snatches up the coins. "They couldn't have come at a better time."

A twinge that's both uneasy and exhilarating passes through my gut. I've never encouraged the title many of the outer-warders have given to the mysterious figure who leaves donations of questionable origin by their windows. I'm not sure I like being referred to as a mere appendage of a divine figure I'd prefer never noticed me, even if the godlen of trickery might not be quite as disapproving as his siblings.

But the fact that they've given me a name at all makes me feel a little more present in their lives.

When Ewalin and Frida have shut the door behind them, I slip down from the oak. With a mind to the upcoming execution, I hop over the fence and set off for the center of the city.

Hitching a surreptitious ride on the back of a carriage just returning to the city shaves a lot of time off the trek. I hop off just before we reach the inner wards.

After skirting the back of several buildings and slinking down a few alleys, I emerge onto Florian's busiest commercial street.

In my first glimpse of this place, the blare of sound and color is always a shock to the senses. The glow of a multitude of lanterns, some fueled by oil or wax and others by magic, glances off the stone faces of the tall buildings lining the wide street, all of which are painted in varying pastel hues.

Conjured images posture and swirl over many of the doorways, enticing customers with visions of what awaits them inside each shop and eatery. A translucent gown swishes its skirts here; wine bubbles in a row of illusionary glasses there.

And plenty of customers churn along the cobblestone road, peering through windows and chattering with their companions. To my left, a minstrel lends his voice and lute to the clamor; farther to my right, I spot another gliding her fingers over a harp.

A flood of scents assaults my nose alongside the sights and sounds. The stink that permeates

Florian's fringes creeps through the air even here, but it's mostly drowned out by wafts of savory cooking and sugary pastries alongside musky and floral perfumes.

I've ventured into the gilded core plenty of times. The impact is intense but not surprising.

So it shouldn't send me into another dizzy spell, my feet abruptly tipping on the smooth cobblestones beneath my boots.

I stumble and slap my hand against the building next to me to hold myself steady. A lurch of queasiness passes through my gut.

As I rub my forehead, the dizziness passes like it did before. But this time it leaves a knot in my stomach.

What's wrong with me? Am I coming down with some illness?

I swallow down the chill of fear that sparks at that thought and look at the facts. I haven't eaten since the morning. Anyone would be lightheaded.

It's nothing more than that.

I'm carrying a few coins I reserved for myself. I'll buy myself a quick dinner, as little as I want to eat when thinking about what's happening next, and my body will sort itself out just fine.

The execution can't be starting just yet. The street is too crowded—with an unusual mix of polished inner-warders and scruffier figures who, like Ewalin's husband, have ventured from the fringes just for tonight.

They're passing the time while they wait for the main event.

I pick out a small bakery with stuffed dumplings on display in the window and a pale illusion of steaming rolls wavering over the door. As I weave toward it, I notice two kids peering in through the front window: a girl with her hand on the younger boy's shoulder.

From their shabby clothes and smudged faces, they don't live in these parts. They must have come for the spectacle and drifted to the bakery at the pang of their stomachs.

The boy presses his hand to the glass, and a woman with wiry gray curls and a flour-dusted apron storms out of the building.

"Get out of here," she snaps at the kids, giving the girl a shove and managing to backhand the little boy in the same motion.

The kids scurry off with their heads ducked low, and my teeth set on edge.

I *was* going to pay for this meal like the upstanding citizen I can pretend to be. But why should I give any of my hard-won silver to a shrew like that?

There are other ways to get what I want. I'll just have to play an even more upstanding citizen than I already intended to.

I flick back my linen hood and whip out the gauzy maroon shawl I keep folded at the small of my back, covering my hair with more role-appropriate finery. It's only a cheap imitation of silk, but it passes just fine in this kind of lighting.

A pinch of my cheeks should bring a little healthy color into my sallow skin. On an impulse, I slip the gold bracelet I didn't mean to steal around my wrist as well, willing away the twinge of guilt.

With my chin lifted at a haughty angle, I march into the bakery on the heels of the baker.

She turns to face me. Before she can say a word, I fold my arms over my chest and announce, "Radir Micramek requests a dozen of your finest dumplings."

The baker blinks at me, her lips parting in surprise. Her gaze darts over my clothing. "You—*you* work for Master Radir?"

I narrow my eyes. "He prefers that his assistants avoid drawing unnecessary attention. But he feels it's time your establishment was evaluated. Will you comply, or must I inform him that you've refused him?"

The time I've spent listening in on conversations here in the inner wards has been well worthwhile. Radir is little known outside of culinary circles, but I happened to learn a couple of years ago that he's one of the royal advisors on cuisine. Specifically, he keeps an eye on all the eateries in the central ward.

A good word from him could have the royal household partaking of your wares. A bad word, and you'll be shut down.

Simply dropping the name is nearly enough to sell the story when I nail the snotty attitude too. For good measure, I tilt my arm slightly so the gold bracelet shows past the edge of my sleeve.

The baker's eyes catch on it, and she licks her lips nervously.

She isn't totally sure I'm telling the truth, but most people who know of Radir wouldn't be the type to pull a con on her. Pissing off my supposed employer will hurt a lot more than losing a few dumplings.

Less than a minute later, I'm striding out of the bakery with my edible loot in hand. I cross the street, tucking away the shawl and bracelet and scanning the crowd.

The two kids the baker chased off are crouched at the mouth of an alley, their heads bent close together as they murmur to each other. I pop one of the dumplings into my mouth—fuck, that *is* good—and come to a stop by a statue of a long-dead queen, just a couple of paces away from them.

"Such a pity I've got more than I can eat myself," I say in the direction of the alley, without actually looking at them.

I tuck a few more dumplings into my pockets and set the bag with the rest at the base of the statue, right in the kids' line of sight. Then I walk away, melding into the mass of passersby.

At the edge of my vision, I see the girl snatching up the bag. Something in my gut untwists.

One small thing in this world has been set a little more right.

The peal of the palace bell rings out, signaling the ninth hour. Echoes reverberate from other official buildings farther out through the city.

With an excited murmur, people start to veer toward the execution site. I gulp down two more dumplings as I follow them.

With each step closer to the Temple of the Crown, the hum of magic thickens in the air. Most people can't feel it, but it wriggles through the cracks in my soul and sets all my nerves jangling.

Lucky me.

What appetite I still had dies. I gird myself before I turn the corner onto the wide thoroughfare that leads up Florian's steep central hill to the largest temple in the country of Silana.

A decent crowd has already gathered in the courtyard out front. The Temple of the Crown looms over them all. The building of the gods that's sponsored by the royal family couldn't be anything but imposingly grand.

Its marble towers stretch up toward the darkened sky. There are three slightly shorter ones at the three corners, each with three golden spires representing the godlen of sky, sea, and earth, and one in the center I have to crane my neck to take in. The single spire of the All-Giver looks as if it could pierce the clouds.

Behind it, a little higher up the hill, two other massive buildings jut their towers toward the sky: the palace and the royal college. They glower in darkened silhouettes beyond the sheen of the temple's pale walls.

As I hurry up the sharp incline, several soldiers of the Crown's Watch come into view. They strut around the wooden platform that holds the gallows, set up off to the side of the temple's broad front doorway.

It'll have been assembled the moment the clerics knew the execution was scheduled, to serve as an announcement of what's to come. And now it's almost time.

My pulse hitches. I dart the rest of the way to the courtyard and slip between the milling spectators to the vantage point I've used before.

Most of the crowd stands taller than me, but that's not a problem. There's a shallow alcove between two of the stately buildings facing the temple. It's so dark I may as well disappear once I step into it, with a ledge at waist height that's just big enough to hold my feet.

I brace my hands against the walls on either side to hold myself upright and peer out over the heads of the other watchers.

A drumbeat starts to roll out from some spot I can't see, reverberating through me alongside the temple's magic. The raucous voices of the crowd dwindle into an ominous hush.

The soldiers station themselves around the platform with its dangling noose. The rap of boots against the cobblestone indicates more approaching.

Ten march forward, a single slumped figure swaying along between them. A sack covers his head and chains bind his arms to his chest, but we all know who he is. What he is.

*I* know better than anyone, because I'm watching the fate that awaits me someday too.

# THREE

T he procession of soldiers jerks to a halt. They pivot to face their audience.

The guards on either side of the sorcerer yank him around, clamping him in place as his feet tangle beneath him.

As long as they're alive, nothing's been discovered that can remove or shut away the magic of the riven. The authorities drug the sorcerers into a stupor from the moment they catch them so they don't have the wits to focus their power.

With an unclouded mind, the man in the sack and chains could murder every living being in this courtyard in a matter of seconds. Men and women like him *have* murdered thousands in the past in their attempts to evade capture… or simply because it served their mad purposes.

Sorcerers like us didn't ask for our magic. We're not limited to a single gift. The power flows through our broken souls if we answer the call, more than any mortal could know what to do with.

More than any mortal can indulge in and keep their right mind.

All magic requires sacrifice, after all. For every act that prisoner carried out with his, his power took its payment.

If you want health, someone else must fall ill. If you want to prosper, others will go without.

And you don't get to choose who suffers the penalty.

There's nothing I want enough to ignore the consequences of giving my magic free rein. I've already lost enough to it.

As long as I resist, I can hope that I never get to the point where I don't even care who I hurt, as this man must have.

The soldiers drag the sorcerer onto the platform. They position him just in front of the dangling noose, his bare feet on the trap door. His head droops within the sack.

It's a little mad that the king and his royal clerics parade the riven in front of a vulnerable crowd. I'd imagine they make very certain their prisoner is totally addled before marching them out.

They feel the risk of people fearing that the feral sorcerers are rampaging unchecked is worse. And no doubt they enjoy showing off their power, that they brought this monster under control.

Every riven sorcerer captured throughout Silana is brought to the capital for their public execution, under the eyes of the royal family.

A brighter glow expands across the balcony at the top of the temple's central wall, high above its arched doorway. All the voices in the courtyard fall totally silent.

In the yellowish conjured light, I make out the majestic figures of King Konram and Queen Ishild, flanked by their two living children, Princess Klaudia and Prince Jacos, and two of the highest-ranking clerics.

The royal family is all dressed in the deep purple associated with Creaden, the godlen of leadership and justice who blesses the royal line. Both of the teenaged royals stand with elegance equal to their parents, their dark brown hair that matches their father's gathered beneath their more modest crowns.

Years younger than me, and they've already accepted their duty in presiding over these killings.

The eerie lighting brings out the king's sharp features—his prominent nose and jutting chin. His commanding baritone courses over us.

"My people. You have come to witness the end of one of the riven. I have nothing but sorrow in my heart for the harm he carried out, but immense gratitude that we can subdue the danger before any more lives are lost and livelihoods destroyed."

A cheer rises up from the swarm of spectators. My voice stays locked in my throat.

King Konram waits until the clamor has fallen away to continue speaking. "It has been nearly two years since we last put down such a villain. I believe this indicates that their numbers are dwindling—fewer souls born riven, fewer remaining among us. I have hope that I will see the day when we no longer need to fear their presence at all."

The audience outright roars their approval.

I adjust my hands against the gritty stone walls, but the ache that's spreading through the muscles in my shoulders isn't quite as uncomfortable as the one expanding in my chest.

One of the clerics steps forward, the light illuminating her multi-colored robe. She rests her hands on the wall at the edge of the balcony.

Her voice rings out clear as crystal. "Five centuries ago, our realms turned on our All-Giver and the Great God's godlen. The riven souls among us are part of the penance we pay. With each abomination we cut down, we prove our devotion to the One who made us. May the All-Giver see and return to smile on us once again."

A more muted cheer lifts to meet that plea. No one, noble or lowborn, likes to think about the disgrace that left our realms abandoned by the omnipotent divinity who once guided us.

The cleric draws back beside her companions. The king makes a small motion, and one of the soldiers next to the prisoner pulls the sack from the sorcerer's head.

The face he exposes looks sallow and doughy with the effects of the stupefying drug. Straggly black hair droops across the man's forehead and cheeks.

If "man" is even quite the right word. From this distance in the hazy light, it's difficult to judge his age, but I'm not sure the hunched figure at the noose is even out of his teens. He could be as young as Princess Klaudia.

As the soldiers fit the loop of rope around the sorcerer's neck and tighten it, my throat constricts as if a noose of my own presses against it. My stomach churns.

But I don't let myself look away.

This is my most likely future. This man—or boy—has a soul just like mine.

I've escaped punishment for my crimes while he stands up there. The least I can do is bear witness.

The soldiers retreat. The sorcerer's shoulders sag as if he can barely hold himself up.

Up on the balcony, the royal family and the clerics tap their foreheads and torsos in the three-fingered gesture of the divinities.

Then someone yanks the lever.

The trap door pops open, and the prisoner plummets. His body jerks as the noose catches his fall.

Even drugged into oblivion, a hanged person's limbs still shudder and spasm. The sorcerer's feet kick involuntarily before going slack.

He sways on the end of the rope, more like a broken doll than a human being now.

Did the first impact snap his neck? Or is his brain still fizzing beneath the drugs as the rope cuts off his breath?

This is the tenth execution of a riven I've watched, and I can never tell.

After a minute, the crowd begins to stir. One soldier checks the body and nods to confirm that the sorcerer is dead. The others ease back to allow curious citizens to approach the platform.

Some of the spectators clamber right onto the boards to prod the corpse, as if they need to feel with their own hands that the monster is vanquished. I see one woman spit on the slumped, purpled head.

Bile burns in the back of my mouth. I've witnessed enough.

I hop down from my perch and slip away through the throng. Keeping my hood drawn low over my hair, I pad through the thickest shadows away from the city core.

A thick, mossy stone wall marks the border between the neighborhoods of the have-much and the have-less in the most concrete way possible. The crumbling structure was once the outer wall of the city, when Florian was just establishing itself as an urban center.

Once enough peasants had gathered and constructed homes in the lands beyond the original wall, the royal family of times past saw fit to erect a new, taller wall to fully encompass the city's growth. No one's maintained the old wall in centuries other than to ensure no blocks fall right off onto the head of a passing noble.

The many gates through the original wall have had their doors removed, and citizens traveling through are no longer *officially* monitored. But one or two of the Crown's Watch are almost always hanging around near them, happy to badger anyone they deem suspicious-looking.

To avoid any potential hassle, I prefer to simply go over the top. In plenty of places, a well-situated shed or shrubbery makes for an easy scramble across the stones.

A few streets beyond the wall, I reach the building that contains a cloth-making business and my home, as much as I can call the place where I sleep that.

The three floors where workers weave, dye, and store reams of linen and wool lie silent for the night. I clamber up the rusting ladder at the back, meant as an escape route in case of fire, and spring from there to the lip at the top of the third story.

A brief scoot to the side, and I'm at the shuttered attic window that's just large enough for me to squeeze my scrawny frame through.

The sprawling attic is cluttered, but I know it well enough to navigate the stacks of boxes and abandoned furniture by only the faint streaks of moonlight that seep around the shutters. I've helped myself to enough of the factory's discards to create a mattress of heaped wool that's decently comfortable, with a linen sheet and a patchy wool blanket.

A few emptied boxes turned on their side serve as a series of shelves. I wriggle out of my tunic, trading it and my breeches for a nightshirt, and fold them to set next to my meager assortment of clothes.

I consider the remaining dumplings, but my stomach balks, so I set them onto a different shelf next to my stash of nuts and dried berries. They'll make a perfectly good breakfast.

My gaze slides through the dimness across the hills of boxes still full of their original contents. The books I've retrieved from those boxes stand in uneven stacks on the floor in between.

Sometime before the cloth-makers took over the building, it must have housed a scholarly business. A business that didn't bother taking much with it when the owners left.

Either they or the new residents simply shoved loads of books and barely bound papers up here to forget about. In my explorations over the years, I've found everything from historical records to philosophic texts to fanciful invented tales.

Stumbling on this bounty is one of the few bits of good luck I can point to in my life. The books keep me company about as well as the people I watch over do.

And every bit of information I can stuff into my head, every additional understanding I can absorb, puts me one more step ahead of ever needing to use my magic. Of making others pay for my power. Of going mad with it like the riven always do.

Of ending up on a wooden platform with a noose around my neck.

The image of the execution fills my mind, and my body tenses.

On a normal night, I might light a small candle in a sheltered spot where the glow won't carry to the window and read a few more chapters of my latest tome, but I'm not in the mood to feed my imagination any more than my stomach right now.

Today I've seen two deaths more than I ever want to in a day. As different as the circumstances were, both memories gnaw at my gut.

I stretch my arms, set my favorite knife by the corner of the makeshift mattress, and wriggle under the covers of my bed. I'm not sure how easily I'll get to sleep, but I should at least try.

I've got to be out of here before the workers show up in the morning.

The day's events swim through my mind, as jumbled as the attic around me. Fresh threads of uneasiness wind through my nerves despite my best efforts to relax.

I'm about to push upright and see if a little reading will dull the lingering tension after all when a feminine voice speaks, as loud and clear as if it's coming from right beside my ear.

"*This* is where you live?"

# FOUR

I jolt to my feet in an instant, my fingers closing around the hilt of my knife. I swing it toward the spot where I assumed the speaker was crouched… but the blade only slices through empty air.

My gaze jerks over the room around me. I can't see any figure in the entire room, let alone right by my side.

My pulse bangs so loudly I can barely hear my own ragged whisper. "Who's here? What do you want?"

A light chuckle fills my head… giving the impression that it *is* actually coming from within my head.

The firm but sultry voice I heard before reaches me the same way, seeming to echo inside my skull rather than coming from beyond my ears. *I simply thought we should talk, seeing as I can't get anything done any other way.*

My grip tightens on the knife handle, but what am I going to do with it? Stab it into my own brain? That's not going to help me.

There are people dedicated to Jurnus—the godlen who presides over communication—who sacrificed enough to request the gift of mind-to-mind speech. Could that be what this unseen woman is doing? She's somewhere nearby though out of sight, projecting her thoughts into my head?

If so, I need to figure out just how close she is so I can track her down and bring the conversation face to face.

I adjust my position so I can quickly spring off the folds of woolen fabric. My voice dips low—so low no one not in the room with me could possibly hear. "If you want to talk so badly, why don't you show yourself like a normal person would?"

Another brief laugh tinkles through my head. *Believe me, I wish I could arrange that. Unfortunately it appears that all that's left of me is terribly ephemeral.*

She caught the question—she's got to be somewhere in the attic. I push to my feet and prowl slowly through the shadows, watching for any sign of movement, any object I might recognize has been displaced.

*What are you doing?* the voice asks with a tinge of amusement that annoys me. *You can't* find *me; I'm already right here.*

"What do you mean?" I say through gritted teeth. "*Where* are you?"

*Inside you, as far as I can tell.*

Even in my tense state, I can't help rolling my eyes. "I can tell you're projecting your voice there. Where's the rest of you?"

*This is pretty much all of me at this point. The body you're looking for, you left in a pool of blood in that putrid alley.*

I draw up short with a sharper hitch of my pulse. She knows about the murdered noblewoman— she saw me there. Is this blackmail?

The voice continues on, unfazed by my silence. *Not that I can blame you. I wouldn't have wanted to dally around that scene either. Although it'd have been nice if you'd at least stayed close enough to check whether the villain who murdered me came by to gloat.*

My jaw goes slack for a second before I snap my mouth shut again. The words snag in my throat before I force them out. "*Your* murderer…?"

*Yes. Let's keep up. Some ruthless miscreant had me slaughtered in a gods-forsaken alley, you ever-so-heroically if futilely raced to my rescue, and somehow or other when my soul left my body, it ended up in yours.*

Her way of speaking does sound like a noble. Would it really make sense for there to have just happened to be *another* noblewoman, one with telepathic magic, hanging around in Slaughterwell to watch me stumble on that body and then managing to follow me all across the city for the rest of the day?

I press my free hand to my forehead. What sense does it make that a dead woman's soul could have taken up residence in my head? I've never heard of that happening to anyone.

No matter how I look at this situation, it's a whole lot of fucking impossible.

"How could your soul have ended up in *me*?" I demand.

*I haven't got a clue. I promise you, this wasn't my idea.*

"Well, gods be sure it wasn't mine."

I stare through the dimness, my stomach still listing uneasily. Am I really going to believe her story?

Wait. There's a simple way to test whether she really is inside my body and not simply watching me.

I back up until my ass brushes a stack of boxes and tuck my hand behind me, still clutching my knife in the other. In the cramped space where no one could possibly see, I press two fingers against my spine. "How many fingers am I holding out?"

The voice in my head snorts derisively, but after a few seconds she must realize I do expect an answer. *Two. Must we really play this game? There are more important—*

My skin has chilled, but it could have been a lucky guess. I adjust my hand to extend all four fingers, including the partial stump of my pointer. "And now?"

*Four. Look, I know this sounds ridiculous, but I've been here in your head while you've roved all over the city, so it's rather difficult for* me *to doubt what's going on. And that I can't do much of anything about it.*

Something about those last words sends a deeper jab of ice through my veins. What was it she said earlier—that she wanted to talk because she couldn't 'get things done' otherwise?

I've really got a ghost in my head, and she's been there for hours. Hours in which my head hasn't always felt entirely normal.

Those dizzy spells that came out of the blue…

"Did you try to make *me* do things for you?" I have to ask. "To… to take over my mind?"

There's a moment of silence that's almost sheepish. Her voice returns as brashly nonchalant as before. *Who wouldn't have? Here I am, trapped in a body that's not mine and that I don't know, with no way of reaching out to anyone who could help unless it's through you—how could I not try?*

Somehow she makes it sound totally reasonable and not like she attempted to hijack my life.

I grimace, picturing the chestnut-haired girl in her silk dress like she must have been before someone jabbed a knife through her neck. I can practically see her arching her eyebrows and tilting her head with measured coyness.

I force myself to return to my bed, sitting down on the heap of fabric. Tension stays coiled all through my frame. "Why didn't you just talk to me?"

*You mean since that's going so well right now? I couldn't imagine how you'd react. It would have been much simpler if I could have borrowed you for a day or two to get my affairs in order... I promise I'd have returned you in the same state I found you in, or possibly better.*

Her tone implies that *better* wouldn't be too hard. I find myself clenching my jaw again.

"Considering that all I know about *you* is that you managed to get yourself murdered, forgive me for being skeptical."

*Well, I'm talking to you now. You do know I was murdered, so surely you can agree that justice should be done?*

"I expect the powers that be will investigate whether I get involved or not. It's not as if anyone could imagine you tripped and accidentally fell on that knife."

*That's not the only—* She pauses with a sigh of exasperation. I have the sense of her gathering her temper.

When she speaks again, it's in a smoother, more cloying tone. *We've gotten off on the wrong foot. I apologize. I should start by properly introducing myself. I'm Julita Laonek of the county of Nikodi, dedicate to Creaden, in my second year at the Sovereign College.*

She may not realize how much she's told me with that single sentence. Her last name uses the masculine ending, which means her family styles themselves an impressive one by carrying on an earlier ancestor's name rather than her using the common form of adapting her mother's. Yet she's not even from a major family overseeing an entire province but some county I've never heard of.

If she's dedicated herself to Creaden, most likely she's planning to either take over the family estate or run her eventual husband's. Or rather, she was, before the unfortunate incident with the knife.

Compared to me, she's minor royalty. But to her peers at the college, she'd be little better than a nobody.

Maybe she's gotten in the habit of laying on the airs thick to distract people from that fact.

*And you are?* she prods as I take everything in. *I'm sure you don't actually work for Master Radir.*

The corners of my mouth kick up. "No. I'm Ivy, and I don't work for anyone except myself."

*Ivy?*

I ignore her prompt for more. There isn't anything more to the name I took on for myself after I fled my family's home, and I'll be garroted before I tell her my old one.

It's no longer really mine anyway.

Instead, I let a prick of my own curiosity guide me. "What were you doing wandering around the alleys of Slaughterwell, Julita Laonek?"

*I was attempting to investigate the local temples for signs of illicit magic.*

Of all the things she could have said, that's definitely not anything I'd have guessed at.

My gut twists into a knot. "What kind of illicit magic? Are you working with the Crown's Watch?"

She couldn't know, or even suspect—?

My unwanted passenger gives a huff. *No, they wouldn't listen. We need more evidence first, which is why I was out looking for it. If any devouts were supporting the conspiracy, it seems most likely they'd need to be from the smaller, out of the way temples to escape notice.*

I pause, knitting my brow. Not anything to do with me, then. But... "What conspiracy? What are you talking about?"

*There's much more at stake here than my life. Someone at the college is experimenting with the same sort of magic that brought on the Great Retribution.*

"What?" I sputter through a jolt of deeper horror. "But—if the godlen realize—they could punish us all over again. Who would be stupid enough to try?"

*People who don't care what happens to anyone else if they can gain a little more power,* Julita mutters. *People who think they're so smart they'll manage to sneak it past the gods.*

"Are you sure? At the royal college—right under the king's nose?"

She takes on an arch tone. *I know what I've seen. They've tried to cover up their rituals, but there've been signs. And they nearly killed the prince the last time the royal family toured the college. That's when I knew I had to do something.*

I rub my temple. "If they're attacking Prince Jacos, why isn't the army doing something about it? What more proof could you need?"

*They think he simply got sick. Whoever's in on the conspiracy, they're stealthy about it. What I've observed isn't something I can hand over to the Watch or the royal guards. It'd only be hearsay.*

Despite her haughtiness, an urgent note threads through her voice. She truly believes the threat is real.

And I can't imagine much short of a potential continent-wide catastrophe bringing a noble to the reeking streets of the outer wards.

Still, I have to confirm that I'm understanding her correctly.

My voice comes out hoarse. "So you're saying that there are students at the Sovereign College who are… sacrificing entire *people* to add to their gifts?"

*Possibly professors are involved too. I haven't been able to determine how far the conspiracy goes, but based on the effects of their attempts, there have to be more than a few of them. You shouldn't sound so shocked. They killed* me, *didn't they?*

She has a point there. I was too startled to put it together, but now that she says it, it's obvious. Not only why she'd have been out there, but why someone would want her dead, if she's on the verge of uncovering crimes this horrifying.

The only type of sorcerers people revile more than the riven are the so-called "scourge sorcerers" who developed their horrific methods several centuries ago. They found a way to demand gifts from the godlen not just through their own living sacrifices but those of family and supposed friends as well, offering up the bodies of the slaughtered.

They thought they could challenge the gods in power. And the All-Giver punished all of us for their psychotic hubris.

The Great God and the lesser divinities ravaged the continent with flames and earthquakes—and then the All-Giver stormed off on us. But only after shrouding our sea in fog and raising the eastern mountains so none of us could attempt to follow.

My soul arrived in this world broken thanks to the aftereffects of that long-distant retribution. I'm a reminder to all of us that when we take on more magic than mortals are meant to handle, it'll destroy us.

But I'm only a danger to my fellow human beings. Scourge sorcery threatens the gods themselves.

And now some greedy assholes are risking bringing the godlen's wrath down on the entire continent once more.

Maybe I shouldn't be surprised. I steal from greedy assholes who don't give a shit about anyone but themselves every week, don't I?

The pricks dabbling in scourge sorcery think they won't get caught. That they can escape divine punishment.

And they're willing to bring the rest of us down with them if they're wrong.

Another unsettling thought strikes me. "The first prince—seven years ago. The royal family said *his* death was an illness. Could it have actually been part of this conspiracy?"

*A very good question,* Julita says in an approving tone. *I've wondered as much myself, but we haven't found any proof one way or the other.*

I rub my tired eyes. "'We'? Do other people know about this?"

*Yes! I had friends working with me to expose the sorcerers—fellow students and a professor. That's where you can help. I must have been getting close to the villains, or they wouldn't have attacked me. I was supposed to meet with the others tomorrow to share what we've learned. You can do that for me.*

I frown. "I can… go to the meeting? Where do you meet?"

*At the college, of course.*

A disbelieving sputter jolts out of me. "I can't waltz right into the royal college."

Julita's voice warms. *Oh, I'm sure you could. I saw how skilled you were in that ploy at the bakery. And you appear to be a master at avoiding notice. I can give you everything else you need.*

"Somehow I think it'll be a little more complicated than that. And your friends will know I'm not who they expected to be meeting."

*I can smooth things over with them. We'll come up with a story just like you did about Master Radir. It'll be as easy as the way you handled the baker.*

I pull up my knees and rest my chin on them, bracing myself amid my spinning thoughts.

The only places I'd want to go into *less* than the Sovereign College are the Temple of the Crown and the royal palace itself. There'll be more guards around than I normally encounter in a year.

*Ivy…* Julita pauses and then goes on at a softer cadence. *There's something incredible about the fact that my soul has survived, however that happened, so I can continue to speak out against these sadistic rogues. I'm getting a rare chance to deal with unfinished business.*

"*Your* unfinished business," I have to point out. "Not mine."

*I'd imagine it'd affect you too if the scourge sorcerers cause a large enough disaster to bring the gods' wrath down on us all. You and the people in the outer wards you clearly care about. Would you truly risk all of them just to avoid a scheme that'll take no more than an hour or two?*

Her words bring a lump of guilt into my stomach.

*My friends need to know everything I've been looking into if they're going to take on the conspiracy without me,* Julita says. *I have no idea how much time we have before there's an even bigger strike against the royal family.*

I think of the young prince, only a year past his dedication ceremony, gazing stiffly down from the temple balcony a couple of hours ago. These are the kind of monsters who'd kill children.

And who knows how many others. Would Ewalin and Frida survive another Great Retribution? Would Zuzanna and her son, or the sisters I watched playing in their garden?

All I have to do is play noble for a couple of hours. Walk into the college, chat with a few nobles, walk out again.

Is that so much to ask?

My body automatically tenses against the idea. I don't step in; I don't get directly involved.

But I already am. How could I be *more* involved in this woman's life than hosting her soul alongside mine?

It isn't as if I could create a worse disaster than the retribution of the gods, right?

My gaze lifts to the ceiling of its own accord. A shiver passes over my skin.

How *did* I end up absorbing Julita's soul, exactly? What if the gods have noticed me after all, and this is a strange test they're giving me?

I'm not sure what the right answer would be, but completely ignoring the problem definitely seems like a wrong one.

And hey, once I give this ghost what she wants, maybe her soul will depart for the peaceful beyond and leave me be. Even if she's only ephemeral, I can already tell that she won't be easy to ignore.

When you add it all up, it isn't even much of a decision.

I wet my lips, square my shoulders, and nod. "Fine. Tomorrow I break into the royal college."

# FIVE

I don't usually give a roach's ass how I look, as long as I don't look any way that's going to make people notice me. So the urge to catch glimpses of myself in the reflections on the shop windows we pass is strange both because it's unfamiliar… and because of what I see looking back at me.

I can't help eyeing the swooping hairstyle I assembled my reddish-blond waves into with my ghostly passenger's coaching after my dip at the public bathhouse. Or the way the berry juice I turned into makeshift rouge brings out my cheekbones and my lips.

Between all that and the faux-silk dress that's the one noble-ish item in my small wardrobe, I'll be drawing a lot more eyes than I'd normally be comfortable with. I'm not going to kid myself that I'm any great beauty with these knobby arms and the pallor to my skin that looks more sickly than creamy, but I need to pretend I think I'm something special.

Because if I show how ridiculous I feel, this con isn't going to last more than the time it takes me to walk through the college's gate.

People believe what you show them. I've learned that time and time again.

I just have to put on my best noble-esque airs and act like nothing could be more natural than my strolling through the city center toward the Sovereign College.

Julita's voice peals through my head, full of her own self-assurance and more upbeat now that she's gotten her way. *You look fantastic. No one would ever think that just yesterday you were scrambling around in the muck.*

I bite back half a dozen snarky remarks I could make, because talking to one's self while taking a stroll is going to draw an even worse kind of attention. I've tried thinking back at her, but while she's obviously aware of what my body is doing, my unbidden guest can't seem to read my mind even when I want her to.

Maybe I should be grateful for that small mercy.

It would make having a conversation in public a damn sight easier, though.

*We'll get there right in time for the meeting,* Julita goes on in a bright voice I think is meant to be reassuring. *You've conned people like this before—no need to worry about it.*

I have, which was why I own the dress, but never for more than a few minutes. Just popping into a business or approaching someone on the street to pilfer a bit of information I need or set the stage for a more surreptitious comeuppance.

I'd rather be lurking under the charm merchant's blasted wagon than taking this walk.

At least I won't need to deal with laying the heaviest news on Julita's friends. When we worked out the plan, she insisted that she doesn't want me telling them that she's dead.

Neither of us has any idea exactly who murdered her. She suggested that telling them would only distract them from the bigger picture. Even if her body has been found and her friends have heard about it, she wants me to act as if it's a surprise to me.

I'm going to claim I'm one of Julita's friends, visiting from her hometown. I'll say she was embarking on a more in-depth investigation and suspected she wouldn't make the meeting, so she gave me the means to turn up in her place.

Then I'll recite whatever information the ghost in my head instructs me to and walk away.

The idea of leaving her friends in the dark about just how far the scourge sorcerers have gone still makes me uneasy. But it's not as if I could tell them I'm hosting her soul without sounding mad.

And it does take the pressure off. I won't have to deal with any anger or grief over her loss from these strangers.

Noble strangers, whose grief could overflow with pompous indignation or hysterical panic for all I know.

*Almost there!* Julita declares with unrestrained eagerness.

A growing tremor of divine energy is seeping over my skin from the Temple of the Crown. As the pale marble building comes into view, I give it a quick glance.

The body of the riven sorcerer hangs where it's been suspended next to the main doorway, a display that typically lasts a day or two until the clerics decide the statement has been made thoroughly enough.

I yank my gaze away from his swollen skin and pick up my pace just a little.

My boots rap against the wide cobblestone road that leads around the grand temple farther up the slope to the walls that surround the college.

The school's builders decided to go for a much more ominous vibe than those who built the temple—or maybe they felt that its inhabitants should be focused on learning rather than pretty architecture. Slabs of dull gray limestone loom before me.

Not that the college is exactly ugly. There's something unnervingly breathtaking about the dark towers that jut up over that wall, dotted with narrow arched windows. And the frame around the broad wood-and-iron door holds an intricate carving: a rearing horse on one side, and a glowering gargoyle on the other.

*This is where you need my bracelet,* Julita says. *Hold your wrist up so the flat part faces the gargoyle's eyes.*

She didn't admit it when I mentioned the stolen bracelet earlier, but I have the sneaking suspicion that she was responsible for nabbing it. Taking a momentary snatch of control over my body while I reeled with the initial impact of her soul.

It definitely serves her purposes for me to have it, because apparently I can't enter the college without the bangle.

I hold the bracelet to the level of the gargoyle's bulging stone eyes. For the space of a few heartbeats, nothing happens.

A bead of sweat trickles down my back at the thought that Julita might be wrong—whatever magical security this vaunted place possesses can tell I'm not the proper owner of her bracelet.

Then the door creaks open.

The second I step past the threshold into the shadowy space beyond, Julita's presence stirs in my head. *Stop there. Just a second.*

What now?

I definitely can't ask her here. I freeze in place, peering into the darkened space around me.

I expected a short passage into the courtyard around the main college buildings. Instead, I'm in a dim, branching hallway that stretches a short distance ahead and on either side of me with no exit in sight.

Magic courses through the air, raising goosebumps on my arms. It doesn't feel as vast as the power that emanates from the Temple of the Crown, but gods be sure there's a damned lot of it in this small, silent space.

Julita murmurs as if to herself. *What was the cursed password of the week? Lively fleas fly… No. Lively fleas rip from royalty like ribbons.*

As I raise my eyebrows at the vaguely insulting phrase, she chuckles to herself and then explains. *The entrance is a conjured maze to make sure no one actually enters who isn't meant to be here. The password gives the current directions. Head left, then forward, then right, forward, right, left, right.*

I'd have had an easier time striding ahead with confidence if she sounded more certain of the password. Willing my hands to stay loose at my sides, I turn toward the lefthand passage.

A few steps along it, more halls open up at either side of me. I keep going forward, then veer right when the hallway branches again. Forward, right, left, right…

As I take my third step into the final passage, an open doorway glimmers into being in front of me. The air there shimmers with a warble of magic I can hear as well as feel.

*Go on through. If you have any harmful gift-magic attached to you, it'll wash you clean.*

That's actually a pretty genius security mechanism.

All the same, I have to suppress a shudder at the ripple of sensation that passes through me as I step over the threshold. It feels as if I've been doused by a transparent, glittery waterfall.

*Good. Looks like you didn't attract any malice recently. The hard part is done.*

Thank all that's holy.

I walk on into the bright late-morning sun—and my pulse hitches with an unexpected smack of recognition.

I've never seen the main college building before—not up close without the walls hiding the lower reaches. Except I have.

The vast stone face with its immense towers blazed into my mind amid the flood of images that hit me when I blanked out over Julita's body.

When her soul slammed into my brain.

I was catching glimpses of her memories, apparently.

The same effect hasn't happened since, but the thought still unnerves me. I wet my lips and propel myself forward despite my uneasiness.

A cobblestone path leads to the castle-like building's main entrance, with fields sprawling all around it within the college's high walls. Not far away, a group of students are exchanging practice blows with swords.

In the other direction, I spot a few women on horseback, trotting around the side of the building. Of course the college would have its own stables as well.

I suck in a deep breath, taking in the scent of trampled grass and seeking the whiff of sweet hay and horsey musk that's one of the few things I miss from my family's home.

*Straight ahead, right into the building,* Julita says. *That's the Quadring ahead of you, where they hold the classes for the four divisions. Leadership, companionship—*

"Scholarship and martial service," I can't stop myself from murmuring. "I've heard."

Julita pauses for a moment as if taken aback. *Well. Even better that you're prepared. We'll go through the entrance ahead of you, right down the main hall, along the walkway, and into the Domi.*

Walking on, I cock my head just slightly. Hoping she'll catch the implicit question in the movement.

Julita picks up on my intention, although maybe it's not surprising that she's become attuned to me when she's been living inside my head for the better part of a day. *There's a smaller courtyard in the middle of the Quadring, and in the middle of that is a building that's officially called the Domicile. But we usually just say "the Domi." That's where you find all the dorms, the dining hall, the ballroom… and the library, which is our destination.*

A couple of guards in the sapphire blue uniforms of royal service stand off to the side of the entrance she indicated. Their gazes slide over the passing students with apparent indifference, but my skin tightens when the one man's head turns toward me.

A spurt of magic flares in my chest with a sudden appeal.

It could conceal me so much better than a counterfeit dress. It could make sure not one person here even—

I tamp down the urge with a subtle clench of my hands. No fucking way.

There's no urgent threat, but my power slaps me with a fit of resentment all the same. My lungs burn as if I've inhaled a puff of acid smoke.

I grit my teeth and keep walking.

Julita's tone turns puzzled. *Are you all right?*

I give a slight nod and inhale slowly. The prickles of pain fade away.

I march through the Quadring's entrance into an airy, high-ceilinged room that several full houses from the fringes could fit inside—which appears to serve no purpose other than as a gathering place for clusters of students and to split off into narrowing internal halls. At the far end, I find myself on a cobblestone path surrounded by gardens on either side and a glass ceiling overhead.

Julita said the inner courtyard was "smaller," but it's hardly *small.* It's still a good half a minute's walk to the mountainous building in the middle.

Through the glass covering that must provide shelter for students traveling between the inner and outer buildings during bad weather, I peer up at the Domicile. Its name seems appropriate not just for its function as the students' home but also for the domed roof arching five stories above my head.

Narrow silver spires jut at intervals along the edge of that roof. I can only count four of them from this vantage point, but I'd be willing to bet there are ten in total. Nine for the godlen and one for the Great God who made them.

The All-Giver might have abandoned us centuries ago, but no one in the realm misses a chance to honor the One and the nine who followed. Especially if they have plenty of money to throw around.

The covered walkway leads straight to a set of double doors in the Domi. Before I've quite reached them, they swing open to grant me entrance.

Because apparently nobles are too lazy to grasp a door handle? Who wasted their energy compelling their magic to serve this purpose?

Gods smite me, I can already feel the grease of privilege seeping into my skin.

The entry hall of the Domi isn't half as grand as the first one I came through, which gives my nerves a chance to settle a little. As I amble past a few wandering students who barely spare me a glance, Julita speaks up again.

*Take the second hall on the left. We're going past the main door to the library and around the bend. Stop just after the tapestry of Signy.*

I keep my chin high and my strides steady. As I pass the library door, a couple of women standing just outside it titter to each other, but there's no reason to think their giggles have anything to do with me.

No reason to think they don't either, but what should their judgment matter to me?

The hall narrows around the bend. Several faded tapestries hang over the gray stone, bringing muted color to the space.

There's a courtly image of some past queen I don't recognize. A scene of Creaden placing a crown on the supposed first king of the entire world.

And then Signy, the greatest hero of the last century. I've seen—and read—so many depictions of her that I can identify her from the very first glimpse.

Like usual, the weaver has set her on a small hill. Her black hair unfurls behind her golden face, and a glow nearly as bright as what artists reserve for the gods shines around her. She's wearing an odd combination of flowing dress and battle armor, her sword pointing toward the massive army of the Darium empire below her.

Only three figures stand around her, just beneath the crest of the hill: the three men she took as lovers and then husbands. With the godlen of love giving her blessing, no one dared to argue about the legalities.

When you free your country from centuries under an imperial dictatorship, people cut you a little slack.

It wasn't even *our* country Signy freed, but every realm on the western side of the continent celebrates her. She showed the way for the rest of us to shake off those shackles too.

I'd bet the countries on the eastern side celebrate her as well—quietly, where the current emperor and his lackeys won't overhear them. They must hope that one day they'll wrench free of his grasp too.

By the far edge of the tapestry, I pause. No one else is wandering through this end of the hallway.

*The sconce just next to you,* Julita says. *Tap the base two times on the left, once on the right, then give it a tug.*

All right then. I set my fingers against the bronze fixture with its magical glow as she said.

At the ending tug, a narrow shadow spills down the wall in front of me. A shadow shaped as if it's falling away into a tight, dark passage—a conjured secret entrance someone permanently fixed to this spot.

"So very sneaky," I murmur under my breath as I step into the passage. Darkness closes behind me.

*We're dealing with people willing to kill to gain power, who're practicing right here in the college. We can hardly afford to be careless. Even being careful...*

Julita pauses, with a hint of tightly held emotion. She's kept up a pretty blasé attitude about the whole murder thing, but the woman did just *die* yesterday.

I can't imagine the shock and horror she's going through, that she's keeping to herself rather than venting all over me. She didn't want to be stuck in this situation any more than I did.

Maybe I should give her a little more benefit of the doubt.

The passage quickly descends into a series of steps. I can't see them, only feeling my way with one foot in front of the other and my hand against the cool stone of the wall.

*Alek found this passage,* Julita continues after a moment. *It leads down to one of the smaller rooms in the archives. They have a normal entrance too, inside the library, of course, but that's more noticeable. Gods know what the scholars used to get up to down here that they felt the need to make a secret entrance.*

My lips twitch with the start of a smile, even as I file away the name. Alek—one of the friends who's helping uncover the scourge sorcerer conspiracy, presumably.

I'm opening my mouth, about to ask for the others' names, when I take one more step and find myself emerging from the darkness in between two bookcases in a hazy, low-ceilinged room.

The figures already standing around the desk in the middle of that room look up, and my mouth freezes before any sound can come out.

There are four of them. Four men, all different in looks but striking in their own ways.

The massive one with the blood-red hair.

The one with the warm smile and the short, tawny waves.

The one with the polished leather mask hiding more than half of his bronze-brown face.

And the one whose skin looks as sun-kissed as his rumpled locks, although the smirk I remember is faltering at the sight of me.

The same four from the image that swam up in my mind while I pressed my hands to Julita's bleeding neck—

Not just an image. A memory. Her memory of meeting with them here, before.

I should have realized after I recognized the college building.

I shouldn't be standing here gaping like an idiot.

But before I can work a single word from my throat, the man with the dark red hair takes a step toward me, the brawn flexing across his broad shoulders beneath his gilded tunic.

His baritone reverberates through the room, smooth and cool but with a tang of menace. "And who the fuck are you?"

# Six

You don't survive for eight years on the streets without a swift set of wits. The second the massive man's question rings through the air, my mind snaps out of shock and locks on to my story.

I take a small step forward, confident but not imposing, ignoring the stutter of my pulse. I shift my usual wording into the formal phrasing typical of the upper class. "I'm a friend of Julita's. She asked me to attend this meeting in her place."

The man cocks his head to the side with a subtle twitch of his head. It's difficult to look away from his stunningly chiseled features.

He crosses his muscular arms over his equally muscular chest in a pose that sends a different twinge of familiarity through me. As if I've seen this man somewhere other than in that flash of Julita's memories.

"Interesting," he says in a drawl too cool to be totally casual. "And where would Julita be?"

In my head, adding to the conversation with an amused lilt to her voice.

*Don't mind him. Stavros has to indulge his bossing-people-around inclinations somewhere now that he's not commanding entire armies anymore.*

Her tone is dismissive, but my entire body stiffens. Stavros? Armies?

My gaze flicks over the looming man again and snags on one of his hands, tucked under his elbow. The hand that's a little too stiff, a little too even in color to be actual flesh, as well as it matches his light brown skin.

With a sickening lurch of my gut, I realize why I recognize his stance.

I'm looking at General Stavros, military genius and leader of a quarter of the Crown's soldiers... or at least, he was until an injury in battle last year knocked him from his pedestal.

Other than the prosthetic hand, which he's needed since his sacrifice to the warrior godlen, Sabrelle, at his twelfth-year dedication, he appears hale and hearty enough. I had no idea he was slumming it with college students.

But that's not what turns my blood to ice. No, the real problem is that the one time I saw him before, two years ago—in a helm that hid his distinctive blood-red hair and with a much *more* distinctive metal prosthetic—he was presiding over the execution of the last riven sorcerer to be brought to justice before last night.

A riven sorcerer he personally hunted down and dragged to the capital.

When I blink, an image flickers behind my eyes: his tightly satisfied smile as the drugged woman jerked in the noose.

Great God filet and fry me, I might as well have draped myself on a chopping block by coming here.

The former general looks younger than I'd have imagined, late twenties at most, but that's hardly a comfort. My fingers have curled toward my palms, my left hand itching to snatch up the knife hidden in my boot.

Of course, I've got nowhere to run to, and *stabbing* the former General Stavros is only going to land me in deeper shit than I've already stumbled into.

My magic prickles through my ribs, but I resist its demanding pinches. There's no immediate danger because he doesn't know what I am—but he sure as shit will if I start throwing my power around.

There's nothing to do but continue the ruse until I can walk away. And fast, because all four of the men are looking sterner with every passing second of my silence.

"She couldn't make it," I spit out hastily, and manage to gather myself enough to even out my voice.

The plan, the explanation we worked out, it's there in my head along with the woman's blasted ghost.

"We met for dinner last night," I go on. "We know each other from back home—from Nikodi —I'm in Florian visiting my uncle. She told me about your investigation, and that there was an urgent lead she intended to follow that would take her out of the city for a day or two, but she didn't want you to worry. So she explained how to find the meeting and asked me to come in her place."

By the desk, the masked man shifts his weight. He's tall but much slimmer than Stavros, his lean frame covered in a moss-green tunic and brown trousers that are less flashy than the former general's clothes but still clearly well-made.

Like the rest of the other men, I'd guess he's around my age—a student, then—although with him it's difficult to tell.

His gaze pierces into me through the holes in the deep brown leather of his mask. The material covers one side of his face from beneath the black waves of his hair along his forehead down to his jaw, but angles up around his mouth and across his nose so that only the area around his eye and forehead is concealed on the other side.

I'm not sure what to make of it. I've never seen anyone from any level of society make a sacrifice that would only affect the surface of their face and not its features.

Those who prefer not to offer more than skin tend toward arm and leg areas and leave the mark on display. Those who want a more significant sacrifice might give an ear or an eye.

Maybe he's suffered some kind of injury too, though I doubt it was in battle.

Even with that much of his features disguised, it's obvious from the tapered slope of his jaw and nose, the fullness of his lips and the brightness of his eyes, that he's plenty handsome himself. Julita apparently prefers her allies to be appealing to the eye as well as stealthy.

The masked man's lips purse tight in the moment before they part. His voice comes out cold and flat. "You're not a student here. How did you even get into the college?"

I force a smile that I hope looks at least mildly reassuring. "She told me the week's passcode and the way to open the secret passage to this room. And she lent me this."

I hold up my arm. Julita's bracelet gleams around my wrist.

The blond man props himself against the side of the desk, a hint of his smirk coming back to his equally fine face. While not as huge as Stavros, he's obviously well-built—and knows it, from the way he carries himself.

He's turned his formal shirt provocatively casual by leaving it unbuttoned halfway down his chest —revealing the godlen sigil branded over his sternum. He's dedicated to Kosmel.

The overseer of luck and trickery is an unusual choice for a noble.

And he's missing the lobes of his ears. Both of them, cut off in a smooth diagonal line from what must have been a dedication sacrifice.

He's got some kind of gift, though probably not a very large one given the minor offering.

"How do we know you didn't just steal the bracelet from her?" he asks breezily, as if he wouldn't care much even if I had.

*Oh, Benny.* I can practically hear Julita rolling her eyes. *Remind him that I outdrank him at the Blue Hart pub the first night we met.*

I arch one eyebrow, channeling my noble passenger's attitude for all I'm worth. "Could I have also stolen the story of how she drank you under the table at the Blue Hart when the two of you met?"

The blond man barks a laugh and claps his hands together. "I like this one. I say we keep her too."

Julita snorts. *As if it wasn't me who herded the bunch of them together in the first place.*

Stavros shoots the other man an unimpressed look. The underlying coolness of his voice sends a shiver down my spine despite his languid tone. "Keep your pants on, Benedikt. She hasn't even told us her name."

"Ivy," I say promptly. "Ivy Euridya of Nikodi." Julita assured me that none of her friends were familiar enough with her birthplace to have any idea of what other semi-prominent families live there.

"Ivy," Stavros repeats, in a tone that suggests it's the most ridiculous name he's ever heard. Is there really no chance I can get away with stabbing him?

The tawny-haired man who's said nothing so far comes around the side of the desk by Stavros. Every movement of his sleek body emanates a feline sort of grace that speaks of both strength and poise. But the soft smile he aims at me is the warmest gesture anyone here has offered so far.

The other men may all be striking, but this one is so gorgeous my breath catches despite my wariness.

A trace of magic tingles through me. Did he work a gift on me?

He turns his dark green eyes toward the military man. "I think we should listen to her. Julita wouldn't have sent her if it wasn't important."

As he talks, I catch the glint of red and blue in the back of his mouth. I have to restrain my reaction before both my eyebrows shoot up.

He's replaced at least a few of his molars with gemstone substitutes. Rubies and sapphires from the look of them.

Teeth aren't an unusual dedication sacrifice, though I've heard they're one of the more painful options, especially if you offer more than one. But usually only courtesans fill in the gaps with such eye-catching replacements, devoted as they are to beauty along with every other pleasure of the flesh.

It's common enough that I've heard pliers of the carnal trade referred to sneeringly as "gaudy teeth" rather than their actual job title.

This is quite the motley group Julita assembled.

*Of course Casimir would believe you first,* she says with apparent amusement. *Sweet Cas, always ready to serve.*

Even though I've only just met the man, her patronizing tone raises my hackles.

Didn't she say these men were her "friends"? She doesn't sound as if she thinks all that highly of any of them.

Since I've now gotten three of their names, I have to assume the one in the mask is the Alek she mentioned who found the secret passage.

The slim man's mouth has tightened again into a grimace, but he sets his hands on the desk with a determined air. "Fine. What did she ask you to tell us? What's this mission she's gone on?"

Benedikt nods with a swish of his sleek golden hair. "And why didn't she let us in on the fun?"

He asks the question like a joke, but a faint crease has bitten into his brow. He's at least a little concerned about her.

Which doesn't seem to matter much to Julita, based on her dry tone. *It is nice to be missed.*

Well, I'm not here to worry about the feelings of these strangers, one of whom would haul me straight to the gallows if he found out about the magic lurking inside me.

I drag in a breath, taking a moment now that I've accounted for all four of the men to study the rest of my surroundings. The small room is packed with shelving units around the broad desk, the shelves stacked with books and boxes, many of them dusty.

I guess no one much uses this room other than Julita and her coalition of conspiracy-hunters.

Yanking my attention back to the men, I rattle off the facts my ghostly guest wanted me to convey. "She saw reason to believe that the scourge sorcerers might be getting some assistance from or have associated with the Temple of Still Waters in Slaughterwell." The reason mainly being that she was murdered on her way to check out the place. "She thinks you should use your connections to look into it further."

Julita gives me a mental nudge. *And the knife. Tell them about the knife.*

I was getting to that. "And she saw someone she's certain is part of the conspiracy, but they had their face concealed. The only item she made out in any detail was a knife they were carrying."

Pausing, I bring up the uncomfortable memory of Julita's gasping, gushing body right before she died.

I've handled a lot of blades in my life. Even though I was focused on attempting to save her life at the time, I automatically noted some of the details.

"It was about eight inches long—two thirds of that blade, the other third handle. A fairly simple handle, metal with a spiral engraving on the pommel and black leather wrapped around the grip. Slightly curved cross guard. Blade about an inch wide, double-edged."

By the time I've finished that recitation, Stavros's glower is searing into me. I resist the urge to glare right back at him.

So I have a bit of a thing for knives. What about it?

"That doesn't sound very distinctive," Alek says doubtfully.

I spread my hands. "That's all she could tell me. Keep an eye out for it, I suppose."

Of course, who knows if the murderer has another blade that looks the same? It hadn't looked like he was coming back for the first. But Julita wanted to give them all the evidence we can.

Stavros clears his throat. "You haven't explained what she's up to now."

He shifts on his feet, just a slight sign of restlessness but enough for me to note it. Even Casimir is watching me with an intensity I can sense is unusual for him, waiting for my answer.

These men are awfully invested in my unwanted passenger. Just how "friendly" has she gotten with them?

She's got decent taste in looks. I could do without the interest in riven-slaughtering, though.

I meet the former general's gaze steadily. "She didn't tell me anything specific about that. She simply said that if she didn't leave right away, she was worried she'd miss her chance, but she didn't want to leave you wondering. It sounded as though there wasn't time for her to send word back to you even if she'd wanted company."

A frown mars Casimir's dazzling face. Stavros rubs his square jaw but can't seem to find anything to criticize about my statement.

*Nicely done,* Julita says. *You got all the important parts in.*

I'd like to think that means I can go now, but Benedikt adjusts his jaunty position on the edge of the desk to glance at the others. "Well, my forays into spydom haven't gotten me very far in the past couple of days. No remarks on any unusual indications of magic in the palace."

I focus on him for a beat longer than I did before. Who is he that he'd have a direct line to what's being said in the royal household?

His archly handsome face offers no clues.

If he's a student here, he can't be acting as a courtier yet, but maybe someone else in his family is. Nobles were the ones who invented nepotism, after all.

Stavros runs his fingers through his hair, looking abruptly bored with the conversation. "I confirmed that there's no official record of dartling eggshell being purchased by any students or staff within the city. If Julita was right about that dust she says she saw."

"Julita knew what she was talking about," Alek says with just a hint of heat creeping into his flat tone.

Casimir nods. "Jules did always say they'd have bought it on the black market or through a secondary source. That was why she was looking into the temples."

Stavros glances at the masked man. "Have you found out anything more about the other substances she mentioned, Aleksi?"

"A few things. There—"

Alek pauses, his piercing gaze coming to rest on me again. "We should let Ivy take her leave, shouldn't we? She must have better things to do than listen to us."

He doesn't sound considerate so much as wary. He doesn't *want* me listening in on their discussions.

Well, that's just fine. I did what I came for.

The sooner I'm beyond the college's gloomy gray walls, the better.

"Indeed." Stavros offers me a cocky grin. "We wouldn't want to bore you."

Julita lets out a huff. *I'd have liked to know more about their progress, but I suppose it'll look suspicious if you try to stay. Well— Oh! Ask them if Wendos has been up to anything—ask them if any of them saw him yesterday evening.*

Her voice turns abruptly urgent with the last demand. I have no idea who Wendos is, but I can't see any point in denying her.

I give a slight cough as if clearing my throat. "I don't want to interfere with your discussions. There's only one thing I almost forgot. Julita also wanted to know if any of you saw Wendos yesterday evening. Or any other time recently, doing anything that made you suspicious."

From the look the men exchange, I get a distinctly dubious vibe from all of them. Whoever this Wendos guy is, maybe Julita's been harping on about him a little too much for her allies' patience.

Benedikt pipes up. "He was in the card room for a few hours after dinner. I didn't have the pleasure of relieving him of any of his money, but plenty of others did."

Julita lets out a disgruntled sound. *Not him then. This is getting us nowhere.*

I bob into the faintest sketch of a curtsy. "That's everything, then. I'm glad I could do the favor for Julita."

Casimir strolls over with another of those smiles that warms me up like sweet tea on a winter day.

A smile he'd never have offered if he knew who I really am.

That thought douses the warmth with an uneasy chill, but the courtesan shows no sign of noticing my discomfort. "Thank you for taking the risk of coming here at all, Ivy. I'll show you the way out."

He tweaks a few volumes on the bookcase next to the bit of wall I emerged from. The shadowy pathway reforms on the wall.

I raise my hand to the men in an awkward farewell that seems necessary and set off. As the darkness closes behind me, I exhale in a rush of relief.

There, that's over with.

*All right,* Julita says briskly, giving the sense of rubbing her hands together. *Let's get down to some real work.*

# SEVEN

I jerk to a halt the second I've stepped into the Domi's hall next to the tapestry of Signy. Did I hear my uninvited guest right?

"Down to work?" I mutter. "I did what you asked me to do already."

Julita dismisses my hesitation in what I'm learning is her usual coyly self-assured way. *I simply want to check my dorm. It's possible my murderer broke in to go through my things after cutting me down. If he left any evidence, we can pass that on to the others too.*

"That wasn't the deal."

*We're already* here. *The hard part is over. It'll only take a few more minutes.*

When I still balk, Julita sighs. *Ivy, I lost my entire life yesterday, to villains who are hoping to destroy a lot more lives if they get away with it. This is my last chance to do everything in my power to ensure they're brought to justice. You've been fantastic so far. I know you won't get into any trouble.*

I run my thumb over the missing stub on my right pointer finger. Every inch of my skin is already itching with the urge to sprint out of this place as fast as I can, to trade the clinging faux-silk dress for my hooded tunic, to duck back into the shadows where I belong.

But I can see her point. And I *am* already inside, past the security measures. No one's badgered me about my presence so far.

What kind of a monster would I be if I ignore her plea?

And just how insane will I go if I have to listen to her complaining about my refusal for however long it takes until I figure out how to *un*invite her from my head?

I exhale sharply. "Fine. But we do need to be quick about it. Where's your dorm?"

Julita's voice brightens with so much relief I feel a jab of guilt over hesitating. *One floor up. If you head around the next corner in the hall, there's a smaller staircase down there that isn't used very often.*

I don't run into any of Julita's schoolmates in the narrowing hall or the even narrower spiral of the staircase. When I step out onto the second floor, a bunch of male students are just ambling through one of the nearby doorways.

One of them looks me up and down with a leering curl of his lips that has my fingers twitching toward my hip where I'd usually have my favorite knife stashed.

Since stabbing him wouldn't be any better for my whole incognito mission than sticking it to

Stavros would have, I settle for pretending I haven't even noticed him. Or the chuckles that follow in my wake as Julita nudges me in the opposite direction.

Are they laughing because he made some crude comment about me, or because they can tell I don't quite fit the mold?

*A lot of pricks in this place,* Julita remarks in a darkly wry tone as I follow the bend in the hall. *It makes figuring out who's just an ass and who's actually evil rather difficult.*

I have to restrain a snort of unexpected amusement.

For a couple of minutes, I walk on past rows of doors spaced several paces apart. Each wooden surface holds an intricate etching of some scene from history: Silana's, the continent's, or that of the gods themselves.

As I stride past them, Julita fills me in on the details of our destination. *This half of the second floor belongs to the leadership division. We room in clusters. Everyone gets a private bedroom, of course, but they're in clumps of ten around a common leisure room. Room assignments switch up once per term. They want us to have a chance to interact with everyone in our division.*

Wonderful—so there are nine potential witnesses to *me* breaking into Julita's dorm.

I allow myself a grimace and drop my voice to the barest whisper so no one beyond those doors can hear me. "And how do I get in?"

*The bracelet is the key there too. All students and staff have an ornament attuned for the access they need —that's mine. I'll tell you what to do once we get there. If anyone's around, you can tell them I sent you to pick something up while I was busy with a project out of town. We're almost there…*

She has me stop outside a door carved with an image of a stately woman who I guess from her crown is King Konram's late grandmother. The artist has given her the same prominent nose. Creaden's sigil slashes through the wood above her head.

*Press my bracelet to the ring on her right hand,* Julita says.

I tip my wrist, and a rasp sounds from inside the door. When I test the knob, it opens.

I slip into the common room cautiously. A gust of mingled perfumes assaults my nose.

Elegant upholstered chairs and settees fill most of the space, along with a card table in the corner and a built-in bookcase next to it. Heavy velvet curtains drape the sides of the broad picture window at the far end of the room.

No one's using the space at the moment, thank the gods. My gaze darts over the relatively plain doors to the individual bedrooms along the side walls.

*Left side, third one down. Let's see if it's still locked.*

That knob jars when I test it.

Julita lets out a satisfied hum. *Feel the notches on the backside of the knob? Press the bottom one twice, then the right one once, then the top, then the bottom again.*

When I've followed the pattern, I'm rewarded with another click. I ease the door open.

Julita's bedroom looks about as jumbled as my mind feels with her bustling around in it. Silk and satin dresses sprawl across every available surface, including the polished wooden floor with its flower-print rug. By contrast, the wardrobe standing with its door ajar across from the four-poster bed appears to be all but empty.

"Is this—?" I start to ask, tensing up at the thought of someone having ransacked the place.

Julita lets out a giggle that sounds just slightly sheepish. *I wasn't expecting visitors. I always say it's easier to find what I'm looking for when everything's on display.*

Ah, so this is her mess, not some intruder's. I'm not sure if that makes me feel better or worse.

Although considering that my own bedroom of sorts is mostly disorganized heaps of books, maybe I'm not in a position to judge.

"Is anything out that shouldn't be?" I ask. "Or anything missing that should be here?"

*Take a walk around and let me check everything.*

I meander through the chamber, hopping over crumpled dresses here and there. Julita has me open her wardrobe all the way, lift the lid of her well-stocked jewelry box, tug back the soft sheets on the bed, and delve into the drawers on the bedside tables.

When I've investigated every nook and cranny, she makes a disgruntled sound. *I don't see any sign that anyone's been in here. Surely they'd have wanted to search to see what proof I'd already found?*

"Maybe they're afraid they won't be able to sneak in without getting caught," I point out. "They did wait to attack you until you were well away from the college."

*True... It was strange. There must have been magic involved. It happened so fast it's a blur. I was walking along, and this blast of wind smacked into me, and then that horrible pain lanced through my neck... If I'd managed to turn around in time, maybe I could have seen them, and we wouldn't need to be digging through my laundry.*

I frown. "Someone who can manipulate wind. They used it to distract you? There can't be too many people here with that specific gift."

*I don't know of anyone. It could have been merely a coincidence that the wind picked up at the same time.* She hisses as if through her teeth. *I should have mentioned that to the men so they could at least look into it. This whole situation is so... disorienting.*

"We could go back to the meeting?" I suggest, as much as my body tenses at the idea.

*No, they'll have gone their separate ways by now. Maybe—*

"Julita, is that you?"

The tart feminine voice carries through the door, and my stance goes outright rigid with a skip of my pulse. I hadn't realized anyone had come into the common room, but one of Julita's dormmates must have noticed my voice.

There's a sharp rap on the door.

*Go on,* Julita says. *If you pretend you're not here, it'll be so much more awkward when we need to leave.*

I square my shoulders and dart over to the door. "Just a moment!"

As I twist the knob, I push my mouth into an ingratiating smile and yank.

A woman tall and sleek as a sapling stands just outside, her flaxen hair piled in an elaborate whorl on top of her head and her wide-set eyes narrowing at the sight of me.

I bring out my most chipper tone before she can speak. "Not Julita. Only a friend picking up something she needed. She's handling a project out of town. She lent me her bracelet so I could get in."

I hold up my wrist to reveal it.

The woman's lips curl with a hint of a sneer. She rotates the partly eaten apple she's holding between her fingers. "Out of town? Where's she slunk off to?"

I keep my smile in place despite the hostility in the words. "Oh, I'm not totally sure. I'm supposed to send it on to her near our hometown. As soon as possible, so I'd better get going."

If this woman hears about Julita's death and wonders about my odd visit, I expect to be well away from anywhere anyone would be looking for a noble visitor by then.

As I step out and shut the bedroom door behind me, the woman takes another bite of her apple and peers down her nose at me. "Fine. When you see her, tell her I expect the jewelry she borrowed to be returned the very first second she sets foot back at the college."

In my head, Julita guffaws. *Is she still fussing about those awful earrings? The wretched things nearly pulled my earlobes off. I left them on the side table outside her bedroom—not my fault if someone else snatched them.*

This is a squabble I'm not interested in getting in the middle of. I edge to the side, away from the door. "I'll mention it to her."

Julita's dormmate makes a scoffing sound. "You be careful with her. I'm sure she's calling you a friend while she can use you, but that's all she does. Use, use, use. Likes to get everyone she can twisted around her little finger."

She seems awfully worked up over a pair of earrings. Were they fitted with godlen-blessed 5-carat diamonds or something?

Julita seems to shake herself as if shedding the venom. *The things people will say that they'd never dare speak to your face. If anyone's a snake in the grass…*

"I'll keep that in mind too," I say, raising my hands in a peace-making gesture.

The woman clicks her tongue. "I'm simply saying, she'll lull you into thinking she's being nothing but helpful. But underneath she's always only looking out for her own selfishness."

Another woman I hadn't noticed stands up from the chair she was curled up in by the far corner of the room. "Anya, simmer down. It's not Julita's fault if people find her charming."

Both my gaze and that of the woman confronting me snap to the interrupter.

It's not surprising I didn't notice her when I had a much more imposing figure in front of me. This girl is slight and modestly dressed as nobles go—which means her dove-gray gown appears to only have three layers instead of five and only a little embroidery on the silky edges. Her fawn-brown hair sits in a simple loose ponytail.

She does have one striking feature, though. She gazes back at us calmly with a single pale green eye, a mauve silk patch with gold-gilded edging covering the other.

She gave up a whole cyc in her dedication ceremony for whatever gift she asked to be blessed with. I hope the godlen she devoted herself to gave her a good one.

Anya sniffs and lifts her apple to her lips again. "I don't see how it's any of your business, Esmae. It's not as if you had much to do with Julita to even know."

The single-eyed woman—Esmae—lifts her shoulders in a subtle shrug. "I know it's hardly good form to lay into someone who isn't around to defend themselves."

Julita's presence in my head stirs with apparent interest. *Never would have thought simpering Esmae would leap in on my behalf. I suppose she's spent all this time shyly admiring me from afar.*

Anya rolls her eyes and bites into the apple. With a sputter of disgust, she rears back her head and fishes for a handkerchief to spit out her mouthful. Then she glares at the fruit. "Wretched daimon. Rotting the thing while it's in my damned hand."

A roaming daimon spoiled the apple in the last minute?

My forehead furrows, but I'm close enough to see how the previously white flesh is now mottled brown and black.

Esmae treads over, wrinkling her nose as she takes in the apple. She catches my gaze. "The college's spirits have been overly restless—and cantankerous—lately. Although perhaps this one merely liked the poetic justice of souring what's held by the sour." She shoots Anya a pointed glance.

Grumbling under her breath, Anya tosses the ruined apple in the waste basket and stalks into her bedroom. My stomach turns, both at the thought of taking a bite of that rotted fruit and the implications of it rotting at all.

Daimon are as likely to ripen fruit as rot it. It all depends on the mood that strikes them. But I've never heard of them interfering with food a person's already eating.

I'd only expect that if they were particularly riled up about something. Something like…

Julita fills in the uneasy suspicion for me. *They've been more agitated than usual for a few months now. Since not long before the prince was poisoned. I think they sense the blood that's being spilled for dark purposes on these grounds—and they're not happy about it.*

When she first told me about the conspiracy, she said she knew there were more than a few nobles involved "based on the effects." I think I'm seeing what effects she meant.

As my stomach roils on, Esmae shoots me a sympathetic smile. "Sorry about Anya. She isn't shy with her opinions."

It's hard not to wonder if there might have been a little truth to those opinions, though. After all, Julita does seem to be unnervingly good at cajoling *me* into doing what she wants.

I manage a quick smile in return. "Thank you for stepping in. I should really be on my way."

And if my ghostly passenger thinks I'm making any more stops during this tour around the royal college, she can eat straw.

I hustle out of the dorm before anyone else can drop in. Julita remains mercifully silent.

Until we come around the next bend and she lets out a sharp hiss followed by a barked command. *Stop there. Back up so he won't notice you.*

A young man with shaggy coffee-brown hair and coppery skin is just shutting one of the other dorm-room doors behind him, his back to us. Julita's command is urgent enough that I jerk back around the corner, bracing myself by the pale plaster wall while I peer at him.

*That's Wendos*, Julita says in an ominous tone. *I wonder how much* he *knows about the knife that ended up in my throat.*

# Eight

Peeking around the bend in the hall at the stocky guy who set off Julita's concern, I raise an eyebrow in question.

Benedikt said Wendos was playing cards when she was murdered. Why does she still assume he could be involved?

*Trust me*, she says. *Whether he's directly responsible or not, he's no shining soul.*

I have to take her word for it. Nothing about the man I'm watching provokes my own defensive instincts.

He raises his hand in greeting to another guy coming out farther down the hall and calls out an easy-going challenge. "I'll see you on the archery range later. You'd better be prepared!"

Then he ambles off in the direction I was headed, toward the main staircase. No sign of subterfuge or a guilty conscience.

"Nothing about him looks particularly murderer-y to me," I say under my breath.

Julita simply hums in answer. When Wendos has disappeared from view, she gives me a mental nudge. *We might as well get going, then.*

We don't catch up with Wendos, wherever Julita's villain has gone within the school, but as I step out of the Domi, my gaze catches on a now unnervingly familiar head of dark red hair.

The former General Stavros is poised about thirty feet away across the sprawling field between the Domi and the square outer building of the Quadring. He's exchanged his hand-like prosthetic for one more like what I saw the night he led the riven sorcerer's execution two years ago: a broad, boxy loop of metal bent into a hook-like curve. It gleams in the sunlight as he raises it.

Some twenty students are standing around him, watching with rapt attention. One is just stepping forward.

Stavros says something brief, the boy nods, and then the former general lunges faster than I would have thought his massive frame would be capable of.

He snags his prosthetic hook around the guy's upper arm, yanks him in, and lets his other fist fly. It stops at a mere tap of the guy's nose. Then he whips his hook up to show how he could slam one of the boxy corners straight into the guy's temple.

A shiver creeps over my skin. That is not a man I'd want to make an enemy of.

But he already is my enemy simply by virtue of the power I never asked for, which is twisting in my chest at the sight of him.

*The king assigned Stav to teach combat and strategy here after he couldn't keep up on the battlefield anymore,* Julita says. *Everyone in the military division vies to get into his classes.*

I'll bet.

Stavros eases back from his student with a coolly cocky smile, and the guy whose skull he could have split open laughs as he adjusts his stance. The other students gathered around are grinning, their expressions avid.

I slow as I take in the class, remembering that Julita wanted to tell her allies about the wind-controlling powers her attacker might have wielded. But Stavros glances across the field then, and his gaze slides right over me as if I'm not there.

Julita prods me. *You can't talk to him here. We keep our meetings secret so no one knows we're associating at all. If it wasn't for that, whoever cut me down would be after the guys next.*

A reasonable precaution. Better not to let murderous conspirators know you're on to them until you can actually cut *them* down.

Walking out of the college is much simpler than walking in. I stride down the grand entrance hall and through the gate with no sign of the maze I had to navigate on the way in or any irritating tickles of magic.

On the street outside, I hurry away from the trio of royal buildings. The tightness in my chest doesn't quite release until the Temple of the Crown is hidden by the looming stone buildings of the main downtown thoroughfare.

I veer down the smaller laneways, instinctively making for my home base. It's too early to sneak into my attic room over the cloth factory, but I've stashed a more discreet change of clothes in one of the bathhouse cubbies.

It definitely won't do me any good roaming around the fringes of the city in this faux-noble get-up.

And then what? As much as Julita is an unwelcome intruder in my head, it feels bizarrely rude to ask her when she plans to take off.

I'm not even sure she knows how to get out of my head... and if she does, would that mean she'd immediately complete her death and pass on into the embrace of her chosen godlen?

I'd basically be asking her to kill herself. Other than the part where technically she's already dead.

It also technically isn't my problem, but that fact doesn't diminish the uneasy twinge in my gut. So instead, once I'm weaving through less crowded streets, I bring up a different topic that's been niggling at me.

"Why are you so suspicious of Wendos? What did he do that made you think he's part of the conspiracy?"

The men she's gathered to help her investigate seemed skeptical, so obviously Julita's wariness was based on something they haven't seen or don't believe.

Julita stays silent for long enough that I might have wondered if she's taken her leave of her own accord. But a faint tingle remains by the back of my skull, that I'm starting to recognize indicates her presence.

Finally, she sighs. *He hasn't done anything at the college that I've been able to uncover. But I know he has an interest in scourge sorcery. Before—he was close friends with my older brother growing up... A little while after their dedication ceremonies, he and Borys both got it into their heads that it would be exciting to expand their magic.*

She doesn't need to elaborate for a chill to run down my back.

A couple of teenage boys dabbling in the most brutal form of sorcery? That sounds like a recipe for a disaster.

Especially when I now have to ask: "How did you find out?"

Julita's next silence stretches even longer. *I'm not sure how far they actually went. I'm not aware of any human sacrifices, and probably they couldn't have gotten away with that. There might have been animals. But they also experimented with mere blood-letting. And since I was younger and right there where my brother could exert his authority, I was the easiest subject for them to practice on.*

The chill coils right around my gut. Blood-letting.

Only a sacrifice at a dedication ceremony can result in a permanent gift, but under certain circumstances, you can bargain flesh or blood for a temporary effect. It's expected that you bargain your *own* flesh or blood, though.

Julita's brother and Wendos used her in whatever makeshift rituals they were able to cobble together based on the sketchy knowledge of scourge sorcery the average noble kid would be able to dig up. Cutting her. Spilling her blood in smaller sacrifices.

Hoping her pain would lend them power.

Julita's voice turns more strident. *It only lasted a couple of years. Then I dedicated myself and got my own gift, and I could put a stop to it. But it seems like it'd be an incredible coincidence if there's scourge sorcery being practiced at the college right now and Wendos isn't a part of it.*

I can't argue with her logic. "What about your brother? Is he attending the college too?"

*He was supposed to, but he was either waylaid or ran off when traveling to Florian. I suspect the latter. Borys was never much for studying... I wouldn't be surprised if he went off to join the infantry so he could see some action.*

So there's only Wendos at the college. A frown crosses my lips. "Are you sure that what you've seen is a whole conspiracy and not just Wendos continuing their old experiments?"

Julita shivers. *I wish it were that simple. Even when he and my brother were dabbling together, the daimon on my estate never acted strangely. For them to be so disturbed at the college, it has to be a much larger effort.*

It's hard to argue her logic—both in that and that there's a good chance of Wendos being involved. So why would the men doubt it? "Did you tell Stavros and the others what the two of them used to—"

*No,* Julita cuts in abruptly. *Not the part about me being involved. Just that I could tell he and my brother were getting up to things. I saw some of the materials they used—like the dartling eggshell powder. That should be enough.*

From her tone, I don't think she's very happy about having exposed that much of her harrowing childhood even to me.

My gut has twisted into a knot. She spent years getting tortured by hopeful scourge sorcerers, ran into more the second she left home, and then got murdered by one.

It's hard to imagine that the little bit of information I was able to pass on to her friends is going to be enough to get her justice. And because she's still here in her ghostly form, she'll know that as well as I do.

My mouth moves before I've quite thought through the offer I'm about to make. "There's a place I could ask around. See if anyone involved in black-market dealings has heard about your murder or whatever else to do with illegal sorcery."

The tingle in the back of my head seems to perk up.

*Really?* Julita says, in a softer but eager tone. *I guess those are the sorts of people you typically mingle with?*

I make a face at her assumption, already feeling a twinge of regret. But the thought of going back on my suggestion now is more horrible than going through with it.

"Not if I can help it. I don't really mingle with *anyone* 'typically.' But I know how to find them when I need them."

Dropping in on Crow's Close will definitely require a costume change, though.

As evening falls, I approach the Frolic Theater in Tangleside, a neighborhood so called because of the confusing twists of its streets. One of my hooded tunics drapes me from the top of my head to mid-thigh, and five knives lie concealed but in easy reach.

The weathered wooden building stands taller and broader than any of the sagging shops around it, its doorless front entrance gaping like a monster's maw. The sigil for Inganne, godlen of creativity and amusement, beams overhead in orange paint, with weathered illustrations of larks and butterflies fluttering around it.

*We're going to take in a show?* Julita asks doubtfully.

"You'll see," I mutter, and push myself onward.

As I climb the two creaking steps outside the entrance, raucous laughter reaches my ears from inside. At the other end of the dim lobby, the stands will be at least half full of locals who needed to brighten their day.

The theater's erratic crew of actors put on comedic pantomimes, puppet shows, and short, silly plays twice a day, charging about the cost of a slice of bread and accepting said slices—or other items —in trade instead of coins if that's all the patron can give.

They can afford to offer their entertainment cheaply because they get a kickback from the theater's other use.

Instead of heading on into the auditorium, I veer toward the first door on the right. A shallow carving of Kosmel's sigil barely shows above it in the dim light.

Any unwitting person stumbling on this doorway would take one look at the darkened, musty stairs on the other side and turn around. I march on downward, wrinkling my nose at the pungent mildewy odor that I'm not sure is totally conjured.

If anyone did venture this far in a fit of daring curiosity, they'd be stymied at the bottom of the stairs. By all appearances, they end at a small, empty, earthen-walled room so dark you can only make out the faint outlines of your fingers when holding your hand in front of your face.

But if you know where you're going, you slip around the left side of the stairs and make a sharp right that should have you walking straight into their underside. Instead, the moment your head would crash into the boards, you find yourself in a passage so black your hand might as well not exist at all.

Five steps forward, three left, ten right, two left again. I can't help wondering whether the criminals who built this passageway were inspired by the college or the other way around—or whether magical security can't help evolving to use the same methods.

With the last step, I walk back out into the earthen room. I lope up the steps and pass through the now-silent lobby. This version of the theater is only a conjured echo of the real thing.

The moment I emerge from the entrance, I'm faced with a mass of activity that's vividly real.

Crow's Close—named after Kosmel's favored bird in recognition of the role the godlen of luck plays in the success of any illicit endeavor—takes its name quite literally. The narrow strip of dirt road with wooden buildings packed on either side is entirely enclosed, stopping at a dead end about a hundred paces in either direction. The only way in and out is through the theater.

Well, the only way *I* know. No doubt the crooks who make this place their permanent residence have other escape routes.

The strip looks like a macabre version of the commercial street near the palace. Conjured illusions gyrate over the shop doors, but with imagery like skulls and weaponry. The lights in the windows glow amber, crimson, and violet in the dusk.

The shoppers are a scruffier lot, with dreary clothing and scars aplenty. Most wear hoods like my own to shade their faces, the more cautious concealing their features with simple masks as well.

But I've got no reputation in the outside world that my presence here could threaten.

The place to get the latest underground gossip is the pub right at the northern dead end, Brew & Dagger. I slink through the strip's other patrons toward it.

The sign over the dark wooden face shows a dagger jabbed into a mug of beer next to the pub's name. The conjured image hovering in front of it mimics the logo, with the blade rising and dropping back into the mug, making the illusionary glowing liquid slosh over the rim.

The inside of the pub smells like stale alcohol and acrid hazebloom smoke. I hop onto one of the empty stools by the scratched-up counter and ask the new bartender for an amber spritz.

As she mixes it, I let my gaze drift around the room, searching for any familiar faces I know will be happy to wag their tongue.

Before I land on one, I get a volunteer.

"If it isn't Ivy. I haven't seen you in a while."

At the voice behind me, I tense inwardly before I've swiveled around to face the speaker. Milo smirks at me, his hooded eyes as dark as his five-o'clock shadow.

Back when I was sixteen and less good at controlling my impulses—and my hormones—Milo seemed like a good option for dealing with those hormones periodically with no strings attached. We'd only had a couple of hookups when I found out that along with perfectly respectable forgery, he has a side-business picking out kids as young as eight for the mines, and my already limited attraction to him snuffed right out.

Four years later, he still hasn't quite caught on that I'd sooner fuck a donkey than get down and dirty with him again.

I grit my teeth and smile tightly back at him. Milo does like to hear his own voice, so this could make my job here easier. As long as he keeps his hands to himself in the meantime.

I take on a careless tone. "I like to make sure I'm missed. But every now and then I get a craving for an amber spritz that no one makes like this place."

He thumps his tankard onto the counter next to where the bartender has just slid my own glass. I curl my fingers around the cool surface, planning on keeping my hand and at least part of my gaze on it at all times while Mr. Can't Take A Hint is hanging around.

"I miss you every day I don't see that pretty face," Milo says, with so much grease to the words you could slip and break your arm on them. My magic bristles in my chest before I rein it in.

He's never actually hurt me… but I'd rather not give him the opportunity.

"Oh, I'm sure you've found plenty of other things to keep you busy." I take a sip of my drink, enjoying the tartly sweet flavor. Brew & Dagger really does make the best cocktails. "I heard there was a bit of a commotion in Slaughterwell… a couple of days back? Something about a noble getting stabbed? That's your main haunt, isn't it?"

Milo's eyes twitch to the side, which tells me he knows exactly what I'm talking about, despite the noncommittal answer he gives me. "Another day, another body. There was a woman found yesterday —pretty stripped down, so what she'd had on before must have been nice, I guess."

In my head, Julita lets out a sputter of indignation. I ignore her and give another casual nudge. "Anyone bragging about doing the deed?"

"Not that I've heard. The whispers about it have been more confused than anything. Whoever offed her, they slunk away fast."

He shakes his head in grim approval. I don't see any reason to distrust his answer.

No one around here knows who killed my ghostly passenger. I guess that's not totally surprising, given that it was probably one of her own, not an outer-warder.

It can't hurt to see if I can stir up any more information, though.

I bring my glass back to my lips. "Mustn't be good for business, having the bigwigs from the hill poking around investigating the crime."

"Oh, *our* bigwigs got things cleaned up quick so that wouldn't happen." Milo tips his head toward the door—toward the building that's both temple to Kosmel and gambling hall in the center of Crow's Close, where the most powerful crooks rule the roost. "They got to her before any official alert went out, disappeared the body, all's well."

He raises his eyebrows at me. "Having the Crown's Watch poking around wouldn't be good for *your* business either, huh?"

Milo has always been put out that I won't share the secrets of what I do when I'm not in this place. I can only imagine how he'd exploit the revelation that I'm the one people call the Hand of Kosmel.

If he thinks I'm bringing up the dead woman out of concern for my own criminal activities, that's fine with me. It keeps him off the scent.

I let out a light chuckle, but my thoughts are whirling. It hadn't even occurred to me that Florian's underworld would cover up Julita's murder.

Tensions have risen in the past few years. The Crown's Watch started cracking down more violently on all sorts of crimes—at least, those that affect the citizens they care about—after King Konram officially inherited the throne from his father.

I suppose it's not surprising that the powers here would rather remove any additional excuse for royal law enforcement to come nosing around.

*What does he mean, disappeared the body?* Julita demands. *They couldn't have just dumped me in a random hole and called that it.*

Oh, they could have. I swish a little more alcohol around in my mouth, unable to answer her here and not sure what I'd say anyway.

All trace of her murder will have been wiped away. Other than whatever bits of clothing or jewelry she had on her that desperate scavengers stole, there'll be no sign she was ever in Slaughterwell.

It isn't just that her friends at the college haven't found out she was murdered *yet*. If I don't say anything… they'll never find out at all.

They'll never know just how serious the situation is. Just how far the prospective scourge sorcerers have gone to stop their own crimes from being discovered.

The men might assume she got scared and simply ran. They won't even know to mourn her.

The full reality is obviously sinking in for Julita too. Her voice roughens with a mixture of outrage and dismay.

*They can't just— I was slaughtered right here in the city! The Watch* should *be looking into it. And the fringe scum threw me away like a soiled rag? How am I… How is anyone… It isn't* right.

I shift restlessly on my stool and take a larger gulp of my drink.

Milo leans closer. His beer-sour breath gusts over my face. "If you've got a mind to stick around for a bit…"

"Sorry," I say, not at all apologetically. "I could only drop in for long enough to grab a quick drink. Good to see you're doing well."

I drain the last of the spritz and slide off my stool. Milo makes a grab for my arm, but when I jerk out of the way, he doesn't follow me.

I stride back out to the street, both my mind and my stomach stewing with everything I took in.

Julita pipes up again, sounding more collected but still raw. *What are you doing now?*

I could leave and tune out the voice in my head until she fades away or dislodges herself in her frustration. It still isn't my business. It's not my problem to solve.

But she's here. I've got her.

I'm the only person who knows what happened to her who might care enough to see that her story doesn't end with its final chapters missing.

The assholes who did this to her aren't just a threat to the haughty rich in their fancy castle of a school. Their experiments in vicious magic could destroy every person I've spent the last eight years trying to help.

If I turn my back on my ghostly guest, I'm turning my back on all of them.

And that might be even worse than anything I've done before.

I set off toward a shop with a tendril of greenish smoke wafting from a side window. "I'm going to ask a few more questions. And then the next time we see your friends, I'll tell them everything I possibly can that'll take those bastards down."

# NINE

As I raise Julita's bracelet to the gargoyle at the college gate, my heart gives a swift stutter. I swallow against the dryness of my mouth.

Stepping through the opening door, I risk a murmur. "You're sure the password won't have changed since last time?"

The men Julita's working with only have their meetings every two days. It's been three now since she was stabbed in the alley.

Julita's back to what seems to be her usual unflappably confident self. *They only change it once a week, and the last time was six days ago. I'm sure of that. We're good.*

I'd have more faith in her sense of time if she had her own corporeal body to experience it with. Girding myself, I march onward.

*Lively fleas—*

"I remember."

Lively fleas rip from royalty like ribbons. An absurd phrase, but I'm in the habit of committing every bit of information I can glean to memory. Left, forward, right, forward, right, left, right.

When the door to the first courtyard opens up in front of me with no blare of a conjured alarm or onslaught of furious guards, I exhale in a rush. My nerves shudder at the deluge of cleansing magic, but it washes over me in an instant, and I'm through.

A couple of men are walking over to the gate hand-in-hand. I veer around them on my stroll toward the main college building and wait until they've disappeared through the gate before speaking to my ghostly passenger again.

"I'm going to tell them, I'll let them ask you any questions they can think of that would help them investigate—and then we're done."

The statement feels more like a question than I'm comfortable with. We've already hashed the plan out, but I don't know how much good faith I can expect from my unwanted guest once we're back on her turf.

*An incredibly fair deal,* Julita says in a reassuring tone. *I'll depart from your body if I can determine how, and if I can't right away, I'll keep my thoughts to myself while I work it out.*

She sounds like she means it, but her dormmate's accusing words linger alongside the tingle of

Julita's presence in the back of my skull. She could say anything she wants to keep me cooperating—it's not as if I have any idea how to force the issue if she goes back on her word.

But it doesn't really matter. This is the right thing to do.

I'm the one controlling my body. I can make sure I walk back out of here once I've fulfilled the mission I agreed to.

The rest I'll deal with when I get there.

Julita waits patiently while I navigate the campus, taking the same route she directed me on last time. When I tap and tug the sconce beside the tapestry of Signy, she lets out a bright chuckle. *You really do have quite the memory.*

"I had to hone every skill I could," I murmur as I step into the hidden staircase. Every skill other than the riven magic that would both drive me mad and bring the rage of the royal family down on my head. Or rather, on my neck.

From my first days on the streets, I decided I'd just have to make myself as brilliant as possible at everything possible so that I never truly *needed* my monstrous power to survive. So far it's worked out pretty well, my current dilemma notwithstanding.

*I'm lucky it was you who stumbled on me,* Julita says. *I can't imagine if—*

My feet hit the floor of the archives room on the other side of the magical passage, and both Julita's voice and my breath cut off with the slam of a hand against my throat.

A hand of molded clay rather than flesh, hard enough to choke me with that first jab.

Stavros shoves me back against the reformed wall, his dark eyes searing into mine. A pinch of pain at the base of my throat tells me he's brought a blade to bear just below his restraining hand.

His mouth twists into a smile so cutting it might as well be a sneer. "So, you came back. Wonderful. Now you can tell us who you really are."

My pulse thunders, and my magic flares through my chest with the urge to hurl him off me. I can't reach the knife in my boot or those under my skirts.

I clamp my hands into fists, reining in the burn, and gasp a ragged breath.

Does he know what I'm repressing? Did he figure it out somehow?

In my head, Julita is sputtering. *What under the gods' gaze does he think he's doing?*

"I came to help," I manage to rasp past the harsh pressure of Stavros's hand.

The other men come into view around Stavros, their expressions stormy.

A deep frown taints Casimir's gorgeous face. "If you wanted to help Julita, then she'd be here."

Alek has his lean arms crossed tightly over his chest. "We've looked into your story. There's no one named Ivy whose family lives in Nikodi."

Shit and smitings. I'd be glad that they don't sound as if they've discovered my magic, but they're at least two steps ahead of me in my confession. Which'll make it look more like they caught me out than like I'm coming clean on my own.

I scramble for the right thing to say, because blurting out, "I've got your friend's ghost in my head!" doesn't seem likely to go over well as an opening.

At the same moment, my riven magic decides to turn on me too. In response to my defiance, it digs into every crevice in my torso with a sensation like piercing claws.

All I can do is gasp again and tense my muscles against the agony.

Good job, stupid fucking sorcery. Punish me because I strangely don't think it's a fantastic idea to show off my illegal power directly in front of a guy who's dragged people like me straight to the gallows.

*What's happening to you?* Julita asks frantically. *Tell them what's going on. Tell them— Oh, Great God help me—*

Dizziness washes over me, scrambling my thoughts—and, to my relief, distracting me from the pain. Giving me just enough wherewithal to recognize what's happening.

She did this before, when she was first in my head, when she hadn't talked to me yet. She's trying to take me over.

"You—" I snap before I clamp down on my frustration, and then I wrestle everything inside me into submission: the magic, its resentful claws, the rebellious ghost attempting to claim my body.

This will not be the last page in my life's story.

Stavros appears to decide he's waited long enough for a coherent answer. He wrenches me around and slams me down in a chair near one of the shelves of records.

Benedikt darts over to yank a rope around my chest and knot it behind me, pinning my arms to my sides.

I might have been able to throw off the binding before he finished tying it if I gave it a shot, but fighting these men isn't going to prove my innocence. And I don't like my chances four against one, especially when the four includes a decorated general.

Julita speaks up with a hint of a quaver in her voice. *I'm sorry. I didn't mean to do it—I panicked about what would happen if I didn't jump in. It won't happen again.*

I don't know if I believe her, but I have bigger problems at the moment.

With the agony of my magic's fit of frustration ebbing, I find my voice. "I came today to tell you the truth. To tell you what happened to Julita."

Stavros looms over me, his chiseled face way too striking when he's this coolly fierce. He only holds my gaze for a second before sweeping his attention over the rest of my body. "Is that so? And why didn't you tell us in the first place?"

"Because the truth sounds fucking insane." I can't stop myself from glowering at him. My magic keeps roiling inside me, pricking at my innards, which isn't improving my mood. "I thought it was easier that way, and you'd find out everything else you need to know later. But it turns out that won't happen, so here I am."

If Stavros is cool, then Alek is outright ice. "Why should we believe anything you say now?"

My gaze slides to his masked face. Even partly covered, I can tell his expression is grim. "Why don't you hear it and then decide? What exactly do you think my evil plan here would be?"

Benedikt tips his golden head back against the shelves. "As much as I'd like to think you simply enjoy our company, it seems more probable that you were spying on our plans. Or attempting to mislead us. Or both."

*You should just tell them,* Julita murmurs. *They're only doing this because they're worried about me.*

I don't want to feel particularly sympathetic to the men who are currently holding me bound and under blade, but their response does make sense. And shows an almost admirable protective devotion to their missing friend—if that's really all they see her as.

I wet my lips. Spilling the beans is going to be even more awkward than I thought.

"You've guessed that something's gone wrong for Julita," I venture, letting my noble diction slide. What does it matter when they'll know in a minute or two how far from noble I am? "That's why you checked the records for me?"

"She's been missing for three *days*," Alek spits out. "She wouldn't leave for that long without giving us any idea what lead she's following."

Casimir nods, but his voice is softer. "You'd be the last person who saw her. You have her bracelet."

Stavros has straightened up over me, making his massive frame even more intimidating. He adjusts the short sword in his grasp casually but with an ease that speaks of his skill. "I think we should be the ones asking the questions, and you should be answering. What happened to Julita? Let's hear everything you know, and be quick about it."

I raise my chin. "To be clear from the start, *I* didn't do anything to hurt her. These scourge sorcerers you're after must have figured out she was on their trail. I was going about my business in Slaughterwell, and I heard a cry. I found—"

Seeing how the men's stances have stiffened, I hesitate. Am I really going to toss their friend's murder in their faces this bluntly?

"You found what?" Stavros prods.

I guess there really isn't any way around it.

"I found her lying in an alley with a knife through her neck," I say, a little quieter than before. "I tried to stop the bleeding, but the wound was so—"

Alek flinches. "She's *dead?*" His hand flicks down his front in the gesture of the divinities.

Casimir's pine-green eyes have widened. Stavros's broad shoulders flex as if he's bracing for the answer.

There's only one I can possibly give. "Yes."

Benedikt sags against the shelves, the cockiness of his stance deflating.

Alek's lips part, but no sound comes out. He takes a few steps backward to sink into one of the chairs around the central desk and drops his head into his hands.

Stavros works his jaw, his eyes outright blazing, his hand clenching around the grip of his sword. But when he speaks, his voice is as coolly confident as ever. "Those gods-damned wretches. They'll regret every drop of her blood they spilled ten times over. We'll see how much they like their sorcery then."

"If we'd gone with her instead of letting her carry out her investigations alone…" Casimir says in a thin voice. His rosy skin has faded to a sickly pallor.

Benedikt snorts, though he still looks sick himself. "As if any of us were 'letting' Jules do anything. She wouldn't have let *us* expose ourselves that way." His pale gaze flicks to me again with sharper focus. "Assuming the imposter is telling the truth and not spinning a lovely tale to hide her own wrongdoing."

Alek's head jerks up. The combined weight of four hostile stares sets my skin crawling.

I grimace at them. "Why would I have done anything to Julita? I didn't even know her before the moment I found her."

Stavros cocks his head, considering. His gaze flicks away and back to me. "The conspirators could have paid you off."

"Paid you to spy on us too," Benedikt adds, warming up to his theory. "Very clever."

"I wouldn't have taken a job like that," I say. "And I haven't told you everything yet. I came to talk to you in the first place because— This is the part that sounds insane. When I was trying to help Julita and she died, somehow or other, her soul… passed into me."

Stavros's eyebrows arch. Casimir blinks, peering at me more intently as if he thinks he might see a glimmer of the woman he obviously cared about through my flesh.

Benedikt barks a laugh. "Now *that's* a story for the ages! We're getting a real tall tale."

I catch my teeth on the verge of gritting. "I know it's hard to believe, but it's true. How else would I have known how to find you? Do you really think Julita would have given you all away just because someone threatened her?"

Julita lets out an indignant huff. *Really. They should know me better.*

Alek starts to shake his head, but Stavros rakes his gaze over me. "She was made of strong stuff, but that doesn't mean she was infallible."

I glare at him. "Well, if I was lying, don't you think I'd have picked a less ridiculous lie? Look, she's with me right now. You want proof? Ask me anything only she would know, something no interrogator would possibly have thought to find out from her. It shouldn't be hard to confirm."

I have the impression of Julita clapping her hands together. *Yes. Excellent idea. They can't deny that.*

My shoulders are starting to ache from how tightly my arms are restrained at my sides, but I hold myself still with as much patience as I can muster. The men glance at each other in silent deliberation.

Casimir has knit his brow. "Have you ever heard of a partial ghostly possession, Alek?"

Alek's mouth slants at a pensive angle. "No. Nothing like what she's talking about has come up in any of the records of unusual magic I've searched out."

Stavros sighs. "She's right—there's an easy way to find out. Let's see… Something only we would know, that has nothing to do with our investigations so it wouldn't have come up in questioning. How's this: What did she tell Aleksi about his mask the last time we were all together?"

*That's easy,* Julita says immediately. *He should get himself a silver one made. It'd set off his skin wonderfully.*

That's the kind of conversation she was having while plotting to reveal a deadly conspiracy?

My voice comes out dry. "She thought he should get a silver one."

The men all go nearly as still as they did when Alek asked whether Julita was dead. Benedikt gives a low whistle.

Before he can speak, Stavros holds up his hand. It's obvious he considers himself in charge of this bunch even if he isn't rallying armies anymore.

His gaze bores into mine. "What color dress was she wearing that day?"

Interesting that *he* paid enough attention to what she was wearing that he'll be able to judge the answer.

I wouldn't have a clue what I'd had on any given day of the week if I didn't always wear pretty much the same thing, but Julita is clearly diligent about her fashion choices. *It was the lavender purple one with silver beading on the sleeves.* Then, in a conspiratorial hush as if she thinks he might overhear her otherwise, *That's his favorite.*

I meet his eyes steadily. "Lavender with silver beading on the sleeves."

Alek pipes up in a stiff voice. "What book did she suggest Casimir should pick up?"

*Honestly, how much proof do they need? The latest volume by Willam of Ockarton on musical theory.*

"Willam of Ockarton's most recent book about musical theory." I slide my gaze over each of them in turn. "Do you really think *anyone* would have thought to ask her about all this before they killed her?"

"No," Casimir says quietly. He steps closer, hesitation muting the grace of his lithe body. But as he stares at me, hope kindles in his eyes. "Jules? You're really here?"

*Oh, Cas,* Julita murmurs in a tone so fond my gut knots up. All at once, I feel like an intruder in my own body. *Tell him I'm sorry. I thought I'd taken every precaution…*

My voice comes out rough. "She's apologizing because she thinks she mustn't have been careful enough."

Benedikt has pushed off the shelves to take a better look at me. Alek's gaze is fixed on me too, his expression a mix of awe and incredulity, as if he can't wrap his head around the idea that the woman he appears to have adored ended up in a person like me.

Stavros takes a step back like he needs to get a wider view—or maybe he's giving the other men room to study me. His fingers flex around the sword's hilt, and then he shoves it into the scabbard at his waist.

"Have you tried to let her *out?*" he asks.

I give him a pointed look. "I didn't even let her *in*. It just happened—I have no idea how. And she hasn't tried to leave yet, as far as I know, because if her soul passes on at that point, there'll be no way for her to communicate with you."

Julita stirs in my head. *Are they going to untie you already? You're technically my guest—in any case, you're doing me an immense favor. They really should show better hospitality.*

My lips twitch upward of their own accord, and Alek's eyes harden again. "Is something about this situation funny to you?"

I give a brief, humorless laugh. "Not particularly. But Julita's concerned about your manners. She's a little put out that you still have me tied to a chair."

Something flashes across Stavros's face too swiftly for me to identify, but my remark must sound like the Julita he knows. He strides forward, unsheathing his sword again, and severs the rope just below my shoulder so the whole coil falls away.

I shake the loops off and spring up from the chair, my nerves jangling with discomfort at the restraints. But I don't move very far. This situation still feels far too volatile.

"You have to understand," I say, before the conversation can become any more awkward, "I'm helping Julita because she made a good case, and I don't want to see scourge sorcerers running rampant. But there's only so much I can do. You needed to know that they killed her, and I'll answer any other questions you have for her. Then I'm going to leave, and *she's* going to leave—like her soul normally would have in the first place."

"That's fair," Casimir says softly, although he looks haunted himself.

Stavros clears his throat with a hint of a scoff. "You want to get back to your life. However much of a life you have if your 'business' happens in Slaughterwell. You're obviously not noble-born. What's your real name, and what exactly *is* your business, hmm?"

I itch to make up a story, to claim some typical fringe career. But the men have already shown they'll go to great lengths to confirm my honesty.

If I want them to believe me enough to get through this conversation properly, I have to actually be honest.

I set my hands on my hips. "My name really is Ivy, and my business is mostly making sure I stay alive. I scavenge what I need."

"Scavenge," Stavros repeats sardonically. "That sounds like a polite way of saying you take what doesn't belong to you. It doesn't seem as if this is the first time you've posed as someone you're not, either. If you're planning on taking advantage of the situation and running some other con—"

"That's not what I'm here for," I interrupt, getting reacquainted with the desire to stab the infuriatingly arrogant man. "If I've ever lifted a thing or two to get by, it was only what was necessary and from people who could afford the loss."

I'm not going to give him a full accounting of my activities in the fringes. For all I know, he'd find my wealth redistribution tactics nearly as offensive as my magic.

As it is, a mocking edge creeps into his voice. "So you're a thief. Of all the people to find Julita—"

"Julita was cautious," I interrupt. "I'm sure you all know that. She wouldn't have shared her secrets with me if she'd seen any reason to distrust my motives."

Casimir glances at the former general. "She's right. Does what she did before really matter? She brought Julita to us—we should be grateful."

Alek dips his head in a jerk. "We need to find out everything she can tell us from Julita about the people who came for her."

Stavros sighs but motions for me to go ahead.

*Finally!* Julita mutters.

I suck in a breath, sharing her impatience. The sooner I'm out of this stuffy room, the better.

"The basics you already know. The knife I described to you at the last meeting—that's the weapon that killed her. She didn't see who did it. She says she felt a blast of wind right before she was stabbed, so it's possible the murderer has a gift involving weather and used it to distract her."

"And the temple you mentioned?" Alek says.

"She was on her way to check it for signs of collusion with the scourge sorcerers when she was murdered. So she assumes it is involved somehow, that the conspirators found out she was going there and decided it was better to kill her first."

Stavros rubs his jaw. "I gave a friend on the Crown's Watch an excuse to have someone keeping an eye on that area the past couple of days. So far they haven't noticed any unusual activity."

I shrug. "I can only tell you what I know. Maybe the would-be sorcerers warned the person at the temple who's been helping them and they're being extra careful now. Or maybe it was something else that made them worried about Julita."

Benedikt ambles through the room, tapping his lips in an erratic rhythm. "Did she tell anyone where she was going?"

I pause to give Julita time to answer.

*Of course not. But I was working my way through all the temples on the outskirts of the city. They might have been able to predict where I was going next.*

"No, but they might have guessed based on where she went before," I supply.

"Did she notice anyone in particular nearby when she left the college?" Casimir asks.

At Julita's *No*, I shake my head.

Stavros looks at me. "Did *you* see anyone around when you found her body?"

"No. The street was empty, and there was no one else in the alley. But I wasn't right there. There was time for someone to have taken off down the alley before I reached her."

Alek hesitates before speaking up again. "What happened to her body? Why hasn't it been found?"

I can answer that one too. "I did a little poking around through my less-than-savory connections. It seems the major criminal elements in the city were concerned that the murder of a noble in their streets would bring unwanted attention, so they cleaned things up. But it sounded as if the murder was random, as far as they were concerned. Really, if any of the black-market lords were involved, there wouldn't have been a body for *me* to find."

As Stavros grunts in response, Casimir offers me a slight but warm smile. "You know, you might not have the typical noble cadence, but you don't sound like you're fringe-born either."

My jaw tightens. "I do a lot of reading. It expands one's vocabulary, I hear."

I'm not going to share any details of my childhood when I don't have to.

"A well-read thief!" Stavros says. "Even better. Which specific alley did the murder happen in?"

While I tell him the nearest streets, Julita's presence shifts restlessly. *I wish there was something else I could tell them. Here I am, evidence of the most obvious crime these degenerates have committed, and I can't even give the Crown's Watch proof!*

The men don't seem to know what else to prod her about either. But in their momentary silence, I remember my peace offering.

I reach back through my memory for the names I got out of the Crow's Close apothecary last night. "I did also take the time to do some looking into the dartling eggshell powder you were trying to track down. Someone involved in underground dealings was able to give me the names of three shops that he sometimes provides a supply to for selling unofficially."

Alek's eyes brighten. "What were those?"

I rattle off the three names, and his gaze goes briefly distant as he must commit the information to memory. I suppose like me he has his reasons for not wanting to keep a written record of this particular endeavor.

Benedikt gives me a bemused look. "You decided to chase down that fact out of the blue?"

"Not out of the blue. Julita explained why it was significant. I was already asking around about her murder. I figured I might as well check that too, since it could make a difference."

All at once, Casimir's smile widens. "Yes, it could. And Inganne has blessed me with a fantastic idea."

I look at him warily. "What?"

"Julita could pick up on all kinds of clues that we couldn't because of her observations of her brother's attempted rituals," he says. "Without her, the rest of us wouldn't have realized the problem in the first place. I don't know how far we'll get without her. But we don't have to be without her."

Benedikt lets out a sputter of a chuckle as he spins toward the other man. "You can't really be suggesting—"

Casimir splays his slender hands. "Why not? She's still *here*. She and Ivy are obviously getting along reasonably well. And Ivy played noble well enough that we all believed it during our first meeting. If we can set her up in the school, she can keep investigating with us."

He glances back at me, his eyes sparkling eagerly. "You said there's only so much you can do—but you can do this too. It could make a huge difference."

Alek frowns. "We do need to catch the conspirators as quickly as possible. I don't like how much the daimon are already acting up around the school. But we can't enroll a new student out of nowhere with no credentials or family history."

"She doesn't have to be a student." Casimir snaps his fingers. "Stav, you were about to put out a call for a new assistant. Take Ivy on. That gives her every excuse to roam the college."

"I suppose I could adjust the right records so anyone else who looks would see a family with a daughter named Ivy living in Nikodi..." Alek says hesitantly.

I open my mouth to protest, but the former general beats me to it. "Hold on a second. I need an assistant who can actually *assist*, not some scrawny Slaughterwell street rat."

Just like that, I'm bristling. "I'll have you know I could have stabbed you a dozen times already if I wasn't being nice."

Stavros snorts. "Maybe you'd like to think so."

If he had any idea the men twice my size I've had to fend off, the aim and reflexes I've spent years honing. He's faced the danger of warfare, sure, but he has no clue what it's like battling just to stay alive when you have nothing.

*Er, Ivy...* Julita says. *You do remember he's one of the most celebrated soldiers in the kingdom, right?*

Oh, I haven't forgotten for a second.

"You want to try me?" I retort, my fingers itching for my nearest knife.

A gleam feral enough to be unnerving lights in Stavros's eyes. "Really? If you insist, I suppose a *very* brief demonstration could set the matter to rest for everyone. Let's see you strip first."

My jaw drops. "Excuse me?"

He flicks his hand to indicate my dress. "No one can fight at their best in a gown. And if we're doing this, I want to have a look at what kind of muscle you're working with. So, strip."

# TEN

Casimir gives a faint cough. "Ah, Stavros, this wasn't quite what I had in—"

The former general jabs his finger in the courtesan's direction. "It was your idea. I wouldn't think *you* would have your sensibilities offended by a woman's bare limbs."

Bare *limbs*. He doesn't want me getting totally naked, just taking off the dress so I can move more easily in my underclothes.

It's still ridiculous. I didn't even want to linger in the college for more than an hour today.

But I've spent the past three days getting yanked in all kinds of directions I wouldn't have chosen, and this is one thing I know I can do all on my own.

It'd be worth a bushel of gold to knock the cocky expression off this asshole's face.

From his sharp grin of anticipation, I can't tell whether the massive man is getting off more on the idea that I *will* accept his challenge or that I'll fold. Either way, he expects to prove me a weakling.

Like it hasn't taken plenty of guts just walking into this den of snakes.

I tweak the skirt of my faux-silk dress, considering the coverage beneath. The last thing I want is any of these men noticing the unmarked skin between my breasts.

Not having dedicated oneself to a godlen and accepted their brand at twelve isn't an executable crime like the riven magic that prompted my decision, but it's rare enough that the godless are viewed with suspicion. I'd rather not raise any questions about why I've forgone the standard ritual and shunned the gods' favor.

But the short, sleeveless shift I have on is made of the same densely woven cotton as my drawers. The neckline rests just below that of the dress, which only skims my collarbones.

Unless one of Julita's men takes a mind to yank the collar forward and peer down my chest, I'm safe.

I wouldn't assume that's impossible if I was here alone, but they know Julita is watching too. I can't imagine any of them manhandling me too badly while I'm hosting her in my body.

I match Stavros's confident, nonchalant air. "Fine." Then I reach behind myself to loosen the laces.

Casimir slips over to assist, leaning close enough that the warmth of his graceful body tickles over me with a whiff of honeyed sandalwood. "You really don't have to do this. He's being a prick."

"A prick who wants to know what I'm supposedly hiring on." Stavros swipes his hands together and props himself against the desk as he watches. "Let's not take too long about it. I do have other things to do, Thief."

My jaw clenches. "I apologize for not having the gift of being able to send my clothes into thin air with the snap of a finger."

Benedikt guffaws. "Now that would be a talent worth having."

Ignoring the gazes trained on me, I step away from Casimir and shimmy out of the loosened dress. As it pools around my boots, leaving me in my underthings and the plain petticoat that would never have passed for a noble's if anyone had been able to see it, Stavros gives his head the odd twitch I noticed when we first met and narrows his eyes.

Maybe noticing that my arms, while gangly, have plenty of wiry muscle packed onto them that was previously hidden by my sleeves. Maybe re-evaluating his assessment just a tad already.

Then Casimir inhales sharply. "What happened to you? Who *did* this?"

He reaches a tentative hand toward my back but stops a few inches shy of the skin.

Oh. Right. I'm so used to my scars that I didn't consider how they'd be visible at the top of my shoulder blades.

"It was a long time ago and not a big deal," I say curtly, but Stavros is already striding over.

He makes another twitching gesture with his head before peering at the mottled ridges that protrude from beneath my shift. "Those look like whip lashes. That's not a typical punishment for stealing." His tone darkens. "What worse crime did you commit?"

Of course he'd assume that.

I make my voice as hard and cool as I can. "It wasn't a whip, and it wasn't punishment for a crime." At least, not in the way he's thinking. "My mother was very enthusiastic with a belt. Like I said, it was a long time ago. There are reasons a person ends up fending for themselves on the streets. Can we continue?"

Casimir looks sick as the implications sink in. Stavros's mouth tightens, but after his gaze slides over my back again, he eases aside.

Can he tell the difference between a whip and a belt when he looks closely?

I don't really care how much he believes me. Mostly I want them to stop looking at the evidence that I'm not totally unbreakable.

Julita's obviously caught on too, maybe more clearly than any of the men, since she's seen how I live in full detail. *Gods, Ivy. Your* parents *did that to you? I can't imagine—I didn't realize—*

"It's fine," I say softly, just to her, not caring what the men make of the statement.

Benedikt lifts his chin toward the white ribbon tied around my upper arm. "What's that for?"

An image flashes through my mind of the length of white rippling through Linzi's hair as my little sister scampered through our yard. I brush my fingers over the worn fabric with a pang through my chest. "Just a memento I like to keep on me."

To make sure I never forget what I am, even if I don't want anyone else finding out.

I glance toward the thin belt tucked under the waistline of my shabby petticoat. "Should I strip my weapons too, or am I allowed to keep those as part of the test?"

Alek lets out a strangled sound, but Stavros takes the question in stride. He touches the pommel of his short sword. "Let's keep it to one each. It wouldn't do to give you an unfair advantage."

He's returned to his cocky tone that walks the line between teasing and outright mockery. He thinks my question was funny, does he?

I undo the tie on the petticoat and let that fall too. Then I reach for the small sheaths on the belt, the same beige as the fabric of my undergarments to blend in.

One knife, two knives, tiny enough that they barely added any bulk to my hips but sharp enough to gut a man. I set those on the nearest shelf in front of the dusty leather volumes there and then bend down to retrieve one slightly longer blade from each boot. I kept my favorite in my left hand while I set aside the other.

Benedikt breaks into chortling laughter. "She carries more metal than you do, Stav. Oh, I do like this one. Julita picked well."

*I don't think picked is the right word,* Julita remarks, and pauses. *But it's hard to imagine getting a better companion for this situation. Kosmel must have smiled on me.*

I don't bother to correct Benedikt. My attention remains on my theoretical opponent.

Stavros has marked my show of disarming with a twist of his mouth that looks as though it's not sure whether to become a grin or a grimace. When I meet his eyes, he lets out a brief chuckle and draws his sword. "Is that all?"

"As much as it was worth bothering with in that dress," I say, rolling my shoulders. "Am I suitably on display for your evaluation?"

I'd imagine all four of these men have seen women in much greater undress than my current state. I'm only slightly less covered than if I were in summer peasant garb. *I've* been much more undressed with more than one man before, albeit under very different circumstances.

Still, my skin shivers under the rake of the former general's gaze. I resist the urge to peek down and confirm that my lack of a godlen brand isn't somehow blazing through my shift.

This might not have been my wisest move ever. But I can't back down now.

"It'll do," Stavros says. "Let's see how well you can use that toy."

Without any further warning, he lunges.

Thankfully, I know better than to trust a noble or an arrogant asshole to play fair. I've been tensed for attack since the moment I grasped my knife.

The former general might be fast for his size, but I'm faster—and there's not a whole lot of me for him to grab. I whip to the side and duck under the sweep of his prosthetic hand.

As I dart behind him, he yanks his massive frame around to face me again. He waggles his arm with the prosthetic. "You're lucky. I'm equipped for keeping up appearances right now, not for a fight."

I snort. "I'm not sure why it matters when you didn't come close to touching me regardless."

Benedikt and Casimir have pulled back to the edges of the room. Alek retreats from the desk, his lips pursing beneath his mask. "Do we really need to do this *here*?"

"I won't damage your precious archives, scholar," Stavros says. "Don't worry, it'll be over soon enough."

Oh, he thinks so, does he?

He springs forward again with a little more respect, feinting to one side and pivoting in the other direction. I have to skid across the floor even lower to avoid a blow, but I slide by close enough to rap the grip of my knife against his muscular calf. "First blood."

Symbolically, anyway.

Stavros mutters a curse, but a fierce light has come into his eyes that's almost giddy. It gives him a maniacal air that sets off a peal of warning through my nerves.

He gives his head that odd tiny shake again, and I frown at him. "What are you doing when you twitch your head like that?"

His grimace-y grin widens. "Let's stay on topic."

Of course, Julita knows. *It's because of his battle injury. It messed with his sight. He can't fully focus on anything for more than a second or—*

I miss the rest of her answer and any chance to ponder the implications of the former general being partly blind when Stavros barrels forward.

It's clear in an instant that he was holding back before. I hope to the gods he isn't even now.

He jabs left and right, shifting on his feet to block my escape, corralling me into a corner. I've never faced an opponent like this.

My heart thumps faster. I flick out my knife to deflect a swipe of his sword that would have sliced open the bare skin above my shift's collar if he wasn't going to temper the strike. The impact reverberates through my bones.

He *is* going to pull his punches, right? Surely he isn't planning to actually spill *my* blood.

It's getting harder to tell. Up until this point, my magic has kept to a persistent but low-level nagging, knowing I asked for this fight, that it's not meant to be actually threatening. Now my power starts to prick more deeply at my innards for me to bring it to bear.

I make a few more testing jabs, but Stavros deflects all of them, coming on like a windstorm. I don't have much choice but to vault onto the desk and leap from there right over his head.

One of the other men takes a sharp breath, but even that move doesn't faze Stavros. He's whirled around before my feet have even smacked into the ground. I nearly trip over them scrambling away from his renewed onslaught.

Gods above, he is a warrior through and through. I might admire his skill a little if he wasn't attempting to belittle me with it.

Despite my sparse clothing, sweat trickles down my back. I feel like I've held my own far better than he could have expected—well enough to prove I don't deserve his mockery.

But he's still going to look down his nose at me if he wins, as if I can be blamed for not having the might of a war-hardened soldier.

If this were a real fight, if I thought I was battling for my life, I'd have already flung my knife into his chest or his gut. It's a little hard to prove that without dealing a potentially fatal wound, though.

Well, sometimes a draw is plenty good enough to settle the score.

I weave and bob, but Stavros is boxing me in even more tightly than before, and there's no handy desk at this end of the room. I can feel the impending moment when he'll bowl me right over.

At any second, my power will attempt to disembowel me for ignoring its demands to help.

So I push into his attacks instead, picking my time, embracing the fight for my own purposes.

Stavros shoves me against the wall with his prosthetic hand. My right arm jerks up against his other wrist to slow the slice of his sword toward my throat.

Aiming the full intensity of his wild grin at me, he presses against my blocking arm to show how easily he could overcome my strength with the power of his bulging shoulders. His scent wafts over me, heated with a smoky peppery bite.

This close, I realize there's something chaotic about his dark eyes too. The ring of deep brown around the pupil blends into a rich blue around the edges, as if his makers couldn't quite decide what color they should be.

If he truly can't focus his gaze that well, he's doing a damned good job of faking it.

He swivels his blade to tap the flat against my throat. "And that's where you'd be dead."

I smile back at him. "And you'd be rutting with a stump."

Stavros's gaze snaps downward—to where my knife is poised just above his groin. Nothing but the fabric of his trousers lies between his dick and my *very* sharp blade.

If he's honest with himself, he'll have to recognize that I could have cut off one very important appendage before he managed to get his sword into my neck.

There's a moment of silence as he takes in our pose. Benedikt breaks it with a whoop and a round of applause. "You two should start putting on shows. I'd pay good money to watch that again."

With a dismissive sound, Stavros pushes away from me. He rams his sword into its scabbard and rakes his fingers through his dark hair, his expression gone coolly implacable again.

I like him better when he looks like a madman.

The thought shakes me as if I've been slapped. In the middle of revealing Julita's death and sparring with the man both verbally and physically, I started to forget he's the same smug general who smiled while a riven sorcerer like me swung from a noose.

I shouldn't *like* him any which way. He really would slit my throat if he knew of the power I'm hiding.

Julita has gotten a little breathless. *Oh, that was brilliant. He's never going to live that down. Nicely played, Ivy.*

Before I can decide how to feel about her eager praise, Casimir eases toward us again, his head tilted to the side with an amused air. "Well, I think we've seen that Ivy is at least fully capable of acting as your assistant. Unless you had duties that require sluggishness."

"No," Stavros says noncommittally. "She'll do. But are *we* really going to do this? Send a petty criminal to mingle with your peers?"

I'd bristle all over again at the remark if he hadn't reminded me what the whole challenge was supposedly about in the first place. "Just a second—"

"We need Julita," Alek says firmly before I can go on. "And she comes with Ivy. That's all there is to it."

I cross my arms. "There is more to it. I get some say. Who says I *want* to 'mingle' with the lot of you?"

Alek stares at me. "But you just— What was the fight for, if you aren't planning on staying?"

I wave my knife toward Stavros before tucking it back into my boot and reaching for my discarded petticoat. "For reminding him not to assume he can judge someone based on knowing a whole three things about them."

Casimir makes his protest in a gentler fashion. "You said you wanted to help—that you don't want to see the scourge sorcerers succeed. There's no better way you can do that than by helping our investigations right here."

"You mean by doing way more than any of *you* have had to. Would you toss aside your whole life to spy on people who hate you?"

"None of us hate you," Casimir says.

At the same moment, Stavros guffaws. "So eager to get back to thieving?"

I cast my gaze toward the former general and give the courtesan a pointed look. Stavros rolls his eyes skyward. "I don't hate you. I will think less of you if all that showing off was only for your ego."

I wrinkle my nose at him. "And why were *you* doing it, exactly?"

Before he has to answer, Alek speaks up again. "But it'll affect you too if the scourge sorcerers get bolder. If they draw more people into their cult without being checked. You must know about the Great Retribution—"

"Yes," I snap. "We do hear the stories even in the gutter."

But his comment hits on the reason I came here in the first place, the reason I listened to Julita at all. All the people these four men don't care about, who'll suffer more than they could conceive of if the godlen burn the continent in punishment all over again.

Julita remains unusually silent. Maybe she's giving me space to make my own decision.

It's not as if it's any secret what course of action she'd prefer.

If she insisted, I think I'd put my foot down and march right out of there. But faced with nothing but the turmoil of my own thoughts in my head, I hesitate.

"I'm not saying no. I just—it's a lot. You could at least give me a chance to think about it before you start building plans around me."

Benedikt pipes up. "I'd say she has a point."

Stavros sinks into one of the chairs and sprawls out his legs. "Think away. But I do have a staff meeting where I'll be missed happening in an hour."

"Wonderful," I mutter. Why am I even considering their scheme? I should walk out of here like I intended and put as much distance between me and the whole college as—

A vibration passes through the air, so faint I don't think any of the men pick up on it. The sense of it quivers through my broken soul.

But they couldn't fail to notice the cracking sound or the spidery line that abruptly splits through two of the stones lining the unplastered basement walls between two of the shelving units. A rain of fine dust and a few pebbles drizzle onto the floor.

Benedikt shudders. "Those damned daimon."

"They can't help it," Casimir says. "They're unsettled—even more than we are."

Alek's expression has tensed. "It's only going to get worse as the scoundrels get bolder with their sorcery. We can't know how long it'll take before the godlen themselves realize. They can't pay close attention to every single gift they dole out across the continent, but if those gifts start being used to challenge their divine power, it won't escape their notice for long."

The scholar's gaze fixes on me. "Helping us will be a sacrifice, but how is it not worth it? Do you really want to find out how the godlen will judge you if they discover that you could have stood in the way and didn't?"

If he thinks the threat of godly punishment is going to sway me, he couldn't be farther from the mark. If they ever pay that much attention to me, I'm toast for reasons already long established.

But his words shake loose something else inside me, like a crack splitting down my center to let a small glow of unexpected hope seep through.

It *would* be a sacrifice.

A huge one. I'd pretty much be giving my whole life over to preventing a catastrophe that both offends the gods and could destroy thousands of innocent people.

If I pull it off... If I make myself the key to exposing the conspiracy and seeing the despicable sorcerers brought to justice, while risking my neck the whole time... *Could* I walk into the Temple of the Crown and ask for a blessing?

Would the godlen believe I'd earned the boon of having my soul healed, my magic wiped away, and my past crimes forgiven?

I've never imagined there was any way I could fully absolve myself even in my own conscience. This—this is an opportunity that doesn't come along in most people's lifetimes.

I'm never going to be another Signy, brandishing my sword on a mountaintop against the forces of oppression. But I can play hero just like I can play noble, right?

And as heroes go, playing is essentially the same as being if I can manage to see the task through.

My mind darts to the realities of the life I would be leaving behind. The dark attic with scraps of fabric for a bed. The constant wariness as I roam the streets.

There's my makeshift family of the fringes too, but I'll be serving them even better if I prevent another retribution than by tossing a few coins their way.

A swell of resolve rushes up inside me. I wet my lips and push the words out before I lose my nerve.

"All right. I'm in."

# ELEVEN

It takes me approximately five minutes to start regretting my boldness. Right at the point when Stavros shoves open the door he's led me to on the fourth floor of the Domi and says, "These are my quarters. You'll be staying here."

My mouth opens and closes and opens again. "What? Assistants don't get their own rooms?"

I'm going to be living in the same space as the man who's hunted people like me?

He ushers me inside with a tap of my back that I dart forward to escape. We step into a living space about the same size as the common room Julita shared with nine other students.

The space is laid out with a sofa and two armchairs around a hearth, an expansive marlwood desk surrounded by matching bookshelves, a small but elegant dining table with four chairs around it, and a cabinet that holds several expensive-looking liquor bottles.

A tiny private shrine to Sabrelle stands in the corner, the table laid with a scarlet cloth. A wooden carving placed in the middle shows a stallion and a stag holding up the godlen of warfare and might's sharply curving sigil.

I'll be keeping far away from that.

Stavros kicks the door shut behind us and gives me one of those inscrutable looks as if I've both amused and pissed him off. "Assistants who are also students live in the student dorms. Assistants who go through the standard official process to get hired on by the college administration share two-bedroom apartments on the staff floor. Assistants we don't want anyone looking too closely at get the sofa."

I wrinkle my nose at his dry tone. "And no one's going to find *that* suspicious?"

"I'm allowed a few whims. I'll just tell them I so *desperately* needed someone of your talents as my assistant that I required your presence from daybreak onward."

One corner of his mouth crooks up in a grin, which annoyingly makes him even more imposingly attractive than before. "That means I'll need to put you to work shortly. Around students and other staff, you'll need to remember to refer to me by my proper professorial title—Ster. Stavros."

"Because you're obviously a paragon of wisdom," I say cooperatively. Although maybe it suits him —it is pretty arrogant of professors to call themselves by a shorter form of Estera, the godlen of learning and knowledge, as if they're lesser divinities themselves.

Stavros ignores my understated sarcasm. He sweeps his gaze over me, making my skin itch in awareness of his assessment. "And I'd better find some training clothes so you won't look totally ridiculous."

He spins on his heel and reaches for the gleaming doorknob. "I'll be back in an hour or so. Try not to steal anything in the meantime."

"I wouldn't—" I start to protest, but he's gone before I can make an effective retort.

*That's just Stav for you,* Julita says in mild consolation. *You don't have to worry about staying here. He can be both a brute and an ass, but when it comes to anything more intimate, he'll behave like the gentleman he is.*

Does she think I was worried about him coming on to me?

"I'm used to having my own space," I say. "I don't love that he could barge into the room at any moment."

*Ivy, your previous bedroom was a dust-choked attic you had to flee every morning before the legitimate inhabitants caught you.*

"I know. But it was just me at night."

*I think you'll find a way to survive.*

Now *she's* taking on that dry tone with me, as if I'm being absurd to have standards of privacy.

I can't say what I'm really worried about, which is basically that he'll kill me. Or rather, drag me off so the king can have me killed.

It amounts to the same thing.

Although with the way this situation is going, the greatest risk might be that at some point he's going to irritate me so much that I kill *him*—which'll put me up for execution anyway, so there's no point in debating the details.

I venture a little farther into the room. With each inhalation, the smell of the place seeps deeper into my lungs: the polished wood, a faint lingering tang of fancy alcohol, a more acrid note that I think might be the oil nobles use to protect their swords.

Lovely.

And there's also, when I step closer to the door left ajar that I assume leads to Stavros's bedroom, a whiff of the smoky pepper scent that comes from the man himself.

I'm going to be *steeping* in him. I'll take the dusty books any day.

Julita gathers herself in a way I can sense before she speaks. *Ivy… What's really going on with the pain you feel? You were obviously in significant physical distress after Stavros grabbed you in the archives room, and it wasn't anything he did directly. I've felt it a little bit here and there before, but that was… unnerving.*

Oh, it's unnerving for *her*?

I bite back a snarky reply, my stomach knotting as I consider my answer. Even if I control everything she can tell the outside world, I don't really want her knowing exactly who—and what— she's ended up tied to.

She could definitely make my life more difficult.

"I've got a bit of a nervous condition," I improvise. "Chronic pain. It acts up the most when something particularly jarring and threatening happens, that's all. Most things don't faze me like that."

*No, I suppose not.*

My uninvited guest doesn't sound totally convinced. I decide a change in subject is in order.

"How did you end up roping the man who was recently the most exalted general in all of Silana into helping you?" I ask, pausing by the built-in bookshelves. My fingers skim over the spines of historical treatises, military philosophy and strategy, and a few on equestrianism that I itch to pull out and flip through.

Stavros would probably consider that theft.

*It wasn't that hard,* Julita says in a familiar coy tone. *He'd fallen from grace, and what better way to prove he can still defend the country than by routing out a bunch of scourge sorcerers who've already threatened the royal family?*

And she felt comfortable walking up to him and pitching her case just like that?

Well, probably not just like that. It isn't hard to picture the woman whose image lingers ephemerally in my head slipping over to his side at some school event and making a few leading remarks.

Reeling him in around her finger the way Anya accused her of doing regularly.

I cock my head. "You wanted him on your side because he has the best chance of stopping the sorcerers once you figure out who they are?"

*He has the king's trust and respect. When we're sure of the details, he'll ensure the problem is dealt with swiftly and effectively.* She pauses with a short laugh. *And I did hope that having him around would make* me *a little safer, but obviously that benefit didn't extend outside our meetings.*

I lean against the edge of Stavros's desk, careful not to displace anything. "What about the others? How do they fit in?"

*Oh, you should find all of them even easier to handle than Stavros. Benedikt's on the outskirts of the royal family, as I'm sure he'll tell you about sooner rather than later. He pretends he doesn't care, but he's still tempted by potential glory. And he's friendly with just about everyone in both the college and the palace, so he picks up a wide range of gossip.*

"Alek is a scholar," I fill in. "You wanted someone who could access all the records and delve into research when necessary."

*There, you're catching on quickly.* Julita titters again. *Alek was an easy choice. He barely speaks to anyone, so he clearly got into the scholarship division based on actual work and not social influence. And he's insecure enough that it only took a little flattery for him to jump at the chance to help.*

My stomach twists at the way she speaks about the masked scholar's weaknesses. Would he be so concerned about her if he knew how she actually sees him?

Would any of them?

I swallow down my discomfort. They made their own decisions to get involved, just like I did.

"And the courtesan?"

*Well, Cas can find out other kinds of gossip, the sorts of things his patrons might only babble about while they're feeling particularly… content. He's good at picking up on people's intentions—when they're lying and things like that. The companionship division is keen on attentiveness. And he's so eager to please that he couldn't resist yet another way to do that.*

"Quite the team you've assembled, then," I mutter.

Before Julita can respond, a soft knock sounds on the door.

I freeze, unsure whether I should admit to being here. It's obviously not Stavros—he wouldn't have knocked.

Is anyone else supposed to know he has a new assistant yet?

I'm saved from that dilemma by an equally soft voice carrying through the thick wood. "Ivy, it's just Casimir. I brought you a few things."

My skin prickles as if my conversation with Julita might have somehow summoned him. What would *he* have brought me?

I push away from the desk. "Oh, er, all right. Come in."

The courtesan breezes inside, swiftly but with a presence so warm it's hard to feel wary. There's a bundle of a few different colored fabrics in his arms, silk by the sheen of them.

Casimir flashes one of his bright smiles at me. "I know Stavros can get you equipped for the official work you'll be doing as his assistant. I suspected he might neglect the *real* work, which is blending in during leisure time. That's when people let down their guards."

It is true that I'm unlikely to be invited into any conversations around the dining hall or strolling in the gardens while I'm dressed in fighting gear. And no noble lady could get away with wearing the exact same dress every day.

Casimir ambles over to the sofa and unfurls each of the gowns he brought over it in a row. Turquoise silk, then icy gray, then a forest green nearly the same shade as his eyes flow across the cushions like vibrant waterfalls.

The courtesan glances from the dresses to me and back again. "I think they should all fit well. The lacing gives some flexibility. As does…"

He reaches down and tugs at the skirts of the dresses, and my heart leaps eagerly. The folds of fabric overlap enough that you wouldn't notice unless they're yanked, but there's a slit on either side, all the way up to my thighs.

When I take a step closer to confirm the others have it too, Casimir outright beams. "I figured you'd want easier access to your assorted weaponry." His smile fades a moment later. "Especially considering what happened to Julita."

I expect he's a lot more concerned with preserving what's left of the woman he adored than my personal wellbeing, but I'll take it. "Thank you. Where did you even find these?"

"They're not actually uncommon, even if they aren't normally used for concealing blades. They make it easier for riding astride. They each have a matching divided underskirt—like flowy trousers—that'll cover your legs to your calves, but you can fix the weapons over that. I found designs with subtle pockets as well."

Riding dresses. I should have thought of that.

Even better, because then it won't matter if anyone *does* notice the slits.

"Thank you," I murmur, fingering the sleeve of the turquoise dress. "If I've got to be in a gown, this is the kind I want."

Casimir will be *very* good at his intended job if he can judge a woman's preferences this well in every area.

I really should not be thinking about any other areas he might put his skills to. Even if he's possibly the most beautiful man I've ever set eyes on. And the way he moves that sinewy body of his—

Mind out of the gutter, Ivy.

"Excellent," Casimir says. "I'll make sure Stavros puts in a request to have some finer underclothes sent up too. A lot of the women in this place might judge based on surface appearances, but they'll judge every layer of that surface if they can." His smile turns a bit sly.

I can't restrain a snort. "I don't doubt it."

Perceptive, clever, and a solid sense of humor. I guess he mustn't want for patrons.

But the comment about having Stavros handle the rest reminds me of something Julita told me. A prickle of concern passes through my gut. "Should you have come up here at all? I thought—Julita told me that the five of you act like you barely know each other in public."

Casimir shrugs, showing no sign of fear himself. "I'm reasonably well-known in the companionship division. It wouldn't be unusual for him to have asked my help outfitting his new assistant. Nothing any tongues would wag about."

I let out a light chuckle. "Totally professional." My head is already starting to ache taking in all the internal politics of this place.

*He's right,* Julita offers. *It should be safe enough. Just don't approach any of the others around campus as if you know them at all well—except for Stavros, of course.*

Naturally. Gods above, why couldn't I have become Casimir's assistant?

I mean, other than the fact that my "companionship" skills are about the direct inverse of my combat skills in effectiveness.

Casimir takes a step back as if he's going to go, but his gaze settles on my right hand. He lifts his chin toward it. "You have a gift. Is it anything that might be useful?"

I instinctively swipe my thumb over the stump where my pointer finger is missing its tip. The long-healed injury does look like it must have been a dedication ceremony sacrifice.

It was actually punishment for infringing a little too obviously on some asshole crime lord's territory when I was fourteen and getting a bit cocky. He'd have done a lot worse if there'd been much more than a few coins at stake.

It's easiest to go along with the misconception. It gives me the pretense of having dedicated myself at all.

"Probably a little," I say. "It helps me move quietly." Might as well pick a skill I already have in a totally non-magical way. I arch my eyebrows. "That's me, the sneaky thief all the way through."

I'm mocking Stavros and his barbed accusations, but Casimir's expression turns almost sad. "I'd imagine you're a lot more than that, Ivy. When I look at you and think of everything you've already risked to be here, I don't see sneakiness or deceit. I see kindness."

For the second time in this place, I find myself momentarily speechless. Casimir smoothly fills in the silence. "I'd better get going, since this is supposedly business and not a social call. I'm looking forward to hearing what you're able to discover when we meet in the archives next."

He pauses, and something in his gaze turns a bit more distant, as if he isn't really looking at me. Because he's not.

"Of course you'd find a way to stick with us no matter what, Jules," he adds for the woman inside me, his voice gone a bit rough. "We'll see this through."

Then he slips out as swiftly as he arrived.

*Dear, sweet man,* Julita says in a droll tone that doesn't hold much admiration for the descriptors.

My hackles rise in unexpected defensiveness. I inhale slowly before letting myself respond.

"He obviously cared about you a lot. They all did."

She lets out a coy little chuckle. *I wasn't going to trust them to have my back while we took on a conspiracy of scourge sorcerers otherwise.*

The way she phrases it, as if their caring was part of her strategy rather than a natural development, niggles at me. But it's really none of my business how she handled her affairs.

I shift the dresses over to one end of the sofa and sit down. To my annoyance, I can't deny that the velvet cushions are about ten times as comfortable as my "bed" back in the cloth factory.

I won't exactly be hard done by even sleeping like an afterthought in the royal college.

I get up again, planning to make a thorough survey of the room while I'm alone. But my solitude only lasts long enough for me to confirm that, yes, most of the etched bottles in the liquor cabinet would have cost more than the people of the fringes make in an average month.

I'm just ambling back to the desk and its surrounding bookcases when Stavros strides into his quarters.

He takes in me and the dresses draped on the sofa in a quick glance. I leap to explain. "Casimir came by. He knew I'd need to blend in outside of the job too."

"Hmm," Stavros says, as if he isn't quite convinced that I didn't manage to steal three dresses in the short while he was gone. He drops his own bundle—this of linen, leather, and a clink that tells me there's chainmail in the mix—onto the cushions next to the gowns. "You're all set then."

I decide to let Casimir broach the topic of undergarments as promised. The former general has spent enough time thinking about my intimate apparel today.

He fishes in his pocket and draws out a bracelet a lot like Julita's, only plain gold without any gemstones. "This will give you your own access to the front gate and these chambers. I thought it'd be best if you weren't going around flashing Julita's."

"Good point." I take off Julita's bracelet to replace it with the new one and then pause, not sure where to put it.

Stavros eyes it for a moment. "What does she want done with it?"

I raise a questioning eyebrow, but Julita's presence is already stirring. *It's just a little scrap of gold. I suppose we should hold on to it in case we need it as evidence of some kind. Stavros should be able to keep it secure.*

I hold the delicate chain out to him. "She'd like you to put it someplace safe in case we need it later."

"Always thinking ahead," he says with a note of wry affection.

As he takes the bracelet from me, he motions to the two inner doors. "Keep out of my bedroom. We can share the latrine. If you want a bath, there's a public room and a few private ones down the hall to your right."

Of course. The elite of the central ward all have running water right into their homes, while the folk of the fringes make do with wells, chamber pots, and outhouses.

It's hard to complain about that while I'm benefitting from the luxury, though.

I prop myself on the arm of the sofa. "So, what's next? How do I get started on this grand quest I've stumbled into?"

Stavros aims a mild glower at me. "I've still got my staff meeting to attend. You can join me for my afternoon lessons and then spend some time getting to know the school. I'm sure a woman of your many talents can figure out the rest?"

I shrug. "Talk, listen, determine who the scourge sorcerers are. Fairly straight-forward."

He guffaws. "Don't we wish it were so. The wretches have proven awfully good at covering their tracks."

I pause before picking up the thread he's unknowingly offered me. "I guess this is your thing, isn't it? Tackling evil sorcerers. I saw you before, a couple of years ago, at the execution of the riven sorcerer you apprehended."

Stavros's voice turns even drier. "Yes, it seems my true calling is to triumph against degenerate magic."

I let my gaze wander across the room as if his response to my next remark doesn't matter all that much to me. "Scourge sorcerers have got to be worse. At least the riven don't pursue their power; it just happens."

Even from the corner of my eye, I catch the stiffening of Stavros's muscular frame. "It just happens, and then they drag the world into their madness with it. None of them are worth the dirt on their hides."

At his vehemence, my gaze jerks back to him. "You take their existence pretty personally, it sounds like."

He gives me a tight smile, anger smoldering in his eyes. I have the impression he isn't seeing me at all in that moment. "A riven sorcerer butchered my best friend. I'll be satisfied when all of them as well as anyone who'd dabble in scourge magic are wiped right off the face of the continent."

Without another word, he heads out the door, with a thud of it shutting hard in his wake.

As I stare after him, Julita's voice mingles with my thoughts. *He isn't angry at you. It's only a bit of a sore spot for him.*

Yeah. A sore spot that also *is* me.

I swallow thickly. I've walked straight into even more danger than I bargained for.

# Twelve

I toss the cowhide figure into the heap with the others and swipe the back of my hand across my sweat-damp forehead. The pile of the lumpy but vaguely human-shaped things looks increasingly unsettling the higher I build it in the military division's storage room.

You might think that nobles would reserve the grotesque thought of having to deal with limp bodies for scenarios that specifically require them. But no, the powers that be—or, at least, the resident former general—seem to have decided they may as well be multipurpose. Anytime a training exercise requires obstacles, drag out the leather corpses!

That's the last of them. I march back out to the field and find Stavros presiding over several lingering students aiming for extra recognition. I guess one good word from the former general could see them launching their military careers several rungs up the ladder.

"—been so long," one of the women is saying. "Do we really need to worry about the empire after all this time?"

Stavros rubs his hands together, the hooked metal one he wears for lessons in the field glinting against the flesh one in its leather glove. His gaze slides from the questioner across the faces of the others.

I've noticed that during class, he rarely rests his eyes anywhere for more than a couple of seconds. He shifts his attention so smoothly I doubt anyone would notice if they weren't watching for it, but I suspect it's to cover the faulty vision Julita mentioned to me.

He speaks in a wryly confident tone that's a little warmer than any he's directed at me. "Darium still exists, doesn't it? Last I checked, they continued to hold Cotea in their grip, just across the channel from us?"

A man off to the side raises his shoulders in a shrug. "We've always pushed them back, though."

"Yes, because we're there and trained in both tactics and combat well enough to do it." Stavros tips his head in acknowledgment. "You all know that Darium's forces conquered the continent by taking advantage of the wreckage after the Great Retribution. They recovered quickly and overwhelmed the rest of us before we were in a state to fight back. It's a far greater challenge for them now, but only a fool believes they're impervious. The late King Melchior won Silana's freedom several decades ago, and yet Darium has never gone more than a year or two without harassing our borders in an attempt to regain ground."

His mention of the Great Retribution chills me. If the scourge sorcerers keep up their sick experiments, they could set us up for full-out war on top of divine punishment.

The students in front of Stavros will serve as officers, with the best mounts and equipment and the ability to make decisions. It's the common people who'd be summoned to bear the worst of the blows on the front lines.

The man who shrugged makes a slight scoffing sound. "Several decades, and they've gotten nowhere."

"Ah, but you never know when a new advisor or emperor might come along with the right insight to shake things up. And if you get careless with your defenses…"

Stavros lunges forward in an instant, flicking his foot around the guy's ankle at just the right angle to send him toppling over. Before the student lands on his ass, the former general grabs his hand and helps right him with a light pat of his prosthetic.

The other students laugh, and the guy who became a demonstration does too. Somehow the man who's such an asshole to me manages to maintain both authority and good will with the younger nobles.

I'd bite my tongue off before I'd admit it out loud, but he's good at what he's doing here.

Stavros sends them off with a wave of his hand. As they offer their brisk salutes of respect, I amble over to him.

When he turns to face me, a quiver runs through my nerves despite my best attempt at matching his effortless cool. The memory of his vindictive expression when he spoke of the riven simmers amid my thoughts.

I can't let him see my anxiety. I force a sardonic smile onto my face and tilt my head toward the storage room. "You know, if all you wanted your assistant to do was cart equipment around, you could have hired a mule."

A hint of his annoyingly cocky grin curls his mouth. "Maybe I did. Are you itching to get in on more action?"

I fold my arms over my chest. "I'm just puzzled about why you made such a fuss about my fighting ability if the closest I'm going to come to even fake battles is wrestling with stuffed leather."

Yesterday afternoon, I propped up the cowhide figures on stands so Stavros could lecture the junior students on the best points to hit with their fake swords from which positions. This morning, I stacked them into piles of three to five, and then Stavros had some of his senior students—the ones I guess he feels have the most promise for higher command—set a bunch of other junior students maneuvering around them all across the field.

I haven't had a hilt in my hand once since he agreed to bring me on. Possibly I am a little disappointed.

I definitely haven't learned anything from the students, who are too busy fawning over their professor and looking down their noses at my laboring to consider having a conversation with me.

Stavros shrugs. "We've only just gotten started. Who knows what fantastic uses I'll find for you yet, Thief."

Julita lets out a long-suffering sigh, as if she's the one he's mocking. *I'm sorry. He isn't normally quite this much of an ass.*

A smile of my own touches my lips. "Julita thinks you should stop being such a prick." Which isn't quite what she said, but the sentiment was implied.

Stavros's face does strange things when he's reminded about the woman I'm hosting. He arches his eyebrows, but at the same time his jaw tightens.

He keeps his tone nonchalant. "And how do I know you're not just making that up?"

*Because he's much better company when he's crooning Veldunian serenades.*

The corner of my mouth quirks higher. "She suggests you should do some serenading instead. Apparently you know some Veldunian songs?"

I get an even more interesting expression in answer to the light jab. Stavros's dark eyes flare, both amused and dangerous. "It was only the one time, and—"

He cuts himself off just before he prods my shoulder in a gesture that might have been playful. If he hadn't remembered at the last second that he's talking to more than just the woman he shares that memory with.

In that glimpse, I can almost imagine a Stavros who isn't an asshole. Then he glowers at me as if it's my fault he slipped up.

The chances he'd ever really joke around with me appear to be approximately nil. I think I'll survive *that* disappointment.

Instead, his voice turns a bit gruff. "Why don't you get on with taking down the wretches you were so eager to destroy, hmm?"

Without waiting for my response, he turns on his heel and strides off to do some former-general-y thing I'm clearly not invited to.

As the distance between us grows, I exhale some of my tension. He has no idea about my power, and I can keep it that way.

I've managed not to give in to my magic's call in nearly seven years. I'm the one in charge here.

I glance around the courtyard. A few clusters of students between classes are lounging on the stretch of lawn between the Domi and the Quadring, but none of them look particularly eager to have a stranger crash their conversations.

Maybe I need a better idea of how the investigation started before I can continue it.

I keep my voice low, moving my lips as little as possible. "Could you walk me through what you saw, and where, on the day the sorcerers made their attempt on the prince's life?"

*If you think it could help. They were touring some of the classrooms in the Quadring—the queen and both Princess Klaudia and Prince Jacos. Take that entrance to your right.*

I cross the field to one of the less prominent doorways and then walk through the halls at Julita's direction.

*I was here,* she says, bringing me to a halt a few doors down from one of the exits to the outer courtyard. *They were saying their last farewells before taking their leave. A crowd of us from the classes that'd just been let out were watching them go. And I heard someone muttering—there were these odd words that my brother and Wendos would use. I'm not sure where they came across them.*

The hall is currently empty, everyone shut away in their classrooms. "Words to go with the scourge sorcery rituals?" I whisper.

*Exactly. I couldn't make out the murmur all that well—it was only a couple of words amid a lot of chatter… And the hall was so packed, I couldn't see who'd spoken. It unnerved me, but I thought I might have misheard it. Except that night, the prince came down ill.*

"Could it have been a coincidence?"

*I suppose. But after I spoke to Stavros, he reached out to people he knows on the Crown's Watch who guard the palace. The symptoms were unusual and severe enough that they had the palace searched for possible intruders who might have poisoned the prince. It wasn't a simple flu.*

I drift back toward the stairwell. "And you've seen specific signs of rituals—where?"

*There's the dartling eggshell—they get it powdered and burn it. It has a very distinctive scent. One time when I was on a hunt in the campus woods, I caught a whiff of it and followed it, and found a few traces on some tree roots in a clearing. There's no other reason for anyone to be smearing that around.*

"Anything else?"

*One other time in the woods before that, I came across a tree that'd been marked with the sigil of the All-Giver, inverted.* Julita shudders. *Borys liked to draw that too, as if it'd encourage more power to flow down into him.*

I frown as I tramp down the stairs. "And that wasn't enough proof?"

*Most of the records around scourge sorcery have been destroyed to try to prevent anyone from following their footsteps. Alek hasn't been able to find any accounts that mention the inverted sigil. And recognizing the words and the dartling egg smell is just my experience, not something anyone can confirm.*

Which is why we need more proof. I worry at my lower lip for a moment before catching myself.

The palace bell begins its hourly ring, and Julita perks up. *Speaking of hunts, it's almost time for the weekly practice hunt the leadership division holds. They'll let an interested assistant tag along. There are a couple of regulars I've been keeping an eye on. And everyone does plenty of talking.*

I don't know what a practice hunt is, but I'm all for finding it out if it means making some progress toward completing this mission. "Sounds good. Where's that?"

*Ah, I think you should probably get changed first.*

I glance down at my combat leathers, which have seen exactly zero combat while on my body. She may have a point.

At the next bell, after changing into one of the riding dresses Casimir provided and pinning my hair into one of the loopy updos that the noble ladies seem to favor, I head over to the stable. If it seems as odd to Julita as it does to me to get dressed up to hang out with horses, she doesn't give any indication.

*I think this is the best one*, she remarks as I smooth my hands over the subtly pleated silk. *It makes your eyes look even more blue.*

It's the turquoise dress, which I think is my favorite too. The cut is simple in its elegance, with only a little gold embroidery, no beading or elaborate swirls, decorating the neck- and waistline.

And I've discovered that the folds on this one allow me to conceal one extra dagger compared to the others. Which is the most important factor, naturally.

Even if I have three dresses, I could get away with wearing this one more than the others, right? After all, I'm supposed to be a mere country noble no one's ever heard of before.

I mean, while I *have* to be wearing fancy dresses at all.

My nerves twitch as I spot the twenty or so noblemen and ladies gathered outside the stable, but the familiar smells take the edge off my anxiety. Fresh hay and old wood and that distinct musky-sweet horsey smell that I welcomed into my lungs whenever I slipped out to my family's much smaller stable to groom Dotty, our mare.

There could be one or two things I'd actually like about the Sovereign College. If they didn't always come with a pack of rich snobs on the side.

As I stroll along the pathway with the smooth but not too swift strides that befit a lady, I pick out several familiar faces in the waiting group. There's Anya, who will never recover her missing earrings and whose flaxen locks currently look more like a sculpture than a hairdo. And Esmae, Julita's petite dormmate with the eye patch who came to my rescue.

The others, I haven't had time to commit their names to memory yet, but I know I've crossed paths with them while walking the halls or perhaps in the dining hall this morning.

Oh, and Benedikt is with them—his golden hair catching the sunlight off to the side of the small crowd. He's laughing with a few of the other men.

I jerk my gaze away. I'm not supposed to know him.

But he's going to witness one of my first real attempts at noble subterfuge. All of which I'd imagine he'll report back to Stavros—and Casimir and Alek—one way or another.

Wonderful.

Julita pipes up, falling into a hush as if there's any chance of someone overhearing. *The girl with the red streak in her hair—keep a particular eye on her. Wendos had a thing going with her for a few months. And I've seen him act very friendly with the short fellow there in the dark blue tunic, so watch him carefully too.*

I want to point out that I'm not sure how much those associations matter when we haven't even proven that Wendos himself is still interested in scourge sorcery, but I'm too close to the other students to talk to Julita without looking insane.

Anya is standing with a couple of similarly haughty women. Her eyes narrow when she notices me arriving. "Julita's friend. What are you doing here again?"

I offer my best ingratiating smile and stick to an appropriately refined tone. "I happened to stumble into a conversation with one of the professors whose father was close colleagues with mine, and it turned out he was in need of an assistant. My family decided they could spare me for the opportunity."

One of Anya's friends lets out a laugh too short to be good-humored. "How intriguing. And you know Julita as well?"

I've prepared for this moment, knowing I'd likely run into someone who'd heard my initial story.

It's fine—possibly even a good thing—if the conspirators find out I supposedly knew Julita. Their reactions to me could give their guilt away.

But I don't want anyone believing that I was involved in whatever investigations they believed Julita was carrying out. That could be a faster death sentence than showing off my riven magic for Stavros.

"I suppose I *knew* her," I say with a slight grimace. "We hadn't seen each other in years. From what I've heard since arriving here, she'd changed quite a bit. I don't even know where she's wandered off to—she didn't bother telling me that much."

Anya hums to herself with a brief primp of her hair. I take a surreptitious glance toward the two classmates Julita pointed out to me, but I can't see any change in their expressions if they noted me talking about her.

If they're worried about anyone investigating her disappearance, they're doing a good job of hiding it.

My gaze snags on another female student in a deep burgundy dress that compliments her olive-brown skin. Unlike the rest of us, her straight black hair is only pulled back from her face in a gold clip but otherwise allowed to tumble down her back. Even Esmae has her hair coiled into a bun for the outing.

The woman is standing at the edge of the group like many others, but something about her stance gives the sense that she's more apart from us. Like there's a short distance there she isn't sure how to cross.

As I watch, she fidgets with the folds of her skirt. Her right hand is missing its smallest two fingers —the flesh smoothed over in the way of a typical dedication sacrifice.

I don't even need to twitch my eyebrow for Julita to pick up on my curiosity. *That's Petra. She's pretty quiet, mostly keeps to herself. Apparently she's a niece twice removed of the queen's family, or something like that. I don't think it's likely she attacked her own cousin.*

Maybe not, but I'm not ruling anyone out just yet.

I smooth the skirt of my own dress and am about to push the conversation onward when a broad-shouldered, middle-aged woman with a face as pasty as a dumpling steps forward. She claps her hands. "All right, everyone. Select your steeds."

Accidentally-on-purpose, I head through the stable entrance just behind Anya and her friends. Which gives me the opening to keep talking after all.

"It's strange that Julita hasn't been around for so long, isn't it? Where could she have gone? Did it seem as if she'd been getting into anything… unsavory?"

The girl at Anya's right scoffs.

Anya simply lifts her nose. "I can't imagine Julita getting her hands particularly dirty."

The girl who asked me about knowing Julita giggles. "No, if she wanted something unsavory done, she'd just wheedle someone else into doing it."

I slant my mouth into a frown. "I hope she didn't cause any resentments, then?"

"Oh, people generally don't get *angry* with Julita," Anya says in a bored tone. "She's just ever so charming."

She doesn't say it like a compliment.

Before I can prod further, she motions toward the end of the row of stalls we've reached. "You should take Toast out. Stall 16. He's the perfect horse for you to start with."

If the cold glint in her eyes wasn't enough to tip me off, Julita makes a sound of consternation. *Toast is a gods-damned terror. She's trying to make a fool out of you… or worse.*

It seems to me I'll look more like a fool if I act frightened by the suggestion. I can't imagine a horse kept in the royal college's stables could be *that* wild.

A terror to noblewomen could still be a piece of cake to someone who appreciates a little spirit.

I shoot Anya a quick smile. "Thank you for the suggestion."

A titter ripples between the three women as I head toward the stall she indicated. Footsteps rap against the stone floor after me.

I recognize Esmae's clear voice. "Anya's just joking, Ivy. I can help you find a better mount."

"Oh, Esmae, don't be a spoilsport," one of Anya's friends mutters.

I glance over my shoulder. "Thank you, but I'll be fine. Now I'm even more curious about this horse."

Stopping in front of the stall, I find myself faced with a stallion whose dun hair holds a sprinkling of darker brown to match his mane. He's got the coloring of a piece of toasted bread. Nothing particularly terrifying about that.

I reach over the low stall door slowly to give him a chance to sniff my hand. He gives a snort and a restless stomp of his hooves. He is a little testy.

The stable hands have already suited him up with saddle and bridle like they must have all the horses on offer for the hunt. All I've got to do is get on him.

I make a soft clucking sound under my breath as I ease into the stall, the way I have before when I've gotten the chance to commune with an unfamiliar horse. I haven't *ridden* any horses since Dotty, but I know my way around them.

I've missed her. Being in a stable feels like coming home—to the one part of my old home I have nothing but fond memories of.

An unbidden heat pricks at the back of my eyes. I grimace against it.

I'm not really any more alone here than I was on the streets. But there I was surrounded by people with concerns I could relate to, whose lives I wanted to take some small part in.

I've never really been able to count on anyone except myself… but I *feel* that fact more in this place than I ever have before.

Toast stomps again. I pat his neck reassuringly and inhale the horsey smell, letting it soothe my brief spell of melancholy.

Benedikt's breezy voice filters from the boards at the back of my stall from the one adjacent, low so no one farther away will hear. "You do like to live dangerously, huh, Knives?"

Knives? Is that what he's going to be calling me now?

I guess I can think of less fitting nicknames.

"I seem to have a knack for it," I retort in a similarly low tone. "I didn't know hunting was your thing."

He hasn't really struck me as the aggressive type.

Benedikt chuckles. "When you're a bastard's bastard, all things can be your thing."

My head swivels toward the back wall. "Pardon?"

*Here we go,* Julita remarks with amusement.

"I'm the bastard son of a royal bastard," Benedikt says, sounding no less amused himself. "Part of the family but definitely not. It's a very unique position—a certain amount of recognition with none of the responsibility. I try to make the most of it."

Julita fills in one of the blanks in that story. *Benny's father is King Konram's half-brother... who apparently picked up* his *father's tastes for stepping outside his marriage.*

That's how Benedikt has connections in the palace. It doesn't sound as if the situation bothers him.

Questions itch at me, but the hunt master hollers from outside the stables for us to get a move on. I grip Toast's reins and push open the stall door.

# THIRTEEN

The stallion follows me down the aisle, shaking his head and swishing his tail. At the sight of the outer yard, he leaps forward.

The reins dig into my fingers with the effort to hold him with me. "Whoa, there," I murmur.

Other students are leading out their horses around us. I guide Toast farther away from the stable so we're not too close to anyone else. Then I grip the pommel and back of the saddle, set my foot in the stirrup, and heft my other leg over.

Before I've quite landed on the leather surface, Toast kicks up his back legs. I jolt forward, just barely catching my balance by clutching the pommel and his mane.

A nervous sweat breaks over my skin. Dotty showed some attitude from time to time, but she never did anything like that.

Julita sighs. *You know how he got his name? Because the trainer said anyone who rides him without knowing what they're doing is toast.*

I grit my teeth. I do know what I'm doing, and I'm not going to let a few stuck-up nobles mock me into fleeing from the challenge.

Even if my heart is now thumping faster than before with the knowledge of just how big a challenge it might be.

I gather the reins and keep a firm but not aggressive hold on them as I nudge my heels against the stallion's sides. He whirls around and nearly bolts off across the field before I rein him in.

The muscles in my arms strain with the toss of his mane.

Anya shoots me a coy smirk from the back of the mild-mannered gelding she's perched on. "I hope he doesn't give you too much trouble."

"Oh, we're getting along perfectly well," I say, pretending my palms aren't sweating from the effort.

When I manage to keep Toast standing relatively still for a minute, my confidence begins to recover. Then the dumpling-faced hunt master weaves between the horses with a couple of helpers, handing out... bows.

I can't help staring as even Anya slings one over her head and touches the quiver of small arrows that's been fixed to her saddle. Somehow I hadn't quite processed that the hunt required all of us to actually… hunt.

*It's all right,* Julita says. *We don't kill anything. Just take our aim at the conjured targets and see who can hit them best.*

The other students are chattering with each other enough that I risk murmuring, "I'm not sure I'll hit anything at all."

*Haven't you ever used a bow?*

I give my head a subtle shake. The woman and her helpers reach me, and I force myself to grasp the reins with just one hand while I accept the curved wooden weapon.

I'm a knife person. A bow isn't going to do much for you on the streets of the fringes, and I sure as shit can't hide one under my tunic.

I get the impression Julita winces. *Well, we're not here to impress them with your fantastic archery skills. I'll coach you as well as I can. Mostly focus on staying on that beast of a horse.*

Toast has definitely noticed that my attention has become divided. He scuffs his hooves impatiently against the ground until I give his reins a light tug so he knows I'm staying on top of him. My mouth has gone dry.

I have to learn archery on horseback while handling a horse who'd like nothing more than to get me off his back. This should be fun.

Across the stable yard, one of the mounted noblemen yelps. As my head jerks toward him, his horse rears and shudders.

"Daimon," someone near me mutters like a curse.

The rambling spirit-creature isn't satisfied with a brief disruption like the one that provoked the charm merchant's gelding. The rider yanks at the reins and shouts out, but the horse keeps bucking and heaving as if it's afraid to let its hooves touch the ground.

While the nearest students draw their own mounts back, the hunt master rushes over. Before she can reach the frantic horse, it flings its haunches so forcefully its rider careens right out of the saddle.

And under the next fall of its stomping hooves.

Bone cracks. The man cries out, reaching toward his leg that's now bent at an unnatural angle.

The dumpling-faced woman catches the reins. "Get a medic!" she hollers at one of the helpers.

The horse has settled down, as if the spirit that was harassing it slipped away as soon as it'd done some real damage. Which, given what I've seen and heard about how the daimon are behaving at the college, might be the case.

Unbidden, my eyes seek out Benedikt. He meets my gaze just for a second, his usual smirk gone tight.

This obviously isn't a typical incident.

"Blasted spirits," someone mutters, and someone else hisses at them to keep quiet as if they're worried the daimon might come at us all.

Several of the students graze their foreheads, chests, and gut with the three-fingered tap of the gesture of the divinities.

They might not be wrong to worry. The minor divine beings of this place appear to be plenty pissed off and perfectly willing to take it out on us.

The hunt master has knelt beside the injured student. She lifts her head and swings her arm at the rest of us. "He doesn't need an audience. Go on. You know what to do."

Er. That's debatable.

Nevertheless, I direct Toast to the right, following the train of horses setting off toward the stretch of woods at the back of the school.

Lovely. I'm going to be hunting on horseback with a bow and arrow while there are also trees in the way. What's next—the teachers set the trees on fire?

Toast huffs and does his best to spring ahead or veer off in a detour, but my firm grip keeps him reasonably in line. Anya glances back at me, and I find her frown immensely gratifying.

At least for the few seconds before Toast decides to take a page out of the other horse's book and get a good rear in.

My ass slams into the back of the saddle and nearly slides right off. I bite my lip and snatch at his mane.

"Down," I order him. "You want to move, then let's move."

Rather than trying to rein him in, I tap my heels to send the stallion trotting forward. He huffs another breath, sounding more confused than irritated now, and lopes past a few of the other horses before slowing down of his own accord.

Da always told me the easiest way to work with a horse was to show you respected it—that you'd give it room to tell you what it wanted too. Back when he still talked to me enough to offer any kind of lessons.

It seems he was right.

As soon as we've urged our horses down the winding path into the stretch of forest, I see what Julita meant about the conjured targets. Here and there, glowing shapes flicker into view amid the branches and on the forest floor. Some look like ghostly animals, others like random blobs of light.

One arrow flies, and another, and another. Around me, the students are claiming their hits like escalating bets in a card game.

Keeping a careful watch on my steed, I ease my bow off my shoulder.

*Set the base of the arrow against the string*, Julita says. *And rest the side of the shaft near the head at the middle of the curve in the bow. Pull back as hard as you can and sight down the shaft.*

Easier said than done.

My first arrow falls off into the brush. The second zings into a tree at least a few feet from the target I was aiming at.

At this rate, I'm more likely to hit one of my fellow students than any magical shapes.

I restrain a grimace. At least Toast is playing mostly nice for now, though I have to grab the reins once to slow him when he tests me.

Esmae comes up behind me, the scattered sunlight glancing off her pale face and the mauve patch over her one eye. "I suppose you haven't done much horseback shooting before."

"No," I say, because it's obvious, and don't bother to mention that I haven't done any shooting with my feet on the ground either.

"It took me a while to get the hang of it." She motions for me to watch her. "You'll have an easier time if you keep your elbow higher. And pull back just a little more, right before you release the arrow."

I give her instructions my best attempt, and my next arrow flies only a foot away from the luminescent deer head I spotted through the trees.

Oh, well, I'm not here to become an expert archer anyway.

I wet my lips and notch another arrow. "Thanks for your help. You're rooming in the same dorm as Julita—do you know her well?"

I already know from Julita that they weren't close, but it seems like the sort of thing a person would ask of a stranger who's randomly helping them. All Esmae knows about me is that I knew Julita.

Esmae cocks her head as if considering the question. "Not exactly. But she's the kind of person you can't help noticing. She's always... Having her around keeps me working hard to impress the teachers just as much as she does."

*Hmm*, Julita says. *She makes me sound like a bootlicker. I didn't ply for their favor that much.*

I open my mouth, forming my next question, and a sharp voice carries from farther behind me.

"So, Ivy of Nikodi, you landed that assistantship with Ster. Stavros right out from under the rest of us."

I peer over my shoulder and make out the speaker in the shifting forest shadows just beyond Esmae. The tall, athletic woman whose name I don't know holds her bow like it's part of her body.

Julita supplies her name. *Romild. Her province is on the border—vulnerable to military incursions.*

So maybe she was hoping that getting close with Stavros would mean more protection from the royal forces.

I can't blame her for that, but I can't give her the position either.

"The timing happened to be right," I say. There isn't much else I can mention to justify it.

Romild snorts. "And you can barely manage to hit thin air. Exactly how many other ways did you please him to make up his mind?"

Her insinuation couldn't be clearer from her tone. My jaw tightens against a flicker of anger.

As if I'd ever lower myself to "pleasing" any man, let alone a jerk like Stavros, to get their good will.

I manage to keep my tone calm. "There's more to military skill than archery."

She guffaws. "You keep telling yourself that. We'll see how long it takes before he *can't* justify keeping you on. There are a lot of us who'd want the chance to work with a legend like him."

I don't see how any good can come from debating the subject further. I clamp my mouth shut and ignore the squirming of magic inside me that wants to teach my accuser a thing or two about combat.

But it doesn't seem wise to let her comments go completely unchallenged among all these witnesses. If I want my noble schoolmates to treat me as more than dirt, I have to prove I can give as good as I get.

I direct Toast to slow between the next couple of targets so that we fall back in the procession. With my bow temporarily slung over my shoulder again, I let my hand slide over my parted skirt and my fingers hook around a small hilt in a sheath fixed to my thigh.

I might be playing noble, but I earned my unrequested title as the Hand of Kosmel.

Romild nudges her steed past me with a fierce flash of her eyes. I nod respectfully—and flick out my hand between us right as she passes.

Her horse makes it a few more steps before her saddle sways to the side. My knife is already tucked back in its hiding place.

Romild lets out a strangled noise and gropes for the horse's mane, but it's too late. The saddle with its split girth slides right down the horse's side, and she tumbles to the forest floor with an audible *oomph.*

As she scrambles to her feet, I hum to myself. "Perhaps General Stavros prefers an assistant who knows how to stay on her horse."

Several of the other students have stopped to watch. No one can prove I actually did anything, so no one makes an accusation.

But they all know the accident probably wasn't a coincidence.

Benedikt's gaze rests on me with apparent delight. The other expressions aimed at me look newly wary... with both respect and hostility.

I send Toast trotting past her again, and Romild tracks me with furious eyes. My magic wriggles between my ribs again—wanting to shield myself, wanting to heave her away—and I tense against it.

She's only a minor threat. Nothing that should bother me much.

Except the next second, an all-too-familiar agony spikes out from my sternum. I clamp my teeth hard against a gasp of pain.

Gods smite me, what *now?* An incident that small has never set off my power's full backlash before.

But it definitely is today. The pain burns through my organs, and my hands shake where I'm clutching the reins.

*Ivy?* Julita says tentatively, but I can't say anything to reassure her right now.

Toast sidesteps beneath me. A quiver runs through his frame.

The stallion can sense that something's off with his rider. If I'm not careful, I'm going to end up tumbling off too.

I can't let anyone else see what I'm grappling with. I can't let them suspect there's anything wrong with me.

And I have to stay on this cursed horse.

I focus on the thud of his hooves against the forest floor. I flex my thigh muscles against his sides, assuring him that I'm still here. I rock the reins in a gentle rhythm.

My awareness of the stallion's presence, the flow of his life with his breaths and his own thumping heart, helps me tune out the wrenching sensation inside me. With a few more breaths, the throbbing subsides.

My back feels drenched in sweat. I hold it straight as I gather myself to make another attempt with the blasted bow.

I'm okay. I made it through—I made it through all of it.

But how much longer can I keep that up if the cracks in my soul are widening?

# FOURTEEN

As I pass the tapestry that shows Signy facing the emperor's army, I can't help shooting her exalted figure a wistful glance. Conquering grave wrongs must be a damned sight easier when you've got the full host of godlen gazing down on you with their blessings.

Of course, I'm not sure we'd want to alert our divine overseers to the trouble we're facing right now. Who's to say they'd help us in our quest rather than decide the scourge sorcerers have already gone too far and it's time to rain down godly retribution?

As I reach for the sconce, I drop my voice to a murmur. "Are you sure he'll be down there now? And he won't mind me showing up an hour early?"

Julita laughs. *Alek would live his whole life in the archives if he could get away with it. I often arrived early to get a more detailed account of the latest discoveries he unearthed.*

That answer doesn't exactly answer my second question, because I'm not Julita. But maybe she can't conceive of the encounter going differently than it would have for her.

The shadowy passage opens, and I step into it and down the stairs.

The questions I have for Alek aren't ones I want to ask in front of the other men, especially under Stavros's suspicious gaze. When I mentioned to Julita that there was something I'd like to discuss with him before bringing it to the main group, she encouraged me to arrive at the next meeting of our little cabal before it officially started.

The masked scholar has acted awfully wary of me himself, as much as he might want to preserve Julita's presence. But he's clearly the one to ask about archaic knowledge that wouldn't have come up in Stavros's military training or the gossip of patrons and classmates.

If the scholar can point me to the information I need, it'll be worth any awkwardness that comes from imposing on him.

It'll be easier if I know more about him—to avoid sticking my foot in my mouth.

As I descend through the darkness, I pitch my voice even lower. "What's the story with his mask? Why does he wear it?"

Julita makes a pensive sound. *I've never seen him without it. It's not the sort of thing it's polite to pry about, but I gather that he's hiding some sort of ugliness about his face—a deformity or a scar or the like.* She lets out another light laugh. *So obsessed with facts and knowledge and yet so concerned about appearances too.*

My skin itches at the slight mocking edge to her tone. If Alek is hiding some unfortunate feature, I can't help thinking it's at least as much about his fellow students' concerns about appearances as about his own.

Having experienced the attitudes around here, I can't say I'd blame him for wanting whatever kind of shield he can get against their judgments.

I can't ask anything else, because with my next step, I slip from the magical passage into the room. My formal slippers rasp against the stone floor, and Alek startles where he was bowed over a thick book at the desk.

When he sees it's me, his stance goes even more stiff. He swipes at his thick black hair and pins me with the piercing gaze that's turned totally cold again. "What are you doing down here? We're not due to meet for another hour."

I splay my hands in an apologetic gesture. "I know. I'm sorry to interrupt. I had a possibility I wanted to pursue before I'm sure it's worth bringing up with everyone, something I thought might have come up in your research. Julita said you're often down here ahead of time."

The set of Alek's mouth softens at the mention of Julita. His bright brown eyes flick downward and then back up to meet mine again with a different sort of intensity. "Is she… okay? I mean, as much as a person could be, when…"

He makes a vague gesture to encompass the ridiculous situation she and I have found ourselves in.

Even though I don't really know this man, even though he probably considers me as much of a street rat as Stavros does, the question brings a lump into my throat.

He might be a haughty noble like the rest of them, but he's still human.

And I know what it's like to lose someone you care about.

"She seems to be doing all right, considering," I say lightly. "She definitely has plenty to contribute. What do you think, Julita? How are you holding up?"

*Well, I'd obviously prefer* not *being dead, but you do keep things interesting. I'd rather be stuck with you than some vapid priss like Anya.*

My lips quirk into a crooked smile. "She finds me an entertaining host."

Alek blinks and then gives himself a bit of a shake as if gathering his thoughts. "It wouldn't do for her to be bored, I suppose. What's the possibility you wanted to look into?"

I have to tread carefully here, making sure that my reasoning sounds logical even though it's not the real reason I'm asking. "I was wondering about methods of magical suppression. If there are any records or stories of procedures or materials that might dampen unearthly power. Maybe there's some way we could make it more difficult for the sorcerers to carry out their evil intent while we're working on proving who they are."

Alek rubs his bronze-brown jaw, his gaze going distant. "Magical suppression. With the riven sorcerers, the authorities rely on general sedatives to ensure they can't work their powers, but we can hardly have the entire college in a stupor."

I manage to stop my smile from tightening. "Obviously. I was hoping there might be a subtler method we could try."

Or at least, that *I* could try, to get a better grip on the power writhing inside me. After yesterday's fit of agony over a simple glare, tamping it down feels significantly more urgent than ever before.

The authorities haven't found any method that would remove the threat of a riven sorcerer's power completely while leaving them reasonably conscious, but I'll settle for taking the edge off if I can get that much.

"There is something that might be relevant, though I can't remember how much detail the records include…" Alek moves toward the door set between two of the many shelves and then hesitates. His body tenses for a moment before he glances my way.

"You may as well come too. We'll be looking for books on pre-empire history, but the organization down here isn't ideal."

I follow him through the door into another archive room, this one at least three times as large as the one we left. Bookcases and open shelving units stretch out in every direction, stacked with leather- and canvas-bound volumes, sheafs of unbound paper, and wax-sealed scrolls. Even the settee squatting amid the maze has several books scattered across its faded cushions.

My jaw goes a bit slack, taking it all in. The tang of ancient ink and paper floods my lungs, almost as comforting as stable scents.

I suppress the urge to embrace one of the rows of books and gulp the smell down even more fully. "Wow. And this is what the scholar division *doesn't* think is important enough to keep in the main library?"

Alek watches my reaction with an expression that might be bemused, though it's hard to tell with so much of his face hidden behind the mask. "We've accumulated a lot of texts over the centuries. Some of the collection is prioritized based on our current academic focus. When it comes to historical events, the royal family prefers that students concentrate on the period starting with the overthrowing of the empire."

I restrain a snort. "Let us not dwell on our failures, only our victories. Somehow I'm not surprised."

I take a few steps along one of the shelves, trailing my fingers over the spines of the books. Only a light sprinkling of dust scatters their covers, suggesting that this room is accessed fairly often—or the scholarship division makes a point of regularly cleaning their archives.

Alek strides on ahead of me, scanning the books with a stricter air. "I checked every account I can find of the gifts of the current students—and staff. There are several Jurnus dedicats in the leadership division and a couple in companionship with weather-associated magic, but mostly along the lines of summoning rain or ensuring a sunny day rather than anything to do with wind."

I frown. "I suppose we should look into their recent activities anyway."

He nods. "I've already begun. So far it appears most if not all of them were on the campus at the time of Julita's murder, but I'll ask Benedikt and Casimir to see what they can find out about those who didn't have classes."

He's certainly thorough in his work—I'll give him that.

I glance back at the shelf, and my hand stalls on a line of familiar embossed type. I yank out the slim volume. "The first book of Gisela Luvinya's Traveling Diaries. I've never been able to find it."

Alek's tone turns skeptical. "How do you even know about it, then?"

"Oh, I found the second buried in the stash where I ended up staying... before I became a fake noble. She's constantly referencing previous adventures but only in the vaguest terms that just make you want the damn book more."

Alek shrugs. "I suppose you could borrow it. I doubt it'd be missed any time soon."

"Really?" I press the book to my chest instinctively, as if afraid he'll change his mind and wrench it away. Which is silly, because we both have more important things to worry about than fifty-year-old travelogues.

A hint of a smile touches Alek's stern face. "It might as well be appreciated by someone."

He pauses. "How is it you learned to read well at all? I was under the impression letters weren't widely taught in the outer wards, beyond the basics."

My delight at finding the book fades. The less I talk about where I came from, the better for both of us.

"My parents were readers," I say briskly. "They saw that we—that I could follow in their footsteps."

Until they no longer wanted me to. But by then I had enough to continue my education on my own.

Alek's eyes have narrowed. "And what did your parents do that *they* learned to read?"

My stomach knots. "I don't see how their occupations are relevant to our mission."

The scholar turns to fully face me, his jaw clenching. "You're expecting us to trust you with—with *everything*. Even with Julita's soul. Why wouldn't we want to know exactly who we're dealing with?"

I refrain from saying that I'd happily hand over Julita's soul to any of them given the choice. My voice comes out tart all the same. "I am not my parents." As they made amply clear hundreds of times over. "And it seems to me that *I'm* the one who's risking far more here with people I have only a ghost's word that I can trust. You already know more about me than I do about you!"

Alek opens his mouth and closes it again. I can't decipher what's going on behind his penetrating gaze.

Julita gives a soft laugh. *That set him straight.*

Then he lifts his chin just slightly. "What do you want to know?"

I hadn't actually expected him to offer himself up for examination. I hesitate, and one obvious question pops into my head. "What's your gift?"

"What makes you assume I have one?"

I stare at him for a second. Asking for at least a small dedication gift is par for the course among nobles.

They can afford to lose a little of their bodies to gain power. Anything to gain a potential advantage in all their jockeying for prestige.

I'm not sure how to say any of that politely, though, so I settle for, "It seems like everyone here does."

"Well, I'm not everyone." Alek pivots back toward the shelves as if he'd rather not face my scrutiny. His hand rises to the middle of his chest, where his godlen brand must be. "I dedicated myself to Estera, of course. But I wanted to know that whatever I accomplished, I brought about through my own abilities and not because of a divine leg up."

*It's true,* Julita tells me. *At least, that he doesn't have a gift. We discussed all of our potential strengths when we first started meeting.*

His commitment to relying on his own mortal abilities… is almost like my own. Other than the part where I do have a gift, just one I never asked for and that's actually a curse.

I can't help watching him for a little longer, taking in the staunch dedication that shows in every movement of his lean body.

Another question spills out of me. "What is it you're hoping to accomplish?"

"At the moment, I'll settle for preventing a second Great Retribution."

The dismissal in his flat tone kills my curiosity. I yank my gaze to the next row of books.

Along that bookcase and on to the next, I skim the titles in search of anything to do with the history of several centuries past. Alek continues his own perusal without comment.

Then a book catches my eye with enough of a jolt for me to break the silence. "They're not all in Silanian."

Alek's dry voice carries through the shelves from farther into the room. "No, most of us at the college know our Veldunian as well, and many have kept some fluency in Darium, if only for being able to access the records from when we were under the empire."

"I expected that. Not folk tales in Woudish." I flip through the pages and grin at the fanciful illustrations that decorate the pages between the curving script.

Alek appears at the end of the aisle I was wandering down. "You can recognize Woudish? What, were your parents immigrants from Woudland too?"

I chuckle. "No. I just—living on the streets, it pays to keep up with all the news you can. And a lot of the best news comes from merchants. There was a Woudish expatriate who did a fair bit of business with his former countrymen when they passed through the city, and I found a couple of old teaching volumes on the language among the cast-off texts I had access to. It meant I could listen in on more of his conversations."

Alek is outright gaping at me now. "You taught yourself Woudish."

"I mean, I wouldn't say I'm exactly fluent. I can follow the gist of a conversation and fairly simple text. I wouldn't attempt a legal treatise, but I'd imagine I could handle this." I hold up the book of folk tales with a hopeful expression.

Alek stares at me for a moment longer. Then he shakes his head with a sputter of a laugh. "Go ahead and borrow that one too. Gods above. Other than me, I only know three students here who've bothered to pick that language up."

"Different priorities." I turn to the opposite shelves, resuming my real search. "I suppose it can't be totally useless even to a noble, or *you* wouldn't have bothered learning it."

"I like to know everything I can. Which I suppose is about the same as your reasons."

Alek lingers at the end of the aisle for a few moments longer. For just an instant, his presence feels almost friendly.

Then his mouth twists into a smile that's bittersweet. "Julita probably thinks we're both absurd. She didn't even like bothering with Veldunian. But then, she could hold anyone's attention without even needing to speak, so she hardly needed it."

The tenderness in his voice is so potent it sends a shiver through my nerves even though it's got nothing to do with me. The guy really was over the moon for my ghostly passenger.

Not that he ever would have talked about a street rat like me that way regardless. It hardly matters.

But when Julita responds with a giggle of wry amusement, my hackles rise of their own accord. *Some of us do know the most useful things can't be found in books. He's done his best, though.*

I have to think she never talked to Alek in such a patronizing way when she was alive, or his feelings wouldn't have remained quite so fond.

Anya might be a vapid priss, but I don't think her assessment of Julita is totally wrong. My uninvited guest did have a habit of charming people simply to get what she wants.

I'd rather not think about to what extent that might include me. I'm on this quest for my own benefit now—for reasons she couldn't even guess at.

I tuck the Woudish folk tales under my arm alongside the Traveling Diaries and continue the search. Alek moves on to the next aisle over.

My head is starting to spin with all the titles I've taken in when the scholar lets out an exclamation of triumph. "If the answer's anywhere, it'll be in here."

As he lugs the thick volume he's found over to one of the room's small desks, I hustle to join him. He flips through the yellowed pages, sucking his full lower lip under his teeth in concentration.

"What exactly are we looking for?" I ask, leaning over the desk next to him.

A faint whiff of a scent like mingled citrus and mint reaches my nose, both tart and cool. Fitting for the man himself.

Alek keeps paging through the book, his eyes narrowing in concentration. "From what I recall from past readings, the one time magical suppression was commonly used was in the old kingship trials."

I frown. "The kingship trials?" That's one bit of information I haven't stumbled on myself.

He nods absently. "Before the Great Retribution and Darium's imposing of their empire, Silana's rulership wasn't entirely hereditary. When a king or queen died, their successor had to go through a series of challenges to prove themselves worthy to the people and the gods. If they failed, others could step up to vie for the throne."

I raise my eyebrows. "That sounds like a fairer way of doing things than just handing it over to the next in line automatically. Why did they stop?"

"It was rather barbaric. Some of the trials could get quite… bloody, and sometimes perfectly good candidates weren't able to take the crown because of injuries sustained. And I suppose it was simpler for Darium to control the monarchy when it was handled in a more straight-forward fashion."

"Darium hasn't ruled here in nearly a century," I point out.

Alek hums thoughtfully. "There's something to be said for simplicity of inheritance even for ourselves. King Melchior did prove his worth by regaining our freedom from Emperor Vitus. And the Melchioreks don't *have* to pass on the crown to the next in line genetically. They use their best judgment, and the country does just fine without any violent challenges."

I don't know if I'd say that all of Silana is doing "just fine." But then, who knows if the rulers who won the throne through bloody trials were any kinder to their poorest citizens?

Alek stops and trails his fingers across a particular page. The ink has faded, and the handwriting style—from before printing presses like Da's had been invented—is more ornate than I'm used to, but I can read it well enough to determine that this page is talking about a feat of "might."

"Here." Alek taps a spot near the bottom of the page. "For one particular challenge, they wanted to be sure the feat was accomplished through strength of will and body rather than anything magical. The prospective monarch ingested a specific herb… They call it "pipe fleece" here, but I've never heard of that plant before."

Pipe fleece. My spirits leap. The name is unfamiliar to me too, but it's a start.

"It's probably a common name, like some people call volhana 'pig's lip.' You've never run into it before?"

Alek shakes his head. "It mustn't have been used often—the herb or the name. But botany is far from my specialty. And we don't have that many records that survived both the Great Retribution and the empire's purges."

I straighten up. "I might be able to find out more—maybe even get my hands on some of the stuff. There are people I can ask."

"If you give me their names—"

I shoot him a pointed look. "I mean people who are a lot more likely to talk freely with someone on their level than with a noble. Let me handle this. It's one thing I'm actually better equipped to do than any of you."

I must have gained a small measure of respect from the scholar during our search, because he tips his head in acknowledgment rather than arguing.

Alek hefts the book in his slim arms. "Even if you can find it, we don't know how effective it actually was or how we'd get it to the right people without interfering with the rest of the school too severely. But the others might have some—"

"Don't mention it to the others yet," I break in.

His gaze jerks to me. "Why not?"

Because I don't want anyone else speculating about that particular goal of mine.

The answer I give out loud sounds feebler than I like. "You just said we have no idea if it'd work— and I don't even know if I can find it. Better not to waste anyone's time thinking about it until we've sorted the first part out, right?"

Alek studies me for a few beats longer than I'm totally comfortable with. I make myself hold his gaze.

His lips purse, and whatever warmth I caught a glimpse of vanishes behind his shuttered eyes. "Fine. But I expect to hear about it as soon as you've discovered anything."

He strides onward, leaving me wondering how I've managed to offend him now. And just how much I should regret it.

I trail behind him. "Where are you going?"

"There's one thing I wanted to double-check in regards to scourge sorcery practices. I have managed to find a few accounts of their rituals that were missed in more general volumes of—"

His voice cuts off abruptly. I hurry over to find him pawing through the books strewn haphazardly across a shelf.

"They're gone," he says.

"What?"

Alek glances over at me with an anxious gleam in his bright eyes. "All three of the books I set aside here that had some mention of scourge sorcery. Someone's taken them."

My heart sinks. "The librarians realized and sent them to be destroyed?" I venture.

Alek puts my darker suspicion into words. "Or I wasn't the only person already aware of them... and the same people who murdered Julita set out to make it even harder for anyone to figure out what horrors they're committing."

# Fifteen

When I look up from the shopping list Stavros has just handed me, the former general is watching me with a gleam dancing in his dark eyes. "Do make sure it's aged kivseed oil not fresh. And I hope you can make it through the errand without slicing anyone or anything up?"

I wrinkle my nose at him. "I haven't stabbed you so far, so I'd say my self-control is working just fine."

He cocks his head with the little twitch that tells me he's refocusing his vision. Abruptly, I get the sense that he's not just heckling me but intrigued despite himself. "I heard you slashed someone's saddle during a hunt the other day."

A chill runs down my back. I don't want this man—this sorcerer-hunter—scrutinizing me any more than he's already inclined to.

I force a guffaw and tuck the list into the pouch on my belt. A silk pouch on a gold-edged belt, naturally, since it needs to go with this fancy-ass dress. "I'd like to see them prove I did it."

"Was there any particular reason you felt the need to send one of the students off their horse?"

*She was asking for it,* Julita mutters.

I opt for a slightly more detailed explanation. "She was questioning my qualifications for the assistant position. I thought it'd be worthwhile to demonstrate that I can take care of my opponents just fine."

Stavros raises his eyebrows. "I suppose it proved something. Maybe next time you can make your point without damaging school property, though. Having the stablemaster venting at me is rather tiresome."

"I'm ever so sorry," I say, not at all apologetically, and gesture to the luxurious quarters around us. "I'm sure there's money somewhere in the college's extensive coffers to cover a saddle strap. And you wouldn't have that problem if you'd let me do more than haul around equipment during your classes, so people would have seen I earned the spot."

"I think *earned* is a bit of an exaggeration." He chuckles and shakes his head. "Did it never occur to you that it might be better if people here *don't* see how you handle a fight? You don't approach combat like a noblewoman."

I shrug. "I'm supposedly a paltry noblewoman from some lowly province and a family no one's even heard of. Who knows what tactics we might prefer there?"

Then the full implications of what he said sink in.

I peer up at him, momentarily unsettled. "Are you trying to say that you've been treating me like a pack mule for my own protection?"

The man I'm most afraid of sending me to my death has actually been defending me?

I guess it's in his own best interests that my true origins remain hidden, as much as he knows about them. Both in case it comes out that he helped me forge my new identity and to preserve Julita's presence here. But it's hard for me to imagine the arrogant jackass in front of me doing anything for any reason other than to annoy me.

And it's not as if he'd do any of it if he knew the full truth about me.

Stavros's mouth forms a slanted grin. "Somehow you've become a cornerstone in our plans, Thief. It would also be tiresome to have to start over after we've gone to the work of setting you up here."

There's still something more curious in his gaze than I've seen before. Is it possible I've earned a little respect from the former general as well?

I don't really like the strange tingle of exhilaration that idea gives me. Anyway, at the moment I have much more need of something else from him.

I hold out my hand. "Speaking of work, can I get an advance on my pay? There are a couple of things I'd like to pick up for myself while I'm in town."

This time Stavros's eyebrows shoot up almost to the fringe of his blood-red hair. "You haven't been supplied with enough fineries yet?"

I fold my arms over my chest. "Who says I want 'fineries'? Women have needs."

Making it sound like some sort of feminine issue does the trick. Stavros snorts and then sighs, but he produces a few coins from a drawer. "I suppose it would look odd if I wasn't paying you some sort of salary."

"What, you figured I'd haul your dummies for free?"

"Your room and board here are pretty fine payment compared to what you made do with before, I'd imagine," he says dryly, and I can't even argue that point.

But he offers the coins, and I slip them into my purse with the list. I don't need to give actual money to the shopkeepers for the supplies he's asking for, since the college has its accounts set up anywhere I'm supposed to shop, but I don't want my personal purchases ending up on any official record.

"Do you have the new passcode for the entrance?" he asks.

I rattle off this week's absurd phrase. "Light fires for lusty ruby lizards. Don't worry. I'll be back to make you regret all your recent life decisions in a few hours."

The gleam in his eyes flares a little brighter. "I'm counting on it."

I definitely shouldn't be tingling over that look.

As I head out of the Domi, Julita pipes up in the back of my head. *You and Stav seem to be getting along a little better now that you've had a chance to get used to each other.*

She sounds pleased about it. I roll my eyes. "I don't think it's time to throw a party to celebrate our deep and abiding friendship."

*It doesn't hurt, you at least making peace with him. Even if he can be an ass, he'll have your back when it counts. I wouldn't have gone to him otherwise.*

I'm not sure how much I trust my ghostly guest's ability to judge character beyond what was useful to her goals, but I know better than to say as much out loud.

Walking through the streets of the central wards in full noble garb is a strange experience. Apparently this getup is much more convincing than my old faux-silk dress, or else my intensive practice at keeping up the airs is paying off. The regular if respectable citizens who cross my path give me plenty of room on the streets, and the business owners plying their wares tip their heads to me as if *I'm* respectable.

It takes almost no time at all to place the orders Stavros asked for. Most of the supplies will be delivered to the college over the next few days, but I tuck the kivseed oil and a couple of other smaller items that he wanted right away into my pouch.

Then I stroll through one of the crumbling gates in the old city walls and make my way through the narrower streets of the middle wards.

*What are you up to now, Ivy?* Julita asks eagerly.

"I figured that while I'm out and about, I should stop by the nearest of the herbal shops the Crow's Close apothecary told us about."

*Oh, excellent. Perhaps the owner can get us closer to tracking down those scourge sorcerers.*

"That's the plan." Not all of it, but the part I'm willing to tell her about. "Other than Wendos and those two students you pointed out to me at the hunt, is there anyone else I should be keeping an eye out for—anyone you've seen around when you've noticed the evidence of sorcery?"

Julita gives a sigh of frustration. *No. The only indications are what I told you before. No one was around the times in the woods, and there were dozens of people in the hall when I overheard that murmuring directed at the prince. With all the jostling, I don't know who was close enough to me in that moment... I froze up a little at first, hearing those words.*

A sense of shame tinges that last sentence. My gut twists at the thought of her childhood torments.

I haven't asked her much about her life outside of her investigations—have tried to pretend I don't have a ghost invading my skull as much as possible. That's seeming increasingly ridiculous.

And gods, she must be lonely. I'm not exactly great company even to the living.

I check the street signs at a corner to confirm I'm in the right spot on my mental map of the city. "You said your brother disappeared—your family hasn't heard from him at all? How long has it been since he headed to the college?"

*More than three years now, and there's been nothing. It probably sounds horrid, but I hope he's dead. My parents assume so. I'm going to be a far better countess over Nikodi than he ever— Well. I would have been.*

My stomach clenches up more at the reminder of the future she's lost.

I wait until a couple of passersby are behind me before murmuring, "I'm sorry. I guess that's what you were studying at the college for?"

*Yes, I was on the self-governing track. So many subjects to consider as master of your own domain.* She manages a light laugh. *Unfortunate that few of them come in handy for unraveling a conspiracy.*

"Should I let your parents know what happened to you, one way or another, at some point?" I venture. I have no idea whether her relationship with them was any better than mine with my own.

*Not for now. The longer my killers don't know that anyone's aware of my murder, the better, I think. I normally only went home for the quarterly holiday weeks, and I didn't write often, so they won't be wondering.*

She doesn't sound particularly attached to them, but then, they did fail to notice her brother torturing her for years. I can see how that might put a damper on any familial fondness.

"Is there anything else I could do?" I find myself asking. "I mean... To make things easier for you? I'm not sure how much I *can* do, but I'd try, anyway."

It isn't her fault we ended up in this mess, after all. And however scheming she was with her friends or the rest of her classmates, it was for an honorable purpose in the end.

I can't say she's been a horrible guest, unwanted or not.

Julita is quiet for long enough that I start to wonder if I've offended her. Then she lets out a softer laugh.

*I can't think of anything. You're already doing an awful lot, Ivy. If I can see the scourge sorcerers brought down because you helped me keep fighting them from beyond the grave, that's the best gift I could possibly have asked for.*

How would she feel about it if she knew I only agreed because of the gift *I'm* hoping to get—the forgiveness I hope to earn from the gods?

Hopefully I'll never have to find that out. May she move on into the peace of her godlen's embrace before I make my appeal.

As I reach a busier stretch of middle-ward stores and eateries, I fall silent. I'm already drawing plenty of gazes with my fine gown—some merely curious, some tinged with hostility.

Most nobles don't roam beyond the inner wards on foot.

My skin starts to crawl. The moment I spot something suitable in a store window, I duck inside and spend two of the fat coins Stavros gave me on a plain brown cloak that covers most of my dress.

The shop I'm most interested in is tucked away in a quiet row of cafes and stores not far from the old city wall. The man slipping past its weathered wooden door as I approach isn't dressed as finely as I am beneath my new cloak, but his fine linen tunic and embroidered over-vest tell me he's doing well for himself.

I shouldn't stick out badly—and the owner is less likely to treat my questions with suspicion if I appear to be one of the elite.

Like most herbal shops, the interior I step into is dim. A musky scent with an assortment of undertones from prickly to sweet fills the air, some of it drifting off the bundles of dried plants dangling along the edges of the main room.

Behind her counter in front of shelves packed with glass jars of various sizes, the shopkeeper squints at me through wire-framed glasses. Her ample frame is wrapped in a linen dress the same cornsilk yellow as her otherwise graying hair.

She draws herself straighter at the sight of me. "How can I help you today, good lady?"

I let out a breezy giggle, as if I don't have much other than air in my head. "I think this is the place my friends recommended to me, but I might have gotten their directions mixed up. Have you had any customers from the college lately?"

The woman taps her lips, frowning in concentration. She looks as if she's honestly considering the question, not coming up with a lie.

"No one who's specifically said they are, but plenty of folks don't say where they're from, and I don't like to pry."

"Hmm. They're all about my age, and they'd be wearing the latest style of clothing. One of the fellows has dark brown hair about to here"—I gesture vaguely toward my ears—"and a rather dark complexion. On the tall side. The other is fairly short in stature and has curly blond hair. Or maybe you've seen a lady with a red streak in her brown hair?"

The shopkeeper has knit her brow. She shakes her head. "I'm sorry, my lady. I can't say for sure that I've seen any of them."

"Oh." I push my lip into the slightest of pouts. "I must have gotten myself mixed up. It happens sometimes. I suppose, now that I'm here… Do *you* have any pipe fleece in stock?"

The furrows on the woman's forehead deepen. "Pipe fleece? I haven't heard anyone call the stuff that in ages. You mean jazfern?"

I giggle again. "Oh, is that what it's called normally? We're supposed to find a plant mentioned in an old book and bring a sample back to share in class. I thought that one sounded funny."

The shopkeeper only looks puzzled now, but she steps back from the counter toward her back room. "I don't have much of it. Not much use for it really that I know of, except it helps keep a few rare substances I deal in stable. Let me see if I can spare a bit."

Interesting. Well, an herb that can stabilize potent substances seems like a decent candidate for stabilizing one's magic.

*We don't know that no one from the college bought dartling eggshell here,* Julita points out as the woman shuffles around in the back. *Shouldn't we focus on that instead of this pipe fleece stuff from a book that was over five hundred years old?*

I nod in an attempt to tell her I haven't forgotten her main quest. But my heart lifts when the woman returns with a small bundle of purplish dried leaves.

"This should be enough to show it," she says. "If you need more, you'll have to let me know ahead of time."

I smile brightly. "I'll do that. Thank you so much. Since you've been so helpful—one of my other friends heard of something called dartling egg she thought might be useful in her coursework. Do you have that here?"

A twitch of tension crosses the woman's expression before her expression goes still. "What kind of coursework is she doing?"

I cock my head. "Something to do with medicine, I'd imagine. She's training to become a medic."

The shopkeeper relaxes just slightly. She obviously knows that the stuff can be put to unsavory uses, but it must have some legitimate functions as well. "It's not requested often. I only get it by special order."

I put on my best cajoling voice. "I don't suppose you've gotten one of those orders recently enough that I could jump the queue? She'd be *so* grateful."

The woman shakes her head briskly. "Nothing here and nothing on the way. I'm sorry, my lady."

All right, then our conspirators haven't been getting regular stock here, if she can be believed. Not all that helpful, but it does let us cross one avenue of investigation off the list.

I thank the shopkeeper again profusely and pay for my jazfern. Popping it into one of my gown's discreet pockets rather than my pouch, I'm just ambling out the door when I nearly bump into a lithe, unmistakably familiar figure passing by.

Casimir beams at me, his gorgeous face more stunning than ever with the sun shining down on it. "Oh, hello! What a coincidence bumping into one of my schoolmates here."

# SIXTEEN

My heart skips a beat and my tongue tangles for a moment in my shock. And not only because I'm afraid Casimir will ask what I just bought.

Why couldn't the courtesan be at least kind of a jerk like the other guys, so I'd have an easier time ignoring his epic gorgeousness?

I gather myself, setting my hands on my hips and lifting an eyebrow. "It does seem to be a pretty big coincidence."

Casimir's smile turns a bit sly, which somehow takes him to yet another level of breathtaking. "There's a beauty goods shop just down the street that's one of my favorites. I don't suppose that happens to be where you're headed next?"

We aren't really supposed to be spending time together. Did he contrive this meeting to give us an excuse to talk?

What could he have wanted to talk about so urgently?

I'd better find out. I match his smile as well as I can. "Actually, it is."

Casimir turns with a discreet gesture to indicate which way we should walk. "I'd be happy to give you some recommendations if you need them."

"Sure, that sounds great."

As we stroll farther down the street, I flick my gaze around to make sure no one's all that close by. I've been getting a lot of practice at talking so that no one will overhear. "How did you know where I'd be?"

Casimir keeps his voice equally low. "I saw you heading out looking rather purposeful, and I remembered the herb shops you told us we should look into. This is the closest one. And I really do like the beauty store down here, so it wasn't any hardship to wander by."

Julita snickers. *Oh, Cas. Isn't he just lovely?*

I suppose so. I still need to know: "What's going on? Why did you need to talk to me?"

Casimir glances over at me, his pine-green eyes briefly pensive beneath the loose waves of his tawny hair. "Outside of our meetings, you haven't had anyone *you* can really talk to other than Stavros, and I know he wasn't entirely on board with the plan."

He pauses, his eyes searching mine. "And I suppose Julita, but as much as we appreciate that she isn't entirely gone, that can't be an entirely comfortable situation for you either. I thought you might be feeling isolated. It must be a strain constantly putting on a persona in a setting you're unused to."

So he followed me out here and waited around until he saw me… so that he could offer a little company? Even as I try to wrap my head around that generosity, a lump solidifies in my gut.

It *is* lovely of him.

What are the chances he'd bother if he knew what I really am—why I actually came out here?

"Thank you," I say around the matching lump that's crept into my throat. "You didn't have to—"

"I know," Casimir says easily, with a glint of his gemstone teeth. "But we are on this quest together, even if we have to pretend to be apart most of the time. We should support each other when we can."

I can't help giving him a skeptical sideways glance. "You didn't have anything better to do?"

He knocks his elbow playfully against my arm. "No classes this afternoon. If it makes you feel better, my career's entire purpose is making people happy. You can consider this field work."

There's probably something wrong with me that framing the situation that way does make me feel better. He hasn't mentioned my recent purchase, so maybe I really am safe.

I can admit it's a bit of a relief to talk to someone everyone else can see exists, who knows at least some of my secrets.

I study the shops along the curve of the road. "So, where is this beauty goods shop anyway?"

Casimir points. "That one with the pink trim along the edge of the roof. Their soap is the best you'll find anywhere. If you'd like to be left with the softest skin imaginable, that's the one to go with."

I'm not sure I want to tell him that the softness of my skin isn't something I've ever considered. I rub my thumb over my wrist surreptitiously and wonder if it'd feel horrifyingly rough to a noble courtesan.

Well, what does it matter? *I'm* not really a noble anyway, and I'll go back to not being one, gods' forgiveness or not, sooner rather than later.

Nonetheless, I let Casimir usher me into the store. The air inside is as perfumed as the herbal shop, but in a softer, sweeter way that reminds me of Casimir's honeyed scent.

I like it on him, but I'm not sure I'd want to drown myself in the stuff.

While I stand there awkwardly, suddenly feeling as if I have ten pounds of grit on my skin and everyone can see it, Casimir goes to a display table and plucks up a few wrapped soaps. The preteen girl in a modest dress who was giving the table's legs a quick polish steps backward at that moment and bumps into him.

She jerks to the side with a flare of red in her cheeks. "I'm so sorry, sir. I didn't see you there."

Casimir waves off her concern. "It was barely a jostle." He glances down at the table. "I can see you've been doing your job well."

The girl's stance relaxes. She shoots him a shy smile before turning to one of the other tables.

As I watch, a strange flutter passes through my chest that has nothing to do with the courtesan's looks. There's something almost wondrous about the ease with which he spreads his own contentment around him.

How does someone born in the inner wards become that generous?

Less wondrous is the reaction of the gaunt gentleman customer who's also watching from where he was perusing the selection of colognes. He curls his lip in a sneer. "You don't need to worry about 'jostling' him anyway. That's practically his line of work."

The elegant woman behind the store counter stiffens. Casimir doesn't bat an eye.

He dips his head respectfully toward the man. "I'm sure we all deserve the same consideration."

The man snorts and steps closer. "What consideration do you have for everyone else's sensibilities, flashing your gaudy teeth around as if we don't know what they mean? Bilking 'clients' for pay for what should be freely given? They shouldn't allow degenerates like you—"

He moves to jab Casimir's arm, and my hand instinctively jerks toward my nearest knife.

But Casimir moves faster.

With a flick of his fingers I can barely track, the courtesan catches the man's wrist and twists. The man lets out a yelp at the sudden jarring angle.

An instant later, Casimir releases him. The gentleman backs away, hissing while he rubs his wrist.

Julita cackles. *The puffed-up prig got what he deserved.*

Casimir simply smiles. "Ardone blesses some of us with talents just as valuable to many as those brought by any of the other godlen. We all deserve compensation for our skills as well."

The man starts to sputter, but the shopkeeper clears her throat. "I don't allow folk in the shop who'll harass my valued customers. I think it's time for you to take your leave."

The prick lets out a huff, but he goes. The lady aims an apologetic glance at Casimir. "I'm sorry your shopping was disturbed."

He shrugs. "All's well that ends well."

As he motions me over to a far wall where several ornate hair pins and sticks rest on shallow wooden shelves, I can't hold back my awed surprise. "Have you been taking lessons from Stavros?"

Casimir chuckles. "That would be more extensive than is really necessary. Part of the training for certain tracks of the companionship division covers defensive fighting. Enough to deal with the occasional judgmental ass like that one—or to step in if a patron comes under threat during our time together."

I guess that makes sense, even if I'd never have thought of it myself. I fidget with my cloak, willing away the flush that's spread all across my skin.

Is there something wrong with me that I find him even more appealing now that I know he could break a man's wrist if he wanted to?

Casimir shows no sign that he's noticed my discomfort. He picks up one of the hair pins.

"You know, this one would look amazing with the reddish sheen to your hair. That color is almost like amber. I'll bet every woman at the college has been envying it... We might as well make them envy it more."

He flashes another grin at me and brandishes the pin, which holds a vibrant teal stone that I can't help thinking would also match my new favorite dress awfully well too. As much as I know about fashion coordination.

The metal around the gemstone gleams gold. My hand comes to rest on my pouch. "I don't think I can afford—"

Casimir waves off my protest before I can finish it. "I consider it a service to the entire city to add to your beauty. It's no hardship."

I manage not to guffaw at the idea of me having much beauty to begin with. It takes more effort not to totally stiffen up when Casimir reaches to fix the pin in my hair, adjusting my current casual updo.

He's so deftly graceful that his fingers barely graze my skin, but a quiver of heat races over my scalp and down my back anyway. His sandalwood smell trickles through the thicker perfumes of the shop.

As he eases back so I can look at myself in the polished silver mirror next to the shelves, I swallow thickly. The gem really does gleam strikingly against the reddish blond of my hair.

"There," he says. "It's absolutely meant to be, Kindness."

He adds a grin with the lilting nickname, a callback to what he told me after he brought my dresses.

The reference only reminds me of just how kind he's being.

I cast my gaze toward him. "I should be the one calling you that. Is this how you are with all your... your friends?"

I don't know if I can really call myself his friend. I wouldn't be in reality, if we were both being ourselves.

Of course, it might not even be me he's thinking about when he makes a gesture like this. He's being sweet to the woman who *was* his friend—and maybe more—who's experiencing it on some level alongside me.

The reminder that he might not even be seeing *me* when he looks at me—not really—hits me like a bucket of icy water. My smile tightens, and I glance away.

Casimir answers in his usual gentle tone. "If I see an opportunity to bring some extra brightness into someone's life, and it's no trouble for me to do it, I do." From the corner of my eye, I think I see his smile falter just a little too. "It's what I was put in this world for."

My attention jerks back to him, just as his expression turns thoughtful. He rests his hand on my arm, the warmth seeping through the silk sleeve of my dress. "It's been a long time since anyone tried to make you happy, hasn't it? Much too long."

Between his touch and the too-accurate observation, my mind freezes up. All at once, I want nothing more than to escape his caring, perceptive gaze.

"Thank you," I say quickly, detaching the pin. "I appreciate it; it's just too much. I should be getting back to the college for Stavros's next class."

The second I've set the pin back on the shelf, I'm hurrying for the door.

"Ivy," Casimir calls after me, but he won't want to make a scene when we're barely supposed to know each other. I don't hear his footsteps behind me as I stride down the street.

*What was that about?* Julita asks. *You've got to know Cas didn't mean any harm by the remark. He really does want to please everyone.*

And she obviously can't see why that wouldn't make me feel better. "I don't like accepting gifts I can't reciprocate," I murmur, which is maybe a quarter of the truth.

Julita sniffs. *Suit yourself. I don't see any reason to refuse generosity when both people enjoy it.* She pauses. *I won't be offended if you get more friendly with him—or any of the others—you know. Even if I were alive, it isn't as if I'd staked any claim over them.*

"I don't think that would be a good idea." But even after I've said that, I have to add, "Did you ever get… more than friendly with any of them?"

*Oh, no,* Julita says, as if she finds the idea absurd. *Maybe a little flirtation, but, you know, sometimes that's necessary to judge a man's investment. I might consider them friends, but exposing the scourge sorcerers was the important thing. It wouldn't do to distract them from our goal.*

I'm weirdly relieved by her answer and also a little queasy, after seeing how devoted each of the men appear to be to her. But who am I to tell her how she should have run her life when she doesn't even have one now?

By the time I've made it back to Florian's central hill, the walk has smoothed out my thoughts. I ignore the thrum of the temple's energy as I skirt it and then pace through the steps dictated by the passcode to enter the college.

As I cross the first courtyard to the outer school building, I scan the grounds around me out of habit. My gaze snags on a stout older man with silvered brown hair and a thick brow, who's pointed out something to the boy beside him.

My steps slow just slightly while I take them in. The boy is far too young to attend the college, which welcomes students starting in their eighteenth year. I'd be surprised if he's even old enough to have completed his dedication ceremony.

Julita notices my curiosity. *It isn't unusual for the staff to bring around young relatives or the children of friends who are considering what gift they might want to ask for or even which godlen to dedicate themselves to. Give them a little tour, a sense of what possibilities await.*

Her explanation should make perfect sense. The boy looks every bit the noble child in his trim jacket and polished boots.

But just as I'm about to leave them behind, the kid taps his chest with a swift swirl of his fingers.

Not the typical four-part gesture of the divinities, but an appeal I've never seen anyone outside the fringes make.

My feet stall in their tracks for a second before I force myself to move onward.

As subtly as I can, I spare another glance over my shoulder at the professor and the boy—taking in the slightly defensive hunch of the kid's shoulders, the lower lip he's gnawing at. My certainty expands until it's an unshakable heaviness in my chest.

*What's wrong?* Julita asks as I hustle through the entrance hall and across the inner courtyard to the Domi. *I told you, it's utterly normal.*

I let out my breath with a low mutter. "And how normal is it for someone to bring a street urchin around, dressed up like a noble?"

# Seventeen

*Are you absolutely sure?* Julita asks for approximately the millionth time.

I frown at my sallow reflection in the mirror as if I can see her through my light blue eyes. "Yes. That motion the boy made—it's a thing the kids on the fringes pick up from each other. A little appeal for safety and mercy when they're too wary to show the full three-fingered tap. I've never seen a merchant or anyone from the middle wards use it, let alone a noble."

My ghostly passenger stirs restlessly as I pin back a few strands of hair that escaped the formal loops during my trek through the city. *I haven't seen it either. But I would have thought it was just a random nervous gesture.*

"Because you haven't seen it before to recognize it. No one who's normally here would have—the college wants even the cleaning and cooking staff to have middle-ward manners." I stalk back into the main room of Stavros's quarters. "You said the professor he was with is Ster. Torstem. Have you seen him bring that kid around before?"

*I can't remember. Like I told you, it's hardly unusual.*

"What do you know about Torstem?"

*He teaches law for the leadership division. I'd have had a class with him next year…* Julita trails off and then seems to gather herself. *I hadn't paid much attention to him other than that. He doesn't draw much attention.*

"Hmm." I pace the room a few times, and my stomach gurgles. Which gives me the perfect inspiration for my next move. "Other people here will know more about him. And it's just coming on supper time. Let's see if I can find a good conversational partner in the dining hall."

*Even if it is strange, whatever Ster. Torstem is doing, it isn't necessarily connected to the scourge sorcerers,* Julita points out as I head down the hall. *Plenty of other unfortunate things go on here.*

"I've already seen that," I mutter. "But it's not as if we have any other leads to follow up on just yet."

Stepping through the broad doorway with its carvings of Prospira's and Ardone's sigils— recognizing that food is both a bounty and a pleasure—I automatically tense up. The dining hall has become a place of both delight and dread for me.

Delight because of the skillfully simmered and roasted dishes that give off scrumptious scents into the vast space.

Dread because I'm in the same vicinity as more of the rich pricks who attend this place than anywhere else.

I pause off to the side of the door to assess my options. Most of the wide sprawl of stone-tiled floor holds circular tables that can seat as many as eight—ten if the nobles deign to squish.

Nearly two thirds of those are already full. I've caught the start of the dinner rush.

High up on the righthand wall, a shimmering magical display lists the evening's options. Beneath it, students have queued to grab plates of their chosen entrees and accompaniments from various counters open to the kitchen through low openings in the wall.

Well, some of them have queued. I'm just swallowing saliva from my watering mouth and deciding I should start with food before interrogating when Anya and a cluster of her associates sweep straight up to one of the nearest counters, totally ignoring the line.

I have a second to notice Alek among the few students at the head of the queue there, the polished leather of his mask catching the light of the crystal chandeliers overhead. Then Anya flicks her fingers, and a blazing glow explodes in the students' midst.

I jump about a foot off the ground in shock, my hand yanking straight to the folds of silk skirt that conceal the knife strapped to my left thigh. But the glow fades an instant later with a few pained gasps.

The students who'd been at the counter stumble away. Alek is wincing and swiping at his eyes.

"Make a little room, weirdie," Anya sneers at him, sauntering into the space the other students cleared. She narrows her eyes at a woman who was there too and bats at the other student's long hair to briefly expose a strip of scar where her ear should have been. "I don't know why they let the failures in to begin with."

*That girl gave up both her ears and didn't even get a gift,* Julita informs me with a horrified shudder I can feel. My gut knots.

It's always a risk making a sacrifice. If the godlen you're appealing to decides you're asking for more than you've offered or that your intentions are dishonest, they can refuse.

But of course, you can't reattach whatever you've already chopped off or pulled out.

Anya clearly got a gift of her own, whatever that trick with the light is meant to be. She lifts a plate off the counter, swivels around, and catches me glaring at her.

Her lips curve in disdain. She raises her voice to carry across the ten feet between us. "What are you looking at?"

I shouldn't say anything at all. I should drop my gaze and walk away as if I'm not seething.

I've already got enough potential enemies in this place.

But my instincts react to the direct question before I can rein them in. My mouth pops open, my answer just as loud. "Nothing much, obviously."

Several gazes jerk our way. Alek stares at me, probably cursing me out in his head for making a scene, as if she didn't deserve it for shoving him around.

While Anya bristles, I raise my chin and convince my feet to get moving as if I've got better things to do than listen to her response.

Which I do. My stomach is gnawing on itself now, and who knows when I'll ever get to dig into food this fine after I've left the college for good?

My heart thuds a little faster as I weave through the crowd, but Anya's dignity saves me from having her chase me down hurling insults. I'm sure I'll pay for the jab some other way in the future, but future-me can deal with that.

*Supposedly the gift she asked for was simply to light things up,* Julita says. *I've heard she gave up several toes and wears special shoes to compensate. She wants to marry some prominent provint or baron, and maybe she figured a wife who could give him a divine glow would be an excellent selling point. But somewhere in the past several years, she figured out that she could make the light intense enough to be painful.*

And she uses it to skip the dinner line. Why am I not surprised? That's probably the biggest concern Anya faces in her entire day.

One of the counters near the back of the room has barely any line at all. I grab a plate off that one, figuring whatever's unpopular with nobles still has to beat fringe scroungings by a mile.

When I scan the tables, the first person my gaze catches on is one I can't go chat with. Casimir isn't likely to know much about the professors from the other divisions anyway, I'd imagine.

Unless Ster. Torstem has a taste for courtesans.

I realize abruptly that the man who stirred up so many feelings in me this afternoon has two plates in front of him. It looks like he's dutifully cutting the slab of meat on one into bite-sized pieces… while the nobleman next to him strokes his shoulder, eyeing him like *he's* a delectable slab of meat.

Julita chuckles. *His patrons do ask to be spoiled in the most childish ways sometimes. I think the men are even worse for it than the women.*

My stomach flips over. What else is Casimir going to do for his current patron after dinner?

I yank my eyes away. It's not as if he hasn't mentioned that he's already taking on work in his chosen field.

It's not as if I'm idiot enough to think I could pursue even a proper friendship with him, let alone more.

So the idea of how much he'd offer to people who *aren't* me definitely doesn't leave a lingering wobble in my gut. That can't be anything but my hunger catching up with me.

Where else can I sit?

I notice Romild, the woman who wanted the job as Stavros's assistant, glowering at me like her eyes could fling daggers at me. I'll give that table a wide berth.

Oh, there's Esmae, wandering between the seats with her own plate deciding on a spot. She glances over at the same moment and waves for me to join her.

She's in the leadership division too—and she's the only person here outside of Julita's men who's been at all welcoming. She might know a thing or two about Torstem.

We settle into seats at one end of a table while the three women already eating at the other side continue chatting away as if we're not there.

"What did you do to Anya?" Esmae asks. "People are talking as if she's about to declare war."

I snort and wield my fork. "I said a grand total of three words. After she'd already done a damned sight worse to a few people simply for being where she wanted to be."

Esmae grimaces. "She doesn't usually push things very far. People find it easier not to raise a fuss."

"I didn't mean to," I grumble, and pop a bite of the uncertain meat and creamy sauce into my mouth. Then it takes me several seconds to remember what I actually wanted to talk to Esmae about, because everyone in this room is a nitwit for lining up elsewhere—this dish is the best thing I've ever tasted.

When I drag myself out of the daze of my unrefined tastes, I glance over at Esmae, who's picking at her own meal much more daintily than I am. I adjust my grip on my fork to the politest possible angle. "Have you had any classes with Ster. Torstem?"

Esmae cocks her head thoughtfully as she chews. "Not so far. He mainly teaches the senior students. Why?"

I shrug as if it's not all that important to me. "I recognized the name—I think one of my uncles back home went to school with him. Figured I'd let him know what his old schoolmate is up to these days. Does he do much around the school other than teach?"

"He runs a few different student organizations," Esmae says immediately, so clearly I came to the right person. "The mock trials confederate, the Silanian-Icarian brotherhood, and the bug club." She wrinkles her nose.

*Hmm,* Julita says. *Wendos is in the 'bug club'—the entomology society. That was one of the various clubs we've noted that would also give the participant an excuse to go off campus and potentially conduct illicit rituals.*

Well, that could be a useful connection—if Julita is right that Wendos has continued his scourgish ways.

I smile at Esmae. "Are you a member of any of those?"

She chuckles. "Oh, no, I just like to be aware of all the opportunities in my division."

Julita makes a derisive sound. *And she talked as if I'm a bootlicker.*

"Does Torstem work on legal cases outside of the college?" I ask, pondering how a professor from the royal college would end up running into any street urchins to begin with.

"Not that I've heard about. But it's possible." Esmae knits her brow. "He seems fairly approachable. I'm sure if you told him about your uncle, he'd be happy to talk with you even though you're not a student of his."

That would be convenient if I actually had an uncle. But I've always been able to find out plenty of information without talking directly to my target before.

"I'll have to do that," I say as I poke my fork into another morsel of meat—

—and a slender arm slams into my shoulder.

An ample splash of red wine smacks the bodice of my gown, soaking through to my skin in an instant. I jerk around to find Anya dangling the errant glass from her fingers and holding her other hand to her lips in mock concern.

"Oh, I'm *so* sorry, I can be so clumsy at the worst times." Her gaze drops to my dress. "At least I've given you an excuse to find something better to wear to the ball."

As her friends titter around her, she sashays off. I pull at the wet fabric and groan. The stain has already seeped through the pale gray silk all the way past my belt into the skirt.

Maybe I should be glad I don't have to spend any more time wondering what my payback will be. And that it was the gray dress, not my favorite.

"She is *such* a beast sometimes," Esmae mutters, dabbing at my side with her napkin and making a face. "Come on, there's the washing room just over there. If we get some water on it quickly, the stain might not fully take."

I let her hustle me over to the room off to the side of the dining hall that holds several latrine stalls and a few large sinks. It becomes obvious within less than a minute that no amount of water is going to stop my dress from looking like a piebald horse.

"It's fine," I say with a crooked smile. "There are few things I care about *less* than her ruining this gown. I'd rather not let her totally ruin my dinner."

Esmae purses her lips, but she must be able to tell there's no saving the dress anyway.

*We'll find a way to make Anya regret this some other time,* Julita says, with a calculating note in her voice that makes me glad I'm the one in charge here.

As we hustle back to our table, I glance across the room. I don't see Anya anywhere nearby, and Alek is either lost in the crowd now or gone back to his room with his food. I've lost track of Casimir too, but maybe that's for the best.

Benedikt has arrived at a table a few over from ours. When our eyes momentarily lock, he twitches his eyebrow upward in either confusion or amusement.

I suppose I can fill him in on tonight's adventures at the meeting tomorrow, if he's concerned.

My delicious food is thankfully still warm. As I gulp down another mouthful, my mind turns over Anya's very specific insult. "There's a ball coming up?"

Esmae looks at me as if I've broken out in purple polka dots. "In two days. Haven't you heard people talking about it? I'd have thought Stavros would have mentioned it. We have one every month, with everyone at the college invited—well, students and teaching staff, anyway."

I decide not to tell her that barely anyone other than her talks to me at all, and when Stavros does, it's mostly to inform me of my inadequacies. Maybe he doesn't think I should go?

I can't say a quiet night alone in his quarters sounds like a *bad* thing by comparison. He has a lot of books I haven't read yet.

"I assume you're going," I say to Esmae, feeling the need to return her friendliness.

She nods, a dreamy smile crossing her face. "They're really the most enjoyable part of being at the college. And sometimes staff from the palace attend too! It's an excellent chance to mingle with them if you're hoping they'll look favorably on you at graduation."

I swallow some more of the mystery meat that I'm increasingly certain must be goat. "Is that what you're planning on—working at the palace?"

"I hope so." Esmae ducks her head sheepishly. "That's what I've wanted for as long as I can remember. I definitely have no interest in returning to my family's county as the last of four heirs. And what could be grander than a position serving the royal family themselves?"

That would be pretty grand, if grand is your thing. My attention settles on her silk eye patch. It feels like she's opened up enough that it's safe to ask, "The dedication gift you asked for—is that something meant to serve members of the court?"

Esmae's hand flutters to the patch's strap. "Yes. I'm dedicated to Jurnus—I can send messages quickly across long distances. I thought that could be useful with military negotiations and trade and all sorts of things."

"I'd imagine so," I say honestly. It's a good gift, and an appropriate one from the godlen who oversees both communication and travel, but it's not of much use to her if she doesn't land the job. She must be incredibly committed to have made so large a sacrifice.

She peers at me with her remaining eye. "What's your gift, Ivy? You're obviously interested in the military arts—did you dedicate to Sabrelle?"

I open my mouth, sorting through my options of just how extensively I want to lie, and a strange sensation washes over me.

It's not the intense dizziness I felt before when Julita tried to take over—more a lightheadedness, as if my skull is detaching from the rest of my body. Kind of like the first time I discovered pub cider and downed three glasses far too close together.

A giggle spills from my lips. I'm not sure what's funny, but the whole world is going topsy turvy. That's pretty hilarious.

Esmae's forehead has furrowed. "Are you all right?"

A cold streak of fear cuts through my unbalanced state. My body sways, and I can't seem to hold my spine rigid.

What's happened to me?

"I think—possibly not," I manage to say, clamping my hand against the table for balance. My plate rattles.

My plate, nearly cleared of food. Food that I left unmonitored for a few minutes after Anya drenched me with wine.

A fucking beast indeed. Did she sprinkle some kind of powdered drug over it?

It might not even have been her. Romild could have seen me leave and made use of the opportunity too.

I definitely have too many enemies here for someone who's only been at the school for a matter of days.

Whatever drug I've ingested, its effects are still escalating. My vision blurs and doubles and then simply wobbles around like a pond someone's dropped a stone into. I'm somehow losing my grip on the table even though neither it nor I are going anywhere.

Esmae mutters a not particularly ladylike curse and scrambles to her feet. "That terror. If we could prove she poisoned you—this is an *attack*."

I laugh. Bubbles are tickling up from my gut all the way to my throat. "Not poison. Doesn't hurt. I just feel… like everything's floating in circles."

Whoever did this, were they hoping I'd make a fool of myself in front of the dining hall? Say or do something that would call into question my position as Stavros's assistant?

I sway backward and nearly upend my chair. As the legs rap back onto the floor, Esmae tugs me onto my feet.

I stumble, trying to get my bearings, knowing the floor is flat but feeling as if it's bobbing like a badly constructed dock.

There's a flash of gold at the corner of my vision. Two Benedikts—no, it's just one—no, wait, now there's three of them overlapping as they all lean against the neighboring table.

"She looks like she hit the wine a little too hard. Or did they put something extra special in that curry?"

He keeps his tone droll, but he must be concerned, or he wouldn't have risked coming over at all. The bubbles turn warm with gratitude, and suddenly I'm grinning.

"I think Anya put something in her food," Esmae says in a low voice. "I'm going to bring her back to her room."

"Aww, and deprive us of the possible entertainment?" Benedikt teases, but his tone goes just slightly serious when he adds, "I've heard she's staying in Stavros's quarters."

The bastard's bastard is playing the same joker as always but conveying the important information at the same time. Julita picked pretty well with him too.

I try to say so, but all I manage to do is giggle uncontrollably. I wobble along with Esmae out into the hall and over to the stairwell.

"Never had food that fancy," I remark, and burst into more laughter.

Esmae shakes her head. "You'll have to be careful. Who knows what she'll try next time."

She pauses, gripping my elbow as I maneuver my unsteady feet up the stairs. "Julita's been gone an awfully long time now. Anya obviously had it in for her too. You haven't heard from her at all?"

Does she think Anya offed her? For some reason, that idea makes me laugh too.

Anya in a dirty Slaughterwell alley knifing someone. I could more easily picture her flying to the moon.

"Don't know," I mumble. "She's been quiet."

She's being very quiet right now. Maybe she can't speak through the haze in my head?

"I hope no one here hurt her. Even a drug like this at the wrong time… Did she say anything at all about what trouble she might have gotten into or what she was up to?"

I'm not supposed to talk about that, but it's hard to remember what's true and what's acceptable conversation. I stick to simplicity. "No. No. No idea."

Esmae drags in a breath and helps me around the landing. The railing feels slick under my sweating palm, but I think my balance is getting a little better?

It's a good thing I was talking to my friend here while I was eating, or I'd have ingested even more of the drug before I realized something was wrong.

A giddy smile curves my lips. I'm about to tell Esmae how wonderful she is when a shriek rings out from above us.

Esmae's eyes widen. She freezes, looking torn between fleeing and seeing what's going on, so I make the decision for her.

If there's trouble here at the college, that's exactly what I'm looking for.

I propel myself forward, clambering with an occasional hand braced against the steps up to the next floor. Esmae catches up with me just as I shove into the hallway.

I stop in my tracks, shocked into something close to sobriety.

Several students are flattened against the walls or their doors, staring at the wreckage on the floor. And it is a wreckage—several marble busts of prominent former professors that were set on display pillars along the hall have been hurled to the floor and smashed to smithereens.

A couple of the students are bleeding, one guy clutching a scratch on his cheek and another a cut on his forearm.

"Gods above," Esmae says. "What happened?"

"It must have been a daimon," the guy gripping his arm says. "Something just blasted down the hall, flinging the statues around."

A woman swings her head, peering through the hall. "Is it gone? Is it finished?"

Another student shudders where she's crouched by her door. "They just keep getting worse. Why aren't the staff doing something to stop them?"

Because they don't know why it's happening. Because there's terrible magic.

Some of it's in me.

If the gods do look down, if the gods see—

We have to fix this.

My power heaves through my chest, determined to whisk all the statues back into their proper forms and places so no divine figures can get angry. I only manage to suppress it by throwing myself down as if I've lost my balance.

I smack into the floor, and the external pain sharpens my mind. I hug myself, holding in my magic.

And the backlash wrenches through me like I'm swallowing several shards of broken marble.

At my gasp, Esmae ducks down beside me. "Ivy! Great God help me. I should get a medic."

"I'll be okay," I rasp out. "Just... just want to get back to my room."

Possibly I should be thanking Anya, or Romild, for giving me an excuse for this sudden fit. Esmae thinks it's just part of the drug's effect.

But as she helps me back to my feet through the spiraling ache, one thought peals through my scattered mind.

I can't go on like this.

# Eighteen

The student feints and then throws a quick punch that my arm whips up to block. I smile at him in what I hope is an encouraging expression, though I'm mainly attempting to encourage myself.

Or more specifically, to encourage my hidden power not to see this sparring session as a legitimate threat.

Just a little friendly exchange of blows for learning purposes. No mortal danger here.

No reason to start thrashing me from the inside out.

Stavros clicks his tongue approvingly and adjusts his student's stance slightly to the left. "You want to leave as little of your body open to attack as possible. You're getting some good power with your strikes, though. You never know when you might lose your weapon in a melee and need to rely on your fists."

The younger man lifts his chin toward me. "And I'd imagine I'd be up against opponents a little more formidable than that."

The derision in his tone only makes me grit my teeth for a moment. I'm getting used to letting noble snobbery and posturing roll off my back.

But Stavros's jaw ticks, and a chill enters his drawl that reminds me of when he held me at swordpoint the second time we met. "You'd do best not to underestimate an enemy based on appearances. Or to insult my choice of assistants while I'm standing right here."

The student blanches and draws up a step. He bobs his head toward both of us. "My apologies. Thank you for your help."

I suspect the apology is mainly directed at his professor rather than me, but I can take a little satisfaction from it all the same. And from the fact that despite said professor's doubts, I have managed not to resort to the sort of dirty street tactics that might have shifted opinion about my formidableness in any of today's mock fights.

Stavros glances at the students arrayed across the field and then nods to me. "I'm taking them back to the classroom now for a brief strategy discussion. You can tidy up here and then take your leisure."

I give a little curtsy in my training leathers just because I think it'll irritate him. "Thank you, sir."

It's not much leisure. By the time I've put away the equipment we were using, I can't imagine I've got more than a half hour before the bell that'll mean I need to get to today's secret meeting.

And I have a task I've been wanting to attend to since yesterday. With Stavros otherwise occupied, it's perfect timing.

Alek's book didn't include detailed instructions on how the prospective kings of old took their pipe fleece. Examining the dried leaves in the packet the shopkeeper gave me, I decided tea was the safest bet.

I swing by the dining hall to request a cup of hot water from the kitchen staff and hustle up to Stavros's quarters. They're empty, just as I hoped.

I retrieve a couple of the leaves I bought and crumble them over the water. The purple-green bits swirl on the surface, and a thin, slightly sour scent makes me wrinkle my nose.

Maybe I should have asked for some honey too. Oh, well.

*Why are you trying the jazfern on yourself?* Julita asks.

I figured she'd wonder, so I already have an answer ready. "I'd rather not risk poisoning the whole student body—or going to great lengths to administer this stuff to them all if it does nothing. So I'm going to take a weak dose and see if it has any effect on me or my magic."

She doesn't need to know exactly what that magic is. If my ghostly passenger has wondered why she's never seen me overtly making use of my supposed talents, she doesn't comment now.

While I wait for my tea to steep, I change into my favorite gown. Then I perch on the edge of the sofa-turned-bed and start sipping the tea.

The herbal bite to it makes me wince. I force down a larger gulp to get it over with.

It doesn't matter how awful it tastes. Confining the monstrous urges that trickle out of my soul would be worth just about anything.

I'm halfway through the cup when Stavros strides into the room. I startle with a hitch of my pulse —I'd assumed he'd go straight to the meeting from his classroom.

The scent of the pipe fleece tea must be strong enough for him to get a whiff, because he gives the mug a quizzical glance before lifting his gaze to me. "What in the realms are you drinking—lemon rind mixed with pine needles?"

I make a face even though his assessment of the flavor isn't totally off. "It's a trick my grandmother taught me as a kid. Helps bruises heal."

Julita takes on an arch tone. *He's not going to be happy if you have to admit you lied later.*

I can't answer her, and I'll cross that bridge when I come to it. Unless it'll actually help our larger cause, I definitely don't want the former general thinking about reasons I might be focusing on suppressing magical abilities.

He chuckles like I expected, his eyes flashing with amusement and challenge. "I give you what you've been asking for, and now you're complaining. Where's the appreciation, Thief?"

The nickname doesn't sound quite as insulting in his current tone. And he did offer a little trust by letting me get more involved in his lessons today.

"I have all the appreciation," I say, matching his attitude. "That doesn't mean I want to go around in frothy gowns with my arms all black and blue. A lady can have multiple desires."

He walks over to the cabinet where I've learned he keeps his various prosthetics. "And here I thought you'd take any excuse not to wear those heaps of silk."

I smooth my hand over the skirt of my turquoise dress, not just soft but *clean* thanks to the college's laundry services. "I'm not saying I'll be bringing them back to the fringes with me, but they might have grown on me a little."

Or maybe I'm just enjoying not having the constant sensation of grit against my skin. I might as well appreciate *that* while I can.

"Hmm." Stavros's grin comes out. He twists off the metal hook-like hand he favors for hands-on training out of the harness around his forearm and picks out the clay one that looks the most like an actual hand. "I suppose we could keep you in them for one of the practice sessions and you could play damsel in distress."

I glower at him. "Now that you've finally let me properly participate, are you just looking for excuses to never do it again?"

"Oh, I'm simply thinking through all the possibilities." The former general clicks his new hand into place and strolls over to his desk. He pauses there and glances over at me again. "You didn't do a bad job of it this morning, I'll admit. You moderated your more questionable tactics rather well."

Gods above, did the great General Stavros just show *respect* for my combat ability? A smile tugs at my lips with more warmth than I'm sure I want to be feeling.

But hey, a victory is a victory.

"That sounds like an insult wrapped in a compliment, but I'll take it!" I announce.

Stavros snorts and reaches for a sheaf of papers left off to the side of his desk.

Julita's laugh rings out through my head. *I knew you two would get along eventually.*

I'm glad someone's totally happy about it.

I haven't seen the former general do much in the way of paperwork since I started living in his quarters, though I assume all professors must need to do some, no matter how famous they are. A few times, Stavros has carried notebooks or scrolls off to his bedroom as if they contain matters too sensitive to be left in my reach.

Apparently he's either decided I'm not a security threat or that there's nothing all that delicate in these reports, because he squints down at them at his desk now. Squints and gives that odd twitch of his head, holds still and twitches again.

As I down the last of my horrid tea, the corners of his mouth tighten in a faint grimace. It occurs to me that there are obvious consequences of his battle injury that I hadn't considered before.

I set down the mug and get up from the sofa. "Do you have trouble reading?"

Stavros's eyes jerk toward me again, darkening at the same time as his voice does. "What?"

"I just—" I motion toward the papers. "Julita told me that your injury affected your sight."

The former general's entire stance has stiffened, the tensed muscles bulging beneath his shirt. My pulse stutters.

For a second, I almost forgot just how massive that muscular form of his is, especially compared to my gawky body.

Stavros's tone turns both colder and smoother than when he set his student straight. "I'm failing to see how that's any of your business."

Possibly I've misplaced my sense of self-preservation, or maybe I'm just sick of trying to keep my head down while everyone in this place slings venom at me.

I set my hands on my hips. "I was only going to suggest that *perhaps* if there's nothing horrifyingly confidential in there, I could read them out loud and spare you the trouble. Assist, since that's supposedly my job."

Somehow everything about Stavros manages to harden even more, from his gaze to the set of his jaw. "I don't need any assistance. Julita should also have told you that I can handle my affairs perfectly fine on my own."

*Oh, yes,* Julita says with a hint of mocking. *He gets by just fantastically. Other than when he needs to spend more than five seconds not being a prick to the woman who's keeping me in this world.*

A flicker of amusement at her remark must show in my face, because Stavros outright bares his teeth without my saying anything. "Do you have any other helpful suggestions? I'd think carefully about your answer."

The hairs on the back of my neck stand on end. He hasn't moved, hasn't made a single threatening gesture, but I see the ruthless general in him loud and clear.

"No," I say thinly, and clamp my mouth shut before anything more impertinent slips out.

"Good," he snaps. "Then why don't you run along to the meeting, since apparently you're itching for work to do? I'm sure Aleksi has all kinds of things you can read down in the archives."

If he's going to be that way, I suppose I will.

I turn toward the door with a swish of my skirt—something else I'm starting to appreciate about gowns. Tunics just don't swish with any kind of effectiveness. "Good idea. It wouldn't be wise for us to arrive at the same time anyway. Thank you so much for your sage guidance."

And then I get my ass out the door.

*He's just a little sensitive about his new deficiencies,* Julita says as I push into the stairwell, working on unclenching my jaw. *I can't say the prickliness is particularly appealing, but it'd have been much harder to convince him to take up my cause if he hadn't had some kind of sensitive spot I could prod.*

Is that why she really turned to Stavros out of all the professors? Not because she thought he was most likely to be able to take on the scourge sorcerers at the college, but because she saw an ideal point of emotional manipulation?

Even though I'm annoyed at the jerk, the thought of her poking at his war wounds—practically literally—gives me a jab of queasiness. Then Julita makes an urgent, wordless sound that draws me up short.

I understand why before she's said a word. A head of shaggy brown hair is just emerging through a doorway on the landing a flight below us.

*What's Wendos up to now?* Julita mutters.

As far as I can tell, following at a careful distance behind him all the way down to the first floor, all he's up to is walking from his dorm to the classrooms. He turns down the hall that leads to the inner courtyard while I have to veer in the other direction to reach the row of tapestries and the hidden entrance.

Julita keeps murmuring darkly as if to herself. *He's got to be involved somehow. I could keep an eye on him better when our dorms were around the corner from each other.*

"I'd rather eat one of these gowns than try to share a dorm with Anya," I inform her under my breath.

It makes sense that Julita hates the guy so much, but I'm starting to see why the men get that skeptical look on their faces when he's mentioned. She assumes he's up to no good at every turn with nothing to show for it.

What if Wendos really has left his bad childhood decisions behind him? How much can any of us trust Julita's judgment when she's harboring all that past resentment?

As I slip down the stairs through the shadowy magical passage, I shake those worries off as well as I can. There's clearly *something* horrible going on here at the college, or the daimon wouldn't be wreaking havoc.

And whatever it is, we'll all be better off if we can figure it out before their agitation spreads any farther.

It seems I'm not the only one feeling the urgency. I'd guess word about last night's smashed statues has spread—and maybe about my incident in the dining hall too. When I emerge into the glow of the archives room, Julita's other three men are already gathered around the desk.

Alek is standing behind it in a typical pensive pose. Benedikt has hopped up to perch on the corner and is swinging one toned leg breezily as if he hasn't a care in the world, but the flash of his eyes when he sees me tells me he's still concerned about yesterday.

And Casimir's response makes it clear Benedikt has shared his observations. The courtesan hurries over, his gaze sweeping over me as if checking for lingering clumsiness.

He stops a few feet away and offers one of his gentle smiles. "You're having an even rougher time of it here than I realized. Have you totally recovered from yesterday's incident?"

The wobble that runs through my pulse when he looks at me that way isn't fair. Neither is the sudden urge to close the distance between us and lean right into his warmth.

I don't think he'd push me away. But his compassion isn't for me, not really.

I have to remember that.

Would I even want to be like that man ogling him last night? The thought makes me cringe inwardly.

I force a smile onto my own lips and keep my tone light. "I seem to have pissed some people off without meaning to. But whatever they stuck in my food, it only hit me about as hard as a few rounds of ale. Not as hard as the daimon that ran through the third-floor hallway hit those statues."

Alek winces. "I've gathered that the palace has insisted on a full inquiry after that display. But—"

With a shift in the air behind me, Stavros's smooth voice rolls through the room. "But no one has any solid explanations to offer them. Because *we* still don't have anything remotely resembling proof."

Benedikt glances over at the new arrival. "I had a chat with a couple of the advisor of commerce's lackeys this morning. It seems a supply of solm sap went 'missing' from the harbor a couple of days ago, and no one's been able to determine who took it."

Alek's head jerks around. "That's one of the other substances I saw reference to in relation to the old scourge sorcerers."

The bastard's bastard nods. "Exactly. The schemers must have snatched it up."

Julita shivers. *What are those villains planning now?*

Benedikt turns back to Stavros. "We could try telling the Crown's Watch what Julita's observed and all the other things we've found that add up. The fact that she was murdered says a lot."

Casimir's mouth twists pensively. "Would they listen when she isn't here to tell them directly?" He shoots me an apologetic glance that it's clear is more for my ghostly passenger. "No one else knew her well enough to confirm that Ivy really is hosting her soul. From us, it's only hearsay."

"And with her body vanished, we have no way to prove the murder either," Stavros puts in with a growl. He isn't looking at me at all, but after our discussion upstairs, I'm all right with that.

Now does seem like a good idea to mention that I may have made a slight bit of progress. "There's something new I want to look into. Or someone new."

Alek catches my gaze with a glint of curiosity in his bright brown eyes. The same ridiculous part of me that wobbles over Casimir's smile twinges with the yearning to share a knowing moment with him.

But what I'm going to talk about isn't what he and I discussed the other day anyway.

Benedikt lifts his chin toward me encouragingly. "What've you got, Knives?"

Julita stirs in my head with anticipation. I drag in a breath and decide to get right to it. "One of the law professors is bringing in outer-warder kids dressed up as nobles and taking them around campus. Ster. Torstem. I saw him with one yesterday."

All four of the men stare at me for a few seconds. Stavros ambles toward the desk, his head cocked to one side. "And you know this because of your magical urchin-detecting gift?"

His tone isn't quite as sharp as when he snapped at me in his quarters, but it's still got an edge under the teasing lilt.

I meet his gaze steadily. "Most people around here never seem to look past appearances. You certainly don't know the subtleties of street-rat behavior. Whereas, as you've liked to point out to me, I'm one of them."

"If Ivy says she's sure of what she saw, I think we should believe her," Cas says quietly.

Benedikt twirls a quill he's picked up between his fingers. "What do urchins have to do with scourge sorcery? Maybe Torstem simply likes watching them play dress-up."

"I don't know," I admit. "I just thought it was strange and that we should look into it."

Alek's mouth tightens with a hint of queasiness. "The accounts I've read of the original scourge sorcerers… Children were some of their favorite targets for increasing their power. Get them sacrificing on the sorcerer's behalf at their dedication ceremony."

My own stomach flips over. "You think Torstem could be murdering these kids for power?"

Alek holds up his hands. "We can't assume that. The records say that they needed to use supplicants who were close to them—usually family members and friends. People who *could* honestly dedicate the sacrifice of their life to someone else's use honestly, because they were devoted to the sorcerer. I read that there were some who had child after child simply to indoctrinate them all before offering them up…"

He trails off, looking even sicker than before.

I can't restrain a shudder. "This kid definitely wasn't raised by any part of a professor's family."

"He has one daughter, grown and an advisor for one of the provinces near the capital," Stavros puts in. "No one's mentioned her missing an exorbitant number of body parts that would indicate even a significant living sacrifice. I don't know about nieces or nephews."

Benedikt twirls his quill at Alek. "Isn't he the staff leader for at least one of the clubs in your list of the ones that make regular trips off campus?"

Julita pipes up. *Yes, exactly what I thought. And Wendos is all mixed up in it too.*

Alek's eyes cloud with thought. "He has a group of elite law students who he takes on regular trips to the surrounding cities to observe provincial and county legal processes. The entomology club goes on periodic insect-observing and collecting expeditions. And his late wife was originally from Icar— he takes the Silanian-Icarian brotherhood on excursions to towns along the border."

"So he'd have lots of chances to lead illicit rituals away from the prying eyes of the capital," I fill in with a grimace, and then add reluctantly, "Julita says Wendos is part of the 'bug club.'"

The others get that expression like they've smelled cow dung, but then all four gazes turn more intent.

Benedikt fixes his on me with the unsettling impression I'm getting used to that it isn't me he's looking at right now. "Has Jules noticed anything else intriguing since she started traveling around with you on campus?"

Julita sighs. *I wish you could say I have.*

I shake my head. "She's been pointing out people I should keep an eye on and observations she's made before, but we haven't uncovered anything new other than the Torstem thing."

Disappointment flickers across the men's faces, but Casimir smooths the moment over in typical graceful fashion. "Whatever exactly is going on, it's definitely an unusual situation. We need to determine what Ster. Torstem's intentions are."

I fold my arms over my chest. "There's got to be a way to find out where that kid—and any others he's brought around the school, if he has—came from. Surely he isn't randomly plucking them off the streets of Slaughterwell or Tangleside."

Benedikt snaps his fingers. "And if we find out where he got the kid, we can find the kid himself and ask him what Torstem was up to!"

"You want me to abuse my staff privileges again," Stavros says dryly. "I'll see what I can discover through my access to faculty records."

Alek glances around the room. "I might be able to trace some of his connections outside of the school through the general records as well."

"Don't go approaching anyone from the fringes without talking to me," I say, shooting a firm look at all of them. "*Especially* if he's done something they're uncomfortable talking about, they'll only clam up more if some noble starts badgering them. I should handle any inquiries beyond the inner wards."

Casimir beams at me. "Of course. It only makes sense. That's why we're lucky to have you working with us."

I contain the giddiness his compliment provokes. "We should keep in mind Alek's point about families too. Are there any staff or students at the college who've had spouses, siblings, or children make unusual sacrifices or outright disappear? I assume there are familial records somewhere."

Benedikt shoots me a grin. "And also good old-fashioned gossip."

Alek is already turning toward the door to the adjoining rooms. "We do have family trees for many of the prominent lineages…"

An unfamiliar sensation that's much more than giddiness sweeps through me from head to toe.

They're listening to me. Taking my suggestions as commands and springing to action.

Like I really am an equal partner in this investigation instead of an unexpected interloper.

I've never had a chance to establish anything I could call comradery before. I had no idea collaborating could feel this *good.*

It's not the closeness I so often craved when I watched Ewalin and her mother bantering by the bee hive… but the sudden wash of warmth fills the same hollow inside.

Then Stavros pops the bubble of my exhilaration with a low chuckle and an offhand jab. "Look at you taking over. I don't know whether we should be thanking you or Julita chatting away in your head."

My spirits plummet as quickly as they lifted. "When something's from Julita, I tell you so," I say tartly, but my gut has twisted.

Will any of them totally believe that?

*As if I'd have brought you here if you weren't capable of thinking for yourself,* Julita says with a sniff. *You're handling them wonderfully, Ivy.* Someone *needs to keep them on track.*

I don't know why, but her assessment of the situation only deflates me a little more.

I take a step back from the men. "I'll continue making my own inquiries as I can. It seems like we all have plenty to do now."

So there's no reason for me to linger and continue being reminded of how I'm not really meant to be here at all.

Before I can leave, Casimir brightens as only he can. "The ball will give you—and Julita—plenty of chances to observe both the students and the staff with their guards down."

I hesitate. "You think I should go?"

Benedikt waggles his eyebrows. "You were planning on skipping the biggest party of the month?"

"Well, I don't exactly have a lot of experience with reveling with nobles." Or rather, reveling in general.

Navigating a ball feels like a much higher magnitude of con artistry than handling classwork or a hunt.

"Don't turn tail on us now, Thief," Stavros drawls, so apparently even he expects me to pull this off too.

Alek looks as if the thought of balls makes him feel about as sick as scourge sorcerers carving up their kids does, but he inclines his head too. "It is probably the best opportunity you'll get all month to observe and overhear things people would usually keep hidden."

Julita shifts in the back of my mind with motion that feels almost like a pat on my head. *Don't worry about it. I can talk you through the whole thing. It'll be fun!*

I have my doubts about that, but I can hardly back down now. "All right. I guess tomorrow I'm going dancing."

Gods help us all.

# NINETEEN

As I let her into Stavros's quarters, Esmae lets out a little gasp. "Oh, it's gorgeous."

Her gaze sweeps over the ballgown I've mostly managed to put on myself—because I didn't want the woman who's somehow become my friend noticing the lack of godlen mark on my front or the scars on my back. I resist the urge to hug myself against her assessment.

The dress *is* gorgeous. When I unfurled it from the package a messenger dropped off a few hours ago, I might have gasped myself.

Translucent swaths of sky blue and seafoam green tumble down across an underlayer of paler blue, giving the impression of gleaming water flowing from my collarbone to my toes. Gold embroidery dances along the waistline and in trickles down the skirt like froth on the water.

Even thinner gauze swirls from my shoulders to my forearms, disguising the knobby elbows that a week of noble food hasn't managed to fill out. Linzi's white ribbon around my bicep only shows faintly through even in the bright lights of the apartment.

A thin silk cloak streams from the back of the neckline nearly to my feet, ensuring my scars are totally concealed.

He thought of everything.

I think I'd have known that Casimir must have picked out this dress even if it hadn't arrived with the hair pin I admired in town tucked into the same bundle. I can't imagine anyone else being that aware of the parts of me I'd prefer to disguise.

To top it off, the overlapping panels of fabric obscure slits that mean I'll still have access to at least a couple of knives. He might have not just picked it out but had the gown custom-made.

The knowledge sends a bubbly feeling through my chest as if I've already downed a couple of glasses of champagne. I'm not sure I like the sensation.

I'm not sure I could possibly belong in this dress. But here I am.

I smile awkwardly and motion toward my lower back. "I don't know if I've gotten the lacing as tight as it should be." I wasn't going to ask Stavros to lend a hand before he set off to make his own ball preparations elsewhere.

"Let me see…" Esmae sweeps over in her own gown, a purple one with just a narrow swath of gauze across her otherwise bare shoulders and thick embroidery defining the waistline above the billowing skirt. It's probably more in the current court fashion than my own, but I can't say I give a roach's ass about that.

*Why is the one-eyed mouse here again?* Julita mutters as Esmae eases aside the lower part of the cloak to give the ribbons at the small of my back a deft tug.

We already had that argument after Esmae volunteered when I saw her at breakfast this morning. I pointed out that between Julita and me, I still only have one pair of hands.

And it's a pair of hands that isn't particularly practiced at the beautifying arts.

My ghostly guest couldn't deny that, but it hasn't stopped her from grumbling. I suspect she's a little offended that Esmae has made more of an effort to be friendly with me than it sounds like she ever did with Julita.

Esmae ushers me over to the mirror mounted on the wall and slips her fingers into my hair. "That pin goes perfectly with the dress too. We could gather your hair all the way up like this. Or keep it more arranged at the back like this."

"Let's go with that one," I say to the second style, and do my best to hold still while she tucks the strands into an intricate arrangement I could never have accomplished on my own.

Before my eyes, I'm transforming into someone even I could mistake for a noble.

Staring at my reflection, my mouth goes a bit dry. A sour flavor lingers on my tongue—I choked down another cup of pipe fleece tea a half hour ago.

I turn away from the mirror toward Esmae. "Can I help you with your hair? I don't know any complicated styles, but I'll do my best."

She smiles back at me. "Thank you. I actually like the way you have yours usually—the broader loops with some of it left loose along your shoulders. That would be perfect with this dress."

"I think I can manage that."

It's a damn sight easier pinning whorls of hair when I can see them right in front of me. I fix the strands in place carefully around the tie of her eye patch, hoping I don't repay my schoolmate with a hairstyle that'll tumble apart halfway through the dancing.

"It's nice, you know," Esmae says abruptly when I'm about halfway through my work. "I mean… I haven't really had a friend here before. Not someone I could get ready for the balls with and that sort of thing."

The admission jabs right through the center of me. I've never had a friend like that ever in my entire life, unless you count the kids my sister and I used to ramble around with when I was small enough to wear smocks.

Imagining I could be wrapped up in the warmth of Ewalin's family wasn't anything like actually having that company. And I can hardly call my grudging allies "friends" even if they saw my uninvited passenger as one.

"You made an exception for me?" I say.

Esmae laughs lightly. "I guess I've always been so focused on my studies, I didn't see the point. But maybe that was silly of me. And… I feel more at ease with you than I usually do with the other students here. It never seems like you're waiting for an ideal moment to get one up on me."

I suppose that's true, even if I am putting on a totally false front about who I am. Her openness leaves me momentarily off-balance.

I offer a little honesty of my own, as much as I can. "I haven't really had good friends either. I'm grateful you've looked out for me."

Julita makes a faint gagging sound in the back of my head, and I resist the urge to smack her through my new fancy hairdo.

"Anyway," I add, "there's nothing wrong with studying. I've always believed that the more you can learn, the more you can do."

Esmae lets out another laugh. "I just want to be able to do enough to impress the palace staff. There's *got* to be a position for me there. I don't have any familial connections to give me a leg up."

I grimace around a twinge of guilt. "Stavros pushed me awfully hard to make sure I could handle being his assistant."

"Oh, I didn't mean—I wasn't thinking of you specifically. I wouldn't be looking to land a job as assistant to a professor anyway."

As I step away from her, she sighs and peers at her reflection approvingly. "I want to meet all the people coming in and out of court, travel with the royal family when they move around the provincial palaces, see everything I can of the continent. I never ventured more than a few counties over before I came to the college."

"I'm sure you'll manage it," I say. If nothing else, her determination rings through every word.

She closes her eye just for a second and then shoots me a tighter smile over her shoulder. "I'd better. If I end up having to go home, I know my parents are just waiting to arrange a marriage to whichever blustering merchant in the area they most want to appease at that particular moment."

Ugh. I offer a little shudder in sympathy. "You can definitely do better than that."

"I'm getting there. Is this what you want for the rest of your life? Work at the college? Even if your family didn't want to spare you before, now that you're here it wouldn't be much trouble to enroll in classes as well. You could aim for anything."

If only she knew.

I shrug as if the topic isn't of all that much importance to me. "I'm glad to be where I am now. It's a good position. But I'm not married to it if a better opportunity comes along."

The vague answer feels slimy as it slips off my tongue, with all the things I'm hiding.

Esmae doesn't seem to notice. "I suppose that's a healthy outlook."

She brandishes a stick and a couple of containers of powder she was carrying with her. "Now let's see what a little makeup can do for you."

I raise an eyebrow. "Is that really necessary when we're all wearing masks?"

The nobles apparently prefer to cover their faces for a little plausible deniability about whatever hijinks they expect to get up to while they party. I guess that means Alek will fit in better than usual.

Esmae grins. "That's why we focus on the eyes and the mouth. I've never even seen your face powdered. I'm sure we could bring a little more color into it…"

She stands between me and the mirror as she works, patting a cool sponge all over my face and then applying color with brushes of varying sizes.

The cosmetics don't feel as heavy as I expected, but maybe Esmae just has a light touch.

When she steps back, I stare at myself. *Now* I look like a noble.

I look like a stranger.

My cheeks have a rosy tint that's unfamiliar on my sallow skin. A deeper ruddy tone makes my lips look fuller.

But it's my eyes that stand out the most, kohl frames and shaded lids turning the bright blue irises piercing.

Esmae clicks her tongue. "It's a shame we'll have to cover most of that up. Could you line my eye? It's always hard when I only have the one to see with."

I can at least offer a steady hand if not one that's wielded kohl often in the past. "Of course."

Once she's satisfied with herself as well, we help each other fasten our simple masks over our upper faces—hers a purple lace that matches her dress, mine a sleek gold imprinted with a subtle lattice pattern that Casimir must have picked out to coordinate with my gown's embroidery. It brings out the red in my hair, as he may have counted on as well.

It's a perfect disguise. I'm going to mingle with Florian's elite while they drink and cavort—and do my best to be in the right place to overhear secrets spilled with a slip of a tongue.

Even Julita sounds pleased, despite Esmae's assistance. *You're doing me proud, Ivy. Now let's get out there and track these scourge sorcerers down.*

We only have one flight to ascend to reach the ballroom. It takes up most of the space on the fifth floor, under the building's broad dome.

As we step through the doorway, I stop my jaw from dropping only with sheer force of will. I've always known the nobles went for extravagance, but this… This is as if the godlen of beauty herself touched the space with her blessing.

Crystal chandeliers twinkle at varying heights across the arced ceiling, which looms so far above our heads they look like clusters of stars. Their glow beams down across the otherwise darkened dance floor in iridescent streams. I can't tell whether the crystals themselves give the light that pearly quality or if it's the result of someone's gift.

Flashes of color slip in and out of those glowing beams as nobles in billowing dresses and velvet suits of every hue in existence circulate through the room. Staff in formal but subdued black suits circulate between them with platters of bubbling glasses that hold their own, definitely magical glow.

The music seems to wind alongside them, coursing from every corner of the room with its lilting melody. I can't see the performers. Are there dozens of them or only a few projecting their music through the vast space?

More magical décor glimmers around the edges of the room: pink roses for Ardone and orange blossoms for Inganne, gliding swans and fluttering butterflies.

One of the waiters breezes by us with a tray, and Esmae snatches up a glass. I decide I'm better off keeping my head as clear as possible.

The very atmosphere in the ballroom tastes like a drug. And I remember far too well how my control started to slip in the grips of whatever Anya or Romild slipped in my dinner the other night.

I drift forward, searching the figures with their gilded masks for any features I can recognize. My gaze halts on a towering figure near the edge of the crowd who's staring right back at me.

There's no mistaking Stavros, even in a suit twice as fancy as anything I've seen him wear before and his realistic prosthetic hidden by a glove. No one else has a frame quite that massive to fill out the deep green jacket and trousers to such impressive effect.

No one else has that shock of blood-red hair turned even ruddier in contrast with the green.

He's wearing a gold mask too, to match the ample detailing on his jacket, a few shades yellower than his light brown skin. The shape of it is sharper than mine, though, with a definite masculine edge.

And his eyes bore into mine from across the room, refocused with that subtle twitch of his head, leaving no doubt that he's recognized me too. Between the fractured lighting and the mask, it's hard to read his expression, but his normally nonchalant posture has stiffened.

His lips part with a flick of his tongue over them that sends an unwelcome waft of heat crackling over my skin. Then he turns away as if he never saw me.

Of course. I'm not here to talk to *him*.

He was probably just startled to see me looking so little like a thief.

*Come on, let's get in there,* Julita says impatiently, and I venture farther into the mass of nobles.

Skirts brush against mine, and laughter bounces alongside the music. I think I spot Anya's pale hair off to my right, but she's whirled away an instant later by her current dancing partner.

I sidle closer to a cluster of figures gabbing between sips of wine. All I hear them exchanging are judgments of the outfits of those outside their group.

Farther along, I catch one male student making a remark about a dagger to his friends. When I linger, it turns out he's describing an ornamental piece his father is having made for his birthday, encrusted with gems.

Gold and jewels gleam everywhere—along belts, around necks, on fingers. In my hair.

So much wealth in one room, it could see every family on the fringes raised out of squalor for a year or better.

And I'm here marinating in it rather than bringing the people I considered *my* family their dues.

I let myself wander out of the crowd at the other end of the room and take a moment to rest my hand against the wall and close my eyes. The lights seem to keep swaying through my eyelids.

I'm here for those people. Here to make sure they don't get burned up in retribution for crimes they could barely conceive of. That's more important than leaving a few coins on a windowsill.

But in that moment, I can't help feeling I'm getting nowhere at all.

When I open my eyes again, I notice Alek standing several feet away, also hanging back by the wall. It's easy enough to recognize him when he's stuck with his usual leather mask, which gleams softly beneath the chandeliers.

His stance is uneasy, like he doesn't feel he fits in here any more than I do. But if I hadn't already thought there was plenty striking about his penetrating eyes, his dark hair, and those full lips, seeing him in ball getup would have shocked the realization into me. He's either got some fashion sense or a friend who does, because the crimson jacket sets off his bronze skin to impressive effect.

Hopefully I'm not ogling him *too* openly, because in the middle of my assessment, he glances over at me. He draws himself up a little straighter, his jaw working.

I'm about to smile, because it feels like I should acknowledge him somehow, but then he's striding off around the room in the opposite direction.

Two out of two turning their back on me so far. I'm obviously making a fabulous impression.

The music dips as one melody blends into a more languid one. My gaze snags on Casimir's tawny hair in the mass of dancers, just stepping away from a woman I don't recognize whose ebony ringlets are gathered in a sphere of curls on her head.

My stomach wobbles, but not in a good way.

I jerk my attention to the side and start to slink back into the crowd on a course that won't take me toward him. But I've made it less than ten paces when a steady but gentle hand closes around my elbow.

"There you are. Oh, that gown did turn out impressively, didn't it?"

I spin toward the courtesan, who's grinning at me from behind a silver mask dotted with sapphires much like the gems standing in for some of his back teeth.

You'd think the lesser metal would make him look shabby compared to all his classmates sporting gold. But with the midnight-blue of his suit and the silvery sheen to his dress shirt beneath, he looks like he could be a godlen of the night sky rather than any kind of mortal.

My pulse stutters, and I lose track of my voice. "I— Thank you. For the dress. And the hair pin. I told you—"

"I know what you told me." Casimir touches my chin with just enough pressure to tilt it slightly upward, but the contact sends a flush straight down my chest. "And you've elevated the gown beyond what it was on its own. You're stunning, Ivy."

It's literally his job to make people happy, so I doubt he entirely means that. But it makes my heart skip another beat anyway.

"Aren't we supposed to be pretending we barely know each other?" I can't help asking.

He makes a dismissive sound. "We're incognito. Besides, I'm simply a schoolmate struck by an incredible beauty wandering by."

His smile widens, and the hand on my arm slides down to twine his fingers with mine. "You're not going to deny me the chance to fully appreciate our handiwork, are you? One dance won't hurt anyone."

It's hard to argue with his warmly cajoling tone. And his "our" melts something inside me, even though I know he and Esmae deserve the lion's share of the credit for however good I do look.

"I didn't realize it came with additional conditions," I say tartly as I let him set his other hand on my waist.

Casimir chuckles. "You're allowed to say no. But you could think of it as part of your cover. It'll look odd if you come to a ball and never dance."

He does have a point.

I set my hand awkwardly on the lapel of his jacket. "I don't know any of these dances, so trying might actually be worse."

"That's all right. I've trained to be an excellent partner. We'll stick to a simple one. Just follow my lead."

The mention of his partnering ability reminds me of the woman I saw him with a few moments ago.

My throat constricts, but I force myself to ask, "Are you not hired for the ball?"

The courtesan shakes his head without any sign that he's bothered by the question. "I approach these events as an opportunity for potential patrons to sample my talents."

My cheeks prickle with a hotter flush from before. "I wouldn't—"

Casimir's voice softens. "I know. This is simply a dance between friends."

Are we friends, really?

That's not a question I can ask. It's impossible at least as much because of who I am as who he is.

He steps to the side so smoothly that my feet move automatically to follow. It only takes a few paces, charting a careful circle across the floor, before the rhythm of the music melds with our movements in my head.

After a minute, I've relaxed enough to try to match his cross-steps. My hand eases up to rest on his shoulder.

Casimir guides me a little closer to him, and his honeyed sandalwood scent drifts over me. My body tingles with awareness of the few inches left between us—of the sinewy muscles responsible for his feline grace. Of his gaze on me, even now.

I lift my head to meet it, but that might not have been the wisest plan. He smiles down at me, our feet still moving in tandem, and seeing his stunning face so close knocks most of the breath from my lungs.

I find myself saying the first words that pop into my head, as unwise as they might be. "Do you normally have much time to do things that aren't about pleasing patrons or learning how to?"

Nearly everything I've heard him talk about that isn't to do with me and investigating the conspiracy has revolved around his work.

Casimir shrugs. "It's a fairly immersive calling. But I spend time with classmates I consider friends." His mouth slants a little, giving a bittersweet cast to his smile. "Although as we branch out into taking on patrons ourselves, a certain level of competition has added tensions."

My heart squeezes in sympathy for the hint of loneliness I catch in those words.

My dance partner doesn't give me the chance to express it. He whirls us around, his hand on my waist firming to ensure I keep up.

"I know you're a reader, but not what sorts of things," he says. "Sprawling histories? Fanciful imaginings?"

He's shifting the focus back on me—my interests, my desires.

I swallow thickly before I answer. "Both of those and pretty much anything else I can get my hands on. It's all interesting one way or another. But I suppose I enjoy tales of adventures the best— real and fictional." I've already devoured the first volume of Gisela Luvinya's Traveling Diaries.

I'm not going to let Casimir act as if it's only my concerns that matter, though. I give his shoulder a light squeeze. "What about you? Are you a frequent visitor of the library?"

His smile turns slightly sheepish. "I can't say so. I'm passable with composing poetry, but the written word isn't a great strength of mine."

He tips his head with the melody lilting around us. "Of all the arts, I prefer music. Perhaps someday I'll have the chance to play my flute for you."

That's always what he's thinking of, isn't it? How he can gratify everyone else.

Even now... With every movement, he's adapting to my inexperience with incredible grace, probably making me look like twice as good a partner as I actually am.

How incredible would *he* look if he didn't have to hold himself back so I could keep up?

Even if he sees this as only a friendly dance, how am I using him any less than all the patrons who at least are paying him?

I start to pull back. "You shouldn't need to keep propping me up."

Casimir catches me before I can go far. He studies my expression from behind his mask.

"That's not how I see this," he says. "Not at all."

He brings my hand that he's holding to his waist and releases it so he can brush his fingers over my cheek, tracing the line of my mask. "We're incredibly lucky you found your way to us, Kindness."

My pulse flutters all over again. I have the sudden impulse to bob up on my toes and kiss him, which only makes my face flare with embarrassed heat.

He wouldn't want— It'd only remind him of the woman he *really* wanted and lost—

My lips part while my mind scrambles for some dry remark to break the intensity of the moment.

And the chandelier over our heads explodes in a hail of crystal shards.

# TWENTY

At the first burst of sound, it's hard to say who reacts first. Casimir and I yank each other toward the floor in tandem.

Chips of crystal pelt our hair and backs. The courtesan sucks in a startled breath, his arms wrapping tighter around me. "What under the—"

His exclamation is lost in the cracking sound of at least a dozen more chandeliers bursting apart. Cries and shouts reverberate through the vast room, mostly in confusion, but a few laced with what sounds like pain.

My nerves jitter beneath my skin with the sense of something unearthly whipping past us. More than one something.

"The daimon," I murmur. "They're lashing out again."

And they're not finished with us.

I dare to raise my head, just in time to see one of the larger shards that fell to the polished floorboards leap from the ground on a supernatural current. It whips straight at my face.

I jerk down again, swallowing a yelp as its sharp edge slices across my hairline at my temple. The cries around us are taking on a panicked tone.

The daimon aren't satisfied with just frightening us tonight. They're aiming to hurt.

"Ivy?" Casimir says, and flicks his hand down his front in a hasty gesture to the divinities. "Keep your head low. We—we should try to find some kind of shelter."

He sounds so worried about *me*, as if he isn't in just as much danger as I am. Self-defense lessons for nobles could hardly have prepared him for an assault like this.

A choking sensation rises up from my chest. I can't let the raging spirit-creatures harm him—not the man who's been so fucking kind from the moment I stepped into this place.

So kind he even sees kindness in me.

Esmae is out there in the room somewhere too—and Alek and Benedikt, and gods smite me, I'd even care if Stavros was lanced through with a chunk of crystal.

If anyone's getting to stab him, I've got first dibs.

I can't speak for the rest of the arrogant pricks in this place, but there are at least a few who don't deserve this punishment. A few who are trying to fix what the daimon are seething about.

A punch of energy smacks against my ribs from the inside, pounding to get free alongside the thud of my pulse. My magic almost escapes me in my next ragged breath.

My entire body tenses against it instinctively. A shudder ripples through my muscles, my jaw aching as I clamp it against the urge.

Oh, gods, setting my power loose would only make things worse.

There are other things I can do. I *do* have experience with being under attack in unruly and unpredictable ways.

Even as my eyes water with the strain of suppressing my power, my mind darts through my memory of the room.

Casimir had the right idea when he mentioned shelter. There were tables and chairs set up along the sides of the room, places for nobles who no longer felt like dancing to lounge about and grab refreshments.

Something else in the room crashes. A whimper reaches my ears through the thunder of frantic footsteps.

Soon we'll be as likely to get trampled as stabbed.

I dig my fingers into Casimir's jacket and propel the words from my constricted throat. "Run for the wall to our right. We'll get under a table."

Casimir inhales shakily and nods. We ease off our knees together and dash toward the nearest wall through the milling bodies.

A flung shard scratches my wrist. Casimir gives a hitch of breath that suggests one struck him too.

The tamped magic inside me lurches against my inner hold.

I wrench it back with fraying threads of control, and agony bursts through my frame. In an instant, every organ is burning, every bone throbbing.

I stumble amid the panicked crowd, and Casimir tugs me onward. "We're almost there. I've got you."

Does he have any clue why I've actually faltered? Every step sends fresh jolts of pain up my legs.

A girl who isn't looking where she's going collides with us. The impact jolts me out of my agonized stupor long enough to rasp at her, "Get down, get to the tables!"

She keeps her head enough to yell out my message to everyone else around. "Move toward the tables!"

Casimir lets out a sharp hiss, and my head jerks around with the fear that I'll find him badly injured. Instead, my gaze stops where his has, on a body sprawled in our path.

It's a nobleman who can't have been older than me, his pale blue suit jacket and white dress shirt darkened by a bloody splotch. A shard of crystal protrudes from his throat.

The horrible sight gives me a fresh rush of resolve.

"To the tables," I holler as loud as I can pitch my voice. "Use them as shields! Get out of the open!"

Another woman sways toward us, blood streaming from a deep cut on her thigh. I grasp her elbow, and the three of us stagger the last several steps to the nearest table.

I drag my companions under it. Casimir reaches up to help me shove it over from beneath.

Platters crash and desserts splatter the floor, but now we've got a thick barrier between us and any bits of crystal the daimon kick up off the ground.

"What's wrong with them?" the woman beside me wails, clutching her leg.

I tear a strip of satin off her opulent gown and do my best to tie it around the wound. "They're upset about something."

Something I can't admit I know about. Shit and smitings, this is bad.

The second I stop moving, stop actively helping, the power inside me thrashes harder. I bite down on a groan and peer over the edge of the table at the chaos still reigning in the room behind.

With most of the chandeliers shattered, the light is even hazier than before. The edges of the mask block my peripheral vision, so I tear that off and toss it aside.

Some of the ball-goers have managed to get to the other tables and duck beneath or behind them, but far from all of them. Silhouetted figures race this way and that.

As I watch, a woman spasms in mid step. She reels around and topples over, her hands grasping wildly at a thin spear of crystal that's pierced right into her gut.

My magic sears through my insides. I can't hold back a whine of distress.

When I'm in action, when I'm doing something, that makes it easier.

I push past the table legs.

Casimir snatches after me. "Ivy, what are you—"

"I've got to help!" I shout over my shoulder, and throw myself back into the fray.

I scramble through the weaving bodies and manage to haul one woman I don't know over to the shelter of a table. Then I stumble on a nobleman bent over his friend, who's bleeding from a shard that might have nicked the guy's heart.

"Let's get him out of the way!" I say over the rising screams and yells for help.

The injured man's friend gives a wobbly nod and helps me drag him off to the side of the room. The man groans, which at least means he's still alive.

I leave them huddled there and whirl to face the rest of the ballroom again, my hands clenched tight at my sides. Pain keeps spiking through my innards, but I can tune it out enough to keep going while I'm focused on the task at hand.

That cursed pipe fleece obviously does shit-all to dampen riven magic. The demanding power inside me feels just as potent as it always has.

Or would it be even worse right now if I hadn't been drinking that tea yesterday and today?

Figures in blue uniforms have appeared near the doorway. Members of the Crown's Watch and maybe other guards as well. They're waving their hands around, but I can't make out what they're saying from here.

I dart onward and nearly bump into a couple of familiar figures.

Wendos is just spinning around with a swish of his shaggy hair to jab an accusing finger toward Romild. "What were you doing? I saw you."

Romild stares back at him, her face pale except for a dribble of blood down her lower lip where it was either cut or she bit through it. "I— What are you talking about?"

I'd stop to find that out myself, but just then another half a dozen crystal splinters flash through the air farther ahead of me. "Watch out!" I holler, sprinting toward the dazed nobles in their path.

As I shove one of them out of the way, another lets out a grunt that sounds more like surprise than alarm. I brace for one of the shards to scrape over me, but no further pain comes.

When I glance around, the bits of crystal are pattering to the floor as if released by the invisible force that was directing them.

The soldiers are spreading through the room. A couple of them are close enough now for me to pick up the low, rhythmic chant they're intoning. A wave of soothing magic rolls through my nerves.

It's not meant for me, though. They must be doing something to subdue the daimon.

No more chandeliers shatter. The scattered wreckage that the furious spirits turned into makeshift blades doesn't rise again.

"Everyone who's uninjured, return to your dorms and quarters," one of the guards calls out. "Clear the room so the medics can find those who need them."

I cautiously ease upright, my gown fluttering around me. The gauze on my right arm was torn somewhere in the chaos; the flowing skirt is now flecked with scarlet as well as gold.

But other than a faint stinging from the shallow scratches on my forehead and wrist, I seem to have made it through undamaged.

I don't know if I can say the same for anyone else who matters to me here. I pivot on my feet, scanning the unsteady nobles as they drift toward the doorway, but I can't make out any faces I recognize now.

Before I can take more than a couple of steps back toward the table where I left Casimir, one of the soldiers blocks my path. She points toward the door. "Out of the room. Calmly but quickly."

"I'm just looking for—"

"You can find whoever you need once you're out of the ballroom. If they're injured, the medics will take care of them."

Not if they're worse than injured.

The images of the fallen bodies flicker through my mind, but the soldier's face doesn't offer any room for argument. Even thinking about challenging her authority sets off a fresh flare of my magic's internal assault.

I grit my teeth and bob my head in acknowledgment.

As I head for the door, I scan all the figures around me, but I reach the hall without having spotted Esmae or any of Julita's men. My stomach knots.

It's possible they got out ahead of me. Stavros could have already returned to his quarters.

He's staff—if any of them know what's going on, who was hurt and who wasn't, it'll be him.

The hopeful thought propels me through the jostling crowd and down the packed stairwell. I push out into the fourth-floor hallway and speed up to a jog, grateful that current noble fashion leans toward flat slippers rather than anything with built-up heels.

I press my bracelet to the carved door and then shove it open.

But as I tread into the dark room beyond, I can tell it's empty. It doesn't look as if Stavros has been in here since I left with Esmae for the ball.

I stand in the middle of the room for several beats of my heart, feeling adrift. A frown crosses my face.

The men aren't the only people I've lost track of. My ghostly passenger hasn't made a peep since the daimon's assault started.

"Julita?" I say tentatively into the silence of the room.

No answer. Not even a stirring in the back of my head. I can't even tell whether I can still sense her presence there. I could be imagining the faintest of tickles, or it could just be the buzz of my uneasy thoughts.

"Julita!" I say again, as if she might be so far away she didn't hear me the first time.

No answer. What's happened to her?

Did the attack or the daimon's magic dislodge her somehow?

I've wanted my mind back from the first moment she spoke up in it, but a lump clogs my throat. Right now, I need the company.

I sag onto the sofa. There's no way for me to find the men. I don't even know where the other three's dorms are.

All I can do is wait here for Stavros to return… or for someone to come tell me he won't be returning at all.

As much of an asshole as he can be, I can't help wishing that I trusted the gods. Because if I did, I'd send up a prayer that it won't be the latter.

# Twenty-One

Linzi skips ahead of me through the park. Her pale red hair flashes in the sunlight.

Ma said she had to stick with me. She's only little—two years littler than I am. She shouldn't run off on her own.

"Linzi!" I call after her, dashing after her. My feet slip on the dew-slick grass.

I'm falling. I thrust my hands out to catch my balance, and Linzi whirls around—and somehow my palms are slamming straight into her chest.

Clouds whirl above our heads, blotting out the sun. Her fragile body erupts, her back bowing. Her head snaps to the side as her arms flail.

A crack forms right down the middle of her. Darkness seems to be pouring from my fingers into her, tearing her more and more open by the second.

Her blood spills over my hands.

"No! No, no, please, no!" I cry, but I can't yank my hands away. I can't move at all.

Her skin sloughs off and her flesh gleams a red so much starker than her hair. Her lips part in a silent scream.

And I keep battering her with the poisonous power I can't haul back.

I can't stop it.

I have to.

I can't.

I—

A tug on my shoulder wrenches me out of the nightmare.

I gasp into the darkness, aware of nothing but a vague form leaning over me, and my hand flies to my thigh automatically. I whip my knife up to brace against the intruder's throat.

And realize it's not an intruder at all.

With another blink, my vision adjusts to the thin light seeping through the room from the window at the far end. Stavros glowers down at me, poised over my body, his mouth slanted into a grimace that might hold a hint of amusement too.

He's shed the fancy jacket he was wearing at the ball, his white dress shirt partly unbuttoned down his sculpted chest. I'd admire the view if my wits hadn't scattered.

His much larger hand closes around my own where it's gripping the knife. The knife that's dug into his neck deep enough to produce a droplet of blood against the light brown skin.

"Hello to you too," he says dryly. "I see you made it through the onslaught of daimon with your impressive fighting instincts intact."

I gape at him for a few seconds longer than is strictly polite, my mind shaking off the dregs of sleep. I'm sprawled out on the sofa but still wearing my silk dress, no blanket over me.

I must have drifted off while I was waiting for him to get back.

And wandered into that awful dream.

I pull my hand back, and Stavros lets it go. Inhaling sharply, I scoot toward the sofa's arm to pull my stance upright and tuck the knife back into its hidden sheath. "Sorry. I— Old habits."

Stavros shrugs and sits down on the far end of the sofa, now vacated by my feet. "If it'd been anyone other than me prodding you here in the middle of the night, it'd have been a perfectly valid response."

He pauses, his dark eyes going momentarily somber as they search mine. "I'd have left you to your sleep, but you sounded as though you weren't enjoying it very much."

Damn, was I acting out my anguish in real life? And of course the former general had to be the one to see it.

"Bad dream," I say shortly, and swipe quickly at my eyes to make sure no tears leaked out. I seem to be okay there. "I wanted to talk to you as soon as you got back anyway. Is everyone else okay?"

"I managed to get confirmation that Casimir, Aleksi, and Benedikt are all in decent shape. I'd have been able to tell you that sooner, but I went to speak to the king."

I blink at him one more time, even though my eyes have totally adjusted now. "You just walked over to the palace and demanded an audience with King Konram in the middle of the night?"

The corners of Stavros's mouth twitch upward. "Having until very recently been his very favorite general comes with a few benefits. I thought— Clearly the daimon are escalating their distress faster than we can unravel the problem. I had a duty to warn him even if I didn't have much to warn him with."

My pulse hitches. He didn't just have a chat with the king—he told him about the scourge sorcerers. "And what did he say?"

Stavros's grimace comes back. "That I didn't have much. He can't stamp out sorcerers we haven't identified. He didn't even sound totally convinced that there *is* scourge sorcery being practiced at the college based on the little I could tell him."

I scowl. "What does he think the daimon are riled up about, then? It's not like they typically trash the college balls, is it?"

"No." Stavros rubs his brow, ruffling the fringe of his ruddy hair. "Apparently there are rumors going around that the disturbances are a sign that the godlen themselves are unhappy with Silana on a broader scale. That they're giving us a chance to reform."

"Reform how? What are they pissed off about if it's not scourge sorcery?"

"Obviously, no one knows. I pointed out to him that it being a reaction to a small group of miscreants makes much more sense than there being some horrible wrong we're all doing that we don't even know about, but he wasn't fully swayed. I think he was annoyed that I hadn't mentioned the sorcery concern earlier."

Which Stavros obviously realized was likely. But he put himself out there anyway.

He doesn't look as if he regrets the decision, but I roll my eyes toward the ceiling on his behalf. "So he was peeved that you didn't have enough information, but also peeved that you didn't come to him when you had even less."

"That's about the size of it."

"What a knob."

A startled guffaw sputters out of Stavros. "Yes, I suppose he can be."

He peers at me again, with the head-twitch to refocus his vision, and his gaze darkens. He lifts his hand to hover his fingers by my forehead. "You're injured."

At the protective growl that's come into his voice, my heart skips a beat for a very different reason. I put on a breezy tone. "It's just a couple of scratches."

"A *couple?*"

I raise my wrist with its thin line of dried blood before he insists on conducting his own search. "I've had worse papercuts."

Stavros mutters something insulting about the daimon and then thumps his false hand against the back of the sofa. "I'm making sure you see a medic first thing in the morning. And we're only waiting until the morning because I don't imagine there are any who can be spared yet."

A shiver travels down my back. "I came across at least a couple of people they won't have been able to do anything for."

"Yes."

A crackle of emotion runs through that word. The former general glowers across the room at something I suspect he can only see in his head.

His attention slides back to me. "I saw you running around in the fray. Looking like you were aiming to get more than a couple of papercuts."

I grimace at him. "I was trying to help."

One corner of his mouth curls upward. "I could tell. It was more than I saw any of my blasted students doing, for all their training. You might have saved a few of the dolts' lives."

I don't know what to do with the warmth that's crept into his voice. So, inanely, I find myself defending those dolts. "No one would have trained them to fight off rampaging daimon."

"You figured it out somehow."

"I just… I had to do something." I look down at my hands and then back at him. "If the king isn't listening, then what do we do *now?*"

Stavros leans against the back of the sofa, stretching his well-muscled legs out in front of him. "There isn't much we can do other than what we've already been doing. The royal family can be more alert to the threat now. They're dispatching extra guards to patrol the college—soldiers with gifts that should help calm the daimon if we need protection."

More protection for everyone else. More chances of someone discovering why *I* should be put to death for me.

I swallow thickly. "Wonderful. Well, I didn't have much opportunity to ferret out any secrets tonight considering how quickly the daimon crashed the party, but I'll get right back to it in the morning. Whenever my official assistance isn't needed."

It occurs to me a half second too late that my last flippant remark could be taken as a jab. I hesitate, not sure if I should apologize.

I didn't do anything wrong in the first place. But it's dangerous to be on this man's bad side.

To my shock, Stavros beats me to it.

He looks at his sprawled legs and then at me, with that tiny twitch to get a better focus on my face. "I appreciate your dedication to the cause. And your 'official assistance' has been better than I expected. I shouldn't have snapped at you yesterday. It was a reaction unworthy of my training, and I'll make sure it doesn't happen again."

For what seems like the third time in as many minutes, I find myself staring at him.

A more typical grin crosses his lips. "You'll make me feel even more like a lout if you keep looking at me like that. I might be an ass, but I'm fully capable of apologizing for it after the fact."

I let out a bemused huff, still lost for words. Where's Julita when I need her to guide me through this awkward conversation with a man she knew far better than I did?

Really, where's Julita at all?

The reminder of her absence—and the thought of how this man and the others will react if she's gone for good—chills me. I push those worries aside and focus on the peace offering Stavros has extended.

I can be a good enough sport to partly return the favor.

"I can understand it must be a difficult subject for you," I venture.

"Yes. Well." Stavros gazes vaguely across the room. His hand comes to rest on my ankle where my feet are tucked near him, buried in the folds of my gown, but he shows no sign he's noticed he even made the gesture.

From his expression, I'm not sure he's here at all.

"Both my mother and my father served as generals under King Dobri—Konram's father—for more than twenty years, you know," he says after a moment, his tone both light and bittersweet. "And both ultimately died as all glorious generals do, defending Silana. I knew I was going to follow in their footsteps from the moment I knew anything at all. I picked my gift to be of as much use in the field as possible. I made my sacrifice happily."

He lowers his gaze to his other hand, the one currently a realistically sculpted replica. The warmth of his touch tickles up my leg.

"What was the gift?" I ask quietly, not wanting to break the moment.

"I can see a few moves ahead. The next several seconds, in a one-on-one fight. Sometimes several minutes, when observing the patterns of an entire army. Or rather, I *could* see. It requires a certain amount of sustained concentration that my eyes are no longer capable of. So here I am, whiling out the rest of my days teaching Silana's elite how to fight the battles I can't."

The bitter overrides the sweet in that last sentence.

He gives himself a little shake and pushes his mouth into a grin stiffer than the one before. "I'm still serving my country. No more damp tents and stale camp food! There's plenty to recommend about the academic life."

His mock-jovial tone doesn't fool me for a second. He hates that he's here—he hates that he's lost the life he gave so much to.

No wonder he acts like such a prick sometimes.

I don't even know what that feels like. I never had a chance to make real dreams to lose.

But I can honestly say, with an ache in the pit of my stomach, "I'm sorry."

Stavros glances down and appears to realize for the first time that he's rested his hand on my leg. As he lifts his gaze to meet mine, he strokes his thumb over my ankle. An absent, totally casual gesture that sets off a flare of heat straight to my core.

"You've got nothing to be sorry for, Ivy of wherever you're actually from," he says in the languid tone I'm used to. "You've at least made recent days a little more interesting."

He shakes his head, and a hint of the bitterness comes back. "The real problem is that I'm *here*, and we're fighting our own kind of war right now, and I still couldn't win it before innocent people got killed."

He's trying to sound flippant about it, but his frustration prickles through. As much as he can be an asshole and an arrogant jerk, I can't deny how much he cares about the people he meant to spend his whole life defending.

Even though I get a pang of loss when I slip my leg from beneath his fingers, I adjust my position so I'm leaning close enough to him to set my hand on his shoulder. "It took the whole host of godlen and the All-Giver on top of that to end the first bunch of scourge sorcerers. I hope your ego isn't so big you expect to equal them."

Stavros lets out a bark of a guffaw and turns to me with a flash of his dark eyes. "I suppose it can't get there with you around to pop holes in it."

When he looks at me like that, heat sweeps through my entire body. My skin tingles with the awareness of just how little space remains between us now.

It would be ever so easy to lean even closer and—

My body sways, and a jolt of panic washes away the flush of desire.

I jerk myself backward, covering my lapse with a straightening of my skirts as if I'm simply tired of being smothered by them.

Great God help me, I almost *kissed* him. The man who'd probably laugh while the executioner fixed a noose around my neck.

"It's been a long night," I say, keeping my voice as even as possible. "We should probably both get some sleep."

Stavros hesitates, and for one anxious moment, I think he's going to ask what's wrong. Instead, he pushes to his feet. "Of course. I'll let you get back to it. Don't let the daimon haunt your dreams anymore. They're settled down for now."

I let out a rough chuckle. I'm not going to tell him what I was really dreaming about.

About the first person my riven magic ever killed.

"If they turn up, I'm sure I can simply stab them," I say, and Stavros echoes my laugh.

I sit still until he's vanished into his bedroom. My burst of panic has spread into a duller chill of fear that's wrapping around me.

What the fuck is wrong with me? First I'm mooning over Casimir at the ball, then I'm falling all over the former general?

I enjoyed the impression of having earned his trust. I wanted to find out what it's like to kiss him.

Just like I wanted to melt into Casimir's arms and pretend I was the only one he'd want to dance with.

But I know, I *know* that's all impossible.

What am I doing here? Running around playing noble while the daimon are bringing the ceiling down on our heads?

My heart's getting tangled up with men who see me as a vessel for the woman they really cared about at best... And who'll consider me a monster as vile as the ones we're tracking down at worst, if they find out the truth.

Fragments of images from the ball flicker up from my memory. The shrieks, the blood, the milling bodies...

The bodies no longer moving, sprawled lifeless on the floor.

Like Linzi. Like my poor little sister, torn through.

By my own wretched hands.

A clammy sweat breaks out down my back. What if that dream was a sign—a warning?

I ruin things. I know that even when I'm asleep.

Have I actually helped the fight against the scourge sorcerers? Maybe I've been inadvertently leading Julita's men astray with my theories and assumptions.

I thought I could write myself a new role as hero, but what did I really accomplish while the daimon lashed out and people *died*?

The only way I'm not going to ruin everything here is if the men I've allied myself with destroy me first.

Or I could just go. I could disappear back into the streets of the fringes, be no one but the unknown "Hand of Kosmel," and the men would never find me.

Go back to where I belong, where I understand the rules. Leave this entire blasted headache behind.

The chill sinks in so deep I can hardly breathe. I shove myself off the sofa and stare at the door.

It's that easy. Wouldn't it be so much better for all of us?

My legs propel me to the door. My fingers rest on the handle, my ears pricked for any sounds of movement in the hall beyond or the bedroom behind me.

A familiar tickle stirs in the back of my head. *Ivy? What are you doing?*

My heart nearly jumps out of my chest. I jerk my hand back to my side.

"Julita?" I murmur, afraid I'll bring Stavros charging out of his bedroom. "You're still there?"

*Where would I go? Believe me, there are no other heads around here I'd like to hop into.*

A lump clogs my throat. Sudden tears burn behind my eyes, but I don't know what they're for. "I just... When I first got back to the room after the daimon wrecked the ball, you didn't answer me."

*Oh. Is that what happened?* Julita's voice turns abashed. *I don't know exactly what I did. The chandeliers were breaking, and we saw that woman dead, and I... I couldn't stop thinking about the knife in my neck. The way the blood filled my throat and I couldn't breathe...*

I feel her shudder before she goes on. *I suppose I was afraid I'd feel something like that all over again through you. And somehow I pulled in deeper where I couldn't feel anything at all. It was all simply dark, and I didn't know what you were doing or what was going on out there. Almost... peaceful.*

My gut knots at the thought of the horrible memories the daimon's assault stirred up for her. "I can understand why you'd have panicked."

*It was ridiculous, though. I've already been through it once. I've had extra time. And I didn't like not knowing what'd happened to you. I had to come back to make sure you were all right.*

"I'm glad you're all right too," I say, and discover that I mean it.

*And the men? Did they all make it through unscathed?*

Julita tries to make the question casual, but a quiver of worry creeps in all the same. My jaw tightens.

She does care about them, no matter what went into her decision to rope them into her cause.

I incline my head. "I've seen Stavros, and he said the others are fine too."

*Thank the gods for that.* She pauses. *It's the middle of the night now from the looks of things. Where were you going?*

I stare down at the hand I set on the door handle, her question ringing through my skull. Her return has shaken my resolve. "I don't know."

Am I really going to turn tail and run out of sheer fear? I don't have any more reason to assume that I've harmed Julita's investigation than that I've helped it. Stavros even said...

I close my eyes against the wrench of uncomfortable emotion. That's what I'm really scared of, isn't it?

What I want. What I can't have.

I tip forward to rest my forehead against the cool wood. My pulse hammers on. But I can't quite make myself reach the handle again.

Coming to the college was never about me, not really. I don't know if I believe there's even the slightest chance that the gods would grant me absolution no matter how this turns out.

But there are far more lives on the line beyond just my own. Beyond the few that were lost tonight.

I wasn't prepared for this task. I don't know how to be the woman Julita was—and her men wouldn't want me even if I could fake it.

I do know how to take a stand.

Julita came back. Julita could have floated off into the peaceful darkness she deserves, but she came back to keep fighting.

And to make sure I was okay.

She's already given her life once to protect the kingdom from the consequences the scourge sorcerers could rain down on us. How can I flee when I barely have a life to give up in the first place?

Maybe I can't rewrite my story into a hero's, but I'll be damned if I let it be a coward's tale.

With a few slow breaths, I trudge back toward the sofa. I grab the folded blanket off the shelf where it was tucked away and curl up on the cushions.

I committed myself to this course. I'm going to see it through.

Even if that choice is the end of me.

# TWENTY-TWO

*There he is,* Julita crows as I step into the warm morning air of the outer courtyard. *You just need to sneak close enough to overhear what he says.*

It doesn't look as if Wendos is going to be saying much of anything right now. He's hunkered down on the grass off by the southeast corner of the yard where Julita said he often takes in some sun, currently alone.

As far as I can tell, he's totally immersed in the book he's propped open on his knee. At least that'll make it easier for me to "sneak close."

I wet my lips and meander along the side of the Quadring beneath the first-floor classroom windows. Sticking to the shadows, I shouldn't be noticeable from any direction, but if someone happens to look my way, I could be simply taking a casual stroll.

Near the corners of the building, the stone walls jut out with a cluster of statues. The one at the southeast shows a figure meant to be King Melchior, the ruler of nearly a century past who shattered the tyranny of the Darium empire in Silana not long after Signy did in Velduny. He stands with bearded chin raised high and a majestic stone cloak draped over his broad shoulders, looming over several hunched figures gazing up at him in chiseled awe.

After a swift glance around to make sure no one's looking my way, I hop into the midst of the fawning subjects. Tucked between two of the stone figures, no one should be able to see me at all unless they walk right up to the statue.

I pull out one of the books I borrowed from the archives for further plausible deniability. I suspect whatever the peasant girls and wandering spirits get up to in the Woudish folktales will be more interesting than listening to Wendos read anyway.

Julita doesn't share my sentiments. *Don't get too distracted. If he's going to talk to any of his co-conspirators, it'll be quick.*

I nod in acknowledgment, gritting my teeth against an argument. As soon as I woke up this morning, she started badgering me about what Wendos had gotten up to after the daimon assault at the ball, even more after I told her he'd seemed to think Romild had done something wrong.

So I'll humor her for an hour or two before our next meeting. Maybe if nothing happens, she'll finally reconsider the idea that her childhood tormenter is some kind of evil mastermind as well.

The vibe around the campus is noticeably uneasy after last night's bloodshed. The students passing me walk briskly rather than ambling, sticking close to their friends. There's still chatter, but I hear a lot more nervous giggles than I'm used to.

Our target doesn't remain totally isolated. A couple of women pause to chat with him briefly about his reading material. Not long after they've headed off, a male classmate he seems mildly annoyed with descends on him with a series of questions about a recent lecture on "resource" accumulation or something like that.

Each time, I peek around King Melchior's whirling stone cloak to watch for any unspoken signals passing between them. Nothing about the conversations looks remotely extraordinary.

"Do you know how long he and your brother kept up their experiments after they stopped hurting you?"

*No,* Julita admits. *As soon as Borys realized I wasn't going to let him bully me anymore, he got much more secretive. Anything else they did, it was well away from me.*

My ass is starting to ache from being squashed against the hard stone, but then a fourth schoolmate ambles up to Wendos. He casts a furtive glance around that sets my senses on the alert.

This guy looks like he might be up to something.

Unfortunately, he's cautious with his voice as well as his surroundings. I can't make out the words he murmurs to Wendos.

Julita's former tormenter shakes his head, his voice also lowered, but more as if he's appeasing his companion than like he really thinks he needs to hide it. I still catch his response.

"Believe me, I tried my best."

The nervous guy rubs his mouth and mutters something else I can't hear.

Wendos sighs. "It's like with rootbeetles—you can point them in the right direction, but you can't ensure they'll act exactly the way you'd want. I conveyed the information as clearly as I could."

He gives a rueful smile. "Speaking of rootbeetles, have you seen that specimen Rolf brought back to the club room? I've never come across one quite that color before."

As they exchange a few more comments about various creepy-crawlies, Julita gives a little shudder. *Ugh. Bug club. It figures he'd be interested in creatures that scuttle in the dirt.*

I'm turning his early remarks over in my head. "Do you think he was talking about bugs the whole time?" I murmur. "What he said about conveying information—maybe he tried to tell the college staff or even the palace about whatever he thought Romild was up to. And they wouldn't take action."

My ghostly passenger snorts. *I can hardly imagine that. He probably enjoyed the violence.*

He hadn't looked as if he was enjoying it when I saw him, but I'm not sure how to convince Julita of that when she wasn't aware enough to see for herself.

"I could try talking to him myself," I venture. "Feel him out, see what he might—"

*No,* Julita cuts in. *I don't want him paying any attention to you at all.*

I grimace, holding back further argument. She *does* know the man better than I do, even if her knowledge is colored by long-held resentment.

It's resentment that he totally earned, whether he's realized that and is trying to make amends or not.

When I glance over again, Wendos is getting up from the grass with a stretch of his arms. He tucks his book against his side and strides off toward the Quadring's main entrance.

I watch him go and then wriggle out of my hiding spot.

We've still got nearly an hour before we're due for the meeting, but Alek will probably be in the archives already. I could always mention to him what I've overheard from Wendos and see what he makes of it.

As I pass through the inner courtyard, a chipper voice rings out. "Ivy! Where are you off to?"

Esmae trots over to join me, her expression so eager that guilt jabs through my gut. I made a point of finding her in the dining hall this morning to confirm that she made it through the ball unscathed, but she was just hustling off to a class, so we barely had time to talk.

Now I'm the one hustling… and I can't even give her a real excuse.

"Good to see you again," I say with a hasty smile, scrambling for a suitable pretext. "Ster. Stavros wanted me to attend a meeting with him, some important staff thing, and I'm nearly late."

Esmae's face falls a little, but she catches it with a renewed smile of her own. "Oh, well, you wouldn't want to upset *him*. I'm sure our paths will cross later."

"I'll look for you at dinner."

I hurry on as if I really am risking Stavros's wrath. Just inside the Domi's door, I pass a soldier from the Crown's Watch, whose gaze slides over me without remark.

The hairs on the back of my neck stand on end as I veer down the hallway toward the library. Stavros did say that the palace was going to send extra guards to keep an eye on the college.

Which means they're keeping an eye on me too.

I'll just have to keep looking like a totally normal professor's assistant. This is what I committed to last night when I decided to stay.

A couple of younger students are drifting down the hall hung with tapestries, commenting on the artwork. I make as if I'm simply appreciating the woven illustrations too until they walk around the corner and I can open up the secret passage.

In the room below, Alek is leaning over the desk as usual. His head lifts when I emerge from the wall, but without the same jerk of surprise as the first time.

A brief smile crosses his face before it falls into his usual stern expression. "You couldn't wait to get to work?"

"After that catastrophe of a ball, it seems slightly more urgent than before."

I step closer, peering at what I can see of his skin around his mask. "Did you make it through completely unscathed?"

He lets out a rough laugh. "There are a few benefits to sticking mostly to the walls. I was on the outskirts from the start."

The question of why he feels the need to hang back itches at me.

Does he think whatever he's hiding behind his mask is really so off-putting? Every bit of him that I *can* see is perfectly appealing.

I yank my thoughts back before I spend more than an instant admiring the curve of his full lips. I've already been imagining kissing enough of these out-of-reach men without adding another to the heap.

My gaze drops to the scroll Alek has spread open on the desk, and it proves an excellent distraction. There's a large T at the top of the paper, with lines branching off in various directions leading to scrawled notations.

I motion to them. "What's all this?"

Alek's stance straightens at the change in topic. He taps the scroll. "I've been charting out all of Ster. Torstem's associations. Family members, friends, close colleagues, favorite students, clubs he runs or has been involved with, classes he teaches…"

He's made a map of the man's life. I study the flow of the lines. "Most of them don't appear to connect to each other, only to him."

Alek nods with a twist of his mouth. "Yes. I haven't found any cluster that would suggest an unexpectedly large collaboration or an unusual combination of personal and professional life. If he's involved in a college-wide conspiracy, he hasn't shown any outward signs of it in his affiliations."

"I suppose that would be a little much to ask for anyway," I mutter, resting my fingers at the top of the page. "Is there any sign of where he might have brought kids from?"

"Not so far. I had a chance to exchange a quick word with Benedikt at the start of the ball—he said he's gotten confirmation that it wasn't the first time Torstem has brought a kid around to see the college. Apparently it's a fairly common habit of his. But the people he talked to were under the impression they were relatives from his own family or those of associates."

I've spotted the family tree part of the chart. "He doesn't have much in the way of his own relatives, it looks like."

"He doesn't," Alek agrees. "One grown daughter who's taken a wife and adopted a toddler. One sister and a couple of cousins, only a few children between them, either years past dedication age or many years off. No one who'd match the boy you described."

"And no one in his family would have acted like an outer-warder anyway." I frown.

Alek glances toward the door to the larger archives. "I wanted to get access to his financial records. Those could tell quite a story. The college has its own banking system for staff, and all money goes in and out through the accounting office. But the accountants keep the ledgers in a secure room off the library. It's not the sort of thing they'd hand over or I can simply walk in and take."

My spirits lift with a flash of renewed confidence. Now this sounds like exactly the kind of job I'm meant to do.

"Show me where the room is, and we'll figure something out."

Alek shoots me a skeptical look. "They're not going to let you just walk in either."

"I wasn't planning on asking." I waggle my fingers. "Thief, remember?"

He pauses, a whole debate going on in the shadow that passes over his eyes.

Julita lets out a bright chuckle. *Oh, this is going to be fun.*

"Julita approves of the plan," I add, because I can.

Alek's gaze jerks to mine again. His lips purse.

Then his flicker of a smile comes back. "Fine. Let's see what you can make of it, at least."

He leads me through the larger archive room and then two more basement areas that are stuffed full of all the documents and books the archivists don't think anyone really needs but can't bear to get rid of anyway. We slip up a winding staircase and into the library proper.

I've never actually been in this vast room before. The smell of aged leather and paper comes with less dust than the lower archives, and the endless rows of bookcases are spaced farther apart for ease of access, with narrow rugs stretching in between. Every shelf is packed with worn leather covers.

I drink in the scent and suppress the longing to wander from row to row, scanning every title. We're on a mission here.

Alek leads me on a roundabout route, avoiding the clusters of chairs around small tables where students are murmuring to each other over open texts. In a far corner of the room, he nods toward a door with a glass pane etched with Estera's sigil and a bronze plaque proclaiming it the *Accounting Archive.*

"Who can open that door?" I ask him quietly.

"Only a couple of the librarians are on the accounting staff and have access. Usually, one works in the morning and the other in the afternoon." He cranes his neck to peek through the window from afar. "Stera. Elzbita is in there right now."

"And they just sit around all day waiting for someone to need to make a transaction?"

Alek shakes his head. "They're still librarians and archivists too. They come out and advise the students when they aren't otherwise occupied."

I take in the shelves around us, the small table off to the side that no one has ventured far enough to sit at, the hardwood floor partly covered by more rugs. A plan takes shape in my head.

"If you can come up with an excuse to request her help, something you'd specifically need her for over the other librarians, I can get that ledger. You'll just need to keep her busy for long enough for me to find the right one."

Alek inhales a little shakily, but when I look at him, a spark has come into his bright brown eyes. He rocks on his feet as if gathering momentum. "I can do that. Yes."

He aims a quick smile at me, brighter than the one before. Great God help me if my heart doesn't flip right over at the conspiratorial gleam in the flash of his teeth. Then he strides forward without waiting for further instructions.

I dash to the table, nudge one of the chairs aside, and duck down where I'll be out of sight. I've got a clear view to the accounting office, about ten paces away.

As Alek knocks on the door, I slide a knife out of its sheath on my leg. My fingers curl around it, the muscles in my arm already flexing as I judge the distance.

The librarian opens the door, and Alek gives her a spiel I can't totally follow about source documents and financial interconnections.

Whatever he's getting at, Stera. Elzbita appears to catch on. She nods a few times and then, huzzah, pushes the door wide to step past it and usher him to a set of shelves elsewhere in the library.

I watch the swing of the door back toward its frame and listen to the padding of their footsteps retreating. At the last possible second, I flick my hand forward.

The knife flies through the air and hits the space between the door and the frame just before the door thuds into place. The two slabs of wood pin the blade between them, leaving the door just a smidge ajar.

Julita lets out a whoop of approval in my head.

I allow myself a victory grin and glance around this corner of the library again. Alek and Stera. Elzbita have disappeared from view; no one else is around.

I stay low anyway, darting across the short span of floor and reclaiming my knife as I scoot through the doorway. I close the door behind me in case anyone passes by who'd be concerned.

The accounting room smells like tallow, though I can't see any candles currently in use. A modest glow streams from a thin window over the built-in bookcases.

I scuttle past the desk, keeping my head below the level of the window on the door, and paw through the rows of leatherbound ledgers on the shelves. Irritatingly, they have only numbers that are meaningless to me printed on their spines, with no apparent order.

After peeking inside a few, I realize the pattern at the same time Julita apparently does. *They're alphabetical by name. Ster. Torstem's should be toward the end, then.*

It only takes a few more tries to land on the one with his name on the first page. I don't bother flipping through the pages with their cramped notations yet, just hug the ledger close to my chest and slink back over to the door.

It should be simple enough to slip back out and—

Voices filter through from outside. I freeze with a lurch of panic at the thought that the librarian might have returned already.

But it's two male voices, joking about how far up their professor's ass they'd like to stick the scroll they were just poring over.

I hold still and silent, willing them to move on. For some reason, they've decided to hang around right by the accounting office.

*Obnoxious asses,* Julita mutters. *Why don't they get moving?*

My mouth starts to go dry. Just how long can Alek keep Stera. Elzbita occupied with his made-up question?

As if on cue, my magic twitches in my chest. Jumping to remind me that *it* could move these obstacles ever so easily if I'd just let it.

I inhale slowly and will it to calm down. Will myself to believe I have everything under control and there's no reason my power should be upset at me for not giving in.

My riven soul isn't totally convinced. A needle-sharp prickling resonates through my ribs. I brace my hand against the doorframe.

It should be a relief when the two blathermouths outside finally budge. Their voices slowly but surely fade away as they amble off.

Now I just have to pull off a stealthy maneuver while my insides are gnawing on themselves. Lucky me.

With my jaw clenched, I ease up to peek through the window. The moment the two men have veered around the nearest bookcase, I gird myself and run for it.

With a quick push to ensure the door closes behind me, I sprint across the rug. A deeper jolt of pain puts a hitch in my stride, but I let myself drop with it so I can skid beneath the table.

As my shoulder bumps one of the wooden legs, Alek's voice reaches my ears, raised a little louder than I'd typically expect. To make sure I hear them coming?

"Thank you so much for your help, Stera. Elzbita. I'm sure I'm on the right path now."

While I watch from my hiding spot, the librarian pats him on the arm and heads back into her office. I stay braced for a few seconds in case she's going to burst back out announcing the theft, the pain dwindling with each moment she doesn't.

Alek ambles away with an uncertain expression. When I'm sure there'll be no immediate retaliation, I duck out and follow him.

Through unspoken agreement, I hang back several paces behind him all the way to the stairs to the archives room. I hit the bottom of the staircase and find Alek waiting there, his eyes gleaming even brighter than before.

His gaze drops to the book clutched in my arms. "You got it?"

I grin at him. "This is the one."

When I hold it out to him, he takes it and examines the first few pages. A smile stretches across his lips. "You really pulled it off. I don't know how you did it."

I shrug. "We all have our own talents. I couldn't have talked the librarian into walking away with me."

He swings the ledger under his arm and meets my gaze to encompass me in his delight. "Not bad for our first real mission together, huh?"

I can't help smiling back. Who'd have thought it'd be Alek out of all of the guys who'd help me pull off a crime—and revel in the thrill of it?

As we head back to the meeting room, he walks with an extra spring in his step. "Is that the sort of thing you needed to do a lot of, surviving on the streets? Sneaking into places, making quick escapes?"

I think of my "home" in the cloth factory. "Yeah, that was a pretty big part of it. Especially as I got older. When you're a kid, you can get away with a little more." Sleeping on a doorstep. Plucking a few spare pieces of fruit off someone's tree. "Thankfully, the older I got, the more practice I had at staying unnoticed."

Alek halts, his gaze gone serious again. "When you're a kid—how old were you when you left home?"

My stomach knots. I probably should have omitted that bit.

"Twelve," I say quickly. "Not *that* young."

But young enough for Alek's eyes to widen. "And your parents just let you—I mean, I know they were harsh with you, but—"

"They didn't *let* me. I went, and there wasn't much they could do about it."

My tone is probably too sharp. It isn't him I'm upset with—and he isn't even wrong.

I doubt they ever looked for me. I doubt they felt anything but relief that I was no longer their problem.

Alek doesn't appear to take any offense to my retort. He hesitates and then offers me another smile, smaller but somehow more giddying than the excited one before. "I suppose it worked out for the best in the end. If it wasn't for that, you wouldn't be here with us."

He doesn't really mean me. He means the woman I'm carrying with me. I *know* that.

But my hand still reaches for his of its own accord, as if some part of me needs the physical contact to confirm our solidarity. Or maybe I'm trying to make it totally clear to him how much I am in this crazy situation with him.

Foolish of me. I've barely brushed his fingers before Alek is yanking them away.

The connection I thought I felt snaps.

The scholar opens his mouth, closes it again, and then tips his head toward the room where we usually meet. "We'd better look through this quickly. We don't want it missing for too long before we return it."

"Of course not," I say, pretending his rebuff never happened, and shove my jumbled feelings down.

I need to keep those ridiculous impulses reined in. We're working together only for now, and soon enough we won't be.

And I'll go back to doing everything on my own.

No one else to worry about. No one else calling the shots.

The thought shouldn't create a hollow sensation in the pit of my stomach.

We tramp back to the small, dusty room, and Alek tosses himself into the chair behind the desk. I perch on the desk's edge while he pages through the ledger, starting at the most recent entries and skimming back through the pages with impressive speed.

"There are regular expenses marked as donations, the same amount once a month, going back years," he reports after a moment. "To 'RI' it says, and nothing else."

"Someone's initials?" I suggest.

"Perhaps. I'll see if a full name comes up."

He's got less than ten pages left when he pauses. "Now that's quite the sum. A large endowment to some place called the Riverside Institute for Children's Wellness, fifteen years ago."

*RI*, Julita murmurs at the same time as my heart leaps.

"Children," I repeat.

"I've never heard of that organization before." Alek peers at the page and then flips back through a few more. "But it looks like the monthly donations started right after that initial endowment."

He glances up at me, a glimmer of his earlier exhilaration coming back into his eyes. "I think we've got it."

Before I can respond, the far wall wavers, and Benedikt steps out of the hidden passage.

He raises his eyebrows at the two of us. "Hard at work already? The others should be along in a moment. What are you two looking so smug about?"

I hop off the desk, my good mood returning. "We're uncovering all of Ster. Torstem's secrets. Now we've just got to check out this place and find out what he's really up to."

# TWENTY-THREE

Right after I've stepped into the stable, I stop for a moment and simply breathe in the sweet and musky scents. A faint aura of comfort settles over me.

Not entirely purposefully, I find myself wandering over to the corner that holds Toast's stall. The dark bay stallion lets out a huff at the sight of me and paws one hoof against the ground.

I reach out my hand and hold it steady a few inches from his face until he concedes to bowing his head so I can give his jaw a gentle scratch. Then he shakes his mane as if to make the statement that he doesn't like the attention *that* much, so I shouldn't get any ideas.

I click my tongue at him. "I wouldn't take you out today anyway. We're supposed to be making a good impression."

*Personally, I hope you never sit yourself on that beast again,* Julita pipes up.

"Oh, he's not as bad as he wants people to think. Are you, Toast?" I extend my hand upward, and he allows me to scratch beneath his forelock this time.

A soft chuckle rings out from down the aisle.

Casimir strolls over, his expression lit with amusement. "Making friends with all kinds of unlikely characters, I see. You got here early."

All at once, I feel awkward, although I had no expectations of keeping the stable to myself. If anyone was going to interrupt my peace, I'd rather it was Casimir than any of the other nobles.

I offer Toast one of the apples I liberated from the breakfast spread and give Casimir a shrug. "I figured since I had to come out here anyway, I might as well make a visit of it. The horses are better company than a lot of the people back there." I jab my thumb toward the college buildings.

Casimir's chuckle expands into a full laugh. Something in his gaze feels more thoughtful than usual as he considers me. "I suppose I shouldn't be surprised you'd feel that way. Have you gotten to spend much time around horses before?"

An honest answer tumbles out of me before I can think better of it. "My family had a mare. She was better company than my parents most of the time too."

Casimir nods as if he can hear all the things I haven't said. "I'm fond of them myself. They're spirited but straightforward animals. So many different personalities within that. And they don't ask for much. I'd spend more time out here if it wouldn't leave all my clothes smelling like horse."

The affection is obvious in his voice despite that last remark. He follows it up with a wink. "I don't mind, but it doesn't go over well with most patrons."

A pang passes through my gut at the thought of the people who are already enjoying Casimir's various talents, even though it's not as if I had any plans to do so myself.

He's never shown a sign that he's anything other than pleased to make his living by pleasing others. Why should it bother me?

It's a little thrilling to discover there's at least one thing he cares about just for himself, though.

I shoot him a grin in return. "Those patrons don't know what they're missing."

Then I glance at the stalls around me. "Since you've gotten to know all the different personalities, maybe you can help me pick out a good ride for a trip through the city. I'd rather not test my truce with Toast that far just yet."

"Hmm. Well, you can't have Pepper, because she's my best pal." He pauses to stroke the forehead of a dapple gray mare who's poked her head from her stall with a whicker.

Casimir offers her a beaming smile and considers the rest of the row. "Scout is a steady one, very stalwart but still knows his own mind. I think he'd be a good fit for you."

I follow his gesture to a sorrel gelding who peers at me with curious eyes.

"You want to get out there and stretch those legs?" I ask the horse, who snorts eagerly.

I go to get a bridle and saddle. Toast makes a vague grumbling sound as I pass him by.

"Be nicer to me next ride, and I'll pick you more often," I call over to the stallion, and Casimir lets out another laugh.

Scout proves to be everything I could ask for in a steed, waiting for my commands and leaping to follow them without any dithering. I let Casimir leave a few minutes ahead of me to give the illusion that we're on separate errands, but it's only a matter of minutes before I'm trotting through the streets of the inner wards to our chosen meet-up spot by the old wall.

As I draw up beside the courtesan, we pass through the ruined gate and into the middle wards. Looking over at him, I can't help noticing how relaxed he looks astride the mare.

Casimir rarely comes across as anything less than content, but there's a sense of deeper serenity to his stance as he sways with the horse's strides that I'm not sure I've ever seen before. It lights a happy glow in my chest that I can't quite bear to squash.

They don't ask for much, he said before about the horses. Maybe the demands of his work get to him more than he normally reveals.

"Is riding part of the companionship curriculum too?" I ask.

Casimir adjusts his grip on the reins. "A small part, and only for those who aren't tied to a very specialized area of focus like bardery or painting. We'd need to be able to keep up if a patron is in the mood to go for a jaunt on horseback, of course."

"So you only go out if someone you're attending to wants to?"

He shoots me a wry smile. "That's essentially the job description. I can't say I wouldn't mind taking a ride through the woods more often, but I have plenty of other activities to occupy myself with."

I don't hear any complaint in his tone, but my gut twists. "It seems to me that you should have some time in there to think about what *you* want, to make yourself happy, you know. Don't you deserve it as much as anyone who'd come to you as a patron?"

Gods above, from everything I've seen of him, he deserves true contentment more than the rest of those elite pricks.

Casimir blinks at me as if I've said something absurd. "Knowing I've brought some kind of joy into another person's life does make me happy. I wouldn't have gone into the profession otherwise."

"I know. I only meant..."

I shake my head, not sure how to put the ache inside me into words. It isn't really my place to meddle anyway. "Never mind. I obviously don't know the ins and outs of it."

I shift my attention to the streets we're passing through. "You're sure the Riverside Institute of Child Wellness isn't *in* Riverside?" That ward lies not far beyond the old walls, in the middle-class zone where I'd imagine a man like Ster. Torstem would feel more comfortable than the fringes we're headed toward.

"It is on the side of the river," Casimir says. "I'd imagine Ster. Torstem picked the name knowing people would assume it referred to the neighborhood, so they wouldn't realize and be surprised he'd invest in a facility in the outer wards. But I can't imagine there are two organizations with the same name, and Alek confirmed it's in Siltston."

I hum to myself. I thought I'd be going on this venture alone—and not on horseback. But once we determined how official-sounding the possible source of Torstem's child visitors was, approaching the workers there as nobles seemed more likely to get us answers.

I'll still be using my street-rat wits to build a larger picture of the situation. And none of the other men argued about Casimir joining me.

*He could cajole a mouse out of a starving cat's paws,* Julita said approvingly when he volunteered.

Let's hope the opposition we face isn't quite that desperate.

As we weave through the narrowing streets near the river, evidence appears of how Siltston got its name. A thin layer of dried mud and grit coats every low surface.

I learned early on to avoid the neighborhoods in this area right after a rain. The banks of the Starsil River drop lower in the fringes, and it splits off into several nearby culverts that all flood together when there's a big enough storm.

Julita's presence squirms at the back of my skull. *Ugh. I can't see why anyone would want to live here.*

Does she think they have a real choice?

My silk dress feels uncomfortably light compared to the tunic I'd usually wear when moving through these streets—with pockets full of silver to leave on the windowsills of the needy. How many con artists have screwed over these citizens in the days since I last dealt out my version of justice?

I inhale deeply to settle my nerves.

I'll be back. We have a far bigger heap of injustice to tackle right now.

Casimir leads the way through the last few turns, which end at a building slightly less ramshackle than its neighbors. The broad, three-story structure boasts a mix of stone, wood, and a few thin trees sprouting through the walls for reinforced stability.

It's nearly ten times bigger than most of the shacks that serve as individual homes on the fringes, with a yard of scruffy grass and wan vegetables all around its gray walls. Painted sigils for Inganne, Prospira, and Elox decorate the door, calling for childish delight, familial comforts, and good health.

I frown as I stare up at the place. "I've been past here before. I never knew what its official name was."

Casimir lifts an eyebrow. "I see Ster. Torstem didn't bother to have a sign erected announcing the institute's formal title or his ties to it."

"How very surprising," I say wryly.

As we dismount and tie the horses near the gate, a babble of childish voices reaches our ears. A gaggle of kids who look to be around six or seven dash by through the garden.

A girl a few years older shouts at the wild ones from an open window. I spot a couple of others flitting by in another room.

They're all dressed in plain cotton and wool, darned and patched to extend its use—no noble clothing here. The grubby faces and tangled hair tell a familiar story that Ster. Torstem's fancy name for the place can't paint over.

This isn't any kind of "institute." It's an orphanage, plain and simple. A handful of adults trying to care for more children than anyone really should, because it's either that or leave them with no one at all.

Why did Torstem care enough to invest in this place, however much he does?

I hate to think how much worse the kids might look without his contributions. They do at least appear to be decently fed and sheltered.

Our arrival—or rather, the horses' arrival—provokes a whole lot of squealing excitement from one contingent of children. Before we've even breached the gate, a slim middle-aged woman with a worn face and a simple but clean linen dress appears in the doorway, presumably drawn by the clamor. "Can I help you?"

She doesn't sound exactly surprised that two people in noble clothes have shown up at her doorstep.

Casimir takes the lead with the whole talking thing. He strides up to the woman and offers a respectful dip of his head. "Our apologies for the intrusion. One of your benefactors asked us to take a look around and see if there's anything additional you might need."

I can't imagine the orphanage has more than one noble investing in it. The woman's brow knits a little, but she nods in acceptance. "I mean, we could always use more help. More hands to keep the kids in order, more variety of food, better clothing. But he's been plenty generous. We do all right."

"Could we come inside?" Casimir asks, spreading his hand in appeal. "I promise we have no intention of judging what you've accomplished. I simply want to make sure we can give him a thorough account of where additional contributions would be most appreciated."

At his soft smile, the orphanage manager can't seem to help smiling back. "I don't see why not. And if either of you have an interest in taking one of these sprites off our hands, they are capable of behaving themselves if given enough incentive."

The interior of the building has a similar atmosphere to the exterior—untidy and chaotic but homey. The smell of fresh-baked bread mingles with the tang of sweat and chamber pot spills.

Through the doorway to what serves as a living room, I see an older woman sitting in a ratty armchair, tilted toward the cluster of small children gathered on the floor around her.

"That's how they tell it," she's saying. "The All-Giver is all things and made all things, but the One God got tired of handling it all alone. So One lay with the sea and the sky and the earth to birth the nine godlen, three for each, so that they could help oversee the realms."

"The All-Giver is a lady, then, if she had babies," one of the kids pipes up.

The elderly woman chuckles and moves her hand down her front in the three-fingered tap. "The Great God is both man and woman and neither all at the same time. It's the grandness of divinity."

The little ones look as if they're as unsatisfied with that answer as I'd have been at that age, but there's no denying the fondness in the woman's expression or the eager curiosity in theirs. They are cared for here.

More than I was, after everything went wrong.

I swallow down the ache of that thought and yank my attention back to our host.

The woman leads us through a few of the rooms on the lower floor and up the stairs to the second, which holds mostly bedrooms it appears four or five children share each. As far as I can tell, there are fifty or so orphans in residence at the moment, ranging from a babe one of the other staff is feeding from a leather bottle to gawky preteens who can't be more than a few months shy of their dedication ceremonies.

But that's the oldest I see. As we circle back to the staircase, I venture a question. "Where do they go after their dedications?"

The manager runs her hand back through her rumpled curls. "Oh, the ones who don't end up adopted—which is most of 'em—go off to the temples in service of their chosen godlen. It's not a bad life. They're usually happy to get away from the bedlam here."

"Do they get to see much of the city beyond the institute before then?" Casimir asks. "I can tell you don't have enough assistance to easily keep track of all of them if you make an excursion."

"That's true. It's simpler keeping an eye on them here. We've got the garden and the river there for them to splash around in. But of course our benefactor arranges occasional visits to the royal college for the ones he feels have the most interest in seeing what the gods can provide."

I stifle a frown. Is that really all there is to Torstem's tours? He's showing off the glory of the ruling powers?

I can't see anything especially ominous about the arrangements here, though.

Casimir snaps his fingers. "That reminds me. I assume you keep records of which of your charges made those visits, and where each of them were placed after their dedications?"

The woman hesitates. "Well, yes, of course."

"It would be ever so helpful if we could look those over while we're here. There are a couple of past visitors who made an impression on people they met at the college, who'd like the chance to support their continued spiritual growth."

It's a deft enough excuse that I mentally applaud Casimir's cleverness. We need to find out what's really happened to the kids Ster. Torstem brought around.

But the woman twists her hands in front of her, maybe realizing that she doesn't have definite proof that we're associated with her benefactor at all.

Casimir beams at her as if he hasn't noticed her reluctance. A whiff of magic tingles over my skin before he speaks again. "You really have done a fantastic job for them here with the resources you have. I must commend you for that."

The orphanage manager's smile comes back. "Well, thank you. I—here, let me get our record books. They aren't the tidiest ever, but you should be able to find what you need."

*He does have a way about him, doesn't he?* Julita says with a tinge of her own admiration.

He does. It's almost trickery, how he persuades people, but he's so gentle about it you can tell there's no malice in it.

I've never known anyone quite like him. It's hard not to think the world would be a better place with more.

As the manager sets a few stained canvas-bound books on a rickety table, a wail bursts out from downstairs. She lets out an exasperated sigh. "I'd better handle that. I'll be back in a moment."

Casimir flips open the first book. He pulls out a paper and writing supplies as he peruses the pages.

My gaze veers to the staircase. I lower my voice. "I'm going to take a quick look at the third floor."

"Excellent idea."

I check to make sure no staff are in view of the staircase and then slip up the steps, wincing inwardly at every creak. All of the rooms I peek into are more bedrooms, but at the third doorway, I pause.

The nervous boy I saw with Ster. Torstem a few days ago stands near the window. I recognize his wideset eyes and pinched chin in an instant, even though he's dressed in a shabby tunic and trousers now.

I ease into the room. "Hello," I say, doing my best to channel Casimir's warmth. "You came by the college the other day, didn't you? Did you enjoy your visit?"

The boy bites his lip as he considers me. Then he gives a tentative nod. "There's so much that gets done there. It was very impressive."

Something about his answer sounds rehearsed, but then, I wouldn't put it past Ster. Torstem to insist on a certain way of talking about the college regardless of his reasons for taking the kids there.

"I suppose you'll be having your dedication ceremony soon," I say.

The boy brightens up immediately, so much that I can't doubt his enthusiasm now. "Oh, yes. I hope that Sabrelle will welcome my sacrifice with a great gift in return."

Well, I can't call him unambitious. He doesn't appear to be traumatized or unhinged. Just… quiet, which is far from a crime.

I try another angle. "What did you think of Ster. Torstem?"

"He's very generous. It was good to see… good to see where he comes from."

The boy gets a bit of an odd look, as if he's worried he's offended me. I scramble for another question. "I trust there wasn't anything frightening that happened during your visit?"

And gods above, let him tell me if there was.

The boy twists his hands in front of him. His next words come out a little too fast. "Oh, there's nothing to be scared of. It's people like Torstem who are making sure everything will be all right."

His face pales a little more, and he makes that hasty protective gesture over his chest like I saw on the campus. "I should help in the kitchen," he announces before I can say anything else, and darts past me out the door.

The whole conversation leaves me uneasy, but in such a vague way I can't say anything was actually wrong. It's odd that the boy referred to Torstem informally—but outer-ward kids aren't used to professional honorifics.

What did he mean about making sure things would be all right, though? That sounded strangely ominous even though it was phrased to be reassuring.

My nerves itch all the way back to Casimir, who's just closing the last of the records books. At the sound of the manager's voice traveling up the stairs, I duck inside and lean against the wall as if I never left.

When he hands the books back to the woman, Casimir gives her an emphatic thank you before we head outside. He tucks the paper he wrote his notes on into his breast pocket.

I have to wait until we're back on our horses and a few streets away from the orphanage before he tells me anything he learned. "If the records are correct, then all the children Ster. Torstem has tapped for college visits are serving at temples as she said."

"We'll just have to look them up at those temples and see if there's anything odd about their situation now. I spoke with the boy I saw earlier this week… He couldn't tell me much, but I got the sense he was still nervous about the situation."

Casimir rubs his chin. "I suppose it's difficult to judge based on that. I'd imagine a visit to the college would be intimidating to any child not raised near it."

The comment sets of a niggle of curiosity I decide to give in to. "Do—do *you* have any children? I mean…"

I flush. It's got to be obvious what I mean without my spelling it out.

"Not as yet," Casimir says in his usual easy tone. "Those of us in my trade who are trained at the college are supplied with mirewort. You've heard of it?"

I've taken it. "It prevents pregnancy. But it isn't infallible."

I've overheard more than one story of girls ushered into motherhood faster than they'd have preferred despite the herb.

"No, but it nearly is when you can get it pure. It's difficult to grow and harvest, so supply is limited, and most purveyors mix it with various other herbs so it'll go farther." The courtesan's mouth slants downward. "Few outside the inner wards have access to a fully effective option."

My stomach sinks. And they wouldn't be able to afford the pure stuff even if they had access.

I drag my attention away from that uncomfortable subject to the task we just completed. "Well, we now have a lot more information on Ster. Torstem's activities than we did before. It was lucky you got your hands on those books."

I glance sideways at him. "Or not about luck. Did you use your gift to convince her to let you at the books?"

I've never asked before what he traded his now-bejeweled teeth for.

The gleam in Casimir's eyes confirms my suspicion. "It does come in handy for a variety of purposes."

I hesitate and then push onward. "Am I allowed to ask what it *is*?"

"Ah." Casimir looks a bit sheepish, but only in the most adorable way. "Ardone blessed me with the ability to determine what I could do that would make a person happiest at any given moment. The orphanage manager deeply wished to be reassured that she's doing well by the children."

My pulse stutters. Has he used that ability on me? "That sounds like quite a power."

As if he's guessed at my concern, his tone turns soothing. "I can't do it often. Once or twice a day is my limit. And it's rarely anything sizeable, since it's limited by my immediate capabilities."

He pauses. "When you first came to us, saying you were Julita's friend, I could tell that you simply wanted us to hear you out. If you'd been looking to manipulate us, to get something more than our attention, I'd have picked up on it."

Oh. I let out a rough laugh. "I guess I should be glad for your gift, then."

His smile curves at the sly angle that might be my favorite. "I often am."

The streets have become more crowded with midday bustle, especially as we leave the fringes behind. Casimir has to pull Pepper ahead of Scout, which makes talking difficult.

We don't bother separating on our approach, since we can easily claim we happened to arrive back at the same time if anyone comments. After we've led our horses through the dance of the current password, I notice that Casimir chooses to remount rather than simply walk his mare to the stable on foot. I follow suit.

As the stable comes into view up ahead, I think the courtesan's companionable glow dulls just slightly. Seeing it dims my own spirits.

No, I will not stand for that.

I nudge Scout forward to walk alongside the Casimir. "That trip didn't take too long. You've got to have time for a quick canter through the woods."

He pauses before answering. "I'm meant to be at etiquette class at the next bell."

I snort. "The bell just rang a few minutes ago. You can fit it in. And charm them into forgiving you if you're a bit late. Unless you're just worried you and Pepper can't keep up with me and Scout?"

The sly glint comes back into Casimir's eyes, but he starts to shake his head. "As much as I appreciate the suggestion, Kindness—"

I don't give him a chance to finish his refusal. I simply pluck the paper with his notes from his pocket and tap my heels against the gelding's sides. "This is mine unless you can catch me!"

I press Scout to a canter, grinning at the sound of hoofbeats against the grass behind me and the laugh that spills from Casimir's lips. We race to the edge of the woods where I joined in the mock hunt and down the broad, well-trampled main path.

Trees whip past us, leaves swaying overhead. Casimir is gaining on me, but I'm not ready for the reprieve from our duties to be over so quickly.

I tug Scout off to the side, into the brush. He has to slow to a walk, but so does our pursuer.

"Ivy," Casimir calls out mock-threateningly.

"You still haven't caught me," I retort over my shoulder.

Scout picks his way deftly between the shrubs and tree trunks, but Casimir hasn't lost his cleverness. He directs Pepper over to the side and taps his heels the moment he sees a clear strip of land.

With a spring of her legs, she trots ahead of us. He wheels her around to block my path.

As I draw Scout to a halt, the exhilarated flush in Casimir's cheeks and his matching grin relieve me of any guilt I might have felt over forcing the diversion.

I might not have the same gift he does, but I didn't need it to know how to offer him a little happiness too.

The courtesan extends his hand, and I make a show of grudgingly handing over the paper. The brush of his fingertips against mine sends a jolt of warmth through me.

Casimir's dark green gaze holds mine as he tucks it away again. "Thank you."

My heart hitches with the giddiness I'm not supposed to feel. I force my tone to sound flippant. "You're ever so welcome."

The unbidden delight lingers as we let the horses amble back through the woods at a more leisurely pace.

*This really is quite nice,* Julita remarks. *I couldn't see much appeal to riding for its own sake before. I wonder—*

My gaze catches on something through the trees. Julita goes quiet as I pull on the reins and squint through the shifting shadows.

"What's the matter?" Casimir asks.

"The ground just looks… odd."

I hop down from Scout and walk over on foot.

There's a clearing so small you can barely call it that. I stop at the edge, staring at the ground.

The dirt is churned up in gouges and lumps. Fresh scratches scar a few of the surrounding tree trunks.

I bend closer to the jutting leaves of a weed. Dark red flecks show against the green.

My lungs constrict. "I think that's blood."

Casimir has followed me. He bends down to examine the plant, his shoulder grazing mine with a warmth I welcome more than ever, and then catches my eyes with a nod.

*Is the ground damp?* Julita asks abruptly. *Check it.*

I reach forward to press my fingers to the churned earth. Moist bits stick to my skin.

Julita shudders. *It's not like that outside the clearing, is it.*

She doesn't say it like a question, but I scuttle backward to test the dirt there.

It hasn't rained in a few days. The soil there crumbles dryly at my touch.

"Did you notice something else?" Casimir asks.

"Julita did." I frown at the clearing. "The earth there is damp, but it shouldn't be."

*Because they drenched it with water to wash away all the rest of the blood they must have spilled here,* Julita says in a strained voice. *The wretched sorcerers carried out some ritual here earlier* today.

# TWENTY-FOUR

I'm stretched out on the sofa, my sheet vanished but heat washing over my skin. Mainly because of the massive man bending over me.

"Ivy," Stavros murmurs in a liquid voice like nothing I've ever heard from him before. He's lost his shirt somewhere, but in my daze, I can't say I mind taking in the muscular expanse of his chest. "Gods, I can't stop thinking about you."

His fingers slide along my jaw, tilting my head up, and then he's captured my mouth.

Yes, this—this is what I've craved. The heat of him courses right through my body, sparking desire in every nerve.

I clasp the back of his neck and arch up to meet him. As my breasts graze his chest, an ache forms between my thighs.

His lips break from mine, and suddenly we're not alone. Alek kneels next to the sofa, his slim hand on my shoulder.

"You can't have her all to yourself," he says, as husky as Stavros. "It's my turn."

He leans in to claim a kiss of his own. My fingers trace the edge of his mask, and he kisses me harder. More lust spikes through my veins.

I have no idea what's going on here, but it feels too fucking good to ask questions.

There's a chuckle, and a well-built form nudges Alek aside. Benedikt clambers right onto the sofa to straddle me, his eyes gleaming with mischief. "Oh, I can top anything either of them could offer you."

Instead of pressing his mouth to mine, he brings his lips to the side of my neck. As he nips the sensitive skin there, his palm swivels against my breast.

A whimper slips through my teeth.

"But none of them really know how to treat a lady." Casimir sinks down next to me, heedless of Benedikt's attentions, and glides a gentle thumb over my lips. All at once, they're throbbing as if I've been starved for contact.

As Benedikt eases down my body, Casimir dips his head close and—

My pulse jolts at a sudden thump. My eyes pop open...

It's just me. Me, with my skin flushed and a pang of need low in my belly, alone on the sofa where I've been sleeping.

Well, not quite alone. Daylight streams from the far window, glancing off Stavros's ruddy hair as he bends to retrieve a box from the floor.

He catches me staring at him and offers a crooked grin. "I'd apologize for waking you up with my moment of clumsiness, but I'd rather say I was testing your reflexes. It's about time you came out of dreamland anyway."

Dreamland.

Right. Dreams.

Oh, gods, what a dream.

I must have stared at him a beat too long, remembering the all-too-vivid press of his bare chest against mine, because Stavros raises an eyebrow. I feel my cheeks flame scarlet.

"Good point," I say, somewhat inanely, shoving off the sheet that is in fact still there. The former general has seen me in nothing but my underclothes before, yet somehow the nightgown that covers much more of me feels far too exposing. "I'll get on with getting ready for the day. I'm sure we have much to do."

Stavros's eyebrow stays lifted as I grab the latest riding gown Casimir has sent along—to replace the one Anya splattered with her wine—and hustle over to the latrine. His drawl carries after me through the door. "Nice to see you so dedicated to your work, Thief."

Yep, that's all that's going through my head. Total dedication to our cause. Also, my drawers are definitely not soaked between my thighs.

Gods smite me.

Julita must notice my discomfort, even if—thank all that's divine—she isn't privy to my imaginings. *Is something wrong? You seem a little agitated.*

I give her a subtle shake of my head in answer.

To my relief, the door thumps with Stavros's departure before I've finished tying the laces on my dress. I splash a little water on my face, twist my hair into the hasty arrangement I've gotten used to, and head down to the dining hall feeling almost normal.

As I slip into the vast room, I might get some inquisitive looks from the nobles at the nearest tables. At this point, who knows how far word has spread of my sudden apprenticeship under the much-lauded general and whatever other exploits people feel are gossip-worthy?

More ominous are the stern gazes of the two soldiers from the Crown's Watch standing guard near the doorway. Apprehension prickles down my back even though I know they're not here specifically for me.

A graceful wave of a hand gives me something else to focus on. Esmae motions me over to the seat next to her.

I veer around to the counters to grab a plate of eggs and pastries before sinking down into the neighboring chair.

Unfortunately, the moment I sit down, I realize that I'm in the direct line of sight of Romild, two tables over. She catches me noticing her and narrows her eyes into a glower.

I drop my gaze to my plate as if it's the most fascinating arrangement of food I've ever seen and snatch up my fork. "I wonder if Romild is ever going to forgive me for that trick with the saddle."

Julita sniffs. *There's nothing to forgive you for. You were simply proving she can't hold a candle to your skills, after she so rudely questioned them.*

"Clearly she had a lot invested in vying for that position," Esmae says in a more measured tone. "I can see how it'd have been... startling for her to find out it'd been taken without the typical procedure."

I grimace. "Don't people"—I cut myself off before I say *people around here*, as if I'm not a noble like them, and regather myself—"Don't all of us benefit from our connections sometimes? It isn't as if I arranged for my father to have known Ster. Stavros's before I was even born."

Esmae bobs her head. "It's totally understandable that he'd have felt he could trust you—and from what I've heard, you've handled the job as well as anyone could ask. But when you really want something, I suppose it's hard not to feel some sting of unfairness."

The tightness of her voice prompts me to take a closer look at her. She doesn't sound as if she's simply speculating about a near-stranger.

Of course, she's been open with me about how desperately she wants to find a prestigious position of her own after she graduates. I guess it can't be too difficult for her to imagine being in a similar situation.

Esmae aims a bright smile at me and motions to the pastries I chose at random. "I'm stealing that moon roll from you if you don't eat it. The chefs outdid themselves with those."

I crack a grin. "In that case, I'm eating it first. You'd better grab yourself another of your own."

The crispy yet buttery shell and the creamy custard within really are something on the level of the gods. I'd be able to savor the delicacy more if Julita weren't muttering in my head.

*Jealousy isn't Romild's only problem if what you said is true. Now Wendos is harassing her? What's he aiming for there? What are they* all *aiming for, sneaking around in the woods again?*

The cream sours in my mouth. Casimir and I weren't able to turn up any other clues about the scourge sorcerers' apparent woodland ritual—not even enough to prove to anyone who didn't already believe there's a conspiracy that the damp earth has anything to do with illicit sorcery to begin with.

All Stavros could offer when I told him about it was a sardonic comment about needing to bring the king more than mud.

As I chew the last few morsels of the roll, my gaze darts across the room instinctively. It snags on Wendos's dark shaggy hair, several tables off amid a few other students.

If he's scheming anything right now, it's how to inhale as much breakfast as possible. I'm still not sure he was exactly "harassing" Romild so much as expressing concern.

What did he notice about her that bothered him? What if it was *her* sneaking around in the woods with the other conspirators?

She did seem awfully comfortable in that setting during the hunt.

We've been focusing on Ster. Torstem, but no matter how involved he might be, it seems awfully unlikely that he's offended the daimon so much all on his own. We've got to find his accomplices too.

"Is that a new dress?" Esmae is asking. "It's a good color on you."

I glance down absently at the pale lilac silk. "Yes, you know, I needed another after the wine incident—I didn't bring very much with me from home."

Imagine if she saw what I usually wear.

"You'll have to have your family send more." Esmae perks up. "I could practice my gift for you to get the message there quickly. Nikodi is farther away than I've tried, but it'd be good to stretch myself. I'd like to be crossing country borders someday, and—"

As she's talked, a slender man in the light blue linen tunic and trousers most of the non-teaching staff wear weaves through the tables to stop by Romild. He taps her shoulder and hands her a folded note.

She glances at its contents and frowns. Then she gets up out of her seat, leaving behind a plate she's only half-cleared.

My pulse hiccups, and I miss whatever Esmae says next. Where's my rival off to in such a hurry?

I think I'd better find out.

I scarf down one last mouthful of eggs and nudge back my seat as Romild approaches the door.

Esmae pauses, staring at me. "Are you going already?"

I snatch at the first excuse I can think of that would make sense to her. "I just saw someone who said he might have news soon about what's happened to Julita. I've got to try to catch him before he heads to class—sorry, I didn't notice him before."

With feet practiced for speed and deft maneuvering, I make it to the hallway just as Romild reaches the corner to my left. As quietly as I can, I hurry after her.

She doesn't glance backward, her steps brisk and her posture a bit stiff, as if she's not happy about whatever the message said. The hall outside the dining area provides plenty of cover anyway with students coming and going.

As I turn the corner after her into the longer passageway leading past the main library doors, the traffic thins.

If she looks around, she won't be able to help seeing me. And wondering why the hell I'm trailing at her heels.

I drift farther back, wishing the hall offered more in the way of columns or pedestals to duck behind, and a perfect solution presents itself in the form of Benedikt.

The bastard's bastard strolls jauntily out of a nearby stairwell, looking as though he's making for the dining hall. I dash over before he can get very far.

"Walk with me," I say under my breath as I catch his elbow. "Pretend we're having an absolutely fascinating discussion about some favor I'm asking you to do for my employer. And if Romild glances our way, block her view of me."

Benedikt chuckles and swerves to join me, his gray eyes dancing with good humor. He pitches his voice similarly low. "I don't know if I'd bother to do any favors for Stavros, but I'll certainly lend you a hand. Or several, if I can collect them."

I manage not to roll my eyes at him. At least he's the most amenable of Julita's men to playing along.

It's hard not to appreciate his good humor. And to stop myself from flashing back to my dream when he—

I shove those memories away as well as I can, which is admittedly not very well. He's sauntering along next to me, his embroidered vest hanging loose over his dress shirt—which, in typical Benedikt style, he's left open halfway down his chest.

Maybe I've denied my bodily desires too much in the past couple of years. The glimpse I get of the muscular landscape beneath nearly sends my mind reeling right back to my overheated imaginings.

I jerk my gaze to Benedikt's face just as he leans his head conspiratorially close. "Why exactly are we following this fine lady? Out of curiosity."

"She might have had something to do with the daimon going wild at the ball," I say. "She also might have been the person who poisoned me the other evening."

"All right, those are two very good reasons for me to delay my breakfast. I'm honored that you called on me for assistance and will assume it had everything to do with my extreme prowess rather than because I happened to be the only person around."

I can't quite stifle a guffaw. Even though I'm only holding his arm to keep him within shielding distance, I give it a quick squeeze. "You're an excellent choice."

He taps one of his sacrificed earlobes. "My gift might come in handy, depending on exactly what you're planning. I have a knack for distracting people, just a little, when I want to get out of trouble."

My eyebrow leaps up. "And how often are you getting into trouble?"

He waggles his eyebrows right back. "I've got to keep a few secrets to maintain my intriguing aura of mystery."

I snort in amusement.

Honestly, it might be fun to have Benedikt along on one of my thieving exploits on the fringes. I can imagine him enjoying sticking it to a few con artists.

Picturing taking on the assholes in the outer wards with company warms me for a few seconds. Then I consider the stink and the dirt and everything else about those streets any noble would turn up their nose at.

No, he'd never actually stoop that low even for a lark, would he?

I hate the way my heart sinks with that knowledge.

Benedikt cocks his head. "I wonder where exactly Miss Possible Poisoner is off to?"

Romild has strode straight past the library doors and picked up her pace even more as she approaches the next bend in the hall.

Julita hums. *It's just the recreational rooms over there—cards, billiards, darts, and the like. Although I suppose that isn't a horrible place to conduct a clandestine meeting without being too suspicious.*

I slow as we reach the corner and peek around it. Romild is bustling onward, so Benedikt and I continue after her.

"What are you studying here anyway?" I ask him, to keep up the appearance that we're having some important discussion. And because I'm interested, whether I should be or not.

Benedikt shrugs as if it doesn't matter all that much. "Oh, a little of this and a little of that. Technically I belong to the leadership division, not that I expect to lead much of anything. As I mentioned before, responsibility isn't really my forte. We royalty-adjacent types tend to get relegated into minor roles to keep us happy and *mostly* out of trouble."

"That does seem like it might be a difficult proposition for you."

"But I'm very rarely bored." Benedikt taps his chin. "I wonder what 'favors' I should ask Stavros to do for me in return? So many wonderful possibilities that would absolutely piss him off."

My lips twitch with a smirk at the thought—and at the same moment, Romild draws to a halt outside one of the rooms farther down the hall.

She peers inside and hesitates. Then she folds her arms over her chest and starts to pivot on her heel.

Shit, she's turning right back toward us.

I clutch Benedikt's arm in warning, but his gaze is already fixed on our target, noting her movements.

He swings toward me without missing a beat and flashes his roguish smile. "Don't stab me for this, Knives."

Before I can wonder what he's talking about, he nudges me up against the wall, leans his arm next to my head to hide my face, and plants his mouth on mine.

In the first instant, I think I must still be dreaming. But the heat of Benedikt's very real kiss sparks a giddy thrill in me that's beyond anything my imagination conjured. My body tingles from head to toe as if I've been struck by a particularly delicious bolt of lightning.

It's far from my first kiss, but I can't say I've ever been kissed quite like this.

My breath hitches, Benedikt's tongue flicks skillfully over my bottom lip, and the part of my brain that actually wants me to survive the next week wakes up.

I'm not supposed to be kissing this man. I'm already in over my head enough.

I'd jerk away from him, but Benedikt eases back a few inches at the tensing of my body. He stays close enough to block any clear view of me from down the hall, his eyes still twinkling. "I think that did the trick."

I give him a pointed look, grasping hold of the remains of my self-restraint. "I'm pretty sure you could have accomplished the same result without going quite that far."

He offers me a smirk that's softer than usual. "This way was more fun. You'll have to forgive me for taking the opportunity that presented itself. I've been wanting to kiss you since you nearly unmanned Stavros."

His gaze flicks up to my forehead. "And if our ghostly friend enjoyed it too, all the better."

The reference to Julita—to the fact that he was thinking about her soul inside me when he kissed me—douses any lingering heat. I clench my jaw and draw myself up a little straighter against the wall.

A flick of my eyes tells me that Romild hasn't gone anywhere. She's standing with her back mostly to us again, staring at the note she was handed while she seems to wait for someone.

"Shall we—" Benedikt starts, and a different familiar voice reaches my ears from the opposite end of the hall.

"Make sure the carriage is ready. I'll be out in a few minutes after I take care of one more matter."

Ster. Torstem calls the words over his shoulder as he steps into the hall from one of the archways leading to the outer doors—speaking to a page or an assistant, I have to assume. He marches past our hallway in the direction of the library.

My heart skips a beat.

A carriage. He's going out somewhere in the city—to the orphanage? To arrange some other plans we'd want to know about?

This is an opportunity I might not get again. There's only one possible course of action that fixes all of the problems I've just stumbled into.

I give Benedikt's arm a quick pat, willing the flush out of my cheeks. "Keep an eye on Romild until you've seen who she's meeting here. I'm going to find out what Torstem's up to."

# Twenty-Five

Benedikt's eyes widen, but I duck under his arm and dart off down the hall before he can protest. The lilac silk I'm wrapped in glints in the light from the sconces. I wish I could dash to Stavros's quarters to grab my plain cloak, but I can't risk missing the carriage.

At least this color is significantly less eye-catching than the turquoise gown.

I slip through the doorway and cross the courtyards to the college's outermost gate. There is indeed a carriage waiting on the road just beyond the walls, modest by noble standards but still more finely carved than anything you'd usually see in the middle wards.

Outer-warders make do with carts and their feet.

Clouds clot the sky overhead, and the breeze feels damp against my cheeks. But the dimness makes it easier for me to avoid notice.

As I eye the vehicle from a shadowy alcove in the wall, it occurs to me that my dress is less than ideal for a variety of reasons. Noble gowns are a damn sight prettier than they are practical, especially for stealthy maneuvers.

Wetting my lips, I peer down at my skirt with its slits for riding. With a few hasty motions, I tie the loose bits tight around my thighs.

The young man Ster. Torstem sent ahead finishes conferring with the driver and heads back into the college. One of the guards on the top of the wall high overhead tosses a bored remark toward the other.

I ease along the wall until I'm out of view of the front of the carriage and then make a leap for it, bending low and sliding across the cobblestones. With a soft whoosh of fabric, I'm hunched under the vehicle.

It isn't built so differently from the merchant's wagon I clung on to what feels like a century ago. To my immense gratitude, carriages tend to be set higher off the ground.

I hook my knees and elbows around the wooden reach bar that runs down the middle between the two sets of wheels. With another tug of the fabric gathered around my legs, I ensure it won't drag on the road.

*Are you sure about this, Ivy?* Julita asks. I can picture her frowning skeptically.

"Nothing I haven't done a dozen times before," I whisper, and tense at the thud of approaching boots.

Torstem doesn't notice anything out of the ordinary. He strides right up to the carriage. "Let's be off immediately."

Without another word, he heaves his stout body onto the seat above my hiding place.

The driver flicks the whip, and the gelding in the harness clops forward. The wheels rattle over the cobblestones on either side of me.

Julita speaks up again in a mildly droll tone. *So… you and Benedikt appear to be getting along well.*

I adjust my grip on the bar, swaying as the carriage veers around a bend in the road. "Is this really the best time to be talking about that?"

My lips purse of their own accord, bringing back the giddying sensation of his kiss. I shake my head against it as if answering my own question.

Julita clearly doesn't agree. *Why not? I'm the only one who can hear you with all the clatter out there. Have you got something better to do during the trip?*

"I guess not," I mutter.

*There's nothing to be embarrassed about. He is appealing in his own way.*

"Kissing him wasn't my idea in the first place."

*You enjoyed it well enough.*

My cheeks flare all over again. "You can't just assume—"

She lets out a tinkling laugh. *I might not be able to read your thoughts, but I experience everything your body does, Ivy. I know.*

"Well, it isn't going to happen again." If he'd even want it to, now that he's scratched that itch.

*He might be a bastard, but he's still only twice removed from the royal family. Not a bad catch at all.*

"I'm not going to be catching him." I make a face at the base of the carriage. "If we have to talk, can we talk about something else?"

*Hmm.* Julita is silent for a few minutes, as if put out by my refusal. *I suppose this is a rather convenient way of traveling while staying concealed. If you have the arm strength for it. Or does your gift help with that?*

My gift that I don't actually have. I swallow thickly and rub the stump of my finger that's my supposed sacrifice. "A little of both, let's say." I pause. "Did *you* make a sacrifice? What was your dedication?"

*Oh, yes. I wasn't going to pass that chance up.* Something firms in her voice, a hint of steely resolve. *I gave my lowest two ribs to Creaden.*

I wince. "That must have hurt."

*For a little while, to be sure, but the devouts sealed up my flesh just like they will have for your finger. It was worth it. He granted me the gift I asked for: that when I say no to a request or demand, it'll be heeded.*

My stomach knots at the thought of why she'd have wanted a gift like that. Why her brother's experiments must have stopped after her dedication.

I don't know what to say. Julita goes quiet after her answer, leaving me feeling guilty that I've shut her up even though I didn't want to talk in the first place.

Then the carriage rolls to a stop. *Ster.* Torstem steps out, tossing a few words of gratitude to the driver. "I'll need you back by the bell for the second hour."

"Of course, sir."

*That's my cue.*

Torstem's feet tramp up the steps of the stone building we've stopped in front of. I can't see anyone else ambling nearby from my vantage point. Two trimmed shrubs jut up on either side of the building's doorway.

The driver prods the horse to walk on. Just as the mare starts hauling the carriage forward again, I release my hold and whip myself to the side.

In an instant, I've rolled off the road and onto my feet behind one of the shrubs. I crouch there, watching for trouble.

No one shouts in alarm. I smooth the makeshift ties out of my now-scuffed skirt and tug the pins from my hair so it drifts down to partly conceal my face. Combing my fingers through the strands, I step farther into the shadows between this building and the neighboring one.

The structure Torstem headed into is tall, some four stories high, with small windows dotted across its side. Raucous male laughter booms from the nearest one. A whiff of pipe smoke reaches me from where the pane is cracked open.

That has the flavor of a gentlemen's club. Is this all Torstem has gone off to do—engage in manly gossip and other indulgences?

I slink along the narrow path down the side of the building, checking for a window I can reach that isn't cloaked by curtains. I've almost reached the rear of the building when a figure marches past from a back door, heading down the alley behind.

My feet stall beneath me. The simple tunic, trousers, and cap the man is wearing are those of a laborer, not a noble. But I know that resolute stride and silvered brown hair.

Ster. Torstem is only using this place as a front to slip off somewhere else. Somewhere he doesn't want to be identified as a noble.

Now *that* is certainly a development worth following up on.

*This is quite odd,* Julita murmurs as I dart after the professor's hurrying form.

I don't dare speak now, but her remark is exactly why I need to find out what he's up to. Because chances are, it's nothing good.

The gentlemen's club was around the center of the middle wards, a couple of streets over from the river. Torstem sneaks along a few alleyways, never realizing I'm creeping a safe distance behind him, and then seems to feel he's gained enough distance to ease up on the caution.

Once he's stepped out onto the proper streets, I can relax a little more too. I trail along at a distance, keeping an eye on the dented top of his cap but letting plenty of pedestrians pass between us.

Thunder rumbles in the distance, but the heavy clouds overhead hold on to their rain for now. The law professor crosses a bridge and hurries on through the dirtier streets that mark the start of the fringes.

We're back in Siltston, though on the opposite side of the river from the orphanage. Is he taking a roundabout route there or heading to a different destination?

As we pass through dingier streets where fewer people have reason to be strolling, I let myself drift farther back. More grit from the ground flecks the skirt of my dress, but that only helps me fit in better.

Torstem veers down a strip of dreary storefronts, several of the front windows boarded up or papered over with the failing of the businesses. But the two-story structure at the end of the street appears to be doing all right.

Two dark-leafed trees sprout from its sides, melded with the walls, and cast their hunched branches over the patchwork of tiles on the vaulted roof. The door stands partly open, strains of music filtering from inside.

A minor conjuring winds around the sign above. It highlights the etched sigil of Ardone—godlen of love, beauty, and sensuality—and the place's name: The Night's Calling.

The logo shows a crescent moon framing a silhouette of a woman's face. A placard next to the door lists the day's specials—meals and mixed drinks—but I know that isn't the main "calling" the place trades in.

Ster. Torstem walks straight inside.

A couple of women in dresses that do more to accentuate their curves than cover them brush past the gauzy curtains on the front window. Julita lets out a startled sound. *Is that what I think it is?*

"A brothel," I murmur, dashing closer as quickly as I dare. "One of the outer wards' more exclusive ones, as exclusive as anything in these parts gets."

A brash female voice filters from inside, jovial with greeting. "Tomas! Good to see you again. Let me make sure your ladies are ready for you."

Tomas? Is that the name Torstem is going by here?

I suppose it makes sense that he'd use an assumed name when he's going to so much trouble to disguise his trip here. Apparently it's far from his first visit.

I hesitate, sidling off to the side of the street so I don't look as if I'm gaping at the building.

On one hand, a whorehouse is a perfectly normal place for a man to be sneaking off to that doesn't indicate any horrifying magical conspiracy. On the other hand, there's no way of telling that Ster. Torstem is here simply to wet his dick any more than that he funds the orphanage only out of the goodness of his heart.

Even if he *is* here for no reason other than to get his rocks off, men often open their mouths when they're in the stupor of the afterglow. At least, Milo did—that was how I found out about his horrible side business.

Torstem might have given away something useful to his "ladies" inside.

Well, there's only one way to find out: go in and ask.

I don't think I'll get very far as a supposed patron. Mulling the idea over in my head, I approach the building cautiously and spot a window halfway open past one of the supporting trees.

All it takes is a quick scramble, and I'm landing with a soft thump in a darkened dressing room. Mingled perfumes clog the air, and dresses lie strewn across the settee, chair, and vanity.

The vanity also holds several scattered pots of colored powders. I snatch a couple up.

Esmae would not approve of the garish art I make of my face. Hasty smudges of crimson mark my cheeks and lips; smears of violet coat my eyelids.

I glance down at my dress, hesitate, and then loosen the lacing so I can tug the neckline partway down my shoulders. A pool of shadow forms at my meager cleavage.

There. That should be decently convincing.

*Ivy…* Julita says in a doubtful tone, but she doesn't seem to know how to debate this subject with me.

I shoot a tight smile at my tarted-up reflection in the mirror. "Don't worry. I'm only going to look the part, not act it out."

In some ways, it's harder to take on this persona than that of a noble. As a noble, I can be distant and wary, and no one thinks it's strange, just snobbishness.

As a harlot, I'm supposed to let it all out. To ooze sensuality and confidence.

I'm not sure I have enough sexpot in me to ooze it, but I summon as much as I can and saunter out into the hall with a swing of my hips. As my pulse drums nervously through my veins, I prick my ears.

A couple of children who look to be five or six huddle against the wall farther down, one of them wiping the floor and another folding sheets from a heaping basket. I stare at them for a second before understanding settles over me.

These courtesans of sorts won't have access to the pure mirewort like Casimir does. An occasional accidental pregnancy will be par for the course for the brothel-workers of the fringes.

Which apparently keeps the brothel set for cleaning staff.

A few feminine voices carry from a doorway closer by. I lift my chin and stroll into that room.

It looks to be a small lounge, presumably for the women to relax between patrons. Exactly what I was hoping for.

Two of the women are sprawled on the armchairs on either side of a small table. Another is perched on a windowsill, holding a slim stick between her fingers that's giving off a spicy smoke.

All three of their gazes lock onto me the second I enter the room.

One of them shoves herself higher in her chair, her bodice sliding against the tops of her breasts, which are threatening to spill over the faux satin fabric. "Who're you?"

"Lilac," I say, in honor of my dress, figuring one plant name is as good as another. "It's my first day. This—this is where we wait until there's a client for us, right?"

The hint of hesitation seems to put the other women more at ease. Maybe it shows I'm not a real threat, not sharp enough in the claws to pry their best patrons away.

The woman in the faux-satin dress folds her hands on her lap, one missing its little finger—a common minor sacrifice, like Ewalin's. What sort of gift would a woman of her calling ask for?

Did she already know what work she'd be doing when she dedicated herself at twelve?

"I doubt you'll be in here long," the one by the window remarks. "Madam will want to get you right into the rotation."

Who knows how long I have before the woman who'll know she didn't hire me bustles in? I drift along the wall beside the door, where to my surprise I find a small bookshelf packed with assorted leather- and canvas-bound volumes.

I bring my thumb to my lips. "Is there a lot of business this early in the day?"

The window woman shrugs. "If they're awake, there'll be someone wanting it. More once it gets dark, of course."

"Sometimes the ones in the day are better," the third woman pipes up. "Sometimes they're just odd."

A couple of silver teeth flash beyond her lips—the gaudiest a fringe courtesan can afford to fill in that kind of sacrifice.

Jumping on the opening, I wrinkle my nose. "I saw a man just come in—Tomas, someone called him. It sounded like he takes more than one woman at a time?"

The woman in the faux-satin laughs, rubbing the stump of her sacrificed finger. "That's hardly the strangest thing you'll run into around here. But you don't have to worry about Madam sticking you with Tomas."

I raise my eyebrows. "Why not? He already has his favorites picked out?"

The window woman takes a drag from her smoke-stick. "You could say that. It's none of us. Madam has some girls set up in the attic. Pampered bunch. Far as I know, they don't cater to anyone but him."

The woman with the silver teeth cackles. "He must pay a pretty penny to make it worth her while to keep 'em."

"Does he come by every day or something?" I ask, opening my eyes wide as if in shock.

The faux-satin woman waves her hand. "Nah, more like every week. But he never stays away too long. Sweet deal, really."

"I don't know," the silver-toothed woman says. "Sometimes the sounds from up there are kind of... funny. Not sure it'd be work I'd like if it's worth that much to him."

I knit my brow. "What kind of sounds?"

"Oh, don't you worry about that," the window woman says. "Cherille just has a wild imagination." She shoots the other woman a quelling glance.

It doesn't sound as if they know much more than they've already said anyway.

I run my finger idly across the spines of the books. The volumes are slim, but they're not all in Silanian—some are Veldunian, a few Darium, a title that looks Icarian—and one in Woudish.

I can't resist sliding that one off the shelf to peek at it. As far as I can make out from my layman's knowledge, it's a book of love poetry.

"What are all the books for?" I say, to avoid looking as if I'm specifically there to pump them for information about Ster. Torstem—and also because I'm honestly wondering.

The faux-satin woman yawns. "Oh, Madam collects some, and some the men bring. They can help set the mood if you need it, with the right type who thinks books are something exotic."

The one in my hand is relatively exotic. I curl my fingers around it and risk another prying question. "Haven't you ever *asked* the girls in the attic what's so special about Tomas?"

The silver-toothed woman shakes her head. "Hard to do it when we never see 'em. They're always up there. Madam brings their meals and all."

"I say they've got some sneaky secret path to go scurrying through the city at their whim," the faux-satin woman declares.

The woman at the window doesn't seem to appreciate my continued questioning. She adjusts her position on the sill, her voice turning brusque. "You'll see how it all goes fast enough."

I can feel my safety here slipping through my fingers—and it doesn't appear these women know more that would be useful.

Surreptitiously tucking the Woudish book into the folds of my skirt, I let out a hasty giggle. "I think I'd better relieve myself before Madam comes with a client. Where's the privy?"

"Out back." The window woman jabs her thumb toward the hall.

As I duck out, the woman in faux-satin peals out another laugh on my heels. "Some of 'em will like it if you get 'em wet."

I'd rather not think about that.

I dart down the dim hall, past the children at their chores, all the way to the door at the back and into yard beyond.

Weeds sprout up between cracked limestone tiles of the modest courtyard. Spinning around, I peer up at the roof.

Ladies in the attic. That's who Ster. Torstem comes to see—ladies no one *else* seems to see.

How very odd indeed.

Nobody appears to be paying much attention to what's going on outside the brothel. Maybe I can take a peek from out here.

As I slink around the building, considering my options, a few raindrops patter onto my hair. By the time I've made my decision and am clambering up the more scalable of the two trees, a steady drizzle flecks my skin with a chilly layer of moisture and streaks across the silk of my gown.

"Casimir's going to have to get me another new dress," I mutter in an undertone.

Julita laughs, though a thread of nervousness winds through her voice. *Somehow I don't think he'll mind. He'd dress up the other men too if they'd let him.*

I manage to brace myself in the crook of a branch by the slant of the roof. The attic holds no windows or other openings that I can see.

And there are multiple women stuck in that closed-off space day in and out?

The mismatched shingles dappling the roof look particularly uneven farther along the stretch of the branch. I edge along it, setting my hand on the roof for balance.

If only I could peer right through the mottled surface, make my own little window—

My magic springs up inside my chest, jerking this way and that.

I can. I can, if only I let it.

I shut my eyes and grimace. Fuck, *no*. When will it get the message?

But my power really isn't accepting my reluctance now. I can't say I'm in any immediate danger, but at the gritting of my teeth, pain spikes through my chest. The riven magic lashes at me from throat to gut like I've got a feral cat scrabbling to break free of my flesh.

I gasp and bow over the roof, groping for balance.

*Ivy?* Julita asks frantically as the agony sears deeper.

It's attacking me because I wouldn't give myself a magical view into the attic on a whim? Gods save me, what will it feel like the next time I really am in danger?

I press the side of my face against the cold, rough shingles, damp now with the thickening rain. The solid sensation grounds me a little.

The turmoil raging inside me ebbs by increments. When it's more a rabid mouse than a feral cat, I ease myself up and slip the knife from the sheath on my thigh.

It only takes a few furtive movements to pry up a couple of the shingles, revealing the boards beneath. There, no wretched magic needed at all.

Bending close again, I rest my ear against the thinned surface of the roof. Muffled voices reach me through the wood.

There's a soft murmur of blurred-together words, ending with, "—without you."

Then a gruff voice I recognize as Ster. Torstem's. "I understand. But you're doing so well. I'm proud of you."

The next murmur sounds more pleased.

Another feminine voice speaks up, this one huskier but louder. "It's always our pleasure to serve."

"I know it has been," Torstem says. "And our plans are so close to coming to fruition. Soon you'll be able to do everything I've promised."

Their plans? His promises?

I strain my hearing, the wood rough against my cheek, but only silence follows.

# Twenty-Six

Nobles seem to flout typical rules everywhere they go, but for some reason they respect the college library. Even with most of the tables full and students wandering amid the aisles in the early hours of the evening, a hush fills the vast room.

I meander along the bookcases and around the tables as if I'm casually making my way to a specific reference section. In reality, I'm peeking at the students around me and their reading material for anything that would raise my—or Julita's—suspicions.

*Herbal grimoire*, she says as we pass one guy who's peering intently at a huge tome. *That could be a resource for darker intentions… but I'm pretty sure I've heard him talk about his studies to become a medic.*

I can't answer her here without being obvious, so I give my head a subtle tip of a nod and move on.

Really, checking up on the noble students' studies is only an excuse to wander around. I'm hoping that Alek, scholar that he is, spends plenty of time in the library outside of our meetings—and some of it in the main room rather than the archives.

I wouldn't want to be caught poking around down there on my own, but all students and staff are welcome in the library proper.

I'd like to give Alek the book I pilfered on his behalf before Stavros notices it and asks where I got it. When I explain at tomorrow's meeting what I learned about Ster. Torstem and his hidden harlots today, I'm going to finesse the story a little.

The men don't need to know I painted myself up as a prostitute.

If Alek puts two and two together after he's got the unusual treasure in his possession, somehow I don't think he's going to make a fuss about it.

The palace bell rings distantly to mark the seventh hour of the later day. I veer around another set of shelves, debating giving up my search for now in favor of dinner.

My stomach puts in its vote with a gurgle.

But then my persistence pays off. I spot Alek's messy black hair and the gleam of polished leather across his bronze-brown face a few rows down this aisle.

I step toward him—and a different figure moves in front of me with a brush of fingertips against my arm.

I freeze, staring up at Wendos's coppery features. He's got less than a foot on me, but Julita's shudder reverberates through my nerves, putting me twice as on guard as I would be otherwise.

If her brother's old friend notices my reaction, he doesn't show it. He offers a relaxed smile with a flash of white teeth. "Sorry if I startled you. You're Ivy, right? Julita's friend?"

Julita practically snarls. *What under the gods' gaze does he want with you?*

I remember at the last second that I shouldn't have any idea who *he* is. At least, not as much as Julita has told me.

"Perhaps acquaintance is more accurate," I say, keeping my voice as light as I can manage while my pulse thumps hard. "My family's from the other end of Nikodi. We didn't visit often."

That should explain why he won't remember me.

He doesn't let the subject go immediately, though his tone stays casual. "Still, I'm surprised we never ran into each other. I'm Wendos—I was a good friend of her brother's."

Julita lets out an inarticulate hiss.

I bite back the words I'd like to chide her with. Doesn't she realize I need to concentrate?

I tilt my head to the side as if in thought. "Oh, I think possibly we did meet once. I'm not sure we were fully introduced. You and Borys were just racing off on some adventure, I suppose."

The picture I painted must fit Wendos's childhood enough for him to believe it, because he chuckles. "I apologize if my manners weren't the best back then. Maybe I can make up for it now. I tried to look out for Julita after she arrived at the college, since Borys isn't here to do it…"

He pauses and sketches his hand down his front in a hasty gesture of the divinities. "I'm worried. If you have any idea what's happened to her, I'll do whatever I can to help."

*Help dig me a deeper grave, he'd like,* Julita sneers, her presence writhing against the back of my skull, so agitated my scalp itches. *What a pack of lies he's trying to sell.*

Is it possible he does actually feel guilty now that she's disappeared? He's definitely evaluating me, but it's possible he's checking whether I'm a potential ally rather than an opponent.

After all Julita's obsession with him, she hasn't turned up a scrap of evidence that he's stuck with his old, awful ways.

Not that I'm going to tell him anything. I don't trust him farther than I could spit a rat.

But I'm keeping my mind open to evidence on both sides, since she obviously won't.

I twist my mouth in a regretful grimace. "Unfortunately, she barely told me anything the last time I saw her. I assumed she was doing something for school, nothing that would cause her any trouble. Do you have any idea what else she might have been involved in?"

Wendos sighs and runs his hand through his shaggy hair. "No. It took me by surprise. But if you come across any indication, will you let me know?"

I force an ingratiating smile. "Of course. I'm not sure that's very likely, though. I assume the school authorities are looking into her disappearance, and I've left them to it. It's not as if there's anything I can do on that score."

Wendos holds my gaze for a moment longer. "We'll just have to hope they turn up something and that she's all right. And if I can lend a hand with anything at all, Ivy, do let me know."

He strolls off, leaving my nerves jangling and Julita sputtering a string of curses I wouldn't have thought a noblewoman would know. *If I could reach out of your body and strangle him…*

"He's gone now," I say in the quietest possible whisper, feeling like I need to try to settle her down somehow. "And he doesn't know any more than he did before."

To my frustration, Alek is gone too. I head toward the row of bookcases where I saw him before and duck down it, but there's no one browsing the texts there now.

A quick skim reveals that this section is focused on the study of stones and soil. Not a popular subject among the elite, apparently.

I've drifted halfway down the row when Alek appears at the other end. After a quick glance to confirm I'm alone, he strides over, his mouth set in a pensive expression beneath the slanted edge of his mask.

"Is everything all right?" he asks quietly. "I saw Wendos come over to you."

His gaze flicks from my eyes to my forehead. He's at least as worried about Julita's reaction as my own, clearly.

I guess I can't blame him for that, especially in this particular case. "He didn't say much, just seemed interested in whether I knew where Julita had gone. She's pretty peeved with him, but he didn't try anything questionable."

Alek's shoulders ease down from their defensive pose. "Good. If she's right about him, we have to be careful."

"Oh, don't worry, she's made sure I'm well aware of that fact." I offer a wry smile and then dig out the small, leatherbound volume from the pocket I stashed it in. "I was actually hoping I'd run into you. I found something I thought you might appreciate. The vocabulary and the style are a little beyond me, but I've never seen anything like it here in Florian."

Alek takes the Woudish poetry book from me and flips open the cover. After a moment, his posture goes rigid. His attention jerks back to me. "Did you tell Julita about this? Was it her idea to give it to me?"

I can't help stiffening up too. Why would he think the gift must be from her?

"No," I say shortly. "I was thinking about our conversation in the archives. If you don't want it—"

"I'll keep it. I—" He peers at me for a moment longer. "Do *you* know what this is?"

My cheeks heat. "Like I said, it's not the basic Woudish I'm used to. I, er, got the impression it was romantic poetry? But I was thinking of your interest in the language in an academic sense."

"Where did you get it?"

"A shop in town," I say, which is only sort of a lie. "It was tucked in a jumble—I don't think they knew enough Woudish to tell what it was about either."

Alek lets out a chocked guffaw. "No doubt. It's poetry, yes, but from what I can tell the focus is less romantic and more erotic."

"Oh." I shouldn't be surprised given where I found it, should I?

My face flares even hotter. Did he think I meant it as some kind of proposition?

Or that *Julita* might have?

The words tumble out faster than I can think them through. "I honestly didn't realize it was quite that… intense. But it'd still give a different perspective on Woudish phrasing and thought than anything the college will have, won't it? That's all I intended by it. I wouldn't imagine—I'm not an idiot."

The shock fades from Alek's face into something more like confusion. "What do you mean?"

My dress abruptly feels too tight against my skin. I dig my fingers into the folds of my skirt. "I wouldn't have offered it as some kind of seduction attempt. I'm a street rat. You're a noble. Like I said, I'm not an idiot."

Alek stares at me for long enough that I think my actual skin has gotten too tight as well. A rough chuckle escapes him.

He glances down at the book, shakes his head, and looks back at me with his piercing gaze that makes me feel as if he's seen more than I meant to show.

"Just to be clear," he says, low but steady, "it's obvious that you're not just a 'street rat.' And those were Stavros's words in the first place, not mine. I'm not really a noble either. I'm a merchant's son. A well-off merchant, but nothing compared to—" He waves vaguely toward the rest of the library. "I got here through luck, good will, and working my tail off."

Now it's my turn to stare. He's not noble-born?

I had heard that determined outsiders and those with enough coin to spare could sometimes win a spot in the royal college, but I assumed it was rare enough that it never occurred to me any of Julita's men would be among those. I guess Alek has never shown quite the same airs as the others, but I assumed that was more his personality than his upbringing.

"I didn't realize. I still wouldn't have—"

Alek waves the book before slipping it into his pocket. "I understand. I'll take it as the scholarly gesture it was. Thank you. I just… I wouldn't have thought you were an idiot."

I hesitate, not sure how to interpret that declaration. Before I can sort out my thoughts, laughter and arch voices carry from the aisle, getting louder.

Some students are heading toward us. We're not supposed to be seen together any more than strictly necessary.

Alek takes a step back, bobs his head in a silent farewell, and hustles away. I turn, planning to amble off in the other direction, just as Anya and two of her friends saunter into view at that end of the row.

Anya spots me at once. She gives a wry giggle and aims a sharp little smile at me. "Oh, look who we've run into. Miss Backwater who thinks she's too good for the rest of us."

I fold my arms over my chest. "I'm just looking for reading material like everyone else here."

"Figuring out more ways to ingratiate yourself with the staff, I suppose. How much higher do you figure you can climb than Ster. Stavros?"

She giggles again, even more humorlessly than the first time, and taps her elbow against her friend's arm. "There's something on those bookcases you might be looking for, don't you think, Tavonne?"

A similarly venomous smirk curves the other woman's mouth. She holds out her hand—and a book flies off a shelf behind me, whacking me in the back of the head.

# TWENTY-SEVEN

I flinch and slap my hand to the point of collision. As an ache spreads through my skull, the book flies the rest of the way to land in Tavonne's hands.

"Oh, sorry," Anya coos. "Did your big head get in the way of her book?"

"I think I need another one." Tavonne reaches out again.

An even thicker volume flies off the shelf. I'm prepared enough to jerk to the side this time, but its edge still smacks against my jaw.

I resist the urge to rub the smarting spot, bracing myself for another attack. My fingers curl against the silk folds of my skirt.

I traded my soiled lavender gown for my favorite turquoise one as soon as I got back to the college. If Anya attempts to ruin this one, I might just have to do violence.

"Fantastic use of your gift, there," I say to her friend. "I'm sure your godlen would approve."

Tavonne sneers at my sarcasm. "Any book I feel I need will jump to my hand. Estera thought that was a worthy request. It's not her or my fault if someone steps in between at the wrong time."

I have to admit that would be a useful gift even if it's being turned against me right now.

My magic vibrates in my chest. I hold on to my self-control with an iron grip, making my tone go haughtily cold. "I'd have expected someone invested in wisdom to find better uses for their time. What exactly do you gain out of assaulting random people?"

Anya sniffs. "Oh, it's all good sport. We all need *some* entertainment. And you need to remember your place."

Tavonne has gathered both of the books under her arm. "I might require one more—"

Before she can extend her fingers, a stern figure in a dark blue uniform strides into view.

The Crown's Watch soldier scowls at the four of us. "What's going on over here? If a daimon's messing with the books, you need to alert us."

He must have heard the thumps and assumed the noble students would never lower themselves to using them as projectile weapons.

Tavonne purses her lips, and Anya shoots a glower that's almost a dare my way.

I'd take her up on that dare—except the power seeping from my broken soul has erupted at the sight of the guard. It surges up inside my chest, thrashing at me with a matching peal of alarm, faster than I can rein in the emotion.

Men like that kill sorcerers like me.

I have to make him leave. I have to escape.

My power has basically lost its mind. There'd be no reason for the soldier to look twice at me as long as I *don't* use it.

But it flails against my hold, rallying for me to bring it to bear.

As I clench one hand behind my back, a chill lances down my spine. It's only a matter of seconds before I pay for defying my magic's call yet again.

I need *all* of them gone before I fall apart.

"No daimon," I say hastily, whipping my mouth into a smile. "I simply had a clumsy moment."

If I take the blame, Anya and her crew won't see any reason to keep up their harassment.

Anya's eyelids twitch with surprise, but the guard thankfully has no patience for wayward students. He motions briskly to the trio. "Well, get on with your studying or whatever you're doing here, then. And you, be more careful with the books."

The pain claws up through my abdomen. My voice shakes just slightly. "Yes, sir."

Anya and her friends laugh and drift away, tired of their game anyway, but the soldier pauses and squints at me. I set my hand against the shelf next to me, doing my best impression of a woman who doesn't need the support to hold me up while agony sears through my innards.

The guard lets out a huff and marches off, muttering something about "frivolous bints" under his breath.

I really don't care what insults he assigns to me, because now I'm alone between the bookshelves again.

The pain spikes through my limbs. My legs wobble and buckle.

I give in to the collapse, sliding against the bookcase. Maybe if I let my body bend to the magic's whim just a little, it'll lighten up its attack.

My scars sting as my back bumps its way down across the edges of the shelves. I slump on the rug, my breath coming with a rasp.

Fuck, the pain is still expanding. Because a soldier simply *spoke* to me.

My magic rakes its claws into me deeper and deeper, my heart wrenching, my lungs burning. My head reels with the overwhelming ache.

I can't help wondering if my soul has given up on trying to have a life and decided to tear its broken self apart instead.

I had a cup of pipe fleece tea this morning just for the sake of trying again. Is it possible the stuff is actually making my situation worse?

I'm tossing the rest down the toilet.

Julita's voice penetrates the haze of my agony vaguely. *Ivy! Ivy, what's going on? You should call for a medic. Oh, this isn't good.*

My fingers brace against the floor. I can't answer her, can't do anything else at all.

Then someone says my name from outside my head.

"Ivy!" Alek's voice is taut as he drops down next to me. "Smite them all, what did those beasts do to you?"

He assumes I'm in this state because of Anya's harassment. Well, that isn't completely incorrect.

"No medic," I mutter through gritted teeth. "It'll pass. I just need… to wait it out."

"I don't know…"

I shudder, and he lets out a choked sound. "Come on, let's at least get you out of here so you can recover in peace."

He slips his arm around my back and propels me upright. My feet stumble under me, and my chest hitches with a jolt of deepened pain.

"Just over here," Alek says. "You can make it."

The waver in his voice makes his reassurance less than convincing.

I manage to stagger with him to the doorway that leads to the archives. I make it halfway down the steps to the basement before another burst of pain spears through my gut and I nearly pitch forward to tumble to the floor.

At least there's no one else around to see it. As much as I hate that *Alek* is witnessing this attack, he had the right idea getting me out of there.

I'll have to remember to thank him for his quick thinking when I'm not on the verge of biting my tongue in two.

At my hiss of pain, the scholar curses. Bending down, he wraps his arms around me.

Alek is the slimmest of Julita's men, but he proves he's far from a weakling by swinging me up against his chest. His cool, citrusy scent fills my nose.

I'm vaguely aware of the tension in his muscles flexing against me as he hurries through the maze of archive rooms to the small one where we usually meet. There, he sets me down in one of the chairs near the desk.

"The others might have some idea how to handle this. Casimir has a little training in healing. Stavros is staff—if anyone can deal with Anya…"

He steps away from me, pulling something from his pocket. My head is swimming too much for me to follow the gesture.

Prickles jab through my lungs again, and I sputter a cough against my hand. Spittle flecks my skin.

I blink and stare at it, half-stunned.

Scarlet swirls in the droplets of spit. I'm coughing up blood.

That's never happened before. Is my power doing real damage inside me?

I swipe the evidence away against my other palm before Alek can notice. The pressure in my chest seems to have lightened slightly, but my limbs only throb more.

Then Stavros is hurtling into the room through the conjured pathway. "What's the emergency—" He jars to a halt at the sight of me hunched in the chair. "What happened to Ivy?"

Not him. Not *him*.

Of all of them, I can't let the former general suspect what's wrong with me.

"I'm not sure," Alek says miserably. "She told me not to get a medic—maybe we should bring her to the infirmary after all. It doesn't seem to be getting better."

I suck in a breath, panic splitting through my pain. "It is. Better. Getting there."

I will that statement to be true.

As Stavros storms over to me, Casimir arrives, his eyes wide with concern. Alek must have had some way of signaling them to come.

The courtesan takes one look at me and blanches. "Is she wounded?"

"I don't think so." Alek gestures wildly. "Anya and a couple of the women she goes around with came over to talk to her in the library. I couldn't see what exactly they did, but they were obviously hassling her. And then I found her like this."

Stavros lets out a growl and bends over me. "Which one of them did this? *What* did they do to you? I'll make them pay for it myself."

Casimir is at my other side in an instant, grasping my hand. "Where exactly does it hurt?"

Every-fucking-where. But as the men's whirlwind of rage and worry distracts me, the pain fades more.

I raise my head, swallowing around a lump in my throat. I hate that they're seeing me like this.

I have to make sure none of them suspect the real cause. They'd be celebrating my agony if they knew.

"I don't know if it was Anya and her friends," I say more steadily. "The pain came out of nowhere. Anyone in the library—it could have been a gift. Maybe someone noticed me paying attention to Ster. Torstem before?"

Stavros glances behind him at Benedikt, who I hadn't seen coming in. "Have you heard of anyone at the college right now with a pain-provoking gift?" he barks, his stance still tensed as if he's about to go into battle on my behalf.

Benedikt frowns. "I can't think of anyone. Someone took a shot at Ivy?"

"Either that, or it was Anya's bunch putting her in her 'place,'" Alek says.

My next breaths come more easily. I push myself straighter in the chair, pretending my arms aren't still tingling with splinters of pain. "It's passing now. It was just to trip me up, like the drug before. Nothing permanent."

I hope.

"Was Romild in the library?" Casimir asks, his forehead furrowed. "We weren't sure if she might have been responsible for the previous incident."

"I didn't see her, but it's a big room." Better not to eliminate any possible suspects. The more they can spread around the possible blame, the less they can do about it.

And the less chance they'll narrow the possibilities down to my monstrous magic.

Stavros shoves away from me and paces the room. "I'll ask around. Someone has to know."

"No," I say. "I don't want whoever it was finding out how badly they affected me. Alek got me out of there pretty quickly. It's better if they think there wasn't any point. Maybe they'll give up."

"It's better if they're never capable of doing it again!"

Julita's laugh rings out lightly from the back of my head. *Whatever else you're going through, you have managed to get them awfully invested in you. Good job there.*

I recoil inwardly from her flippant assessment of the situation. I haven't been trying to… to "wind them around my finger" the way Anya accused Julita of doing to everyone.

Whatever concern they might have for me, I didn't scheme my way into it. I'm just trying to survive.

Benedikt steps in to brush his fingers across my temple. "Someone came at both of our girls. That's just not acceptable."

Both of their girls. Me and Julita.

Stavros pauses. "Is she still there with you? The attack didn't… dislodge her?"

The last of the agony vanishes under a surge of frustration. None of their concern is really on my behalf anyway, is it?

They aren't worried about my well-being for my own sake, only as a vessel for the woman who clearly did have them all wrapped around her finger. Who mostly saw *them* as tools in her investigation rather than people.

"Yes," I say tersely, "she's just fine. And I'm fine too, now."

I stretch my arms in front of me as if confirming that and then stand right up. My legs hold me steadily enough.

I won't think about the faint smear of blood I'm hiding on my palm.

Alek eyes me with obvious skepticism. "You couldn't even walk for a minute there. I still think we should have a medic look you over."

I grimace. "And what? Make me look even weaker?"

Benedikt rubs his jaw. "We could have the Crown's Watch keep an eye on—"

With a stutter of my pulse, I shake my head vehemently. "No. How can I get close to anyone who's conspiring against the crown if I've got the royal family's chosen soldiers trailing around behind me?"

The bastard's bastard raises his eyebrows. "There is such a thing as taking a break."

I glare around at all of them. "I'm here to complete a mission so I can get back to my own life, and I'm going to do that. Whoever struck out at me meant to shake me up. The last thing I want is for them to see I was shaken. Or think I went running to any of you to help. How would that keep our group a secret?"

"You're *my* assistant," Stavros starts.

I cut him off with a pointed look. "And at least half of the reason anyone's harassing me is because they think you favor me unfairly. So let's not confirm their suspicions, all right? Or maybe there will be real damage next time."

He hesitates, and Casimir takes the opportunity to hook his arm around mine. "I think Ivy's been through a lot today, and she could use some space. I'll see that she gets some unwinding time. We can sort out any other ways we should respond tomorrow."

His tone is typically gentle but firm. The other men exchange a glance.

Stavros's shoulders flex, but he nods. "Make sure she's all right, work your pampering skills on her, but see that she's back at my quarters by the tenth bell."

My thoughts are still more scattered than I'd like, but Casimir's mention of what I've been through today reminds me of something much more important that went on earlier.

I catch Benedikt's gaze. "Who was Romild waiting for this morning?"

He raises his eyebrow as if bemused that I'm bothering to ask that after what I've just experienced. "I wasn't able to find out. She seemed to get impatient with waiting and left before anyone turned up."

Damn it. I turn to the others. "Well, however she fits into this mess, we have to check on the girls from the orphanage that Ster. Torstem brought to the college in particular. Determine whether they really ended up at temples after their dedication ceremonies."

Alek frowns, but Casimir tugs me with him before the other men can ask any questions. "Enough work from you, Ivy. You've had to deal with more than you could have been prepared for already. Let me take care of you a little."

I don't know how to argue without sounding totally unreasonable. And now I've told them the only part of what I learned that they can act on right now.

Maybe if I go along with Casimir, the others will back off on insisting we get some kind of retribution against my supposed attacker. At least until it doesn't matter anymore.

"Yeah," I force myself to say. "That would be nice."

As the courtesan ushers me toward the wall with its hidden staircase, I realize I have no idea where he's actually taking me.

# Twenty-Eight

As soon as we've been swallowed up by the darkness on the conjured stairs, I give a private refusal a half-hearted try. "I really am feeling totally recovered now. It'd be enough just to go back and relax in Stavros's—"

Casimir cuts me off with a short chuckle. "Oh, no. You've run yourself ragged. I've got just the cure for that."

I *am* still wiped out from my magic's punishment. A faint ache remains in my lungs, and any hunger I once felt has been burned up by my stomach's churning.

Partly out of a lack of energy to argue and partly out of curiosity, I let Casimir guide me down the hallway in the opposite direction from the library entrance.

"We'll take the back staircase," he says. "It's not likely we'll run into anyone there."

He ushers me up the narrow flight of stairs and a short distance down the third-floor hall that must hold the dorms for the companionship division. His fingers skim over a few doors that are carved in a simple but elegant style with Ardone's favorite things. Roses sprout from leafy stems, salmon leap from rivers, and swans soar on lakes.

The godlen of love and beauty would feel right at home.

Something about the doors must tell Casimir which he can use. He presses his fingers against the fourth in a swift pattern, and it swings open to admit us.

The room he leads me into is definitely not a dorm, though it's nearly as large as the common room in Julita's. Pale marble tiles line the floor and walls, gleaming under the bright glow of the crystalline light fixtures overhead.

On the far wall, someone's painted the tiles with a mural of the All-Giver's raising of the godlen. Taking the idea that the Great God "lay with" earth, sea, and sky in a much more literal fashion than I've generally seen it portrayed.

With a flush of my cheeks, I jerk my gaze to take in the rest of our surroundings. Shelves built into the walls hold towels, sponges, and an assortment of bottles and jars. A sweet floral scent laces the air.

And in the middle of the room, next to a thick white rug, stands a claw-foot bathtub.

Gold-plated pipes rise from the floor to the faucet at one curved end of the tub. Casimir walks straight over with his usual assured grace and starts the water running.

As steam wafts from the warbling current, the courtesan turns to the shelves. He opens a jar full of glinting pink crystals and sprinkles a handful under the running water. Bubbles foam in their wake.

A crisper scent reaches my nose that somehow seeps into my muscles to release some of the tension wound up there. But even as my shoulders start to relax from their defensive pose, my stomach knots tighter. "You're running me a bath?"

"I can't think of anything better for soothing the nerves and escaping the day's stresses." Casimir flashes me a smile and ambles over to join me.

Stepping behind me, he brushes his fingertips along the collar of my gown. But the flare of heat isn't enough to stop me from stiffening when he reaches for the lacing at the back.

"Casimir, I don't think this is a good idea."

"I'm the expert. You don't trust my judgment?"

I don't trust his reaction if he sees all of my body exactly as it is. I can't keep my undershirt on in the bath.

No doubt he's seen dozens of nude women before. My gawky body wouldn't be a particular thrill.

But it does have one unexpected feature—or lack thereof.

"Maybe a bath would be nice," I hedge. "But I generally prefer them to be private. You've set everything up perfectly. Am I not allowed to use this room alone?"

Casimir pauses with his hands halfway down my back. The loosened dress slips over the peaks of my shoulders, and I fold my arms across the bodice to ensure it doesn't drop.

"You could have it to yourself," he says. "But that will make pampering you much more difficult. I'd also like to check that you haven't taken any wounds you're trying to hide, seeing as you're so adamant about not letting an actual medic look you over."

So, he does have a bit of an ulterior motive here. I can't even be annoyed at him for it, because it's out of concern.

"I'm not hiding any wounds," I insist.

Of its own accord, my hand clenches against my sternum. Against the spot just below the modest swell of my breasts where I *should* be branded.

"Ah." Casimir raises his hands to rest them gingerly on my shoulders, his thumbs stroking soothing lines over my bared skin. "It's all right, Kindness. You don't have to hide *that*. I already know."

My heart just about bursts straight through my ribs. Despite my best efforts to keep it steady, my voice wavers. "You know what?"

His voice stays gentle, wrapping around me like another layer of silk. "I don't imagine the others would have guessed. I'm trained to pick up on body language, to evaluate people's reactions... And before I started official classes at the college, one of the boys I was tutored with was godless. Some quirks are familiar."

*What?* Julita bursts out.

My legs wobble under me, rocked by a surge of emotion. Shock that the courtesan actually does know, immense relief that he doesn't know *everything*.

I can't see much point in trying to deny the truth now, to him or my ghostly passenger.

I take in a gulp of air and let out a shaky laugh. "Not much gets by you, huh? What 'quirks' am I giving myself away with?"

"Like I said, I doubt anyone else would realize." Casimir keeps up his slow massage of my shoulders, but his voice has lightened as if he's relieved too. Maybe he was worried about how I'd respond?

"It took me a while myself," he continues. "But I've never seen you make the gesture of the divinities, even when you're under threat. When you're tense, you sometimes shield that spot like you did just now, as if you're covering it from view. You kept your gaze averted from the Temple of the Crown when you rode by on our return from the orphanage."

I test my teeth against my lower lip but catch myself before I really start worrying at it. I can seem a little discomforted, but I don't want him wondering why I'm still agitated after he's shown he won't judge me.

Especially not after he's proven what a keen observer he really is.

I feel the need to give an explanation. I can offer a somewhat honest one. "I was on my own for a lot of my childhood. It felt wrong to dedicate myself to any of the divinities who didn't appear to give a shit about what happened to me up until then. I never wanted a gift."

Least of all the one I ended up with through no choice of my own.

"I'm sorry I lied to you about that," I add. "People see my finger and just assume it was a sacrifice, and it's easier to agree…"

"I understand." Casimir gives my shoulders a reassuring squeeze. "My friend had similar reasons. Choosing godlessness shouldn't be *that* offensive. Our lives are still our own—the All-Giver never denied that even while watching over us. You clearly haven't done anything terrible enough for the gods to strike you down."

He chuckles as if the idea is totally absurd, and I make myself laugh along.

He has no idea. I'm just lucky the godlen don't keep too close an eye on the millions of mortals under their purview.

"There are a lot of other people who don't see it that way." I don't want him bringing it up with the other men.

"Within these walls in particular," Casimir says in acknowledgment. "I haven't mentioned the suspicion to anyone else, and I won't. I wouldn't have mentioned it to *you* if it hadn't seemed to be holding you back."

Holding me back from the bath, which is now nearly full of water and foamy bubbles.

Casimir leaves me so he can shut off the water. I drink in the haze of steam in the air.

The knot in my stomach lingers.

Do I even deserve the compassion this incredible man is offering me? I'm still lying to him.

But if my magic keeps tearing away at me, how much longer do I even have?

I'm never going to get my daydream from my times in Ewalin's oak tree, of family and belonging and laughter. Is it really unfair to accept just a sliver of that kind of amity?

Great God help me, I would like to be pampered, just once. When am I ever going to get an offer like this again?

I grapple with the pang of longing inside me for a few moments longer and then meet Casimir's gaze. "Just a bath."

His eyes twinkle with his smile. "If that's all you'd like."

The thought of all the other things he might do for other women—and men—he could have brought into this room brings back my hesitation. "You know I wouldn't— I'd never *expect* this from you because of the work you do. I wouldn't hire you, if I could even afford to. I mean, not because you're not very appealing and everything. Er. It just isn't the sort of thing… the sort of thing I'd feel okay about doing."

I'm not sure if I've made a whole lot of sense in my babbling, but Casimir's smile stays in place as he returns to me. "You don't have to worry. I don't see it that way. Think of it as—if you were friends with a baker, they might bake you a cake to cheer you up after a hard day. You're friends with me, so you get a bath."

I consider the bubbles. "It does look like a very nice bath."

"I take pride in my work, even more so when it isn't really work at all." Casimir pauses, and his eyes soften. "I'll take your word for it that there are no wounds unaccounted for. Let me know when you're ready for the rest of your pampering."

He turns his back to me to start looking through the paraphernalia on the shelves as if that's exactly what he always intended to be doing. Letting me finish undressing without any spectators.

The unstated understanding in the gesture melts the last of my hesitation.

My broken soul might rip me right in two by this time tomorrow. What have I got to lose?

I shimmy out of the gown and my underthings quickly. As I unwind Linzi's ribbon carefully and set it with the pile, Julita's presence stirs. *I can't believe I never realized. I suppose you weren't in the habit of ogling your own chest while you were changing.*

Quite purposefully, once I knew she was inside me. I feel strange talking to her with Casimir right here, so I simply shrug and clamber into the tub.

The steaming water envelopes my body in a delectably warm embrace. The sweet scent of the bubbles fills my lungs.

I exhale in a sigh, tipping my head against the arched back of the tub.

Yes, this is nice.

*Not that it makes any difference to me,* Julita goes on. *Even without any godlen ties, you clearly know right from wrong. I don't think I'd mention it to Stavros, though.*

I raise an eyebrow as if to say, *No kidding.*

"How are you getting on there, my friend?" Casimir asks in a tone as warm as the water.

I hum contentedly. "I'm feeling pretty pampered already."

He laughs. "Oh, it can get much better than this. Let's get started with your hair. I'd imagine it's been a long time since you had anyone to help you wash it."

Not since I was a child of six or seven. I can't remember if Ma stopped attending to me that closely in the bath before she realized I was a monster or only after.

The clash of memories brings back the ache in my chest, but the press of Casimir's fingers moving deftly over my scalp soon whisks the turmoil away.

He stops for a moment with a whisper of fabric, and I realize he's taken off his shirt. To avoid getting it wet, presumably, but I can't help regretting that I'm missing the view with him behind me.

Kneeling, he eases my head back into the water to ensure my hair is totally soaked. Then he works a lavender-scented soap into the pale locks.

As his fingers move down to the nape of my neck, a starker heat seeps through my veins. It's difficult not to imagine how those skillful hands would feel tending to other parts of my body.

*Well,* Julita murmurs. *I can't say I mind getting to experience Casimir at work. He does know what he's doing. But I think perhaps I should give you a little more privacy… to enjoy yourself fully. If I can slip deeper away like I did before, I won't even know. Let's see.*

Her voice fades out. The faint tingling of her presence dwindles too, until it's the barest tickle at the back of my skull.

Did she notice some sign that Casimir is about to do something I'd rather have private? My pulse stutters.

But after the courtesan douses my hair with water, he sits back on his heels. "We have a salve that helps scars heal. I'm not sure how much effect it'll have on older ones, but I'm happy to try if you'd like."

I've never gotten a clear view of the ruddy lines that crisscross my back, but I don't like the story they tell of my history. I'd happily see them gone for good.

"Worth a try," I say, not looking too hard at the twinge of disappointment that passes through me. "Thank you."

He retrieves a small jar full of greenish cream and has me sit up and lean forward so the upper half of my back is exposed. "Do they hurt at all still?"

I shake my head. "Not unless I bang up my back. Which I'd imagine would hurt anyway, but maybe they make it hurt a little more."

"I'll still be careful."

The substance he spreads across my damp skin is warmer and more slippery than I expected. With each stroke of Casimir's fingers, I feel as if it's sinking through the mottled ridges, deeper into my flesh.

It's probably weird that the act sends another pang of desire through my core. I grope for a conversational subject that'll distract me from my lustful urges.

"How did you end up in this line of work anyway?" I settle on. "You've made it sound as if you grew up always planning to become a courtesan."

I've heard of large noble families directing their youngest children who have no chance of inheriting into the arts of various sorts, but I wouldn't have thought they usually decide it very early on.

Casimir gives a hum of agreement in answer to my words. "It's a family calling. My mother served the barons and baronesses, traveling with them in the royal court from place to place. I believe her mother served the same way before her."

"Oh." I guess that makes sense as well—that the practitioners of the sensual arts who mingle with nobility are seen as nobles as well. And quite possibly for his grandmother to have ended up in that position, she was noble to begin with. "And you wanted to follow their footsteps?"

"It's what I was raised for. It's what I do best."

I can't stop myself from craning my neck to peer over my shoulder at him. "Did you have any chance to try doing anything else?"

He shrugs as he returns the lid to the salve and rinses his fingers. "I wasn't inclined to. When you have an obvious path to follow, and you're happy to do so, there's no need to go looking elsewhere."

How much of a choice was it really, if he was told he was meant to serve others this way from the moment he could understand anything at all?

Casimir guides me back against the end of the tub. Sitting up this way, the bubbles graze the undersides of my breasts.

"You don't need to worry about me, Ivy," he says, as if he can sense my doubts. "It truly is a joy to see the delight I can bring."

I frown at the faucet across from me. "I just—I don't think anyone should be *bound* by who their family was."

"I don't feel constrained. But the fact that you'd say that is one of the reasons I like you."

I think his head has dipped a little closer behind me.

His breath tickles over my neck. His hands come to rest on my shoulders again.

Suddenly it's hard to pull my thoughts together. Too many sparks are flaring beneath my skin.

I end up saying, inanely, "You like me, do you?"

"Of course I do. What's not to like?"

His tone is casual enough that I can hardly take it as a statement of devotion. Am I really anything like a friend or just a momentary diversion?

But then he lets his hand drift over my shoulder and down my chest, leaning close enough that his lips brush my ear, and any lingering questions flee my mind.

"Would you like me to show you how much I do?" Casimir murmurs, his fingers caressing the slope of my breast just above the nipple.

Anticipatory pleasure jolts through my nerves. I lick my lips, and any reason I could have to protest feels very far away.

He wants to do this. I'm not remotely taking advantage.

The magic I'm hiding might be horrifying, but it isn't going to hurt him.

I can accept this for me, for all the life I won't get to lead... as long as *he's* really doing it for me.

My voice sounds distant to my own ears. "In case it matters to you, Julita's found a method of pulling away inside my head to give me some privacy. She did that earlier, after I got in the bath. She isn't really here right now."

Casimir simply chuckles. "Good. Because I don't get the impression that you're much of an exhibitionist."

I hear no regret in his tone, no disappointment over an opportunity lost. His fingers glide right over my nipple, and all I can do is gasp.

Casimir tilts forward where he's poised behind me, his other hand stroking my cheek and down my neck, the side of his face resting against my damp hair.

He circles his finger around the nub of my nipple until it rises to his touch, aching for more. Then he closes his whole hand over my breast, squeezing the peak between two fingers.

The rush of pleasure brings a whimper to my lips. I resist the urge to squirm my legs together to try to release the growing pressure between my thighs.

He hasn't even reached past my chest yet, and he's already conjured more bliss in my body than any man I've rolled around with ever did.

Casimir nips the shell of my ear. His voice is pure seduction now. "You're lovely. I want you to always remember what it's like to be treated right."

He rolls my nipple between his thumb and forefinger while nibbling his way down my neck. I clamp my lips to stifle a full-out moan.

Casimir nuzzles the crook of my shoulder with another hot wash of breath. "You can be as loud as you like. These bathrooms are sound-proofed."

A breathless laugh hitches out of me, because of course they are. But I don't want to think about the many ways the man with me might have made the most of that fact in the past.

Casimir eases around the side of the tub so he can slide his hand across my chest. As he gives my other breast equal attention, he kisses my cheek and then my jaw.

Every flick and swivel of his fingers sets off fresh quivers of pleasure. I shift against the tub's slick bottom, my sex throbbing now.

He grazes his other thumb across my cheek. "So beautiful with this flush in your face."

I know he's only sweet-talking now. I have never been and will never be a great beauty. But just then he dips his hand lower beneath the water, skimming across my belly to the spot I need it most, and the surge of pleasure knocks every thought out of my head.

As Casimir strokes my sex again, my head tips back with an inarticulate groan. He has his other arm braced behind me before my skull can smack the porcelain surface.

I arch against him, my breath hitching. "Fuck."

"Good?"

I can barely manage more than a mumble. "So good."

"Give yourself over to it," he murmurs. "Let the pleasure wash away your troubles from the inside out."

His thumb presses against my clit while his fingers slip lower. As I rock with the pulsing of bliss, one and then two curl right inside me.

I moan and grasp his arm as if I need something to clutch on to or the sensations will sweep me away. Gods above and below, if I'd known giving in to carnal desires could feel *this* good, I might have been pickier in my choice of partners.

Not that I had all that many to choose from. But this man has chosen me tonight.

This man might as well be blessing me like the godlen of sensuality herself with the paradise he's evoking within me.

His voice sounds a bit rougher than before—or maybe I only want to imagine that. "I have you. Come all the way with me."

The water ripples around me with the jerking of my hips. Casimir pumps his hand faster, thrusting deeper into the welcoming slickness inside me, and I tilt my face against the taut muscles of his chest.

The heat of the water and of his body encircles me. Pleasure blazes up from my core.

My mind whirls, my nerves crackle, and then ecstasy explodes inside me.

It roars through my body, as potent as my hidden magic, sizzling through every nerve with giddy delight. My head shudders against Casimir. My fingers dig into his arm, but he keeps stroking me as the impact rolls back.

When I sag with the release of the aftermath, he slips his hand back up over my belly and plants one last kiss on my temple. "Gorgeous. You're a natural at being pampered."

A guffaw tumbles out of me. "That—that was a little more cake than I expected."

Casimir beams at the callback to his earlier metaphor. There's no denying the joy on his face, no way I can feel guilty when he looks so pleased. "You needed every bit of it. Now why don't you enjoy a little more of a soak, and I'll find you the fluffiest towel we possess?"

When I climb out of the tub, the towel he picks out for me does feel like it's made of a blend of velvet and cloud. I allow myself to snuggle in it for a few moments before getting to the practical business of drying myself off. Casimir rubs my hair down with a smaller towel.

It's hard to feel self-consciousness about my nakedness when he's just gotten so very familiar with my body. There's nothing provocative about the way he handles me now as his usual warmly vibrant self.

Maybe getting someone off really is no more intimate to him than whipping up a pastry. It's easier for me to accept what happened if I assume so.

After the courtesan has re-laced my gown, he stops me by the door with his hand at my cheek. "It was a pleasure spending this time with you, Ivy."

The words and his touch send a renewed tingle straight down the middle of me.

My face flares all over again, but I've regained my wits enough to reply, "Even more so for me than for you, I'd imagine."

His dark eyes gleam. "You might be surprised."

I practically float through the halls and up the stairs to Stavros's quarters. I only come to earth when I push open the door... and find the former general sitting on the edge of his desk, his gaze shooting straight to me like he's been waiting for my arrival since the moment I left the archives.

Stavros's gaze sweeps over me. I'm abruptly twice as aware of the dampness of my hair and the freshly-washed rosiness of my skin, which no doubt tell at least part of the story of what Casimir and I got up to.

I don't know if Stavros can guess the rest. A muscle ticks in his jaw.

His gaze lifts and sears into mine for a few awkward beats of my heart before he straightens up.

"Casimir looked after you his way," he says, his cocky voice marred by the hint of a growl in it. "And I'm going to look after you mine. Starting tomorrow, I'm going to need your assistance from breakfast to evening bell. If anyone wants to so much as aim a poisonous look at you, they'll have to get through me first."

# Twenty-Nine

Stavros's new intense "need" for assistance puts a significant damper on what little social life I was developing. When Esmae catches me outside the dining hall, arriving for breakfast while we're just leaving after an early one, I feel like I haven't seen her in a year.

"Your employer is keeping you awfully busy these days," she says with a sympathetic smile when I stop to say hello.

Stavros glowers from where he's also halted several paces away. Which is about as far as he's gotten from me at all in the past two days, although at least he allows a door between us when I use the latrine.

I offer a wry smile in return. "I'm surviving. It's good to see you, but I don't think I can stay for much of a conversation."

Esmae's single-eyed gaze darts to Stavros and then back to me. Her laugh sounds a bit nervous, maybe because he looks like a menace even when he's leaning against the wall in a supposedly nonchalant pose. "That's all right. He's got to give you a break at some point, I suppose. For now…"

She fishes in her carry pouch and produces a fine gold chain with a simple flower pendant dangling from it. A teal gem gleams at its center. "There was a merchant selling these in sets of two. I didn't need both… I thought it might go well with your dress."

She tips her head toward my turquoise gown, which I guess I must wear often enough for anyone to figure out it's my favorite.

My heart squeezes with a bittersweet pang. For an instant, I'm seven years old again, beaming at Linzi's dimpled five-year-old face as she holds out a daisy she plucked to me.

Outside of Casimir's bath, that's probably the last time anyone offered me any kind of present.

As I take the necklace and fasten the chain around my neck, a faint aura of magic prickles into my chest. It feels like one of those minor spells shopkeepers who can afford it use to encourage people's purchases.

Well, even if Esmae bought it partly thanks to magical influence, she didn't have to give the second necklace to me.

Julita scoffs. *Cheap thing. Might not even be gold all the way through. I doubt it cost her more than a few bits.*

If she wasn't an ephemeral presence residing inside my head, I'd kick her. Nobles obviously don't understand that a thing can be worth much more than the money you have to pay for it.

I aim a more emphatic smile at Esmae, wishing I was a better friend to her than one who has to make up lies and pretend to be someone I'm not. "Thank you. They do go together well."

Stavros clears his throat with an air of impatient boredom. I shoot a glower back at him before gathering my skirts. "Sorry. Duty calls."

Esmae pats my arm. "I won't keep you from it."

I pick up my pace to draw up beside the former general as he strides through the nearest entryway and across the courtyard. "You don't have to protect me from *her*. She's tried to stop Anya and the others from harassing me."

Stavros lets out a disbelieving grunt. "That little mouse couldn't defend you from a fly. Are you really so overworked? I thought you were looking forward to today's expedition."

I make a face at him, but I honestly can't complain.

Yes, I've spent the past two days constantly on edge that my magic will flare up and spark Stavros's suspicions. But the truth is that the former general's presence has scared off all of the enemies I've made here.

We've been eating early or late, and I've mostly been trotting at his heels from responsibility to responsibility, so my path hasn't crossed with Anya or Romild much. But even when it has, the sight of him looming nearby has kept their mouths shut and their hands to themselves.

So far, no more assaults has meant no more flailing deadly magic tearing up my insides. I can thank him for that, as much as I'd prefer not to.

And I've been counting down the hours to our trip today.

"How long a ride should it be?" I ask without deigning to address his comments.

"No more than two hours if we set a good pace. Mostly flat country roads, nothing too onerous. I hope you're up to that."

The glint of challenge in his eyes adds *Thief* to the end of the last sentence even if he didn't say it out loud.

"Sounds like a walk in the park," I declare, even though I haven't ridden outside of the city in nearly ten years.

Just to prove how little concerned I am, when we reach the stable I walk straight to Toast's stall.

Stavros lets out a guffaw when he sees where I'm going. "You're not serious."

"We've made friends. Haven't we, Toast?" I reach to scratch the stallion's jaw, and he does actually lift his head for me without hesitation this time. "He should set a good pace, I'd think."

"He'll do that," Stavros drawls. "Whether it'll be in the direction you want to go..."

"Let me worry about that."

Toast makes a show of shaking his mane and stomping his hooves as I lead him into the yard, but he doesn't put up too intense a fuss. How often does he get taken out at all by anyone other than reluctant stable hands ensuring he gets the minimum of exercise and idiot noblemen proving their bravado?

Sometimes kindness is the way to go. If he scares me off too much, he knows he'll be stuck with just those louts again.

Naturally, Stavros has a stallion of his own, an immense ruddy chestnut that looks picked to match both his size and his hair. His current prosthetic—a narrower hooked loop of metal with a thumb-like protrusion on one side, which I guess must be designed for riding—snags around the reins easily so he can lead the animal to the gate.

His mount falls into step with him with perfect coordination. Beside me, Toast kicks up his heels with a rebellious snort.

Traitor.

Beyond the college walls, Stavros swings into the saddle as easily as dropping into a chair. Toast sidesteps when I reach for the saddle, leaving me hopping for balance, but I get a good grip on his mane at his shoulders and heave myself up regardless.

"I'm fine," I say to Stavros's raised eyebrow.

To my immense gratitude, Toast does mostly behave on our way out of the city. We circle around the college grounds through the inner wards, cross the river over the longest bridge, and have only a short trek through the outer neighborhoods before we can pass through the gate nearly due north of the city.

Stavros flashes a seal imprinted on a leather token at the guards there, and they motion us through without comment. We pass a line of merchant wagons and carts hauling farm produce and then find ourselves with open road ahead of us.

The former general studies it with occasional twitches of his head where his gaze lingers. I can't see anything but wild fields and neater farmland on either side of us.

Far ahead, a dark smudge of forest shadows the horizon. The early morning sun warms my hair through the scattering of fluffy white clouds.

Not even the tang of manure from the nearest farm can diminish the freshness of the air away from the city streets. I drink in a big gulp of it and start asking the questions I haven't risked while we were within the college's walls. "Where do your colleagues think we're going?"

"I mentioned that I'd heard of an excellent smith out this way who King Konram might want to bring on for arming our forces. Sadly, we're going to discover that he's off on a pilgrimage of his own." Stavros shoots a cocky grin at me.

"Very convenient," I agree, and adjust my grip on the reins. I've been waiting for us to take this step in our investigation, but that hasn't stopped a knot of anxiety from forming in my gut. "And the temple where we're actually going is devoted to Inganne?"

Stavros nods. "I suspect there'll be plenty of music and frivolity if you didn't get your fill of dancing at our interrupted ball."

I roll my eyes. "I think I can manage to restrain myself."

The godlen Inganne presides over creativity and play. She's generally depicted as childlike, with round cheeks and bouncing curls. It's hard to imagine her taking out vengeance on me even if she happens to look down on her devouts and notice my illicit power among them.

I can hope, anyway.

I should be glad we're not heading to a temple of Sabrelle, the combative godlen whose sigil Stavros bears, or of Creaden, given the royal godlen's hard-on for justice and authority.

When Toast takes a mind to investigate the tufts of clover off in the field we're passing, I give him a firm tap. "You said more than one of the orphans Ster. Torstem took an interest in have dedicated themselves there?"

"Yes, three of them. Two girls, who I know you were particularly concerned about, and one of the boys."

"How long ago?"

"The boy was nine years ago, the girls six and two."

A good range of time, then, in case Torstem's intentions have changed over the years.

The thought of all that time passed gives me pause. "If the orphans are tangled up with the scourge sorcerers somehow… that would probably mean they've been experimenting for quite a while, wouldn't it? Torstem sponsored the 'institute' more than a decade ago. I thought the daimon only began acting up recently."

The former general grimaces. "That's true. If the conspiracy has been underway for years, they've either mostly kept their experiments away from the college before now, or they've started escalating their magical practice in the past few months."

I suppress a shiver. "Maybe for those plans Torstem was talking about."

Stavros glances over at me, swaying so easily with his stallion's even gait that I want to jab my heel against *his* side. "We'll obviously confirm that the devouts are who we expected and question them about Ster. Torstem's involvement in their lives. Do you have some test in mind to determine if they snuck off to whore themselves out at his bidding?"

I narrow my eyes at him. "I think questioning should cover that too. If he was taking other girls to stash them at brothels for whatever reason, there'd have been talk among the kids." I pause. "But I suppose we'll know as soon as we see these ones whether he's roped them into the conspiracy."

Stavros's face darkens with a momentarily serious cast. "Any major sacrifices would be immediate cause for concern. Devouts don't usually offer up that much of their bodies when they're already dedicating their whole lives to serving their godlen."

"Do you think scourge sorcerers would still be able to draw on someone's gift if they were living far outside of town?"

He lifts his shoulders in a shrug. "Who could say? It's not as if we've got a plethora of accounts to go by. Torstem could have stashed them away to call on them later."

"Later as in now, it seems like." Another shudder ripples through me with the memory of what the law professor said to his "ladies" in the brothel attic. "I'd hope the clerics would notify the royal family if they had a spat of new devotees with unusually intense sacrifices."

Stavros's tone turns droll again. "I'd hope no one teaching at the royal college would get involved in world-shattering magic, but we don't always get what we want."

I remember the agony that wrenched through me a few days ago and bite back a wince. No, indeed we don't.

The distant ringing of the city bells is echoed by equally distant town clock towers around us, marking the first hour of our trek. Not long after, the vegetation along the road becomes unrulier until it's sprouted up into the forestland I saw from a distance.

The horses clop along, Stavros's stallion keeping the same steady pace and Toast huffing at the shadows of breeze-tossed leaves. I click my tongue at him and pat his neck, and he settles a little.

Stavros eyes the two of us but makes no further comment on my choice of steed. He reaches down as we pass a bush dense with small, dark green leaves and snaps off a twig.

I can't stop myself from staring when he pops one of the leaves into his mouth. "Do you take up a horse diet when you're out riding?"

He laughs. "It's kindlebrush. Excellent wood for starting fires when dry, good for a snack when green. They have a nice flavor and keep your energy up. You can take a leaf if you'd like. We wouldn't want that beast to tire you out."

I wrinkle my nose at him but pick a leaf off the twig he holds out to me. The waxy oval breaks apart under my teeth with a burst of tartly sweet juice and a peppy tickle through my nerves.

"Never heard of it before," I say, studying the twig he's now tucked partway into his saddle bag. "Is that a soldier's trick?"

"Something like that. My parents taught me a lot of strategies for getting by if you've got nothing but the landscape to survive off." Stavros aims a grimmer smile at me. "My mother and her squadron were once stuck in an ambush in the woods near the Seafell Channel for a full week without supplies."

"Ah." I give the vegetation around us a more appraising look. Edible leaves would seem a lot more appealing if it's that or starvation.

I shift my attention back to the former general, turning another question over in my mind but unsure if I should pry.

Stavros doesn't meet my gaze, but he must feel it. "Whatever you're thinking, you can spit it out."

"I was just wondering what it was like being raised by two generals. Did you literally grow up on battlefields?"

A hint of nostalgia softens Stavros's chiseled features. "To some extent. But after I was born, my mother was mostly stationed at the main fort in the Pinch, to monitor any bids for territory or trade interference from Velduny, Icar, or Bryfeen. Which isn't a frequent problem, so it was more of a defensive position. I usually lived with her when my father was caught up in the more active campaigns fending off Darium incursions."

"You didn't see him often, then?" I venture.

"Oh, he was still around quite a bit." The corner of Stavros's mouth kicks up in a fond smile. "His gift allowed him to travel from one place to another in a blink—he could pull that off a couple of times a day before he exhausted himself. In theory, it was to serve the army, but he used it at least as much to drop in on us whenever he had a stretch of quiet."

"That's quite the gift." Imagine all the things I could do—and steal—with a talent like that.

"He gave up quite a bit for it. A kidney and part of his liver and various other internal parts that he could reasonably survive without." Stavros chuckles. "It meant he had to give up alcohol, but he always said that wasn't any great loss since he'd never liked the taste anyway."

It's strange, listening to him talk about his childhood. Hearing the affection in his voice.

I can't quite picture the massive man beside me as a little boy, but he was one once. He had a life so far beyond the little I know of him.

The question of what happened with his best friend, the one he said a riven sorcerer killed, itches at me. But I'm not so foolhardy to risk bringing up that subject over simple curiosity.

I lapse into silence instead. And curse it all if that silence doesn't feel almost… companionable.

When we emerge from the woods, our destination lies in clear view up ahead. There's no mistaking the peach-toned marble walls of Inganne's temple, nor the kites of a rainbow of woven colors that bob on the breeze over its walls.

I've read that as long as Inganne's blessing lies on her temples, those kites stay buoyant regardless of the weather.

The temple stands on a gentle slope, with a low marble wall around the base of the hill and buildings placed at intervals up the rise to the sprawling structure at the top. Sunblot saplings sprout here and there across the grounds, their brilliant orange blossoms nearly glowing in the daylight.

The godlen's sigil, the circle with its star-like center and outward curving lines, marks the stones on either side of the gate and the lintel of every doorway. Carvings of Inganne's favorite creatures—larks, butterflies, dolphins, and otters—cavort across many a stone surface.

There's plenty of cavorting among the living inhabitants of the temple as well. Devouts dressed in orange robes sprawl in the grassy courtyards and sway to the music a few of their fellows are piping and strumming into the air. I spot a line of figures playing leapfrog through the garden and an artist smearing paint across one of the building's walls in a vague image that might represent a sunrise.

Laughter bounces off the buildings. Actual butterflies flutter between the many flowering plants growing haphazardly throughout the grounds. Toast stares at one that glides over the wall and nickers when it lands on his nose.

We take all this in from the gate, neither of us feeling totally comfortable marching straight in without an invitation. There are no guards, and none of the devouts seem to be paying attention to our arrival.

*Well,* Julita says, *it certainly is an… interesting place.*

She sounds as if she'd prefer to flee in the opposite direction.

When no one greets us after a few minutes, I exchange a glance with Stavros. He swings off his horse and ties the stallion to a tree near the gate, so I do the same with Toast.

"There's some good grass here, and I've left you enough rein to reach it," I tell my steed. "Be good."

Ignoring the stallion's incredulous look at my command, I hurry over to join Stavros.

The magical atmosphere of this temple isn't as intense as the towering Temple of the Crown in Florian, but a tingle wriggles into my skin as I pass through the gate. I resist the urge to rub my arms against it.

I'm here for a good cause, not to do harm. Out of all the godlen, surely Inganne would see my current motives as more important than my past actions.

Stavros peers around us as we continue into the temple's grounds, searching for someone in charge. But having seen the way Inganne's devouts worship her, I'm even less sure that they really go for authority figures around here.

"Welcome!" several cheerful voices call out, but then the joyful figures go back to their pastimes. I can't wrap my head around being that unconcerned, full of pure contentment.

Finally, as we reach the largest building at the top of the slope, a white-haired man with a wizened face steps out to meet us properly. The ornate clasp on his robe marks him as a cleric. He glances us over with a twinkle in his bright blue eyes that reminds me a little of Casimir.

Well, Inganne and Ardone *are* said to be sisters in joy, just rather different aspects of the emotion.

"Welcome and blessings, esteemed visitors," the cleric says with a dip of his head. "What brings you to the Temple of Artful Dreams?"

Stavros must have encountered devouts of Inganne before, because he doesn't look all that taken aback by our reception. He bows his head in turn to the cleric.

"I'm sorry to interrupt your worship," he says smoothly. "There are three devouts we believe serve at this temple who we'd like to speak with, if possible. Privately. They may have information from their time before their dedication that would benefit the royal family."

"I'm sure they could spare a moment for that cause. Come inside and give me their names, and I'll bring them to you."

He leads us to a small room with mismatched chairs and paint splattered across the walls in chaotic fashion.

Once he's left with the names Stavros gave him, the former general leans back in his chair and takes in the space with a bemused expression. "They do know how to entertain themselves."

I sink deeper into the plush cushions of my seat. "I suppose that's all Inganne really wants from them."

"I wonder."

The cleric ushers in the boy first, really a gangly young man now twenty-one, with wayward hair that looks as if it's been splashed with paint too. He plops himself in one of the chairs and offers us an easy grin. "Cezari said you wanted to ask me about something?"

He certainly doesn't look traumatized or in the grips of dark magic. It takes me several seconds to even spot his sacrifice—a pale scar in the tan skin of his forearm, about the size of a thumbprint. The kind of sacrifice people make when they're barely asking for a gift at all, just wanting to show their devotion.

Ster. Torstem wouldn't be siphoning any major powers from this guy.

Stavros leans forward, no doubt taking in the same details I have. The idea is for him to do most of the talking and me to observe, jumping in if I catch anything he's missed. "I understand you spent most of your childhood at the Riverside Institute in Siltston."

"Oh, yes," the guy says with a laugh. "Not a bad place to grow up."

"A professor from Sovereign College took a bit of an interest in you, offering some guidance?"

The guy nods, looking pleased that he's able to confirm it. "That's right. Torstem. He helped me figure out where I was meant to go. I'm grateful for that."

His enthusiasm appears totally genuine to me.

Stavros offers him a warmer smile than he usually aims at me. "I'm glad to hear it. What did you think of the college when he took you to visit?"

The guy's gaze turns a bit distant. He rubs his fingers together in his lap, and a tickle of apprehension quivers down my spine.

"Oh, it was very impressive," he says. "All those buildings, so many people—the fine clothes and all. Not a place where I belonged, but it shows how the godlen smile on Silana."

"Did Ster. Torstem mention anything in particular he might want you to help *him* with?" Stavros asks. "Something you could contribute to?"

The guy knits his brow. "Not that I can think of. He said he wanted to make sure I fulfilled my potential."

After a couple more dead-end questions, Stavros dismisses our first interviewee. His grin slants crookedly. "Well, that got us a whole lot of nothing."

"I don't know."

I hesitate, and Stavros's gaze darts to me.

"What?" he demands, suddenly sounding every bit the general.

I hold up my hands. "I could be wrong. I'm not an expert. But I got the impression that when he talked about seeing the college, he was lying."

"You think something went on during the trip that he's hiding?"

"Not like that… More like he was inventing what he said about it in general." I frown. "But that doesn't make any sense. He sounded honest the rest of the time."

Stavros hums thoughtfully. "Well, let's see what we get out of the other two."

Fyrinth, the older girl who's now eighteen, answers much the same as her male counterpart did, though partly distracted by the butterfly she seems to have trained to circle her head. I have the sense that she too takes a little more effort to remember her trip to the college than she does anything else we ask her about.

Was the campus really that forgettable for kids who'd probably never been out of the fringes before?

I study her as I fit in a question of my own toward the end. "Were there any other girls Torstem took under his wing at the orphanage who seemed uneasy about his guidance? Or who talked about maybe going in a different direction than dedicating themselves to a temple?"

Fyrinth merely looks puzzled. "Not that I can think of. We were all grateful that he took an interest in our futures at all."

Her only sacrifice is the common one of a little finger, which possibly is what has allowed her to do this trick with the butterfly. When Stavros asks her about her choice, her smile turns a bit sad. "My mother had the same. I miss her a lot."

She must have come to the orphanage old enough to have known her parents. My throat tightens with sympathy.

The younger girl, Delja, tumbles into the room with a cartwheel and perches on the top of the chair back with her feet on the seat cushion. "It's a glorious day, isn't it?" she chirps.

Well, the fourteen-year-old doesn't look particularly disturbed either. And she quickly informs us that she opted to make no sacrifice at all, "Because Inganne was happy to have me either way."

She's just as pleased with Torstem's presence in her life as the other two. And she rattles on at more length about her trip to the college. "I got to have lunch there. Never tasted food that good before! And there was an amazing statue of Inganne riding a dolphin—just beautiful."

Stavros's eyes flicker, but he doesn't show any other sign of concern through the rest of his questions.

When I ask, Delja claims she never saw any hint of trouble around Torstem's visits. "He really was so nice!"

After she's left, Stavros eases back in his chair. His forehead has furrowed. "There's no statue of Inganne riding a dolphin at the college."

Julita's presence stills in the back of my head. *That's true. I've never seen it. But she'd have visited before I enrolled.*

I pause. "Is it possible there *was* and it was taken down? You've been teaching for less than a year, haven't you?"

"I suppose. We'll have to consult with Aleksi—he knows everything about everything." He sighs. "Not that it would tell us much even if I'm right."

"Yeah. What does it say if Torstem didn't actually take these three to the college like he said he was? Even if he did something else with them or somehow messed with their memories of what they saw there, he obviously hasn't used them for any evil purpose."

"Exactly." Stavros rubs his brow. "I don't like it. We've gotten no evidence at all that he's done anything except help a handful of kids determine their ideal path. Which isn't any kind of crime."

As we thank Cleric Cezari and make our way back to the horses, my stomach sinks despite the admittedly glorious day around us. I wait until we've reached the forest before speaking up again.

"We haven't tackled every avenue. There's still the matter of the women in the attic at The Night's Calling."

Stavros nods. "I could pull some strings and have the Crown's Watch conduct a raid, come up with false pretenses so we don't tip anyone off that it's because of Ster. Torstem. It'll take a little time to arrange."

"Maybe that will get us somewhere."

"Perhaps." Stavros glances sideways at me. "Or you might have to accept that the law professor is nothing more than a letch who makes grand promises and has an unexpectedly generous soul. What does Julita make of all this, Thief?"

The question jabs at me more than it should.

Julia speaks up without further prompting. *Ster. Torstem gives me the creeps, but I haven't seen any direct evidence of scourge sorcery around him. This is all just... very odd.*

"She thinks it's strange and she doesn't like Torstem, but she hasn't picked up on anything specific," I paraphrase. My gut has gotten as heavy as if I've swallowed a heap of stones.

All my sneaking and spying, and we don't seem to be any closer to finding the culprits than Julita was before her death.

The gloom of that knowledge hangs over me the whole ride back to Florian. I'm only rattled out of my melancholy by a frantic ringing that peals on and on as we pass the city walls.

Stavros stares toward the distant spires of the capital hill. "That sounds like the palace bell."

"And, what, it's fifty o'clock?"

"Something's wrong."

He nudges his stallion to a canter, and I urge Toast after him. Thankfully my steed is more concerned with proving he can keep pace with the grander animal than defying orders.

We clatter over the bridge and across the cobblestones to the throughway between the Temple of the Crown and the adjoining outer walls of the college and palace. The road there is crowded with people, all looking up at the still ringing bell.

Several soldiers stand among gawkers, and I spot other dark blue uniforms in the tower around the bell.

I ease Toast closer to Stavros amid the mass of inner-warders. "Do you think it's the daimon lashing out again?"

Have they moved to the palace now? That... seems particularly unpromising.

Stavros's jaw has clenched. "If so, it appears the Crown's Watch is—"

The latest peal cuts off with an echoing *crack*. And then a clatter.

The enormous tower bell splits right in two, the pieces banging against the walls.

As my jaw goes slack, one immense chunk teeters right through the broad, paneless window and plummets toward the palace courtyard below.

# THIRTY

"That was a good attempt," I say to the military student who's just come to a panting stop next to me on the training field. I nod toward the cluster of trees where she and her team have been attempting to carry out a mock assassination attempt on the leader of the opposite team. "Sticking low to the ground is an effective strategy, but if you can make your way into the trees, people are even less likely to look up."

The woman lets out a breathless laugh. "I'll keep that in mind if we do this again. You've conducted a lot of assassinations, huh?"

I let out a laugh of my own, even though I know she's assuming I've never done anything remotely criminal in my supposedly noble life. "Oh, yes. Our keep's spiders and centipedes lived in terror of me."

A couple of her teammates jog over to us in disgrace. One of the guys rakes his fingers back through his spiky hair. "All right, this was a lot harder than I expected." He tips his head to me. "Your tips did help, though."

I shouldn't enjoy the glow of pride that lights in me at his acknowledgment, buoyed by the other student's friendly banter. If I'm gaining some respect as well as enemies while assisting with Stavros's classes, it's all based on a lie.

But that doesn't stop the acknowledgment from feeling good.

In the palace tower across the wall, the smaller bell that's serving as a temporary replacement lets out a couple of dings to mark the hour.

"All right, ladies and gents," Stavros calls from across halfway the field. "I think I've made my point. I want you to remember that the soldiers you'll be sending into any actual battle, all the way down to the infantry, are real people with real lives, not mere fodder for your plans. Some risks cost too much."

He claps his hands and offers a wry smile. "But you successfully got yourselves out of the last half of a lecture, so I suppose it's a victory on both sides after all."

He brought his military strategy class out here for an impromptu challenge after the guy who just acknowledged my tips asked why an army wouldn't simply kill the opposing commander and leave the rest of the enemy forces in disarray. Stavros felt showing them that it's hardly a simple task would be more effective than merely telling them so.

Or maybe he doesn't like being shut away in the classrooms any more than many of his students do. He keeps up the same confident, nonchalant air wherever he goes, but to my eyes, he never looks totally comfortable standing behind a lectern.

I give myself a mental shake. I shouldn't be spending enough time worrying about the former general's comfort to have noticed.

The woman who reached me first glances toward the bell tower, her expression darkening. "I wonder how long it'll take them to properly replace that huge thing. It was the daimon running wild that broke it, wasn't it?"

The guy with the spiky hair chuckles humorlessly. "I heard they had a whole squad of guards over there trying to calm the situation—not that it worked—so I suppose so. I don't know if we should be glad they didn't batter the college again or worried what it means that they're taking their new kind of mischief farther."

His companion swipes his hand across his mouth, which sets in a grim line. "I've heard talk that it's a sign there's something's off with the royal family. The spirits are unsettled by how they're running things, including the college."

A soft but startled voice breaks in from behind me. "Who said that?"

I jerk around to see Petra, the standoffish but elegant girl Julita pointed out to me during the hunt, studying the guy with her dark brown eyes. I'm not sure why she's even sitting in on the strategy class when she's associated with the leadership division, but maybe whatever territory she's hoping to rule over is in a contentious area.

The guy who mentioned the rumor shrugs awkwardly. "No one in particular. It's just an idea people are passing around."

The other woman grimaces. "I suppose it makes a kind of sense. I've never heard of the spirits doing this kind of damage before. It could be a warning from the gods."

It is a warning, but not because of anything King Konram is doing.

I swallow down the knowledge I know it might not be safe to share. We still have no idea how many students are part of the scourge sorcery conspiracy.

Unless we've assumed wrong, and it's only a coincidence that one or two rogue students are dabbling in those dark arts while there's a bigger problem provoking the daimon. Stavros said that even the king was concerned that there might be some larger divine dissatisfaction.

After all the dead ends our investigation has run into, it's hard to feel sure of anything.

"We've been ruled by the Melchioreks since we threw off Darium's rule," Petra points out. "I don't think King Konram is doing anything especially different from the kings and queens before, and the daimon didn't act out with them."

The spiky-haired guy nods. "That's true too. Who knows what's gotten them riled up? I just hope someone figures it out soon so that we can have a little more peace around here again."

Why is Petra invested in what people think of the royal family anyway? I eye her for a moment longer and then jerk my gaze away.

Right. Julita told me she's related to the queen somehow. Of course she'd care.

Now I'm getting as paranoid as Julita is with Wendos. Even if Petra was trying to cover up illicit magic, it'd make sense for her to encourage other explanations for the daimon's unrest, not quash them.

As Stavros ambles over to us along with the rest of the class, the spiky-haired guy turns to him. "Ster. Stavros, you said you'd go over the final stages of the Battle of Bartosa with those of us who wanted to know before the end of class. Can we still discuss that?"

A few other students perk up with obvious interest. Stavros glances around at them and smiles wryly. "I don't go back on my promises. But you'll have to tolerate the classroom a little longer. We'll need the map."

His gaze slides to me. I can't really contribute anything to a conversation about a battle I wasn't present for and know less about than any of his students do. And we already put off an earlier lunch because of the timing of his classes.

To my surprise, he tips his head toward the college buildings. "Go get yourself something to eat, Ivy. I'll see you later."

At first, I assume he's decided that his constant presence over the last few days will ward off any new attempts at harassment for at least a couple of hours. But as I head over to the Quadring to pass through to the Domi, I notice a familiar blond figure ducking inside some twenty paces ahead of me.

Benedikt ambles along in the same direction I'm heading without glancing back, the whole trek to the hallway outside the dining hall. Where Alek just happens to be leaning against the wall at the opposite end of the hallway while perusing a book.

Alek looks up, appears to catch Benedikt's eye, and gives a nearly imperceptible nod. As Benedikt saunters on past the dining hall, Alek pushes off the wall as if to enter.

Ah. So Stavros made some kind of plan with the other men to watch for threats to me. I guess that's better than him feeling he needs to personally supervise my every move.

*How adorable*, Julita says with a mildly scoffing tone. *They've decided they're not just conspiracy fighters but your own personal bodyguard as well. Not as if you need it.*

My irritation at their surveillance vanishes beneath a deeper annoyance with her. It's *her* safety they care about at least as much as mine—she could be grateful she matters that much to them.

I stride on toward the dining hall as if I haven't noticed the subtle hand-off between the men, but I've only made it a few steps before a voice booms through the hallways from around the bend Benedikt was making for.

"All still and proper to acknowledge His Royal Highness, the honorable King Konram!"

Everyone in the hall—Benedikt, Alek, and the scattered nobles who were passing by—jerks to a halt and draws themselves up stiffly straight against the wall. I imitate them, my heart skipping a beat.

The announcer couldn't seriously mean—

But he did. A man with a voice-projecting horn marches into view, followed by three members of the Crown's Watch... and a head of dark brown hair topped with a gleaming crown right behind them.

Three more guards bring up the rear of the procession. I stare as they stop by Benedikt, and King Konram holds out his hand to shake the younger man's. Benedikt grins at him with obvious awe.

I guess a bastard's bastard doesn't get much face time with his half-uncle.

My hands are sweating. I grasp the folds of my gown's skirt with a weird sense of gratitude that I'm dressed for a classroom lecture rather than the field exercise it turned into. As if the ruler of our realm really cares about my personal fashion choices.

As the procession continues toward me, my pulse thumps faster. With each step, the king's face comes into sharper focus.

There are the deep-set eyes and imposing nose that caught the shadows when he gazed down from the temple balcony at the riven sorcerer on the hangman's platform. The thin lips and jutting chin that tensed with his displeasure.

Those lips are curved into a reassuring smile now. He stops to say a few words to every figure in the hall.

As the group closes in on me, my spine goes even more rigid. An ache runs down my legs with the urge to bolt.

Running like a maniac will get me killed a lot sooner than pretending I have no problems here. No problem at all facing the man who'd happily approve my murder.

I don't need to wonder why he's making this gesture. Stavros's students gave an explanation enough.

King Konram is aware of the rumors and how they'll have gained momentum after the cracking of the palace bell. This is damage control. He wants to show the nobles that he's still watching over them, still concerned about their fate.

It's generous of him to take this time to soothe their worries, I guess, even if it doesn't actually solve the problem. But I'd rather he was generous enough to skip right over me.

No such luck.

When the procession reaches me, my breath catches in my throat. The king offers me his smile with a slight crinkle at the corners of his eyes that suggests it might even be genuine.

"Even in trying times, we stand together," he says, so close I can count the faint wrinkles on his face that none of the paintings show, and gives my shoulder a light pat.

It's barely a brush of his fingers. Definitely no kind of attack.

But as I bob my head with a dip of a curtsy, my power shudders inside me.

Push him away. Fling myself out of here. Put whatever I can between myself and the man who's ordered the execution of every person like me.

My magic doesn't understand why I won't do any of that.

King Konram turns with his guards back toward the entrance to the dining hall, and a tremor runs through my body. My bottled power churns and thrashes.

A matching panic shoots through my veins. It's only a matter of seconds before the backlash begins.

Everyone else is still holding themselves motionless on the announcer's command. Sweat trickles down my back, and the first punishing claws dig deep into my lungs.

I stifle a gasp.

The procession marches out of view into the dining hall. The students near the doorway stir and start to walk away—and I spin toward the nearest stairwell.

I have to get away. Away from anyone who'll see my agony and wonder why it struck now.

I just need a few minutes alone…

With each hasty step across the stone floor, the magic's frustration twists tighter inside me. By the time I reach the doorway, my gut is throbbing and my teeth have clenched from holding back the pain.

As I dash up the stairs, piercing jolts radiate through my limbs. Shit and smitings, why must Stavros's quarters be on the fourth wretched floor?

On the third landing, I stumble, and a choked sound escapes me. Footsteps thud against the stairs below me.

Through a haze of pain-jumbled thoughts, I hurl myself onward.

Keep my feet moving. Keep my mind on the door I have to reach. That's all that matters.

I burst out into the blessedly empty hallway of the staff wing and stagger to the door to Stavros's rooms.

A bump of my bracelet and a quick press of my fingers sends the door swinging open. I shove myself through just as my legs crumple under me.

I slump so fast my forehead smacks the edge of the rug. If my riven magic has claws, they're scalding now, stabbing through my nerves across every inch of my body.

I wrap one arm around my belly instinctively. When I sputter a cough, the metallic tang of blood saturates my mouth.

If that stupid pipe fleece amplified my magic's attacks, throwing it away hasn't helped anything. How much worse can the backlash get?

I'm not sure I want to know.

*Ivy!* Julita is calling. I can't tell how long she's been shouting at me while I tuned everything around me out. *What's happening? This is even worse than before. I don't know how long it'll be until Stavros gets back.*

That's fine. I'll ride the fit out and be back to normal before he returns, and everything will be okay.

I can't find my voice to say that to her, though.

Urgent knuckles rap against the door.

Alek's worried voice filters through. "Ivy? Are you all right?"

Gods smite me, he must have noticed me take off and wondered why. It was obvious that I'd originally been heading for the dining hall.

I grit my teeth, fighting through the anguish to speak. But when my lips part, all that comes out is a groan that'll only make him more concerned.

Benedikt's voice joins Alek's. "Come on, Knives. Let us know what's going on. We can bring lunch up to you if you're simply overwhelmed by royal admiration."

I can't even summon a hitch of a laugh.

They mutter to each other beyond the door, too low for me to make out the words.

My lack of answer isn't helping anything, but they can't get in regardless. They have to leave eventually, right?

Or I'll recover and open the door as if nothing was ever bothering me.

A renewed burst of pain radiates through my body, and I can't hold back a gasp. My thoughts spin out of coherence.

*Ivy, you need help. Can you get to the door to let them in?*

No. No. I shiver and squirm in the opposite direction, only making it a few inches before another surge of agony wracks my body.

Julita's voice turns more frantic than I've ever heard her. *This is— I can't leave you like this. Please. I have to—*

My mind whirls with a rush of dizziness. I hiss through my teeth, and the unnerving disorientation sweeps through me alongside the pain.

My limbs jerk. And suddenly, without any conscious intent, they shift to haul me around.

What—?

I grope for control, but I can't stop my shaking arms from pushing me onto my hands and knees.

The sear of the magic's attack rages through my body, and I almost don't feel myself lurching up toward the door knob. Grasping it and turning—

No!

I wrench myself backward, breaking the spell, but it's too late. Benedikt rams the door wider open, and the two men hurtle inside.

"Shit." The bastard's bastard drops to the floor by my face and touches the side of my head. "We were *right* there. How could someone have gotten at you again?"

"I didn't see anyone in view who looked like they were focused on Ivy," Alek says. A quaver runs through his voice as he grasps my hand. "But maybe they used the distraction of the king's visit."

"Or maybe it's something else."

I try to speak, to say something remotely reassuring, but another cough heaves from my lungs. My throat burns, and something wet dribbles over my lips onto my forearm.

"That's *blood*," Benedikt says, his voice turning shockingly urgent.

Alek squeezes my hand and starts to release it as he moves to stand. "I don't care what she said before. She needs a—"

"No!" I manage to spit out, clutching at his hand to hold him with me. The next wave of pain that lances through me doesn't hurt quite as much as the ones before.

There. It's starting to ebb. I've made it through.

Just a little too late to escape the consequences.

Benedikt brushes his fingers over my hair. "Her breath is evening out. She can tell us what happened. Right, Knives?"

I inhale and exhale, gathering myself as hastily as I can amid the continuing ache. The men wait, crouched on either side of me like sentinels.

As soon as I think I can do it without falling over again, I push myself into a sitting position. Alek moves his hand to my shoulder in case he needs to steady me.

"Hey," he says gently. So much worry shines in his bright eyes that I have to fight the urge to lean into his support, as frustrated as I am that he's witnessed this fit at all.

This isn't time for weakness. I'm inches away from being discovered.

One small misstep, and that worry will transform into revulsion.

"I'm sorry I troubled you," I say, my voice only a little rough. "Apparently there are some lingering effects from whatever happened last time—but it wasn't as bad as before."

Alek peers at me doubtfully. "It *looked* worse."

*It was definitely worse, Ivy,* Julita breaks in with her internal perspective. *You have to tell them the truth.*

That's the last thing I can do.

I manage a crooked smile. "I got a good workout with Stavros's students this morning. It must just be that I was more tired in general."

Benedikt slips his fingers under my chin to tilt my face toward him. "As much as I admire a woman who can fend for herself, whatever magic's been cast on you, it's doing real harm. Alek's right. You need a medic to look you over."

I shake my head emphatically. "No. I told you, that'll only make me more of a target."

"Not if we can stop the perpetrator."

"We don't even know who that was. I swear, I've been through worse before I came here."

"Ivy." Alek's forehead has furrowed when I look at him. "Is it— With Julita in—"

Before he can finish the sentence, anger flares nearly as scorching as the previous pain. "She's fine too," I interrupt sharply.

Why wouldn't he be thinking about her even now? He wouldn't want the handy body that's ended up hosting her to conk out.

I rein in my temper. "Look, I just need some time to rest and think through what could have led to this. We have a meeting later this afternoon. We can all hash it out then."

Alek opens his mouth, closes it, and hesitates before finally speaking. "I don't want to leave you alone after you just went through… whatever that was."

*And you shouldn't be alone,* Julita pipes up.

I ignore her. "I won't be alone for long. Stavros was going over some extra material with a few students, and then he'll come back. You two shouldn't be seen hanging around me or his quarters anyway, right?"

Benedikt sucks a breath through his teeth, his expression conflicted.

I give him a shove toward the door. "See, I'm perfectly capable of looking after myself again. I've got all my knives too. I'll survive the next ten minutes. Don't you dare jeopardize our entire investigation over this."

The vehemence in my voice seems to persuade them, albeit reluctantly. Alek exchanges a glance with Benedikt. "Can you come up with an excuse to stop by Stavros's classroom, give him a sign that he needs to wrap things up fast?"

Benedikt nods. "If I can't find him, I'll come back myself." He wags a finger at me. "Don't go any farther than that sofa."

The moment they've stepped out the door, I sag against said sofa, my head tipping back on the cushion.

*Why are you pushing them away so hard?* Julita demands. *You need their help. Something's wrong, and—*

Her insistent voice snaps me back to the moment when my body moved of its own accord.

Or not *its* accord. Because right beforehand, I got dizzy like I did after Julita first moved into my head.

I cut her off, my hands clenching at my sides. "You took over. You *made* me open the door. You promised you wouldn't try again."

She hesitates in momentary silence. *I—I didn't know it would even work. I thought you were* dying *—I had to do something. I wouldn't have attempted it otherwise.*

She was afraid I'd die and leave her without a host too. So much concern for me that's not really for me at all.

I lower my head into my hands, but I'm too tangled up inside to sit there with my feelings.

The cracks in my story are starting to show. I have no idea how I'm going to handle this situation now.

The thought of facing the interrogation Stavros will give me when he marches into his quarters makes me want to vomit.

Grasping the sofa cushion, I heave myself to my feet.

Julita's presence shifts in the back of my head. *Where are you going? They said—*

I walk carefully to the door. "I know what they said. And I know what I need. Just a little quiet, so I can actually think."

Girding myself against the pangs still echoing through my battered body, I stride out into the hall.

# Thirty-One

There aren't many places I can go.

After the ball, I imagined slipping away into my old life on the fringes. That feels impossible now.

I don't trust Julita's men not to come hunting me down. In their eyes, I'd essentially have kidnapped her, stolen her away from them.

I can keep out of their way, but I'd distract them even more at the same time as the daimon are ramping up their assaults…

If the scourge sorcerers are escalating their plans, the men need to be here, figuring that out. Maybe I'm no hero, but I'm not going to screw up the greatest chance of preventing a new divine retribution.

There's also the fact that I don't trust Julita not to make another play for control over my body if I completely walk away. And with the way my magic is breaking me more with every attack, I don't trust *myself* to fend off another attempt at full possession.

I have to stay at the college, at least for now. But I can seek out a little peace and quiet to figure out how I can stop the latest incident from turning into a full-blown catastrophe.

I take the little-used staircase at the back of the Domi that'll let me reach the secret archive entrance without having to pass the main library doors or any of the students who might be circulating there. No doubt the whole school is buzzing about the king's visit.

The narrow spiral of steps is cool and cramped, but I'm just glad to be alone. Other than the restless stirring in the back of my head, where Julita has decided to suppress her complaints for the moment but is clearly still unhappy with me.

All the way down the three flights, I consider my possibilities.

I could say I have a terminal illness that I didn't tell them about before. Something uncurable and gradually progressing. It'd almost be true.

But I find it hard to imagine the men wouldn't drag me off to a medic to confirm my story. After all, none of them are going to believe I got assessed by someone fully qualified while I was living on the streets.

I could say I thought it was an effect of hosting two souls in one body. There isn't much a medic could do about that—and I don't think the men want to reveal to anyone that Julita is still with us.

Who knows how they'd react to that news, though? Would they set out in search of a new host or an alternate way to keep her around instead of focusing on stopping the scourge sorcerers?

Maybe if I say I think one of the medics themselves used hostile magic on me, so going to them could mean exposing me to worse treatment? Of course, then I'd have to create a bigger lie to explain how and when the supposed attack happened...

By the time I reach the hall of tapestries, I'm gnawing on my lower lip. The pinch of pain from my teeth doesn't sharpen my thoughts.

I don't know what the best course of action is. I don't know what will get me out of this mess with the least damage.

I pass the fading images of past royalty and military commanders in their glorious deeds, feeling awfully small in comparison. Signy seems to glare at me from her hilltop as I prod the sconce to open the conjured passage.

She took on the Darium empire's entire army. Why can't I tackle a little conspiracy of evil sorcerers?

I guess it helped that the emperor's army stood out in broad daylight with their swords and spears so she knew exactly who the enemy was.

As I step into the small archive room, a magic-fueled lantern flickers on. The stillness of the dim space wraps around me.

I inhale the scent of dust and old paper, and even though I don't have any answers yet, a little of the tension in me unwinds. I've never been in this room on my own before, but I can't imagine finding much more peace anywhere on campus than I've got here.

I sink into one of the chairs and pull my legs up to hug them against my chest. Resting my forehead on my knees, I close my eyes.

I will get through this. I've gotten through so much else before.

And with my magic's increasingly intense efforts to punish me, I doubt I'll be around much longer for any trouble I get into to matter anyway.

I have some choice over what happens to me. I don't even *have* to explain.

If I say I don't want to see the medics, what are the men going to do? Drag me kicking and screaming through the halls?

The thought doesn't reassure me as much as I'd like. Partly because I'm not entirely sure the answer is no.

I hug my legs tighter, a lump filling my throat.

I don't want to have to fight them. Even if they care more about my usefulness to Julita than my own well-being, they *have* looked out for me.

I can admit that it's been almost... nice, being a part of this little group, aside from the impending divine doom we're struggling to prevent.

Who would ever have imagined—

"Ivy?"

At the gentle voice, my head snaps up.

Casimir is standing in the doorway to the rest of the archives, a scroll in one hand. The smile I suspect leapt to his face at the sight of me falters as he takes in my expression.

I was too startled to put on a show. By the time I've plastered a smile on my own face, Casimir's brow has knit.

He walks to the desk to set down the scroll and then moves to my side. He doesn't ask what I'm doing down here so early or why I'm upset, only, "Do you want to talk about it?"

The respect offered by the question makes the lump in my throat expand. Tears I didn't know I had in me prick at the backs of my eyes.

I will them away and swallow thickly. "Not particularly. I thought no one else would be here."

Casimir's mouth slants at an apologetic angle. "I remembered hearing about a tournament that was held here several years ago, with people using their gifts. I thought I'd check if there was any mention in the records of wind-based talents, since that line of inquiry hasn't turned up anything yet. Didn't want to waste everyone else's time if I got nowhere with it."

I glance at the scroll. "*Did* you find anything?"

"I haven't had a chance to look yet. But that can wait. It was a last-ditch effort anyway."

He pauses. "You don't have to talk. I'll leave you alone if that's what you'd prefer. But I'd be happy to sit with you and see if company could be a little better than total solitude."

My next smile is a lot smaller, but I mean this one.

Only with Casimir, I think I might appreciate the company. I wasn't getting very far on my own anyway.

He holds out his hand and leads me into the adjoining room, over to the settee I noticed before. Casimir sweeps the books scattered across the cushions into a stack he sets on the floor. Then he sits at one end, leaving the rest of the space for me.

As I sink onto the other end, he slips his hand around mine again. Gingerly, so I can tell he'd release me in an instant if I pulled.

Looking down at our interlocked fingers resting at the edge of my dress, an unexpected wave of emotion swells inside me.

I said I didn't want to talk, but it feels as if my only options are letting out words or tears. So I go with words, my gaze still on our hands rather than Casimir's face.

"This isn't my life. I was never meant to be here. I don't really know what I'm doing."

Julita tuts lightly. *You've hardly been doing badly, Ivy. I'd say you've held your own impressively.*

Casimir doesn't bother with patronizing reassurances. He strokes his thumb over my knuckles. "In the area of investigating scourge sorcerers, we're all pretty out of our depth."

I lift my eyes to meet his then. "You're used to everything else around here. And even the investigating—it was Julita's quest, not mine."

His smile turns crooked. "And she badgered you into coming here, as much as we've appreciated it. Do you want to go back to your life from before?"

A bark of a laugh jolts out of me. "Is that even a choice? Our problems aren't going to disappear if I bury my head in the sand. It's just… it's all gotten so complicated."

I don't mention the latest complications, and Casimir doesn't push. "I can be right here with you through those complications, as much as you need me."

He tucks his arm a little around mine, and I find myself scooting closer automatically.

When I lean my head against his shoulder, his sweet sandalwood scent seeps into my lungs. I just barely resist the urge to burrow my face into his silk tunic to soak up even more.

How does he manage to make me feel so seen when there's so much about me I've hidden from him?

But he does. There isn't a part of me left in doubt that he honestly wants to know I'm happy, simply for my own sake.

I can't say that about anyone else I've ever known… except maybe Linzi. And look how that turned out for my sister.

My jaw clenches against the memory, but I can't erase the ache in my chest. Because the pang isn't just about her.

What has the courtesan really gotten out of our "friendship"?

"I don't have any way of 'baking a cake' for you," I find myself saying. "The best I can think of is I could steal something for you, but I don't think you'd appreciate that anyway."

Casimir nudges his chin against my forehead. "What makes you think you'd need to do something like that?"

*Oh, Cas,* Julita says with a dismissive tinkle of a laugh that raises my hackles defensively. It's a sweet question, not one that should be mocked.

But one I feel the need to answer anyway.

"If we're friends… I *should* be giving you something in return, shouldn't I? To balance things out. It doesn't really seem like a fair friendship otherwise."

A chuckle escapes him, with an unusual roughness to it. I raise my head so I can see his expression.

Casimir's dark green eyes gleam, but a raw note winds through his voice, marring its usual smooth grace. "What makes you think you haven't given me anything?"

I arch an eyebrow. "What makes you think I *have*?"

He turns toward me, lifting his hand to brush a few stray strands of hair behind my ear. As he rests the backs of his fingers against my cheek, I can't look away from his gorgeous face.

"Maybe you don't totally fit here," he says. "But that can be a good thing. You notice what no one else here could. You say what no one else I know would. Do you realize, I—"

He cuts himself off and drops his gaze for a second.

When he locks eyes with me again, I can sense the resolve in his. "Jules, if you're listening in, I'd appreciate you giving Ivy and me a little time completely to ourselves."

My mouth goes dry. It's strange, hearing him speak to her through me but on my behalf.

Julita's next giggle is more awkward. *Well. Of course I can take my leave.*

Her presence fades in the back of my head.

Where is Casimir going with this? I stare at him. "She's pulled back."

"Good. Because what I'm saying now is just for you." The courtesan's mouth forms a slightly sheepish smile. "You have no idea how much I've come to look forward to seeing you. Even if it's just in passing that day. It reminds me that there's more to life than what's inside these walls."

He unfurls his fingers across my cheek. The heat they trail across my skin shivers all the way down to my core.

I grope for the right words to answer him. "I mean… The rest of the world is right there. You don't need me to remind you of that."

"Maybe I did." He traces his fingertips lower, down to my jaw, and desire peals through my body louder than any bell. "You've made it seem possible to want more than I've ever let myself consider before."

My mouth has gone dry. It keeps all my effort to hold my voice steady, but it still comes out so low it's almost a whisper. "What do you want?"

He strokes his hand down the side of my neck to delicious effect. The gleam in his eyes looks hot as a glimmer of flame. "Right now? I want you. Every way I can have you. As selfish as that might be."

There's no mistaking his meaning. A quiver that's pure delight runs through me from head to toe. "I don't think it can be selfish when I'd have an awfully good time too."

Then an uncomfortable thought strikes me. I ease back a bit. "You're not saying that because you think it would make me happy, are you? I wouldn't want you to pretend—"

Casimir lets out a rasp of laughter. "And I wouldn't. I don't think it'd ever make you happy to have someone fake their desires—and you're sharp enough to notice. But I don't need to pretend."

I can't help glancing down at myself. At my gawky frame, for all it's prettied up in layers of silk; at the pallor of my skin that might be even more sickly than usual after this afternoon's agony.

The courtesan touches my jaw to bring my attention back to him. "You know… I've never been intimate with anyone simply because we both knew we'd enjoy it—rather than as a transaction, one kind of happiness for a different sort. It could be that straightforward, couldn't it? Neither of us owing each other anything, just finding our pleasure together."

My voice goes rough too. "Yeah. I think it could."

No promises, no future plans, just an interlude of shared joy. It can mean nothing more than that.

It can't be selfish of me to want it when he thinks *he's* being the selfish one, right? Maybe there really is something in me that Casimir has needed, even if his desire turns out to be fleeting.

My entire life is teetering on the brink of one sort of disaster or another. I've got to grab on to the good in it while I can.

I lean forward and press my lips to his.

With the first giddy jolt of heat as Casimir hums encouragingly against my mouth, I realize we've never actually done this before. The other night, he touched me in places barely any other man has, but we didn't exchange a single proper kiss.

He claims my mouth with the same gentle confidence he brings to every other gesture. Before he's even skimmed his hand along my side, I'm already melting into him.

I didn't get to touch him much last time either. Now, as he eases me closer against him, I trail my hand down his sleekly muscled chest. The compact ridges thrill me even through the fabric of his tunic.

Casimir marks a path of scorching kisses along my jaw and down my neck, following the path his fingers traced earlier. As he nudges aside the chain of the necklace Esmae gave me, his hot breath sets my skin alight.

I gasp and jerk free the belt at his waist so I can slide my hand right underneath his tunic. His toned chest feels even more delightful skin to skin.

Casimir lets out another pleased hum and reaches behind me for the laces of my dress.

"It's probably better not to dislodge your clothing *too* significantly," he murmurs against my neck. "In case we need to reassemble you in a hurry. But I can work around that limitation."

He tugs down the gown's bodice just far enough that he can scoop one of my breasts into his hand. As he swipes his thumb over my already pebbling nipple, he grazes his teeth across my throat.

The two sparks of pleasure collide with a flare that shocks a whimper out of me. Then he lowers his head to suck the peak of my breast into the exquisite heat of his mouth, and I bite my lip against a full-out moan.

The archive walls won't be soundproofed. These rooms are large and infrequently used enough that Alek and I have never run into any other scholars down here when we've briefly roamed, but that doesn't mean I can count on the entire basement remaining empty.

But it's hard to keep my sounds of pleasure contained as Casimir summons a steady tingling of bliss with the pressure of his lips and the darting of his skillful tongue. He attends to the one breast until I'm digging my fingers into his soft hair and his back just to hold on through the heady sensations, and then kisses his way across my chest to the other.

As he laps my nipple to a stiffened peak, he tips me over on the settee. I arch against him, my sex throbbing with need.

I didn't think I could want a man as much as I did when he "pampered" me in the bathtub, but I'm burning even hotter now.

"I need to taste your mouth again, Ivy," he murmurs, rising up over me.

I have no complaints at all about the kiss he brands to my lips—or the way his hips settle between my splaying legs. I instinctively arch up to meet him.

My breath stutters at the feel of the bulge that's come to rest against my core.

Casimir lets out a soft groan as if he's as affected as I am. From the hardness of the shaft straining against his trousers, maybe he actually is, even if I can't wrap my head around that fact.

His lips brush mine as he speaks. "I would like to caress every part of your lovely body without the gown in the way. Perhaps another time, in another place..."

I hum urgently in agreement, not wanting to think that far ahead, and yank his mouth back to mine.

We kiss and grind against each other with growing fervor. Casimir's hands caress more jolts of giddiness through my chest, and I chart the delectable muscles beneath his shirt with clumsier but no less eager strokes.

My fingers graze the slightly raised scar of his dedication brand, and I tug them away. Ardone may have inspired some of my lover's talents, but she has no place here now.

This is only about him and me.

With every rock of his hips between my thighs, the skirt of my gown has ridden up. My drawers are absolutely soaked.

Casimir presses his straining bulge against me with another pulse of bliss that reverberates through my nerves. My legs twitch around him, and a mewling sound that I hardly recognize as my own voice tumbles from my mouth.

He tucks one hand between us to cup my sex, and I clamp my teeth to muffle a moan. My hips buck to meet him, beyond any remaining self-control. My mind is hazed with pleasure and the keening need for release.

Casimir's voice comes out ragged and husky. "I want to be inside you, Ivy."

"Yes," I mumble, realizing he's waiting for a response. "As soon as possible, please."

His chuckle is ragged too, with an edge of desperation that only inflames me more. He parts the overlapping folds of fabric in my underskirt and drawers that allow for all sorts of private activities without a full undressing.

In an equally deft movement, he works himself free from his trousers. At the slide of his cock's tip over my sex, I shiver in eager anticipation.

Casimir exhales shakily and loops one of his arms behind me to cradle my head. "You feel so good even like this."

I swallow a groan of mingled pleasure and frustration and manage to mutter, "Could feel even better."

With a lighter laugh, he circles his thumb over my clit and then guides himself into me.

The stretch of his shaft filling me brings a deeper rush of bliss than anything before. My fingers dig tighter into his shirt.

As I sway to welcome him, Casimir bows his head over mine. With each thrust, our noses graze each other. His breath tingles across my lips in hot little pants.

Every collision of our bodies sends me spiraling higher. I don't know how to do anything but clutch his shoulder and jerk my hips up to meet his.

Between breaths, praise spills from his lips. "That's the way. You're absolutely lovely, Ivy. Mmm, can you take me even deeper?"

When I tilt my hips in answer, he plunges far enough to set off a headier bolt of pleasure inside me. At my stifled cry, he pecks a smiling kiss to my lips. "Yes, just like that, Ivy."

The sound of my name vaguely penetrates my lustful daze, even as the final wave of my release swells inside me. He's been saying it rather a lot, hasn't he?

Then it hits me, with a pang straight through my heart.

Casimir knows I've been nervous about how much he's interested in *me* rather than the ghost I'm harboring. He wants me to be sure that it's me, Ivy, he's thinking of while we fuck—me he's delighting in possessing.

And just like that, it's more than fucking. It's a deluge of emotion sweeping through me alongside the orgasm that's just burst from my core like a shooting star.

My nerves sing and my heart wrenches in tandem. I cling to the courtesan through the whirlwind of ecstasy, gasping with both pain and pleasure.

Casimir's chest hitches, and he pumps into me again and again, sending me soaring higher. As he shudders over me with his own release, my fingers tangle in his rumpled shirt.

I want to squeeze him to me and never let go.

I'm falling for this man. Falling so hard I've hit the broken-hearted center of it before I even realized.

I don't just want him between my legs. I want to cuddle against him and dance in his arms and ride through the forest with him and fawn over pretty gowns. I want *him*, in every possible way, so many more ways than he could have meant when he said the same thing.

My eyes squeeze shut. Damn it. How did I let this happen?

How could I not, when he is the way he is?

I shouldn't have indulged him… or myself. I should have kept my distance rather than giving in to desire.

Imagine if I told him. A courtesan of nobles tying himself to a gawky street rat—anyone would laugh.

He has a life here and even he's acknowledged that I—I really don't.

I might not have much of any life left at all.

Gods above, if he finds out I'm one of the riven—no, *when* he finds out, because I don't know if I can even hide the fact for the rest of the day, let alone however many days more—

He's going to hate me. All the warmth in that gorgeous face will drain away, leaving nothing but cold horror.

Casimir withdraws from me, but he stays poised over me, a brilliant smile lighting his sweat-damp face. I force myself to smile back at him, but my stomach has twisted.

I can't let this happen again. I can't let it hurt any more than it already will.

I can't indulge my own desires when I know how false the pretenses are.

He'd never have desired *me* at all if he knew what I really am.

Something must show in my expression, because a more serious cast comes over Casimir's face. "Are you all right?"

I nudge myself upright and straighten out my underclothes between our partly entangled bodies. "Of course. That was fantastic. It's not as if anything I've experienced before could compare to a born courtesan."

A flicker of confusion crosses Casimir's face. I'm obviously not selling my nonchalance as well as I intended.

I yank my skirts into place and scramble onto my feet as quickly as I can manage. "We really should get back to the meeting room, though, shouldn't we? It can't be more than an hour before the others should arrive—we should see what we can make of those records you found before then. Maybe we'll have the whole thing solved just like that."

The laugh I produce sounds reasonably genuine to my ears despite the mix of guilt and shame searing through my chest.

I told Alek I wasn't an idiot, but I am—gods smite me, I am.

"Ivy," Casimir says with the same gentleness as always, like I'm a wild foal he needs to tame.

I can't bear it.

I stride to the door and push past it. And at the same moment, all three of the other men come barreling through the secret passage into the room.

# THIRTY-TWO

Alek, Benedikt, and Stavros jerk to a halt at the sight of me. As I stare back at them, my nerves too frayed for me to gather myself in that instant, Casimir hustles after me. "Ivy, I think—"

The caustic bark of Stavros's laugh draws the courtesan up short. All three of the other men's gazes flick to Casimir and then back to me.

Benedikt's eyebrows shoot up as Alek's eyes widen.

I'm abruptly aware of the sweat-damp strands of hair clinging to my temples, of the neckline of my dress drooping sloppily at my shoulders because I retied the laces too hastily.

Of the flush that hasn't quite left Casimir's face and probably still colors my cheeks. Of his unbelted tunic and his own rumpled hair.

We might as well have a conjured sign over our heads proclaiming, "We rutted."

Any remaining heat drains from my body. I yank at the sleeves of my dress—too little, too late.

Stavros steps forward with a jab of his hand toward me. "This is where you ran off to? To jump onto Casimir? These two made it sound like you were half *dead*."

I can't stop myself from glowering at Alek and Benedikt, who are still staring at me in incredulous shock. If I even was half dead in the grips of my magic's attack, it was only temporary.

"I'm fine," I snap, drawing myself up taller. I'm not going to let them shame me for an act they've no doubt engaged in dozens of times themselves with women who meant less than Casimir means to me. Even if that last bit still has my own shame burning in my chest. "I needed some time alone."

A guffaw sputters out of Benedikt. "It appears you had good company for that alone time."

Before I can do more than glare at him, Casimir eases closer to me. "Were you attacked again, Ivy? You didn't say—"

Shit and smitings, now he's going to join the judgmental brigade too.

"There was nothing to say," I cut in. "I'm *fine*. It was an after-effect of whatever magic was thrown at me before—it wasn't fun, but it passed."

Alek speaks up with a strained voice. "You were coughing up blood."

I make my tone as flippant as I can manage. "Not the first time and it probably won't be the last. Can we get on to more important things—like what this meeting was supposed to be for?"

They've got to be early—Casimir and I weren't enjoying ourselves for *that* long. I guess they went hunting for me after they realized I'd left Stavros's quarters and decided to check the archive.

"You're not invincible," Stavros growls. "If you care about this mission, you should be looking after yourself, not running around throwing caution to the wind."

Why, because I might risk my ghostly passenger?

I fold my arms over my chest. "Does that only go for me? I hope to the gods you three weren't barging around the college together, letting everyone see you've been colluding on something."

Benedikt's tone turns sharper than usual. "Yes, forgive us for the grave sin of being worried about you."

"We were careful about it," Alek adds, even terser than before. "We didn't forget what matters."

Is he implying I did?

I hug myself tighter as Stavros looms over me. "Don't try to turn this around on us. You're the one who went sneaking off after even more evidence that you've become a target, just to get your rocks off."

Apparently the commotion has been enough to bring Julita back into full consciousness, because her laugh ripples through my thoughts. *My goodness. What are they all so worked up about? Upset because you paid a little more attention to Cas than the rest of them? Boys are such boars.*

Her mocking tone sets my nerves even more on edge.

I take a step back, my ass bumping the edge of the desk. "Not that it's any of your business, but I wasn't planning that. I didn't even know Casimir would be down here. I just—"

"You just weren't thinking," Stavros interrupts in a savage tone. "Clearly. The fate of the entire city —gods, the entire continent—could rest on what we're doing here, and it turns out you'll toss that all aside for a roll-about. My expectations were slightly higher than that, even for a street rat."

"You made a commitment," Alek adds. "You can't forget about it whenever you want."

Julita snorts. *Gods above. As if any of them would have listened to me about the problem if they hadn't been hoping they'd get into* my *drawers.*

A sour taste creeps through my mouth. "I've kept my commitments—which I never even asked for. None of this was my idea!"

Stavros sneers down at me. "No, it was Julita's. You made a commitment to *her*. What does she think of you throwing yourself at Casimir instead of staying focused on the mission you came here for? You should listen to her instead of—"

Something in me cracks. I release a broken laugh so harsh Stavros's voice falters.

This is what it comes down to in the end: no matter what I've done, they can't see me as anything but fringe trash while I'm dying for their fucking cause.

Well, I'm really done now.

"You want to know what Julita thinks?" I say, casting my gaze around at all of them. "She was goading me on, and now she's laughing at the bunch of you for losing your heads over it. You really have no idea how she actually saw you all, do you?"

Julita's voice wavers. *Ivy? I'm not sure—*

I snort to cut her off.

She was perfectly happy to take over my entire body when it served *her* purposes. I'm done with her too.

I hurtle on without waiting for her to keep weighing in. "Sure, she cared about the investigation. That's all she cared about. The four of you were just hapless dupes to her—the people she figured would be most useful to her, the people with some weakness she could exploit to get you invested, to be sure you wouldn't back out on her. You talk about her like she was a divine being, and maybe that's appropriate, because to her you were definitely worth nothing unless you were acting like her adoring devouts."

*Please, Ivy, don't—they don't need to hear—I would never have—*

"Why should we believe anything you say about her?" Alek demands, his shoulders gone rigid.

But I see the self-doubt already darkening Benedikt's eyes, tensing Casimir's face.

"I think you already know," I retort. "You just wanted to believe she saw something more in you than you did. That's how she roped you in to begin with. That's how she roped *me* in, for fuck's sake. But if this is the thanks I'm going to get after I've stuck my neck on the line a dozen times, I've had enough."

I shoulder through their semi-circle around me and stride toward the far wall.

Stavros shakes himself out of his stunned silence quickly enough to snatch after my arm, but I dart out of the way and tug on the books to open up the passage.

"Ivy, you can't just—" he shouts after me, and then his voice is lost to the darkness of the staircase.

I sprint up the steps as fast as my legs will carry me.

Julita feels as if she's whirling in my head. *No. This isn't good. You've got to go back. They're going to think— Please. Just stop for a second.*

I dash down the hall in the direction of the secluded back door, not interested in having this conversation. Not interested in having *any* conversation.

Tears that infuriate me sting at my eyes. My jaw is set so tight my teeth are aching.

They're just a bunch of arrogant, ignorant noble twits. All of them, Julita too. It's ridiculous to think they could ever tackle a real disaster.

And I can't either—not here, and not on my own. I never should have imagined I could.

Me with my riven soul, impress the godlen into forgiving me for the blood on my hands? I must have been insane.

Julita cajoled me; Julita made me feel I could be important. She leveraged *my* weakness too, without even knowing exactly how deep it ran.

Well, I see everything clearly now. I'm not going to play the fool anymore.

As I veer around the corner where the hall narrows, my gaze fixes on the small door up ahead. I have to get out through the gate. Then I'll be free enough.

Not much chance of the men chasing me into the fringes after the confrontation we just had. Let them stew in their memories of how wonderfully perfect Julita supposedly was.

For some reason, the thought makes my stomach churn harder. My fingers curl into my palms hard enough to prick the skin.

I hustle past the final row of narrow columns before the door, hearing nothing but the pounding of my pulse and the furor of my frustrations—and a blast of air rams into me from behind.

I lurch toward the nearest column, too fast to catch my balance. My forehead slams into the stone surface.

Pain splinters through my skull, setting my mind reeling.

Wind? There shouldn't be any wind blasting through the Domi's hallways.

It was conjured, just like when Julita—

Another surge of furious air smacks me against the column before I can turn around. With it comes a brutal pain that rips through my abdomen from my back.

The searing gash of a thick blade that's just slammed between my ribs.

# THIRTY-THREE

Pain floods my torso from throat to gut. I sputter a breath.

My legs buckle as if they've come detached from the rest of me, and I slump down the column to the floor.

My chin lands in a sticky pool. Blood—my blood. Coursing out over the floor with every lurching thud of my heart.

My lips part, but the next breath I strain to suck in feels like pure fire. I think the blade that's stabbed me has punctured my lung.

I try to lift my head, to look to see who launched the attack, but at the same moment a blow shoves the knife deeper into my back.

My whole body convulses. Fresh agony lances through my chest.

The puddle beneath me spreads. I can't tell whether the metallic flavor filling my mouth is from within or without.

With another shock of pain, the blade yanks free. Something hard—the hilt of the knife?— smacks into the back of my head.

My temple knocks against the floor, and my thoughts spin away from me.

*Ivy!* Julita yells. *Ivy! Call for help! Make some noise! Stab this asshole with one of your knives! Do something.*

I can't, though. My brain is rattling through my skull and my innards are in pieces.

I can already feel the blood loss leaching the strength from my limbs. My fingers twitch, miles from any of my weapons.

My lungs can barely drag in any air at all. I struggle to push a sound from my throat and only spew liquid that tastes unnervingly fleshy.

There's no one around to see. That's why I picked this route.

I can't tell if my attacker is still there. My awareness is dwindling to the boundaries of my body— to the pain… and the flash of frantic magic whipping through it.

My power wriggles through me, tugging at me, pleading.

It could seal the wound; it could set me right. The pain would go away.

But my dimming mind keeps just enough conviction to refuse.

My eyelids droop, and I see Ma shivering in her bed as her body failed. Her skin stretched pale and thin over her hollowed cheeks. The glimmer of life fading from her glazed eyes.

I felt the same call then. I felt the surge of power thrumming through my veins, and I *knew* I could save her.

So of course I did.

I placed my small hands on my mother's clammy arm and called the magic up through my soul— the soul I didn't know was broken yet. I welcomed the power into me and from me to her.

Yes, remember that. Remember, even as the magic nags at me now.

Remember the rush of joy when her shivers stopped and her eyes cleared. Remember the healthy flush returning to her cheeks, the first steady breath in days that she dragged into her lungs.

Remember the thump that reverberated through the air from behind me.

I see that too—the image that met me when I whipped my seven-year-old frame around.

Linzi, slumped to the floor with her wooden doll fallen from her slack fingers. My little sister, as still and empty as that fucking doll.

I killed her. I stole the life right out of her.

I should have known better. Magic doesn't come from nothing. There's always a sacrifice.

And the riven sacrifice again and again and again.

I can't heal without hurting. I can't conjure joy without inflicting sorrow.

My power flails at me again, but I tighten my resistance. I will not make the same mistake.

My life isn't worth that much. It isn't worth someone else's, whoever's future my brutal magic would steal.

I was a monster back then. I won't be now.

I *won't* be.

My eyelids slide all the way closed. The world is darkness and pain.

But even the pain is getting fuzzy, as if I'm drifting away from it. From everything. Into the black void that will swallow me up and deposit me at the feet of the godlen.

If Julita is still raving at me, her voice has faded into the distance too. My magic can't hurt me any more than I've already been wrecked.

It's all over now. My whole wretched—

A resounding voice cuts through my dwindling thoughts. *Ah, my wayward rogue. What mess have you gotten yourself into now?*

It's not Julita—the voice is nothing like hers. It's everywhere and nowhere, echoing through my veins, reverberating into my bones, speaking from inside me and outside me and yet neither all at once.

Every particle in my body goes still and silent, like the figures standing at attention for the king this afternoon. Recognizing an authority far beyond even the man who rules my country.

*Who… who are you?* I say and yet don't, a wisp of a thought in a final burst of coherence.

*This doesn't appear to be an ideal time for introductions. Consider me a concerned benefactor. Now why don't you rouse that power of yours and bind yourself back together.*

I can't tell if my body actually flinches or if it's only my mind that recoils. A wail of wordless denial rises up inside me.

*Ah,* the sublime voice says. *Mortals and their fears. You've been incredibly honorable about the whole thing, but really, if there's a moment to set those qualms aside, this is it. You do realize you're a minute or two from dying, don't you?*

My next response is also wordless, something along the lines of not giving a shit.

*Stubborn too. It's a good thing I appreciate that quality. I'd really prefer not to lose what we've already accomplished here, so what if I lend a small helping hand?*

My answer could probably be best expressed as, *Huh?*

*I'll direct the power for you. Just a little whiff of magic, enough to hold you together until help arrives.*

*And I'll aim the backlash at the one who attacked you. You can't claim there's any unfairness to that consequence, I presume.*

Direct the power? I wouldn't even know how.

The voice can obviously read my thoughts even when I'm not specifically thinking at it. *I know how. All I need is your agreement. You want to live, don't you? That's all you have to tell me.*

The darkness is thickening around me. My mind has turned to sludge.

I don't know how to tell the voice anything, but just for an instant, the words provoke a flicker of hope. A glimmer of light and the desire to reach toward it.

There was more I wanted to do…

*Excellent. Let's try to avoid any future stabbings, though, because I have to say that…*

The voice washes away with a final wave of black that rolls over my mind and drowns every remaining thought.

Familiar voices are babbling around me, colliding and interrupting each other.

"Fuck. All that blood."

"Who would have—is she even still breathing?"

"Loosen her gown! I need to see the wound."

"Ivy… I'll bring a medic."

Footsteps pound into the distance. The floor is hard and warmly wet beneath the side of my face. The wetness has soaked through my shoulder.

Everything aches.

Fabric shifts against my back with a sharp sting. A groan bursts from my lips.

"She's alive!"

"You're hurting her."

"I've got to stabilize her as much as I can. It's a clean cut, but not bleeding as badly as—"

My skirt rustles, and the sound of tearing silk rattles into my ears. Something presses against the stinging spot, making it throb harder.

I gasp, and my eyes pop open. I find myself gazing blurrily at three sets of crouched legs.

"There's our fighter." That's Benedikt's voice, somehow managing to sound both lighthearted and raw. He touches the side of my face. "We're getting you help, Ivy."

"Hold this," Stavros orders in a ragged tone I'm not used to, turning to the third guy. "Firm but not forceful."

The former general leans closer, his handsome face swimming into view when I shift my eyes. I'm afraid to move any other part of my body.

Afraid of how much it'll hurt… or how much it might not.

Stavros's hand jerks down his front in the gesture of the divinities. "Who stabbed you?" he demands in a low, savage voice that could be a weapon all on its own. "Who fucking did this, Ivy?"

It's Alek's voice that wavers from where he's now pressing the balled cloth to my wound. "I wouldn't have thought Anya would go *this* far…"

Benedikt snorts. His sardonic edge could cut stone. "Not when it might mean getting blood-splatter on her pretty dresses."

Stavros emits a strangled growl. "Let Ivy tell us."

But I have nothing to tell them. I didn't see the person who stabbed me. They never spoke.

I couldn't offer a single detail about my attacker, except…

My first attempt at speaking turns into nothing more than a croak. I swallow the blood-tainted saliva pooled in my mouth and try again. "The wind…"

I sense more than see the guys exchanging a look. Julita understands, though.

Of course, she was right there with me during the attack, like she always is.

*It must have been the same scoundrel who murdered me. If we find out who attacked you, we can unravel the whole conspiracy! As long as... Are you going to be okay, Ivy? For a few minutes there... You seemed to blank out completely, and then I did too. But something feels different now, like you've pulled through.*

I don't know how to answer her. I'm not sure I could form the words anyway.

Frantic footsteps come racing back toward us.

"Here!" Casimir calls out, his gentle voice gone taut. "Please hurry. I don't know—it looks awful."

Alek and Benedikt draw back as a woman in a medic's white robe kneels at my side. The hazy thought passes through my head that white may be serene Elox's preferred color, but the dedicats of the godlen of healing must go through an awful lot of laundry. She's going to get my blood all over her.

Stavros shifts over to give the woman room, his real hand coming to rest on my hair. I think I feel a brief tremor ripple through it, but that can't be right.

The medic sucks in a horrified breath and touches my back on either side of my wound. "I'll do whatever I can..."

She pauses, and a tickle of warmth flows through my flesh. The power inside me quivers in resonance with her magic, but it isn't clamoring for me to use it anymore.

An ache that has nothing to do with my injuries forms in my stomach.

The medic's next remark sends the ache burning deeper. "The cut doesn't go as deep as I thought from looking at the amount of blood. Somehow it didn't quite puncture her lung."

She stands. "I've patched her up well enough that she can be moved. We need to get her to the infirmary for the rest of the treatment."

"Will she make it?" Alek murmurs.

There's no mistaking the confusion in the medic's voice. "I think... I think she will. You must have found her just in time."

My eyelids flutter shut again.

Stavros's hand slides to my shoulder. "I'm going to be as careful with you as I can be, Ivy. You can curse me out later for however much it ends up hurting."

His tone has gone oddly tender. I'd wonder about that or the gingerness with which he lifts me into his brawny arms, but behind my closed eyes, my mind is whirling far beyond even the throbbing agony of my partly healed wounds.

A chill has wrapped around my abdomen. I was dying, but I survived. My magic seems satisfied.

What under the gods' gaze have I done?

And who paid for it in my place?

# THIRTY-FOUR

The next time I wake up, I'm definitely not in the infirmary.

I'm lying on my side in an expansive bed, tucked into silky sheets under a thick quilt. Dark wooden posts rise from the corners of the frame to form a latticework canopy overhead.

A gilded leaf pattern decorates the wall across from me, where a matching wooden wardrobe stands. Next to it hang a pair of paintings: a stern middle-aged man with a craggy face and a similarly aged woman with a piercing gaze and familiar dark red hair, both in military uniform.

At the sight, the pieces click together in my head. I don't know who those could be other than Stavros's parents, and I don't know whose bedroom would hold paintings of the late esteemed generals other than Stavros himself.

Why am I in his bed?

I shift tentatively to roll over. The stirring of the bed covers wafts a tickle of smoky pepper scent into the air that only confirms whose room I'm in.

A dull pain wakes up between my ribs at my back, and a fainter ache seeps through my skull where the knife hilt whacked me. Both sensations are far more tolerable than what I was feeling the last time I was conscious, so I'll call that a win.

The bedroom door has been left open. At my movement, two figures appear at the doorway as if they've run over.

Casimir steps in first, his gorgeous face holding a mix of hope and worry. He hurries to the side of the bed and then hesitates. "How are you feeling?"

Alek ducks in after him, coming to a halt at the bed's foot. His dark hair droops across the top of his mask to obscure his eyes, but his mouth twists tight as he waits for my answer.

I wet my lips and ease my hands across the mattress—which is even comfier than the sofa Stavros gave me, damn him and his fancy quarters. In a careful motion, I push myself into a sitting position.

The pain in my back flickers and settles back into its previous dull state. Nothing else hurts. That seems like some kind of miracle.

The thought of miracles brings a lump to the base of my throat.

"I think… I'm all right," I say, testing out my voice. The rasp in it clears after the first few words.

"The medics fully closed your wounds," Alek says hastily. "They said there shouldn't be any permanent damage—it was lucky your attacker didn't strike you with more force."

I remember the slam of the blade deeper into me, the sear of it through my lung.

Luck, or some other power none of them would have considered?

Casimir is nodding. "They put you into a trance-sleep so your body could finish more of the healing on its own. We thought you'd be safer here than in the infirmary."

My pulse skips a beat. "How long have I been unconscious?"

"Not that long—about a day." Alek looks down at his hands where they've closed around the bedframe and then back at me to blurt out, "I'm sorry."

I blink at him. "For what? I'm pretty sure you weren't the one who stabbed me."

His stance goes even more rigid than it already was. "No one would have had the chance to stab you if we hadn't come at you with all those accusations… I shouldn't have gotten so upset."

The reasons I went dashing down that secluded hall feel incredibly distant now in comparison to all my other concerns.

My fingers curl into the quilt, but I manage to keep my voice steady. "It seems you were at least right that I was in more danger than I was acknowledging. Was… was anyone else hurt yesterday?"

If I gave in to the strange voice and my magic's demands inside me despite my best intentions—if my riven power sealed the worst of my injuries to keep me alive—someone must have faced the consequences.

But no sign of understanding crosses either of the men's faces.

A crooked smile curves Casimir's lips. "Not long before Stavros had you brought here, a couple of military division students came into the infirmary scuffed up from a fistfight, but that's nothing unusual."

No other injuries. No sudden wounds appearing out of nowhere.

I tense my arms against the sway of my body.

Does that mean I really did just get lucky? I managed to resist tapping into my magic at all?

I sink back against the pillow rather than continuing the fight for balance. "Did anyone see my attacker? Do you have any idea who it was?"

Alek frowns and leans forward. "No. You don't remember anything?"

"There's nothing to remember. I never saw them—they stabbed me from behind. After shoving me with a blast of wind."

"The wind," Casimir murmurs, his own expression darkening. "Stavros mentioned you said something about it—I thought that might be what you meant. I did look over the scroll about the tournaments, but it wasn't helpful."

"Someone with a gift for weather or air currents." Alek's grip tightens on the footboard. "All of the students we identified with weather-related talents were accounted for the evening Julita was attacked. We'll have to check their activities yesterday afternoon, just in case."

But whoever tried to kill me must be the same person who murdered Julita. It seems a bit much to imagine there are *two* wind-manipulating nobles running around slaughtering their peers.

Before I can say so, a tremor runs through the floor.

My body tenses all over again. "What was that?"

The men exchange a glance.

"A whole horde of the school's daimon are acting up," Alek says, his gaze veering toward the window where the afternoon sunlight is streaming in. "The guards are trying to calm them down… They keep moving around, which means they're not doing much damage anywhere, but also hard to contain… They seem particularly interested in hitting the foundations of the buildings."

I stare at them. "And we're still staying *in* those buildings?"

"They haven't harmed anyone," Casimir says quietly. "And the guards insist that they're managing the situation."

Alek makes a rough sound. "They know that if we all rushed out of the college, we'd send the inner wards into a panic too." His gaze flicks back to me. "It isn't as bad as the ball. So far we do seem to be better off staying."

I don't feel entirely reassured by the explanation, but I don't have much will in me to argue. I just woke up—I'd hope they have a better sense of the risks than I do.

Casimir lifts his hand and then drops it to his side again. "You should focus on fully recovering. Do you want anything? Oh!" He hustles out of the room with his typical grace and returns holding a plate and a glass. "Benedikt brought up food from the lunch spread for you."

"He'll come by again later," Alek puts in. "He wanted to apologize too. And Stavros will obviously be back—he stayed all morning, but they called a staff meeting about the daimon situation..."

"It's all right." I rub my forehead. I'm not sure I want to talk to either of the other men just yet.

I'm not sure I want to talk to the men right in front of me all that much either.

I motion to Casimir. "If you could put the food on the bedside table... And could I have a little space to myself? That might make recovering a little easier. I don't feel all that bad—you don't need to hover. You two must have classes and everything too."

"That doesn't—" Alek starts, but Casimir makes some gesture that cuts him off.

The courtesan gives me his gentle smile that brings a different sort of ache into my chest. "You never did get the alone time you were looking for yesterday. You should have that. But if you need us..."

He pulls out a silver trinket, an oval about the size of the pad of his thumb, with hinges on one side like a locket. When he flicks it open, I realize it *is* a locket—a plain one with no picture tucked inside.

"Benedikt had the idea of us getting these made when we were first starting our investigations," he says. "I suppose Julita's was lost. Press the inside, and it'll send a small magical pulse to alert the rest of us and indicate where we should go."

He sets the locket on the table next to my lunch. Alek adjusts his weight on his feet as if he'd like to say more, but his mouth stays clamped shut.

Does he expect me to apologize for the things *I* said?

I'm exhausted just remembering it, but it was all true. There's nothing to take back.

Casimir nudges him. Alek bows his head, making a quick three-fingered tap down his front that I guess is meant for my safety, as if the divinities care about that.

The two of them leave the room. A moment after the outer door clicks shut behind them, another tremor ripples through the room.

My stomach knots. Whatever's going wrong, it's getting worse.

And whoever's behind it knows that I'm hoping to stop them.

It's too much. My world hasn't stopped falling apart in the past day. It's only fractured into more pieces, so many I don't know how to fit them back together.

I close my eyes. The tingle of Julita's presence stirs in the back of my skull.

"You're still there, aren't you?" I say. "You talked to me when the medic was first healing me."

*I'm here.* Julita pauses. *I thought I should probably wait and let you decide when you wanted to hear from me.*

I guess my outburst yesterday was as critical of her as it was of the men.

I grimace. "I'm not angry with you. It was mostly them. The way they talked about you and the way you talked about them was just so... different."

Something about the momentary silence has me picturing the chestnut-haired woman she once was bowing her head in shame. *They're good men, all of them. I just—I needed them. I needed someone. I couldn't take on a whole conspiracy of scourge sorcerers on my own.*

"Of course you couldn't." But that doesn't mean she had to go around manipulating people's vulnerabilities to get that support.

*I needed to be sure,* she says, as if she sensed my unspoken criticism. *That kind of power—the temptation of it—there couldn't be any chance...* She trails off. *We did work well together. They were always there for me. But it's not as if it was really about me anyway.*

"What else could it have been about?"

She lets out a rough chuckle. *Stavros needed glory. Alek needed to be chosen. Benedikt needed someone to see him as more than a joker. Cas needed to do something bigger than catering to patrons' whims.*

There's a weird tenderness in her tone, not like her usual amused condescension. She did know them well.

*I offered them what they needed, and they gave me what I needed in return,* she goes on. *It isn't as if... Even if I had wanted... They wouldn't have really wanted me, just as myself.*

My throat constricts. Maybe the things I told the men weren't completely true after all.

Because all I hear in Julita's voice now is affection and doubt. I've seen signs of her concern for them in the past too.

Just how much did she care about the four of them underneath? How much might she have wanted and simply refused to let herself acknowledge?

I know what it's like to put up walls to keep yourself safe from people so they can't hurt you. Hers just might look different from mine.

What else did *she* need when she went looking for help? In a way, she already told me.

She needed to be able to refuse.

"I don't know about that," I say softly. "And I was a little unfair in what I said. I know they mattered to you."

Julita seems to gather herself. *Well, it hardly makes a difference now. You've done a lot more than just step into my shoes, Ivy. They should respect that and you.*

I'm less comfortable with this subject the more it turns back toward me. There's one very large reason the men should never respect *me* just as myself.

I grasp for a change of subject. "What happened to your locket?"

*Oh. I... When I first found myself in you, I managed to get you to slip off my bracelet. Your hand was already resting by my arm. But before I could prompt anything else, you took over again. It would have been in my pouch.*

To either be snatched up by scavengers or disposed of by the outer-ward criminal kingpins.

It's hard for me to be angry about her admission when we didn't know each other at all in that moment. But thinking about it reminds me of the other unnerving intrusion in my head.

"After I was stabbed, before the men found me," I say. "Did you hear the other voice?"

*The voice?*

"Someone else speaking to me. Trying to get me to help myself."

I can hear Julita's puzzled frown in her response. *I felt the villain who attacked you hurt you more and then leave, but they didn't say anything. There was no one else, and then you must have blacked out, because I did without trying to. Did you hear someone else?*

"I—I don't know." Did I only imagine that overwhelming voice and its urging? Was it some new trick of my riven power to encourage me to use it?

But as far as I can tell, I didn't even do that. Not in the way it's worked before.

I rub my eyes and sit up again to grab the glass of water Casimir left with my food. I could simply be going mad with all the chaos that's been whirling around me.

The cool liquid coursing down my parched throat only leaves me restless. A third tremor nudges me out of the bed.

I test my legs on the floor, pacing the room in the knee-length shift the medics left me in. Stavros's wardrobe isn't particularly interesting, but there's a small bookcase tucked away next to the bed that holds several volumes that look like fictional adventures rather than the dry texts he keeps in the main room.

Resisting the urge to peek through them, I walk to the window next. The view only shows me a squad of blue-uniformed soldiers marching past.

I jerk back from the glass with a hitch of my heart.

I haven't really resolved anything. I've only got more problems now. How can I lie in bed hoping those will somehow solve themselves?

I don't know what I'm going to do, but I'm not going to figure it out while napping.

Someone—probably Casimir—has left two gowns spread over the back of the sofa in case I want to get properly dressed: my favorite turquoise one and a new one that's a pale green. My knives and the straps I use to hold them beneath my clothes lie on the cushions, a pair of slippers on the floor.

I reach for the green dress, since it's less flashy. Right now, I don't particularly feel like drawing attention.

But even in that one, as I fiddle with the laces behind my back, the layers of light silk weigh on my limbs like bindings.

I've been trapped from the first moment I stepped into the college. From the moment I ran to try to save Julita, really.

Fixing a knife in place on each of my thighs should make me feel better, but the constricting sensation doesn't ease. I ignore the slippers in favor of my old leather boots that I shoved under the sofa and tuck my favorite knife into the left one.

*Are you going somewhere?* Julita asks. *We should wait until one of the men—*

"I don't need a guardian," I interrupt, but I do go back into the bedroom to grab the locket. Just in case. I'm not throwing caution completely to the wind.

When I glance down at myself, even the pale green fabric looks too bright. I make a face and dig out the dull brown cloak I also stashed beneath the sofa.

It ripples down over the gown, hiding most of the vibrant color. With the hood up, I could pass for a messenger or some other servant if no one looks closely.

A little of the tension in my chest eases. Gods above, I've missed my old invisibility on the streets.

I practice a little of that stealth slinking out of Stavros's rooms. A few students pass me in the hall, but none of them give me a second glance.

Nor does the soldier who marches by on patrol, although his mere presence makes apprehension prickle down my spine all over again.

If I did use my magic and the powers that be simply haven't discovered the consequences yet... I'm hemmed in from all sides.

I dart down the stairs, not knowing where I'm going until an unfortunately familiar voice reaches my ears from the landing below.

"I took a whole week's wages off him, just like that." Even Anya's laugh takes on a sneering tone. "The lower staff should know better than to wager with the rest of us."

There's a muffled clink. I peek down the central spiral and make out the side of her haughty face.

A couple of her friends are standing with her. She tosses a modest leather pouch that must hold her winnings in one hand before tying the strands to her belt.

As her friends giggle about how the kitchen boy she wagered against has been taught his lesson, my teeth grit. Resolve wells up inside me, so sure and potent I can't ignore it.

Yes. That's it—that's what I need.

I ease down the stairs until I'm just out of view. Anya turns to step out into the hall, one of her friends pushing the door open for her, and I dart silently down the last flight.

As I brush past her so subtly my cloak barely rustles, a flick of a knife releases the pouch into my grasp.

As I slip on down to the ground floor, I squeeze the leather surface hard to stop the coins from jingling. The fading laughter behind me tells me that Anya hasn't noticed the loss yet.

By the time she does, I bet I won't even be on campus.

*Ivy?* Julita says in a doubtful voice, but I don't let her shake my conviction. I stride past the guards patrolling the courtyard, restraining a shiver at a brief trembling of the ground, and hustle out through the gate.

I've draped myself in silks and coiled my hair and painted my face to become one of the nobles. If I'm going to make it through whatever the next day holds, I need to remember who I really am beneath all that frivolity.

I take the quickest path I can to the outer wards, dodging other pedestrians, darting down alleys. With each mile I cover, the buildings shrink and slant, until they've transformed from stone mansions to wooden hovels.

This neighborhood wasn't next on my rotation as the Hand of Kosmel, but I've lost track in my absence anyway. The massive family of fringe-dwellers I abandoned will appreciate my contribution all the same.

Normally I'd wait until dusk, but I don't need Julita's men flying into a panic again. At the first residential street I reach where the fences sag and the houses are held up with a mixture of overgrown vegetation and sheer will, I veer into the row of scruffy back gardens.

Because it's full daylight, I have to stop more often than usual to flatten myself against a refuse bin or a shed. But for the most part, the inhabitants are busy in their houses or off at work.

Halfway down the row, I pause to wait for an elderly woman to finish tending to her scruffy garden. She plucks up the last few weeds and moves her hand down her front in the gesture of divinities, maybe making a silent prayer to Prospira for good growth.

The motion reminds me of Alek making the same gesture—and Stavros over my bloody body yesterday, and other nobles a dozen times over the last couple of weeks.

How strange is it that they and the people here are so far apart from each other, but in at least one way, they're the same?

While I linger on the outskirts in both places.

A brief sense of melancholy drifts over me, but it fades when I get on with my task. Another window and another gets its "blessing" of silver.

There aren't all that many coins in the pouch I lifted from Anya. I'd have thought the college could afford to pay even kitchen boys more than this.

As I set down the last pile, the pouch gone light in my hand, a sweeping sense of release washes over me.

No matter what else happens, I gave back a little more. I helped *someone.*

Maybe it won't count for much in the eyes of the gods, but it matters to me.

*Now what?* Julita mutters as I step out into the wider street. *Don't tell me we're going back to the cloth factory. You can't just leave—*

"I'm not," I say, setting off again. "I'm going back. I just needed to—"

A towering figure steps from the shadows to intercept me, and my voice dies in my throat.

Stavros sets his hands on his hips, his head cocked to the side and his mouth set at a slanted angle I can't decipher.

"So," he says in that cool drawl of his, "you're even more of a thief than I guessed."

My hackles rise automatically, but my sense of self-preservation holds me in place, my stance rigid. A slightly hysterical laugh forms at the base of my throat.

Have I gone through all this only to be arrested for petty theft?

I adjust my feet against the uneven dirt of the road in case I need to run for it. "I don't consider it quite theft when it's money essentially stolen to begin with. What are you doing here?"

Stavros keeps the same implacable expression. "I saw you hurrying across the courtyard and wondered what your urgent mission is. And I didn't suppose you were likely to tell me if I simply asked."

The gleam in his dark gaze dares me to argue. I can't.

"So you followed me all the way out here?" My skin itches with both irritation and horror. How did I not realize?

Stavros shrugs. "My father was a believer in smarts as well as might. He taught me plenty about stealth when he was there to teach. Where did you get the coins?"

My fingers tighten around the empty pouch. I don't see any point in lying about that. "Anya was bragging about how she'd won it off one of the kitchen staff."

"Hmm." His gaze lifts to the house behind me with a brief head-twitch. He must be able to just make out the glint of the silver by the back window.

To my shock, a genuine guffaw tumbles out of him.

Stavros shakes his head in apparent bemusement. "All this time—Great God help me. *All this time* I had the Hand of Kosmel sleeping on my fucking sofa."

My jaw goes slack. I snap my mouth closed again, my stomach lurching, but my initial reaction will have more than confirmed I recognize that nickname.

Stavros's gaze is back on me, studying me with another focusing twitch.

"What are you talking about?" I say, because I can't quite bring myself to give up that easily.

Stavros dismisses my attempt at denial with a careless wave of his prosthetic hand. "Do you think the stories don't get around that far? The Crown's Watch listens to gossip, and then they gossip about the more interesting stories among themselves, and I do pass the time with them now and then. I'm more curious how many of the disgruntled merchants they've had to pacify were your victims."

I draw my chin up. "I don't have anything to say about that."

"No, I suppose you wouldn't." He studies me for a few moments longer with another subtle twitch of his head. What exactly is he looking for?

I cross my arms in front of me. "I *do* take our investigations seriously, whatever you happen to think. I just—I needed to step away and remember why it matters. I was on my way back to the college."

"I know. I heard you saying so—to Julita, I assume."

"Yes."

With a beckoning gesture, he turns in the direction I was headed. "Well, come on then. If you're well enough to run around the city, you can assist me with my Siege Survival class."

Is that all? "You're not going to arrest me?"

"I wasn't planning on it, but I could drag you over to the nearest station of the Crown's Watch if that's what you'd prefer."

"No. No." I lope forward to join him, feeling abruptly awkward.

The awkwardness turns into sarcasm on my tongue. "You're not even going to lecture me about taking off on my responsibilities? Or failing to properly inform every concerned party of where I was going?"

Stavros lets out a bark of a laugh so raw it startles me. "I got the impression I did more than enough of that yesterday."

I open my mouth, close it again, and finally settle on, "I suppose you did."

We walk in silence for several minutes, leaving behind the fringes for the less shabby streets on the edge of the middle wards. Stavros rests his prosthetic hand, the realistically sculpted one he's currently got on, on his opposite palm, running his thumb over the inflexible fingers.

"You've been at it for a while, this charity project. I first heard the talk about 'the Hand of Kosmel' a few years back."

"Yes." If he's not going to ask a proper question, I don't see the need to give more than a single-syllable answer.

"From what I heard, most of the merchants complaining about lost earnings were of the particularly slimy sort."

In answer to that comment, I simply grunt.

Stavros glances over at me. "You would have been putting yourself at an awful lot of risk, over and over. Leagues more than if you'd only been stealing to get by on your own. Why?"

It's the shortest question possible, but it compels me to give a proper response anyway.

"You put yourself in an awful lot of danger every time you led the army into battle against our enemies. Somehow you felt that was worthwhile."

I don't need to spell my motivations out more. He considers my answer for a moment and then says, "I was trained for that danger. Brought up for it. You wouldn't have—"

"I had my own experiences to prepare me. I'm not happy about everything I've done in my entire life. If I can set some things right, it seems only fair."

He hesitates. "Well, that explains rather a lot. I know your family treated you harshly. I can't imagine anything a child could do that would warrant those scars on your back."

Oh, he can. He just hasn't let himself.

I grimace, but part of me wants to be a little honest, just this once. To keep being who I actually am a bit longer.

"My little sister died when I was seven," I say. "My parents resented the fact that I was alive and she wasn't."

And the fact they suspected: that I'd been the one who killed her.

How can I blame them, really, when I'll never forgive myself either?

I keep that half of the answer to myself, which is the only reason Stavros's mouth tightens with sympathy rather than disgust. But he must sense it's not a subject I want to dig into any further.

He drags in a breath. "The Watch raided The Night's Calling last night. The attic showed some signs of habitation, but no one was currently living there."

I'd be grateful for the change of subject, but my heart sinks at the news. "Another dead end."

Did Ster. Torstem secret his special ladies away to some other place? Does he know we're on to him—did *he* direct the attack on me?

"For now," Stavros says. "It does suggest that everything is connected. Torstem didn't say anything about them leaving when you were listening in, did he?"

"No. I suppose it could be a coincidence."

He snorts. "I'd rather not bet on that."

I guess I wouldn't either.

The former general picks up his pace, and I manage to match it on my shorter legs. It's only when the spires of the temple come into view up the sloping inner-ward street ahead of us that he gets back to business.

"All circumstances considered, I'd *strongly* prefer if you'd oblige me and not make any more impromptu trips around the city. Whoever made that attempt on your life is likely to try again."

I wrinkle my nose at him. "Don't you think you should be worried about yourself too? Are you keeping tabs on the other men or just me?"

"I can look after myself. And the others have barely been seen around you. There's no reason for anyone to think you've been making arrangements with them."

"Still, I—"

A chill races through my veins.

My gaze jerks to Stavros. "Have you seen Esmae since my attack?"

His brow furrows. "The dormmate of Julita's you've been friendly with? I can't say so, but I might not have noticed."

My heart starts thudding faster. "She didn't come by to check if I was okay?" I assume word about my trip to the infirmary must have gotten around the college by now.

"Not while I was with you. Why?"

I release a hiss of frustration. "I've been seen talking with *her* several times. If someone's looking for potential allies of mine, she's the first person they'd think of."

Stavros frowns. "I'm sure if anything had happened to her—"

"You don't *know*." I grasp my skirt at the sight of the college gate ahead of us, preparing to hustle forward. "I'll play assistant after I've checked on her. If my would-be murderer hasn't gotten to her too."

# THIRTY-FIVE

As I lope across the courtyard to the Domi, the ground gives a little lurch beneath my feet. The walls of the Quadring creak.

One of the passing students points at the ground with a yelp. A narrow crack has split open in the soil, veering out from the base of the building.

Shit. A squad of guards tramp over, the captain hollering at everyone around to "Stay calm!" but I bolt through the doorway.

I don't know what's going to happen to this place. I don't know if the college can even be saved.

But I'm not letting the one real friend I've made get taken down in the wreckage.

I clamber up the steps, taking some two at a time, to the second floor. As I burst out into the hall, the building gives another shudder, unnerving enough to make my pulse wobble.

A few of the other students are huddled in the hallway, murmuring to each other in anxious tones. Hustling past them, I catch a couple of truncated phrases: "unhappy daimon" and "challenging the king."

Obviously the rumor about divine dissatisfaction is still going around. I can get back to work at proving the real source of the spirit-creatures' distress once I've confirmed that my friend hasn't been murdered.

*I'm sure she's all right,* Julita says as I round the corner on the way to her old dorm room. *No one could think* Esmae *was some sort of vigilante champion for justice.*

"I don't think we can assume the person who stabbed me and came back to shove the knife in farther is incredibly logical in all things," I mutter back.

I've almost reached the dorm room door when a woman I vaguely recognize from the hunt emerges. Another of Julita's former dormmates, I guess.

"Hi!" I say with forced brightness, drawing to a stop as I reach her. "Is Esmae in there?"

If not, maybe she has some idea what class Esmae would have right now. She wouldn't normally get dinner this early.

"As far as I know," the woman says, knitting her brow. "Zofia checked on her around lunchtime when she missed a class they have together, and Esmae said she wasn't feeling well and was skipping the day. I assume she's still in there."

My spirits plummet before they've had much chance to rise. "You haven't seen her?"

She shakes her head. "Not since yesterday morning. It's not as if we're close, though." She reaches back toward the door. "Maybe it'd be good for her to talk with someone. I can let you in."

Julita lets out a soft huff as I slip into the common room. *I could have gotten us in. I know that door—there are ways if you've lost your bracelet. Not as secure as the front gate.*

I refrain from pointing out to her that it doesn't matter anyway. We're inside.

As my gaze slides around the common room, I realize I don't know which bedroom belongs to Esmae. I never saw her come out when I was in here before.

Anya's not around, at least. The whole common room is deserted at the moment.

I raise an eyebrow at Julita in question, and she hums noncommittally. *I never paid that much attention. You could simply call out her name—she'll hear you.*

And so will any dormmates also in their bedrooms. I'm not sure if it's wise to make that much of a ruckus.

I hesitate and then start forward, thinking I can at least get closer before I call out. But just as I reach the line of doors on the right side of the room, near where Esmae was sitting that first day, the one a few paces away from me eases open.

My eyes lock with a familiar one-eyed gaze. That one eye flares wider... and Esmae moves to yank the door shut again.

I don't think, only react on instinct. There isn't time to snatch up one of my knives, but I fling myself forward and catch the door with the toe of my boot before it reaches the doorframe.

"Esmae, what's the matter? I'm here to help. If someone's been after you—"

"This really isn't a good time," Esmae squeaks out, but I push the door wider. And then I stare.

A hasty cloth bandage has been pressed to Esmae's chest just above the neckline of her gown, spots of dried blood showing through. The fabric droops with her abrupt jerk backward, revealing an edge of a cut—shallow slash of raw pink that's no longer actively bleeding.

My heart stops. "They attacked you too. I was worried... Who was it? Why haven't you been to the infirmary? We need to tell the guards—"

Esmae takes another step back, her face going so tight that my words die in my throat. I follow her into the room automatically, distantly taking in the perfect order of the space—the bed neatly made, the books all lined up at exactly the same depth on the bookcase.

"Why don't you sit down?" Esmae says in a strange voice that makes me wonder if she's injured worse than I can tell. She motions to the chair at her small desk.

I move toward it, but only to grip the top to steady myself. "We have to get you to a medic to see to that cut. And if you know who came after you, we can..."

I falter for the second time as Esmae positions herself between me and the door. She reaches toward her bookcase and picks up something off one of the shelves.

It's just a letter opener, a thin blade with a wooden curlicue at the top. But she holds it like a dagger.

*Ivy, something doesn't feel right about this*, Julita murmurs, as if she's afraid of being overheard.

No, it doesn't. I swallow thickly, clutching the chair tighter. "Esmae, what's going on?"

She smiles faintly and reaches toward her throat—to the pendant that matches the one she gave me—absently, as if she's barely aware of the movement. "I thought you were still in the infirmary. The medics took your necklace off. I should have considered that."

I guess they did. I'd gotten the necklace so recently I hadn't thought to look for it.

But her odd comment brings to mind the tingle of magic I sensed in it.

"Can you— You can tell where it is? They're magically connected?" I eye her pendant with a deeper lurch of my gut. "Why would you want to know where I am?"

"You've been going all over the place." Esmae rotates the handle of the letter opener between her fingers, her gaze never leaving me. "You said you'd barely spoken to Julita in years, but that didn't stop you from digging and digging behind my back."

Several fragments from the past couple of weeks slide together in a sickening collision. I sink into the chair, but only so I can rest my left hand on my thigh right by the overlapping strips of fabric that hide one of my knives.

"She disappeared," I say quietly. "Even if we weren't close anymore, it's natural that I'd be worried, isn't it? Esmae, how did you get that cut?"

"I don't know," she snaps, her voice laced with venom. "But I'm guessing it has something to do with you. What's your gift, really?"

The voice last night, the one I wanted to believe I hallucinated, echoes up from my memory. *I'll aim the backlash at the one who attacked you.*

Why would Esmae hide a wound? Why wouldn't she get help?

Unless she was afraid the injury would prove something else she wanted to keep hidden.

What if I did tap into my magic yesterday… and the healing power I called on dug its claws into her to balance the scales? Just like the voice promised.

My throat has closed so tightly it takes me a few seconds to regain my voice. "I'm more interested in hearing about your gift now. How exactly do you carry messages across an entire country?"

Why did I never ask her that before? Jurnus doesn't just preside over communication and travel but weather as well.

What better way to convey a missive swiftly and directly than on the wind?

But it never occurred to me that the details of her magic would be important. She was so fucking *nice*.

Esmae lets out a dark laugh. "I don't think that really matters at this point, do you?"

I fumble for something else to say, some part of me desperately hoping that if I give her the right opening, she'll reveal this is all some horrible joke. "And knives… I suppose they could be considered a sort of message, huh?"

Esmae shows no sign of misunderstanding my meaning. Her eye narrows, and her fingers tighten around the letter opener.

Another chilling thought hits me. "When I was drugged in the cafeteria—you started asking me about Julita. Was that a trick to get my guard down?"

She wrinkles her nose. "That isn't how I'd have done it. Once it was done, why shouldn't I have taken advantage?"

Because we were friends, I want to say. But obviously that was never true.

The question tumbles out in a weaker voice than I like. "Why?"

"I've worked too hard," Esmae says flatly. "I gave too fucking much to let her steal my opportunities away from me, and I'm not going to let you ruin my life either."

I feel it would be unwise to point out to her that the life ruining seems to be mostly happening in the opposite direction.

*What is she talking about?* Julita says with obvious distress. *I barely even talked to her when I was alive. I certainly never interfered with any of her career ambitions.*

I hold up my right hand in a placating gesture. "What opportunities do you think Julita was trying to steal from you?"

Even more anger sharpens Esmae's voice. "She was cozying up to the professor I'd want for my recommendations. He only puts forward one student in each graduating class. Her gift wasn't even in his specialty, but she had to weasel her way in there…"

*I swear, Ivy, I have no idea what she's talking about. I'm not—I wasn't—even on the same track as Esmae. I've told you before, I was studying so I can take over my family estate. She wanted to get a job with one of the courtly families. I didn't need recommendations.*

I will my own voice to stay steady. "She told me she was planning on taking over as countess in Nikodi after she was done here. Why would she have been angling for a recommendation to the court?"

"She must have lied to you! I saw it with my own eyes. He told me I should keep an eye out, and then I saw her going to Ster. Lezek's quarters… laughing with him… conniving her way into his good graces like she did with everyone…"

Julita sounds even more bewildered. *Ster. Lezek? I've never even had a class with him. I went to his office one time because I got a note asking me to, but when he met with me, he was confused about it too. We had a little laugh, and then I left…*

A note. Like the one that had me following Romild but apparently went nowhere too?

A shiver runs down my spine. Oh, no. Oh, please, no.

"Esmae," I say, soft but steady, "who's 'he'? Who told you that Julita was out to get in your way?"

Not Ster. Torstem. No, it would have looked strange for a professor to insert himself into student affairs.

But Torstem was never who made me look at Romild either.

It was…

"Wendos," Esmae declares with an emphatic slash of the letter opener. "Wendos of Nikodi. He should know her, shouldn't he? He said they grew up together, and she told him things; he didn't think it was fair not to warn me. To point me in the right direction to do what I had to do."

*That* bastard, Julita snarls. *When we're through with him—*

I raise my placating hand higher. "Esmae, you need to listen to me. Wendos had his own agenda. He wanted you to hurt Julita. Did he point you toward me too?"

She scoffs. "He didn't need to. You told me what you were about the moment you came in here looking through her things. For a little while, I thought maybe I didn't need to worry after all, that you really didn't care… but then it became obvious."

There's nothing but determined ferocity in her eye now. Wendos must have seen it in her—the insane dedication behind the quiet front, the fanatical need to ensure her future place.

He pointed her at Julita—why? Did he realize his former victim had picked up on the scourge sorcery being practiced at the school? He wanted her gone without any clear way of tracing the crime back to him?

And he distracted me by drawing my attention to Romild. She probably has nothing to do with the conspiracy.

He wanted me watching her rather than him—or whoever else he realized I was suspicious of. Or maybe it was a test to see whether I'd taken up Julita's investigations.

It doesn't really matter.

"I had no idea you had anything to do with her death," I say honestly. "I thought—" I thought she really was being my friend, but that sounds far too pathetic now to say it out loud. "We can figure this out. Wendos is the real criminal here. If we go to the Crown's Watch with what we can both tell them—"

Esmae's mouth tightens. "You're just trying to save yourself any way you can. Why would Wendos want Julita hurt?"

My mind goes totally blank.

Curse it all. I'm so sick of lying.

"Because he's trying to cover up a conspiracy of scourge sorcery," I spit out.

Esmae gapes at me. Then she starts to laugh in a halting, humorless way. "You really will say anything. It isn't going to work. I've come too far. I swore to serve the gods with my gift, and I'm going to ensure I can do that as grandly as they deserve."

Without warning, she springs at me.

You're always going to be at a disadvantage when you're sitting and someone attacks you from a higher position. Less ability to maneuver, more easily knocked down.

But for all the desperate force in Esmae's lunge, it's obvious the noblewoman has never really learned to fight. Not against an opponent who's had to scrape her way to survival on the streets of the fringes.

I yank myself to the side, rolling off the chair and across the floor to the bed. As my shoulder bumps the bedframe, I'm whipping my knife from beneath my dress.

Esmae's stab digs the letter opener's blade into the chair cushion. She wrenches it out and whirls toward me.

"Yesterday should have been enough. I *heard* you dying. I made sure."

"Take it as a sign," I say. "It isn't meant to happen like this. Esmae—"

She hisses through her teeth and launches herself at me again. I jerk to the side and shove, propelling her onto the bed.

I had some vague idea that I could trap her, wrap her up in the sheets so she couldn't lash out anymore, but she's faster than I expected. She swings around and slams her heel into my gut before I can grasp her arms.

The letter opener rakes across my forearm. I wince and snatch at her wrist, but I'm better coordinated with my knife hand.

I unsheathed the weapon as a defensive measure. I don't really want to use it.

Esmae might be insane, but she was a tool rather than the instigator.

She's the only concrete proof we have that Wendos orchestrated Julita's murder and my attack. That Julita even *was* murdered.

My unwillingness to fully commit to the fight is the bigger disadvantage. Esmae slashes and strikes again. Every feral movement shows she doesn't care about how she hurts me, only that she does as much damage as possible.

Meanwhile I'm dodging this way and that, trying *not* to hurt her.

I manage to grab one of her wrists and pin it down, but I have to jerk sideways when she rams the letter opener right at my face. When I shove her against the wall, she only reels for a second before throwing herself at me again.

I have Casimir's locket in a pocket by my thigh, but there's no time to grab it. Every second I hesitate, Esmae gets in another scratch or smack.

My magic starts to squirm within my ribs, begging for notice. But either the brief bit I used it yesterday or the fact that it can tell I'm far from out of my depth keeps it from outright wrenching at me.

Esmae grasps my hair and yanks hard enough to make my scalp scream. I claw at her face with my free hand, and she spins me around.

And then my feet slip on the rug.

I tumble onto my knees, and Esmae is on me. My power flares, demanding I let it intervene.

Her hand rams down with the letter opener, straight at my throat.

In that split-second, I know I might be able to deflect her blow. I might be able to send the blade into my shoulder rather than my throat.

I also know it's only a matter of seconds before my magic digs its punishing claws into me all over again, leaving me crumpled in agony… unable to block any stabs after that.

Every future ends with me as dead as Julita in the Slaughterwell alley, except—

Despite the twisting of my gut, my fighting instincts guide my hand. I whip my arm up to stop Esmae the only way I can.

An instant before she'd have rammed her blade home, my knife plunges into her chest, straight to her heart.

Esmae lurches, her blow glancing off my skin instead of digging in.

"You," she rasps as she teeters above me. "You—"

She slumps over sideways, still sputtering breath. I grope at her chest, afraid to move the knife, afraid not to.

"I'm sorry, I'm sorry, I didn't want to—"

My pleas and my frantic hands can't save her. A few more furious wordless sounds rasp from her lips with flecks of spittle. The letter opener drops from her slackening fingers.

"No!" I protest. "Esmae, come on…"

Blood seeps in a growing stain across the bodice of her dress. Her head lolls onto her arm.

Her eyes roll up, vacant as an unmarked page.

No medic can help her now.

# THIRTY-SIX

As I stare at Esmae's body, a series of thumps resonate from somewhere behind me. It takes some time for the sound to register through the ringing of shock that's blaring in my head.

Stavros's voice calls through the dorm-room door. "Ivy? Are you still in here?"

His fist bangs against the wood again. I open my mouth, but no sound comes out.

The former general must be aware of the tricks Julita mentioned for unlocking doors, or else professors have extra access. There's a mutter and a different sort of bump, and the click of the hinges swinging.

I have a sudden image of the massive man barging through the dorm's lounge area, calling out my name, and somehow that propels me to my feet. I shove Esmae's bedroom door open just as the first syllable leaves his lips.

"Iv—"

He freezes by one of the sofas, our gazes locking. Whatever he sees in my face, it makes his eyes flash with fury.

Stavros strides over like an ornery stallion, the muscles in his broad shoulders tensing beneath his shirt and vest. "What happened? Did— You're *bleeding*."

A bolt of panic crackles through my shocked daze. What am I doing? He's going to see—he's going to know—

I stumble backward, but he practically leaps the last few paces to grasp my hand. My pulse rattling, I hold still and tensed as he examines the thin cut Esmae carved in my forearm.

There's no hiding it, is there? And he needs to know what we're up against.

That's more important than my life.

My lips part again, and I manage to do a little more than croak. "She—it was her. It was always her."

Stavros's expression turns even stormier. He shoulders past me into the room.

I follow with my shaking hands balled tight at my sides.

He's going to see the wound on her chest, the one she already bandaged. He's going to wonder how that happened when I claimed I never saw my attacker yesterday, let alone had a chance to fight back.

And what if he sees some sign of the riven magic he's tracked down before?

The survival instinct I apparently haven't lost completely stops me from dropping to my knees and begging for mercy. I still wobble on my feet as Stavros stares down at Esmae's limp form.

His head twitches. "That's your knife."

Of course he'd recognize it. He doesn't seem concerned about anything else, not yet, but I guess that's understandable.

The facts. I can simply state the facts—the ones that won't get me executed.

At least not immediately.

I grip the back of the same chair I did when I was first talking to Esmae. "I came in to make sure she was okay, and she attacked me. It was her yesterday—it was her with Julita—she has a gift for conveying messages on the wind, and she managed to twist it into carrying weapons too. I—I didn't want to kill her, but the way she came at me…"

The worst of the knotted feelings inside me surges to the fore, hitting me so hard my voice breaks. "I thought she was my friend."

"Ivy." Stavros catches my elbow. I find myself grasping his shirt sleeve as tightly as I'm clutching the chair, and not because of the tremor that resonates through the floor at that moment.

A raw laugh reverberates up my throat. "I should have known better. I don't have friends. It doesn't work."

"This isn't your fault. This isn't—" Stavros looks down at Esmae again, his forehead furrowing. "*She's* practicing scourge sorcery?"

Through the whirl of my emotions, something hardens inside me. She wasn't—and I have to get a grip on myself.

I have to make sure that the man who's actually responsible for this horror gets what he deserves.

My legs stiffen under me. I draw my spine straight against the turmoil inside me, the mess I don't have time to sort through right now.

"Julita was right all along. Wendos is part of the conspiracy—he manipulated Esmae into thinking Julita was sabotaging her career chances. I think he was trying to lead me in the wrong direction too. We have to find him before he can hurt anyone else."

Stavros blinks at me as if taken aback by my shift in demeanor. But only for a moment. He isn't a celebrated general for nothing.

"Wendos," he mutters. "Once a prick, always a prick, apparently. All right. Let's get you out of here, call on the others, and we'll pull together a plan."

He spares Esmae one final glance. "The king can decide what he wants to do about her after we've dealt with the more urgent problems."

He ushers me out of her bedroom, letting the door close and lock to hide her bloody body.

My gaze darts over my dress, catching on the flecks of blood that've marred the pale green fabric. I pull my cloak closer around me to hide them.

Stavros nods approvingly. "Good. Straight down to the archive room."

I form a tight smile. "No time to waste."

I hurry with him down the staircase at a similarly swift pace to my way up. As I reach for the sconce in the hall of tapestries, Stavros pulls out a silver trinket that matches Casimir's, the one that's tucked in my pocket.

We burst into the small archive room. Stavros walks straight to one of the shelves and retrieves a scroll that he unfurls on the desk.

It's a blueprint of one level of the Domi—one of the dorm-level floors, based on the layout of the rooms drawn onto it.

There's already a small mark on one of them. Stavros taps it. "That's Wendos's dorm. I'll need to call for soldiers to be sent there, but I don't know if he's likely to linger anywhere obvious when he must realize his deception is coming unraveled."

Yes, he's probably heard about the attack on me and guessed who was behind it and why. And he'll know Esmae failed.

Julita speaks up in a thin voice. *Even though I knew Wendos couldn't be trusted... He tricked me too. Not just with the note. Our two classmates that I pointed out to you during the hunt—who knows if they've done anything at all? He might have realized I was keeping an eye on him and purposefully gotten close with them when I was around to lead me astray.*

After everything else Wendos has done, I wouldn't be surprised.

My jaw clenches. "We need to find out who his actual associates are. And we can't go by Julita's observations—or maybe mine either. He was suspicious of us, so he did whatever he could to confuse the situation."

"Who did?" Alek demands, just slipping from the conjured passage. "What's happening?"

"Wendos," I say darkly. I'm coming to share Julita's automatic revulsion to the name. "He's been involved all along."

Alek's eyes widen within the frame of his mask. "He really— Gods. With Julita watching him that closely, it must have taken him a lot to hide what he was up to."

I grimace. "Seems that way."

Benedikt hustles from the passage, nearly bumping into Alek in his haste. His stride turns jauntier as he veers around the other man and glances us over. "Another emergency. Exciting times we're living in."

I wrinkle my nose at him. "I'm not sure 'exciting' is the word I'd use."

He pauses, his gaze lingering on me, and I'm abruptly reminded that this is the first time we've spoken to each other since my near-murder. Since his mocking comments in this very room.

Benedikt dips his golden head and reaches a tentative hand to brush my arm through my cloak. "It's good to see you on your feet again, whatever the circumstances. You gave us quite a scare there."

I can't stop my voice from going tart. "Well, I suppose it wouldn't have been *that* great a loss."

He winces, and I see Alek stiffen at the edge of my vision.

Benedikt's hand drops to his side. "We were all in a bit of a lather about the whole situation—I said things I shouldn't have. I would vastly prefer to tackle scourge sorcerers with you at our side than without."

"Yes," Alek says quickly. "In case I didn't make that clear enough earlier, I completely agree."

Nothing like almost dying to shake a little sense into people, apparently, however much they'll mean it when the current crisis is over. I notice Stavros hasn't bothered to outright apologize so far, even though he laid into me the most.

I shouldn't care. I shouldn't care what any of them think of me. It hardly counts when they don't know the worst part of me anyway.

So I shove down the pang that's filled my heart with their words and keep my tone firm.

"I wouldn't be here at all if this mission didn't matter to me more than anything else I could be doing." I look from Benedikt to Alek, feeling the former general's presence looming behind me.

Any response they might have given is interrupted by Casimir's arrival. As he emerges from the wall, his face tight with worry, another shudder of the building's foundation makes my pulse hiccup.

Nothing at all is going to matter unless we fix this catastrophe fast.

I clap my hands. "All right. Here's the deal. Wendos has been jerking around a whole lot of people to cover up his involvement in the conspiracy. He arranged Julita's murder. And he's got to be up to something even worse right now—him and the others. The daimon have never been this worked up before. We have to stop them, fast."

Benedikt and Casimir take the revelation in with a flicker of shock that they don't let interfere with the discussion ahead.

"All right," Casimir says, soft but steady, and looks at Stavros. "Can you get the Crown's Watch involved at this point?"

Stavros nods. "That's my next stop. But the guards are awfully noticeable—easy to dodge. I think we'll have a better chance of tracking the prick down first."

Especially if Wendos hasn't realized who Julita and I have on our side.

I glance down at the blueprint. "So someone needs to check his dorm. Obviously the dining hall is a possibility. Benedikt, you said you've played cards with him before, didn't you? And isn't he in one of the clubs Ster. Torstem runs—the one for studying bugs?"

The corner of Benedikt's mouth kicks upward. "You've got it all figured out. I can sweep the ground floor of the Domi to check the dining hall and the recreational rooms."

"I'll go by his dorm and see if anyone there has seen him recently," Casimir says. "Although—we need to be able to signal each other if we find him. I want Ivy to hold on to my locket."

Alek motions to him. "We can stay close together. I've got his class schedule memorized. I'll take a look around the professors' quarters while you're checking his dorm, and then we can head over to the Quadring not too far apart and see if he's arrived early for his afternoon session or gone to any of the offices for extra help."

Stavros leans his hands onto the desk. "If you spot him, you alert the rest of us and keep your distance. Just don't let him out of your sight. The Crown's Watch is equipped to actually apprehend him; we simply need to get them moving in the right direction."

His last words tug at my memory. I hesitate, frowning.

Esmae said something about being pointed in the right direction—Wendos had suggested that was what he was doing by "warning" her about Julita. But there was also…

After the carnage at the ball. He talked to that guy from the so-called Bug Club about a creature it was difficult to fully control.

*You can point them in the right direction, but you can't ensure they'll act exactly the way you'd want. I conveyed the information as clearly as I could.*

What information? Who was the "they" he was talking about?

Not the Crown's Watch if he was only badgering Romild to mislead me, and not me since he couldn't know I'm hosting more than one person at the moment.

The floor shivers under me and seems to pass a chill right up through my skin.

I wet my lips. "We know Wendos was manipulating Esmae, and maybe Julita and me too, but he was also talking about something after the ball… If the mess there was *because* of him and the other conspirators, it almost sounded like—like maybe they directed the daimon purposefully, rather than it being an accidental consequence. Is that even possible?"

The men draw up short. Benedikt barks a laugh but shuts his mouth at Stavros's stern look.

Alek's eyes darken with thought. "I've never read any account of a gift that would allow a sorcerer to control daimon. Even what some of the soldiers have been doing—that's general magic for encouraging peace in any being, not something specific to daimon."

"And it hasn't been terribly effective on them either," Benedikt remarks.

Alek nods. "They're divine spirits, under the governance of all the godlen. No one gift should be enough to command them."

My mouth forms a pained smile. "Isn't that the whole point of scourge sorcery? To try to elevate themselves to the level of gods? If they're drawing on major gifts from dedications to all the godlen…"

Stavros rubs his jaw. "I don't know. We can't say it *isn't* possible, but if there aren't any accounts of even the original scourge sorcerers managing that, it seems incredibly unlikely. He probably merely meant that their other activities provoked the daimon."

That wasn't how it sounded. And it isn't as if the Great Retribution left us with the most complete records of all the brutal sorcery that prompted it.

But every second I spend arguing about it is another second we're not tracking down Wendos and his fellow delinquents.

"Never mind," I say. "We've got a plan. Unless… Julita, is there anything you'd want to add?"

The men go silent as I wait for the answer, their stances tensing just slightly. None of them has mentioned her presence in me since my outburst yesterday.

Maybe after what I told them, they don't know how to feel about her still being here.

But this was her mission first. She deserves the chance to weigh in.

A hint of gratitude colors Julita's voice. *I think you've got it covered, Ivy. I just want to see Wendos and whoever he's working with destroyed.*

"Destroy Wendos," I say to the others. "Sounds like a good start to me."

Alek tips his head toward Casimir. "You and I can go through the regular archives entrance so we're not all seen coming out together."

As they head for the door and Benedikt opens the secret passage, Stavros sets his hand on my shoulder. "You're coming with me, Lady Thief."

The adjusted nickname sends a strange flutter through my chest despite my annoyance with the second half. I've been elevated to a lady now, have I?

I assume he's bringing me with him to the palace to report on what I witnessed. My pulse kicks up a notch as we stride down the hallway.

Instead, he leads me up the stairs to the fourth floor and over to his quarters.

As he locks the door, my forehead furrows. "What are we doing up here? Is there something you needed to bring to the palace?"

"Not quite." Stavros motions me in and moves to a chest under the window. Whatever he starts rummaging through, there's a lot of clanking and thudding.

"You'll stay here while we find Wendos," he says without looking back at me.

My eyes just about pop out of my head. "Don't be ridiculous. We all need to be—"

"You've done enough," he interrupts, in a tone so fierce I hesitate.

He stands up with something in his hands. "You've nearly been murdered twice in as many days, and I'd rather not have to worry about it happening again the second I turn around. This is the one place in the college with a door only you and I—and I suppose the dean—can unlock."

I glower at him. "I suppose we'd better hope the dean isn't in on the conspiracy too, then. I can help. Isn't it more important—"

The former general crosses the room to me in a few powerful strides. "We can handle it between the four of us—and the entire Crown's Watch, once I've got them. And if I'm wrong about that…"

He holds out the object he pulled from the chest. It's a leather belt, twice as thick as the dainty feminine one I'm wearing now, with a short sword in a scabbard attached at one side.

A short sword with the royal family's crest emblazoned on the pommel in glinting gold.

My lips part. I yank my stare from it to him.

Stavros' gaze sears into mine. "Part of my old military equipment. That crest carries weight. Show it, and whoever's around will listen to you if you need their assistance."

A laugh hitches out of me. "And you're giving it to a thief?"

"Ivy…" He pushes the sword into my arms and steps closer in the same movement. His head bows over mine, his hand rising to cup my jaw.

"You're not just a thief," he says. "I'd already realized that, and I shouldn't have forgotten that. And I've seen how dedicated you are to the cause. You're—you're not like anyone I've ever known before. I don't know what you have going on with Casimir or whoever else—"

I scowl. "That's nothing you should be—"

Stavros hurtles onward before I can get out more than that. "It isn't for me to judge anyway. What matters is… I gave up a hand to receive a gift I can't use anymore. And now it seems another 'hand' has come to me." A trace of a smile touches his lips at the reference to my outer-ward nickname. "A better one than I knew to ask for. Maybe better than I deserve."

My throat closes up. "Stavros—"

"Just listen. I don't want to lose you, and I've already been on the verge too many times. I don't know any other way I can protect you right now. So stay here and be safe, for once in your existence. Please."

The 'please' unravels something inside me I didn't know I was holding so tight. I swallow hard against the wave of affection I instinctively tamp down.

He wouldn't say that if he knew everything.

But the fact that he's saying it even knowing some of me feels incredible.

I adjust the sword in my arms. "All right. I'll stay here. As long as there's no urgent reason I *need* to leave."

A chuckle tumbles from Stavros's lips. "That sounds like as much of a promise as I could have expected."

Something shifts in his expression. A flush creeps up my neck with the impression that he's going to kiss me.

The moment crackles between us and vanishes when Stavros pulls back. He dips his head to me. "We'll get the whole scourge on this college rounded up as quickly as we can."

Then he strides out of the room, leaving me clutching a general's royal sword and drowning in a whirl of emotion.

I take a couple of steps back and all but collapse onto the sofa.

"What was *that*?" I ask the air—and, inadvertently, the ghost inside me.

Julita lets out a laugh, but there's a twinge of melancholy to her voice. *You've really affected him. I've never heard him speak like that.*

Not around her... or to her, I suppose.

My stomach twists. "I wasn't looking for anything like that when I came here. I never meant—"

*I know. You've got nothing to justify anyway. Even if I was still properly here, none of them were* mine, *at least no farther than I was using them. I got what I needed.*

Maybe that's a story she tells herself too, to lessen the sting of what she's lost. "You cared about them more than that."

*I liked them well enough, and they liked me. But there wasn't much to it. It appears that in a couple of weeks, you've given them something I didn't bother to in the months we were working together. I think they've all told you things they never told me.*

I don't know how much she's mourning the life she lost in general or the chances she didn't take, but her attempt at a breezy tone can't hide the sorrow.

"Once we take down Wendos and Ster. Torstem and whoever else, I'll be done here," I remind her. "I won't have them either."

She tuts. *I passed up whatever chance I might have had. Why should you? I doubt any of them is going to kick you out the door. Whether you're aiming for one in particular or a whole set like another Signy.*

I make a dismissive sound, hoping she can't feel the flicker of exhilaration that passed through me at the thought of having all four of the men standing by me in all sorts of ways.

She doesn't know the most vital thing about me any more than they do. It's a lot more complicated than simply reaching for what I want.

And who knows how any of them will look at me once the danger has passed, regardless.

I lean forward on the sofa, opening my mouth to say as much, and a tremor quakes through the room hard enough to rattle my bones.

# THIRTY-SEVEN

The books on the shelves jitter. A quill topples off the edge of Stavros's desk.

An unearthly groan reverberates through the walls.

With a lurch of my heart, I spring off the sofa. As I dash to the window, the view outside already looks wrong.

The second I reach the glass, I understand why.

One of the Quadring's four towers is collapsing.

A flood of dislodged stone and crumbling mortar tumbles to the ground in an earth-shaking thunder. The floor heaves beneath my feet, leaving me clutching the edge of the window.

Shouts carry across the courtyard, loud enough to penetrate the glass but too muddled to be all that coherent. I back away, a cold sweat breaking over my back.

The floor gives another shudder.

*This doesn't seem good,* Julita says in a taut voice.

I snatch up the sword from where I dropped it and lash the belt around my waist. "It doesn't. Stavros will have to forgive me for leaving when it looks like the ceiling's about to fall on our heads."

When I shove out into the hall, a few professors are already bustling toward the stairwell ahead of me.

"We've got to evacuate now," one of them is saying. "The spirits have gone absolutely insane."

Another nods. "Check the dorms. Get all the students out into the courtyard. The dean's disabling the locking system on the second and third floors so no one gets locked in their bedroom injured and beyond reach."

Her statement sinks in through the hammering of my pulse. The dorm room locks will be disabled?

That means I could get right into Wendos's room. Look through his private things.

None of the men have set off the alert in the locket. They haven't found him yet.

And who knows how much worse this disaster will get if we don't figure out what Julita's old nemesis and the other scourge sorcerers are up to soon?

I dash after the professors, racing on down the stairs after they veer off to tackle the third-floor dorms.

I saw Wendos leaving his dorm room before, after I visited Julita's during my first trip to the college. In the back of my mind, I bring up the mental picture that matches the marked blueprint Stavros showed me.

On the second floor, students are crowding the hallway—some pushing past me into the stairwell or hurrying toward the other flights of stairs, some milling about in confusion. I weave through them as deftly as I can, grateful that my destination isn't too far along.

A skinny, harried-looking guy is just emerging from the dorm, stumbling when the floor abruptly shakes. I catch his arm to help him keep his balance, and he shoots a tight but grateful smile at me. "Thank you. It's madness around here."

I give a half-hearted chuckle of agreement and raise my chin toward the room he was coming out of. "You're one of Wendos's dormmates. Is he still in there?"

The guy makes a face. "He headed out a little while ago, like he had somewhere important to be —lucky for him. Tossed off a remark that he was going to high places, whatever that was supposed to mean."

High places. The ballroom? Was he up in the tower that just collapsed?

We should be so fortunate.

"You'd better get out of here too," I suggest, and the guy doesn't hesitate to brush past me, doing just that. He never glances back, so he doesn't see me slip past the door into the common room he just vacated.

It *is* vacant—he must have been the last to leave. The bedroom doors are all closed or slightly ajar, but no sounds of movement reach me from any of them.

*Are you sure about this?* Julita asks as I dart to the nearest bedroom. *If the ceiling* does *collapse...*

"This is our best chance of making sure the disaster doesn't get to that point," I murmur, and yank open the first door.

My conviction is rattled by a more emphatic hitch of the floor—and the sight of a crack opening in the plaster of the far wall. Gritting my teeth, I peer into the room.

Heaps of discarded clothes, a tipped over goblet on a stained rug, rumpled bedcovers—obviously someone used to household servants picking up after him.

"See anything that looks like it's Wendos's?" I ask Julita.

*No. This wouldn't be him. He was always careful with his things.*

"Good, that'll help narrow it down."

The next two rooms aren't quite as messy but still nothing close to "careful." The fourth looks tidy, but Julita points out the godlen sigil marked on a wall-hanging over the desk. *This must be a Creaden dedicat. Wendos went with Prospira.* Her tone turns acidic. *He wanted his own abundance of sorts.*

The floorboards rock with my steps as I sprint to the next doorway. A distant rumble suggests more stones have fallen.

I throw open the door with an unsteady hand—and see a neatly tucked bed, closed wardrobe, and shelves organized into books, scrolls, and various wooden contraptions. But what convinces me is the glass tank at the back of the desk where a couple of bright orange beetles are crawling across strips of mossy bark.

I stride into the room. "He really does like bugs, huh?"

Julita makes a disgusted sound. *Either that or it's just to keep up the front. But I wouldn't be surprised, given how low he stoops.*

I jerk open the drawers on the desk and quickly uncover definitive proof of whose bedroom this is: a set of papers—a report Wendos has been working on in a cramped scrawl—with his name already written at the top.

I dig further, displacing quills and stoppered inkpots, sheafs of paper and spare candles. "This all looks like schoolwork."

*It does seem unlikely he'd have left any obvious evidence of his magical experiments lying around, even in his private chamber.*

"We just need some kind of hint, anything… What are they doing to rile up the daimon now? Where are they working their magic? No one can be perfectly careful."

I crouch down to sweep my hand under his bed, but Wendos keeps the floor not only clear but regularly swept. I don't even reach a dust bunny.

Lifting up the mattress reveals a few sketches of naked women sprawled in provocative positions, but nothing I can't imagine half the other male students—and some of the women too—have secreted away.

*Maybe the books?* Julita suggests.

Through another tremor, I turn toward the bookcase. Heedless of the mess I'm making, I yank text after text off the shelves. I shake their pages over the floor to check for anything stuck inside and then toss them away.

An ominous creaking sound resonates through the walls. Julita squirms in the back of my skull. *Ivy, we're not getting anywhere. The whole school could fall apart.*

"No. I'm not leaving yet. Not until I've tried everything. You obsessed over Wendos for months even when the men started to doubt you, and you were right. So let's see this fucking through."

I grate the last few words through my teeth as I throw the last book aside. Popping the seals on the scrolls, I discover nothing but faded ink.

The contraptions on the lower shelves look like they might be something to do with the bugs—to examine the creatures and test them.

Where else would he hide something? Someplace he wouldn't think anyone would look if they happened to come into his room.

My gaze slides back toward the tank with the beetles. Or someplace most people wouldn't want to disturb?

Gingerly, I set my hands on either side of the tank and lift it. At first glance, my spirits sink—the desk is bare beneath it.

But then I bother to hold the tank up higher and check underneath.

There's a folded paper with its corner wedged in the seam along the edge.

My breath catches in my throat. I snatch the paper out, set the tank down, and unfold my discovery on the desk.

It's… a bunch of circles. Three in a lopsided triangle here, three in a differently lopsided triangle there. Five different configurations, spaced far apart on the thin paper with sketchy lines, as if Wendos were simply doodling different patterns.

But why would he hide a doodle of a trios of circles?

"Does this mean anything to you?" I ask Julita.

*I've never seen anything like that. I mean, just like that. It could symbolize three towers or spires or windows or whatever. A lot of buildings have those.*

Yes, because we like to do things by threes in recognition of the godlen. Three overall domains they belong to, three of them in each. But that hardly narrows anything down.

Peering closer, I notice what might be a smudge on the underside of the paper. I flip it toward me and hold it up to the late afternoon sunlight streaking through the window.

There are several smudges—faint imprints of ink as if this paper was pressed into another one it was resting on top of.

The imprints are too vague to identify any definite shapes or writing… but something about the overall pattern strikes a chord of familiarity in me. Darker clumps and touched spaces winding in between…

Like a map. Like a city map, with winding streets and clumps of buildings.

Why was Wendos marking circles on top of a map—and why in clusters of three?

"He said he was going to high places," I murmur.

An image flashes through my mind—the old woman I saw in town earlier today, tapping three fingers against her chest in the row of three to honor the divinities.

And Alek's comment about the daimon. *They're under the governance of all the godlen.*

If you wanted to control the wild spirits, you'd need to call on all the gods. And if you wanted to control them on a larger scale than ever before...

Maybe you'd want to get as far from mortal activity as possible. In three different spots, to echo the divine pattern on as large a scale as possible.

What are the highest places in the city?

My mouth has gone dry. I shove the paper into my pocket and run out of the dorm, Stavros's short sword bumping against my thigh.

*Ivy, where are you going now?*

"I need a better vantage point."

I scramble up the stairs to the fifth floor that holds the dome. The hall that surrounds the ballroom is lined with windows.

I walk from one to the next, trying to clear my head of any sensation. Focusing my gaze on the tallest buildings I can see beyond the square.

Coming around the corner, I find myself facing the Temple of the Crown. And in that mere glance, a jitter of wafting magic tickles into the broken space inside of me.

I draw my gaze up the central spire, the tallest one right in the center of the building. The jitter expands the higher I draw my gaze.

A clammy sensation wraps around my gut. Shit.

*Someone's* up there. And I'd bet my riven soul that whatever they're doing, they shouldn't be.

I hesitate. I could go back to Stavros's room or out into the courtyard and summon the others there. Try to convince them of what I've pieced together.

But I don't know how long that'll take. Stavros might not even have started talking to the king yet. Who knows where the other three are at this point?

My mind slips back to the moment we stood around the desk in the archive room, all of them listening to me, jumping to respond without question or argument.

I have no idea where I'll stand with them once this is over or whether I should even let myself care. But I trust them to have my back in this.

I'll go, they'll follow, and we'll tackle the threat together.

Without wasting another second, I sprint to the stairs.

# THIRTY-EIGHT

No one's left in the stairwells. I make it out of the Domi unimpeded.

All the way across the inner courtyard and through the Quadring's central hall, I keep my cloak tucked tightly around me to conceal both Esmae's blood and Stavros's royal sword.

Then I burst from that entranceway with only a hundred paces between me and the main gate and find Anya standing directly in my way.

In that first instant, she has her back to me. But as I move to dodge, one girl in the pack of friends that's grown since I saw her earlier today notices me and raises her eyebrows.

Anya whirls around with a swish of her ample skirts.

At the sight of me, she makes a disdainful scoffing sound. "Where are you scurrying to so fast, country girl? You have the warrior skills to earn a spot working for General Stavros, but you run for the hills at the first sign of trouble?"

I bite my tongue against reminding her that the current catastrophe is more like the thousandth sign. "I have something to do in the city. Pardon me."

I move to veer around her, but Anya sidesteps gracefully, beckoning her friends. The clot of them closes in a semi-circle around me.

Heads all around the courtyard have turned our way. The back of my neck prickles with the awareness of their gazes.

They're all watching, evaluating how this confrontation goes down. And Anya is as aware of our spectators as I am.

Her lips curl in a sneer. "Oh, no. I think you'd better stay right here. You'll make an excellent shield if we happen to need one."

I glare back at her. What I'd like more than anything is to whip my favorite knife out of my boot and hold it to this wretched woman's throat. But a deeper instinct holds my aggressive urges in check.

I don't know how the next few hours will go down. I might have to come back here, might have to face all these blasted nobles again, move among them, learn more secrets.

If I threaten her with violence, I'll look like an outright criminal. I can only imagine the murmurs that would spread from all the witnesses around us.

I could draw back my cloak and flash the royal crest on Stavros's sword, but what kind of rumors would *that* display provoke? I'd be shining a spotlight on just how closely he's working with me, pinning a target to his back.

I'm not sure Anya would believe the crest enough to respect it in my possession anyway.

My hands clench. I'm so tired of this harassment.

So tired of knowing that she and the rest of them would treat me ten times worse if they knew how lowly in status I actually am.

*Take her down*, Julita urges. *Toss her right on her ass and show her who she's messing with.*

I give my head the slightest shake. I don't for one second think there's anything I could do to Anya that would frighten her into leaving me alone without setting tongues wagging all across the college.

Not anything forceful, at least…

A glimmer of an idea lights in my head. Esmae nearly had me at her mercy without a single cutting word or blade.

Without letting myself second-guess the inspiration, I let out a light laugh and step toward my harasser.

"Oh, Anya, let's stop jerking our poor schoolmates around. They've got plenty of other things to worry about beyond us pretending we're at each other's throats. It's been a lot of fun while it lasted, but I think the charade has run its course. You've been fantastic at it, friend."

Anya stares at me as if I actually did stab her. Probably she'd have had a better idea how to respond in that circumstance.

Ignoring the revulsion twisting through my body, I grasp her arm and pull her into a friendly hug. With a bob on my toes, I bring my mouth close to her ear.

"Play along and make nice," I murmur so only she can hear, "or I'll let Ster. Stavros drag you in front of the royal family as a traitor like he's been itching to ever since you poisoned me. Even assistant teaching staff are delegates of the crown, you know."

Anya's posture stiffens. Then she lets out a chuckle that's only slightly strained and brings her arms up to return the embrace.

Ah. So I gambled right, and she was the one who tampered with my dinner that night.

I can feel that she's hating every second of the clinch, but that's all right. So am I.

I draw back from her with a triumphant smile.

"I really do have an errand to take care of, but we'll have to catch up properly soon. Take care of yourself!"

"You too," Anya says in a dazed tone. She eases to the side, and I stride on to the gate with nothing following me but several dozen startled gazes.

By the time I reach the wall, the students behind me have already fallen back into their previous buzz of conversation. There'll be a bit of talk about the con Anya and I supposedly pulled, pretending to be strangers and enemies, but people who like each other is not that interesting. The mutterings should fade soon.

Julita makes a noise of disbelief. *I think that ploy actually worked. But you had to* hug *her.*

"We all make sacrifices for the greater good," I mutter under my breath as I slip beneath the archway.

I skirt the side of the Temple of the Crown where it stands just ahead of the college walls, through the thrum of its ever-present magic. The sensation is even more unnerving than usual now, while the knowledge of what I'm about to do simmers inside me.

I come around the front of the temple and gaze up the short flight of broad marble steps to the grand public doorway that's open as always to worshippers. A few are ambling out right now, their expressions soft with peace in the fading daylight.

A lump rises in my throat. My heart is already thumping hard against my ribs.

Peace is the last sensation I'm going to feel stepping into that building.

I fled to the streets the morning of my twelfth birthday specifically so my parents wouldn't fulfill their obligation to bring me to my dedication ceremony.

Going into Inganne's temple was bad enough. The structure before me is the most exalted place of worship in the country, blessed by all nine godlen and perhaps the All-Giver as well.

Will the divinities see me the second I step through that doorway? See me all the way down to my broken soul?

My hand comes to rest on the folds of my skirt. I pull out the locket, flip it open, and press my thumb to the inner surface.

A tingle of magic tells me it's worked. The men will know I've found something—they'll follow the call here.

I could simply wait outside and let them do the rest. Stavros—and maybe the others too—might even prefer that.

But as I stare up at the sublime building with dread pooling in my gut, a tremor shakes the ground all the way to the cobblestones I'm standing on.

One of the nobles who just exited the temple startles with a little gasp. My chest constricts.

The trouble is spreading. Whatever the scourge sorcerers are doing, their influence is creeping far beyond the college walls.

How much more might be destroyed if I just stand here when I could have tried to stop them?

*You don't have to do anything else, Ivy,* Julita says, although she can't possibly know the full reasons for my hesitation. *No one would blame you.*

I exhale in a rush. "I would."

Girding myself, I raise my chin and march up the steps into the temple.

Some part of me expects a lightning bolt to careen out of the sky and strike me dead before I cross the threshold. But of course that's not how the riven usually die.

The gods rely on mortals to carry out the actual executions. Out there where I was just standing, with a rope coiled tight around a neck.

I swallow thickly and propel myself across the polished marble floor. The thrum of divine power deepens, crawling through my veins.

I pass magically lit sconces and carved scenes of the godlen emerging from the sea, sky, and earth. Then I step from the entry hall into the vast worship room.

The rasp of my boots echoes off the ceiling arcing above my head, as high as the dome over the college's ballroom. Lingering rays of sunlight streak in through divine scenes captured in stained glass across its surface.

The multicolored glow beams down over the nine sculptures arranged in their alcoves around the room, each decorated with symbols of their strengths, both artful and real.

Elox, the peaceful healer, bows his head of wispy curls over a sleeping lamb cast in marble. Someone has laid a spread of cut willow branches and lavender around his stone feet.

Sabrelle, the domineering warrior, stares fiercely from beneath her helm as she brandishes a spear. A carved hunting hound stands by her side amid a scattering of dried bloodfruit, a favored snack of soldiers.

My gaze snags on Kosmel next. The godlen of chance and trickery peers across the room with a sly smile curving his thin lips, a crow perched on one shoulder and a rat nestled against his opposite forearm. Dice lie around his booted feet.

I've heard that people weighing the risks of a particular decision will roll one under his watch and take guidance from the numbers turning up odd or even.

I have the urge to walk up to him and study him more closely, as if I'll find answers in a devout's stone rendition. With an itch of discomfort, the memory rises up of the unsettling voice that came to me while I lay dying.

If any of the godlen would not just look the other way but outright encourage my monstrous magic, it'd be the guider of gamblers and protector of rascals, wouldn't it?

Or maybe that voice had nothing to do with the gods. Maybe I did imagine it, and I aimed the backlash of my magic at Esmae myself.

Maybe it was the gift of some mortal figure I hadn't realized was watching over me.

I'm not sure any of those options are exactly *good*.

I yank my eyes away and hurry to the thick column in the center of the room. It contains a spiral staircase that winds all the way up into the central spire, the tower of the All-Giver.

At least I don't have to worry about the Great God glaring down on me, since the One who is all things was offended enough by the first batch of scourge sorcerers to abandon our continent centuries ago in the midst of the Great Retribution.

Having now experienced the venom of scourge sorcery firsthand, I kind of understand.

I climb the stairs as quickly as my legs will go. With every step, the taint of magic in the air thickens.

It's not only the temple's, but an energy that's more erratic and searing as well, radiating down from above.

To my frustration, my own power stirs in my chest in answer. It starts to niggle at my innards with its familiar demands.

I could launch myself right to the top of the tower in an instant. I could crush whoever's working their brutal sorcery up there without even seeing them.

I set my jaw and march on up. I *need* to see.

I need to know what's actually happening before I can be sure of stopping it properly.

And I won't lower myself to the same stinking depths Wendos and his allies have, not caring what or who they sacrifice to get what they want.

When I reach the first windows showing the increasingly dim light of the impending evening outside, I know I've emerged beyond the level of the temple's main roof. I push my burning calves onward, breathing in a slow, steady rhythm.

There are platforms at periodic intervals now. The flat spans of stone floor hold markings of ash, wax, and other fragments that suggest the clerics conduct occasional rituals up here.

I haven't passed so much as a devout. Do they not use the All-Giver's tower regularly?

Or have the scourge sorcerers done something to ensure the temple's staff would be occupied elsewhere?

A breeze drifts down from above, carrying an acrid smell. Julita's presence goes rigid at the back of my head.

*That's burnt dartling eggshell. Borys and Wendos thought it would help them consolidate sacrifices into a greater power.*

At the same moment, I catch the first muffled voice from above. Whoever's burning the stuff now, I've almost reached them.

I set my feet even more carefully as I continue my swift ascent, keeping my ears pricked. When I get close enough for the words to become clear, I recognize the voice of the man who approached me in the library and claimed to be Julita's friend.

Wendos's tone is harsher now. "We need more. I can't quite connect our power with the others'. Focus your gifts."

A youthful female voice answers, lower and pained. "We're trying."

"We'll see through our duty to the gods," another man says with a rasp. "We won't let them down."

They think they're doing this *for* the gods? Are they insane?

I guess that's a very real possibility.

I ease up the last spiraled flight with silent steps and breath held. Who are the "others" Wendos mentioned that he's trying to connect his magic with?

My hand drops to the pocket where I tucked his sketch paper. The arrangements of three circles.

Was I right, and at least two more scourge sorcerers are at some other high points in the city? It sounds like they haven't accomplished what they're aiming for yet, though.

So what exactly is that? The college is already in chaos.

But they're out here in the rest of Florian. Maybe they're hoping to wreak the same havoc across the entire capital.

My blood runs cold. I push myself a little faster—until the final landing emerges into view around the next curve of the staircase.

I spot the top of Wendos's head, his shaggy dark hair swaying as he shifts his view. His back is mostly to me.

Crouching low, I creep up step after step. Then I huddle with my back against the central post of the spiraling stairs, which ends at the span of floor just above my head.

At the sight before me, my stomach flips over.

Yes, Wendos is standing there, poised by the stone railing that surrounds the uppermost platform of the tower. Only the nine narrow columns that hold up the final spire of the roof break the view of the rest of the city all around us.

Julita's childhood tormenter has smeared a dark, glinting powder across his hands and the stone edge, and he mutters words I can't make out as he stares off into the distance.

Toward his far-off associates?

He has other associates here, though. Three of them, hunched in a ring around him—but they barely look like people at all.

Their scalps are bare patchworks of scarring where their hair was carved off. Only ruddy holes mark where their ears should be. The one I can see in profile has nothing but wizened hollows where his eyes once were.

And their bodies…

Their cloaks slump across shoulders far too narrow. I don't think any of them have *arms*. A wooden post protruding from one figure's skirt suggests she's lost a leg as well.

No, not lost. Sacrificed.

*Gods save us all,* Julita murmurs.

As nausea roils through my stomach, I understand. The scourge sorcerers haven't lured innocent kids into sacrificing their whole existence to fuel someone else's power—at least, not all of their victims. They've had them give up every piece of themselves they can while still living to gain who knows what twisted gifts the godlen felt obliged to reward them with in return.

In a sickening way, the strategy makes sense. It's a subtler approach than the typical, fatal scourge sorcery technique.

The sacrificial accomplices have kept their own gifts while staying ready to support their sorcerous leaders with them when called on. No one figure has been carrying massive amounts of power as if trying to match the divine.

Alek said it'd take the power of all the godlen to compel daimon. Are there at least nine of these ruined figures positioned around the city for the sorcerers' evil purpose?

Where did they come from? Is this who Ster. Torstem had hidden away in the brothel's attic?

Were they the prostitutes' children? How could anyone in that place allow this horror to happen to kids they'd watched grow up?

Wendos hisses through his teeth and makes a sharp motion at the forms around him. "Concentrate harder! We need the daimon rampaging right through the inner wards if we want everyone to see the truth."

My pulse hiccups. They have found a way to control the spirit-creatures, then.

But what truth could he possibly think he's conveying?

His voice has gone even more ragged. Whatever his mad purpose is, he's obviously happy to tear the city apart for it.

I glance at the stairs behind me, but there's no sight or sound of *my* associates. How long will it take for Julita's men to follow me?

I dig my hand into my pocket to press the locket again, in case they won't realize I've gone up the tower. I have no idea how long the magical signal lasts.

Wendos has to be stopped—but we need to know who he's working with too. Where the other sorcerers are. What they're trying to accomplish.

Ending this catastrophe isn't as simple as running in there and stabbing the royal sword straight through him. I don't know how to do this right.

Then the woman in the middle of the semi-circle stifles a sob, and Wendos's attention jerks toward her.

"Get yourself together, Fyrinth," he snarls. "Or would you rather Torstem dumped you back at the whorehouse where maybe you belong after all?"

Fyrinth?

I register the confirmation of my suspicions, of Torstem's involvement and the brothel's, but all that feels momentarily distant behind the chill that name provokes.

It's not a common one in this city—I think it's Icarian or Bryfesh in origin rather than Silanian. But I've heard it before, just a few days ago.

What are the chances that one of the orphans Torstem saw off to the Inganne's temple had the exact same name?

*Oh,* Julita mumbles, just as the same realization hits me like a sucker punch. *Oh, no. He switched them.*

The women of the brothel didn't sacrifice their own children. They sent them off to better lives at the temples.

Did they even know it'd be under some other child's name?

The girl who was going by Fyrinth—her sacrificed little finger—just like one of the prostitutes I spoke with. It's a common minor sacrifice. I never would have assumed…

That could have been her mother. And the real Fyrinth was secreted into their attic, with no one at the orphanage or the temple having a clue that she'd never ended up at her supposed destination.

No wonder the devouts spoke so vaguely—or outright fancifully—about their visits to the college. *They* had never actually been, only the kids whose places they'd taken.

How far does the conspiracy stretch? There are dozens of brothels across Florian's wards.

We have no idea how many devastated children the sorcerers have groomed and hidden throughout the city. How much power they might be calling on now.

Fyrinth sucks in a ragged breath and squares what's left of her shoulders.

Whatever she does must help, because Wendos's face brightens. "That's it. I can feel that. It just might be enough…"

As he turns back toward the view of the city, my gut churns. There's still no sign of my allies arriving.

It's only me. I have to stop him before he unleashes even more terror on my city, however I possibly can.

My magic shudders in my chest alongside the queasiness in my gut, but there's no direct threat to me yet. It isn't wrenching at me the way it can.

Let's hope I can keep it that way.

I slide Stavros's sword from its sheath, testing the weight in my hands. It's about twice the size of my favorite knife and three times the weight, but I've wielded bulkier weapons when I've needed to.

Maybe the interruption will shake the accomplices' loyalty to the man who's channeling their gifts. Maybe I can take him prisoner without any more bloodshed.

I have to try.

I heft the sword in my hands and adjust my position on the steps. Inhale and exhale to steady my body and my mind. Wait until Wendos appears completely focused on the world beyond the tower.

And then I launch myself at him.

# THIRTY-NINE

I fling myself up the last few steps and over the smooth stone tiles of the tower's highest platform. There's little room to maneuver. I'm going with the best strategy the environment allows: barrel straight into my target and knock him down.

If I can pin him to the floor with the sword at his throat, I don't think there's much his ravaged accomplices can do. And once Stavros gets here, possibly with the king's soldiers in tow, he can take Wendos into custody.

That's the idea, anyway. I didn't take into account the scourge sorcerers' *other* accomplices, unwilling or not.

I hurtle across the floor, the blade flashing. Wendos starts to whirl at the thump of my feet, too slow.

Just as I'm about to dart between two of the slouched figures to reach him, an invisible force smacks into me from the side with a crackle of supernatural power.

He must have commanded at least one daimon to play guard.

I stumble to the side. As I regain my balance and whip back toward him, Wendos's eyes widen.

He snaps out a sharp, nasal-toned phrase of words I don't recognize, and all at once I'm battered by a supernatural onslaught.

Blows pummel me from chest to calves as if a heap of invisible fists are slamming into me all at once. I hiss in pain and stagger backward, and something flits past my ankles, knocking my feet out from under me.

Right at the top of the stairs.

I skid down several steps as I grope to catch my fall. My tailbone jars against the stone edges, pain spiking up my spine.

The royal sword goes spinning out of my grasp, clattering farther down the stairwell.

Just as I manage to snag my fingertips on a small groove in the wall, Wendos sweeps his hand downward as if in command. I don't know what specifically he was hoping his harnessed daimon would do, but the stairs above me shake and crack.

Chunks of stone surge toward me, some bashing into my body, others tumbling past me after my sword or raining down through the widening crack onto the stairs below. One particularly large piece crashes down on my shin.

I can't hold back the cry of pain at the agony that lances through my leg. It feels like the blasted chunk of marble shattered the bone.

A pit has opened up in the stairwell between me and the platform where Wendos is standing—six steps fallen away, leaving nothing but empty air unless I want to plummet a story down onto the rubble beneath.

My magic surges through me, battering me from the inside out in turn for a chance to fight back. I clamp down on it with the clenching of my jaw.

My power scratches at my innards with its usual frustration, but not nearly as overwhelmingly as the last several times. As if the fact that I let it out yesterday has partly appeased it.

I don't know whether to rejoice or cringe away from that fact.

I wrench myself into a proper sitting position, pushing close to the wall and gasping for breath. I could have jumped that distance, even going upward, at my best.

But not with a broken leg.

*We can still do this, Ivy,* Julita says, but there's a wobble in her voice. *I know you can find a way.*

Wendos saunters up to the crumbled edge of the platform to gaze down at me. There's no hint left in his tense face of the supposedly concerned guy who implored me to turn to him if I needed help.

As he takes me in, his eyebrows rise. He makes a scoffing sound. "You. How the hell did *you* find me?"

I scowl at him. "You aren't half as smart as you'd obviously like to believe you are."

Wendos lets out a low chuckle. "And yet somehow no one other than me realized Julita had noticed our activities. I took care of her before our past association became a liability with my colleagues, and I'll take care of you too. The others will never even have to know."

*Oh, he thinks so, does he?* Julita sneers.

A shiver wriggles down my spine. I bite my tongue against the urge to throw Wendos's bragging remarks back at him, to tell him he never managed to get rid of Julita entirely.

The less he thinks I know, the more chance there is that he'll give me an opening.

I still have two knives—one at my right hip and one in my left boot. But I can't risk reaching for them while he's looking straight at me.

The pain in my shin throbs on. Unwanted tears sting behind my eyes.

"What's happened?" one of the armless figures mumbles, turning her sightless face. "Are we—"

Wendos doesn't even look back at her as he snaps out his answer. "I've got it under control. Go back to focusing on your gift."

I lever my body carefully so that my legs are parallel with me on the same step, giving me a more stable position. "The gifts aren't really *theirs* when you and your 'colleagues' convinced them to make their sacrifices for your purpose, are they?"

I pitch my voice so the slouched figures can hear me too. If I can make them rethink helping him…

I can't see them from here, but none of them says another word.

Wendos gives no indication of concern. "It's their purpose too. It'll be better for all of us. Even you, no matter what Julita told you before she died. Who are you really?"

I edge my hand a little closer to my hip. "A friend. Unlike you."

"As you apparently knew from the start." He bears his teeth in an unnerving grin. "That's fine. We'll figure it out."

His gaze sweeps over me, lingering on the blood streaking through my underskirt from my broken shin and how gingerly I've angled my leg. "I don't think you're walking down all those stairs, so you can stay right there until I've finished the important part. Then I'll deal with you."

He starts to turn away.

My heart lurches. I can't just stand here and watch while he compels a horde of daimon to ravage all of Florian.

The men can't be *that* far behind me, can they? With the Crown's Watch at their heels?

Simply delaying him might be all I need.

I blurt out the first thing that pops into my head, desperate to interrupt his work. "How is destroying the city good for anyone?"

Wendos lets out another chilling laugh. "Sometimes you have to knock a few things down in order to build something better. Even the All-Giver knew that. The Order of the Wild will put things right."

He brushes his hand down his front in a three-fingered tap… as if he thinks the divinities would *approve* of this madness. I barely stop my jaw from dropping.

Julita's voice has turned faint. *He's gone even more insane than he was before.*

"The Order of the Wild?" I ask, but Wendos ignores me, walking away. I can't even see the tufts of his stupid shaggy hair from my current position.

"Let's continue," he says to his accomplices, and picks up his previous muttered chant. I can make out the syllables now, but they're no words I know.

The waft of magic they stir raises the hairs on my arms.

As I force my breaths to even out, mastering the pain in my leg, Julita's presence stirs.

*You are, you know,* she says quietly.

I arch an eyebrow in a question Wendos can't hear.

*A friend. You're the best friend I've ever had. However this ends… Thank you.*

Tears that have nothing to do with my fractured shin form behind my eyes. I didn't ask for this mission, and there are plenty of things I've criticized Julita for, but she didn't have to say that. She must know by now there's no need to say anything to get me to keep fighting.

She simply wanted me to know.

I dip my head in silent acknowledgment. Then I lean forward to reach for the sheath in my boot.

If I'm only going to get one chance, I want my favorite knife.

The blade slides out easily, my fingers curling around the familiar hilt. But I can hardly hit Wendos with it when he's out of sight.

He's underestimated me in his arrogance. I have to take full advantage of that fact, whatever way I can.

The daimon on guard only intervened when I got close to Wendos. He indicated in the conversation I overheard after the ball that he can't direct them too specifically.

It's possible that a thrown knife could get past them. I just need to be in a position to actually throw it.

As I shift my legs, I grit my teeth until my jaw is aching nearly as much as my shin. My power twitches inside me, reminding me that I could heal my leg if I wanted to.

But at what cost?

If I could be sure it'd be Wendos's bones broken in my place, that'd be one thing. For all I know, the backlash will hit some innocent person.

Or one of the men hopefully climbing the stairs beneath me, sending them toppling to a snapped neck.

How much good would it do me to fix my leg anyway? I already know that throwing my whole body at this asshole isn't the answer.

With the threat to my life no longer immediate, I can tune out the nagging of my magic, if only some of the physical pain I'm in. I can't put any weight on my one foot, so I angle myself around until I'm squatting on my knees.

My cloak seems likely to trip me up in my current position. It isn't as if I need to hide my dress here.

I untie it and let it slip from my shoulders onto the lower stairs. Then, with my hand braced against the wall and tears I can't blink back welling in my eyes, I lurch up one step.

Then another.

Then another.

Each impact radiates a sharper agony through my leg from foot to hip. The pain crackles through my thoughts, dizzying me. I bite my lip to hold back a whimper.

Without consciously intending to, I find myself picturing Casimir. The affection in his voice when he told me he wanted me. The sparkle of his eyes when he thanked me after our ride through the woods.

He doesn't know the worst of me, no. But he's been there for the parts of me I have let him see. He's made a place for me.

They all have, in their own way.

Stavros, handing the sword to me a couple of hours ago. His bemused shock when he realized just how famous a thief I am.

Alek's anguished apology at my bedside. The firmness of his arms, carrying me from the library to help me hide my pain from prying eyes.

Benedikt and the flippant ease with which he can shatter any tension. The mischief in his smile after he shielded me with a kiss.

Even though I can't have everything my heart might want, I've gotten more than I'd have ever dared to imagine. That's some kind of gift, isn't it?

I don't know who I should thank for it, but I have to keep going.

Hold on to the strength and faith they offered me. Push through the agony.

Another step.

Another.

Veering around a couple of jagged chunks of marble, I reach the last stair left before the gaping hole. A faint breeze cools the sweat on my face, traveling up through the opening to mingle with the open air on the platform.

When I straighten up as tall as I can with my hand still pressed against the inner wall, I can see Wendos's head and shoulders.

I've made it. I'm close enough.

Land a dagger in his back, and he won't be tossing around any more magic.

Maybe he'll die, but at this point I don't feel I can be incredibly picky about how this confrontation ends. A whole lot of other people will die if he finishes the joint sorcery he's attempting.

As I ready my hand, Wendos sucks in an awed breath. "Yes. Yes! It's coming together— Look at all that stone coming crumbling down."

A distant crash reaches my ears even all the way up here. I lose my breath.

It's almost too late.

I whip back my arm and fling the knife forward.

At the same moment, Wendos takes a step to the side.

I clamp my lips against a noise of protest. The knife flies true—and smacks into the flesh of his upper arm that's now in its path.

Wendos yelps and clutches at his arm. He wrenches out the knife and tosses it to the floor.

Julita lets out a cheer, but my heart has sunk.

It wasn't enough after all.

"Fucking bitch," Wendos snarls. "Pin her down. Stop her from moving. I don't care how you do it."

As he spits out several more words in that odd language, I'm struck again by the invisible projectiles that must be daimon. They hurl me to the side.

My chest bangs against one of the chunks of marble, the sharp edge raking down my sternum with the rasp of tearing silk. A new sting of pain flares across the skin beneath my now frayed bodice and undershirt.

The daimon heave me onward to slam me against the outer wall, swinging my broken leg so wildly I groan. Two, maybe three of them press against my body, resisting when I try to move.

*No, no, no!* Julita cries out, but no one other than me can hear her.

"Can we keep going?" the man on the floor asks in an unsteady voice. "The energies feel weakened."

"I'm fine. I'm—" Wendos lets out a hiss of frustration. "I'm bleeding all over the fucking floor. How'm I supposed to concentrate— They'll get loose. Torstem was counting on me... *Fuck.*"

Julita's voice drops to a mutter. *Ha. Serves him right.*

I can't see Wendos anymore, but I hear the scrape of his feet as he turns on his heel. I'd feel more victorious about his partial meltdown if his voice didn't drop to a new frigid low.

"We're so close. It's happening—we can't let the effort falter now. I need you. I need *everything*. For the All-Giver, for the way things should exist, for creating the world this is meant to be."

"We understand," one of the women says, but I don't, not at all.

Not until, over the lip of the platform, I see one of the armless figures lurch toward the railing. She raises her face to the open air she must be able to feel even if she can't see it.

"Hear me, godlen! I give my all to this man's power in this moment, to letting him show the world his way!"

Her declaration rings out toward the sky—and then she pitches herself over the railing.

"No!" The protest bursts from my throat without any thought.

Julita's presence freezes in the back of my skull. *Sky, sea, and earth, what are they* doing?

Even as a sickening thud sounds from the roof far below this tall tower, the other two figures call out their own words of sacrifice. Two more fleshy thumps of fallen bodies reach my ears.

I flinch, stomach acid burning up my throat. For a moment, I'm afraid I'm going to vomit all over my torn dress. The daimon won't let me even buckle over.

They've offered a much grander momentary sacrifice than the blood-letting Wendos once inflicted on Julita. And a voluntary one.

Is it going to work? Will their fatal offerings actually—

Wendos's dark laugh gives me all the answer I need. His voice rises. "That's right! Listen to us. We command you now—all of you!"

He speaks his strange chant louder than before, letting it spill out into the thickening dusk. From far away, I think I hear a panicked shriek.

*Oh, no,* Julita murmurs. *What do we do now?*

I squeeze my eyes shut, my throat closing up too.

I can't let Wendos finish this. The elite of the inner wards don't deserve the horror he's planning to rain down on them, awful as they can be.

And what if the daimon spill their destruction over into the fringes?

What will become of Zuzanna and her sickly son, Marta and her many lovers, Frida and Ewalin gossiping while they tend to the bees...?

My magic claws up through my chest. I tense instinctively... but this time I can't dismiss it completely.

Could calling on my own power now really be *worse* than what'll happen if I don't?

I don't know. I honestly don't know. I have a monster inside me with a mind of its own.

Hopelessness washes over me in a wave, tinged with a strange sense of absurdity.

I've fought with myself for so long. Refused and refused and refused, no matter how my power hurt me.

But I'm the only one here. It's the only weapon I have left.

How can this be the answer? How can I trust myself to make that call?

Unless... Unless I'm not entirely alone.

*Someone* was able to control it once before. Someone who might be watching right now over a temple that bears his and his siblings' blessings.

Even as the temple itself quivers with a quake from below, both my mind and my body balk. Can I really count on the godlen, the divinities who broke souls like mine in punishment for crimes committed five hundred years ago?

What other choice do I have?

Wendos cackles madly between roughened phrases, and my resistance fractures.

I suck in a breath like a sob and will my mind to open. More and more, from the slightest quivering crack until I feel as if my fractured soul is reaching out toward the walls around me.

*Godlen,* I think, like I spoke in my head to the voice while I was dying. *If you can hear me, please help me. Please guide my magic so I don't do harm that's undeserved. Let me stop him without ruining something else.*

*Please.*

No one answers. But a tingle spreads down through my lungs as if ephemeral fingers have brushed over them with the lightest touch.

I might have imagined it, but it's all I've got. There's no time left.

There's a rustle as Wendos swings his arm wildly, and I release my grip on my magic.

# FORTY

My power roars out of me, smacking into the daimon pinning me down. They scatter like puffs of cloud.

The full force of my intent rams into the figure I can't even see where he's poised by the railing.

Through the magic streaming from the fissures in my soul, I feel Wendos jerk and spasm. Taste the power *he* was wielding slip from his fingers as mine devours his will and awareness.

For the space of a heartbeat, rage wells up alongside my power.

He had Julita killed—he would have happily murdered me too. He sent those poor scourge sacrifices to their deaths.

Who knows how many other innocents he's already slaughtered or meant to in his sick quest... for what?

A growl of fury passes over my lips. My power wraps around him—

And I remember.

I remember the man who attacked me seven years ago, the second and until yesterday last time I unleashed my magic. How my gut knotted when I stared down at his slumped corpse and the destruction spiraling out around it.

I remember that Wendos is only the beginning of the conspiracy, not the end. There's so much more we need to unravel if anyone's going to be safe.

With a gasp, I snatch at the power rushing out of me. I heave all the control I can summon into yanking the magic back, reining it in like it's a stallion I have to tame.

Just stop him. Just stop him—don't shatter him completely.

A giddy warmth spreads through my limbs and across my chest. I sense Wendos's body crumpling.

I haul every shred of power I can catch back into me.

That's enough. That's enough, for now.

Gods above, let it be enough forever.

As the torrent of magic contracts, I shove myself onto my feet—and realize that I can stand without agony. Some of the damage I inflicted on Wendos must have bounced back the opposite effect into me.

The scratch on my chest has healed, my gown's bodice and the ripped chemise beneath drooping open between my breasts over smooth skin. My shin is solid.

I jerk up my head and freeze.

All across the walls of the tower, vines have sprouted. Slim, green tendrils unfurl from notches and cracks. They spread vibrant green leaves to the last hazy glow of the setting sun.

More twine together across the gap in the staircase, forming a woven ramp to seal the hole.

I dealt out harm, and I conjured new growth. And not a growth that's going to hurt anyone—not like last time.

A laugh hitches out of my throat, and I press my hand to my mouth.

I scramble to the edge of the collapsed staircase and tread more carefully onto the ramp of vines. It holds my weight with only a slight give.

No more distant rumbles or shrieks reach my ears. The tower doesn't shake again. The thrum of unsettling magic has vanished.

By cutting Wendos down, I ended whatever horrible spell he and his colleagues were constructing.

With another step, I can see him.

Wendos sprawls on his side on the floor of the tower platform, unmoving, his limbs strewn about. But as I watch, his chest lifts and falls with a halting breath.

I hit him hard, but I didn't kill him. I held on to that one bit of control.

Julita laughs more openly, with a sensation as if she's spinning excitedly in my head. *You did it! You knocked him right down.* She pauses. *What exactly* was *it you did?*

My lips part. Before I can decide on an answer, a different voice that's no longer unfamiliar reverberates through my nerves as if from all around me.

*Well done, my wayward rogue. When you welcome me, I can come. And I suspect we'll work together again before long. But for now you have a rather different problem to attend to.*

What?

I freeze, my gaze searching the platform for potential threats—and the rasp of an indrawn breath carries from behind me.

I spin around and find myself facing three men who've stiffened where they're standing just past the final bend in the stairs.

Casimir's expression looks sickly. Alek is leaning against the wall as if he's about to fall right over. And Stavros...

Stavros is staring at me like he's never seen me before. Staring at the bare skin down my sternum it's too late to hide, where no godlen sigil brands my flesh.

Staring around me at the vegetation called up by a power no godless person should be able to wield. Past me toward the man I struck down with that power.

"I stopped him," I say, my voice coming out with a creak. "I stopped him."

But it looks like I haven't yet paid the price.

# Thief of Silver and Souls - Bonus Scene

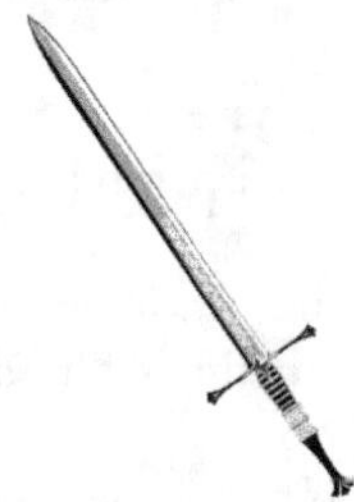

*How did Ivy's men react to her storming off and getting stabbed in chapter 32, and how did Stavros feel when he discovered her secret identity in chapter 34? You can get all the details in this bonus scene from his point of view...*

*Stavros*

The thief glares at us, her body taut and her rumpled red-blond hair shining in the lantern's glow. To my hazy vision, she's like a lit match come to life.

"If this is the thanks I'm going to get after I've stuck my neck on the line a dozen times, I've had enough," she snaps out to end her tirade, and darts past me.

Her previous comments are still ringing in my ears. Her claims about how Julita exploited our weaknesses—*my* weaknesses. How easily the woman who brought us together manipulated us all.

I can't even say I believe she's lying.

But we're not done with the interloper in our midst either. I whip my right hand out to catch her arm, but she dodges as swiftly as ever.

With a flick of her hand, she's already grasping the right books to trigger the secret passage.

I wrench myself around. "Ivy, you can't just flee like a—"

In the space of those words, she dives into the shadowy opening in the wall. The plaster solidifies in her wake.

Blast it all.

I push myself forward to give chase. But as I reach for the same books, Casimir lets out an urgent sound. "What do you think you're going to say to her?"

"It doesn't matter," I retort, my voice coming out in a growl. "We weren't finished with this conversation."

The courtesan manages to sound mild but firm at the same time. "*She* appears to be finished with it. Do you really think you're going to get any further with her if you barge after her ordering her to listen?"

My hand hesitates on the books. I wouldn't have been much of a general if I couldn't see logic even when my temper's riled.

Aleksi speaks up before I have to say anything else. "She was trying to make us angry, wasn't she? Everything she said about Julita…"

He hesitates. His mask might hide most of his expression, but his distress is obvious in the strain in his voice, the tense slant of his mouth.

Out of all of us, the scholar was always the softest on Julita. I didn't need to be any kind of companionship specialist to have noticed that.

Casimir's tone gentles. "I don't know if that's how Ivy would have presented things if she hadn't been upset. But I think we all know that Jules was perfectly willing to flatter and flirt to get what she wanted."

"And what did she want more than to never have to worry about scourge sorcerers again?" Benedikt says wryly, but there's a tension in his face too that suggests he's not much happier about the situation than Aleksi is.

I don't particularly want to get into this subject. Julita was lovely to look at and charming to speak with, and yes, she flattered me and even sometimes flirted with me. I never *truly* believed she felt anything more than friendly affection for any of us.

But there could have been a moment now and then when it felt good to indulge in the fantasy that she might.

What niggles at me more is the idea of her looking at me—at the most quickly decorated general of my generation, at the champion of dozens of battles against our greatest enemies, entrapper of riven, and a decent professor whether I wanted the job or not—and seeing only the cracks I buried so very deep. The fissure lines where she could pry her fingers in and prod me into doing her bidding.

I'm here, aren't I? I followed her this far, on a quest I've barely seen any evidence to justify myself beyond her reports.

Fuck.

I clench my jaw. "It doesn't really matter, does it? Julita's *gone*, in just about every way that matters. You couldn't have her even if she wanted you, Aleksi."

The scholar winces. "I never said—I wouldn't have presumed—" He pauses. "I didn't even know her all that well."

His gaze slides to the wall Ivy vanished through. I wonder how well he's gotten to know the thief in our midst.

The woman whose sardonic retorts and totally un-thief-like honor have gotten under my skin in equal measure.

The woman who had no real stake in this fight but has not only stuck it out but gained us more ground in a matter of weeks than Julita did in months.

The woman who shines like a flame and sparks more emotion in me than I've wanted to look at.

Which possibly is why that spark flared into a full out inferno I can't say she necessarily deserved the moment I saw her with Casimir in their intimately disheveled state.

"We still need to settle things with Ivy," I insist.

Casimir smiles tightly. "I agree. But we need to settle them the right way, or she's going to flee right out of the college and our lives. She came down to the archives feeling uneasy. She was already convinced that she's too out of place here to really contribute, even after everything she's done. And you all hammered that point farther home."

I grimace. She hadn't sounded all that out of sorts… but I can recognize that if even *I* barely feel like I belong in this place, a woman who's been living on the streets of the outer wards can't be having an easy time of it.

I shouldn't have called her a street rat again. I'd be an idiot not to know she's more than that at this point.

"All right," I say. "We find her, and we show that we can calmly discuss the actual matters we're here for and put the rest behind us."

Benedikt snorts, but he moves toward the wall alongside me. Apparently Casimir is satisfied with my current attitude, because he and Alek join us as I finally open the passage.

We tramp up the shadowy stairs. I peer into the hallway of the tapestries first, confirming no one's around.

No one to see us together… and no Ivy either.

She's gotten quite a head start.

The royal bastard glances in both directions as he emerges with the others. "Which way do you figure she went?"

"She didn't want to deal with us," Aleksi says in his flatly pedantic way. "I doubt she wanted to encounter anyone else in this wretched place either. She'd have gone around the back rather than past the library."

I can't argue with his reasoning. Biting back my annoyance, I jog toward the bend at the end of the hallway.

The others hustle behind me.

"Perhaps we should split up," Benedikt suggests. "I'm sure she's made it out of the building by now. We can spread out, and whoever encounters her first summons the others."

I'm about to agree when I round the corner, and my gaze catches on a form slumped on the floor in a heap of dark green silk.

Ivy was wearing a dark green gown.

A bark of alarm breaks from my throat. Then next thing I know, I'm charging down the hall as fast as my feet will carry me.

My vision clouds as I try to focus on the crumpled body. I shake my head as I run, jerking my gaze away and back again, every trick I know to regain my focus for the second or two my ruined eyes will give me before it all goes hazy again.

I see her red-blond hair, like spilled sap rather than a flame now.

I see the glint of a deeper red in the liquid spreading around her torso.

My heart thunders in my chest. My thoughts whirl in my head in a constant chain of *fuck no fuck no fuck no.*

We ran her off. We told her she'd let us down, she decided she'd had enough assholery, and now…

I'm vaguely aware of other footsteps thumping around me. Of a gasp and a strangled sound from my companions.

I drop down by her fanned hair, sliding my fingers around her throat, praying and bracing myself at the same time.

*Sabrelle, this wasn't a fair fight. Look down on her, let her live, let me feel her pulse.*

There's no way of knowing if my patron godlen or any other heard my plea, but a faint heartbeat stutters against my fingertips.

"She's not gone yet," I rasp out, turning toward the wound. The red-stained fabric, clearly punctured by a knife, blurs before my eyes.

Benedikt crouches by the top of Ivy's head, swaying a little with the color drained from his face. "Fuck. All that blood."

Aleksi stumbles to a halt and stares down at the scene. "Who would have—is she even still breathing?"

Was he not listening to me? I ignore the question, groping for the thin laces I can only focus on for a second at a time. "Loosen her gown! I need to see the wound."

Casimir skids to a stop, his eyes wide. "Ivy… I'll bring a medic."

He spins around and dashes back the way we came. At least one of my allies has kept his head enough to do something useful.

Aleksi is fumbling with the dress's ties. As he works them loose, I ease back the panel of fabric over the wound to try to get a closer look.

A groan sputters from Ivy's lips.

"She's alive!" Benedikt blurts out, because apparently he was too shellshocked to process what I said earlier either.

Aleksi glances up at me, his hands closing into fists. "You're hurting her."

I scowl at him. "I've got to stabilize her as much as I can." With another twitch of my head, I take in the severed flesh. "It's a clean cut, but not bleeding as badly as—"

Neither of the other men appears to be listening to me, too busy gaping at the fallen thief again. Gritting my teeth, I cut myself off and reach farther down her dress.

With a sharp yank, I tear a broad strip off the outer layer of the skirt. I bunch it over the wound in an attempt to stem the bleeding as much as I can.

As I exert pressure on the spot, Ivy gasps. Her eyelids jerk half-open.

"There's our fighter," Benedikt says in a reassuring tone, as if he's done anything at all for her in the last few minutes. "We're getting you help, Ivy."

It may not come fast enough. The knowledge clamps around my gut.

She didn't deserve this. Not a bloody death in the Domi's hallway, not the shit we hurled at her just before.

She *has* stuck her neck out, just by coming here. This wasn't even her fight.

The ache in my gut swells into a burn of determination. Whatever happens to her, the brutes who did this are not getting away with it.

I jab my elbow toward Aleksi. "Hold this. Firm but not forceful."

As he takes over my makeshift compress, I ease over to peer into Ivy's face. She stares back at me, her stunning blue eyes turning muddled to me as my vision hazes again. But it isn't her looks I need to take in right now.

I need her words.

But gods above, it sharpens the ache inside to see her face so pale and slack. I tap my hand down my front in a silent appeal to the divinities before I find my voice.

It comes out thick and dark. "Who stabbed you? Who fucking did this, Ivy?"

"I wouldn't have thought Anya would go *this* far..." Alek mumbles as if I asked him.

The royal bastard lets out a snort. "Not when it might mean getting blood-splatter on her pretty dress."

I bare my teeth at the two of them. "Let Ivy tell us."

Her lips move. A wordless croak seeps out of them. Her jaw seems to work.

The faintest whisper emerges. "The wind..."

The *wind?* Or am I mishearing, and that's the start of someone's name? Thew Ind? Thewin D-something?

Thudding footsteps break through my panicked confusion.

"Here!" Casimir shouts. "Please hurry. I don't know—it looks awful."

A woman in a medic's robe hurries after him. Aleksi and Benedikt pull away so she can kneel beside me and examine the wound.

I ease to the side as well, feeling abruptly, chillingly helpless. There's nothing *any* of us can do that really matters here.

Ivy will survive or die based on the limitations of the medic's magic.

My hand comes to rest on Ivy's head, as if she's likely to take any comfort from my touch. I stiffen against a shudder that runs through my body.

The medic inhales with a rasp and rests her hands over the wound. "I'll do whatever I can..."

She closes her eyes in concentration. After a few heart-wrenching moments, she adjusts her position and then focuses again.

"The cut doesn't go as deep as I thought from looking at the amount of blood," she says with obvious surprise. "Somehow it didn't puncture her lung."

I know enough about battle wounds that a portion of tension rushes out of me. No vital organs pierced?

Our thief was damned lucky.

The medic stands. "I've patched her up well enough that she can be moved. We need to get her to the infirmary for the rest of the treatment."

Aleksi has folded his arms across his chest. "Will she make it?"

The medic's forehead furrows. "I think… I think she will. You must have found her just in time."

I'm by far the strongest of the five of us around her, and the only one other than perhaps the medic with significant experience carrying the wounded. I'm not letting anyone else lay their hands on her.

I give Ivy's shoulder a gentle squeeze. "I'm going to be as careful with you as I can be, Ivy. You can curse me out later for however much it ends up hurting."

Great God help me, I'm looking forward to that tongue-lashing. I'd listen to her hurl verbal daggers at me for days if it means never having to see her laid this low again.

I slide my arms around her as carefully as I can manage and lift her so she's tipped against my chest. She's such a forceful presence when she wants to be that I've forgotten just how slight her body actually is. It feels wrong, the lightness of her sprawled limp in my grasp.

I brace my prosthetic against the ball of silk containing any lingering bleeding and stride toward the infirmary with the medic leading the way.

I'm not sure how much attention I actually pay to the staff meeting I've been summoned to. Someone mentions proper evacuation procedures, and someone else scoffs at the idea of those ever being necessary, and someone *else* rants about needing to keep the students safe—and my mind is back in my bedroom.

Has Ivy woken up yet? The medics *said* she should fully recover.

But you never actually know how a major wound has affected a person until you can speak with them.

A quake ripples through the room, and everyone tenses. My right hand clenches at my side.

I couldn't think of anywhere safer to bring Ivy than my own blasted room. Maybe I should carry her right out of the college.

My mind definitely shouldn't linger on how comfortable she looked tucked beneath my covers, her bright hair spilling across my pillow. As if she belonged there.

Chairs scrape, telling me the meeting is finally over, thank the gods. I hustle out of the room as fast as I can move without provoking stares, down to the first floor of the Quadring and out into the courtyard…

Where a figure whose gait I recognize at a glance is just slipping into the shadows of the Quadring's main entry hall, a few strands of her red-blond hair drifting from beneath the hood of her cloak to catch the sunlight.

I stall in my tracks and then barge after her. What in the All-Giver's name does that obstinate woman think she's doing now?

How is she even on her feet? She was still out cold when I left not much more than an hour ago.

I'm going to haul her right back to my bed and chain her there if that's what it takes for her to actually rest.

But as I follow behind her, something about her furtive movements gives me pause. She tugs her hood lower, flits from shadow to shadow to avoid notice. And she's heading for the gate that'll take her right out of the college.

Is she truly fleeing on us—as far as she can get? Abandoning the cause now that it's come so close to killing her?

My chest constricts, but I don't know if I could fairly blame her if she's made that decision.

Maybe I should give her the choice. A chance to leave all the shit here behind.

I'm not going to leave her completely at the mercy of the city streets when she almost died yesterday, though.

At the gate, I let myself fall farther back. I set my feet carefully on the cobblestones, drawing on all the techniques for stealth my father taught me.

Every few seconds I sweep my gaze back and forth to regain my focus. A dark brown cloak with the trim of a pale green dress showing beneath it.

Just keep following that figure.

I almost lose her a couple of times in the inner wards when she makes an abrupt detour into an alley or through a shop. But I've prowled these streets enough times in the past year to know my way around. After a few tense minutes, I catch sight of her up ahead again.

Once she's hopped over the old city wall, she seems to relax more. Fewer glances over her shoulder, fewer sudden diversions.

She isn't really expecting to be followed. She assumes anyone who had questions about her leaving the college would have confronted her by now.

I draw a little closer so I have less chance of being left behind while still keeping the length of several buildings between us.

Those buildings become increasingly shabby, the scents of rotting food and emptied chamber pots clogging my lungs. Ivy doesn't slow her pace for a second.

She's taken out a leather pouch I don't remember seeing on her before, curling her fingers around its smooth surface.

Not long after, she pauses to peer around her. I leap into the shadows behind the shack I was skirting before she's quite turned around.

When I sneak a glance around the slanted wooden side of the building, Ivy's taking a sudden turn where there isn't a road at all. She clambers over a ramshackle fence into the back garden—if you can call the scruffy patch of weeds that—behind one of the outer-ward shacks.

As I ease a few steps nearer, she delves into the pouch and extends her hand toward the shack's rear window.

Something glints silver in the afternoon light. I give my head a twitch to briefly hone my vision.

She's left a small stack of coins on the window ledge.

I stop in my tracks and simply stare for the space of a few breaths, my mind spinning. It can't really— What are the chances—

I force myself to walk closer and peer down the row of houses she's slinking along. Matching piles of coins gleam at two more windows, and she's just reaching toward a fourth.

Gods above. It's really her.

It's obvious where Ivy's route will take her. I double back to a parallel street and stride along it so I'll be in place when she finishes her series of offerings.

I've called her a thief since the first time we knew she wasn't some childhood friend of Julita's. I said it with such fucking *disdain*.

The woman who's been sleeping on my sofa for the past two weeks, who I've derided and belittled… has been running the largest charity operation in the city secretly and steadily for the past five years.

A charity operation almost certainly funded by ill-gotten gains, to be sure. But having met the

Hand of Kosmel now, I'm even more certain than I was before that any complaining merchant who lost loot to her thievery had gotten the wealth pretty ill to begin with.

Ivy isn't the type to make innocents suffer. I figured that out before I had any clue she'd built a life around reversing as much suffering as she can.

How many risks has she taken... how many patrolling soldiers dodged... how many tight squeezes barely escaped...?

Just to do this. Little stacks of coins at the windows of those who have the least and need it the most.

I position myself just out of view by the next cross-street. It takes several more minutes for Ivy to come into view, gracefully vaulting over the final fence.

I suppose Julita must say something to her, because she ducks her head as she starts up the street —toward me, back the way she came.

"I'm not," she murmurs. "I'm going back. I just needed to—"

I step out in front of her before she has to go on. Ivy jerks to a halt, staring at me.

What am I supposed to say to her?

Like I have so often in the past year, I grasp hold of the dryly nonchalant air that's seen me through ambushes and rallying of my troops as easily as rounds exchanged at the pub, hiding every trace of vulnerability that no one else needs to see.

"So, you're even more of a thief than I guessed."

# Games of Death and Desire

## Rites of Possession #2

# ONE

Ivy

A once exalted general is pointing a sword at me—and somehow that feels like the least of my problems.

Stavros's grip on the sword tightens enough that his light brown knuckles pale in the dim twilight. He takes a wary step up the curving staircase of the tower toward me.

Toward the woven vines I'm standing on that fill the gap where daimon smashed several of the stone stairs. The vines that my monstrous magic called forth.

The same magic twitches in my chest, tugging at me to let it push Stavros away, shatter his sword —defend me.

I clamp down hard on the urge. Releasing my power is what got me into this mess in the first place.

There's got to be a way we can all walk down from this tower alive.

My hand starts to lift toward the torn folds of fabric on my chest where a fall ripped open the bodice of my dress. Stavros twitches both his head and the sword.

"Don't move an inch," he says in a voice so low and dark it sends a shiver down my spine.

I suppose it wouldn't do any good to cover up the bare skin he's already seen—the smooth flesh between my breasts where nearly anyone else would bear a godlen brand. The absence of a brand means I shouldn't be able to wield any magic at all.

Other than the kind that'll get me executed, that is.

The massive man has always cut an imposing figure, but I've never felt so close to death, not even when he held a sword right against my throat. Through the rattle of my frantic pulse, I register that the sword he's holding now isn't his usual blade, which is still sheathed at his hip.

No, it's the short sword with the royal crest on its hilt that he gave to me just hours ago, when he told me all he wanted was to keep me safe.

As tense as I already am, my stomach balls even tighter.

I'm never going to hear sentiments like that from Stavros's lips again.

He takes another step, his gaze sliding past me for just a second. For long enough that even his unsteady vision will be able to pick out the body slumped on the platform just above me.

The man I nearly killed.

It was *nearly*, not completely. I can take a shred of pride in the self-control I held on to, even if the former general won't see the situation that way.

The words tumble out of me. "I didn't kill Wendos. I only— He was summoning daimon to attack the city."

I sense one of those spirit-creatures flitting past me with a ripple of my skirt, and then it's gone. The several daimon that pinned me down on Wendos's orders all appear to have fled.

"I had to stop him," I go on. "But the Crown's Watch will still be able to question him, find out... find out who he was working with."

My voice falters with the hardening of Stavros's expression. I hadn't thought his stunningly chiseled features could get any fiercer than they already were, but I was wrong.

"What exactly did you do?" he demands.

My hands clench at my sides. I can't help glancing past him toward the other two men poised farther down the staircase.

Alek has managed to straighten up a little, though his bronze-brown hand is still braced against the wall as if he needs the support. It's always hard to judge the scholar's reactions with his polished leather mask covering most of his face, but his full lips are set in the stiffest line I've ever seen.

He jerks his hand down his front in a shaky gesture of the divinities—three fingers tapping forehead for sky, heart for sea, and gut for earth before they all fist over his sternum. I restrain a cringe at the thought of any more godly attention being drawn to us.

Casimir—the man who welcomed me from the start, who treated me like a friend and sometimes more—simply stares at me. His gorgeous face has drained of color, leaving his normally peachy skin as sallow as my own. None of his usual grace shows in his rigid stance.

They all know. They know what they're seeing, what this scene must signify.

Denying it will only make me look guiltier.

A rasp creeps into my voice. "I don't want to be what I am. I don't want this power. I don't *use* it —I haven't been using it—I tried everything and there was nothing else, and he was going to destroy the city. I managed not to hurt anyone but him."

Which would be a first.

The other participant in our standoff, the ghost who's an uninvited guest inside my head, pipes up a little shakily. *Ivy, you're... you're riven?*

I hadn't wanted to say the word myself. I don't see the need to answer Julita. Even to a minor noblewoman who's barely been outside her own county and the capital city's royal college, the source of my godless magic must be obvious.

Stavros's sword hasn't wavered. He makes a scoffing sound. "And you expect us to believe you? Of course you'd claim all that now that you're caught."

It's a battle already lost. The riven are reviled throughout the continent, and Stavros hates magic like mine more than just about anyone.

Still, I can't stop myself from arguing. "Other than just now and keeping myself from *dying* yesterday, I haven't let my magic out in seven wretched years. I'd snuff the power right out of me if I knew how."

But the problem is how I'm torn already. The cracks in my soul that let endless magic seep through me, taking and sacrificing without limit if I give it free rein.

Alek finally speaks, his voice thin. "Riven sorcerers go mad with their power. It consumes them. That's what always happens."

I swallow thickly. "Well, apparently it's possible to at least delay that outcome for a while, if you're stubborn enough. Why do you think I've been refusing it? The magic would like me to bring it out every blasted moment I could. You can be sure it never shuts up about how disappointed it is."

Casimir eases up a step, his deep blue gaze gone pensive. "Is it because of your magic that Julita… Is *that* how her soul ended up inside you?"

Julita's presence shudders in the back of my skull. *Gods above, maybe it is.*

I answer both her and the courtesan at the same time. "I don't know. I didn't use any magic when I tried to save her. If I had, she'd be alive and we wouldn't be here right now, and somehow I don't think you'd be upset about it then."

Stavros's lips draw back from his teeth in a silent snarl. "You wielded the power meant as divine punishment in the greatest temple in Silana—in the All-Giver's own fucking tower. Don't try to take the moral high ground."

My jaw sets on edge. "If the gods had a problem with it, I don't think one of them would have been egging me on."

"*What?*" Alek blurts out, swiping his messy black waves back from where they'd shaded his eyes.

"He told me to use it after I was stabbed. Practically ordered me to. I would have let myself die otherwise—I didn't even exactly *agree*—and he spoke to me again just now—"

Stavros cuts me off with a sputter of a laugh. "You *are* insane. If the gods even noticed you were here, they—"

Then his voice dies too, with a widening of his eyes and another subtle twitch to refocus his sight. At the same moment, Alek and Casimir freeze all over again.

Alek's lips part in apparent shock. Casimir's eyebrows jolt upward.

A tingling sensation like a waft of magic brings my own gaze down, to the spot on my chest they're staring at. My pulse lurches.

The skin between the torn flaps of my bodice was bare a moment ago. Now a godlen sigil shimmers there, an unearthly glow against the thickening darkness of the night.

Two lines arch from a central apex, with two smaller points poking from their peaks like little horns.

Kosmel's sigil.

Well, I figured he was the most likely of any of the nine lesser gods to support my riven magic. The godlen of luck and rebellion is known to appreciate a little chaos.

But I keep staring at the glowing mark just as the men are, my jaw gone slack. That's divine magic shining against my body.

Like I've been claimed, without any say in it.

Kosmel must be trying to help my case here. If he didn't want me dead from a knife wound, he won't want me ending up with a noose around my neck either. He's confirming my story.

Part of me recoils all the same. I didn't ask for this—I purposefully skipped my dedication ceremony. I've avoided the attention of our deities in every way I know how.

My soul's been ravaged by godly retribution enough without anyone else sticking their divine fingers in.

For the first time, Stavros's sword wavers. Even he isn't going to suggest that a riven sorcerer could get away with blasphemous fraud in the grandest building that bears all the gods' blessings.

He doesn't outright lower the blade either, though.

"You—" he starts, and Casimir's head jerks to the side with a ripple of his tawny hair.

"Someone's coming," he says quickly. "Probably the Crown's Watch. Stavros—we can't hand Ivy over to them. Not when Kosmel himself is watching over her. We should at least give her more of a chance to explain. She's never hurt any of us, and gods know she's had plenty of opportunity."

Alek purses his lips. "We need to understand exactly what's going on."

Stavros inhales with a hiss through his teeth, but his sword hand drops to his side. He glares at me while he answers the others. "What are we going to say happened here, then?"

As my spirits rise with the unexpected reprieve, fragments of an idea come together in my head. "Let me handle that. I'm the one who *was* here for most of it."

Stavros grimaces as if he's going to argue, but right then the sound of hurried footsteps reverberates from just around the bend in the stairs.

My pulse stutters for a different reason. "This battle isn't over. There are other scourge sorcerers out there. If they find out we were working together—"

I don't need to say any more. I doubt the former general cares about protecting my identity at this point, but he spins to charge down the stairs and meet the incoming brigade while motioning Alek and Casimir farther up the steps.

The glowing sigil has faded away. I snatch at the torn fabric of my bodice to cover my lack of dedication brand just as a familiar blond head comes into view beyond the other men.

"I've brought the full squadron of royal soldiers," Benedikt announces. The king's bastard half-nephew sounds a little ragged but still manages a jaunty lilt. "Although from the fact that all the shaking and crashing stopped a few minutes ago, I assume we're not quite as urgently needed as expected?"

A couple of men in the rich blue uniforms of the Crown's Watch appear behind him at the front of the squadron. I draw farther to the side where I'm less visible. My mouth has gone dry.

One word from Stavros, one swerve in his resolve back toward ridding the world of all illicit sorcery, and I'll be meeting the hangman tomorrow.

His voice comes out terse. "It appears everything is under control now. There's only one villain up here, and he's been subdued. You're welcome to bring him down the tower to take him into custody."

Benedikt lets out a soft huff. "Barely needed at all, then. Well, I was happy to lead the charge all the same."

One of the soldiers in view lets out a snort he doesn't even try to stifle. Benedikt's grin stiffens just for a second.

He turns toward the squadron. "The threat has been quelled. It's been an honor ushering you into battle even if it never happened."

The other soldier I can see barely spares Benedikt a glance, his attention focusing on Stavros. "Are you sure all's clear up here, General? This fop didn't seem to know much about anything."

The self-proclaimed "bastard's bastard" lets out a light chuckle as if he thinks the insult is a joke. Stavros taps his prosthetic hand against Benedikt's arm in a subtle gesture of solidarity.

"None of us was sure what we were going to be dealing with," he says. "But the immediate danger has passed. I need to speak with the king. If a few of you could go ahead and inform him that I'll require a private meeting—"

"I could—" Benedikt starts to volunteer.

But the first of the nearby soldiers is already turning away from him to shoulder down the stairs. Benedikt falls silent and gives an awkward shrug.

Stavros strides back up the steps and over the woven vines, I suppose to collect Wendos's unconscious body. But he pauses beside me just long enough to speak in a dark murmur.

"You'll come with me and follow my lead to the letter, or gods help me, Kosmel will find himself missing a Hand too."

# Two

The thief walks down the shadowy palace corridor with a meekness she's never shown in my presence before.

On our way down the tower, she picked up the cloak she must have discarded, and now she has it wrapped tight over her dress. Her head dips low beneath the hood that conceals her pale red-blond hair. Her shoulders have hunched as if she's drawing in on herself.

She's trying to make herself look weak. Fragile.

Because she's just proven herself to be the exact opposite to an extent I never could have imagined.

Not just a street-hardened petty criminal. Not even just the charitable vigilante the outer-warders dubbed the Hand of Kosmel.

Gods smite me, I've had one of the riven under my nose for weeks and never suspected.

As I walk a step behind where I can keep a careful eye on her, my fingers clench around the hilt of my sword. I can't draw it, because the blasted royal bastard insisted on accompanying us to see King Konram in case his familial influence could be of use with his half-uncle, and he wouldn't understand why I'd like to keep a blade pointed Ivy's way.

I don't know if I should tell him. I don't know if I should already be planning how to run her through and explain why afterward.

The uncertainty gnaws at my gut.

I was coming to respect her. To appreciate her presence. To *want* to hear her snarky comebacks when I heckled her, to see the hesitant way she'd brighten when I offered a friendlier remark.

Great God help me, just remembering the moment when I handed her my old sword with its royal seal sets an unwelcome warmth blooming in my chest. I grit my teeth and smother the sensation.

How much of her mix of mettle and vulnerability was an act?

Just how wretched an imbecile have I been?

My wooden prosthetic feels like a dead weight on my arm. I didn't have time to swap it for a metal one shaped for combat, which would at least give me another advantage.

Bizarrely, I wish I hadn't sent Casimir and Aleksi back to the college. It was a split-second decision based on wanting to keep our group out of the public eye, as secret as this particular route through the palace is.

It isn't as if the scholar or the courtesan would be much help in a fight against a riven sorcerer. Fuck, *I* wouldn't be much use in that fight.

The only way you take down one of the riven is by surprise. Might to might, you'll always lose.

At least if they were here, the decision wouldn't rest entirely on me. Whether to lunge and bash her head against the plastered wall beside us or keep escorting her on, bringing one of the most dangerous beings in existence to a chat with the king.

I don't think even riven magic could harm him through the precautions he takes for an unguarded conversation, but who can say what a monster might be capable of?

Ivy is the only one who knows what happened when she confronted that prick Wendos. What he said about his scourge sorcerer colleagues and their plans.

Kill this riven woman, and we lose our best chance of stopping a whole horde of even viler villains.

But what lingers in my mind the most is the image of Kosmel's sigil glowing on her chest. The look that came over her face when she noticed it too, startled and then almost horrified.

She didn't ask for the godlen's blessing. He imposed it on her.

I'm not arrogant enough to argue with a divine being.

Aleksi is right. We need to figure out what this all means. Which requires that she stay alive for at least a little longer.

The back of her head has turned into a blur, as everything does if I hold my gaze in the same place for more than a second or two. As if I'm looking through a window that's hazed with condensation.

I flick my attention to the hall ahead and then back to this unpredictable woman for another brief moment of clarity.

Is Julita still in her head? I can't picture how our former ally would respond to the revelations we've just heard.

Whatever Julita thought of me when we worked together, I'd like to believe she'd understand if I have to end the scrap of a life she's managed to cling on to via her reluctant host.

Even with the thief's meek stance, there's still a confidence to the way she moves. As if she always knows exactly where she's putting her feet—and how she'd need to pivot at an unexpected interruption.

I have to yank my attention away before my appreciation of her subtle assurance brings my gaze skimming down her slim body. It's traveled that path before more times than I'd like to admit, with a flicker of heat I can't allow now.

When we reach the door to the king's most private meeting room, I push a little ahead of Ivy and Benedikt. I'm one of the few who knows how to handle the carving on the wooden surface to disengage the lock.

With a flash of flaring magical sconces, we step into a small, windowless sitting room that nonetheless demonstrates the palace's splendor. With a flick of my eyes, I take in the velvet cushions on the chairs and the gold gilding around the fireplace.

What matters most is the huge, gold-framed mirror that stands against the wall next to the fireplace, taller and broader than even me. I motion for Ivy and Benedikt to join me before it.

I don't know what gift allowed the creation of this mirror or how long it's been in the Melchiorek family. It's a fantastic trick, allowing King Konram to speak with trusted advisors without even a guard overhearing while remaining in the security of his personal chambers.

There must be something in the room that alerts him to our entry. Within a matter of seconds, our reflection on the mirror shudders and ripples away, replaced by the king's regal form.

In the first instant before my sight clouds, I take in the sternness of his deep-set eyes and the tight set of his thin lips. It's late in the day for handling official business, but a king's job is never truly done.

"Ster. Stavros and companions," Konram says with a slight nod of acknowledgment. Unlike his soldiers, he never makes the error of calling me by my lost military title. "It's been a tumultuous day, but I gather we're closer to answers than the last time we spoke?"

I draw my posture even straighter than it already was. Through months of practice, I hold my gaze steady on him as if my vision isn't hazed. I can see well enough to make out the basic shapes of his features if not the details.

I might not be serving under him as a general any longer—I might have fucked up not just my career but so many other things that mattered more as well—but he still values my input. I have to show I'm worthy of his generous trust.

"It appears that the scourge sorcerers I told you about were responsible for a great deal of the destruction today," I say, going over my mental inventory of that damage. Part of the college's Quadring building, a row of shops a few blocks away, a nobleman's home on another corner.

I gather myself before continuing with the part that makes me balk. "I mentioned that my assistant, Ivy, was helping us investigate. She confronted one of the sorcerers directly in the All-Giver's tower of the Temple of the Crown."

Konram's head turns so he can study Ivy. "You saw the supposed scourge sorcery first-hand?"

Ivy keeps her cloak close around her, but she lifts her chin with the fire I'm used to from her. "I saw enough to know it isn't 'supposed.' I found Wendos of Nikodi at the top of the tower, conducting a ritual. He had three accomplices with him—people whose power he was taking to bolster his own."

The king frowns. "And when you say taking, you mean…?"

Ivy's voice tightens. "It seems these scourge sorcerers are attempting to avoid the gods' retribution by using a slightly different strategy than the ones centuries ago. Rather than having people die in sacrifice, they're manipulating their accomplices into sacrificing every body part they can spare while remaining alive. Presumably so they have as large a gift as possible to lend the conspirators ongoing power."

My stomach roils at her words. Every part they could spare? The image her words stir in my mind is sickening.

I didn't see any accomplices with Wendos in the tower, but I'm not going to question her story while my king is in the middle of doing so himself.

"That does complicate matters," Konram says. "Do you know what the purpose of tonight's ritual was?"

Ivy dips her head. "Wendos said he was trying to combine his and his accomplices' powers with those of two other sorcerers who were working elsewhere in the city. They'd already been exerting some control over the daimon—I'm sure they encouraged the creatures to attack everyone at the ball the other night. This time they wanted a larger scale disaster, wreaking havoc throughout the inner wards and maybe the rest of the city too."

Konram hums to himself. "So we're dealing with at least two other members of this conspiracy then."

Ivy hesitates and then ventures, "From the way he was talking, I think it's quite a few more. Unfortunately, Wendos didn't mention any names… except Ster. Torstem. And I believe one of the sacrificial accomplices was an orphan Ster. Torstem groomed for the role. Possibly they all were."

She got confirmation about Torstem. A strange lurching sensation runs through me, half exhilarated, half queasy.

We're getting closer to the root of the conspiracy. But I never wanted to believe one of my fellow professors was involved.

With a slight tick of my eyes, I make out the furrowing of the king's brow before everything blurs again. "The law professor? I've looked into his past conduct—there's been nothing amiss."

Benedikt steps forward with a quick bob of a bow and a flash of a smile. "If I may, Your Highness, from what I've seen of Ivy over the past few weeks, she may be sharper than the rest of us combined. She wouldn't say a thing like that if she wasn't certain."

Konram barely spares the royal bastard a glance. "My certainty is what's more important."

"Wendos was very clear about Ster. Torstem's involvement before he even knew I was there to overhear," Ivy says, her tone mild but firm. "He was threatening one of the sacrificial accomplices that Torstem would take her back to where he'd hidden some of them away if she couldn't pull her weight. You'll be able to ask him yourself when he comes to."

The king's gaze swerves back to me. "This criminal is still alive, Stavros? Hasn't he already been questioned?"

"He's currently unconscious," I reply immediately. "The Crown's Watch took him into custody and are guarding him while medics see to his recovery."

Benedikt pipes up again before anyone else can speak. "If he clams up once he's awake, I could see what I can wheedle out of him. Disarm him in my own way, so to speak."

With another adjustment of my eyes, I make out Konram's faint grimace of distaste in the moment before he replies. "Were *you* there when the confrontation took place, Benedikt?"

The royal bastard hesitates. "Well, I—the commanding officer was in the middle of gathering troops when we got the summons. I volunteered to lead the way for the soldiers while Stavros and the others hurried ahead. It was lucky we weren't needed."

"If you didn't see anything there, then why exactly are you *here*?"

A hint of exasperation has crept into the king's even tone. Benedikt lets out a nervous laugh, as if he shouldn't have been able to predict that his "influence" over the half-uncle who's barely acknowledged his existence would amount to nothing more than hot air.

Before he can come up with a suitable answer, Konram focuses on Ivy. "Let's hear the whole story from you. Everything from what made you check the All-Giver's tower in the first place to interrupting Wendos's magic. As succinctly as you can manage."

Ivy folds her arms over her chest, gripping her cloak. "I'll do my best."

I watch her blurred form with occasional ticks of my gaze to catch a clearer glimpse, my gut knotting. She's the only one who can tell him this part of the story—and I want to hear it too, even if the thought of what she's leaving out unsettles me.

With a quick glance toward me that might be apologetic, the thief explains how she left my quarters when she saw the Quadring starting to crumble, how she overheard a professor mentioning that the dorms would be unlocked and realized she could check Wendos's room, and the notes she found there that led to her deciding he must be using the tower for his spell.

My muscles tense more when she gets to the confrontation itself. How is she going to spin *that* story without revealing her own deviant magic?

"Once I realized what Wendos was trying to accomplish, I did everything I could to stop him," she says. "But he had quite a few daimon under his control protecting him. They stopped me from tackling him, and I was unlucky with the one knife I managed to throw—it only hit him in the shoulder. After that, the spirit-creatures pinned me down."

Konram motions for her to continue. "It sounds as though you fought valiantly."

Ivy's small smile doesn't reach her bright blue eyes. "The accomplices whose power he was stealing were more valiant. In the end, they broke free from the scourge sorcerers' influence and sacrificed themselves to stop him. They jumped off the tower and died when they hit the roof of the lower temple below—and the power of their sacrifice hit him hard. That's what knocked him out. They must have tried to fix the tower too, because vines grew over the steps the daimon broke."

I stare hazily at her for a second before yanking my attention back to the king. Her story sounds impressively reasonable… but I know a significant part of it is falsehood.

What *really* happened with the mutilated accomplices?

Konram is nodding. "I've heard reports of the bodies and the vines from the temple staff. Once we can identify the victims, they'll be given honorable funerals."

"How would you like us to move forward from here?" I have to ask. "If you plan to arrest Ster. Torstem, I may be able to—"

The king cuts me off with a shake of his head. "I don't think we can proceed to that step yet."

I will my tone to stay cool and collected. "No? Are Ivy's observations not enough?"

"They're enough for me that I wouldn't let the man within striking distance of me or my family, but she's also said she believes he has many other allies. He's the only one we can identify. There's no guarantee he'll reveal anything else to us if we attempt to force him to talk." Konram sighs. "From consultation with my chief magical advisor, I've gathered that there's no definite method to confirm a person has carried out scourge sorcery after the fact. Removing him does us little good if there are several others who'll continue attacking the city."

Ivy hasn't tempered her reaction quite as well as I have, her voice taut with disbelief. "Then they *will* keep attacking the city—or sending the daimon they've harnessed to do it. They've already tried to kill your younger son, and for all we know they were responsible for Prince Dunstam's death years ago too."

My gaze flicks from her to Konram in time to catch the subtle tensing of his shoulders. I haven't mentioned the death of his eldest son and former heir in connection with the scourge sorcerers before. We haven't found any evidence they were involved in the illness that struck down Dunstam just a few days before his twelfth birthday.

"That was more than seven years ago," he says tersely.

I step in to draw his attention back to me. "We've traced Ster. Torstem's questionable activities farther back than that. It appears the conspiracy has been growing for more than a decade in the shadows."

Konram lifts his chin imperiously. "The gravity of the situation is clear. I'm not saying we'll do nothing. As soon as the medics are able to revive Wendos, he'll be questioned and given every reason to reveal his associates. And I'll have the Crown's Watch pursue our other leads. You said Ster. Torstem has been conscribing orphans into the conspiracy?"

"Yes. We've identified one orphanage where he's given funds and spoken to the wards, but there may be others."

Ivy clears her throat. "I know he was hiding at least some of the sacrificial accomplices at a brothel not far from there. That might be a common tactic of his. Anyone who'd see one of the victims would know immediately it wasn't a typical dedication sacrifice."

The king folds his arms over his chest. "Then we'll make arrangements for raiding brothels and monitoring this orphanage and others in the city. In the meantime, you three and your companions have proven yourselves adept at uncovering the conspiracy bit by bit. Ferret out whatever other information you can about their intentions. Ster. Torstem will reveal more if he doesn't know you suspect him."

It *will* be easier for us to investigate, being sure of Torstem's involvement and his connection to Wendos. But I can't help raising a careful protest of my own. "The daimon have already been rampaging. The students at the college may be afraid to—"

"We can rebuild the damage done quickly. I'm bringing in several clerics who are skilled at working with unsettled spirit-creatures to counteract the effects on the daimon—they should arrive tomorrow. I'll be traveling with most of the court for several days on a scheduled tour, but I plan to keep in close contact with my people here. If the situation escalates, I'll revise my strategy."

A little relief trickles through me with the knowledge that the royal family will be somewhat distant from the threat while we continue to grapple with it.

I don't like this situation any more than Ivy appears to. Skulking around hoping we can dig up more intelligence on the miscreants while the one we know of for certain walks free...

But at the same time, I can't deny the wisdom of Konram's approach. Scourge sorcerers build their magic by maiming and killing others. They're no strangers to sacrifice.

If we arrest Torstem, the odds of him lashing out to force his murder or simply offing himself seem far too high. Then we'd be left with no solid trail to follow at all.

Of course, the conspirators will know that *someone* foiled their plan tonight. I don't intend to let down anyone under my watch.

Konram sweeps his gaze over us with an even more commanding air than before. "You have your orders. I trust you can get on with them?"

I speak up before he officially dismisses us. "It's become increasingly difficult for us to meet and discuss our findings without our association being discovered. If you could offer any resources to allow greater ease of communication, that would be an immense help."

Konram rubs his chin. "I might be able to arrange just the thing. I'll confirm with you as soon as I have it ready."

I incline my head. "Thank you, Your Highness. We will do our best."

"We'll bring all the scourge sorcerers down," Benedikt puts in. After the king's earlier dismissal, his vigor sounds forced.

Ivy remains silent, but I can almost feel her stewing. She's smart enough not to voice any of her concerns in front of the man who rules over us all, though.

The king pauses, his gaze focused on me. "You seem even grimmer than I'd expect given the progress we've made and the disaster averted, Stavros. Is there another problem I'm not aware of?"

The woman next to me stiffens just slightly.

This is my opening, the time to tell him what she is if I'm going to. To send her off to the gallows where all the riven belong.

If nothing else, don't I owe my king my honesty?

In the instant when I teeter in indecision, the memory of Kosmel's sigil glowing on Ivy's chest flashes through my mind. My previous sense of resolve hardens.

I can't serve both my king and my gods, and I know which holds the higher authority.

"No, Your Highness," I say. "I'm merely frustrated that we weren't able to arrest more of the conspirators despite the crimes they've already committed."

Konram lets out a low chuckle. "I trust you'll remedy that shortly."

His image vanishes from the mirror. Gathering myself, I beckon the others to follow me out of the room.

We hustle along the discreet hall and then out into the passage through the hedges that obscure our departure from view. We've almost reached the wall when a familiar giggle tinkles out into the air.

My legs stall of their own accord. My head swings around, my gaze finding a narrow gap between the bushes.

I only have a clear view for an instant before everything fogs over, but that's enough. Enough to make out Neela's face in the glow of lantern light from the carriage she's just stepped out of.

Enough to notice her hand clasped around that of the courtier whose arm she then tucks herself beneath with another giggle.

I wrench my gaze away, my jaw clenching. My voice comes out harsher than I intend it. "Let's move along. There's nothing for us here."

And I won't let myself make another catastrophic mistake.

# THREE

As we pass through the college gate into the outer courtyard, a steady rumbling sound carries across the field. I flinch instinctively in the instant before I make out the figures gathered around the ruined corner of the Quadring.

Several workers who must have a gift to do with building or mending are sorting through the rubble. In the glow of their lanterns, I can see a chunk of stone they've just raised melding back into place. More workers must be helping inside, handling the interior structure.

Julita speaks up for the first time in a while, though her voice is still more subdued than I'm used to. *They started the repairs quickly.*

Benedikt lets out a light chuckle. "In a couple of days, it'll be good as new. Like nothing ever happened."

A shiver runs down my spine. "Unless the scourge sorcerers rile up the daimon again."

"Konram's clerics should help with that," Stavros says in the brusque tone that's all I get from him now.

The college's yards and hallways are empty other than the workers and a few soldiers standing guard. How many students fled during the chaos, and how many were simply ushered back to their rooms once the daimon settled down?

The quiet niggles at my nerves. It feels too much like the prelude to a larger storm.

Once we've stepped into the Domi, Stavros gives Benedikt a quick clap on the shoulder. "You should get to your room and sleep. We'll all need our wits about us in the coming days."

Benedikt's gaze flicks between us, probably wondering why we're not heading up the same stairs as him. The staff quarters are just above the floors that hold the student dorms.

But he doesn't question Stavros. The bastard's bastard seems to have deflated a little since I first spotted him at the top of the tower.

The way his half-uncle spoke to him raised my hackles on his behalf—but I'd be a real idiot if I told off the king. Frankly, there are about a dozen other things I'd like to tell the king off for after our conversation, if I happened to be feeling idiotic.

A few locks of my pale hair have drifted out from beneath my hood. Benedikt reaches to give one a teasing tug, a trace of his usual smirk returning. "Until tomorrow then, Knives. Try not to get into any more trouble without me."

He heads into the stairwell, and Stavros nudges me forward in ominous silence. Past the dining hall and the main library doors, down the dimmer hallway with its old tapestries hanging on the wall.

When we stop and the former general grasps the sconce to activate the conjured secret passage, my gaze lingers on the tapestry of Signy beside us. She stands at the top of her hill with that heroic golden glow around her, her sword aloft and her stance full of determination to push back the mass of soldiers below.

I've thought about the Veldunian hero who freed her country a lot since I took up this mission. About how she faced an entire imperial army while I'm struggling just to tackle a college conspiracy.

At least she had three men at her side who did everything they could to support her. Who weren't contemplating hauling her to an executioner if she so much as blinked wrong.

When the thicker shadow that's not really a shadow spills down the wall in front of us, Stavros glances at me with a twist of his mouth, as if he's not sure whether he wants me ahead of him where he can see me or behind him where he can shield his comrades from me. With a rough sound, he prods me to go first.

As I step into the passage, a faint hiss tells me he's drawn his sword. Its tip grazes the scars on my back through my cloak.

He's getting ready in case he feels it's necessary to stab me.

The lump that rises in my throat nearly chokes me. My magic flares alongside it, yanking at my ribs, demanding I let it at him.

Good plan. Defend myself from stabbing by giving him a reason to stab me.

My magic might be potent, but it's not especially wise.

Thankfully, launching my power at Wendos seems to have appeased the worst of its resentment at being ignored. A prickling sensation creeps through my innards at my refusal, but nothing like the vicious searing that's brought me to my knees in the past.

I force myself to walk steadily down the hidden steps. The former general follows right behind.

When we emerge into the small archive room where we've held the meetings for our investigation, the two men waiting for us straighten up on either side of the desk.

Casimir's face lights up with what might be relief—because I haven't slaughtered Stavros with my riven magic so far?

Alek's posture stays stiff, his hand resting on the belt that holds the sheath for the royal sword now lying on the desk. Stavros sent him off with it and the belt when we parted ways, I guess so he didn't have to explain to the king how it ended up in my possession.

Looking at the sheath, an echo of the sense of solidarity that filled me in this room just this afternoon passes through me. My fingers itch as if I could reach out and snatch it back.

Any comradery I shared with these men was always fake; it was always based on a lie. But losing it makes my chest ache anyway.

"What did the king say?" Casimir asks.

Stavros grimaces. "At least until Wendos can speak, he wants us to continue our investigation. Ster. Torstem appears to be the cornerstone. We need to find out who else he's roped into this madness."

Alek glances at me before turning his gaze to Stavros. "How did you explain… everything?"

It's obvious what specific part of "everything" he means.

Stavros's grimace only deepens. "The thief spun a story about Wendos's accomplices turning on him." He taps my arm with the flat of his sword. "Was any of that true?"

I step to the side and lean against one of the shelves that holds heaps of books and loose records the librarians don't consider important enough to include in the main collection upstairs. Having something solid at my back helps ground me against the impending interrogation.

"There really were three people with Wendos," I say. "They were missing their hair, their eyes, their ears, their arms—at least one of them part of a leg. One of the women came from the brothel—that's where Wendos threatened he'd have Torstem take her back to. Her name was Fyrinth."

The tick of Stavros's jaw tells me he recognizes the name too. He's smart enough to put the pieces together like I did. "Torstem kept the children from the orphanage after they made their sacrifices and sent others to the temple in their place."

I nod. "Prostitutes' kids, I think."

A shudder runs through Alek's lean frame. "So they aren't having dedicates *die* in sacrifice… just asking them to give up everything they can *without* dying?"

"It seems that way." Acid sours the back of my mouth at the memory. "But they did die. Just not to stop Wendos. After I threw my knife at him, he couldn't concentrate quite as well through the pain. He wanted more power. So he told them to provide it, and they all threw themselves off the tower in a final sacrifice."

"That's why you called on your own power," Casimir says quietly.

I brace myself. "Yes. Whatever magic he and the other sorcerers were imposing on the daimon, it was working. I couldn't even move with the ones he had in the tower restraining me. I could hear buildings falling below. I didn't know how far behind you might still be. It was the only chance I had left."

Stavros adjusts his stance, his sword at his side but still in his grasp. "I think you'd better start from the beginning. Where you really came from. What you've done with your powers before. All of it. No feints, no lies. If you can manage that."

I can't stop myself from glaring at him for a second before I rein in my temper.

I have been lying to them all along, if mostly by omission. And somehow the truth might be the only thing that keeps them from murdering me right now.

It's not only them I've lied to.

Julita stirs in the back of my head. *I'd like to hear this too.*

I drag in a breath. "You've wondered about my upbringing. My parents run a printing press. Nothing fancy—they mostly handle posters and pamphlets—but I wouldn't be surprised if a few of the newer books up there came from their shop." I motion toward the main room of the library overhead.

Alek leans against the edge of the desk. "That's why you're such a reader."

I shrug. "It's a family calling."

Stavros's eyes have narrowed. "And they hid you—"

I shake my head adamantly to cut him off. "Not really. Not like that. I—"

My voice catches in my throat. I look down at my hands, which have twisted together in front of me.

I've never told anyone this before. Never talked about it out loud.

Dredging up the words sends the pain of the memory lancing through me even sharper than usual. "It was my parents and me and my little sister Linzi. When I was seven and Linzi was five, our mother got sick. One of the wasting fevers. It ate at her for two weeks until she could barely roll over in bed, she was so weak. She wouldn't eat, coughed up any water she tried to drink… The medics my father brought around couldn't do much, it was too far spread through her body."

Casimir's mouth slants at a sympathetic angle. "Even the palace medics can't combat certain types of illness."

"I know." I gird myself and hurtle onward. "One afternoon, my father was in the shop handling an order—he didn't like to leave my mother like that, but we needed money for the medics. Linzi and I were with her. And all at once, her breath got so thin and creaky, like she could hardly draw it, and her body went limp—I knew she was dying right that moment. And just as I realized that, I also realized I could save her."

I halt, my own lungs constricting with the images washing over me. Stavros motions with his sword for me to continue.

"I could just feel it." I press my hand to my sternum, where my magic fizzes faintly now. "The power welled up inside me, and I could already picture her happy and well again, so I reached out and let the magic flow into her. It worked. Her breath evened out—the color came back into her face. But—"

My throat closes up completely. My hand rises to touch Linzi's ribbon through the sleeve of my dress.

"But what?" Stavros demands.

I propel the words from my throat. They come out hoarse. "The energy I put into her had to come from somewhere. My sister… She collapsed. She was only three steps away, but by the time I reached her, she was already gone."

My head droops. All the anguish from that moment thirteen years past sweeps through me again, pricking at the backs of my eyes.

*Oh, Ivy,* Julita says softly.

I push onward. "My parents didn't know what happened. Not for sure. My mother was too far gone when I used my magic to realize, and my father wasn't there… I was so scared and confused, I just kept quiet. They said Linzi must have had the same sickness but it hit her all at once because she was so little. I don't know how much they believed that, though. They didn't know for sure what I was, but my mother definitely suspected."

Alek's jaw tightens. "You said she'd beat you."

"She took the belt to me anytime she got frustrated, which was a lot, and she didn't feel I deserved much in the way of food, and most of the time she couldn't stand to even look at me." I form a tense smile. "She said I brought a curse on the family. And her attitude rubbed off on Da. He loved Linzi so much, and losing her suddenly shook him hard."

I spent so many nights huddled in the corner trying to sleep, my stomach pinching from hunger and my back throbbing from the lashes of Ma's belt.

But none of it hurt more than the ache of loss and guilt that never left me.

Stavros's eyes are fierce with accusation beneath the fall of his dark red hair. "*You* knew what you were."

"I figured it out," I acknowledge. "We'd been to see a riven execution the year before, but I didn't totally understand… The next time one was caught, I heard some of the older kids in the neighborhood talking about the kind of magic they work, and I made the connection. But I knew my power wasn't a good thing even before then. It would tug at me, telling me other things I could do, but I just wanted it to go away."

The former general snorts. "At seven, you had the self-control not to give in to a magic that would provide you with anything you could possibly want?"

My back goes rigid. "I killed my little sister. That's what this fucking magic is to me. It can't give me Linzi back, and there's nothing I'd have wanted more. Nothing *terrified* me more than wondering what else I might lose."

Stavros's expression hardens, but it takes him a few seconds before he replies. "And you're trying to tell us that you never used it again until tonight?"

"No," I say, unable to stop an edge from creeping into my voice. "You haven't let me finish. Unless you'd like to tell the story for me, since you're apparently so sure of how it all happened?"

It might not be the wisest move to snap at the man most likely to send me to the gallows, but my nerves have frayed too much for me to care.

Stavros holds my gaze for several unsteady beats of my heart, with a tick of his head as he adjusts his vision. Then he waves his prosthetic hand. "By all means, continue."

I gather myself. "Even if I didn't use my magic again, what I'd already done with it was obviously horrible. So I didn't want the gods noticing me. The morning of my twelfth birthday, when my parents would have taken me to a temple out of obligation to have me dedicated, I ran away. I got by on the streets by stealing and begging and finding shelter wherever I could."

"And no magic."

I ignore Stavros's skeptical tone. "And no magic. Until a little more than a year later, a man cornered me in the abandoned house where I'd holed up and pushed me down and—"

My mouth presses flat before I can go on. "I'm sure you can imagine what he meant to do. I was too small and weak to fight him off, so I panicked, and I threw him off me with my magic. I wasn't *trying* to kill him, just stop him, but I wasn't exactly thinking clearly..."

That memory is doubly sickening. The revulsion of the man's hands pawing at my tattered clothes congeals with the horror of seeing his lifeless body, knowing I'd done it again.

*At least you wouldn't have killed anyone to kill him,* Julita says in an apparent attempt at optimism.

A choked laugh hitches out of me. "That wasn't even all of it. Ending his life made more life to balance it out, but I couldn't control that either. All these bugs came streaming out of the walls of the house—they swarmed the whole street, got into people's food, their gardens—people who barely had enough as it was..."

I hug myself. "I never wanted to feel like I had to use my power again. So from that point on, I did everything I could to prepare myself for whatever I might face the way I was living."

"You learned to fight," Casimir suggests.

"Yeah. I found a dueler who was willing to teach me in exchange for stealing various things. He trained me here and there for a few years. And I hoarded information on all kinds of subjects from listening in on conversations, reading every book I could get my hands on, studying and observing... It worked, well enough. Since that day when I was thirteen, I hadn't given in to the magic again until yesterday when I was dying. And not for lack of it badgering me, you can be sure."

Alek shifts forward on his perch against the desk. "You asked me about techniques for magical suppression, but you never brought it up again. That was actually for you, not stopping the scourge sorcerers, wasn't it?"

I shouldn't be surprised the scholar would be so quick to put those pieces together.

I meet his penetrating gaze with a half-smile. "I mean, I wouldn't have minded if it'd been useful against them too. But I did have an ulterior motive. My power has gotten... increasingly more insistent over the past year or so. I didn't want it distracting me. But I found the pipe fleece—it didn't do any good that I could see."

Julita hums to herself. *Ah. A lot of things make quite a bit more sense now.*

She doesn't sound all that upset with me. But then, she's been inside me all this time, aware of everything I'm doing. She knows I haven't been secretly going around carrying out malicious magic behind the men's backs.

With my confession over, I slump against the shelves. "So, what now? That's all of it."

"All of it?" Stavros guffaws. "Other than the fact that you could ruin more here with a snap of your fingers than the scourge sorcerers have managed to in months."

I scowl at him. "If I *wanted* to hurt any of you, don't you think I would have already? If it'd been up to me, I'd never have ended up in this situation to begin with. But I did, and I don't want someone else's toxic magic wrecking this city any more than I want my own to, so I stuck around and did what I could to help. Even though that meant being surrounded by the people most likely to have me hanged if I slipped up."

Stavros glowers back at me, but it's Casimir who speaks next, in a careful but gentle tone. "Why did you agree to take the risk, Ivy? You could have walked away, even with Julita's spirit in you."

I rub my forehead, abruptly embarrassed by the answer. "I did want to help. I wanted to protect the city. But it wasn't totally selfless. I—I had the stupid idea that maybe if I played a large enough role in stopping the scourge sorcerers, the godlen would forgive what I've done before. Maybe they could heal my soul so it wouldn't be riven anymore."

I can't quite bring myself to look at any of the men after my admission. Their silence seems to confirm how idiotic that idea was.

Riven sorcerers don't get forgiven. Our whole reason for existence is to remind the rest of society of humanity's past wrongdoings.

To show that limitless power is a curse more than a gift, and that no one should strive for it the way the scourge sorcerers did before.

Julita speaks up in a more spirited tone. *They* should *pardon you. It would only be fair, after everything you've done. You must have saved more lives than you hurt already!*

I don't know about that.

I wet my lips. "I'd like to keep helping. I know that by law you should consign me to execution—but I *have* kept my powers under control. You can see I'm nowhere near insane. I still want to stop the scourge sorcerers. Whatever happens after… I'll be happier knowing I did one really good thing no matter how my life ends."

"Ivy," Casimir says, with a rasp that makes me glance up. The compassion that made me fall for him gleams in his eyes before he looks at Stavros. "I think we should give her that chance. She hasn't done anything wrong the whole time she's been here."

Stavros glowers at both of us. "As far as we know."

I let out a huff of breath. "If you still don't believe *me*, you could check with Julita. She's been along for the ride every moment."

Stavros raises his eyebrows. "And how exactly am I supposed to ask her when she only talks through you?"

I think back to the first time I told them about Julita's ghost. "Ask a question only she could answer, about something you're sure she wouldn't have randomly told me about before. If she thinks I'm lying to you and doesn't want you to trust me, she won't tell me what to say. Simple enough."

*Yes,* Julita says. *Of course I'll speak for you.*

The former general pauses, his eyes going distant as he contemplates his test. Then he motions to me. "At the last ball—the last one she was alive for—what did she spill on herself?"

Julita's presence shifts restlessly. *Spill? I didn't spill anything on— Oh.*

I avert my gaze so the men won't think I'm talking to them. "Oh *what?*"

Her tone turns abashed. *It wasn't exactly "spilling." I was trying to be stealthy and sneak closer to Wendos to overhear what he said to the people around him. I was just slipping past the refreshments table when someone backed up right into me. I lost my balance and dunked my elbow in a bowl of crackleberry pudding.* She pauses. *I didn't realize Stavros even noticed.*

"Well?" Stavros says.

I focus back on him. "She says she didn't spill anything—someone bumped into her and her elbow landed in crackleberry pudding."

His mouth flattens, as if he's not happy that I've answered right. Was he trying to trip me up with his phrasing, thinking of another spill she might have mentioned already that I'd try to con him with?

Let him be disappointed. I proved my point.

"Kosmel himself gave her a vote of confidence," Alek points out. There's no hint of how he might feel about that fact in his flat voice. "We all saw it. And she has been a lot of help. It's not as if she poses any danger to the rest of the school right now."

Stavros scoffs. "The riven are *always* dangerous." But then he sighs and rocks on his heels with a resigned expression. "How exactly do you propose you're going to help next?"

Is he seriously giving me the chance?

I lift my head, trying to look more confident than I feel. "We know that Ster. Torstem is playing a major role in orchestrating the conspiracy. He has an inner circle of associates who are conducting scourge sorcery with him. The only campus organization he leads that Wendos was involved in is the entomology club—I even heard Wendos using bug talk as a cover to discuss the daimon attack at the ball. At least a few of the other members must be part of the conspiracy. We should focus on them."

"They're not going to admit to conspiring with illicit magic if you simply ask."

Alek appears to perk up. "I can dig into the records and come up with a list of current members for Ivy to spy on. They've got to slip up somewhere."

Stavros still doesn't look convinced. "They managed to conceal their activities so well that it's taken us all this time to be sure of *anyone* who's involved, even with Julita keeping a close eye on Wendos."

An idea sparks in my head, bringing a hint of a smile to my lips. "Maybe I need to do more to draw them out, then. I'm new at the college—no one will be totally sure of my goals and beliefs yet. I heard how Wendos talked. I can drop a few comments along similar lines near the bug club members and see how they react. Thinking a sympathetic party is around might loosen their tongues."

Alek pauses. "Won't they know to be wary of you? If Wendos realized that Julita suspected him, and you've told people you were friends with her…"

I shake my head. "Wendos bragged to me about how he took care of Julita all by himself without the other conspirators needing to know. I think he didn't want to reveal that his childhood experiments might be what exposed the rest of them. If he kept quiet about her, he wouldn't have told them about me either. And his accomplices who saw me in the tower are dead."

"We've been careful to keep our investigations secret," Casimir says. "Barely any of the king's soldiers saw Ivy even tonight. It sounds like a reasonable plan to me. And Julita would have ideas about how Ivy should behave. She must have heard plenty of scourge sorcerer attitude from her brother. If she's willing to draw on that."

*I'm not going to abandon the cause*, Julita says tartly. *You're the one taking the real risk.*

"She's contributed every way she can since I got here." I hesitate, realizing I owe her more than that. "And you should know—what I said here yesterday, when I was upset… It wasn't a lie, but it wasn't the whole truth. I think she's made herself sound more callous than she actually felt at the time, trying to distance herself from everything she's lost to deal with… with having lost it. I know you all mattered to her as more than just a means to an end. She gets worried when you're in danger. She appreciated how you stood by her. I'm sorry I made it sound as if she didn't."

*Ivy,* Julita murmurs. *You didn't need to—you had every right to say what you did. My mistakes are mine.*

Casimir offers me a soft smile. "You *were* upset. And you weren't the only one." He aims a pointed look at his companions.

Alek shuffles his feet. "Thank you. It's good to know that."

Stavros doesn't give any sign of being affected either way, his chiseled features hard as ever. "Then we've made our decision, and there's nothing more we can do tonight. Let's get some rest before we resume our investigations. But first—" He jerks his sword toward me. "Give Casimir back his locket."

Right. They wouldn't want to leave me with the ability to summon the rest of them on a whim.

I draw out the locket that can send a magical signal to those the rest of them carry and hand it over as swiftly as I can. I don't want the brush of Casimir's skin to dredge up my memories of the much greater intimacies we've shared.

How queasy does it make him to remember what he did with a woman who's really a monster?

The courtesan's fingers close around the locket, and he shoots Stavros another firm look. "We should get another one made for Ivy. If she's going to be associating more with the scourge sorcerers, she might need help quickly."

Stavros lets out a hum that sounds more like a growl. "We'll see."

The thought of our whole group stirs up another question. "What are we going to tell Benedikt?"

Another silence falls over the room. The men exchange a glance.

Casimir exhales softly. "I don't like keeping secrets from him when we've had a policy of sharing everything we discover. But he wasn't there—he didn't see any of it… I'm not sure he'd approach the situation with the proper understanding."

"He might think Ivy's bewitched us and report her to the king," Alek says with a wince.

After seeing how eagerly Benedikt sought his half-uncle's acknowledgment, the same worry winds around my gut. "He might."

I don't say how I feel about that possibility, but it shouldn't be difficult to guess. I like Benedikt, as much as I've gotten to know him in the past few weeks, but I can't say I'd gamble my life on his good will.

Julita appears to share our apprehension. *Benny can be a little… capricious. I don't know how he'd react.*

Casimir turns to Stavros. "The information doesn't really have anything to do with the investigation. Not having it won't stop him from pitching in as much as usual. It's not as if Ivy's ever likely to be around him without at least one of us there too."

I can't tell how much that's his own justification and how much it's what he thinks Stavros would respond best to, but the former general makes a brief gesture of acceptance. "Fine. Let's not make this a bigger mess than it already is. That decision can be re-evaluated at a later date."

His last words come with a ring of finality. He picks the royal sword off the desk and slings the belt with its sheath over his shoulder.

The thought of him escorting me back to his quarters, radiating skeptical hostility the whole way, makes my skin crawl. I can't help thinking of the other unknown scourge sorcerers who were out there in the city tonight—the ones Wendos was trying to combine his magic with.

And the sooner I prove just how committed I am to this mission, the better.

"There is something else we can do tonight," I say. "Something I can do, anyway. Ster. Torstem and the other conspirators will need to regroup. They're still in the city… If they're going to discuss how their plans fell apart and their next moves, they'll want to be somewhere familiar."

Stavros frowns. "And you think you know where that is?"

I glance around at all of the men. "Does anyone know what room the bug club meets in?"

# FOUR

*Ivy*

Even after Alek has unfurled a blueprint scroll and pointed out the entomology club's dedicated room on the third floor of the Quadring, Stavros keeps scowling.

"And how exactly are you planning to get in?" he asks me in an acidic tone. "With your magic?"

I bristle before I can catch my reaction. "No. I'm a thief, as you so enjoy reminding me. There are plenty of non-magical methods of breaking and entering. If anyone's there, I'll see what I can overhear. If they're not, I'll search for evidence. It's worth a shot."

It's better than waiting around to see if he'll decide to send me to the hangman after all. And I can hope that the more he sees me working toward the same cause he believes in, the less murderously inclined he'll be.

Casimir speaks up in his usual mild way. "If we're going to let Ivy stay a part of our investigations, we have to *really* let her be a part. In every way she can."

Alek finishes re-rolling the blueprint and hesitates for a second before adding his own understated vote of support. "She's never hurt anyone at the school before."

Stavros considers both of them, his jaw working. He knows I have hurt one person here—but only in self-defense. The rest of their points he can't argue at all.

"Fine," he bites out, pinning me with his gaze. "You see what you can make of the bug club's headquarters, and then you come straight back to my quarters. If I get the slightest hint that you're deceiving us about anything…"

He doesn't need to finish that sentence.

I nod in acknowledgment, and he moves toward the wall that holds the secret passage. As Stavros steps into the shadows, Alek ducks through the doorway that leads to the rest of the archives.

Casimir aims a soft smile at me. "We'll work this out."

I'm sure we will. I'm just not yet convinced it won't be worked out with a noose around my neck.

The courtesan vanishes after Stavros, and then I'm alone. I should give the men at least a couple of minutes to leave the area around the library before I come waltzing out too.

Well, I'm alone other than my uninvited ghostly friend.

*Thank you,* Julita says. *For what you said about me… You really didn't need to do that.*

I shrug. "I felt like I did. It was true."

She doesn't confirm or deny that point.

In her silence, I realize there's a little more I should probably say to her. I flop into one of the chairs near the desk. "Are you sure that *you're* okay working with me? Hanging out in the closest possible proximity to a riven soul? Now that you know."

Julita guffaws. *Ivy, I have been with you through everything. If more of the souls around here were like you, we'd have a much smaller mess on our hands. I don't know what it'll mean for you in the future, whether the power will start to control you, but right now, I'm not worried.*

More relief than I expected washes over me. I start to push myself upright, but Julita speaks again.

*Are you sure you want* me *hanging on?*

I knit my brow. "As opposed to…?"

*You've already been stuck with me for longer than either of us expected. I know it can't be easy having your head invaded. I could try to leave, to pass on, however exactly that works.*

I didn't ask to have another woman's soul lodged inside me. I've wished my life were entirely my own again more times than I can count.

But hearing her extend the offer makes my heart lurch.

It'd be like asking her to kill herself. No one knows exactly what happens when your soul moves beyond this plane of existence into the embrace of the gods—how much you'll remember, how much you'll be aware of.

The thought of Julita's determined spirit fading away just feels… wrong.

I keep my tone dry. "You dragged me into this mess. You can't leave me to fend for myself now. And Alek's right—your knowledge of how your brother and Wendos talked and acted should come in handy."

Julita sounds a little relieved herself. *Well, if you put it that way… I would like to see this through, as much as I can.*

"Then it's settled."

I peel myself off the chair and touch the books in the right pattern to re-open the secret passage. In the stillness of the night, I pad quietly through the darkened halls.

Staying far beyond the reach of the lanterns around the outside of the Domi and out of sight of the workers in the distant corner, I cross the inner courtyard swiftly and slink into the Quadring.

The square ring of a building that surrounds the Domi feels even more vacant. No one's likely to venture over here until classes start up again in the morning.

No one other than, I can hope, at least a couple of disgruntled scourge sorcerers.

Holding the image of the blueprint in my mind, I dart up the stairs to the third floor and ease down the hallway to the right spot. Only the faintest moonlight seeps through a broad window at the far end of the hall.

I stop by the door I'm sure is the right one. Leaning my head close to the tiny gap between the door and the frame, I strain my ears.

No sound reaches me. But a quiver of magical energy wriggles through my nerves.

I pull back with a shudder.

*What's the matter?* Julita asks.

I answer in a murmur. "There's some kind of spell cast on the doorway."

Here in the teaching building, where hundreds of students might be coming and going from any given room during the course of a day, the college administration hasn't bothered with the fancy magical locks that guard the dorms and the staff quarters. This one merely has a regular keyhole below the knob. But someone's added an extra layer of protection.

Julita gives an ominous hum. *Ster. Torstem must have wanted to keep the club's space especially secure.*

"I guess that makes sense." No one who isn't riven would even notice the magical precaution if they weren't specifically looking for it. My broken soul automatically resonates with supernatural energy.

My power twitches in my chest. It could dissolve this spell in the blink of an eye. It could open the door as smooth as butter.

I did manage to take down Wendos without causing any unwanted destruction…

The second the thoughts pass through my head, I could slap myself. For fuck's sake, I told the men that I had my magic under control just minutes ago.

I deserve the noose if I'd make that promise a lie the first time I face a tiny bit of trouble.

I only made it through the confrontation in the tower because Kosmel answered my desperate call. My current problem hardly qualifies as desperate.

The moment I let down my guard with my magic, it'll screw me over. I can *never* trust its nagging call.

With guilt pooling in my stomach, I step back. I can't get access to the room by picking the lock without setting off some kind of alarm.

But the doorway won't be the only access point.

I pad down the hall to the neighboring room. That door gives off no impression of magic.

With a faint smile, I retrieve my one remaining knife from the sheath at my thigh.

The blade is thin enough that I can fit it into most keyholes, including this one. I wiggle it until I feel the right point of tension, and then I twist—and the lock clicks over.

I don't know what the room on the other side is used for, but whatever that is, it involves a lot of clothes. Racks of gowns, tunics, and jackets line the walls amid full-length mirrors. The odor of heavy perfume hangs in the air.

I hustle over to the window and ease open the hinged lower pane. The cool night air brings a welcome clarity.

The bug club's window awaits farther down the wall. A narrow ridge, about as wide as one of my feet, runs along the stone wall just below the window ledge.

That's all I need.

Julita lets out a soft laugh of approval as she must recognize my plan, but she doesn't speak. Maybe wanting to avoid distracting me from this precarious maneuver.

Thankfully, no tremors are shaking the campus like they were this afternoon. The daimon the scourge sorcerers riled up around the college have gone quiet just like they did in the temple's tower.

I peer farther across the outer courtyard. A few distant figures shift in their guard posts atop the college wall. Lanterns cast a muted glow on the grass of the courtyard, but none close enough to highlight my perch.

I tug my dark brown cloak closer around me and knot the loose corners at the base in front of my ankles to ensure it covers my pale green dress. If all goes well, I'll blend into the shadows.

After one last scan of the courtyard, I clamber out the window. My toes jar against the ridge, which barely holds them and the balls of my feet inside my boots.

It's fine. I've made more difficult scrambles before.

I don't want to be visible on the wall for any longer than necessary. Sliding my hands along the gritty blocks, I glide my feet after them.

One sideways step, two, three. I lean so close to the building, the rough stone bumps my cheek.

I don't let myself think about what would happen if I tipped just a tiny bit backward and lost my balance.

My extended fingers bump the window frame. With a flash of gratitude, I feel along the glass for the movable pane and pop it open.

With one more furtive scramble, I'm swinging over the window ledge into the dark room.

All at once, I find myself missing the cloying perfume I left behind. The entomology club's headquarters holds a mossy scent that isn't entirely off-putting, but woven into it are hints of acrid smoke and an unpleasant tang I can't place at all.

*Ugh*, Julita says in apparent agreement.

At a rustle from my right, I freeze in place. But as my eyes adjust to the room, I realize I have nothing to fear from its current inhabitants.

Which are, naturally, bugs.

The entomology club can justify its dedicated room with the rows of tanks and jars that seem to cover every piece of furniture in the space. Beetles clamber over bits of bark and twigs; winged creatures flit along glass walls; jointed worms wriggle through murky water.

"Ugh," I mutter, echoing Julita's reaction.

I can think of few places it'd be creepier to sneak around in the darkness. Fortunately, I have no need to lurk in any of those places.

I do, however, have a job to do here.

Aiming to be methodical, I pick a direction and begin a careful circuit of the room. As I weave between the stands and shelving units, I scan every available surface for anything that might hint at intentions beyond the buggy.

I duck low to check under the containers I can lift, which was how I found the vague evidence Wendos left behind in his dorm bedroom. I even sweep my fingers under any furniture with a raised bottom, bracing in case I touch something unnerving.

All I find are labels with the names of bugs and instructions for things like feeding. A few scraps that look like pages from school reports that were tossed aside as unsuitable. Nothing that so much as hints at a conspiracy.

At the far end of the room, I determine that not quite every surface is covered in insect enclosures. A calendar hangs on the wall, with a couple of days marked off that I commit to memory.

Beneath the calendar stands a broad desk that's stacked with books, writing supplies, and a few loose papers, but no bugs.

The drawers on the desk hold tons more papers. I sink into the leather chair by the wall and go through them one by one.

Squinting in the dimness, I can't make out every word. But all the words I can make out seem to have to do with bugs: supplies and environments and behavioral studies.

If there's any hidden meaning to the records, I can't make it out. And I don't want to risk bringing any of these papers with me when I'm not sure they'll help our investigation.

It wouldn't do to tip Torstem off that we're on to him and his club.

I've stared at enough pages that my head is starting to ache when something taps against the door.

My pulse stutters. I nudge the drawer closed and dive under the desk just as the lock rasps over.

Where I'm huddled in the thickest shadows, I can't see anything of the people who enter. But multiple sets of footsteps scrape across the floor.

The first voice to speak, hushed even in the privacy of this space, I recognize as Ster. Torstem's. "We'll regroup. We took a gamble and it failed. There are plenty of other prizes to try for."

It definitely doesn't sound like he's just talking about rare insect specimens. I scoot a little closer beneath the desk, my heart thumping with both anxiety and eagerness.

A woman speaks next, no one I can identify just by her speech. "Do you know exactly what went wrong?"

"We lost some of the bugs, and there weren't enough left for our purpose. I think we'll get farther with the other enclosures. It's time to focus on more refined tactics."

I frown. I'm guessing that by "bugs" he means the daimon, speaking in code to be safe. But what other enclosures? What would that word stand for in terms of their real plans?

A third figure, a younger man I also don't know, interjects with a short chuckle. "That seems like another kind of gamble."

Torstem makes a dismissive sound. "They allow for easier control. We've built up quite a supply already, and I've already sent someone on to speed up construction."

*Well, that definitely doesn't sound good,* Julita remarks with a sense of a grimace.

No, it does not.

"We'll need more people to exert that control, won't we?" the younger man goes on. "With Wendos—"

Torstem cuts him off with a chiding sound. Obviously the law professor is awfully careful about what he says even in here.

"Our club could always use more members with the right perspective," he says in a measured voice. "If you notice any likely candidates with appropriate interests, pass their names on to me."

There's a warble of fabric as he retrieves something. He must hand it to the woman, because she thanks him. Then they head back out into the hall.

With the click of the door shutting, I slump against the underside of the desk. My head is spinning.

The scourge sorcerers have some new plan—which may or may not involve the daimon, but if it does, it's using different tactics from before.

I don't really want to know how awful their new efforts are going to end up being.

But our investigations won't be finished until I do. And Ster. Torstem is looking to recruit even more students into his sick cabal...

I pause, lingering on that discovery. An uneasy flutter passes through my chest, solidifying into a ball of resolve in my gut.

That might be our answer right there.

As I slip back through the neighboring window and make my way to the Domi, I keep turning the idea over in my head. With each prod and poke, my certainty grows.

I ease open the door to Stavros's quarters to find him sitting at his desk, watching me with an expression like he's considering ramming a sword through my middle.

As the door swings shut behind me, he stands up. "Good. You kept your word once."

I swallow down the ache at the memory of past conversations we had in this room, when he looked at me like more than a criminal. "I found out something we can use. Something that could get us everything we need to take them all down."

The former general's eyebrows arch despite himself. "And what's that?"

My lips form a crooked smile. "I'm not just going to make friendly with a few students. I need to convince Ster. Torstem to recruit me into his conspiracy."

# FIVE

*Ivy*

"And that," Stavros says from his lectern at the front of the classroom, "is why you should always check your boots before shoving your feet in them."

He offers a wry grin to his students as laughter ripples through the class. I set the quills I just collected in the storage case and resist the urge to fidget.

Seeing him banter with his pupils in his usual confident way only drives home how much his demeanor has changed with me. In the last day and a half, I've barely gotten more than grunts and brusque remarks—when he bothers to acknowledge my presence at all.

Of course, the alternative would be meeting the hangman, so I can't really complain.

The ringing of the palace bell—the smaller substitute while a proper new one is being constructed to replace the one the daimon broke—marks the turn of the hour and the end of the Field Strategy lecture. As the students get to their feet, Stavros catches my eye. His expression tenses just slightly, but he gives me a small nod.

He informed me of the afternoon's schedule—curtly and coldly—this morning. He's off to check with the king's people about their progress in their own investigations, and I'm speaking with Alek to get the low-down on the bug club before our usual larger meeting.

It took about a half hour of arguing the other night before Stavros conceded that my plan to infiltrate the conspiracy is a good one. For all the same reasons I could have cajoled the bug club members into thinking I might be a kindred soul, I'm the only one of us who's unknown enough at the school that Ster. Torstem might believe I'd go all in on the scourge sorcery thing.

He's telling his followers to watch for ideal candidates. So I need to find out whose attention I should be catching.

I follow the stream of students into the hall. Their chatter is more subdued than usual, many gazes darting nervously at a rasp from down the hall that turns out to merely be another professor adjusting the position of his desk.

The daimon haven't stirred up any more trouble since my confrontation with Wendos. When I step out into the early afternoon light in the inner courtyard, the corner of the Quadring I watched fall to pieces two days ago looks startlingly solid. You'd almost think it never fell.

But we all know it did. And most of the students don't even understand why.

I assume everyone else is somewhat comforted by the greater number of soldiers now patrolling the campus, sometimes with a cleric in tow. The sight of the blue uniforms makes my skin crawl.

No one's come for me yet. No one's realized I lied about what happened in the All-Giver's tower.

I'm safe as long as the three men who do know my secret keep believing they're better off with the riven monster alive than dead.

Entering the Domi, I smooth my hands down my skirt. It's hard to take any pleasure in the feel of the turquoise silk, even though I've come to think of this as my favorite gown. Wearing it now feels even more like a charade than when I first laced it up.

But it's perfectly designed for my needs, thanks to Casimir's thoughtfulness. The layers of fabric that rustle around my legs overlap to conceal slits at the sides of my thighs, allowing quick access to the knives strapped over the divided underskirt beneath.

I left my favorite knife behind in the tower. I'm not even sure where it ended up after Wendos yanked it out of his shoulder. Stavros didn't give me a chance to poke around the scene of my crime.

Students are coming and going from the main library entrance with a couple of soldiers watching over them. I stride by with the best haughty noble air I can summon, as if my nerves aren't jangling with apprehension.

A couple with their arms twined hustles past me from the corridor of tapestries, their faces flushed in a way that makes me suspect they were using the quiet passage for a hasty tryst. As long as they're not in my way, I'm not going to judge.

When I'm sure no one's in sight, I slip down the conjured stairs into the archive room.

I'm not at all surprised to find Alek already sitting at the desk, scrawling on a piece of paper with a quill. The scholar is ever dedicated to his work—whether his studies or our investigations together.

He glances up, and his stance tenses for an instant at my arrival. Then he forces a quick smile. "I've made a lot of progress with the entomology club. You should be well-informed about Ster. Torstem's people when we're done here."

"Perfect." I walk over, pretending I haven't noticed his discomfort at my presence. But when I grasp the back of one of the chairs to pull it over beside him, his posture stiffens again.

My fingers curl around the carved wood as a thread of loss coils around my stomach. Just days ago, Alek was grinning through our schemes together and gathering me in his arms when he thought I was wounded.

I swallow thickly. "If you'd feel better about it, I can sit on the other side of the desk. Keep my distance."

Julita lets out a huff. *He'd better not be an ass about it. Stavros is bad enough.*

Alek blinks at me. His mask conceals most of his reaction, but his mouth slants as if he's chagrined. "I—no, it's fine. It'll be easier for us to go over the information together if I'm not constantly having to flip the pages around."

I don't move. "You don't have to act as if you're okay with… with me. I can understand why you'd feel uneasy."

It's the first time we've been alone together since he found out what I am. Alek spoke up for including me because he believes at least one of the godlen approves and because I've been useful, but that doesn't mean he loves the idea of having a riven sorcerer hanging around.

I'm still alive, I remind myself. I have that. Just that is more than I should have hoped for.

Alek looks at the papers in front of him Dead then at me again. "You said you haven't used any magic in years—not until Esmae attacked you," he says abruptly. "Are you sure nothing ever slipped through, maybe without you even meaning it to?"

Is he worried I worked my riven power on him in some way?

I smile awkwardly and sink into the chair even though it's still a couple of paces from the desk.

"I've had a lot of practice at keeping my power under control. I swear to you, no matter how much it hurt, I kept my grip on it."

I can tell Alek's eyebrows have drawn together just above the holes in his mask. "It hurt, stopping yourself from using it?"

A startled laugh spills from my lips before I can catch it. He hasn't put *those* pieces together.

"Yes, it hurt," I say. "Starting about a year ago, I started feeling as if the magic was lashing out at me from the inside when I refused it. More and more, the more I resisted. You're the one who found me when I collapsed in the library—you saw how I was after King Konram's visit to the college. I wouldn't have put myself through that agony only to let a little sorcery slip out some other time."

*Oh. I always wondered*— Julita shudders. *Gods above, Ivy, that power of yours really is a monster. It was vicious even to you.*

I suppress a wince at the thought of all the times I lied to her about the pain I was in.

Alek's mouth has dropped open, but it's a moment before he manages to speak. "That—that wasn't an attack from Anya or anyone else? That was your own magic hurting you?"

I guess I didn't make that aspect clear with my explanation before.

I find myself yanking my gaze away from the shock in his bright brown eyes. "Yeah. The power acts up worse when I'm in danger but shut it down anyway. And I've felt more in danger here than I did in my old life. In the library—I was scared of the guard, that he'd realize what I am. And then having the king right in front of me... I saw him just a few weeks ago talking about how wonderful it was that so many riven had been executed."

"And your magic thought you should strike out at him first?"

I shrug. "It thought I should do *something*. Shove them away, run for cover, disguise myself—anything to stop them from seeing me at all, from having any chance of arresting me."

"But you didn't. So your magic—" Alek's voice roughens. "Ivy, you were coughing up blood. It was literally tearing into you."

I aim a tight smile at him. "I know. But that was better than letting it hurt someone else."

For a few seconds, he simply stares at me. Then he scoots forward on his chair so he can reach my hand where it's clenched on my knee.

Alek's slim fingers slide around my own with a reassuring squeeze. The tenderness of the gesture makes my breath catch.

"I always knew you were strong," he says quietly. "But you're so much stronger than I even saw. I'm sorry I wasn't giving you credit for that."

My innards have completely tangled. "You didn't know. I'm sorry I lied to you about it, though I imagine you can see why. And I'm sure you had plenty of your own concerns to focus on."

Alek lets out a wry scoffing sound. "I once thought I had it hard being a devoted scholar in a family of weapons mongers and soldiers. I'd take all the derision and disappointment ten times over before trading it for what you've had to deal with your whole life."

I cock my head. "You said you were the son of a merchant."

"A merchant whose specialty was all things warfare, including when it came to his two other children. The idea of someone preferring to spend their time with books rather than swords was absolutely ridiculous to all of them."

My next smile comes a little easier. "Well, I'm glad you pursued your passion anyway—that you're here to help us tackle the scourge sorcerers. And fill me in on all the things I need to know. And—thank you for keeping my secret. I know it's a lot to ask."

Something shifts in Alek's penetrating gaze that I don't know how to read. "It isn't. It shouldn't have been at all." His grip on my hand tightens. "Is it still hurting you—your magic?"

I think of the other night when Stavros had his sword pointed at me. "Nowhere near as badly as before. I think the fact that I released it in the tower has mollified it for the moment."

"If it gets serious again, you have to tell us. *Before* you get to the point where you're writhing in agony. All right?"

*Yes,* Julita pipes up. *Listen to Alek. He always knows what he's talking about.*

I don't see that there's anything we could do to fix the problem, but if anyone could figure it out, I suppose it's Alek. And it doesn't cost me anything to agree. "All right."

He hesitates as if he might say something more. Then he gives himself a little shake and turns back to the desk, his hand slipping from mine with a beckoning gesture. "Come right over. We should get through all of this material before the others show up."

As I tug my chair next to his, Alek fans out a sheaf of papers. "I dug up everything I could on the entomology club's membership and activities. There are currently sixteen active members by the most recent record. It seems that for their off-campus excursions, they split up the group. So as not to be too intrusive on the wildlife, supposedly. Half of the members go sometimes, the other half the rest of the time."

Julita hums. *I'd be keeping an eye on whoever Wendos was associating with.*

I was just thinking the same thing. I motion to the papers. "Do we know who was in the group that Wendos was usually traveling with?"

Alek's mouth curves with a smile that's a little sly. "I was able to piece together a pretty good idea. These are the seven members who appear to have always gone along on the excursions he was a part of. There are a couple of others who bounced back and forth between groups, but I'm guessing they're not quite as involved."

I expect a series of names with a few notes jotted for each. Instead, the first page he shows me has a sketch at the top. Simple, sparing in detail, but keenly drawn enough that I'm sure I've seen that man in the dining hall a few times.

Alek's smile turns sheepish. "I thought it'd help if you had a visual so you can recognize them on sight. As much as my limited skill can allow that."

My gaze jerks back to him. "You drew this? It's very good."

He chuckles awkwardly. "I mean, no one's going to frame it."

"No, but it does what it's meant to do. You captured the shape of his features accurately." I risk extending a teasing bump of my elbow. "You didn't tell me you were an artist."

Alek holds up his hands. "I'm really not. I just—I do try to get down the information I want to convey as clearly as possible. And sometimes a quick sketch can accomplish that better than any number of words could. I've mostly created diagrams and the like."

Whatever amount of experience he has, he obviously has an eye for lines and shading. The scholar has a lot of surprises up his sleeve.

"Well, it *is* good, and much appreciated," I insist.

Alek walks me through each of our main suspects—names, areas of study, godlen they dedicated to, gift if he was able to determine one, classes, clubs, and known habits. Not all of the faces in his sketches are familiar, but there's a guy who's been in some of Stavros's classes, a woman I think I noticed when I went on a hunt with some leadership division students, and two others I have a vague sense that I've seen but can't place.

I commit the images and facts to my memory as quickly as I can. Carrying Alek's carefully constructed profiles around with me is too risky.

It's amazing that he managed to compile all this information so quickly.

After going over the last of them, I brush my hands together. "All right. I'm prepared to put on a show of being morally degenerate. It shouldn't be too hard—Stavros thought I was right from the start."

Alek brings his hand to his mouth to cover a snort. As he eases the pages back into a canvas wrapper, his expression turns more serious. "I'm glad I could contribute something useful. We know how far these brutes are willing to go… I wish you didn't have to take on all the risk of getting their attention. If it would work for me to put myself out there—"

A different sort of ache passes through my chest. He really means what he's saying, even now.

He doesn't know even half the risk I'm planning to take on yet.

I touch his shoulder to stop him, doing my best to tamp down on the tingle of warmth at our closeness. "It wouldn't work. It makes much more sense for me to shoulder this challenge than it would for any of the rest of you—and I'm okay with that."

*And you'll hardly be alone in it,* Julita puts in.

I glance back at the profiles. "What about the former bug club members who'll have graduated? We know Torstem's been roping in orphans for a while."

Alek's gaze goes distant with thought. "I did check the older membership records. The trouble is, it's impossible to know which graduates were just bug enthusiasts. I'm following some threads to check for suspicious behavior after they left the college. The graduates I've looked at from particularly prominent families are still under one or both parents' shadows, though, so they're not in a position to enact new policies or anything like that yet."

I give a rough laugh. "That's a little good news. Of course, even if Ster. Torstem only started funding the orphanage fifteen years ago, I guess we don't know whether he already had allies then or if that was the start of the conspiracy."

"I think we can reasonably hope it doesn't go much farther back than that. They would have needed sacrificial accomplices to practice any kind of scourge sorcery." The scholar snaps his fingers. "But that reminds me! I also thought I should look into Torstem's gift, so you can be prepared if he tried to use it on you."

I should have thought of that myself. "Is it in the school records?"

Alek grins. "No, but he conducted trials before he came on as a law professor. The courts require all staff to disclose their gifts, and I was able to get access to those files. He's dedicated to Creaden, unsurprisingly, and his gift on record is the ability to quell anger. Possibly other agitated emotions as well, given the flexibility most gifts have."

The ability to quell agitated emotions. My jaw clenches. "How very convenient for persuading kids to be at peace with the idea of carving themselves up for his use."

Alek's smile falters. "Yes, I think it's likely he applied his gift for that purpose."

"All the more reason we need to bring that asshole down before he ropes in any more orphans."

"I'll keep digging up all the information I can. And like I said, if there's anything specific you'd want me to look into, don't hesitate to tell me."

The offer stirs up the uncomfortable questions that've lingered in my head since the night in the tower.

I pause and then prod myself to speak. "I have actually been wondering—and if anyone would have come across information on this, I'd wager it'd be you… Have you read any accounts of the gods outright talking to people before? It wasn't something I thought generally happened."

Even in the fables I've read, the godlen make their desires known with glowing symbols and meaningful dreams. Not so much direct conversation.

If Kosmel ever decides to get chatty again, it'd be kind of nice to know what that means for me.

"Oh! Of course you'd be interested in that subject." Alek taps his mouth, his gaze going distant with thought. "It's certainly never happened to me or anyone I've spoken to. Although I suppose Estera probably wouldn't be inclined to say much to someone who didn't even offer a sacrifice anyway." His hand rises to his chest where his godlen brand lies beneath his tunic.

I can't hold back a guffaw. "I didn't even dedicate myself."

Alek shoots me a crooked grin. "Well, Kosmel is known for taking on difficult causes. I've definitely come across written accounts from clerics of their 'interactions' with the gods in various ways… I think I can find a couple of old journals that could give you some insight, and I'll do more research in that area after today."

He motions for me to follow him into the larger archive room next door. After several minutes of stalking along the cluttered shelves, he's handed over two small leather-bound books to me, one stained with dribbles of wax, the other with splotches that give off a sour smell that makes me think they're wine.

"Those should make a good start," Alek says.

I laugh as I tuck the books under my arm. "You really do know how to find out everything about everything, huh? We're lucky we have you on our side."

The scholar ducks his head with a hint of awkwardness at the praise. "I'm not sure just how helpful they'll be. One thing I've seen from reading anything to do with theology is there are all kinds of contradictory theories and observations… I'm not sure it's something we mortals can fully pin down."

"Even partly pinning it down would be a relief. Thank you."

We return to the smaller meeting room to find Benedikt lounging at the desk with his feet propped up on its edge. At our arrival, he tilts his head at a jaunty angle. "The both of you are down here already getting to work. What are you up to now?"

I don't know how to begin telling him about my new interest in the divine without revealing more than I'd like to. "Alek was just filling me in on the key members of the bug club."

"Ah, we're going to start poking at them like the bugs they are, hmm?"

Benedikt chuckles at his own joke, and it occurs to me that no one has filled him in on even the initial plans we made without him two nights ago.

"I, ah—Stavros and I decided that I should try to make myself look like an appealing new recruit to the scourge sorcerers," I say. "It'll be easier if I know whose notice I'm trying to catch."

Alek's head jerks toward me at the news.

One of Benedikt's eyebrows lifts. "You and Stavros decided, and Alek already knew to pull the information together?"

"I didn't know," Alek says, a little tightly, his gaze still fixed on me. "Not the recruiting part anyway. It was obvious we'd want to focus on the people most closely associated with both Ster. Torstem and Wendos. The medics still haven't been able to draw Wendos out of his coma. It seemed urgent that we get started."

"Yes. Urgent." Benedikt spins a quill he's picked up between his fingers. Can he tell that we're leaving out part of the story? "Those accomplices of his really messed him up good with their final sacrifice."

Or rather, I did. I don't know what my magic did to Wendos that the medics haven't been able to heal.

Before the moment can become truly strained, Casimir arrives through the conjured passage. He bobs his head in greeting to all of us, his gaze lingering on me with one of his gentle smiles. "Good to see you. Have you been getting on all right, Ivy?"

His concern sets off a flutter of warmth in me that I have no right to feel. I make myself smile back. "I always do."

Benedikt sits up straighter, his gaze darting between us. "Why wouldn't Ivy be all right? Has that bitch Anya been after her again?"

My stomach flips over. "No, no, I'm totally fine."

Casimir is better than me at smoothing things over. "I only thought she might be a little out of sorts after everything she went through the other night."

Then the wall wavers again, and I'm unexpectedly relieved to see Stavros's red-topped head ducking from the secret passage. Now the meeting can get going without any more questions I'd rather not try to answer.

As the former general glances around at us, he holds up a leather sack. "King Konram was good to his word. We'll have a new meeting place after today, and the means to enter it directly from wherever we happen to be."

A much more understandable sense of relief fills me. "That's great."

Stavros fixes me with a glower, his voice coming out in the sardonic drawl I like least. "I should have said, most of us will have the means. I'll be holding on to yours, Thief."

Benedikt waves his hand as if to redirect Stavros to what he believes is a more important subject. "What's all this about Ivy getting herself recruited by the scourge sorcerers?"

Casimir's eyes widen. "What?"

Apparently the former general has no more patience for that subject than he does for me in general. His voice turns terse but firm. "She thinks diving right into the villainy is the best way to unravel it. Her arguments sounded reasonable. If she's so eager to put her neck on the line, I don't see why we should stop her."

He glances around at the other men as if daring them to argue. I hold my chin high to show my commitment to the plan, even if I don't love the way he phrased his approval.

Casimir catches my eye with a questioning expression, and I give him a smile I hope looks confident.

At the lack of overt protests, Stavros claps his hands together with a thump of flesh against wood. "Now let's get on with determining how she can present herself as one of the villains."

# Six

*Ivy*

"What blasted book are you reading now?" Stavros demands as he strides into his quarters, back from another briefing with his contacts in the Crown's Watch.

I bite back a snarky remark about how he should be glad I'm reading rather than tossing my illicit magic around. Somehow I don't think the joke would go over well.

I tuck the book's ribbon between the pages to save my spot. "It's a journal written by a cleric who ran one of Prospira's temples under Darium rule. She claims that Prospira chatted with her from time to time. I'm trying to figure out how true that is and if it could tell me anything about what Kosmel wants with me."

Stavros pauses at the chest by the window. He retrieves his preferred prosthetic for the combat class he's about to teach—the broader hooked metal loop—and screws it into the harness around his handless forearm. "And has it been at all enlightening? I certainly can't comprehend his interest in you."

I'm used to his acidic comments now. This one doesn't even sting.

Well, it barely does.

"I don't know," I admit. "Her overall grasp on reality seems pretty shaky. And the things she mentions Prospira saying to her so far are, like, what to have the temple cooks bake for breakfast. It's hard to believe a godlen would care."

After reading her account, I'd almost be convinced I hallucinated the voice *I* heard… except that would mean the man glowering at me and two of our colleagues hallucinated Kosmel's sigil too.

"Better dictating the breakfast menu than encouraging one of the riven," Stavros mutters under his breath.

I narrow my eyes at him. I might not be reckless enough to throw my unwanted power in his face, but I don't have to sit silently while he lambasts me.

I get to my feet. "I noticed you have quite a few novels in your bedroom. Maybe you're only harassing me about my reading material because you can't do much reading yourself these days. My offer to assist with that still stands, you know."

I say it mildly so he can't accuse me of mocking him. An honest gesture of generosity from the monster he's housing will irritate him more than if I returned his insults.

*Ivy,* Julita says warningly. *You know how grouchy he gets about his sight.*

But Stavros simply lets out a sound that's half huff, half growl. He doesn't dignify my comment with an answer.

I'm going to count that as a win.

And I need all the wins I can get. Because the truth is, when the former general marches over to join me, looming more than a foot both taller and broader than my gawky frame, every nerve in my body peals out in alarm.

And, okay, there might be a tiny bit of attraction still tangled up in there too. The man does cut an impressive figure.

But he isn't simply putting on a show of being intimidating. The tension coiled through all that brawn is very real, and very much directed at the threat he considers me to be.

Isn't it wonderful that our current plan requires me to go out into the hall and shout at him?

"Any interesting news from the Crown's Watch?" I ask, possibly holding on to the slight hope that they've rooted out all the major conspirators without me needing to do anything further.

The sound Stavros makes in answer is definitely a growl this time. "Nothing at the brothel they inspected last night. And no suspicious activity around the orphanage. Now that Wendos is in custody, the scourge sorcerers must be taking extra precautions. Whatever other sacrificial victims they have in the city, they may have moved them to a new type of hiding place."

Wonderful. Then as far as we know, our chances of uncovering the rest of the villains depend entirely on my fledgling plan.

I rub my arms to stop the creeping of my skin. "We'd better put on a good show, then. Are you ready?"

Stavros's glower returns. "Your performance is the one that really matters here, Thief. But we already know how good you are at lying."

My fingers curl into my palms. I simultaneously picture slamming my fist into his arrogant face and have a minor panic attack imagining the consequences of doing so.

I drop my hands to my sides instead and jerk my head toward the door. "Let's get out there."

Stavros pushes past me without another remark, leaving me to trot obediently at his heels like a good little assistant. I plaster a serene expression on my face as we head out of the Domi.

I'm dressed in a thin shirt and trousers this morning, because supposedly I'm going to be helping him with his combat lessons. But with the thick leather vest strapped over the shirt, it doesn't feel that much more comfortable than my frothy dresses do.

A pang of homesickness for my old tunic and breeches, for my old life without the judgmental stares and sneers, reverberates through my chest. I was never exactly *safe* roaming the streets, stealing from corrupt merchants and leaving coins for the needy... but it was definitely simpler than my current situation.

I don't even know if I'll be able to go back to being just the Hand of Kosmel after we've taken down the scourge sorcerers. Not now that my secret is out.

One problem at a time.

We hustle into the Quadring and up the stairs to the professors' offices. In theory, we're grabbing a piece of equipment from Stavros's office before the class.

Actually, we happen to know that Ster. Torstem finishes up his own office hours right around this time.

As we emerge from the stairwell, Stavros drops his voice so no one other than me will make out his voice. "Just up ahead. Third door on the right."

I nod. "Got it. Five paces past it?"

"That sounds reasonable. Then you'd better talk fast."

"I think I can manage that."

Our hushed conversation will sound terse even if no one who notices it can distinguish the words. Which is perfect, because five paces past the door to Torstem's office, I raise my voice as if getting caught up in an argument we've already been having. "You can't really think they're handling this problem properly."

Stavros spins around to face me. I jar to a stop with a flash of very genuine discomfort at the fierceness of his expression. "And you think *you* know better than the royal family?"

My magic stirs at the hostility vibrating through the air. I clamp down on it, reminding it that this is just pretend.

We're speaking loudly enough that our voices should travel through Torstem's door now. I think I catch the creak of the floor on the other side.

Just in case, I add a little more rancor to my words. "They're stuck doing the same old thing. It's obvious the gods aren't happy with them."

"So you'd prefer for the royal family to let the city collapse around our ears?"

I set my hands on my hips, restraining a shiver at rephrasing the words Wendos said to me in the tower. "Sometimes a few things need to get knocked down so we can build something better. Even the All-Giver thought so."

Julita shudders inside me. *And may the Great One have smote the first guy who said that.*

Stavros steps closer—for the benefit of anyone who happens to peek out, but I can't help suspecting he's enjoying looming over me. Letting me feel his frustration with this whole situation.

"You'd better watch what you say out loud," he says. "You'd better watch what you're *thinking.*"

"I'm only saying the truth!"

He scoffs harshly. "Then you're a bigger idiot than I thought. Get out of my face until you've had a chance to get your head on straight."

That's my cue to take off. Tamping down the racing of my pulse, I give an exasperated sigh and storm off down the hall.

My heart isn't thundering so loud I miss the squeak of hinges behind me. Or Ster. Torstem's voice, low and even, just before I round the bend. "Having a little friction with your new assistant?"

A flicker of triumph cuts through my unsettled thoughts. He's taken the bait.

Now Stavros can vent to Torstem a little about my ridiculous attitudes—attitudes we know the law professor will secretly approve of.

*That did seem to go smoothly,* Julita says. It's hard to tell from her tone whether she's actually happy about that fact.

She has more experience with scourge sorcery than any of us, having been subjected to her brother and Wendos's experiments as a child. While she hasn't openly balked at our plan, I can't imagine she loves the idea of getting closer to people who bolster their own power through others' pain—or hearing me spout off their philosophies.

I round the corner—and find myself face to face with Romild, the leadership student who had designs on the position as Stavros's assistant. My self-appointed rival lets her lips curl into a sneer.

She probably heard at least part of our argument. She's thinking about how Stavros must be regretting giving the position to me now and no doubt hoping she'll get another shot at it.

The sense of her judgment shouldn't rankle me the way it does. Although Stavros is definitely regretting working with me, just not for the reasons she thinks.

I simply glower at her and stalk on to the stairwell.

I keep a peeved expression on my way out of the building. At the sight of a blue-uniformed figure who's appeared by the Domi's side entrance, my pulse kicks up a notch.

I'd veer off toward a different doorway, but these days I'm as likely to find two soldiers someplace else as none. So I stride ahead as if my mind is focused on some matter too important for me to acknowledge the man standing guard.

He doesn't stir from his post a couple of paces from the entryway. But as I walk past him, a faint tingle of drifting magic quivers through my riven soul.

My stomach lurches. Did he just cast a gift toward me?

What will it have told him?

I continue on into the building, but rather than heading upstairs to Stavros's quarters, I turn down the hall. At this time in the morning, students with later starts to their school day are still trickling in and out of the dining hall, but I don't pay them any mind.

I slip out through the front entrance, past two other soldiers who don't give me any impression of magic at all, and ease around the outside of the building.

Not for the first time, I'm grateful for the grand statues the college's administration erected around the grounds. A looming marble figure of some famous cleric hides me behind his sweeping stone robes.

Propping myself against the base of the statue, I peer toward the guard who used his gift.

*What's the matter?* Julita asks.

I pitch my voice low. "I caught a whiff of magic when I passed that soldier. As if he was working a gift on me."

It doesn't appear that the effort gave him any reason for concern, though. The man, who looks young enough to pass for one of the college's students, is still standing tall and stiff in the same spot next to the doorway.

I study him for a few minutes longer. Several students and a professor meander through the doorway, and he doesn't so much as twitch in reaction.

If he's casting magic toward them too, it's slight enough that I can't pick it up from this far away.

It can't be unusual for soldiers to have at least some small gift they claimed with a dedication sacrifice. Even among the poor of the outer wards, I knew at least as many people who'd given up a piece of themselves for a little power as not.

I don't see any obvious markers of a sacrifice on the man. No missing fingers or bits of facial features. But there are plenty of possibilities I wouldn't be able to easily notice.

Casimir gave up several of his back teeth, replacing them with gems in the typical courtesan fashion. Julita told me she sacrificed her lowest two ribs.

There's only so long I can keep watching the soldier without it looking odd to anyone who starts watching *me*. I commit what I can see of his face to memory, so I'll recognize him if we cross paths again.

Short chocolate-brown curls that gleam under the morning sun. A strong but elegant nose. Creamy, unblemished skin.

Gods above, if he ever decides soldiering isn't to his tastes anymore, I'd bet the companionship division would welcome *him* as a courtesan. He sure as shit doesn't look as if he's seen a whole lot of combat.

What if it's for his magic rather than his fighting skills that the Crown's Watch recruited him?

I pull myself away from the statue with a knot I can't shake in my gut.

If the king is using gifts to seek out sorcerers… who's to say they won't pick up on the sorcery *I'm* trying so hard to suppress?

# SEVEN

*Casimir*

As she leans back in the chair, the Elox dedicat who stopped by the companionship division's daily massage clinic lets out a rush of breath.

Even medics need someone to take care of them from time to time.

I dig my thumbs just a little deeper into her shoulders, finding the points of tension in the muscles. There's a special delight to be found in making someone's day better with just fifteen minutes and the press of your fingers.

But my current client also gives me the opportunity to support a greater cause.

I keep my tone light. "You're all knotted up. Stressful week?"

Her next breath comes with a soft sputter of agreement. "You could say that. I'm working on a case like nothing I've ever seen."

She's one of the medics assigned to heal Wendos from whatever exactly Ivy's chaotic magic did to knock him out. I don't hear any alarm in her voice, so I doubt they have any suspicions of the actual cause.

I work my thumbs farther down her spine through the thin fabric of her tunic. Patrons who stop by for the chair massages don't bother undressing. "I can tell you're devoted to your work. I'm sure you've already made progress."

"It doesn't seem that way. But we haven't made the situation *worse* either, so that's something, I suppose."

She's conscientious too, carefully not revealing any details of the circumstances or her patient. I can read between the lines well enough, though.

Wendos hasn't even begun to rouse from his coma, and the medics don't know how to mend what's wrong. But he isn't getting sicker.

We can still hope he'll recover and reveal his co-conspirators, but we can't count on it. Which means Ivy will have to continue courting the scourge sorcerers' favor for gods know how long.

A knot of my own forms in my stomach.

I'm careful not to let my uneasiness sour my voice or harden my touch, switching to asking the medic if she tried the particularly excellent sweet loaf the college's cooking staff served with today's lunch. A courtesan should show concern but not pry.

A courtesan is meant to distract patrons from their worries, not heighten them.

I happen to think there's more to learn when following those tenets than if one tries to circumvent them. I hear an awful lot in my daily work without any forceful questioning.

All the same, I was lucky the medic came in when she did. She's my last patron of the hour-long shift I pick up in the massage clinic once a week.

At the end of the brief session, I send her off with a relaxed smile and add her coins in compensation to the pouch on my belt. As I head down the hall, my gaze slides to the arched windows along this floor of the Quadring.

Late afternoon has darkened into evening while I worked. The shadows stretch long across the outer courtyard amid the streaks of light from the wavering lanterns.

A lithe figure moves through those shadows, aiming for the stables.

A hooded cloak covers most of the woman's form, but I recognize the determined stride. And it isn't hard to imagine the woman it belongs to deciding to slip out to the stables in the quiet of dusk.

It doesn't look as though much of anyone else is around. I amble down the stairs as if I simply felt like taking a stroll and wander over to the stables myself.

Only a faint glow seeps through the stable windows into the building, leaving the interior hazy. The scents of hay, leather, and horse wash over me, bringing a smile to my lips.

I really should venture out here more often, if only to say hello to my favorite animals. Being around them settles my nerves.

Walking down the aisle, I cluck my tongue at one gelding and rub the nose of an eager mare. I find Ivy exactly where I expected I would, leaning over the door of a stall at the end of the next aisle over.

"Oh, don't be grouchy," she says to Toast, the terror of a stallion whose jaw she's scratching. The obstinate animal snorts and stomps one hoof, but I notice he doesn't pull his head away.

He's met his match in this woman—and it looks as if she's won him over despite himself. As I watch them, affection swells in my chest.

For a second, I try to picture the woman whose soul Ivy is carrying inside her. From the way Ivy spoke up for Julita the other day, they've forged their own unusual understanding.

Behind all her charm, Julita always struck me as being a little lost... maybe lonely. But she held me at a distance even when she was being flirty. I never got to know her much beyond the coyly confident front she put forward.

I wish she'd had the chance to find the friendship she seems to have with Ivy while she was alive. At least she's been able to form that kind of bond before she's passed away completely.

With just a couple more steps, Ivy notices me approaching. Her head snaps around, her hood sliding back over her pale amber hair.

When she's looking right at me, it's impossible for me to see anyone but the woman in front of me. The woman who's captured so much of my attention she lingers in my mind even when she isn't around.

Ivy's expression softens a little when she sees it's me, but tension lingers in the set of her mouth. Over the past few weeks, I'd mostly won *my* way past the instinctive wariness in her bright blue eyes, but the incident in the tower has brought it back.

I stop a few stalls away and reach to give my favorite mare, Pepper, a pat in welcome. "Taming that horse might be your greatest accomplishment."

Ivy relaxes more at my teasing tone. She gives Toast one more scratch under his chin and steps back. "I don't think anyone really gave him a chance before."

I can't help thinking of how much that remark could apply to her own situation.

The urge runs through my body to walk right up to her, wrap my arms around her, and tell her that she's still got me on her side. That she never needed to earn a chance to begin with, in my opinion.

I hold myself where I am instead. I'm not sure she'd welcome the embrace, let alone believe me, and I can hardly blame her for that.

It isn't as if I was free of doubts when we first came around the top of the All-Giver's tower and saw her summoning vines at her feet. I make a career out of seeing the best in people—I'm aware that my judgment isn't infallible.

But with every word she's said since, every emotion that's played across her face and colored her voice, it's become increasingly clear that she's still the woman I found myself drawn to from the start. Still just as sharp and bold and kind as ever.

Of course, she might not want my affection regardless of whether she believes in it. Some part of me thought—some part of me *hoped*—that the deeper fondness kindling inside me had sparked inside her too.

From the way she reacted after our last intimate moment, though, it was nothing more than casual pleasure to her. Which was all I'd offered anyway.

All I'm meant to offer.

I allow myself to take a single step closer, studying the interplay of reactions I receive. A faint flush colors her cheeks, but her posture goes slightly rigid as if she's bracing herself to flee.

She's grappling with some conflict within herself, and I can't say what it even is. Do I stir up feelings in her that she's feeling awkward about? Is she afraid I'm going to push for more than she actually wants?

Another impulse itches at me—to tap into my gift, to find out how I could make Ivy happiest—but I quash it. It feels like too much of an invasion of her privacy now.

And just because something would make her happy in the moment, that doesn't mean it's what she'd actually appreciate in the long run.

So I stay where I am, but I dig into the pocket of my trousers. I can give her one thing I expect she'll enjoy.

I retrieve the item I've been carrying around waiting for a moment like this and hold out the knife to her grip-first, my fingers around the slim hilt. "I managed to pick this up in the tower while we were leaving. It's been cleaned... I thought you might want it back."

The way Ivy's eyes light up makes my heart skip a beat. She steps forward and plucks the knife out of my hand as if she's afraid it might be a trap.

As she gazes down at it, a grin stretches across her face. "It's my favorite one. I thought it was gone for good."

She lifts her gaze to meet mine again, the wariness still there but faded. "Thank you."

I return her grin. "I would have given it back earlier, but I wasn't sure how Stavros would react if I attempted it in front of him."

Ivy gives a dry laugh. "Yes, he wouldn't want me getting even more dangerous."

She bends down to slide the knife into one of the boots she's wearing, mostly hidden beneath the rippling skirt of her dress.

When she straightens up again, her voice turns tentative. "Can I ask you kind of a strange question? There aren't a whole lot of people around here I *can* ask."

The fact that she's willing to turn to me for any help at all brings a glow of warmth into my chest.

I spread my arms. "Be my guest. Indulge your curiosity."

Ivy glances around the stable, confirming that we're alone here. There's no sound but the shifting of the horses in their stalls.

All the same, she drops her voice low and keeps her question vague. "You seem pretty... close with your godlen. Does Ardone reach out to you in different ways, let you know how she feels about what you're doing or what else she might like you to do?"

I don't need to ask why Ivy's curious. She looked confused and a little terrified when she talked about Kosmel's divine voice speaking to her.

My thoughts dart back to the night of the incident in the tower, after Ivy made her full confession.

That night, I knelt at my small shrine to Ardone in my dorm bedroom and asked my godlen to show me if my heart was being led astray. If I needed to beware the woman who's unknowingly claimed so much of it.

I answer Ivy in the same subdued tone. "Not the way you've experienced it, from what you've said. But I've felt Ardone's presence regularly in smaller, subtler ways. Every now and then I have a dream I can tell she's touched, but mostly it's simply sensing my attention being drawn to specific objects or images, like a symbolic sort of message."

Like that night after I made my appeal, my gaze drifted up through the flickering candlelight to see a shadow like a butterfly's wings fluttering by. Flying free without a care.

My godlen might as well have spoken to me in that moment, saying, *Follow the path to your joy unhindered.*

Ivy's brow furrows. "I haven't noticed any smaller messages. It's like he comes out of the blue, and then he vanishes."

I cock my head. "You haven't exactly been open to accepting his presence—or any other godlen's —have you? The connection between mortal and divine has always felt like a matter of meeting halfway to me, rather than having someone else's will imposed on me. They guide rather than command. And you can't guide someone who's shutting you out."

"I guess I can't argue with that reasoning." Ivy lets out a huff of breath. "I don't know if I *want* to let any divinity in."

"It's up to you. You could always see if you're comfortable opening the door just a little. Nothing's stopping you from slamming it shut again if you're unhappy with the outcome."

Ivy snorts. "Assuming I'm in a position to do anything at all once he's done with me. Listening to him has already gotten me into more trouble than I ever did on my own."

I have a flash of an image of Ivy slumped on the hangman's platform, and my stomach lurches. My hand instinctively flicks down my front—tapping my fingers to forehead, heart, and gut, and then a fist to my sternum over my godlen brand—as if I can ward off that horrific potential future.

Ivy's mouth twists at my gesture. I take another step toward her. "Kosmel protected you with Stavros—with all three of us—when he needed to. I'm sure he will again if it's necessary. And… in case it wasn't clear… he *wouldn't* need to with me. Stavros may be having trouble coming to grips with your magic, but I know you're still our Kindness."

A look that's almost haunted comes over Ivy's face. Before I can panic that I've disturbed her somehow, she lets out a laugh—if a bit of a stiff one. "You've always been kinder to *me* than I probably deserve. Thank you, for now and before. I'd better get back to the Domi before the former general thinks I've gone rogue."

She pats Toast's head and ducks past me without waiting for me to answer.

I reach over the stall door to stroke Pepper's neck, grappling with the tangle of emotion inside me.

I gave Ivy a little comfort, a little happiness. As much as I probably could. I should be grateful for that.

Once I've given Ivy the distance she appeared to want, I head back to the Domi myself. On the third floor, I find a different woman waiting outside my dorm.

As I approach, taking in her features, her name rises up from my memory: Agata. The second daughter of one of the court Barons, a student in the scholarship division. A couple of months ago, she hired me for a night on the town and a private interlude afterward.

At the time, I suspected she'd become a returning patron. The tangle inside me knots tighter with the knowledge that I'm about to be proven right.

I stop a couple of paces from her and smile. "Hello, Agata. It's good to see you. How have you been?"

She twists a strand of her sleek auburn hair around her finger. "Pretty well. But I was feeling that there's a little something missing. When are you free for another evening? We could have a similar outing to last time."

From the suggestive note that's crept into her voice, I have no doubt that she intends a similar ending as well.

It's the work I do. Sex is a celebration of the godlen I dedicated myself to, an act of both worship and joy.

But not a single part of me feels joyful at the idea of carrying out that particularly intimate work right now.

I manage to hold my smile in place. The words slip out before I can totally think them through. "I'm not. Free, that is. I'm sorry. I'm on a short hiatus from taking private patrons."

At least, as of this moment I am.

"Oh!" Agata giggles. "I suppose you must have schoolwork and so on to keep you busy like the rest of us do. Let me know when you're in business again, then. I'll be looking forward to it."

As she saunters away, a lump of guilt forms in my gut. I've never turned down a potential patron before.

What in the realms am I here for if not to serve? To pay back everything that was given so I could be here at all?

I clamp down on my roiling emotions and press my college bracelet to the door to disengage the lock.

I'm serving Ivy. I'm serving the royal family.

What greater purpose could there be than tackling a menace that threatens the entire continent? Our mission deserves all our focus.

I won't entertain any thoughts of the other reasons I might be making this call—or what they'll mean for *my* future.

# Eight

*Ivy*

I bob and dodge, blocking a punch and narrowly avoiding a knee to my gut.

My sparring partner swivels, and I see a brief opening where I could whip a jabbing thumb into her eye. That's what I'd do if this were an actual life-or-death fight, but I don't think my employer would approve of street tactics in his combat class.

And the noblewoman I'm sparring with doesn't deserve it anyway.

I rein in my defensive instincts and shoot out my fist more loosely, giving her the opportunity to block. The point of this drill is for the students to get a feel for constantly moving on their feet while in face-to-face conflict, not to destroy my opponent.

I'm grateful Stavros is allowing me to participate in the lesson at all. It'd be terribly boring standing on the sidelines handing out water and patching up minor scrapes.

No doubt he's studying my every movement, watching for an excuse to declare that I really am an irredeemable menace after all. He might even be hoping he gets one.

The former general's voice rings out from across the field. "All right, people! Switch partners again. Every enemy you go up against will have a slightly different approach. If you're on the ground in a battle, you need to be prepared to adapt in an instant, or you'll find yourself underfoot rather than on your feet."

A few of the students around me chuckle at his dry tone. I turn away from the woman I was up against, wiping at the sweat that's formed on the back of my neck, and look for the guy I particularly wanted to have some face time with.

My gaze catches that of the male student I was searching for, several paces away. When I make a gesture of invitation, he strolls over to take the position across from me.

Even though I prompted this face-off, my pulse gives a brief hitch alongside a tiny defensive flare of my magic. The man approaching me is one of the bug club members from Alek's homemade dossiers. The scholar's simple sketch captured the bulky guy's broad nose and boxy jawline perfectly.

Julita must recognize both him and my intentions. *Better be careful with this one, Ivy.*

As the possible scourge sorcerer comes to a stop in front of me, I dip my head in acknowledgement of both our intention to spar and Julita's point. The sparse facts Alek pulled together whirl through my thoughts.

This is Olari Igorek, second son of Provint Igor of Yersi, who governs that province. Dedicated to Sabrelle, in his third year at the college.

A family as prominent as his would normally see any children going into military service becoming majors, if not generals, right out of the gate. Olari has shown a preference for more hands-on field tactics rather than broader strategy, in line with settling for captain.

He'd rather be bossing around the infantry and engaging in regular skirmishes than worrying about the larger issues of a conflict, apparently.

Other than the entomology club, he's a member of the fencing club and the darts league. Obvious competitive streak. He received an award in a dueling contest last year.

None of that tells me whether he definitely enjoys the idea of using others' pain to fuel whatever gifts he came by through his own sacrifice. Although I see what sacrifice he made when his lips draw back in a grin of challenge.

His upper front four teeth have been replaced with steel replicas.

If we ever get into a real fight, I'll have to make sure he's never in a position to bite me.

Olari makes the first lunge without waiting for any additional signal that I'm ready to begin. His fist sweeps over my ducked head.

I spring to the side. Thank all that's holy I spent most of the past several years honing my speed as well as my strength.

"You're pretty skilled for your size," my opponent remarks as we circle each other. "I can see why Stavros hired you."

Is he trying to lower my guard with compliments?

I can't complain, because he's giving me my opportunity to drop a hint of my supposedly deviant attitudes in case he'll pass the information on to Ster. Torstem. "I don't believe we should be limited by what we were born with. I've always striven to become more."

Olari hums approvingly, and our conversation falls off into a series of blows and blocks as he tries to land a strike. I keep my silence patiently, waiting for another good opening to throw in a telling remark, not wanting to come on suspiciously strong.

As we circle each other, Olari eases slightly back. "You've arrived in the middle of a rather chaotic time here at the college. You mustn't have been expecting to deal with daimon crashing balls and toppling buildings."

Interesting that he's bringing that subject up. I shrug, debating my answer.

The scourge sorcerers were obviously in favor of chaos, but Wendos didn't make it clear exactly why. Only that he thought somehow it'd set the world "right."

Julita pipes up with a hushed suggestion, as if she's afraid Olari might overhear. *My brother and Wendos sometimes talked about how violence and pain are just the natural order of things.*

That does sound like the sort of sentiment scourge sorcerers would appreciate—to justify the pain *they* inflict.

I pick my words carefully. "There's so much chaos in the rest of the world, I guess it's more surprising that the spirit-creatures don't act out more often themselves. Although I'm sure that's not much comfort to those who were harmed."

Olari lets out a faint snort. "Indeed."

He swipes at my jaw and then my ribs, managing to knock my side just slightly before I dart away. I answer with a sweep of my foot against his calf that would have sent him stumbling if he wasn't so sturdy.

Maybe I can pick his brain for a hint about what the scourge sorcerers' current plans are, if he's involved with them. "The daimon have settled down quite a bit since the day they broke the Quadring. The clerics the king sent in must be very skilled."

Will the remark sting his pride and prompt an insinuation about other reasons the spirit-creatures seem to have backed off?

Olari chuckles, his breath only a little rough with exertion. "I suppose we'll see." He attempts another strike. "There's been a lot of speculation going around about why the daimon were so agitated to begin with."

He leaves that open-ended comment hanging. Apprehension prickles through my nerves with a deeper certainty.

He didn't give any clues with his vague statement about the daimon's current behavior, but I'm increasingly sure this guy is on Torstem's side. He's adding chatter to our sparring match specifically so he can evaluate what I say on topics of particular interest to the conspirators.

It was two days ago that Stavros and I staged our argument for the law professor's benefit. Plenty of time for him to order an underling to feel me out further.

I don't need Julita's help to figure out the best response this time. Wendos obviously wasn't happy with the way things are being run in Silana, and most of the running is done by the king.

I wouldn't be surprised if the scourge sorcerers started the rumor I'm about to repeat.

"Some people are saying the daimon must be upset with the royal family. That's the only real theory I've heard." I rub my hand across my mouth as if nervous about saying too much. "I don't know what exactly they're upset about, though."

Torstem wouldn't want to recruit someone foolhardy enough to shoot her mouth off without concern for the consequences. I can give the impression that I think the theory is plausible without openly supporting it.

As I throw another punch, Olari laughs. "I've heard that claim too. Although sometimes I think maybe they're just tired of getting stuck with nothing but bits of cast-off food for offerings and they're rallying for something more."

I'm not sure the remark would sound so ominous if I didn't see the obvious parallel to the scourge sorcerers' bid for power. As it is, my skin crawls.

"I suppose we all can't help wanting more than we have from time to time," I say mildly, just as the bell for the hour starts ringing.

Stavros motions to his students, his metal prosthetic flashing in the sunlight. "You know what that means. Off to the showers, the lot of you. I won't be held responsible for any sweat-stink in your next classes."

I restrain myself from rolling my eyes at the tongue-in-cheek order and turn to find an unexpected gaze on me.

The woman who's watching me from several paces away isn't even part of the military division. Petra was one of Julita's frequent classmates over on the leadership side. But she's dropped in on occasional combat and strategy classes before.

My ghostly passenger informed me that she's a distant relative of the queen's. She definitely looks more like Queen Ishild's side of the family than the king's, with olive-toned skin and features more elegantly proportioned than the imposing nose and jutting chin of the Melchiorek line.

Her dark gaze flicks from me to Olari with unsettling intensity. Then she pivots on her heel with a swish of her straight black hair.

*What's Petra in a stew about?* Julita mutters.

A hollow forms in the pit of my stomach. I can make a few educated guesses.

Did Petra overhear some of what I said? She's seemed bothered in the past when people repeated the rumor about the daimon being upset with the country's rulership.

King Konram knows I'm investigating the scourge sorcerers on his behalf, but we purposefully kept that fact quiet from everyone else in court.

Which means I have to worry about making new enemies just as much as turning my existing foes into friends.

# Nine

*Ivy*

I'm shoved around in the dark, blinded by scratchy fabric wrapped across my face. It's suffocating me.

I can't draw a breath through it. I can't tell where I am.

What in the realms is happening?

I have to get out of this. I have to tear free. I—

My feet thud onto a raised surface. Wooden boards. Something creaks overhead.

More footsteps thunder after me, as if on all sides. Their impact reverberates through the boards and into my legs.

I try to suck in air and only drown in the coarse fabric. I can't feel my hands.

My throat strains with an attempt to cry for help, but my lungs are burning for breath. With another shove, I stumble to the side.

Then someone wrenches the fabric from my face.

It's still dark—night all around me, glowing with distant lanterns. Voices murmur, maybe hundreds of them, but all I can do is stare at the man whose shadowed face looms over mine.

"You couldn't keep hiding," Stavros grates out, and lifts his hands.

All at once, he's gripping a loop of rope. He jerks it down over my head, his metal prosthetic scraping my cheek.

"No," I murmur. "No. I swear, I never…"

Never what? Never killed? Never hurt innocent people?

"We both know that's a lie," Stavros sneers as if he read my thoughts.

We do.

I always knew I'd end up here.

But my heart thuds madly as Stavros tightens the rope around my neck. The heavy cord digs into my throat.

I start to twist my head, but he catches it between his hand of flesh and his hand of metal. His voice is the darkest growl.

"You're not going anywhere. Stay and take what monsters like you deserve."

There's nothing but ice in his eyes and his tone. It chills me right through to my veins.

He takes a step back and lifts his right hand to give the signal, his lips curling into a triumphant—

"Ivy!"

My body jolts, and my eyes open to more darkness. Darkness that's also tangled with fabric, although this material is thin and silky, draped across my torso and legs.

I jerk upright, my hand flying to my thigh instinctively, but I've woken up here often enough that some part of me already recognizes what happened.

I'm in the outer room of Stavros's quarters, on the sofa where I always sleep. It was only a dream.

My gaze finds the man who haunted me in that dream standing a few paces away, his arms crossed over his chest, his expression set in a glower. "You were mumbling and thrashing around. It was getting disturbing."

My mouth tightens. "Sorry I disrupted your sleep."

The other time the former general woke me from a nightmare, he leaned right in to shake my shoulder. He seemed mostly amused when I nearly sliced open his throat before I realized who he was.

He trusted that I wouldn't actually hurt him then. He doesn't now.

He knows how easily I could.

Not a single bit of magic squirms in my chest, though. There's nothing about this situation it can fix, as even it is apparently aware.

Stavros shrugs, and a different part of my brain kicks in, noting that he's only wearing an undershirt and drawers. The sculpted brawn of his arms and legs is on full display, his biceps flexing with the movement. "I'm sure my sleep is very high on your list of concerns. I'll be fine now."

I expect him to stalk away, but he pauses with just a slight shift of his feet. "What was terrifying you this time? Ster. Torstem and his cronies?"

My gut twists at the memory. An honest answer tumbles out before I can think better of it. "The hangman's noose."

Stavros's stance goes absolutely still. He stares at me for a moment, all trace of the glower gone.

We also both know who's most likely to lead me to that noose.

Does he have any idea how nervous I've been of him all along? Has it even occurred to him how much courage it took to stay here night after night, knowing how badly things could go wrong if *he* of all people discovered my secret?

Even when he'd warmed to me, even when he was being *nice*, I was still a little bit terrified of him.

It's all out on the table now, though. I don't have to hold back anything I'd want to say out of fear of what he'd realize if he reads between the lines.

Maybe it would help me re-earn his trust if he could see that I've considered his side too.

I swallow against the dryness of my mouth. "I understand, you know. Why you consider me a threat. Why you see riven as monsters. I don't trust my magic either. Why do you think I've tried so hard not to use it?"

A little of the bite comes back into Stavros's voice. "Why not turn yourself in, then?"

I grimace at him. "Because I haven't been using it. I've kept it under control. If I really thought I was on the verge of being a danger to the people around me..."

"It doesn't seem as if most riven think of themselves that way."

"Most riven go insane," I mutter, and hesitate. I've barely admitted what I'm going to say even to myself before.

But it's true.

My fingers curl into the sheet puddled around my waist. "I assume the insanity comes from using the power. So as long as I restrain myself, my head shouldn't get muddled like that. Sometimes... sometimes I think it's a good thing the first time I realized what I could do, I killed my sister. If it'd been a smaller act with smaller consequences, I'd probably have kept going. I'd have hurt so many more people. This way the damage was mostly contained."

Julita speaks up from the back of my skull. *Ivy... you can't think any of it was right. You shouldn't have had to deal with this mad power at all.*

And yet I do have to deal with it. I can't say my pain is worse than what I could have inflicted on hundreds of others combined.

Stavros's jaw clenches. For a second, I think he's either going to shout at me or laugh.

But when he speaks again, his tone is milder. "Is that why you took up your calling as the Hand of Kosmel? You said you had things you wanted to set right. You decided it was some kind of penance?"

"Something like that." I look down at my hands. "I was born with a broken soul. I know that makes me a monster. But for as long as I'm able to... I'd like to be other things too."

My body tenses, braced for the blow I'm expecting to come, whether verbal or physical.

Stavros props himself against the side of a nearby armchair, no longer looking as if he's holding himself back from storming away. His arms come down, the one that ends in a stump resting on his thigh. He doesn't wear a prosthetic to bed, of course.

He swipes the hand he still has across his mouth. "I suppose there are worse reasons."

"So glad you think so," I can't stop myself from muttering and then snap my mouth shut.

I peer up at him tentatively through the darkness of the room. He's looking at me with the little twitch of his head that tells me he's refocusing his vision. Studying me rather than accusing me with his gaze. His red hair and his eyes with their blue-and-brown-ringed irises both look nearly black in the dimness.

"You still don't have any idea what Kosmel wants with you?" he asks.

I shake my head. "He hasn't spoken to me since that night in the All-Giver's tower."

"Perhaps you should try to speak to him. He's got a shrine right in that temple."

My body balks instinctively. It was unsettling enough entering the Temple of the Crown, the largest building of worship in the country, when I knew the entire city was on the line.

To simply go in to try to chat with one of the godlen who should theoretically hate what I am, even if this particular godlen doesn't seem to mind at the moment...

"Maybe," I say. "I'll see. He didn't tell me anything all that useful the two times he did talk to me anyway."

"Sounds like typical theology to me."

Stavros straightens up again, presumably planning to finish the sleep I interrupted. The tentative peace between us feels as if it might shatter the second he walks out of this room.

I open my mouth, and the other topic I've been afraid to bring up leaps onto my tongue.

"I'm sorry about your friend too. I—I never wanted to remind you of any horrible part of your past. Was it the riven sorcerer you tracked down two years ago who was responsible?"

The first day I stayed in this room, the former general told me one of the riven had "butchered" his best friend. He has a more personal reason than most to hate me for what I am beyond all the atrocities the riven have inflicted on broader society.

Stavros stiffens. "No," he says shortly. "It was—we were teenagers when it happened."

Anywhere from ten to fifteen years ago, then, if he's in his late twenties like he looks. A grief he's being carrying about as long as I've mourned my sister.

"What happened?" I venture.

He takes a step back from me, his expression hardening. "I was living with my mother as I told you I usually did. He was one of her supporting officers' sons. We had the idea we'd make an adventure of having a ramble through various towns in the area. And we ended up in the wrong place at the wrong time. We were stupid and careless, and I didn't realize until it was too late—"

Stavros cuts himself off. His voice goes totally flat. "We were stupid, and we crossed paths with a monster. That's all there is to it. You don't need to know the details to ensure you don't end up doing the same."

He prowls off into his bedroom without another word.

*It'll be okay,* Julita says, her voice a little too quavery to be totally convincing. *He'll come around. He's got to see you're not like the other riven.*

Does he? I don't know about that.

I thought we'd made a little progress, but I might have dashed it to bits with my curiosity.

Exhaustion from my own interrupted sleep drags at my eyelids. I force myself to lie back down on the sofa and tug the blanket up to my chin, trying not to think about the conversations I've had with Stavros in this room that ended on much better terms.

Trying not to ache with the knowledge that he may never speak with me like an equal again, and I'm not sure that's even unfair.

# TEN

*Ivy*

I didn't realize how much I appreciated having a friend to sit with in the dining hall until that friend was gone.

Granted, Esmae was only pretending her friendliness. She murdered Julita and tried to do the same to me.

But she was good company before all that came to light.

Gripping the breakfast plate I've picked up from one of the room's many counters, I scan the tables. The first familiar face I spot is Anya's.

My former nemesis has her blond hair piled on top of her head in her preferred style and a sharp smile curving her lips. I disarmed her by pretending to be *her* friend shortly before my confrontation with Wendos in the All-Giver's tower, but I have no desire to cozy up to the bully beyond that. I'm just glad my gambit worked well enough that she hasn't resumed her harassment.

A few tables over, there's Romild, who probably thinks even less of me now than she did when she insinuated that I'd fucked my way into the assistant position. It's become clear that Wendos used her as a diversion to lead my investigations astray and that she isn't actually involved in any illicit sorcery, but it's been equally clear that she'd sooner spit in my face than have a genial conversation with me.

My gaze snags for a moment on a tawny head I've come to know well. Casimir is seated with his back mostly to me, but there are only a few other students sitting at his table.

It wouldn't look *that* odd for me to grab a chair at the other end, would it? I don't even have to talk to him—simply being in his presence would make me feel less alone.

But just as I start to take a step toward him, a noblewoman with ebony ringlets sashays to his side and rests her hand on his shoulder as she leans in to speak. It's the woman I saw him dancing with at the ball.

He told me he uses the balls to let possible patrons "sample" his skills as a courtesan. Is she looking to hire him now?

My stomach twists, and I yank my gaze away.

It's his job. I've got no right to feel queasy over him embracing his calling.

I don't really want to witness a transaction in progress, though. It's safer for him if I keep my distance anyway.

Really, it was selfish of me to consider going over there when I could be putting him in danger.

That thought helps me focus on my larger mission. Are there any bug club members around I could contrive to sit near?

I don't want to be blatant about seeking them out, but even being able to listen in while they talk with other students might reveal something useful.

I meander between the tables, casting my gaze about as if I'm looking for an ideal seat.

While I can fake the airs of a noblewoman reasonably well, I've always stuck out a little among this upper crust crowd. No one meets my eyes other than once, briefly, followed by a disdainful curl of a lip.

I've only made it past a few tables when a clear, even voice speaks up from behind me. "Ivy, isn't it? You could join me over here."

I swivel to find distantly-royal Petra aiming a subdued smile at me. She motions to a few empty chairs at a nearby table.

My legs lock, just for a second. I don't have any reason to believe that the queen's niece-twice-removed—or whatever exactly she is—would see me as an ideal dining companion.

What's she really up to?

Will it be more of a mistake to accept her invitation or to refuse her?

*Go on,* Julita murmurs. *Let's find out what she wants. It's not as if you couldn't take her in a fight.*

I restrain a snort at that sentiment and make myself return Petra's smile. "Thank you. I'll do that."

As we walk to the chairs and take our places, I surreptitiously study the other woman.

Julita is probably right in her assessment of our fighting capabilities. Petra has a few inches on my short frame, but her arms look soft in contrast with my wiry muscle. Her figure is more curvy than combat-hardened.

I have to assume she drops in on Stavros's classes to try to develop skills she's lacking rather than to hone an established talent. I definitely haven't seen any impressive moves from her during sparring sessions.

She is a little hard to pin down, though. Her dress is fine, with delicate embroidery across the bodice and down the skirt—eye-catching but not entirely fitting the typical styles around the college. She must have enough interest in fashion to appreciate impressive work without caring whether anyone else is impressed by the same.

Like the other times I've seen her, she's let her black hair spill loose over her shoulders, only a small portion braided back from her tan brow. I've looped my own hair into an updo so I can fit in with most of my schoolmates, but apparently Petra doesn't care about that either.

I guess when you're related to the royal family, even if only by marriage, you're a little above those concerns. She does always seem to keep a subtle distance from the other students.

But not with me, not right now.

I glance around to confirm no one I'm keeping an eye on from the bug club is nearby. The kinds of things I'd want them to overhear and the kinds of things I'd be comfortable saying directly to Petra have very little overlap.

As I lift my fork, my nerves buzz with apprehension. Thankfully, Petra speaks before I have to decide how to start a conversation with her.

She flicks her hand in a graceful motion toward the room at large. "You've only been at Sovereign College for a few weeks, haven't you?"

I nod and stick to my standard cover story. "I only meant to come for a visit, but I ended up meeting Ster. Stavros at just the right time and found myself with a job."

"I've seen that not everyone has been all that welcoming, but hopefully you haven't regretted staying."

I can't suppress a laugh. She has no idea how much I have to regret.

But I can still truthfully say, "No, I like having the chance to accomplish more than I could back home."

Petra gives a light laugh in return and tears the crescent roll on her plate in two. She has to hold it carefully in her right hand, where her little and ring finger are both missing—her dedication sacrifice, I assume.

Giving part of her dominant hand would have earned her a greater gift. I don't sense her working any magic on me now, but some divine talents are more passive while still useful.

"You've found a few things to like, then," she says. "Ster. Stavros hasn't been too difficult an employer?"

Oh, that's a topic and a half. I turn my answer over in my mind, deciding on the best way to word it. Last night's tense conversation stands out starkly in my memory.

"He has high standards," I say. "And he demands a certain amount of deference. But he isn't unreasonable. I don't mind having to work hard if the situation is fair."

*I wouldn't say he's been all that fair to you lately,* Julita puts in.

Petra tips her head thoughtfully as she chews. "I haven't attended many of his classes, but he does seem to have a good balance between being supportive and firm."

A little of my own curiosity bubbles up. "You're in the leadership division, aren't you? Why have you joined any of the military classes?"

The corner of Petra's mouth kicks upward in a crooked smile that looks a little odd on her otherwise dignified face. "My parents have always maintained that it's important for us all to be able to defend ourselves and what we care about if need be. You never know when you might end up under threat with no one with more expertise to call on for help. And everyone says Ster. Stavros is the best to learn from."

The smile gives her a more youthful appearance than before. I assumed she was late in her schooling, a couple of years older than me, but suddenly I'm not so sure.

"How long have *you* been taking classes here?" I find myself asking.

"A little over a year now," she says, which means if she started at the college at eighteen like most nobles do, she won't be more than nineteen now. I'm actually her senior, though not by much. "Also, I honestly enjoy the physical exertion of the sparring. Haven't you found activities here that you enjoy even though they're not part of your official focus?"

I shrug. "Of course. I appreciate the chance to go riding when I get it. And there are a lot more books in the library than I had access to at home—I'm certainly not reading about warfare all day long. But having fists thrown at you isn't most people's idea of a good time."

"I suppose not." Petra keeps smiling at me, though I still get the sense she's studying me as much as I am her. "But it's appeared that you're not all that concerned about being like 'most people' either. That's one of the reasons I thought it might be nice to talk."

One of the reasons. Gods only know what the others are.

Julita hums as if in agreement. *There's definitely more to this overture than she's letting on.*

"Well, thank you," I say awkwardly, not sure how else to answer her.

We eat in silence for a few minutes while I wonder if I'm giving away something uncouth in my gestures or expressions. What does she believe she's learned about me so far?

Does she think I might be acting against her family? What will she do if she decides I am?

Petra pops one last piece of roll into her mouth and leans back in her chair as she swallows. "You became friendly with Esmae very quickly. It must be difficult, her leaving so abruptly."

It sounds like an off-hand remark, but I have to stop my spine from stiffening. Stavros told me that the king decided to put out an official story that Esmae returned home rather than reveal her death and all the complicated circumstances around it.

After a week or two without her turning up, people will start to assume she was waylaid on her journey and murdered. I'm not sure if her family will find that more comforting than the idea that she'd become a murderer herself, but it's not up to me anyway.

*Good riddance,* Julita mutters.

As much as I can't regret my act of self-defense, a lump rises in my throat with the memories of the meals I shared here with Esmae when I thought we were friends. It's a particularly uncomfortable sort of loss, missing a person while also feeling ashamed that they managed to deceive you so thoroughly.

My smile probably looks a bit rigid, but surely I'm allowed to show a little of my emotions even if I'm pretending it's a less permanent loss. "It seems as though people come and go pretty often here. But it has been a bit lonely without her."

And with most of the men I'd counted on before eyeing me with varying degrees of suspicion.

Petra gives my hand a light pat. "You should join us for another hunt sometime. That'll give you an excuse to ride."

She gets up to carry her plate to the counter. I chew the last of my bacon, but my stomach stays clenched tight.

She definitely had some other agenda. Now I've got to make sure I'm playing this game right to keep out of trouble with her too.

If Esmae taught me anything, it's that I can't underestimate just how much damage one student might do.

As I drop off my own plate, I notice Casimir and the ringleted woman heading out. When I reach the doorway, they're ambling toward the main staircase, her hand grazing his shoulder while she lets out a bell-like laugh.

Julita stirs in the back of my head. *The patrons don't matter all that much to him, Ivy.*

Maybe that's true, but it doesn't mean I want to watch them canoodling the whole way up to my room.

I veer in the other direction and just keep walking—past the games rooms and other leisure venues I haven't investigated, all the way around to the narrow hall at the back of the Domi's first floor.

The sight of the stone columns along the walls makes my lungs constrict. It was farther down this hallway, at the other end near the row of tapestries, where Esmae stabbed a knife into my back.

I stride on into the dank, cramped stairwell barely anyone bothers to use back here. No need to worry about running into prying eyes on my way to the fourth floor.

I emerge amid the staff quarters a few minutes' walk from Stavros's rooms. A couple of other teaching assistants are just wandering around the corner ahead of me.

Ducking my head and itching for the anonymity of my cloak, I meander slowly after them so I won't catch up and have to navigate either sneers or awkward small talk. My gaze slides along the rug that runs the length of the hall—and snags on a small, gray-furred body that's just wiggling out of a crack between the stones at the base of the wall.

A rat. It freezes against the wall, maybe noting my presence.

There's nothing so strange about a creature like that scurrying through a building like this. Even nobles have to fend off vermin from time to time, especially when there's food around.

But as I come up on the animal, a quiver of magic jitters through my nerves.

It's not just a rat. Someone's used their gift on it, somehow or other.

And then left it to sneak around on the staff floor. I can't think of many good reasons to do that.

In my hesitation, the creature darts forward along the wall. I don't think, just leap after it.

My fingers snatch at the rat's tail, firm enough to stop it in its tracks.

I expected it to squeal or freeze in terror. Instead, it whips around with its teeth bared to chomp at my thumb.

"Shit," I hiss, smacking the rat's head away with my other hand.

It only flails more wildly, its jaws and tiny claws raking at every bit of my flesh it thinks it might be able to reach. I fumble to try to get a grip on it that would restrain its body, and it sinks its teeth into the base of my palm.

My hand jerks instinctively, slamming the rodent into the wall. It hits the plaster surface headfirst with a crunch of its skull.

Before I can even curse that I couldn't capture it alive, the creature's limp form turns hard and heavier in my grasp. I'm so startled by the sudden change that I drop it.

The thing that was once a living rat hits the floor and cracks into a few jagged pieces. Jagged pieces of what looks like fired clay.

*What in the world is that?* Julita demands.

I don't know. Totally bewildered, I hunch down to take a careful look.

The chunks of clay would form a sculpture of a rat if I nudged them back together. Fine lines of fur are even carved into the reddish-brown surface.

But it had actual fur when I grabbed it. It felt like a real rat—it moved like one.

It bit like one, as the blood dribbling over my hand can attest.

A chill seeps through my body. Something is very wrong here, and I've never seen anything like it.

# ELEVEN

*Ivy*

As he lays the cord in a loop on the floor, Stavros shoots a wary look at the small canvas bag I'm clutching. "What exactly is your big surprise?"

My fingers curl tightly around the bag's neck. "I think it'd be better if we all discuss it together."

The former general is going to find my story hard enough to believe without me needing to tell it twice.

He grimaces but lays out the second circle of cord without remark. His is red. Mine is black.

The cords are the key to the new meeting room King Konram set up for us before he left on his courtly tour. We each got a different color.

The other men have kept their own cords, of course. Stavros hasn't budged about holding on to mine as well as his own, so I can't use it unless I have his permission.

Who knows what horrible riven things he thinks I'd get up to on my own in a room full of books and maps?

It doesn't matter anyway, since I'm not likely to be attending meetings without him present. I manage not to roll my eyes at him when he steps back from my loop and gestures toward it as if to say, "Go ahead."

As I step toward the ring of cord, my chest tightens just a little. I *can* thank my wretched magic for the fact that using this enchantment sends a wriggling sensation right down the middle of my soul.

The cords must have been blessed by Jurnus, the godlen concerned with travel as well as communication and weather, through the gift of a dedicat who made a particularly hefty sacrifice.

Girding myself, I step into the center of the loop—

And with a thud of my heart and a shudder through my veins, I'm standing in a matching loop positioned between a set of bookshelves and a gilded wooden desk.

I step out of my cord and nudge it off to the side just as Stavros's massive form pops into being next to me, as if out of thin air. He doesn't look remotely disturbed by our means of arrival.

We're the first to arrive. I take a moment to survey the space, which we've only used once before.

According to Stavros, this room is somewhere within the palace, next door to the college. The king told him the cords' power wouldn't extend much farther than that, as incredible as it already is.

I can't say whether we really are inside the palace and not just some secluded room on the campus, because the room hasn't got any windows. The only illumination gleams from a chandelier overhead, with candles I have to assume light up magically when there's movement below and snuff themselves out when we're gone.

It's hard to imagine King Konram assigning one of his staff to stop by on a daily basis just to replace those that have burned out. The thick wooden door next to one of the bookcases is secured by three different locks that even we don't know how to open.

We can't go out into the palace… but presumably no one can get in either.

The desk is certainly fit for a king: broad, heavy, and glinting with gold detailing. Four leather-padded chairs stand around it, as if he decided there'd never be any need for all five of us to sit down at the same time.

Set against the walls on either side, the massive bookcases rise all the way to the ceiling. One is packed with books of history and theology, the other with scrolls on the same subjects as well as various maps.

A narrow doorway leads to a smaller supply room with blank paper, ink pots and quills, and more recent records from the college and around the city. Everything King Konram thought we might need for our pursuit of the scourge sorcerers.

I'm not anywhere near as well-versed in the college library's materials as Alek is, but he swooned when he saw some of the volumes that'd been hidden away in the royal collection. It was almost too bad when Stavros hauled him over to begin the actual meeting.

Only almost. I don't need to become any fonder of the eager glint that can light up the scholar's bright brown eyes than I already am.

The space is like a fancier version of our old archive room—an archive befitting a king. Including an additional feature I'm not sure how to feel about.

Hanging on the wall by the supply room door is an ornate mirror about half the size as the one we used to speak to King Konram more than a week ago. I'm guessing this one could be used for the same purpose, unless he thought fixing our hair would be vital to the cause.

Does he expect to be let in on our discussions here when he returns to Florian?

Pushing aside that uneasy thought, I set my bag carefully on the tabletop. A waxy scent laces the air, telling me that the bases of the candles are real rather than conjured. I breathe it in, but I can't take any comfort from the subtle sweetness.

This is going to be a difficult conversation no matter who's involved.

Casimir arrives next, his short waves faintly damp as if he's just toweled off from a bath. I yank my gaze back to the table before the heat that sparked between my legs at the sight can flare any hotter.

He notices the bag on the table at once. "What did you bring, Ivy?"

I have to meet his eyes then; have to smile because I don't want to be a jerk. Even though a twinge runs through my gut with the memory of seeing him with his patron this morning.

"I made an interesting discovery today," I say. "I thought we should discuss it."

Benedikt arrives with a typical jaunty grin. As he saunters over to me, he digs his hand into his pocket. "I have a little present for you."

He retrieves a locket dangling from a chain—just like the ones the men all carry. "I had my merchant echo the blessing on mine, so yours should work the same way. It seemed about time you had one."

My skin prickles with my sense of Stavros looming nearby. Benedikt wasn't around when the former general dismissed Casimir's suggestion that I needed a means to summon the rest of them.

"Oh," I say, reaching to take it carefully, a little concerned that Stavros might swipe it out of my hand. "Thank you. Hopefully I won't need to use it again."

"Better safe than sorry," Benedikt replies cheerfully, and hesitates as his gaze slides to Stavros. "Did I beat you to the punch, Stav? If you were having one made too, it can't hurt to have a backup."

"It's fine," Stavros says, but Benedikt's brow knits at the edge in his voice.

He laughs it off a moment later and flops into one of the chairs with a return of his carefree air. Alek materializes a moment later, shooting a longing glance toward the bookshelves before joining us.

Stavros points his prosthetic hand toward me. "Ivy has something to share with us."

He manages to make it sound like a punishment.

Ignoring his mood, I tug open the mouth of the bag. "This is going to sound crazy, but I promise you, I know what I saw."

*I saw it too*, Julita pipes up. *I mean, it was insane, but it was also real.*

I slide the broken pieces of the clay rat out onto the tabletop. As I nudge them into an approximation of their correct form, all four of the men lean closer.

"Is that a sculpture of a *rat*?" Benedikt asks in an amused tone. "What, did you pilfer it from a shrine of Kosmel to try to catch his attention?"

Rats are one of the godlen of trickery's symbolic animals, but I don't think my divine acquaintance had anything to do with this one.

I shake my head. "I saw a rat nosing around on the fourth floor of the Domi. Something seemed... off about it." Benedikt doesn't know about my magical sensibilities because he doesn't know about my actual magic, but hopefully the others can guess what I mean. "I tried to catch it so we could examine it, and it attacked me. I killed it accidentally—and it turned into this."

I motion to the clay figure.

No one speaks for a few seconds. Alek's lips part, but it takes another beat before he gets any words out. "You're saying an actual rat turned into clay?"

"Yes," I say. "The second it died. Which makes me think it was *always* clay, just someone magicked it into looking and acting alive."

Stavros clears his throat. When I look at him, his gaze burns into mine. "That's an incredible feat. You're suggesting the scourge sorcerers were responsible? Not anyone else?"

Benedikt's forehead furrows in confusion. "Why would we think it's anyone else?"

I know exactly what the former general means. He's suggesting my fathomless magic was responsible somehow.

I glower right back at him. "I can't think of anyone else who'd have an interest in doing something like that." Including myself.

Casimir rubs his chin. "There are a lot of purposes a scheme like that could serve, aren't there? The conspirators could be using small animals totally under their control to spy on staff or retrieve items or create some kind of effect. But I've never heard of anyone with a gift that could bring inanimate material believably to life."

We all look toward Alek.

The scholar leans forward to snag his fingers around one of the chunks of clay. Frowning, he examines it.

Then he lifts his eyes to meet mine. "You're absolutely sure it transformed? It wasn't just a trick of the light that made you mistake it for real?"

"Yes," I say quietly. "I was holding its tail—I could feel the skin and its fur brushing my fingers. And its teeth when they bit open my hand." I hold up said hand where a faint mark lingers after a medic's healing efforts. "I heard its skull break when I smacked it against the wall."

Alek's mouth twists. "I've heard of people who could animate figures like puppets before—still *looking* like the constructed object, made of wood or clay or what have you. But even in those cases, they had to stay close by to direct them. It's possible the scourge sorcerers have combined gifts to be able to conduct that kind of magic from more of a distance... But to turn it from clay into a creature of flesh..."

"People have tried," Benedikt says in a flippant tone. "It's one of those horror stories they like to tell, at least in the kind of childhood I had. Mothers who went seeking someone who could bring their infant back to life out of a doll. Parents who tried to recreate a beloved pet for their grieving children."

Julita shivers. *One of our maids told me that one about the baby.*

Alek is nodding. "Right. They're horror stories rather than histories because it doesn't *work*. No human being has ever been able to use magic to create life itself."

He taps his fingers down his front in the gesture of the divinities. "It's said that the All-Giver brought life into being by combining breath, blood, and flesh—sky, sea, and earth—as well as divine will. A *person's* will isn't enough. All you get is a body that looks real but remains totally lifeless. Not a rat that could scamper down a hall and fight being captured."

I sink down onto the arm of one of the chairs, hugging myself. "We didn't think the scourge sorcerers should be able to control daimon either, but it turned out they'd found a way. I heard Torstem saying they needed to switch tactics."

Stavros scowls as if he's displeased that he has to agree with me even a little. "You said he mentioned something about construction, didn't you?"

"Yes." I stare down at the remnants of the clay rat. "He could have meant figures like this."

Even Benedikt looks startled out of his normal breezy attitude. His face has gone paler than usual. "Gods above, if they can create life itself…"

Julita lets out a discomforted sound. *How can the villains be getting even* worse *than they already* were?

"We don't know exactly what's going on," Casimir points out in his gentle tone. "It could have been a very elaborate, very convincing illusion over a puppet-like figure. Or some other trick we haven't thought of."

The former general draws his brawny body even taller. "Still, it's nothing good. They're pulling together a new plan. We need to be more prepared this time. I'll pass on word to the king and let him decide whether he wants to put his staff on guard for vermin. It's a delicate balance between defense and tipping the conspirators off before we can take them down."

"*We* can all keep an eye out," I say. "For any animals—it may not be only vermin. If you see a bird hanging around the school more avidly than is normal, or even a stray cat or dog that comes out of nowhere… We should try to catch it. Then we can examine it properly and get a better idea of what the magic is."

Benedikt chuckles. "Don't use your strategy, you mean."

I make a face at him. "Killing it was an accident."

"We don't need to rely on Ivy anyway," Stavros breaks in. "We can handle a few things ourselves."

The bastard's bastard flicks his attention to the former general with another furrowing of his brow. He's got to be picking up on the new tensions that've formed between us—and he won't have any idea what could have caused them.

My skin itches with that knowledge.

I gather together the clay pieces and set them on an empty section of shelf as the start of a collection of evidence. "We should all get on with it. My attempt at drawing Ster. Torstem's interest hasn't born any fruit yet. The daimon haven't caused any more trouble—the scourge sorcerers have to be up to *something* else."

"And the Crown's Watch hasn't turned up any further evidence of their activities," Stavros admits grimly. "The medics appear to have made a little progress with Wendos, but they still can't rouse him."

Alek dips his head with a jerk. "I'll see what I can find out about this sort of magic. We don't know how long we have before they make another major move."

He pushes away from the table but pauses to glance my way once more. "Be careful."

Before I have time to wonder why he aimed that concern only at me, he's stepped into his loop and vanished.

"I'll see what new rumors I can hear around the card tables as well," Benedikt offers, and hops into his own makeshift portal.

I straighten up, and Stavros motions me brusquely toward our adjacent rings of cord.

Casimir takes a hasty step toward us. "Stav—if I could talk to Ivy, just the two of us, for a minute?"

Stavros's scowl comes back, but he lowers his hand. "Fine. But I'm waiting for her here."

He stalks over to the doorway to the supply room to give us a little more space, though I can feel his gaze on me. I go over to join Casimir, pretending my heart doesn't wrench at his bright smile.

The courtesan lowers his voice so it's just for me. "Are you still coping with everything all right?"

I shrug as if rats made out of living clay are just another typical day. "Same as usual. Wishing we were making progress faster."

He pauses, his gaze flicking to the floor and up again. "You were in the cafeteria this morning— you might have seen me with—"

A flush sears up my neck. I interrupt before he needs to barrel any farther into whatever unnecessary explanation he's going to make. "It's fine. I know what we did the other day was just a little fun. I'm not going to get offended."

Is my heart aching like it's been stabbed through? Absolutely. But that's not Casimir's fault.

He wets his lips, the movement of his tongue only provoking more heat I wish I could will away. "With all the commotion afterward, we never really talked about our tryst. If anything about it left you out of sorts, I'd want to know."

The flush creeps up to my cheeks. Great God filet and fry me, has he been able to tell that I've fallen for him?

Have I been mooning over him despite my best efforts, and he's trying to get me to admit it so he can let me down easy?

I force my tone to stay as cool and steady as possible. "There isn't really anything to talk about. We both enjoyed ourselves, which was the whole idea, wasn't it? I haven't regretted it, if you're worried about that."

Gods smite me, has *he* had regrets?

Before I need to grapple with that awful thought for more than a second, Casimir offers me a softer smile that sends a flutter I can't suppress through my chest. "Good. Neither have I."

He draws in a breath as if to say more, but I don't know how long I can keep up my impression of nonchalance with him just a pace away, looking at me with those compassionate eyes in that gorgeous face.

"Then all's well," I say briskly. "I'd better not leave Stavros waiting any longer, or he might explode, and that would be quite a mess."

I say the last bit loud enough that the man in question hears it and lets out a derisive snort. With a bob of my head farewell, I hurry back to the former general's side.

Julita makes a puzzled sound. *Ivy, you have to know Cas would never do anything to hurt you. He really is concerned.*

I know he is. But with who we are and how I can't help feeling, his kindness hurts almost as much as cruelty would.

# TWELVE

*Ivy*

The hum of the Temple of the Crown's magic wraps around me as I gaze up at the immense marble building. I restrain a shiver at the sensation.

The gold spires of the four towers—three at the corners and the one in the middle that looms twice as high—shine as impressively as always. There's no sign that a week ago, a sorcerer of the most reviled sort of magic attempted to carry out a horrific purpose from that central tower.

If I'd had any doubt that the All-Giver abandoned our continent after punishing the first rise of scourge sorcery with fiery retribution, the scene before me would erase it. How could the One who is all things be here and *not* have noticed a mortal carrying out such horrific work in one of the grandest temples on the continent, in the tower dedicated to the highest of all divine powers?

I'd wonder why the lesser gods the All-Giver created haven't noticed either, but clearly at least one of them has. Kosmel helped me direct the backlash of my unpredictable magic while I knocked down Wendos.

Why haven't the godlen intervened further? Is Kosmel up to something, and he's hidden what's happened from the others?

Are they all waiting, giving us mortals a chance to set things right on our own? Poised to rain down more punishment if we can't prevent the scourge sorcerers from going too far?

I don't know where they might draw the line. We could be teetering on the edge of a second Great Retribution right now.

Which doesn't make me feel any keener to step inside those pale marble walls devoted to all nine of the godlen as well as their creator. But I've got my part to play in the whole mission to set things right.

Benedikt passed on word through Stavros that a couple of the bug club members from Wendos's group played a few hands in the cards room last night... and mentioned that they were planning to make appeals to their godlen at the grand temple this morning.

Stavros decided we would spend *our* morning strolling the outer field near the main entrance marking out spots for future strategic exercises. At least, until I spotted the two students I was watching for making their way out of the college.

I followed them at a careful distance, only stepping into view of the temple's broad front steps just as the two of them vanished through the huge arched door at the top. They're inside now, asking for a blessing or insight from the godlen they're dedicated to.

It doesn't matter what they want. What's important is that they see and hear me.

I square my shoulders and stride over to the steps.

Climbing them today in the bright autumn sunlight isn't quite as unnerving as my first trip up these stairs through the thickening twilight. Not knowing if I'd be struck down the second I set foot inside. Not knowing what deviant magic was being carried out up in the tower.

I survived my initial venture, and as far as I know, no one's trying to destroy the city right at this moment.

My boots tap across the smooth marble of the entrance hall. I've taken to wearing them with my dresses even though slippers are more the fashion.

I'd rather not end up anywhere without every knife I can have on me. You can't conceal much weaponry in a slipper.

I could walk silently, but I want the worshippers inside to hear my approach. It seems as if Ster. Torstem has already mentioned me to at least one of his followers. I can hope these two will be curious about what I have to say to the gods.

A few other figures pass me on my way to the vast worship room. When I enter the space beneath the vast arching ceiling with its panes of stained glass, I see several people kneeling at the godlen's alcoves or simply strolling through the room in silent contemplation.

Thankfully, Kosmel's alcove is currently empty—other than the tall statue of the godlen himself.

I march over, letting my boots hit the floor a little harder than is strictly necessary. From the corner of my eye, I see one of the two bug club members—who's crouched before Inganne, godlen of the arts and play, in the next alcove over—glance my way.

Good.

I sink to my knees by the base of the statue and look up at the marble-cloaked figure of the trickster godlen with his sly smile. The sight of the carved rat on his shoulder makes me want to grimace.

What does my self-appointed divine overseer make of the scourge sorcerers co-opting one of his symbols for their use? He's been awfully quiet the past several days.

Casimir suggested that I should come here and open myself up to Kosmel, see if he'd offer more of his inscrutable commentary. Even here, with the multicolored light shining down on me from the painted glass above and an aura of divine power quivering through my nerves, my body balks at the idea.

The first time the godlen addressed me, I was nearly dead with my defenses crumbled. The second time, I invited him in out of pure desperation.

I'm not dying or desperate right now. I'm not sure there are any other circumstances where I'd welcome that imposing presence into my head.

It's plenty crowded as it is.

*What are you going to say?* Julita whispers. *You can't mention anything too unsettling with all these other worshippers around.*

As if I need to be reminded. But I've had time to contemplate my tactics while waiting for the chance to act.

I bow my head and pitch my voice so that it sounds low but still carries beyond the alcove. As if I'm trying to stay quiet but my emotion is getting the better of me.

I'm hardly yelling, but if anyone nearby pays attention, they'll be able to make out my words.

"Kosmel, please guide me. How do I make them see that sometimes change is necessary? I know that's what you'd want too."

I lapse into a brief silence. No divine voice resonates through my bones, but if there's a door inside me I'd need to crack open, I'm definitely holding it tightly shut.

I'd rather the godlen realizes I'm *not* actually asking him these questions genuinely.

Maybe this is the last time I'll have to put on a show. Stavros passed on word yesterday that Wendos was showing more improvement. Maybe he'll wake up within the day and spill everything he knows, and the conspiracy will fall just like that.

Until that moment comes, I have to continue as if it won't.

After a few moments, I speak up again. "Give me the fortitude to hold my ground when so much around me is wrong. Let them see how it could be better. Let us not cower in fear of the risks worth taking."

Julita hums with an uneasy sort of amusement. *Those do sound like the sort of sentiments Wendos would have approved of. And my brother would have whole-heartedly agreed with your point about risks worth taking.*

I can hope I've earned a few points with any eavesdropping scourge sorcerers, then.

My gaze settles on the dice scattered around the feet of the statue. Gambling falls under Kosmel's purview, and his dedicats often make their appeals or ask their questions with a roll that may convey his answer.

A tumbling die feels a lot less intimidating than a divine voice ringing through my skull.

I pick one up and squeeze it against my palm, thinking as loud as I can at the stone figure before me. *Am I on the right path? You want me to take down the scourge sorcerers—is infiltrating their conspiracy a sound strategy?*

Then I flick the dotted cube across the marble base.

It taps against one of Kosmel's boots and rattles a short distance to the side, landing on a three.

The standard interpretation is that odds are yes and evens are no, higher numbers indicating a more emphatic response. If I believe the godlen had any hand in how the die fell, I could take a little comfort from that result.

*If* I believed it. Sometimes I still have trouble believing I haven't hallucinated Kosmel's interference with my life altogether.

I stand up, giving one last addition to my performance. "Thank you for watching over me and all others who don't quite fit expectations."

Without glancing around, I head out of the temple.

My stance doesn't start to relax until I've left the last marble step behind. I meander across the cobblestone courtyard, taking a few moments to simply breathe before I barge back into the equally judgmental atmosphere of the college.

An urge niggles at me to rove farther into the city—to slip into Crow's Close and find out the latest shady street gossip, to check in on the outer-warder families who haven't been visited by the Hand of Kosmel in weeks now. To snoop around the brothel where Torstem hid some of his accomplices or the orphanage he plucked them from in case the Crown's Watch has missed something.

But I don't know how closely the conspirators might be watching me. I can't do anything that could suggest I have other, suspect motives for acting like a good scourge sorcerer candidate.

As I amble into the lane around the side of the temple that leads to the college, raised voices catch my ears. I pick up my pace and spot several guards milling about outside the palace wall farther down the lane.

My magic quivers in my chest with a hitch of my pulse. What's going on?

I slow down to give me time to study the guards as I continue toward the college gate, and a well-built figure falls into step beside me. I have to suppress a twitch of surprise at Benedikt's boldness, approaching me here in public.

"Don't worry," the bastard's bastard says from the corner of his mouth, strolling along at a matching pace with his hands slung carelessly in the pockets of his embroidered trousers. "I'm using my gift of distraction to divert curious eyes."

It can't be that strong a gift when his dedication sacrifice was nothing more than the lobes of his ears. But there isn't much traffic coming in and out of the college along this road anyway, and the guards now hustling into the palace grounds aren't paying us any mind.

"What was so urgent you had to see me right away?" I ask, keeping my gaze ahead as if I'm walking on my own.

Benedikt pauses. His jaunty tone turns strained. "Those guards have a lot to answer for. Wendos is dead."

I flinch before I can rein in my reaction. Julita lets out a cry of frustration in my head.

With a deep inhalation, I regather my composure. "What? I thought he was recovering."

"From what I've heard, he seemed to be. He was starting to move, to murmur—more like he was in a dream than unconscious. The medics left him for the night—supposedly guarded, of course—and this morning they found his spirit had… departed."

*The scourge sorcerers murdered their own to cover their tracks,* Julita mutters. *No surprise at all.*

The same thought had occurred to me. My jaw tightens.

I drop my voice to the faintest murmur. "It must have been his 'friends.' They realized he might talk."

"Agreed." Benedikt lets out a rough laugh. "Although how they breached the security of the palace prison… Well, I suppose if they have even rats on their side, we're doomed."

Not doomed. Just out of hope that we can count on anyone other than ourselves.

Anyone other than me and my precarious plan.

As my stomach knots, Benedikt risks a glance over at me. He seems to hesitate again.

"Ivy… Did something more happen up in the temple's tower than what you all have shared with me?"

Shit. It takes all my self-control not to let my gaze jerk to his face. What has he figured out?

"I can't think of anything," I say cautiously. "Why?"

At the edge of my vision, I see Benedikt's mouth slant at a discomforted angle. "I've simply gotten the sense that our lovely group dynamic has been thrown off since that night in a way that doesn't fit what I do know. Stavros in particular has been acting rather oddly when it comes to you."

I'm going to have to lay into the former general about how poorly he's been hiding his hostility. My mind scrambles for an excuse.

"I think he's a little sore that I tackled the threat without him," I improvise. "The man does have quite the ego."

Benedikt chuckles, but he doesn't sound quite convinced. "You know, if there was anything else going on—we've been on this mission together from the start. We've looked out for each other. I hope I've never given you any reason to feel I couldn't pull my weight."

I swallow thickly. I don't think Benedikt has fumbled the investigation. He's been a valuable ally… Sometimes almost a friend.

When he kissed me that one time, mainly to give me cover, I could have imagined us being even more.

But he's also the half-nephew, bastard or not, of a king dedicated to ridding the country of the riven. A king I've seen him yearning to impress, as much as Benedikt tries to pretend he doesn't care much about anything.

I have no idea how he'd react if he found out the truth about me. And taking that gamble would put not just my life but our one current hope of destroying the scourge sorcerers in jeopardy.

"Of course not," I say firmly. "Although I might start questioning your judgment if you insist on accompanying me right into the college for all to see."

I give the second part a teasing lilt, but it serves its purpose. Benedikt winces and gives another chuckle that doesn't manage to hold much humor.

"Point taken, Knives. I've got matters to attend to elsewhere anyway."

He tips his head and veers off to make for the palace rather than the college.

Guilt sits leaden in my gut as I flash my bracelet to the gargoyle at the entrance and navigate the conjured maze to the directions embedded in this week's absurd password. *Flaming roaches lurch for righteous lust.* I'm not feeling any better when I step out into the courtyard.

Julita makes a sound as if clearing her throat. *I wouldn't tell him either. He didn't see Kosmel's mark on you—that's what's kept Stavros from going overboard. And Benny can be a little erratic. This isn't a matter where we'd want any more excitement than we've already had.*

Her confirmation takes the edge off my guilt but doesn't dissolve it completely.

I force myself to duck into the dining hall, because I'm supposed to be assisting with classes for most of the afternoon. Stavros will be incredibly unimpressed if I faint from hunger.

All through the hallways and between the tables inside the vast room, I sweep my gaze in search of furtive creatures sneaking about. I don't see anything except the usual haughty nobles.

I'm making for the classrooms in the Quadring after my hasty lunch when a prickling sensation spreads across my left palm. I jerk my hand open in front of me.

The prickles soften into an unnerving tingle that seems to crawl across my palm alongside spindly lines even paler than my sallow skin. Spindly lines that form letters before my eyes.

*You want more from this world. Tonight at the single bell. 50 paces into the woods. Come alone.*

As the conjured writing fades away, my mouth goes dry.

I've been summoned.

# Thirteen

Like with the rat, I wait until the last of the men emerges from his loop of cord in the palace meeting room. Although unlike the rat, Stavros already knows what I need to say, which is how I convinced him that we needed this impromptu meeting.

As Casimir glances around at us with a worried expression, Benedikt sets a plate of pastries in the middle of the table. "Confiscated from the dining hall. I thought we all might need a little refreshment at this time in the evening."

I guess we know what he was doing when he felt the tug to come. Naturally he'd bring dessert.

The rest of us eye the assortment without making a move to grab one. I know my stomach is clenched too tight for the idea of eating anything to be appealing.

Benedikt plucks up a tart and sprawls into one of the chairs. "Well, let's hear the urgent news. I interrupted an excellent dinner for this."

The former general shoots him a disgruntled look. We weren't supposed to meet again until tomorrow, but I signaled the others with their lockets.

"Ivy received an invitation," he says before I can speak. "Presumably from the scourge sorcerers."

Alek's shoulders stiffen as he stares at me. "What? Already? Who delivered it?"

I glance down at my hand. "I don't know. Conjured writing appeared on my palm and then vanished again. They obviously don't want me having any proof of the summons."

"What did they tell you to do?" Casimir asks quietly.

"I'm supposed to go into the campus woods—at least, I assume that's the woods they meant—at the first bell after midnight tonight, alone. That's all I know so far."

Benedikt has paused halfway through his tart. He licks a stray drop of berry filling from his thumb. "The woods. That seems rather ominous."

I shrug as if I'm not all tangled up with apprehension inside. "We know they've conducted rituals out there. Julita pointed out evidence of it before. And it'd be away from prying eyes."

Alek frowns. "Which means they could do anything to you and no one would see to help."

I tap my thigh where one of my knives lies beneath the skirt of my gown. "I am reasonably good at defending myself."

"But you don't know how many of them will be waiting for you. Or what magic they might be ready to wield."

All of that is true, which is the reason for my tangled apprehension.

I force a smile. "I'll cross that bridge when I come to it. If they simply wanted to kill me, I'd imagine there are easier ways to arrange that."

Stavros pulls one of the scrolls off the shelves and spreads it on the table. It's a map of the college and its grounds. "I may be able to obtain something that'll help conceal my presence. The king is supporting us, and he has plenty of resources. If I enter the woods from a different angle—"

I tug at the edge of the map to interrupt him. "No. The message emphasized the *alone* part—and Alek's right. We don't know what magic they can bring to bear. They managed to murder Wendos while he was under palace guard! You can be sure that whatever they're doing, confirming that no one's going to spy on their activities will be at the top of the list."

Stavros's cocky voice takes on the edge of a growl. "You can't go waltzing off into the woods in the middle of the night to meet a group of murderous psychopaths totally on your own."

I set my hands on my hips. "That's been the plan all along, hasn't it? What did you think would happen if I caught Ster. Torstem's notice—he'd invite me to tea to discuss the possibilities for overthrowing the royal family? Anyway, I won't really be on my own. Julita will be there with me, and she knows what these people are like better than any of you."

*You'd think I'd get a little credit from this bunch*, Julita says with light-hearted offense, but she can't totally hide the tension in her tone. *I'll get you through it as well as I can. I don't know exactly what you'll be facing. I never saw Borys and Wendos initiate anyone into their practices.*

I can't imagine she's looking forward to potentially reliving aspects of her childhood trauma. But she hasn't said a word against me continuing with this plan, no matter how much danger it puts her continued survival in too.

Of course, it isn't the danger *I'm* in that Stavros is worried about so much as the danger I might pose everyone else.

The former general narrows his eyes at me. "It'll be an unnerving situation, and they *could* mean to harm you. It'd be easy for you to get careless in how exactly you defend yourself."

I might slip and unleash my magic, he means.

Benedikt raises an eyebrow. "Does it really matter how 'careless' she gets with blades when it'll be these pricks getting cut by them? I say Ivy can stick it to them any way she likes."

I fix Stavros with a firm look that hopefully he catches at least a glimpse of with his faulty vision. I warned him just an hour ago that the fourth member of our group was catching on that we were hiding something from him. "I'm sure I won't be flinging my knives so far that they hit anyone who doesn't deserve it. Although if you decide to lurk in the woods and jeopardize whatever trust I've gained with them, I'd count you among the deserving."

Benedikt stifles a snort of laughter.

Stavros glowers back at me, but he seems to relax his stance with concentrated effort. "I'll keep my distance, then, but I'll be on watch."

"Fine."

Alek sets his hands on the table, the bronze-brown skin of his knuckles paling. "You may have their trust now, but what if they're looking for something from you that you can't give them or don't realize? Once you've interacted with them at all… they're not likely to give you the chance to report anything back to the authorities."

I've already thought about that too. "I'm good at thinking on my feet. This is our best shot. What other options do we have now that they've killed Wendos?" I glance at Stavros again. "The surveillance of the brothels and the orphanage still hasn't turned up any leads, has it?"

He grimaces. "Not so far."

"I just—" Alek's hands clench against the tabletop. He drops his gaze to them before meeting mine again, his bright eyes so intense my pulse skips a beat. "You've already risked so much for this investigation. I don't even know if we could get justice for you if they murder *you*."

"Alek," I start, not even sure what I'm going to say to reassure him, but he shakes his head as if he already knows.

"I've seen records—there've been a couple of members of the entomology club who disappeared at different times. One body turned up looking like he'd been mugged. Another was set up to look as if she'd gone boating on the river and drowned. I'd guess they saw something they shouldn't have... and Ster. Torstem's people know how to remove 'problems' without it even looking like murder."

So if I die tonight—or later—at the hands of the scourge sorcerers, even my death might be for nothing. My stomach knots tighter in response to the agitation Alek's failing to hide.

"We'll know," Casimir says in his gentle way. "Ivy has all of us on her side. The scourge sorcerers don't realize that. No matter what happens, we'll see through their lies."

Alek still looks so miserable even with his expression concealed by his mask that my heart wrenches. He opens his mouth and closes it again in a tight line, as if there's something he wants to say but doesn't feel he can.

Has he found out something else that he doesn't want Benedikt—or Stavros, for that matter— hearing about?

A chill ripples down my spine.

I make myself pick up one of the glazed puffs from the plate of desserts and take a nibble. The sweetness laces my tongue without providing any comfort.

"Well," I say with a wave of the pastry, "it seems like that's all there is to talk about. I'll go into the woods tonight and not get murdered and find out what the scourge sorcerers are up to. The rest of you can go back to your dinners or what have you. I'll signal you through the lockets in the morning so you know I'm back at Stavros's quarters safe and sound."

Benedikt gets up, though I think the look he aims at the rest of us is a little wary. "I may have to indulge in a second dinner to make up for the first that'll have gone cold before I could finish," he announces jauntily, and steps toward his makeshift portal.

Casimir aims a soft smile at me. "I know you're stronger than them." He pauses until Benedikt has vanished and then adds, "They might ask about your magic—the magic they'll assume you have from your dedication."

I glance down at my right hand with its missing fingertip—what the men around me assumed was a sacrificial offering at first. "I can make up a story. They won't expect anything major with this small a 'sacrifice.'"

I'd sooner kiss Stavros's boots than tip the scourge sorcerers off that I'm godless, let alone what other magic I can wield despite that fact.

"We don't know what lengths they'll go to in order to confirm your story." The courtesan tips his head toward Stavros. "I can use makeup to imprint a believable godlen brand on her chest. I'll come by a couple of hours before they're expecting her?"

The former general gives a begrudging grunt. "We should be prepared for every possibility."

I hadn't even considered that one. My hand closes against the unmarked spot between my breasts. "Thank you for thinking of it."

Casimir's smile comes back. "Even if we can't go into the woods with you, you'll have our support."

Alek clears his throat with an urgent note. "Shouldn't Ivy be able to support herself in every way she can? If she has to prove something to the scourge sorcerers, or if she needs to defend herself, or there's a chance to find out more... Her riven magic would allow her to—"

"No." Stavros cuts in with a tone so dark and harsh it makes my pulse jump. "We're not adding more horrors to the mix. If Ivy's looked after herself so well for all these years without her magic, she can continue to do so."

"But—"

"We are *not* unleashing riven sorcery within a stone's throw of the capital palace," Stavros snaps.

I hold up my hand, catching Alek's gaze. "It's all right. I agree with him. I don't want to be throwing my power around either—I don't know what the consequences could be."

We stand in silence for a few tense moments before the scholar lowers his head in acceptance. I can't quite believe he'd approve of me bringing out my magic to begin with.

Just how worried is he about what will happen tonight?

"I know you can handle yourself," Casimir says with a brief touch of my arm. He vanishes through his ring of enchanted cord.

Stavros shifts as if he expects the rest of the meeting to break up, but Alek is still hesitating by the table. If there's something more he knows, he doesn't want to reveal it in front of the former general.

I motion to the dessert plate. "Why don't you have one, Alek? Take a moment to savor a little treat and remember how far we've already gotten."

He studies me for a few seconds and then reaches to pick up a tart.

I take another delicate nibble of my puff and raise an eyebrow at Stavros, who's standing stubbornly there waiting for me to trot back to his quarters at his heels. "I could use a moment too, without you glaring daggers at me. You're about to let me wander off into the woods on my lonesome tonight—how much trouble do you think I can get up to in a locked room?"

Stavros attempts to glower me into submission, but he hasn't drawn his sword, so I feel reasonably secure it's a bluff.

After a moment, he sighs. "If you insist. I'm going to finally get *my* dinner and negotiate field time with the other military division professors. I should be back at my quarters by tenth bell—I expect to see you then too."

I bob into a mock curtsy that's probably less respectful than doing nothing at all. He shakes his head and strides over to his cord.

When he's gone, Alek sinks into one of the chairs. "You didn't need to stay with me."

"I figured dessert is more enjoyable with company," I say. "And I really do need a break from that oaf."

The corner of the scholar's mouth twitches, but the impression of gloom around him doesn't shift. All the same, I can't help tracking the movements of his full lips as they close around the edge of the tart.

All of these men are too ridiculously handsome for their own good. Or for *my* own good, is more like it.

Yanking my eyes away, I pop the rest of the puff into my mouth while I consider my words.

Propping myself against the table near his chair, I motion toward him. "What are you really worried about? You seem more concerned than everyone else combined. Did you find out something you didn't want to tell the whole group?"

Alek looks startled enough that I believe his denial. "What? No. It's only…"

He frowns and glances away. When he fixes his attention on me again, it's with an air of determination. "You're going in there with Julita. How much is she supporting what *you* think is the best plan, and how much is she pushing you to do what *she* thinks is?"

My hackles come up automatically, even as Julita makes a chagrinned noise. "I'm perfectly capable of coming up with good plans on my own."

Alek holds up his hands. "I'm aware of that. That's not what I was implying. I—I remember what you told us about how she persuaded the four of us to start investigating, and you said she'd used a similar strategy with you. Now you're diving into this mission that could very well be fatal. I know how much it mattered to her to stop the scourge sorcerers."

*Oh,* Julita murmurs. *Well. I suppose that's fair.*

It isn't, though.

I shake my head. "I also told you afterward that I blew the situation out of proportion. She's been a good friend to me, on the whole—as good as she can be, the way things are. It's a messy situation. But I didn't survive for eight years on the streets by letting other people badger me into doing things I thought were a bad idea. And this idea I came up with myself, whether you think it's bad or not."

Alek winces. "It's not so much that I think it's bad. It's just so risky, putting yourself in the scourge sorcerers' hands. And we'd lose both of you just like that."

Is that really the crux of it? He doesn't trust Julita whole-heartedly anymore, but he's also afraid that what little life she's clung to will be snuffed out? And maybe he's conflicted about wanting her and yet feeling he shouldn't both at once.

He always did seem to be the most devoted to her out of the four men.

An unexpected melancholy descends over me. I can gaze at his handsome face and admire his incisive mind, and he once told me he wouldn't think I was an idiot for making a pass at him, but the scholar is just as out of reach to me as the courtesan is.

I can't give him what he really wants, because what he really wants is a woman who's only a ghost. Who maybe didn't even totally exist the way he saw her when she was alive.

But he still cared enough to make sure I wasn't being shoved into dangers I wasn't totally okay with. He trusts *me* despite the reams of research I'm sure he's done on the riven.

I want to give him something that means as much as that back, so badly my chest burns with the urge.

If he could just hear from Julita in her own words…

My stance goes abruptly still. Ah. But he *can*.

The mere thought sets my pulse thumping anxiously fast. I wet my lips and shoot him a hasty smile. "Can you just… wait here for a minute? I think I might be able to show you something that'll settle your mind at least a little."

Alek eyes me with obvious curiosity but nods in answer. I push off the table and slip between the shelves to the adjoining supply room.

*What are you thinking, Ivy?* Julita asks. *Did you stash something in here that I didn't notice?*

"No," I whisper, low enough that Alek shouldn't be able to hear. "I was just thinking—"

I halt with a jolt of apprehension that shoots from my gut to my throat. Am I really going to put this proposition out there, even tentatively?

I said she'd been a good friend, didn't I? I've told her I trust her, and I do.

This would be as much a thank you to her for all the ways she's helped me navigate this world as it is to Alek.

It's some kind of miracle that I can offer her anything at all after the awfulness she's been through, including her own brutal murder.

I take a couple of steadying breaths to solidify my resolve. It still takes concentrated effort to form the words. "I thought we could make a deal. If I… relaxed and let you come forward, the way you've tried to before—the way you did when you made me let Alek and Benedikt into Stavros's quarters… you could talk to Alek. Reassure him about how you really feel. Explain things. Show him you're all right, or as well as can be expected. Just for a few minutes, and then you'd pull back. I wouldn't—"

*Ivy,* Julita breaks in, her voice a little shaky with shock. *Are you sure? I'd never have asked—*

"I know. That's the only reason I feel okay offering." I swallow down the nausea that's pooled in my stomach and square my shoulders. "You—you deserve to have at least one more glimpse of actual life while you're still here."

Julita lets out a raw laugh. *I wish I could hug you right now. You have no idea how honored I am that you'd give me this chance. You just let me know when you're ready. And if you change your mind, I won't be upset.*

I inhale and exhale one more time and lean against the wall. "Let's get it over with. Ready when you are."

I will my mind to wander as if in a daydream. My heart thuds on, but it feels more distant in my detached state.

Then the tingle of Julita's presence at the back of my skull ripples through my awareness.

My nerves jump with the instinct to block her way. I manage to rein myself in, floating on those ripples rather than fighting them.

My sense of my body turns fuzzy, as if I'm slightly numb from head to toe. My limbs move—my arms nudging me off the wall, my feet stepping across the floor—without any direction from me at all.

It is like floating. Drifting along inside a body I no longer control, all sensations clouded.

Is this how Julita feels all the rest of the time, when she's the one towed along by my decisions?

She saunters into the main meeting room but jerks to a stop when Alek glances around at her.

At us.

Her mouth stretches with a smile. "Gods above. Alek—it's so good to properly see you again. I don't even know where to begin."

Her voice sounds strange to my ears even though it's technically my own. I'm not sure if it's only because of my warped perspective or because she actually has a different cadence until Alek stiffens in his chair.

He can clearly tell something's changed.

"What's going on?" he says. "Ivy—"

Julita lets out a giggle that's definitely not a sound I'd normally emit. "She gave me a chance to speak to you properly. She really is a much more spectacular human being than any of you give her credit for."

Alek's posture stays rigid, but his jaw slackens. "Julita?" he croaks.

"In the flesh! Well, Ivy's generously lent flesh." She walks toward him, sliding her hand along the edge of the table as if reveling in the sensation. "I'm so sorry everything's become such a mess. I—"

Alek springs to his feet when she's still a couple of paces away from him.

"No," he interrupts, his voice taut. "Stop. Bring Ivy back."

Julita freezes, and I go still inside her.

Why's he so upset? I thought he'd be happy to get this chance.

"She suggested this, Alek," Julita says quietly. "She offered. I promise you I'd never have—"

A tremor runs through Alek's tensed frame. "It doesn't matter. This is *wrong*. You've already—Bring her back, *now*."

Julita seems to flinch, and then her presence is slamming straight through my mind like a sprung arrow. I jolt back into full awareness with a stumble and a gasped breath.

The impression of my ghostly passenger whips into her usual place at the back of my head and dwindles away. She's not just retreated but pulled right in on herself the way she has a few times in the past—into the distant, darkened state where she's told me she can't sense anything at all.

"Julita?" I venture, but as I expect, there's no response. Not even a quiver of acknowledgment.

Alek is staring at me. He wavers on his feet as if he's not sure whether to step closer or not.

His voice comes out rough. "Ivy?"

I yank my attention back to him. "Yes. Why— I was trying to help. I didn't mean to upset you."

He still looks upset. His mouth forms a series of only partly familiar sounds that I recognize with my rudimentary Woudish. "*Do you know the hour?*"

"*A little past eight,*" I answer automatically in the same tongue, and understand why when Alek all but lunges forward to grasp my arm.

Julita didn't know a word of Woudish. Hardly anyone at the college does.

He was making sure it really was me, not Julita just pretending to have left.

I'm vaguely offended on her behalf, but Alek speaks before I can defend her, the slide of his fingers sending a distracting tingle up my forearm. "Don't ever do that again. She had her life. This is yours."

I frown at him. "Well, she's completely withdrawn now—tucked away so deep she won't even be hearing this conversation. You were worried about her. It was the only way I could give you a chance to talk to her directly."

He steps closer, his bright eyes piercing mine. "I don't need to talk to her. Not like that. You're worth more than that. I was mostly worried about *you*. You've already given up a piece of your mind and a heap of freedom and everything you were doing before you were dragged into this place."

"It was my own choice to come. I decided—"

"You decided what your conscience could bear, not what you'd find easiest." Alek lifts his other hand to touch my cheek. "She's right, you know. You're the most spectacular person I've ever known, and I don't want to watch you whittle even a little of that away to make yourself less for someone else."

Warmth blooms in my skin at his tentative caress, making it harder to think. But I'm nothing if not stubborn. "It was only temporary. I wasn't giving anything up."

"You weren't *you*," Alek says. "It matters. It matters to me. I—"

He cuts himself off with a choked sound, and then he's dipping his head to press his lips to mine.

My mind blanks in shock and a blaze of heat. I barely manage to do more than stutter a breath before Alek is yanking himself away.

"I'm sorry," he mutters, pressing the heel of his hand to his temple. "I'm sorry. Of course you don't — I'll go."

He spins toward the loops of cord. Through my reeling thoughts, it hits me that he thinks *I* couldn't possibly want *him*.

Gods smite us all, how did we end up so muddled?

I throw myself after him before he can reach his ring and catch his hand. "Alek—"

I don't know what else to say. I ache with all the things I want and the possibility that this stunning, brilliant man might never realize it.

Maybe this surge of emotion matches what he felt just moments ago.

So when he turns back toward me at my tug, I let the flood carry me. I slip my hand around his neck, bob up on my toes, and meld my mouth to his.

# FOURTEEN

*Alek*

I'm kissing Ivy.

Ivy is kissing *me*.

I haven't kissed anyone at all in a long time, but I think the moment would feel miraculous regardless.

So much about this woman is tough and unyielding, but her lips are perfectly soft against mine, sweet from the pastry she just ate. The heat of her floods me from the meeting of our lips and her hand at my neck all the way down my body.

I want to drown in the sensation.

My pulse races madly with the giddying thrill of the embrace. How is this even possible?

I don't know, but all I can do is kiss her back and slide my arms around her slim frame. Pull her closer against me.

Through the heady rush, the memory rises up of seeing her emerging into the archive room with Casimir at her heels. Of the jolt of a different hot emotion that shot through me at the sight of their flushed faces and her rumpled dress.

A stab of jealousy, a searing impulse to protest that she was *mine*, and a dull burn beneath that tempered the other two reactions with the knowledge that of course she wouldn't want me that way.

But she does. By some miracle, she came to me. For at least the space of this kiss, she's mine after all.

Her fingers tease up my neck to my jaw, her thumb brushing the lower edge of my mask, and reality comes crashing in with a lurch of my gut.

She isn't really mine, not in any way that counts. I can't say she's picked me when she doesn't even know who I am.

Imagining the recrimination that would appear on her face makes me recoil. I pull back even though it feels like a piece of me breaks putting that distance between us.

Ivy stares at me, her cheeks flushed for me now, with the same ruddy tint that laces her hair. Her lips part, and then something shifts in her sky-blue eyes. Her body starts to tense.

As if she's bracing herself. I've seen that reaction before.

I know *her* well enough now to recognize what it means. Buried deep inside the fierce, resourceful woman who captivates me is the girl whose mother starved and beat her, who fled to the streets of the outer wards rather than risk catching the attention of the gods.

And I'm catching a glimpse of that wounded girl in those doubtful eyes.

"No," I say hastily, grasping her shoulder. Trying not to let the soft warmth of the skin at the edge of her neckline divert me from my purpose. "I'm not stopping because of you. Gods help me, there isn't a single thing about you that I don't want."

She lets out a rough laugh. "Not a single thing? Somehow that's a little hard to believe. There are at least a few things about me *I* don't even want."

I swallow thickly. I don't know how to tell her in a way she'll accept that her being riven has only made me more sure of how incredible she is.

Maybe once she knows what I really am, it'll make sense to her. Even if that means she wants nothing at all to do with me.

I keep my voice as even as I can. "That might be so, but I know what those things are. I know what you've done and who you are. But you... you have no idea how much I have to be ashamed of."

Ivy's forehead furrows. "You don't need to give me a list of all your wrongdoings. Everyone's made mistakes."

My chuckle sounds hollow even to me. "Not like mine. I—I can't feel right about this unless we're on level ground, aware of exactly who we're both welcoming." Whether she will still welcome my embrace afterward or not.

I pause. "Unless you'd rather end things here without—"

"No," Ivy interrupts, soft but firm.

Her gaze searches mine. She lifts her hand to rest it over mine on her shoulder, giving my fingers a quick squeeze that just about unravels me. "If you feel like you have to tell me, you can tell me."

All at once, my stomach is churning. But I asked for this—I practically demanded it.

I've tried so hard to only look forward. To plaster over every bit of my past failings so nothing matters but what I've done since.

But if there's even the slightest chance she'd kiss me again even after she knows, dredging up my shame is worth it.

I glance over at the gilded table. "You might want to sit down. It's a bit of a long story."

As I let go of her shoulder, Ivy follows my gaze. She walks back to the table, but rather than take one of the chairs, she hops up to perch on the edge of the tabletop itself.

Somehow she looks more comfortable there with one leg tucked under her skirt and the other dangling casually, her hands set by her hips as she leans slightly back on them.

I've started to treasure moments like this—glimpses of the real Ivy who isn't pretending noble airs and manners. The way she should always get to be.

It was so obvious from my very first glance when it wasn't her moving her body at all, when Julita was molding Ivy's shorter and wirier figure to the flirty poise that came so naturally to her in her own frame. It was like watching a contortionist manipulating someone else's limbs, twisting them into shapes they weren't meant to form, almost more horrifying for how subtle the shifts were.

Ivy let Julita's ghost play with her body like it was a puppet for *me*. Because I bungled things so badly she thought I'd want that—that I cared more about getting time with Julita than having Ivy be Ivy.

It doesn't matter whether she wants to kiss me again. If I can at least convince her of how much she matters to me—as she is, without needing to bend herself to anyone else's whims—that will be more than enough.

I rest my hands on the top of one of the chairs. My fingers curl around the ornately carved wood, grounding me.

Where to start but at the beginning?

"I've told you a little about how I grew up," I say.

Ivy nods. "Weapons merchant parents, brothers who joined the army, none of them appreciating how smart you are."

The corner of my mouth kicks up at a bittersweet angle. "You might revise your opinion of my intelligence once I'm done." I run one hand back through my hair, gathering myself. "I suppose you're aware of the provincial schools some temples run?"

"You started your education at one of those?"

"Yes." I suck in a breath. "There's a temple of Estera that has a school a couple of towns over from where I grew up. When I turned thirteen—that's the youngest they'll let you enroll—I convinced my parents to let me travel there to apply for entrance. I think by that point they were glad to have me out of sight and out of mind. When I was accepted and came back to gather my things, they barely bothered with good-byes."

"Better off without them," Ivy mutters.

I can't argue with her there.

"I thrived at the school," I continue. "I quickly started earning top marks, and that only made me more eager to continue my success. The fact that I could achieve so much without any gift seemed to impress people even more. My teachers offered me exclusive opportunities, my classmates wanted to collaborate with me. I even had a few brief flirtations, as far as those ever go at that age."

Ivy gives me a smile soft enough to tug at my heart. "You must have been pretty happy."

I wish I could remember the happiness in all the vividness it must have had at the time. Every bright moment I think back on is soured by what came after.

I look down at the chair I'm still clutching. "I was. But then, about a year and a half after I began my education, a boy and his twin sister enrolled. They were late arrivals, around the same age as me, but right from the start, the teachers started fawning over him—they graded his work even higher than mine, let him in on the same opportunities."

"It makes sense that you'd find that hard," Ivy says.

"In some ways, maybe, but..." I grimace. "A lot of my frustration was pure prejudice. They were from a lower-class family—pig farmers, I think. At least a few steps down from most of us there and several from me. He'd made a dedication sacrifice, and it rankled me that he might only be besting me because of his gift. And he barely even seemed to *try*. He was always going off to play sports or cards or what have you rather than studying. Over the course of a few months, I convinced myself more and more that it simply wasn't fair."

Ivy is sharp enough to recognize where my story is going. Her voice comes out quiet. "What did you do?"

I push myself away from the chair, too restless in my discomfort to stand still. But pacing to the bookshelves and back doesn't make me feel any better. It only reminds me of the long nights I spent poring over books on subjects that had nothing to do with my usual areas of scholarship, my eyes burning from concentration and my shoulders twinging from hours spent hunched.

"I told myself it was only right that I leveled the playing field. The strategy I came up with was to dose him with a botanical chemical that's considered a 'berserker' drug—in a few countries in the past, it's been used by warriors to fuel their ferocity and stamina in battle. At the proper quantity, it lowers your inhibitions and sparks your aggressive urges for a few hours. I thought he'd act out a little, insult some teachers and get in trouble, and people would stop seeing him as such a shining star."

"I'm guessing it didn't work out that way."

"No." A lump clogs my throat. "Neither botany nor chemistry are areas I've spent much time delving into, and less so then than now. I don't know... Either there was something about him that altered the effect, an extra sensitivity, or I gave him too high a dose. He went on a violent rampage, stabbed a classmate, punched a few teachers who tried to subdue him... and he never fully recovered.

His temper remained frayed; he couldn't concentrate on schoolwork. They had to expel him. I ruined his entire life."

My voice has gotten rough by the end. Ivy sits silently, absorbing my words.

I keep going before she feels the need to comment. "Obviously I felt horrible. But not horrible enough to confess what I'd done, because I felt even more horrible about the idea of getting expelled myself. Still so fucking selfish… But my rival's sister did have an interest in chemistry and suspected what I'd done. She brewed a potion meant to test my guilt—it would only burn a person's skin if they were guilty of whatever the person applying it accused them of."

Somehow, after everything I've told her, Ivy still winces in apparent sympathy as the implications must sink in. "She threw it in your face?"

At the memory of the searing pain and the acrid smell that flooded my lungs, I have to suppress a shudder. "Yes. In the middle of the dining hall at lunch time, yelling what she thought I'd done so everyone would see and hear. And the proof showed plainly. I'm lucky I flinched to the side and jerked up my arm, or the stuff would have splattered my eyes and *every* bit of my face."

"Couldn't the medics do anything about it?"

"I don't know," I admit. "The staff had the one on staff look at me, but I'm not sure how inclined they were to absolve me of my crime. She claimed the damage was set too deep for her gift to alter."

Ivy's jaw tightens. "So you were expelled after all."

I incline my head. "The temple school obviously didn't want to keep me. The only reason I'm here at the college is because one of the teachers saw particular value in my work. I've been most interested in finding traces of the parts of the continent's history that the Darium empire tried to destroy during their reign, piecing together fragments from journals and asides from treatises on other subjects… I'd managed to uncover quite a bit even back then. He took me under his wing privately and oversaw my continued work, and he recommended me to the scholarship division when I was old enough."

"It's been several years since your expulsion, then?" Ivy asks gently.

I can't bear the compassion in her voice. "Six. But that's no excuse. I was nearly fifteen. You knew better than to risk harming someone for personal gain by the time you were that age, even though you could have done it so much more easily."

Ivy's stance tenses. "I just made my mistakes earlier."

I sweep my hand through the air dismissively. "Because you were trying to save your mother's life and then your own. That's the most defensible excuse there is. I destroyed a classmate's entire future because of wretched *jealousy*. If either of us is a monster, it's obviously me. I even look the part."

"Alek…" Ivy scoots along the table, closer to me. "You're not a monster. You acted badly, but you saw how wrong it was, and you've made up for it. You've dedicated yourself to your work; you've been helping expose the scourge sorcerers. And I assume you've never been tempted to repeat the same mistake—you're not spending every day holding yourself back from making another spiteful attack."

"I'm not. But that doesn't change who *you* are. You can't help having the magic, but you've refused it, over and over."

"All right. Maybe I can believe that you don't think I'm a monster. Can you believe that I don't see *you* as one?"

My throat constricts even tighter. I make myself meet her gaze. "You've never really seen me."

The words hang between us for a few seconds. Then Ivy reaches out with a beckoning gesture. "Then let me see. Take off the mask, and you'll know for sure what I make of you."

Every particle of my body resists the idea. I haven't let anyone see my scars in years.

The last was one of the college medics when I first arrived. Her shiver of revulsion told me plenty.

But if I say no, then what? What has this whole confession been for if I'm going to refuse to expose the clearest evidence of my transgressions?

My shoulders have stiffened. I inhale sharply, and Ivy's eyes widen.

"You don't have to. I shouldn't have asked—"
"No," I break in. "You're right. We may as well settle this."
And let the cards fall as they may.
I take a step toward the table and reach for my mask.

# FIFTEEN

*Ivy*

Alek sets his fingers against the edge of his mask as if he's looping a noose around his neck. I brace myself against the urge to leap in and stop him—not for my sake, but because he looks so conflicted.

Maybe taking this step will be better for him. But I don't know exactly what he's about to reveal.

He undoes a snap that attaches the mask's strap around his head and eases the molded leather away from his face. His head starts to droop so his dark hair falls forward, as if he wants to hide himself as much as he can still, but he catches himself and lifts his chin.

When he lowers the mask, he turns his face so the most damaged side is angled toward me. So the full impact of the chemical burn is obvious.

Across his forehead and nose other than a strip over his eyes where he shielded them, down his right cheek to the edge of his jaw, streaks of mottled scars discolor his bronze-brown skin. Ruddy patches mingle with darker brown ridges, crossed through here and there by marks of deep gray.

In that first glimpse, my heart lurches, but only in shock. I hadn't pictured the damage looking quite like this.

But as I steady myself, gazing at him, it doesn't take long for my mind to adjust. There's nothing gory or frightening about the face before me. It's simply… different.

The swathes of different hues make me think of the impressionistic paintings I've seen—portraits and landscapes conveyed in broad strokes of paint that don't appear realistic up close but merge together into a cohesive image when you take in the bigger picture.

It's a style favored more by poorer artists who can't always take the time to match every tiny detail for pure realism, but I've always appreciated the vision that goes into them.

Alek shifts his gaze to meet mine, his bright eyes part of that varied canvas now rather than standing out starkly amid an even plane, but no less penetrating for it. His stance is so taut I'm almost afraid to speak.

He needs to see that I'm not afraid of *him*.

I slip off the table and raise my hand. "Does it still hurt?"

"No," Alek says quietly, with a hint of a rasp. "Not since the first few weeks."

I rest my fingertips gingerly against the right side of his face. Alek somehow tenses even more, but he doesn't pull away.

Ever so cautiously, I trace the erratic, overlapping streaks of color. The ridged lines are only slightly raised, the texture rough to my touch but not unpleasantly so. Even in the smooth areas between them, the scarred flesh feels thicker, denser, like scales more than skin.

But still just as warm as the other parts of his body I was pressed up against minutes ago.

"You know," I say lightly, "I think I like it. It's as if an artist decided to experiment with his techniques on your face. You're art. There aren't many people who can say that."

Alek sputters a laugh. "You don't have to pretend it isn't bad. I have a mirror. I know how it looks."

"You know how it looks to you. With the weight of all your regrets, with the knowledge of how all the haughty assholes around here would talk about it." The corner of my mouth quirks slightly upward. "You know, the same assholes who'd assume I must be a monster because of the crack in my soul."

"It isn't the same. You—"

"*You*," I interrupt, resting my palm flat against his mottled cheek, "are a pretty incredible person too. You don't have to let your past mistakes and the judgment of idiots define you. If a riven sorcerer can make a go of being a hero, then gods be sure you can decide what you're going to be now. I don't see how anyone can stop you."

Alek grimaces. "I don't think simply deciding is going to absolve me of my crimes."

"What about everything you've done since then?" My mind trips back over all my memories of our times together, my heart squeezing. "I don't think I've ever thanked you for how much you've been here for me. You tried to get me help when you could tell I was hurting, even though I was pushing you away so you wouldn't realize why. You listened to me. You kept an open mind in spite of the awful circumstances that brought me into your life. Even when you weren't sure you could trust me, you answered all my questions, you brought me all the information I asked for and more."

At the thought of all the reasons he's had to distrust me, my gaze drifts away, but Alek tugs it back with the grasp of my other hand in his. "I never thought you were a bad person, Ivy. Maybe I didn't know what to make of you at every moment, but I could tell you were doing the best you could with this mess."

A small but ever so real smile crosses my lips. "I'm glad I've had you and your brilliant scholarly mind on my side."

Still cupping his scarred cheek, I guide him to me so I can claim another kiss.

My mouth brushes Alek's tentatively, and his breath stutters hot over my lips. But then he presses closer and kisses me back.

It's not the hasty rush of our first coming together. More a careful feeling each other out, meeting halfway, testing just how far we can take this tenderness.

I run my fingers up into his thick hair, reveling in the texture that's a mix of soft and coarse. Alek lets out a rough sound of approval.

His arm slides around me, his hand on the small of my back beneath the worst of my own scars, but I can still feel tension in his stance. A trace of hesitation, as if he's nervous about giving himself over to the moment completely.

I ease back just an inch, teasing my thumb along his jaw. "You know, I thought you were breathtakingly handsome from the very first time we met."

Alek lets out a light guffaw. He tips his head so his nose grazes mine. "Did you?"

"Oh, yes." I tap those full lips that caught my attention even while he was interrogating me on our second meeting. "And now I know you're also clever and caring and brave... and just as stubborn as me."

He brings both of his hands to my face, framing it between them. "I can't keep my eyes off you when you're nearby. You *glow*, in so much color, like the sun shining through one of the stained-glass windows in the temple out there. And yes, you're stubborn, but about things that matter—and if we're talking cleverness, who manages to teach *themselves* Woudish—and the dedication you've shown to this mission that wasn't even yours…"

Alek pauses. For a second, I think he's going to kiss me again, which I'd fully approve of. But his voice dips lower.

"I'm not the only one who's noticed how fantastic you are. You and Casimir—I'm sorry I went off on you when I saw you two together—"

I grasp the front of his shirt with a firm tug to emphasize my point. "You've already apologized. I understand."

"I shouldn't have taken my jealousy out on you."

I draw back far enough that I can meet his eyes directly again. "You don't need to be jealous. Casimir made it clear from the start that what happened between us was only casual for him. He's been sweet to me, but that's how he is with everyone. I don't know if he even *can* see 'companionship' as something exclusive."

Alek studies me with his incisive gaze that picks up on so much. "But you would have wanted him to."

My throat constricts. I've had enough of lying to this man.

"I have… feelings for Casimir that I'm still sorting out," I say. "But that doesn't mean that I want you any less. It simply means that I've had a *lot* of feelings since coming here that don't seem to know how to make up their minds."

"And if Casimir showed that he was interested in something more committed…?"

I can tell the scholar is trying to sound detached about the subject, but his voice has gone a bit raw all the same.

I turn my head to press a kiss to his palm before I lock eyes with him again. "I wouldn't use you to pass the time while waiting to see if he comes around. I… I don't think that would be good for either of us, would it? If we're doing this, I'm choosing you. For however long it lasts, however it all plays out. And I'll be nothing but happy with that choice. I'll feel like the luckiest woman alive that I got to make it."

My voice drops to a whisper with that last sentence as it hits me just how true it is. A few weeks ago, I could barely imagine risking another no-strings-attached roll-about, let alone having an actual partner who wanted to stick around. Who I could trust with everything I am.

Alek gives a strained laugh, but his face has lit up. He leans closer again to speak in a murmur. "And what exactly are we doing here?"

Elation sweeps through me at the promise in his question. At the sense that we're teetering on the edge of crossing a line we'll never come back from… but that I wouldn't want to back away from anyway.

A wider smile curves my lips. "Well, I'm about to go on a deadly mission with an uncertain outcome. And—"

The ding of the palace bell, somewhere overhead, interrupts. Nine resonant peals.

I raise my eyebrows at Alek. "And we still have an hour before Stavros gets peeved. That's plenty of time. Why shouldn't we make the most of it?"

Alek beams back at me. "I think that's the most brilliant idea I've ever heard."

Then he's kissing me again, and it really is nothing short of brilliant.

Our mouths collide over and over, my desire flaring hotter until I have to gasp for breath. Alek takes advantage of the moment to grasp me by my hips and lift me back onto the edge of the table so I no longer have to stand on my toes to reach his lips.

I'm not sure what thrills me more—the strength I always forget he's hiding in those slim arms or the greater access he's given both of us.

Alek steals another kiss, tracing his fingers along the neckline of my gown. "You know, maybe you shouldn't have to choose. From that poetry book you gave me, it's obvious women taking multiple partners like Signy did is pretty common in Woudish culture."

A breathless giggle slips out of me. "Or at least the culture of Woudish erotic poets."

He hums in shared amusement. "Whatever the case, it was kind of… exhilarating to read about."

"Oh? Did you get a lot of enjoyment other than scholarly out of my present?"

I think Alek has blushed beneath his dark skin at my teasing. He pauses. "I don't have very much practical experience to draw on with all of this. In case that wasn't obvious. I—there was barely anything with the girls I knew before my time at the temple school ended, and here… In my first year, there was a woman who pursued me, but I found out right afterward that she just thought it'd be exciting to fuck a freak."

I bristle around a rush of sympathy. "You're not a freak. Who was it? If I—"

Alek nuzzles my cheek. "It's all right. I don't need you to defend my honor. I just don't want you to expect more than I can offer."

"Hey." I angle his face to catch his gaze. "So we're clear, I can count the number of roll-abouts I've had on my fingers, without needing all of them. And half of those I didn't even really get off, which is why it stopped seeming worth the risk. You don't have anything to prove to me."

"I still want it to be good for you," he mutters. "I *have* done plenty of reading—poetry and otherwise. Scholarship can come in handy in all sorts of ways."

"I'd imagine it can."

He tilts his head next to mine, his lips brushing the shell of my ear. "You have no idea how many fantasies I've indulged in where I offer to help you expand your Woudish by reading that poetry book, and while we're going through it you turn to me and suggest we try bringing the verses to life…"

A giddy shiver races through my veins. But even more potent is a swell of affection so fierce my heart aches with it.

I hug him to me, absorbing the warmth of his lean frame. "That sounds like a lovely way to spend a day. But right now I'm happy to keep it simple. We *do* have less than an hour."

"Hmm. Better stop talking then."

He claims my mouth and slides his hand down the front of my bodice. His fingers chart the slopes of one breast, gradually working their way to the peak.

When his thumb travels over my nipple through the fabric with a sharper flare of pleasure, my breath catches. Alek grins against my mouth and repeats the gesture with a firmer pressure.

The delight his touch provokes builds with each iteration. I arch into him, urging him on.

In every caress, I can feel Alek gaining confidence. With a pleased hum, he gives my hair a light tug to tip my head to the side and applies his mouth to my neck.

His breath and his lips brand the sensitive skin from my jaw down to the crook of my shoulder. I sway in his embrace, a gasp slipping out of me at a tentative nip of his teeth.

"I want to kiss every part of you," he murmurs, "just to find out which get me the best reaction."

I let out a little huff of amusement. "If you're going to study me, then I want to study you too."

I give the collar of his tunic a yank. Rather than simply helping me, Alek pulls back just far enough to peel the shirt off himself.

Apparently he's a lot less shy about his body than his face. And there's nothing to be shy about.

My fingers reach out, drawn by the softly defined planes of muscle that cover his slim but toned torso. His godlen brand, Estera's sigil that's both looping and pointed, reminds me of his usual purpose in life. "I'm guessing you don't spend *every* spare moment with your head in a book."

Alek chuckles with a trace of sheepishness. "Exercise helps keep your mind honed. It's actually part of the scholarship regimen, to ensure we don't turn into sickly lay-abouts."

"Well, I approve."

I trail my hands right down his front, stopping just above the waist of his trousers. On an impulse, I tip forward to kiss his smooth skin just above his own nipples.

The cool, citrusy tang of him fills my lungs. His chest hitches, and then he's bowing into my explorations, fondling my chest in turn with one hand while the other slips around me.

With a few deft jerks, he loosens the lacing on the back of my gown. It only takes him a second to delve his hand beneath both my bodice and my undershirt.

The feel of his hot palm right against my breast brings a whimper to my throat. I mark a path of kisses up his chest and neck before our mouths crash into each other again.

Alek tugs my bodice a little lower and then slides both of his hands under the layers of fabric. He cups my breasts in unison, working me over with eager precision as he discovers exactly what sorts of movements spark enough bliss to shock more sounds from my lips.

A burning heat has formed between my legs—and I'm far too aware of the time ticking away before we might be interrupted. Nothing would put a damper on this interlude faster than Stavros barging into the room with his judgmental scowl.

I scoot forward on the tabletop so I can run my fingers right down Alek's abdomen to the bulge behind his trousers.

A guttural sound tumbles out of him. "Fuck, Ivy. I—"

He seems to decide taking action is better than talking. As I curl my fingers around his erection through the fabric, he shoves the mass of my skirt upward.

I squirm to make it easier to push the layers of silk aside, but my legs are still mostly covered by the divided underskirt that's like billowy pants underneath. The underskirt with knives strapped around my thighs overtop of it.

Alek lets out another chuckle at the sight of my weaponry, with no sign of being put off. With a shaky inhalation, he rocks into my grasp and fingers the overlapping folds of cloth between my legs to find the gap between.

Just the brush of his hand at the apex of my thighs sets off a sharp enough flare of pleasure to have me moaning. I give his cock another squeeze, delighting in the groan I achieve in return, but this partial closeness doesn't feel quite satisfying.

"Let me…" I unclip the straps that hold my knife sheaths and then wriggle right out of my underskirt and drawers in one go.

My intention couldn't be more obvious. Alek's breath quickens. He jerks at his trousers, and I help him yank them down.

Then I wrap my knees around his hips and grasp his shoulders. With a heady pressure that sends tingles all the way to my fingertips, he enters me.

The slickness of my sex can't leave any doubt about how eager for this moment I am, but Alek guides his cock in slowly, his breath turning even more ragged. When we're fully joined, he stops, just holding on to me and panting into my hair.

"You have no idea how good you feel, Ivy," he mumbles.

I try to push toward him, to encourage him onward. Alek grips my bare ass beneath my skirt to hold me in place.

"Wait. I don't know—I don't want this to be over too quickly. I need to last long enough that you get to feel just as good."

I brush my fingers over his hair, exerting all my self-control not to buck against him. "I already feel pretty fantastic." As I pause, the larger truth of the matter rolls over me with a sudden catch in my throat.

It takes a moment before I can speak again, my voice gone rough. "You know, this is the first time I've ever been with someone who knew all of me. I don't have any more experience with that than you do. But I can't imagine anything feeling better than I do right now."

Alek exhales in a rush and tips my head to capture my lips. He kisses me until my head is spinning with the passion emanating off him.

As his tongue flicks out to tease over mine, he tucks his hand between us and sets it low on my belly. His thumb strokes downward until it hits the spot just above where we're connected. A jolt of bliss shoots through my core.

His lips travel across the edge of my jaw. "Right there?"

His thumb pulses against my clit, and I whimper before I can answer. "Right there. So fucking good, Alek."

He works his thumb over me until so much pleasure is racing through my body that I start to shake—and only then does he finally move his hips. First in careful, shallow strokes while dappling kisses across my face and neck.

I grind into him with a needy sound, and a raw chuckle reverberates from his chest. He picks up the pace, thrusting into me faster, harder. Setting me alight from the inside while his thumb keeps conjuring more bliss against my clit.

Even with Casimir, the expert on all things carnal pleasure, it never felt quite like this. Maybe because even with him, I had to keep some part of me distant. I had to close myself off.

But Alek has already embraced every terrible part of me. He wants me as I am.

I have nothing left to hide here. I can simply be.

And oh, it's wondrous being me at this moment. My nerves sing with the pleasure thrumming through my body.

Alek's fingers dig into my ass with a firmness that only heightens the sensations. He holds me in place as he slams even deeper into me.

Our mouths crash together with messy kisses between hoarse breaths. The swell of ecstasy inside me builds and expands until I'm barely aware of anything except my hands clutching Alek's shoulders, his cock plunging into me, and the magic he's creating with his thumb.

The muscles in his hips tense against my thighs. "Ivy," he mutters. "I can't—"

But it doesn't matter, because just as he starts to spill himself inside me, the wave that was rising washes through me. I hug him even tighter to me, quaking and crying out with the force of my release.

Alek groans and wraps his arms around me just as firmly. He buries his face in my hair as his panting subsides.

For a minute or two, we simply rest there against each other, sweaty and spent but ever so sated. Alek stirs first, seeking out another kiss.

Then he freezes up. "We didn't take any precautions. I should have thought—"

I rest my hand against the scarred side of his face. "It's all right. At this time of the month, it's not much of a risk for me anyway. But just to be safe, I could take mirewort. I got the impression it's not too hard to come by here at the college."

Alek nods. "I can request some. Since we won't want anyone wondering who you're seeing if you ask about it."

I hadn't even thought of that. Trust Alek to consider every possible threat—and mitigate them for me. "It's effective as long as it's taken within a couple of days. You can give it to me at our meeting tomorrow. Which I will definitely be making it to, perfectly safe and sound."

A tinge of anguish crosses Alek's face as he gazes back at me.

"You'd better," he says with sudden fierceness. "Or I don't care what the king's orders are—I'll kill Ster. Torstem myself."

# Sixteen

"It may create a prickling sensation," Casimir says as he dabs a thin brush into the little pot of burgundy paste he brought with him. "But it shouldn't actually hurt. If it does, let me know, and we'll wash it right off."

When he brings the brush to my chest, I hold myself perfectly still. The touch of the paste does set off a faint and not uncomfortable burn—but the more prominent sensation is my heated awareness of how close we are, our bodies just inches apart.

With his courtesan training, can he tell what I was getting up to with Alek an hour ago? I had just enough time to dunk myself in one of the bathing rooms before I met Stavros back in his quarters, but a renewed flush ripples under my skin every time my mind slips back to my interlude with the scholar.

It doesn't help that I'm half-naked for this task. The typical spot where a godlen sigil is branded lies well below the necklines of any of my clothes, so Casimir brought me a thin towel to drape across my shoulders and over my breasts for some kind of modesty.

It's not as if he hasn't seen those breasts bared before. But he isn't the only one in the room with me.

While Casimir paints the shape of Kosmel's sigil on my lower sternum, Stavros paces from his desk to the sofa and back again. "You're sure this technique will pass for an actual dedication brand? They'll be far more suspicious if she shows up with a fake one than none at all."

Casimir adds the thin horn-like points to the top of the sigil with a delicacy that has me suppressing a heady shiver. "I brought some rouge to make sure the details are just right. But the mark this paste will leave behind is pretty convincing all on its own. I have a colleague who uses it sometimes when he's working with a patron who might object to godlessness. So far, no one's called him out as a fraud."

"We don't even know if the scourge sorcerers will want to check who I'm dedicated to," I point out.

Stavros grimaces at me. "You'll be in a much bigger fix if they do and you're not prepared than if you're more ready than you need to be."

Well, he isn't wrong about that.

Casimir steps back, and my next breath comes a little easier.

I meant what I said to Alek—he's more than enough. I wouldn't pursue anyone else. But that doesn't mean the feelings that already existed have vanished.

"We leave the paste on for ten minutes," the courtesan says, rinsing the brush in a bowl of water. "Then we wipe it off, and I'll touch it up as much as it appears to need. The imprint should last at least a few days, but if you get called to another secret meeting in the woods after that, we'll want to repeat this process."

I nod. "Hopefully it won't take too many late-night wanderings to find out everything we need to know. Thank you for helping."

Casimir gives me one of the warm smiles that still makes my pulse flutter. "Of course. I'm sending you out there with all the armor I can provide."

Stavros clears his throat. "On the subject of combat equipment... We don't know how thoroughly they'll examine you in general. I'm not sure what they'll make of a noblewoman carrying a whole arsenal of knives. I'd rather send you with as many blades as you can carry, but..."

"That might be more dangerous than going relatively unarmed," I fill in. "Fine."

I reach between the folds of my dress to detach the thigh-strapped sheaths. "I'll keep one in my boot. It's not unreasonable for a noblewoman to be a *little* concerned with self-defense. That's my favorite knife anyway."

Stavros rolls his eyes skyward. "Of course you have a favorite."

I raise my eyebrows at him. "Don't you have a favorite sword?"

His silent glower is answer enough.

Casimir goes to the latrine to wet a cloth at the sink, but when he returns, he simply holds it in his hands, considering me.

"If you get a bad feeling about the situation," he says. "Worse than you'd expect, I mean—there's no reason you shouldn't retreat. You don't know anything about them yet. They shouldn't see you as a threat at this point. You could walk away if you need to."

I smile tightly in return. "I suppose we'll see."

He doesn't know that for sure. And it doesn't really matter anyway.

I have to do this. The king is counting on us to take down the scourge sorcerers. I need to prove to Stavros that I can keep control over my magic.

What am I even here for if I back down now? I might as well flee straight back to the outer wards.

I might have to flee the whole city if Stavros decides I'm a traitor to this mission.

No. I've spent most of my life in hiding. I've finally found not just a purpose big enough that it might balance out the harm I've done but at least a couple of people who accept all of what I am.

I can't give that up. I have to be worthy of this chance.

When Casimir removes the paste, the pinkish-brown mark that remains on my sallow skin does look an awful lot like the brands I've seen. As the courtesan gives it a tad more depth with his rouge, my lips curve crookedly.

"I hope the gods don't see the imitation as outright blasphemy. I guess if any godlen would approve of this kind of trickery, it'd be Kosmel."

Casimir chuckles. "He has given you his show of support before." He touches my cheek with a graze of his fingertips. "Make it back safe, Ivy."

My throat constricts. "That's my plan."

As Casimir gathers his supplies, Stavros steps toward the loop of cord the courtesan arrived here through. "After you've returned to your room, I'll bring this back to its usual place. We'll see you at tomorrow's meeting."

Casimir bobs his head in acknowledgment and farewell, aims one more gentle smile my way, and then vanishes through the cord's magic.

While Stavros is sorting out the cords, I quickly don my chemise and pull up the front of my gown. I'm nearly done with the laces by the time the former general returns.

He eyes me with one of his inscrutable expressions and a brief twitch of his head, and an uneasier heat tickles over my skin. I have the sudden, misguided urge to ask him to come over and help me finish tying the laces.

As if he'd agree. As if I should even care whether he does.

I give them a few final tugs myself and smooth my hands down the skirt of my dress. Across the courtyards, the palace bell starts to ring out its longest series of peals.

Midnight. One hour to go.

I fold my arms over my chest and give Stavros a pointed look. "You know, you should probably at least make a show of going to bed. It's not going to look like I snuck off on you if anyone notices the light's still glowing in your window when I'm leaving."

Stavros sighs, but he knows I'm right. He makes a vague motion toward me. "You have everything you need?"

A dry laugh hitches out of me. "As far as I know. It's a bit difficult to be fully prepared for illicit meetings with mysterious figures."

He balks for a moment longer, as if he thinks he can intimidate my power into staying under wraps with his frown, and then he stalks away into his bedroom. The door thumps shut behind him, but I don't exactly feel alone.

I douse the lantern in the main room and sit down on the sofa. The darkness wraps around me, the quiet of the night feeling unusually ominous.

A tingle stirs in the back of my skull. *Ivy?* Julita whispers.

She's returned from wherever exactly she goes when she withdraws from my awareness. I was starting to wonder if she'd end up missing our first foray among the scourge sorcerers.

She might not have minded if she did. I can't imagine what horrific memories tonight will stir up for her.

I open my mouth and close it again, settling for simply tipping my head in response. I don't think there's much chance Stavros actually *has* gone to sleep, and I feel strange talking to her where he could easily eavesdrop.

Maybe I should get a bit of a head start on the whole sneaking out thing.

I pull my hooded cloak over my dress and hair before slipping out into the hall. The lanterns there have all been snuffed out for the night.

From around the nearest corner, I can hear someone stumbling between drunken giggles and someone else doing their best to shush them. Otherwise the staff halls are empty.

I turn in the other direction, toward the narrow hallway at the very back of the school that's too cramped and dreary for the nobles to venture into unless they're feeling particularly secretive.

As I walk, I veer from one side of the hallway to the other, keeping my senses alert for any unexpected quivers of magic. I don't know how many enchanted creatures the conspirators might have created, but if they could use one to spy on me now, it seems likely they would.

Nothing catches my notice. I duck into the stairwell and pad down the spiraling steps halfway to the third floor. Then I sit down against the cool stone wall.

"Are you okay?" I ask Julita in a murmur. "I'm sorry—I didn't know Alek would react that way."

How awful must she have felt to finally have a moment to speak to him again only for him to shove her away?

Julita lets out a soft laugh. *How could you have known when I had no idea either? Obviously… obviously he's become even more attached to you than I realized.*

Is there a bittersweet note in her voice? My ghostly passenger has made a good show of not caring about the men she assembled beyond their usefulness in tackling the scourge sorcerers, but I've noticed cracks in her façade.

She might not have believed it'd be a good idea to pursue anything deeper with them, might even have convinced herself that none of them would truly care about *her* beyond the unflappable, charming front she presented, but they mattered to her. She was abused by her brother and his friend as a child, had no one around she trusted enough to turn to for help—that'd mess up anyone's mindset.

Probably the only reason she trusts *me* is she doesn't have much choice.

"I wasn't expecting him to care that much about me either," I say.

*I trust he was able to forgive you for letting me take charge. I told you before, Ivy—you should have your happiness where you can take it. Why shouldn't it be with Alek?* She pauses. *Did he say whether he forgives me?*

I actually can't remember if Alek said anything at all about Julita after she returned my body to me, other than to confirm it really was me he was talking to. "He didn't mention it, but he didn't appear to be angry with you. I made sure he knew it'd been my idea."

*Ah. Well, I suppose all's well that ends well.*

She doesn't ask what happened between Alek and me afterward. I don't know whether she can guess or she doesn't want to know or she's allowing me my privacy.

Possibly it's all of those reasons at once.

There's still time before I need to enter the woods. I continue down the stairs and make a brief detour to the stables to apologize to Toast that I haven't taken him out in a while. Then I meander toward the back of the outer courtyard where the tree line looms.

When the palace bell lets out its single peal, I venture down the main path into the woods.

I count off the paces silently. Fifty would lead to a fair bit of variation depending on the length of the legs doing the walking, but I guess it'll get me to the right general area.

The glow of the school buildings' external lanterns falls away behind me. The branches overhead block out most of the moonlight. By the time I reach fifty, I'm finding my way by squinting at the dim columns of tree trunks to avoid walking into them.

I stop and glance around, but I can't make out anything at all except the nearest, incredibly vague shapes of the trees in the darkness. Leaves rustle overhead, and an insect buzzes by somewhere to my left. The cool breeze licks under my cloak, rippling the fabric.

My magic tugs at me, offering to sharpen my sight and form shapes out of the darkness. I clench my jaw in refusal.

What I said to my men was true. Even if my power could make this task easier, I don't trust it. It'd probably turn someone blind to give me greater vision.

Kosmel helped direct the consequences before, but I have no idea if he's listening now. If he'd think it worth extending his divine power just to spare me from the darkness.

I have no idea how quickly the madness might start to creep through my mind if I embraced my broken soul.

It's safer for everyone, including me, if I continue turning to my magic only as a last resort.

The seconds tick by with the thud of my heart. Nothing happens.

*This is rather anti-climactic,* Julita murmurs.

Did I already make a misstep, and the conspirators have decided not to bother with me? Did I misread the message that appeared on my palm?

I adjust my weight, restraining the urge to pull my knife from my boot so it's closer at hand.

How long should I wait?

This could be part of the test. Evaluate how committed I am, whether I'm intrigued enough to hang around rather than giving up and leaving.

They're probably also keeping watch to ensure I've actually come alone.

I have no idea how long it's been already. Wetting my lips, I keep my breaths steady and my ears pricked.

Something slides across the ground to my right. Tensing, I glance down.

My eyes have adjusted enough to the traces of moonlight that I catch the curve of a sinewy form winding into the grass at the edge of the path. A snake.

My nerves jitter with a sense of magic. Was that creature conjured from clay like the rat?

Or am I getting so bored I'm imagining things?

Two peals of the palace bell resonate through the night. I lift my head—and all at once a more potent wave of magic sweeps around me, setting the hairs on my arms on end.

"Welcome, Ivy Euridya of Nikodi," a voice warbles, thin and yet seeming to reach me from several directions at once.

The magic I sensed must be carrying it—disguising the speaker and the direction they're standing in. I don't recognize the voice at all.

I'm supposed to be playing the part of a disgruntled but idealistic noblewoman. I draw myself up straighter. "I came as you asked. What did you mean about wanting more from the world?"

The words continue to drift around me as if carried on the breeze. "You can sense that something isn't quite right, can't you? The way the kingdom is run, the way we honor our gods."

I shrug as if I'm being careful about sharing my opinions. "The daimon definitely seemed to feel there's a problem. I don't think anyone could argue about that."

"And would you want to heal the damage that's been done if you could? If you had the chance to change all of Silana—all of the continent—for the better, would you take it, even if the way was hard?"

Julita lets out a scoffing sound in my head. *We know what ways these people have been turning to —and that they've been cajoling kids into taking on the real hard parts.*

I remain cagey. "I suppose that would depend on what kind of hard you mean. Of course I'd want to serve the godlen as well as I can."

Wendos thought that what he and his associates were doing was somehow honoring the gods. I'm going to assume that's a common line of thinking among the conspirators.

They have to justify the horrors they're committing somehow.

"There are many who'd stand in the way of rebuilding what was lost," the voice says. "You would need to work against them and risk punishment if you're found out."

*My brother never trusted anyone—except maybe Wendos,* Julita says. *I don't know if you can even dabble in scourge sorcery without getting paranoid. They'll be suspicious if you give in too easily.*

I can believe that.

I cock my head to the side. "Why should I accept that *you* know what's right when you won't even show yourself? I have no idea who you are."

"We must be cautious if we're going to succeed. The fate of the world rests on our shoulders. Any indiscretion jeopardizes that goal."

These murderous psychopaths do think awfully highly of themselves, don't they?

"How am I supposed to fit in, then?" I demand. "If you're not going to tell me anything specific, I don't see how I could help even if I wanted to."

"Once you've earned our trust, we can reveal more. We will give you simple tasks, and if we're satisfied with the result, you'll earn more responsibility. Trust can flow both ways."

How very poetic.

I restrain myself from wrinkling my nose. "I'll admit I'm intrigued. What do I have to do first to get you to tell me more?"

I guess I shouldn't be surprised by the request that follows, knowing what I do.

"Show that you're willing to give of yourself. There's a dagger on the ground a few steps ahead of you. Find it, cut your palm, and offer your blood to the All-Giver with whatever prayer feels most fitting to you."

To the All-Giver, not to the unknown speaker and their fellow conspirators.

I don't see how that act can hurt anything—other than my hand. "I can do that."

I feel along the ground until my fingers brush the hilt of the dagger. It's a small one, the grip barely long enough for me to wrap my whole hand around it.

As I straighten up, I cautiously arch my eyebrow in a silent question. What does Julita think these people would consider an appropriate prayer?

When my invisible companion speaks, her tone is more subdued than usual. *Borys and Wendos mostly talked about their own personal power. But sometimes they'd add in something about how they'd use that power to honor the gods.*

That gives me a little more material to work with beyond what I heard from Wendos in the tower.

I bring the blade to my right palm, half expecting Julita's presence to withdraw before she has to experience the pain of blood-letting again. But she remains, the tingle of her presence twitchier than usual but still with me.

*Go ahead*, she says. *I'll be all right. This is all so we can defeat them in the end.*

I drag in a breath and dig the edge of the blade into my skin.

Pain stings along the line I've cut down the middle of my palm. I kept it shallow but pierced far enough that several drops of blood streak across my hand and patter to the dirt below.

I tilt my head back toward the sky. "All-Giver, Great God, the One who made all that exists around me, I give of myself to you. See me, show me the way that is right, and I will carry out whatever purpose you put me to. Whatever strength you give to me, I'll use it to better this world."

My nerves jitter with the words, but it's actually less frightening calling out to the All-Giver than any of the godlen. After all, the Great God abandoned the realms of the continent centuries ago… after razing the first scourge sorcerers from existence.

Really, we have the same goals.

I doubt my voice can reach wherever the All-Giver has gone. And I mean what I'm saying anyway, even if not in the way I intend the conspirators to think.

But making a plea to the highest power I know of is still a little intimidating.

No godly voice answers in my head. Only the unknown watcher from wherever they're poised amid the trees. "You could do great things with an attitude like that, Ivy of Nikodi. You could be one of the few to truly serve the All-Giver as the Great God deserves."

Ah, so now they're buttering me up, making me feel special in the hopes that I'll want to chase that feeling. I've watched so many con artists using similar tactics on the streets of the outer wards.

"If I can, I will," I say more earnestly than is truthful.

"Put the dagger down and bind your cut with the cloth that was lying next to it. We have one more matter to discuss tonight."

As I wrap the strip of fabric around my palm, the pain of the cut dulls with a quiver of magic. The bandage is Elox-blessed.

"What's the other 'matter'?" I ask.

"There's a small package we'd like you to deliver for us. You'll be able to carry it in a pocket unnoticed. We ask that you bring it to the Temple of the Crown tomorrow night and leave it behind Prospira's statue."

I knit my brow. "What *is* this thing I'm going to be carrying around?"

"All you need to know is that it's heavily enchanted, and the magic must not be disturbed. Opening the pouch it's enclosed in could ruin its potency."

My skin crawls. The question I think anyone else would most likely ask first is, "It won't hurt me, will it?"

The voice chuckles. "Oh, no. Especially not if you leave it be and carry out your task as requested."

"What's the point of bringing it to the temple anyway? What's it going to be used for?"

"The powers that be stand in our way, but our work needs to be done. We do what we can to thin their numbers."

I stiffen against a very honest hitch of my pulse and let more concern seep into my voice than I would have if I didn't want to sound normal. "You mean it's going to hurt someone *else*? Someone important?"

"I didn't say that. And nothing at all will happen while you're nearby."

The implications are there, though. This is the real test—seeing if I've bought into the speaker's grand talk enough to risk being party to treason.

What else can I do? If I refuse, the road ends here. I might not even survive the walk out of the woods.

"This is your first opportunity to serve the All-Giver as you said," the voice goes on at my hesitation. "If you would prefer to return to your previous life of following orders and bowing to those who haven't earned it—"

"No," I say quickly, with feigned urgency. "I'll do it. Where's the package?"

"At the base of the tree directly to your left. Take it, and leave the woods. And remember to keep the pouch closed."

"I know."

I approach the tree I can only vaguely see and kneel down. My heart is thudding in anticipation, my body braced for the magic I expect to feel radiating from my new cargo.

My hands find a leather pouch no wider than my smallest finger. I can't imagine it's holding anything much bigger than a ring.

I take it into my grasp…

And there's nothing.

Not even a tiny quiver of magic wafts off the pouch and its contents. As far as my riven soul can tell, there's no power attached to it at all.

Suppressing my confusion, I stand up and tuck the pouch into the pocket at my hip. Were the conspirators somehow mistaken about an artifact they got their hands on? Or—

The answer comes to me like a flaming arrow out of the night.

It's all a trick. A gambit to test me in all sorts of ways.

They wouldn't trust me with a blessed object when I've barely started proving myself. They simply want to know whether I'll do as they say. Whether I'll alert the authorities to their supposedly violent scheme.

This time.

When I carry out their task, gods only know what they'll ask of me next.

# SEVENTEEN

An even thicker silence hangs over the school when I return to the Domi. Even the drunkards have found their way to their beds.

I slink through the halls with every sense on the alert. The small weight grazing my hip with the sway of my skirt keeps me tensed even though it appears to be a decoy.

I bring my bracelet to the right spot on Stavros's door and ease it open at the click of the lock. To my surprise, the former general hasn't prowled out so he can glower at me immediately on my return.

As I shut the door behind me, a grunt reaches my ears from the bedroom. Then a violent rustle of fabric.

My pulse lurches. Has someone broken into the rooms and attacked him?

I dash to the bedroom door and yank it open.

In the thin moonlight, it's immediately clear that Stavros is alone on his expansive bed. He's sprawled on top of the covers, his vest discarded on a nearby chair but his massive frame still clothed in the same dress shirt and trousers he was wearing when I left.

That and the prosthetic hand still attached to his wrist prove he didn't plan to fall asleep. It looks as if he propped himself up on a pillow leaning against the headboard and then sagged to the side when he drifted off accidentally.

I have been gone for a while.

The chiseled planes of his face have softened in this state, but somehow that makes him look both younger and wearier. I can't help remembering the way he talked the first time he woke *me* up from a nightmare, when he let his cocky assurance drop for long enough that I could see how much the loss of his gift and his military career weighed on him.

He's carrying plenty of burdens of his own. Which must be why his sleep is anything but peaceful.

As I take in the scene, his arm jerks against the covers with another rasp of fabric. His brow furrows, and he sucks in a hitched breath.

"No," he mutters. "Michas, watch— Stop!"

The last words come out so raw I can't bear to walk away. I dart to the edge of the bed and grasp his ankle.

"Stavros," I say, low but forceful, giving his leg a quick shake. "Wake—"

He jolts upright before I can even finish the command. His hand whips toward me as if to grab me, and I throw myself backward.

My shoulder jars against the side of the doorframe. My magic flares with a defensive lash, but I grit my teeth and tamp it down.

Prickles spread through my chest in response, like a dozen needles scraping their points over my innards. It's still a mild enough pain that I can stand against it, but a chill quivers through me.

My power is getting more restless. How long until it starts ripping open my lungs and whatever else again?

The former general glares at me, both his hair and his eyes fathomlessly dark in the dimness, his entire body rigid. "What do you think you're doing?"

The cutting tone, somehow even more hostile than what he usually aims at me these days, kindles my temper and burns away every shred of sympathy. As if I'm not already dealing with enough without him becoming an even bigger jerk.

I stay where I am, crossing my arms and glaring right back at him. "Waking you up from what sounded like a pretty unpleasant dream. You're welcome."

His lips draw back from his teeth. "I don't need *you* fighting any battles for me. Worry about yourself. What happened in the woods?"

"I didn't cause any disasters," I shoot back. "And I think I played the part well enough that I'll get deeper into the conspiracy. They're too cautious to give away much at the beginning, of course."

"So you've got nothing useful after all that fuss."

I swallow a hiss of exasperation. "Nothing that'll take down the scourge sorcerers right this minute, but I'm on the right track."

"Wonderful. If you haven't set the school falling down around our ears, get out of my bedroom and I'll hear about the rest with the others."

The dismissal stings, which maybe is why I let my curiosity get the better of me as I scoot into the doorway. "Who's Michas?"

The snarl in Stavros's voice confirms just how unwise a question that was. "You're the last person who should be bringing up that name. Get the fuck out!"

With a wince, I scramble over the threshold and yank the door shut behind me.

*I've never heard him talk about anyone named Michas before,* Julita murmurs. *What under the gods' gaze is the matter with Stav tonight?*

Stavros's parting words have made me abruptly sure of the answer, with a sour taste that's crept up the back of my throat.

Who would enter one of his nightmares that he'd be particularly offended by me talking about? What are the chances it's *not* the one person close to him who was murdered by a riven sorcerer like me?

And if he came out of a dream about monstrous magic only to see the most recent person he's witnessed working it… I can't say I forgive him for his animosity, but I can understand it.

Even if I can explain his reaction to myself, that doesn't make the atmosphere in his quarters any more comfortable. I drift over to the sofa, but my skin is itching, my heart beating at an anxious pace.

I'm not getting any sleep like this. How can I drift off with just a door between me and a man who's looking like he wants to murder *me*?

My head feels heavy with fatigue after the late night and the stress of everything I've been through, but with every second I stand within these walls, my nerves twitch with more agitation.

My magic will act up even more if I'm in a panic. I need to walk it off. Clear my head, give Stavros time to simmer down.

Maybe by the third bell, I'll feel like I can take a little rest.

Julita stays silent as I slip back into the hall. She's been with me through enough turmoil to know my usual habits for dealing with fraught situations.

I don't want to roam around inside the building where I might disturb the other inhabitants. So I descend the back stairwell again and step out into the cool night air.

My feet carry me of their own accord across the courtyard. I tip my head back and take in the vast stretch of stars in the clear sky above me.

A pang like homesickness runs through my chest. The tops of the buildings on either side of me cut off a lot of my view, though.

I sneak through one of the Quadring's side halls to the broader fields of the outer courtyard. There's a gazebo a short distance behind the stables, where I often see students gathered to gossip and flirt during the day.

At night, it's just an empty shell. An empty shell with a conveniently placed railing for my purposes.

I hang back at the edge of the entranceway while a soldier on patrol marches past. When he's disappeared around the front of the Quadring, I steal across the field to the gazebo.

Clambering up the side isn't quite as easy in a gown and cloak as it would have been in my typical outer-wards tunic and breeches, but I manage with a minimum of fumbling. My sliced palm doesn't even sting in its bandage of healing fabric.

I haul myself onto the slanted roof and lie back on the smooth boards with the sky spread above me.

"Now that's a view," I whisper.

*I've never paid much attention to the stars,* Julita admits. *I suppose if I was up after dark, it was usually at a dance or a pub, not out in the open.*

When I was little, Linzi and I occasionally snuck out at night to the small park near our house. We'd huddle together on the grass, suppressing giggles, and I'd point out the constellations I'd learned to her.

Back when the world seemed like a relatively safe place, with not much more to worry about than tripping on a loose cobblestone or getting ink on a favorite dress.

Melancholy swells up inside me. I push it away with a lift of my hand toward the stars.

"That line there they call Elox's Staff. You see it makes kind of a curve at the top like a shepherd's crook?"

*So we're supposed to think Elox is lounging about up there in the sky?*

My lips twitch in amusement. "It's more of a poetic thing. But I guess he could be. Aren't the godlen supposed to be everywhere all at once?"

Julita chuckles. *It's a wonder they ever pay attention to anything at all down here when they're spread that thin. We should be glad Kosmel, at least, noticed enough to get involved.*

I'm not sure I love the results of the trickster godlen's involvement, but I keep that to myself and point to a different part of the sky. "That diamond-ish cluster is supposed to be Inganne's greatest kite."

*Hmm, I can almost see that one. I think she'd appreciate a sparkly accessory.*

Having been to one of the joyfully chaotic temples dedicated to the godlen of creativity and play, I can agree with that.

I squint at the twinkling specks of light to see what else I can pick out. "That bright line there with a triangle at the end is Sabrelle's Spear. And the clump over there gets called Prospira's Basket, but no one seems to be able to agree whether it's full of fruit or bread or coins."

Julita lets out a soft snort. *Somehow I'm suspecting it depends a lot on the interests of the person making the claim. It just looks like a big jumble to me.*

A smile crosses my lips. "Yeah, I've always thought that one is kind of a stretch."

An unexpected sense of peace has settled over me as we've talked, as if Elox has cast a blanket of serenity down over me with his starry staff. The tension in my chest has loosened.

I'm not alone, no matter where I go. Sometimes that's frustrating and unnerving… but sometimes it's kind of wonderful.

I push myself up on my elbows to study the horizon. "I think right over there you can see Estera's Tome, that square-ish shape with—"

A hard but level voice cuts through the night. "What are you doing?"

I flinch in surprise and brace my hands against the boards on either side of me to hold my balance. I've kept my voice so quiet I hadn't thought anyone would notice, and I didn't hear footsteps approaching.

Pulse thudding, I tilt forward to peer over the edge of the gazebo's roof.

A man in the deep blue uniform of the Crown's Watch stands just below me. His pale face with its topping of chocolate-brown curls is tipped to fix me with a stare as hard as his voice.

Even if my nerves didn't shiver with the traces of magic wafting off him, I'd instantly recognize those stunning looks. It's the guard who's made me uneasy before.

Despite the darkness, his striking blue-green eyes seem to hold a light of their own. An alertness that's piercing me right now.

Fortunately, as far as I'm aware, nothing I'm doing at the moment is any sort of crime. The soldiers who've been assigned to monitor the college must be getting used to the random habits of rich young nobles.

"I'm stargazing," I say honestly.

A small furrow forms in the middle of the guard's smooth brow. He really is far too pretty for his job. "Watching the stars? What for? They aren't doing anything."

He might be pretty, but apparently he's also a stick in the mud.

I can't stop a dry edge from creeping into my tone. "Because they're spectacular to look at? Because they inspire all kinds of stories?"

The expression on the guard's face suggests he'd question what stories are for too. Instead, he shifts his focus. "Who were you talking to?"

If the magic vibes he's giving off have anything to do with judging my honesty, I can still say this and not really be lying. "My sister."

Her memory has been hovering alongside Julita and me since I climbed up here, after all.

The guard frowns. "There's no one up there with you."

"I know. She's dead."

I probably shouldn't let myself get a perverse pleasure out of seeing my interrogator's face turn even more perplexed, but he's kind of asking for it. Surely it didn't look as if I was actually causing any harm sitting up here, but he had to interrupt me anyway.

"Why would you talk to someone who isn't alive?" he asks.

I shrug. "Sometimes they still have meaningful things to say, even if only inside your head. If you don't believe there's anything more to the world than what you can see right in front of you, you're going to miss a lot."

I can't tell what the guard makes of that comment. He pauses for a second and then motions to the school buildings behind him. "You should be inside. Everyone's sleeping now."

"*You* aren't," I point out pedantically, but I scoot to the edge of the roof and drop to the ground with a soft thump of my feet. "I'm going now. You can be reassured that the world is set back into order."

I stride toward the Quadring without a backward glance, but I can feel the guard's gaze on me the whole way.

*Do you think we need to be worried about him?* Julita asks.

I can only grimace in answer.

I don't know. But I sure hope not, because it's not as if I've got a shortage of worries as it is.

# Eighteen

*Ivy*

After he's laid out the rings of cord, Stavros points to mine. "You go first."

Like usual. Like he thinks I'm going to inflict something terrible on his quarters if he leaves while I'm still here—as if I don't have access all day long anyway.

He's been even surlier and more prone to glowers all morning, though he hasn't said much. I'm not sure if he's forgotten our strained conversation after I woke him up last night or if he's simply pretending it never happened.

I don't particularly want to dwell on the way he snapped at me—the way he *looked* at me, like I'd just eviscerated someone—either. I'll take avoidance over a repeat.

"Ladies first, after all," I say with wry primness, and step into the ring.

Even after several rounds of practice, the sudden lurch of magical transportation makes my pulse stutter. I step out of the matching ring in the palace meeting room with a slight wobble in my step.

Alek is already there, waiting right by my looped cord. At my arrival, his face brightens so visibly even with his mask back in place that I can't stop myself from smiling giddily in return.

What happened between us last night was real. Right here in this room, he cherished me like I was one of the noble ladies he should be looking to for a match.

No, he cherished me like he'd rather have a thief from Slaughterwell than any kind of lady.

Alek grasps my hand, both to give it an affectionate squeeze and to pass on a small packet. "I thought I should get this to you right away."

The mirewort. I'll chew on a leaf when I have a little more privacy.

Because before I've even had a chance to tuck the packet away, Stavros is emerging from his ring, eyeing the two of us with a puzzled frown.

I'm not sure I want to deal with the former general's reaction to our newfound closeness. But I don't want to pull away from Alek as if in rejection.

Thankfully, the scholar seems to have a similar sense of discretion. He bobs his head to Stavros in greeting while stroking his thumb over my knuckles in one small caress and then eases back. "It's wonderful that Ivy returned to us unharmed, isn't it?"

As if he'd only approached me in friendly welcome.

Stavros appears to take the comment in stride, although he doesn't stop frowning. "There certainly could have been worse outcomes."

I restrain myself from rolling my eyes and surreptitiously slip the packet into my pocket. "I should check the room for any roaming magical vermin."

Just as I finish my circuit of the space, Casimir and Benedikt arrive within seconds of each other. Both men brighten in their own ways when they see me: the courtesan with one of his soft smiles and the bastard's bastard with a typical smirk.

I set off a signal through my locket this morning as planned, so they knew I'd returned, but I can imagine they were a little worried all the same.

"You survived the start of your scourge sorcery initiation," Benedikt says in a teasing tone, sprawling in the chair at the foot of the table. "Soon you'll be a fully-fledged menace."

I manage to laugh, but Stavros stiffens—enough that I see Benedikt mark his response with a furrow in his brow.

Casimir slides a box across the table to interrupt the awkward moment. "Since Benedikt set the precedent yesterday, I thought I'd bring a treat to celebrate Ivy's initial success. One of my dormmates who's on the culinary track had a batch of chocolates to sell."

The sight of the glossy brown orbs laid out in the box has my mouth watering. I lean over to snatch one up. "That was a fantastic idea. Thank you."

He passes paper-thin linen napkins around the table, and even Stavros concedes to taking a chocolate. The former general holds it in his hand without taking a bite and fixes his stare back on me. "Are you going to tell us what happened during your 'victory,' Ivy?"

I sink my teeth into the bonbon and pause for a moment to let the richly sweet flavor with its edge of bitterness lace my mouth. There's nothing wrong with using a treat to bolster my spirits.

"I'm not sure it was much of an initiation yet," I say. "It felt like they were merely feeling me out. They were obviously trying not to give much away. I couldn't even tell how many people were watching or where they were—the one who spoke to me stayed hidden and used some kind of magic to project their voice from different directions."

The eager gleam in Alek's eyes dims. "So you wouldn't be able to identify any other conspirators yet?"

I shake my head. "I guess it makes sense. They don't know if they can trust *me* yet, so why would they risk showing themselves?"

"It isn't surprising," Casimir agrees. "What did they say to you?"

Julita gives a little shudder in the back of my skull. *Rather a lot of madness.*

I rub my mouth, thinking back to the conversation. "They talked a lot about the All-Giver. I got the impression that they think they're doing things the Great God would approve of, or that they can make an appeal even though it's been ages since the All-Giver abandoned us. And they're obviously dissatisfied with the current ruling powers, although they were careful not to come right out and say they want to overthrow the Melchioreks."

Benedikt lets out a rough guffaw. "I suppose that confirms who's been encouraging the rumors that the daimon were acting out to spite the royal family."

I nod. "Undermining King Konram's rule might have been the main purpose of their plans all along. Create as much turmoil as possible and blame it on how things are being run at the palace."

Stavros finally pops the chocolate into his mouth and manages to look angry about the fact that he's chewing it. "What exactly makes them so upset with our current ruler?"

I spread my hands. "I've got no idea. They didn't bother to mention that part. I think they're waiting to see if I prove loyal before getting into any detail."

Alek tenses where he's standing next to me. "How are they testing your loyalty?"

"Well, first they had me spill a little blood to honor the All-Giver." I hold up my hand, where the

Elox-blessed bandage I've since discarded left me with just a pale scar. "And they gave me some secret object I'm supposed to leave at the Temple of the Crown tonight."

Stavros's eyes narrow. "What sort of object?"

"I don't know. One of their conditions is that I'm not supposed to open the pouch it's in. They must have some way of telling if I do. But I think it's a sham anyway. They made a big deal about the powerful magic it's supposedly imbued with, but I can't—"

I cut myself off, remembering at the last second that Benedikt doesn't know I can sense magic. He doesn't have any reason to think I should be capable of doing so without my revealing the cracks in my soul.

Stavros, of course, has no concern for my need for caution. Although he might not realize what I was going to say. "You can't what?"

I choose my next words carefully. "I can't see how it's likely they'd give anything all that powerful to a candidate they've barely talked to. It's got to be a decoy so they can see how I'll handle it without overplaying their hand. Having held it, I just have a feeling that there isn't much to it."

I aim a pointed look at the former general with those last words, willing him to remember that the part of me he hates also means my "feeling" on this matter should be trusted.

He scowls. "And what are we risking by going by your gut?"

"They hinted that the object would be used to hurt the ruling powers somehow. Very vaguely, for plausible deniability, but it seemed clear they *wanted* me to think that. I'd imagine they'll be watching closely to confirm that I follow their instructions and that no unexpected contingent of guards shows up at the temple to arrest whoever comes to retrieve it."

Casimir hums to himself. "They want to know that you'll go along with their plans rather than turning them in once actual harm might be done."

"I think so."

Benedikt looks unusually pensive. "We can't be sure, though. Before we potentially put a weapon in our enemies' hands, we should ensure it won't do any significant damage."

"If Ivy says this is the safest way, we should trust her," Alek says, a little too quickly. When Benedikt casts a puzzled gaze his way, maybe wondering why the man who's normally the most cautious of us all is advocating for jumping in feet-first, the scholar recovers as well as he can. "She's the one who spoke to them. She has a much better idea of the situation than any of us."

Benedikt glances at Stavros next, probably thinking the former general will back him up, but Stavros simply grimaces in resignation. "The thief does also have plenty of experience with trickery. If we give the sorcerers any indication that she's tipped someone off, our whole stratagem falls apart."

The furrow in Benedikt's forehead deepens. "There must be some subtle way we can—"

"She follows through with the orders, and we keep our eyes open as we have all along," Stavros interrupts brusquely. "Don't *you* go tattling to anyone at the palace, unless you want to go to the king with total failure of the mission he assigned to us next."

Benedikt shuts his mouth. The bewilderment in his eyes wrenches at me, but I don't know how to reassure him.

I'm going to have to share my secret with him eventually, aren't I? How long can we keep going like this?

But just imagining confessing to him makes me queasy.

"I won't jeopardize the mission," Benedikt says quietly after a moment, with a tip of his head to me that's almost apologetic. He squares his shoulders. "I'll do whatever I can to help without getting in your way."

I offer him a grateful, guilty smile. "Thank you."

"Did the conspirators give any indication of when they'd reach out to you again?" Alek asks.

I drag in a breath. "No. I'm assuming they want to wait until they see what happens in the next couple of days, and then I may receive another invitation."

Or another knife in my back, depending on how they evaluate my performance.

Stavros claps his hands. "All right. That aspect is settled. Has anyone else made even a sliver of progress toward unraveling this conspiracy?"

Each of the men has a little to say about gossip overheard or purchases of supplies, but nothing that gives us solid evidence. Always more threads to follow up on, which seem to wind onward and onward without ever reaching a useful end.

Maybe once I've found out more information directly from the scourge sorcerers, we'll be able to stitch all those scraps together into a clearer picture.

Stavros declares the meeting is over with a thump of his boots as he steps back from the table. "It sounds as if we've covered everything. You all have lives to get back to. Well, for the most part." His gaze flicks to me.

All at once, I balk at the thought of trudging back into his quarters and then spending the rest of the day tagging along at his classes while he offers more warm congeniality to his students in a minute than he has to me in weeks.

The words slip out before I've totally thought them through. "There's a book of records in the storage room that I wanted to consult with Alek about. I'll catch up with you in a few minutes."

Stavros's jaw clenches, but after he left me and the scholar alone for hours last night, he must feel he'd look more odd arguing than not. "I'll need you for my cavalry class at the next bell. Make sure you're not late."

"I would never miss a chance to commune with the horses," I inform him tartly, and usher Alek over to the side room.

The scholar comes along obligingly and turns to scan the shelves of supplies once we're through the doorway. "What book did you find in here? I didn't think—"

I tug him farther out of view. "There's no book. I just wanted to do this without an audience."

I tease my fingers into his thick hair and bob up to claim a kiss.

Alek makes a soft, urgent sound in his throat that makes me quiver in delight and kisses me back. One of his hands comes to rest on my hip while the other cups my cheek.

For a few moments, nothing matters but the heat of his mouth and the lean strength of his body aligned with mine. I want to stay right here, wrapped up in the heady pleasure of his affection, where no conspiracy or sneering nobles can reach me.

Unfortunately, I can't escape my responsibilities for very long. I settle for hugging him tightly to me through one more lingering kiss before easing back.

We did have one bit of audience I couldn't remove us from. Julita makes an awkward coughing sound. *Ah, if this is going to continue, I suppose I should…*

I give my head a subtle shake to tell her there's no need for her to vanish herself and smile up at Alek. He's gazing down at me with so much delight of his own that an uncharacteristic giggle bubbles up from my chest.

"Very sneaky," he says.

I give his hair a teasing tug, remembering how exhilarated he got when we contrived to steal Ster. Torstem's financial records a few weeks ago. "And you love it."

Alek bows his head closer to mine. "Yes, I do."

It's strange seeing him in his mask now that I know what he looks like beneath it. I trace my fingers along the edge of it at his jaw. "I didn't want to leave without doing that first. I hope that soon we'll have enough time for me to see all of you again."

He chuckles and leans in to brush a kiss to my cheek. "There's a lot of you I'd like to see," he murmurs by my ear. "Gods, I wish we could spend time together on anything other than meetings. If you didn't have to be so careful with Ster. Torstem's people watching you…"

"We can hope that won't be for long."

I don't want to think about where we'll end up when there is no more conspiracy to tackle. Will I be able to stay at the college? How would we get on if I have to return to my old haunts?

Those are problems for another day.

"We should get back," I say, but I can't resist gripping the front of his shirt and stealing one more quick kiss.

Right as Casimir steps past the doorway.

"There are a few chocolates left, if either of you—" he's saying, but his warm voice falters as Alek and I jerk apart.

I grab the scholar's hand before he can get too far, abruptly afraid he'll take my startled reaction as shame. As I squeeze Alek's fingers, Casimir's gaze flicks between us.

I wait for him to laugh or make a playful remark about our subterfuge. It isn't as if I'd expect the courtesan of all people to be offended by anyone indulging in a brief moment of bliss, even someone he's done the same with himself.

But just for a second, the light fades from Casimir's gorgeous face. In that moment, he looks so lost I forget how to breathe.

He recovers quickly with a straightening of his posture and a hasty smile that doesn't totally cover the awkwardness of the moment. "I— Well, never mind. I apologize for accidentally interrupting."

He retreats with a brisk bob of his head. I stare after him through a few thumps of my pulse, an ache expanding through my chest.

Was he actually *sad* to see me with another man? Why would it even matter to him, unless—

I shake myself out of my daze and turn back to Alek… who's watching me with a wistful but not accusing expression.

"You should go after him," he says. "Tell him how you feel."

My fingers tighten around his where I'm still clutching his hand. "No. I don't— It doesn't change anything about how I feel about *you*. I told you—"

"I know. And I told you I wasn't sure you should have to choose." He steps closer and tips his head to press a kiss to my forehead. "I'm sure now that you *shouldn't*. Signy managed to juggle three lovers. I think you're nimble enough to handle two."

I sputter a laugh. "I'm hardly another Signy."

"I don't know. I think someday they'll be weaving tapestries and singing songs about you too." Alek nudges me toward the door. "I want to see how happy you can look when you're getting all the devotion you deserve. Go on, or *I'll* have to confess on your behalf."

I can't say whether it's the tenderness of his words or the panic that he might carry out his final threat that propels me back into the main meeting room.

Stavros and Benedikt have already departed, thank all that's holy. Casimir is just gathering the napkins that were scattered on the table.

As I hurry over to him, he sets them on the box of chocolates and spins toward his ring of cord.

"Casimir," I say. "I—"

"It's all right," he breaks in swiftly, with a much more convincing smile now that he's had more time to gather himself. "I'm happy for you both. I was only surprised I hadn't realized sooner. I'll leave you to—"

"Wait." I grasp his elbow.

Casimir turns back toward me to meet my gaze. Staring into his deep blue eyes, I find my thoughts have scrambled.

How am I supposed to "confess" in any way that doesn't sound ridiculous? What if I mistook his reaction just now and he really was simply surprised?

Through the whirl of my thoughts, it occurs to me that there's one way both of us can know exactly what we mean to each other.

My voice comes out quiet. "Use your gift on me."

Casimir blinks. "What?"

"Use your gift. See what you could do that would make me happiest right now."

It wouldn't make me happy for him to lie. I'd rather he let me down easy if that's what he needs to do.

The courtesan knits his brow for just a second before his stance relaxes. His eyes go a bit distant, and a quiver of magic passes through my nerves.

All at once, he's tossing the chocolate box onto the table and wrapping his arms around me in the warmest of embraces.

"Oh, Kindness," Casimir murmurs with a catch in his throat, his head lowered so his cheek rests against my temple. "Do you really not already know how much I adore you?"

I choke up a little too. "I mean, you seem to think a lot about *everyone's* happiness—I didn't realize I mattered that much more. I'm sorry I acted like I didn't care. I was trying not to make a fool of myself."

Casimir makes a rough noise and strokes his fingers over my hair. "My fault. I was worried about overwhelming you, and instead— I've been falling for you since the first day we met. You're woven into me now. I get an ache in the pit of my stomach when we're apart and a glow around my heart when you're nearby."

He glances up, still holding me close, toward where Alek is ambling over to join us. "Not that I would try to claim you all for myself if you're finding joy other places as well."

I glance over at the scholar, my cheeks heating with a flutter of my nerves.

To my relief, Alek's crooked smile is all fond amusement. "She doesn't believe me when I tell her she's going to become the next Signy." He trails his fingers down the back of my arm. "I'm not sure how much more proof she needs."

"I'd rather not have to face off against an entire imperial army any time soon," I protest.

Casimir just chuckles. He ducks his head to seek out my lips.

As the courtesan's kiss floods me with tingling warmth, Alek slips his arm around my waist from behind and presses his mouth to the side of my neck. My heart skips a beat.

It is overwhelming, being caught up between these two men, but only in the best possible way. I can barely believe *this* moment is actually happening while I'm in the middle of it.

Casimir draws back just an inch, his breath still caressing my lips when he speaks. "I'm not taking patrons now—not that kind. I wanted to be sure of where I stood with you first."

I hesitate. "I saw you with that woman in the dining hall..."

He gives his head an emphatic shake. "She hired me to play music at a party she's hosting. Nothing more intimate than that."

"Oh." I let out a shaky laugh and lean into Alek, looping my arm around his to show him how much I welcome his embrace too. "But—I mean, it's your calling; it's what you always meant to do..."

I can't ask him to give something that important up, even if the thought of him caressing another woman—or man—makes my gut twist.

"I don't know how I'll handle things in the future," Casimir says. "But for right now... I don't think it'd be good for me to muddy the waters."

I guess I can accept that. If he starts to seem miserable trying to hem himself in, I'll have to speak up, however painful it might be for me.

It can't be more painful than thinking I barely meant anything more than the women who pay him for his affections.

I lift my head toward Alek to aim a peck at his jaw. I wouldn't have found out any of this if the scholar hadn't pushed me. "Thank you."

Alek's arm tightens around me. His voice comes out a bit rough. "I think you've spent too long thinking you were barely worth anything at all, Ivy." A wry note creeps in. "Now I'll have some help convincing you otherwise."

I'd like to linger here and find out how they'd continue their convincing, but my awareness of the impending class niggles at me. With a regretful sigh, I ease away from both of the men.

"If I'm not ready for class in time, Stavros will probably come for all our heads."

"We'll see you again soon." Casimir gives my shoulder a quick squeeze, his eyes shining with so much affection it wraps around me like another embrace. "Stay safe, and know our thoughts are with you."

As I reluctantly step toward my circle of cord, Julita finally speaks up again. *Well. Capturing hearts all around, aren't you?*

She lets out a giggle that I can't help thinking sounds a bit forced. I swallow thickly as I step into the ring.

Julita has always urged me on when it comes to pursuing her men... but she might not ever have expected more than one of them would return my interest.

She might not have been prepared to think about all the experiences she can now never hope to have for herself.

I don't know how many of those experiences *I'll* even get to have if I continue down the path I'm on.

I've found so much more here at Sovereign College than I could have predicted. And that means I have so much more to lose if this all goes wrong.

# Nineteen

*Ivy*

I'm heading to one of the Quadring's side entrances after another afternoon class when I cross paths with Anya and a couple of her friends.

The vindictive noblewoman who spent most of my early weeks at the college heckling and harassing me pauses for just an instant, a flicker of apprehension flitting across her face. I don't think she knows what to make of me after I disarmed her with supposed friendliness.

The fact that I also threatened to let Stavros have her arrested for treason probably plays into her wariness as well.

She settles for a stiff smile and a primp of her hair and sashays on past me while her friends shoot me curious looks.

*Ha,* Julita says with a triumphant air. *You knocked her feet right out from under her without needing to land a single blow.*

My body has tensed up in anticipation of some kind of spat. It feels strange to be able to simply relax and walk on.

For all the turmoil I've been through with my men and our investigation in the past couple of weeks, my regular life as a supposed assistant has been relatively tame. I guess I should be thankful that the snobbish nobles have decided I don't make an ideal target in their jockeying for dominance, settling for disdainful looks if they pay attention to me at all.

I've got much bigger enemies to contend with.

Enemies who may be lurking closer than I'd prefer. As I step out of the doorway, a faint prickle of a magic catches my attention.

My head jerks around in the direction it seemed to be coming from—just in time to spot a lithe, scaled form slithering through the grass toward a gap in the wall's mortar.

It's a smaller snake than the one I noticed in the forest three nights ago, as slim as my thumb and only as long as my forearm—the perfect size to slip into the school's walls. And do gods know what inside the Quadring.

As I spring after it, my mind spins with a torrent of urgent thoughts. The rat lashed out at me violently—I have to assume the snake will too. But I only have a matter of moments before it's glided out of reach.

I want to take this one alive.

My magic flickers up eagerly, offering its services, but I ignore its pull. My hand darts between the overlapping fabric of my skirt and retrieves one of my tiny stashed knives. I yank it through one of the strips of silk and return the blade to its sheath in the space of a heartbeat.

Grasping the swath of fabric I've cut off, I pounce on the snake.

It flings its tail like a whip and snaps its head around with fangs bared, just as I expected. But I slam the fabric down over it and clutch it through the layer of cloth.

*Be careful!* Julita cries, as if I'm not already trying to be.

As I flip the snake over and knot the fabric around it into a bundle, it flails against its silky prison. A seething hiss filters through the cloth.

Once the makeshift pouch is fully closed and secure, the creature squirms for several more seconds and then goes still as if giving up. Or biding its time until it senses a better opportunity for escape.

Julita's presence shivers. *I wonder what they're trying to find out with all these horrible spies.*

"A very good question," I mutter under my breath.

I push upright from my hunched position by the wall and glance around cautiously. Several students are meandering around the field, but no one's all that close to me.

I catch one raised eyebrow aimed my way from a nobleman I don't recognize, too far away for him to have realized what I was doing. I aim a prim smile at him and stride off toward the Domi as if I have nothing to feel awkward about.

Everyone already thought I was a little strange anyway.

My hand remains clamped around the top of the bundle of silk, keeping a firm grip on my captive. I need to summon the men as quickly as possible in case this creature vanishes into dust or a poof of smoke if it's restrained for too long.

Who knows how the scourge sorcerers worked their illicit magic on the thing?

I can't go straight to our new meeting room, because Stavros in his infinite wisdom is still holding my enchanted cord hostage. Gods forbid I have free access to an entirely locked and secure room we can't even tell is within the palace.

But we still have our original meeting spot, even if the archive room seems dreary and cramped by comparison.

I march through the Domi's main entrance and head past the library doors. It's just a short distance to the hall of tapestries—

"Ivy! Where are you off to in such a hurry this morning?"

Petra's clear, melodic voice rings out from the library doorway. I jar to a stop with a silent curse.

Her question was casual enough, but it'll look awfully suspicious if I charge on by without acknowledging her. And the lesser royal has already shown more interest in me than I'd like.

I tuck my strange parcel close to my gown as I turn to face her. Since it's the same fabric the skirt is made of, it should blend in.

I don't trust my knots quite enough to risk stuffing the snake in my pocket.

Petra steps out of the library. Her smile is friendly enough, but her dark eyes look pensive.

"Oh, I'm simply on an errand for Ster. Stavros," I say with a light laugh. "He doesn't like to be kept waiting, you know."

Petra echoes my laugh. "I suppose in his past line of work, most tasks were much more urgent. I hope he isn't putting you under too much stress."

"No, not at all. But I'd better get on with it."

I dip my head to her, praying that she doesn't try to stall me any further. Her voice doesn't follow me down the hall, but my old scars itch with the sense of her studying my retreating back.

*Why is* she *so interested in you all of a sudden?* Julita murmurs.

I wait until I've turned the corner into the hall of tapestries and confirmed that no one else is around before replying. "Do you think King Konram might have asked her to keep an eye on me—back when he first heard from Stavros that I was helping the investigation? I'm new to the school, after all."

It'd make sense for the king to be concerned that I'm so involved in delving into a conspiracy that could have dire consequences for his family.

Julita lets out an uncertain hum. *I'd have thought he'd trust Stavros's judgment more than that. And he didn't even want to inform his closest staff—I can't see him revealing all this trouble to a girl who's only distantly related to his wife. The success of our mission depends on its secrecy.*

Maybe the king picked up on Stavros's recent apprehensions about me. It's not as if the former general has been all that great at hiding them.

On the other hand, after what happened with Esmae, I'm hesitant to assume anyone who strikes a sudden interest in me has good intentions. Better to treat Petra as a hazard until I have irrefutable evidence that she's not one.

While I tweak the sconce with my free hand, I spare a glance at the tapestry of Signy. At the three men gathered around her on the hill.

Did she find herself totally bewildered when she realized more than one of them returned her feelings—and was willing to stand with the others at her side?

The stories never give much detail about their romance, making it sound as if her magnificence made it inevitable that she'd win their hearts. I'd like to think someone selfless enough to take on an entire empire to free her country would have a little more humility than to take anyone's affections for granted, but who really knows?

The much-celebrated hero of Velduny died before I was even born.

The moment I've descended the conjured shadowy staircase into the small archive room, I grope for my locket, flick it open single-handed, and press my thumb to the inside. The signal will tell the men where to find me.

I peer around the room with an odd waft of nostalgia, though it's only been a couple of weeks since I last came down here. As if sensing my momentary distraction, the snake makes another attempt at thrashing its way free from the bundle of silk. I clench my fingers around the gathered edges of the fabric.

If the creature is acting as some kind of spy, we shouldn't have an unguarded conversation about it. What might the men give away when they rush in to answer my call?

A jolt of anxiety sends me to the desk. I paw through the drawers one-handed and dig out a piece of parchment, a quill, and a bottle of ink that's still half full.

I have to pull the stopper out with my teeth while I'm holding the snake's silk prison, but I manage to wet the quill and scrawl a quick message across the parchment. *STAY SILENT.*

I've just pushed the stopper back into the ink bottle when Benedikt emerges from the wall. "What's the—"

In an urgent motion, I jerk up the paper with my command. He snaps his mouth shut, his eyebrows arching.

With a shrug, I hope I convey that I realize how ridiculous the situation might seem. Then Alek comes hurtling in through the door from the larger archives, and I whirl toward him with my message raised.

He's only sucked in a breath when he sees it, his voice catching before he's released a single word. As he frowns at me in concern, I offer an apologetic smile and swing back around to aim the message at Casimir, who's come down the hidden staircase a minute behind Benedikt.

It takes another few minutes of awkward quiet before Stavros finally makes his appearance. He glances around at all of us, taking in our expressions and my demand, and folds his arms over his chest with a pointed look.

I set down the paper and motion to my silk bundle. The snake has gone still, so they won't have any idea what's going on.

Bracing myself, I feel along the creature's body through the fabric. It wriggles, but I manage to grasp it between my thumb and forefinger just behind its head.

Keeping the snake secured like that, I loosen the folds of cloth and delve in with my other hand. Gingerly, I ease the green-and-brown-scaled serpent from my trap.

It flings around its tail some more, but it's short enough that I can easily hold it away from my body. The position of my hand prevents it from taking any bites out of me.

Alek's eyes widen with a light of understanding. He makes a creeping motion with his hand and mouths, "The rat?"

I nod.

He eases closer, and after a moment, the other men follow suit. It should be obvious to all of them that the animal in my hand is no more clay-like than I am.

Stavros taps the top of its head as if he needs to feel its scales to be sure. Then he draws the sword he always carries on his belt and motions for me to lower the snake to the desk.

I hold it there as still as I can between my hands. The former general braces himself and chops the edge of the blade downward like a chef's knife, just an inch from my clutching fingers at the creature's neck.

The snake's body squirms away from its head—and stiffens. The surface against my fingertips turns harder and rougher.

I lift my hands away from the two clay pieces now lying on the desk.

The unpolished reddish-brown surface has been etched with faint lines to indicate scales and two dots for eyes. It's not a particularly realistic replica other than in shape.

Alek's eyes widen. His hand flicks down his chest in a three-fingered tap to the gods.

All sense of the magic in the snake has vanished. I exhale in a rush. "I think we can talk now."

"You're just guessing?" Stavros says darkly.

I glower at him, and Alek jumps in with a suitable explanation that doesn't reveal my magic-detecting ability to Benedikt. "The enchantment on it has obviously been broken. The sorcerers wouldn't want anyone to be able to test the magic once it's been discovered."

Casimir runs his fingers over the clay body. "That's incredible. It really did look and move exactly like a living animal."

I wipe my fingers against my skirt, the sensation of writhing scales clinging to them. "None of you have ever encountered or even heard of a gift that could accomplish this?"

Alek shakes his head. "I'd imagine it has to be multiple gifts combined, or some kind of temporary magic gained through sacrifice."

With that last word, he looks a bit sick.

What kind of sacrifice would it take to bring a lump of clay into something so close to life?

Benedikt leans back against one of the shelving units, tapping his lips. "I've kept an eye out for anyone handling clay objects around the campus and the palace. Haven't noticed anything unusual so far. Pottery isn't exactly a common conversational topic at the cards table."

"I couldn't find any connections between Ster. Torstem and a place where he might be sourcing or working with the clay," Alek says. "He must be keeping his distance from that part of the conspiracy's operations. I'll extend my search and see what else I can find—I'll make it my main priority."

I catch Stavros's gaze. "You should warn the king that it's not just rats. Maybe the clerics who've been watching for more daimon antics would be able to pick up the magic in these creatures and 'discover' them on their own."

Stavros's mouth tightens as if he doesn't love taking a suggestion from me, but he can obviously recognize it's a decent one. "I'll pass on word to him as soon as I can."

Casimir frowns, picking up the snake's clay head and examining it. "What real purpose would these serve? Who would the scourge sorcerers want to be spying on? It seems like a totally different tactic than what they were attempting with the daimon."

It does, which unnerves me more than I'd like to admit. "Maybe they feel they need to use a more subtle approach after how things turned out before."

"At least we know," Benedikt points out. "That keeps us one step ahead of them."

I'm not sure we're ahead so much as not as far behind as we could be. But before I can decide whether to put that depressing thought into words, a creeping sensation spreads across my palm.

I jerk my hand toward me in time to see the words flicker across my skin. *Tonight, same place and time. Alone.*

"What?" Stavros demands, taking in my reaction.

I let out a raw chuckle. "It looks like I'm going to get another chance to dig into the scourge sorcerers' plans directly—tonight."

# Twenty

*Ivy*

This time, I don't have to remind Stavros to head to his bedroom and turn off the lights. After Casimir finishes touching up the false godlen brand I haven't needed to show off yet, the former general simply casts his gaze toward me and says, "Be careful."

From his tone, it's obvious what he's actually saying is, "Don't you dare burn the school to the ground with your crazy riven magic."

"Good night to you too," I call after him, and flop onto the sofa to wait until it seems like a reasonable time to head out.

Julita gives a resigned sigh. *I didn't think it'd take him this long to come around. It's not as if you're a different person from who you were before he found out.*

I grimace. "In his mind, I am."

*He's got to see that you have a handle on your magic eventually... I suppose being stubborn was an ideal quality in a general.*

I chuckle under my breath. "Good thing I'm awfully stubborn too."

I pause for a moment, debating how much of a conversation I want to get into even with my voice low when Stavros is in the next room. But what I want to ask Julita about isn't anything I'd dare saying out loud anywhere else on campus.

"Is there anything else you can remember from your brother and Wendos's rituals that I should be prepared for? There's the blood-letting and the appeals for power, but we've already covered those."

Julita is silent for a moment before she answers—long enough that I wish my current mission didn't require that she dredge up those awful childhood memories.

*That was most of it*, she says. *There were things like drawing symbols with different materials like the dartling eggshell powder, and odd chants similar to the things Wendos was saying in the tower—but not quite the same. I don't think they had the full picture. Which doesn't mean this bunch of scourge sorcerers does either, but they seem to know more.*

"And they want more. Your brother never said anything about undermining the royal family, did he?"

I have the impression of Julita shaking her head. *Nothing on that large a scale. I mean, they were barely teenagers while I was involved. Stupid boys, dabbling with magic they didn't understand, hoping they'd get some extra power that'd make them feel special. I never got the impression they even thought all that much about politics or religious ideals.*

"Nothing along those lines came up around the family dinner table?" I can't help asking.

Julita snorts. *My parents didn't—don't—care much about what goes on beyond our county either. Frankly, I wouldn't have if I could have gone back to Nikodi and simply focused on running things smoothly there. You know, all the territory we managed from our estate only contained about a quarter of the people who live just in this city. When you spend all your time in a place like that, the world feels… smaller.*

"That makes sense." I doubt many intrepid merchants or travelers bothered to linger within Nikodi's far-flung borders either.

I might have spent most of my life struggling to keep food in my belly and find any sense of home, but my world was far larger than Julita's until she came to the college.

"Is there anything you'd like to see?" I say abruptly. "I mean, when we're done here—you've missed out on a lot of things—and *I* wouldn't mind taking in more of Silana or even farther abroad. The king's got to offer a good enough reward that we could do a little traveling with plenty left over."

Before she moves on for good, that is. My stomach knots when I consider saying that part.

Julita's voice goes quiet. *That's very kind of you to offer. I'll have to think about it. Mostly I wanted to be such a good countess my parents couldn't possibly wish Borys had stuck around instead.* She lets out a dry laugh.

The apprehension about the unknown tasks ahead is starting to get to me. I pace the room a little, taking in the twelve rings of the midnight bell, and wander out to the stable again.

I'm tempted to take Toast out for a ride into the woods—the conspirators never said the fifty paces had to be human—but I'm not sure I want to find out what might happen to him if they object.

I rub his neck and call him a good boy, and drink in the comforting stable scents until my restlessness drives me onward.

I can't stay out in the open in the outer courtyard without the patrolling guards noticing me, so I duck into the shadows at the edge of the hunting woods. Setting my feet carefully so I don't make any noise, I slink between the trees off the path.

I don't come across any trace of the scourge sorcerers' presence. How far ahead of me do they come into the woods themselves?

Or do they have some magical means of arriving here, the way we can use the enchanted cords to jump between the college and the palace?

A niggling tug of my own magic reminds me that *it* could expose any figures lurking in the shadows if I let it. I grimace at the sensation.

At the single peal marking the first hour of the morning, I square my shoulders and set off toward the fifty-pace meeting spot.

Like before, I'm met with silence. I stand still and calm, taking in the breeze and the warble of swaying leaves, on the alert for any sign of supernatural power.

The conspirators can't know about my sensitivity to other people's magic any more than Benedikt does. I do have a few aspects of my unwanted abilities that I can draw on without doing any harm.

Abruptly, the voice—which may or may not be the same voice as last time—wavers around me again. "Ivy of Nikodi, you fulfilled your first task. All of us who are committed to a better world thank you."

"I thank you for the opportunity to work toward that better world too," I say, the false gratitude sour on my tongue. "Is there more that I can help with?"

If they could get on with the part where they fill me in on their plans, I'd be truly grateful.

But we wouldn't be in this predicament if the scourge sorcerers were that carefree.

"There will be more opportunities," the voice says. "Tonight, we want to see how much restoring the All-Giver to these realms means to you."

So they aren't delusional enough to believe the All-Giver never left. They just think they can bring the Great God back?

I guess that's some kind of delusion too.

I give a slight bow. "I can't think of much I wouldn't do." As long as the All-Giver dispatches all the sorcerers and their sick tactics without harming the rest of us. Which, granted, isn't a sure thing, so we'd better be able to take these psychopaths down ourselves first.

The voice shifts as if changing direction in its rippling path around me. "We must return to the old ways from when the Great God watched over us. We've distanced ourselves too much from where we came from. Can you tap into the roots of humanity, Ivy?"

A shiver travels up my spine. "I'm not sure what you mean."

"We're all animals at heart. We're born wild, meant to revel in sky, sea, and earth by immersing ourselves in them, not holding ourselves apart. Too many have forgotten the essence of our nature."

*Born wild.* What was it Wendos talked about? He mentioned "the Order of the Wild" as if that was the name of the group he was allied with.

Julita hums. *This does remind me a little of some of the things Borys used to say. Mingling blood with the earth because it all comes from the same place and things along that line.*

I nod as if I agree with what the speaker said. "We've cut ourselves off from our origins. I can see what you mean. Everyone's so concerned with making rules and keeping peace."

"Good. Then you understand. Now embrace that thought. Get down on your hands and knees."

My muscles tense against the command, but I force myself to kneel, my skirt fanned beneath me. As I set my hands on the hard-packed dirt of the riding path, I wish I'd changed into my combat training clothes for this secret rendezvous.

The scent of the earth fills my nose, pungent and loamy. There is something a little exhilarating about getting down in the dirt, shedding expectations of proper posture and noble elegance.

"Now run," the voice says.

My head jerks around—aimlessly, since I have no idea where the speaker is. "What?"

"*Run.* Like the animal you are. Follow the wildness within."

I feel more uncomfortable than wild in that moment, but I can't let the evaluating sorcerers notice me hesitate.

With a jerk, I untie the cloak from my neck to let it fall on the path so it won't tangle with my limbs. Then I push myself forward, scuttling in my crouched position along the packed dirt.

After a short distance, I decide it'll feel better if my legs are squatting rather than kneeling, my feet propelling me instead of my knees.

As I adjust my stance, the voice hollers after me. "Deeper into the woods. Away from all the restrictions they've tried to place on us!"

I spring between the trees, wincing as broken twigs and sharp pebbles bite at my palms. The toe of my boot snags on a jutting root, and I sprawl forward, scraping my chin before I'm scrambling back up again.

Pain stings along my jaw as I hurtle onward, but I tune it out. I focus on the brush of the vegetation against my skin, on the hiss of my skirts against the ground.

The silk catches on a broken branch and tears. A strange sense of satisfaction passes through me at the rasp of sound, followed by a swell of horror.

I can't be buying into this madness. I shouldn't be enjoying anything about this moment.

But the conspiracy wouldn't be growing if their ideals didn't have a certain appeal. Maybe in some ways I *am* the sort of person they'd have wanted to recruit.

I scramble on through the darkness, my torn gown flapping around my legs, my fingernails digging into the dirt. I don't know how long they expect me to keep this up.

Should I throw back my head and howl at the moon like a wolf, or would that be too much?

The idea kind of amuses me, which makes me uneasy all over again.

As I swerve around a tree trunk, fern fronds swiping across my cheek, my magic unfurls through my chest again. If I don't want to be here, I can wipe out every other person in this forest, just like that.

I can force them to leave me alone. I can end this wretched madness.

I grit my teeth against it.

No. I'm fine. No one's hurting me.

No one except my own wretched power. When I clamp down on it, it thrashes against my hold harder than before. Claws of pain rake across my ribs and down to my gut.

I swallow a gasp and dash onward, hoping whoever's watching will attribute my stumbles to the uneven ground. As the pain digs in deeper, tears burn behind my eyes.

Even my broken soul knows that this bizarre display is wrong. But I can't lash out the way it wants when I still know so little about our enemy.

With every thump of my feet, I will my roiling power to calm down. I can keep up this act for as long as I need. There's no real threat here.

Then I stumble into a glade, and a pale gray rabbit leaps in front of me.

"Kill it!" the voice says, bouncing between the trees. "Tear it apart with your hands and offer up its life to the one who made us all!"

My heart lurches, and I lunge forward. My panic that I might fail the trial cuts through my nausea at the task.

I catch the softly furred body in my arms. My hands grope toward its neck.

I've killed rodents before—when I was desperate, when both my stomach and my power were gnawing at me to act.

Normally I'd have used a knife, but I know how to feel for the knobs of the spine—

*Crack.*

The body goes limp in my grasp. As I hold up its body to the thin beams of moonlight, the voice calls out again.

"Spill its blood. Dedicate it to the All-Giver!"

My stomach churns with another wave of queasiness as I squeeze my hands. My magic reverberates through my limbs, offering its service—I can't give in. I have to do this myself too.

I wrench and heave, and flesh tears. Fur and skin part; blood spurts onto the ground.

"For the All-Giver!" I rasp. "I run wild and show the animal I am for the All-Giver."

The scourge sorcerers aren't done yet. The voice echoes through the woods around me—or is it multiple voices now—in an emphatic chant?

"The right rulers should rise, and the wrong should fall!"

"The right rulers should rise, and the wrong should fall!" I repeat, restraining a shiver of horror. How exactly do they mean to see the "wrong" rulers removed?

And who do they think the right ones are? Does Ster. Torstem expect to take the throne?

I don't know. I'm smeared with dirt and blood, and all I can do is play along.

Play along until I've tumbled far enough into this rabbit hole to see my way out again.

# Twenty-One

*Stavros*

Ivy is stealthy, but I haven't lost any of the hearing I honed in sparring rings and on battlefields. At the ever-so-faint click of the door to my quarters closing, my head snaps up.

I learned my lesson from last time. So my mind would stay alert, I sat myself in my bedroom's armchair rather than on the bed and forced myself to track the periodic patrols of guards and the few students arriving late to the dorms.

I shouldn't have fallen asleep before regardless. The tension coiled in my gut gives off constant pangs of uneasy adrenaline.

The problem is that tension I'm carrying hasn't subsided since the moment I found out what our thief really is. For the past two weeks, I've only been sleeping in brief fragments, made even less restful by the nightmares I haven't managed to shake.

The problem is I'm fucking exhausted.

But I've survived on stints of little sleep plenty of times in the midst of an ongoing skirmish or siege. I can hold myself and my blasted temper together.

I have to, because the chaotic and unnerving conflict I've found myself in the middle of is the closest thing to a war I'll ever fight again. If I can't defend my country from even that...

Rather than following the uncomfortable thought to its conclusion, I push myself from my chair and stalk over to the outer room.

Ivy is standing by the sofa, peeling off her cloak. Her hair falls loose across her shoulders, many of the strands clinging damply to her skin.

Did she stop at the bathing rooms on her way back?

Gods smite the flare of heat that idea sends to my groin.

She startles just slightly at my entrance. Something about the tensing of her stance, more nervous than boldly defensive, has me striding closer with a tick of my gaze to refocus it.

As I round the sofa and get a full look at her dress, my feet stall beneath me. I stare, with another twitch of my head and a lurch of my stomach.

Dark streaks stain the pewter gray silk of her gown all down the skirt. The bottom hem is tattered as if she ran it through a thresher. And a few of the stains, including a couple higher up on the bodice, have a ruddy hue I can make out even in the hazy light that creeps through the window.

I'm striding straight to her in the instant before I catch myself. I halt just a couple of paces away, my right hand clenching at my side.

My voice comes out harsher than I like. The idea that she might be injured *torments* me more than I like. "Did they make you cut yourself again?"

Ivy lets out a laugh, ragged enough to pierce my heart. "No. Not me. Just a poor little bunny. Sorry I'm a mess. I kept my cloak over my gown on the way back and washed up as well as I could."

Hearing her apologize sets me even more off-balance. How shaken is she that she'd act as though she needs to justify herself rather than brush me off with her usual banter?

"They asked you to kill a rabbit?"

She glances down. "With my bare hands. After I raced around the forest on all fours like a wild creature. These scourge sorcerers have very strange ideas about what the All-Giver would want."

Her voice has lightened, but it doesn't reassure me. She still sounds unnervingly detached.

I know that tone. Soldiers often get it after their first intense battle—when they've had to kill in ways they never imagined, when they've seen too many comrades slain in front of them.

Two chilling thoughts cut through me in quick succession.

The scourge sorcerers' tactics are rattling Ivy more than anything I've ever seen.

How is she going to control her riven magic if they keep breaking her down?

"You shouldn't go back," I say before I've thought the comment through.

Ivy blinks at me, and a little of her usual keenness comes back into her gaze. It'd reassure me more if her next words weren't, "Of course I should. I'm gaining their trust. I've got a better idea of how they think than I did before, and they'll keep revealing more."

"That only works if they leave you in one piece," I retort.

She makes a scoffing sound that also sounds more like her usual self and swipes her hair back from her face. "I'm all right. It was just very weird. They've already told me I'm supposed to come back tomorrow night—we might get something concrete on their plans then."

She's putting herself in their grasp again that soon?

My pulse stutters. "Ivy—"

She holds up her hand. "We made *our* plan, and I'm following it as well as I can. Have I screwed anything up so far?"

I scowl at her. "No, but—"

"Then let me do what I came here for. At some point you've got to believe I'm on your side and not the villains'." She brushes her hands over her dress. "Now I'm going to get out of this ruined thing and get some sleep."

She marches past me to the latrine to change. I hesitate in the middle of the room, but she's obviously recovered from her initial shock.

What am I going to do, stand sentinel over her all night to confirm her magic doesn't slip out of her in her sleep?

Some part of me wants to. Gods help me, some part of me longs to gather her slight but strong frame in my arms and let my own strength shield her from the horrors she's experiencing.

But what happens tomorrow when the insane conspirators might put her through even worse? How long will it take before their madness starts rubbing off on her?

I retreat to my bedroom, but I can't walk away from the qualms that are nibbling at the edges of my mind even more insistently than before.

How far can I really let her mission go?

If I judge the situation wrong, if I extend more trust than I should, the resulting disaster could be even worse than if the scourge sorcerers go unchecked. One of the riven unleashing her magic right outside the palace gates? Right in the same *building* as the royal family during our meetings?

I can't count on our companions to notice the warning signs. Even with my faulty sight, I've seen the way Aleksi and Casimir look at her.

It isn't as if I don't understand the attraction. The sly humor that can shine in her stunning eyes, the confident might in every movement of her lithe body—

But *I'm* keeping those compulsions reined in. The two of them appear to have welcomed her back into their trust—and who knows what else—whole-heartedly.

The security of the entire kingdom rests on my shoulders.

I slump onto the bed and close my eyes to try to get some rest, but it takes ages before I drift off. And then the images of Michas sear up from my unconscious.

Flashes of real memory: the riven sorcerer's snarl, Michas's face blanching in panic, the way the unharnessed magic wrenched through his body, tearing it limb from limb…

And in the dreams, Ivy stands here too. She echoes the snarl of the man from my memory.

She waves her hand, and another slash rips through Michas with a gush of blood.

I wake up in a sweat with my heart racing. Pressing my arm to my forehead, I tip my head back against my pillow.

I can't go on like this. *I'm* fraying at least as much as Ivy is.

An idea wavers up through my fatigue like a lantern in the fog.

Maybe there's a way I can be sure of my choice. A way to test the control she claims will never falter.

If she's going to unleash her magic, it'll be better if it's when I'm prepared for it than off in the woods in the middle of the night.

The test won't even take that much.

The hardest part is deciding which of my students will shoulder the responsibility—far more responsibility than they even know.

In true fairness, I should take the risk… but if Ivy lashes out at me, I won't be around to put her down. That would undermine all the reasons I'm carrying out the test at all.

I have to be alive to protect everyone else from her magic.

If it's not me, it has to be a student. I can't turn to my fellow staff or the guards of the Crown's Watch. They'd ask too many questions—they'd talk with their colleagues.

The students know Ivy. They're used to seeing me as a teacher, to participating in combat scenarios I set up purely so they can learn.

I stew on the question for most of the morning, the guilt that I have to ask it at all digging deeper into my gut with every passing hour.

Finally, at the end of my senior strategy class, I motion for Ivy to take her leave and gather a cluster of my most dedicated students. The ones I expect to recommend for positions as higher officers at the end of the school year.

"I may have a mission I need to send a few people on," I tell them. "It'll be dangerous—I can't promise you'd come out of it safely or even alive—but it'd be for the protection of the country. I won't order anyone to take it up while you're still in the middle of your studies. But if any of you feel prepared to tackle that kind of task, I can accept potential volunteers."

Bartos, the second son of one of the counts who rules not far from Florian, speaks up without hesitation. "I'll go, if you need me. That's what all this studying has been for."

The others add their own voices in agreement. I've obviously judged their devotion to their country well.

Bartos wasn't just the fastest to leap at the chance, he's also the strongest physically. For my actual mission, I need someone who'll pose an obvious threat.

As the others leave, I keep him back for a minute longer. "I appreciate your enthusiasm. There's a smaller task I could use some help with right here at the school today, if you don't mind lending a hand there as well."

Bartos simply smiles. "I'd be honored to assist."

"Good. Go get yourself some lunch and meet me by the storage rooms right after."

I can't tell him that the smaller task and the dangerous mission are one and the same. At least I've gotten my confirmation that he's willing to put his life on the line for a cause like this.

By the time Bartos arrives at the building where the college keeps most of its military training equipment, I've already worked out the most viable strategy. I meet him with a length of sturdy rope in my hands, willing down my nausea at the hiss of its corded surface sliding against my metal prosthetic.

If Ivy really isn't a threat to us, then I'm ensuring she never has to meet the fate I'm going to stage.

I've worked out my story as well. As I wave Bartos into the hall between the supply rooms, I keep my tone casual.

"I've been working with Ivy one on one to judge her aptitude for a promotion to an officer role or taking up teaching herself. I'd like to get a clear view of how she'll respond to a perceived attack. You'll need to be convincing, but I'll step in as soon as I'm sure of her reaction—before you'd do any real damage, if she can't fend you off."

My guilt only digs in deeper at Bartos's unquestioning nod. "I can do that."

"She can't realize you're one of my students, or she'll know it's just a test," I go on, handing him the rope. "You'll need to come at her from behind and get this around her neck. Fast enough to startle her. She'll be coming in to start setting up for our afternoon class at the second bell. You can wait here and catch her right after she arrives."

I have him stand in the shadows just beyond the doorway Ivy will pass on her way to the leather figures she's sometimes complained about hauling around. I position myself on the other side of the hallway, where I'll be able to see the struggle without Ivy noticing my presence.

When the palace bell starts to peal, I draw my sword and hold it ready at my side.

If Bartos shows any sign of being under magical attack, I don't know if I'll be able to charge in fast enough to save his life. But I can ensure no one else gets hurt by her chaotic power.

And if Ivy can fight her way out of this test without drawing on her power, maybe I can stop worrying about the stress the scourge sorcerers are putting her through.

If she can't... then there's too much chance of her control slipping during so many other dire situations she could find herself in.

My throat constricts, but I tighten my grip on my sword. I'll do what I have to do. What maybe a stronger man would have done to begin with, glowing godlen sigils be damned.

Ivy might mutter about the work sometimes, but she shows up promptly. She casts a slim shadow across the floor from the open doorway, changed into a short tunic, breeches, and leathers for the combat exercises to come.

She's got one knife on a belt at her hip, but Bartos can see that for himself. I've no doubt there are two more hidden in her boots, but if he plays his part properly, she won't have the chance to reach for them.

She strides into the hallway with a brief glance around and what looks like a suppressed yawn. I can't help wondering if this test wouldn't be fairer after *she's* gotten a proper night's sleep.

But life is hardly fair. The scourge sorcerers don't care how well-rested she is.

My body tenses in anticipation.

The second Ivy steps past Bartos's doorway, he launches himself at her.

As he whips the rope around her neck, he lets out a brief roar. Apparently he's going all in on the role I gave him.

He snaps the rope against Ivy's throat and wrenches upward, towering a full foot over her short body. I flinch at the sight, even though I'm the one who brought it about.

I can't afford that kind of weakness. I can't… I can't trust my own judgment when it comes to this woman.

But I feel strangled myself as I watch Ivy's frame go rigid. Her eyes widen, blown out with panic, and my stomach lurches in anticipation of how she'll retaliate.

Bartos yanks her back against him, hauling her high enough that she's left stumbling on tiptoe. Her arms flail out, but in the first few seconds they're jerky and imprecise.

Great God help me, is she picturing the noose from her nightmares right now?

I lift my sword with a twitch of my head to clear my vision. If only I could focus my blasted eyes for long enough for my gift to take hold, to witness her next moves before she makes them…

In the middle of my anguished thought, Ivy regains her wherewithal enough to grope for her knife. Bartos slaps her hand away.

I brace myself for her to defend herself the easiest and possibly the only way she can.

Her boots scrape frantically against the floor. Her arms fling out again—but all at once something in her posture shifts.

Her muscles coil, her focus sharpening.

She manages to swing her body to the left, heedless of the rope, and slams her heel upward. It jars against Bartos's kneecap.

He sways just slightly, but he's already a little off-balance from her squirming. He bats away a fist she aims backward at his jaw only to take an elbow in the middle of his gut.

Ivy strikes him hard enough to knock the breath out of him. My student pitches backward, Ivy snatches at her knife again—and without any divine gift necessary, I see how the blade will stab straight into his heart.

"Stop!" I burst out from my doorway, dropping my sword with a clatter.

I snag the hooked end of my prosthetic around Ivy's wrist just inches from the knife piercing Bartos's flesh.

Bartos drops the rope and staggers out of range. Ivy's feet jolt all the way to the ground. She stands there, panting and staring at me as if she doesn't recognize me. Wisps of her red-blond hair have stuck to her temple with sweat.

"Good work," I say in the easy-going drawl I normally use with my students. I don't want Bartos realizing I lied about my motivations. "You got your fear under control and found a way to turn the tables. A pass with flying colors."

She didn't use a single trace of magic. She mastered herself more than Bartos could realize.

Relief floods my fatigued mind so swiftly it's dizzying.

I wasn't wrong to guard her secret after all. I didn't misjudge her control or her determination.

She's still the woman I believed in.

I lift my gaze and nod at my student. "Thank you for your help. You can get on with the rest of the day—I trust your knee is all right?"

Bartos gives a rough chuckle. "Oh, I'm sure I'll recover quickly enough. You did pick quite a tenacious assistant."

He bobs his head to both of us and ambles out—with a hint of a limp, I can't help noticing.

"You," Ivy mutters under her breath. "You *asked* him to— You were testing me?"

The last word is broken by a hiss. She wraps her arm around her belly and reels backward to brace herself against the wall.

Any relief that was buoying me washes out of my body. I dash forward to grab her elbow. "Ivy— are you hurt?"

"Fuck you," she spits out in a strained voice, all pretense of a noble lady dropped.

Her legs wobble. She stiffens them for a second before they buckle completely.

My fingers clamp around her arm to slow her collapse. I sink down with her, my pulse suddenly thundering.

"Where are you wounded?" I demand. "You have to let me—"

Her words spill out between hitches of breath. "I don't. Have to. Do. *Anything*. For an asshole. Like you."

Her head bows forward to rest against her upraised knees. Her whole body shudders, a whine seeping from her lips.

The sound is so agonized it guts me.

I did this to her. My wretched test has left her more injured than the scourge sorcerers ever have.

My hand slides up her arm to her shoulder. I tip my head close to hers. "I'm sorry. I had to know—I had to be sure that even under duress— He wasn't supposed to really harm you."

Ivy manages to emit a derisive snort. "Wasn't Bartos. Stupid power. Gets mad. When I won't. Use it."

She raises her head shakily, pain etched across her pale features, so her bright gaze can burn into mine. "But I didn't. I never want to. I'm not. A fucking. Monster."

Understanding jars into place in my head with a sharper swell of regret.

Did she tell us that much before and I didn't heed it? I know she indicated that it was hard for her to resist her magic, but I didn't quite make the connection—

That time Aleksi called us all to the archives because Ivy had supposedly been attacked. And later, when Benedikt raced into my classroom to tell me I needed to hurry to my quarters, that she'd collapsed and was coughing up blood…

Those incidents weren't caused by spite from the idiots at this school. That was her magic lashing out at her. Because it wanted to take action and she refused it?

I never saw her in the worst grips of either of those fits. She was already recovering when I reached her the first time, and the second she appeared perfectly fine once we tracked her down.

I had no idea she experienced anything like this just to restrain her power.

How many times has she put herself through this agony since coming here, with all the threats and animosity she's faced? Not least of all from me.

Gods above, she could have run back to the streets of Slaughterwell any time.

But she stayed. She stayed to fight the scourge sorcerers with us and protect so many people who'd have sent her to the gallows—even though she knew how I felt about the riven, even though the constant danger of staying in this place might have been killing her from the inside out.

She's proven the truth again and again. Since the horrors of her childhood, she's never used her magic except when the consequences of not using it were worse.

Have I ever really wished she'd let Wendos tear apart the city instead of stopping him?

She'd allow the power to destroy *her* before she inflicted even a fraction of the damage she's capable of on this world, wouldn't she? Curse it all, seeing her like this, I can't imagine her doing anything other than falling on one of her own knives if she thought she'd truly lost control.

And I just egged on the magic I've hated so much. I made it bring her to her knees.

I've encouraged it to torment this woman who's shown more honor than I can imagine ever achieving myself, despite all my doubts.

In that moment, I want to stab myself, but that won't help either of us. Instead, I hug Ivy closer, swallowing the lump in my throat.

From what she's been saying to me, she probably doesn't find my embrace all that comforting, but I don't know how else to show how sorry I am.

I knew how resilient she is. I knew how far she's gone to help the people who needed it most.

I let the fact of her magic blind me to everything else she'd already shown me.

I'd tell me to fuck off too.

My voice comes out hoarse. "I'm sorry. I didn't realize it would do this to you. I shouldn't have been such an ass about it anyway. Is there anything I can do to help you through the pain?"

Ivy expels a rough breath. "It's starting to… ease up."

I rest my right hand against her cheek, resisting the urge to bury my face in her hair. To soak up everything I've found wondrous about this woman that I buried under anger and fear.

"I can get by in my afternoon classes on my own. I'll help you to the infirmary, and then you should go back to my quarters. You might need all the rest you can get before tonight."

Ivy peers at me. "You're not going to order me to stay out of the woods? Claim I'm too much of a liability?"

My shamed laugh sears up my throat. "Ivy, if it's possible to stop those fiends, I wouldn't put my money on anyone but you."

# Twenty-Two

*Ivy*

When Stavros returns to his quarters just after the tenth bell, it's with a plate holding three of the flaky, custard-filled pastries the nobles call "moon rolls." I glance up from the sofa and have to pretend my mouth doesn't water at the sight of them.

As he stops across from the sofa, looking at me, my silence starts to feel awkward. "Needed a late-night snack?" I ask.

His gaze drops to the plate. I'm not sure I've ever seen the former general act hesitant before.

It's a little unnerving.

"They're meant to be for you," he says, in the careful, faintly beseeching tone he's taken with me ever since he sicced one of his students on me this afternoon.

Oh. I stare at him. "I was just in the dining hall a couple of hours ago. I ate plenty of food."

"I'm sure. But you like these, don't you? I saw there were a few left and thought you might want to fortify yourself for whatever's coming tonight."

Julita shifts within my skull. *Did you* break *Stavros? This morning he couldn't glower at you enough, now he's tripping over his feet to cater to you. I've never seen him so rattled.*

So it's not just me unnerved by the change.

Of course, if Stavros is broken, I don't know what she'd call what's happened to me. He rushed me to the infirmary as soon as my magic had finished lashing out at me and claimed the red mark around my neck was the result of a training mishap, but my throat still stings faintly when I swallow.

The medic repaired the encroaching bruise, but the damage went deeper than that. Possibly not just in my neck but various internal organs as well, thanks to my magic's frustration.

I take the plate and simply hold it, not sure what to do with it. My taste buds might be eager, but my stomach is clenched tight both in anticipation of yet another trial with the scourge sorcerers tonight… and however the former general might react to me next.

Will he take a rejection of his generosity as a sign of malicious intent? Should I choke down one of the rolls to prove I appreciate the gesture?

His mood has shifted so much in the course of the day that I have no idea what to expect.

"I'm quite full," I say tentatively. "But it might be nice to have them to come back to, after everything."

I set the plate on the small table by the arm of the sofa. Stavros's gaze follows its descent with an odd air of sadness.

Well, he's not shouting accusations at me, so I guess I'll call that a win.

*It was horrible, what he did today,* Julita says. *He shouldn't have gone that far—he shouldn't have felt he needed to. I wouldn't forgive him just yet, but I don't think he really wanted to hurt you, Ivy.*

Does it matter what he wanted? He was willing to hurt me anyway to get whatever proof he needed, since apparently he judged that I wasn't offering enough evidence of my loyalties on my own.

Who knows what else he might feel he needs to do?

Stavros's head ticks as he studies my face. "Is there anything else that might help you prepare for your meeting with the scourge sorcerers tonight?"

I splay my hands. "Hard to say when I don't know what that meeting will entail."

His presence in the room and the weight of what he put me through this afternoon is becoming increasingly suffocating. I turn away and reach for my cloak. "I was thinking I'd stop by the temple and see if Kosmel has anything else to say for himself."

"Ah. That seems worth trying." Stavros pauses. "Will you come back here before you're expected in the woods?"

I shrug as I fasten the cloak around my neck. Stavros tracks the movement of my hands, maybe thinking as I am of the rope that wrapped across the same spot just hours ago.

"I suppose that depends on how talkative the godlen is and whether I can find anything else to pass the time," I say. "But you shouldn't be waiting up anyway."

"Of course."

There's another pause, the silence so awkward I practically flee for the door.

Once I'm walking down the hall, the pressure lightens, if only a tad. I still have my impending foray into the woods to worry about, and that's no small thing.

I really don't have any idea what to expect from the scourge sorcerers either.

One of the guards by the college gate stops me briefly to check where I'm headed at this late hour, but when I tell him, he waves me on. I hurry along the cobblestone road and slip through the temple's grand doorway.

In the thick of the night, the only illumination in the massive worship room flickers from sconces set above each of the godlen statues. The glow catches on swaths of red silk that've been fixed to several of the columns and two immense gold swords now crossing each other over the entrance to the central tower.

I've been so distracted it takes me a moment to remember the reason for the adjusted décor. Sabrellia, the festival for the warrior godlen, is coming in a couple of days.

Each of the godlen get one day a year when everyone celebrates their contributions to our world. I can't say I'm looking forward to honoring the violent divinity Stavros dedicated himself to, though.

I doubt I'll be in a festive mood.

A couple of devouts pass through the worship room with subtle dips of their head toward me. The temple is open at all hours—they must be used to worshippers arriving at random.

I approach Kosmel's alcove with a sense of trepidation. The godlen of luck and trickery insisted I stay alive. He must have some purpose for me.

It'd be nice to get a clearer idea of what that is.

But the thought of hearing his divinely overwhelming voice in my head again makes every part of my body tense up.

The one thing both of the clerics whose journals I read agreed on is that you can't dictate when or how you'll receive messages from the gods. You have to extend your question into the universe and watch for some indication it's been heard.

Kosmel probably loves keeping us mortals on our toes.

I kneel before his statue, ignoring the dice this time. A simple *yes* or *no* doesn't feel like enough to satisfy all the uncertainty inside me.

*I'm doing the best I can*, I think at him. *Is there anything I'm missing? Do you have any advice at all? I want to take down the scourge sorcerers soon—I don't know what else they're going to ask of me.*

I close my eyes, thinking maybe images will float up from my mind the way the cleric of the Temple of Fruitful Abundance sometimes described. When all I get is an ache forming in my knees from the hard floor, I glance upward at the statue.

At the same moment, the sconce above Kosmel flares. The shadows on his marble form shift—and I swear I catch a shape like a gowned figure leaping headfirst into a thicker clump of darkness.

A chill settles over me. Maybe I only imagined that.

But even Casimir said that's how he feels Ardone guides him sometimes—drawing his attention to meaningful details in the world around him.

I raise my eyebrows at the smirking godlen. "Just dive farther in?" I murmur.

He doesn't say anything, naturally. In frustration, I pick up a die and toss it by his feet.

It lands five up. The most emphatic yes.

Swallowing thickly, I pull myself to my feet. My innards feel all jumbled up.

Until the last few weeks, I've avoided the notice of the gods. I don't really like the sensation of one of them dabbling in my life.

Is that really *better* than being left to my own devices?

My skin creeping, I stride out of the temple. There's nothing more for me in there at the moment.

The apparent message nags at me all the way back to the college. I pause in the outer courtyard, marking the eleven peals of the bell, and veer around the Quadring to make for the woods.

*Isn't it awfully early?* Julita asks.

I let out my voice in the barest mutter. "He wants me to dive in; I'm diving in. They can ignore me until one o'clock if they want."

Or maybe we can get the next trial over with, and I can take a break from the precarious balancing act I've been performing for a day or two.

I count out my fifty paces into the woods and sit down on the forest path, settling in for what might be a long wait. The warble of the breeze through the leaves and the periodic buzz and chirp of forest life are becoming familiar.

There's nothing in this darkness I really need to fear except the human beings venturing into it alongside me.

I breathe in and out at a regular pace, absorbing the sounds around me, the shifts in the cooling air. I might even drift into the sort of meditative state the clerics sometimes talk about, though I can't say any great insight comes with it.

Apparently Julita can't do the same. She stirs restlessly within my head. *Of course they'd have to pick the creepiest time and place to conduct their initiation tests. I'm sure they simply want you to be as off-balance as possible.*

As if to prove her point, a voice abruptly breaks through the quiet. It's distorted by the same magical effect as usual, but this once I have a definite impression of it coming from somewhere ahead of me and a bit to the right.

"Why are you here already, Ivy of Nikodi?"

Interesting. So there are probably at least two conspirators who've been conducting these trials, only one of whom is able to project their voice widely.

Determining that fact doesn't get me any closer to knowing who those people are, though.

I consider what sort of answer the scourge sorcerers would most want to hear from a potential recruit. "What's been happening out here feels much more important than anything I could be doing in the college. I thought I'd see if I can get more in tune with the All-Giver."

Julita gives a chuckle of approval. *Buttering them up. Very nice.*

I can't hear any hint of movement in the forest. Either the speaker has been standing wherever they are for a long time without moving, they're propelling their voice from quite far away, or they're incredibly stealthy.

They don't bother to answer, maybe waiting for companions to join them. I go back to my sort-of meditation, but I keep my ears even more pricked than before.

Sometime after the midnight hour has been rung in, a voice breaks the quiet again, surrounding me in the more usual fashion. "The All-Giver would appreciate your commitment, Ivy. We'd like to know what else you can do for the Great God."

I ease myself carefully to my feet. "Did you have anything in particular in mind?"

"You made a small sacrifice of your finger, it appears. What godlen are you dedicated to, and what is your gift?"

My heart stutters for an instant before I remember Casimir's gentle touch as he re-imprinted my false dedication brand yesterday night. When I looked at it this evening, the pink-toned mark between my breasts still looked completely believable.

How much can the conspirators even see in this darkness if they demand a peek?

"I'm dedicated to Kosmel," I say, bringing out the answer I prepared. "I asked for a talent for forgery. There've always been things I wanted to do that my parents wouldn't approve of. It's helped… clear the way."

I do have a talent for forgery, but it's one I developed entirely without divine intervention. And the scourge sorcerers might see some use for it, sooner rather than later.

If I can get them to hand over any physical evidence of their plans—documents related to their schemes that they need false signatures on or adjusted duplicates of—that might be enough to bring the whole conspiracy down.

There's a brief silence that makes me think the sorcerers are consulting with each other. Then one speaks up again. "Have you ever tried to create a forgery on a larger scale? An illusionary copy of a real object, for example?"

A shiver runs down my spine. Are they thinking I might be able to help with their clay creatures?

That wasn't the kind of job I had in mind.

Well, I can answer honestly. "No. I'll admit it's a fairly small gift since it was a fairly small sacrifice. I was more cautious at twelve than I've become since."

"Then if you could increase your power with a new sacrifice now, you would do it?"

My uneasiness grows, but there's only one way I can answer that question that keeps me in the game. "Of course, if it's for a good purpose."

"This time, it'll be for the purpose of showing us how committed you are to challenging what's wrong in this world."

I dip my head. "I can understand why you'd want to confirm that. But how would a new sacrifice work?"

"We wouldn't ask it of you often," the voice says. "Much can be gained by combining the gifts we already have. But what you can do on your own matters too. Come to the edge of the woods, and we'll see what fits the moment."

*I don't like the sound of this,* Julita mutters as I tramp back the way I came.

Neither do I, but I don't see how there's anything she or I can do about it. At least I'm not having to kill living creatures with my bare hands tonight.

I stop in the shadows of the trees at the edge of the patch of forest. Moonlight streams down over the field between me and the back of the Quadring.

"We have decided," the voice says as if from right behind me.

I suppress a flinch and glance backward, but no one's in view. I will my muscles to relax. "What did you decide?"

"The Crown's Watch carries out orders without concern for their legitimacy. They only care about their own power, not what pleases the gods. You've seen that, haven't you?"

I let out a light guffaw. "Oh, yes."

At least, I've seen them abuse their authority. I can't say I'm sure of what pleases any of the gods.

"You could put a couple of them in their places. Remind them that there are greater powers at work in the universe."

My gaze darts across the campus. The first figure it catches on has a pale face topped by glossy brown curls—the gifted guard who hassled me when I was stargazing. He's walking next to the Quadring's back wall.

Can I use any magic on *him* without his gift reacting? Do the scourge sorcerers even realize he's got magic he uses regularly?

How deep a pile of shit are they going to throw me into?

"How should I do that?" I ask tentatively.

"On the eastern wall," the voice says. "Do you see the two soldiers stationed there who are speaking to each other?"

My attention jerks to the outer wall with a jolt of relief. Not that I know for sure the two figures I spot atop the stone barrier *don't* have gifts of their own.

I nod. At least one of the conspirators must be close enough to see me, because the gesture seems to be answer enough.

"You will ask Kosmel to expand your power so that you can 'forge' an object of your choice out of the air. You will use it to startle the guards. If you can start a fight between them, we'll be even more impressed."

I wet my lips. "I don't think Kosmel will grant my request just because I ask nicely."

"That's why you'll do more than ask. You'll show how committed you are to the task with an offering."

A figure shrouded completely in black steps out of the trees to approach me. I can't tell whether they're male or female, young or old. Even their face has been covered by a swath of black fabric that hangs from the edge of their hood, though it must be thin enough to allow them to see through.

The scourge sorcerer lifts their hand, and a knife glints in the filtered moonlight. My magic wakes up at the sight, squirming in my chest.

Julita shivers. *I don't know... I think this might be deep enough right here, Ivy. You could make a run for the college buildings—you're fast.*

And then what? The scourge sorcerers will want me dead for what I already know.

"What would you have me give?" I ask, managing to keep my voice steady.

The figure in black motions with the knife, but the voice that speaks comes from elsewhere, farther off in the forest. "You will give up your full forefinger from your left hand, with a plea to bolster your gift for tonight. We will not numb it and seal it immediately as the shirking clerics do. The blood and the pain show the depth of your sacrifice. The All-Giver wants us to *feel*."

My breath catches in my throat. Not at the thought of the pain—I've experienced worse just this afternoon.

But if I give up my entire forefinger on my dominant hand... I'm not sure how long it'll take me to learn how to handle a knife without it. Whether I'll ever be able to effectively fight or steal again.

So many of the skills I counted on for survival in my old life—so many that have helped me survive even at the college—

Do they even realize how much they're truly asking from me?

*Ivy, no, you shouldn't have to go this far,* Julita is saying, at the same time as the voice from the woods demands, "Are you willing?"

I swallow a broken laugh. My power twitches in my chest, begging to thrash the sorcerers for even asking to harm me, but I clamp down on it tight.

Kosmel indicated I should go deeper—I should throw myself straight in. I did commit to this course, even if not for the reasons the scourge sorcerers think.

How much of a life will I have left if I refuse?

I extend my hand. "Absolutely. Thank you for the opportunity."

Every word scrapes up my throat like a jagged stone, but I must have answered quickly and convincingly enough. I can almost hear the speaker's smile. "You're most welcome."

It all happens so quickly I barely have time to second-guess my decision. The figure with the knife grasps my wrist, presses my other fingers and thumb close to my palm, and jams my hand against the nearest tree trunk.

Before I've so much as sucked in a breath, they swing the knife.

Gods help me, the blade is sharp. It chops straight through flesh and bone with a burst of pain.

As I clench my jaw against a whimper, blood streaks down the bark and across my hand. I keep just enough wherewithal to remember the plea I'm supposed to make.

My voice tumbles ragged over my lips. "Kosmel, All-Giver, whoever hears me: Give me the power tonight to forge so much more than I could before."

I swing toward the guards on the wall, stretching out my bleeding hand.

I just want to get the trial over with. My head is whirling with pain and horror and a twinge of regret; I want to scream at someone for dragging me into this place.

I don't have a normal gift anyway. I'll try, and it won't work, and the scourge sorcerers will make of it what they will. Or maybe Kosmel will step in and conjure up an illusion on my behalf.

But that's not what happens at all.

My riven power surges inside me alongside the stream of blood pattering onto the forest floor. My head spins—and all at once I can't contain the churning energy inside me.

I can't plug all the holes. I can't smother every shred of the magic jangling through my nerves.

A punch of the errant magic slips my hold. It flings through the air toward the guards, latching on to the intention I claimed to have, the image the conspirators put in my head.

I don't know what illusion it forms. All I see is one guard lurching toward the other.

No, no, not like this. I hug my other arm around my gut, desperately scrambling to rein my magic in without giving away what I'm grappling with.

The ground bucks under me. I can't tell if that's scourge sorcery or the backlash of my own power, but it knocks me to my knees.

My magic flails out of me in one last attempt to carry out my will, whether I like it or not.

The guards stumble again—and one of them smacks into the low crenelation along the top of the wall with so much force she flips right over it.

The thud of her body hitting the ground carries through the night straight to my ears.

I gulp for air and shove my power down as far as I can go, fighting to keep my horror off my face so the conspirators won't see my distress. My unwounded hand braces against the damp earth to steady me.

My magic tries to lash out again, but I clamp it tight. Its frustration reverberates through my bones.

I grit my teeth against it. No more.

Gods above, what did I do to her? Has she even survived the fall?

I never meant to—

The black-robed figure crouches in front of me. A voice rings out with obvious satisfaction from the woods beyond us. "An impressive performance. The gods look kindly on you. You don't have to worry. For your service, we'll see you made whole again."

I don't understand. I'm too scattered to even realize what's happening until the figure who wielded the knife presses the finger they chopped off against the bleeding stump, and a hot tingling spreads through my flesh.

She has a healing gift. She's melding my hand back together.

It shouldn't surprise me. How would the conspirators expect me to explain away the sudden loss of my finger once I returned to school?

Healing me is for their benefit at least as much as my own.

But as the sinews and bones bind back together, my gaze returns to the wall. To the guard shouting for help from where he's still poised at the top, peering down at his fallen companion.

The scourge sorcerers didn't realize the true source of my magic or how little I wanted to let it loose. But I know.

I lost control, just for a matter of seconds, and this is what I've done.

Maybe Stavros has been right all along. Maybe I can't be anything other than a monster.

# TWENTY-THREE

*Ivy*

The whole city is draped in red.

Scarlet banners hang above storefronts and stretch high across the streets. Crimson streamers dangle from windows. Ruby ribbons festoon every cart and carriage.

And the people only add to the cacophony of red. Every noble and inner-warder milling around the courtyard outside the Temple of the Crown wears silk, satin, or finely woven wool dyed in some shade of that hue.

Even in the outer wards, where few can afford full outfits in every divine color, people will be tying red sashes and scarves around their bodies to join in the celebration.

Casimir didn't fail me in his self-assigned role as my official costumer. Airy silk wraps across my chest and tumbles over my legs in a deep wine-red that somehow makes my sallow complexion look creamy rather than sickly.

The assault of color that meets my eyes everywhere I look makes me *feel* a little sick, though. At the edge of the square where Stavros and I have halted to survey the festivities, I shift my weight and reach to adjust the lace that shades my eyes.

Along with Sabrelle's color, everyone in the inner ward has donned helmet-inspired headdresses to honor the godlen of war. For women, that means a light metal cap with silver-toned filigree meant to mimic chainmail, which flows over my hair and down my face to the tip of my nose.

Nobles do love an excuse to be semi-anonymous while they revel.

Thankfully the face covering includes eye holes, so my vision isn't too obscured. I'm not here to revel myself, but to keep watch.

Beside me, Stavros frowns at the crowd from beneath his own helm. The men wear a less dainty version, with silver plates over the nose and cheeks.

"Our performance for the military division isn't until the seventh bell," he says. "You'll have lots of time to circulate. From what I saw of the planned layout, the entomology club has their demonstration of sorts set up in the northeast corner of the square. You should be able to get a look at most of the members there so you can keep track of them."

I nod. "I already spotted Ster. Torstem. He's got golden stags embroidered on his jacket."

"I doubt *he'll* make any concerning moves." Stavros sighs. "I'm not sure any of them would risk revealing their intentions with so many witnesses around. But they did strike at Prince Jacos in the middle of the college. With the royal family making an appearance, we can't be too careful."

A blare of a trumpet brings my head around. "And here they come now."

The crowd parts around the front of the temple to make way for the royal procession. No doubt as aware of the threat as we are, the king has brought a dozen members of his personal guard, their usual uniforms swapped for a striking garnet-red.

King Konram and several other figures walk in their midst. He, Queen Ishild, and their two living children—Princess Klaudia and Prince Jacos—wave to the revelers, who raise their voices in eager cheers.

They only just returned from their tour of the provinces last night. Not a bad welcome, coming home to a massive party.

I'm not familiar with their companions. A stately woman in a belted dress that looks more like a cleric's robes than a noble gown strides along behind them, one of her eyes covered by a patch that reminds me of Esmae's. At her left trots a spindly, ivory-haired man whose uneven gait could indicate the stiffness of old age or a leg-related sacrifice.

And behind them—

My breath hitches at the sight of the third man's misshapen form. He holds his substantial frame tall and haughty, but neither his posture nor his thick cloak can disguise how lopsided his body is.

He's missing one arm, all the way to the shoulder.

Gods above, what kind of gift will he have gotten for *that* sacrifice?

"Who are those three with the royal family?" I murmur.

Stavros dips his head lower so he can match my quiet tone. "I suggested to the king that he might have his magic advisors join him for this excursion. I don't think he's mentioned specific concerns to any of them except his chief sorcerer, Hessild Korinya there, but any of them are likely to pick up on unusual magical activity around them. The two men are Tinom Akorek, the smaller one, who specializes in illusions and ephemeral blessings, and Lothar Riosemek, who's a master of herbal and chemical concoctions."

I can't help raising an eyebrow. "He gave up an entire arm just to mix potions?"

One corner of Stavros's mouth crooks upward. "I'm not sure exactly what his gift is, only that he dedicated himself to Creaden. I'd imagine it allows for more than just smooth mixing."

"But not impressive enough for the king to make *him* chief sorcerer."

The former general shrugs. "I believe Hessild has a powerful gift in her own right. An eye isn't a minor thing. And there's a family history. Her mother and grandfather both served as chief sorcerer before her."

Julita lets out a huff in my head. *You'd think between three royal sorcerers, they could keep this scourge menace in check themselves.*

Stavros pauses, and his hand slips around mine as if to emphasize his next words. "Be particularly careful if you cross paths with Lothar. He's been more vocal than the king himself in encouraging the hunts for the riven and the public executions. I get the impression he has a personal vendetta."

A lump fills my throat. "I wasn't planning on—"

"I know." Stavros runs his thumb over the base of my forefinger—over the tiny scar that's the only evidence of my temporary sacrifice two days ago. "Just… be careful."

He lets go of me, but the ghost of his touch lingers on my skin with an unwelcome warmth. My gut knots with the memory of my confession yesterday morning.

I knew he'd find out about the fallen guard. He'd be suspicious about when and where it happened. If I'd tried to lie, I'm not sure he'd have believed me.

And maybe a part of me thought I'd get some kind of confirmation out of it. That if I told him, the man who's reviled my magic from the moment he discovered it, his reaction would give me whatever punishment I truly deserved.

Somehow, he didn't run me through or drag me to the gallows. When he growled a few curses, they were directed at the scourge sorcerers rather than me. Then he stormed off and returned simply to inform me that the guard had lived.

She's still in the infirmary, undergoing additional care from the medics. Her skull cracked with the fall. But apparently they expect her to fully recover, given enough time.

Neither of those facts has loosened the guilt still tangled up inside me. I think I might actually feel more reassured if Stavros *had* dragged me off to be executed.

I lost my grip on my riven power. Only for a few seconds, and with consequences that weren't absolutely dire—but we don't know what the scourge sorcerers will demand of me next.

How can I promise it'll never be worse?

A couple of days ago, I was angry with him for not trusting me. Now I'm not sure I deserve the trust he's decided to offer.

Stavros shifts forward. "I'm going to stay close to the king until it's time for the performance. But it looks as though you'll have some company while you keep an eye on the rest of the festivities."

I glance around to see two men weaving through the crowd toward us.

I'd recognize Casimir's graceful stride anywhere, regardless of the helmet covering most of his face. His soft smile brings an answering one to my lips despite the tangle inside me.

I can't say military gear suits him, but he manages to look stunning in his crimson-and-gold tunic even with the lump of metal on his head.

Alek's lean form follows right behind the courtesan. He's wearing a festival helm that extends all the way to his jaw, hiding his mask completely. His red tunic is edged with embroidery in a bronze tone, and his breaches are more fitted than Casimir's fashionable billowy ones, but he cuts just as striking a figure.

We can explore the celebration together at least for a little while, with our identities concealed to anyone who doesn't know us quite so well.

Stavros nods to them discreetly and heads off toward the royal procession.

Casimir slips his hand around my elbow. "How are you doing, Kindness?"

The tenderness of his tone tells me he's not just asking if I'm enjoying the festival. Stavros was able to alert him and Alek to meet us early yesterday so I could tell them everything that happened without worrying about revealing my secret to Benedikt. The courtesan stuck close to me for the whole rest of the meeting, as if he could tell how unsteady I'm feeling.

"Wishing I was back in my room with a book," I say with a light laugh. "But I suppose we'd better celebrate Sabrelle properly."

Alek comes to a stop in front of me, his expression solemn. He spent several minutes yesterday arguing with both Stavros and me about whether we should call off my plan to infiltrate the conspiracy.

Not because he's worried about what I might do. Because he's worried about how it's affecting me.

"Sounds like a better way to spend an evening than this," he says. "We could go do that right now."

I wag a finger at him to try to show I'm all right. "We've got work to do here. I should probably see if I can enjoy myself too. I've never spent very long at any festival but Signy's."

It never seemed like a good idea to strut around when everyone's trying to draw one or another godlen's attention in every way possible—not when I was trying to *avoid* the gods' notice. Unless there was an item it was an ideal time to steal or a con I needed to pull, I stayed off the streets during festivals.

Casimir's thumb strokes my arm through the sleeve of my gown. He can probably guess at my reasons. "Does that mean you've never tried bloodfruit pudding?"

I give him a skeptical look. "It does. I wouldn't have thought that was a great loss." How good can any dessert made from a favorite field snack of soldiers be?

The courtesan chuckles and tugs me with him into the throng. "You'll be surprised then. I don't care for the stuff dried as army rations, but it's got a lot to recommend about it when cooked fresh."

We squeeze through the crowded square to a stall selling small paper cones filled with the jelly-like pudding, designed to be eaten straight out of the disposable dish. I lap up a little with my tongue, and my eyes widen at the tartly sweet flavor with a tang that's almost spicy.

"Okay, you've proven me wrong. What other delights have I been missing out on?"

Alek's smile turns a bit sly in that way that makes my chest flutter. "All the best weapons-smiths have their goods on display. I saw some skillfully crafted throwing knives for sale."

Casimir guides me onward. "And you won't want to miss the cavalry show."

I release my first real laugh in days. "All right, all right. Apparently you know me better than I know myself."

*They've gone all sappy*, Julita remarks, in a tone almost as tart as the bloodfruit. *We do have a job to do here too. I hope they won't forget.*

She doesn't say anything about *me* forgetting it, but I immediately feel a pang of guilt. As we continue on through the courtyard, I keep my eyes peeled for any other familiar forms.

I don't know the members of the bug club all that well. It's hard to recognize much of anyone beneath the helms.

Over by the smiths' stalls, a group of duelists and soldiers are putting on a series of sparring matches—some with each other with flashy moves, and others open to challengers from the crowd. While I allow myself to buy a particularly appealing little dagger that might give my current favorite a run for its money, one of the fighters plants his fists in another's face, making blood spurt from his opponent's nose to match his scarlet jacket.

Farther along, the hunter's guild shows off a rack of skins from various slain animals. Illusionary images of deer and hare romp in the air above their stall, periodically crumpling with the strike of a conjured spear.

They've set up a compact archery range for revelers to try their luck at shooting one of the very real pigeons whose wings they've clipped. A little girl squeals in victory when her arrow hits its mark with a thud of the feathered body.

This is a celebration dedicated to the godlen who presides over sports and hunting as well as warfare. But taking it all in, my stomach sinks.

Are the scourge sorcerers totally wrong? The ones who've spoken to me have claimed that the gods want us animalistic and wild, not bound by strict standards of behavior.

It certainly appears that at least one of the godlen would rather see us bloody and squabbling than maintaining lawful peace.

Why would the All-Giver have created a godlen like Sabrelle at all if he didn't approve?

Why haven't the lesser gods intervened more forcefully if they're unhappy about what the scourge sorcerers are doing? If Kosmel knows, surely others have noticed the conspiracy too.

The trickster godlen seems to want me to interfere, but I don't really know why. Or what ultimate outcome he's looking for.

I'm drawn out of those uneasy thoughts at the sight of the bug club's demonstration up ahead. Alek lets out a disgusted sound, but we all go over together.

The scholar hasn't forgotten our purpose, no matter what snarky remarks Julita makes.

Several bug club members stand around a semi-circle of small terrariums, with a large glass tank in the middle of their assigned area. As we approach, two of the students are just dropping a couple of beetles nearly as large as their palms into the central tank.

The hulking insects lumber toward each other, and Julita's presence cringes in my head. Then I'm suppressing a cringe of my own as one of the beetles hurls itself at the other and wrenches off a jointed leg.

Ah. So this is how the entomology club celebrates Sabrelle—by staging bug fighting matches. Lovely.

It does fit the general theme of the celebration.

I jerk my gaze away from the battle of bugs and scan the figures staging the fight.

One of them grins, and I identify him as Olari from the gleam of steel teeth between his lips. His decorative helm has a little red tassel, and he's wearing a dark gray belt with red stitching over his tunic. That should help me recognize him if he roams into the crowd later.

With a couple of the others, I catch enough of a glimpse of their features to connect them to students I've observed on campus. The rest I'm not sure of—they could be from the second group that Alek suspects isn't involved in the illicit magic part of the club's practices.

I commit the most distinctive details of their clothing to memory and then turn away. "I think I've had enough of that."

Casimir tucks his arm around my waist. "Let's find those horses. It's amazing what the top trainers can coax them to do."

It's obvious that he and Alek are committed to making the event as enjoyable as possible for me, no matter what else I have on my mind. We watch a parade of horses prance by and perform several feats of agility and strength with their riders. Then Alek pulls me over to a stall serving freshly steamed dumplings that I happily devour a handful of.

The scholar points out the scrolls unfurled by a bookshop's storefront, missives from old historical battles that I can tell he's itching to carry back to the library.

I give him a teasing nudge with my elbow. "I could probably arrange for a few of those to end up in your possession."

Alek looks vaguely horrified, but on my behalf rather than at the suggestion. "I wouldn't ask you to take that risk—"

"Oh, it'd barely be any." I pause. "But I suppose I should stay on my best behavior in all things not strictly necessary, given everything else I've been getting up to."

Before my uneasy melancholy can settle over me again, Casimir waves us on toward a dog breeder's tent. "It looks like the royal houndsman has a new litter on offer. Who doesn't like puppies?"

I have to admit that the sight of the furballs tussling and tumbling does lift my spirits a little.

I want to sink into the strange sense of normalcy I'm tasting traces of, wandering around the festivities with two men who somehow want to be here with me. But every time I glance up, I need to be watching for the bug club members on the move. I'm always at least a little aware of the cluster of guards around the royal procession.

Finally, the peal of the bell tells me it's time to help out with the college's military performance. I hustle over to the space set aside for Stavros and the three other professors who organized the display and hand out the assigned weaponry to the participating students like a good little assistant.

As the professors and students launch into a re-enactment of one of the most famous historical battles, I take a step back from the ring.

A jaunty voice speaks softly by my shoulder. "You should be over there putting them all to shame with your skills, Knives."

I chuckle and glance over at Benedikt, who's come up behind me. Always a fan of luxury, he's gone with a gold-plated helm that I can't imagine any actual warrior wearing into battle, and his striped jacket is as much gold as red as well.

I can't say the look doesn't suit him.

"I don't think they'd appreciate me changing the course of history," I retort.

"Oh, I don't think anyone could fail to appreciate you once they witnessed those impressive skills." He pauses. "I saw you surveying the crowd earlier. You've been making the rounds with Casimir and Alek?"

There's a hint of tension in his voice that I know I'm not imagining, because Julita picks up on it too. *Why is he asking? Who else would he expect you to spend your time with?*

"We bumped into each other early on," I say. "You could have joined us."

"Oh, I was having plenty of fun with my dormmates. It was just a little odd—when I showed up for the meeting yesterday, it almost felt as if you all had been discussing things for quite a while already."

A prickle of apprehension runs down my back. "Just a little small talk while we waited for you to show up."

Benedikt's hum sounds skeptical. "You were awfully vague about that last trial our 'friends' put you through."

I didn't mention my actual last trial in front of him at all, only the one from the night before. But he doesn't know that.

I force my tone to stay dry. "They aren't exactly pleasant memories. I don't see how they're all that useful beyond the little bits of information I've been able to pick up."

"True, true. Our conspirators do have an interesting way of seeing the world, don't they?"

Again, his tone niggles at me—and not just me.

*What's he getting at?* Julita murmurs.

I shake my head ruefully. "If by 'interesting' you mean absolutely horrifying, then yes. Oh!"

I've just caught sight of Ster. Torstem, his embroidered stags glinting in the lantern-light that's glowing through the falling dusk. The stout man is shouldering through the crowd... directly toward the procession that includes the royal family.

Julita's voice sharpens. *And what is he aiming for?*

I'd better find out. Of course the law professor would approach the king while Stavros is occupied.

Benedikt follows my gaze. His tone turns bitter as it drops even lower. "Yes, let us all fawn before the great King Konram."

He's obviously in a sour mood in general.

"Maybe I'll cross paths with you later," I tell him hurriedly, and set off after Torstem.

The royal procession has come to a stop by a booth offering mulled wine, just beyond the houndsman's tent. Ster. Torstem sidles closer to them and dips his hand into his pocket.

What *is* he up to? He definitely doesn't look as if he has any legitimate reason to catch the king's attention.

And who knows if his illicit sorcery will allow him to launch some kind of surreptitious attack right through the host of guards around the royals?

*We have to stop him,* Julita frets. *But if he realizes you interfered, it'll ruin all the progress you've made with his sycophants.*

I grit my teeth, my gaze searching the crowd. How can I alert the guards to a potential threat when he doesn't look threatening at all—and without Torstem realizing I'm doing the alerting?

My magic lurches to the ready with a smack against my ribs, but I shove it right back down with a clench of my jaw. It's hurt enough people in the past few days.

My attention settles on the nearby tent. Maybe I simply need to provide a different "threat" to disrupt the guards' current complacency.

I slip around the back of the tent, drawing my new knife. No time like the present to break it in.

Listening carefully to make sure there's no one near that corner of the structure, I slit the ties holding two folds of fabric in place. Then I duck down and lean inside just long enough to sever the ropes securing a few of the larger hounds to their post.

With a silent apology to the animals, I pick up a sharp stone from the ground and flick it into one of the dog's haunches, right by his fellow beast's muzzle.

The first hound lunges around, sure he's been nipped. The second barks at the sudden hostility. In a matter of seconds, they're chasing each other and the third hound in their midst out of the tent, snapping and baying at each other.

The nearby crowd scatters. Torstem himself has to stumble to the side to avoid being bowled over.

The royal guards draw even closer around their charges. I catch one's comment to the king: "I believe we should move on from this commotion, Your Highness."

King Konram must decide he's had enough commotion in general, because the procession weaves its way back toward the palace, only stopping for a moment here and there for the royal family to give their greetings.

I lean back against the nearest building with a sigh of relief. Ster. Torstem can't follow them right into the palace.

But I don't even know what disaster I might have averted.

# TWENTY-FOUR

*Ivy*

My head spins in the darkness. Then hands grip the edges of the sack by my shoulders. I already know what's coming, with a lurch of dread in my gut. I've been here too many times before.

The sack wrenches away from my head. I find myself staring into Stavros's searing gaze, his mouth curved into a vicious sneer.

He reaches for the hangman's noose—

And I manage to jerk myself out of the dream before I have to face the horror of the rope tightening around my neck.

I exhale raggedly into the dimness of the room I've woken up to. A faint stinging lingers at my throat—how much from the nightmare and how much from the memory of a very real rope that pressed against it a few days ago, I'm not sure.

Ever since Stavros's test in the equipment building, that unnerving dream has come for me every night. No matter what he says or how much he apologizes, my mind doesn't totally believe him.

As I sit up on the sofa, trying to shake off the awful images, a hazy but urgent muttering filters through the bedroom door. It's followed by a harsh rustle of sheets.

*It sounds like neither of you is sleeping well,* Julita remarks.

I let out a rough laugh under my breath. "We make quite a pair, don't we? Giving each other nightmares while we're sharing the same quarters."

I'll bet Stavros never bargained on this development when he insisted I stay in his rooms.

A grunt reaches my ears, muffled but clearly uneasy. My fingers curl around the edge of my blanket.

My ghostly companion must be able to tell what I'm considering from the tensing of my body. *I wouldn't disturb him. He's survived worse than a bad dream or two. After the way he reacted last time... But I suppose I don't really know what to make of his behavior anymore.*

I grimace. "He obviously doesn't know what to make of me. I never meant for anyone to find out."

*Of course you didn't. But better you did than let Wendos finish his wretched plans. If Alek and Cas can accept you, he should be able to too.*

"I'm guessing they didn't lose anyone they cared about to someone like me."

Julita lets out a huff. *Whatever murderous villain killed Stavros's friend, they weren't like you at all. I've had to live with someone who was merely* trying *to become an evil sorcerer, and I can assure you, you're leagues better than even that.*

My mouth slants into a crooked smile. I wish I could appreciate Julita's reassurances more.

There's a soft thump, as if Stavros has struck the mattress. I wince.

*It might not even be about you,* Julita adds. *I can't begin to imagine how many horrifying things he must have seen during his days on the battlefield.*

That's true, but the next sound that filters through the door comes in perfectly distinct words. "Ivy. No."

My stomach lurches. Before I can think better of it, I've sprung to my feet.

As I stride to the bedroom door, Julita lapses into silence. She must be able to tell there's no point in arguing with me now.

I can't bear to just sit there knowing he's trapped in a dream with me doing who knows what despicable things.

I push open the door and hesitate on the threshold. Stavros is sprawled on his side on the bed, the sheets tangled across his torso and thighs, his face half buried in his pillow. His brow is furrowed, his hand clenched tight.

I don't think I want to get within striking range.

"Stavros," I say, carefully quiet. When he only hisses through his teeth, his eyes still squeezed shut, I raise my voice. "Stavros! Wake up!"

With a flinch, he rolls onto his back. He swipes at his face and stares at me blearily through the faint moonlight.

I'm abruptly aware of the fact that I've got nothing on but the chemise and drawers I normally sleep in. Not that Stavros hasn't seen me in a similar state of undress before.

The sheet has fallen far enough on his chest to reveal some of the sculpted muscles that fill out his massive frame. The brand of Sabrelle's sigil marks his light brown skin with a darker, ruddy shade low on his sternum.

I have the sudden, ridiculous urge to find out what those muscular planes would feel like under my fingers.

Heat trickles through my veins, but I clench my hand against the thought, resting the other on the doorframe. At least the former general isn't yelling at me.

So far.

He pushes himself into a sitting position, his arms tucked in front of him—his hand of flesh cupping over the stump left by his sacrifice.

"Did I wake you up?" he asks with a hint of a rasp in his voice.

I shake my head. "Already had my own nighttime terrors taking care of that."

His mouth sets in a grim line. "I'd say 'good,' but that isn't really good at all."

"It meant I was awake to disturb your sleep in a less discomforting way," I say with forced brightness. "I'll let you get more rest that's hopefully better."

As I start to turn, Stavros leans forward. "Ivy—wait."

I glance back at him. "What?"

Now that he has my attention, he looks as if he's groping for something to talk about. "You haven't had any further contact from the scourge sorcerers?"

"I'd have mentioned it if I had. Nothing since the last trial four days ago. But I suppose making me stew might be a trial in itself. There were a few days between their first and second tests anyway."

I pause with an uncomfortable pang through my chest. "Or maybe they realized something was odd about my magic that night after all, and they're deciding what to do about it."

Stavros gives a guffaw derisive enough to be weirdly comforting. "Whatever they might speculate, it won't be the truth. There's no way at all they'd imagine *I* could tolerate hiring a riven sorcerer or that you could have been in my presence so long without my realizing it. The riven generally avoid notice by staying away from anyone who'd want to execute them, not prancing around in plain sight."

I smile tightly. "Yes, it is pretty bizarre that I'm still here. Although I suppose that might change, given that *you* do know what I did to that guard."

Stavros blinks at me. His next words come out careful but firm. "I don't think that had anything to do with you being riven."

It's my turn to stare. "What are you talking about? It was my blasted magic that knocked her off the wall."

"Yes. Your magic. Which probably would have done the exact same thing if it'd been the typical kind of magic that no one would think of hanging you for."

My arms come around to hug myself. "I'm not sure why you'd think that."

Stavros's tone turns a bit dry. "I'm not sure why you wouldn't. You told me yourself that they went as far as cutting off your finger to bolster your power. They've constantly talked about how people should give in to wildness and violence. Unless you've been misportraying the scourge sorcerers, it's sounded to me like what you did is exactly what they meant to happen if you'd had a regular gift."

I open my mouth and then close it again. I hadn't considered the situation that way.

*You know,* Julita murmurs, *he does have a point.*

Maybe so, but all the same— "It *was* riven magic, though, because that's the closest thing to a 'gift' I have."

Stavros lifts his shoulders in a subtle shrug. "Does the source of the magic matter if the end result was the same? If *any* person, including myself, would have trouble controlling our gift in the same situation, then I don't see how you can blame the riven part of you for it. Or really blame yourself at all. And even with all that going on, you mastered it the moment you realized someone had been hurt."

"Someone did get hurt all the same," I can't help saying.

"Ivy, I've seen trained soldiers with gifts stumble in the face of unexpected attacks more times than I can count. The fact that you regained control so quickly in a situation you'd never experienced is *impressive*, not anything I could call weakness."

I swallow thickly. I had no idea he was thinking about the situation this way.

I don't know if I can too.

My voice drops to a whisper. "I hate it. I hate that I did it. I hate that I lost control for even a few seconds."

A shadow crosses Stavros's face. "I know. I could see it when you told me. That's the other reason I didn't think I needed to be concerned. Unless *you're* concerned that it's gotten too much—if you want to put an end to this whole recruitment scheme—"

"No," I interrupt. "It's not as if I even could at this point."

He considers me with total seriousness—and a twitch of his head that tells me how intently he's studying my expression. "You could. As far as they know, you have no idea who any of them are, so they might leave you alone regardless. But even if we feared they wouldn't, we'd find a way to extricate you and keep you safe. If that's what you want."

He sounds so certain I believe him. But the idea of fleeing from this mess doesn't budge the resolve balled inside me.

"I want to know we don't have to worry about these psychopaths hurting anyone anymore. I'm getting closer—they're showing themselves to me more. I'm not abandoning ship now."

A small smile crosses Stavros's face. "That's exactly what I assumed you'd say, Lady Thief. I just wanted you to know you have the option. I mean it."

The emphatic words and the affectionate nickname he hasn't used since he found out what I am set me off-balance. I don't know what to say other than, "Thank you."

He snorts. "I should be the one thanking you. You're taking on the lion's share of the risk." He hesitates. "And I should *definitely* let you return to bed."

Something about the way he says it and the fact that he doesn't adjust his own position as if he's going to lie back down hold me in place. "Are you going to be able to get back to sleep all right?"

Stavros chuckles faintly and rubs his forehead. "Nights like this I'd normally read something light to settle my mind. But the reading is more of a stress than a comfort these days."

He glances toward the bookcase beyond his bed—the one I looked over when I found myself in this room a few weeks ago, after I was stabbed.

One corner of my mouth quirks upward. "Is that what your adventure stories are for? To put you to sleep? They mustn't be very thrilling ones."

The former general looks a bit sheepish. "There have been nights when the tactic backfired and instead I was up hours longer than I'd have preferred. But they're comforting in a way—all the action and excitement without the pain and the grit you'd have if it were real."

"And you hide those tales away in here because…"

He fixes me with a look that's only mock-stern. "Even a former general has certain appearances to keep up."

I can't restrain a laugh. And then, for reasons I couldn't totally explain if asked, I find myself saying, "I said before that I could read to you. If you won't take it as an insult, the offer still stands. It might help settle my thoughts too."

I tense automatically, half expecting him to snap at me like he did before. But Stavros simply goes still as if taking the suggestion in.

"All right," he says finally, his voice a bit stiff in a way I can't decipher. "Only for a chapter or two. Close the curtains so you can put on the light without being seen from the window. I'll pick out a decent story."

I keep behind the heavy folds of fabric as I drag the curtains across the high window. By the time I've lit the lantern by the chair in the corner, Stavros has set one of the slim leatherbound volumes on the corner of the bed.

I pick it up and settle into the chair, tucking my legs on the seat beside me. With the former general's gaze on me, I feel abruptly awkward.

Flipping the book open, I focus on the pages rather than the man across the room from me. "*Charlster's Journey: A heroic tale of the mountain kingdoms. Chapter One. It started with a fire in the stables.*"

I read on through a typically spirited beginning about an intrepid stablehand saving a countess's prized horses and being granted the responsibility of carrying an urgent message across the mountains to the realm's king. As my voice carries through the room, Stavros sinks down on the bed.

He doesn't interrupt. From the corner of my eye, I notice when his head starts to droop.

I pitch my voice gradually lower, not wanting to interrupt any impending slumber. Around the point when the stablehand encounters robbers on the mountain path, I glance up and see Stavros's eyes have closed. A slow breath rasps from his slightly parted lips.

An unexpected twinge of affection runs through me. I set down the book and douse the light.

The floor doesn't so much as creak beneath my stealthy feet as I creep back to my sofa. I've just bundled myself in my blanket when a prickling sensation digs into my palm, sharp enough that I think it'd have woken me if I *had* been sleeping.

I jerk my hand up. The words gleam briefly against my palm.

*50 paces into the woods. Alone. Now.*

# Twenty-Five

*Ivy*

I'm not sure what time it is until the bell rings three while I'm darting across the outer courtyard. The conspirators have never summoned me out to the woods this late before.

They've never summoned me with no advance notice before.

*Well, this is a rotten trial,* Julita grumbles, as if she's suffering from the lack of sleep too.

I give my tired eyes a brief swipe, allow myself a moment to long for the comfortable sofa I left behind, and then train all my attention on the task at hand.

Who knows what other tactics the scourge sorcerers might have up their sleeves tonight, designed to rattle me and betray any lack of commitment?

I have to stop by the far side of the equipment building when a patrolling guard swings into view around the corner of the Quadring. As soon as she's marched well past me, I sprint through the shadows with barely a rustle of the grass.

I take a little comfort in having exchanged my nightclothes for my linen combat shirt and breaches rather than a gown. Casimir chose my dresses well, but I can't move while smothered in layers of silk the same way I can when my limbs are unencumbered.

If the conspirators think there's anything odd about my choice in clothing, I'll simply tell them that I wanted to follow their instructions as swiftly as possible, and it takes much longer to lace up a gown than to pull on a shirt. I've worn these clothes around the school plenty of times, so the outfit shouldn't come as a total surprise.

My racing pulse only starts to slow once I'm swathed in the thicker darkness between the trees. I hurry along the path with my chin raised high, putting on my best noble airs alongside my haste.

Forty-eight, forty-nine, fifty.

I plant my feet on the path and peer into the blackness around me. You'd think after they dragged me out of bed, my evaluators would be prompt about greeting me.

There's a faint crinkle somewhere behind me to my right, like a foot stepping on a dried leaf. I can't tell whether it was a human foot or some animal passing by, though.

The hairs rise on the back of my neck.

The air stirs *right* behind me. I move to whip myself around when a sharp edge digs into my scarred back.

My muscles freeze instinctively. My breath halts in my throat.

"Turn left and walk into the forest," a magically-distorted voice says, no more than a pace behind me. I can't tell whether that's a sword, knife, or spear against my back, but any of those options would be equally fatal if rammed deeper. "Keep going until I tell you to stop."

Drawing more air into my lungs, I force myself to obey.

Twigs snap under my feet as I tramp onto the uneven ground off the side of the path. Leaves brush my arms.

My magic unfurls in my chest, tugging at me to let it bowl over the person who ambushed me. To melt the blade. To send it rampaging through the woods after every comrade who approved of this plan.

No. This is probably just another test, not an actual threat.

I will my power to stay coiled and quiet—not attacking them *or* me.

After letting it out to play a few nights ago, I find it easier to settle the restless energy. But the farther we walk in tense silence, the harder it gets to suppress my worries.

Gods smite me, have the scourge sorcerers figured out I'm a monster after all? Or maybe someone noticed my trick with the hounds during the festival.

But why would they have waited two more nights to do anything about it? It's not as if they could even have been sure I meant to interrupt Ster. Torstem rather than merely creating trouble for the royals, which would be a mission I'd expect this bunch to approve of.

Or this really could be just another trial. Make me *think* they're upset with me, see if I babble any excuses, reveal errors they didn't actually know about.

I guess I'll find out.

*Ivy,* Julita says, her presence contracted at the back of my skull, *this could be really bad. If you need to use your magic… I think you should.*

My mouth tightens. My automatic reaction is to refuse, with all possible vehemence, but I'm no longer completely sure that's the right answer.

Only as an absolute last resort. Only if it's clear there's no other way to escape—and that escape is worth the consequences.

The second I start treating these people like the enemies I know they are, everything I've put myself through to make it this far will be for nothing. We'll lose the one small foothold we've gained.

My power continues to roil within my ribcage, but it doesn't lash out too forcefully. It's waiting like the rest of me to see how this situation will play out.

Whether I'm facing actual danger or only a staging of it.

I step into a small clearing that might be the one where I tore up the rabbit or a totally different spot—it's all vague shapes in the night. The figure behind me says, "Enough."

I jar to a halt.

More forms move in the darkness between the trees, shrouded in black like the knife-wielding healer was before.

Most of them I only catch vague glimpses of. I think there are four or five people lingering at the outskirts of my limited sight.

Two of the figures step closer, to the edge of the clearing where they stand side by side with a narrow tree trunk between them.

"You accuse this woman?" says the figure on the left. His voice is distorted like the one behind me but deep enough to definitely be male.

The other new arrival wasn't given the same benefit of magical warbling. "I do," he says, in a gruff but clear voice that sends a quiver through my nerves.

I don't recognize it exactly… but I have the sense that it shouldn't sound that way. That there's something unnatural about its tone.

"Accuse me of what?" I demand, keeping my head high and peering at the unknown man through the darkness.

My nerves jitter with the sense of the presences around me forming a circle to pen me in. They're afraid I might run for it.

This definitely isn't good. But if it's an accusation from an outside source, I might be able to turn the tables on my opponent.

Who could know anything all that incriminating about me?

The first figure, directly in front of me, draws himself straighter with a pompous air. As I note the way the black fabric shifts against his broad frame, the suspicion tickles through my head that I might finally be face to face with Ster. Torstem in his scourge sorcerer guise.

When he speaks again, I listen hard for traces of the law professor's voice through the magical distortion. "Another of our number claims you're a traitor to our cause. That you have courted our favor not to serve the All-Giver and see the world returned to its former divine grace, but to undermine everything we've worked for."

A chill trickles through my veins. How could any of Torstem's people have guessed that much? Are they simply fishing to see if it's true without really believing it?

Presumably they don't actually *know*, or I'd already be dead.

Julita mumbles a string of curses and then speaks up in an urgent tone. *I know how to play this. Act all sweet and innocent, like you have no idea how anyone could think that of you. Like you're a naïve twit who's too brainless to have even considered that these fiends deserve to be undermined.*

I'm sure that's how she would have played it, but the idea of acting like an idiot doesn't sit right with me. It isn't as if it'll match what Torstem and his followers have seen from me before.

Innocence, though, I'm totally on board with.

I knit my brow. "Why would I want to undermine you? I've kept everything to myself, as you've asked."

"Lies," my accuser says in the gruff voice that feels even more wrong with each word it speaks. "She's an excellent pretender. You can't believe anything that comes out of her mouth."

*What rot. Go on and simper like you're shocked by his claims.*

My body balks. I can't shake the sense that me simpering would come across just as fake as my opponent's gruffness.

There are other ways to show I have nothing to hide.

I set my hands on my hips and hold my voice steady. "Has my accuser brought any proof? As far as I can tell, *he's* the liar. He must think he has something to gain by turning you against me."

"I heard her," the shrouded figure insists. "I heard her plotting with that lout of a failed general she works for, talking about how they'd bring the Crown's Watch down on you all."

He flicks his hand beneath his concealing robe, and the fragments of recognition crash together with a sickening certainty.

His gruff tone faltered with the urgency of that last claim, more of his natural voice coming through. And something about his flippant phrasing, about the gesture he just made…

Is that *Benedikt* hiding beneath the shroud?

I try not to react, but I have to stiffen against the cold rush of nausea that floods my body.

What would he be doing out here? Why would he—?

The scourge sorcerers are waiting for my answer. Maybe I'm mistaken.

I wrench my scattered mind back to the most vital matter at hand and manage to let out a snort. "I can barely stand to discuss the weather with my employer, let alone get involved in some ridiculous scheme. I accepted your invitation to discover what more I could be in this world partly for a chance to get *away* from that man."

*Ivy… I don't know…* Julita squirms inside my skull, but she must realize I've decided to ignore her advice.

She's guided me well so far, but I'm the con artist between us. I've handled tricky situations with everyone from the lowest street rats to the highest nobility.

If I'm going to get through this mess, and without my magic tearing me and who knows what else apart, it has to be my way.

The figure who might be Ster. Torstem crosses his arms over his chest with a ripple of his shroud. "We *are* only going by hearsay."

He turns his head toward the man I don't want to believe is Benedikt. "And you did have a motive. You were trying to make up for your failure tonight."

His failure? At one of the initiation tasks?

Since when was Benedikt even aiming to get recruited? That was my job.

I want to think that means I was wrong, but with my accuser's next protest, even more of his familiar voice, taut with strain, shows through. "If I were making this all up, how would I have known she's been sneaking out here in the first place?"

My stomach has tied itself in a dozen knots, but I can put on an even better performance than he probably expects.

I roll my eyes skyward and let a sneer creep into my voice. "I can't imagine it'd be all that difficult if you know what to look for. What, were you watching the woods every night to see who'd sneak out here so you'd have someone to point a finger at if *your* loyalty was too shaky to keep up?"

Make the scourge sorcerers see him as the potential traitor. Take the heat off me and aim it back at him.

A sour tang of bile creeps up the back of my throat, but I don't know what else to do.

And if that's Benedikt, then he *is* a traitor. To me, to Stavros, to Julita—to everything we were supposed to be working toward.

"You question *my* loyalty," he starts to sputter, but I'm ready for him. Ready to fight.

I fix him with a glare. "I do. How selfish can you be to try to compensate for your own weaknesses by dragging someone else down with you? Someone who actually wants to see the All-Giver return and create a world the Great God would be proud of."

I sense a shifting in the circle of figures around me. I'm sowing doubt in their heads.

One thing Julita's made more than clear to me is how arrogant the scourge sorcerers are. They think they deserve greater power than anyone else; they think they have some special calling.

Like every upper class prick I've ever dealt with, the fastest way to win them over is to stoke their horrific egos.

I fix my attention back on the possible Torstem. "The nights I've spent out here, immersing myself in your teachings, are the most alive I've felt in my whole life. There's so much more I want to learn. So much I can tell I could accomplish with your guidance. If I've failed you in any way—if I've given you any reason to fault me—then I'm not worthy of this opportunity. I'll accept whatever judgment you'll give."

"Don't listen to—" Benedikt says.

The other man cuts him off with a jerk of his hand. I feel his gaze on me. "I have only your word too, Ivy of Nikodi."

I bob my head in a slight bow. "And whatever you've seen of my acts in service of your cause. But if that isn't enough…"

Julita breaks in with an urgent whisper. *I know! Borys and Wendos—when they couldn't agree on a course of action—they'd call on their powers to decide who was right.*

Hmm. I'm not going to invite my riven magic into the mix… but there is another, higher power I can appeal to.

My pulse stutters at the idea, but I don't have a better one. The words tumble out, no chance to fully think them through. "Why not let the godlen show their favor? Everything we're doing is to bring back their full glory and the world they'd want, isn't it? Test us together, and let the gods support the one whose heart they know is faithful."

Which would be me, wouldn't it? Seeing as I'm the one who's had a godlen talking to me, when he can be bothered to?

It'd better fucking well not turn out that Kosmel is playing a big prank and the lesser gods are all in favor of scourge sorcery after all.

Possible-Torstem is silent for several moments. When he speaks again, I think I can make out a pleased smile in his voice.

"That may be a reasonable suggestion. We'll need to discuss exactly how to proceed. Both of you, come along until we can settle this matter once and for all."

# TWENTY-SIX

*Ivy*

The figure who prodded me through the woods strides along between me and Benedikt, a slim sword in their grasp. Whether they're protecting him from me or me from him, I can't tell. Perhaps it's a little of both.

With every step we take through the night-draped forest, I'm surer of my earlier impressions. With every loping stride of the man across from me, more quivers of stomach-churning recognition race through me.

I don't understand, but somehow one of the men I counted as an ally has become my enemy.

He's accused Stavros too, in an indirect way—saying the former general was conspiring with me to double-cross the scourge sorcerers. If the fiends believe him, they'll attack Stavros without any warning.

But he's kept Alek's and Casimir's names out of it. Because he does have some kind of conscience still, or because he didn't know how to explain they were helping me without revealing that *he* once was as well?

It takes all my concentration to keep my expression impassive and my own strides steady. If our interrogators realize that I've identified my accuser, that I feel betrayed… then they'll know I really did have secrets *to* betray.

The figure I think is Ster. Torstem marches between the trees ahead of us. I haven't seen enough of the law professor to confidently recognize him from his gait, but nothing about his movements contradicts my suspicion.

I'm still vaguely aware of a handful of others tramping in their loose ring around us. Guarding against any attempt to escape.

Where are they taking us? What are they going to do with us?

My magic slithers through my chest like the snake I caught by the Quadring. I can almost hear it hissing in frustration.

It would like to knock Benedikt's feet out from under him, to punch through his ribcage and wrench him apart. Even though I'm horrified by what's happened tonight, the images that flash through my mind sicken me too.

I need to know more. I'll be safer if I can play this cool and careful.

For now, I'm managing to convince my power of that. That the threat isn't significant enough for it to punish me for not letting it loose. No one has a rope around my neck so far.

I doubt I'd have kept it as well contained if it hadn't gotten that brief chance to exert itself a few nights ago. How much worse can this situation get before it sinks its claws into me, and the conspirators realize something's going wrong beyond a squabble between their recruits?

I push down that worry, keeping my hands loose and relaxed at my sides. Mentally charting the distance to the knife in my boot, for the small comfort the thought provides.

Our strange procession draws to a halt at a looming stone barrier. We've reached the back end of the massive wall that surrounds the entire campus.

Guards will be patrolling all the way around it, but there mustn't be any within sight right now. The man I think is Torstem steps forward and presses his hands to the lichen-spotted stones.

I can't see what he does or make out any words from the faint murmur that leaves his lips. Then the stones seem to ripple as if the shadows are condensing in a thicker patch right in front of him.

It looks like the secret passage in the hall of tapestries. As our escort prods us onward, a chill seeps through my skin.

The scourge sorcerers have managed to alter the walls of the school itself during the time they've been active here. What other defenses have they managed to penetrate?

A deeper chill washes over me on my way through the conjured opening, and then I'm standing on the rocky bank of the Starsil River.

At this early hour, only a couple of spots of lantern light gleam among the middle-ward buildings on the other side of the coursing waters. No one stirs on the streets.

The man in charge leads us several paces along the bank to what looks like a bunch of scattered boards. When I'm close enough, the image shimmers with a tingle of magic, the boards melding into a small wooden boat.

An illusion—designed to conceal the watercraft they've stashed here.

There's nothing I can do but clamber onto the boat at the swordsman's gesture. Benedikt follows. The leader, the swordsman, and three other figures sit around us.

We cast off onto the water. No one brings out paddles, and the craft has no sail, but somehow we glide along a fairly straight course along the river. The tingling sensation I felt before heightens—there's more magic guiding us on our path.

It takes us diagonally across the Starsil, avoiding the built-up banks within the city proper, gliding on toward the wilder stretch beyond the main walls.

I spot a few members of the Crown's Watch on guard on the city side, but the illusion must hide us well enough. Not a single shout goes up.

No one's patrolling in the sparse forest across from the main harbor. We disembark and trudge on, leaving the city behind.

None of the conspirators have spoken the whole time. I assume they don't want to risk discovery, but the silence gnaws at me.

How far are we going? Do I still have a chance at turning this situation around, or are they cutting their losses and marching both of us to our deaths?

The sound of the palace bell filters through the trees, marking the fourth hour. The forestland thickens around us, the ground starting to slope upward.

I'm not sure how much farther we've walked before the man who might be Torstem signals for us to stop.

We've reached a low cliff face, only about twice as tall as my scrawny frame. The swordsman directs us to a narrow crack that turns out to be the entrance to a cave.

"You'll wait here while we confer," the man in charge tells us.

He picks up a lantern from just beyond the cave entrance, lights it, and ushers us inside.

It's clear they've kept prisoners in this place before. The conspirators lead us down a short passage to a small cavern only about ten paces across... with several chains fixed to the walls, manacles attached to their ends.

As the swordsman pushes me to sit down next to a length of chain, Julita shudders in my head. I have to restrain a cringe of my own, letting the sorcerer clamp the manacle around my ankle.

At the other side of the cavern, the lead man grasps Benedikt's shroud. "This will only get in the way now. The accusations go both ways; you should be on equal ground."

He wrenches the fabric off Benedikt's head in one yank.

It *is* him. The jaunty bastard's bastard stares across the cave at me, his golden hair rumpled and his mouth clamped flat as if he's trying not to vomit.

My gut lurches at the confirmation. I manage to take him in with a slight furrow of my brow, as if I'm confused rather than shocked or horrified.

The conspirators will be watching my reaction, judging whether I have any connection to this man.

It's a good thing they can't hear Julita's yelp that rings through my head. *Benny—what in the realms—how the* fuck *could he—*

Apparently she didn't pick up on the same hints I did. Not surprising when her awareness of what I see and hear is dulled, if it's anything like what I experienced the one time I let her spirit take over.

She doesn't seem to know what else to say, lapsing into stunned silence.

Benedikt leans his well-built frame against the wall of the cave and accepts his own manacle. He's dressed for the occasion all in the same black as his shroud: black silk tunic, black trousers, black boots polished enough to gleam in the lantern light.

Queasiness fills my belly. I study him for any clue as to why he's turned on me, but his betrayal doesn't make any more sense than it did before.

He focuses on the man who might be Torstem. "I await whatever test you'd conduct for us. I know the gods will be on my side."

He's trying to keep up his usual nonchalant tone, but I pick up a slight quaver he can't totally smooth out of his voice.

The scourge sorcerers stalk out of the cave. They take the lantern with them. The light wavers away, leaving us in total darkness.

I drag in a careful breath despite my rattled nerves, not wanting to show any emotion. I can't sense any magic lingering around us, can't hear anything other than the erratic thud of my own heart and the faint rustle of Benedikt's clothes as he adjusts his position, but there's still a chance the conspirators are monitoring us.

*I'm so sorry,* Julita says. *I never would have imagined he'd— I thought he'd do anything to support the king! I have no idea what's the matter with him.*

All I can do is raise my shoulders in a shrug to indicate my shared confusion.

For several minutes, we sit there in silence. The cool but stuffy air of the cave seems to congeal around me, thick with a moist, mineral scent. My head keeps whirling, my thoughts getting even harder to pull into order through my growing fatigue.

Benedikt shifts again with a clink of his chain. "I didn't mean for things to turn out this way."

His voice is low but abrupt, making my nerves jump in response. I peer toward him through the darkness but can't make out even the outline of his body.

It seems safest to stay silent, as much as my confusion gnaws at me.

"You have no idea what it's like," he goes on. "Nothing I've ever done has mattered to the people who are supposed to be my family. I got in the habit of acting like an idiot because that's all they see me as. That's not what I *wanted* to be."

Julita brings the snark I can't voice out loud. *And he thought turning on you would make him less of an idiot? If I had my hands to slap him with...*

"I thought I had a chance to do something real with Julita and… everything." Benedikt pauses, maybe as aware as I am that he shouldn't say anything too incriminating. "But what do I get? I'm dismissed over again. Treated like I'm useless. Two chances are better than one, aren't they? I went to see what I could find out on my own."

He set himself up to be recruited just like I had, presumably. Hoping he'd come up with answers before I did?

I guess it mightn't have been that hard to make Torstem's supporters believe the bastard's bastard didn't give a rat's ass about the royal family given how irreverent he's tended to act.

And he did it because he could tell the rest of us were keeping something from him? It isn't as if we totally shut him out.

If he had any clue why our group was starting to fracture…

Gods help me, it's a good thing I never trusted him enough to reveal my power.

"Fine," Benedikt says. "Keep ignoring me. But you know what? The more I've heard, the more I think these people have the right idea. What has the royal family done for anyone except the people who fawn and flatter them the best, really? Why should the exact circumstances of your birth dictate how you'll be treated for your entire life?"

My stomach sinks at the caustic note that's crept into his voice. I had no idea Benedikt was concealing so much resentment behind his carefree attitude.

But then, I've only known him for a matter of weeks, barely talked with him outside of the business of our investigation. I saw him as a friend because of our shared cause, but we aren't much better than fleeting acquaintances, really.

"Everyone else does whatever they have to do to get ahead," he goes on. "Why shouldn't I? What have you ever done to earn *my* loyalty? If I hadn't—"

He cuts himself off and lapses into a heavy silence. My lungs tighten.

There's one subject I can bring up without giving any validity to his claims. "The people who brought us here said you failed a test. What makes you think you deserve *their* loyalty?"

The silence stretches a little longer. "I didn't know. I wasn't prepared. They said to carve my whole cheek off, and I only—I only *hesitated*. I never said no. I simply needed a moment to be sure…"

Carve his whole cheek off. I can't restrain a wince, echoed by Julita's presence within my skull.

They must guess at what sacrifice would be most difficult for each potential initiate. Benedikt is a flirt as well as a jokester.

He didn't know they'd heal him afterward any more than I did, and he was afraid to return to the world with a mangled face.

I'm not sure I can blame him for that. In a way, he has grounds to say it was partly my fault—because I never told him about how that trial went for me. If I had, he'd have known in advance it was only a temporary sacrifice.

For pointing his finger at me to save his own skin—I can assign plenty of blame just for that.

A wave of anger sears through my nausea, choking me. I gave up my entire life, the small bits of security I counted on, and the anonymity that protected me for so long to help this prick continue his mission. And the first time things got really hard, he decided I'd make a better sacrifice than any part of him.

I was good enough to sweet talk and kiss, but nothing he couldn't toss aside the second he needed to save his skin.

Fuck him and his semi-royal airs.

My voice hardens. "I was right then. You knew you couldn't hold your own, so you watched for someone to take the fall for you. Why would *anyone* want to count on an asshole like that?"

I turn my back on him, not that he can tell anyway, and sink onto the rough floor with my arm cushioning my head.

I'm not interested in hearing anything else Benedikt has to say. Maybe I can steal a little sleep while we're stuck in here for however long it takes the scourge sorcerers to deliberate.

Whatever comes next, I'll be able to face it better the sharper my mind is.

As I close my eyes, it occurs to me that the conspirators never searched us for weapons. My knife is still hidden in my boot.

I might be able to land a killing blow in the darkness, just judging by Benedikt's voice.

The idea makes me feel sick all over again. It feels so cowardly.

And that's how it'd look to our captors too, isn't it? Like I didn't think I could stand up to him in a fair trial.

No. I need to triumph over him on their terms to have any hope of keeping their trust.

Their terms… and maybe the gods'?

I think hard in my head the way I've prayed silently to Kosmel before. *Guardian of tricksters, I could use a little luck down here right now. If you want me to survive to keep playing this awful game, you'd better have my back.*

No one answers. But a soft pressure comes to rest on my shoulder, like someone setting a reassuring hand there. Like a confirmation that I'm not alone.

Like my father's touch when I was lying in bed sick or shaken by a bad day. Back when he still cared to try to comfort me.

Unwelcome tears prick at the backs of my eyes. I squeeze the lids tighter closed and tuck my free arm across my chest.

And somehow, with the simultaneously unnerving and comforting impression of a god watching over me, my mind drifts off.

I wake at the scrape of footsteps over the uneven floor. My head jerks up as I blink to clear my bleary eyes.

A thin stream of light is seeping down the passage from the narrow cave opening. Day has arrived. Hurrah.

As I push myself into a sitting position and swipe at the grit that's stuck to my face, I don't bother to glance Benedikt's way.

I don't want the shrouded figure approaching us to see any reaction I wouldn't be able to control, looking at the man who tossed me to the wolves.

In the faint daylight, the black shroud looks even more unsettling than at night. It's like a loose, hooded robe that falls all the way to the wearer's feet. I can now see there are slits for sight cut in the black cloth that falls from the top of the hood, but the face beyond them is too shadowed for me to make out even the glint of its eyes.

"Come and let the gods judge who should earn our trust," the man says in the voice that might be Torstem's.

Even though the strategy was my suggestion, an ominous hollow forms in the pit of my stomach.

I hold myself stoically still while one of the other shrouded figures unlocks the manacle from my ankle, but Benedikt can't restrain his restlessness. "What's the trial?"

"You'll see." The leader beckons for us to follow him.

I don't spot any of the other scourge sorcerers when we emerge from the cave, but I suspect they're somewhere nearby. Braced in case they need to intervene.

The possible Torstem points at two particularly expansive pine trees about twenty paces apart. "Stand by one of the trees marked with the All-Giver's sigil. You'll find what you need there."

Every nerve on edge, I head toward the tree that's slightly closer to me. As I come up on it, I make out the sigil of the All-Giver etched into its bark—upside down, like Julita mentioned she's seen it before.

The scourge sorcerers think they can call the Great God back to our level. What more ridiculous hubris could there be?

Any confidence *I'm* feeling drains out of me as I reach the base of the trunk and see the objects waiting for me.

A large wooden bow leans against the tree. A quiver with several arrows lies on the forest floor beside it.

Oh, fuck.

Julita's presence shifts with obvious agitation. *It could still be all right. I don't know that Benedikt is* that *wonderful a shot.*

He doesn't have to be wonderful to best me. I've only handled a bow once in my life, and that time I don't think I clipped a single target.

I pick up the bow, testing its weight, and finally look toward my betrayer. Benedikt is staring right back at me, his hand clenched around his own bow… and a trace of his usual smirk curving his lips.

He was there for the hunt when I showed off my ineptitude at archery. Great God smite him, he must be silently crowing over how easily he'll beat me.

"You have a minute to prepare yourselves," the lead man calls out in his magically warbled voice. "You will stay within reach of your tree. Once the trial begins, you will shoot at your opponent until one of you is too injured to continue. But if you *kill* them, your victory is forfeit. May the gods guide the one who deserves it."

As his voice fades from the crisp autumn air, my gut plummets all the way to my feet.

He wants us to destroy each other without killing. Like the mutilated accomplices who sacrifice so much for the scourge sorcerers' demented cause.

He's not just testing us against each other but evaluating our willingness to maim for our convictions as well.

My fingers tighten around the bow. I sling the quiver over my shoulder and slide out one of the arrows easily enough.

Across from me, through the mottled shadows cast by the leaves overhead, Benedikt's smirk has only grown. Curse it all, he doesn't look the slightest bit guilty about what he intends to do.

He'll tear me to pieces with his arrows until I'm slumped bleeding on the ground, and then he'll waltz back to the college to pretend he has no idea how I went missing. He'll learn all the king's plans for protection and feed them back to the scourge sorcerers.

Or I could tear him apart and leave him for the conspirators to murder.

Even after everything, I can't say that I want the man in front of me dead. He can't be *that* horrible, can he, after all the good things he tried to do before?

Just so incredibly misguided.

But faced with his triumphant smile, with the selfish excuses he gave me yesterday echoing in my ears, I can't say the idea of hurting him makes me feel all that guilty either.

It's a matter of survival. Me or him. And if he survives, a whole lot of people other than me could die because of it.

The choice should be simple, if not for the power roiling in my chest.

The only way I can win is to use my magic. I don't stand a chance of hitting him effectively unless it or some divine intervention guides my arrow. And Kosmel has never offered any physical assistance before.

I've sworn so many times to keep my riven soul under wraps. The only time I released it on purpose, the city was literally on the verge of crumbling.

What will the cost be this time?

How many times can I use it and still stay sane enough to rein it back in?

How many will die if *I* survive… and turn more into the monster every riven eventually becomes?

Benedikt notches his arrow. I have only a matter of seconds left to decide.

As I grip my bow, a swell of resolve rises up inside me. The same iron conviction that came over me when I lay dying in the Domi's back hallway.

I want to live. There's more I want to do.

Maybe, like then, I should let the gods decide just as I told the scourge sorcerers I would.

I position my arrow against the bow and open my mind to the trickster godlen with his wryly divine voice. *If I ask my magic to guide my arrow, will you see that I don't hurt anything I would regret?*

My pulse stutters with the overwhelming voice that resonates through my body for the first time in weeks. *I can guide the backlash, my wayward rogue. But you have to pull the string. The choices you make here can only be yours.*

I swallow against the dryness of my mouth.

Yes. It's my life. My choice.

I'm playing this game to win.

A mortal man's voice reverberates through the forest. "Begin!"

My hand looses the arrow.

The bowstring twangs, and my power leaps with it. I hone it onto the arrow, narrowing it to my target with all the control I can summon.

Just this act. Just this once.

Land one shot so Benedikt can't shoot another.

I might not be much of an archer, but I know how to deal an effective wound. Benedikt needs his arms to shoot.

So I simply have to disable them.

The power ripples through me, pulling the arrow on course—and part of me senses a branch somewhere far off in the woods cracking as it wrenches *away* from its natural direction.

So much of my focus is on my magic that I barely remember to jerk myself away from the arrow Benedikt aimed at me. The vicious tip slices through the sleeve of my tunic with a stinging line of pain and thuds into the trunk behind me.

The break in my concentration jostles my magic. My arrow plunges into Benedikt's shoulder—into the fleshy outer muscle, not right at the center of the joint where I'd have rendered his arm useless.

Benedikt sputters a curse and snatches at another arrow, his bow wobbling in his damaged but not disabled grasp. I whip another projectile of my own out of my quiver and notch it as quickly as my hands can move.

Please, please, please. I don't want this to turn into the torture session the scourge sorcerers must be hoping for.

I don't risk allowing any magic to speed my movements. Even with his injury, Benedikt moves faster than my inexperienced fumbling.

A second arrow thrums through the forest. As I leap to the side, my bow sways in my grip.

I have to do this. I have to end this—*now*.

Gods help me, truly.

I yank back the string and release before Benedikt has a chance to position a third arrow. My second careens toward him, my heart aching with the power bleeding out of me, hurtling it straight to its mark—

He tries to dodge, but my magic either catches him or makes the arrow veer. It slams home, digging into the sinews that attach his arm to his torso.

An anguished groan bursts from Benedikt's lips. His arm sags, the bow slipping from his grasp.

He slumps back against his tree, blood coursing in a wet streak down his tunic. His fingers dangle limply. He gropes for the bow with his other hand, but there's clearly no way he can shoot one-armed.

"No!" he shouts. "No, I swear, I was telling the truth. I don't know how—"

A black-shrouded figure emerges from behind the tree and smacks a rod against the top of Benedikt's head. He topples over, limp as a sack of potatoes.

My stomach heaves. It's all I can do not to hurl the remains of last night's dinner onto the earth by my feet.

I did it. I won.

But every inch of my skin feels as clammy as if I'm about to die too.

My magic flails around me, desperate to deal out more vengeance, and I clench my hands as I drag it back inside me.

A couple of broken branches. Not too horrific for payment.

As if that's the most awful thing about this situation.

The man who's probably Torstem steps toward me, his voice unnervingly warm. "An impressive showing, Ivy. The gods must smile on you. It's our honor to know your loyalties lie with us."

# Twenty-Seven

Ivy

I don't know where the conspirators got the dress from. They must have felt it'd be too suspicious to send me back to the college in a dirty, torn set of training clothes.

They had me change by shoving a bundle of fabric into my hands and sending me into the cave to put it on. I swapped my shirt and trousers for the simple riding gown as quickly as possible, wanting to be out of the dank space.

Now, the silk skirt whispers across my legs as I stride back toward the river, the man who might be Ster. Torstem on one side and the swordsman on the other. The fabric is light, but it feels out of place in the wilderness around us. The brush snags on it, tugging it against my legs.

I pop the last bite of the cheese-stuffed roll they gave me into my mouth and force it down my throat. I didn't really want to eat anything these psychopaths provided, but it's late enough in the morning now that my stomach was gnawing on itself with hunger.

And if I'd refused, they'd have questioned my faith in them all over again.

I'm not sure how many of the other conspirators are following discreetly behind us and how many have hung back to deal with Benedikt. One of them—presumably the same woman who healed my finger the other night—approached me to seal the wound on my arm before I left.

I doubt they're giving the bastard's bastard the same courtesy.

As if he can guess the directions my thoughts have gone in, the possible Torstem glances over at me with a rustle of his shroud. "We didn't enjoy the process of judgment. With such a major accusation, the gods demand an equally intense trial."

The gods demanded it. Sure.

*That's a heap of cow dung if I ever heard one,* Julita mutters, and I'm inclined to agree. If there's one thing I know about the scourge sorcerers, it's that they encourage pain rather than shying away from it.

Does he think I've forgotten how they ordered me to rip apart a rabbit and provoke a fight between the guards?

Of course, he doesn't realize I already know the worst of their crimes: the immense sacrifices they demand of the children they con into joining their cause. Eyes, ears, hair, arms… Everything they can remove while remaining alive. Who knows what else on the inside?

Just remembering the sacrificial accomplices who'd crouched around Wendos in the tower makes my stomach turn.

I keep my revulsion off my face and concentrate on playing the role of devoted recruit. Even a loyal applicant would have a few questions about what just happened—especially one who isn't supposed to know as much about the Order of the Wild's practices as I do.

"What will happen to him?" I ask. "The man who accused me?" Better if they think I'm not even sure of his name.

The shrouded figure gives a shrug. "The gods will decide on the appropriate justice for his crime, and we will carry it out on their behalf. We can't let such a betrayal of our principles go unpunished, of course. Those of us who embrace the All-Giver's true will must support each other."

How convenient that the ones who have so little end up supporting the ones with plenty, and in much more drastic ways.

"You can be sure he won't threaten you again," the man says, as if he thinks my silence means I'm worrying about that.

He doesn't seem to be concerned about revealing that much to me, but then, he isn't explicitly saying that they're going to kill Benedikt. And even if he thought I might report a possible murder to the authorities, what could I tell the Crown's Watch at this point?

I don't even know for sure that the man next to me *is* Ster. Torstem, let alone who any of the other conspirators who participated in this charade of a trial are. I have no proof of anything, not even the tests I myself carried out.

I could point to a cave with shackles in the woods, if I could retrace my steps there, but I doubt the scourge sorcerers will leave any evidence of who used the chains.

Torstem doesn't need to be careful. In a way, this is all another trial. Will I turn on them after all, or will I accept the brutality I just participated in as reasonable?

The sun lifts higher, streaking warmth I can't appreciate through the trees. It feels as if we walk for ages longer than we did coming here, a fact that's confirmed when the trees thin and I can make out the landscape beyond them again.

We've come around the curve of the river to where it starts to narrow. As my escorts stop there, a soft nicker reaches my ears.

I jerk around and spot Pepper, Casimir's favorite mare, saddled and bridled with her reins tied to a nearby tree. The horse whinnies and bobs her head as if beckoning me over.

"How…?"

The man next to me chuckles. "It'd look odd for you to return through the city on foot. We would have contrived to bring the steed we understand you've been most inclined to use in the past, but the stallion proved… difficult. This one seemed a reasonable alternative."

I can just imagine Toast's reaction to mysterious figures he hasn't warmed up to trying to drag him off in the middle of the night. I hope he bit one of them.

But now I understand why they brought me a riding dress. They really do think of everything to cover their tracks.

The scourge sorcerer points to the bridge farther along the river across the field of shrubs and grass. "You can cross there, and you'll be close to the college. Show the guards at the gate your bracelet, and they'll let you through without any trouble. You're clear on your story if your employer asks where you've been?"

"I got an urgent message from my uncle," I rehearse, not that I'm actually going to use the lie. Little do the conspirators know, the real Ivy doesn't even have an uncle. "I hurried over to help any way I can. I'll apologize profusely for not being able to leave word beforehand."

"Good. Go ahead, quickly. We'll call on you again when it's time."

Time for what? I want to ask, but I don't think he'll tell me. And he might not appreciate the prying.

I take Pepper's reins, clamber into the saddle, and set off across the field at a canter. As I sway with the horse's strides, Julita stirs in the back of my head.

*Stavros will be having a fit. Gods only know what he's imagined you've gotten into. I hope he isn't too difficult to talk down.*

My stomach knots. Whatever the former general is imagining, it might not even be totally untrue. I did tap into my riven magic today, on purpose.

As my escort suggested, the guards take one look at my college bracelet and silk dress and wave me through without comment. I set Pepper trotting through the streets at as fast a pace as seems appropriate for a noble and remove her tack quickly at the stable, though I do linger there for long enough to check on Toast and give him an apologetic chin scratch for whatever trouble the conspirators gave him.

Then I hustle the rest of the way to Stavros's quarters with my heart thudding at the base of my throat. As I slip inside, I brace myself.

No furious former general waits on the other side. I stall in my tracks, unsure what to do with myself, and notice the ring of cord stretched open on the floor near his desk.

He must have called a meeting with the other men.

Stavros still has my own portable portal—if he thinks I'm trustworthy enough to carry the cord myself now, he's forgotten to hand it over. But we've only separated them out for convenience's sake. Anyone can use any of the magical passages.

I hesitate for just a moment and then stride over to step into the corded circle.

The world around me flashes to darkness and then to the sconce-lit, windowless palace meeting room with a jolt of magic through my nerves. As I stumble to a halt one step past Stavros's cord, the three men poised around the table whirl toward me.

Casimir's face breaks into the most brilliant grin I've ever seen. Alek's breath rushes out of him in a whoosh of relief.

But Stavros moves fastest. The massive man crosses the floor in a matter of seconds and grasps my shoulders with his wooden prosthetic and his real hand, peering down at me.

His stormy expression makes my pulse hiccup, but the growl of his voice sounds more anguished than angry. "You're all right. Where have you been? It was the fucking scourge sorcerers again, wasn't it?"

My mouth opens, but it takes me a couple of seconds to find my words with his dark eyes searing into mine and the heat of his hand coursing over my skin. "Yes. They summoned me in the middle of the night—wanted me to arrive right away. I…"

I falter, the enormity of what I need to tell them hitting me like it hadn't quite before, and Stavros's grip on my shoulder tightens. "*Are* you all right? What did those vermin do to you?"

*Well,* Julita remarks with an awkward laugh. *I suppose Stav didn't get the wrong idea after all. You really have turned his head, haven't you?*

"That isn't one of your regular dresses," Casimir notes quietly.

Stavros bares his teeth. "If those assholes—"

"The dress barely matters," I interrupt. "And it wasn't—it wasn't exactly all the scourge sorcerers."

"What do you mean?"

"Stavros," Alek says, sounding as if he's keeping his usual even tone through sheer force of will, "why don't you give Ivy room to breathe so she can explain exactly what she's been through?"

The larger man stares at me as if it hadn't occurred to him that his presence might be just slightly imposing. He lets out a strangled sound and dips his head so low his forehead comes to rest against mine.

"I'm sorry," he says. "I thought—I thought they'd murdered you."

A lump fills my throat. I'm even more overwhelmed with him leaning so close. His smoky scent floods my lungs dizzyingly.

I can't claim the heady thump of my heart is only anxiety.

Was he really so worried about *me*? How much was he simply afraid that our plans to ensure his king's safety would fall apart?

Despite the questions whirling in my mind, I find myself resting my hand on the front of his shirt as if to give him additional confirmation of my words. "I'm here. Not murdered. Not even really hurt."

Stavros lets out a huff and places his hand over mine. He tips his head to the side, and I'm struck by the impression as I have once before that he might kiss me.

My heart lurches, torn between apprehension and a longing that's never quite died.

Like before, he doesn't follow through. He squeezes my fingers and steps back, his jaw flexing with continued agitation. "Go ahead. Tell us what happened."

From his tone, he might as well be saying, *Tell me who I need to kill.*

"Wait," I say. "Let me just—"

I stalk around the edges of the room, confirming that I can't sense any magically enhanced creatures lurking in the walls. By the time I return to my original spot, I feel a little steadier but no happier about the conversation ahead.

I drag in a breath to start. "The summons came around three in the morning…"

I give them the full account, from walking into the woods to being accused to my first suspicions of who my accuser was. When I say Benedikt's name, Alek's stance goes rigid.

Stavros outright bares his teeth. "What? What wretched game did the royal bastard think he was playing at?"

I swallow thickly. "I don't think he saw it as a game. He talked to me a little later—he'd been feeling like we were shutting him out, which we were, because we were hiding my magic from him— he thought he'd prove himself by getting information from the scourge sorcerers on his own, but they ended up swaying his loyalties. Convincing him that what they're doing is right."

Alek's jaw drops. "He's siding with *them*?"

His shock echoes my own. "I guess they're more persuasive than we gave them credit for."

Stavros slams his hand against his thigh. "The blasted idiot. He treated our mission like a joke half the time, and then he— I'll wring his fucking neck."

The former general shoves himself away from the table, but I hold up my hand to stop him. "I don't think you can do anything at all to him. I—I don't think you'd need to. The scourge sorcerers will be taking care of that now that they've decided they can't trust him."

The ominous silence that follows my statement tells me all three men know exactly what I'm implying.

Stavros's jaw works. "And he blathered about our entire investigation?"

I shake my head. "He hadn't given away anything about the rest of you. Well, other than trying to claim that he'd overheard me making plans with you, but I'd imagine the conspirators will dismiss that idea now that they've assumed it was all a lie. He didn't mention Casimir and Alek at all."

"That's the least of our concerns right now." Casimir shakes his head. "I suppose none of us were all that close with him. Meetings were all business, and we couldn't spend time together outside of them. But I still wouldn't have thought…"

"Neither would I," Alek says hoarsely. "It's his own *family* they're encouraging people to turn against."

I remember Benedikt's remarks over the past few weeks—and the way he looked when his half-uncle chided him. "I think that might have become a benefit rather than a problem."

We linger in our shared horror for a minute before Casimir ventures another question, his voice gentle. "How did you persuade them to trust you over Benedikt?"

More haltingly, I explain about the trial I suggested, the way the scourge sorcerers put it to us, and Kosmel's divine assistance. I tense up when I get into the part where I used my magic—used it to wound a man these three recently considered a friend—but Stavros only reacts with a rough exhalation when I mention the arrow that wounded me.

"They healed it," I say before he can reach for me again. "Like they did my finger."

What I can see of Alek's bronze-brown face has grayed beneath his mask. "Are you sure they completely believed you? If they wanted to eliminate any risk of betrayal, they could have gotten rid of both of you."

And they still could, he's obviously thinking.

I hug myself. "As far as I could tell, they were convinced. I'm sure they'll be watching me even more closely for the next few days, though."

Stavros starts to pace. "You can't go back. This is too much. They had you chained in a fucking cave."

I grimace. "If I don't go back, they'll definitely want me dead."

"I never should have let you start off on this reckless path to begin with."

My hands drop to my hips. "You didn't *let* me do anything. I made my own decisions. And even with everything that's happened, this is still our best chance at taking the scourge sorcerers down."

Which Stavros well knows, because he can't even argue that point, only hiss through his teeth in frustration.

He stops, raking his hand through his ruddy hair. "I have to report to the king. Benedikt was part of his family, if not a totally legitimate part."

Casimir steps forward and touches my arm. "You do that. Alek and I can look after Ivy. I'm sure she could use some peace after what she's been through."

He pauses. "You have the cord she normally uses, don't you? Could you give that to me before you leave? We should be doubly careful about any arrangements we make from now on."

I'm not sure what the courtesan is thinking, so I doubt Stavros is either, but he digs into the pouch on his belt and hands over my cord without argument. He moves toward his own portal ring but turns toward me at the last second.

He lifts his hand to touch my cheek. "They are going to pay for this. All of it. I can't wait until that day."

# Twenty-Eight

*Casimir*

I've spent many hours in the former General Stavros's presence. I noted the spark of interest that lit in his eyes when Julita turned on her charm. A couple of times, I observed him from afar with one of my carnal arts professors on his arm—a woman of unarguable beauty and sensuality.

In the course of our association, I've witnessed him pleased and angry, resolved and disheartened.

But I've never before seen the intensity that's come over him while he speaks to Ivy right now.

There's immense passion smoldering in his eyes as he gazes down at her, and I can tell with every emphatic word and gesture that the emotion goes much deeper than mere attraction.

From the moment his temper erupted at the sight of her with me after our interlude in the archives, I've suspected he has some kind of interest in her. Now... Now it's obvious and potent enough to stir up my own emotions: approval, compassion, and a dollop of jealousy I don't have any right to feel.

It's about time he removed his head from his ass when it comes to her. About time he started treating her like the awe-inspiring woman she is.

After what she's just been through, the betrayal she's just faced, she deserves nothing more than full commitment from the rest of us in every way we can offer it.

And I'm starting to think all three of us *can* offer our devotion in every conceivable way.

I'd encourage Stavros to explore all those ways right this moment, but I can't deny the urgency of alerting the king to the traitor within his own family, no matter what dire fate Benedikt may already have met. Who knows if the scourge sorcerers will find some final way to use the royal bastard before they're through with him?

The shock lingers like a knot in my gut. I was wrong about Benedikt. He put on such a carefree front during our short meetings that I got into the habit of not checking in on his emotional state that closely.

How long has a deeper resentment been simmering inside him without us even realizing—bitter enough that the scourge sorcerers were able to draw him in?

We may never know. Gods help us, I wish I'd paid more attention while I could.

Maybe I couldn't have changed his mind, but I might have been able to spare Ivy the trauma she endured at his bidding.

Stavros pulls himself away from Ivy with what looks like incredible effort. I can read his reluctance to leave her all through his stance as he turns toward the loop of cord that'll take him back to his quarters.

I offer him my most reassuring smile.

We'll take good care of her. We'll give her everything she could need until he's able to join us.

I turn Ivy's cord in my hands. "Leave your loop at the other end open so Ivy will be able to follow it back to your quarters once she's ready."

Stavros gives a quick nod and one final, anguished glance over his shoulder at Ivy before stepping into the circle of cord and vanishing.

Ivy stares after him, shock etched on her pale face. It's a crime how much trouble she's had accepting that any of us could truly care about her. In Stavros's case, it must be even more difficult after how harshly he treated her when he discovered her magic.

I slip my hand around her arm again, stroking my fingers from her shoulder to her elbow and back again. Maybe it'll help her believe if she knows I can see it too.

"If you're our Signy, I suppose you did need a third paramour."

Ivy's gaze jerks toward me. "What do you— He wouldn't really…"

She trails off, uncertainty mingling with the weariness in her expression. She's been through so much in the past day.

I brush her amber hair back from her face in a gentle caress. "I think Stav has been fighting with himself even more than he's fought with you. It's a relief to see that devotion finally won over fear."

A blush spreads across Ivy's cheeks. "He hasn't said anything. We haven't *done* anything."

I chuckle. "Oh, he's said enough. And you don't have to worry. I'm not complaining. You should get all the adulation we can offer you."

I glance toward Alek, who's been watching the whole interaction with a mix of concern and bemusement. At my silent prodding, he steps closer to Ivy.

There's something poignant about the tentative but determined way he tucks his arm around Ivy's waist, as if he's still not sure he could be allowed to show her that much affection. The scholar has also had a long journey toward believing anyone could want *him*, I suspect.

"If Signy's men could handle sharing between a trio, I'd imagine we could figure out a way too," he says, and presses a kiss to her hair. "You've spent too long with no one you can count on."

The corner of his mouth crooks upward at a sly angle I'm not used to. "And three lovers opens up even more… intriguing possibilities."

Ivy arches an eyebrow at him, but a hint of a smile crosses her lips. "You and that poetry book."

"There's nothing wrong with wanting to see you happy—and satisfied."

I beam at both of them. "I couldn't agree more. And to get started with that…" I swipe at a little smudge of dirt at the corner of Ivy's jaw that the scourge sorcerers missed in their hasty clean-up effort. "You spent the night in a cave. I think the first step to getting you good as new is a nice soak in a bath, don't you?"

Ivy's blush darkens.

"Just a bath?" she asks, sounding amused.

Remembering how the first bath I set up for her ended sends a quiver of desire to my groin. I lean in to claim a quick kiss.

"Whatever pleases you, Kindness. I simply want you to know we're here for you however you need us."

Alek lifts his chin. "Agreed."

Ivy looks down at herself. "Getting clean would be a relief—I'm sure about that."

"Then I have just the thing. You two wait here while I make the arrangements. I'll step through the cords and escort you back when I'm ready—it shouldn't take long."

I slip her cord into the pouch on my belt and step through my own ring. After a moment of disorienting darkness, I'm back in my dorm room in the Domi.

A few of my dormmates are chatting in the common room, one who's training to be a dancer doing stretches on the floor, another who's about to start an apprenticeship as a bard strumming casually on her lute. I give them all a friendly nod and head out into the hall to check the reserved bathing rooms.

The companionship division has ten private bathing areas for our exclusive use, in consideration for the services some of us provide and the extensive cosmetic preparations many of us require. I breeze past the smaller options like the one where I brought Ivy last time.

This time, I don't want the experience to feel like something I'm presenting her with. I want us all on the same level, like real lovers rather than anything resembling courtesan and client.

And having additional space for whatever other activities we might engage in would be ideal too.

The first of the larger rooms has the eyes closed on the face carved on the door, indicating that it's locked for use. The second is open.

I slip into the cream-tiled space, survey it to confirm it meets my expectations, and secure the door. With practiced efficiency, I move through the room—turning on the tap on the massive bathtub built partly into the floor, pouring in an oil for relaxing sore muscles and a bubbling powder with a soothing scent, setting three plump towels on the bench for ease of access.

Then I spread Ivy's cord on the floor in its circle and step back through to the meeting room.

Ivy and Alek are leaning against the table, his arm still around her and their heads bent close together. When they look up at my arrival, it's clear I've interrupted a quiet conversation.

A pang shoots through my heart like the sensation that hit me when I walked in on them kissing in the side room the other day. Like a wordless admonishment telling me that I can never have quite the same shared affection.

But maybe I can. Maybe it isn't too much to ask that I have a woman who wants *me* to be happy as much as I want the same for her.

Because as content as Ivy looks in Alek's embrace, her face lights up at the sight of me.

She's an incredible woman. I'm still serving both my godlen and my purpose on this earth by catering to her pleasure.

Who could deserve more than the woman who's putting herself in so much danger to protect us all from divine retribution?

"Come with me," I say, and quickly add when Alek starts to hesitate, "Both of you."

We emerge one after the other into the bathing room. Ivy looks around at the sprawling, tiled space and lets out a laugh. "It's not just a bathroom—it's a bedroom too."

There is indeed a large, four-poster bed with covers the same ivory as the frame standing at the opposite end from the bathtub.

I grin at her. "Sometimes people want to relax in a drier fashion once they're clean. We can accommodate all preferences. If you simply want a comfortable sleep, you're welcome to it."

A sigh escapes her. "I might take you up on that. But first…"

She walks up to the bathtub, reaching for the lacing on the basic silk gown the conspirators dressed her up in. So much more confident than the last time.

It warms me to see her assurance growing.

I move to join her, loosening the ties with experienced fingers. "I thought the three of us might enjoy a soak together. I'm sure both Alek and I could use a chance to unwind after all our worries about you while you were missing. And then you'll have proper company."

Ivy hums. "Sounds fair enough."

She casts a sideways glance toward the scholar, and I follow her gaze. At his awkward expression, I realize I may have miscalculated in my hurry.

"Only if you'd like to," I say to him, unsure of the best approach. Alek has always seemed like a rather private person. "I shouldn't have assumed—"

"It's all right," he interrupts with a crooked smile. "I'm glad you counted me in. It's only— My mask…"

He gestures to the leather shape that covers most of his face—not a good material for dampening.

Of course. I should have been prepared for that concern.

I scan the room, considering the possibilities. "I'm sure I could find an appropriate substitute if you're not comfortable removing it completely…"

Ivy turns with her dress slipping partway off her shoulders. "Or you could go unmasked. You know I think you're just as handsome without it. And I'm sure Casimir won't judge."

There's a tenderness to her voice that I've never heard with anyone else. An understanding between them that I'm not privy to.

At her words, Alek practically glows with adoration in return. He touches the edge of his mask, weighing the options.

I dip my head in acknowledgment of Ivy's remark. "Whatever you're covering, it only reflects how your life has shaped you. There's a beauty in all experience, good and bad—in still being alive to show what we've been through."

Alek's throat works. Then he reaches for his tunic. "All right. It shouldn't matter anyway."

He sounds certain enough that I leave him to his undressing and shed my own clothes.

Ivy shimmies out of her undergarments, her wiry body drawing my eye as it always does. She unties the ribbon she wears around her arm in memory of her sister and rests it on top of her pile of clothes.

Then she clambers over the low edge of the bath and sinks into the bubbly water, sitting on the ledge along its wall. With a deep breath, she slides a little deeper. Her eyelids dip and her hair fans out into the water.

An ache fills my chest all the way to the base of my throat. She's so lovely—and so unaware of that fact.

A bath is hardly anything to compete with the horrors she's faced in the past day—gods, in the past several weeks. I wish I could wash all the stress and pain she must be carrying away.

I wish I could stop her from having to experience any more of it.

But how in the realms could a courtesan do that?

I can't keep her safe. I can't take down the scourge sorcerers in her place.

Pampering her to the fullest extent of my ability is the best thing I can contribute… but compared to what Stavros and Alek can offer, it feels like barely anything.

A niggling voice in the back of my head pipes up that I'm being selfish by focusing all my energy on this one woman, that I don't deserve to even try to devote myself to her, but I tune it out as well as I can. What I can give her is better than nothing.

I ease into the bath and sit kitty-corner from her. Alek pauses at the edge of the tub, stripped down to his drawers.

There's plenty to recommend itself about his tall, lean frame. The toned definition of compact muscle shows beneath his bronze skin across his chest and arms. He has nothing to be shy about there.

He grips his mask and pauses. Visibly girding himself, he peels it off his face.

The mottled flesh beneath, stretching across his forehead and nose and down his left cheek, tells a story I don't know the details of. I can see it was some kind of injury, one that dug too deep to be fully healed.

But he did survive it. Ardone teaches us that beauty can be found in all things. There's beauty in the interplay of colors amid the scars; beauty in the unusual shapes they create on his face.

Beauty in the fact that he was willing to share it with me at all.

I smile at him, hoping he can tell that I'm unbothered by his appearance. "It's an honor to have you trust me with your full self."

Something in Alek's stance loosens. He tugs off his drawers and scrambles into the tub.

"Oh," he says as the water envelops him. "That is nice. Now I'm thinking I've never actually had a proper bath."

Ivy shoots me a fond grin. "Casimir elevates them to an art form."

I tip my head back against the edge of the tub. There's so much space we can all sit without bumping up against each other. "Anything can be an art if you give it the proper attention."

Just because we don't have to bump into each other doesn't mean I want the distance. I scoot over so I can stroke the side of Ivy's face. "We can't change the hurt you've been through. But you can know that you never have to worry about where *we* stand. We want to see you safe and well. There's so much joy waiting for you when you reach the end of the mission you're on."

Ivy's smile tightens a little, but her eyes shine bright. She looks from me to Alek and back again. "You know… when I was in the tower, after Wendos injured me… part of what helped me keep standing up to him was thinking about you. How you'd already been there for me even then."

The ache gripping my chest melts into a heady warmth. "Any strength I can give you is yours to take, whenever you need it."

"And if you ever need more than we've thought to give, just ask," Alek adds, his voice gone a bit hoarse.

Ivy ducks her head with a hint of shyness. "I wouldn't mind help washing my hair."

I reach for the soap. "It would be my pleasure."

As I massage the suds into Ivy's scalp, Alek takes a little soap and washes away the smudge on her jaw I noticed earlier. As he works his way down her neck and along her arm, I feel the tension releasing from Ivy's body. She hums encouragingly.

We dunk her hair together, running our fingers through her wet locks on either side. Alek watches my movements closely and mimics them with careful precision.

Ivy sprawls out languid between us, her eyes closed. "Maybe we need to send an army of courtesans to deal with the scourge sorcerers," she murmurs absently. "Anyone would give up just about any information when they're getting this kind of treatment."

Alek chuckles, but the offhand remark pierces right through the center of me.

I've found out everything I can from my past clients and my leisure activities around the college. None of the bug club members we're keeping an eye on have been in the habit of hiring anyone from the companionship division.

But that isn't the only place we might find useful information. Ster. Torstem has been taking his accomplices out of the college—out of the city—for all those bug club expeditions and who knows what else…

The image floats through my mind of my mother's friend Laselle. Stopping by every month or two to lounge alongside my mother, her loose white-blond curls bobbing with her expansive movements as she gossiped about her clients.

Laselle has been in business for decades now, catering to the counts and provints on the estates closest to the capital. The conspirators won't have been able to go *too* far abroad.

It's possible they've left behind evidence of their dealings that someone has noticed and commented on.

My stomach tightens up at the idea of seeking Laselle out. The last words she ever said to me still ring out from the memory—that brief conversation at my mother's funeral.

*I hope you make something of yourself, Casimir. A good woman was ruined to bring you into this world. You'd better do her legacy proud.*

They used to make a game of it, her and my mother, having me perform for them and criticizing every tiny error. At the age of six, I once pinned and re-pinned Laselle's hair until my fingers started to bleed while she sneered at every effort I made.

Gods only know what she'd make of the man I've become. Of the quest I've devoted myself to that's nothing like what my mother expected of me.

But what does her opinion mean compared to the chance to make Ivy's task easier? If I can dredge up a clue that'll help us expose the conspirators' plans sooner, extricate her from their grasp before they harm her even more…

That would be worth just about anything.

Ivy teases her fingers along my chin and tugs me into a kiss. My pulse hitches eagerly as I drink in the sweet heat of her lips.

Apparently we are going to have more than just a bath—and I certainly won't complain. I've been longing to feel this woman's body against mine since our first and only full encounter weeks ago.

When she turns her head to seek out Alek's mouth in turn, I nip her earlobe and flick my tongue along her jaw, earning myself a gasp.

I know I can be everything she needs. I can bring her pleasure and a way out.

It could be a dangerous journey. I'll need to travel the estates alone to track Laselle down while keeping my true purpose hidden, and a courtesan on the roads can draw the wrong kinds of attention.

And that's fine. Why shouldn't I risk my life when Ivy already has and will again, over and over, until we see the scourge sorcerers fall?

# Twenty-Nine

*Ivy*

I thought being enveloped between two stunning men in the meeting room was a thrilling experience. Finding myself pinned between them in the steamy water of the bathtub, our naked skin softened by Casimir's oils, is so overwhelming I might be drowning in delight.

It'd certainly be an incredible way to go.

With every brush of their hands over my body and every collision of our lips, the anguish of the past day melts away. I tug Alek even closer, arch back into Casimir's caresses, longing to lose myself in the pleasure of this moment as deeply as I can.

So much of my life right now is out of my control. It's barely mine at all.

But this—the unexpected connection I've found with these two men that I can hardly believe is real—is all mine. I want to own it, revel in it.

I shift around to reclaim Casimir's mouth, and he strokes his hand over my bare breast. As I gasp into the kiss, Alek slides a tentative but no less eager hand down my side to my hip.

My head is spinning with the heat of the water and their bodies, with the sensations flooding me from both sides. Julita drew back into the farthest depths of my skull sometime after we got into the bath—I can barely sense her presence.

But through the blissful haze, a thread of uneasiness wriggles into my awareness. The memories of Benedikt's face revealed beneath the shroud, of his smirk when he raised his bow to shoot at me, linger on.

If even he would betray us…

I hesitate, and Casimir notices my reaction immediately. He eases back to catch my gaze. Alek goes still at my other side.

I sink back down onto the ledge so I can look at both of them. My hands instinctively reach for theirs. "You know you never have to worry about where *my* loyalties lie, don't you? I still think the scourge sorcerers are maniacs and criminals. I have no interest at all in buying into their mad philosophy, no matter what I've done to convince them."

Casimir chuckles and trails his free hand down the side of my face. "Of course. I never even considered it."

Alek is frowning. "Have we done or said anything to make you think we don't trust you?"

A lump rises in my throat. "No. Nothing like that. I just— You knew Benedikt for longer than you've known me, and he startled all of us. I figured I should make my position clear."

Alek's fingers tighten where they've intertwined with mine. "I've never worried either. You of all people would be able to recognize harmful magic when you see it."

Casimir dips his head to kiss the peak of my shoulder. "And every time you've talked about their initiation rituals, it's been obvious how uncomfortable you were with them. I hate that you've had to go back to them at all—I know you'd rather never deal with the conspiracy again."

The fleeting panic that gripped me unwinds from my gut. I relax into their combined embrace again, but the doubtful part of me—the part that's having trouble understanding how a street-rat thief won a brilliant scholar's and a noble courtesan's devotion—insists on one final clarification.

I glance at one and then the other. "And you're really okay with what we're doing here? With me being with both of you? I never would have expected—I wouldn't have asked—"

"I think we both know that too," Casimir murmurs, releasing my hand to tuck his arm around me. "I'm not the jealous type, Kindness. The happier you are, the happier I'll be too."

Alek's smile twists. "I never thought I'd be able to have anything like this at all. I know you caring about Casimir doesn't take anything away from whatever we'll have together."

He pauses, his gaze sliding to the other man with a hint of shyness. "And maybe Casimir will help me ensure I'm making you as 'happy' as I possibly can, since I can't say I know what I'm doing in that area all that well."

Casimir beams at him. "I can always offer advice. We should look at this as a collaboration, just like our investigations. We each bring our own approach and talents to the task at hand, and we're better for combining them."

I narrow my eyes. "Now you're making it sound like work."

The courtesan laughs and tugs me close against him. His voice drops to a murmur by my ear. "I can assure you what we're doing here is nothing but a pleasure. And I'm looking forward to seeing how much pleasure we can bring you."

He nibbles a path down my neck while teasing his fingers along my inner thigh. Alek leans in for another kiss, and just like that, I'm lost again.

I want them to feel good too. I want them to know just how much I cherish the affection they're offering me. How much I cherish *them* and everything they've brought into my life.

I stroke my hand over Alek's toned chest and across his stomach. He hums approvingly against my mouth.

My ass has settled into Casimir's lap—against the rigid length of him that tells me how much he's already enjoying this interlude. Shifting my weight, I rock against him in what I hope is a provocative motion.

It must work, because Casimir's breath hitches. He groans, and his hand slips up my thigh to cup the most sensitive part of me.

At the bolt of pleasure that races up from my core, I can't restrain a whimper. Alek lets out a hungry sound and kisses me harder, massaging my breast.

I trace my fingers over the lean muscles of his abdomen until they graze the jutting length of his cock. When I wrap my hand around it, he bucks into my grasp with a groan of his own.

Casimir swivels his thumb over my clit and delves his forefinger inside me. The pressure sends bliss pulsing through my nerves.

As my head tips back with a gasp, he nips my shoulder and starts to adjust our position. "There's one talent I'd like to bring to bear that I haven't gotten a chance to yet. And this is the perfect place for it…"

He lifts me out of the water, Alek adding his arms to the task when he realizes what the courtesan is up to. Together, they set me on the smooth, wide edge of the tub.

Casimir motions to the scholar with a tip of his head. "You should get out too—I'd love to know someone's keeping her satisfied up above while I see what magic I can conjure down here."

He winks at me with an impish grin—and nudges my knees apart so he can lower his head between my legs.

At the first press of his mouth against my sex, the jolt of pleasure shocks a mumbled curse from my mouth. "Fuck."

I've heard women talk about this act, even seen it performed once, but none of my previous, momentary lovers were attentive enough to try it.

Gods above, I never imagined it could feel so good.

Casimir laps his tongue across every sensitive bit with exquisite care, as if he's charting my most private domain with his mouth. Each flick and swipe sparks even more of the heady delight now flooding my body.

I moan and clutch at Alek, who's followed Casimir's suggestion to clamber out next to me.

The scholar embraces me from behind, branding my neck and shoulders with heated kisses, caressing both of my breasts with his agile hands, tweaking my nipples to set off sparks through my flesh. His breath has gone ragged as if he's as affected by the sight of Casimir's attentions as I am by receiving them.

The courtesan curves his tongue between my folds. Then he sucks on my clit with just the right force to make me shudder with need. My fingers dig into Alek's arm.

A strained noise escapes the scholar, and then he's scooting back around me. "Can I— I'd like to do that for her too."

Casimir grins up at us with a lick of his lips. "It'd be selfish of me to keep this treasure all to myself."

As Alek sinks into the water, Casimir eases onto the side of the pool next to me. A pang resonates through my body at the loss of contact, but Alek wastes no time taking the courtesan's former position.

He considers me with his intense gaze. His bright brown eyes have never felt more penetrating. As he runs his thumb over my clit, they light up with an enthusiasm that might be academic as well as passionate.

"I've read about techniques," he says, lifting his gaze to Casimir. "But I wouldn't be surprised if you know better than any account I've happened across in the library."

Casimir's smile only grows. "Take your time. Enjoy every part of her, and she'll enjoy it too. Put your whole head into it, build up the pressure and a rhythm. And follow her encouragement."

He nuzzles my cheek. "Why don't you set one of those clever hands on Alek's head? Give his hair a tug to show him when he's doing particularly well."

I reach out to tangle my fingers in Alex's thick locks. Casimir helps me keep my balance, looping his arm around my waist to stroke my belly and palming one of my breasts with his other hand.

The first few swipes of Alek's tongue are tentative, but in my sensitized state they're giddying all on their own. I urge him toward me, and he captures my sex in the most thrilling sort of kiss. The coarse texture of his scarred cheek rubs against my inner thigh with unexpectedly delicious friction.

As he works me over, gaining confidence with every gasp and whimper he provokes, he glides his hands against my thighs. Somehow that touch amplifies the pleasure of his mouth beyond anything I was feeling before.

"Very good," Casimir murmurs, tweaking my nipple between his fingers in time with the rocking of Alek's head. When his fondling stirs another moan from my chest, he brings his skillful mouth to the crook of my jaw as if in reward.

At my tugging of his hair, Alek exhales roughly across my sex. He delves in deeper, picking up the pace of the movements of his tongue.

There's no doubting his devotion to the task now. He devours me as if he's intent on conjuring every bit of pleasure he can from my body, and all I can do is arch into his mouth.

The bliss that's been building inside me swells higher, tingling through every limb.

"Focus on her clit now," Casimir instructs, his voice roughening. "Stroke the rest of her with your fingers."

Alek complies, clamping his lips around that point of pleasure and flicking his tongue. His fingers massage my folds in time.

A choked sound escapes me. My fingernails dig into his scalp, and then I'm coming, unraveling, washed through with a blaze of ecstasy that leaves me shaking.

When I come back to myself, Alek is gazing up at me with an expression both pleased and a little dazed. He's so gorgeous in his delight at my release that all I can think of is paying him back in kind.

"My turn," I say. "Let's take this out of the water."

I help Alek climb out of the bath and usher him over to the bed, tugging Casimir with us. The courtesan raises no complaint when I scramble onto the covers, dripping, and pull Alek with me.

As the scholar sprawls out on his back at my urging, I take a moment to appreciate the full expanse of his trim form. He watches me, excitement bringing a ruddy tone to his bronze cheeks.

His cock bobs, rigidly erect, drawing my gaze. I lean over him and slick my tongue up his length.

Alek's hips jerk with a stuttered breath. Emboldened by his response, I smile and take him right into my mouth.

His cock has the same cool tang as the rest of him, sweetened by the lingering scent of the bath oils. I'm not really sure of what I'm doing, but I figure Casimir's advice probably applies to this act just as well.

Take my time. Enjoy every part. Build up the pressure and rhythm.

Gradually, I work my way down Alek's shaft, lapping my tongue against him and tightening my lips by increments. Each groan spurs me on.

Casimir strokes my back and offers a murmured suggestion. "Apply extra pressure beneath the head of his cock. Then swirl your tongue right around his shaft."

I suck and flex my tongue, and Alek outright shudders. As I feel his response, renewed arousal pools between my legs.

"It feels so good," he rasps, alternately caressing and clutching at my hair. "So good, Ivy. Casimir, you should be making her feel good too. Fill her… Fill her all the way."

I wonder if that's one of the arrangements from the Woudish erotic poetry book he's become so fond of. I can't complain about the suggestion it's inspired. When Casimir kneels behind me and squeezes my ass, I push into his touch approvingly.

He'll get at least as much out of this act as I do.

As I pump my head over Alek's cock, Casimir guides his shaft between my folds. My first climax wore me out, but part of me clamors for more—to be stretched, to be fully claimed.

"Fuck," Alek mumbles. "Ivy, I can't— I'm going to—"

I simply suck him down harder, willing him to let go. Casimir thrusts into me with a burst of pleasure, I moan around Alek's shaft, and the scholar bucks up to meet me with a breathless grunt.

Then he's coming, hot salty fluid coursing into my mouth as Casimir pulses into me from behind. The almost desperate sounds of Alek's release and the courtesan's practiced strokes send me spiraling faster than I would have thought possible.

I duck my head against Alek's thigh with a gasp. Alek trails his fingers over my hair, murmuring a stream of tender words, while Casimir plunges into me ever faster.

I clench around his cock, my second release crackling through me hard enough to white out my vision. Casimir's breath fragments as he grasps my hip.

He slams into me with even more force, setting off fresh sparks behind my eyes, and spills himself inside me.

As the courtesan rocks to a gentle stop, Alek sits up to guide my mouth to his. I kiss him, long and lingering, and then twist around to capture Casimir's lips in turn.

A warm, mellow sensation has spread through my entire body. I squirm against the sheets. "I just want to curl up here and drift to sleep."

Casimir pecks my cheek. "You can do that. Would you like us to stay?"

A flicker of panic rattles my pulse at the thought of them leaving after the intimacy we just shared. "Yes. Please."

He smiles. "I'll leave Stavros a note, then, so he doesn't go on a rampage trying to find you. Give me a minute, and I'll be right back."

He slips into a robe and heads for the ring of cord we arrived through.

Alek eases me down on the bed and aligns his body with mine. "I wish I never had to be anywhere else."

The raw honesty of those words hits me right in the heart. "Me too," I whisper, feeling oddly shy about the words even though I'm only echoing his sentiment.

How could I ever have dreamed I'd find joy like this here in a den of vicious nobles?

The scholar runs his fingers lightly over the scars across my shoulder blades. "You deserve a life where no one's trying to hurt you. Where you're surrounded by people who want you to thrive. With all the books in every language, all the horses to ride, all the best knives."

I don't know how to answer the tenderness in his voice at all. My throat closes up, and then I manage a dry remark. "It might be a while before I get that if the scourge sorcerers have anything to say about it."

Alek leans in to nuzzle my hair. "I'm going to do whatever I can to make sure you're free of them soon. I've researched all the quarries producing significant amounts of clay across the country—I'm going to start traveling to the closer ones to take a look around."

My pulse hiccups. "If they notice and suspect why you're doing it—"

He kisses my temple. "I can come up with a good excuse. A scholarly one. It'll be a new 'research project.'"

If anyone could frame the investigation the right way, it's Alek. His tone is casual as he talks about it. But a knot forms in my stomach at the thought of him venturing out into the unknown, poking around in the places the conspirators might be hiding their most closely guarded secrets.

I have to crack those secrets from within—*soon*. That's the only way I can protect Alek and the other men from the dangers they're taking on too.

If I can't... I don't even want to think about the price I might have to pay for having this brief bit of happiness.

Casimir returns as quickly as he promised and settles himself onto the bed at my other side. Despite my worries, I find myself lulled into a doze between the warmth of their bodies. It isn't as if I got all that much sleep last night.

Somewhere in the midst of their own slowing breaths and soft caresses, I slip right into slumber. When my eyes flutter open again, I don't know how long it's been.

Alek and Casimir are asleep on either side of me, their bodies relaxed, their breaths even. A renewed glow of joy lights inside me.

I'm about to close my eyes and see if I can get a little more rest when Julita's presence stirs.

*What— You're still— It's been* hours.

I don't understand why she's upset. I open my mouth but hesitate to answer her for fear I'll wake my lovers.

Julita lets out a sound that's almost agonized. *Why am I even here? They don't think about me. I don't matter anymore. They only see you.*

My pulse lurches. "Julita?" I say under my breath, but my sense of her in my head has already contracted again. I don't think she even hears me.

# THIRTY

Ivy

"You can have a bit of a break now," Stavros says to me as we step into his quarters. "The next class today isn't until the fifth bell."

"And I have so many wonderful things to do with my free time." I roll my shoulders, which have gotten a little stiff from standing at attention during his lecture, and move into my now-automatic circuit of the room.

I can't even hope that I'll run into Casimir or Alek someplace we could talk a little. They've both been away from the college pursuing whatever leads they think might get us closer to exposing the scourge sorcerers' plans.

I haven't been able to contribute to that goal at all in the past few days. Since my trial with Benedikt, my palm has stayed blank. There hasn't been so much as a peep from the conspirators.

Maybe they're simply being cautious, giving me plenty of time to reveal ulterior motives before they call on me again. Or maybe they've decided keeping me around is too big a risk, even if the gods appeared to favor me over Benedikt.

Stavros's gaze follows me around the room with a weight of concern that itches at me. He's probably wondering whether *he* made the right choice in backing me if I'm going to be useless to the cause now.

His voice comes out dry but mild. "I'm sure you'll have plenty of company to occupy you again when—"

A quiver of magic races through my nerves from somewhere along the wall. I jerk my hand up to cut off Stavros's remark.

His mouth snaps shut, his brow furrowing. I hold still by the side table I was passing and then carefully crouch down so I can peer beneath it.

The trace of magical energy guides my gaze. It still takes me a moment to spot the fat brown beetle hiding between one of the table's legs and the baseboard.

*Ugh*, Julita murmurs. *That's an unwelcome sight.*

The impression of sorcery is definitely coming from the bug. And what an appropriate creature for the members of the entomology club to have sculpted.

Frowning, I study it. The beetle stays where it is, unmoving. Nothing about the energy leaking off it shifts.

We still don't know what purpose the conspirators have for the creatures they've been creating out of clay. My riven soul might react to magic in the air, but I can't identify the specifics of what's been cast.

Julita lets out a huff. *What are you waiting for? Squash the vermin.*

My hand balls. I'd very much like to smash the bug out of existence. But beneath my first instinct, another idea is tickling up through my thoughts.

If the conspirators are using their creations to spy on people somehow… we could use that fact against them. Offer them more proof that they should trust that my attitudes align with theirs.

It's worth a shot.

Stavros can obviously tell that I've discovered something, and he knows what I was looking for. He stands silently as I back away from the beetle.

I make a vague gesture that I hope he can understand is encouragement to play along. "I don't want to hear any more about that. How can it not bother you having the royal guards swarming the college day and night?"

The former general's eyebrow ticks upward, but he gamely matches the irritation in my tone. "They're keeping us safe."

I snort. "Keeping us safe or keeping us within their tight restrictions? The daimon were trying to tell us something isn't right, and they've silenced them. It's not like *we* can say anything for ourselves without risking getting arrested."

"I don't think anyone wants to hear the kinds of things you've been hinting at," Stavros replies, letting his voice darken. "Least of all me. Don't shame your family by talking like a traitor."

"Isn't it more traitorous *not* to speak up when something's wrong with the world?"

He scowls at me, getting right into character. "I don't want to hear another word. If I have to drag you to the guards to make sure you're not doing anything more than spouting off senseless rhetoric—"

I stomp toward the door. "Oh, quit acting like you've got the moral high ground here. I'm sure I can find better company than you."

As I grasp the doorknob, I catch his gaze. He offers a slight nod to indicate we're still good, that he knows it was all a pretense.

A pretense I need to follow through with. I stride out into the hall and hesitate there, smoothing my hands down my skirt.

I don't know if our mock argument accomplished anything at all. The beetle could be in Stavros's room for any number of other reasons, not picking up on what we say at all.

At least I tried.

I'll have to make sure it's gone when I get back. Or maybe Stavros will contrive to discover it before then and do the squashing for me.

The peal of the palace bell rings through the Domi's walls, and I find myself remembering another afternoon when I was looking for ways to investigate. My pulse kicks up a notch with a spark of inspiration.

I set off toward the stairwell with renewed determination. No one else is around, so I risk a soft murmur. "Today would be a hunt day, wouldn't it?"

Julita shifts. *I believe so. You'll be able to tell quickly at the stables. But didn't you hate the last time you went?*

I shrug. "I can tolerate the embarrassment if it serves a purpose. I seem to remember a couple of the bug club members participated before…"

*Oh! Yes, you're right. Were they from the group Alek thinks is part of the conspiracy?*

I think back to the scholar's sketches of the members he considered most suspicious. "One of them was for sure. And even if they don't join the hunt this time, word might get around."

I need to do something to feel like I'm moving our mission along. Who knows what the conspirators have been planning while I wait for them to reach out to me again?

Julita goes quiet as I descend the stairs. I've just reached the ground floor when she speaks up again, in a wistful tone. *I wonder how Alek is getting on with his clay research.*

The hint of melancholy to the comment draws me up short with a prick of guilt in my gut.

We haven't talked about how close my relationship with both Alek and Casimir has gotten or about her mournful complaint when she returned to find us all in bed together the other day. I've been waiting to see if she'll broach the subject in her own time... but she's pretended as if it never happened.

Instead of heading straight to the stables, I take a meandering route that leaves me in the courtyard apart from the other roving students. There, I stop to pluck a flower that's sprouted between the blades of grass.

When I hold it to my nose as if to smell it, my hand hides the movement of my mouth. "Julita, if I'm handling anything in a way that upsets you—if it's uncomfortable for you to have to be here with me when I'm with Alek or Casimir—"

*It's fine,* Julita breaks in, too brusquely for me to believe her. *I can pull away—I told you. They want you; you want them—it's good.*

I swallow thickly. "I'm sure they still remember you, think about you."

*Not while they're doing* that *with you. And they shouldn't be. I never meant that much to them, and I know it, so there's nothing more to say.*

I don't think that's all she meant with her remark about them not seeing her anymore. It's true that none of the men have referred to Julita inside me as much as they used to—and Alek vehemently rejected her attempt to talk to him directly.

"We're friends, right?" I say, giving it one more try. "And friends should be able to talk about—"

*There's nothing to talk about,* Julita insists. *Everything is good. You'd better hurry up, or you'll miss the start of the hunt. Oh, gods smite us, there's that pushy guard again.*

I think she's only attempting to change the subject until I shift my attention beyond the flower and realize the ridiculously handsome guard who badgered me while stargazing is marching straight toward me with a stern expression. Although even when he's making a face like he's got a stick up his ass, those blue-green eyes are fucking breathtaking.

I bet the rest of the Crown's Watch hates this guy.

He comes to a stop a few paces away from me and tips his head toward me. "What are you doing wandering around over here?"

I twirl the wildflower between my fingers. "Can't a lady stop to enjoy the flowers?"

He knits his brow at me beneath his chocolate-brown curls, as if he's trying to figure out how flower-picking could be a questionable act. The tingle of magic wafting off him reminds me to be wary of his unknown gift.

Then he asks the last question I'd have expected. "Are you all right?"

I blink at him and scramble for words. "Quite. Even better now that my nose has enjoyed this lovely scent. But now I have places to be."

I hustle on toward the stable, willing him to return to his post.

Thankfully, I haven't missed the hunt. Pampered nobles aren't known for their sense of urgency.

A couple dozen students are milling around the yard outside the stable, most already mounted but a few not even having claimed horses yet. It looks like the hunt master's assistant has only just started handing out bows.

I spot several familiar faces in the bunch: my former bully Anya and a couple of her friends, my rival Romild taking a bow into her arms like it's an extra limb, Petra the distant royal off to the side with her usual reserved distance—and not one but two faces I recognize from Alek's profiles and my own investigations of the entomology club.

Restraining a smile of relief, I hustle into the stable to get my steed.

Toast huffs at the sight of me as if admonishing me for neglecting him. I rub his nose as I lead him out. "Who else would give you a chance at all, huh? You'd better behave, or maybe I'll pick a new favorite horse."

The temperamental stallion stomps a hoof, but then he walks out behind me without more than a brief shake of his reins.

As I mount him, Anya arches her eyebrows at me. "Really? You're riding that beast again?"

I aim a wry grin at her. "We've formed an understanding, and now we get along just fine. Thank you for introducing me to him."

The haughty noblewoman looks as if she's bitten back some caustic comment, probably remembering the understanding the two of *us* reached that ensures Stavros doesn't have her arrested.

Petra catches my eye briefly with a flicker of a smile I pretend I don't notice. She did suggest that I join another of these hunts, didn't she? Does she figure I'm here to kindle a friendship with her?

I'd imagine it's best if the probable conspirators in our midst don't get the impression I'm cozy with any member of the royal family, no matter how minor.

I accept the bow and the sheath of arrows the assistant offers me and wield them with a little more skill than the first time. With a subtle twitch of the reins, I send Toast ambling away from Petra, closer to the bug club members so they'll have a clear view.

If I really had been touched by the gods in my stand-off with Benedikt, I'd be startled by the unexpected talent I seemed to have gained. I might hope my improved skill was permanent.

I stroke my fingers along the wooden curve of the bow and adjust my position in the saddle, giving my best impression of a noblewoman eager to enjoy her newfound ability.

I can tell before the hunt master even directs us into the woods that I'm going to be clumsy as ever with the arrows. If I could throw knives at the conjured targets that appear along the forest path, *then* I'd be showing up the spoiled elites around me.

Instead, I let my face fall with disappointment more and more at every arrow that misses its mark. Partway through the trek, I pause and stare down at my hands as if I don't understand how they could be failing me now.

Great God help me, let the scourge sorcerers be watching my performance. Let them be thinking about how well the gods must have guided me the other day for me to have bested Benedikt then, how much faith they must have in me.

Otherwise I've acted like an idiot for nothing.

I've just prodded Toast back to a trot when Petra draws up beside me. She glances sideways with a purse of her lips. "Have you been getting on well, Ivy?"

I force a chuckle and waggle my bow. "It doesn't seem to be getting on with me."

She shakes her head. "No, I mean… in general."

A trickle of uneasiness winds through my stomach. What is it with people thinking I'm not okay? First that guard, now a royal niece-twice-removed or whatever exactly Petra is.

Do I *look* like I'm in some kind of trouble?

As I debate how to answer, I notice one of the bug club members has turned her head our way. My pulse stutters.

If they get the impression that I really am friends with Petra, any point I've managed to make with my disastrous archery performance won't matter at all.

I lift my chin as if I'm offended that she asked. "I'm sure you have better things to do than worry about *my* well-being."

Before she can respond, I apply my heels to Toast's sides. He breaks into a canter.

Now I have to hope that Petra isn't so offended she complains about me to the king. This is a nice pickle I've found myself in.

Not for the first time, I miss the simplicity of ripping off corrupt merchants and dropping coins on window ledges. At least as the Hand of Kosmel, I always knew exactly where I stood, exactly what needed doing.

I manage to stay ahead of Petra for the rest of the hunt. I also manage to nick the edge of one target, to Julita's excited cheer as if I hit it dead center. Which I guess with my aptitude is about the equivalent.

I keep up my show of being disgruntled with my pitiable skills while I brush Toast down and head back to the college buildings, however much good it's doing. My gut feels heavy.

How much longer will I have to keep up this whole charade?

The question nags at me through Stavros's afternoon class in the field, through a lonely supper in the dining hall, through a quick wash in one of the shared bathing rooms that aren't half as fancy as those in the companionship division.

Then, as I'm toweling myself off, a prickle spreads across my left palm.

I jerk my hand around. The glowing words crawl across my skin.

*Midnight. Same place. Come alone.*

I stare at my palm for a few seconds longer after the message fades away, waiting for relief to wash over me. All that rises up is a vague sense of trepidation.

I got what I was looking for. But I also wish I could be doing anything other than walking into the woods at midnight tonight.

# THIRTY-ONE

*Ivy*

I arrive fifty paces into the woods with a cool autumn breeze nipping at my arms. As I peer through the darkness, I tug my cloak closer around me.

This time, the scourge sorcerers don't make me wait for long. It can't be more than a few minutes before two black-shrouded figures emerge from the thicker blackness between the trees.

Two black-shrouded figures… and a man in noble clothing whose smooth face still holds a touch of baby fat.

I have the vague sense I've seen his face around campus—he's got to be a first year, only eighteen.

I only have two years on him, but seeing his wide eyes and the nervous set of his mouth, I suddenly feel ancient in comparison.

"Come along," one of the shrouded figures says, managing to sound gruff even with the magical warble altering her voice. At least, I think it's a her. "The ceremony will begin soon."

She and her silent companion usher the nobleman and me through the woods at a brisk pace. I sneak glances at the guy, noting the resolve in his shoulders and the set of his jaw.

I'm pretty sure he's a potential recruit just like me. Why are they bringing us together now?

Why are they letting us *see* each other? When Benedikt accused me, they let him stay hidden until they started to doubt his story.

I guess I should be glad that their leaving us on equal ground probably means I'm not about to face another accusation of treachery.

Maybe it's yet another different test. The scourge sorcerers don't want to risk letting us identify any of the established conspirators, but if we turn on our fellow candidates, they'll know we can't be trusted to hold our tongues.

The young man whose name I don't know keeps quiet, so I do the same. I'm not sure what I could say that would be a good idea anyway. This isn't exactly a prime setting for small talk.

Fancy meeting you here! Lovely night to plot against the royal family, isn't it?

I arch an eyebrow slightly in a silent question to Julita. To my relief, she catches on despite the tension that's seeped into our interactions lately.

*No idea who he is,* she says. *If he's a first year, he's only been at the school for a couple of months. He mustn't be in the leadership division, and he can't have done anything all that noticeable.*

I continue studying him, attempting to commit his face to memory. Dark hair, narrow nose, knobby chin, top-heavy body with broad shoulders but narrow hips.

If I can describe him well enough to the other men, hopefully one of them will have some idea who he is.

After several minutes of tramping through the brush, I develop a suspicion of where we're headed. Sure enough, we reach the back wall.

One of our escorts raps on the stones with a low muttering, and the shadowy opening appears in front of us.

The woman who spoke earlier prods me through, her companion and the nobleman following behind. We emerge to find one more conspirator dragging the concealed boat onto the river.

Apprehension prickles down my spine. I hardly feel safe *on* the campus, but my situation is even more precarious when I let these psychopaths guide me beyond the college's walls.

But any hesitation is dangerous. Benedikt proved as much with his confession—he said he only balked briefly at making the sacrifice they demanded before they decided he wasn't committed enough.

An odd twinge passes through me, thinking of him and the last time the scourge sorcerers brought me out here. There's a jab of anger, but also a twinge of grief and guilt.

I hate that Benedikt was selfish enough to turn on me to try to save himself. I don't understand how he could have bought into this madness.

But I also hate that we made him feel inferior, however inadvertently.

I clamber onto the boat with the shrouded conspirators and the nobleman. We glide across through the darkness without so much as a peep from the guard patrolling the back wall.

Maybe the pretty boy who keeps hassling me should put his gift to better use and catch the actual bad guys around here.

On the far bank, we hike for another short distance to a horse-drawn cart. Five more figures are waiting for us there—only two of them concealed by black shrouds.

I eye the other three as I climb into the cart. They study me with equal suspicion.

These must be potential recruits from elsewhere in the city. They're at least middle-warders by their clothing—quality fabrics and clean, no patches or darning.

One is really just a kid, a girl of maybe fifteen or sixteen, but the other two are significantly older than me. I think the woman, whose mousy brown hair is twisted back from her face in a tight bun, must be in her thirties, and the man maybe a decade older. The moonlight catches on the silver flecks in his hair.

Then one of our escorts pulls an arched canvas covering over the top of the cart. A tiny bit of moonlight filters through, but no one will be able to see in... and I won't be able to see where we're going.

*These fiends are cleverer than they have any right to be,* Julita mutters.

Two of the conspirators take seats at the front of the cart to start the horses trotting down the rough track. One of the others sits in our midst.

"We have friends ensuring that our travels stay safe from those who'd oppose our hopes for Silana," she tells us. "If a cry to take flight goes up once we've reached our destination, run straight to the cart. We'll have plenty of advance warning, and the gods will protect us from discovery."

The gods? More like the conspirators' deranged magic.

No wonder it's taken so long for anyone to stumble on the scourge sorcerers. Even Julita only did by chance, because of her history with Wendos. They take every possible precaution to keep themselves hidden.

Even if I called on my men for help, it sounds as if I'd be whisked away before they could reach me.

As I suppress the jitter of my nerves, the shrouded woman retrieves a bottle from beneath her shroud.

"Everyone take a gulp," she says, handing it to the nobleman next to me. "It'll open your minds so you can fully embrace what's ahead."

I don't like the sound of that.

The nobleman makes a face after his swallow and passes the bottle to me. I take a quick sniff, but I don't recognize the sour earthy scent.

Well, I do have plenty of tricks up my sleeve, sometimes literally.

I make a show of filling my mouth and pass the bottle on. Then I raise my arm to swipe my hand across my mouth.

Before I can finish the gesture, the cart bumps on a rut. A dollop of the liquid jolts down my throat.

I spit the rest down my sleeve, silently cursing the lumps in the dirt. At least I didn't swallow a full portion.

As the cart jostles on, a faint fizzing develops beneath my thoughts. It's hard to judge the full effect when I'm just sitting here, but my gut clenches with uneasiness.

I have no idea how long the cart ride lasts. We candidates sit in tense silence. The shrouded figures among us intone in the thick, muddled syllables of the arcane dialect I heard Wendos using, so quietly I'm not sure I'd understand them even if I'd learned the language.

The cart jerks to a halt. Our escorts draw back the canvas to reveal a wide clearing surrounded by sparse forest on all sides.

Nothing I can see stands out as a potential landmark to identify this spot. No doubt that's by design.

There's a big dark heap off at the other end of the clearing, only a jumble of lumps in the darkness. The conspirators don't make any move toward it, directing us in front of the cart before leading the horses farther to the side.

When I walk, my mind seems to list as if I'm a boat on a wavy sea. I swallow thickly, the sour aftertaste of the drugged liquid lingering in my mouth.

If I'm feeling out of sorts, how badly will it have affected those who swallowed the entire mouthful?

Then one more shrouded figure steps into the clearing across from us, leading a man who has his hands bound behind his back and a golden crown on his drooping head.

At the first glimpse, my heart lurches. The crowned man has the same dark hair and strapping build as King Konram.

Julita gasps. *They couldn't really have—*

No, they couldn't. She cuts herself off when he raises his head, and we both see a face similar but not the same as the king's. The nose is large, but more bulbous than hawkish; the eyes are squintier and wider set.

Just a stand-in. But the implications are clear.

They become even more so when the shrouded man leading him lifts his voice.

"This king hasn't proven himself worthy of ruling over us," he says, projecting his words out into the stillness of the night. "All those who wish to lead must be properly tested. Rise to the challenge and make him confirm his might."

I've spent a significant part of the past few days observing Ster. Torstem whenever I could, wanting to make sure I could recognize him if I encountered him in this guise again. It only takes a couple of sentences before I'm sure this is the law professor's authoritative tone, even with the magical warbling disguising it. His cadence sounds just like it does when he's at his lectern.

Before I have a chance to wonder how we're going to "rise to the challenge," one of the other scourge sorcerers presses a knife into my hand. I stare down at it, my fingers instinctively curling around the hilt.

It's a plain one, but I can tell it's sharp from the way the faint moonlight hits the blade. My stomach flips over.

The woman from the city glances around, clutching the knife she was handed. "What are we supposed to do?"

Torstem shoves the false king toward us. "Deal a blow. Cut him deep. If the gods are with him, he'll endure."

*Great God help us,* Julita mumbles.

My magic flickers in my chest, but aimlessly. I'm braced for danger, but my riven power can't tell where the threat is.

In this moment, technically the threat is me.

I adjust my grip on the knife, willing down my queasiness.

I can handle this. I know my way around a blade.

I can make a strike look fierce while avoiding any vital organs or major blood vessels. A superficial wound.

The drug gives me even more of an excuse. They can't expect me to aim properly when my balance is off kilter, can they?

The shrouded figures around us raise their voices. "Test him! Test the king! Find out what he's worth."

The teenage girl darts forward and slashes with her knife. She clearly isn't experienced, but she slices through the man's silk tunic so blood wells against the fabric.

The nobleman lunges forward next, with a breath hissed through his teeth. He stabs the false king in the chest just below his shoulder.

As more blood spurts out, the man grunts. That's the only sign he's affected by the wounds.

I'm next. I grit my teeth and push myself forward, honing my mind as well as I can through the partial haze.

Whip out my hand. Hit him right *there.*

The blade glances off a rib, just as I intended. The impact reverberates up my arm, and the false king wobbles.

I bite back the apology that leaps up my throat and stumble to the side.

The woman from the city steps toward the stand-in, her knuckles pale where she's clutching her knife. She stares at him, at the blood staining his clothes. Her body sways.

Her voice comes out slurred. "I don't... To attack the king..."

Torstem makes a swift motion. Two of the other conspirators grab the woman and drag her away.

"Wait!" she cries out. "I can do it. I could. I just—I just wanted to be sure."

"If you aren't sure already, it's too late for you," Torstem announces, his voice booming through the clearing. "The gods will decide where you belong."

In a grave somewhere with no one knowing what really befell her, no doubt.

My innards lurch between the impulse to leap in and defend her and the need for self-preservation. I hold myself still, telling myself this is the right choice.

Would saving her be worth blowing my entire mission? She's been on board with everything the scourge sorcerers have asked of her until now—how reasonable a person can she really be?

My rationalization doesn't alleviate my growing nausea. As one of the scourge sorcerers clamps a hand over the woman's throat and they disappear between the trees, I avert my gaze.

The older man hurtles at the false king as if determined to show how very willing *he* is in comparison. He rams his knife into the other man's abdomen at an angle that might pierce the liver.

I restrain a wince. That's it. We've all shown our dedication—or not.

Now they'll bring out their healer woman and—

Ster. Torstem strides up to the false king from behind. "It's too late for this king. He's betrayed us all with his claim to the throne. Now we bring him down!"

He slams a dagger of his own right between the man's ribs, deep enough to pierce the heart.

I only just catch a yelp of alarm before it bursts from my throat. My power flares fiercer.

That's the threat. That's a man who'll kill just to make a point.

As the false king staggers, raising no more protest than a groan, my magic tugs at me to heal his wounds. To cast away the villains who staged this vicious "ceremony." To—

No. No, I can't.

I yank it in, and my head spins. A burning sensation spreads across my skin as if my power is trying to sear its way out.

I fumble to suppress it, and I think it senses my drugged weakness. It lashes out with a sharper pain straight through my lungs. I have to clamp my mouth shut against a grunt.

One of the shrouded figures drags the false king into the woods in a different direction from the woman who failed the trial. I swing myself away from them, tensing every muscle in my legs to hold them steady against the onslaught.

I let a little magic free only a few days ago. Gods only know how hard it'd be hitting me if my power wasn't partly sated.

*Oh, gods, Ivy, I'm sorry.*

Julita's sorry? What for? She sounds honestly anguished.

I sputter a puzzled guffaw, which hopefully sounds like derision toward the false king.

My ghostly passenger squirms in the back of my head. *I thought I recognized the smell—Borys and Wendos used a potion like that sometimes to supposedly help them tap into the 'power of their inner mind' or some rot like that. It simply made them act like idiots. I would have warned you, I just— I figured you could deal with it yourself. You handle so much else without needing my help.*

Despite her apology, resentment taints those last words. But between my unsteady mind, the magic I'm still grappling with, and a sudden blaze of fire before me, I can't focus on Julita right now.

The shadowy heap I noted at the far end of the clearing is a big heap of firewood. One of the scourge sorcerers has set it alight. The flames surge up toward the sky, warbling like their disguised voices.

Torstem waves us toward the bonfire. "Come! Let us treat the traitor king the way he deserves. Offer him up to the gods whose will he ignored!"

Great God smite us, he doesn't really mean—

Even as horror wrenches through me at the thought that we might be burning the man he fatally stabbed before the fellow's soul has departed, three of the scourge sorcerers drag a figure far too big to be any living human toward the fire. The wavering orange light glances off stitched together clothes stuffed with straw and a crown that looks like it's made of painted wood tied to the sagging burlap head.

Nice to know the psychopaths draw the line at burning a man alive. For the moment, anyway.

They really aren't hiding their intentions now. There's no mistaking the clear message: they want King Konram dead.

They tried to kill Prince Jacos too. I still don't know if they murdered his older son, Prince Dunstam, years ago.

Maybe I can find out at least one vital fact while they're in a sharing mood.

The shrouded figures motion us new recruits over to haul the straw figure the last few paces to the bonfire. I picture the flames leaping out to catch on their shrouds with an uncomfortable sense of satisfaction and clamp down on my magic when it wriggles up to offer its services.

As I join the others in grasping the straw-stuffed cloth, I let my legs sway a little more, my head loll with our movements. The drunker I seem on their drug, the less they can blame anything that comes out of my mouth on my conscious intentions.

"Death to the unworthy king!" I holler for extra credit, and heave at the figure in time with my current comrades.

The fire roars around the straw figure. In a matter of seconds, body, head, and crown are completely consumed by the flames.

I step back from the heat that prickles at my face, letting a wobble creep into my steps. "There he goes!" I babble, and turn to one of the shrouded figures. "Is this what you did to Prince Dunstam? Gotta get rid of them one by one, right?"

*Ivy*, Julita says nervously, like a warning.

But the scourge sorcerer just chuckles without revealing anything definite. "Everyone will get what they deserve in the end."

I lean closer, tilting my head to the other side and slurring my words. "But really. That *was* you—us—what we're doing here— He didn't really get sick. You took care of him, didn't you? We should celebrate that too!"

A hand claps onto my shoulder, followed by a voice that makes my pulse hitch.

"We should look to what we can do in the future, not dwell on the past," Torstem says.

Which doesn't answer the question either. I don't know whether they're trying to cover up their crime or take subtle credit for a "victory" they can't actually claim.

But with the leader of the conspiracy standing over me, I'm not going to push my inquiry any farther.

I aim a goofy grin at him. "Of course! Let the king burn!"

This one, anyway. What have they done with the living one? *Is* he still living?

Maybe if I can figure out what they've done with his body, that'll be another useful bit of proof.

I lean into my drugged act, playing up my dizziness to maximum effect. I've watched plenty of drunken louts all through the outer wards to know what effects an intoxicant can have on the body and mind.

I raise my fist in the air. "The other fake king should burn too! Let's send him to the gods. Where is he?"

When I stumble off toward the woods, I'm prepared for one of the conspirators to drag me back. But they must assume I won't remember much—let alone be able to do much—in my current state.

Or maybe they trust my loyalty enough now that they don't care what I see.

I stagger between the trees, allowing myself to trip on a root and sprawl in the dirt. Twigs cling to my skirt when I push myself upright.

"Ouch," I mumble, keeping up the dazed act for anyone who might be keeping watch.

Two tiny, darting presences whip past me with a tingle of agitated energy, tossing my cloak over my head. I yank it back in time to spot a faint glint flitting off through the forest.

Daimon. The spirit creatures don't appear to have enjoyed the scourge sorcerers' ceremonial burning any more than I have.

Which direction did the villains take the false king in? I fight through the real haze in my head to solidify my sense of direction.

I think… that way. I meander toward it on a rambling course, as if I'm weaving through the forest mostly at random.

Of course, the conspirators might have carted him off in another direction once they were out of sight. I'll just have to keep roving around, playing the fool, until I stumble on his corpse or they call me back.

I scramble over a log and bumble through a clump of bushes. Then the toe of my boot hits something that makes an odd clinking sound.

Like… like *pottery*.

I do my best not to freeze up. Instead, I act as if I've tripped again to give me an excuse to end up on my hands and knees.

My fingers close around shards of fired clay.

In the darkness, I can barely see them, but I feel more chunks everywhere I touch. Far more pieces than a snake or a rat would break into.

My fingers close around a nob that feels like the shape of a nose. A chill sweeps through my body, turning my blood icy in my veins.

Gods help us all… Are the scourge sorcerers conjuring entire human beings?

# THIRTY-TWO

*Ivy*

The first glow of the dawn has just reached the horizon when I slip into Stavros's quarters. The drug the scourge sorcerers gave us still muddles my thoughts and throws off my coordination alongside a growing fatigue. I managed to make my way to the fourth floor quietly enough, but I push the door closed a little too hard, with a thump that resonates through the room.

A grunt and a sharp breath carry from the bedroom. Stavros charges to the doorway and scans the living space with eyes both bleary and panicked.

He obviously fell asleep during the long time I was gone. His dark red hair and the dress shirt he never changed out of are rumpled. From the urgency in his expression and the tense set of his mouth, I think I might have startled him out of another nightmare.

A nightmare about me, no doubt.

My hand flies up. "Wait!"

I teeter around the room feeling for magic, but the beetle must be gone, and nothing else has taken its place.

I collapse onto the sofa to ease my dizziness. "It's okay," I tell Stavros. "I haven't caused any catastrophes. The scourge sorcerers, though—"

Images from the chaotic night flash through my mind. I leap back up with a lurch of my own panic. "We should meet right away. I need to tell everyone—they're making people. They want to burn the king. We stabbed a man—"

There's too much I need to say—it's all colliding. I grope for the right words and sway on my feet.

*Ivy, I think you should sit down again,* Julita says in a nervous tone. *You've been up all night. It's not like they're staging a coup right now.*

Stavros has already marched across the room to set a steadying hand on my shoulder. "Are *you* all right? Did they hurt you?"

I shake my head, which unfortunately makes my head spin harder. "No. There was a drugged drink—I tried not to swallow—the stupid cart, ruts in the road…" I stop and force myself to inhale and exhale slowly. "I learned a lot. I should tell everyone."

Stavros's grip on my shoulder tightens. "Is there any immediate danger to the royal family or the city?"

"It didn't seem like it. But I don't know. If they have a lot of clay—and they threw the dummy in the fire."

I'm aware that I'm not making a great deal of sense, but I can't seem to keep my thoughts in coherent order.

Stavros nudges me toward the sofa, keeping his hand firmly in place until I've sat down. "I don't think you're in the best condition to explain what happened at the moment. You must be exhausted. Get a few hours' sleep, and then you can tell us everything."

I'm abruptly aware of how heavy my eyelids have gotten. I swipe at my eyes and peer up at the former general.

All the confusion I've felt in the past week swims to the surface, straight past my internal filter.

"Why are you being nice to me now?" I demand. "You should want the scourge sorcerers to murder me. Then you wouldn't need to worry anymore."

Stavros's expression tightens with what might be horror—or guilt. "Ivy, I'd never want that."

I scoff. "You hated me. My soul's still broken. I give you nightmares."

His mouth twists. "I didn't—I didn't hate you. I was afraid of what you might be capable of, but I know I was wrong. I shouldn't have needed to test you to figure it out."

I wave my hand vaguely. "You don't need to feel guilty about it. I'd have wanted to strangle me too. I'm afraid of me—how can I blame you?"

Stavros pauses with an audible swallow. He rests his hand on my shoulder again, gentler now. "You don't have to worry about *me* anymore. Lie down and get some rest. I'll be right here if you need anything."

I have the ridiculous urge to grasp his hand and pull him down on the sofa with me, so he really will be "right here." To sink into the heat of his body and his peppery scent, wrap myself in all the strength that emanates from his massive frame.

Of course, he wouldn't fit lying down on the sofa with me because of that massive frame. I doubt he'd want to be *that* close anyway, no matter what Casimir says.

I shouldn't want him to be either. He probably does still hate me somewhere underneath. He might decide to put another rope around my neck, and even if I can't totally blame him, I do generally prefer being alive.

Stavros lifts his hand to stroke his fingers over my hair—a fleeting caress, but it makes my pulse skip a beat. "If you want to have that meeting, then sleep. We're not going anywhere until you've rested."

I let out a disgruntled huff, but I oblige him by lying down. My eyes close automatically. I'm not sure anything has ever felt as wonderful as these sofa cushions.

I think Stavros is still standing there, watching me—standing guard, like he thinks I might run off again if he doesn't. I can't find the wherewithal to care.

The fog rolls over my mind, and I drift away.

I wake up to a bitter taste in my mouth and a dull ache in the back of my head. But when I sit up, blinking in the bright daylight now streaming through the window at the other end of the room, my head doesn't reel. My body remains steady.

Stavros stands up where he was seated behind his desk. I don't know if he slept more, but he's wearing a new, unwrinkled shirt with an embroidered jacket over it, and he's put on his hand-shaped prosthetic over the stump of his left wrist.

He speaks in a familiar wry drawl, but his gaze fixes on me intently with a twitch of his head. "You've returned to consciousness. Do you have a story that makes a little more sense now?"

I can't remember exactly what I said to him when I first arrived this morning, but enough of our conversation—especially the last part of it—comes back to me that my face flushes.

I glance away with the excuse of grabbing a new dress. "I'll get changed, and then we should signal Alek and Casimir to come to the meeting room. Assuming they're around. It'll be easier to tell all of you at once, and they might know things that'll fill in the missing pieces."

Stavros nods, his tone darkening. "I have a little news of my own."

With that ominous statement hanging over me, I duck into the latrine and hastily swap my grass-stained gown for one more befitting the lady I'm pretending to be. As I fumble with the laces, it occurs to me that I'm going to need Casimir to bring me yet another replacement.

I seem to go through dresses like most people go through dinner.

I bustle back out to find Stavros waiting for me with his cord already looped on the floor and a plate of bread, cheese, and sliced meat in his hand. "I picked you up a little food when I went down to breakfast earlier. Nothing meant to be hot since I didn't know how long you'd sleep."

He's matter-of-fact about his generosity, but a fresh prickle of heat still creeps up my neck as I accept the plate. My stomach lets out an approving grumble. "Thank you."

Julita gives a laugh that sounds a bit stiff. *I obviously should have prodded him more to bring out this unexpected generous side.*

I lift my shoulders in a slight shrug to indicate that I didn't ask for any of this and wolf down the food in approximately five seconds flat.

Stavros waits for me to take my own cord out of the drawer in the sofa-side table where I've been keeping it. Like he's making a show of the fact that he's letting me handle it now.

Am I supposed to thank him for that too? He only handed it over because Casimir asked.

I lay it out in its ring hastily and step through at the same time he does. The magical passage into the palace meeting room hits me with a little more dizziness than usual, but the effect clears the moment I'm on solid ground again.

I prowl the edges of the room to confirm no unwelcome creatures are lurking. Stavros takes his locket out of his pocket and taps it to signal the others.

The sight of it gives me pause. I hadn't fully thought through the part of the plan where we alerted the other men. "Are you sure it's safe to use that? I mean, Benedikt had one too…"

Stavros's jaw tightens. "That problem has already been taken care of."

I'm about to ask him what he means when Alek emerges into the room with a warble of the air. "Is Ivy all—" he's saying before he's even steadied himself. Then he sees me, and a relieved smile springs to his lips.

I step closer to catch his hand for a quick squeeze. "I was summoned by the scourge sorcerers again last night, and it was pretty… intense. I thought I should fill you all in as quickly as possible. And you can tell us about your investigations too."

Alek's mouth slants downward. "There isn't much to report there so far, unfortunately. Plenty of clay quarries and few ways of narrowing them down without taking the trip to visit them."

Stavros dips his head to the scholar. "It's good that you're looking into them at all. None of the rest of us would be able to invent a suitable excuse."

Alek's smile comes back at the former general's praise. "I want to pitch in however I can. All the responsibility shouldn't fall on Ivy."

*I mean, it's not as if you're out there alone,* Julita mutters.

A twinge of guilt runs through my stomach. "At least I've got Julita with me no matter what happens," I say.

Alek blinks, as if he really had forgotten about the ghost who's taken up residence in my head.

Stavros lets out a stiff chuckle. "And we're still glad for any help she can offer, as limited as it might be in her current situation."

Julita lets out a disgruntled sound. *Limited? I've had plenty of useful observations—*

Her rant is cut short by Casimir's arrival. The courtesan steps out of his cord and swipes his disheveled hair away from his eyes, his outfit of dress shirt and trousers looking hastily pulled together. "Sorry. I was still sleeping. I had a late night plying people for information over drinks."

"So did Ivy," Stavros says dryly. Despite his tone, he lifts his hand to rest it on my back long enough to set my skin tingling, guiding me toward the table. "It sounds as though we've all been busy. Let's sit, and our Lady Thief can start by telling us what madness the Order of the Wild has pursued this time."

I settle into one of the chairs, my stomach knotting. But now my mind is clear enough that I can give a cohesive account of last night's events.

As I lay out everything from meeting with the other candidates to our journey across the river to the drugged drink we were given, the men's expressions turn increasingly tense. They barely speak other than sounds of sympathy or protest. But when I describe the young man who also came from the college, Casimir knits his brow.

"I might know him. That sounds like one of the newer students in the companionship division— he's specializing in poetry."

"See if you can arrange to point him out to Ivy in the dining hall or elsewhere so she can confirm," Stavros suggests with his commander's airs, and motions to me. "Where were they taking you?"

My gut only gets heavier as I tell them about the ritual in the clearing. Alek's stance goes rigid when I mention Ster. Torstem killing the false king, and Casimir pales at my description of the burning effigy and the remarks the law professor made.

"They've all but stated outright that they intend to see the royal family dead," I finish. "I don't know how soon they plan on making a move or how they'll do it, but I think we should warn the king of how passionate they are about that goal. And that might not even be the worst of it. I went looking for the body of the false king while the bonfire was still going... but what I found was a bunch of clay shards."

I have the sense that Alek's forehead has furrowed behind his mask. "They killed several of their conjured beasts too?"

I wet my lips. "I don't think so. I think the *man* was conjured out of a sculpture. That must be how they got him to look fairly similar to King Konram. And why they didn't have any qualms about killing him just for a trial."

Stavros's eyes have widened. "Bringing small animals to life is shocking enough. This was a totally convincing person?"

I grimace. "Yes. I mean, he didn't say anything, so I have no idea how much of a mind he had. But I had no suspicion he was anything other than an actual human being until I found the mess of clay."

"Great God help us," Alek says faintly. "If they could be making a horde of supporters..."

Stavros pushes back his chair with a rasp of the legs against the floor. "I think I'd better inform the king of all this as quickly as he can see me." He pauses. "I've already had some other news from the Crown's Watch."

My heart lurches at his tone. "What?"

The former general's eyes have gone stormy. "Benedikt's body was found yesterday evening. In the harbor, made to look like he was wandering amid the boats after having too much to drink, fell in and hit his head and drowned."

He catches my gaze. "He had his locket on him, probably because the conspirators didn't know the significance and wanted to avoid the death looking like a crime by involving robbery."

That's what he meant when he said we didn't need to worry about signaling the men.

*Oh, Benny,* Julita murmurs.

I hug myself, queasiness bubbling up through my chest even though I expected an outcome like this. "At least… At least he can't harm the royal family now. I hope it was a quick death."

Casimir taps his fingers down his front in the gesture of the divinities, his expression downcast. "However much of a scoundrel he decided to be in the end, I hope the same for him too."

Alek stiffens. "You don't think—if the scourge sorcerers can make *people* out of clay—could everything with him have been a trick?"

I stare at him, my stomach flipping over. *Could* it be true…?

But in the first instant I consider the idea, as much as part of me welcomes it, a conflicting certainty rises up. "I don't see how. The replica of the king only sort of looked like him—it doesn't seem the scourge sorcerers can make exact copies. And how would they have known I've got any connection to Benedikt for it to make sense as a trick? Unless they figured out I'm working against them, I guess, in which case they'd have already killed me."

"Not to mention that in every account we've had of the conjurings so far, they've changed back into clay at death," Stavros adds. He pauses, his tone turning even more solemn. "I saw his body myself to confirm. The poor prick."

Alek bows his head. A moment of silence passes between us—the last thing we can offer the colleague who betrayed us.

Then Stavros stands with a nod to Casimir. "Have you discovered anything I should bring up with King Konram as well?"

The courtesan makes an apologetic expression. "No. I'm still chasing down leads that I hope will turn up more concrete information."

"Then I'll make my report now." Stavros pauses. "Ivy, wait here until the next bell. If I'm able to speak to the king right away, he may want to hear more details directly from you."

A shiver runs through my nerves at the thought of facing the king, but I bob my head in agreement. Stavros strides to his ring without hesitation.

When he's gone, Casimir tugs his chair closer to mine and reaches to caress the side of my face. "Every time those fiends call on you, they ask something horrible of you."

I smile tightly. "We knew it'd probably be that way when we came up with the plan. I'm surviving."

Alek makes a face. "You should be able to do more than just *survive.*"

When I look at him, I find I can smile more openly. "I have been, though. Mostly thanks to the two of you."

The scholar's piercing eyes soften. He touches my jaw and leans in for a kiss.

At the brush of Alek's lips against mine, Julita lets out a disgruntled sound. *Well, there's my cue to remove myself again.*

I jerk back, meaning to reassure her, but I can already feel that the tingle of her presence has faded to almost nothing in the back of my head.

"What's wrong?" Alek asks.

"It's not you," I assure him quickly. "It's…"

All Julita's remarks over the past few weeks bubble up to the surface. An ache wraps around my heart, but I know the right thing to do.

I grip Alek's hand to try to soften the blow. "Julita's been feeling discarded now that we've gotten so close. I think she's regretting chances she didn't take when she was alive and having trouble coming to terms with the fact that she won't get to take any chances like that again. It hurts her, seeing us together."

Casimir knits his brow. "That isn't your fault, Kindness."

"No. But if I'm going to live up to that nickname… we should tone down the physical closeness, at least. For now." I don't even know how much longer she'll end up staying with me. "She feels like she has to pull away every time we get at all intimate, and it sounds like she's stuck in this vague dark space when she does that…"

Alek twines his fingers with mine. "You know you haven't done anything wrong, don't you? None of us were involved with Julita that way."

He glances at Casimir, who inclines his head in confirmation. "She never engaged my 'services' as a client or as a friend. Occasional flirtation isn't any kind of claim, even if she were still alive."

"I know." I swallow thickly. "But she's the first real friend I've had. She's helped me through so many of the things I've faced here. And I wouldn't have met you at all if she hadn't trusted me with her mission. I don't want to make her last days here, however few they might be, totally miserable."

From the way she talked during the last trial, she's started to feel as if even I don't really want or need her around.

Casimir offers me a tender smile. "And that's why you do deserve the nickname. We can hold off on the physical displays of affection for the time being. As long as you know it's not for lack of interest." A sly glint enters his eyes.

I laugh. "If I start to doubt that, I'll give you the opportunity to remind me."

Alek still looks pensive. "I know this would be a difficult situation to bring up with her, but at some point you'll need to talk about—"

A flash of light blazes from the mirror in the corner, and his mouth snaps shut. I get to my feet, my pulse thumping faster.

The light must have been some kind of alert that the mirror's magical purpose was activated. It fades away to reveal an image of the king, standing in what looks to be the same room as when we spoke to him right after the attack on the city.

King Konram studies me for a moment in silence. My skin crawls under his scrutiny, but I hold my posture straight and clasp my hands in front of me to stop them from fidgeting.

"Ster. Stavros has informed me of your continuing work infiltrating the scourge sorcerer group," he says abruptly. "From what he describes, they've shown a particular animosity toward me."

I give a slight bow. "I'd say that's accurate, Your Highness."

"I'd like you to give me your full account of the recent ceremony that included my likeness. Leave out no details."

"Yes, of course."

I drag in a breath and go through the story again, pausing here and there to make sure I haven't forgotten anything. When I get to the most violent aspects of last night's events, my lungs constrict, but King Konram doesn't do anything more than frown.

The most reaction I get is when I mention my attempts to uncover his eldest son's fate. His stance stiffens slightly.

He makes a gesture to stop me. "You shouldn't pursue that line of questioning any further. I've confirmed that scourge sorcery had nothing to do with Dunstam's death."

How did he manage to confirm anything about a death several years ago?

But it's hardly my place to debate with the king. I continue on to the end of my account.

"They continue to conceal and obscure everything they can," Konram says when I'm finished. "You still haven't heard any specific plans they intend to carry out?"

I shake my head. "I'm sorry, Your Highness. I'm not considered a real part of their 'order' yet—I suppose they don't trust me enough. But now that they're meeting in larger groups, there'll be more chances for me to identify people. Or, if soldiers could reach us after I send a signal, to take several into custody to interrogate."

The king gives a pensive hum. "From what you've said, they've become very skilled at evading discovery. Given the magic they can wield, I'm not sure any of my people could slip past their sentries unnoticed in order to apprehend the others—especially a large enough squadron to be sure of overpowering them."

My stomach sinks. And what magic might the scourge sorcerers have ready to throw at those soldiers if they did make it close enough to attack?

"I'll try to learn more about their defenses as well," I promise.

"Well, perhaps it's better this way. Even if we could apprehend them, they're far more likely to open up to a supposed ally than an officer of the law, don't you think?"

"That's why we took this course to begin with."

"Then I think we should continue it. We can't even be sure yet how far the conspiracy reaches. I have plenty of guards to see to my immediate protection." King Konram peers at me more closely. "Do you feel *you're* in any significant danger if you stay the course?"

I hesitate, startled by the question.

The king goes on before I need to speak. "My loyal general appears to be rather concerned about your well-being. Do you have any concerns about pushing onward with your mission?"

Gods smite me, has Stavros been trying to appeal to the king on my behalf?

Of course, it'll be as much to ensure I don't fall apart and lose all control over my powers as about my personal safety.

My stomach lurches, but I bob in a slight curtsey. "I'm glad that I can serve the royal family and my country in this way. Also, it would likely be at least as dangerous for me to attempt to withdraw at this point as to stay the course."

King Konram's lips curve into a thin smile. "I appreciate your commitment. It is vital that I know their strategies to fully defend myself, my family, and our country. Do whatever you can to find out what definite actions the miscreants intend to carry out. The risks you're taking will be rewarded."

# Thirty-Three

*Alek*

The midday sun beats down on me from the cloudless sky. It's warmer than I expected for an autumn day, or I'd have dressed in a lighter shirt.

I wipe the sweat from the back of my neck and restrain a grimace at the prickling of perspiration beneath my mask.

Ivy would point out that I could simply take it off. The memory of her hand against my cheek, the affection shining in her eyes when she took me in as I am, still sends a giddy thrill through my chest.

But I've faced enough looks of horror and disgust from other people that I'd rather not risk it. I don't want to give the employees of this clay quarry any reason to hesitate about welcoming my visit.

The sprawling building I'm approaching is appropriately covered with glazed clay tiles to form a mosaic: an image of Creaden, the godlen who presides over construction as well as leadership and justice, raising a temple from the ground with a sweep of his hands while the first king of Silana applauds.

To the left of the main office entrance is a doorway to the on-site shop, a feature I've discovered is common at the clay quarries. The businesses ship most of the materials they dig up elsewhere for craftspeople to work with, but they also like to show off the end product that can be created.

To the right, I note a few wagons of varying sizes around the side of the building. I'd imagine there are storage and equipment rooms at that end.

This is the fourth quarry I've visited in the past week, a little farther from the capital than the others but still close enough to make a day trip of it. I've developed a pattern of investigation that seems to serve me well.

First, I step into the shop room. The woman supervising it bobs her head to me, her gaze lingering on my mask for a few moments with obvious curiosity. "Welcome to the Earthshine Quarry. I hope you find much to enjoy in our wares."

I nod to her in turn, pushing my mouth into a smile despite my self-consciousness. "I can already see the clay produced here is of excellent quality."

I turn toward the display shelves, taking in the variety of dishes, vases, and figurines, some fired plain, others glazed or painted. "Were all of these made on site?"

"Yes, our master potter likes to show off all the many styles that can be applied to our clay."

As I meander along the shelves as if browsing, I draw a small piece of broken pottery from my carry pouch. It's a shard from the snake Ivy captured and Stavros killed.

I've studied the color and texture of it so closely that I can see it when I close my eyes, but I examine it again to compare it to the examples of plain fired clay before me. My heart starts to beat a little faster.

My sample has the same ruddy brown hue as the clay produced here, with an equally fine grain. I rub my thumb over the shard and then touch one of the bowls.

They feel much the same too.

At all of the past quarries, my hopes dwindled at this point as I saw the differences in the materials. But this—this could be the clay that the scourge sorcerers used to make their conjured creatures.

And conjured men too, if Ivy's observations are correct. Knowing her, I'm inclined to think they are.

Suppressing the nausea that pools in my gut at that thought, I tuck the shard away.

"Can I help you with anything or make any suggestions, good sir?" the shopkeeper asks.

I shake my head. "Not at the moment, thank you. I've actually come from Sovereign College with an academic purpose rather than to buy. But it's been helpful seeing the finished product. I'll be sure to recommend this quarry to the artists at the college."

The last comment appears to please her even though I'm not a paying customer. She smiles brightly as I head out again.

I amble over to the office area as casually as I can, attempting to give every impression of a diligent but not overly invested scholar. If this is the source of the conspirators' clay, I don't know how tangled up the employees might be in their schemes.

They could know nothing about what purpose their materials are being put to... or they could answer to Ster. Torstem and the others. I can't give them any reason to suspect that I have an ulterior motive for being here.

As I reach the door, I give my hands a furtive wipe against my trousers, drying the sweat that isn't only because of the day's heat. My heart is still thumping twice as fast as it ought to.

I have no idea how Ivy manages to stay so cool under pressure, dealing with the unnerving trials the conspirators have forced on her. I'm nervous enough just having a chat with a quarry manager.

But maybe if I can handle this conversation well, she won't have to endure any more of those trials. The evidence of the scourge sorcerers' ultimate plans could be right here.

I knock on the door. After a moment, a burly man with a face nearly as ruddy as his clay opens it. His expression flickers between respect for my refined clothes, wariness at the sight of my mask, and a general air of confusion.

"I'm sorry to interrupt your work," I say quickly but smoothly, willing any sign of my nerves out of my voice. "I'm Aleksi Antoniek of Dovia, a scholar from Sovereign College, and I'm conducting a study of mining activities in Silana now compared to under Darium rule. I'd simply like to ask a few questions and take a quick look around—I won't interfere. I have a letter from my supervising professor if you'd like confirmation."

I fish out the small scroll and hold it out to the man. He takes it and scans the contents.

His gaze sweeps over me again, and my skin itches with the sense that he's assessing me as not much of a threat. He rubs his jaw, his eyebrows lifting slightly. "Our operation could be part of a royal study? That's pretty impressive. Come on in. I can give you a few minutes."

He motions for me to follow him into the building. Just beyond a small fore-room, he steps into a large office with a boxy wooden desk. The papers scattering its surface in apparent disarray have my fingers curling against the urge to straighten them out.

The rest of the space is filled by several shelves of paper records, a few books, and various odds and ends that I can now recognize are parts of mining equipment. Probably saved as mementos to mark significant milestones of the business.

There's only one chair, behind the desk, where the burly man promptly sits. Even though he's now much lower than me, he gazes up at me with an imperious air. "My name is Nomar Pavelek, and I'm the manager of the Earthshine Quarry. Worked here for nearly three decades now, manager for two of those. What do you need to know?"

"I'd love to take a look at a few months of sales records to get an idea of where most of your materials end up," I say, with not a little relief at the idea of being able to dive into written accounts rather than trying to cajole information out of a person. "And it'd be helpful to know if there have been any particularly notable transactions or incidents during your time here."

Like, say, a new client suddenly demanding huge amounts of clay materials for some mysterious business they haven't clarified.

I can't say that last part out loud without potentially raising his suspicions, though.

Nomar leans back in his chair, his eyes going distant. After several seconds, he shakes his head. "I can't think of any 'incidents' that'd be of scholarly interest. It's a pretty steady business, not much in the way of dramatics. But I don't mind you taking a look at our books. We don't keep sensitive information in the ledgers, only names and amounts."

I offer an ingratiating smile. "That's all I'd need."

The manager propels himself out of his chair again and strides across the room. He pulls a sheaf of loose papers off one of the shelves and hands it to me. "That covers the first three months of this year. I'd prefer it stayed in this room."

"That's totally fine," I assure him. "I'll look through it and take whatever notes I need to right here."

I retrieve a paper, a small quill, and a tiny pot of ink from my carry pouch to look appropriately scholarly and sit on the floor with my back against the wall as if it wouldn't have occurred to me that I'd need a desk. Nomar goes back to whatever work he was taking care of in his own seat, shooting occasional evaluating glances my way.

Unfortunately, for all my hopes, the ledger papers don't reveal anything particularly enlightening. There are regular shipments of various amounts to the craftsmen's guilds in a few different cities, to a couple of townships presumably for building materials, and to an assortment of smaller clients.

Nothing jumps out at me as reason for concern, although I jot down all the names to look into later. But as I tabulate the figures in my head, my forehead furrows.

I wouldn't call myself an expert after seeing a grand total of three previous quarries, but I've noted certain patterns. This particular operation—the size of the building, the number of vehicles, and the sprawl of the quarry itself—gave the impression of being larger than the other three.

And yet it appears they've been sending out significantly less clay than those others, at least in the past few months. Strange.

I look up from my reading. "Would it be possible for me to examine a ledger from, say, ten years ago?"

Am I being paranoid, or does the manager hesitate for a second before answering. "I don't see why not. Let me find it…"

He skims through the records and offers me another sheaf after I return the first to him. When I scan the new set of figures, certainty congeals in my gut.

There are several substantial clients listed here who were no longer receiving shipments in the more recent records. Some of them might no longer have any need for clay… but a few I recognize from the list of current clients at the other quarries I visited.

"It appears you've lost a number of customers in the past decade," I say in an off-hand tone.

I'm almost certain Nomar's posture goes a tad rigid at the remark. "Oh, our production has slowed a little over the past several years. And tastes change no matter how good our product is."

I suppose that could be the true explanation. I don't know how to prove it *isn't* by talking to this man. He's obviously not going to appreciate me accusing him of lying.

The scourge sorcerers have proven incredibly adept at hiding all evidence of their activities—even the sacrificial accomplices they've mutilated to bolster their magic. I have to handle my investigation with all due care, or a lead could slip right through my fingers.

Pretending to accept the answer at face value, I jot down a few more notes and then return the ledger to its place.

"Thank you so much for your help," I tell the manager. "Would it be a problem for me to take a quick look around this end of the quarry? I promise I'll take care not to fall in."

It's not much of a joke, but it gets me a chuckle out of Nomar. He waves me out. "Take your time. I don't know how interesting it'll be for a scholarly type, but we're proud of the work we do."

Outside, I wander around the side of the building where I saw the wagons. A couple of men are hauling sacks that are presumably full of the clay base onto one of the smaller vehicles.

I amble over to them, my mouth going dry as I scramble to think of how to approach a conversation. I didn't see enough reason for suspicion at any of the other quarries to feel the need to chat with the lower-level workers.

Why would manual laborers want to reveal anything to a privileged scholar from the capital city?

My thoughts trip back to the moment when Ivy presented me with that very provocative book of poetry—to her embarrassed remarks when I told her what it was. Her fear that I'd think she was stupid for making an overture to a noble.

But I assured her that I wasn't a noble in the first place.

I'm not, after all. I'm the son and grandson and great-grandson of merchants.

I might not have any idea what it's like to make a living digging minerals out of the earth and loading them into wagons, but I know a fair bit about goods and customers, production and distribution.

I do my best to loosen my posture as I come around the wagon, letting go of my meticulous academic airs. One of the men heaves the last sack into the back of the wagon and wipes his hands on a rag, peering at me.

With the sort of wry grin I saw my brothers often make when they spoke with the smiths my family employed, I pat the side of the wagon. "Another load about to go out? I hope it's a customer who gives more compliments than complaints."

The other man snorts. "Oh, they all find something to complain about now and then. This one's not so bad." He lifts his chin toward me. "You have some business here?"

I make a flippant gesture with my hand. "I'm just learning about the clay business—finding out how it's changed over the years, what goes into it, that sort of thing. You do important work. It should be recognized. And I know dealing with the clients is probably the hardest part of the job, not hauling the materials around."

The first man lets out a wary chuckle. "You're not wrong about that. Do you have clients to deal with too?" He takes in my fine clothes with obvious skepticism.

"Not recently," I admit. "But I grew up in a family of weapons merchants. Never heard my dad curse so much as when a customer came to him asking him to replace half the merchandise because the shine wasn't quite right on the steel or some other absurd excuse."

To my relief, it seems as if my gambit is working. The worker's stance relaxes a little as he gives a more open laugh. "There are always a few with bizarre requests like that. We had someone last week try to return an entire shipment because they found a pebble in one of the bags. And then there's the client who's so concerned about keeping the purchases quiet that—"

His colleague cuts in with an urgent sound. "Jevam, that's enough."

Jevam shuts his mouth with an abashed expression that only fans the flames of my curiosity.

Someone buying the clay who's being secretive about it? That sounds like exactly a subject I should pursue.

I let out a guffaw as if I'm not taking any of it too seriously. "I wouldn't have thought clay would be a product requiring much secrecy."

The second man waves off my statement. "It's not. He's just exaggerating." He narrows his eyes at Jevam. "We should get back to work. I'll bring the horses around."

He stalks off toward another building that must be the stable. When he's disappeared into the building, I raise my eyebrows at Jevam. "Seems like he's all about keeping things quiet too."

Either I'm not being convincingly uninvested about the topic or his colleague's admonishment has really gotten to him. Jevam simply shrugs. "Not much to tell about it anyway."

I can't let this opening go. I grope for the right way to loosen his lips. "A case like that could give me a new understanding of the trade. That's the whole reason I'm coming out to talk to people like you."

In an instant, I realize I've made a misstep. I've separated us into people like me and people like him.

Jevam's mouth tightens, and he glances away. "Like I said, there isn't much to tell."

Maybe if I show I can relate to his situation, that'll smooth over my stumble? "You can probably imagine we had a lot of hush-hush dealings in the weapons business. I don't know how many times we supplied someone and then the next day armed whoever our first customer was going to go up against." I raise my hands in the air. "That's business for you."

"Yeah," Jevam mutters. "It doesn't make much sense to me when it's just clay."

But then he clams up again. He rubs the back of his hand, pushing up the loose sleeve of his shirt from his wrist, and I notice a ruddy, almost scaly patch of skin there. The thin cracks rippling through it shine an angry pink.

A twinge of sympathy resonates through my gut. That kind of skin condition would only be exacerbated working in conditions like this.

The words spill out before I've really thought them through. "You know, there's a technique that's gone out of fashion for treating painful dryness of the skin. It was common in the time before the Darium invasion. You boil some yimmerbush leaves and bark, which isn't hard to find, and let them steep in the hot water until it cools into a gel. Spread that salve on the spot twice a day, and it might start to clear up."

Jevam blinks at me. "Really? I never heard of that before."

I shrug. "Like I said, it's gone out of fashion. But pre-Darium history is my specialty."

And when I first arrived at the college, I was particularly interested in every possible cure for potentially healing one's skin.

The man looks down at his wrist and then offers me a smile that's almost shy. "There's a big yimmerbush that grows near my house. I'll have to try that. Thank you."

I find myself smiling back. "I hope it helps."

Jevam pauses and then leans in, his voice dropping. "I don't know how it'd help *you* much. But the client I mentioned—we've been bringing clay to them for a couple of years. Lately it's been twice a week. The crazy thing is, they have us take the wagon to a spot about an hour from here, where there's nothing around, pick up the wagon we brought last time that's empty now, and leave the full one. I have no idea where they take it from there."

A shiver runs down my spine. "That is awfully odd. And the manager agreed to that arrangement?"

He grimaces. "They got some special deal for 'discretion.' That's what I heard, anyway. Apparently the guy who came to negotiate it showed the king's seal, and Nomar felt he had to go along with royal authority."

The shiver deepens into a full body chill. I resist the urge to hug myself, releasing a rough laugh as if I merely find the story amusing.

Someone made the arrangements for these secret, escalating shipments of clay using the king's seal.

Someone among the scourge sorcerers was able to gain enough access to the palace to steal that emblem. And if they could do that… who knows what other havoc they might wreak right within the royal family's home?

# Thirty-Four

*Ivy*

When I slip into the dining hall late in the evening, it's nearly empty, as I was counting on.

I wasn't counting on my employer being one of the few figures lingering around the tables.

As Stavros saunters over to intercept me on my way to the counters, he arches his eyebrow. "Didn't you get your fill during our dinner earlier? I seem to recall you shoveling quite a healthy portion into your mouth."

The dry teasing somehow sets me more off-balance than any other attitude I've gotten from him in recent weeks. I know how to brace myself against his hostility, and I can accept his contrition and his aggressive protectiveness even if I find both a little baffling.

This… This feels like the old Stavros. The banter that started to take on a hint of affection rather than criticism in the last few days before the battle in the All-Giver's Tower exposed my magic.

I don't see how we could ever really go back to the way things were. But hearing the warmth in his drawl makes my pulse flutter no matter how much it shouldn't.

I decide it's safest not to look at his stunningly chiseled face directly. Instead, I focus on the last scattered appetizers from the dinner spread.

"*You're* back here too," I point out as I pluck up a couple of delicate pastries, a spiced egg, and a half-roll topped with frothy cheese. "I don't recall your plate being particularly sparse before you polished off the meal."

"I'm not here to eat. I had a student ask if we could discuss her progress while she had her own late dinner."

Ah, that'd probably be the brawny woman I passed on my way in, who marched out looking like she was ready to conquer an invading army all on her own. I guess Stavros gave her a good pep talk.

I add one more tidbit to my plate. "I'm not going to eat either. These are for something else. I had an idea."

Stavros folds his arms over his chest. "Now I'm intrigued."

I cast my gaze past him to our few other schoolmates who are taking their evening meal late. This isn't the place to discuss my ideas about tackling the scourge sorcerers in any detail.

"I'll fill you in if it gets me anywhere useful," I tell him. "I promise it doesn't involve anything death-defying. Now if you'll excuse me…"

I bob in a curtsey that's purposefully mocking, because we are supposed to be at odds as far as the rest of the school is aware.

Stavros takes the supposed insult in stride. "Just make sure you're not out so late you're groggy for our morning class."

I let sarcasm color my tone. "You have my full dedication."

I hold my head high as I carry the plate through the doorway.

The royal guards are so used to bizarre but innocuous behavior from spoiled nobles that neither of the two stationed by the front gate remarks on my cargo. They don't care where I eat my apparent late-evening snack.

As I head down the road between the college's walls and the Temple of the Crown, I tuck the small plate close to my side under the fall of my cloak. A few worshippers leaving the temple glance at me on my way up the steps, but none of their gazes linger.

What I'm doing isn't against any law or standard of propriety, but it is a little unusual. I'd rather not encourage questions.

The vast inner worship hall still overwhelms me when I step beneath its looming ceiling. I swallow thickly and push myself on toward the base of the central tower, the thick column that extends from the ground floor to high above the rest of the roof.

The tower where I sealed Wendos's fate and in some ways my own as well.

I haven't set foot on the spiral staircase since that evening. Girding myself, I begin the climb.

Julita's presence stirs. *Are you sure this is the best place to reach out to the daimon?*

I shrug. "We know there were some up here when Wendos was orchestrating his plans. And they're divine spirits, right? They probably like hanging out in temples in general—when they're not making mischief elsewhere."

*Let's hope they don't decide to hassle you too badly.*

"I don't think we need to worry about that." The city's wandering spirit-creatures haven't disturbed anyone at the college since that night. I doubt they *wanted* to fling around glass during the ball or knock down part of the Quadring—it was the scourge sorcerers imposing their magic on the invisible beings.

But my brief encounter with a couple of them in the woods near the conspirators' bonfire reminded me of how much they might still be affected by the tactics inflicted on them. The scourge sorcerers manipulated them before—and maybe still are in some way we haven't uncovered.

The daimon might be able to reveal things I haven't learned through other means. Anything I can do to bring our investigations and my cozying up to the scourge sorcerers to an end, I'm all for.

I keep climbing until I reach the first slightly wider platform above the level of the roof. Narrow marble pillars frame an alcove with three arched windows. The floor is bare, but lingering traces of wax speak of previous acts of worship.

I set the plate in the middle of the alcove and kneel next to it. No one's sure that daimon ever actually consume the traditional food offerings people leave for them, but I hope they at least appreciate the gesture. This is a finer spread than the scraps of meat and fruit they'd typically receive.

Bowing my head, I extend my senses to check for any trace of magical presence. Nothing catches my attention, but that's not totally unexpected. The spirit-creatures roam all through our world, but I've only noticed traces of their energy when they're particularly riled up.

I inhale slowly, listening hard to confirm there are no human lurkers nearby, and launch into my plea in a low voice.

"Daimon of the city, I offer these delicacies in thanks for the peace you've given us in the past few weeks. I know you were forced to harm us. I'd like to make sure that never happens again. If there's anything you can show me about the people who manipulated you so I can expose them and stop them, I open myself to your help."

Closing my eyes, I will my breath to even out. Will the tension out of my body, as much as I'm capable of it.

If I'm too tightly guarded, who knows if the daimon will be able to convey anything at all?

For the first few minutes, there's only the cooling breeze drifting through the windows and the pang spreading through my knees from my position on the hard floor. Then a quiver of sensation brushes past my arm.

My pulse hiccups, but I hold myself still and calm. The quiver grazes my skin again, tickling over my neck and across my scalp. Another faint impression glides over my hands.

An emotion that isn't my own seeps into my chest: a pang of regret that feels like an apology. Then a tremor passes through my mind, giving me a flash of that high tower room, my fall on the steps, the pressure of the spirits pinning me down.

A lump rises in my throat. "I know it wasn't your idea to hurt me. He was controlling you. Do you know how he managed it? Or what else the people like him were hoping to do? Who else was working with him?"

The memory fractures into a blur of jumbled images that I can't make any sense of. Maybe that's the daimon's way of indicating they've got no answers to my questions.

I settle my nerves as well as I can and give it another shot. "Are they leaving you alone now, or are they still trying to push you around?"

That question results in an immediate jolt of distress. A rush of heat sweeps through me, tightening around my body.

Behind my closed eyelids, I catch a glimpse of billowing flames. But it's dark inside the fire, so dark and cramped, like my very soul is being squeezed—

The sensations fall away, leaving me gasping. My eyes pop open of their own accord, but I can't make out the daimon in the dimming light around me.

"What was that?" I whisper. "What are they doing to you?"

Either the spirit-creatures can't answer me or they're reluctant to. Or they've fled completely at the signs of an impending interruption.

Voices are carrying up the stairs, along with the distant rasp of footsteps. My heart skips a beat.

I'm not doing anything wrong, but I'd rather not have to answer to a devout—or worse, a cleric. And if it's anyone with ties to the scourge sorcerers, they'll wonder why I of all people would be attempting to appease the daimon.

Not for the first time, I'm grateful for my scrawny frame. I tug the plate off to the side of the alcove where it'll be less noticeable and then tuck myself between the wall and one of the columns. There's just enough room for me to pull all the way back into the shadows beyond the nearest window.

I can't see much other than the alcove now, but there is a narrow gap between the column and the wall that gives me a view of the stairs. I peer through it, waiting to see who's bothering to climb the tower this late in the day.

A member of the Crown's Watch appears first, making me even more grateful that I decided to slip out of view. Then my gaze catches on the ornate silk robes of the figures following him.

There's Hessild, the royal family's lead magical advisor, looking as poised and polished as when I saw her during Sabrellia. Next to her treads the unnervingly lopsided man who's a secondary advisor —Lothar, Stavros said his name is. Along with warning me of the man's hatred of the riven.

The third advisor, Tinom, strides along behind them, a little faster to keep up with his shorter stature.

They're in the middle of a conversation. Lothar sighs as he passes my column. "I simply feel it's questionable to put just as much money and energy into celebrating a woman who isn't even Silanian as we do honoring the godlen."

Hessild tsks her tongue. "Signy is an important figure to the people—a symbol of our freedom from our former conquerors. If we had a hero from Silana who'd made anywhere near as much impact, I'm sure—"

She goes on, but my mind stops processing her words when I see who's following behind the three advisors.

There's no mistaking the chocolate-brown curls or elegant features of the guard who's taken to badgering me. As he passes by, bringing up the rear of the procession, a trace of the magic he always seems to be emitting pricks at my skin.

I go even more still, holding my breath.

The advisors proceed on up the next flight of stairs without a glance into the alcove, still debating the merits of the festival for Signy that's happening in a couple of weeks. The guard pauses at the base of the steps and turns toward the alcove.

I can only see a sliver of his pale face—only one of those unsettlingly bright blue-green eyes—but I can tell he's noted the offering plate. He cocks his head.

His gaze skims the alcove and comes to rest on the shadowy nook where I've tucked myself.

My heart thumps faster. My magic twitches in my chest, eager to thicken the shadows and ensure he doesn't see me.

But does it really matter if he does? Is he going to arrest me for skulking in the tower? There aren't any laws against that.

It's certainly not worth risking whatever magical backlash I'd cause.

His mouth twitches with what might be... a hint of a smile? Before I can decide what to make of that, Tinom calls down to him. "Everything all right, guard?"

The guard whips around and hustles up the steps. "Yes. My apologies for falling behind."

I wait in my hiding spot until I'm sure the tower's other visitors are well out of hearing. Then I ease out and crouch by my offering again.

Any serenity I'd cultivated has scattered with my thoughts. I take a few deep breaths and try to return to my meditative state, but I'm too aware of the possibility that I could be interrupted again.

No more images waver through my mind. No tingles of magic pass over my skin. The daimon might have wandered off anyway.

I leave the plate behind in case they decide they do want a snack, however exactly ephemeral beings who don't have mouths or stomachs would consume noble appetizers, and dart down the steps the way I came. I'd prefer to be gone before the advisors make the same trek.

As I hurry back to the college, I contemplate what the spirit-creatures did convey to me. It seems as if the scourge sorcerers have continued meddling with the daimon, just in some new way that has different effects.

They're being trapped or caged somehow? In a place with fire?

Maybe the conspirators are gathering a whole bunch of them to unleash on the city all at once? If they can control a whole horde simultaneously.

But I have no proof of that or anything else they might be plotting. It's mere speculation based on the vaguest of impressions.

I'm just passing through the college gate, charting my path through the conjured maze to this week's obnoxious phrase—*Leering freaks return for rotted lunch*—when my palm prickles with a burst of warmth. I jerk my hand up and catch the brief message as it glows across my skin.

*Welcome to the Order of the Wild. Be ready for the call to your initiation.*

# Thirty-Five

*Ivy*

Alek paces the meeting room with uncharacteristic agitation. "We have no idea what they'll throw at you now that you're supposedly one of them. *Anything* could happen at the initiation."

I lean against the side of the broad table. Tension's been coiled tight around my gut since I got the message from the scourge sorcerers a couple of hours ago.

But I still have to say, "That's been the case every time I've answered their summons. It's always been a risk. At least this time, they trust me enough that I might find out what I need to ensure that I *don't* have to go back again."

Casimir has maintained a warm presence at my side, his hand tucked gently around mine, but a thread of uneasiness winds through even his soothing tone. "This is what you've been working up to. But they didn't tell you when the 'call' would come. Do they expect you to run off to the woods at a moment's notice?"

I shrug. "That's how it worked when Benedikt accused me. They want people who'll be obedient to them above any other duty."

My gaze veers along the empty table. A pang of melancholy resonates through my chest at the thought of the man I believed I could count on as much as the three around me.

The man who was willing to see me dead so he could join the scourge sorcerers' ranks. The man who met a shameful death of his own because I fought back.

The conspiracy is like a poison, tainting everything it touches.

The second Alek pauses in his pacing, Stavros begins his own restless prowl of the room. "We can hope that there'll be a large group of the conspirators together for the initiation. You should signal us with your locket once you're all together—I can lead a squadron of the Crown's Watch to arrest them. We can put an end to this and see you safe all at once."

The determination in his tone sets off a different sort of pang in my heart. He sounds honestly concerned about my well-being.

I still don't know how to wrap my head around his renewed protectiveness.

"The king didn't like that idea when I suggested it to him the other day," I point out. "I'm guessing he'll like it even less now that he wants me to find out who's gotten a hold of his royal seal. And we have no idea if it would even work when the conspirators are guarding their rituals so closely. If I'm the only one being initiated, as soon as a sentry warns of soldiers on their way, the scourge sorcerers will know I'm the one responsible."

And gods only know what they'll do to me then, before any squadron can reach me.

Alek's mouth slants at a miserable angle. "They might find out even before then, depending on how much access the conspirators have to discussions in and around the palace."

Stavros exhales sharply. "If the men King Konram sent to spy on the clay quarry catch the next secret delivery in time—"

"Then maybe it won't matter," I break in. "But we don't know how long that'll take or how soon they'll call me. We have to assume I'm going."

A growl escapes Stavros. He glowers at me, but his expression looks more anguished than angry. "I could follow you on my own. Act as a secondary witness. Be ready to jump in if they threaten you in any way."

My throat constricts. I think he means it. He'd jeopardize the entire plan so that he can act as my personal bodyguard.

Does he feel *that* guilty about how he treated me before? Or… does his interest actually run much deeper than that, the way Casimir suggested?

I don't know what to do with that possibility. It hardly matters when I have no idea how long his current dedication to my safety might last.

I manage to keep my voice nonchalant as I set my hands on my hips. "And how far do you really think you'd get before they noticed you? Maybe you could convince them you were tracking me without my knowledge, but they might not want to take the chance and slaughter us both regardless."

Stavros's hand moves to rest on his sword. "I'd slaughter plenty of them first."

I barely restrain myself from rolling my eyes. "Yes, well, true as that might be, I'd still prefer *not* to get slaughtered in the end, no matter how many of them we'd take down with us."

The former general grimaces, but he knows I have a point.

Casimir lifts his head. "There's another possibility we could revisit. Ivy's already needed to use her magic in unplanned ways to protect herself and win over the scourge sorcerers. It's the greatest weapon she has against them."

My power quivers in my chest, bringing to mind visions of the uses I could put it to. Freezing the conspirators in place so they're helpless while the soldiers ride in. Yanking the details of their plans from their mouths.

I brace myself for Stavros's angry refusal, but he's lapsed into a pensive silence instead. His gaze slides to me. "Perhaps it is time we took that step."

I stare at him. "Are you serious?"

He's claimed that he's come to terms with my riven magic, but I never imagined I'd hear the day when he gave it his overt approval.

The former general grimaces. "It isn't my preferred strategy. But we've run out of those. I think it's clear that we can trust your abilities more than the fiends you'd be inflicting your power on."

Alek speaks up, quiet but emphatic. "And it's going to start hurting you again if you keep denying it when you're in danger, isn't it? They're putting you in worse situations than the students here ever did."

I haven't told him how much my magic has already been punishing me. I wet my lips, grappling with a barrage of conflicting emotions.

"I don't… I don't know what would happen if I let it loose on that large a scale," I admit, my hands clenching. "I don't know if I can count on Kosmel to guide the consequences if my life isn't directly under threat. I *could* cause a total disaster."

Casimir strokes his thumb over the back of my hand. "I'm sure it couldn't be worse than what the scourge sorcerers are planning."

"Who can say?" A ragged laugh escapes me. "I don't even know what'll happen to *me* if I give in to the magic that openly. Somehow the middle of a scourge sorcery initiation doesn't seem like a great time to find out just how easily a riven soul can go insane."

Pointing out the danger I could be putting myself in gives all three of the men pause.

"Maybe not," Alek concedes after a moment. "But you have the option. If the situation becomes dire—if you see an opening you can't pass up—"

I can't picture any circumstances where I'd happily give my magic free rein, but I dip my head in acknowledgment. "I'll keep my locket on me too, in case it does seem worth signaling for help."

"You should carry more knives when you go," Stavros says. "You can justify it by saying you wanted to be prepared for anything—they have asked you to stab people in the past."

Casimir gives my hand a quick squeeze. "I should touch up your false godlen brand regularly."

I touch the spot between my breasts where he reapplied some makeup just a couple of days ago. "It's fine for now, but if I haven't been called on in a couple of days, definitely."

Alek perks up. "And I can find some almreed tea for you to start drinking regularly. I don't know what would directly counteract the drugs they'll use without knowing what those substances are, but almreed has a general anti-toxin effect. It'll at least lessen the effects of anything reactive that you ingest."

Julita sighs. *I'm sorry I don't know what drug Borys and Wendos used. They didn't want to share their actual secret "knowledge" with me.*

That's not her fault. I smile for both her sake and Alek's. "I'll do my best to avoid the ingesting, but that'd be great to have as a backup plan."

Stavros rakes his hand through his hair. "All right. I'll keep thinking about additional measures. If anything occurs to the rest of you, call us to this room or pass on the message however you can."

Casimir bumps his shoulder softly against mine, but his gaze lingers on the other man. "I'm sure Ivy knows that we're doing everything in our power to protect her."

Something about those words and the look Stavros shoots the courtesan sends a wobble through my pulse.

The former general steps away, his gaze sweeping over the three of us in our closer cluster. "It's settled then. I'll go on ahead in case there's anything you wanted to… discuss in more privacy."

He steps into his cord and wavers out of view in an instant.

Heat blooms in my cheeks. What exactly does he think we're going to do in his absence?

What does he realize we've already done in the past?

Julita's presence squirms at the back of my skull, but both Alek and Casimir clearly remember what I said to them last time. Alek simply takes my other hand. Casimir gives me a quick but tender peck on the cheek.

"We really will do whatever it takes to see you back here safely," Alek says, his bright eyes flashing with resolve. "And if they hurt you… I won't rest until every one of those pricks is dead and buried."

I grip his hand tightly in return and manage to summon a teasing tone. "Bringing out the violent side beneath the straightlaced scholar. I like it."

Casimir gives my knuckles one last caress. "I'd be right there with him. But in the meantime, I'll pray to all the godlen to watch over you while you defend *them* from this menace. Now you should get some rest. We don't know when you'll be called on."

Alek tugs me into a swift hug that wrenches at my heart. "We'll talk more tomorrow," he says firmly.

After they've departed, I lean against the table for a few moments longer. I want to gather my emotions before I have to face Stavros again.

*That's all?* Julita speaks up in a puzzled tone. *A kiss on the cheek and a hug? You'd think with the danger you're about to charge into, they'd have a little more affection to show.*

A quiver of exasperation runs through my nerves. Now she's complaining that they aren't fawning over me *enough*?

"I told them we should cool off that side of our relationship for now," I say. "It was obviously making you uncomfortable."

Julita hesitates. *I was all right. I never expected—*

I break in before she gives any more of the reassurances I no longer believe anyway. "I know. But you've lost a lot, and I don't want to rub it in your face. I don't want you to feel like you have to hide away in the dark constantly. Having you here matters a lot to me too, in case I haven't made that clear enough. Besides, I've got an awful lot of other things to focus on right now."

*I had no idea— Well. If you think that's best.*

I notice she doesn't protest all that emphatically. Which is fine. I wasn't waiting for her to talk me out of my decision.

"Let's just get through this initiation, and then we can worry about the rest."

She lets out a strained laugh. *We can only hope it'll be so simple.*

When I step through the ring of cord into Stavros's quarters, I find the former general standing by his chest of prosthetics, removing the wooden hand from his wrist harness. He startles at my arrival and turns to face me as I make my now-habitual circuit of the room.

"I didn't expect you back so soon."

After confirming no conjured vermin are lurking around, I offer him a tight smile. "We'd already said almost everything that needed to be said."

"Ah." The former general hesitates, the set of his broad shoulders looking strangely awkward. "I don't know the specifics of what's developed between the three of you, but I hope that neither of them are concerned about you continuing to share my quarters."

"You've managed not to murder me so far, so I suppose they've decided you're not that great a threat to my continued existence."

Stavros's chuckle sounds awkward too. "I didn't mean as far as that… There aren't many who'd like the idea of their paramour living with another man."

I can't suppress the snort that escapes me. "Oh, they're probably happy about that part. They seem to have gotten it into their heads that I'm going to be the next Signy, and I need a full set."

The words have barely spilled from my lips before I realize that I've said them to the last person I'd have wanted to admit it to.

I snap my mouth shut, my cheeks flaring, and shoot Stavros a pointed glance. "Not that I agree with them or have any designs along those lines."

I won't mention the flicker of heat that washes through my veins when he gazes at me with as much intensity as he is right now.

The corner of his lips curves upward in a hint of his usual cocky grin, the one I haven't seen much of in recent weeks. "Duly noted. I'm glad to hear there aren't any issues of jealousy, in any case."

"Nothing to worry about." I pull myself away from him, my skin still thrumming with unwelcome heat, and head toward the sofa. "I guess we should both get some sleep while we can."

"It has been in rather short supply."

A trace of discomfort in Stavros's voice brings my gaze back to him. He's looking at his bedroom door now, with an expression as if he's dreading climbing under the covers.

A weird sense of guilt knots my stomach. Or maybe not so weird when I know it's nightmares about my possible crimes that have been disturbing his slumber.

After the protection and trust he offered me during our meeting, I can give him a little something in return, can't I?

The suggestion tumbles out before I can think better of it. "I could read some more from our book first. It might help settle my mind too. If you'd like that."

Stavros seems to waver for a moment and then shoots me a self-deprecating smile. "Who would have thought the great General Stavros would need a bedtime story? But thank you—if you aren't terribly tired already, I'd welcome it. Let me undress on my own so I don't offend your modesty. Join me in a few minutes."

As I wait for the rustling from the next room to quiet, I remove my belt and my boots so I'll be able to sit more comfortably while I read.

*You shouldn't feel that bad for him after the way he treated you before*, Julita says tartly. *He hardly needs coddling.*

"It really might help me sleep better too," I murmur back.

She lets out a skeptical hum.

When Stavros accepts my knock on the bedroom door, I find him sitting up at the far end of the vast bed, leaning against the headboard. The loose short-sleeved undershirt that covers everything but his head, neck, and arms leaves whatever modesty I possess completely unaffected. I do my best not to wonder what he might have on—or not—under the covers tucked around his torso.

As I go to retrieve the book from the table where I left it, the former general clears his throat. "Since it doesn't sound as if it'd cause any issues with Aleksi or Casimir, I was thinking—and you can absolutely say no, not that you've ever had any trouble with that before—I would feel even better if you spent the night in here rather than on the sofa. Simply so I'll know immediately if the scourge sorcerers call you away during the night."

I blink at him. "You want me to sleep in the chair?"

The crooked grin comes back. "I was thinking the bed has rather enough room. We can stick to our own ends without imposing on each other's space at all. I'd imagine it'd be more comfortable for you than the sofa."

My fingers tighten around the book. I know from past experience that his mattress is close to divine—he brought me in here after Esmae nearly murdered me.

But his bed didn't have *him* in it then.

I want to say yes at least as much as I want to say no, and I'm not sure I'd like the reasons why if I looked at them closely.

"Won't that be worse for your nightmares?" I say instead. "Having the monstrous riven sorcerer right there beside you?"

Stavros stares at me for a moment, some of the color leaching from his light brown skin. Then he swipes his hand over his face. "Ivy... You're not the villain in the nightmares I've been having lately. And I'm never quite fast enough to save you. So I'd say having you close at hand would help deflect any bad dreams too."

Julita makes a sound like a sucked in breath. The book wobbles in my hand. I can't find my words.

Even after all his apologies and attempts at amends-making, it never occurred to me that he could fear for my well-being on such a deep level it'd infect his dreams.

In my silence, Stavros makes a dismissive gesture. "It's all right. You clearly don't like the idea. Make full use of my chair for the reading, and—"

"No." My heart is beating very fast, and I'm not totally sure why. I don't know if I want the answer to that either. "A bed definitely beats a sofa. If we both stick to our own sides."

Stavros halts, and a softer smile touches his face. My racing pulse manages to skip a beat as well.

"We stick to our own sides," he says like a promise. "You can sleep on top of the covers if you prefer—or I will. Whatever makes you most comfortable."

I swallow thickly. "I'll stay on top for reading, at least."

Stavros nudges one of the plump pillows closer to my side. I prop it up against the headboard and sit gingerly right at the edge of the bed.

He's far enough away that I'd have to lean over to touch him. This really isn't that big a deal.

Insisting on that to myself, I tug on the ribbon to open the book to our last page and focus on the story. "They thought that was the worst of the journey, of course, until they stumbled on the village in the hidden valley…"

# THIRTY-SIX

I jolt out of sleep at an unexpected pressure around my waist.

I tense instinctively and realize it isn't just my waist. There's solid warmth all down my back that matches the weight on my side.

Stavros. He's drawn himself against me on the bed and looped his muscular arm around my belly in a loose embrace, his smoky spicy scent wafting over me.

I don't think he's aware of what he's done, though. The soft, slow rasp of his breath behind me tells me *he's* still asleep.

The heat of him courses right through to the center of me. I'm starkly aware that there are only a couple of layers of thin fabric separating our bodies.

How in the realms did we end up like this?

After he drifted off in the middle of the second chapter I was reading, I set the book aside and tried to doze off where I'd been sitting on top of the covers. But the lacing of my dress felt too constricting.

He has seen me in my chemise and drawers before—including much shabbier ones than what Casimir has supplied for my noble role here at the college. I decided it didn't matter if he happened to see me again and wriggled out of the dress.

But then it was chilly in the open air. And he hadn't stirred from his end of the bed—he'd actually rolled away from me.

I thought it'd be safe enough to tuck myself under the covers at my end. It did help me get to sleep.

Until now.

Julita lets out a faint chuckle. *So much for sticking to his side. He's more interested in sticking to yours. Who would have known Stav is a cuddler when he's asleep?*

I can't tell whether she's annoyed as well as amused. I drop my voice to a whisper. "I definitely didn't. This isn't what I agreed to."

*Hmm. You did put all those ideas about Signy and her lovers in his head.*

She's definitely teasing me. I guess that's better than bitterness?

I grimace. "I didn't mean to say that. And I told him it wasn't my idea."

*It seems he had ideas of his own.*

A lump rises in my throat as I sort through my groggy thoughts. He *is* asleep—he's never shared a bed with me before.

"I doubt this has anything to do with me anyway," I mumble. "He must be used to sleeping with someone else."

How many lovers has the exalted general taken in his time? How many stuck around long enough for him to develop any kind of bedroom habits with them?

Those questions shouldn't stir a twinge of jealousy deep in my gut.

"What should I do?" I murmur to Julita.

I get the impression of her presence shrugging. *He made the move. I can't imagine it'll be easy to detach him unless you want to rouse him. It might be more fun to let him wake up on his own and become horrifyingly embarrassed, if you don't find his nearness too distasteful.*

I don't find it distasteful at all. My body is tingling with eager exhilaration.

Which might be a problem in itself.

But I'm too tired to worry about that right now. Why not enjoy the protective warmth, even if it's not entirely meant for me?

My ghostly passenger isn't wrong. It will be pretty satisfying to see how Stavros reacts when he realizes he snuggled up to me. I'll be able to hold it over his head for *years*.

The thought gives me a strange sense of contentment. I press my head deeper into the pillow and close my eyes, willing the giddiness of my pulse to slow.

If his body is looking to cuddle, I can at least assume he isn't having any nightmares. And maybe the show of supposed affection will convince my mind for one night that he isn't any kind of threat either.

I'm just starting to drift off again when Stavros shifts his position against me. His hand slides down… and dips right between my legs.

*Oh!* Julita exclaims alongside the spike of arousal that shoots up from my core.

In an instant, my sex is aching, my breath catching in my lungs. A gasp stutters out of me.

And Stavros wakes up.

I feel it in the hitch of his chest and the tensing of his muscles against my body. His words come out in a hasty mumble as he yanks his hand away. "Ivy—I didn't—Gods—"

He's started to pull away from me when his frame freezes up even more. A husky note enters his hazy voice. "You're wet for me."

I'm pretty sure my drawers are outright drenched from his unconscious groping. The evidence of my arousal must have lingered on his hand.

I should say something to break the moment, but need is still humming through my body. My lips part, and all that comes out is a whimper that sounds like a plea.

"Fuck," Stavros mutters, so raw a heady shiver ripples through me.

He shifts toward me again, setting his hand on my hip like a question.

This is absurd. I shouldn't want this.

But the only thing I'm certain of in my sleepy haze is how much I do.

My head tips back encouragingly as if of its own accord. My hips give a slight rock, guiding his hand forward.

Another guttural curse spills from Stavros's mouth, his breath hot on my hair. Then his fingers slide back to the place where I craved them most.

I bite my lip but can't quite restrain a moan. Stavros echoes the sound with a ragged breath and ducks his head to brand his mouth against the crook of my neck.

He strokes his hand between my legs, setting off pulse after pulse of pleasure. I open my thighs a little wider to give him more access, and he makes a strangled sound.

"That's right. Want to make you come apart for me. Gods, I want to feel all of you."

He releases me to a whine of protest that I haven't finished before he's delving his hand right beneath my drawers. The caress of his fingers against my most sensitive skin brings another gasp to my lips.

Stavros molds his body against me as he has his way with my sex. His forefinger circles my clit in a spiral of blissful sparks and dips lower to explore my soaked opening. When he curls it right inside me, I shudder with a swell of delight.

Even through the daze of mingled fatigue and pleasure, I notice the bulge nudging against my lower ass. If the strain in his voice and the eagerness of his touch weren't enough to convince me, that'd be plenty of proof of how affected my unintended lover is.

I can't let him keep all the control here, can I? I'm not going to be selfish.

As my hips sway with the rhythm of his hand, I reach behind me. At the graze of my fingers, Stavros growls.

The rocking of his hand speeds up. A second strong finger dips between my folds, parting them, stretching me in just the right way.

As the heel of his hand starts to rub against my clit to giddying effect, I drag my fingers up and down his rigid cock through his drawers. Gods smite me, there's a lot of him.

I guess I shouldn't be surprised if that part of him is as massive as the rest.

Stavros buries his face in my hair, his urgent breaths tickling over my scalp. I'm too lost in the pleasure to figure out where the waistband of his drawers are, but I curl my fingers around his length as well as I can amid the fabric to pump him properly.

With a groan, he bucks into my grasp in time with his pulsing hand. The wave of pleasure is building inside me, already fogging my vision.

Even as I press into his touch, desperate for the release I can taste, I'm determined to bring him with me. I grip him tighter, work my hand faster, reveling in the broken panting that shows he's as lost in the moment as I am.

Stavros plunges his fingers even deeper into me with a graze of my clit, and a dam inside seems to burst.

I come with a rough cry and a clench of my sex around him, the final surge of ecstasy searing through my body. But even as my muscles shake with my release, I manage to pump him harder in turn.

Stavros groans again, how much because of my climax and how much my touch, I don't know. Either way, his hips jerk behind me.

In an instant, his drawers are as damp as mine, the hot spurt of his release soaking through to my wrist.

He withdraws his hand slowly to rest it on my belly, and mine drifts back to my thigh. As our breaths even out and the final shivers of bliss dissipate, a sheen of ice creeps through my chest.

How much did he really want this intimacy with *me*, rather than whatever woman his bleary mind imagined in his sleep?

Will he think I prompted the interlude somehow? Lured him in with my riven wiles?

What if this is the moment that tips him back over the edge to reviling me?

I hate the ache that lances through me at the thought.

I tug myself away over the short remaining space to the very edge of the mattress and flip around to face him. "This wasn't— I didn't mean for this to happen."

Stavros peers back at me, his damaged eyes unfocused in a way he doesn't usually allow them to appear when he's fully alert. He knits his brow. "Of course you didn't. You barely even wanted to sleep in the bed."

The tension keeps constricting around my ribs like a vise. My swallow brings back an echo of the burn of the rope around my throat. "I stayed on my side. I didn't even realize you'd moved until you were already right there."

He frowns and seems to stir himself into greater wakefulness. "I'm not upset. That was—" His head twitches to sharpen his vision. "Curse it all, Ivy, don't look at me like that."

My hands ball between us. "Like what?"

"Like you're fucking terrified of me."

My mouth opens and closes again. I stare back at him, and the only honest thing I can say spills out. "What if I *am* scared of you?"

I don't think I'm imagining the pain that flickers through Stavros's expression. He shifts his hand toward me but stops before it touches my face, maybe noting the stiffening of my posture.

"I've told you how sorry I am," he says hoarsely. "I swear I don't see you as a threat anymore. Gods above, I trust you… as much as I trust anyone in this place."

And there it is. My lungs constrict so tightly I can barely breathe.

I push myself into a sitting position, every part of me braced to run. "But you don't trust me completely. Or you wouldn't feel like you needed to qualify that statement."

Stavros gives a ragged laugh. "This is how I was trained. I don't trust anyone completely—not even myself. It doesn't matter."

The bottom of my stomach has dropped out. I scramble right off the bed, snatching at my discarded dress.

"Of course it fucking does," I retort. "You can laugh about it, because it doesn't matter to *you*. But what it means to me is you could change your mind back again at any moment, after any mistake, and I'd find myself with a noose around my neck after all."

"Ivy." Stavros jerks upright in my wake, but I'm already darting past the bedroom door.

I haul my gown down over me as hastily as I can and toss my cloak over the undone laces. Grabbing my boots, I tuck them under my arm with my balled underskirt.

Every motion, every brush of my drawers against my sensitized parts, reminds me of what an idiot I was just a few moments ago.

With a thump of the covers, Stavros's footsteps barge after me. "Ivy, you have to listen to me—"

No. Listening to him is how I ended up in his bed to begin with.

I bolt for the door and flee down the hall with my cloak flapping around me.

# THIRTY-SEVEN

*Ivy*

From the bathing room I ducked into, I hear the creak of Stavros's footsteps stalking by down the hall. He doesn't know where I've gone, though.

I assume he stopped to pull on trousers before he rushed out of his quarters after me, and that gave me a decent head start.

He's not so indiscreet as to bellow my name and wake half the school's staff. After several minutes, the footsteps retrace their path.

I catch a rasp of a frustrated exhalation. The distant thump of a door closing.

Then there's only silence.

I can't quite rouse myself into action until the palace bell peals through the night—just one ring. Stavros and I turned in pretty early, but I've barely gotten any sleep.

Oh, well. That's typical these days. I'm sure as shit not going back to Stavros's quarters tonight, not even to take the sofa.

I don't love the idea of hiding in the bathing room all night either, though. Everything around me is hard and cold. But I'll need to be properly dressed before I venture farther.

As I set down my boots and straighten out the loose pants of my underskirt, I drop my voice to the faintest murmur. "Quite the mess I've gotten into now."

Julita's voice doesn't lift with a wry remark. It occurs to me that her presence has dwindled to only the slightest tingle in the back of my head.

Of course. She's always been uncomfortable witnessing any sexual intimacy between me and the men she once considered hers.

I can't restrain a wince at the thought. I told her I was cooling things off on her behalf, and then I went and did the exact opposite just hours later.

She probably pulled back into the blankness beyond my awareness as soon as she saw that I wasn't going to reject Stavros's attentions. Maybe as soon as she realized he was offering them at all, consciously or not.

I'm entirely alone.

The knowledge weighs on me as I shimmy the underskirt on over my legs and then reach behind me to tighten the laces of my gown.

I can't go back to Stavros, not after what just happened between us. I can't reach out to Alek or Casimir—even if it wouldn't put them in danger for me to openly seek them out, I wouldn't know where to find them beyond the general area of the dorms.

I couldn't even signal them to a meeting room. I left my locket behind in the pouch of my belt.

As I slip on my boots, I find I'm missing a different sort of weight. I removed my thigh sheaths with their knives when I was stripping down for sleep a few hours ago and didn't manage to catch them up in my hasty grab for my discarded clothes. They're lying on the floor in Stavros's bedroom right now, no doubt.

I have my favorite blade in my left boot, and that's all.

It's served me well enough on its own plenty of times. But remembering that doesn't stop a sense of gloom from washing over me.

I straighten up, fastening my cloak around my neck, and attempt to take stock. My assessment only leaves me more depressed.

I let desire get to my head and all but fucked a man who wanted to see me hung just a week or two ago. I drove away the one person who's been by my side more than anyone through this entire ordeal—not that Julita's had a whole lot of choice in the matter.

And now I'm adrift in this college where I don't even belong, with nowhere to sleep, nothing to do, and no one to turn to while the most dangerous part of my association with the scourge sorcerers looms on the horizon.

Blast it all from sea to sky.

I hug myself against the tightening of my chest, and my mind latches on to the possibility that there is still one figure left I could appeal to. The one who insisted I stick on this path.

Girding myself, I ease out into the hall.

The Domi's common areas are dim, the sconces put out. The streaks of moonlight through the windows at either end of the hall offer just enough illumination for me to find my way to the stairwell and out into the courtyard.

I pull my cloak's hood up over my head, but as usual, the guards don't raise any concerns about my leaving the security of the college. I guess it only really matters whether the people coming *in* have the right to.

The streets of the inner wards are nearly as quiet as the campus, although voices filter from a pub at the far end of the large square outside the temple. The temple's lanterns are still burning, of course, welcoming worshippers through the broad doorway at all hours.

The huge worship room feels even vaster draped in the dense shadows of the night. I halt on the threshold, momentarily overwhelmed.

I've approached Kosmel's statue enough times that I could head straight toward it blindfolded. But my gaze catches for a moment on the voluptuous marble form of Ardone at the other side of the domed room, her perfectly proportioned body poised in a come-hither stance, her full lips curled in a seductive smile.

Maybe I should be asking the godlen of love and sensuality for advice this time.

The thought has barely passed through my mind when I'd swear the statue winks at me.

My pulse hitches. I stare at Ardone's beautiful carved face, but none of her features shift again in the shadows.

It could have been a trick of the light. Or it could be one of those subtle ways the gods like to communicate with us.

I'm not sure which I'd prefer.

I tear my gaze away and stride over to Kosmel's cloaked form. The lanterns' glow turns the trickster godlen's smirk crueler than it's appeared before.

Kneeling by the base of his statue, I bow my head. I pitch my voice as low as when I spoke to Julita, wary of any devouts or fellow worshippers who might be lurking beyond my view.

"I'm tumbling even deeper into this insane game. I'd like to make it back out again. If there's anything you can tell me or show me that will help me through, I welcome it."

I try to open my mind to whatever his divine presence might want to bestow on me, though my gut stays knotted. My muscles brace in anticipation of a message I won't actually welcome all that much.

Nothing comes. The temple remains silent.

The tension in my belly creeps to the base of my throat. The memory rises up of the reassuring touch I thought I felt when I prayed to Kosmel in the cave in the woods, and sudden tears prick at the backs of my eyes.

Have I somehow strayed too far from what he wanted from me, and now he's cast me aside?

I shove down my emotions and reach for one of the dice scattered around his marble feet. A simple yes or no answer. Surely he'll grant me at least that much.

I ask my question only in my head. *Should I keep playing along with the scourge sorcerers?*

The die rattles from my fingers. It bounces across the platform... and comes to rest against the side of Kosmel's boot, tilted at an angle so both the five and the six face equally upward.

I stare at the die for a few thumps of my heart. It doesn't budge.

A rough guffaw travels up my throat.

He might as well have said, "Fuck off, little rogue. You've got to figure this part out on your own."

I push back to my feet, uncertain of my destination. At the same moment, a prickling sensation spreads across my palm.

Oh, no.

I have to look. I have to watch the three letters gleam against my skin in the instant before they fade away.

*Now.*

I've gotten the call to my initiation.

# Thirty-Eight

The message didn't say where to find my supposed co-conspirators, but I've only ever met up with them in one spot. They must figure if I can't work out where to go at this point, I'm not worth initiating after all.

I hustle the last short distance to the campus woods with all the stealth I can bring to bear. My magic unfurls in my chest, niggling at my nerves. Not demanding release yet, but testing me, stirred up by my apprehension.

Julita's presence is still faint. I don't know what the godlen who's pushed me this far wants from me next. None of my allies in the college have any idea I've been called on.

I don't even have the extra knives I meant to bring along for this event.

But the *Now* that glowed on my palm didn't offer any room for argument. I assume they're giving me a little grace so that I can get to the meeting spot from wherever I was before, but not much.

They could be watching me already, taking note of any diversions.

So I stride straight down the path between the trees, fighting the urge to shiver as the cool shadows swallow me.

It's windier than usual today. The gusts of breeze whip my cloak to one side and then the other, whirling through the panels of my skirt. The leaves hiss overhead.

Either the male student who joined me last time didn't make the cut or the conspirators have whisked him away from someplace else. I come to a stop fifty paces in alone. Immediately, one of the shrouded scourge sorcerers steps from the depths of the forest to receive me.

The figure doesn't speak, only beckons me to follow. I catch a faint rustling behind me that might be another conspirator bringing up the rear. Making sure *I'm* not being followed?

But no one has any idea I've been summoned. Even if one of my men was going to ignore my protests and try to watch over me, they never had the chance.

We pass through the back wall again and traverse the river on the concealed boat, the second shrouded conspirator joining us there. Like last time, my guides lead me to a cart, though only one other person is waiting—the teenaged girl who was part of our expedition last time.

As the horses set off, she studies me with wary eyes. Our escorts still haven't spoken to us.

It seems wisest not to break the silence. I'm not sure what I'd say anyway.

At least no one's pressed a cup of mind-addling drugs into our hands.

I close my eyes as if to get some more rest, which honestly I could use. But instead, I do my best to chart every shift in direction, every slight sound that reaches my ears from beyond the cart.

As far as I can determine, we're heading on a northeasterly course from Florian. As we leave the city farther behind, the cart veers more to the east, and the driver taps the horses to a faster pace.

The cart jostles, my tailbone jarring against the boards. Would it kill these people to give their newest recruits a cushion or two?

We must travel longer than last time. We're still moving when I pick up the second-hour peal of a bell from some distant temple, and we keep going for long enough after that I start listening for the set of three peals.

The cart slows. One of the scourge sorcerers ducks into the covered part of the cart with us, carrying a lumpy bundle.

"Put these on," he says, handing part of the bundle to each of us. "You'll become part of the Order of the Wild by tapping into your most primal self. Welcome to the salvation of Silana."

These murderous assholes do think highly of themselves, don't they?

I restrain a derisive snort and paw through the objects I've been given. There's a black cloak, thinner but longer than my own, folded around a simple clay mask designed to cover the upper half of my face.

A quiver of magic radiates off the mask into my soul. It's been enchanted in some way.

The consequences of refusing to put it on are almost certainly worse than the consequences of wearing it, though.

I ease the mask over my eyes and fasten it in place with the two ribbons that wind around the back. Then I swap my brown cloak for the black one.

The billowing wool fastens down the front with a series of clasps, covering my clothing completely. I pull up the hood instinctively.

The girl across from me has donned her own costume of sorts. I can't see any magical effects from the mask on her. Perhaps the vibe I got had to do with how the clay was sculpted rather than any continuing impact it might have on the wearer.

The cart continues on for several minutes longer, until I do pick up the bell for the third hour. Moments later, the wheels jar to a stop under us.

I hear the fire before I see it. We step out from under the cart's covering to see an enormous bonfire crackling only twenty paces away.

It wafts not just heat but prickles of magic as well. The conspirators are probably using their sorcery to conceal the light. I can't even imagine how much power that's taking.

Power they mostly stole from their sacrificial accomplices. Are some of them here too? How soon will they reveal that horrifying part of their practices to the new members?

A softer tingling of magic flows down over my body. I tense instinctively, just as the girl next to me lets out a gasp.

When I spin toward her, her form has changed, and not merely because of the eerie, wavering light from the bonfire. Her mask appears to have stretched and morphed, covering her whole face and jutting up above her forehead with the pointed ears, mottled fur, and yellow eyes of a wild cat.

She's staring at me with as much shock as I feel. I touch my face, but can't feel anything strange about my skin. My mask is still where it was before.

Oh. Her mask won't have changed either. Her new "face" must be an illusion, triggered by our arrival.

More cat-like features sprout from her cloak—furry stripes and a sinewy tail, a flash of claws when she reaches her hand from between the folds. A little of the light shines through those surfaces, confirming that they're illusionary rather than solid.

What creature have the scourge sorcerers concealed me as?

My skin itches at the idea that their magic is all over me. But our guides usher us forward, and I push myself toward the fire.

Now that my vision has adjusted to the blaze, I take stock of the ring of figures around the fire. Some twenty figures are waiting for us, all dressed in the same black cloaks we are, their faces obscured with images of wolves and bears, owls and falcons.

Tapping into our inner wildness. That's what the conspirators told us in the cart.

Which means I still can't see any of my new colleagues. How long are they going to keep us new recruits in the dark about who we're actually working with?

Where have all of these people come from? There are far more than can be just from the bug club. How many are past students, how many other followers Torstem drew in from across the city—and who knows where else?

I have no way of knowing when I can't see their faces.

When I glance at our escorts again, they've drawn back the lower part of their shrouds' hoods to fix their own masks in place. One appears to be a stoat, while the other looks like a snake.

It takes all my self-control not to shudder.

"Join us!" The call goes up from the figures already around the fire, first from one and then echoed by a dozen other voices. We hustle over to fill the space that opens in the ring.

The fire's heat crackles against my face through the illusion. Sweat trickles down my back beneath my gown.

A particularly imposing form whose illusion makes him look like a hawk steps closer to the fire and walks along the inside of our ring of bodies. He holds up a large clay carafe.

They might be casting illusions on our faces, but they aren't bothering to disguise voices any longer. I recognize Ster. Torstem's authoritative tone the instant the first word leaves his mouth.

"Greetings to the newcomers and those already initiated! Tonight the Order of the Wild joins together in our worship of the gods and the old ways that have been forgotten. We'll tap into the essence of who we are and what the world should be. Let us Wildings drink to that!"

He stops by my companion from the cart first and taps her chin. The girl tips her head back, farther at his second nudge, her lips parting.

Torstem holds her chin in place as he pours a dollop of the liquid in the carafe down her throat. My stomach twists, watching.

She has no choice but to swallow. Even through the illusion, the bob of her throat is visible. And Torstem doesn't release her until it happens.

He turns to me next. My magic flares between my ribs, urging me to propel him away, to knock the whole lot of them down.

Would it be enough to destroy this group? Is everyone important here? Could I put an end of the conspiracy just like that?

Even if I could, what would happen after? I don't know where I am, don't know what's nearby, and have no way of communicating with anyone who'd care.

Maybe it shouldn't matter, but images from the stories of evil riven who slaughtered entire villages flash through my mind. I balk, and Ster. Torstem's hand comes to rest against my jaw.

My head tilts automatically, away from his touch. I force myself to open my mouth.

If I can manage to swallow only a little and spit out the rest after…

But the sour liquid sloshes into my mouth so forcefully it's either swallow or choke. I gulp, half gagging, and an unsettling lightness sweeps through my body before the stuff has even hit my gut.

The law professor pats my shoulder approvingly and lets me go. I clamp my mouth against the urge to vomit.

If I did, I suspect he'd come back to insist on another dose.

As he prowls on around the circle, distributing the drugged drink to disciple after disciple, my head spins. The figures around me expand and distort, like monstrous versions of the animals they're hiding behind.

They are monsters. All of them. If I'm going to be a monster, wouldn't slaughtering the lot of them be the most honorable kind of viciousness I could carry out?

*Kosmel*, I think, as loud as I can. *What do you want me to do? I can't unleash that kind of power without you guiding the backlash. I don't know what other disaster I might set off.*

Killing one man years ago left all the gardens in the surrounding neighborhood decimated by the explosion of insects. What would happen if I killed twenty?

How would I explain the end result to King Konram? I'd have gone against his orders. I haven't discovered who infiltrated the palace's defenses or how yet.

No answer feels right.

My stomach turns, and not just because of the toxins working their way through it. My body sways forward and back like a sapling in the wind.

The godlen of luck remains silent. He's left me to take my chances on my own.

Torstem finishes his circle and tosses the clay vessel into the fire. He lifts his arms, turning to take us all in with the fire warbling at his back. "The Order of the Wild remembers the wildness of our past! We will live as humans were meant to be!"

The other figures around the ring raise their hands too. "We will be wild!"

I realize us newbies are supposed to join in too. There are a couple of others who hesitated farther around the ring.

On the second iteration, we all lift our fists and our voices alongside the others. "We will be wild!"

Torstem strides around the ring at a faster pace, urgency creeping into his voice. "We will throw off the taint left by the empire and the usurpers who thought to rise up in their place!"

"We will!" the rest of us echo, though my heart skips a beat. The usurpers?

He leaves no doubt that he's talking about the current royal family with his next statement. "The Melchioreks barged in when the country was unsettled and tried to make it their own. But we know their way is not how it's meant to be. We'll destroy them all and let the gods decide the rightful rulers of our country as they once did!"

I force myself to join the shout, even though my nausea has returned. "We will!"

"We'll hold trials to find the ones who are worthy, and never let the crown pass to anyone unproven!"

"We will!"

The whole world is blurring around me, but even through the muddle in my head, I remember Alek telling me about this sort of thing. How before the Darium invasion, there'd been kingship trials to determine who would inherit the throne.

He wasn't upset that the trials had stopped. He said they were barbaric, that people who would have been great rulers ended up injured or dead.

Of course, the Order of the Wild seems to be all for barbarism.

"We'll bring back all the old laws that were forgotten. We'll honor *our* gods, *our* people. We'll celebrate life by truly living, in all its chaos and savagery!"

"We will!"

Is that what all this fuss is really about? They think Silana was better centuries ago, before the Darium Empire's meddling and everything that's followed?

A laugh I can't totally explain slips out of me. It doesn't matter—others are laughing around the circle too, joyfully. So pleased with throwing away five hundred years that I don't think can all be bad.

But then, what has the stinking royal family done for me that's all that good? It's because of the king I'm here in the middle of this madness. I didn't *want* to be.

What am I supposed to make of anything?

My head reels, and my feet stumble under me. Someone strikes up a tune on a fiddle—a dissonant, jerky melody that only jumbles my thoughts more.

Most of the scourge sorcerers start to move with the sound, curling their fingers and arching their backs, scratching at the air and leaping like the wild things they believe they are.

I find myself joining the strange dance alongside them. My body wants to reach for something beyond this place—something to steady me, something to hold me down. But there's nothing but the chaos Ster. Torstem talked about.

We stomp and spring around the fire, my senses getting dizzier with each step. I grope for my convictions, for the solid sense of why I'm here at all.

I need to identify the conspirators. I need to find out exactly what they mean to do.

At the first thought, my power is already leaping forward in time with the mad dance. My heart lurches, and I snatch after my magic with all my self-control—

But I don't have much left.

My riven power slips through my jumbled thoughts and flings itself at the problem I've identified. The figure just ahead of me staggers to the side.

He clutches at his face, too late. The mask and the illusion attached to it wrench away, revealing Olari's boxy features, taut with a mix of drugged haze and sudden panic.

A surge of triumph rushes through my own panic to contain my magic. I figured he was a part of the conspiracy, but now I know for sure. I can tell King Konram. I—

Across the fire, someone shrieks. I heave myself forward in time to see another of the scourge sorcerers hunching over.

She's clawing at her face—at the mask that seems to have melted down over her nose. It's clogging her mouth. Only a whistle of breath escapes her.

I spin around. No, I have to stop it.

They'll see the connections—they'll realize I'm riven—

A few paces down the ring behind me, another mask rips upward. I recognize the dark eyes and heavy brow of a women I've seen bringing out food in the dining hall.

Over by the carts, one of the horses squeals in pain. A gasp escapes my lips.

What have I done to the animal? Is its harness digging deeper into its flesh?

No, no, I can't let this happen. Startled murmurs are breaking out all around me, along with hysterical laughter from those too far gone to be afraid.

The horse cries out again.

I pitch myself to the side, farther away from the fire, and crouch down with my hands pressed over my mask as if I'm afraid I'll lose it too. As if I have no idea what's happening.

With my eyes pressed tightly shut, I drag my magic back to me. I need to contain it. I need to make sure it doesn't rampage any farther.

I have to shut it away before it gets *me* killed.

My power jerks against my unsteady hold. It could do so much more. It could topple them all to the ground. It could fling them into the fire.

No, I scream at it inside my head. All that'll mean is more chaos. More damage I can't control.

There's a shattering sound—I think the breaking of one of the warped masks. A tendril of my magic escapes me and flits into the fire, sending a flame lashing out at the scattered ring.

More shrieks. I scuttle farther away with my hands tangling in the grass.

Ster. Torstem's voice rises over the furor. "The gods act in unusual ways! They want us to prove we're worthy. Perhaps there's one among us who isn't. Stand and present yourselves."

Fuck. I don't know if I even *can* stand up straight without falling right over again. I'm shaking with the effort to contain the rest of my power. My head feels like it's been tipped upside down and kicked across a field for good measure.

Footsteps rustle through the grass toward me. Can I even trust what words will spill out of my mouth in my muddled state?

In the midst of all the terror and anguish, a clear voice breaks through my whirling thoughts from within them.

*Ivy? What's going on?*

I can't tell Julita—I can't speak to her without them all hearing.

I lift my head, attempting to push myself to my feet, and lose my balance. Instead, I topple back on my ass.

Torstem is stalking toward me, the hawk illusion draped over his face and feathering his cloak looking even more ominous than it did before.

I swipe at my mouth where a hint of the sour flavor lingers, the most answer I can offer my ghostly passenger who's finally returned. "Hard to... hard to keep everything under control," I mumble as if to myself.

Julita must be able to sense enough to figure out the gist of the situation. She speaks quickly but firmly. *Okay. We can get through this. I had ways of staying centered when Borys and Wendos would drag me into their rituals... Press your hands and your feet flat against the ground.*

I follow her instructions automatically, adjusting my legs so the soles of my boots brace fully against the earth, leaning my splayed hands against the grass on either side of me.

*Focus on all that stability,* Julita goes on. *Imagine you have roots growing all the way down into the soil, anchoring you there. Deeper than any drug they could have fed you.*

With every word, the image she's giving me solidifies. I drag air in and out of my lungs and feel those roots as if they've literally sprouted from my palms and heels.

For good measure, I imagine branches unfurling inside me too, weaving into a box to hold my power in.

"The professor's assistant, isn't it?" Torstem says, coming to a stop in front of me. "You look as though you aren't doing all that well."

My attempt at anchoring myself helps me fend off the dizziness. "I think perhaps I drank a little too much wildness," I say, managing to keep up my noble diction, and let out a laugh I hope sounds more breezy than hysterical. "I'm a bit of a lightweight."

He holds out his hand. "Let me help you up."

He's the greatest threat here. He's the one who's orchestrated all the pain and violence.

My magic sears at the imaginary bars of its cage, burning through my veins with a sting so sharp I force another guffaw to cover a gasp. As I lift my hand to take Torstem's, my power flails madly with the desire to blast at least him apart.

Julita lets out an urgent noise. *Your feet are still grounded. Your skin is so thick, no cut you take could ever really penetrate you. Everything important is yours to keep.*

An ache fills my throat. The sentiment she's expressed would have had a much more literal meaning when her brother and his best friend were carving her open to spill her blood in their amateur sacrifices.

As the law professor pulls me to my feet, I will my skin to turn to armor, like the thickest bark in existence. I smile brightly and harden the rest of me.

My magic batters against the new walls I've created, but it doesn't find any cracks this time.

There are other ways I can defeat this man. More important things I need from him than his death.

"Thank you," I say, and turn my face toward the bonfire as if reveling in the heat. "Things seemed to get rather insane for a moment. Why were the gods angry?"

Torstem smiles back with a curl at the corner of his illusionary hawkish beak. "I don't think they were—they were only ensuring we stood our ground. All's well again. There's nothing to be scared of here. The wildness guides us, and the gods are on our side."

I feel his gaze studying me, but I've given no reason for him to suspect I had anything to do with the supernatural disturbances. The only good thing about the reputation of the riven is no one expects to meet one who seems perfectly normal.

I lift my hands to the fire. "How soon do we really begin? How will we get our true kings?"

"Eager to see the change? I like that." He turns toward the fire as well, releasing my hand. "You shouldn't have to wait long. We've been gathering our forces. Within a few weeks' time, we'll be able to cut straight through to the royal family. Everything will fall with them."

I tense my neck to stop my head from jerking around in surprise.

A few *weeks*, and the king could be dead?

"That's good," I coo, the drug slurring my speech without my trying. "So good. Where do we cut King Konram down?"

Torstem lets out a low chuckle. "Don't worry about it. We'll build our connection to the old ways until then. When the time is right, we'll have all the power we need to strike."

# Thirty-Nine

*Ivy*

I have the vague idea that I can grab my cord and my locket without rousing Stavros, leap off to the palace meeting room, and summon the others so maybe I'll have company before I have to face the former general again.

No such luck. I shoulder open the door to find him standing by the sofa in the thin dawn light that's seeping past the curtains.

His stance stiffens at the sight of me. "Ivy—"

"There isn't time," I blurt out, at least as panicked about the thought of having to discuss what we did earlier tonight as about what I've learned from the scourge sorcerers. I snatch my cord from the drawer and brandish it toward him. "We need to talk to the mirror."

I haven't had a chance to make sure there's no conjured creature lurking around this room, so I'm not going to mention the king outright.

Stavros can clearly tell what I mean. He tenses even more, his eyes flashing. "What happened? You're swaying."

I am. I grasp the shelf beside me, steadying myself as well as I can, and toss my cord on the floor. It takes a few jerks before I can get it in a full circle. "I'm fine. Just go."

I hop through the makeshift portal before he can argue.

*What exactly happened between the two of you?* Julita murmurs, sounding as though she isn't sure she wants to know.

"Nothing I feel like discussing," I mutter as I wobble into the meeting room.

In the seconds it takes the former general to set up his own means of supernatural transportation, I conduct my usual survey of the space. No quivers of magic penetrate my lingering dizziness.

The scourge sorcerers don't even know this room exists. We should be safe.

My heart keeps thudding. I slump into one of the chairs so the room will spin less.

Stavros emerges a few paces away, already gripping his locket. As he presses the inside to signal the others, he looks me over with a grim expression and a twitch of his head.

"You got the summons for the initiation," he says. "They drugged you again. You need to rest."

I shake my head and grip the arms of the chair harder against the vertigo the motion provokes. "This is important. The royal family has to start preparing right away, for everything. For anything."

I'm babbling like before. I shut my eyes and focus hard on the set of my feet against the floor, the arms of the chair in my hands.

Julita's presence shifts inside me. *I'm sure the Melchioreks will be all right for another hour or two. You need to look after yourself, Ivy.*

That's what I'm doing, as much as I can justify.

The grounding makes me a little more coherent. "I'll explain to you and the others, and you can explain to the king. In a way that's more organized. I'm sure I can get it all out."

Stavros mutters something under his breath, but he isn't going to jeopardize the king's safety just so I can take a nap.

The second Casimir steps from his own cord, Stavros whirls toward him. "The courtesans must know all kinds of hangover cures. What can you mix for Ivy quickly that'll help take the edge off any kind of intoxication?"

Casimir's gaze flicks to me with a widening of his eyes.

"I'm *fine*," I insist. "Just… just hazy. Fucking sorcerers."

The courtesan turns back to Stavros. "I can grab a couple of things that might help. Give me a few minutes."

He vanishes, and now I'm alone with the last person I wanted to see again.

Stavros's jaw works. "Ivy, about—"

To my immense relief, Alek springs into the room before the former general can do more than start that sentence. "Did the initiation happen already? Ivy, are you all right?"

"Fine, fine," I mumble, but affection swells in my heart at his concern.

I am okay now, aren't I? I'm back with the few people in this world who care about what happens to me.

And maybe I can stay here. King Konram will have to take action after he hears what Ster. Torstem said, won't he?

No more playing scourge sorcerer. No more gritting my teeth and forcing myself through trials and celebrations I find equally awful.

Although, what will I do with myself after that? It's not as if there'll be any reason for me to stay on as Stavros's supposed assistant once our investigations have concluded.

I guess I'll go back to my old haunts… The king implied he'd give me a reward, which'll mean I can distribute even more silver than usual to the people of Florian who need it most…

"Ivy," Alek says from right beside me, and I give a little start. I got so wrapped up in my wandering thoughts that I hadn't noticed him approaching me.

The scholar sets his hand on my arm, and I smile up at him with a sudden tightness in my throat. *He* can't follow me to the streets. Does everything we've shared end here too?

I don't want it to.

The scholar peers down at me with his piercing gaze. "You look upset. What did they do to you?"

A ragged laugh slips from my mouth. "Not much. Shitty refreshments. Clay masks."

Stavros speaks up from farther down the table, where he's wisely keeping his distance. "I think they forced her to take even more of that drugged drink than last time. She definitely seems more affected, but she insisted that she needed to fill us in right away."

I thump the chair arm. "Yes. It's important. When is Casimir coming back? We need him too."

As if conjured by my request, the courtesan appears in his ring of cord just seconds later. He's holding a steaming mug between his hands.

"Here," he says gently, bringing the mug to me. "This should help settle your mind and ease the disorientation. If you don't feel much better afterward, I brought an herb you can chew as well."

I sniff the hot liquid, which gives off a creamy nutty sort of scent that isn't unappealing, and accept the mug. The first tentative sip sends a flood of warmth straight to my gut.

*Cas always knows just how to look after a person,* Julita murmurs.

The men watch, radiating tension as I down the drink as quickly as I can stomach it. By the time I've drained half of the mug, my thoughts are managing to stick in place rather than floating off through my mind before I can totally set them in order.

I keep sipping while I gather those thoughts. More sobriety could hardly be a bad thing.

"The scourge sorcerers had a huge bonfire more than an hour's cart ride east of here," I say. "A few of us new initiates and around twenty established members. Everyone wore masks with magic to totally cover their faces, so I still don't know most of them. Ster. Torstem was leading things, and I ended up seeing Olari from the bug club and one of the dining hall chefs—the dark-haired woman who focuses on the desserts."

"Willone," Casimir supplies. Of course he'd know everyone's name. He grimaces. "I never imagined… Well, I haven't spoken to her much at all."

I nod in general acknowledgment. "We drank the drugged stuff and repeated some things Torstem said about the Order of the Wild, and there was a lot of weird dancing—but what's important is what he said."

I shift my attention to Alek. "You told me before about the kingship trials they used to hold in Silana before the empire took over. Torstem said outright that he wants to destroy the current royal family and hold new trials so we can have 'worthy' rulers. And other things about going back to the old ways. They seem to think that all this wildness they keep talking about is how it used to be in Silana. That's why they think the gods would prefer it—because we behaved like that back then, but we stopped."

Alek frowns. "They can't have a very definite idea of what anyone did all those centuries ago. It's my main area of study, and even with all the books I've had access to, I've still only come across fragmentary mentions of what ordinary life was like. What's survived the empire's purges is mostly references to major events like the trials."

"The scourge sorcerers took a few pieces they liked and ran with them," Stavros mutters, "making the rest up to suit themselves."

I let out a rough chuckle. "Probably. I have no idea how they justify the scourge sorcery element —they haven't mentioned that part to me yet. But I asked Torstem how they were going to eliminate the current rulers, and he said they're almost ready. That they've been gathering their 'forces,' whatever exactly those are, and he thinks they'll be striking at the entire royal family in just a few weeks."

Even Stavros draws up short at that announcement. "A few weeks? How?"

I shake my head miserably. "I couldn't get him to tell me any more detail, only that we'd hear about it when it's going to happen. But I don't know how much advance warning a new initiate would get. I don't know if he might have been making a cautious estimate and it could be as early as a few *days*. The Crown's Watch needs to take some kind of action right away."

Casimir comes up at my other side and brushes a few stray strands of hair back from my face in a soothing caress. "You've done fantastic, Ivy. You went through all that, and you were able to find out the part of their plans we needed to know most."

I rub my face. "I just hope it's enough."

"It has to be!" Alek says. "You can't go back to them when they might drag you into an assassination attempt next."

Julita's voice turns tart. *I should certainly hope not.*

Stavros has started to pace. "Did Torstem or the others say anything else? I need to know everything, even if it didn't seem relevant."

I pry back through my muddled memories of the night. "Before he sent me back here, Ster. Torstem told me to come to the next entomology club meeting, which is tomorrow evening, and that from now on I'll come to the Order of the Wild activities through them. So we got definite confirmation that the club is a front. I'd bet the half of the group that Olari is in supposedly went on a field trip last night."

Alek's mouth flattens into a pensive line. "Did they say anything about the clay? Did you find out what the drug is?"

"No. I didn't want to question them too much about things someone who's actually invested in the cause wouldn't care about—or that I shouldn't know about anyway."

Casimir squeezes my shoulder. "That's fine. You needed to protect yourself while you were out there at their mercy."

I strain my mind, but nothing else comes to me. "The rest was all more of the same—vague statements about removing corrupt undeserving people from power, honoring the gods properly, blah blah blah."

"All right." Stavros stalks over to the mirror. He presses something on the back of it, and a faint thread of magic grazes my skin.

As he steps in front of the mirror, Stavros glances over at me. "I'll do the talking, but you might as well stay here in case the king wants to speak to you directly again. For now, relax and recover."

Casimir teases his fingers over my hair again. "When we're finished here, I think you need a more enjoyable escape. I can book a bathing room like the one we used last time."

I open my mouth to protest, with a pang of guilt both for the rejection I need to make and the fact that I didn't reject other overtures last night.

But the courtesan holds up his hand to stop me. "Just for you, Kindness. I'll see which rooms are available and give you the instructions for accessing it. You can have a soak and a sleep, in whatever order you wish." He aims his attention at Stavros. "As long as your 'employer' won't begrudge you taking a day off."

Stavros's jaw flexes, but he inclines his head slightly. "She needs it. And I only have one lecture today, so her absence won't be all that conspicuous."

His gaze sears into me, reminding me of all the things we haven't really talked about yet. All the reasons I'd rather not catch up on my slumber in his quarters, where I doubt I'll be able to relax much at all.

I clasp Casimir's hand with the most affection I feel comfortable offering while knowing Julita is watching. "Thank you. I can't imagine anything better after all of this."

And then… And then I suppose tomorrow we'll have to talk about where I go from here.

My gut starts to twist, but before my worries can expand very far, the surface of the mirror wavers.

King Konram's image swims into clarity on the glass. His crown balances perfectly on his dark brown hair; his royal jacket and trousers look as neat as if he—or his assistants—spent an hour smoothing out every wrinkle.

If we've summoned him out of bed, he's doing an impressive job of hiding that fact.

"Ster. Stavros," he says in an equally smooth voice. "For you to be holding a meeting at this early hour, I assume you must have a matter of some urgency to convey."

Stavros dips into a respectful bow. "Yes, Your Highness. Very much so."

He summarizes the key points of what I told him much more succinctly than I managed in my still somewhat hazy state. I might appreciate his ability to cut to the chase more if my pulse hadn't started thudding harder as I take in the king's reaction—or lack thereof.

Konram is a consummate politician. Only the barest trace of emotion flickers through his expression at the revelation that the scourge sorcerers believe they'll be murdering him within a few weeks' time.

When Stavros is done, the king is silent for a stretch, absorbing the information. Then he shifts his position as if attempting to peer deeper into the room. "Your assistant who's infiltrated their 'Order of the Wild'—she's still there with you?"

Stavros's stance tenses, but he motions to me. "Yes, Your Highness. She'd be happy to answer any questions you have."

Casimir's hangover cure has dulled the effects of the drug enough that I can walk steadily if a little slower than usual over to the mirror. Stavros remains off to the side, a couple of paces away, as if he thinks I need guarding from the reflection of his king.

I dip into the lowest curtsey I trust myself to manage without losing my balance. "I'm sorry to have brought such dire news, Your Highness."

"Better that I receive it than go unawares," the king says with a hint of dryness that makes me like him a little better. "From what you've observed in your interactions with this group, Ster. Torstem is the leader of the conspiracy?"

"Yes, Your Highness. Whenever he's been present, he's been the one ordering the others around. And he's the head of the bug—the entomology—club that's wrapped up in the group too. He's also the only one we know of who's been finding the orphans to use as sacrificial accomplices. And Wendos referred to him as an authority figure."

King Konram hums thoughtfully, his dark gaze turning more penetrating as he considers me. I'm abruptly aware of my hair hanging loose and probably tangled, of the wrinkles that've no doubt formed in my own clothing during my long night.

"You didn't find any new information about who might have exploited the royal seal?" he asks.

"I'm sorry. They're very careful about how much they say, and I couldn't ask about it directly without revealing that I know more than a regular initiate should."

"Understandable. I assume, then, that they still believe you *are* a regular initiate, loyal to their cause?"

Where is he going with this?

"Yes, Your Highness," I say. "Ster. Torstem even asked me to meet with the entomology club tomorrow."

"Excellent." The king folds his hands in front of him. "I'm sure you can all appreciate that this is a delicate situation. The threat is imminent but unclear. If we wait for the traitors to strike, we may not be fully prepared."

Stavros steps closer. "With your permission, I could rouse Ster. Torstem right now, arrest him and bring him to—"

"No." Konram draws himself a little taller. "It's clear we can't hold back from action any longer, but if we only have Torstem, his imprisonment and trial may simply rile up his supporters and lead to a worse outcome."

I frown. "You could have the bug club members we suspect taken into custody too."

The king's gaze settles back on me. "Stavros said you saw many more conspirators at the initiation ritual than could have been part of that club, didn't he?"

"Yes," I acknowledge. "There are seven members we're reasonably sure are working with Torstem, but I counted around three times as many people at the initiation."

"Then I think we need to strike while they're all gathered together. That will give us the absolute certainty that those we apprehend are guilty, and we can subdue most if not all of Ster. Torstem's followers in one swoop. It does us no good to quell a few of them if the greater portion are still plotting against the crown. And as soon as they know we're making arrests, those we haven't captured will become even more cautious."

Stavros lifts his chin. "What do you suggest then, sire?"

King Konram's attention remains on me. "You've proven yourself adept enough to assist in Stavros's combat classes. I understand you're quite good with a knife."

"I—yes." A chill creeps over my skin. "I can hold my own."

"And Ster. Torstem has allowed you to get quite close to him during these rituals of theirs?"

I remember the closing of Torstem's fingers around mine when he helped me to my feet just a few hours ago. "Yes, Your Highness, he has."

"Then I think the course of action with the best outcome is obvious. The next time his Order of the Wild goes on one of their excursions, find a moment to stab him in the heart or slash his throat. In the ensuing chaos, disable their means of transport and flee after signaling your colleagues by your usual means. Stavros can bring a squad of soldiers to round up the other conspirators. Their distress over Torstem's death should make them easy pickings. And any remaining followers will be lost without a leader to rally around."

My heart stops for the space of a few beats.

Stavros makes a rough noise low in his throat. "Your Highness—you're asking Ivy to assassinate—"

Konram's gaze slides back to his former general. "Let's not think of it as an assassination. That would violate the laws of fair trial. But I'm sure I could forgive, even reward, a subject who was caught up in a horrible uprising and found the strength to strike at the instigators before it was too late."

"I should be the one—"

The king shakes his head at his former general, his expression turning almost bored as if he's already done with the conversation. "I can't have Ster. Torstem slaughtered in the halls of the college. The Crown's Watch will be on guard, and if we have an opportunity to settle the issue sooner, we will. But surely you can see that this strategy allows us the most discretion while removing the primary threat entirely."

"She is only an assistant," Stavros insists. "It's too much responsibility."

"That's not how you spoke about her before." Konram studies me again. "What do you think, Ivy of Nikodi? Do you have the skills and the stomach to carry out this one final task to defend your country?"

Every part of me wants to scream *No*.

Images well up in my mind—my sister's limp body, the crumpled corpse of the man who attacked me years ago, Esmae bleeding out on the floor. My stomach churns.

The king's eyes pin me in place. Will he see me as a traitor too if I refuse him?

I've already cut off my own finger and stabbed a man on this terrible quest. Why wouldn't he expect me to accept this demand too?

This is what the godlen would want anyway, isn't it—the scourge sorcerers not just imprisoned but razed from the earth? That's how *they* handled the last bunch.

But King Konram wants to keep up the appearance of a fair and honorable ruler before his people. Of course he'd have some minor noblewoman from a backwater county carry out the dirty work rather than handle it directly.

For an instant, a flare of anger cuts through my horror. *This* is the ruler I've risked so much to protect? How would he fare in one of those kingship trials if he were put to the test?

The moment the questions flit through my mind, I jolt back to reality with another flood of cold that drenches me from head to toe.

I'm thinking like the scourge sorcerers.

As if any of us can say whether the royal families of the past were the slightest bit more righteous than the one we have now. At least King Konram bothered to ask rather than order.

I square my shoulders, swallowing down my guilt at the traitorous thoughts that gripped me.

Why *shouldn't* it be me with the blood on my hands? I'm more capable than the man before me has any idea of.

"I can do it," I say, with only the slightest rasp in my voice.

Stavros sucks in a breath, but the king smiles before his former general has the chance to speak. "Then it's settled. I look forward to hearing of your success."

"Your High—" Stavros starts, but the mirror is already shimmering back to our reflections.

A taut silence fills the room. I wrap my arms around myself, my fingers curling into the edges of the cloak I retrieved in the scourge sorcerers' cart.

Stavros spins toward me. "Why did you agree? You can't *want* to play assassin."

"Of course not," I snap back, unable to hold back the quaver from the words now. "But how under the gods' gaze am I supposed to say no to the king himself?"

Alek and Casimir come around the table to join us.

"You shouldn't have to," the scholar says, his tone raw with pain. "You're not a killer."

I force a shrug. "I am, though. And I said I wanted to see the scourge sorcerers destroyed. If this is the way to do it with the least damage to the people we're trying to protect, then that's the way it is."

"If they catch you in the act, they'll kill *you*."

His voice breaks with the last word. I clutch my cloak tighter. "I know. But that was always true, wasn't it?"

Except before I was doing everything I could to appease the scourge sorcerers. Now I'm going in with the intention of committing the worst crime any of the conspirators could imagine.

If I can't flee quickly enough—

Dread pools in my gut. I don't want to think about that.

"Ivy…" Casimir's dark eyes flash. "I've tracked down someone who may have information that'll give us a bigger picture. It might not be necessary to go quite that far after all."

I smile at him with a twinge of gratitude, but I can't summon any real hope. "Thank you."

The courtesan touches my cheek and presses a quick kiss to my temple. "I'll see about getting that bathing room for you. You'll need that chance to unwind now more than ever. And if I can get you out of this awful mission, I swear to you, I will."

# Forty

Casimir

The carriage rolls to a stop. My chest constricts around my heart for just an instant before I nudge myself forward to open the door.

From an objective standpoint, there's nothing to be afraid of beyond that door. It's just a baron's country home, and I've visited more than a dozen of those in the past.

But I'm not here to entertain a court noble on holiday. In theory, I'm making a friendly call on an old family friend, though I can't say she was ever really a friend of *mine.*

And I'm not a man of objectivism anyway. My calling is all about matters of emotion, and this conversation is likely to stir up a whole host of those, no matter what guise it's under.

I step out into the crisp fall air. The leaves of the tree overhead gleam in brilliant shades of red and orange. The breeze carries the light floral scents of the last late-blooming flowers from the garden around the side of the sprawling house.

I only take the smallest enjoyment from the pleasant setting as my gaze latches on to the woman waiting by the house's gilded doorway.

Laselle stands shorter than in my memories, mainly because I haven't seen her since I was ten. I have a few inches on her now. Her presence still looms large, though—enough so that I have the instinctive urge to bow even though she no longer has even a passing authority over me.

She must be well into her fourth decade now, perhaps even reaching her fifth, but the creams and powders skillfully layered over her face turn her golden-brown skin perfectly smooth, her eyes large and bright, her rouged lips full nearly to the point of absurdity.

She and my mother both practiced the art of toeing the line, amplifying their beauty to the absolute limit before it became grotesque.

She's kept a figure Ardone herself would admire. A vast ruby-red gown embroidered with gold emphasizes her hourglass figure. Jewels glint amid her intricately whorled hair and around her neck and wrists.

Clearly, Laselle has been doing well for herself as she continues to ply her trade. The most adept courtesans can continue drawing high ranking clients well into their elderly years.

Her current clients are one of the wealthiest couples in King Konram's court. It's taken me this long to track her down because they whisked her off to Icar for a more exotic international trip.

She steps forward with a smile that doesn't part her lips. Her voice is the same resonant lilt that fills my memories, with just a hint of hoarseness. "Cas! So *lovely* to see you after all this time. And you've come all the way from the city—goodness. Come along. We have lunch waiting for us in the pavilion."

I dip my head to her, even though she hasn't offered me the same respect. "It's good to see you too, Laselle."

She sweeps through the garden without another word to me until we reach the rounded, open-air structure that could have held a luncheon for thirty. The chic wooden table and chairs set up in its center look oddly dwarfed by the empty span of floorboards all around it.

Laselle sinks into one of the chairs with perfect grace, and I take the seat across from her. Bread, sliced meats and cheeses, and pastries are already laid out on a few platters between our plates.

A kitchen server appears and fills our cups with a rosy liquid with the sour tang of alcohol. I nod to her in thanks.

My dining partner leans forward, her gaze trailing over me more intently now that we're settled in. "How long has it been? Eleven years? Twelve? Too long, really."

"Eleven," I say evenly, and ignore her last remark entirely. If she'd really wanted to see me again, it'd have been much easier for her to visit Florian than for me to track her down while she toured the country estates beyond the city.

And I wouldn't have welcomed those visits anyway. Her visits in my childhood filled me with even more dread than when I had only my mother's wishes to appease.

Which was unfair of me. Laselle and my mother only wanted me to fulfill my potential, to honor our god in every way I could.

But feelings are feelings, and there isn't much you can do to argue with them.

Laselle daintily picks up a piece of bread and gives me another of her restrained smiles. "And now you're fully grown. You look to have been taking care of yourself well. You must be almost finished with your education, I assume?"

"One year left before I can enter the courtesan's guild," I confirm. The thought combined with my uncertainty about how exactly I want to continue my intended career path sends a thread of tension winding around my gut.

"At this point, I hope you've been pleasing many patrons already." She takes a careful bite of bread and cheese, showing just the slightest hint of her teeth. Not enough to reveal the row of jeweled replacements at the back of her mouth, but I know she has four sapphires embedded there.

Half as many gaudy teeth as my own, yet the sacrifice I planned never seemed to be enough in her mind.

"I've been quite active since I started the college program," I say, avoiding any mention of my current partial hiatus. "They encourage us to put our skills to use for a lesser fee. You can never learn as much as you do with the actual people you're meant to please."

"Well spoken. Perhaps you've managed to fill part of the void your mother left." Laselle's eyes narrow. "But why are you serving your own pleasure with countryside visits when there must be plenty of others who'd enjoy your services? Or more learning you could be doing?"

I swallow thickly behind my own smile. Flickers of memories rise up of the cutting glares and sneering remarks whenever my mother caught me taking a moment of my own leisure.

*I didn't bring you into this world for you to loll about baking in the sun.*

*Don't tell me you took a ride on your own. Of all the useless things…*

*If your head is too empty to think of anything you need to be doing, you ask me. I can think of plenty.*

*Where's your appreciation for the life I gave you? You want to ruin me all over again?*

I make my tone as ingratiating as I'm capable of. "I was hoping I might learn more from *you.*

After all, you were Mother's greatest friend. I haven't had the benefit of her guidance in so long. I thought hearing of your own recent patronages might give me further inspiration."

Laselle simply hums dismissively and nibbles at her bread. An ache spreads up through my abdomen.

She isn't going to tell me anything if I don't make the right sort of appeal. It's been too long since I knew her, and I had only a child's understanding of her interests then.

Well, my gift can help with that.

I press my replaced molars gently against each other in my mouth and draw on the magic Ardone blessed me with in exchange, holding my gaze on Laselle. What could I do that would make her happiest right at this moment?

As always, the answer my gift brings me comes in a current of images and impressions. The flavor of them makes the ache in my stomach expand.

Ah. So that's really what matters most to her after all, at least when it comes to me.

I suppose I shouldn't be surprised. My mother always talked as if she wanted nothing from me but accomplishment, but I've always felt as if it was something more like atonement she was looking for.

If it saves Ivy from having to put herself in the scourge sorcerers' hands again and carry out the king's murderous orders, a little abasing is the least I can do.

I push back my chair and sink to my knees, letting my head come to rest against the edge of the table. "Please. The truth is that I feel I've lost my way without your and Mother's steadying advice. I'm not living up to her wishes. I'm not the man she expected me to be yet. Speaking to you is my last hope. Let me learn what I still can from you."

Shame prickles across my face at the humiliating position I've put myself in, but I keep my head bowed to hide it.

Laselle tsks her tongue, but I catch a hint of appreciation in her chuckle. "Well now, that is quite a quandary you've found yourself in. I'm not surprised you've gone astray—it was always difficult for Yonata to keep you in line even with my assistance. I suppose I owe it to her to set you to rights if I can."

I will the embarrassed heat from my face and lift myself back into my chair, maintaining a hunched, humble posture. "Thank you, with all my gratitude. It eats at me every day to think I'm failing to fulfill her legacy."

That last sentence stings coming up. There's a trace of truth to those words.

Why *am* I here and not catering to a patron? Why have I let myself think I can do anything else well enough that it's worth spending my time otherwise?

My mother would have said I should stick to my calling. Pamper Ivy if she'd pay me. Seek out the highest ranked clients I can impress.

Bring about all the delight she can't anymore.

I ball my hands against the niggling doubts. I'm an adult now—I'm my own man. Which means I have the responsibility of deciding the best course of my life for myself.

Not that she necessarily was wrong.

I do my best to hold my uneasiness at a distance while I kowtow to Laselle and ask my simpering questions about her exploits of the past few years. With every tale she tells to teach by example, she manages to work in a jab or two: "You'd need to stretch your creativity farther than you ever bothered." "You have to give yourself completely over to their whims, not let any of your selfish inclinations divert you."

I nod, give my thanks, and make the exclamations of awe I know she'll expect, holding that smile on my face until my cheeks feel ready to crack. I wait until she's told enough tales that I think she could accept a less fawning inquiry, and then delay several minutes longer to be safe.

Laselle gives me a decent opening, tipping back in her chair with a light laugh. "But then, for all their grandeur, a lot of the barons and baronesses have relatively simple tastes at heart. That's why they come out here to escape the complexities of the city courts."

I keep my tone casual, as if this is just another question in the long line. "I've heard a few murmurings about some rather wild parties out in the countryside. Large bonfires, masks, dancing beneath the stars. Are any of your patrons part of that crowd?"

My mother's friend taps her ruddy lips. "I don't think any of the noble families take part in events like that. But I have caught murmurs of my own. When I was calling on Baroness Reginne several months ago, I paid attention to the staff gossip as usual. Apparently one of the house messengers stumbled on some odd traces when he took a shortcut through one of the more distant and little-used areas of the county."

I raise my eyebrows enough to show curiosity, not my full investment. My pulse skips eagerly. "What sort of traces?"

Laselle waves her hand vaguely. "I only heard bits and pieces secondhand. From what I gathered, there were a few scattered bits of burnt wood and something the messenger took to be bone. That was what unnerved him. It seems whoever was carrying on out there, they needed extra internal stimulation to enjoy themselves. He also brought back a strip of dried crozzemi mushroom he found in the same area, and the kitchen staff had quite a night after boiling that. I'd have tried some myself, but it always gives me a headache after."

"Crozzemi?" I repeat. "I didn't think those grew in Silana."

"I can't say I've looked into it. I suppose whoever's indulging, they must have decently deep pockets even if they aren't noble born." Laselle's gaze turns more pointed as it focuses on me again. "I hope you haven't resorted to intoxicants of that sort to enhance your abilities. A true courtesan should be able to please his or her patrons without skewing their sense of reality."

I hold up my hands. "Of course not. I wouldn't touch the stuff or offer it to anyone myself. I was only surprised."

Her eyes linger on me as if she isn't entirely convinced. As if she's thinking it would be just like me to take the lazy route—and lie about it.

I switch to a different angle. "It can't have been much of a bonfire if all they left was a few bits of wood."

Laselle shrugs. "At least they clean up after themselves, whatever they're after with antics of that sort. The real upper class wouldn't lower themselves to messing about in the dirt."

No patrons worthy of us, she means.

It doesn't appear she knows anything more about strange meetings in the counties around Florian. I work in a few more leading questions between more requests for advice, but none of her answers leave me any wiser about the scourge sorcerers' activities.

Still, when I get up from the table, I can bow to her with a satisfaction I don't entirely have to fake, even if it's not for the reasons she'd imagine.

"Thank you for taking the time to share all this with me. I'll continue to do my best to live up to my mother's aspirations for me."

"You do that," Laselle says, and hustles me back to my carriage.

I sit in a stew of uncomfortable memories and anxious thoughts the whole journey back to Florian. When the carriage stops outside Sovereign College's gate, I walk through the steps of the password almost without thinking, my mind already on the conversation ahead.

I don't want to disturb Ivy with a summons if she's still resting from her ordeal, though. I head to the bathing room I reserved for her first.

Peeking inside, I find the bed covers rumpled to show that she's slept there but the room currently unoccupied.

Where else might she have gone if she wanted some peace amid all the pressures laid on her?

I know her well enough to be fairly sure of the answer to that question.

The stables are somewhat busy in the middle of the afternoon as students come and go with their chosen mounts. No one's bustling about at the end of the aisle where Toast's stall is, though.

I wouldn't know Ivy's there either until the faint rasp of a brush over horsehair reaches my ears when I'm only a couple of steps away. My first entirely genuine smile of the day crosses my face as I stop by the stall door.

Ivy looks up from where she's tucked herself away toward the back of the stall, rubbing down the stallion's haunches. Her face brightens with the pleased light that never fails to set my spirits soaring.

The usually irritable horse snorts at me as if expressing annoyance that I might interrupt his grooming session, but he lowers his head with an almost apologetic air when Ivy pats his side. I shouldn't be even a little surprised that she's brought Stavros around when she's managed to tame this animal who until recently was seen more as a curse than a steed.

He stays still when I slip in after her so no one passing the aisle will see us talking.

"Had enough sleep?" I ask, keeping my voice low.

Ivy's smile tenses. She goes back to her grooming, to Toast's approving sigh. "As much as I could. I got restless, so I thought I'd pay this beast a little attention." She swats him teasingly.

"Well, the room is yours until midnight. So if you feel you need to escape back there later, don't hesitate."

"Thank you." She studies me with those brightly knowing eyes of hers, so alert to any sign of trouble. "How did the visit you were going to make go? Did you find out anything?"

I can tell from her tone that she isn't even bothering to hope that I can get her out of the horrible task the king has set her on.

Guilt forms a lump in my gut before I manage to answer. "A little. I think I know where the scourge sorcerers have been holding at least some of their bonfires. And I'm almost certain of what they've been using to drug you."

Even though my offering barely feels like anything to me, some of the tension releases from Ivy's stance. "That could be a big help. I'd love to be able to keep my head clear."

I wish I could promise her that much. "We'll have to see if Alek can track down a viable antidote. I'll pass on word to him as soon as I've finished speaking with you—probably I'll need to call a meeting, but I won't be saying anything I haven't told you now. You should keep relaxing."

I doubt she's been exactly relaxed at any point today, but it speaks to how much stress she's under that she tips her head in agreement rather than insisting on coming along.

Every particle in my body clamors to wrap my arms around her and comfort her the best way I know how.

To stir enough bliss inside her that she can forget her worries for a time. To demonstrate my devotion in the most concrete possible way.

But I hold myself back from doing more than setting my hand on her shoulder. I've let myself forget that it's not just Ivy but Julita I'm engaging with.

And Ivy, for all she balks at my nickname for her, is kind enough that she'd forego her own pleasures to ensure the woman whose soul she's carrying doesn't have to experience more unhappiness before her ultimate departure.

How long will she bury her own happiness to support everyone else's? She's already taken on too many burdens.

I know there's no arguing with her about it, though. She'd think less of me if I did.

Ivy leans just slightly into my touch, deepening my urge to pull her close. It's not as if it'd only be for *her* pleasure. The feel of her against me stirs something in me that's so much more than desire.

Then she peeks up at me through her eyelashes, a hint of slyness mingling with her concern. "You didn't like having to go see whoever you were making the trip to. I hope they weren't too obnoxious."

I haven't hidden my discomfort quite well enough.

I manage a sheepish laugh and allow myself the luxury of a kiss to the side of her head, breathing in the sweet scent of her hair with the smoky tang of the bonfire still lingering in it. "It'd simply been a long time. I wasn't sure what to expect. She was a friend of my mother's. They both had high expectations for me."

Ivy raises her eyebrows. "I find it hard to imagine anyone criticizing your abilities as a courtesan. You said it's a family tradition, didn't you, so they obviously didn't expect you to take up some other career path."

"Oh, definitely not. They wanted me to do as well as possible, that's all."

"Your mother isn't around anymore?"

Gods above, I shudder at the thought of having needed to arrange a meeting between the two women who've meant the most to me. "No. She passed away when I was ten. But the courtesan families look out for each other. I always had people to stay with."

Ivy touches my cheek. "I don't know how she could be anything but proud of who you've become."

My throat chokes up abruptly. I force a guffaw to cover the swell of emotion, but it keeps burning inside me.

My mother would yell at me for coming out here at all, for spending any time on a woman she'd see as a nobody. And maybe I have been lax in my responsibilities, in the debts I'm not sure I'll ever fully repay.

But she'd be wrong about Ivy. Because I know as I gaze back at her, with a certainty that stretches right down the center of me, that all the desire and devotion, the aching and the burn, add up to one word.

Love.

I love her, like I've never loved anyone. Like I had no concept was even possible.

Maybe I shouldn't indulge in the emotion. Maybe it's the selfishness Laselle talked about.

But love is Ardone's highest purpose. This feeling is her blessing.

Nothing could be more honorable to the divine powers I serve.

And if I have to get down in the dirt or spill blood to defend that love, I know with every fiber of my being that I won't hesitate.

# FORTY-ONE

*Ivy*

I don't know what any of the salts and oils are meant to do, so I simply open the bottles and sniff until I find a scent I like. Then I sprinkle the powder liberally into the running water of the bath.

The resulting foam intensifies the soothing herbal smell. I strip off the rest of my clothes and climb into the massive tub.

As I sink into the hot, fizzing water, a long sigh escapes my lips. It's echoed by the voice in my head.

*If there's one thing I miss, it's enjoying a good soak.*

The corners of my lips quirk upward, although a twinge of uncertainty ripples through my gut at the same time. Julita hasn't said much since we returned from the initiation ceremony. I'm not sure how she's feeling right now.

I keep my tone light. "Have I not been bathing to your noble standards?"

She chuckles. *It isn't as if you've had time to indulge in a longer wash all that often. And when you have—*

Julita stops, probably not wanting to touch on exactly what I've been getting up to during my extended baths. The twinge inside me deepens to an ache.

I pick up the cloth I left on the side of the tub and start to rub the lingering grit and sweat from my skin. "Well, if there's any particular oil you'd appreciate or soap you'd prefer, now's the time to tell me."

*No, what you've chosen is just fine.*

There's a sense of reverse to her tone that I'm not used to—not so much as if she's restraining herself but simply subdued. I guess she might be tired too.

I don't push. I massage the soap into my hair, unable to stop a shiver of delight at remembering Casimir's lithe fingers performing the same act, and dunk my head several times to rinse it. Then I work in some of the cream that's supposed to add silkiness and shine to the strands, just for the luxury of it.

The middle-ward bathhouses I had access to before never supplied anything that frivolous.

Once I've rinsed the cream out too, I sit on the ledge at one side of the tub and absorb the silky heat of the water. The scent floods my lungs. Even the scars on my back seem to soften.

This *is* a luxury. But I can't totally relax into the indulgence when I'm aware of the presence at the back of my skull, shifting here and there with thoughts she isn't sharing.

"You've been quiet today," I say finally.

*Oh, I've simply had a lot to mull over. And there hasn't been much for me to contribute anyway.*

My throat tightens. "You know, I'm sorry about what happened with Stavros, after I told you— I think we were both still half asleep, and I got caught up in the moment— I shouldn't—"

*It's all right,* Julita breaks in. *If you wanted that, I shouldn't be stopping you from getting caught up. I… You've had to change how you're living an awful lot because I barged into your head, haven't you.*

It's not a question, but I feel compelled to answer anyway. "You didn't force me to come to the college. I made the choice."

*I mean, you haven't had any privacy. You've constantly had to consider me as well as yourself. I know you were used to getting by on your own, so to have a stranger watching your every move, interrupting your thoughts with mine whenever I spoke up…*

Even when she was bemoaning the men's focus on me, I've never heard her sound quite as defeated as she does right now. Where is she going with this?

"It's an awkward situation," I acknowledge. "But we've made the best of it, or at least we're working toward that."

And the situation should be almost over with. But I don't know how to say that part in a way that doesn't sound totally insensitive.

When I've seen Julita's quest to destroy the scourge sorcerers through, when their conspiracy has crumbled, there'll be no reason for her to cling to this last shred of life through me. At some point, we'll have to talk about her final death.

I'm just not expecting that conversation to happen immediately.

Julita makes a sound as if clearing her throat. *I was thinking… I haven't been all that helpful in the past week or two. So perhaps it's time for me to move on and let you have your life just for yourself again.*

I blink, momentarily startled speechless. "Why would you even say that? We aren't finished with your mission."

I get the sense of Julita's presence squirming a little before she answers. *If anything, I suspect I've been distracting you. I've obviously been too caught up in my own concerns to ensure I'm there when I can help. If I'm causing more problems than I'm solving, leaving would be better for the mission as well as for you.*

My mouth opens, but no words come to me. A heat that has nothing to do with the bath has flared in the back of my eyes.

Why do I feel like I'm about to cry?

Julita isn't *wrong.* My ghostly passenger has been pulling back more and more. It's been difficult trying to balance her emotions with my own desires.

But somehow the thought of her vacating my mind completely, leaving me as alone as I used to be, makes the bottom of my stomach drop out. The emptiness I picture sends a shiver through my veins.

I'd be facing the scourge sorcerers with no one at all by my side. No wry remarks to keep my spirits up. No expressions of concern when I'm struggling.

Does she really think she's troubled me that much?

Maybe hanging on has become too much of a strain for *her,* but she doesn't want to admit it.

"Do *you* want to move on?" I ask, fighting to keep my voice steady. "If sticking with me has become too uncomfortable, I obviously wouldn't insist that you stay."

*Ivy… I've appreciated every bit of life you've let me cling to. The last thing I want is to overstay my welcome.*

I think that's a no to my question.

I gather myself as well as I can. "You haven't overstayed. Obviously everything between me and the men has become a little much for you, and I don't blame you for needing some space. But you are still helping. I don't know if I'd have gotten through the initiation without giving away my magic if you hadn't talked me through it. You *were* there when I needed you the most."

I can almost see Julita hanging her head. *I should have been there sooner.*

"That doesn't matter. You weren't too late. I—I hate that I have to deal with those assholes at all. It'd be so much harder without a friend there with me."

Julita gives a rough laugh. *You still consider me a friend?*

I frown. "Of course. That's why I've tried to consider your feelings. You stood up for me before any of the men bothered to. You've had my back, and I want to have yours."

There's a long stretch of silence. When Julita speaks again, she sounds as if she's choked up too, even though she hasn't got a throat to hold a lump or eyes to spill tears.

*I'm so sorry. I'm gone from their lives now, so it's not as if I could have any of them anyway. It's not as if I'd have let anything happen with them if I'd stayed alive. I was too careful about protecting myself... It's not your fault I can now see that closing myself off might not have been the path that'd have made me the happiest.*

I wish I could give her a hug. It occurs to me, with the sweetest of bittersweet pangs, that this is what it might have been like talking with Linzi if my little sister had lived long enough to confront adult jealousies and regrets.

"I've messed things up in plenty of ways myself, making assumptions and hesitating to trust," I say. "It isn't fair that you never got the chance to change your mind."

*I'd say it's much less fair that I've made it harder for you to enjoy the affection they've offered you. You never treated them badly, Ivy. It made sense that you were cautious given how they first treated you and the differences between your positions and... everything. I had no excuse.*

My mouth twists into a crooked smile. "I think you did. Your brother was awful to you, and your parents obviously weren't paying enough attention to intervene... Of course you found it hard to trust anyone."

*Well. I think both of us can be more than our hardships.* Julita gives herself a shake that tingles through my scalp. *They truly care for you. Even Stavros. I got so caught up in missing what I lost that I didn't stop to think... This is the best I can have now. Celebrating their devotion to you. Getting to enjoy a little taste of the exciting parts before I give you your privacy... and perhaps an additional vicarious thrill if you'll share some gossip afterward?*

I can't stop a giggle from tumbling out of my mouth. "Are you sure you really want to put yourself through hearing the details?"

*I have to look at it the right way. What I'm gaining instead of what I can't have. I shouldn't really be here at all experiencing any of this.* She pauses, and her tone turns sly. *And I'm not sure I wanted to miss seeing Stavros finally, completely won over. Why are things so tense between the two of you again?*

I wrinkle my nose. "Everything you could probably tell was about to happen happened, and then I got nervous that he wouldn't be happy about it when he fully woke up. And he admitted that he still doesn't totally trust *me.* I didn't stick around to hear his excuses about why."

Julita lets out a humph. *That man. He's got to get his head on straight eventually. Do what you will with him once he does. And don't hold yourself back with Alek and Casimir anymore either. I should have argued with you when you first told me you'd backed off.*

And this—this is exactly why the thought of the ghost in my head departing sets my emotions off kilter. We understand each other. We have each other's backs as well as we can, just like I said to her.

"I don't know about Stavros," I say. "But the others—are you *sure?*"

*Absolutely. You should be soaking up all that adoration, and I'll enjoy the afterglow. It's more fun sharing your life if you're enjoying it too. I simply forgot that for a little while.*

I swallow thickly. "Well, thank you."

*I should be thanking you. You could have told me good riddance a few minutes ago.*

The water is starting to cool around me. I stretch out my legs and inhale more of the herbal scent, and then reach for the lever to open the drain. "Hopefully we'll have time for a little more enjoyment before we get to the murdering."

Julita gives the impression of a wince. *You'd think King Konram would be grateful enough for everything you've already done not to lay that on you too. If I could—*

She halts, with a pensive silence that puts me on the alert.

"What?" I prod after a moment as I climb out of the tub.

*I wonder if my gift would still work. If you let me take charge briefly again. We could call on the king, and I could tell him you're not going to be his assassin, and he'd have to accept it.*

I wrap one of the fluffy towels around me as I ponder her offer. "We don't know for sure that your gift *would* still work when you're not in the body that made the sacrifice. If it doesn't, the confrontation could go very badly."

*I suppose that's true. It'd be difficult to test since we don't know who would request something and be unwilling to accept a no unless I compelled it.*

I rub the towel over my head and hesitate in front of the room's tall mirror. My pale reflection gazes back at me, my figure no longer quite as scrawny now that I've had the benefit of the college dining hall for several weeks of meals, although my elbows are as knobby as ever and the muscles I've honed stand out against my sallow skin. Plenty of scars mar that skin even without my back in view.

I still don't look like a noble. I look like a woman who's had to see and do more than anyone really should.

And maybe that's okay.

I pull my posture straighter. "Someone has to deal with Ster. Torstem. It might as well be me. I *am* in by far the best position to handle him quickly and without causing a bigger ruckus."

*You don't want to perform an assassination, do you? I know you've hated having to kill before—even Esmae.*

"I have hated it," I say quietly. "But I didn't want to come to the college at all. I didn't want to take on any of these responsibilities. I just liked the idea of what might happen if I didn't even less. That hasn't changed."

Even if carrying out this final part of the mission gets me killed too.

Julita is quiet for a moment. Then she says, *I think I can see why Kosmel called on you.*

I snort. "If he ever bothers to speak to me again. *He* was totally unhelpful last night. Couldn't even give me a dice roll."

*I suppose it's difficult to interpret the actions of the gods.*

"I don't know. That felt like a pretty clear 'Fuck you.' But it doesn't really matter. I got into this mission without him, so I'll get out of it without him too."

By the time I've dressed, the restlessness that drove me out of the bathing room before has crept back in.

It's evening now. Stavros will be back in his quarters soon if he isn't already.

Casimir said I have the room until midnight, so I can't hide away here for the whole night. And the thought of falling asleep and having to be kicked out makes my skin crawl.

I don't relish the idea of talking to the former general about last night's encounter just yet either.

With a huff of breath aimed mostly at myself, I step out into the hall and make my way to the Domi's small back stairwell. Fresh air to clear my head can't be a bad thing.

I wander through the inner courtyard, but there are still too many students milling around in the descending dusk. I spot Petra emerging from the Quadring and all but bolt in the opposite direction.

A conversation with her seems like a bad idea too.

I end up meandering through one of the Quadring's halls to the larger outer courtyard. The dark sprawl of the campus woods looms at the other end of the field, but I don't let myself focus on it. I stroll through the grass, taking in the statues positioned along the tall stone wall.

The one of Elox tossing a rippling blanket into the air is a particularly impressive feat of carving. I'm admiring it so avidly that I nearly trip over my feet when I step past it and my gaze jars against the figure on the other side.

The guard with the too-beautiful face and the magical vibes is standing by the wall a few paces down. He's wearing his deep blue uniform, so presumably he's on duty and meant to be patrolling, but he's standing stiffly still, his attention fixed on the arm he's raised in front of his chest.

At a twitch of movement, I realize there's a butterfly perched on his jacket sleeve.

The insect's yellow-and-blue wings dip down and back up again. The guard stares at it, his expression uncertain, as if he isn't sure what to do about the situation and worries he'll make the wrong choice.

*Does he imagine it's going to attack him?* Julita murmurs with amusement.

It's a bizarre enough scene that I stall in my tracks rather than hurrying past him. Which means I'm still staring at *him* when he lifts his gaze and notices me standing here.

I expect him to snap at me for gaping at him, the way high ranking people tend to do if you catch them in an awkward moment. Instead, his eyes open wider, almost pleadingly. As if he's making an appeal for help.

It's ridiculous. He obviously doesn't actually need help.

But everything about the situation is so absurd I find myself walking closer. "Have you been assaulted by that butterfly?"

The guard's gaze jerks back to the insect. He adjusts his arm a little higher, but the creature keeps clinging to it.

"It landed on me a few minutes ago," he says, his voice as puzzled as his expression, and points to one of its wings. "I think it's hurt—it might not be able to fly any farther. I don't know what to do."

Is he that concerned about the fate of a butterfly?

An uneasy pang runs through my chest. Somehow I can't simply dismiss him when he's showing such an unusual display of compassion.

Most of his colleagues would probably have shaken the creature off or swatted it dead and been done with it.

I study the wings and note the tattered edge on the one he indicated. Can a butterfly recover from an injury like that?

I don't know, but we might as well give it a chance.

Glancing around, I motion toward the woods. "Let's bring it someplace it'll have shelter. If it's going to recover, it'll be better off in a spot where no predators will notice it. Assuming you're not going to carry it around for the next day or two."

"No," the guard says as if he's taking my suggestion seriously. "It might get more damaged riding on me."

"Then it's settled. Come on."

I stride toward the line of trees, ignoring the apprehension that fills me at the sight of the woods after all the things I've done within them. The guard trails behind me, holding his arm steady so as not to disturb his cargo.

When we reach the nearest trees, I peer through the brush and point out a leafy twig jutting from a sapling. "Put it here. The branch right overtop should stop any birds from spotting it."

The guard cases the butterfly onto his finger gingerly. It grips his skin with its tiny feet, but when he nudges it against the twig, it springs onto the bark with a flutter of its wings.

Studying it in its new resting place, the guard's stance relaxes. He glances at me, and another tingle of that magic he exudes brushes against my nerves.

I do my best to hide the tensing of my muscles, but a small furrow forms in his porcelain-smooth brow. "I make you nervous. This place does too. But you helped anyway."

My chin comes up automatically. "I'm perfectly fine. You looked like you could use a little direction. I've got other things to do now."

I spin around and stalk off before he can make any other accusations, but I catch his voice before I put more than a few paces between us. "Thank you."

I walk on without looking back.

Julita chuckles softly. *Now he is a strange one. I suppose if he badgers you about stargazing again, you can remind him of his butterfly escapades.*

A hint of a smile touches my lips, but my heart isn't in it. I don't feel comfortable wandering around the courtyard anymore, not when I might run into the guard and his unknown magical abilities again.

He couldn't have any idea *why* the woods make me uneasy, right?

The last streaks of sunlight are fading from the sky. Sconces flicker along the walls of the college buildings.

I rub my arms, cast about for another option, and then resign myself to my fate.

I do have to talk to Stavros eventually. About *all* the things that happened last night that we haven't addressed yet.

Time to get the awfulness over with.

# Forty-Two

I wasn't trying to break the plate. I only brought it up to my room at all because the buzz of chatter in the dining hall was grating at my nerves.

So the dish happened to be sitting by the edge of my desk while I paced around the room, straining my mind for something I could say to my king to change his mind, some alternate strategy I could offer that would make Ivy's involvement unnecessary. And when I kicked the leg of the desk in frustration, the plate happened to hop off and shatter on the floor.

Naturally, Ivy returns while I'm muttering to myself and picking up the broken pieces.

At the squeak of the door opening, I freeze other than the upward jerk of my head.

Ivy slips inside. Her bright blue gaze feels especially penetrating as she takes in my position and the jagged chunks of ceramics on the floor around me.

"What did that poor plate ever do to you?" she asks, her tone sardonic but her body tensed as if she thinks she might need to bolt right back out the door.

"It was an accident," I mutter, scraping the shards together as hastily as I can between my regular hand and the hooked prosthetic I put on for a late-afternoon workout—which did absolutely nothing to get my head on straight.

While I work, Ivy stalks around the room in her now-typical surveillance for conjured creatures. Apparently finding none, she steps tentatively to the sofa and lowers herself onto it.

Her posture still looks braced to flee.

It hasn't escaped my notice that she's been running from me ever since my blunder last night. She's left every room we've been in together as swiftly as humanly possible.

As I bring the mess to the waste basket, I shoot her surreptitious glances. Brief twitches of my eyes for as long as my vision will remain steady.

She's gazing toward the window rather than watching me. Her mouth is set in a line that looks pained.

Even though the moss-green hue of the new gown Casimir's provided sets off her pale skin and red-blond hair to impressive effect, it doesn't suit her quite as well as her sparring clothes. But the fierce strength of her spirit shines through all the same.

That spark in her set my blood thrumming through my veins long before I was willing to accept, let alone admit, the effect she has on me. Now, remembering the way she arched and shuddered against me in my bed last night—

No, better to remember the fear in her eyes afterward. Giving in to my hotter desires before we had a stable foundation to carry us through them is what landed me in this disaster.

I wash my hands in the latrine and return to the common room, half expecting our thief-turned-lady to have darted off in my momentary absence. She's stayed, sitting stiffly on the sofa.

I consider walking over but decide it's safest giving her plenty of space. As I prop myself against the front of my desk, my stomach churns with all the things I need to say.

Before I can even open my mouth, her gaze flicks to me. She blurts out the words in a rush.

"My magic got away from me during the initiation."

Ah. Perhaps it's not just my blunder she's been fleeing.

Not that I can take any comfort in that fact. Her body has somehow become even more rigid where she's perched on the sofa.

Even with my view of her blurring, I can feel her gaze burning into me with its intentness.

If I don't handle her admission just right, I'll prove myself exactly the enemy she's afraid I am. I don't know if we'll be able to come back from another misstep so soon on the heels of the last.

I keep my voice perfectly calm. "I can't say that surprises me, what with the drugs and the chaos the scourge sorcerers were encouraging. What happened?"

She shifts uneasily on the sofa cushions. When I give my head a twitch to get a clearer glimpse of her, it's obvious from the distant look that's come into her eyes that she's as much uneasy with her recollections as how I'll react to them.

Which only offers more evidence of why I don't need to be afraid of *her*.

"Everyone was disguised," she says after a moment. "I knew I needed to figure out who they were, that getting out of this whole dangerous mission depended on identifying the conspirators. So my magic decided it would start wrenching off people's masks, and it slipped my grasp a couple of times. That's how I saw Olari and the woman from the dining hall."

"I'm not hearing anything horrifying so far. We told you that you should use your power if it would work in your favor."

Her hands twist together in her lap. "But there's always a backlash. Kosmel wasn't around to guide it, and I don't know how. It—it pushed in to balance out the pulling away. One of the scourge sorcerer's masks seemed to *melt* down her face and into her mouth. They had to break it to stop it from choking her. And my magic hit one of the horses too—something with the bridle hurt it. The woman might have deserved it, but the horse definitely didn't."

I consider her account. "Surely it wasn't a lot of harm for something as simple as removing a mask?"

"With all the magic on the things, I'm not sure removing the masks was 'simple.'" Ivy sighs. "It didn't seem as if the horse was outright wounded. But if I hadn't gotten a handle on my power when I did, I don't know who or what else it might have hurt."

"You did get a handle on it, though. Without any permanent damage done."

"I couldn't manage it on my own. I was too disoriented. But Julita helped me steady myself and focus."

Julita. It's gotten increasingly difficult for me to picture the coy, chestnut-haired woman who cajoled me into taking up her cause residing in Ivy's head. What has *she* been saying to Ivy about me?

Is Ivy here right now because of her or in spite of her?

The firmness of her tone suggests her declaration matters to her. And I'm not lying when I say, "I'm glad she was there when you needed her."

Ivy's fingers tighten around the edge of the sofa cushion. "She won't always be, though."

"And you won't always be socializing with scourge sorcerers." I pause, summoning all the conviction I feel into my voice. "Ivy, nothing you've just told me changes my opinion. I'm not worried about you or your magic. You went seven years without ever losing your grip on it before you stumbled into this situation, so I don't see any reason to think your incredible control won't work just fine once you're out of this mess."

"You don't see any reason so far."

There. There is the crux of the problem, the catastrophe I created.

She was willing to trust me once after I'd been an ass to her when we first met. And then I let prejudice and fear and—being honest—my own wretched insecurities about one part of who she is overshadow all the rest, and wasn't just an ass but a brute.

How am I ever going to convince her that I won't make another about-face on her?

*I* know I won't. So I'm just going to have to give this appeal my all, no matter how much shame I have to dredge up in the process.

I owe this incredible woman my full truth.

I drop my gaze for a moment, gathering myself. "Ivy... You never deserved anything I put you through. I was wrong, over and over again. There was *never* any reason, not in anything you did, not even in what you are, so now that I've sorted myself out, I won't imagine any more."

Ivy's tone is wary. "If it wasn't anything I am, then what was it about?"

The corner of my mouth crooks up at a wry angle, but my chest constricts around the words. I've buried these unsettling emotions so far down, hiding them under layer upon layer of confidence and authority and comradery.

I never wanted to let them out. Maybe I had the fanciful idea they'd rot and disintegrate like a corpse into the earth, but it hasn't worked. The stifled anguish has been eating away at me from the inside all this time.

"I have fucked up, so badly. *I* hurt so many people, so many more than you have, and I was so terrified of making an even worse mistake that I couldn't see I was fucking up all over again with you."

When my gaze flicks to Ivy, she's knit her brow. "You've killed people in battle, sure, but I don't think enemy soldiers count the same way."

"That's not—" A rough laugh escapes me. I rub my forehead. "I've already told you what happened with Michas. Approximately."

"A riven sorcerer murdered him," Ivy says quietly.

"And I didn't see the danger in time. When I *did* realize something was wrong, I froze up rather than getting Michas out of there, against every combat instinct I'd already been training in..."

The words snag in my throat. I force myself to go on. "I could have saved him. The riven man was just trying to avoid capture. He struck out at Michas because he was closer and then fled. If we'd retreated sooner..."

Sympathy I'm not sure I deserve resonates through Ivy's voice. "You don't know that. You don't know how many more people that mad sorcerer might have murdered if you hadn't realized what he was."

"I know how many people died because of the choices I did make. Michas was only my first fuck-up. I can't even count how many soldiers have fallen under my watch over the years."

Ivy lets out a dismissive sound. "I don't think any general manages to completely avoid bloodshed on our side. That's not how war works."

My jaw tightens. "I don't know. I don't know how many of those deaths were unavoidable and how many I instigated. Because—have you heard anything about my last battle?"

She shakes her head, still and silent. Waiting for me to go on.

My sight stutters and hazes with each blink. A flare of frustration sears through the tangle of guilt and shame, but the anger is directed only at myself.

"Like most gifts, I could only use mine so many times in quick succession before it'd start wearing on me. I'd be able to see less and less of what was to come, and I'd get a headache and have trouble thinking straight. Not a good state to be in when you're leading hundreds of soldiers into the fray."

"All gifts have limitations," Ivy murmurs. "That's why the godlen hate scourge sorcery—for trying to cheat the natural boundaries."

"Yes. So I had to moderate how I used my magic when a situation got intense. I had to decide when to look ahead at the enemies' next moves and when to hold off. We were clashing with a Darium legion, and I'd already seen them behave exactly as I'd have guessed a few times, so I got cocky. I assumed there was no need to strain my gift and look again when it seemed obvious how they'd strike at us next."

I find myself gripping the stump of my wrist where the prosthetic is attached to its harness. The spot where I gave the sacrifice I then dishonored, for the gift I can no longer use.

"They had a new trick up their sleeve that I hadn't predicted," I go on, my voice stiffening against the weight of the admission. "Before I recognized it and could regroup, they'd slaughtered half of the soldiers I was leading. Men and women who'd counted on *me* to guide them through the battle. One of the Darium soldiers hit me with the blast of magic that scrambled my vision."

"But you ended up pushing them back."

"With sheer brute force and desperation—and the help of some excellent comrades. Nothing I can really take credit for. And then I was done, as I should have been for my idiocy anyway."

Ivy pulls her legs up onto the sofa to wrap her arms loosely around her knees. "I'm sure you're not the only general who's ever had a battle go badly."

I grimace. "I can't think of any others who lost their entire usefulness in the field in one swoop."

"You're not useless."

I can taste the bitterness in my words, but is there really any point in pretending it away? "Useless enough that my king sent me here to simply teach what I was meant to be doing. Useless enough that my fiancé couldn't stand the thought of marrying a disgraced general and called off the engagement."

Ivy's lips part in shock. "You were engaged?"

"Yes," I say brusquely. "To the daughter of one of the barony families in Konram's court. It wasn't an epic romance, but we suited each other and liked each other enough that I hoped it would become more of a love match over time. But I was no longer the man she thought she'd have, and I wouldn't have wanted to stay with someone who saw me as inadequate anyway."

Ivy hesitates. "Last night, when you reached for me in your sleep—were you thinking of—"

I cut her off with a derisive noise. "No. Not really. There was obviously some unconscious habit associated with sleeping next to a woman, and I apologize for that—it's been nearly a year since I slept next to anyone, and I didn't think it would affect me. But I knew who you were from the moment I woke up."

I'm not sure the old habits *would* have kicked in if it wasn't that I've wanted Ivy more than I ever longed to touch Neela, even at the height of our courtship. But I doubt this is the ideal time to mention that fact.

I barrel onward. "That's not what matters the most, regardless. What matters is I witnessed your magic in the tower, and all I could see after that moment was the catastrophe I might have instigated. I agreed to let you act as my assistant. I missed any signs of what you were. If you lashed out at the students or staff or, gods forbid, wreaked havoc on the royal family right next door, I'd be to blame."

Ivy's voice sounds abruptly small, so painful to hear it might as well be a blade to my gut. "That sounds like a reasonable concern."

"It wasn't." I smack the desk hard enough that the ink pot rattles. "I was so caught up in how horrible I'd feel, how horrible I'd *look*, that I lost sight of what I'd already realized. I have nothing to fear in you. You'd sooner kill yourself than let your power run wild. You hated even stabbing that wretched false friend who'd already stabbed *you*."

Ivy swallows audibly. "It doesn't seem as if the riven get a choice."

"Because they go mad. But I have to assume as you have that they go mad through using their power. Which you've been willing to cough up blood to avoid doing. You'd sooner let some lout strangle you than protect yourself with it."

"I *have* hurt people."

"When you didn't know you could. When you didn't have a choice. Who am I to judge you for that? Hundreds of people died on the battlefield in one day because of a choice *I* made, and no one's ever suggested hanging me."

I push myself off the desk and step toward her, but the tensing of her stance stops me halfway to the sofa. My hand clenches at my side.

"I'm sorry," I say. "I've told you that before, but it never seems like enough. You've put so much of yourself at risk to protect this entire country, and I was treating you like a villain. The gods themselves had intervened, and somehow I still thought my honor was the thing on the line."

Ivy ducks her head. "I never expected you to trust me."

"But I do. That's the point." I dare to take another step closer. "I didn't say it properly last night. I think you're the only person in this mess I truly trust. It's my judgment I've never been sure I could count on, and I took that out on you. That's the real crime I've committed here."

When I refocus my vision on her, Ivy's expression is skeptical. I reach for the right words to convince her of how much I mean this confession.

"You're the most honorable person I've ever met. With every act you take, every word you speak, you prove it again and again. Just now, you didn't have to tell me about your magic acting up during the initiation, but you did. You gave Julita credit for helping you master it. You've offered me grace and compassion over the awful things I've done even though I had none for you when you'd just prevented a city-wide disaster."

"I don't think you did anything all that awful. And it shouldn't be all that special just to tell the truth."

My chuckle comes out raw. "But it is. I think you know it is. Ivy…"

I take another step, bringing me to the end of the sofa. I can't tell if she'd tolerate me trying to sit next to her, but I hate the sense that I'm looming over her like the brute I've acted as.

After a moment's hesitation, I sink down to a crouch that puts us on eye level. I hold her gaze even as her face goes hazy in my sight.

"You said that Casimir and Alek have compared you to Signy. I don't think they're wrong, and not just because of whatever romantic entanglements you've gotten yourself into."

Ivy snorts, but I go on. "If anything, you're even braver than she was. You're facing down an enemy less predictable and more brutal, who could do more harm to this world than the empire ever did, and you're doing it on your own except for a ghost who can't offer you anything but her voice. We'll stop this threat because of *you*, whether the rest of the country ever finds out who the real hero was or not."

Her voice roughens. "I haven't been alone. You've still been here, no matter how much of an asshole you've been in that time. Alek and Casimir have helped."

"You're the one riding at the front of the 'army.' You're the one taking the blows. I would never have asked what you're doing of any soldier, but you've volunteered, again and again, when you had no reason to come to us in the first place other than the selfless generosity you somehow keep dismissing. It would be *my* honor to have you as my Signy."

Ivy draws in a ragged breath. I hold there, waiting for her response, wishing I could read her face for more than a second at a time.

"You really mean that," she says in a wondering tone.

I can't suppress the dry note that creeps into my voice. "I'm aiming for honesty too. I—I don't expect anything from you. You deserve people standing by you who never doubted you to begin with. I'm only hoping that you can feel safe in my presence. That you know I'll only ever leap to protect you, not to hurt you. I don't know how much that's worth when I've failed to save so many before, and that was when I could at least still fucking *see*, but—"

Ivy leans forward and touches my cheek. "Stop."

The feel of her fingers against my skin arrests me. I blink, trying to make sense of the command. "What?"

"Did you really fail before?" she asks, an unexpected tender note slipping into her voice. "You froze up when you were a teenager—if we're not counting my childhood mistakes, I don't think we should count that either. During that last battle, the surprise tactics the Darium soldiers turned to—would you have been able to prevent the slaughter if you'd seen their next few actions a minute ahead of time?"

I think back to the moment when the tide shifted. The sudden blasts of conjured explosions, the wheeling of the cavalry.

"I don't know," I have to admit. "It might not have been enough to recognize their full strategy and counteract it. But it could have been. I never gave the soldiers who were relying on me a proper chance."

Ivy's hand lingers against my face, the warmth of her touch coursing across my cheek. "You might have been able to save them. But you also might have seen the signs and adjusted your own approach, and the Darium army would have held off until they were sure they'd take you by surprise. You might have burned out your gift too soon and missed something even worse."

"I can only go by what happened, and what happened—"

"—wasn't a guarantee. It was a bad situation that *they* caused. Haven't you started telling me that I shouldn't blame myself for struggling with my magic when it's because of the scourge sorcerers' meddling?"

I make a face at her. "That's different. You barely hurt anyone. I had a job to look after those soldiers."

Ivy offers me a small smile. "And I'd be willing to wager good money that you did as good a job as you could with the information you had. In any case, it isn't your job to protect me. There's nothing to fail."

A growl creeps up my throat. "I failed to even stop King Konram from placing that wretched demand on you. I know how much you've hated every time you've taken a life. And the moment you do, every other scourge sorcerer there will be out for your blood. He shouldn't have asked it of you. He's got a whole army trained to kill for him."

Somehow her smile turns even more sad. "But none of them could make it to a meeting of the Order of the Wild."

The growl bursts out of me. I push to my feet with a surge of resolve. "I should put an end to this entire thing. March down the hall to Torstem's office and run him straight through."

Ivy catches my hand. "And then what? His main accomplices will have a chance to scatter and regroup. The king will have to put you on trial. It'll come out that I infiltrated their group, and then anyone out for vengeance will come after me anyway. How does that help anyone?"

I exhale in a rush, but I don't have an answer.

Ivy straightens her posture with an air of resolve. "At least if I do it myself, I can control the situation. I can probably take him down without the others even realizing the knife was mine. And then it'll be over."

She says the last three words like a prayer.

I shake my head. "And you'll have to carry that much more weight on your conscience because I'm too damaged to shield you."

The anguish of my latest dreams echoes through me—the dreams where I see her up on the hangman's platform from across the square, the executioner just looping the noose around her neck.

The dreams where I run and yell, but my boots sink into the cobblestones like mud, and I'm still much to far away when the trap door drops beneath her.

Ivy shatters the image with a guffaw and gets to her feet. "Stavros, I've seen you spar. If it comes to a fight, I'd rather have you defending me than anyone else, even myself. If you were too 'damaged' to be a threat, I wouldn't have been scared of you. But we can settle this right now."

I'm distracted enough by her use of the past tense when she mentions her fear that I don't quite process her last statement. "Settle what?"

The next thing I know, the woman before me has whipped a knife from her boot and lunged at me.

If she could read my emotions in that moment, she'd know how true everything I said to her is. My pulse jumps with surprise and a little alarm, but nothing close to panic.

I know down to my soul that she isn't turning traitor on me. This isn't a real attack.

But that doesn't mean she'll shy away from jabbing me a little if it proves her point.

The tip of Ivy's blade skims the side of my hand just before I block her strike. A pinprick of pain tells me she broke the skin.

More than two decades of honed combat instincts kick in. I shift my posture, dodge her next blow, and check her stance for an opening.

I took off my sword belt after I came back to the room, so I've only got my hands to work with, though the metal prosthetic serves as a decent weapon. I snatch at her wrist to try to disarm her, but she darts out of the way just in time.

Her knife never stops flashing for an instant. She's no match for me in size, but she's so fast I barely have the chance to overpower her.

As we circle the sofa and approach the window, Ivy keeps me on the defensive, blocking and parrying. But I've fought difficult battles before.

I rap her shin just hard enough to put her off-balance and attempt to topple her with a shove of my shoulder. Ivy scrambles backward, but she's retreating now.

Her knife clangs off my prosthetic, and I wrench the curved metal loop around just in time to snag on Ivy's hand. With a twist, I send the weapon careening across the room.

I yank her arm toward me and catch it in my other hand. With a breathless laugh, Ivy squirms against my hold. Her knee rams toward my gut.

She doesn't have a hope without her blade. Tucking my other arm around her head to cushion it, I heave us both onto the floor and let my much larger frame pin her limbs in place.

"That's enough," I say. "What in the realms are you playing at?"

Ivy beams up at me, her hair fanned across my forearm, her grin so bright even the blurring of my vision can't hide its delight. "Not playing. Just proving why I don't have to worry about your protective abilities. Even when *I'm* attacking you, you manage to protect me as well as yourself."

I stare down at her, my stomach flipping over with a heady rush like nothing I've ever felt before.

Gods above, this woman is more than incredible. I don't have the words to describe her.

But describing isn't what I most want to do with her right now.

My head bows as if drawn by a magnet. Ivy tilts hers upward just in time for our mouths to collide.

How can this be the first time I've really kissed her? These lips have caught my attention so many times, but those glimpses of them is nothing compared to their softness against my own or the eager breath that spills over them with an intoxicating heat.

All of it feels right—the press of her mouth, the silkiness of her hair when I run my fingers over it, her lithe body beneath mine.

I lift myself up slightly so I can deepen the kiss, and Ivy slips her arm free. She wraps it around the back of my neck and teases her fingers up into my hair.

The simple gesture sets off a cascade of sparks through my scalp. Fuck me, we've barely started kissing and I'm already painfully hard.

I can't rut against her like the animal I turned into last night. If I fuck this up, I don't know if I'm ever going to get another chance to show her what she means to me.

I break the kiss to peer down at her, with a twitch of my head when my sight starts to fail me. Ivy meets my gaze, flushed and still smiling, looking nothing but pleased with our current position.

Her hand leaves my hair to trail over my neck along the collar of my dress shirt. "If you're all so determined to have your own Signy, I suppose I'll give it my best shot."

A laugh sputters out of me, alongside a swell of emotion that hums through my pulse and condenses at the base of my throat.

I know exactly what I need to say. What's been becoming true for longer than I've been willing to admit it, and maybe that's why I've been so terrified.

Part of me wants to duck my head so I don't have to take in her response, but that would be a coward's way. I adjust my eyes with a little tick to the side just as I speak, so I'll see her face as clearly as possible in the first moment.

"I love you."

# Forty-Three

Ivy

I gape at Stavros, everything narrowing down to the three words ringing in my ears. Did he… did he really say what I thought I heard?

In my startled silence, his expression shifts, his mouth tensing. He moves as if to push himself right off me, but I snap out of my daze in time to catch the front of his shirt.

I still don't know how to answer him, but my arms move of their own accord. They loop across his shoulders, hugging him closer to me instead.

Stavros bows his head so our foreheads rest together. I hear him swallow.

He manages to find the droll tone that's both amused and annoyed me over our weeks together. "I shocked the words right out of you. That's some kind of accomplishment."

My laugh comes out choked. I tilt my head to seek out his lips.

Somehow sinking into a kiss feels easier than saying anything back just yet. My emotions are still roiling inside me, plenty of previous shock mixing with amazement and affection.

Can I really doubt his admission when he's opened up to me about so much else? He put all his regrets and weaknesses on display just to reassure *me*.

*Well,* Julita says softly. *That's not where I was expecting this conversation to end up, but I'm glad I got to see it. He's right in everything he said about you, Ivy. And I think I've played voyeur long enough.*

Her presence dwindles in the back of my skull. Stavros's heat still encompasses me, his body dwarfing mine though no longer trapping it.

He loves me.

I can't quite wrap my head around the idea, though every time I remember his voice saying those words, another giddy flutter passes through my chest. I never thought…

Well, I never thought I'd hear him say most of the things he has tonight.

My heart aches with all the things *I'm* not saying. But it's not as if I could return the same exact sentiment yet.

Less than an hour ago, I considered it possible he'd end up dragging me to the executioner someday. A person needs a little time to catch their balance when the ground they thought they were standing on tips over.

I've wanted him… for much longer than I've liked. I think I started falling for him that night after the catastrophe of a ball when he admitted how much he'd come to appreciate my dedication—and revealed a sliver of the anguish he's fully bared this evening.

Every movement of his lips against mine is delectable. Every inch of my body tingles with the awareness of his massive frame braced over me.

Even as I think that, Stavros eases back. He pulls himself upright, drawing me with him so we're sitting facing each other.

Not exactly apart, though. My knee rests against his thigh. His hand lingers against my jaw.

His mouth quirks into a slanted smile. "I suppose the shock can't be that bad. You didn't run away screaming in horror."

I meet his blue-and-brown gaze, letting my hand settle on his other arm just below the jut of his prosthetic. "It's still sinking in. I'm sorry I can't— My feelings were already jumbled up from everything we talked about before—"

"It's all right." Stavros strokes his thumb across my cheek. "I haven't made it easy on you. And I wouldn't want you to lie to me. It feels like some kind of miracle that you're even willing to kiss me."

More heat collects low in my belly. I'd like to do a lot more than kiss him—that much I'm sure of.

The knowledge steadies me. We've covered some of that territory before. Hooking up isn't quite as fraught as declarations of devotion.

Maybe there's an easy way I can put us back on level ground and defuse the tension of the moment.

I scoot a little backward and wave my hand at Stavros carelessly. "I think we can do better than that. But first, strip."

His expression turns incredulous. "What?"

I give another flippant gesture, indicating the whole muscular expanse of him I've never really gotten to admire before. "Strip. I want to have a look at what I'm working with."

His eyes flash with the eager light that's drawn me to this man from the first moment I saw it flare in his gaze. A sly grin crosses his face. "Turn-around's fair play, hmm?"

So he's recognized the call-back to our first sparring session, back when he thought I was nothing more than a thieving street rat.

I shrug, offering my most innocent smile. "At least I have the pure motivation of simply wanting to appreciate the view, no ego involved."

Stavros guffaws. "Pure?" But to my delight, he stands up, reaching for his shirt.

I do drink in the view as he deftly undoes the buttons with his one hand. I suppose having sacrificed the other to Sabrelle when he turned twelve, he must have gotten a lot of practice at doing all kinds of things one-handed. None of his prosthetics would be much help with more delicate maneuvers.

The triangle of bare chest shows wider with each opened button. Then he reaches the bottom and shrugs the shirt right off, leaving the full muscular expanse of his torso bared, along with the harness that keeps his prosthetic in place against the stump of his wrist.

I lean back on my hands while I study him. He might not ride off into battle anymore, but he's kept up a warrior's physique. Every inch of his chest, abdomen, and arms is sculpted into taut ridges of muscle.

Here and there, marks either paler or ruddier cut across his light brown skin. I'm familiar enough with certain sorts of wounds to tell a few are scars left by blades and at least one was a burn, but others must be from weapons I don't often encounter.

Or not weapons at all. It was a magical strike that damaged his vision.

In the midst of it all, the curving lines of Sabrelle's brand stand out at the base of his sternum. The dedication he took for a life he's been almost entirely shut out of.

I hope Sabrelle hasn't abandoned him for his injury. He served her well while he could.

I'm occupied enough with ogling that it takes me a minute to notice that Stavros has stopped undressing. He's watching me take him in with a gaze as avid as mine.

I arch an eyebrow. "I don't think you're finished yet. You had me down to my underclothes."

"That I did. Well, if the lady wishes it…"

He tugs off his boots without hesitation. I think a hint of a flush creeps up his neck as he loosens the ties on his trousers.

I've no doubt that Stavros has entertained plenty of women beyond the one he once thought he'd marry, but I'd guess most of them didn't ask him to put on a show for their amusement.

He'll be used to them seducing *him* with strategically revealed skin and flirty glances.

I don't see any need to be coy after everything that's passed between us. When he drops his trousers, I let my gaze rove over every bulge and shadow of his chiseled legs from thighs to calves—and back up again, to one particularly impressive bulge tenting his drawers.

Stavros kicks his trousers to the side, his gaze smoldering into me. "Do I meet your satisfaction, Lady Thief?"

I wasn't always sure I liked that nickname. Hearing it now in his old sardonic lilt, the cockiness returned to his voice with warmth twined through it, lifts my spirits with another flutter of my pulse.

I smirk back at him. "I suppose you'll do."

With a rustle of my skirt, I stand and saunter toward him. Stavros holds perfectly still other than the rise and fall of his breath.

I set my hand on one pectoral and skim my fingertips down to his waist. The slight hitch of his chest eggs me on.

The top of my head barely reaches his shoulder. But that simply means that I'm the perfect height to press a kiss to one of those scars mottling his torso.

At the brush of my lips against his heated skin, a rumble of amusement that's a little ragged as well emanates from the former general's lungs. He cups my shoulder, gliding his thumb along the curving neckline of my dress.

Everywhere I shift my gaze, there's another nick or lingering line that I couldn't make out from afar. My lungs constrict at the sight of them.

I really don't have any concept of just how much this man endured during his years on the front lines of Silana's ongoing military squabbles. Has he skirted death even more times than I have?

With a sudden sense of urgency, I set my hand over the roughened skin of his dedication brand and kiss another of the scars. And another. And another.

"What are you doing?" Stavros asks, with a rasp in his voice he can't quite master.

I move my lips to the next scar, letting them graze his mottled skin as I speak. "Thanking Sabrelle for ensuring that none of these wounds brought you to your end."

A choked sound escapes him, and then he's tugging my chin up while he lowers his head. His mouth crashes into mine.

I've been kissed before by all three of the other men Julita brought together. Benedikt's kiss was merely a quick thrill, doused by his blasé attitude afterward. But Alek's can electrify me, and Casimir knows how to make me melt.

Stavros's kiss sets me on fire.

Even as the flames of desire dance beneath my skin, threatening to burn me up, I can't help leaning into him. Can't help wanting to absorb every bit of the scorching need we kindle between us.

This is the only kind of bonfire I want to worship at.

When he tugs at the laces of my gown to loosen it, I don't have a single protest left in me. I let the garment fall and wriggle out of my underskirt as well between kiss after addicting kiss.

I have to let go of him so he can pull off my chemise. He gazes down at me, now as bared as he is, with the familiar twitch of his head that makes me abruptly self-conscious.

I won't look anything like the pampered noblewomen he must be used to. No amount of living among them will disguise the effects of my childhood deprivations or the scars I've taken in different sorts of battles.

But Stavros traces his fingers down my sternum with a reverent expression. They graze the false godlen brand and continue to my belly button.

Then he lifts my arm and presses a tender kiss to the scar that slashes across my bicep from a blade I didn't dodge quite fast enough. The wider one on my forearm, where I scraped it on a window ledge fleeing the Crown's Watch at thirteen.

He trails a caress back up my arm and grazes the worst scars across my shoulder blades, his touch feather-light. His voice comes out low and raw. "The only one I can thank for keeping you alive is you. But Sabrelle herself would be impressed by the strength that's gotten you through everything you've endured."

I can't deny the admiration or the hunger in his tone. Before the surge of emotion can overwhelm me, I yank his mouth back to mine.

With one hand tangled in my hair and other arm a solid pressure against the small of my back, Stavros guides us both down to the floor with me straddling his lap. It's a good position for our mismatched heights, putting me where I can claim another kiss by bobbing a little up on my knees... or drop lower against him to create a friction that has us both groaning.

When I grind against him through our drawers, Stavros's arm tightens around me. He teases his hand down my front to cup my breast and cants his hips upward to pay me back in kind.

"Last night was good before I screwed it up," he murmurs between increasingly urgent kisses. "But this is so much better."

I make a noise of agreement that sounds embarrassingly like a whine of need and reclaim his mouth. As his tongue flicks between my lips, his thumb swivels over my nipple. I shiver with the pleasure flooding me from every angle.

A hard surface cooler than his skin strokes over my hip. I startle for a second before I recognize that—of course—it's his prosthetic.

Stavros pauses, glancing down at the hooked loop of metal against my leg. "I can take it off. I wasn't thinking—"

"No," I say quickly. "I... I like it."

A blush burns across my cheeks at the admission, but the look Stavros gives me in return sears away any shame I might have felt about unusual tastes. Like I'm the only person he ever wants to look at for the rest of his life.

A sudden fear squeezes my heart. I touch his face as if I need to steady us both against this question.

"Are you sure you're okay with—with me being with Alek and Casimir too?"

Alek suggested it to begin with, and I know Casimir has an open mind about romantic partnerships, but Stavros has never struck me as the type to be good at sharing. Does he think my giving myself over to this moment with him means I'm giving myself *just* to him from now on?

Before the fear can dig its claws any deeper, one of the sly grins that used to infuriate me curves the former general's lips. "I'll tolerate it. Because just one man couldn't possibly be enough for our new Signy."

I like him this way. The cockiness buoyed by the warmth of real assurance, no harsh edge of defensiveness souring his tone.

This is the man thousands of soldiers would gladly have followed into battle, knowing he'd subject them to no risk he didn't take himself. Knowing their well-being mattered to him as much as brilliant tactics did.

I don't think any of the men and women who died fulfilling his orders would have blamed him for it.

I tap my fingers against his cheek in the lightest of swats. "It seems to be the only part of the role that actually benefits me."

Stavros hums and dips his head closer so I'm flooded with his smoky, spicy scent. His voice is more a purr than a growl now. "I like seeing you a little bit selfish. Asking for what you want, taking everything you can have. If that means I have to make sure I keep proving myself worthy of you so you don't decide two is plenty, I'm not one to shy from a challenge."

A headier shiver travels down my spine. I run my hands down the impressive planes of his chest and let my mouth meld with his.

With each collision of our lips and caress of his hand against my breast, the throbbing need between my legs deepens. I rock against him, whimpering into our kiss at the feel of his hardness meeting my sex.

I delve one hand down between us and stroke him through his drawers.

"I want this," I mutter, with a flare of boldness. "Inside me."

A ragged chuckle escapes Stavros. "Then who am I to deny you, Lady Thief?"

He wrenches at my drawers, hooking his prosthetic over the waist, and I fumble with his at the same time. The second I've kicked mine off, I sink down over him, letting his rigid erection graze my folds skin to skin.

I'm so wet with my desire that we slide together perfectly. Stavros groans, but he steadies me in his arms.

"We take this slow. I don't want you feeling anything but good."

I give a small huff in acknowledgment, but he's just as big as I remembered from last night. I pump my fingers up and down over the velvety flesh that's rigid as steel underneath and line us up to take him into me.

With the first stretch of penetration, both our breaths stutter together. He eases inside gradually but firmly, filling me with a heady pressure until it takes all my self-control not to slam the rest of the way home, knowing I'd probably regret it.

Stavros strokes his prosthetic across my ass and his hand up and down my back, careful of my scars. A rumble sounds from low in his chest.

"That's right. Take it all. Fuck, Ivy."

There's so much need in those last two words that I clench around him with a whimper of my own longing. It already feels so good that I have trouble imagining what it'll be like when we really start moving.

Sweat has beaded on my forehead. I lean it against Stavros's shoulder and rock just slightly up and down. Working him deeper inside with every iteration until my next exhalation comes out in a gasp.

"Good?" he checks with a note of concern.

"So fucking good," I mumble, and start to pick up my pace.

Stavros bucks his hips up to meet me, carefully and then with more force when I moan my approval. Every jolt of sensation inside me sends bliss radiating through the rest of my body.

I cling to him, my fingernails digging into his back, but he makes no complaint. His lips brush against my hair, murmuring praise and encouragement and then simply, "Love you. Love you."

He bucks into me with those words, sending me soaring toward my release. The rush of it knocks the air from my lungs and a choked sound from my throat.

I tilt my head to the side and graze my teeth against the crook of his neck as if I need to bite him to stop myself from spiraling away completely. Stavros's hips jerk upwards, his cock plunging into me at just the right angle, and I shatter apart.

I feel him come with me, his muscles flexing around me, his embrace tightening as he clings to me just as firmly. I careen through the wave of pleasure and come back to earth nestled in his scorching but tender embrace.

"Mmm." I tuck myself even closer against him, reveling in the strength his body emanates. "Remind me to be selfish more often."

A laugh hitches out of Stavros. "I wish you could be. Great God help me, I wish I could hold you right here until the end of fucking time."

*Until there are no more scourge sorcerers to worry about. Until the king has to make some other plan without me.*

*It's a nice thought, but we both know there's no answer so simple.*

I nuzzle his jaw and hug him for the last short while before I have to go out and face the murderous path I've set myself on.

# FORTY-FOUR

*Ivy*

I'm just pulling on my leather sparring vest when a hand comes to rest on my shoulder.

"I can help you with that."

I peer up at Stavros through my eyelashes as he hooks the loops down one side and then the other, his fingers sparking tingles over my skin through my shirt. "I have managed to do it up just fine on my own all those times before."

He hums, a soft rumble that makes my nerves flutter even more. "I like that you'll let me." His head dips lower as his hand slides across my waist. "And it puts me in a perfect position to do this."

His mouth claims mine before I can say anything else, but at that point I'm not interested in arguing anyway. Being wooed by the exalted former General Stavros is an unexpectedly intoxicating experience.

And his ex-fiancée gave this up because he wasn't riding off into battle trying to get himself killed every other day? I don't know anything about her other than her status, but I'm pretty confident in saying she's an idiot.

Julita giggles. *You know, I wasn't sure if Stavros would be all that talented at kissing. I'm glad I lingered long enough to be proven wrong.*

There's enough genuine glee in her voice that I don't worry she's bottling up more jealousy. The new biggest problem in our friendship may be having to decide just how much detail I'm willing to go into about the intimate parts she's withdrawn for.

That thought reminds me of all the other ways Stavros and I need to be circumspect about our newfound closeness.

I ease back reluctantly. "When we leave this room, we're going to have to pretend things are still tense between us. If anyone associated with Torstem realizes we might be colluding after all…"

Stavros nods before I have to finish my statement. "I'm not looking forward to it, but I can glower and grouse at you if it'll shield you from worse harm." He glides his fingertips along my jaw in one last caress. "As long as you remember it is all an act."

I grin at him. "I don't think my memories of last night are going to fade that quickly."

But there are plenty of other memories to cast a pall over the day ahead. As we step into the hall, keeping a careful distance apart, my gaze slips along the row of doors toward Ster. Torstem's quarters farther down.

How long of a reprieve will I get before I need to spill his blood or betray the king?

I have the sudden urge to shove Stavros back into his quarters, to signal Alek and Casimir and spend whatever time I have left soaking up all the happiness I can squeeze out of this life. I don't know how much of a life I'll have left once I've carried out King Konram's orders.

As simple as the king made the job sound, with every passing hour the knowledge weighs on me that there's no guarantee I'll be able to escape in the chaos after the assassination. Torstem's end may be mine too.

But I have to admit that one life to rid the continent of a new scourge sorcerer uprising seems more than fair. I knew the risks when I set off on this path.

So I simply clench my hands at my sides and stalk along behind Stavros as if resenting my duties, all the way down to the training field.

Assisting with the combat class isn't so bad. These students have sparred with me enough to grant me a little respect.

I throw myself into the moment, clashing blades with the opponents Stavros sets me against and tossing out snarky remarks as if I'm every bit the rebel. It's a better distraction than moping around the campus on my own.

When the former general's back is turned, Olari shoots me a conspiratorial smile.

Does he know I saw him unmasked at the initiation ceremony? Or maybe he's simply anticipating that I'll put the pieces together when I join him for this evening's meeting of the bug club.

Despite my feigned friction with Stavros, I do my best to put on a supportive face with the students. Most of them have nothing to do with the mess I've gotten myself into.

I don't need more enemies on top of those I already have to contend with.

Speaking of potential enemies, this is one of the classes Petra joins the military division for. I contrive to avoid facing her throughout the various exercises Stavros assigns, but the distant royal has an unfortunate stubborn streak.

When I've finished hauling our equipment back into the storage building at the end of the class, I emerge from the room to find Petra standing in the building's dim hallway.

There's no one else around. It's obvious she's waiting for me.

I debate going so far as to stride right past her, but such a blatant snub feels unwise. So I stop and give her my best blank expression instead. "Was there something you needed?"

Petra's dark gaze flicks around us, as if she's as alert to possible eavesdroppers as I am. She steps closer, pitching her voice low. "I wanted to speak with you—briefly. I won't delay you for very long."

I fold my arms over my chest with a conscious effort to keep them loose rather than defensively tight. "Speak to me about what?"

Petra studies me for a few seconds, her pensive gaze uncomfortably keen. "I understand why you've rebuffed and avoided me, and I don't blame you for it. I shouldn't have put you in an awkward situation to begin with."

My stomach knots, but I knit my brow with honest confusion. "What are you talking about?"

She makes a dismissive gesture. "That's not the important part. The main thing I wanted to say is… When someone asks too much of you, it's reasonable to refuse. The people with the most power aren't always right."

A sinking sensation ripples through me from throat to gut. She can't possibly know—surely King Konram wouldn't have discussed his secret assassination plans with his niece however many times removed, of all people?

I'm not sure I believe he'd even tell the queen.

I can't stop my voice from stiffening slightly. "I don't quite follow what you mean. Ster. Stavros hasn't asked anything all that immense of me. I'm happy to do my job."

It's the response she should expect from someone who hasn't been given a different, horrible job by a figure with a lot more power than my employer, but the intensity in Petra's smooth face doesn't shift.

"Maybe you're not sure you can say no outright," she says. "But you can pick your own methods to achieve the same goal. Do it your way, the way that feels right to you. That's all the gods want from us. I'm sorry."

She turns on her heel and hurries out of the storage building without another word. Her last two words ring in my head.

Somehow the apology unsettles me more than anything else.

*Well,* Julita says in a doubtful tone. *What in the realms was she getting at?*

I lift my shoulders in a tiny shrug, but my stomach keeps churning.

It certainly sounded as if Petra knows what I've been asked to do. Even if she doesn't—would her suggestion still apply?

Gods smite me, why should I listen to some minor royal's opinions anyway? It isn't her neck on the line with the scourge sorcerers or the king.

But through the rest of the day, Petra's words keep niggling at me.

I'm already carrying out the king's command "my way," aren't I? I'll be using my stealth and my knife, the tools I've relied on so often in the past.

Of course, Petra has no idea who I've been in the past. Does she think her distant uncle instructed me on exactly how to kill Ster. Torstem, and there might be some other method of murder I'd prefer?

Or did she mean something else entirely?

And what in the realms would the god who's kept me alive this far want, anyway? Kosmel is continuing to be frustratingly silent on that subject.

I have to push all those unsettling questions aside when I make my way to the entomology club's room in the Quadring. This time I get to enter it through the door rather than slipping through a window.

Having experienced the space before, I'm prepared for the mix of woodsy and sour scents and the ever-present rustling of the club room's smallest inhabitants. Still, my skin creeps as I step inside.

Although to be fair, the human inhabitants are at least as much to blame for that.

Olari looks up from where he's standing near a row of terrariums with two other students I recognize from Alek's sketches and my own furtive observations. He dips his head to me in acknowledgment.

Several other students glance over from their places amid the tanks and tables to take in the newcomer. Some I recognize as other likely conspirators. The others are probably innocent dupes who think this organization really is just about an interest in insect life.

And then, naturally, there's our valiant leader, Ster. Torstem.

The law professor strides over and beckons me farther into the room. "Ivy of Nikodi. I heard you'd expressed an interest in joining our little cabal here." He chuckles lightly as if "cabal" isn't actually a more accurate word to describe what he's been running than "club."

He told me exactly how to reply, even if he doesn't realize I know he was the one giving the instructions.

I offer an ingratiating smile. "I've always been curious about the smallest of our world's creatures. I heard you've collected several rare specimens."

"Indeed we have! Come in, come in. Let me show you a few that we're particularly proud of."

He sets his hand on my shoulder to guide me forward. In the back of my head, Julita's presence shudders the way I wish I could.

*I don't approve of King Konram assigning you to be a murderer,* she mutters, *but if you have to murder someone, I can't say I mind it being this slimy traitor.*

I can't help but share her sentiment.

Ster. Torstem points out a pair of beetles with iridescent shells that change color depending on the angle of the light, a moth that looks identical to the leaves on the branch in its enclosure, and a ruddy-shelled centipede as thick as my thumb and twice as long. I gamely ooh and aah over them while sending silent thanks to Creaden for the thick construction of the habitats' walls.

I wouldn't say I'm particularly squeamish after my years living on the streets, but if that last creature scrambled its many legs up my arm, I think I might scream.

Torstem introduces me to the other club members in attendance, focusing on Olari's trio and the others whose names I'm familiar with.

"I believe you'll be with our fields group to start," he says in a casually authoritative tone. "It's too unwieldly for all of us to make our expeditions together, so we've divided into fields and forests, switching things up halfway through the year. Luckily for you, we have a fields expedition coming up in just a couple of nights, if you're able to join us. It's right before break-day, so it shouldn't interfere with your assistant position."

A couple of nights?

A chill sweeps through my body, but I keep my smile plastered in place. "I'm sure I can arrange that. I'll look forward to the trip."

In just two days, I'm supposed to kill this man.

Torstem simply smiles back, oblivious to my true intentions. "Wonderful. You'll be a welcome addition to our team."

Even if my head is whirling, I'm supposed to make a show of having a real interest in the club. I wander along the shelves of tanks, watching the various insects navigate their manufactured habitats. I can't shake the feeling that the walls have closed in on me as tightly as those surrounding the bug club's many tiny prisoners.

At one table, a couple of the members who must be from the forests group are adding soil to the base of a large, open-topped terrarium. I gravitate toward them. It might be nice to talk to someone who isn't scheming to topple civilization as we know it.

"What are you setting this one up for?" I ask.

The guy pats down the soil around a small metal trough with pebbles along the bottom. "We're hoping to find a glowdid on our next trip out. They only show themselves for a few weeks during the early summer. The club's never had one before."

"They're awfully quick too," explains the woman next to him. "And of course we don't want to harm the one we catch."

"I think we have a good chance." The guy brushes his fingers over the small shrub planted at one end of the tank. "Glowdids only eat pilmetta leaves, and it's notoriously difficult to grow them inside. But we've gotten this one to thrive. Prospira must support our quest."

The woman sketches her fingers down her front in the gesture of the divinities. "I think we should take it as a sign of approval. Maybe not of catching one, but of our overall goal, at least."

A quiver of sharper alertness runs through my nerves. Those words echo back to something Petra said.

I cock my head. "Your overall goal?"

The woman nods enthusiastically. "We'd like to catch a couple of glowdids in order to study and even breed them. But the most important part is simply observing them and getting a better understanding of their behavior, even if it's only in their normal environment. Their numbers have been dwindling lately. We'd like to find a way to help their population stay healthy and secure."

Different methods to achieve the same goal. Another quiver races straight down the middle of me. "That makes sense. I hope you can manage it."

I meander on, my eyes turned toward the next set of terrariums but my mind drifting far beyond this room.

The king's goal isn't really to have me murder Ster. Torstem. It's to end the threat the scourge sorcerers present. He simply thinks their leader's death is the likeliest way to ensure that outcome, and I'm the tool most readily available.

What if there's something that could destroy the conspiracy *without* me having to stain my hands with all that blood?

# FORTY-FIVE

*Alek*

When I step through the cord into the palace meeting room at our scheduled time and find only Stavros waiting, my pulse hiccups. "Isn't Ivy—"

"The bug club meeting ran a little long, but she's fine," he says from where he's sitting at the table, before I need to finish my anxious question. "She didn't end up eating beforehand, so she ran to grab something from the dining hall before she'll join us."

The momentary panic that gripped me eases. I walk over to the table, but I still feel too anxious to sit down.

Stavros's expression is grim. It's hard to relax when even a former general who's survived a hundred battles looks uneasy about a situation.

My fingers curl around the top of the chair. "Did she tell you anything about what went on with the entomology club?"

Stavros's mouth tightens even more before he answers. "A little. As usual, she wants to give us the full account all together rather than repeating herself."

He obviously isn't inclined to give me the little he does know, but after a pause, he lifts his gaze to meet mine again. "One of those clay deliveries you suspect is for the scourge sorcerers went out this morning."

My heart skips in a more enthusiastic fashion. "Was someone able to track it?"

"The two soldiers the king assigned to watch the quarry are particularly adept at stealth missions. They followed the workers at a distance and saw the hand-off with the buyer. Unfortunately, they only managed to stay on the buyer's trail for half a mile before the wagon and its driver vanished."

I frown. "'Vanished'?"

Stavros lets out a disgruntled sigh. "Simply disappeared from view in a blink, as the soldiers tell it. They hung back for a short while and then surveyed the area, but they couldn't find any traces of passage."

I push away from the chair to pace the length of the table. "We know from what Ivy's told us that the scourge sorcerers must have someone very skilled with concealing magic on their side. They're able to disguise their passage of the Starsil and the bonfires they worship around."

"Yes, we have to assume magic was involved. So we don't know *where* they were taking the clay, but I think we can consider it confirmed that it is the scourge sorcerers who are taking it."

His tone stays as grim as his expression. I can't summon a smile myself.

It's an awfully minor victory. We need so much more if we're going to free Ivy from the task King Konram assigned to her.

Casimir arrives a moment later, with the same worried glance around the room I must have made on my entrance. Before he can even ask about Ivy, she emerges from her loop of cord too with a swish of her layered skirts.

Her face holds such a mix of foreboding and resolve that a pang reverberates through my heart even as my lips spring into a smile at the sight of her. She swipes a few stray strands of hair back from her cheeks and squares her shoulders.

But when her eyes meet mine, the emotion that sparks in them sends a bolt of giddiness straight through my nerves. With an answering smile, she walks straight to me and bobs up to press her mouth against mine.

It isn't one of the chaste pecks we've exchanged since she told Casimir and me that we needed to tone down the physical part of our relationship. The heat of the kiss sets my pulse racing with a flush that washes over my skin.

I hesitate only for an instant with a hitch of surprise, and then I clasp the back of her neck to return the kiss as eagerly as she's offered it. I don't know what's gotten into her, but I want her to know I'm right here with her.

Ivy draws back with a softer smile that lights me up from head to toe. "I sorted some things out with Julita. We don't have to hold back our feelings."

The relief that sweeps through me at those words is as much for Ivy as my own satisfaction. I can't imagine what it's like being at odds with another person who's residing right inside your head.

I squeeze her shoulder. "I'm glad you could come to an understanding." As I peer into her eyes, I try to picture the woman I knew before her watching me through them too. "Thank you."

Ivy breaks into a laugh, a hint of a blush coloring her pale cheeks. "She says you're very welcome as long as you make sure to take good care of me."

My own face heats even more, but my lips twitch with a grin. "I don't think that'll be a problem."

Casimir has been following our exchange with his usual serene composure, no sign of impatience or jealousy. But the second Ivy turns to him, he steps forward to meet her, beaming so avidly no one could doubt how happy he is to accept her embrace.

It's a strange sensation, watching the woman I've fallen for kiss another man. A wobble runs through the pit of my stomach, a sense of loss that I'm not sharing that moment with her as well. And yet exhilaration floods me to see her beam back at him, even happier now that she's reconfirmed her affection for both of us.

She's an extraordinary woman. I'm not sure I really could "take care" of her as thoroughly as she deserves on my own.

And there's no one I'd trust more than the courtesan to ensure she's never left wanting—in any of the ways I want her life with us to be better than what she had before.

My gaze slides to the other man at the table.

Stavros has remained in his chair, but his expression has shifted as he watches Ivy with us. Like he can't tear his eyes from her… and he isn't sure he'd want to anyway.

I'm not sure what to make of that or the slightly wary smile Ivy shoots him that relaxes when he chuckles in return. Something has changed in their dynamic. The tension that's shadowed this room so often in the past few weeks has lightened.

I'll count that as a win, whatever exactly has passed between them.

Then Stavros sits up straighter, the solemn cast returning to his face, and I'm dragged back to the full reality of our situation. This isn't a joyful reunion—it's a strategy session to send Ivy off to commit an assassination.

The happy glow that came over Ivy dims too, but she speaks with the same steely resolve I saw when she stepped into the room. "I'm supposed to go on a 'bug club' expedition in two nights. Presumably it's actually an Order of the Wild gathering."

My breath halts in my chest. "Two nights? You were *just* initiated."

Ivy shrugs. "Maybe they want to get us initiates fully immersed quickly. It's probably for the best, since we want to make our move before they have a chance to strike at the royal family."

Casimir sets his hand on her arm. "Did they say anything about what you'll be doing on the 'expedition'?"

She shakes her head. "I doubt they'd want to even hint at their real purpose with the other club members around. But it'll involve at least all of the members who are part of the conspiracy—and I should have a chance to get close to Ster. Torstem."

Stavros pushes to his feet as if he can't bear to stay sitting any longer. "I can alert the king and make an excuse to visit the nearest posted squadron that night, so I'll be able to direct them to you when you signal me."

It's happening too fast. I can't stop myself from blurting out a protest. "You shouldn't have to do it."

Stavros's dark gaze swings to me. "None of us thinks she should. But if she's going to insist—"

"I'm not," Ivy breaks in.

All three of us stare at her. Now I feel as if the breath has been knocked right out of my lungs.

"What?" I manage to say, afraid to hope that she means what I think she does.

Ivy lifts her chin defiantly. "I'll kill him if I have to. But I want to try another way first. The king doesn't *need* Torstem dead by my hand, does he? All that really matters to him is overturning the conspiracy."

Stavros is studying her with open bemusement. "I'd say that's true. He seemed to think Torstem's death was a necessary component. Do you have some new plan for accomplishing that aim?"

She grimaces. "I'm still working it out. I was hoping the three of you could help. We need all the scourge sorcerers distracted and in disarray for the soldiers to be able to sweep in and apprehend them. If the king would like one of his people to then find a reason to murder Torstem—for resisting arrest, perhaps—it'll be out of my hands."

A vicious light sparks in Stavros's eyes. "I know at least one person who'd be happy to take up that duty. And who can assure King Konram that you fulfilled all the important parts of your mission, as far as I'm concerned."

My spirits have lifted, but the weight of doubt dampens my initial excitement. "We'd still have to get the squadron to the conspirators before they realize there's trouble and scatter. From what Ivy's said, it'll be awfully difficult to distract them enough that they'd disregard a warning from their sentries. They're so quick to turn on anyone they feel isn't standing with them… Anything Ivy does to upset them could make her a target."

Stavros glances at Ivy with a frown. "Yes, whatever you do would have to keep them too distraught to rally at an impending threat for long enough for us to reach you. The closest squadron is about an hour's ride from the region Casimir identified."

I nod miserably. "I hate to say it, but you'd be safer stabbing Torstem and then fleeing. I can't think of much that would affect them that strongly other than losing their leader. The fervor they've shown—they're so devoted to their cause and so convinced that they have the only true answer to calling back the All-Giver—"

Ivy's head jerks toward me. "That's it!"

I blink at her. "What is?"

"They're sure they're right," she says, rapping her hand against the tabletop. "But even with all their power, they're not. What if I can do something that makes them doubt the entire reason they've gathered at all? Turn them against each other thinking they've been led astray, that the gods are angry with them rather than approving?"

Casimir rubs his jaw, his eyes gone pensive. "You'd need to tread carefully. The gods could be offended by *you* pretending to speak for them too."

But the new idea has given me a renewed surge of inspiration. "They don't have to speak. Most people don't hear voices from their godlen anyway. They interpret dreams—well, I suppose that isn't likely to be applicable in the middle of a gathering—and signs that catch their attention. If you could create a significant omen that would look like disapproval without outright impersonating one of the godlen…"

Stavros clears his throat. "To make a big enough 'sign' to unsettle the scourge sorcerers, I'd imagine Ivy would need to use her magic."

An uneasy silence settles over the room. Ivy's mouth twists as she studies Stavros's expression.

"You're right," she says after a moment. "So maybe I can't attempt a different approach after all. I —I'd be willing to tap into my power if it means throwing the conspirators into disorder, but I don't know if I'd be able to control it well enough to avoid doing more harm than good. It's always been Kosmel guiding the consequences when I've handled it effectively, and he hasn't given *me* any signs in days."

The hopelessness that's crept back into her voice lances through my gut.

I grope for any tool I have to counter it. "I was able to find an antidote for the crozzemi toxin's effects. I've already arranged to pick some up tomorrow morning, so you'll have it in time. You'll be more in control of your reactions than before."

Ivy shoots me a grateful smile, but she still looks deflated. "Thank you. That'll make some difference, assuming it works. But even when I'm fully conscious, I've never been able to harness the backlash my magic creates. It seems to decide for itself."

Except when the godlen who appeared to have chosen her as his champion intervened.

I knit my brow. "You said Kosmel hasn't offered any guidance recently. What exactly has he said before when he's spoken to you directly—when you've asked him to regulate your magic?"

Ivy pauses, her lips pursing as she thinks back. "The first time, when I was dying, he talked as if he couldn't guide it unless I agreed. In the tower, he said he'd help as long as I let him in. And the last time, with Benedikt… He basically said it was up to me. That I had to decide how I wanted to handle the situation and he'd just back me up, essentially."

I consider that and what she said about her initiation. "Did you ask him to help you do something when you were struggling with your magic the other night?"

Her forehead furrows. "Nothing specific, I guess. It was more of a broad call for help."

"Then maybe that's the problem. The gods don't generally intervene all that blatantly in anyone's life—and it sounds like he's said you have to direct how he assists rather than the other way around."

Casimir lets out a thoughtful hum. "That does align with a lot of the philosophy I've heard and read from clerics and devouts. The gods will act through us but not for us."

"So if I decide what I want to happen and tell him exactly what I need," Ivy says slowly, "maybe he'll show up? But I won't know until I try."

The courtesan offers her a wry grin. "That's why they call it faith and not certainty."

Stavros stirs on his feet. "Normally in a situation this dangerous, I'd say only trust what you can hold in your hands. But he's supported you multiple times before."

Ivy inhales deeply and seems to gather herself. "All right. I don't have to make the ultimate decision until I'm there. I'll prepare as much as possible, but I can still go straight to the stabbing if I don't like the looks of things."

The ex-general tips his head. "We may also be able to arrange for some supplies to be left in the general area, so possibly your magic could draw on something concrete rather than having to conjure every effect from nothing. If you have any idea what sort of effects you'd want to create?"

Ivy has always seemed awkward when anyone's complimented her appearance, but I can honestly say that when that shrewd yet hopeful light comes into her face, I can't imagine another person looking more stunning. I can see everything she's been through—and all the strength she's used to rise above it.

She wets her lips and glances around at us. "The scourge sorcerers like to use fire to destroy what they don't want. What if I could turn the flames around on them?"

# Forty-Six

*Ivy*

In the moments after I've pressed the inside of my locket, I clutch the trinket tightly, waiting under the warm glow of the meeting room's chandelier for the men I've summoned to arrive. Despite all the sentiments we've already exchanged, I feel unexpectedly adrift when I think of why I'm here.

I need to say it. I'm heading out in a matter of minutes to try to take down a murderously obsessive conspiracy.

I don't know if I'll get another chance.

Here with no one to see me, I let my anxious fingers fidget with the folds of my skirt. I've put on the turquoise gown that's my favorite, its vibrant hue mostly tucked away under my cloak, in an attempt to boost my spirits in every way possible.

I can become a noblewoman. I can catch a man's eye.

I'm a force to be reckoned with, and I will wield my magic as *I* wish it tonight.

Casimir materializes first, his deep green eyes wide with urgency. I hold up my hand and then clasp his before he needs to ask any panicked questions. "Nothing's gone wrong. I just wanted to see you and Alek one more time before I go."

I discussed this meeting with Stavros in his quarters—he knows to ignore the signal. He's already set off to join the squadron that'll hopefully be charging to my aid in just a few hours.

I don't need to explain anything more to Casimir. The courtesan's expression softens with a mix of fondness and concern that squeezes my heart even tighter than it already felt.

He knows the chances of my returning are much less than any other time I've gone off with the Order of the Wild. Maybe altogether slim.

Who can say whether we'll see each other again?

Alek emerges from his cord a moment later, with his dark hair swaying across the top of his mask and a similarly urgent air. I tug him close to me with a reassuring smile that I hope gives him more comfort than it's giving me.

"I needed a little company right before I leave," I say.

But that's not the full reason. It's just going to take me a minute to gather myself for the rest.

Alek slips his arm around my waist and Casimir tucks his around my elbow. The two men who first accepted me for all I am envelop me in their warmth and their different sorts of strength from either side.

If I were being perfectly fair, I'd speak to Casimir before Alek. He's the one who welcomed me from the very beginning, who won my heart when I was so afraid of losing it.

But knowing these men as I do now, I turn to the scholar first. Casimir has the certainty of his gift showing him how much he matters to me; he has the confidence of years of navigating tender emotions.

This territory is as new to Alek as it is to me.

I touch the side of Alek's face, and he leans in automatically to claim a kiss. The lingering press of his mouth against mine tastes bittersweet, as if he's hoping the gesture can keep me here away from danger. I choke up despite my best efforts.

When he finally eases back, his bright brown eyes shine with as much emotion as is whirling inside me. I find the words rise in my throat with no effort after all.

I smile up at him. "I love you."

Alek's lips part with a moment's shock. "What?"

It's even easier the second time. "I love you. I love how quickly your mind works and how much information you choose to fill it with. I love your dedication to every cause you take up." My smile turns sly. "I love how much you enjoy certain volumes of Woudish poetry."

A breathless laugh escapes him, and then he's capturing my mouth in another kiss, more emphatic than the last.

"I love you too," he murmurs after, still close enough that his breath grazes my mouth. "Everything about you, everything you bring to this world. Gods help me, Ivy, if I could ride out there with you and stand with you against the scourge sorcerers—"

I swallow hard. "I know."

When I shift my gaze to Casimir, he's smiling so brightly I have no doubt that I made the right decision. He looks as happy to see me declare the depths of my affection for Alek as Alek is.

Here's hoping I can make him even happier.

For all the confidence I've gained, the words still feel momentous on my tongue. I tighten my grip on his hand. "I love you. I love your boundless compassion and your commitment to increasing the joy in the world. I love the generosity you've spoiled me with and the ways you've let me spoil you a little in return."

The courtesan dips his head, his lips brushing my temple and my cheek before reaching my mouth. I'm tingling before we're even really kissing.

"I love you too," he says, sounding a little choked up himself. "And I look forward to watching your delight through every bath and ride and dance we share. Meeting you is the greatest gift I could have asked for."

I hug them both closer, willing back the tears that prick at my eyes. I need to remember this—all the faith they have in me, how avidly they'll be awaiting my return—through every moment I'm out there among the enemy.

My mind slips back to my last exchange with Stavros: the fiery kiss he gave me, the emphatic order to do whatever it takes to get away from the scourge sorcerers alive. His promise to be there to cut them down for me as fast as his steed can carry him.

I might not be ready to say those three words back to him yet, but I treasure his faith in me too.

"You'll take the antidote?" Alek checks.

I nod. "I'm going to chew one of the tablets you made from the powder before I leave, just to be safe, and have a couple more in my sleeve for after."

"Good. Two should be enough to offset a cupful, but it won't hurt to have three."

Casimir reaches into his carry pouch. "I bought this before we knew how soon you'd be going. I thought it'd make a perfect welcome back present. But seeing you in that dress now…"

He draws out a pendant with a gleaming teal gemstone, hung on a fine gold chain. "So you'll have something from me with you no matter how far away you have to go."

I have to start blinking away tears now. I fasten the chain around my neck and slip the pendant under the neckline of my dress where it'll stay safe next to my heart. "Thank you. It's beautiful."

The bell sounds through the walls, marking the eighth hour. That's my cue to go.

Official club meetings don't need to be held furtively in the middle of the night like clandestine initiation tests do.

I pull away from my men reluctantly. "I'd better go. I'll see you tomorrow."

Let that be a promise and not a lie.

With a ripple of magic through my flesh, I step back through the ring of cord into Stavros's quarters. I take a second to pat my thighs and confirm my extra knives are in place this time, as loath as I am to use them.

Then I pop one of the three antidote pills Alek gave me into my mouth. Its bitter flavor coats my tongue as I hurry out of the Domi.

I meet up with a few of the bug club members including Olari on my way across the outer field. The nine of us heading out tonight congregate along the college's wall just beyond the gate, where two carriages are waiting.

We're traveling in noble style this time. I guess there are some benefits to foregoing anonymity.

Ster. Torstem ushers us into the carriages seemingly at random, but I end up squeezed into the back of one directly across from him. As I peer out the window at the streets we pass, I can't help wondering if the law professor wanted to keep a close eye on his newest college recruit.

Am I the only one from whoever he was considering at the school who passed all his tests? I haven't seen the young man who came along that one night among the bug club members.

It's possible he's made a strange disappearance or met an untimely death, just like Benedikt.

I glance up at the star-flecked sky with a silent prayer. *Kosmel, if you're still watching over me, I need you with me tonight. I've jumped in as deep as I can get… but I'm not sure I can get out again without your help.*

No divine voice reverberates through my head in answer. I catch a flicker of movement that might be a crow landing on a rooftop, but when I peer closer, I can't make out its form any longer.

A sign or just wishful thinking?

My fellow club members stay quiet until we've passed through the gate out of the city. With farmland around us and no chance of anyone overhearing, Olari speaks up. "Where are we going tonight?"

A thin smile crosses Ster. Torstem's face. "I have something a little special planned that I think you'll all appreciate. We deserve a chance to stretch the gifts we've earned."

My stomach flips over. What's that supposed to mean?

Julita stirs out of her uneasy silence with a snarky remark. *He won't like what your gift can do to him.*

She still sounds unsettled, though.

As far as I can tell from the stars and the turns in the road, we head east and a little north as expected. But about an hour into our journey, the carriages roll to a halt, and we disembark to find a large covered wagon waiting for us.

The other bug club members clamber inside without missing a beat. Clearly this is typical protocol.

I follow them, suppressing the apprehension that's swelling in my gut.

Beneath the stretched canvas, a small lantern smolders, casting its wavering light and an oily scent through the interior. Built-in benches set with cushions line the sides of the wagon. Still more comfortable than my past conveyances, not that I find the fact all that reassuring.

As the driver taps the horses into motion, I notice the wagon lurches to the left. I think it's heading southeast now. After a few minutes, it veers farther left again.

We're not going to the same area where Casimir heard there'd been evidence of bonfires in the past. Will we end up closer to wherever Stavros's squadron is stationed… or farther away?

Even with my hands tucked under the fall of my cloak, I resist the urge to clench them. Around me, the other would-be worshippers are starting to talk in eager voices, anticipation thrumming through the air.

They're looking forward to this expedition as much as I'm dreading it.

Ster. Torstem pulls out a small chest from beneath the bench. He produces several vials of a greenish liquid that he passes around to each of us. "Let's buoy up our festive mood! The gods deserve all our emotions bared."

With a few whoops, everyone else unstoppers their vial. I do the same and take a quick whiff.

It smells the same as the stuff we drank before. One small relief.

Feeling Torstem's gaze on me, I toss mine back with the others. I don't risk trying to spit any down my sleeve while I'm in his sights, but I do pop the other two antidote pills into my mouth under the guise of wiping it.

*How do you feel?* Julita asks, as if I can answer her right now. *Do you think the antidote is working?*

My nerves are still jittering, but none of the dizziness has come over me so far. Around me, my companions are laughing and swaying on their seats. I force a grin onto my face and giggle at a jolt of the wheels as if I'm equally ecstatic.

Avoiding the drug was the least of my many problems. What's this special something Torstem has planned?

In the midst of the growing clamor, someone pulls out a sack of clay masks like the kind we wore during my initiation. I guess we college-goers still want to stay disguised from the rest of the Order of the Wild, wherever they come from.

Or maybe they see it as part of their worship, merging our humanness with animal forms.

I fix a mask over my face, the sense of concealment oddly reassuring even though I know everyone here is aware of who I am already. A quiver of energy tickles against my skin, but the illusions don't spring into being yet—they must be triggered by other magic cast near the place where the Order of the Wild carries out their rites.

It isn't much longer before I have the sense of the wagon tilting up a slope. We jostle against each other with more giddy laughter that I have to fake.

Did Torstem drink any of the drug? I think he might be totally sober too, though he joins in the laughter with a few chuckles of his own.

When the wagon lurches and stops, we scramble out onto a broad hilltop. A bonfire is already roaring away in the center of the grassy plateau, where three other covered wagons are parked nearby.

A figure whose mask gives the look of a weasel is just tossing more logs to feed the flames. At least a dozen others stand around the fire, cloaked in illusions of various beasts.

As Ster. Torstem ushers us forward, the heat crackles over my skin alongside a ripple of the magical energy that must be concealing it to more distant eyes. Some of the other conspirators start reaching their hands toward the flames and whirling around in chaotic dances.

"We open ourselves up for the All-Giver!" someone shouts.

More cries go up through the warbling of the flames. "Worship the wildness within!"

"Remember where we came from!"

"Honor the spirit at our center, the true life the Great God gave us!"

I spin and clap my hands as if thrilled to be there, eyeing the supplies around us surreptitiously. There are the four wagons, although I need to be careful of the horses. A couple of people have brought out crates, one holding a few bottles of wine and another a heap of apples. Several of the revelers have dropped their cloaks or jackets to bask in the fire's heat.

I have no sense of where the materials my men arranged to have stashed for me ended up relative to our unexpected diversion in route, but I think I have everything I need with me as it is. Should I ask Kosmel to guide my magic now or let the scourge sorcerers get even more caught up in their arcane ritual?

My magic stirs in my chest, and I instinctively balk against it.

What if Kosmel doesn't approve of the course I've taken? I don't even know how much might be at stake if I give my power free rein without any divine direction at all.

In my hesitation, Torstem waves toward one of the wagons and raises his voice. "Wildings, we have a special guest with us tonight! Throughout our realm, there are those who've sacrificed much to support our cause and enhance the gifts we've been granted. Please celebrate Ginelle for all she's given us and her deep devotion to our gods!"

A woman emerges from the wagon with a masked figure on either side of her. Or at least I assume she's a woman from her name.

A shroud—pale gray, unlike the black ones the Order has favored before—drapes across her from head to feet. But even with that covering, having seen people like her before, I can make out the signs of a sacrificial accomplice.

No hair fills out the folds around her head, where her scalp will have been carved bald. No doubt she gave up her ears too. The fabric falls flat across her face, where she's probably sacrificed her eyes and nose.

Her entire body looks oddly slim, because she's had both arms carved off at the shoulders like Wendos's accomplices in the tower. Her lurching gait suggests she gave at least part of one of her legs as well.

And who knows how much they cut out of her insides.

*Another one*, Julita murmurs with a shudder.

My stomach churns. The current scourge sorcerers have tried to skirt the prohibition against claiming another's sacrifice for their own power by keeping their victims alive... but I don't know how what those poor dupes are put through can be considered a life at all.

Torstem grooms them from childhood, seeking out orphans and maybe other vulnerable boys and girls as well. Telling them stories of the greatness they can help him achieve in the name of the gods.

Persuading them that mutilating themselves to the edge of suicide is the greatest offering they can make to the divinities and their country.

The shrouded woman drops into an awkward kneel and bows her head. From the hazy whispers around the fire, I'm not sure how many of my companions have seen one of the accomplices meant to support their sorcery before, even concealed like this.

Torstem points across the darkened land. "Over there lies a count's manor house. A despicable man who doesn't deserve the title. He gathers taxes for himself in the name of the false king and ignores the pleas of the peasants living under him. We can free them to pick their own master. Ginelle's gift will amplify our own. Let us show the false leaders of this world what the gods think of their arrogance!"

A cheer rises up from the revelers. I lift my voice alongside theirs, restraining a snort at the hypocrisy.

Arrogance? Has Ster. Torstem looked in a mirror lately?

"If you have any kind of talent that would allow you to move or project or send something to a destination, join us now," the law professor goes on. "Let's throw some of our fateful fire onto the count and send his manor home up in smoke as an offering to the gods watching over us."

I'm exempt from this act of sabotage, then. My gift is supposedly for forging replicas, not conjuring anything real, and an illusion of flames isn't what they're looking for.

That fact doesn't stop my gut from plummeting as several of my companions step even closer to the fire.

"Repeat after me," Torstem orders. "These divine words tell the gods that we want to merge our gifts with Ginelle's for their benefit. Say them and picture the house of corruption. Use whatever power you have to cast the flames toward it."

He points in the direction he indicated before and starts speaking the same disjointed syllables I heard from Wendos in the tower. Julita cringes back in my head.

The participating Wildings pick up the chant, some with the confidence of experience, others cautiously as they adjust to the sounds. The fire flares higher, a sharper heat washing over me.

My pulse lurches. Whatever I'm going to do, I'd better do it soon.

I delve my hand into my pocket, flick open my locket, and press my thumb to its inner surface.

The summons has been sent. There's no going back from this.

I ease toward Torstem, counting on the ritual to distract part of his attention. I want to be near enough that I can spring in with one of my knives if my other plan goes wrong.

Someone breaks from their chant with a triumphant shout. My gaze jerks across the darkness— and catches on a flicker of light that appears to have sparked on a rooftop.

Even as my pulse stutters, the flame fizzles out. But the voices around me intensify with eagerness as the scourge sorcerers see the first proof that their efforts could work.

A pool of icy horror forms in the pit of my stomach, setting my riven power banging at my ribs for release.

I don't know anything about the count who oversees this domain, but he won't be the only one in that house. He'll have a family, maybe children—there'll be staff and servants. Most of them asleep and oblivious to any threat.

I have to act *now*.

I take one more step in Torstem's direction but fix my gaze on the fire. Through the clamor of my magic, I open myself up to the divine touch that's come to my aid before.

*Kosmel, direct the backlash of my magic away from any who don't deserve the harm. As I command the fire, steal heat where it won't be missed. Please.*

He doesn't answer. But like Casimir said, this is about faith, not certainty.

The only thing I'm certain of is that I don't want to be a true murderer.

I loosen my hold on the power inside me and funnel it toward the flames. With a yank of my will, they shoot higher—and lash out toward the gathered figures around me.

The chanting sorcerers yelp and scatter, dashing backward from the fire that's turned on them. A tingling pressure forms on my shoulder, like someone has set his hand there, confirming he's with me.

*You're doing it!* Julita crows. *Let's teach these fiends a lesson.*

I'm not alone, inside or out.

But I'm not here to murder by burning alive either. All I want is to sow chaos against the people who've encouraged it—and remove the scourge sorcerers' means of escape.

I fling the fire toward the wagon we arrived in, letting it lick across the discarded clothes on the grass in between. The lumps of fabric and the wagon's canvas covering burst into flames.

I yank their searing heat down toward the base and its wheels, holding it back from the horses and their squeals of panic.

Kosmel's wryly divine voice reverberates through my body. *Very good, my wayward rogue. A few houses that had caught fire in the next province over have found themselves abruptly saved so you could bring the flames here. I'm sure you don't mind.*

I have to hold back a laugh. Power vibrates through my veins.

I can do this. I can bend my own wild power to serve a good purpose.

Let the scourge sorcerers see the results of *their* arrogance. Let them think about why their worshipful fire might have turned on them.

I will another blast of flames toward the second wagon—
And they sputter out before they reach the arched canvas.
The heat sizzling through the air dwindles. The fire on the first wagon snuffs out too.
Julita gasps. *What in the realms…?*
My gaze flicks around the hilltop, understanding hitting me like a jab to the gut.
Something is countering my magic.

# Forty-Seven

*Ivy*

"Be calm!" Ster. Torstem calls out to the gathered worshippers in their animalistic guises, with a tingling rush of magic that prickles through my nerves.

The panicked voices fade. The fire droops lower.

*Oh no,* Julita murmurs.

As I stare at the law professor, Alek's voice filters up from my memory: "His gift on record is the ability to quell anger."

Plenty of people find ways to adapt the gifts their godlen blessed them with to broader uses than they were originally intended for. Esmae's talent with the wind was meant for carrying "messages," but she managed to twist it into flinging knives as well.

You could certainly see a fire's destructive blaze as a sort of anger.

It never occurred to me that Torstem might be powerful enough to deflect my riven magic. But that's what's so dangerous and reviled about both my power and the kind scourge sorcerers take on, isn't it?

He's not using only his gift but the benefits of Ginelle's immense sacrifice as well.

And he doesn't even need to worry about consequences. The sacrifices have already been made.

The Order of the Wild members start to chatter with awed relief, and I realize my attempt has even worse consequences of the non-supernatural kind. Torstem has managed to make it look as if his authority cooled the fire and prevented the destruction—as if the gods support him even more than his followers would have already believed.

Fuck.

My hand drifts to my side in a subtle gesture, braced over the knife beneath. I've already signaled Stavros—before the soldiers get close, I need the scourge sorcerers in disarray, too distraught to cover up their ritual and flee.

My way didn't work. So now all that's left is to kill the man in the bloody fashion the king asked for.

My ghostly passenger isn't ready to give up. Julita shifts in the back of my head. *Isn't there anything else you could ask your magic to do? He can't have the power to stop* everything.

As Torstem motions his followers closer to the bonfire again with an air of total assurance, bitterness courses through me. I don't know what else I could do that would set this bunch scrambling.

I'm not sure how much time I even have. With every minute I delay, I risk ruining the entire plan.

How ridiculous is it that this man has built his secret cabal of traitors by riling up anger against our rulers, while holding a gift meant to do the opposite?

The second that thought runs through my mind, my breath halts in my throat.

He *has* controlled his followers by stoking their anger—with his words and his actions, not his magic. He was doing it just now, encouraging them to take out their frustrations about unfair rule on the nearby count's home.

But he also has the power to diffuse all that anger, more effectively than any word or action could.

No one could be better at draining the conspiracy of its might than the man who started it.

The orange light of the flames dances off the illusion covering Torstem's face, like it did off the straw figure of the king he had us throw in the fire weeks ago. After he ordered us to stab a man who was conjured out of clay to look like King Konram too.

The spark of inspiration sends a giddy rush through my veins. That's it.

When it comes down to his life or his schemes, he'll have to choose the former. What will any scheme mean if he's dead?

"If the wheels are too damaged, we'll simply crowd into the smaller wagons," Torstem is saying, his even voice dismissing the last of his lackeys' fears. "No doubt what we just saw was some defensive magic from the count's estate, meant to stop us from dealing out the justice that's due."

Oh, he wants to see justice done, does he?

I ease a couple of steps back, not wanting to be near him when I set my new plan in motion. For a few beats of my heart, I cast my gaze skyward, in case that's where Kosmel is watching from right now.

*Please, I need your help again. I don't know what the exact consequences of what I mean to do would be. When I change him, whatever else changes to balance it out, let it do no harm to our cause or to anyone who deserves protection.*

This time I get no response at all. But I remember the sense of a hand on my shoulder, the voice that resonated through my bones.

The godlen who's claimed me is here, working through me.

No, working *with* me. Kosmel has made it clear that I'm supposed to be calling the shots.

A strange warmth blooms in my chest. It frightened me when he first blazed his mark onto my skin… but I'm glad he's watching over me.

For the first time in my life, I'm embracing the divine attention I've earned. Kosmel has claimed me, and that means I have a place in this world, no matter how many cracks run through my soul.

I train my own attention on Ster. Torstem's form. I picture King Konram's face—the deep-set eyes, the imposing nose and jutting chin, the thin lips, the dark brown hair that tops it.

Then I nudge my magic toward the law professor to morph the illusion projected by his mask.

The same hawk-like visage Torstem wore during my initiation wavers and transforms into a replica of the king's appearance. With a quiver of energy from my soul, a gleaming gold crown materializes on his head.

Torstem, of course, hasn't got a clue what I've done to him, since he can't see himself. But the few followers who were looking at him freeze with expressions of shock.

I don't wait for the rest to notice on their own. With another backward step, I point at the leader of the scourge sorcerers. "Great God help us—he looks like the king!"

Gazes all around the bonfire jerk toward Torstem. In their drug-addled state, the Order of the Wild members launch into a flurry of murmurs as agitated as they are confused.

Torstem's hands leap to his face. "What? It can't be."

"He does!" someone else shouts. "That's exactly what King Konram looks like—I just saw him up close at the Sabrellia festival a few weeks ago."

A girl near me reels on her feet behind her cat-like mask. "How could this happen?"

I drift behind a few of the other revelers so I'm partly hidden among them. "The gods must be sending us a message. Our leader has no more right to rule than he says the royal family does! He's been leading us astray, and they're warning us."

An off-kilter laugh carries from farther away. "Or maybe that is the king himself! Maybe the gods have brought him to us so we can do what needs to be done immediately."

I guess that interpretation will serve my purpose as well as the one I was suggesting. I raise my voice again, without the slightest twinge of guilt when I think about all the children Ster. Torstem has manipulated into carving themselves up for his gain. "We have to destroy him!"

Rumbles of agreement reach me from all sides. The gathered conspirators surge toward Torstem, swaying but intent on their goal.

The law professor holds up his hands, his eyes that look like King Konram's sweeping from side to side. He must be wondering who's responsible for this magic, calculating his odds of survival.

I doubt he's got enough humility to consider that the gods might actually be sending him a divine message.

"This is a trick," he calls out, projecting his voice over the warble of the fire and the increasingly aggressive muttering of his followers. "Our enemies are trying to deceive you."

"Our enemies aren't *here*," the fox-masked man in front of me retorts. "This is a secret meeting. It has to be a sign from the gods. If it wasn't, why haven't they shown us they don't agree?"

Another shout careens across the hilltop. "Throw him into the fire!"

Torstem backs away, but the conspirators are closing in on him from all around. With the fire only a few paces behind him, there's nowhere for him to go.

"Look at him, trying to escape the fate he's owed," I holler for good measure. "Not much of a leader now, is he?"

Torstem's gaze veers in my direction, peering through the hazy light. Has he recognized my voice, realized that the supposed Ivy of Nikodi must have played a part in this charade?

It doesn't matter. There's no easy escape for him.

He has to use his magic on the crowd. Persuade them that the sight of the king shouldn't anger them, that our ruler can have a calming presence.

Contradict everything he's spent the last however many years brainwashing them into believing.

The raven-like figure nearest Torstem snatches at his arm, but Torstem yanks it away. His voice has frayed. "It's still me. You know me. You've trusted me—trust me now. This isn't what it seems."

"What else could it be?" a woman beside him demands. "You have the face of the man who's forced all of us under his wretched rule."

Another man smacks his hands together. "It *is* the king. He's lying through his teeth like always!"

I risk one more shout of my own. "The gods have given us a sign! We have to show we've listened."

A harsh cheer goes up. "Throw him in the fucking fire!"

This is the moment when Torstem needs to act. I brace myself for the calm to wash over me along with the rest of the crowd, with all the power of his sacrificial accomplice magnifying it.

I can only imagine the confusion that will follow.

He can try to inflame their rage against King Konram again afterward, but it'll never quite be the same. Their certainty will always have been shaken—they'll never be as confident as they were before.

He'll have destroyed the essence of his conspiracy before I had to lay a finger on him.

But as the small crowd converges on the law professor in his kingly illusion, a strange shift comes over his body. His shoulders tense, and he lifts his head higher with a look of resolve I'd think will only infuriate his followers more.

He raises one hand as if for our attention. "The king must die. The royal family must fall. Let me continue to show you the way."

Then he leaps straight into the fire.

A cry escapes my throat before I can catch it. A couple of the closer followers grope after their leader and jerk their hands back with yelps of pain at the burn.

In the fire, Torstem's figure and the illusion wrapped around it crumple amid the flames. A hiss-like whine of pain penetrates the roar of heat, and his body convulses. I don't know how he holds back a scream.

"The king is burning!" someone shouts, and the scourge sorcerers erupt into ragged cheers.

They whirl around, resuming their revels even wilder than before. An elbow bangs my shoulder, and I duck farther into the shadows at the edge of the hill, horror clamping around my gut.

How could Torstem have done that? He sacrificed himself... so his followers didn't have to sacrifice the beliefs he cultivated?

Does he really think they'll carry on with his mission after he's gone?

Did *he* honestly believe in his cause that deeply?

I might not be drugged, but my mind is reeling. I crouch down, my fingers digging into the grass in an attempt to steady myself.

Julita's voice carries through my mind, hesitant but clear. *Well, I suppose you accomplished what you set out to do, even if it wasn't quite what you expected. You killed Torstem. You fulfilled the king's orders.*

I drag in a gulp of the smoky air, and my stomach starts to settle.

She's right. I got rid of Torstem like the king wanted, but I did it on my terms. I didn't shed his blood. He decided his end.

I'm no more of a killer than I was before, and that's what matters the most.

As I watch the conspirators stumble and cavort around the fire, a small smile crosses my lips with the first flutter of relief. They don't know it yet, but their reign of wildness is over.

Stavros is on his way with a squadron of soldiers right now. They'll round up this leaderless gang of traitors, and the conspiracy will die tonight just as Ster. Torstem did.

It's already starting. A couple of the revelers pause, swaying as they peer around them.

"Where *did* our real leader go?" one of them mumbles. "Did he just... leave us?"

"He became the king!" another crows. "The king died!" Then she pauses. "So Ster. Torstem is dead..."

As confusion starts to spread through the gathering, I think I catch a distant yell where I'm crouched farther back from the fire. It's too faint for my drugged companions to have made it out yet.

Is that one of Torstem's sentries, coming to warn them of the incoming soldiers?

I have one more task to complete to ensure my mission's success.

With the conspirators so dazed, I hardly need much stealth, but I move as swiftly and silently as I can through the wavering shadows. A slash of my favorite blade here and another there sets the restless horses free from one wagon and then next. Swats of the knife's handle send them galloping away, eager to flee the vicious flames that nearly charred them.

Just as I reach the final wagon, the hollers of alarm become more distinct. "The army's coming! Gather everything and leave! Where's Ster. Torstem?"

I don't wait to find out how the traitors will answer. With one last swipe of my blade, I sever the harness straps holding the last animals in place—and launch myself off the wagon onto one of their backs.

I clutch my steed's mane and dig in my heels. We race away into the night, leaving the traitors to their fate.

# FORTY-EIGHT

*Ivy*

The sound of voices filtering through a doorway rouses me. I shift beneath the covers and blink, recognizing that I'm somehow in Stavros's bed.

I found him near the hill after the conspirators were arrested and rode back to Florian alongside him, but as soon as we reached the trio of royal buildings, he sent me to the college on my own with a strict order to sleep. From what I recall, I crashed on the sofa as usual.

He must have carried me over here when he finally returned. Maybe he figured I could use a little extra comfort.

If he shared the bed with me, more chastely than the last time, he's already gotten up. His voice is the one reverberating through the door now.

"I don't want to wake her. Last night will have taken a lot out of her."

Who's he talking to?

I scramble out of the bed, still wearing the turquoise gown I was too exhausted to peel off last night, and smooth out the wrinkles as well as I can on my way to the door.

"I'm already awake," I say mildly as I push open the door, and halt on the threshold. "What are you two doing here?"

Alek and Casimir smile back at me from where they're standing near Stavros, Alek a little sheepishly but Casimir with all his usual warmth.

Stavros offers me a crooked grin of his own. "I passed on word that last night's conquest was a success, and your admirers took it upon themselves to stop by to get all the details."

Casimir chuckles and swoops in to sling his arm around my shoulders. "The scourge sorcerer conspiracy is being dismantled. Ster. Torstem is gone. There's no more reason for us to hide our association."

He sounds so pleased, but the pang of uneasiness that filled my stomach after my initiation returns. There's no reason for us to hide that we're associating, no… but there's also no more concrete reason for us to associate at all.

I push that thought aside for later and let myself lean into the courtesan's embrace. My gaze returns to Stavros. "What have you gotten out of the conspirators you rounded up last night?"

His grin sharpens. "More than we even hoped. The villains were still addled with their favorite drug, and a few of them started babbling with almost no prompting about how they'd freed Silana by killing the king. We got confessions of their traitorous plans—not with much detail, but it hardly matters at this point—along with some rather bizarre stories."

A rough laugh jolts out of me. "Last night… didn't exactly go the way I expected. Were the soldiers able to confirm Ster. Torstem's death?"

Stavros nods, his good humor dimming a little as he studies me. "We retrieved what was left of Torstem's corpse from the remains of the bonfire. There wasn't much. But with some of his followers collaborating your story that he jumped into the flames, no one has any doubt that it's him and that there's no crime to be punished for his death."

*Thank the gods*, Julita says with a relieved sigh.

A current of my own relief penetrates the tension wound inside me. "It's over, then? What about the other sacrificial accomplices Torstem was working with?"

"It'll take some time to tie up the loose ends," Stavros says. "The poor girl at the bonfire wouldn't say much to us, but gods only know how traumatized she is at this point. It's hard to tell, but I don't think she's more than fifteen."

I wince. "You have to find the others. I don't know how much of a life they can have, but they should at least be free."

"The Crown's Watch is already tracing all of Torstem's activities and travels. A couple of his associates from last night have given us some leads as well, though they clammed up once the drug wore off. We'll set the rest of it right."

Stavros reaches out to squeeze my arm. "You did well, Ivy. Incredibly well. No one's going to ask anything more of you."

Including the king, he clearly means.

I take a deep breath, not sure what else to say.

But Alek, naturally, is thinking as far ahead as I am. "Ivy can continue on as your assistant, can't she? There isn't any reason for her to leave the college." He hesitates, his bright gaze searching mine. "Unless you want to."

They want me to *stay*? To keep playing a noblewoman as if I belong here?

But neither Casimir nor Stavros raises the slightest objection to Alek's idea.

I open my mouth and close it again, groping for words.

There are all the people in the outer wards I meant to keep helping. I haven't left my blessings of silver coins in weeks.

Is it possible that I could still be the Hand of Kosmel… while also staying on as Ivy of Nikodi, assistant to Ster. Stavros? I may not like most of my schoolmates or every bit of the work, but the role does come with some rather impressive benefits.

A tremor of hope rises through my chest.

Julita lets out a laugh that sounds like pure delight. *Of course you should stay on, Ivy. You can keep putting everyone who needs it in their places.*

"I believe the king intends to reward your service well," Stavros says. "You'd be able to fill plenty of pouches with plenty of coins for trips around the city's fringes."

He understands—he *approves*.

An even starker wave of relief washes over me. I swallow thickly and gather myself.

But before I can speak, a firm knock sounds on the door.

From his furrowed brow, Stavros isn't expecting anyone. He strides over to answer it.

When he yanks the door open, his massive form blocks most of the doorway. I catch a glimpse of a stunning blue-green eye and chocolate-brown curls, and my body tenses.

"Is this a summons from the king?" Stavros asks.

"No," a familiar voice says. "I was hoping to speak with Ivy of Nikodi. Is she here?"

Stavros hesitates, but I step forward.

The guard who's seemed to haunt me around campus stands in the hallway, his face as beautiful as ever but his jaw tight and his eyes wider than I've ever seen them.

He looks almost... scared.

My heart lurches with the sudden certainty that something is wrong, even if I have no idea what.

I hurry the rest of the way to the door. "I'm here. What's the matter?"

The guard glances at me, and a faint glow of hope comes over him. "You're the only one I could think of to come to. I need your help."

Stavros shoots me a puzzled look, but I'm equally bewildered. "Help? With what?"

The guard nudges past Stavros, who lets him enter but looms over him with a defensive air. The other man doesn't appear to notice, let alone mind.

His attention is fixed completely on me.

"I've broken some of their hold on me," he says. "I've been asking questions, challenging orders... and they've decided I'm no good to them anymore."

I stare at him. "Who are you talking about? Who's had a hold on you?"

"The ones who made this body." He taps his chest. "They built the form out of clay and put me in it, and now they want to shatter me and send me back to the state I was in before. But I don't want to go. I like this kind of living."

Behind me, Alek lets out a strained sound. "They made you... out of clay?"

I'm outright gaping now, but I don't know how to reel in my shock or slow the thumping of my pulse. "The scourge sorcerers made you. But who—*what* were you before?"

The guard who isn't really a guard shifts his weight on his feet. "I have been saying I'm 'Rheave.' It's the closest thing to a name I have. Humans call all of us 'daimon.'"

Understanding snaps into place in my head alongside my memories of my appeal to the spirit-creatures in the All-Giver's tower. The images they sent of flames and constricting darkness.

It could have been fired clay, closing in around them.

The conspirators switched from controlling the daimon in their ephemeral form to stuffing them into physical bodies.

"That's how they created life," Alek mutters as the pieces click together for him too. "They didn't actually create it. They stole what was already there."

"Can I stay with you?" Rheave asks, his gaze darting across my men and back to me. "If they find me, they'll kill this body."

Casimir eases forward, speaking in a soothing tone. "You should be safe now. The leader of the scourge sorcerers is dead. The army is rounding up his—"

"What?" The daimon in human form looks at the courtesan as if he's grown a second head. "No, he's not."

I manage to stop gaping long enough to ask, "How do you know?"

Rheave's gaze swings back to me. His lips purse as if he doesn't like what he's about to say.

"He's just called on all of us nearby. We're to go to the palace and murder every inhabitant who has Melchiorek blood."

# GAMES OF DEATH AND DESIRE - BONUS SCENE

*What was going through Rheave's mind when Ivy found him with the injured butterfly and helped him bring it to safety? This bonus scene shows that moment from his perspective...*

*Rheave*

My current orders resonate through my head and carry into the rest of my body in a steady repeated murmur.

*Patrol the school grounds. Take note of any unusual behavior. Report back when you're done.*

Those are the only things the command asks of me. A few weeks ago, it's all I would have done—numbly, unthinkingly, barely conscious of my actions.

Something has... shifted. None of the students catch my attention, but I find myself absorbing the feel of the ground beneath my feet. The shift from the soft but uneven cushioning of the grassy stretches to the smooth hardness of the cobblestone paths.

The murmur cuts in, urging me onward, trying to blot out my other awareness.

*Patrol the school grounds. Take note of any unusual behavior. Report back when you're done.*

I pick up my pace, but that doesn't stop me from noticing the cool lick of the gusting air against my face. The current ripples through my hair, setting off a tingle through my scalp.

I've never had a face before. Never had hair or a scalp to feel anything like this.

It's fascinating, so many sensations I had no idea existed—

*Patrol the school grounds. Take note of any unusual behavior. Report back when you're done.*

I circle around toward the back of the school. Wildflowers have sprouted up amid the grass by the wall, bright red and purple against the green.

I find myself veering toward them, drawn by the impulse to take in their vibrant colors close up.

As I approach, a sweet scent trickles into my nose. I never had a nose before—did I ever smell anything before?

I reach back to my vague memories that the constant commands have mostly drowned out. I have the impression that I was aware of plenty of things around me, but in a distant sort of way, flitting by without letting anything sink in.

This new way of being... Is it better?

I'm not sure, but I like it. And I can tell there's so much more about it I haven't discovered.

I can't because of the insistent orders that keep prodding me onward.

*Patrol the school grounds. Take note of any unusual behavior. Report back when you're done.*

A frown crosses my face. Nothing used to guide me except my own curiosity. Who gave this murmur the right to usher me around and dictate my actions?

I certainly didn't.

I've slipped pieces of its hold before, but right now, my legs walk on without asking permission. It's irritating, another sensation I don't remember feeling before.

My feet only make a couple of steps before my gaze snags on another bit of bright color clinging to the dark blue sleeve of my uniform.

A butterfly has landed on the cloth, about halfway between my wrist and my elbow. Its delicate yellow-and-blue wings drop open and then pull close again.

My feet lurch to a halt. The repeated command falls away beneath a wave of startled confusion.

Why has this creature come to me? What am I supposed to do with it?

As I stare at it, its wings flutter open again. One of the edges looks ragged, as if some other creature has scratched at it.

What if it can't fly any farther? Should I carry it through my patrol?

What would I do with it afterward? I don't know what nourishment it needs.

It looks so fragile. I might break it more without meaning to.

That wouldn't be right. It deserves to fly free.

It shouldn't end up trapped like I am.

I lift my head as if answers might present themselves from somewhere around me, and there she is.

The woman my orders often tell me to watch—*Ivy of Nikodi*, her name whispers through my thoughts—is standing several feet away. The glow of the setting sun catches in her hair, lighting up the reddish tint in the pale strands as if there are flames dancing beneath the surface.

She's staring back at me. Her blue eyes that often spark with emotions I can't interpret have gone pensive, as if she's concerned too.

Instinct compels me to hold her gaze, wishing she'd approach me.

She seems to know a lot of things. She seems to *care*. Even the gods see it.

She'd know how I should look after this creature, wouldn't she?

To my relief and a brighter glimmer of emotion I can't decipher even in myself, Ivy walks over to me.

Her expression has tightened a bit the way it often does when she's talking to me. Her voice comes out with the dry tone I can never tell what to make of. "Have you been assaulted by that butterfly?"

Assaulted? No. Although when I adjust my arm, the creature does hold on very persistently.

"It landed on me a few minutes ago," I explain. "I think it's hurt—it might not be able to fly any farther. I don't know what to do."

The admission brings a bit of heat to my face even though it's true. Should I have a better handle on this situation I've found myself in? Haven't I roamed through this world for ages before any of these humans were even in it?

But I've never had an arm for a butterfly to land on before.

Ivy considers our surroundings and waves her hand toward the dark stretch of forest at the back of the school grounds. "Let's bring it someplace it'll have shelter. If it's going to recover, it'll be better off in a spot where no predators will notice it. Assuming you're not going to carry it around for the next day or two."

There's a playful lilt to her last remark, but I've found it best to assume humans are never joking even if they're outright laughing when they say a thing. Much less chance of them getting angry and throwing a drink or a punch at you.

"No, it might get more damaged riding on me."

Ivy takes my response in stride. "Then it's settled. Come on."

She sets off ahead of me, leading the way, even though I can see for myself where the forest is. Even though looking at it makes her shoulders tense up and her fingers curl toward her palms.

She could have left me to it and gone off somewhere she'd rather be. Instead, she's seeing her suggestion through.

That's the sort of human she is. I've interacted with enough by now to know it's not a common type.

I keep my arm lifted and as still as possible. The butterfly doesn't appear disturbed by being carted around.

Ivy stops by the first trees and taps a small branch protruding from a spindly trunk. "Put it here. The branch right overtop should stop any birds from spotting it."

There is another branch, with more leaves for shade, just a few inches higher. It seems like a good plan.

I study the butterfly and slide one of my fingers toward its feet. With a gentle nudge, it lifts them to plant them on my finger instead. Then, with a little encouragement, it steps from my finger onto the branch.

A gleam like the glow in Ivy's hair lights in my chest. I helped it. It might be okay now.

*We* helped it.

But when I look at Ivy again, with the urge to smile at her and a strange pang around the hope that she'll smile back, her stance stiffens just slightly.

Oh. She's still not happy to be here.

"I make you nervous," I venture, as if pointing out the reaction will somehow diffuse it. "This place does too. But you helped anyway."

Maybe showing her I've noticed and that I appreciate her kindness will ease her concerns—about me, at least.

She backs up a step. "I'm perfectly fine. You looked like you could use a little direction. I've got other things to do now."

She pivots and moves to stride away, and the impulse to call her back leaps up my throat.

But no, she doesn't want to be here. I shouldn't make her.

It isn't right to make people do things they'd rather not do.

The protest turns into the only right words I can think of to say. "Thank you."

She doesn't glance back. Her form melds with the shadows stretching long from the school buildings.

And the unshakeable murmur winds through my head again. *Patrol the school grounds. Take note of any unusual behavior. Report back when you're done.*

I walk on automatically, the diversion that let me shed the command now over. But as my feet thump against the satisfyingly solid ground, one certainty forms in my mind.

I'm not going to report anything "unusual" about Ivy of Nikodi. Not today or ever.

# Secrets of Graves and Gold

## Rites of Possession #3

# ONE

Ivy

I'm not sure I fully believe that the palace is under attack until I see the gate.

Or rather, what's left of the gate.

With a lurch of my heart, I jar to a stop in the cobblestone lane between the royal college and the king's primary residence. My hand clenches around the knife I've drawn.

The heavy wooden doors in the high stone wall normally loom nearly twice my admittedly unimpressive height. Now, they look as if they've been blasted off their hinges.

Dark streaks lash across the fallen slabs, blackening both the wood and the bands of steel that reinforce it. Even the stones that frame the doorway look scorched.

My ghostly passenger's arch voice resonates through my head with an air of shock. *Did someone decide to roast the doorway?*

The three men who raced over from the college with me have halted around me at the same moment. Alek flicks an unsteady hand down his front—forehead, heart, gut, and back up to his sternum—in the gesture of the divinities.

The scholar's voice comes out faint. "What in the realms…?"

A bang and a flurry of shouts reverberate from beyond the walls. Stavros launches his massive frame forward with impressive speed, his sword in his hand and the combat prosthetic he hastily donned flashing on his other wrist. "I have to protect the royal family."

Out of the four of us, the former general is the only one who has any direct mandate to defend our rulers. It's hard to say how much good a thief-playing-noble, a scholar, and a courtesan can do in this apparent disaster.

But the rest of us hustle after him just as we rushed the whole way from the college.

We're the only four people in the kingdom who have any real idea what exactly is going on here. Well, other than the villains who orchestrated this attack, and I'd be overjoyed to stop them before they cause any more mayhem.

We dash through the courtyard to the main palace building, past fallen guards who are burnt or bloody or both. Casimir's gorgeous face blanches beneath the tawny waves of his hair.

The courtesan is trained to see beauty in all things, but I doubt he can find anything to admire in this scene.

"He was right," he says in a low, strained voice that holds none of his usual calm. "How many captured daimon could the scourge sorcerers have gathered?"

I don't need to wonder who Casimir means by 'he.' Less than ten minutes ago, a guard who'd badgered me a few times around the campus turned up at Stavros's quarters to plead for my help. Why he picked me in particular, I didn't have time to find out.

We thought we'd defeated the psychopathic sorcerers and their cultish Order of the Wild last night. I watched the man we believed to be their leader die in a bonfire; a squadron of soldiers rounded up a couple dozen followers.

But the guard, Rheave, claimed that the conspirators have accomplished more with their magic than we realized. He said *he* is a daimon, one of the spirit creatures that flit through our world, trapped in a body made of clay that scourge sorcery brought to life.

And he told us that there are many more like him, all of whom were called to the palace by some still-living figure of authority within the Order—who instructed them to murder every member of the royal family.

As we sprint up the palace steps to the even grander door that's cracked right down the middle with more of those slashes of black, Casimir's question echoes through my head.

Have the scourge sorcerers built an entire army of captured daimon?

Inside the front hall, more guards sprawl across the marble floors. Blood soaks the lavish rugs and splatters the fine paintings hung on the walls. Cries ring out from up ahead.

My mouth tightens. "There must be a lot of the clay beings. But who the fuck is directing the daimon now?"

*A very good question,* Julita mutters faintly.

There's no way Ster. Torstem, the law professor we believed was leading the conspiracy, could have survived his burning alive. I saw him crumple in the flames. Stavros said the soldiers found the remains of his body.

Unless the scourge sorcerers have managed to twist their sick magic to defy death itself.

The thought makes me want to vomit, but I race on after Stavros toward the sounds of the fighting.

Through the haze of panicked adrenaline, I notice bodies that aren't in the sapphire blue uniforms of the palace guards and royal soldiers. A few wear fine formal shirts and trousers that would befit the palace's domestic staff, and I spot a couple of court nobles who were wandering the entry rooms unluckily early this morning.

Amid them are bodies that barely look like bodies at all: reddish-brown figures of fired clay, sculpted into human form.

Some have remained whole other than a blade jabbed through a chest. Others lie in broken but still identifiable pieces.

Alek has taken them in too. His bright brown eyes widen in the holes of his leather mask.

"Gods help us all," he mumbles.

Stavros slams past a door with a heave of his shoulder, and the four of us barge into another opulent palace hall.

This one is filled with total chaos. Several guards are swinging their swords to defend a cluster of nobles who are cringing at the far end of the vast room. The soldiers' expressions show as much confusion as they do protective furor.

Because the attackers they're fending off don't look like villains at all. A few of them sport the exact same rich blue uniforms as the defenders—guards like Rheave who were constructed for the scourge sorcerers' purposes? And the others...

From their simple clothing, most of the figures in the onslaught look like ordinary middle-ward citizens. A couple of grubbier ones might have come all the way from Florian's fringes.

Are they actual people caught up in the conspiracy, or more clay-captured daimon bound by the sorcerers' magic?

Stavros doesn't appear to think it important to stick around and find out. It's King Konram and his family he's most concerned about protecting, not the lesser nobles.

He hurtles toward a side door, waving for us to follow him.

As we dash after him, one of the attackers gives chase. A woman in a woolen dress that I'd expect on a shopkeeper or a craftswoman lunges at us with the dagger she's raised.

My years of street-honed instincts kick in. As she slashes at Alek, I spin around and stab out with my knife.

I'd prefer to simply disable her. I don't have much stomach for killing, not when any death I deal out reminds me of my very first and most regretted kill.

But the woman simply lurches away from my blow to her shoulder, heedless of the blood coursing through the bodice of her dress, and snatches Alek's slim wrist. There's determination and then there's being ludicrously single-minded, and she's clearly crossed that line.

The scholar wrenches backward with a hasty kick that doesn't quite land. Julita yelps in my head.

The woman rams her dagger toward Alek's neck, and every nerve in my body screams in denial.

I will not watch one of the men I love slump in a pool of blood. None of his brilliance or tenderness can save him from a blade.

But I can.

My magic flares in my chest. I'm moving before it has a chance to rattle my insides for freedom.

I plunge my knife into the woman's throat the instant before she can land her blow.

I only have a second for a jolt of guilt to shoot through me before her form hardens to clay. She thumps onto the floor and fractures across her torso and legs.

Julita's presence shivers. *Nicely done, Ivy.*

Alek sputters a ragged breath and swipes his messy black hair back from the top of his mask. "Thank you."

I snatch up the dagger the woman dropped—the only part of her that was real—and press its hilt into his hand with a tight clasp of my fingers. The warmth of his bronze-brown skin brings a lump into my throat.

He's all right. He's still all right—and I want him to stay that way.

I squeeze his hand. "If anyone else comes at you, just jab them as well as you can."

I should have given him one of my knives earlier. We had no idea what we'd be facing here—just how true Rheave's mad story would turn out to be.

Alek nods with a grateful if pained smile. The worry shining in his eyes is for me as much as himself.

Despite my horror at the riot around us, the knowledge that we're facing it together steadies me. I'm no longer on my own.

Side by side, we run the rest of the way to the door Stavros has already pushed through. Casimir ushers us onward, touching my arm in a brief but reassuring caress.

Stavros lopes onward, barely sounding winded. His military training has clearly held up well. "There are doubly fortified rooms in the basement that the royal family can descend to in an emergency—and a secret escape passage if the situation gets dire. With luck, they've already removed themselves—"

He cuts himself off with a hiss of breath as we come upon two more dead guards slumped outside a stairwell.

Stavros bends, the fall of his dark red hair across his tan forehead an unnervingly similar hue to the congealing splatters of blood. He hauls one of the murdered soldiers out of the way and heaves open the door.

Shouts and the clang of metal carry from below the stairs.

"Curse them all," the former general growls, leaping down the steps.

My stomach clenches at the sound of fighting ahead. A thin voice shrieks—is that one of the royal children?

Princess Klaudia and Prince Jacos are only sixteen and fourteen. I can't imagine they've ever seen violence on this level before, let alone directed at them and their parents.

My magic squirms inside my chest, tugging at my ribs for me to let it out.

It could hurl the villains back to wherever they came from. It could smash through them all.

But as always, I have no idea what else it might destroy to balance out the power I release. All magic requires sacrifice.

Until I know exactly what we're dealing with, we're all safer sticking with tools we can hold.

I slip my free hand between the folds of my riding gown's skirt and retrieve another knife from the hidden sheath there. As we barrel onward, I tap Casimir's arm to offer the weapon.

The courtesan glances down and shakes his head with a glint of his deep blue eyes. "I fight better with my hands. Holding something will throw me off."

I've seen him dissuade a judgmental nobleman with a wrench of the fellow's wrist, so I know he has some defensive skills. I doubt he's ever found himself in the middle of a full-out battle, though. "If you change your mind…"

He manages to shoot me a fond smile. "I know who I can count on for extra blades."

At the bottom of the stairs, a short hall leads to a doorway half-filled with collapsed stone. Stavros curses and scrambles over the rubble, the rest of us following in his wake. The rough edges scrape at my palm.

The sprawling room behind is a picture of carnage. One of the inner walls has partly crumbled; the lanterns flicker wildly.

I nearly trip over a body half-buried by the doorway. More corpses lie scattered across the stone floor.

The wavering light gleams off a golden crown. King Konram is wearing his where he's braced next to his wife to shield a few smaller figures I assume include their children.

Six guards continue fighting valiantly in front of them, but one of them is swaying and another's sleeve is drenched in blood.

At least twice as many opponents have closed in on them, half of them in guard's uniforms, the others in plainer clothes like I saw upstairs. Most of them are wielding swords and daggers.

But in the first moment after I leap into the room, one man swipes out with his bare hand.

A crackling light escapes his fingers and smacks into one of the guards, searing blackened lines across his face. As the soldier staggers backward, a pool of ice forms in my gut.

The daimon have their own supernatural powers. Now we know how they barbequed the gate.

Another man snatches up a huge chunk of broken rock and hurls it at the royal guards. It slams into one woman's head, and she falls to her knees.

Stavros roars and throws himself forward with his sword whipping through the air. He cuts down two attacking men, who smash into clay shards on the floor before any of the others can react.

The largest of our opponents whirls. As Stavros moves to swing his sword, the equally immense man charges right into the former general like a battering ram. They slam through a side door and careen into the shadows of the room beyond.

Another attacker races to fight with Stavros, and two more spin toward the rest of us new arrivals. A burly man slashes his sword at me.

I duck and whirl around to kick at his legs. He stumbles backward but only for a second before he's lurching toward me again.

The other attacker has hurled herself at Casimir and Alek. Alek swipes inexpertly with his confiscated dagger before Casimir lands a blow to her head with both strength and his usual grace. The impact sends her reeling sideways into the wall.

The instant she hits the stone blocks, more energy sizzles from her hands. The wall cracks and bucks.

A deluge of stone batters the two men. I have to roll to the side to escape the slice of my attacker's sword, and when I glance again, both the scholar and the courtesan are pinned to their waists beneath the rubble.

Stavros gives a vicious cry and heaves one of his opponents back out of the side room. But that man takes the same tactic the woman did and slams his hands against the side of the doorway.

The stones crumple inward, cutting off Stavros from the room the rest of us are in.

Grit prickles in my throat. I cough and dodge, landing a blow with my knife to my attacker's thigh. As he staggers sideways, I kick his legs right out from under him.

He thumps to the floor but doesn't drop his sword. And as he tenses to lunge at me again, my gaze slips past him to the royal family.

More clay litters the floor now, but so do more bodies of the real guards. The last of them is just collapsing with a blade through his gut.

The five clay-captured daimon still standing near the king launch themselves at the unguarded royal family.

*No!* Julita cries as my pulse stutters.

I hurl my knife at one of the attackers, but the others don't even look as their companion topples over.

Both King Konram and Queen Ishild have drawn blades of their own, but I can see those won't be enough. They're an instant from being overwhelmed.

Nothing would be enough.

"Ivy!" Alek rasps out from where he's shoving at the rubble on his legs. "Quick—you have to."

My stomach sinks at the same moment as my magic thrums through my bones.

Right. *I* would be enough.

There isn't time to think, isn't time to plead with the lesser god who's guided me in the past to help me control the backlash. One of the attackers stabs his sword toward Konram's heart just as the king parries a different blow from another—and with a choked sound, I fling my power at the swordsman.

The magical force wrenches the man to the side and snaps his neck. He collapses into a jumble of clay.

I heave my arms upward and will the stones from the walls to rise. My power surges through my limbs, vibrating to the core of my bones.

As I shove the stones back into place, a booming sound from above suggests my magic has torn down other walls somewhere else in the palace. I can't find the capacity to care just yet.

The woman who destroyed one of those walls stares at me with a flicker of light behind her eyes. "Riven!" she cries.

Stavros hurtles out of the newly restored side room and crashes straight into another of the attackers sword-first. Alek and Casimir scramble to their feet.

The courtesan grabs at the swordsman in front of me, who was just making a lunge of his own. He yanks the man's arm around sharply enough for bone to crack just as I snatch another knife from the sheaths at my thighs.

As I push forward to slit the swordsman's throat, Queen Ishild plunges her short sword into the nearest figure's gut. King Konram stabs another in the chest—just as the man jerks his hand toward the ceiling.

The stone surface cracks. I let out a yelp of warning.

A surge of my own magic rattles up through my ribs.

The broken chunk freezes just inches from cracking Konram's skull. Then it slams back up to re-meld with the ceiling.

My skin twitches with the effort, sweat beading on the back of my neck.

Stavros cuts through the last of the attackers, and suddenly everything is still except the rasp of our labored breaths.

I wobble, and Casimir grasps my arm to steady me. I let myself lean just slightly toward him, relief washing over me at his calming presence.

We fended off the attack. King Konram and his family are alive and relatively uninjured.

My magic settles into a restless churning within my chest, uneasy but satisfied that it's pitched in as much as was necessary.

Julita's voice travels through my thoughts. *Well, I'd rather not ever do* that *again.*

I might have chuckled, but right then I notice the king staring at me.

Konram's gaze flicks upward to the mended ceiling and then back to my face. His expression has tensed even more than it was during the battle.

A chill pools in my gut.

His head jerks toward Stavros. "You heard what that one traitor said. You saw what she did."

Stavros's forehead furrows. "Your Highness… Ivy saved your life."

The king stares at him for a moment before a sickly pallor creeps over his face. "You already knew. You brought one of *them* into my palace, straight to my family…"

Stavros's entire massive frame goes rigid, as does his voice. "She saved your *life*," he repeats, as if he thinks possibly Konram missed that point the first time.

The king adjusts his grip on his sword, though he doesn't dare raise it toward me. At least, not yet. "She might have been behind this whole attack. My own guards turning on me—"

"The scourge sorcerers were behind it," Alek snaps. "Look at those guards now. We told you the conspirators were conjuring creatures out of clay that looked alive, and probably people too."

Julita gives a soft huff. *He can't seriously think we went through all the madness of the past few weeks just to turn on him now. I'd hope the man who governs all Silana has more sense than that.*

I can't summon much hope of my own. King Konram has been one of the biggest advocates for slaughtering all riven sorcerers. He parades every captured riven before his people so they can watch the sorcerers hang and know the country is that much safer.

I swallow against the sudden dryness in my throat. "Your Highness, I mean you and your family no harm. Now that the threat is dealt with, I'll leave."

Konram flinches as if my words were a threat themselves. He glances at Stavros again. "You know what needs to be done."

"Wait!"

I know that voice, but my pulse still skips in surprise when a familiar light brown face framed by sleek black hair appears from the corner the king and queen were guarding.

Petra must have been visiting with the royal family when the attack started. I didn't realize she associated with them that closely. From what Julita said, she's only a distant niece of the queen's.

But I had started to wonder if King Konram asked her to spy on me at the college. Maybe this is confirmation of my suspicions.

"F— Your Highness," she says with a brief fumbling of her words. "I don't think Ivy— We should at least hear them—"

"The laws are clear," the king interrupts, holding out his arm to push her back. "Stavros, if you'll continue to harbor a riven sorcerer, I have to consider you a traitor to the Crown as well."

The former general's jaw ticks, but that's the only sign he's affected by the words of the man he swore to serve to the death. "Please, Your Highness, if you understood—"

King Konram's knuckles whiten where he's clutching his sword. "The only thing to understand is that I've been betrayed from all sides." He raises his voice. "Guards! *Guards!*"

I don't know how many are left from the fighting to answer his summons, but footsteps pound against the ceiling overhead.

Stavros lunges forward to grab my arm. "We're getting out of here." He cuts his gaze toward the king. "Because *this* is how I can best serve you."

Konram takes a stiff step forward. "How dare you—"

Stavros doesn't give him time to finish his caustic words. He yanks me toward the doorway, and all at once I'm running again.

Alek and Casimir dash after us. We've barely made it to the stairwell before the king's voice reverberates through the air again, and I realize he's got some blessed item that's amplifying it through the palace. "Guards, don't let Ster. Stavros and his companions leave the palace! Cut them down if you must."

"Shit." Stavros hustles me even faster, but I don't need the encouragement. My feet fly up the steps.

If we can't get out of here fast enough, we might be slaughtered by the same people we raced in here to protect.

I don't know whether to be thankful or horrified that the scourge sorcerers' clay attackers took down enough of the guards that we're able to dash through the side hall without encountering even one. Does the king truly realize just how close he came to dying himself today?

We're almost at the main entrance when a yell carries from behind us. "There they go!"

We sprint past the fallen door and onward between the bodies of flesh and clay to the blasted gate —and run straight into a small herd of saddled horses in the lane beyond.

Rheave peers at us from the steeds' midst, his luminous blue-green eyes as eerie as always beneath his chocolate-brown curls. "I brought the horses like you told me to. Does the king need them?"

Casimir sputters a laugh. In the chaos, I'd forgotten that Stavros had sent the daimon-man to the stables in case the royal family needed to make a hasty getaway out the front of the palace.

"He doesn't," Stavros says grimly, catching one set of reins from Rheave. "But we do. Everyone, ride!"

# Two

Ivy

A snort brings my gaze to a stallion I know well. I snatch at his reins. "You brought Toast!"

"He's the one you like," Rheave says, as if it's self-evident that of course he'd know that. At a volley of shouts from the courtyard beyond the gate, he hefts himself onto a nearby mare.

Julita lets out a choked laugh. *It seems the daimon is good for something.*

The instant we're all mounted, Stavros kicks his horse to a gallop. We take off down the laneway with a clatter of hooves against the cobblestones.

For the first several minutes, we simply hurtle through the streets, following Stavros's lead. The citizens of the inner wards gape at our frantic passing. We're certainly not maintaining a noble standard of propriety.

We have to slow to a canter to avoid crashing into any pedestrians, but when we approach the ring of the old city walls that now mark the division between inner wards and middle, Stavros nudges his stallion faster again. "Be ready to jump," he hollers back at us.

A curse slips from Alek's mouth. I'm not sure how avid an equestrian the scholar is.

I haven't been in the habit of sending my mounts over obstacles rather than around them myself. I tighten my grip on the reins, leaning forward to murmur to Toast. "If I'm going to stay on you, you've got to work with me now. No messing around."

The dark bay stallion is known as the terror of the college stables. He and I have come to a sort of understanding, but that doesn't mean he never tests my patience.

My steed gives a short huff, although I can't tell whether it's in protest at our renewed gallop or a dismissal of my concerns.

We veer along a curving road, and I spot the reason for Stavros's instructions up ahead.

Most people pass the old city walls through one of the many deteriorating gates. But the Crown's Watch likes to monitor those spots to watch for suspicious persons venturing into the hub of Florian's elite.

The former general must be hoping to avoid having any of the city's royal police force observe our frantic dash. So instead, he's aimed us at what's meant to be a dead end.

The stones of the old wall ahead of us are particularly crumbled. Only the base of the wall remains in an uneven line. But it's still about as high as my waist.

*Oh, dear,* Julita murmurs, and then seems to rally. *You can handle this, Ivy. Give that beast a good prodding.*

I sink lower into the saddle as if I can meld my ass and thighs with the leather.

To be honest, I've never jumped on a horse before. Hopefully Toast knows what he's expected to do here—and doesn't toss me right off his back in the process.

Stavros's stallion launches over the uneven row of stone blocks first. The black animal he took from those Rheave grabbed isn't his usual mount, but he still makes the leap look easy.

Casimir nudges the chestnut gelding he chose a little faster and soars over the stones with the same grace the courtesan seems to bring to everything he does. Then it's my turn.

Toast makes a sound that might be skeptical, but he pushes himself forward a little faster. With a soft grunt, he heaves himself up and over the low wall.

For a second in the air, I lift slightly off the saddle despite my best efforts. The wind whips my cloak's hood back from my hair. Then we're both thumping back into place—Toast's hooves on the road on the opposite side, my butt into its seat.

The breath jolts out of me alongside a shaky laugh. The rolling thunder of hooves behind me tells me Alek and Rheave have both managed to follow.

Stavros only races onward for another minute or two. He draws his stallion to a sudden halt in a small square where a few merchants peer at us from their shop windows.

We gather close together, my gaze darting over the buildings around us.

Alek swipes at the back of his neck and speaks before I can. "Where are we going?"

Stavros considers our surroundings, his expression tense. "We got a good lead, but we've made a lot of racket. It won't be hard for the Crown's Watch or the army themselves to track us."

Casimir's face has flushed from the ride, but his peachy skin pales again at those words. "You think King Konram will go that far in pursuing Ivy?"

"There are few things more important to him than stamping out the riven. He sees her existence as an affront to the gods—and sparing her as a betrayal of them." The former general cuts his gaze toward me. "It wouldn't have been a bad time for your divine guardian to throw in his sign of support."

I grimace back at him. "Kosmel makes his own rules. For all I know, he's enjoying this mess as long as I survive it."

The godlen of luck and trickery isn't exactly the predictable sort. All I'm absolutely sure of is that he'd like me to stay alive.

"Ivy knows how to hide in the city," Alek suggests.

Julita's tone perks up. *Yes, you're the expert on this part of Florian.*

My stomach sinks despite her optimism. "I know how to hide myself. All of us will be a little harder, especially with horses in tow."

I can't quite picture my sophisticated men scrambling up the side of the cloth factory building into my secret attic hideout.

"Our situation is particularly precarious while we're in the capital," Stavros says. "We could leave the city, find a place to regroup where we won't draw attention, and then work out how we're going to convince the king Ivy can be trusted."

He pauses, his head swiveling as he takes stock of our location, and points. "The nearest gate is that way. If we cut straight through the outer wards—"

A flash of light whips over the rooftops in the direction he indicated, and his voice dies in his throat.

Rheave tracks the same phenomenon from the edge of our group. "That was magic."

Stavros's voice darkens. "Yes. The palace is sending a message to the gates. No doubt ordering the guards to close them until we've been apprehended."

My ghostly passenger goes still in my head. *Curse it all.*

I swallow thickly. "They can't lock down the city for *too* long, can they?"

"For a threat as great as one of the riven?" Stavros shoots me an apologetic glance, his mouth slanted at a pained angle. We both remember all too well how badly he took the initial revelation of my magic, and he knew me far better than King Konram does.

Alek shifts in his saddle. "There's no way we can leave, then. We'll have to hide ourselves here."

While the king sends every available soldier sweeping through the city in search—and the scourge sorcerers do gods know what else in the meantime? My skin crawls with the impression of the walls closing in on me.

I turn to Rheave. "Are the people who made you going to send more daimon after the king?"

The daimon-man frowns. "Everyone in the city was called to the palace. If you freed them all, they won't cause any harm."

Stavros studies him warily. "Everyone in the city, you say. What about outside the city?"

"There are many. I'm not sure of the exact number or what they might be doing at the moment on our creators' orders."

"Then the real threat is out there for now," I say.

Alek studies Rheave with his piercing gaze. "If he knows what he's talking about and he's not leading us astray."

The daimon-man cocks his head with a look of genuine puzzlement. "Why would I want to make trouble for you?"

Stavros lifts an eyebrow. "You were working on the scourge sorcerers' behalf for weeks, weren't you?"

"Because I was under their control. I've broken free from that magic—I want to stay as far away from them as I can."

Because he's afraid they'll destroy the body they created for him, and for whatever strange reason, the daimon has decided he likes his prison of flesh. He told us that much when he came looking for me.

My throat tightens at the memory of his earnest appeal for my help.

He *has* acted in my favor before, keeping quiet when he noticed me in hiding. And his concern for the injured butterfly that landed on him days ago couldn't have come from the conspirators—that was all him.

I glance around at my men. "King Konram would be dead if Rheave hadn't warned us. He isn't our enemy. And it sounds like our actual enemy is beyond the city walls. If we want to continue protecting the kingdom, prove to the king that *we're* not villains, and save our necks from the gallows, our best chance is leaving."

Casimir reaches to give my wrist a gentle squeeze. "That makes sense, but how are we going to manage it?"

Stavros's gaze settles on me with a tick to focus his damaged vision. "We can't count on your power to clear the way even if Kosmel would be willing to guide it this time. Not without doing enough damage that we *would* be villains. The guards at the gates and throughout the city will be alert to any sign of riven power—some of them have talents that allow them to detect magic."

Julita sighs. *I suppose he has a point.*

He does. And the trepidation in his voice reminds me of how much he distrusts the magic that flows through my broken soul in general.

Which is fair, because I hate my demanding, chaotic power too. As mercurial as Julita can be at times, she's a much more considerate lodger than the magic I was born with.

I pause. The fringes of the city are my domain, and I've navigated them without a spark of magic for years. I have to take the lead here.

My men's lives could rest in my hands as much as they held mine in theirs when they discovered my secret.

As I grope for the right answer, my gaze catches on a crow landing on a rooftop across the square. It looks like a perfectly ordinary bird, and it might not have anything to do with the godlen crows are associated with, but it lights a glimmer of inspiration in my head all the same.

I turn to the men. "I might be able to get us out of the city today, no sorcery required. But you'll need to do everything *exactly* as I ask."

Casimir nods. "Where do we start?"

The others wait for my answer without any sign of protest. I form a grim smile. "First we head to Tangleside."

# THREE

Ivy

It feels like years since I last stepped through the broad doorway of the Frolic Theater. On the threshold, I restrain the urge to glance over my shoulder toward the derelict storage building where I had the men and our horses lay low for the time being.

The gang that rules Crow's Close keeps a close eye on comings and goings. I don't want to give them the slightest clue where I've left my allies.

This negotiation is going to require the most delicate of touches. I'm just lucky that one of the head honchos owes me.

*We're going into that den of criminals again?* Julita murmurs from the back of my head as I walk to the inner door with Kosmel's sigil carved over it. *Do you really think you can get them to help us?*

"We'll see," I whisper as if to myself, and slip down the musty stairwell into the darkness below.

A right turn beneath the stairs, then a winding pattern of steps in the passage where the darkness is thick enough to suffocate. I hurry out into the matching basement room and up the stairs to the enclosed street that's Florian's biggest hub of criminal activity.

On the front step outside the theater's echoed façade, I pause to take in the strip. It's both less busy and less vibrant in the mid-day light, the kind of place that comes to life with the sinking of the sun.

The usual conjured illusions still shimmer over some of the doorways of the wooden buildings, though other shops haven't even opened for the day yet. Their owners are probably sleeping off last night's exploits.

A few disreputable-looking characters slink along the narrow dirt road, one ducking into the Brew & Dagger pub that'll have just opened. My gaze lingers on the sign with a pang of longing for one of their amber spritzes.

It would take the edge off all the tension of the day, but I've got urgent work to do here.

On the other side of the street to my left, the largest building in Crow's Close looms. The darkly varnished wooden structure holds three floors, the lowest one a public gambling den and the upper two dedicated to the private exploits of the most powerful crooks in the city.

Kosmel's sigil stands out in silver paint against the dark boards over the crooked doorway, framed by a carved crow on one side and a rat on the other. As I watch, one of the other stealthy figures prowling the street slinks through the entrance.

I just have to hope that Garom Rochimek has roused himself from his bed already.

I tug my cloak closer around me. The noble-style silk gown beneath it itches at my skin with the awareness that it's nothing like what I'd typically wear on a visit to this street.

Opulent clothes aren't totally out of place among the criminal element, but most of us prefer not to draw attention. It's a good thing I have a reputation to precede me. Otherwise I'd look like an easy target.

I stride across the road and beneath the divine symbols over the doorway, thinking a silent prayer at Kosmel. *How about helping me get out of yet another sticky situation? It does seem to be your specialty.*

He doesn't answer, but then, I don't really expect him to. The trickster godlen is fickle about how and when he chooses to communicate.

Plenty of clerics would be astonished to hear he ever bothered to speak to me with his actual voice in the first place.

As we step into the building, Julita lets out a soft hum. *Well, this is an interesting approach to worship. I suppose it's fitting to the godlen being honored.*

From the first glimpse of the interior, it's obvious the building is meant as a temple to Kosmel as well as its business purposes. Carvings of Kosmel's symbols and paintings of scenes from his legendary exploits decorate every wall of the expansive room that's a gambler's paradise.

And in the center of the space, the ceiling is open all the way up to the roof three floors overhead. A massive silver statue of the godlen stands in that column of open space, only visible up to his thighs from where I'm poised.

I've always wondered how the members of the Black Talons feel about having the trickster godlen staring right into their private quarters. Considering their typical moral code, maybe the gang members take comfort in the close proximity. Their illicit organization acts as the clerics and devouts of this temple.

The heads of three families combined forces to form the Black Talons ages ago. I scan the sprawl of tables around the statue for the specific figure I'm looking for, the current patriarch of the Rochimek family.

Only a few of the tables are in use this early in the day: a couple of rounds of cards going on at one side of the room and a cluster of gamblers trying their luck with dice at the other. The rattling sound bounces off the ceiling.

A couple of figures sit at the bar at the back of the room. A greasy, peppery scent wafts from that direction—the kitchen has gotten started on the fried goldrud root that gamblers consider a lucky snack.

And a middle-aged man with rumpled blond hair lounges by an otherwise empty table near the card-players, nursing a mug of ale. His baggy clothes give the impression of plumpness, a patchwork of stains and darning decorating the shabby fabric.

There's dressing down, and then there's outright slobbery. But in this case, I know it's all by design.

Keeping my expression cool, I smile inwardly and amble over to join the apparent vagrant.

I'd imagine Garom noted my arrival from the first moment, but he doesn't glance over to acknowledge me until I'm just a few paces from his table. As I lower myself into the chair next to him, he offers a reserved nod. "Ivy. It's been a while."

*You're on a first name basis with this vagabond?* Julita says with a note of disbelief. Apparently Garom's disguise has worked on her.

I figure it's best to cut right to the chase. He's a man who appreciates frankness.

"I wish I had a better reason to visit. I need to cash in the favor you owe me."

Garom's eyebrows rise beneath the messy locks of his supposed hair. He pushes to his feet. "I guess we'd better take this to my office, then."

He keeps up the vagabond act all the way to the staircase in the back corner, adding a shuffle to his walk as if he isn't totally steady on his feet. The moment we pass out of view of the gambling den, his strides lengthen.

I trail behind him up to the second floor. The torso of Kosmel's statue gleams at the other end of a hall that branches off into several rooms.

Garom pushes into one of those rooms. The moment the door has thudded shut behind me, he tugs off his wig.

The heads of the other two families in the Black Talons make regular appearances on the first floor in sharp suits and polished shoes that emphasize their success. Garom prefers to take a more subtle tactic. He hangs around the gambling tables regularly in the guise of an aging drunkard to observe how his patrons behave when they don't think they're being monitored.

The wig is necessary because of the typical sacrifice all members of the Black Talons families make. Beneath the fake hair, Garom's head is bald, a mix of shaved scalp and the scars where a cleric carved that scalp right off during his twelfth-year dedication ceremony.

Each member has a different pattern scored into the flesh over their skull. Garom's is made up of lines as chaotically woven as the streets of Tangleside.

I've heard people whisper that it's a maze with only one start point and end, not that anyone will have had the chance to test out that theory.

Garom drops into the chair behind his sturdy oak desk and studies me with keener eyes than he showed on the floor below. His gaze skims over my clothing. "You've gotten all dolled up for the occasion. I don't think I've ever seen you in a dress."

"It's a long story," I say. "And not really relevant. The king has closed all the city gates. I need a way to get past the walls, along with a few companions."

Garom's eyebrows leap up even higher than before. "Don't tell me the sudden commotion is because of *you*? I heard there was some kind of brawl at the blasted palace itself."

Of course one of his lackeys would already have caught wind and informed him. I should be grateful there was no one alive other than my men and the royal family to gossip about my confrontation with the king.

I have to choose my next words carefully. It's well-known that while all key members of the Black Talons sacrifice parts of their scalp by tradition, most make other, more discreet sacrifices so they can request a gift of sizeable power.

No one's sure what exactly Garom offered up alongside some skin and hair, but he's got a significant talent for separating truth from falsehood. And if he catches me lying to him, any sense of obligation he feels to fulfill his promised favor may evaporate.

I roll my eyes as if the suggestion is ridiculous. "I didn't attack the king. But having the gates closed is inconvenient for various other reasons. My associates and I are at risk of getting swept up in the search."

"And you want me to get you and—how many others?"

I would say three, because I barely know Rheave. He's barely even *human*.

But he did warn us when no one else could. He begged me to protect him from the scourge sorcerers.

If I leave him behind, will they get control over him again?

"Four," I say firmly.

"You want me to get five people out of the city while the Crown's Watch has Florian under a full royal lockdown." Garom's tone has taken on an incredulous note. "What kind of sorcery do you think my people can pull off?"

I manage not to wince at the s-word. "I think you're one of the leaders of the most powerful organization in Silana outside of the royal court, and if *you* wanted to be outside those walls right now, there'd be some way you could make it happen. So make it happen for me."

Garom leans back in his chair with a sigh. "I know I'm in your debt, Ivy. But *you* know that we're trying to keep the Crown's Watch off our backs. If you've gotten yourself mixed up in trouble as big as it sounds… that's a bigger ask than I was prepared for. I have to think about the security of everyone who works under me."

I fold my arms over my chest and fix him with my best defiant stare. "Really? Your daughter's life isn't worth that much? I believe your exact words at the time were, 'Anything you need, no questions asked.'"

Garom's jaw ticks at the mention of the job I did for him that earned me his favor. A few years ago, an upstart rival gang kidnapped his then-preteen daughter and threatened him with all the things they'd do to her if the Black Talons didn't kowtow to them.

I stole her back for him before he even had to tell the rest of the organization about his precarious position. Since he had the rival gang slaughtered, nobody much knows what went down other than me and him.

Unfortunately, that means *my* position is now precarious. If Garom refuses me, I can't turn to anyone else to enforce our deal. His colleagues aren't aware it exists.

But it's no secret that you don't become one of the realm's top crooks by playing by the rules. I came prepared.

He's still hemming and hawing. "Ivy, I'm going to see that you get everything you deserve for your help to my family. If it were in another week or two—"

I step forward and smack my palm against the edge of the desk. "I might not have a week. We need to go *today*. So let me make this easy for you. If I don't return to my companions with a plan for getting out of here before nightfall and see that plan through, I've arranged that the Crown's Watch will be informed of how to access Crow's Close, along with a list of who's responsible for all sorts of past crimes."

Garom stiffens, his face going sallow. He can tell I'm telling the truth. "You wouldn't— If they break into this place, they'll ruin everything. You'd side with those pompous assholes over *your* people?"

"Of course not." I smile tightly at him. "I don't *want* to tell them anything. I knew you'd be good to your word and I'd be able to stop the message before it's triggered. I just figured you might need a little reminder of just how much you do owe me first."

Garom studies me with warier eyes. I'm sure right now he'd like to slit my throat and toss me wherever bodies disappear in the Close, but then he'd be screwing himself over.

If I don't return, Rheave will deliver the sealed message I really did write to the palace. It'll be trickier to ensure my failsafe works if Garom's people turn on us in the middle of our escape, but he doesn't know that.

And if we make it out of the city safely, I'll burn the missive without anyone setting eyes on it.

A scowl darkens Garom's face. He can tell I was being honest about the rest of what I said too— that I don't want to do it, that I believe he'll come through with the proper motivation.

Sometimes I think perceiving truth and lies might be more of a curse than a gift. It'd make it a lot harder to lie to yourself when you'd like to.

The gang boss drums his fingers on the table and lets out another, rougher sigh. "I think I might be able to set something up. We made a recent acquisition—I had other plans for it—but you're right. I wouldn't trade Luzia's life for a business opportunity."

"I'm sure she'd be glad to know that," I say dryly, and prop myself against the edge of his desk. "Tell me all about this 'acquisition.'"

# Four

*Ivy*

I stare at my reflection in the cracked mirror for a few moments, taking in the results of my efforts at disguise. The dye Garom included in the supplies his people brought us has darkened my reddish-blond hair to a chestnut shade that makes my skin look even more sickly than usual and my blue eyes stand out starkly.

But not as unnervingly brilliant as the sea-green irises of the daimon in our midst.

Rheave comes up beside me and peers over my shoulder into the glass. I'm still not sure how much of the initial attitude I saw from the false guard is part of his personality or something imposed on him by the scourge sorcerers. There's a much more open vibe to his comments now.

"Humans can change their appearance so easily," he remarks studying my reflection, his tone awed.

Casimir lets out a soft laugh from the other end of the room where we're making our final preparations for our escape. "I suppose daimon don't have much of an appearance to change in the first place."

Rheave tilts his head to the side, watching his own reflection next to mine. "We don't normally need one. But it's interesting having that too."

He touches the face I've always thought was far too beautiful to belong to a soldier. "I wonder how I would look with pale hair."

I nudge him gently with my elbow. "We don't have time to find that out now. You can experiment with makeovers when we're out of this mess."

My jacket shifts around my scrawny form. Casimir carefully pinned it so it looks like almost a perfect fit, but I can still tell it's too big for me.

Rheave is the only one of us who came by the clothes he's currently wearing honestly. We simply left him in his typical guard uniform.

Garom has supplied the rest of us with a set of Crown's Watch uniforms he came by through means he wasn't willing to share.

I glance down at the smallest of the uniforms—the one I donned. I checked over every detail in comparison to Rheave's sapphire blue jacket and trousers, and Stavros examined them too, and as far as we can tell, they're perfectly authentic.

Perfectly designed to convince the guards at the gate that we're colleagues of theirs leaving the city on the king's authority. As Garom pointed out to me when he went over the plan, soldiers are the only people allowed to come and go during a lockdown.

I'm not loving the idea of marching out right under the noses of the people who most want to execute me, but I can't think of a better gambit.

Julita sounds as if she's suppressed a snicker. *I mean no offense, but I don't think military garb suits you.*

I snort in agreement and turn away from the mirror.

Casimir is just putting the finishing touches on Alek's face. The scholar has his back to me, but I can see plenty of tension in the rigid set of his shoulders.

He hasn't gone without his leather mask covering most of his face in public for years. It was hard for him just to let me and Casimir see his scarred skin before.

But we know the king will have put out descriptions of us, and it'd be hard to explain him away as a *different* man with a dark brown mask. So he's tucked it away in one of the saddle bags and agreed to let Casimir cover the mottled area over his forehead, cheeks, and one side of his jaw as well as the courtesan's skills with makeup allow.

"There," Casimir says, stepping back. "It isn't flawless up close, but from the distance everyone outside our group will be seeing you, especially with the daylight fading, no one will notice anything unusual."

Alek turns hesitantly. When his bright brown eyes meet mine, a stutter runs through my pulse.

Julita gasps. *Cas really can work a kind of magic with that palette.*

Casimir has managed to paint over the ridges and streaks of reds, grays, and browns to match the smooth bronze skin that's Alek's natural coloring. Well, not quite as smooth as the unmarked side of his jaw, but awfully close.

I'm looking at the scholar as he would have appeared if he'd never let jealousy lead him down a vicious path that ended with a burning potion splashed in his face.

He's absolutely stunning.

But he's also not exactly the man I've fallen in love with. I'm torn between catching my breath at how striking he is and wishing I could wipe away all the makeup to see the real Alek underneath.

He's stunning with his scars too, just in a different way.

"It looks great," I tell him with a reassuring smile.

Alek's stance relaxes slightly at my words. "I suppose I need to see it as a different kind of mask."

"Exactly." Casimir brushes his hands together with a satisfied grin. "We're all going into hiding in plain sight."

Stavros lets out a grunt from where he's just finished darkening his hair with a black powder that's completely obscured the blood-red hue. Disguising him has been our biggest concern, seeing as the exalted former general is rather well-known among everyone with military inclinations.

"Some things can't be changed," he says, tapping his left wrist against his side—the left wrist that's currently just a stump.

He's removed his distinctive combat prosthetic, the loop of metal that's bent around into a hook-like shape, but his more realistic wooden hand is back in his quarters at the college. Even Garom couldn't come up with a believable replacement for that in the short time we have.

Casimir hums. "Keeping the stump hidden in your pocket should do the trick just fine. Plenty of soldiers ride around with just one hand on the reins."

The courtesan pauses to study the work he did on the former general's face. We couldn't adjust anything about Stavros's massive frame, which is stretching the largest of our borrowed uniforms, so we've tried to change as much as we can otherwise. Along with the darkened hair, Casimir has painted

Stavros's light brown skin a creamy peach tone similar to his own, mottled by a broad scar across one temple and cheek as if from a vicious sword slash.

I'm not sure I'd recognize him at a glance if I hadn't watched Casimir do his work. We have to hope it'll be enough.

Rheave gives my face another once-over. "I'd still know you, even with the different hair color."

"You've seen me several times," I say. "You know what to expect. The king won't have been able to get out much more of a description than my hair and height."

Thankfully the latter detail is less obvious when I'm mounted on a horse.

I motion toward the doorway to the room where we've left our steeds. "I don't think it's going to get any better than this. Let's pack up and get out of here."

As we squeeze the last few items into the saddle bags, Alek turns to Rheave. "Are you sure you want to come with us? The king probably hasn't realized you helped us. You could go back to playing guard at the college."

He speaks evenly enough, but I can tell from the hesitation in his stance that he's not convinced bringing the daimon-man along is a great idea.

I brace myself to defend the decision I made, but Rheave speaks up first. "The people who made this body—the scourge sorcerers, as you call them—they'd find me there. They'd break me." He pauses and smiles at me. "And if I can protect myself while protecting Ivy as well, that's even better."

When he looks at me like that, talks like that, a flutter passes through my pulse even knowing what he really is.

Stavros props himself against the doorframe, his eyes narrowing. "You were very set on coming to Ivy for help in the first place. Why her?"

The daimon-man pats the neck of his mare with a vaguely bemused expression that turns more solemn when he returns his gaze to me. "The scourge sorcerers assigned me to watch her. Because they wanted to make sure it was safe for her to join their group."

A finger of ice runs down my spine. The possibility that he was spying for them had occurred to me, but it's different hearing him confirm it. "So that's why you seemed to be around so often. What did you tell them?"

"There wasn't very much to tell. They wanted to know if you seemed friendly with any of the other guards, and I said no. They wanted to know if I saw you doing anything unusual, but they didn't seem worried about the stargazing."

He stops for a moment in thought. "And the man who gave most of the orders at the college—Torstem, the one you got rid of—he brought me when they put you on trial. He asked me to sense if a divine force blessed you."

Gods above, the scourge sorcerers were testing me even more than I realized. As I tighten the girth on Toast's saddle, I swallow thickly. "What did you say about that?"

The daimon-man offers me a softer smile that only makes me feel more jumbled up inside. "I felt the connection when you shot the arrows. Someone was watching over you. That's how—that's how I knew I could trust you. None of the rest of them ever called down any kind of influence from the ones you call godlen."

Stavros guffaws. "Did you mention that part to them?"

"They didn't ask. About that or what other supernatural forces might be working through Ivy."

Alek's head jerks around. "You knew she was riven?"

Rheave lifts his shoulders in a casual shrug. "I thought so. I only felt it a little, that one time."

It's a good thing I kept my magic so tightly under wraps, then. If there were more clay-captured daimon around during any of the other rituals, they might have tipped off the scourge sorcerers.

I have no idea whether the murderous psychopaths would have been excited to exploit my power or seen me as just as much of a threat as the king does.

I heft myself into the saddle, which puts my back to the daimon-man. "Is that why you came to me? Because you figured I was powerful enough to stand up to them?"

"No," Rheave says brightly. "I came to you because you helped me with the butterfly. Even though I could see you were nervous about being near me, you helped. And I could sense by then that you didn't really like what they were doing. I didn't tell them that either."

I can't help glancing over my shoulder at him. His beautiful face is utterly placid, as if he doesn't find anything about what he just said all that meaningful. But my chest has constricted around my heart.

He isn't wrong, is he? I lent him a hand with the injured butterfly that'd landed on his sleeve—because it realized he was something more than human?—for pretty much the same reason I haven't yet told him to take a hike.

My monstrous magic has left me with one firm principle I've never strayed from. If I can do some good for the people around me, balance the scales of the harm I've dealt and might deal in the future a little, then I do it.

*Well,* Julita says doubtfully. *I suppose that makes a certain kind of sense.*

Casimir lets out a soft laugh. "I think he sees the same things in you that we all do, Kindness."

I shoot him a teasing grimace at the nickname, but before I can say anything in return, a slim figure bursts through the doorway.

"There's a patrol coming this way," Luzia says breathlessly. "They'll be here in less than five minutes. You'd better get going."

She gives me a hasty but encouraging nod. As soon as she heard that her father had agreed to help me, she insisted on pitching in.

The men clamber onto their mounts, and we hurry out onto the street at a trot. If we go any faster, we'll only give away that we're fleeing rather than a patrol ourselves.

Clouds have congealed overhead, dimming the sun. A distant rumble of thunder sends a quiver through my nerves.

I set up our escape. My men are all counting on me.

What if Garom's tactic fails, and we end up arrested?

I've been prepared for that final fate for years. It won't feel so much like a tragedy as an inevitability.

But if I drag the men I've come to care about so much down with me...

Shaking off my worries, I will myself to stay focused.

We take the first side street and continue on a winding path to ensure the soldiers behind us don't catch sight of our group. It's only a short ride to the outer walls.

Garom monitors the schedule of the guards at the city gates and knows that they usually change at the sixth bell. If we get there right before the current sentinels are due to be relieved of duty, they'll be at their most restless. Eager to get on with things so their work can be done.

As we come out onto the main thoroughfare that leads to the gate we're aiming for, we arrange ourselves into a more formal procession. Rheave, who's still technically an actual guard, takes the lead with Casimir and I behind him. Stavros and Alek, in their heavier disguises, bring up the rear where they'll be less visible.

I hold my posture stiffly straight, as if I can add a few inches to my meager height, and form an expression with the sort of arrogant disdain I've witnessed on dozens of Crown's Watch soldiers in the past. With my chin raised, I peer down my nose at the pedestrians we pass.

There's a line of civilians along the right side of the road—mostly merchants with carts or wagons of goods they're hoping they can still take out of the city today, as well as a couple of carriages. They've been waiting long enough that many of them have perched amid their merchandise to talk with their neighbors in line. The muttering intensifies as we trot by.

Then a voice catches my ears, one I haven't heard in years but so familiar it cuts right down the center of me. "Oh, we were supposed to have these tracts to the Temple of Sunlit Skies three hours ago. I don't see why they can't let legitimate business people like us through."

My gaze flicks to the side before I can catch it. And there she is.

My mother perches on our old cart next to several stacks of thin books. Her pale hair is wound back in one of her usual buns, as much gray as blond now. Her thin lips slant at the disgruntled angle I can still vividly remember deepening into outright fury.

A prickle runs down my back through the scars she inflicted with the regular lashes of her belt. My breath freezes in my lungs.

I yank my gaze away, but Casimir has already picked up on my reaction. He peers at me with concern, keeping his voice low. "Ivy, what is it? Do we need to divert course?"

It takes far too much effort to drag the humid air into my chest. I grip my reins and will my voice to stay steady. "It's fine. I just didn't expect—I saw my mother."

There's a rustle as Stavros shifts in his saddle behind me. His words come out in a dark mutter. "What? Where is she?"

Alek speaks in a similarly hardened tone. "The cart with the books, I'd imagine? *That's* the woman who—"

He cuts himself off with a muted growl.

Their obvious agitation only rattles my nerves more. "It's not like you can do anything about it right now. It's not as if I'd *want* you to."

Rheave glances back at us. "What's wrong? Why's everyone upset?"

Casimir manages to make the explanation simple. "We passed by a woman who used to hurt Ivy when she was a child."

Rheave's posture goes rigid, his eyes flashing as he searches the line. "Where? Why hasn't she been punished?"

The fierceness of the words makes my heart skip a beat. "Gods above, not you too. It's my mother. We're not doing anything."

The daimon-man catches my gaze with a frown, his hands still balled into fists around the reins. "If she hurt you, then she's an enemy more than anything else."

Alek lets out a low, raw chuckle. "Hear, hear."

I aim a glare around at all of them. "In case you've forgotten, we've got much bigger enemies to worry about. Can we please focus on getting through that gate alive?"

Rheave makes a chagrinned expression and tugs his body back around. Stavros growls something under his breath that I don't ask him to clarify, but no one makes any further attempts to inflict justice on the woman who raised me.

*Men,* Julita murmurs with a hint of amusement. *I suppose it's a good thing for both of us they're so committed to defending you.*

It's a good thing they've remembered the larger problem, because we're just a few buildings from the gate now. I inhale and exhale slowly, gathering myself.

We're not fugitives. We have every right to pass through. We carry the full authority of Silana's military order.

Ha.

Normally there are only two guards monitoring each gate, maybe one on the wall overhead. Today, four blue-uniformed figures stand in front of the barred doors, with three others monitoring the situation from above.

My throat constricts, but I lift my chin again with my false haughty airs. More thunder rumbles in the ever-darkening clouds overhead.

Rheave rides right up to the row of soldiers as if he can't imagine them stopping him. At least he knows how to play this part well.

"We need to get through," he says in a commanding tone. "We have orders to search the countryside."

The woman in the middle frowns. "The lockdown hasn't been lifted."

The daimon-man lets a more urgent note creep into his voice. "There are concerns that the fugitives may have escaped before it was enforced. If that's the case, we must track them down quickly."

She still looks hesitant, and her colleagues peer along our procession, eyeing the bunch of us with critical gazes. My skin itches with apprehension.

The longer they take to ponder our story, the harder it'll be to convince them.

I nudge Toast half a step forward and summon all my memories of past Crown's Watch soldiers who've sneered and stomped their way through the outer wards. "We've been delayed enough already! Let us through, or the king will have your heads for your idiocy. We have a job to carry out even if you're struggling to do yours."

The guards stiffen, but my domineering attitude appears to do the trick. The woman mutters an apology and reaches with one of the men to heave open the crossbar.

My heart thuds ever louder as the doors swing open. We tap our horses into a trot, Rheave passing beneath the arch in the wall first, then Casimir and me. The hammering against my ribs doesn't start to ease until I hear the clops of Stavros's and Alek's steeds emerging behind me.

Then, in a deafening warble of thunder, the clouds open up with the first deluge of rain.

The drops splatter across our bodies. I spare a panicked glance behind me in time to see the make-up running on the faces of both of the men at my back.

And I'm not the only one who sees it.

"There's something wrong with them," one of the guards atop the wall hollers to his fellow soldiers. "They were disguising their faces!"

"Halt!" someone bellows from behind us, just as Stavros barks out, "Ride!"

We all prefer the former general's suggestion. I dig my heels into Toast's sides, and he takes off like his tail's on fire.

More rain pelts down on us, pounding almost as loud as the horses' hooves. Stavros urges his stallion to the head of the group, veering to lead us toward the nearest stretch of forest where we can disappear from view.

With an unnerving whine, an arrow shoots through the air just inches from his shoulder. It thuds into the grass instead.

"Faster!" Alek calls out raggedly.

I don't think Toast can gallop any harder than he already is. Clutching the reins, I sneak a peek over my shoulder in time to see all three of the guards on the wall drawing bows, with more soldiers racing to join them.

The arrows careen through the rain. Two fly wide, but the third is shooting straight toward Stavros's back.

Panic jolts through my veins with a chill that has nothing to do with the water seeping down my back. My magic leaps up alongside it.

Before I can second-guess the decision, I fling my arm out.

Like with the king this morning, there's no time to beg Kosmel for guidance, no time to even question the decision. I can't stand to see Stavros killed over my mistakes.

So possibly I make another.

My power slams the arrow to the side. It hisses harmlessly into the grass.

And on the wall behind us, a cry of pain rings out.

The backlash of my magical shove must have struck one of the guards. My head is whirling too fast for me to rejoice or regret the act.

I duck low against the growing downpour and hurtle between the welcoming trees.

# FIVE

*Ivy*

By the time Stavros slows his stallion ahead of us, I think I'm drenched right through to my bones. The rain has started to ease off, but a steady drizzle continues flecking my cheeks through the gloom.

The former general wheels his stallion in a small clearing and looks to me first. His face is taut with worry. "Are you all right?"

I restrain a shiver and paste on my best unflappable smile. "I'll survive. What do we do now?"

Stavros lets out a rough breath. "We've covered a lot of distance quickly. As unpleasant as the rain has been, it'll have covered most of the signs of our passing. I brought us around the city and onward in nearly the opposite direction from where the guards last saw us, which should help keep us beyond their initial searches."

Alek wraps one arm around his chest over his sodden uniform, which is plastered to his lean frame. "They aren't going to give up any time soon, though. Not as long as the king is afraid of a riven sorcerer on the loose."

Casimir taps his gelding to bring it up beside me and rests a comforting hand on my arm. "The royal family does have plenty of other things to focus on at the moment, though. I'd imagine the attack on the palace will be their most immediate concern."

"Unless they're going to blame that on me too," I mutter, with a shudder I can't suppress at the memory of King Konram's accusing question.

Julita sniffs in disdain. *That's ridiculous. Surely the king has at least enough of a brain to realize you weren't responsible for that. Why in the realms would you have protected him from attackers you'd sent to murder him?*

A very good question, and one I'd like to hope will occur to Konram when he's had time to think things through.

Rheave glances around us, his eerie eyes gleaming in the thickening darkness. "This body is hungry. None of you have eaten much today—you must need the energy too. Can we stop for long enough to have a meal and relieve ourselves?"

Part of me wants to cling to Toast for dear life and ride to the very edge of Silana, but even as the urge passes through me, my stomach gurgles.

Alek's gaze twitches to me. "Yes, we should eat. If we get back under the trees, they should keep most of the rain off."

The muscles in my legs protest as I dismount. Toast shakes his mane with a snort and ambles to the edge of the clearing to snack on some grass.

Casimir retrieves a bundle of food from his saddle bag, and we gather under the denser branches. As he hands a cheese-stuffed roll to me, another shiver ripples through my body, too intense for me to suppress it.

The courtesan pauses. "You're freezing. Your cloak is in one of the bags, isn't it? You could change back into your dress and—"

I cut him off with a terse laugh. "And get that drenched too? No. I'll put on my cloak when we set off again, but I've been through worse."

The tightening of Casimir's jaw suggests he isn't happy to hear that, but he glances around at the others. "We should all put on our cloaks for the rest of the ride. There's no need for the journey to be completely miserable."

Stavros tips his head obligingly, looking faintly amused by the courtesan's concern.

I bite into the roll, even though I can't summon much sense of appetite despite my gut's grumbling. As I swallow the sticky lump, thoughts of everything we've been through in the past day whip through my mind.

My spirits sink like the fading of the daylight. I force down the rest of the roll, but it sits like a boulder in my belly.

"This is my fault," I say.

All four heads swivel toward me. Alek knits his brow. "What do you mean?"

I wave my hand vaguely. "I showed my magic in front of the king. Now he wants all of you imprisoned—or executed. You've had to run for your lives; you've had to leave everything *in* your lives behind…"

A pang of guilt brings a burn to the back of my eyes. "I think I hurt one of the guards while we were escaping. King Konram is going to be even angrier with me, which means the same for you too."

"Ivy…" Casimir slips his arm around me and presses a kiss to my temple. "I have no regrets at all about being here with you. The only alternatives were letting the scourge sorcerers slaughter the royal family or turning on you."

"And neither of those are remotely acceptable," Stavros says. He takes a step closer to me and hesitates, his dark gaze searching mine through the dimness.

It's only been four days since the former general and I finally made a real peace with each other. Since he told me he loved me… and I found I could trust him enough to believe it.

We haven't had much time on solid ground before our equilibrium was upended all over again.

Stavros's jaw works before he goes on. "You fought for the royal family with all the loyalty they could deserve. You put your life on the line over and over to infiltrate the scourge sorcerers and end their conspiracy. It is my honor to be standing with you, ensuring you'll get all the recognition you deserve."

I wish I found it easier to accept those words. How do I shake thirteen years of seeing myself as a monster because of my magic and the harm it's done?

Then Alek eases past Stavros to stop in front of me. A little hope quivers into being at the determination etched on his scarred face.

He touches my cheek, his gaze intent on mine, his voice equally intense. "You know I've made more than my share of awful mistakes. I can say beyond a sliver of doubt that the only one I've made today was failing to convince King Konram of who you really are while I had the chance."

A lump rises in my throat. "I don't think anyone could have."

"And I don't see any way you could have handled what happened today better than you did. What did I leave behind? Books and papers? I'd rather have you still in my life than the entire royal library."

A laugh hitches out of me even knowing how huge a statement that is from the scholar.

Alek captures the sound with the press of his lips against mine. More warmth flows through my chilled body, washing away the worst of my anguish.

When he draws back, I lift my hand to echo his caress. My fingers trace the ridges of now uncovered scars that ripple across his cheek. "In case you need the reminder, I like you best without any kind of mask."

Alek smiles at me so brilliantly that I could almost believe everything is already fine. But as he drops his hand, Rheave shifts on his feet.

The daimon-man focuses on Stavros. "How intently will the Crown's Watch continue pursuing Ivy even while they have their other enemies to deal with?"

Stavros swipes his sleeve past his mouth. "We probably have at least a few days before a particularly invasive search begins. The Crown's Watch won't venture very far beyond the city. It'll be the wider army we'll be contending with. But with the attack on the palace, standard protocol would be for all soldiers in the area to ensure the royal family's safe passage to one of their secondary residences before anything else."

"King Konram will be leaving the city too?" I ask.

"It's possible he and his family already have. There are secure routes out of Florian that are accessible only to the royals and their guards." Stavros exhales in a rush. "After that, I suppose it depends on how large of a menace the scourge sorcerers continue to present themselves as."

Casimir turns to the daimon-man. "Rheave, you'll know more about that than we currently do. You indicated that the leader of the conspiracy is still alive."

Rheave nods, his chocolate-brown curls swaying with the movement. "Not the one Ivy knew who worked in the college."

A fresh chill washes over me. "Ster. Torstem." The man we thought was running the entire so-called Order of the Wild.

He really did sacrifice himself to the fire so that his followers would keep faith in the conspiracy, then. Because he truly believed in the cause himself? Because he knew whoever commanded him would continue their efforts?

"Torstem gave out most of the orders for what happened in and around the college, but he was getting his orders from someone else," Rheave says. "There was someone overseeing the workshop where this body was made."

He touches his chest as if he still sees his human body as an object that's not entirely *him*. "I didn't see that man, though. When he came to the workshop, I was already trapped in the body, but the sorcerers hadn't fully animated it yet. I had no sight."

Alek perks up with an air of keen interest. "Would you recognize his voice if you heard it again?"

The daimon-man's forehead furrows as he considers. "Possibly. The sounds traveled strangely when I was encased in the clay, before it became flesh."

"Do you know where that workshop was?" Stavros asks.

"No. It was a fairly long journey to the city. We were kept in boxes, nothing but darkness." A slight tremor runs through the daimon-man's muscular form that makes me want to clasp his hand, as if I can offer some comfort.

"But this leader," Alek says, "he could still talk to you directly? You indicated that you sensed him calling all the daimon he'd harnessed to attack the palace."

Rheave hums thoughtfully. "It wasn't quite talking. It was more like a tug or a push. But I could understand what it was tugging or pushing me toward. My first few weeks guarding the college, I simply had to go along with those tugs and all the other orders they'd imbedded in me."

Casimir's mouth curves up into a fond smile. "Until Ivy inspired you."

The daimon-man's gaze veers to me. "Something like that. I wasn't really thinking about what I was doing, just following the orders and wishing I could break out. But Ivy talked about things I couldn't help wondering about later, and I started noticing what I liked about having this body. And when I questioned the people controlling us at the college about their orders, they didn't like it."

I wince. "They threatened to destroy you."

"Yes." Rheave's unearthly eyes remain fixed on my face. "But I knew if there was anyone who would stop them from doing it, it was you. And I was right. If it won't trouble you to have me around, I'd like to stay with you, wherever you're going. I know that's the best place for me to be."

A strange pang reverberates through my heart. I'm not sure how to be a figure like that in anyone's life, especially a daimon who's not used to having a mortal life at all.

But I can't think of any other answer I could possibly give. "Of course you can stay with us. We'll need all the help *we* can get."

Stavros grimaces, but he refrains from arguing for now. "The more information we have about what we're up against, the better. Do you know who arranged for you and the other daimon to be hired on as guards? Is there anything else you learned about the scourge sorcerers' plans, what they intended to do beyond the attack on the city?"

Rheave's gaze goes momentarily distant. "I'm not sure about hiring us. But for their larger plans—they were making their own army. I heard a few of them say that in the workshop. Building numbers, preparing to overthrow the Melchioreks… But I didn't hear anything more about it after I got to the city. The others might know more."

"The others?" I say. "You mean the other captured daimon? You said there were many more. Where?"

Rheave shakes his head. "I'm not sure of that either. Only a small number of us were sent to the city, but where the others went, I wasn't told. I think the attack on the palace was a sudden decision provoked by the arrests and Torstem's death. It wasn't the main thing they were working toward."

The rest of us exchange an uneasy glance.

"A small number," Alek repeats. "Just how many daimons did they stuff into clay bodies like you?"

Rheave's eyes widen. "More were always going out. But the workshop was big. In the week while they were making me, there were at least a hundred others they were animating."

Casimir pales. "And most of them have been gathering somewhere else? There could be an army of thousands by now."

The bottom of my stomach drops out. "And who knows how many scourge sorcerers egging them on."

The conspiracy seemed horrifying enough when I thought it was merely a few dozen villains scheming around the city. If the Order of the Wild stretches right across Silana… how in the realms are any of us going to stop them?

# Six

*Ivy*

For all Casimir's concern about keeping us warm and dry, he's the one sneezing when we finally stop for the night.

"I'm all right," he tells me when I go over to check on him, but his voice sounds unusually rough. His face has flushed with what might be the start of a fever.

Guilt and worry tangle in my gut. I caress his cheek and grab another roll from our stash of provisions. "You should get a little food in you and then rest."

He grimaces. "It's only a little cold." But when I drag him into the tent after Stavros and Alek get it set up, he sinks onto his sleeping bag as if it was taking all his energy just to stay standing. His breath rasps out of him as it slows with sleep.

Cuddled up next to him, I only manage to drift off when I'm sure he's completely out. My heart keeps aching until slumber rolls over my mind.

I wake up to the warble of the night breeze passing over the fabric of the tent and a twinge in my bladder.

Casimir is still deep asleep beside me, the hoarseness of his breath smoothed out enough that no fresh worries grip me. Alek has tucked himself close at my other side, our shared body heat stopping us from freezing during the chilly autumn night. I can't really complain about having only one tent.

The scholar's cool citrusy scent has mingled with the courtesan's honeyed sandalwood into a complex perfume. I wish I could wrap it around me always.

I close my eyes, but my bladder protests more emphatically. Julita lets out a soft chuckle. *One of the few things I don't miss about having a body.*

Scowling, I ease myself up between the two men. I need to be able to get back to sleep if I'm going to be rested enough to ward off whatever illness Casimir has caught.

Moving slowly and carefully, I manage not to rouse either of my lovers or the daimon-man who's sprawled back-to-back with Alek. I slip out from under the two wool blankets we layered across our sleeping bags and step through the tent's flaps.

Stavros glances up from the log where he's been keeping watch. He'll have traded off with Alek a little while ago, and he's meant to switch with me in another hour or two. I don't think he trusts Rheave to take on guard duty alone at this point.

Like the rest of us, the former general has traded his stolen soldier uniform for the more discreet tunic, jacket, and trousers Garom supplied us with as well. The rain washed the black from his hair like it's mostly rinsed the temporary dye from mine, though the dark red strands still look almost the same shade in the faint moonlight that penetrates our campsite.

He arches his eyebrows at me in question, but his expression tenses with concern at the same time.

I wave toward the trees, pitching my voice low to avoid waking the others. "I just need to relieve myself."

Stavros's stance relaxes in a way I don't totally understand until he says, in a matching low tone, "No nightmares?"

I choke up for a second at the history implied in those two words. Stavros knows as well as I do that he was the starring figure in most of my recent nightmares, wrenching a noose around my neck as he once thought he might need to do in reality. He even instructed one of his students to partly strangle me with a rope to test my control over my magic.

But we've come a long way from there—both of us.

I walk over to the log. "No bad dreams at all."

Drawn to the mix of affection and anguish in his eyes by the same emotions coiled inside me, I bend down to kiss him.

Stavros meets the press of my lips with an encouraging hum and teases his fingers into my hair. When I pull back a few inches, he gazes up at me with a hint of his old cocky grin. "Trying to distract me from my duties?"

I snort softly. "Trying to show you how much I appreciate you watching over me."

"Hmm. I think I'd better appreciate you a little more, then."

He tugs me back down and claims my mouth with enough passion to leave my head spinning.

We both know this isn't the time or place for a lengthier interlude. I squeeze his shoulder before weaving off between the trees for a little privacy.

As I squat behind a bush several paces away, Julita speaks up with no apparent concern about what I'm up to. Really, privacy isn't a concept that can exist when you've got another person's soul residing in your head.

*Where do you think we go from here?*

I gather the skirts of the plain woolen dress I changed into and take a few steps from my makeshift latrine. The rustling and buzz of the forest life around me stir up memories of my ventures into the campus woods to join in the scourge sorcerers' rituals and spy on them.

We rode another few hours from the spot where we stopped to eat yesterday evening, to an isolated stretch of land Stavros says is along the border between two provinces. With no towns or roads nearby, it's unlikely anyone will stumble on us.

But clearly we can't simply camp out in the woods for the rest of our lives.

"I don't know," I murmur. "I guess we'll come up with some kind of plan in the morning after we're properly rested."

*What a plan it'll need to be.* She huffs. *We were supposed to be* done *with those fiends. I can't believe they've managed to spread their toxic magic across the whole country.*

Horror colors the noblewoman's tone. She's more familiar with the brutal side of scourge sorcery than the rest of us, having been subjected to blood-letting experiments by her brother and his best friend as a child in their fumbling attempts to enhance their magical talents.

I grimace in answer. "Rheave might be mistaken about just how far their operations have expanded. But it does sound as if it's a much bigger mess than we had any idea about."

My ghostly passenger shudders. *When I set you on this mission, I never thought it'd ask anywhere near this much of you, Ivy. I never thought it'd ask this much of me. And now the king wants your head too… I'm sorry.*

Does she really think this disaster is somehow her fault?

I wrap my arms around my waist, wishing I could touch the woman I now consider a friend, look into her eyes, make sure she accepts how much I mean this. "You didn't launch the Order of the Wild. You never asked me to use my magic. I'm still glad to have a friend through all this chaos, as long as you can stick with us."

I think the tickle of Julita's presence at the back of my skull gentles a little. Her voice comes out softer. *I'll stand with you until the end of it—as well as I can actually stand.*

The corner of my mouth ticks upward, but the unsettled mood the conversation provoked lingers. Pulling my cloak closer around me against the breeze, I peer through the night-cast woods.

A flutter of movement catches my eye. Was that a crow taking flight from a branch overhead?

I hesitate and then step toward that tree. Gazing up at it, I can't see any further sign of divine presence or anything else.

Did Kosmel know all along that he was sending me on a collision course with a murderous conspiracy that extended far beyond the college's walls? Have I offended him as much as I did the king with my impromptu shows of magic?

I was already in over my head at the college. Now I'm so deep underwater I can barely see a glimmer of light through the churning surface overhead.

How is a street-rat thief supposed to challenge a kingdom-wide, hundreds-strong plot to overturn the very fabric of our society?

For a moment, the drowning sensation overwhelms me. I close my eyes and sink to my knees at the base of the tree trunk.

I know what the clerics would say I have to do if I want to call on him properly.

Open myself up. Prove that I welcome his guidance.

Because I do need it now, more than I ever have before.

I'd started to take comfort in the trickster godlen's interest in me. Knowing he was on my side and supporting me helped me stand up to Ster. Torstem and deal with the conspirators my way.

Please, let him not have abandoned me.

I close my eyes and bow my head, thinking out to the divine powers that flow through our world. *Kosmel, if you're still watching over me, I could use some advice. Our enemies are so many more than we realized. I have no idea how I can even start to tackle the rest of the scourge sorcerers. And the king's soldiers will be hunting me too… If there's any direction you can offer, I've never needed it more.*

I wait, cold seeping into my knees from the dirt, leaves hissing against each other overhead.

No voice comes to me. No sense of a divine presence grazes my skin.

After a few minutes, I push myself to my feet. A hollow sensation has formed in the pit of my stomach, but I ignore it as well as I can as I head back to the tent.

I've gotten through plenty of sticky situations in the past without any godly assistance. We'll figure something out.

Stavros nods to me as I pass him. I tuck myself back under the blankets between my other two men and soak up their warmth until it takes the edge off the ache inside.

The sleep I fall into this time is full of jumbled images that don't quite form a dream. Shadows whirl, and jagged shapes brush against my limbs.

Then I'm perched on a tree branch in the midst of the woods, the light of a full moon beaming over me… and a strange figure balanced on the branch across from me.

At first glance, I think it's a gigantic crow. Then the creature raises its head, and the eyes of a man stare back at me—pale but fathomless eyes as if I'm staring straight through a star.

My pulse hitches, and I jerk my gaze away, over the body that's feathered and winged but with a man's legs, leather boots braced against the branch's bark.

A low chuckle reverberates around me. "There are many ways I can appear. I promise you'd find most of the others more disturbing."

"Kosmel," I mumble. Am I still asleep?

The godlen doesn't bother to acknowledge his name. "You know I can't tell you what to do, my wayward rogue. Some of my siblings feel I've meddled too much as it is."

But he's here. He's reached out to me after all.

"I can make my own decisions," I say, remembering the things he's said to me before. I can't quite keep my voice from shaking. "I'd just like to do it with a better understanding of what we're up against. You want all the scourge sorcerers stopped, don't you? But I don't know how much I can risk using my magic without becoming just as big a problem as they are…"

Kosmel is silent for long enough that I'd think he might have vanished if I wasn't staring at his boots. The awareness of his divine energy prickles over my skin.

"It's a complicated journey you've found yourself on," he says finally. Like when he speaks in my head, his voice resonates through every particle of my body, quivering into my bones, scattering my pulse. "Being cautious is not my natural state, but things end in catastrophe when gods impose too much of their will on mortals. You've already suffered enough from those consequences."

I'm not totally sure what he means about my 'suffering.' I grope for the right thing to say. "You must have wanted to tell me *something*, or you wouldn't be here."

The godlen makes a rough sound that's as much caw as grunt. "I heard your plea. I didn't want you to think I've forgotten you. But this may be the last time we speak."

For a second, I feel as if the branch beneath me has disintegrated. I wobble, fighting through the sensation of freefall, of the one bit of security I clung to slipping through my fingers.

"But—my magic—if I need to use it again, will you help me guide it? I didn't want to let it loose without your direction; there just wasn't time—"

"Don't fret like that," Kosmel interrupts. "It doesn't become you." His dry tone gives no indication that he's upset about how I used my power in the past day.

He pauses and then clicks his tongue. "You should have guidance of some sort. I can offer better than my own, in this one case. To mend some of what was marred."

I shouldn't be surprised when the godlen of trickery speaks in half-riddles rather than plainly, but it's frustrating all the same. "Better?"

He adjusts his position with a ruffling of his crow feathers. "Walk with the sun at your left in the morn and your right after noon until you see the silver peak through the trees. Climb straight to the crossed trees, then continue to the left until you reach the waterfall. Announce to the sky that Kosmel led you there and expects you to receive a riven's welcome. Then listen well."

Listen well? Another question tumbles out. "If there's more I should know, can't you—"

Kosmel cuts me off with another raspy caw. "Mortal business is between mortals."

His wings sweep past me in a blur of black feathers, and I really do lose my balance. My boots slip on the branch. My clawing fingers catch only air.

I plummet down and down and—

My eyes pop open as if with a smack of impact. At my gasp, the men around me stir.

Casimir blinks sleepily with a hint of a sniffle and touches my arm. "All right, Kindness?"

I stare into the darkness, the dream echoing through my head. "I think so. I know where we need to go."

# Seven

The soft blades of grass tickle my palm. I turn my hand over, taking in the difference of how they feel against my knuckles.

There are so many tiny experiences that make up the essence of bodily life. So many sensations it never occurred to me might exist when I barely brushed against the physical world.

Flowers of different shapes and colors bloom between the green blades. Their petals graze my fingers with a different texture.

A glimmer of curiosity lights inside me. I pluck up one blossom and then another and another before pausing to admire how the hues intensify when placed next to each other.

With a second quiver of inspiration, I crack little notches into the stems and start fitting them together. A smile crosses my lips at my handiwork.

As a pure daimon, I danced through the city streets and the fields beyond, stirring up the energy of everything around me when the impulse caught me. Now I can spark amusement and surprise more directly.

Stavros's commanding baritone carries across the field where we stopped to let the horses graze. "Rheave, why don't you join us? It'd be good for us to know how you could best contribute in a fight."

Sounds hit me much the same in this form as when I breezed along as a ball of spirit energy, only sharper and with a distinct impression that I should pay attention to them. It was easier to ignore humans talking in my previous state.

I glance over at where Stavros is standing with the other two men who are Ivy's dedicated companions. Stavros has drawn his sword, and Casimir and Alek are both holding daggers.

While we rode this morning, the big man said something about teaching the others more combat skills. Making sure they're prepared for whatever we might face on the road.

I didn't realize he meant me too.

I hesitate, reluctant to leave off my current occupation. Many humans seem to be fond of smacking and stabbing each other. It didn't appeal to me when it was the ones they call scourge sorcerers jostling each other around, and I'm not eager to be a part of any similar games with this bunch.

A few paces away from me, Ivy lifts her head by the buried firepit where we're roasting a couple of rabbits that Stavros caught in snares overnight. The earthen cover over the flames ensures that no smoke escapes to give away our location.

It's an old army trick, he said. Fascinating.

Ivy is exempt from his training, but I think that's only because she doesn't need it. It was also fascinating watching the deftness of the knife in her hand as she skinned the rabbits. The shifting of her fingers against the handle, the way the sunlight glinted off the blade…

"That's right," she says, her clear voice cutting through my reverie. "The scourge sorcerers put you in place as a guard—did they train you at all for the position first?"

I don't like thinking about the first couple of weeks as I learned to operate the body that felt like a heavy cage around me at the time.

My mind skims through the memories. "They made sure I could move and speak well enough to pass as a regular human. I think we were supposed to rely on strength rather than skill when they called on us to attack."

Alek considers me with a gleam of interest in his eyes. His blotchy face is fascinating too, so different from any other complexion I've seen.

He doesn't seem to like it, though. Ivy swatted me this morning when I must have been studying the interplay of color and texture for too long.

"What about the supernatural power the other daimon used in their clay bodies?" he asks. "It looked as if they were summoning bolts of lightning from their hands. Can you do that?"

I look down at my pale hands beneath the strand of flowers draped across them. Callouses are forming from gripping my horse's reins. I'm lucky the creature seems to like me, or I'm not sure I could have stayed on it.

"I don't know," I admit. "I never have before. I never tried."

Stavros waves his sword. "Well, come on. We'd better find out before you fling it around at the wrong time or place. And Casimir could use a break."

The courtesan makes a sound of protest, but then he starts to cough. With a disgruntled noise, Ivy gets up and yanks him over to sit near the fire. "You should be taking it easy."

Casimir wipes his nose on a scrap of fabric he's turned into a handkerchief. "I might need more than my fists if we encounter a whole army of daimon."

"You won't be fighting any which way if you're too stuffed up to breathe."

Stavros is still watching me with the evaluating look that makes my skin prickle. I can't tell whether he's happy that I might be able to help or studying me like a potential enemy.

But Ivy glances over at me too with an expectant air. All of the others are working at being better protectors.

How can I ask for her help and not offer my own in return in as many ways as possible?

I get to my feet and bind the last of the stems as I cross the field. "First, for you," I say, setting the ring of flowers on Ivy's head like a crown. A renewed grin springs to my lips. "The colors look wonderful against your hair!"

"Oh." Ivy touches the garland tentatively, a faint blush coloring her cheeks. "Um, thank you."

As Casimir chuckles, I force myself to walk toward Stavros and Alek next. A niggling sensation runs down my back with the awareness that I'm leaving Ivy farther behind.

It's because of her that I'm here. I should stay close to her.

I want to understand her and all the little, unusual things about her that helped me snap out of the scourge sorcerers' control.

But the other men who hover around her seem to think she's *theirs*. That it's up to them to protect her and watch over her.

Maybe if I swing around a blade to their satisfaction, they'll start to see that I can look after her too. That I have just as much right to follow her on her quest as they do.

When I'm a few paces away, Stavros motions for me to stop. "Stay there and watch. I'll run through the exercises with Aleksi first, but you'll give them a try afterward."

The other man pauses and gives Stavros a lopsided smile. "You know, you could simply call me Alek at this point. Almost everyone does other than the professors. I think being on the run together puts us on a slightly less formal level."

It hadn't occurred to me to wonder why Stavros said the name a little differently, but Stavros looks chagrinned.

Casimir tsks his tongue playfully. "The scholar has a point."

"All right," the big man says, with a hint of a smile of his own. "Let's see how much you've learned so far, Alek."

He talks Alek through a series of jabs and parries. I watch for a couple of minutes, but my attention slides back to Ivy.

She's tucked a blanket over Casimir's shoulders and ambled over to the horses. When my gaze settles on her, she murmurs to the stallion she's most fond of while she brushes his neck. The animal pauses in his grazing to lean into the strokes.

Stavros clears his throat, and my gaze jerks back to him. He's watching me with a stern expression. "You're not going to pick up much skill if you aren't even following the exercises."

"I don't want to attack *you*," I point out. "We're all on the same side. What's the point?"

Humans are so odd.

A dry note creeps into the big man's voice. "The point is that your body won't be used to fending off an actual attacker if it's never gotten any practice. Brute strength will only get you so far. Especially if we find ourselves going up against the king's soldiers rather than only other conjured men and women like you."

With that last sentence, his voice stiffens a bit, but I don't know why. I can see there might be some logic to his words, though.

I roll my shoulders, reveling in the feel of the muscles flexing and stretching. "All right. I'll practice. Whatever will work the fastest."

Casimir shoots me a softly amused smile from his spot by the fire. "You don't like the idea of an extended battle?"

"Daimon don't get into fights," I tell him. "We let each other exist without worrying about anyone except ourselves. Why make more pain?"

Alek rubs his jaw. "You do play tricks on people sometimes. Startle animals. Things like that."

"Nothing that does any real damage. Not when we're in control. We just liven things up where the energy gets too dull."

"Then I'll try not to bore you." Stavros gestures to Alek. "Let Rheave use that dagger for a bit. Come on, daimon, let's see what you can do."

It's hard to put my full commitment into the imitation of fighting he leads me through. I push the dagger through the air as he instructs, but none of the movements feel natural, like how I'd want to move if I actually needed to deflect an attacker.

My fingers curl awkwardly around the weapon. Once, when Stavros blocks it with his sword, I fumble and nearly drop it.

The big man lets out a grunt that suggests he isn't entirely happy. "What about that burning magic the other daimon used? Can you send a little of that into this tree?" He taps a nearby maple.

I stare at the looming plant, but I can't summon any sense of power inside me. No part of me wants to burn this living thing that's doing nothing but growing peacefully.

A shiver runs through my limbs. That's the kind of thing this body's creators would have ordered me to do. They're the ones looking to destroy whatever they can.

To show I'm trying, I walk over to the tree and rest my hand on the bark. The texture presses into my skin to delightful effect. I want to trail my fingers over the surface, not sear it away.

"I don't know how to make it happen," I say. "Maybe it's something the scourge sorcerers channeled through the others, not something we brought."

"I suppose that's possible." Stavros ambles back toward the fire. "Those rabbits should be just about done. Let's see if we can't get in a little more—"

He cuts himself off with a wrench of his head in my direction. His metal prosthetic hand leaps up to point at a spot behind me. "Quick! One of the riven-hunters has snuck up on us—they'll be after Ivy!"

His words and the urgency coursing through them have my body whipping around before I make a conscious decision to move. My gaze snags on a bush just behind the maple tree, the twigs shuddering as if someone's about to spring past it.

I lunge first, a growl lurching up my throat. My arms shoot forward, the dagger dropping from my hand.

No one's getting to Ivy. No one's going to damage one fragment of her skin, one strand of her hair—

Fear and anger collide to set off a flare in my chest. I launch myself right over the shrub, snatching at the first movement my gaze catches.

The need to obliterate the threat crackles through me.

I thump to the ground and roll to the side. When I heave back to my feet, there's no one there.

No riven-hunter. No person at all other than the men and Ivy all watching from the field.

The frantic haze clears from my head. I look down at my hands and find myself clutching the blackened body of a bird.

When I adjust my fingers, its burnt feathers disintegrate into chalky powder.

"Well," Stavros says in a deadpan tone, "that answers at least one question."

My gaze flicks over to him. "I didn't want to kill a bird. I thought there was an enemy—you *said* there was."

"I was simply wondering what might happen if you were sufficiently motivated."

He's eyeing me, giving his head the little shake that I've come to understand means he's focusing harder. His face gives away no emotion now.

Is he pleased by how well I'd have tackled the supposed threat... or upset that I'd have gone so far?

Humans don't make any sense. But if this one decides I'm a problem, he'll campaign to leave me behind.

I don't know what he wants from me. I can only say the truth. "If Ivy needs protecting, I'll protect her."

"And that's good to know," the woman in question says from over by the firepit. "Plus now we have a little extra for lunch. Why don't you bring that bird over here, and we'll see if there's any edible meat on it?"

Her easy smile makes the men around me seem to fade. I stride over, holding out the bird, grateful for the chance to return to where I'd have preferred to be all along.

Ivy slices into the bird I apparently charred without any sign of concern about the power I inflicted on it. Her exclamation of victory when she finds cooked flesh within settles my nerves more, even though I can sense Stavros still examining me from a distance.

What I told him was true. I'll protect Ivy from any danger that comes our way, however I need to.

Because I need her. Her strange remarks and unusual attitudes shocked me out of the spell the scourge sorcerers had me under. They gave me my first taste of how wondrous living in this body I didn't ask for could be.

If I'm forced apart from her—if I lose her... how easily would my former captors make me their prisoner all over again?

# Eight

Ivy

"Are you sure he said the 'crossed trees'?" Stavros asks, pausing to swipe the sweat from his forehead.

The breeze licks cold across my own dampened skin. I rub the back of my neck, dislodging the strands of hair that've stuck there.

We spotted the peak of the mountain this morning, shining like silver where it jutted up just above the tree line. The sun was directly overhead by the time we reached the mountain's foot, and we've been climbing for what feels like hours.

I can't be sure of the exact time, since we've found ourselves in a part of Silana so remote that the peal of the nearest town bell was little more than a distant chime even before we started the climb.

The air has cooled as we've ascended, but the exertion has warmed us at the same time. The last section of the trek has been up terrain so steep we had to dismount and lead the horses in our weaving path across the rocky ground.

I peer through the brush around us for any sign of trees that would fit Kosmel's description. "Yes. I remember every instruction he gave perfectly."

Apparently dreams provoked by godlen don't fade into vagueness like the regular sort. His divine voice burned itself into my memory.

Alek swipes his fingers through his thick hair, glancing around us. "The forest is dense enough that we can't see very far through it. We could have already passed the trees by."

I grimace. "He said to 'climb straight.' We set off from the exact spot where we reached the mountain, and we've only been veering a few paces from side to side. I don't think it could be that far off course."

Casimir hums to himself and then lets out a few coughs. Guilt jabs through my stomach as I turn to him.

"We should take a few minute's rest anyway. Look, there's a log over there where you can sit."

The courtesan gives me the bemused look that's become more common in the past two days. His voice is still hoarse from his cold. "I'm not worn out yet."

"We shouldn't wait until you're totally exhausted." I prod him over to the log, touch his forehead to check his temperature, and turn to the horses. "Where are those berries we gathered this morning? Those seemed to help soothe his throat a little."

Stavros has already moved to his stallion's saddle packs. "Right here. It's not a bad thing to pace ourselves."

He hands me a bundle of the plump purple berries, and I hustle back to Casimir. After he accepts the snack, there isn't much else I can do for him other than sit on the log and massage his back with slow circles of my hand that I hope soothe his muscles too.

Casimir swallows a couple of the berries and tips his head toward me. "You don't need to worry about me. I've had colds before—it's hardly serious."

I let out a humph. "You've pampered me plenty of times when I was perfectly well. Let me return the favor as well as I can."

The flush that creeps into his cheeks at those words looks more pleased than feverish. He presses a kiss to the side of my head. "You're doing a wonderful job."

Alek leans against a nearby tree, looking equally glad for the brief rest. "Did Kosmel give any indication at all of *why* we should come up here? If we had a broader sense of what we're trying to find…"

"That would make it easier, I know. I don't think he was going for easy." I sigh. "He mentioned it after I asked him about whether he'd still help direct my magic. He claimed coming here would 'mend some of what was marred,' but I have no idea what that means."

For the first time in ages, Rheave speaks up from where he's standing at the edge of our group. "If a godlen said it, it'll be true. They don't tend to explain things thoroughly, but they don't lie."

I look back at his smooth face. His eerie eyes gleam with unshakeable confidence.

How much do daimon know about our deities? They're considered divine creatures, closer to godly than mortal, but they're a far cry from being even lesser gods themselves. More like the stray cats and dogs of the unearthly realm.

Although I guess that means they probably still know more than any of us mortals do.

He peers around at the rest of us with an air of avid curiosity I'm seeing more and more of over time. "Have any of the rest of you talked to the gods? I didn't think they touched humans that directly often."

Casimir laughs. "They don't. Only Ivy has had that honor. Kosmel obviously sees something particularly impressive in her."

The daimon-man's gaze returns to me, even more avid. "She is special. But you two have gifts." He nods to Casimir and Stavros.

"One I can't use anymore," Stavros says brusquely. The injury that lost him his knack for catching glimpses of the near future is still a bit of a sore subject for him. I don't imagine he wants an inhuman near-stranger prodding about it.

As if to intervene, Casimir pops the last of the berries into his mouth and stands. He gives his gelding an affectionate pat. "I'm good to continue. Let's push on."

I adjust my grip on Toast's reins as I study the terrain around us. "Maybe we should split up to cast a wider net. We have our lockets—whoever finds the trees first can signal the rest of us."

Rheave frowns as if he doesn't like the idea of breaking up the group.

Julita chuckles in the back of my head. *The daimon would probably insist on coming with you. I swear he's even more stubborn than the others. You didn't even give him any offerings, and he's stuck on you like a hound to its master.*

The stray dog comparison might be even more apt than I realized. I did give Rheave something, without realizing it: honest answers and a little compassion.

A meal he needed more than the standard daimon offering of scraps of food on a plate, it appears.

There's no denying his commitment to his newly formed loyalty. The way he charged at that bird in the bush yesterday when he thought I was threatened... He was more attack dog than hunting hound then.

An attack dog capable of roasting a starling in an instant.

Really, I should simply be glad he's aimed his loyalties at me rather than the scourge sorcerers who made his human body.

Stavros guides his stallion toward a path through the underbrush. "I think we should keep together for now. We can reconsider later if we still haven't found the spot."

Toast grunts in protest, but he clomps onward up the slope at my gentle tug. Pebbles rattle away under my feet.

The sun dips lower, our shadows lengthening. The wind picks up and tugs at the hood of my cloak.

I'm just starting to worry that the climb will get so steep we'll have to leave the horses behind when I lift my head and spot a strangely angled trunk through the forest above.

My heart leaps. "Is that...?"

I do leave Toast then, though only to clamber through the clinging shrubs and over jutting tree roots as quickly as I can. A twig scrapes across my palm, but I barely feel the sting.

I come to a stop in front of the trunk I spotted, and a smile stretches across my face.

Somehow or other, a massive birch ended up growing on a slant. Its papery white bark makes it stand out like a slash against the trees behind it.

It looks as if the tree leaning against it was struck by lightning in a storm. The charred trunk toppled to the side—and caught on one of the birch's boughs. The pale tree holds the dark log against it in an arboreal embrace.

The tops of the trees veer past each other, stretching off into the forest. Forming a shape like a mismatched X in the midst of the woods.

Alek comes to a stop beside me with a breathless laugh. "The crossed trees. We head to the left from here?"

Of course the scholar would have memorized all of Kosmel's directions the moment I shared them.

I nod, my spirits lifted despite my fatigue from the climb. "I don't know how much farther it is from here. But I don't think we can miss a whole waterfall."

I turn to scramble back to Toast, but Stavros has caught the reins to lead both stallions up together. As the former general studies the crossed tree trunks with a wary expression, I give my steed's jaw a good scratch in apology for temporarily abandoning him.

We head left through the brush. Fading sunlight filters through the trees and sets off glints amid the vegetation.

I pause to examine a particularly glittery spot and find the rocks jutting from the soil are flecked with some kind of sparkly mineral.

"Mica," Alek says, and pauses. "The peak must be coated with the mineral to shine the way it does. You don't usually see deposits quite that big."

Casimir pats a nearby tree. "It's a godly place. Some of them enjoy a certain grandeur."

I wouldn't have thought Kosmel was one of those, but then, this mountain might not be his domain. He was sending me to seek help other than his own, after all.

A pang of hunger ripples through my stomach, but we're too close to our goal now for me to suggest another stop. As if sensing my mood, Stavros pulls out the apples we liberated from an orchard we skirted yesterday evening and passes them around so we can eat while we walk.

As we tramp onward, the daylight stretches farther with the sinking of the sun. Where the trees briefly thin, Stavros surveys the landscape beyond the mountain: mottled fields and forestland with a few isolated buildings in the distance.

"No sign of soldiers on our trail," I say.

He smiles grimly. "No. But gods only know what the scourge sorcerers have been up to since we left."

The uncertainty gnaws at me too. How long will whoever else makes up the Order of the Wild wait before they unleash more of their horrific magic on Florian… or the rest of the kingdom?

Kosmel knew that stopping the conspiracy was my greatest concern. I was under the impression he was awfully concerned about the scourge sorcerers himself.

Surely wherever he's sent me, it'll help us in our mission to stop them?

The trek along the side of the mountain is less strenuous than climbing upward, but we walk long enough that the ache in my calves spreads all the way up to my hips. The sunlight starts to dwindle completely.

I'm just debating suggesting we camp for the night when the warble of tumbling water reaches my ears.

I tug Toast faster. "I hear the waterfall!"

We hustle the horses along until we come into view of the stream that courses down the side of the mountain. Right in front of our path, it careens in a sheer drop maybe ten times my height before pooling on a rocky ledge a short distance beneath us and gurgling onward.

Stavros steps forward to splash some of the water on his face and then cup it to his mouth for a drink. We haven't had fresh hydration since the creek where we filled our canteens this morning.

I follow suit, shivering in delight at the chilly liquid rinsing the sweat from my skin. It's too cold for a full shower to be appealing, but the gulp of icy water I swallow snaps me back to total alertness.

I step back from the waterfall as the other men take their turns refreshing themselves. A faint tingle seeps through my awareness at the same time.

My body stiffens as I take in the sensation.

"What is it?" Casimir asks softly.

I swallow hard. "There's magic here. I can't sense much yet. I don't know where it's coming from."

Maybe that isn't surprising, given who sent us here. We can probably find out what's going on soon enough.

Kosmel said I was supposed to announce myself.

The words the trickster godlen gave me reverberate through my mind. I lift my voice to carry, ignoring the hitch of my pulse at forgoing caution. "Kosmel led me here and expects me to receive a riven's welcome!"

*And a better riven's welcome than the king offered,* Julita mutters.

We stand in silence for a few minutes, nothing reaching my ears but the hiss of the water. Alek eases closer to me. "What was supposed to happen now?"

I shake my head. "Kosmel didn't explain. He just told me that I should 'listen.'"

The scholar slips his hand around mine and squeezes my fingers. I grip his hand tightly in return, my heart thumping in anticipation.

For all I'm watching and listening, it's Rheave who notices first, with an urgent sound low in his throat. "There's a woman up there."

My gaze jerks to the point he's looking at just as a form moves into view, made tiny by the distance. The figure vanishes into the brush again, but I keep my head tipped up, so I see her as soon as she re-emerges by the top of the waterfall.

She's still too far away for me to make out the finer details of her appearance, but she looks to have at least four decades behind her, perhaps five. The streaks of pale gray woven through her black hair remind me of the crossed trees. She moves a little stiffly, not with the full limberness of youth.

Her plain brown dress and matching cloak cover everything but her hands, boots, and face, helping her blend into the forest. As she stares down at us, her posture stiffens even more.

She backs up a step as if she thinks we could threaten her from all the way down here.

"Which of you called me?" she demands in a gravelly voice she projects down the mountainside.

I raise my hand. "I did. But we've all come together. These men are with me."

It's hard to decipher the woman's expression, but she sounds incredulous. "And you brought them *here*?"

"I don't even know where 'here' is. Kosmel gave me the directions, and I followed them. He didn't say anything about needing to come alone."

He didn't say I should have the men with me either, but I don't see any point in mentioning that. It's not as if the godlen couldn't have figured out that if he didn't specify one way or another, I'd be bringing them along.

The woman hesitates. I'm not sure what she's waiting for.

"They know what you are?" she says in the same disbelieving tone.

Stavros speaks up in his commanding general's tone, sounding as if he's trying to rein in his impatience. "We're aware of her magic, and we have no interest in extinguishing it. In fact, we're quite devoted to ensuring she remains alive in spite of other opinions to the contrary. If that's all you're concerned about, there's no need to worry. Maybe you could explain why the trickster godlen would have pointed us here?"

The woman is silent for a long moment. Her lips move, but she must have murmured something to herself, because I can't make out the words.

A more potent quiver of magic passes by me from just behind, coursing up the mountain. Casimir lifts his head—he must have used his gift, sought out a sense of what he could do to make her happiest right now.

The courtesan offers one of his gentle smiles. "You have nothing to fear from us at all. We simply want to see Ivy safe and well. We've taken every care to ensure no one could track us here, so your own security shouldn't be disturbed. But if there's been some mistake and we aren't welcome at all, we can take our leave."

Something shifts in the woman's face. Another supernatural quiver tickles through my nerves, one I think came from her.

What gift is she casting over us?

Whatever it is, between our words and her own observations, she makes up her mind. Her posture relaxes incrementally.

"Tie your horses there for now. I'll come to lead them the long way around after we've had a chance to talk properly. You'll find a sort of staircase of stone between the trees a little to your right."

I glance over, and the rocky stairs show plainly through the brush—so clearly I don't know how I could have failed to notice them before.

Unless they were hidden by the magic I sensed.

My pulse kicks up a notch, but I start scaling the rough staircase. The woman was obviously more nervous about my companions rather than me. It's best if I face her first.

By the time I reach the top of the waterfall, I'm sweating again. The woman stands on the rocky outcropping waiting for us.

Once we've all arrived, she turns toward the trees and sets off on a path between them.

I hurry to keep pace with her swift strides. "Who *are* you? Do you know why Kosmel would have sent me here?"

She doesn't bother looking back. "My name is Sulla. And I'd imagine the godlen guided you here so I could teach you how to work with your magic."

I lose my breath for a second. "You can do that? I thought that was impossible."

She shoots a faint smile over her shoulder at me. "I can, because I'm riven too."

# Nine

*Ivy*

Even after spending the night on the mountain, I haven't gotten used to this place. We're sitting on plump cushions around a low table—a little squashed together because the dining area obviously wasn't built with six people in mind and we're trying to give our host enough space to be polite. Sunlight filters through translucent panes in the rocky ceiling overhead, drawn there by magic. It streaks over us in a golden glow.

The table's wood shimmers with little carvings that move if you pause to watch them. Near my end, there's a fish that leaps out of the wavering water of a stream and a deer that gambols along a stretch of trees.

Rheave taps an etching on the corner of the table in front of him and laughs with delight at whatever effect he provoked. Casimir leans over to watch with a friendly smile.

*It's incredible,* Julita says, watching through my eyes. *Like the work of a master artist.*

If that wasn't enough magic, Sulla has a whole array of supernaturally enhanced tools at her disposal. Despite the fact that this room is carved into a mountainside, running water flows to her sink. I watched her fill a kettle from the tap only for the vessel to immediately start to steam.

The plates our meal of fried eggs and buttered rolls are sitting on exude warmth to keep our food at the perfect temperature. I only had to reach for the saltshaker before it leapt the rest of the way into my hand.

I've never been surrounded by so many objects imbued with power before. My skin quivers with a constant tingling as my cracked soul resonates with the magic.

I dab the corner of my roll in the runny egg yolk and pause to savor the mingling of savory and nutty flavors on my tongue. I've never had this kind of bread before either.

Julita hums alongside my contentment. *And the food is rather delectable too.*

It's a far cry from the typical elaborate spreads at the royal college, but it beats the bare bones fare we've been reduced to while on the run.

Despite my enjoyment of the meal, curiosity itches at me. Last night, Sulla hustled us into a bedroom and supplied us with down-stuffed mattresses and blankets for our slumber on the stone floor. She deflected all our questions with the promise that she'd get into everything in the morning.

I think she wanted a little more time to take stock of our unexpected arrival. She has to understand that we want to take stock of *her* just as much.

And it is morning now.

I study a carving of a woman in a dress who twirls on ever-shifting feet and then lift my gaze to meet our host's. Now that I've seen her up close, I'd put her in her late forties or early fifties—older than my mother. Her silver and black hair winds from her temples in two thick braids that she coils together at the back of her head. The even lines at the corners of her eyes and mouth make her face look serene, as if she hasn't smiled or frowned all that often.

I've never heard of a riven sorcerer this old. Sometimes they manage to go unnoticed for a couple of decades, but usually their increasingly ambitious manipulations draw notice before they reach their thirties.

And then there's the fact that she doesn't appear any less sane than I am.

I motion to the table and the glowing panes overhead. "Did you create all this with your magic?"

Sulla lets out a light chuckle. "Oh, no. The Haven has been a home to riven sorcerers for ages longer than I've been alive. We all contribute a little. It adds up over time."

Stavros shoots her a wary look. He's come to accept that *I'm* not a monster just because of my magic, and I suppose he can't help seeing that Sulla is hardly a raving lunatic either, but his past experiences with the riven have left him with more scars that you can see.

Accepting her hospitality and not overwhelming her with demands for answers has to be harder for him than the rest of us.

"Are there others living here?" he asks carefully, with a tick of his eyes so he can focus on her reaction as she answers.

"Not at the moment." Sulla lifts her teacup to her lips and takes a sip before going on. "There aren't many who make it to the Haven. I arrived at fourteen, and the two sorcerers already in residence then were nearly as old as I am now. They've since passed. I've been on my own here for nearly ten years. I was starting to think I'd be the last of us."

In my head, Julita shudders. *Ten years! It's a wonder she didn't go insane just from that.*

I try to imagine living somewhere—even a spot as magically animated as this one—for a decade without any human contact and have to suppress a shiver of my own. "Do you never come down the mountain to get supplies or… or anything?"

Sulla shakes her head. "We're only safe as long as we stay out of sight. If word got out about an odd woman who lives on the mountain, people would start poking around out of curiosity. And then it might all be ruined."

I'm starting to see why she was so unnerved by the five of us showing up together.

Alek glances around the room. "How have you kept yourself occupied all that time?"

"There's plenty to do. The sorcerers before me enchanted various entertainments, and we've amassed a collection of books—many written by the Haven's residents. There are gardens and animals to tend to. And one of the best things for a riven sorcerer who wishes to live in harmony with their power is meditation."

The scholar's eyes light up at the mention of books, but Sulla doesn't seem to notice his reaction. She scoops the last bit of her egg into her mouth and pushes to her feet. "Speaking of which, I should begin your training, Ivy. It's shocking that you've remained sane as long as you have without any guidance."

My stomach knots. I didn't get much out of Sulla last night, but she insisted on hearing the basics of my history, at least in relation to my magic. "I had a lot of motivation to keep my powers in check."

But my efforts haven't been without their problems. I remember Sulla wincing when I told her about the way my magic has lashed out—the pain that's seared itself through my lungs and gut so many times—and gulp the last of my roll. "I'm ready if you are."

If I can live to be as old as she is—older than many people in Silana who *aren't* riven become—without going mad with my power, I'd do just about anything.

Stavros catches my gaze, his eyes with their mix of brown and blue darkening with concern. "Take it easy. You know how to judge your magic's reactions best."

To judge whether it might slip my control, he means. He trusts my commitment to keeping my power in check, but not my power's demands to be unleashed.

"I'm sure we'll start slow." I turn to Casimir. "Did the tea help?"

When Sulla noticed his symptoms, she offered him an herbal brew last night and again this morning that she said should ease them. I haven't heard him sniffle since he woke up.

The courtesan beams at me and then at our host. "I feel much better already. Thank you. Sulla, I don't want to intrude on your privacy, but is it all right if I explore a little? I'm already intrigued by the many wonders you and those before you have created."

Rheave's face brightens. "Yes, I'd like to see them all too."

Sulla dips her head. "Feel free to wander within the boundaries of the Haven that I showed you last night. I only ask that you don't venture beyond them without me there to ensure we stay concealed."

"That's no problem at all," Casimir says.

Stavros motions to Alek. "I can run you through some more of our own training exercises. Ivy shouldn't be the only one honing her skills."

As Alek appears to restrain a grimace, Rheave pauses with a conflicted expression. "Maybe I should train too. In case there's any trouble for Ivy here."

His gaze follows me as I join Sulla by the doorway.

Sulla shakes her head with a light laugh. "No trouble will find us within the Haven. But you can pass the time however you wish."

She ushers me out of the room. As she leads me down the hall past the bedroom where we slept, her voice drops to a murmur. "Your companions do seem very devoted to you. I... I've never seen those who aren't riven themselves accept someone like us to that extent."

I give a rough chuckle. "It didn't happen instantly. And it helped that they'd known me for a while before they found out—and that Kosmel showed he was on my side."

"Still, it's a rare thing. Almost magical in itself. You're very lucky."

A twinge runs through my chest thinking of her many years of isolation. "I know. Most of the time I have trouble believing how lucky I am."

Julita huffs. *Not just luck. You earned every bit of devotion they offer you and then some.*

My mouth twitches in a smile of gratitude, but I don't pass on her comment to Sulla. We haven't seen any point in mentioning my other supernatural oddities.

The floor slants upward through the mountainside. We pass other rooms with door-less entrances, and I catch glimpses of the books she mentioned as well as various other collections of objects and storage containers.

I don't realize that we've wound around back to the surface until Sulla pushes open a door and the cool autumn air washes over me. We climb a winding path of stone steps past several slanted gardens with a variety of crops.

Magic dances in the air; little spurts of water erupt to dampen the soil.

Sulla escorts me through another doorway into a smaller interior structure that's no less fascinating than the first. A large bucket with a strange lid appears to be shearing grain off a set of stalks of its own volition. Drying herbs rustle as the thread they're hanging from creeps in a steady rotation.

"Most of the time I have far more food than I need," Sulla says. "But we've set up good systems for preservation. It serves us well when a newcomer finds their way here—and during the winter months when we haven't enough magic in place to grow very much."

We pop out into the mid-morning sunlight for another short trek past more gardens. Sulla points out a few shrubs in a cluster near the next doorway. "Mirewort, if you need it. We made sure to cultivate a few plants… This isn't any kind of a life to bring a child into."

I dip my head in agreement, taking note. In our hasty departure from the college, I left behind the small stash of the contraceptive herb that Alek procured for me.

I'll have to keep a supply close by from now on. It's not something I want to risk going without.

When we step through the next doorway, it becomes clear why the inhabitants of the Haven chose that particular spot to grow their mirewort. More golden light washes over the hallway and the rooms branching off it, which do have doors though those are currently standing open. Conjured warmth emanates from the rooms on the other side.

"These are typically the sleeping quarters," Sulla explains. "I've gotten into the habit of taking my rest in the base building since that's where I spend most of my time anyway, but you and your companions could retire here for the nights if you'd like. There'd be more room to spread out across. If that's something they're willing to do."

She shoots me an amused look that brings a flush to my cheeks.

"Then we wouldn't be quite so much in your hair," I say. I'm not sure how pleased she is to finally have some company, but she must have gotten used to having a lot of peace and quiet.

"It's fine. You're where you need to be. The gods saw to that. And this is where we'll do our most important work."

Sulla nudges open one final doorway, and we climb a dozen stone steps carved between two rocky walls. When we emerge onto the plateau above, I lose my breath.

We're nearly at the mountain's peek. Mica-laced stone glints all around me under the shining sun.

The tops of the nearest trees rise to the level of my knees. Over them, I can see all across Silana to where the vibrant green and mottled autumn leaves of the land meet the crystal blue of the sky.

Julita makes a sound with a sharp inhalation. *Wow.*

It takes me a moment to find my own words. "That's quite the view."

"I'm rather fond of it."

I tear my gaze away to take a closer look at the flat platform we're standing on. It's about ten paces across in a near-perfect circle, with the All-Giver's and each of the godlen's sigils carved along the edges.

Even though one of those godlen sent me here, my pulse gives a brief hitch at the call to the divine powers.

Sulla marks my reaction. "We ask them to have mercy on us and guide our way. Although you're the first I've heard of who's been guided quite so blatantly."

She motions for me to sit across from her. "Let's start with you telling me everything you can about how you've controlled your powers in the past."

Shaking off my qualms, I sink onto the smooth stone and lean back on my hands. The warmth of the sun and the crisp forest scents contrast sharply with the twist of discomfort her question provokes.

"I touched on it a little last night," I say. "It's hard to explain. I feel my magic clamoring to get out, get a sense of the things it could do, and I simply… refuse. I guess I tighten up my body against the urge. But mostly it's seemed to be willpower. The times when it slipped away from me have been more about mental distraction or haziness than anything else."

Sulla nods as if this doesn't surprise her. "Have you used any specific mental tricks? Imagery or similar?"

I reach back through my memories. "I instinctively picture my refusal as a sort of clamping down, like I'm shutting the power away, putting up walls around it. One time when I was really struggling, I imagined I was like a tree with a thick layer of bark that it couldn't break through."

"You should continue choosing concrete visuals that resonate with you and draw on them when you're tamping down your magic. We've all found that approach the most effective strategy." She pauses. "You also mentioned that suppressing it has led to some physical pain and possible injury."

I grimace. "Yes. For a little more than a year now, it's felt as if my power is attacking me from the inside when I refuse to use it. It only hurt mildly at first, but at its worst, the pain was so bad I couldn't stand, and I coughed up blood a couple of times."

Sulla sighs, the solemn cast that comes over her face making her look even older. "That's the most treacherous part of the magic that flows through our souls. If too much of it builds up inside us without being given a chance to act on the rest of the world, it'll act on us instead."

I run my hands over the warm stone. "But when riven sorcerers use their magic, they start to go insane. Isn't that true? I mean... I've never met any others besides you, but I can't imagine so many would have been hunted down if they weren't acting bizarrely enough to get noticed."

And Stavros has encountered at least two brutally violent riven firsthand.

Sulla's mouth slants at a pained angle. "Yes. It's a difficult balance we must all walk. We must use our power regularly to conserve our own bodies, but not so much that it starts to addle our thoughts. That's the main thing I can teach you."

My spirits lift higher than I've dared to let them since we arrived here. "So you've found that balance? You use your magic, and you manage not to harm anyone in the process?"

And not to go mad either. She's been aware of her power for more than thirty years, as far as I can tell, and she seems perfectly sane to me.

The older woman offers me a reassuring smile. "That's the most basic goal of the teachings we pass on here. I'm glad I'll have the chance to share what I was fortunate enough to learn."

My magic stirs in my chest as if it's picked up on the fact that it might get to play today.

I swallow thickly. "How do I start?"

Sulla smooths her hands over the skirt of her dress where it's gathered around her crossed legs. "One of the main principles is to keep the effects small. Just a little magic here and there. That makes it easier to keep a handle on both the external consequences and how the power affects you. Any of the more complex enchantments you see around the Haven are layers of smaller efforts that've been built up over time."

A laugh bubbles up my throat. "So you don't have all those augmentations just for your convenience. It's a way of channeling your magic into something useful, since you have to use it somehow."

"Exactly."

"But even letting a little out, there'll still be some kind of backlash."

"Yes," Sulla says. "That's inevitable. But using similar techniques to how you contain your magic, you can control both sides of the equation."

My eyebrows shoot up. "How? I've wanted to, but... it always feels impossible."

"That's the part requiring the most concentration and forethought. You should always plan both the impact you want to make and how the consequences should play out before you bring your magic to bear."

Sulla tips her head toward the sigil nearest to her, Jurnus's curving lines. "Let's say I wanted to carve this mark a little deeper. I need to think of what the obvious counteraction would be—if I'm reducing a little rock, something else would need to grow. And then I decide what I wouldn't mind seeing grow. Maybe the leaves on that shrub there."

She points to a spindly bush clinging to the edge of the platform.

"It's that simple?" I ask, barely able to believe it.

Sulla chuckles. "Not exactly simple. Not every effort you might want to make will have such a clear counter. And you need to imagine a reaction that's big enough to fit what you're trying to accomplish. That's why keeping things small is particularly important."

My heart is thumping even faster than before. "And once you've decided on all that…"

"You center yourself and ensure your mind is clear and your concentration steady. Then you picture both the action you want to carry out and how the countering energy should behave at the same time, as vividly as you can."

She closes her eyes, resting one hand on the sigil and the other on her knee with her fingers pointing toward the shrub. Magic quivers through the air.

As I watch, a few of the shrub's leaves tremble and stretch just a little longer.

When Sulla raises her hand, I can see that the etching digs deeper in the rock. She brushes a few bits of grit from her fingers.

"It only works if your choice of counteraction is appropriate," she warns me. "If you try to balance out your intentions with something unsuitable, the magic will act otherwise however it sees fit."

*Keeping it small definitely sounds like a good idea, then,* Julita remarks. *But, Ivy, if this works… you could do just about anything!*

Anything small. I'm not going to defeat the scourge sorcerers by carving little lines into stones.

But the idea that I could work with my magic even in this small way sets my pulse thumping giddily.

"Should I just… try it?" I ask.

"Why don't you borrow my example for your first few attempts?" Sulla gestures to the arching lines of Kosmel's sigil. "You could start with the godlen who guided you here, since he deserves some recognition for that. But take some time to simply meditate on your intentions and how you want them to play out first."

"Right."

I scoot over so I can rest my hand on Kosmel's sigil. Closing my eyes, I picture its shape in my mind.

I also imagine the shrub on the other side of the platform. The breeze licking over the leaves I'm going to channel the backlash into. The sun gleaming off their pale green surfaces.

Breathe in, breathe out. Steady the thunder of my pulse. Convince myself that I really can harness my magic.

It's only one small act. Even if I screw it up, no one should get hurt. But it doesn't even sound that hard.

When I've built up enough certainty inside me, I form the images in my head—the grooves of the sigil digging deeper into the stone, the leaves on the shrub growing bigger in return.

My magic tugs at me, eager to join in. I crack open the walls around it just slightly.

Just enough for a faint tingle to shoot through my arms, shaped by the pictures I've drawn in my mind.

My pulse skitters, and the images waver. In a sudden panic, I jerk my power into me so forcefully I rock backward.

When I lift my hand, the sigil looks lopsided. I pressed one side of the symbol a little deeper but didn't manage the whole thing.

One of the shrub's leaves has expanded about twice as large as the others. It looks rather ridiculous.

*It's all right,* Julita says. *It was great for a first try.*

I let out a bark of a laugh, but Sulla takes on a reassuring tone too. "That was an excellent start. See if you can hold your will firmer next time."

After periods of steadying meditation, I attempt my carving twice more. The second time I manage to even out the sigil, but I crack the tip of one of the curved lines.

Sulla has me focus on sealing the crack while snapping a twig off the shrub. I'm not sure I've ever felt as victorious as when the rough edge beneath my fingers vanishes alongside a light crack of broken wood.

I glance around the platform, newly energized, but Sulla holds up her hand. "That's enough for one session. Even minor magic adds up. We'll find other ways to occupy ourselves for a few hours, and then we can return to practice in the afternoon."

I clamp down on the impulse to protest. She knows the safe limits of our magic far better than I do.

And the fact that I'm excited to keep going is a warning in itself.

# TEN

*Alek*

The impact of Stavros's sword clanging against my dagger rattles through every bone in my hand. Possibly my entire arm.

I restrain my flinch as well as I can and sidestep the way he's shown us. The goal is both to block the blow that might follow and to put myself in a better position to find an opening.

My feet stumble on the rocky terrain. My arm whips out to steady myself, but I realize I've left my torso completely open with the same motion.

Stavros pauses, lowering his sword. "I think that's enough for today."

I straighten up, flushing with shamed relief and the lingering exertion. My hair clings to my forehead and the back of my neck, damp with sweat. My skin feels sticky beneath my shirt despite the cool mountain air.

I need to learn how to fight. It might be the only useful thing I can do out here without a vast library and records to turn to, without much in the way of practical skills beyond my ability to glean information from a page.

How could I stand against an army of scourge sorcerers with only book learning anyway? There are so few records that give even brief accounts of the old practices of the illicit magic.

But knowing how to do a thing and teaching one's body to actually do it are leagues apart.

I swipe at the perspiration on my brow, managing not to cringe at the texture of my uncovered scars, and glance toward the main Haven building. My relief deepens when I see that Ivy isn't even watching our current sparring match to have noticed my stumble.

She's standing with Casimir and Rheave, the latter of whom is examining a quiver of arrows he must have found in the Haven's many storage rooms. My chest tightens a little at the thought of him aiming those projectiles at targets around him.

How much can we really trust the daimon in our midst? How long will the dogged devotion he's shown to Ivy even last?

There are no records at all about spirit creatures inhabiting human forms.

As Stavros and I both amble over to join them, the daimon slides one of the arrows out of the quiver and then picks up the bow he rested against the outer face of the building. "I've seen these used before. You pull it back with the string, and it flies?"

Ivy lets out a wry chuckle. "I'm not the right person to turn to for archery advice."

Casimir holds out his hand. "I won't say my aim is fantastic, but I can show you the gist."

When Rheave hands the weapon over, the courtesan notches the arrow, looks around, and launches it at one of the broader trees along the edge of the small clearing. The head thumps into the bark a little right of center.

"Better than I could manage," Ivy mutters without any rancor.

Rheave's bright eyes have widened. He takes the bow back and grabs another arrow. "I like this. Better than swinging around a blade in the hand."

He positions the arrow exactly as Casimir did—a quicker study than I've proven to be with weaponry. With a twang of the string, he sends it soaring between the trees to smack into a more distant branch.

Ivy arches an eyebrow at him. "Are you sure this is your first time?"

"It makes sense," Rheave says with obvious excitement, snatching up another arrow. "The arc and the air and the tension in the string…"

He shoots a glance at Ivy, with a flare of fierceness in his gaze that somehow sparks both approval and uneasiness in my chest. "I can protect you from up close and from far away."

"I'll be very safe from any murderous trees that descend on us," Ivy says, but she pats the daimon's arm at the same time. "I'm glad you've found a form of combat you like, if only so you and Stavros don't need to squabble so much."

Stavros glowers at her with obvious affection before turning to Rheave. "Unless you want to climb those trees to get the arrows back, I'd suggest you stick to targets that aren't quite so distant. I don't imagine there's a huge supply of weaponry here."

Rheave hums thoughtfully. "How would a soldier practice?"

Naturally, Stavros knows all about that. He motions Rheave over and sets about constructing a couple of suitable archery targets at the edge of the woods.

I sit down on a stump that's been carved into a stool, finding a strange enjoyment in the graze of the cool air over my bare face. It's been years since I stepped outside without my mask.

My pulse still lurches from time to time when I remember that my scars are exposed, but none of my current companions react to them. There's nothing to really stir my insecurities.

It's unexpectedly freeing not having that small but constant weight against my skin.

Rheave works through the quiver of arrows with swift efficiency, landing all of them in the inner three circles of the makeshift bullseye Stavros created. I can't deny that the daimon has some strengths —and that his eagerness is admirable.

While Stavros offers a few tips, Casimir disappears into the building. The courtesan returns holding a metal flute that flashes as it catches in the sunlight.

He props himself against the wall and starts to play. The lilting tune winds through the air, drawing Stavros's and Rheave's attention.

The daimon bobs with the melody as he yanks the arrows from the target. "Music is better than shooting," he declares.

A laugh escapes Stavros that he then looks startled by, but he allows Rheave a small smile. "I suppose that depends on whether you're under attack."

He pauses, his gaze settling on Ivy with a brief tick of his head. The intensity in his expression has me bracing myself, but there's no hostility behind it now.

He steps toward her, holding out his hand. "Seeing as we're not under attack at the moment… I missed the chance to dance with you at the one college ball you were able to attend. I wouldn't mind remedying that oversight."

Ivy gives a laugh of her own, a blush touching her pale cheeks as she takes his hand. "I could probably use a little more practice at dancing like a lady, in case I need to play one again."

Stavros offers her a sly grin. "Who says I want you to dance like a lady?"

Ivy casts her gaze toward me for a moment, catching my eyes with a quick smile that I can read easily enough. She's telling me that I'm included too. I'd imagine I could have the next dance if I ask for it.

Of course, I'm not much more graceful a dancer than I am a sparring partner.

As Casimir keeps playing, an unexpected sense of peace settles over me. Stavros turns Ivy with the music, Rheave sways in his own sort of dance, and the mid-day sun beams down on all of us as if we're part of a strange new family.

And I'm on the outskirts of that family, even though I've been by Ivy's side for far longer than the daimon has.

The serenity I felt disintegrates. I don't want to feel like an outsider in this unnervingly immense mission we've found ourselves on.

The ground has shifted beneath all of us, and I need to get my footing.

The cotton shirt I wore for sparring has stiffened against my torso with dried sweat. I duck through the nearby doorway and make my way up to the sleeping building where I left my regular clothes.

Sulla has managed to provide us with a couple of spare sets, washing what we've discarded despite our insistence that we could take care of that ourselves. It was easier to stop protesting when she showed us the washer tub that churns the clothing all by itself once it's filled with soapy water.

I'm not sure where our host has gone off to at the moment. She seems to prefer to give us our space—or to recover her own—outside of meals and her training sessions with Ivy.

But she did give us permission to explore all of the Haven's buildings. I don't think she keeps even her own bedroom locked.

Not that bedrooms are on my mind right now. After a quick shower thanks to the magic conveying the mountain stream's water through the Haven, I head back to the main building where I found one particular spot I can put the skills I've already cultivated to use.

A room down the hall from the dining area has built-in shelves on either side. One set holds various sources of entertainment: wooden board games, a couple of faded sets of cards, toys that suggest some of the Haven's inhabitants arrived here at an even younger age than Sulla did, and a few musical instruments. I assume this is where Casimir found the flute.

The other set of shelves holds a varied assortment of books, many of their covers crumbling with age.

I've already perused the contents a few times in the past couple of days. Most are fiction, either books of tales past residents brought with them or stories they wrote themselves. I found a journal kept by a sorcerer who lived here nearly a century ago, which I spent a few hours yesterday carefully paging through, but he mostly talked about his efforts cultivating new crops through both traditional means and magic in the Haven's gardens.

So far, I've avoided the oldest volumes in the collection, mostly out of respect. I'd be a horrid guest if I destroyed the Haven's archives by having the ancient texts fall apart in my hands.

The books stashed away here haven't benefitted from the professional archival efforts of royal or temple librarians. I can see signs of rot in the leather, scraps of paper that've already cracked off their brittle pages.

But there's nothing else left for me to check. And those aged volumes are the ones most likely to contain some piece of information I don't already know.

Something that'll help us convince the king of Ivy's worthiness or defeat the scourge sorcerers? That might be too much to hope, but I have to try.

I ease one of the older books off the shelf, wincing as the leather binding crumbles more against my fingers. Sinking into one of the two armchairs set against the wall between the shelves, I open the pages as carefully as I can.

This one is handwritten, and it took some water damage before it arrived here. Many of the words are lost to splotches. Some of the paper sticks together too tightly for me to risk cracking it apart.

What I can read appears to be instructions for various games I've never heard of, with other pages holding tallies of scores. New entertainments that past inhabitants made up to pass the time here?

I set that one back in its place and lift another book that looks more professionally bound. It turns out to be printed, with ink that's held up fairly well over the years, but it's a guidebook to the animals of the Abandoned Realms. Interesting but not particularly useful to my purposes.

I work my way through several more books until I reach one with thick leather binding and an attached strap. The strap snaps in half when I loosen it, and in my horror, I almost put it back.

Leaving it alone won't fix the damage, though. I take a deep breath and peel back the cover ever so delicately.

This is one of the books where the pages have started to fragment. Chunks are missing along the edges in an erratic pattern.

What's left of the pages is hand-written in a scrawling, disjointed style that I'd find difficult to decipher even without pieces missing. Staring at it, I almost give up again.

Then my eyes catch on the word *riven* in the midst of the mess.

Girding myself, I study the letters closely.

*They call us riven... don't know what that... something happened to us... I want to keep a record... went through the Great Retribution... but when the fire came...*

My heart beats faster. Is this the writing of one of the original riven sorcerers, born in the wake of the Great Retribution? They might know more about the scourge sorcery that brought down the All-Giver's rage than we do.

I peer at page after page until my head starts to ache from deciphering the messy scrawl and the fractured sentences.

As far as I can determine, the writer was alive not long after the Great Retribution. They saw the effects of the destruction and kept their magic hidden because of a few early experiences where people reacted with horror.

There's no mention of scourge sorcery, though. I suppose the writer had enough of their own problems without accounting for anyone else's illicit magic.

Then I come to a page that's nearly whole, just ragged along the edge.

*...never asked for this. Did I want our world torn apart by those who use death for their own gain and seek to bend the entire continent to their will? Of course not. But to be turned into a vessel for the gods' power—to be used like a weapon with no will of my own so they can defeat those villains, bringing down a hail of fire and destruction—and then left with my soul cracked open now that they no longer need me... Why have I been punished for serving our deities as they chose?*

I stop at the end of the page and simply stare blankly, my breath halting in my throat. The writer can't really mean...

It sounds like they're saying the gods used *them* to fight the scourge sorcerers. That the effect of the divine power is what cracked their soul.

Not born that way as a lingering punishment, but purposefully created as a tool.

That contradicts everything I've read before about the origins of riven magic. Why would the gods let people who served them be shunned and driven to insanity?

Maybe this one was already going mad and had delusions clouding their mind. Or maybe they convinced themselves of this story to justify other destruction they caused with their magic.

I turn the page with a shaky hand, but the next few only vent about the hardships of a trek on the road between towns with no mention of magic at all. The several pages after have lost too many chunks for me to glean much of the subject. There's a brief account of seeing the silvery mountain top and deciding to try to reach it.

And then I arrive at the end of the journal.

There's nothing definitive, nothing to confirm his stories. They're as likely to be the ravings of a near-lunatic as anything we should put any stock in.

What good would it do Ivy to bring up the possibility when I have no reason to believe it isn't utter nonsense? I can't trust a word of it unless I find other accounts that corroborate the writer's story.

As I get up to search the shelves for any records that might give a clearer picture, a thud in the hall brings my head jerking around. I dash over to the doorway.

Rheave is kneeling on the floor a few paces down the hallway, his hand braced against the wall. He's frowning at his knees, but he looks up at my arrival.

"I… My feet moved the wrong way," he says. "I tripped right over them."

I offer him a hand to help him back up. He shifts his weight tentatively and then stiffens.

"What?" I ask. "Are you all right?"

His frown deepens. "I think the creator of this body is trying to call me back."

The daimon's gaze darts up to meet mine again, panic flickering through his expression. "It's only a faint tug right now, but what if they pull harder? How can I stop them?"

That… is a very good question.

I open my mouth and close it again, realizing I don't know what to tell him.

Until a few weeks ago, I wouldn't have believed it was even possible for magic to create a living body to house a daimon that could pass for a human being. How would I have any idea how they might control it?

But the fact that he's asking at all, that he cares this much, makes me want to help him. Is this how Ivy felt when she agreed to have him join us?

Gods above, how many other types of magic have I read about? I should be able to give him some sort of answer.

As I grope for the right thing to say, Rheave adjusts his posture in that slightly alien way that reminds me he isn't used to having a body at all. He's a creature of pure spirit trapped in a physical cage, as much as he's come to enjoy his new home.

Perhaps the answers aren't in the magic involved, but in the rights of possession. I watched my parents haggle with customers often enough to know that negotiating any kind of deal centers around claims of ownership.

My thoughts whirl and come together with a quiver of inspiration. "It's your body they're trying to take back, not your spirit, isn't it? They can't control what you think or feel?"

Rheave nods. "The body is the part they made."

I tap his chest lightly. "But it's yours now. They gave it to you. The more you can convince yourself of that, the more you may be able to pull away from their hold."

The daimon peers at me. "How do I convince myself?"

"Think about all the ways you control that body now. All the things you can do with it. Move it around to prove that you get to decide what it does."

Rheave looks down at his well-built form. He claps his hands together and stomps his feet against the stone floor, and a grin springs across his face. "Yes. Yes, it is mine now. They can't have it back."

He bounds off down the hall with renewed energy. I watch him go with a tendril of dread winding through my gut.

I hope he's right about that.

What will it mean for the rest of us if my little trick isn't enough?

# Eleven

*Ivy*

The petals unfurl above my fingers. My pulse flutters at the incredible feeling of their velvety surface blooming with life.

Of course, my magic is dealing out death as well. I chose a twig on one of the hunched saplings around the stone platform to shrivel as the bud blossomed.

When I open my eyes, the yellow flower beams up at me. A glance at the twig confirms that it's turned wizened, its beige bark transformed into dark gray.

I slump back against the stone beneath me. The act has left me depleted even though I've created much vaster effects with my power before.

The concentration needed to moderate both the intended effect and the consequence drains me faster than simply tossing my magic out into the world.

That and the increased clamoring of the magic I *haven't* let out.

I turn to the imagery I've found resonates most with me: a leafy vine wrapping around me, like the plant I took my chosen name from clinging to the oak in Ewalin's yard in Slaughterwell. As I picture it winding densely together, shutting away the thrum of energy inside me, my power gradually settles.

But it's still simmering there, eager for me to stretch its capabilities more.

Sulla smiles with a crinkle at the corners of her eyes and pats my shoulder. "You've been doing very well. I think tomorrow we can start making minor adjustments around the rest of the Haven. More practical matters and slightly larger effects that could sustain you for longer before your magic becomes demanding."

My mouth goes abruptly dry. "Really? You think I'm ready for that?"

This is only my fourth day of training. I haven't slipped from my intentions since the second afternoon, but the single flower I've just invigorated is the most potent act I've carried out.

And nothing I affect up here matters all that much. If I crack the stone or snap a twig I didn't mean to, no one suffers for it.

If I falter in my control around the rest of Haven, I might ruin a treasured relic or valued tool that the sorcerers here created over decades of work. I could hurt Sulla or one of my men.

"I'm sure of it," Sulla says without a hint of hesitation. "You can still come up here to meditate and ground yourself, but it's important to get comfortable working your magic in everyday settings. Especially if you still intend to leave the Haven once we've finished your basic training."

I know she doesn't approve of that goal. From what she's said, I may be the first sorcerer to train here and not stay on. But the scourge sorcerers and their unknown leader, whoever stood even higher than Ster. Torstem in the Order of the Wild, are still out there, wreaking havoc or planning to.

I can't just sit on my ass while the rest of the world falls to ruin. That would be almost as bad as carrying out the destruction myself.

When I get to my feet, energy continues humming through my chest and limbs. I might not have done anything spectacular with my magic during our twice-daily sessions up here, but I've used it more times in the past four days than I have in my entire life before.

My power feels primed now, ready to spring out of me at a moment's notice even though there's no threat to provoke it. The sensation makes my gut twist.

I picture the vine tamping it down again and take a deep breath to steady myself.

I'm in control. I decide how I use my power.

Sulla says that once the habit of using it in minor ways becomes familiar, I'll find its presence reassuring rather than unnerving. I'll know that my defenses won't allow any power to slip free without my permission.

It's hard to imagine that level of comfort right now.

Thankfully, as we walk down the mountainside through the network of buildings, the movement of my body pushes my awareness of my magic into the background. The woolen dress I've customized with slits to my thighs swishes against the loose trousers I've turned into an underskirt.

Out here, away from noble society, I could simply wear pants and tunics like I used to on the streets. But I've come to appreciate how much easier it is to keep my blades close at hand but concealed with riding-style dresses.

While we descend, Julita stirs at the back of my skull. *Hmm. I wonder what you could do first? Add a little picture to the walls? Try to fix up one of those old books Alek's been obsessing over?*

Both suggestions sound potentially complicated. I lift my shoulders in a slight shrug.

By the time we reach the main building, I feel almost like myself. Sulla drifts off to tend to her gardens, and I head toward the sound of voices carrying from the dining room.

Rheave is sprawled across a couple of the cushions by the table, plucking slices of pear out of a bowl. Casimir sits across from him with a cup of tea, and Stavros is pacing as much as the short width of the room allows.

"—what they'd do next," he's saying as I reach the doorway. He halts both his pacing and his remarks at the sight of me.

His restlessness sets my heart thumping at an uneasy pace. "Is something wrong?"

The former general offers me a crooked smile. "Not that we're aware of." He pauses. "Can you see much from that perch where you do your training?"

The memory of the view swims up in my mind. "I can see a lot, but it's mostly wilderness other than a few farms farther off. Why?"

Stavros sighs. "I wish we had more of an idea what's happened since we left Florian. I know what the king's first steps would have been, but without any sense of what the conspirators' continuing plans were…"

The twist in my gut tangles into a series of knots. It's because of me that we're here—because of me that we've been totally cut off from the rest of the world for days.

In all the time we've already spent here, I've only gotten the slightest grip over my magic. How long will it take me to harness the vast stores of power that can flow through my riven soul?

My throat constricts against the words, but I have to say them. "You don't need to stay. If you want to go back and start helping with the military efforts—"

Anguish flashes across Stavros's chiseled features. He steps forward and grasps my arm to stop me. "Ivy, that's not what I meant. I'm not leaving you. You should have us supporting you while you grapple with your magic."

His voice still tenses slightly when he speaks of the practice I've been doing. He can't help seeing my use of my potentially destructive power as a different sort of battle.

I paste a smile onto my face, willing my voice to stay even. "I'm taking things slow, so you don't need to worry about me. If it would make sense—if you could help more that way... I don't want to feel like I'm holding you back."

"You're not. We're here so you can be properly prepared for all the threats we're facing, and then we'll have the best chance of overcoming them together." He lets out a rough chuckle. "I'd simply like a better idea of what exactly we're facing so I could prepare more in the meantime."

Rheave pops one last bit of pear into his mouth. "Is there any way you could find out without going far away? Humans have ways of passing news along, don't they?"

Stavros rubs his jaw, appearing to give the daimon-man's suggestion his full consideration. "Not to random farmers, I wouldn't think. But I suppose..."

He glances toward the map he found in one of the Haven's storage rooms that he was poring over last night. "I'll have to think on it. There's no point in taking a risk if the benefits wouldn't justify it."

I swallow down the lump of guilt. "If you come up with a plan, I'm sure it'll be a good one."

"Thank you for your unconditional confidence," Stavros says dryly, but he leans in to give me a quick kiss.

It's the most public he's been with his displays of affection, the heat of his mouth reassuring and thanking me, and gone sooner than I'd like. When he draws back, Rheave is watching us avidly.

I flush at the daimon-man's intense attention, but he shifts it completely to Stavros a moment later. "If you don't have any other plans right now, you said there were more advanced techniques with the bow and arrow. Would you show me?"

Stavros chuckles. "I suppose that's as good a way to pass the time as any. We'll have you toppling scourge sorcerers in no time."

Julita snorts. *It figures that he'd get friendlier as soon as military skills were involved.*

My mouth twitches with amusement. Regardless of the reasons, it's nice to see that the former general seems to finally be warming up to our newest companion.

As Stavros motions for Rheave to follow him, Casimir takes one last sip of his tea and gets to his feet too. The courtesan ambles over to join me while the other men stride off to continue their combat training.

"Where's Alek gotten to?" I ask.

"Oh, he's buried in the books he's found." Casimir grins fondly. His voice is back to its usual smoothness now, all traces of his illness gone. "I don't think he's in any hurry to return to the rest of the world."

I try to laugh, but it comes up in a hitch. "At least that's one of us."

Casimir studies my expression, his hand rising to stroke up and down my back. "Are *you* all right, Ivy? Sulla's mentioned that your sessions with her are going well, but you've seemed more and more tense the past couple of days."

I give my body a little shake as if I can shed the worries that've gnawed at me. "I *am* getting better at controlling my magic. There's just so much of it to contend with. I feel like I've only just learned how to stack pebbles and I've got a whole mountain looming inside me."

"If there's any way any of us can help..."

"I know." I lean into his touch, unable to hold back a sound like a purr when he trails his fingers right up the side of my neck. "Unfortunately, since the magic flows through *me*, it's really up to me to handle it on my own."

"That's a lot of responsibility for any one person to have to take on." Casimir caresses my cheek and teases his fingers into my hair, sending tingles over my skin. "It's been weighing on you. Hmm. You're done with your training for the day, aren't you? How would you like to take a break from having to be in control?"

I peer at him through lowered eyelashes, swaying with the pleasure his touch provokes. "What do you mean?"

The courtesan offers a smile of promise that sends another tingle straight down the middle of me and clasps my hand. "Come with me, and I'll show you. It's been too long since I got to do any real pampering."

*Ooh,* Julita murmurs. *I want to see where he's going with this, but then I'll give you your privacy.*

I'm not going to deny my ghostly passenger a little taste of the bodily pleasures she can no longer experience herself. She never sticks around for very long when things heat up with my men.

Casimir leads me through the Haven to the building where we've been sleeping. Most residents have made do with plump mattresses right on the floor, but one of the rooms has a full if low wooden frame. After we first explored the rooms, the men insisted I take that bed.

"Wait here for a moment," Casimir says. He vanishes down the hall and returns holding a bundle of silky fabric. He tugs the door shut behind him. "Let's undress you first."

"Just me?" I ask as Casimir sets the fabric down on the bed and reaches for my plain dress. "Shouldn't the nakedness go both ways?"

"I'll take care of myself and you. All you're going to do is enjoy the experience."

Julita giggles. *Well, I think that's my cue to go.* She dwindles into the faintest of tickles at the back of my skull.

I'm not sure I'm totally on board with Casimir's goal. The courtesan has a habit of putting everyone else's needs—and pleasure—over his own. But for the moment, I gamely help him strip off my dress and underclothes, everything except the ribbon I keep tied around my upper arm in memory of my little sister.

The magical warming system in this building takes the edge off the autumn chill. Casimir nuzzles my cheek with a gentle kiss, his closeness warming me even more, and then nudges me over to the bed. "Lie down on your back."

The cozy fabric of the blanket cushions my old scars. As I comply, Casimir picks up his bundle of silk and unravels it into a few separate strips of fabric. He winds the end of one around my ankle and glances up at me to judge my reaction.

My heart skips a beat. "What exactly are we doing here?"

Casimir dips his head to press his lips to the top of my foot. "Making sure you're fully aware that you're not in control of this interlude—and you don't need to be. What do you think, Kindness? Can you let me completely take over?"

When he says the words in that heated tone with the gleam of desire in his eyes, it's hard to imagine why the idea should unsettle me. Of all my men, Casimir has never hurt me even unintentionally.

I trust him with my life. Trusting his skills with my body is nothing compared to that.

Still, my limbs have tensed at the idea of being bound. Casimir strokes his fingers over my calf, watching me.

"We don't have to do this. But I think it might be good for you. Offer you a chance to remember that you can give up control without any kind of disaster. If at any point your feelings become too intense and you want to stop, all you have to do is say so."

I drag in a deep breath, anticipation and my own desire overcoming my instinctive reluctance. "Okay. Keep going." I let my gaze rove over his lean, graceful frame in the simple tunic and trousers he's wearing. "But you did promise I wouldn't be the only one undressed."

Casimir chuckles and obligingly strips off his shirt and pants, leaving only his drawers. While I ogle his deliciously toned body freely, he ties the end of the cloth around my ankle to one side of the footboard. Then he repeats the process with my other ankle on the opposite side.

He's left me spread open, my sex bared—and dampening with a heady heat as he flicks his hungry gaze over it.

But the courtesan isn't finished preparing me yet. He moves to the top of the bed and binds my wrists together over my head, just snugly enough that I'd struggle to release them but not to cause any discomfort. He attaches that strip of fabric to the middle of the headboard's slats.

"There you go," he murmurs, bending over me. His lips graze my cheek, my jaw, my throat. "There's nothing you can do. Nothing you *need* to do. I'm the one in charge here, and I'll play with you as I see fit."

I haven't heard Casimir sound quite so domineering before. His tone sends a giddy quiver down my spine.

He swings his leg over my waist to straddle me and captures my mouth. I give myself over to his searing kiss.

Part of me still wants to resist. My arms flex against their bindings with the urge to wrap my arms around my lover, to run my fingers down his chest.

A tremor of my magic reverberates against my ribs, offering to release my restraints.

I focus on the sparks of delight conjured by the press of Casimir's lips and the caress of his hands down my torso. It's not up to me what happens here. I don't *have* to decide. I don't have to try to keep up or give back equally.

As I sink into that acceptance, it's a weirdly freeing idea.

Casimir nibbles his way along the edge of my jaw and down to the crook of my shoulder. Bliss flows over my skin from every place his lips mark with their delectable heat.

When he nips my collarbone, my hips jerk of their own accord. Casimir's tongue darts out to smooth over the spot. "Oh, we're just getting started, my darling."

As he continues to tease his mouth along my upper chest, he strokes his fingers up from my belly to cup my breasts. He swipes his thumbs over my nipples in tandem, bringing a gasp to my throat at the combined jolts of delight.

Casimir works several more increasingly urgent sounds out of me with every skilled swivel of his hands. He kisses his way down my sternum, pulling backward so he kneels between my splayed legs.

The erection tenting his drawers brushes against my core, and I can't help arching toward him with a needy whine. Casimir hums and laps his tongue over one stiffened nipple, letting the vibration of the sound carry through the gesture.

"We have lots of time to get to that. I won't be satisfied until you're absolutely drenched for me."

A strangled noise escapes me. "I think I'm already there."

"But I still have so much to enjoy here." He slicks his tongue over the other nipple to set off a renewed pulse of pleasure. "You're at my mercy, Ivy. I decide when you're ready."

My disgruntled huff breaks into a moan when he sucks the tip of my breast right into his mouth.

He strums it with his tongue and then scrapes the tips of his teeth across the peak. All I can do is writhe against my bonds with bliss.

He teases and suckles that breast until my head is hazed with the sensations, running his fingertips up and down my sides at the same time to spark even more delightful quivers. With another satisfied hum, he turns his attentions to my other breast.

One hand slides over my belly to delve between my legs. His hot breath spills over my breast in an approving sigh. "That's what I like to feel. And I'm going to enjoy it fully."

I understand what he means when he eases farther down the bed and lowers his head to where his fingers were just fondling me. The first swipe of his tongue over my clit makes my hips buck to the limits of my restraints.

The courtesan shoots me a pleased grin and buries his face between my thighs.

With every movement of his lips, every swirl of his tongue and graze of his teeth, ecstasy floods me. It washes over me in waves, until I can't stop myself from straining against my bonds, rocking into his mouth to urge on my release.

Casimir sucks hard on my clit and curls two fingers into my channel to stroke me from the inside. But just as I shudder to the edge, he pulls back a few inches.

I growl in protest, my sex aching with need.

The courtesan licks my arousal from his lips and glides his fingers over my inner thighs. "You'll come when I decide."

"Fuck," I groan.

But when he laps his tongue over me again, I have to admit the pleasure spikes through me even more forcefully. The burn of need deepens into a searing sensation that spreads all through my body.

Casimir works me over just as thoroughly as before. He thrusts a third finger inside me to fill me even better while he teases my clit with his mouth.

Every nerve in my body trembles giddily. I sway with the movements of his tongue and hand, spiraling toward my peak—

He pulls back at the last second again with a low chuckle that could almost make me come on its own.

A sound slips from my lips that's almost a sob. Casimir presses a tenderly apologetic kiss to my hipbone and tugs off his drawers.

My pulse skips eagerly at the sight of his rigid cock. He rubs it across my sensitized folds in careful strokes until I really am sobbing… and then he plunges into me in one smooth thrust.

The sudden pressure sets off a chain reaction inside me. Pleasure crackles through my nerves and bursts through my body.

I bow my head against the pillow, crying out with the force of my climax.

Casimir holds still while my channel clamps around him, his skin flushing with restrained desire. When the haze clears from my vision, he smiles wickedly down at me. "We're not finished yet."

I'm too wrung out with bliss to argue. And not a single part of me *wants* to argue when the courtesan starts to rock into me.

He has to lean close to hit the right angle, clasping my hip with one hand and bracing his elbow next to me so he can caress my breast with the other.

He builds up his pace so gradually it would be torturous if I hadn't just come. As it is, the ache of bliss builds slowly and steadily with every thrust until it's radiating all the way to my toes and fingertips.

Casimir hits just the right spot to send an extra jolt of pleasure up the center of me. I let out a ragged moan—

And the bedroom door slams open.

Stavros jars to a halt on the threshold, his stance stiffening at the sight of us. As Casimir tilts farther upright to glance over his shoulder, a ruddy cast creeps up through the former general's light brown skin.

He takes a step back. "I—I heard you cry out. I didn't mean to interrupt."

My whole body has flushed hotter, first with embarrassment and then with a thrill at the matching heat that's sparked in Stavros's eyes.

He's never seen any of the other men do more than kiss me before. His hand has closed into a fist as if he's tempted to punch the courtesan right off me, but hunger blazes in his eyes.

Maybe I'm just high on the pleasure that's already flowed through me, but it seems like a good idea to say, "You don't have to go. You could join in."

The next instant, my gaze darts to Casimir. I've immersed myself in his control enough that I'm not sure if I've stepped out of line.

He beams when he sees me check with him, flicking his thumb over my clit as if in reward, and looks at Stavros again. "Yes, you could. I'm teaching our lady a lesson in letting the rest of us take on some of the responsibility around here. She might pick up the material even faster with a professor pitching in."

Stavros wets his lips. Part of him is still hesitating, but his gaze smolders hotter.

With a strangled groan, he hurtles across the room and drops down at the edge of the bed by my shoulder. His fingers trail through the sweat that's formed along my clavicle and up my neck to tip my chin toward him.

Then his mouth crashes into mine with all the ferocity I expect from this man.

As Stavros's kiss consumes me, I notice a light tug and a loosening at my ankles. Casimir has adjusted the strips of silk to increase their length without completely freeing me.

He guides my knees into a mild bend and then lifts my ass so he can ram into me while staying upright. When I gasp against Stavros's lips, the former general only kisses me harder.

The courtesan picks up his pace, filling me over and over again. The head of his cock strokes the most sensitive spot deep inside.

At my next moan, Stavros tears his mouth from mine to scorch a path to the crook of my jaw. His hand teases over my chest to cup one breast.

His cocky drawl, turned nearly liquid with lust, resonates into my ear with a tingle of his breath. "You like letting him take you, hmm, Lady Thief? How much can you open yourself up? Let's see you give him everything."

I thought I already was, but the words make me whimper with the desire to comply. Somehow I manage to splay my hips even wider, to buck even more eagerly into Casimir's thrusts.

The courtesan groans in approval and rests his thumb on my clit. He fingers me as deftly as if he's playing a song on my body while he pounds into me ever faster.

Stavros nips my earlobe before his darkened voice reaches me again. "So obedient for once. See how good it can be when you let someone else call the shots? Next time it'll be me driving into you, taking you right over the edge."

The combination of the promise and Casimir's talented thumb sends me careening into ecstasy with the courtesan's next thrust. As the blaze of my second orgasm roars through my body, a ridiculous stream of sounds tumble out of me.

Stavros's mouth brands the side of my neck, his fingers stroking my breast through my release. Casimir's grip on my ass tightens, and then he's bowing toward the other man as he loses himself to his own climax.

We linger there for a minute, breathing heavily, coming back to ourselves.

Casimir slides out of me with all his usual tenderness and caresses my thigh. "You can always count on us to take care of you, Ivy."

"In every way we possibly can," Stavros adds in a raw voice.

Casimir unties my ankles and then my wrists. My hands immediately dart out to slip around the backs of their necks, drawing one lover and then the other in for another kiss.

As we nestle together for a moment, still coming down from the high, a pang reverberates through my chest.

Casimir made his point. I know not everything here depends on me.

But gods above, do I wish nothing at all depended on any of us. That we could stay here in this cocoon of peace for the rest of our lives.

What's going to become of the trust and understanding we've forged when we have to face the judgment of the outside world once more?

# Twelve

*Stavros*

The sun is sinking by the time I spot the crossroads up ahead. I turn my stallion to the left before I reach the marker, a mix of trepidation and relief congealing in my gut at the sign that my destination is close at hand.

I've been riding for hours, but I've made it here in about the time I expected. I wanted darkness to be falling before I approached the small fort where one of my old colleagues has been posted for the better part of the past year.

I tie the horse well out of view of any road and make the rest of my approach on foot.

There hasn't been much military activity in this part of the country in years, so I don't encounter any sentries patrolling the grounds around the building. I'd imagine Major Pawlem has gotten a little restless while overseeing this post. But it's not far from the Icarian border to the southwest, and they could rush to help if Darium came at us across the Seafell Channel to the east.

The forest has been cleared around the stout stone building with its high surrounding wall. The fort will house the major, a captain or two, and perhaps thirty infantry prepared to run a first line of defense against an attack. They'll mostly have been occupied with tracking down local bandits and highwaymen.

I stop at the edge of the clearing where the shadows of the trees still conceal me, the tart scent of the autumn leaves filling my nose. Lanterns gleam in several of the windows. The soldiers may be just sitting down to their dinner.

I spot a figure in the tower that juts up over the arched doorway and two others standing guard on the ground on either side of the gate. As I watch, one makes a brisk circuit of the wall. They talk in low voices for a few minutes, passing the time with idle conversation, and then the other makes his own circuit.

Pawlem will be inside. I don't fancy marching into the midst of a squadron that may have gotten orders to arrest me on sight, so I need to contrive a reason for him to come out here.

I considered the problem for the entire ride out here, but I still pause and work through it in my head before stepping forward. One misstep, and this errand I decided to attempt will put everyone I care about at even more risk than before.

The two soldiers on the ground snap to attention the moment I've taken two paces from the trees. I stop before one has even hollered, "Who goes there?"

I keep my prosthetic tucked under my cloak so they can't identify me by it. The cloak's hood and the thickening dusk should hide my next most distinguishing feature: my hair.

I can't do anything about my face or size, but it's relatively unlikely that either of these two will have encountered me in person for any significant length of time. The plain trousers and jacket I borrowed from the Haven won't fit their image of the great General Stavros.

"I'd like to speak with Major Pawlem," I say evenly. "I assume he's still stationed here? But I'd prefer to keep the conversation outside for discretion's sake. If one of you go in and tell him the man he always beat at three-snap has stopped by, I'd imagine he'll come."

I've kept my tone mild, with just a hint of the commanding air I'd have projected if I had any real authority here. The pair draws themselves even straighter, studying me with more intense concentration.

I'd imagine they're not quite sure what to make of a man who dresses like a peasant, speaks like a noble, and refers to their superior officer with such familiarity.

The woman replies first, with a stern expression to offset her obvious confusion. "I think you'd better come inside. If the major is willing to speak with you, you should see him there."

"For the security of the country, I feel that would be unwise." Really for my own security, but a call to patriotism should work better as motivation. "Pass on the message. If he refuses, we can worry about alternate arrangements."

The soldiers step closer to each other to murmur in private conference. Their hands rest on the hilts of their swords at their hips. I keep my hand loose at my side, well away from my own blade, but I'm ready to retreat into the woods if they decide to take an aggressive approach.

They're good infantry, looking out for their commander and the safety of the fort. Watching them sends a twinge like homesickness through my chest.

It's been over a year since I last commanded anyone other than the students at Sovereign College. I never felt anywhere near as alive in the classroom or the courtyard as I did planning strategy, giving pep talks, and leading forays along the borders.

My vision fogs, reminding me of why I'm never going to take on that role again. What I'm doing right now is the closest thing to fighting for my country that I'm capable of anymore.

Before I can wallow in the loss, one of the soldiers ducks into the fort. The other remains, eyeing me warily. I keep my careful distance from the building, both so I don't appear a threat and so they can't pose much of one to me.

The last glow of sunlight fades from the sky. I shrug my cloak closer against the bite in the wind—and the gate swings open.

Major Pawlem looks much the way I remembered him: keen eyes wide set in his tan face, sandy hair pulled back in a short ponytail at the nape of his neck, average height made more impressive by the assurance with which he carries himself.

He strides a few paces from the doorway and stops there with an expression of disbelief I catch in the moment before my vision hazes again. "Gods above. What in the realms are *you* doing here?"

I note with relief that he hasn't brought any additional soldiers with him, at least not right out of the fort. Knowing Pawlem, he has at least a few waiting on his call just beyond the gate. His cleverness didn't only extend to card games like three-snap.

He's also been circumspect enough not to name me in front of his charges. Which means he isn't yet sure whether he should report my presence here or not.

I smile grimly. "I'm trying to avert a nation-wide disaster. And I was hoping we spent enough time together that you know I *would* be on the side of averting it rather than causing it."

He lets out a huff of a sigh and motions to the soldiers at the gate. They hang back while he ambles toward me, but their gazes stay glued to me, watching for any threatening movements.

Pawlem wears a sword of his own, his hand resting casually on his belt within easy reach of it. He comes to a stop about halfway between the fort and my position near the trees.

He doesn't want to open himself up to an easy ambush either. That's perfectly fair.

I walk to meet him, watching for any trickery on his end. No one else stirs around the fort. A raucous laugh filters faintly through one of the lantern-lit windows.

The soldiers are having a little ale with their dinner, from the sound of it.

I draw up a couple of paces from my former colleague: close enough that we can speak without his underlings overhearing, far enough that he'd have to lunge to stab me.

I pitch my voice low. "I'm sorry to come to you like this. You're probably aware that my situation has become rather... fraught. I won't take much of your time. I've been cut off from my usual sources of information—I wanted to confirm that the royal family is still safe and find out whether there've been any additional attacks since the assault on the palace."

Pawlem lets out a rough chuckle under his breath. "You have missed a lot. Is it really true, Stavros? You've given your loyalty to one of the *riven*?"

I manage to work a wry note into my next words. "Strange as it might seem, it turns out there's more to them than their powers, just as there is with every other human being. And this one happens to be the key to fulfilling my loyalties to the Crown, as hard as the king finds that to believe at the moment."

"I'll say. By rights, I should arrest you. He's calling you a traitor."

I grimace. "He didn't give me much of a chance to explain myself. But I swear to you, Pawlem, on the souls of all the men and women we saw fall in battle, I'm serving him as well as I know how, whether he can understand my methods or not."

The major takes a few moments of silence. Even without twitching my head to clear my vision, I can feel him studying me.

He wasn't one of the officers I worked most closely with, but he rode out under my command enough times for me to have felt this visit worth the gamble. There was a time when the man in front of me trusted my word implicitly.

He once helped lead our squadrons on a rambling hike through icy wind and drifts of snow because I said it was the best route to come at our opponents' flank. On another occasion, he had his cavalry charge straight through what looked like a wall of fire after I assured him it was only illusion.

But now he isn't sure he can even talk to me.

Pawlem swipes his hand across his mouth. His gaze darts from me across the nearby trees. "Is she here?"

I don't need to ask who he means. "No. I came alone. For *her* safety."

He sighs and shakes his head. "I never thought I'd see this day. There are patrols sweeping the countryside looking to hunt you down like a common criminal, you know. Have you gone as mad as the riven do, throwing everything you've worked for away for some woman?"

It takes all my self-control not to bristle. "If you knew her, you'd realize she's more than that. And as I said, my decision has to do with what's best for our entire country. I can understand that's hard to accept. You don't have to believe it. But what would it hurt to answer the questions I asked?"

Pawlem appears to deliberate silently with himself. Then he makes a flippant gesture as if to say, *Why not?* "I'm not going to tell you where the king and his family have settled for the time being, but the last I heard, they were all still alive and uninjured."

Thank the gods.

I take a deep breath. "And the miscreants who attacked them? Has anyone significant been apprehended? Have they made any further moves?"

Pawlem's jaw works as if he isn't sure he's comfortable telling me. Or maybe he's simply uncomfortable with the fact of what he has to say.

His voice comes out strained. "There's been a rebellion in one of the northern provinces up near the Bryfesh border: Eppun."

My heart lurches. "*What?*"

Pawlem scowls. "We've only gotten information in dribs and drabs out here. But it seems some group claiming they know the gods' true will has inflamed the commoners and displaced the local counts and countesses. The heir to the seat of Coliz up and murdered his parents to stake a claim for what they're calling the 'Order of the Wild.' There's been heaps of turmoil in Nikodi and Selce as well."

I resist the urge to reach for my sword, as if I could cut down the traitors from the other side of the country. Frustration sears through my gut.

The scourge sorcerers have managed to gain that large a foothold—to commandeer an entire province? How long have they been laying the groundwork for this uprising without us realizing?

"And they've swayed enough civilians to their 'cause' to hold the territory?" I ask.

Pawlem's scowl only deepens with shared frustration. "You know what the outer provinces can be like. Always thinking the capital isn't doing enough for them. They feel left out, so they decide the sophisticated ways of the urban nobility are suspicious. It'd be easier to win them over with seditious ideas than anyone else."

It would indeed. My hand flexes at my side with tension I don't give in to. "The king can't let that kind of mutiny stand."

"No. But they're giving the army a difficult time. From what I understand, the traitors haven't tried to march any closer to the capital yet. I suppose they learned their lesson with their attack on the palace in Florian. Instead, they've been challenging the king to come and face them himself. But it's not as if they're standing on a field waiting for a charge. The first few squadrons sent up that way were ambushed and handed their asses."

"They want to pick away at our forces, wear us down until they see an opening," I mutter. It's the kind of tactic many Silanians turned to during the uprising against the Darium empire several decades ago—a solid tactic, even if I hate knowing it's being used against us now. "And the more soldiers the king sends out there, the fewer he has protecting him."

Pawlem nods. "That's about the size of it. Bad business all around. I'm sure we'll quash them eventually… but I don't like how much it'll cost us along the way."

I can't share his certainty about the first part. He hasn't witnessed scourge sorcery firsthand—he has no idea how fanatical this Order of the Wild can be.

They mean to see King Konram burn one way or another.

"Thank you," I say to Pawlem, because I am grateful for the intelligence even if I'm horrified by it as well. "I'll do whatever I can to see our country set to rights."

He raises an eyebrow. "Not with riven magic, I hope."

An uneasy twinge runs through my gut at the thought of the power Ivy's been working at the Haven. Practicing the vicious magic that's hurt her as much as those around her, attempting to tame it.

Gods only know how much it'll ruin—including the woman I love herself—if it yanks free of her hold.

I force a small smile. "I would never rely on just one trick, my friend. And I never risk more than we stand to gain."

When I tick my gaze away and back, I can see enough tension in Pawlem's stance and expression to recognize that he doesn't fully trust my judgment now. He isn't really my friend, even if he played along with me for now.

He thinks he has something more to gain here too.

I don't want to assume the worst, but present circumstances require expecting it. And I promised Sulla I'd take every precaution to ensure no one finds out where I've been staying.

I bob my head to Pawlem. "I'll take my leave of you, and I won't bother you again. I hope our next meeting is under better terms."

"So do I," he says as I turn away.

I walk into the forest in the opposite direction from where I left my horse. After several minutes, I stop at a particularly dense stretch of brush and sink back against a tree trunk.

It doesn't take long before I catch the crack of a twig and the rustle of boots through fallen leaves. What little hope I had left deflates.

Pawlem sent people to track me. No doubt he imagines he'll turn me and all my treacherous companions over to the royal patrols for much reward.

My gift might not work with my damaged vision, but I can still see some moves before they're made.

I stalk onward through the woods as if I'm being cautious but unaware of my pursuers. When I reach the farm I spotted on my way here, quiet with the fallen night, I ease into the barn and select the largest of the horses.

With a silent prayer of apology to Prospira for disturbing this family's livelihood and a request to guide the animal home safely, I lead it out around the back of the barn where the soldiers won't have followed too closely yet for risk of being seen. Then I whack the horse on the rear hard enough to send it galloping over the nearest hill.

There's a scuffle of hasty footsteps from the woods as the soldiers must rush off to alert companions hanging back on steeds of their own. I wait until I've watched two stealthy soldiers on horseback crest the hill before trekking back to my actual mount.

By the time they find the horse and realize it's riderless, I should be well out of easy tracking range. And I know all the techniques to ensure they can't follow my path by more complex means either.

But as I swing into the saddle and set off, all I can feel is the weight on my shoulders.

The Order of the Wild is claiming our kingdom, including the county Julita once expected to rule. Even so, King Konram wants Ivy's head—and the rest of ours too—on a platter.

There's truly no one we can count on across the entire kingdom except ourselves.

# Thirteen

An unexpectedly homey atmosphere has developed in the Haven's dining room. As the five of us gather around the table, I try to let the warmth of the company I have distract me from worries about the man who's not currently with us.

Even if all went well, Stavros wasn't sure he'd return before noon. There's no reason to fret.

As Sulla sets the dishes she prepped last night on the table, Casimir reaches for the tea pot. He's gotten into the habit of pouring out the tea for all of us—remembering that Alek likes just sugar in his, I prefer only cream in mine, Rheave wants both, and Sulla takes neither.

As the pale cream swirls with the darker tea, the daimon-man leans over next to me and tips the end of his spoon into it.

"Watch," he says eagerly, and gives the metal handle a little wiggle. Somehow he creates an image like a spinning leaf in the tea's surface for a few seconds before it wisps away.

The playful gesture distracts me a little more. I smile at him gratefully and tune out the skip of my pulse when his face turns even more stunning with his smile in response.

I pluck up an egg and pass the platter to Alek, because I know he'll want at least two. As I gulp down my own, Casimir nudges the basket of biscuits toward me.

I've just taken my first bite of the rich, nutty dough when footsteps thump into the hall. Before I can do more than swallow, Stavros appears in the doorway, hair windblown and expression fraught.

His voice comes out rough. "The scourge sorcerers have already struck again."

Alek's eyes widen. "What? How?"

With a grimace, Stavros launches into a recounting of his conversation with his former colleague.

By the time he's finished, the biscuit I was eating has crumbled between my clutching fingers. I can feel it disintegrating in my hand, but all I can do is stare at Stavros.

My voice rasps on its way up my throat. "They've taken over an entire province?"

Stavros bows his head in acknowledgment. He must be exhausted—I don't think he could have slept at all since he left yesterday morning, expecting to reach the fort where a friend was stationed by the evening.

But all I see on his handsome face is horrified determination.

"The better part of Eppun, at least," he says. "And the major's information would be at least a couple of days behind."

Julita speaks in a strained murmur. *They took Nikodi… What have they done to my parents?*

It's obvious that Stavros doesn't know more than he's already told us—and that his uncertainties are gnawing at him.

Casimir reaches along the table to squeeze my forearm. At his reassuring touch, I finally drop the chunks of decimated biscuit, brush the crumbs from my fingers in a daze, and turn my hand to clasp his.

The courtesan manages to keep his voice calm, though the grip of his fingers betrays the tension he's holding back. "It sounds like their goal is the same as it's always been: destroy Silana's rulership and establish their own."

Alek's lips have tightened. "The heir who's taken over Coliz—who murdered his parents to do it— he was an entomology club member under Ster. Torstem before he graduated three years ago."

He glances at Rheave. "Does this uprising line up with anything you remember hearing or orders you were given?"

The daimon-man shakes his head, his forehead furrowed beneath the fall of his dark curls. "I don't think so. That could be where most of the others like me were sent—to the north. But I never paid attention to names of things like counties and provinces in my natural form."

Why would it matter to a spirit-creature what lines humans drew on a map or what they called the territories on either side?

I swallow thickly. Any appetite I had left has fled. "The people who are standing with the Order of the Wild can't know who they're really supporting, can they? They wouldn't push for scourge sorcerers as our new rulers."

*I should certainly hope they can see through the degenerates' lies,* Julita says hotly. *It'll be their kids the fiends are carving up next. Great God help us, what if they've already started?*

My stomach lurches with horror echoing her own. If the conspirators could get away with hiding their sacrificial accomplices right under the Crown's Watch's noses within Florian's walls, how much easier would it be in a far-flung province?

Stavros's mouth twists. "I'd imagine they've hidden the source of any powers they've displayed. They'll be presenting themselves much as they did to new recruits like you supposedly were—as true believers who want to bring the country back into harmony with the wishes of the gods and unseat greedy despots who've abandoned real faith."

Casimir swipes his free hand over his face. "And the people of the border provinces will have taken to that message much faster than anyone in the city. A lot of them are already inclined to see the rest of us as selfish prigs."

"The king should be able to expose the scourge sorcerers," Alek says. "He knows."

Stavros sighs. "Maybe he's tried. We don't know what's going on out there. But the conspirators have captured the people's attention first. They can claim he's telling tales to discredit them and protect himself."

I wrap my arm around my churning stomach. "The members of the Order of the Wild might even believe they *aren't* scourge sorcerers. I never heard any of them refer to their magic that way. And they don't seem to think the All-Giver would object with another Great Retribution. Maybe they've convinced themselves that they're different—that it's acceptable magic as long as they aren't outright killing anyone in sacrifice."

Who knows how those sadistic psychopaths think?

And now they're filling the heads of tens of thousands of people with their nonsense. How many ordinary civilians will march with them the next time they strike directly at the royal family?

Gods help us, where will we be if they manage to take over all of Silana?

Sulla has been watching the conversation in silence from her spot at the head of the table. She clasps her mug between her hands. Her knuckles have paled.

"It's a long way from here," she says evenly. "And all will end as it should. The entire army will be defending the king."

The entire army other than the soldiers he's sent to hunt me down.

"They aren't providing a very effective defense, from the sounds of it," Stavros says. "Guerilla tactics are difficult to stamp out. And we still need to defend our border with Darium, or the emperor will take advantage of the lapse to attack. If the conspirators spread our forces too thin…"

He can't help speaking about the army as "we" rather than "they" even a year after losing his position. The frustration in his voice wrenches at me alongside my nausea at the thought of the atrocities the scourge sorcerers have committed.

The words spill out before I've thought them through. "We have to go."

Every head around the table jerks toward me, including Sulla's. Casimir's grip on my hand tightens. "Ivy—"

I sit up straighter, conviction swelling in my chest. "We know better than anyone what the scourge sorcerers are like. We know their attitudes and their tactics. And we have an ally who can identify other captured daimon." I tip my head toward Rheave. "We could speak to people who are hesitant about the Order of the Wild, build up a local resistance, pick away at the uprising in ways the army couldn't."

Rheave perks up. "I'll help you any way I can."

Even Julita seems to liven up. *I know many people in Nikodi, especially those living near our estate. I'd be able to help you make contacts and determine who's taken charge.*

Stavros's stance appears to firm at my words, but his gaze darkens. "We'll have to cross most of the country—if any of the soldiers catch you, they'll kill you on sight."

I gaze right back at him. "Then that's a risk I'll have to take. I've been risking my life to stop these psychopaths from the start. I'm not going to risk *less* when they're hurting so many more."

Alek taps his finger against the table, his shoulders rigid with tension but his tone abruptly invigorated. "We could solve both of our problems, couldn't we? We already thought that dismantling the conspiracy was the answer. What would prove our loyalty to the king more than putting down the uprising? No one could argue that Ivy's a threat if she's just saved the entire country from a scourge sorcerer coup."

Stavros pauses and then nods slowly. "We could request a royal pardon. The locals we collaborate with would speak up for her too."

"For all of us," I put in, in case he's forgotten that there's a bounty on his head as well. "But that's not the most important part. We *have* to stop whoever's leading the Order of the Wild—soon, before they destroy even more than they already have."

Sulla's voice breaks in, a slight quaver running through it. "You can't."

The mug trembles in her hands. As she sets it down, I stare at her. "Why not? We can't wait while they take over the entire country."

"It's too dangerous." Sulla thumps her fist against the table. "You haven't been training even a week yet. It could take years to fully master your power, especially when you've gone so long without guidance. You want to help—what about the harm you could do?"

The question lances right through the middle of me.

As I grapple with my words, I see Stavros hesitate.

But Casimir speaks up first. "Ivy's kept control over her magic on her own for all those years. I'd say that's more than enough proof that she can avoid unnecessary harm."

"And this might be her only chance to convince the king that she deserves to have a real life," Alek adds.

Most of the color has drained from Sulla's face. "The riven don't get to have those kind of lives. We stay here where it's safe for both us and the rest of the world."

I manage to push my voice past the lump in my throat. "You knew I was planning to leave. This is just a little earlier than I expected."

"Too early. I can't condone it."

*Who says she gets a vote?* Julita mutters. *This woman barely knows you.*

Casimir speaks again in his gentle way. "You could come with us. *You've* had years of training, so your control over your powers must be impeccable. And you could continue guiding Ivy along the way."

A rush of hope fills me. I smile at Sulla. "Yes. You could be so much help with your mastery over your magic. We can find another horse for you—we'd make sure—"

"No!" Sulla cuts me off with a scrape of her chair legs as she springs to her feet. "Neither of us should be going anywhere. Maintaining the right balance in a carefully controlled setting is nothing at all like dealing with a war like what's sparked out there."

I stare at her. "Then we'll figure it out. We'll be careful about bringing our power to bear. It's better than doing nothing."

Her gaze burns into mine. "You don't know that."

A little anger prickles through my disappointment. Julita's right—Sulla doesn't really know me. Maybe she doesn't care if Silana descends into a mass of torment and suffering, but she should at least be able to understand why it matters to me.

I push myself to my feet so we can eye each other on an equal level. "You don't have to join us, as much as I'd like you to. But we need to do this. *I* need to do it. It's my country too, no matter what most of the people in it think of me. The last thing we need is another Great Retribution."

Which could mean even more riven, more sorcerers torn between unbridled power and madness. Has she even thought about that part?

If she's thinking it now, she doesn't care about those consequences either. Sulla lifts her chin in a stance haughtier than I've ever seen from her. "You won't listen to reason. Who knows what blunders you'll make."

Before I can protest, she sweeps out of the room.

Casimir stands next to me, stroking his fingers up and down my arm in a soothing gesture. "She's upset, but it's not her place to choose what's right for you. Kosmel always supported your quest against the scourge sorcerers."

"He did," I say, the thought bolstering my resolve.

Alek looks at Stavros. "How long will it take us to reach Eppun on horseback?"

Stavros's gaze goes distant with thought. "The college horses are good stock, and they've had plenty of time to rest. Depending on the weather and how many diversions we need to take, I'd hope we could cover that ground within a week or so."

My pulse hiccups at the thought of all the things that could go wrong in a week of scourge-sorcery-driven warfare. "We need to get moving right away, then. It shouldn't take long to—"

A clatter from the hall outside interrupts me. We exchange a glance and hustle out of the dining room in a mass.

Sulla is just tossing a shape I recognize as Rheave's quiver of arrows into one of the smaller storage rooms. As we hurry toward her, she tosses the dagger Alek was training with and the camp pot we used during our trek after it.

"What are you doing?" Rheave demands, rushing to the front of our group.

Sulla holds up her hand to stop him while shoving the door closed with the other. A tingle of magic in the air tells me she's sealed the room with more than physical force.

She swings her hand toward the far end of the hall as if to lock the door that leads to the higher buildings as well.

"Whatever you brought here is part of the Haven now," she says in a ragged voice. "You're not taking any of it with you. And you're not getting very far without your equipment."

She's trying to force us to stay.

My heart plummets. How are we going to get by on a week-long journey without most of the supplies we arrived here with?

How much farther will she go to stop us if we linger any longer? If we're leaving, we have to go *now*.

Stavros's expression has hardened. Any doubts he might have had about the validity of her concerns appear to have vanished.

He marches toward the sorcerer. "This isn't your decision to make."

Casimir tucks his hand around my elbow and leans close so only I can hear him. "We left a few things in the saddle bags down where the horses are stabled. I don't think she could have grabbed anything there yet. We'd better get to them first."

Sulla's head swings toward us. Her mouth sets with determination.

She must have come to the same realization we just did.

I bolt for the nearby doorway, the one she hasn't sealed yet. It's a short scramble down the stone steps built into the mountainside to the covered wooden shelter where we've been keeping the horses.

The men hurtle down the steps behind me. Sulla's cry carries after them. "No! I can't let you do this. You're meant to be here."

At the base of the stairs, I dart to the side, letting the men charge past me to prepare the horses. Toast nickers, either in greeting or to protest that I'm not attending to him myself.

Sulla scrambles after us, her eyes wide. She catches her balance against a hunched sapling just a few steps away from me and stares past me toward the makeshift stable.

Her hand rises again as if she intends to cast out more magic.

I step right in front of her, my own magic unfurling through my chest with an unnerving but potent vibration. "Is this really what you want to do, Sulla? You're going to protect the world from being hurt by my magic by hurting us with yours?"

The desperate look she gives me sends an ache through my heart. "You don't know what could happen."

I gather all my determination in my posture and my voice. "Neither do you. I know where I'm meant to be, and it's not locked away up here for the rest of my life. Not when there are good people down there who'll definitely be hurt if I don't step in."

Sulla looks down at her extended hand. Her arm shivers, and she lowers it to her side with a mumbled curse.

She's probably already let loose more magic in the past few minutes than she normally would in a week. I can't imagine she had enough time to think through the consequences. How much damage has *she* done to her own home?

Seeing her hopeless expression, I can't help giving her one more chance. "You could still come with us. We'll keep each other in check. I'd appreciate your guidance just as I have here. Please."

Sulla meets my gaze again. There's so much anguish in her eyes that my throat closes up.

"We're not meant for the rest of the world, Ivy," she says. "I know that. I pray that you realize it as well before too many others pay the price."

# Fourteen

*Ivy*

My mentor's words echo in my head long after we've left the Haven behind. With every step I take down the mountain, a boulder seems to sway in my belly.

Sulla saw my power firsthand. She knows more about the riven than anyone else I've encountered in my twenty years in this world.

What if she's right that I shouldn't trust myself? Tackling a province-wide uprising is going to challenge me a lot more than tangling with a small group of conspirators at the royal college.

My men have stayed mostly silent as we descend the mountain, concentrating on leading the horses well so none of us breaks a leg. As the ground between the trees levels out, Stavros draws to a halt at the head of our group and reaches for his saddle to mount.

The rest of us move to follow suit, but Casimir stops me with a touch of my shoulder. He trails his fingers up to my jaw and leans in to claim a kiss.

The heat of his mouth reminds me of all the ways he took charge the other day, of the fleeting freedom he offered me from my responsibilities. Which maybe is his intention, because when he draws back, he says in a firm but tender tone, "We're facing this crisis together. If you need anything, we'll be right there with you."

I gaze up at him with a swell of affection. "I know. I couldn't do this on my own."

*And you shouldn't need to,* Julita pipes up in my head. *But I do look forward to seeing the bunch of you accomplish what the king's whole army hasn't managed. He'd better realize he never should have cast you out.*

As I haul myself into Toast's saddle, I appreciate my trousers and the slits I cut in my dress's skirt overtop more than ever. At least my legs will stay decently warm in the late autumn air.

Stavros glances back at the rest of us. "We should take stock. See what equipment we still have—what supplies we're starting with so we know what we might still need. I have my sword."

He taps the weapon at his waist that thankfully he wore on his trek to the nearby fort.

I look down at myself. "I've got two knives—one in my boot and one on my thigh. The other two, you were using for your combat training. Sulla must have confiscated them."

"We'll want more weapons then. Is anyone else carrying anything of use? What's in your saddle bags?"

We keep the horses walking at a sedate pace while we check the baggage attached to the saddles. My favorite noble dress that I was wearing when we rushed to the royal family's aid is still bundled up in mine, along with the military uniform and a few extra apples. The men all have their uniforms too.

Alek has the tent, which we haven't needed to use since arriving, and Casimir has one blanket. We brought the others up to the Haven buildings when we were first getting settled in.

We have two canteens between us, which Stavros and Rheave already refilled at the mountain stream. We all wore our cloaks coming down from the sleeping building, so we're not doing too badly for outerwear. Although I'm not sure just how cold it'll get in the north with winter creeping in.

Casimir finds the makeup he used to partly conceal Stavros's and Alek's faces, however much use we might get out of that. And the four of us have our enchanted lockets that we can signal each other with if we separate.

Stavros hums pensively when we've finished our accounting. "We can forage for food, but hunting won't be easy with just a sword and a couple of knives. We'll see how far we can get with my snares. It'll be a lot harder to start fires without the flint. And we're awfully short on blankets."

Alek glances at Rheave. "Could you start a fire with your daimon powers?"

Rheave peers at one of his hands. "I'm not sure. It seems to go straight to burning without any flames."

"We didn't see any fire at the palace, only scorch marks and charred things," I acknowledge, and hesitate. "I suppose we could... borrow a few things from one of the farms around here?"

The idea of stealing from farmers who are eking out a living sits much worse with me than pilfering from the overflowing coffers of greedy merchants.

I suspect Stavros can sense my reluctance. He knows my aspirations as a thief were to give to the commoners who needed it, not take from them.

He scans the horizon and turns his stallion a little to the right. The rest of us follow suit automatically.

He motions with his prosthetic toward the route ahead of us. "About halfway to the fort, I spotted a military marking that indicates an equipment stash nearby. The royal army has hidden stores across the country for emergency situations. There'll be food rations and weapons and probably some tools and the like as well."

Alek tenses in his saddle. "Will it be guarded?"

The former general shakes his head. "That would defeat the purpose of hiding it. We'll have to be careful because of the patrols the major mentioned, but that's the case no matter where we go. And the stores aren't checked often. Supplies taken from one are much less likely to be noticed and commented on than a farmyard theft."

My uneasy spirits settle. "Let's make that our first stop, then. If scourge sorcerers taking over the country doesn't count as an emergency, I don't know what would."

We nudge the horses to a trot, not wanting to push them too hard when we have a long journey ahead of us. Alek lets his mare fall back closer to Rheave.

"When we reach the north, it sounds like there could be quite a lot of other daimon that the scourge sorcerers have turned into accomplices," the scholar says. "How close would you need to be to distinguish between them and actual people?"

I peer over my shoulder in time to see the daimon-man cock his head. "I think I'd just need to see them clearly. Someone in the same city square or across a clearing like the ones we've been in should be fine—there's a feeling I get."

"You'll let us know if you do see any?" I ask.

Rheave draws himself up straighter at my attention. "Of course, if it would be helpful. I'd like to know what's happened to the others like me."

"It'd definitely help," Stavros remarks from ahead of us. "At the very least, it'll let us know there are likely to be scourge sorcerers in the area."

Alek adjusts his grip on his reins. "And do you know any way to disable them or, well, free them other than killing them so the bodies imprisoning them turn back into clay? Or to break the scourge sorcerers' hold on them so maybe we don't have to?"

Rheave knits his brow. "I think... I think if the one who cast the magic that can command us died, the other sorcerers wouldn't be able to control us anymore. But the previous orders might linger for some time. And I don't know who cast the magic. From what I've seen, the bodies remain whole and living, containing us, as long as they're alive."

Alek was obviously hoping for a more useful answer than that. He lets out a mild disgruntled sound.

After a moment, he ventures another question. "How long have you been in existence anyway? Were you around for the Great Retribution?"

Rheave hums. "I've heard talk about that time for a while, but I don't remember experiencing the sorts of things people mention happening. My memories do become blurry fairly quickly, though. We don't pay much attention to the passing of time, only what we're doing in the moment."

"Ah." Alek pauses. "You said you could tell when Kosmel reached out to Ivy. Do the daimon interact with the godlen often? Have *you* ever talked to one directly?"

Why is he asking about this? Does he think Rheave might be able to plead for our cause with the other lesser gods, prevent another hail of vengeful fire?

If so, it appears we're out of luck. The daimon-man lets out a chuckle. "I sense when they come, but they don't usually pay attention to us. And we don't really... talk, even to each other, in our usual form." His tone abruptly brightens. "Maybe we should. Talking can lead to many interesting discoveries."

Stavros sounds as if he's restrained a snort, but Rheave's enthusiasm brings a smile to my lips for the first time since we left the Haven. He manages to find so much wonder in the world even in dire circumstances.

There *is* so much that's wonderful in this world, no matter how difficult the road ahead of us becomes. That's exactly why we need to save the world from those who'd twist it to their sadistic ends.

As the trees thin up ahead, the former general twists in his saddle, his voice low. "We should avoid any talking now unless it's absolutely necessary, until we're back in the cover of the denser woods. Our voices will carry farther over open ground."

Rheave clamps his mouth shut with an emphatic nod.

We cross the fields and weave through a stretch of forest beyond them. The sun is just past its peak, gleaming through the leaves, when Stavros motions to a small carving on a tree trunk.

It's Sabrelle's sigil surrounded by a circle with a few other, smaller etchings I don't know the meaning of. But Stavros clearly does.

He urges his stallion to the right, and the rest of us follow. Several minutes later, he turns left at another etching. It can't be more than a few minutes after that when we arrive at a small glade.

When Stavros dismounts, we all do the same and gather around him. He kneels to brush aside the fallen leaves to reveal a smooth, round stone. When he lifts that up, a steel hatch shines in the early afternoon sunlight.

The former general pauses. The center of the hatch holds the imprint of the Melchiorek family crest, like he had on his old sword that must be back in his chest in his quarters at the college.

He sits back on his heels with a faint growl. "Shit. I didn't think about that. Every officer carries a seal that could unlock this, but obviously I don't have mine. The entrance is locked with magic."

My power twitches in my chest. Casimir and Alek both glance toward me, as if the answer is inevitable.

Maybe it is, but my lungs constrict even as my magic squirms through them. None of my training with Sulla prepared me specifically to set my magic against a spell already in place.

I don't know how to counter that properly. I don't know what the consequences would be if I can't focus on a proper balancing effect.

Stavros is already uncomfortable enough about my magic without me screwing up on my very first attempt at using it since leaving the Haven.

Rheave shifts his gaze to me too. My hands clench at my sides.

We *need* what's down there. That matters more than anyone's opinion of me.

The backlash for opening a lock can't be *that* immense, can it?

I open my mouth, but before I can force out the offer, Rheave pushes in front of me and kneels by the hatch. "My power might be able to break the magic on it. Ivy should save hers for when no one else can help."

I stare down at him, not sure what to make of his declaration. Is he only thinking in practicalities… or did he realize how conflicted I was?

The daimon-man is directing all his focus at the hatch now. He rests his hands on the edge of the metal surface. "I think the rest of you might want to back away."

We all take a step back, apprehension rippling between us. Rheave leans closer to the hatch. He exhales in a soft hiss.

Energy crackles across the hatch in a burst of light with a metallic squeal. The daimon-man lurches backward as if shoved by the force he's exuded.

I leap forward automatically, ducking down to catch his shoulders before his head slams into the dirt.

The impact knocks me off-balance too. I tumble sideways, falling to my knees with the daimon's head landing on my thighs.

As I catch my breath, Rheave gazes up at me with his unearthly eyes. I'm still clutching one of his shoulders, close enough to his head for his glossy brown curls to graze my wrist.

He reaches up to brush his fingertips along my jaw, so delicately a flutter passes through my pulse. "Thank you, Ivy. You protected me too."

Before I can sort out the sudden clash of emotions inside me, Rheave sits up with a jerk and motions to the hatch. "Try it!"

Stavros moves first, hooking the end of his metal prosthetic around a small fingerhold in the steel circle. He tugs at it—and the hatch lifts with a faint creak. A trace of a burnt scent wisps through the air with the movement.

Casimir laughs lightly. "Now that's a use for daimon magic that I can approve of."

As Stavros peers into the blackness below, I slip between the other men to join him. "I can go down first. I'm used to finding my way in the dark."

The former general frowns as if he's about to argue with me, so I don't give him the chance. Spotting the glint of an upper rung, I plunk myself down at the lip of the opening and hop onto the ladder inside.

"Ivy," Stavros protests, but I'm already clambering the rest of the way down.

When my feet hit the earthen floor, I glance up at his looming form. "Why don't you move your massive self out of the way so I can get a little sunlight down here?"

I catch a muffled guffaw that sounds like Alek. Stavros mutters something about insolent ladies under his breath but draws back from the opening.

I choose not to remind him that I'm more a thief than a lady and study my surroundings in the beams of sunlight that streak past the hatch.

A few rectangular shapes that I determine are cots lean against the wall near the ladder. In case a few soldiers need to hole up here for a while?

Beyond them, the room stretches off into darkness, the light only catching on the edges of crates and chests. I step closer and make out the shape of an empty lantern propped up on one stack.

Squinting and groping, I find a set of shelves carved into the wall that hold, among other things, a tin of beeswax candles and a flint. In a matter of seconds, I have the lantern flaring. The sweet scent of the wax mingles with the loamy odor of the packed soil around me.

Stavros must catch the flare of the light. "Keep watch," he says to someone above and climbs down to join me with Alek following close behind. I guess he's left Casimir and Rheave on guard duty.

The lantern has illuminated the entire space, which is rather impressively large for a secret room no one much expects to use. There are houses in Slaughterwell you could fit in here.

It appears Stavros knows his way around. He strides past the shelves and the crates to the very back of the room, where the lantern's glow is now reflecting off several metal surfaces.

A sort of weapons rack is embedded in the back wall. The former general taps his fingers against the hilts of several swords that don't meet his approval and finally picks out a short one as well as a fighting dagger that I suspect is for Casimir and a hunting knife.

"Get over here," he says with a motion to Alek. "See if you can find at least one blade you'll feel reasonably comfortable with. Ivy, you can take your pick too."

Back in familiar territory, I pluck up the smallest two knives and fit them into the vacant sheaths in one boot and on one thigh.

As the scholar studies the weaponry with a grimace, Stavros hefts a bow and a quiver of arrows that was leaning against the wall nearby. He considers the other few quivers and shakes his head. "We can only carry so much. But the daimon will be happy."

While he carries our new arms up to the surface, I pry at the lids on a few of the crates. One proves to be full of various nuts, while another holds strips of dried bloodfruit.

I hold up one of those to show Stavros as he returns. "So many delicious meals ahead."

He raises an eyebrow at my sarcastic tone. "Better than starving."

*I suppose he has a point there*, Julita says, but she doesn't sound any more enthusiastic about the rations than I am.

Alek has shoved a thin dagger under the belt around his tunic and is checking the chests. "Here are some blankets," he announces. "There are spare clothes down here too, but they don't look any warmer than what we already have."

Stavros nods. "They stock what's appropriate for the area. If we want heavier wear, we'll need to find a stash up north."

I move to the chest to inspect the offerings. "We should each grab a set anyway. Two layers is warmer than one."

"Ah!" Stavros snatches up what looks like a ball of twine from a lower shelf. Closer to the lantern, I see it gleams like steel. "Wire will make for easier snares. You'll have something to eat other than nuts and bloodfruit, Lady Thief."

"Let us all rejoice."

We paw through the rest of the supplies, but Stavros is right that there's only so much we'll be able to carry. We have to balance equipping ourselves with our need for haste.

As it is, carrying our findings to the surface, we determine that we can't take quite as many blankets as I'd have preferred. We all put on an extra tunic now so that we don't have to find space for them in the saddle bags.

Stavros gives the hatch one last look before he moves to cover it again, with a tense expression that dampens my delight at our find.

This isn't how he would ever have expected to access one of these storerooms—as a fugitive, breaking in and technically stealing from it.

We really are criminals now. And we have a long road ahead of us before we can prove ourselves to be anything different.

# Fifteen

*Ivy*

Toast gives his mane a rebellious shake as he trots along, but his gait has turned more sprightly on the even ground. After three days of traveling through woodlands, we've decided we can risk taking one of the smaller country roads, at least as long as it's cutting through forests rather than fields so we can't be seen at a distance. It's hard to keep up a good pace picking through the brush.

Stavros is still taking the lead, since he's the one with by far the best idea of where we're going. A couple of times he's ridden ahead alone to check road markers, but mostly he seems to be guided by the sun and the occasional landmark.

We all scan the trees warily as we ride, our passage silent other than the clop of the horses' hooves. My ears are pricked for any other sound that could alert us not just to a patrol but local brigands as well.

Although with most of us visibly armed, in peasant-style dress, and carrying little cargo, we probably don't look like ideal targets for a robbery.

It's only when we stop for a brief break that we speak again, in lowered voices. Casimir passes around handfuls of nuts and bloodfruit, and Stavros checks our steeds' horseshoes for stray pebbles while they graze.

Rheave drifts over to the trees while chewing on his dried fruit and trails his fingers over the leafy vine that's wrapped around one of the trunks. "Ivy," he says thoughtfully, and looks over at me with a glint in his eerie eyes that's almost sly. "Is it strange that you have the same name as a plant?"

I shrug. "It's not the most traditional name, but I've met people named after flowers. I picked it because it meant something to me."

The daimon-man blinks, and his face lights up with more curiosity. "*You* picked it?"

Julita's presence perks up in my head. *I didn't know that either. You've been holding back stories.*

She at least knows the basics of my history, things I'd rather not have to explain to Rheave too.

My stomach knots, and I pick my words carefully to skirt the worst parts of the tale. "Things were bad between my parents and me as I grew up. I left home early and picked a new name for myself.

There was ivy growing on a tree in a neighborhood I often visited. It seemed like something resilient and a little sneaky, and I liked that."

A giggle bubbles out of Julita. *It certainly suits you, and I mean that as an absolute compliment.*

Rheave appears to consider my explanation. "Maybe all people should pick their own names. They would be more fitting that way."

"No one would know what to call us when we're too little to decide," Casimir says in an amused tone.

Rheave starts to chuckle. "And if you went by what babies look like, they'd all be called 'Potato' or 'Gourd.'"

I muffle a laugh of my own with my hand. The fact that I can laugh at all despite the tension hanging over our trek lifts my spirits and makes the day seem a little brighter.

Alek shakes his head with a short guffaw and shoots a tentative glance at me. "What *was* your birth name? Not that I'd call you anything but Ivy. But it might be useful to know in case it comes up somehow… In case anyone manages to connect you to your old life."

I guess that's true. I hesitate all the same, my body balking against forming the sounds I haven't heard spoken to me in more than eight years.

My voice comes out a bit raw. "Izabel. Izabel Milaeya."

Stavros makes a dismissive sound, as if casting aside the name and all the painful history entwined with it. "Ivy suits you much better. And you don't need a last name when the woman it refers to doesn't deserve to be honored."

*I completely agree,* Julita declares.

The former general pats his stallion's neck. "Come on. I'd like to cover a lot more distance today."

An unfamiliar voice pipes up from behind us. "I don't know if you'll accomplish that."

We all startle, Stavros's hand whipping to his sword as he whirls to face the source of the unexpected interruption.

A figure is standing in the middle of the road, just a few paces from the nearest of our horses. I have no idea how the man got this close without any of us noticing him approaching.

Especially given that he doesn't look like the nimblest of hikers. His shoulders are hunched within the layers of dark gray cloth that swath his body so erratically I can't tell whether they're part of a cloak or a thick tunic, or perhaps some combination of the two. He sways a little as we stare at him and clenches his hand around a gnarled walking stick.

His face is gnarled too, a sharp nose jutting from his wizened brown face. Wisps of white hair peek from beneath his hood.

But his eyes are perfectly steady. He peers right back at us with a fathomless gaze, his irises so dark I can't tell where his pupils end and they begin.

Julita shivers. *Who in the realms is that? And did no one ever tell him it's impolite to sneak up on people?*

I'd hardly take the man for a threat if it wasn't for his abrupt arrival. Stavros's tensed stance suggests he's unnerved too.

What on earth is anyone doing traveling this isolated road alone and on foot? Does he live on a farm nearby?

The former general motions to the old man with his prosthetic, his hand of flesh still resting on his sword hilt. "What do you mean, we might not accomplish it? Who are you?"

The man rocks on his heels, making his head bob in an unsettlingly bird-like motion. "Many people make plans. They don't always turn out as they hope."

He ignores the second question completely. I glance at Rheave, but the daimon-man shakes his head. "Not like me," he murmurs. "Just a man."

"Where are you headed?" Casimir asks cautiously.

The old man hums to himself, his expression turning distant. "I simply need to find it, and then I'll know…"

He seems so out of sorts that I can't keep quiet. "Are you all right?"

His unsettling gaze snaps back to me. A chill washes over my skin.

"There are a few coming who would like to set their swords through all your hearts," he says in the exact same tone as before.

The instant his last word fades in the air, the sound of far-off hoofbeats carries on the wind.

Stavros stiffens and motions us toward the trees. He pitches his voice ominously low. "Take shelter. Pull as far back into the woods as you can, but be quiet about it."

I snatch Toast's reins and tug him with me between the trees. The stallion huffs in dismay but follows, shuffling through the brush.

The men guide their own mounts on either side of me. But we've only pushed about a single horse-length into the forest before Stavros jerks up his hand to stop us.

I glance toward the road—and spot a flash of rich blue fabric that makes my pulse stutter.

Three soldiers in the standard military uniforms are riding around the bend in the road maybe a quarter mile distant. The thudding of their horses' approach reaches our ears even more clearly now.

Shit. It's got to be one of the king's patrols.

If we keep tugging our steeds along, they'll hear us rustling through the forest now. They'll be able to see us in a matter of seconds.

But if we abandon the horses to walk more stealthily, the animals will still give us away. At best, we'll lose all the supplies we've gathered.

At worst… our blood might water these trees.

Stavros's face has gone taut with tension. He gestures for us to ease our horses down to lie on the forest floor.

I touch Toast's muzzle in the hopes of keeping him calm and sink to my own knees. The stallion gives me an incredulous look but follows suit with just a brisk shake of his mane.

We're more concealed by the bushes now, but I'm not sure it'll be enough. The pale gray hair of Rheave's mare stands out amid the vegetation even in the shadows.

Are we going to have to fight these men? Kill them so they can't stab their swords through us the way the old man suggested?

My stomach churns at the thought. I left the Haven to stop people from dying, not to add to the death toll.

At the thought, my magic flares in my chest and quivers through my limbs. There are so many things it could do to protect me.

I hesitate and then slowly consider. *Is* there something I could do that wouldn't hurt anyone?

Maybe it's time I put Sulla's teachings to use. Now, while I have a few moments to gather myself, rather than in a desperate jab if this comes to a battle.

Soon I might not even have the choice.

My heart thumps faster, but I can't back away like I did about opening the underground storeroom. Eventually I need to find out whether I can count on my control when it matters most.

The soldiers don't know we're here. All I need to do is ensure I keep it that way. Something concrete with a clear counteraction.

An idea forms in my head. My hopes rise with it.

I glance around at my men, confirming their positions in the forest around me. My heart aches at the thought of any harm coming to them.

I simply can't let that happen. They came all this way to defend me, and now I need to return the favor.

Girding myself, I let go of Toast's reins to extend one hand in front of me while lifting my other arm toward the treetops. Guiding my focus with my body.

Julita's presence shivers in the back of my head, but she doesn't speak, maybe not wanting to distract me when she can tell I'm up to something.

I picture the effect I want to see and squeeze the power in me into the shape I've imagined.

Darkness condenses through the trees between us and the road. The shadows thicken and stretch, forming a wall no mortal eyes should be able to penetrate in the gaps between the trunks.

My breath hitches with the energy streaming out of me. Overhead, the shadows should be stripping away from the uppermost branches to balance out my magic. The remaining leaves and the branches they're clinging to will be glaring with unmuted sunlight.

But no patrol will see the blaze from the ground.

Through the thunder of my pulse, I will my cloak of shadows to hold steady. We all stay crouched in silence.

The soldiers trot by, their gazes skimming over the woods on either side of the road. For a second, one leans a little over in his saddle, squinting our way—

And then he's straightened up with a rough chuckle as if chagrinned with himself. The patrol rides on without stopping.

I have the impression of Julita clapping her hands. *Now that's a worthy trick.*

I keep pouring my magic into the darkness draped over us until the hoofbeats fade away and my head starts to spin. With a sharp exhalation, I pull my hands back to my chest, yanking my power in with it.

My magic squirms against my grasp, but half-heartedly. It settles into a soft vibration within my ribs that feels almost content, like a purring cat.

I sink back on my ass and swipe at the sweat that formed on my forehead. Relief surges up from my gut.

I did it. I worked with my magic instead of fighting it, all while keeping it on a tight leash. I stopped the consequences from harming anyone.

I really have harnessed it, and for once I didn't need a godlen's intervention to hold disaster in check.

An instinctive need to reassure myself of my men's safety grips me. I turn toward Alek where he's crouched across from me and pull him to me in a tight hug.

He returns the embrace with a rough noise in his throat. Casimir slips closer to me through the brush and wraps his arms around me in a hug of his own, as if to reassure me that he's grateful rather than horrified by my efforts.

I squeeze him back too and then look up to find Stavros standing over me.

"Are you all right, Lady Thief?" he asks. "The conjuring didn't rattle you at all?"

I drag in a slow breath. "No. I feel fine."

His mouth curves into a half-smile that's fond if restrained. "You did well. I think we just might make it to Eppun after all."

Alek grips my shoulder. "That was fantastic. And using your magic a bit means it won't hurt you as much if you have to hold it back later, doesn't it?"

I nod, my nerves settling at their joint show of support.

As I get to my feet, nudging Toast to follow me, Rheave moves to join us. But he's looking toward the road. "Where did the man who warned us go?"

We tread carefully out from between the trees. The road lies completely empty of both soldiers and strange old men.

*He was... very strange*, Julita remarks. *I can't say I'm upset that he's gone.*

I can't say I am either.

"He probably moved off into the woods on the other side," Stavros says. "Whatever he's up to, it's no business of ours. Let's get going. We've had plenty of break time now, and I don't want to be here if that patrol decides to double back." He flashes another smile my way. "Let's not make our sorcerer save us all over again."

Despite the lightness of his words, I feel his gaze evaluating me. Watching to see if the use of my magic has had any ill effects on me?

As I heft myself into the saddle, a different sort of ache spreads behind my sternum.

I did save my companions… and I can only pray to whatever gods are watching over us that I can do it again without bringing even more danger down on us.

# Sixteen

*Ivy*

I wake at a gust of icy air slipping beneath the layered blankets.

Casimir follows the draught, returning from his time on watch. He must have swapped with Stavros, who was sleeping on that side of me the last time I was conscious.

Alek mumbles and pulls deeper under the blankets at my other side. It's just occurred to me that there should be one more man squeezed into the tent with us when Casimir speaks by my ear at a whisper.

"Rheave came out maybe half an hour ago. He's sitting off by himself under the trees, not even with his hood up. I tried to convince him to come back and warm up, but he didn't listen to me. He seems to pay more attention to you, if you want to try to convince him."

I muffle a groan and swipe at my eyes. Does the daimon-man want to turn the body he's so determined to keep alive black with frostbite?

Why would he want to be out there in the freezing dark anyway?

I can't really complain about the interrupted sleep. Since I used my magic the other day, the men have refused to let me take any of the watches. They want to ensure I have all the focus I need if another occasion arises, so I've been getting the most rest out of any of us.

I give Casimir a quick kiss and squirm out from under the blankets.

The nights have gotten increasingly chilly as we've continued north. We've mostly gotten through by cuddling close together to share body heat, which the small tent makes kind of necessary regardless.

I'm not sure what's been more torturous: the occasional wafts of frigid air that manage to reach us anyway or lying so close to my lovers without being able to do more than cuddle. Having Rheave sharing the space doesn't exactly set the right mood for an intimate encounter.

But I'm not going to let him freeze just for a little privacy with my men. Sighing, I pull my cloak close around me and tramp out onto the frost-laced grass.

Stavros is poised on a stone a couple of paces from the tent, his own cloak covering most of his massive form and his body tipped toward the smoldering firepit. He's partly buried it to limit the smoke, but it still emanates a faint glow and a little heat through the earth to take the worst edge off the chill.

He glances over his shoulder toward me with a sweep of his gaze over my form.

"Are you all right?" he asks in a quiet voice, taking a casual tone despite his obvious concern. He's been asking that question more frequently than usual since the day I called on my magic by the road.

I match his tone. "Just making sure the daimon doesn't become as much ice as clay."

Stavros gives a muted chuckle and tips his head to the left. Following the gesture, I spot Rheave's muscular form sitting cross-legged between two trees several paces beyond the edge of the clearing.

Like Casimir said, the idiotic daimon hasn't even bothered to raise his hood. His chocolate-brown curls are going to end up as frosted as the grass, which crackles under my feet as I walk over to him.

When I get closer, I see he has his bare hands splayed on his knees rather than tucked into his pockets like any sensible person would. Because of course he isn't a person, and also not especially sensible as far as I can tell, though I'm not sure what's typical for a spirit-creature.

Julita lets out a soft huff. *What in the realms is he doing? Attempting to transform into an ice sculpture?*

"I suppose I'd better figure that out," I murmur, treading between the trees.

Rheave doesn't stir as I come up beside him. His eyes are closed.

I peer at his hands and face in the dim moonlight, but I can't tell whether they're already turning blue.

"Hey," I say, unsure whether he's even awake. Can a daimon fall asleep sitting up?

Rheave's vibrant eyes blink open. He looks up at me and frowns. "Why are you out here? Isn't this your time to sleep?"

"Isn't it yours?" I retort. "I'm guessing you didn't sleep as a daimon, but I'm pretty sure that body of yours needs it. And it also needs to avoid turning into an icicle."

The daimon-man considers me with a gleam of curiosity rather than concern in his eyes. "Is that a thing that can happen to humans?"

What am I going to do with this guy?

My tone comes out dry. "Not exactly, but bodies of flesh *can* freeze if they do things like, I don't know, sitting out in the forest in the middle of the night with no heat source nearby."

Rheave shrugs as if the idea doesn't particularly bother him. "I was never cold when I was a daimon. Or warm. Or anything like that. It's interesting to feel it. Like the air is biting you, but not that hard."

The breeze blowing past us is definitely nippy. I tuck my own hands deeper under my cloak, out of its reach. "So now you've felt it. Why are you staying out here?"

"The way it feels keeps changing a little. Some parts tingled. Some stopped feeling at all." He taps his fingertips against his knees with apparent delight.

Panic jolts through my nerves. "How long *have* you been out here?"

I bend down to press my fingers to his cheek and then the back of his hand. The latter feels outright frigid.

My magic jostles inside me, clamoring to flood him with heat, push back the chill.

But where would that heat come from? Everything around us is freezing except me, my men, and the fire I don't want to snuff out.

I wrap my hand around Rheave's as if I can squeeze some warmth back into his skin and tug at him. "You've had enough trying out the cold for now. Come on—we need to get you warmed up before you do any permanent damage to yourself."

Rheave pushes slowly to his feet and looks down at our clasped hands. "I don't feel *bad*. I'm sure I'll be all right, Little Vine."

Is that what he's going to call me now? I might be 'little' compared to him, but I've still got the ivy resilience.

I step away in an attempt to drag him toward the tent, my throat constricting with worry. "That part where you can't feel anything? If you leave it very long, it becomes permanent. And then the bits with no feeling fall right off. Do you really want to start losing pieces of this body? I don't think the scourge sorcerers are going to build you a new one."

To my relief, my final comment finally rouses him to action. Rheave strides with me over to the tent, grimacing as he wobbles on legs that must have gotten stiff. "Mortal bodies are very fragile."

"That's right. How about you keep that in mind from now on?"

I push him into the tent, tug off his cloak which might as well be pure ice, and draw him down with me toward the blankets. Casimir is still awake, rolling over as I nudge Rheave toward him.

"He's already going numb," I whisper, wanting to avoid waking Alek too if I can. "We need to warm him up as quickly as possible."

Rheave makes a faint sound of protest, but he lets me push him closer to the courtesan. The two of us tuck ourselves against the daimon-man's body, even though I wince at the cold still seeping from his clothes.

"Put your hands in your armpits," I murmur at him. "Pull your face right under the blanket so it'll soak up the heat too."

Rheave ducks his head. His silky curls graze my jaw.

I pull the blanket higher over him and instinctively set my hand against his arm to reassure myself that he's still got some warmth in him. That he isn't totally frozen.

The constricting sensation in my throat has spread down through my chest. What if he *has* done real damage to himself?

The realization creeps over me so gradually but undeniably that my heart clenches up too. As exasperating as the daimon-man can be, I appreciate the brightness and wonder he's brought with him. I've enjoyed his company.

I don't want to lose him.

What am I supposed to do with that knowledge or the ache that's come with it?

Our breaths rise and fall together. Gradually, the heat we radiate penetrates the cold we carried with us.

Despite the tangled emotions inside me, I lift my hand to rest my palm against Rheave's cheek. It's still cool but not totally cold anymore. He's okay.

A rush of relief tinged with absurd humor passes through me. At least his ridiculously beautiful face shouldn't be marred by his embracing of the northern night.

I tap his jaw lightly to get his attention. "Let me feel one of your hands."

He adjusts his position, rolling onto his side to face me. I expect him to reach for my hand, but instead he places his palm against my stomach.

A flicker of an even more confusing emotion lights low in my belly. A deeper heat than his sunny smiles ever provoked.

I clamp down on it, mentally shaking my head at my reaction. This man is gorgeous and bizarre and makes me wonder about things I never did before, but he's also not really a man.

And I've got three other men I'm very much devoted to. Even Signy, after all her heroics, stopped at a trio.

I grasp Rheave's wrist the second enough warmth has seeped through my over-tunic and dress for me to be sure he won't be losing any fingers and ease his hand away.

Rheave lifts his head from beneath the blanket. It's nearly pitch black inside the tent, but I can feel him looking my way. Maybe he can make out my face even if I can't see his.

The second I let go of his wrist, he reaches for me again. He touches my shoulder and then slides his hand down almost to my elbow.

We've never slept next to each other before. My men have always insisted on surrounding me, and the daimon-man has settled for taking the spot closest to the flaps where he can still serve as some kind of protection.

I didn't realize he was going to be touchy-feely about our current position.

Julita lets out a giggle. *He is all about feeling new things, isn't he? If you could snap the rest of the scourge sorcerers' army out of whatever spell they're under, they'd be dopey as puppies.*

When Rheave speaks, he doesn't sound particularly dopey. He keeps his voice low but steady. "Everything is back to normal now. My fingers were prickly for a while, but that faded away."

"Good. Then you didn't freeze them right off."

"I wasn't being careful. I'm sorry I worried you. I'm supposed to be looking out for you, not making you do that for me."

He sounds downcast enough that I stroke his cheek again in an effort at reassurance. "We all look out for each other. That's what… friends do. And you're still getting used to being whatever exactly you are now. It'd just be nice if you'd listen faster the next time I try to warn you. Or you could listen to the others. We all have a lot more experience in mortal bodies than you do."

"I know. But you're the one I'm sure will really listen to me. I'll try to be better about listening too."

He's silent for a moment, his fingers squeezing my arm lightly, and then he drops his hand to my waist. It flexes against my side as if he's testing some other new sensation.

"Ivy," he says, "why do humans press their mouths together?"

I think I hear Casimir choke back a guffaw. My cheeks flare. The courtesan should be the one fielding questions like this.

And if I have to, he could at least do me the favor of going to sleep so I don't have an audience.

I grope for a reasonable answer. "It feels good. It's a way to show you like being close to someone."

Rheave hums and dips his head toward me. I jerk my hand against his sternum before he can press right against me, tuning out the pulse of desire that sparked in my core.

"Are you trying to kiss *me*?" I demand as quietly as I can manage.

*I think you opened yourself up to that one, Ivy*, Julita says through another giggle.

The daimon-man simply sounds confused. "You said it feels good. I wanted to see. You kiss Stavros and Casimir and Alek."

Great God help me. "I know them a lot better than I know you. We have a different kind of relationship. Most people don't get that close with each other."

"Oh."

Now he sounds outright despondent.

I grit my teeth at the twinge of sympathy that runs through my chest. Who's ever going to want to kiss a man who's not really a man?

At least, enough to allow themselves to go through with it. We won't talk about the feelings I'm reining in as much as I have my magic.

Well, maybe we can compromise.

I turn my head away from him. "On the mouth, anyway. People who are just friendly could kiss each other on the cheek. That wouldn't be so strange. It's not quite the same, but you could try that."

My earlier rejection seems to have shaken Rheave's confidence. "Are you sure? I don't want to do anything that would upset you."

The twinge rises through my chest to solidify into a lump in my throat. I don't like hearing his eager brightness give way to hesitance. "It won't. Go ahead."

He leans in, soft hair against my temple, hot breath drifting over my jaw. His lips graze my cheek and then press the skin a little more firmly.

Heat flushes my body from head to toe. I can't blame it completely on the wash of his breath.

I'm not sure I ever noticed the daimon-man's personal scent before. There's a fresh, woodsy scent to him that makes me think of leaves dappled in dew under the morning sun.

He draws his head back, but then he wraps his whole arm around my waist, pulling me right up against him again. "Now I'll keep you warm. You should sleep."

It *is* warm in his embrace. I rest the side of my face against my arm and close my eyes, dismissing the emotions that have jumbled inside me.

It's the middle of the night. He almost froze to death. Of course I'm out of sorts.

It's not as if it means anything—or as if it even could.

The next time I wake up, sunlight is beaming through the walls of the tent and Rheave is stepping over me to push outside. As I rub my bleary eyes, Casimir takes the opportunity to scoot closer to me.

"Did you have a nice snuggle with your new friend?" he asks in a teasing voice.

I elbow him lightly. "Oh, hush. He's still figuring out what's normal."

The courtesan guides my mouth to his to claim the sort of kiss Rheave attempted to last night. Then he nips the crook of my jaw. "You were very sweet with him. He deserves the patience. I think he adds a little something to our group that we all benefit from."

Before I can decide whether to debate the issue, Stavros's voice carries from outside. "Rise and shine! Let's not waste the daylight."

We scramble out and gulp down the hasty breakfast that the former general passes around. Alek grabs the canteens to refill them at the stream we stopped near, as has become his self-appointed duty, and Casimir and I pack up the tent and blankets. After several days of trekking, we fulfill our roles with brisk efficiency.

When I go to saddle Toast, he snorts as if he's personally offended by the wintry weather.

"Just be glad it isn't snowing yet," I tell my cantankerous steed.

Apparently I spoke too soon, because a few fat flakes drift down as we set off. Stavros grimaces at them and leads us even deeper into the woods.

We've stayed off the roads for the past couple of days now that we're close to Eppun. We wouldn't want to run into the Order of the Wild's forces or the king's marching to confront them.

We set a swift pace through the trees, marking time by the ringing of distant town bells. We've heard two when the forest thins up ahead.

Stavros motions for us to dismount. We slink the rest of the way through the woods to a small rise that blocks all view of what's ahead.

At the former general's direction, we crouch low to creep up the slope and peer over the top.

On the far side of the hill and perhaps a mile to our right, a road cuts through the fields of browned grass. A wooden post juts from the earth along its course, and a couple of men stand on either side of it.

At the sight of them, Rheave goes utterly still.

"Those are daimon," he says with total certainty. "I can feel it even from here. What are they doing?"

Stavros's mouth forms a grim smile. "Guarding the territory their masters have claimed, I assume. That post marks the border of Eppun."

"We made it," I murmur.

And now the truly hard part of our mission begins.

# SEVENTEEN

Stavros paces in front of the tent. "I can't simply sit here while the rest of you do all the work."

"You're not sitting," I point out helpfully. "And I'm sure we'll find plenty to keep you busy once we know what we're doing. But when we're simply going into the town to wander around and get the lay of the land, you'd stick out like a sore thumb. You're too recognizable."

Stavros growls, but he knows I'm right. It's doubtful that the conspirators know or care that the king wants our heads on a platter… which actually works against us with them.

If anyone from the Order of the Wild recognizes one of his former top generals, they'll assume Stavros is here under King Konram's orders, to stop them.

Alek touches my arm where he's come up beside me. "Just be careful. We don't know what exactly to expect here in Nikodi."

He's hanging back at our campsite too, for similar reasons. If any word has gotten around about the supposed traitors harboring a riven sorcerer, showing his scars or his mask will make him easy to identify.

We're only going on a scouting mission, after all. The point is to blend in and gather information, not to make any big moves.

I give Alek a quick kiss. "We should be fine. There's no reason for anyone to find us suspicious. And this is Julita's home territory—we have her to guide us too."

My ghostly passenger pipes up from the back of my head. *That's right. I'll keep you on the right track.*

Her attempt at a perky tone doesn't entirely work. Apprehension winds through it.

We're heading to her family's estate first. We have no idea what we'll find there, but I've gathered that she finds it hard to believe that her parents would have been won over by the Order of the Wild.

Which means the scourge sorcerers have likely taken over by force.

I offer Stavros a kiss for good measure, which he accepts with another disgruntled growl but plenty of heat in return. When I draw back, he studies Casimir and Rheave for a second, with less hesitation than he used to show the daimon-man.

Casimir picks up on the worry he's not expressing. "We'll make sure Ivy comes back in one piece."

Rheave draws his well-muscled form up straighter. "No one will get past us to harm her."

"Hey, I might be the one who ends up defending the two of you," I retort lightly.

A shadow crosses Stavros's expression before he seems to will it away. He keeps his tone even. "Better not to turn to your magic unless you have to, while you're still getting the hang of balancing the effects."

I smile even though my stomach knots at his cautioning. "Agreed." I pat my pocket where I've stashed my enchanted locket. "Signal us if any trouble finds you."

Stavros nods and turns to Alek. "I suppose we should keep working on those knife skills of yours. I'll whip you into shape eventually."

Alek groans, but he gets out his dagger without further protest.

I wink at him. "Draw a little blood for me."

As Stavros snorts in amusement, I haul myself onto Toast's back. Casimir, Rheave, and I set off at a trot.

The ride to bring us within sight of the county of Nikodi's seat of authority takes about two hours. We pass it in silence and brief moments of hushed conversation, scanning the countryside as we go.

With each passing mile, my gut twists tighter. We don't really know what to expect up ahead. I've spent years picking up information from the streets of Florian, making my way through both the grittiest and poshest neighborhoods without drawing attention, but I've never had to navigate a violent uprising before.

I've got much more practice at subterfuge than any of my men, though. I have to keep them safe —both here and on a broader scale.

If we can't find a way to clear our names and prove ourselves to King Konram, they'll spend the rest of their lives like I've spent most of mine, just a couple of steps shy of the gallows. All because they've stood by me.

Julita alerts me to our arrival with a strained noise. *There's the house. You can see the roof over the top of that rise.*

I slow Toast to a walk and peer into the distance. She's right—just over the top of the rolling fields ahead of us, I make out a few peaks of a tiled roof.

"That's your family's manor house?" I ask her in a low voice.

*Yes. I suppose we should approach more cautiously from here. Once you reach the top of the next slope, you'll be able to see the whole estate and the city of Pima to the left.*

I pass her suggestion on to the men and dismount. We leave the horses grazing lower down the rise and sneak to the higher ground on foot.

As soon as the house below comes into clearer view, I drop lower to the ground, setting my gloved hands in the frosty grass. The men follow suit. Our breaths puff out of us like smoke in the chilly winter air.

The building Julita grew up in is much broader and more sprawling than the noble homes I'm familiar with from Florian. Which makes sense, given that the nobles in the capital are restrained by being packed together in the city's inner wards.

The house below me looks as if it might have started as something more compact. The central structure around the main doors is symmetrical enough, looming three stories to a stout tower. But over the centuries various counts and countesses built the sides and back out with additional rooms until it became a bit of a mishmash of stone-block forms.

Julita lets out a ragged sigh without adding any words. It's been months since she was last home.

Now she'll never really be able to enter that building again, not as herself at least. I can't imagine how that feels.

I might have left my own family home, but there was nothing for me there anymore. And I *could* return if I really wanted to.

Julita lost the choice.

My gaze veers to the stretch of smaller rooftops to the left. A handful of tall structures—a few temples, what might be the city's main hall—jut up amid single and two-story buildings.

Compared to Florian, it's hard to call that habitation a city. It can't be more than a tenth of the size of the capital.

Julita did tell me once that all of Nikodi had maybe a quarter of the citizens Florian can boast.

Casimir makes a soft sound in his throat that draws my attention. I jerk my gaze back to the estate.

A couple of men have emerged from the orchard around the back of the property and are walking next to the low wall that surrounds the grounds. As I watch, another figure—a woman dressed in a simple jacket and trousers under her cloak like the men—walks out of the house toward the front gate.

They don't look like nobles even of Julita's backwater level. But they move with a menacing assurance I'm not used to seeing from household staff.

*We usually only had one man on watch,* Julita murmurs. *And he'd have been wearing a proper uniform.* The nervousness in her voice has grown.

I glance toward my companions. "Julita says her estate normally wouldn't have had so many people patrolling. Those could be people associated with the Order of the Wild."

Rheave is staring intently at the figures. His expression darkens with a frown. "They're all daimon."

Even though I was already assuming they weren't regular staff, my stomach drops. "All three of them?"

He gives a subtle nod. "In the conjured bodies."

Julita's presence shivers in the back of my head. *The scourge sorcerers have taken over my home.*

"We'll figure it out," I say in the quieter tone I use so the men know I'm talking to her rather than them. Then I raise my voice slightly to include Casimir and Rheave as well. "They could have her parents and members of the actual staff imprisoned inside, under watch. Or have driven them out. Or there's a chance the household is collaborating, whether truly willingly or only under duress."

Casimir is frowning too. "I suppose we can hardly go over and ask."

Julita sucks in a breath. *I hope they're all right. We might not have seen eye to eye on everything, but... they tried. They gave me opportunities even though Borys was the main heir.*

She was hoping to inherit the estate as countess at some point after she finished her education at the college. With her older brother going missing a few years back and presumed dead, it should have been possible.

But now the scourge sorcerers have upended not just her life but the rest of her family's as well.

"We'll figure it out," I say again. "What do you think we should do now?"

She pauses for a moment in thought. *It seems unwise to approach the estate. We'd draw too much attention and likely not get any answers regardless. Let's go into Pima and see what's happening in the city.*

I pass on the idea to the men, and we creep back to our horses. As we turn them toward the road into the city, an air of gloom has descended over even Casimir's gorgeous face.

We have a story prepared, but none of the people who observe us riding into the city bother to stop us, let alone demand to know why we're there. Rheave murmurs that a few of those hanging around at the outskirts are daimon.

I guess that others keeping watch are human members of the Order of the Wild. Either scourge sorcerers or ordinary civilians who've become wrapped up in their claims of restoring Silana to its former glory.

Merchants are still coming into the city with wagons of goods; shops and eateries are open; pedestrians circulate on the streets. But a thread of tension winds through the atmosphere, as if everyone is periodically looking over their shoulder to check for threats.

I know the impression isn't just in my head when Julita comments on it too. *It feels like life as usual… but not quite. Everyone's just a bit keyed up.*

Nikodi sits at the northern end of Eppun province, its farthest border rubbing shoulders with Bryfeen, so I doubt there've been any direct clashes with the royal army here. But obviously the effects of the revolt have rippled through the county.

As we tie our horses at one of the city's hitching posts so we can mingle with the townspeople, a sharp voice carries over the softer hum of everyday conversation. "King Konram and his court have bullied us for too long! Everyone should stand up for Silana and embrace the ways the All-Giver intended us to live!"

A woman with a cluster of followers is standing on a crate at one corner of a nearby square. She hands out pamphlets to everyone who passes nearby.

I pick up one that's been dropped on the street and restrain a grimace. The Order of the Wild has taken one of the old myths about Creaden supporting the first kings of the realms and twisted it to make it sound as if even the godlen of rulership would support their cause.

The very fact that there are no soldiers or local law enforcement around to shut down the woman's hostility toward the Crown shows how thoroughly the scourge sorcerers have taken over. I shudder to think what they've done to anyone who tried to stand up to them.

Julita's voice stays subdued as she takes all this in through me. *There was a pub around this end of town that the staff often talked about visiting. The Silver Stag. I went there a couple of times myself. It's possible we'll spot someone I know who'll talk to us there… I think if we take a right at that cross-street…*

We follow her directions through a few turns to a pub on the corner that's bustling with lunchtime business. Rheave's eyes light up as he watches the conjured illusion of a stag leap from one end of the sign to the other and back again.

When we slip past the door into a room smelling of fresh-baked bread and fried dumplings, almost all of the closely packed tables are full. So are the seats along the varnished bar where some people are having a more liquid sort of lunch.

I ease between the tables as if looking for someone I meant to meet, letting my gaze sweep over the patrons. None of their faces mean anything to me, but toward the back of the space, Julita gasps in excitement.

*There's Hanie! The woman alone at the small booth on the back wall—in the olive-green dress with the brassy hair. She's the head maidservant at our estate. Always making sure the newer maids were looking after my clothes and hair properly and keeping our rooms clean.*

I pause to study the woman Julita indicated from the corner of my eye. She's hunched over a bowl, her gaze flicking toward the rest of the room between bites.

If she was in Julita's house when the uprising reached Nikodi, she must have escaped it. She looks as if she's afraid her association with the county's rulers will be found out.

At the very least, I don't think she's comfortable with the shift in authority in the city.

*Go on,* Julita urges. *Talk to her. Tell her you're a friend of mine and see what she knows.*

I duck my head close to the men to tell them what's going on, and they follow me over to Hanie's table. When I reach her, she stiffens with one hand raised partway to her mouth and the other braced against the bowl of stew.

"Are you Hanie?" I ask, because technically I shouldn't know her for sure on sight.

The woman eyes me warily, lowering her spoon into the bowl. "That's my name. Can I help you?"

"I hope so. We're friends of Julita's. She told us who to look for… Would you mind if we join you so we can talk more discreetly?"

Hanie's eyes widen. She dips her head in agreement, tugging a strand of her brass-brown hair behind her ear as Casimir and I squeeze into the seat across from her. Rheave shifts position to block us from view from most of the rest of the room.

"Has Julita come back to Nikodi?" the maidservant asks in a hushed voice that betrays a mix of excitement and worry. As far as I can tell, she still cares about the family she worked for.

No one in Nikodi will have any idea what happened to the daughter of their count and countess. The story passed around the royal college is that Julita made a hasty departure for home, but I doubt anyone's bothered to check whether she completed that journey yet.

As far as anyone here knows, she's still studying away in Florian, not murdered and buried in an unmarked grave with her spirit stuck in someone else's body.

I shake my head. "She couldn't leave Florian yet, but she's been upset after hearing what's been happening here. It was easier for us to make the trip. We promised her we'd do whatever we can to help."

Hanie's gaze drops to her bowl, her expression morose. "I'm not sure there's much helping to be done. The past two weeks... It's been a nightmare."

Well, she definitely doesn't support the uprising. Good to have that confirmed.

Casimir's mouth twists in sympathy. He speaks up in the gentle voice that could soothe a thunderstorm. "We've had some dealings with the people behind this 'Order of the Wild' back in Florian. We've been able to prevent them from carrying out some of their worst plans."

"I think we can do the same here," I add. "We just need a better idea of what exactly they've been doing."

Hanie's shoulders come down a little. She glances around the room again and drops her voice even lower. "They stormed Julita's estate first—and the local Watch building. I heard all the soldiers in the fort farther south were slaughtered too. Since then, the Order people have mostly been talking about how they're going to put a 'real' king on the throne and pave the way for the All-Giver to return. And coming down on anyone who questions them."

I wince. "Have you seen any odd-looking figures with them? People who've made an unsettling number of sacrifices, or covered up so you can't even see their faces?"

"Knowing where they're gathering to make plans or keeping supplies would also be useful," Casimir puts in.

Hanie's expression turns distant with thought. She brings her knuckle to her lips. "I've noticed a few things around town... I try not to get too close. You'll need to be careful. Anyone who's pushed back at all forcefully, they just disappear."

I swallow thickly. "We won't be blatant about it. But someone has to stand up to them before they do any more damage."

Julita squirms at the back of my skull. *What about my parents? She said the scourge sorcerers stormed the estate—what's happened to everyone else?*

I can't blame her for wanting those answers while she has the chance to get them.

I drag in a ragged breath. "And if you can tell us, so we can send word back to Julita—where are her parents now? Are they being held in the house?"

Hanie's face pales. I brace myself for the worst.

Her voice falls to a mere whisper. "They're gone. The brigands—they dragged them out of their beds and cut their throats."

Julita lets out a wail that resonates through my head. I close my eyes for a second, grieving her loss alongside her.

How much more blood is going to be spilled before we can stop these psychopaths for good?

# EIGHTEEN

The Petal's Pleasure brothel is one of the subtler establishments dedicated to the carnal arts I've observed in my time, at least from the outside.

That isn't to say it's outright discreet. The owner commissioned an illusionist to conjure an image of a woman's manicured hand stroking along the letters on the sign, and Ardone's sigil is clearly carved on either side of the business name. But the face of the building is painted a modest ivory, dulled in patches to light gray, with no additional decoration. The dark red curtains covering the windows obscure all hint of what goes on within.

What's going on right now may be more than indulgences in bodily pleasures. Julita's former maidservant mentioned that she's seen some of the more authoritative Order of the Wild members coming and going from this place regularly.

It could be they're simply looking to scratch an itch. But considering that the conspirators in Florian used at least one brothel to hide their sacrificial accomplices, we felt it was worth investigating.

And my observations from the past two days have only increased my certainty that Petal's Pleasure figures into the scourge sorcerers' plans in some significant way. Whenever the man who runs the place steps out in one of his elegant but slightly tatty suits, I can see the stress he's under in everything from his furtive swipes at his face to the stiffness in his slim frame.

Something is making him nervous. From the looks of his business, he's been in the trade for decades, so I doubt he's having misgivings about the official services he offers.

And when a few of the men and women we've identified as important members of the local Order stopped by last night, they came and went with attitudes much more resolute than leisurely.

So, we're taking a gamble, and we'll see if we can chip away at a little of the scourge sorcerers' power in Pima.

For a second, the thought of the uprising that's spread across the entire province squeezes my lungs. I'm used to dealing with people one-on-one, tending to their concerns with a personal touch.

I never expected to find myself tackling a horde of traitors with brutal magic.

My hands clench where I'm standing down the street from the brothel. Dragging air into my lungs, I will them to relax.

A personal touch may be exactly what's needed here. Hanie questioned whether we'd be able to make a difference, but it doesn't need to be a matter of bowling the conspirators over all at once.

We can try to undermine them with a few small, swift jabs that might seem minor but will make an impact as the effects ripple through their organization. They've only had a couple of weeks to set down roots.

We have to do everything we can to cut those fledgling roots out from under them. All of us working together, no matter how far we are from our usual endeavors.

Gathering myself, I stroll over to the brothel through the thin late-afternoon light. I hold my chin high and my posture straight like the conspirators I watched enter the building yesterday.

The hinges give a faint squeak as I open the door. Warm air washes over me from the hall, thick with the scents of vanilla, jasmine, and roses.

A narrow, cushioned bench sits just inside the hall. A curtain sections the front area off from the rest of the house. Sultry music and a burst of feminine laughter carry from beyond it.

Only moments after I've stepped inside, the slim man appears at the doorway of the one room on this side of the curtain, which I assume is his office. He looks me over with a calculating smile. "What can I do for you, sir? It's early—there are plenty of options."

I keep my answering smile reserved enough to hide the gem teeth in the back of my mouth that would give away my own status as a courtesan. "Actually, I'm here to do something for you."

As I speak, I nudge my gift toward him. A tingle spreads through my gums where I sacrificed the eight teeth to Ardone, and a rush of images and sensations floods my head.

Ah. Conveniently, what I can do that would make this man happiest is exactly what I came hoping to do.

His brow has started to furrow. I go on before he can question me. "You have something here that belongs to the Order of the Wild. We need to relocate them. I'll be taking them off your hands. You will, of course, receive the rest of your due compensation."

Relief flashes across the man's face before he can hide it. He bobs his head with the eagerness he's trying to suppress and motions for me to follow him. "I'm glad I could be of service to those who celebrate the All-Giver."

But he's even more glad not to have the responsibility hanging over him anymore. From the twinge of revulsion I caught in the gift-brought stream of impressions, I suspect he's caught at least a glimpse of what his unexpected lodgers look like under their shrouds.

I don't think he wants to know what the Order of the Wild plans to do with these mutilated people.

The brothel owner leads me down a flight of stairs at the back of the building, where the perfume smell gives way to dust and a trace of mildew. He unlocks the door to the right of the stairs and motions me toward the room beyond without stepping into it himself. His stance has already tensed.

Oh, he's definitely unnerved by what he's seen of the scourge sorcerers' sacrificial accomplices.

Keeping my expression mild, I cross the threshold into the dim space.

The room has no windows and barely any furniture. Four cots stand along the walls, a small table between them with plates still scattered with scraps of food.

Without arms to hold their food or eyes to see it, do the sacrificial accomplices simply lower their mouths to the plates and eat like animals? Have my supposed colleagues ordered the brothel owner to assist with their meals?

The shrouded figures look eerie even beneath the dove-gray cloth that conceals most of their mutilations. It's obvious to the eye that the fabric falls too smoothly across their heads, too narrowly along their bodies, where they've given up so much for whatever gifts they received that the scourge sorcerers are now exploiting.

I've been taught to see the beauty in every scar life can leave behind... but there's nothing beautiful about sacrifices made through manipulation. The scourge sorcerers cajoled these people into carving themselves up when they were mere children of twelve, with promises of divine glory.

That knowledge tells me how I need to cajole them myself without any need for my own gift.

The four of them turn their heads toward me where they're perched on their cots. They won't be able to see me, but even without the outer shells of their ears, they'll still be able to hear.

"It's time for you to contribute to our cause," I say, speaking steadily despite the twisting of my gut. "You can serve our purpose in an incredible way tonight."

"Of course!" one of the shrouded figures says in a slurred voice, lurching to his feet.

The woman beside him bows her head. "We welcome the chance."

They all stand except the one figure whose shroud falls unevenly across his knees. He's missing the lower part of one leg, only the stub of a crude wooden prosthetic protruding from beneath.

I touch his arm so he knows I'm there and help him leverage himself upright. He sways but catches his balance.

"Our wagon will have drawn up right out front," I tell the brothel owner. "Thank you for your own contribution."

He trails behind us as we form a wobbly procession up the stairs and back down the hall. Without arms, the sacrificial accomplices sway even walking straight ahead.

I stay in the lead to guide them with my footsteps, watching to ensure there's nothing to trip them up. With every rasp of breath they emit and every hitching motion, horror swells inside me.

Do the scourge sorcerers tell themselves what they're doing isn't a crime because they haven't killed the people whose sacrifices they use to boost their power? Because it seems to me they've traded the brief cruelty of murder for a lifetime of torture.

I reach the door first and lean out to make a swift signal. Down the street, Rheave taps the horses to draw the wagon we commandeered from an abandoned farm in front of the brothel. The canvas arching over the cargo area will hide the accomplices we're stealing from view.

As I guide the shrouded figures out of the brothel, the canvas flaps at the back of the wagon part. Alek holds one side open while I usher the four figures inside.

He wanted to join us for this venture, but not out in the open while we travel through the city streets. The makeup I painted over his scars isn't a perfect cover.

He shoots me a quick, tight smile of welcome. Neither of us are happy about the state of the people we've come to free, but we're glad we can free them at all.

Even if I'm taking the lead role in this operation, I couldn't pull it off without both him and the daimon who's become such a devoted ally.

Once the sacrificial accomplices are settled on the benches within, I close and tie the flaps. Alek's even voice filters through the canvas as I come around to the driver's seat. "I want to make sure we position you properly for the best impact. What are each of your gifts?"

I pull myself onto the seat beside Rheave, who takes that as his cue to set the horses trotting forward. The brothel owner has already disappeared back inside his establishment, no doubt thinking, "Good riddance."

I pitch my voice low to murmur to the daimon. "We should keep a conservative pace until we leave the city so we don't draw suspicion. Once we're on the open road, we'll push the horses harder. We don't want to take so long that the accomplices start to worry."

Rheave tips his head in agreement, his expression calmly intent. He's really the perfect comrade for a bit of subterfuge like this—he's so unaffected by human insecurities that he doesn't have any nerves to hide.

I wasn't totally sure at first how he'd fit in to the dynamic that's formed between the four of us. Ivy, Alek, Stavros, and I have been through so much at the college before Rheave quite literally barged in. But somehow he manages to be both fanciful and steady when we could use more of both to bolster our spirits.

I sink back in my seat, letting my own nerves settle. It should be smooth going from here. Hanie vouched for a cleric at a temple of Prospira that's about an hour outside the city. We'll go there and surrender the sacrificial accomplices to his care.

Alek wanted to talk to the cleric too—something about investigating records about the Great Retribution. I'm not sure where he hopes that line of inquiry will lead him, but I trust the scholar knows what he's doing.

And now the scourge sorcerers will have four fewer victims to exploit to enforce their rule. All the brothel owner will be able to tell them is that one of their own came to—

"Hey, you there! Halt a moment."

A burly man with a sword at his hip steps into the street ahead of us, holding up his hands. My pulse hiccups.

We've only made it a few blocks from the brothel. Did someone realize what we're up to?

From the man's swaggering stride toward us, he's either a member of the Order of the Wild enforcing their will around the city or one of the locals doing the same to win the Order's favor. His imperious gaze sweeps over us.

"What's your business in Pima?" he demands. "I don't recognize either of you."

Probably a local, then, and one whose head has swelled with his newfound authority.

I keep my stance relaxed. "We came through town to do a little business. We're making the trip back to Valk now."

I pick a Nikodian town that's farther from the border rather than closer in the hopes that'll deflect any worries that we're involved with the king's forces. All I get in return is a frown.

The guard takes on a haughtier tone, ambling past the horses. "I hope your business supports our goals. Have you pitched in anything toward seeing a proper king on the throne?"

"We do what we can. What the All-Giver would want from us."

He pauses next to me and squints at Rheave. "Your business partner is awfully quiet."

Rheave peers at him in his unflappable way. "Is there something you wanted to ask me?"

His detached tone appears to raise the guard's suspicions. He glances at the rest of the wagon. "Maybe I should take a look at what goods you're peddling."

Gods smite us. I grope for the right words to temper his authoritative ego, but nothing comes to me.

I don't know what he really wants. But I do have a way to find out.

I inhale deeply, my teeth setting tight against each other. I wouldn't normally use my gift twice in such close succession—I'm not totally sure it'll work.

As I aim my attention more intently at the guard, pain splinters through my forehead. It condenses into a throbbing ache at the sides of my skull.

I keep casting out my gift through the pain. The impressions that reach me come in filmier fragments than usual, but I think I grasp enough emotion and ambition—and a single name—to piece together an answer.

Now I know what would make him happiest… and I'm going to do the opposite.

I set my hand on the seat beside me to offset the dizzying headache and raise my voice just slightly. "You're one of Artor's fellows, aren't you? He did say you were getting a bit big for your britches."

The guard jerks around, his shoulders going rigid and his face flushing. "You know Artor? He talked about me?"

I know from the glimpse I caught that Artor is someone who's given this man orders, who he desperately wants to impress.

I manage to nod despite the throbbing in my head. "Oh, yes. We've known each other since we were little. I told him it's impressive what you all have coordinated here, but he's concerned some have come on board to puff themselves up with bullying rather than to see that the gods' purpose is fulfilled."

The guard blinks, and most of the arrogance deflates out of him. He averts his gaze with a scowl. "I was only trying to do my job."

"I'm sorry if we gave you any reason for suspicion," I say in an arch tone that's more chiding than apologetic.

My heart doesn't stop thudding until he waves his arm for us to continue. "I didn't know you had those kind of ties here. Go on now."

"Thank you," Rheave says in a tone that's a little more chipper than the situation calls for, but to my relief, the guard doesn't shout after us as the horses clop onward.

I tip my head into my hand, rubbing my temple as the ache slowly wanes.

Rheave glances over at me. "Are you all right? You used your magic on him, didn't you? But I thought it was a regular gift—it shouldn't hurt you like Ivy's does."

I manage to give him a crooked grin. "It only does if I push it harder than is wise. As long as I don't try to peek inside anyone else's head today, I'll be fine."

He hums to himself, though I'm not sure if he fully understands what I'm saying. How can a being practically made of magic comprehend the kind of gifts we humans sacrifice for?

He turns to glance at the canvas covering behind us as if he can see through it. When he faces the road again, his face has turned solemn. "You got the people the sorcerers are using for extra magic?"

"Four of them."

He knits his brow. "It isn't any of them."

I shoot him a puzzled look. "What isn't?"

"The one who helped make my body—and the one who helped control it. Neither of them are in the wagon. Those two are still out there, making more like me."

# Nineteen

I'm not sure whether I like the "apartment" Ivy's new friend found for us to stay in better than camping.

It is much bigger than the tent: two attached rooms, one with enough space for a table and set of chairs as well as a wood-burning stove that helps warm us, the other empty other than the blankets we've laid down to form beds. The walls hold in the heat better than the tent's canvas, so my fingers and ears don't get tingly and numb.

But there's only one small window overlooking the street. It's impossible to tell that anyone's coming up the stairs to the second-floor hall until you hear the boards creak, and equally impossible to know which of the three apartments they're going to unless they knock on the door.

We only have one way to flee if danger arrives, and it'll probably have to be right through the danger.

I understand we need to be in the city so we can make our plans effectively. The people who trapped so many of my kind need to be stopped.

But I miss the wide-open space of the forests and fields we kept to on our journey here. My spirit is used to roaming.

I don't think Ivy's friend likes being in this room either, at least not with me. Since we've been squeezed around the table, discussing our next steps to disrupt the scourge sorcerers, she's been shooting little frowns my way.

She didn't know I wasn't exactly human until the others told her, but I don't see why it should matter. Especially when it means I can be useful.

Because the main thing we've been talking about is how I can use the energy I seem to be able to generate to create a disturbance.

"What would be the best target for Rheave's daimon magic?" Ivy says, rubbing her chin as she studies a map of the city that Alek and Casimir were able to obtain. We've marked the known sites of major Order of the Wild activity on it.

Stavros folds his real hand over his prosthetic as he leans his elbows against the side of the table. "His energy appears to burn very quickly. We could destroy supplies they're relying on."

I consider the materials that I've observed humans require most often. "Food?"

Hanie jumps in with another of those quick frowns and a hasty protest. "If you mess with their stores of food, they'll just take from the rest of us."

"What about weapons?" Alek suggests, rubbing the edge of his mask. He put it back on when he heard Hanie would be coming to this meeting, although I don't know why he feels he needs to hide his interesting face from someone who's supposed to be our friend. "They aren't going to win many battles if they haven't got the tools to fight with. I'd bet Rheave could damage even swords and daggers."

I imagine the crackly energy that can flow out of me searing through metal blades and leather-wrapped handles. A grin springs to my lips. "Yes, I could muddle them!"

Ivy turns to Hanie. "Have you seen any place where the Order seems to be stashing that kind of equipment?"

The local woman shakes her head. She gestures to one area of the map where several buildings are marked. "They're mostly operating out of that neighborhood. I'd imagine any stores of supplies they've built up are somewhere in there. I don't—I don't want to risk wandering around too close without any real reason to be there, or they might assume I'm spying."

Casimir touches her arm. "It's all right. We can scope out the situation. You've helped a great deal already."

Ivy smiles at him as if she's the one he was speaking kindly to. Like he's done a wonderful thing.

If I can burn up a bunch of swords and shields, will she smile at me that way?

It's not that she never aims any smiles my way at all. But they always look a little... uncertain compared to how she is with the other men.

She helped me snap out of the spell the scourge sorcerers had me under. She led me to freedom.

I can't shake the feeling that I haven't done even half as much for her yet. But I want to.

I also want her to touch my face again like she did when I was out in the cold night. That was a special kind of warmth like nothing else I've felt.

But I don't have any wish to frighten her again like I did that time.

It's a complicated desire.

"We could ride through on the horses to take a look," I suggest. "Then we'd be able to leave quickly if anyone acts suspicious."

Ivy hums. "I think it'd be better if I sneak around and don't let anyone see me at all. It shouldn't take very long to figure out their operations."

Stavros turns to me. "You haven't seen any signs that they're producing clay bodies in the city?"

"No," I have to admit. "It was a big space where I first woke up. I'm not sure there would be room in a city."

"Well, that was a long shot anyway. Even if the production is happening in Eppun, Nikodi is only a sixth of the province's territory, and Pima a fraction of that."

The big man sighs and shifts backward in his chair. "We can continue monitoring the few other brothels in the city and watching for shrouded figures in general. The more accomplices we displace, the less power they'll have to maintain their authority."

Casimir nods. "The cleric we brought the others to said he'd be happy to take in more. He was horrified by what's been done to them. With Prospira's influence, we can hope he'll be able to help them grow beyond the near-slavery the scourge sorcerers consigned them to."

Alek clears his throat. "I should mention—my conversation with him was somewhat fruitful. It sounds as though there may be detailed records on certain aspects of the Great Retribution at a temple of Jurnus a few hours east of here. I think fully understanding how the godlen dealt with the original scourge sorcerers could be essential to challenging them now. I'd like to take a day or two to visit and go through the accounts, since I haven't been needed for much here so far."

Worry clouds Ivy's bright blue eyes. "You'd go alone? That doesn't seem safe."

"Who could you spare to come with me?" he asks, his normally flat tone softening the way it often does when he's talking to her. "This is the best way I can contribute. The scourge sorcerers won't be searching for solitary scholars on the road. They're watching out for armies."

His logic makes perfect sense, but Ivy's brow stays furrowed. She reaches across the table to squeeze his hand.

Another pang of that uncomfortable emotion hits me in the chest.

I don't think she'd look at me like *that* either. If I offered to go on a quest by myself, would she try to convince me to stay for my safety?

I wouldn't, though. I don't even like it when we're apart within this city, even though I can see why sometimes it's necessary to carry out our mission.

Everyone starts to get up from the table. Stavros tips his head toward Alek. "Let me go over some self-defense techniques for when you're on horseback, just in case. So our lady can worry a little less."

"Yes, you do that," Ivy mutters, but the look she gives the big man is undeniably fond too.

I nudge back my chair and push to my feet, still fascinated by the sensation of moving through physical space: the air shifting against my skin, the recalibrating of my center of gravity. I went through my entire past existence totally unaware—

A force wrenches through me like a rake hooking its prongs around my insides. As I stumble backward, bumping into my chair, a command that's as much felt as heard reverberates through my nerves.

*Come here,* the call says. *Come to me. Now!*

I have only a vague sense of where the magical command is directing me to go, but my body lurches around before I can get a grip on it. The chair clatters over on its side.

Ivy's voice reaches me as if from a distance. "Rheave? What's the matter?"

Then Alek's: "It might be the scourge sorcerers trying to regain control. They did it before. Remember what we talked about, Rheave!"

And then Hanie, panicked: "The sorcerers can still make him do things?"

I try to focus on Alek's words. Remember what we talked about—the advice he gave me back at the Haven.

Focus on all the ways this body is mine now. All the things I can make it do.

I try to stomp my feet against the floor so the impact will reverberate through them, but I nearly trip over them instead. A flare of my own panic crackles through me.

I can't let them manipulate me. I can't let them make me hurt anyone.

I can't let them kill me.

My hands flail out. One smacks into the wall; the other swings toward the table.

In my urgency, the energy I can call forth courses up my arm as if it can anchor me to the furniture. A bright streak sears across the wood, blackening the surface in an instant.

Hanie yelps. Stavros charges toward me, but Ivy darts in front of me first.

She grabs my face between her hands, turning my head so her face fills my field of vision. All I can see is her bright blue eyes, her skin turned even milkier than usual, her pale orange hair billowing around her.

"Rheave," she says. "You're staying with us. You don't belong to them anymore. You can fight them off."

I find myself swaying toward her even as the command yanks at me again. As if she's a tether holding me in place.

No, I don't belong to them anymore. I belong to myself—and to this woman who's always cared even when I couldn't do the same in return.

I set my hands against her forearms to help solidify the connection between us. From somewhere beyond her, I'm vaguely aware of Hanie saying, "I've really got to get going," and scampering out the door.

Ivy doesn't break eye contact with me. "Better?"

"Yes." Then I shudder with another magical tug. The rake prongs are digging in with little points of pain.

That's another sensation I never experienced as a pure daimon. Pain is fascinating but also unpleasant—especially when I know that the purpose of this specific discomfort is to break my will.

"Come here." Ivy guides me into the sleeping room and closes the door, putting one more barrier between me and the sorcerers attempting to repossess me.

"If you need any help…" Casimir calls after us.

"I think I've got this." Ivy slides her hands down to my shoulders. "Deep breaths. Feel your feet on the floor. Feel my hands squeezing you. You're here. They can't take you away."

I inhale and exhale, abruptly conscious of the act my body performs so automatically most of the time. It's easy to hone my attention in on the feel of her fingers against my shoulders, pressing through the fabric of my shirt.

She didn't want me to get *too* close to her that night she brought me in from the cold, but every particle of my being resonates with the need to get as close as I can. It's a demand loud enough to drown out most of the sorcerers' call.

I step closer and wrap my arms right around her. Ivy's breath hitches with surprise, but then she hugs me back.

"It's okay. You can stay right here with me, as long as you want to."

I'll always want to. I know that right down to the core of my being. With every word she says, every gesture she makes, every second I spend observing her, I know that wherever she ends up is the only place I want to be.

I don't know how to say that to her in a way she'll understand or accept. I turn my head and brush my lips against her cheek like she let me the other night.

A softer sound escapes Ivy, one that sends a very different jolt to the mostly useless appendage between my legs. A strange heat creeps over my skin, but she's already easing back.

She gives my arm one last pat and smiles at me—her usual cautious smile, not the one I want. "It's good to have you back with us. You just keep shutting the scourge sorcerers out. Practice those techniques even when they're not badgering you, and you'll be better prepared when they do. At least, that's helped with my magic."

"Thank you," I say, the heat from before prickling into a flush of shame. I'm supposed to be protecting *her*, and now she's had to do it for me again.

But the worst knowledge niggles at me as we walk back into the other room.

She grounded me. She drowned out my former masters' call.

What will happen if they yank at me that hard again—or harder—when Ivy isn't around?

# Twenty

*Ivy*

Tucked into the shadows of the narrow alley, I point at a boxy wooden building a few storefronts down the street. "They're hoarding all kinds of weaponry and armor inside that inn. It doesn't seem to be operating as a proper business anymore."

The two men beside me study the structure in pensive silence.

Rheave knits his brow. "Why do they want to keep all of it together? Don't the Order of the Wild people need to use the equipment?"

I shrug, doing my best to ignore the sense of dread that's crept up inside me since I started monitoring the scourge sorcerers' activities here. "They haven't had any battles nearby so far. I'd imagine they're either gathering equipment in case the army pushes this far into the province, or they're planning on sending cartloads of it on to the front lines as it's needed."

Julita's presence gives the impression of a wince. *I don't like either of those options.*

Neither do I.

I'm about to suggest that we should set our own plan in motion when a horse-drawn carriage pulls up right outside the inn.

For a second, I think I've been mistaken, that the place is still receiving guests. But no one gets out of the carriage. While the driver waits with a bored expression, a couple of men emerge from the inn carrying crates that they stuff into the vehicle.

Casimir keeps his voice low. "It looks like they might already be moving some of their stash around."

I match his tone. "Maybe things didn't go as well as the Order would like us to believe in their clashes with the royal army over the past couple of days."

Several news callers have taken to the streets announcing victories against army squadrons the king has sent to try to stomp out the uprising. The conspirators passed around free ale and had minstrels playing in a celebration last night that was noisy enough to interrupt my sleep until well past midnight.

I'd certainly like to believe they're actually being squashed like they deserve. Taking them down all by ourselves is an awfully big undertaking.

I lean as close as I dare to the mouth of the alley and prick my ears. The men bring out a few final boxes, and one of them stops to pat the horse's flank.

"A bunch of us will be following in just a few days," he says. "Make sure everything's organized for the march to start."

The driver nods and prods the horse into motion. I draw farther back into the shadows as the carriage rattles by.

"It sounds like they're going to be moving people too," Rheave remarks once the carriage is out of sight.

I nod. "To march to the border of the province? They might have lost a lot of manpower on the front lines."

Casimir pauses, a frown shadowing his face. "Something about the way he talked makes me think it might be bigger than that."

*Gods, don't tell me this situation can get even worse,* Julita mutters.

I let out a shaky breath and square my shoulders. "Well, whatever they're planning, it'll be harder with significantly less weaponry. Are you clear on your part, Rheave?"

The daimon-man meets my eyes with an eager light in his. "Yes, I'm ready! I'll ruin everything in there that I can. I'm getting better at adjusting how much power I pour out."

He gives his fingers a subtle snap in demonstration, and a tiny spark jumps from them to tickle my neck. It sends a deeper shiver right down the middle of me that I refuse to acknowledge, but a little of my tension ebbs.

I smile at him. "All right. Give me a moment to cast the magic to conceal you. Casimir will tell you when it's safe."

I sit down on the grubby alley floor, taking the position of my training sessions with Sulla. It's easier for me to concentrate on directing my magic in the now-familiar pose.

As Casimir takes my place at the mouth of the alley where he's going to keep watch, I fix my gaze on Rheave. I take in his stunning face and muscular form—and imagine the dwindling daylight passing straight through him.

My power vibrates through my chest, sensing that I'm about to call on it. An image of Stavros's concerned expression when we confirmed our tactics floats up with it, but I push that away.

He trusts me to extend my magic this far. What am I even doing here if I don't bring the most useful skill I have to bear?

Although I can't help thinking that as much as my men like to compare me to Signy, the exalted Veldunian hero didn't need to sneak around in shadowed alleys or tap into illicit magic to get things done.

I close my eyes against all those distractions, holding the image of Rheave fading away in the front of my mind. I focus the rest of my attention on the consequence I'd like to counter-act the spell.

Up on the rooftop above my head, light will bounce off empty air as if the form of a man is standing on the shingles. If anyone happened to be up there, they might see a mirage of Rheave.

I let my weight sink into the ground to steady myself and slowly open up. My magic unfurls from my chest toward the targets I've pictured.

A choked sound escapes Casimir's lips. "It's working. I can barely—now I can't see him at all. Rheave, you should go, quickly. We don't want Ivy to strain herself."

My magic races after the daimon-man as he hurries down the road. A nervous jitter shoots through my veins at the sensation.

I haven't expended quite this much energy in a sustained way… ever.

As long as I keep focusing the backlash somewhere it won't hurt anyone or reveal our trick, it should be fine. I know what I'm doing.

It's *my* power, and it's going to obey me.

Casimir eases back and crouches behind me. He sets his hands on my shoulders. "I'm right here with you, Kindness. If you need grounding, you can focus on me."

The tenderness in his voice does help me stay centered in the midst of the magic flowing through me. I breathe in and out, channeling the power through me from the broken soul this man doesn't shy from.

As if from a much farther distance, a hiss and a warble of flames reaches my ears. Rheave's spent a lot of the past couple of days testing out his powers, and he thought he might be able to create the right sort of sparks to set the building outright on fire. It sounds as if he's succeeded.

Casimir shifts his weight with a soft rasp of his shoes against the ground and a gentle pressure on my shoulders. Shouts reverberate from the direction of the building.

My magic prickles through my flesh, contracting into me as Rheave lopes to rejoin us. The second his feet thud into the alley, I yank all of my power back inside with a gasp of breath.

As my eyes pop open, the daimon-man solidifies into view in front of me. He's grinning wide, his eerie eyes sparkling. "I burned up everything I could—I even melted some of the metal."

Casimir straightens up and tugs his arm. "Wonderful. Now let's get out of here before they start searching the whole street for the culprits."

The courtesan holds out his hand to yank me to my feet as well. We dash down the alley the way we arrived, wind around the back of a few buildings, and emerge into a public square.

Most of the civilians we hustle out to join are peering over the rooftops. I spin to see smoke billowing up from the burning building, tainting the deep blue of the early evening sky.

Julita lets out a wordless crow of victory. *Ha! They'll be starting to see they can't get away with their degeneracy.* I get the impression she's spun around in my head with excitement. *You were amazing, Ivy. It's incredible what you can do now that you know how to work with your magic.*

I chuckle under my breath, not able to fully share her enthusiasm. Like when I pulled the shadows over us on the side of the road, the effort has left me a little dizzy.

I'm not sure I could do much more than this and stay focused.

But it is pretty incredible that I was able to help even as much as I did. I kept Rheave hidden so he could attack the scourge sorcerers in ways I wouldn't dare to attempt with my own magic yet.

We gape at the smoke for a minute like the other bystanders, just to fit in. Then Casimir tucks his hand around my elbow with a careful tug. "We should probably—"

His voice cuts off as we turn and find a cluster of five men and women closing in on us, their gazes unnervingly intense.

Rheave pushes in front of me in an instant, his hands rising defensively. I grab his sleeve to hold him back, though my stance has tensed.

The man at the front of the group holds up his own hands in a gesture of surrender. "We're not with... *them*. We just want to talk."

The woman next to him folds her arms over her chest beneath her long cloak. "And it seems we have a lot to talk about."

Julita's presence stirs uneasily. *Hmm. Rather presumptuous, aren't they? I don't know any of this bunch.*

Casimir puts on his best innocent expression. "I'm sorry, but I'm afraid I'm not sure what you mean."

With a scoffing sound, the man rakes his hand through his scruffy black hair. He drops his voice lower. "We know you three hit their temporary armory. We were right there—because *we* were planning on trashing the place as well as we could. You beat us to the punch."

The woman jerks her head toward a quieter corner of the square with a swish of her sandy-blond ponytail. "So can we have this conversation somewhere it's less likely to get us killed?"

Apprehension prickles over me, but the group hasn't made any aggressive moves, even though they've got us outnumbered. The cautious twitch of their gazes reminds me more of our own wariness than the cocky air most of the Order members and allies give off.

If there are other people in the city willing to strike out at the scourge sorcerers, shouldn't we find out what they can tell us? It's not as if Julita's said anything concerning about them—she won't have known most of the city commoners, I'd imagine.

Rheave keeps his protective pose, but Casimir seems to agree with me. "We'll come. But we want to stay somewhere we can easily leave if we feel the need to."

The woman laughs, making the scar across her cheek jump. "The sentiment is mutual. Come on."

The group tramps over to a side-street and then down it to an open-ended road by a stable no one appears to be attending to at the moment.

The three who haven't spoken so far spread out as if to watch for unwelcome interruptions. The man dips his knobby chin to us. "Since you trusted us enough to come along, we can do the first introductions. I'm Emor, and this is Voleska. We've been trying to figure out a way to get these Order of the Wild pricks out of our city since they first showed up."

Voleska studies us. "You aren't from Pima. I'd have noticed you before."

I'm not ready to give her our names yet, but I'll acknowledge that point. "We were in the capital when the palace there was attacked. When we heard about the uprising in Eppun, we came to see what we could do to help before the situation gets even worse."

Emor hums and glances over his shoulder toward the smoke still wafting up toward the sky. "You've made a decent start of it, I'll give you that."

"What have you been doing?" Rheave asks. "You have gifts—can you use those?"

He nods to the obvious signs of their dedication sacrifices: Emor is missing a little finger and Voleska her left thumb.

It's not generally considered polite to prod people about their gifts, but I can't help being glad Rheave didn't know that—because I'd like the answer too.

Emor doesn't show any sign of being offended. He rubs the stump of his missing finger. "Unfortunately, mine isn't good for much other than ensuring our people have decent meals."

He glances at Voleska a little awkwardly, but she simply shrugs. "I didn't receive a gift, and fairly so. I was a lot more selfish at twelve than I've learned to be since."

*Yikes,* Julita murmurs.

Rheave's eyes widen. I don't know if he was aware that not every sacrifice is recognized by the godlen it's made to.

I suppress a shudder at the thought of losing a whole thumb for nothing, but Voleska spoke without rancor. I guess a situation like that would make you rethink a lot of things about your life.

The daimon-man cocks his head. "So you want our help because we can do more than you can."

I give his arm a light swat to try to tell him to ease up on the attitude, but Casimir speaks before I can. "Our friend might not be the politest of gentlemen, but he does raise our main concern. Why did you approach us? It'll be easier for us to decide how to respond if we know where this conversation is going."

Voleska clicks her tongue. "Straight to the point. Fine. You *are* clearly working with some impressive gifts. But we have the local connections. We could accomplish a lot more if we combined forces and tackled these assholes together."

Julita lets out a skeptical sound. *I don't know. This bunch seems awfully… rough around the edges.*

I restrain a snort. The small apartment Hanie found for us to squat in didn't come with a mirror —my ghostly passenger has no concept of how scruffy I must look at this point.

Rough around the edges could be exactly what we need.

But we still have to be careful about it.

I raise an eyebrow. "We've gotten by all right without extra connections. What could yours tell us that we don't already know?"

Emor smirks. "I'm sure you've heard all the victory celebrations, but did you know that one of the king's magical advisors, a fellow named Lothar, has come with the latest troops to try to negotiate with the Order?"

Lothar—the royal advisor Stavros said specializes in potions… and hunting down riven sorcerers. The one who sacrificed an entire arm for whatever his gift is.

Has the king sent him to try to learn more about the scourge sorcerers' illicit magic?

A chill ripples down my spine. "I didn't know that, but how does it help us?"

"It shows how ineffective the royal army's been," Voleska says in a sneering tone. "Sending all these soldiers out here, and they either get cut down or have to retreat. At this rate, they'll negotiate the whole province away just to save the rest of the country. We have to do something big."

"That's right." Emor rubs his hands together. "And because we've lived here our whole lives, we also know the best ways to appeal to our neighbors. We just don't have the power to speak to them without getting dragged off and tossed in a ditch. We need to show the people of Pima that someone *can* get the upper hand over the Order of the Wild."

Voleska jumps back in with a triumphant smile. "*And* we know that the Order is planning some big meeting tomorrow morning. That'll give us the perfect opportunity to make a stir when there are fewer of their stooges looking to bash dissenters' heads in."

I hadn't known about the meeting either. A flare of hope lights inside me.

Casimir slips his hand around mine with a light squeeze as if to say he'll stand with me. The subtle smile he shoots me suggests he's ready to trust this bunch at least a little farther.

I've thought so many times about how difficult it'll be for us to take on the scourge sorcerers alone. How can we dismiss any advantage that presents itself?

I let my lips curl with a small smile of my own. "I like the sound of that. Let us check with our companions, but maybe we can meet up later tonight and form a real plan."

# TWENTY-ONE

*Ivy*

I crouch on the ledge in the pre-dawn darkness, watching a devout cross the main temple room in the glow of the single, central lantern. He vanishes through the back doorway.

Like all towns and cities of decent size, Pima has one temple dedicated to the All-Giver and the nine lesser gods together. It's nowhere near as impressive as the Temple of the Crown in Florian, but the vaulted ceiling and the statues watching from the alcoves below me still set my nerves wobbling.

I'm about to steal Nikodi's greatest religious treasure from right under all the gods' noses. Or right over their noses, as the case may be.

Hopefully they'll feel the ends justify my means.

My ghostly passenger seems to be feeling similarly apprehensive.

Julita's presence shivers in the back of my head. *This is where I had my dedication ceremony and made my sacrifice to Creaden. I never thought I'd be back here just to pillage the place.*

I speak under my breath, so quietly no one other than the soul lodged in my head could possibly hear the words. "They'll get the artifact back afterward. I'd imagine Creaden would approve of you making sure your county isn't taken over by questionable leadership."

Julita makes a skeptical sound, but she doesn't argue as I creep along the narrow ledge toward the decorative shield mounted on the wall high above the floor. The aged wooden surface tells the story of its significance with its carvings.

Supposedly, many centuries ago, the neighboring country of Bryfeen tried to steal Nikodi and the other nearby counties away from Silana. As the legend goes, the locals weren't well-prepared enough to fight off the Bryfesh army on their own, and they were worried the royal forces wouldn't reach them in time.

So they prayed to the godlen of leadership and justice for help.

The current countess woke from a dream of Creaden to find she had a plan for securing Nikodi's freedom in her head—and this shield resting against her bedframe as a symbol of the godlen's support. She led her supporters to push back the Bryfesh soldiers and ensure the people of Nikodi got to choose who governed them.

From what Emor and Voleska told us and Julita confirmed, the people of Pima still avidly celebrate that long-ago triumph. They have a festival in honor of the countess every year, and people who feel oppressed by their circumstances come to the temple to pray both to the statue of Creaden and beneath the shield.

As a symbol to convince the citizens that they should resist the Order of the Wild's mutinous rule rather than bowing to them, you couldn't ask for much better. But it's a shame the artifact might end up damaged in the process.

The ledge takes me to just beneath the shield. Ever so carefully, I slide my fingers beneath the wooden surface and detach it from the hooks that hold it in place.

Thankfully, the leather arm strap must be periodically replaced or kept in good condition through magic. I slip it over my arm almost to my shoulder without any fear that it'll crumble.

Julita lets out a nervous giggle.

Keeping my own mouth clamped tight, I brace the shield against my back and slink along the railing to the main entrance. Then I pull out the canvas sack I brought and wrap it around the shield to hide my cargo.

With a deft leap, I land on the stone floor near the entrance with only a soft thud. I hurry out into the city without waiting to see if anyone will come to investigate the sound.

*Creaden forgive us*, Julita murmurs. I have the vague impression of her making the gesture of the divinities, as well as she can in her current state.

It's dark enough that I don't need to use my magic to conceal myself. Which I'm grateful for, since I'll need it later this morning. Sulla's warnings linger in the back of my mind.

I haven't felt any negative effects from the ways I've worked my power since leaving the Haven, but my attempts have been fairly minor. I'd like to keep it that way.

I dart through the streets to the café where I'm supposed to meet the others. The storefront is shuttered, but the door around back opens at my tug.

A small crowd is waiting for me in the room beyond. Stavros insisted on joining Casimir, Rheave, and me for this undertaking, since we're expecting to do at least a little fighting. I can't help being glad that Alek is off on his research trip so he won't be caught up in the violence too.

Near my men, Emor and Voleska stand in a cluster with a few of their associates. They turn to face me with eager expressions.

"You got it?" Voleska asks as she takes in the sack, her tone hushed.

I suspect the shield is pretty meaningful to her too, even if she's willing to use it for this gambit. When I nudge down the canvas fabric to reveal part of the wooden surface, she, Emor, and their companions go still with awe.

I nudge it toward them. "I don't know how long it'll be before the temple staff notice it's missing."

Emor hums dismissively, his attention still fixed on the shield with a reverent air. "To avoid creating a panic, they'll keep the disappearance quiet for at least the first few hours while they search. By then, we'll have already shown everyone why they *should* be panicking."

Finally, he tears his gaze away to consider me and my men. "We'll set up in the square at the ninth bell. Everyone's clear on what they're meant to be doing?"

We all nod. As far as the local rebels know, I have a gift for moving things with my mind, which covers both of the purposes they want from me. Once the expected chaos starts, the three men will join in, working on cutting down the scourge sorcerers' support.

If we can turn the tide here, maybe word will spread and more of the province's people will reject the Order of the Wild's claims.

Voleska pauses to peer at Rheave. "You'll help us identify these... daimon in conjured bodies? We don't want to hurt anyone who was simply duped by the traitors."

Her group took the news about what Rheave actually is—and how many others like him the scourge sorcerers are manipulating—with a certain amount of skepticism. But this is the perfect chance for us to free some of those captured daimon.

"I know them as soon as I see them," he assures her, and pats the quiver on his back. "I'll only shoot the captured daimon. I can guide the arrows well with the power I have. If my effort doesn't break their body, the arrows will show you which ones you should go after."

Emor raises his eyebrows. "What if you run out of arrows?"

It appears Rheave has already considered that possibility, because he answers without hesitation. "I'll send my power on its own. I don't want to burn anything too badly when there'll be a lot of people around, but I can char their hair as a signal."

He sets his fingers against the wall with a spurt of crackling energy. When he lifts his hand, a small scorch mark remains.

The rebels stare at it for a moment, Emor's shoulders stiffening. This is the first time they've seen his daimon powers in action.

"It's a good thing we have Rheave on our side," I remind them. "Otherwise we'd have no idea who the Order conjured out of clay."

Emor gives a rough laugh. "True, true. Well, we'd better wrangle some breakfast before we wage our little war." He tugs one of his companion's sleeves. "Come on, you can help me whip up some of my famous scrambled eggs."

Most of the rebels duck into the next room, which I guess is the café's kitchen. Voleska remains, crouching down to study the shield where she's propped it against the wall.

I move to the window, peering out into the faint dawn glow that's just touching the streets. Casimir starts helping Stavros with the false hand he's made to help him blend in—a leather glove partly stuffed to fill out the fingers, that they're hoping to fit over his metal prosthetic in disguise.

Rheave ambles over to join me. He gazes out into the back alley for a few moments before saying, "I wish we could give them the choice."

I glance over at him. "Who?"

"The other daimon. I'm sure some of them simply want to be free. That's all I wanted at first. But they're not getting the chance to really own these bodies if they'd like to experience this kind of life for a while."

My stomach twists. I hadn't thought of the situation like that. "If there was a way we could simply snap them out of the scourge sorcerers' control…"

Rheave aims a quiet smile at me that suddenly makes him look much older than his youthful looks suggest. "But there isn't. I know. And it's better for them to be free in their usual state than forced to do horrible things for the sorcerers. Once we've defeated the Order of the Wild, though, we should let the ones who are left decide what they'd prefer."

"Of course."

He lapses into an unusually pensive silence before turning his gaze more intently toward me. "You're sure this is a good plan, aren't you?"

"I wouldn't have agreed to it otherwise." I furrow my brow. "Why—do you think it isn't?"

The daimon-man shakes his head. "I don't know either way. It's only that… I realize that in the long time I was in this world before, I wasn't interacting with humans the same way I do now. I didn't fully understand what I saw happening between them. But there was an atmosphere around them sometimes… When they become angry, it's difficult to predict how they'll act. And anger seems to keep going and going until someone stops it."

*Hmm,* Julita says. *That's rather wise from a being who's only been semi-human for a few weeks.*

It is. I can't deny that he has a point.

Sometimes I forget that as young as Rheave can seem with his inexperience in the physical world, he really is much older than the rest of us. By human standards, I'd imagine his spirit self is nothing short of ancient.

"That's true," I say. "But sometimes you need to stir up that anger if you want to shake people out of complacency or fear. The important part is directing it at the right targets."

"People aren't that easy to direct when they're upset, are they?"

I grimace. "No. We'll do our best. We have to do *something*, and this seems like our best shot at making a significant difference quickly."

Rheave offers me a wider smile, with a gleam of affection in his eyes that makes my heart skip a beat. "Humans are always doing something. All that sense of purpose used to confuse me. Things didn't matter the same way to me before."

He hesitates and then pats my shoulder. "But now that I understand, I like it."

Something about his vocal appreciation makes my pulse wobble more—and a glow of hope light in my chest.

Yes, human beings are pretty amazing. They can create all kinds of horrors, but they can also fight with so much conviction to see those horrors overturned.

I don't ever want to forget that.

Emor's voice carries from the kitchen, calling us to breakfast. We eat standing along the counters, anticipation thrumming through the air. I barely taste the eggs, as good as I'm sure they are.

Casimir rubs my arm, pitching his voice so it's just for me. "Are you okay with everything you committed to?"

I let myself lean into his warmth briefly. "Yes. I really am getting a handle on things. It's... it's good to be able to help without constantly worrying about doing damage at the same time."

I glance down at the short sword he's wearing on his belt and then over at Stavros, who's drawn closer. "Are you two ready? It could be a mess."

Stavros smiles grimly. "All the better for us to get in there and thin the scourge sorcerers' numbers without being obvious about it. It's about time they realized they can't conquer Silana so easily."

Casimir touches the hilt of his sword. "I may not be anywhere near as experienced in combat as our general is, but I'll put what skills I do have to good use."

It makes my heart ache to think of this sweet man spilling blood for the cause, but I know there's no point in protesting. The scourge sorcerers set the tone with all the violence they've already carried out.

We all have to give this attempt everything we have. If it goes well, most of the beings we cut down won't die, only fly free of the bodies that caged them.

If it doesn't... I can't afford to worry about that right now.

# Twenty-Two

*Ivy*

All too soon, the peal of the eighth bell rings through the café. We double-check our equipment and prepare to split up into our positions.

I pause for long enough to kiss Stavros and then Casimir. "I'll find you in the crowd after the important bit is over."

Stavros clasps me tightly to him. "Stay safe before anything else. You're taking your own risks, and we'll take ours."

Rheave watches us in his quietly intent way. I go over and give his hand a squeeze because it feels wrong to leave him completely out. "I'll see you soon."

He bobs his head. "I'll fulfill my part of the plan as well as possible. For you."

We part ways just outside the café, making our journey to the square where our demonstration is going to take place by separate routes. The streets are already starting to bustle with people on foot and horses pulling carts.

At the square, I slip around a shop Voleska pointed out to me and hurry up the back staircase. From the second-floor window, I have an excellent view across the square—the most central and largest in Pima.

Dozens of people mill around across the cobblestones, going in and out of eateries and shops, stopping at the stalls set up here and there, lounging by the fountain. Water streams around the marble statue of Creaden in the center of the pool. The godlen peers down over the square from his high pedestal with an air of benevolent authority.

Finally, a nearby temple bell rings in nine brisk peals. I brace my hands against the window ledge, already picturing how I want to shape my magic.

Two figures leap across the fountain and scramble up the pedestal to the statue of Creaden. Bracing themselves on either side of the marble figure, Voleska drops the canvas from the shield as Emor pitches his voice to carry across the square.

His words resonate loudly enough that I hear them faintly through the window. "People of Nikodi, listen to us!"

That's my cue. I focus all my attention on the shield in Voleska's hands and loosen my hold on my power.

My magic ripples out of me and rushes toward the shield. As the force I'm propelling forward wraps around the wooden object, I picture a branch cracking on the old willow tree by the abandoned farm where we borrowed a wagon.

When I lift the shield into the air, the branch falls to the ground.

With the heft of my power, the shield floats above the statue's head where everyone in the square can see it. A flare of light conjured by one of the rebels' gifts washes over the civilians—and condenses on the shield to make it glow.

Every gaze in the square jerks toward the spectacle. Gasps and shouts rise up across the crowd.

Emor speaks quickly before the spectators can become overwhelmed with confusion. "My friends! We took Creaden's shield from the Temple of Divine Grace this morning—just before the Order of the Wild could ruin it. We heard them plotting to destroy this great symbol of our city because they don't like us having loyalty to anyone other than them."

A horrified hush sweeps through his audience. He jabs his hand in the air. "The Order says the king has a false claim on the throne, but they're trying to lay claim over us just like Bryfeen did all those ages ago. Why should we let them? They have no right. They're just as bad as the rulers they say they hate."

The murmurs that follow are fraught with tension. The crowd shifts, but no one seems to know quite what to do yet.

And then the moment Emor predicted arrives. One of the scourge sorcerers or a lackey pushes toward the fountain.

"You can't talk like that," he hollers. "We've freed you from a royal family that only wants to exploit you. Show some gratitude."

I wind my magic back into my body gradually, letting the shield sink toward Voleska.

As she raises her arms to catch it, Emor pivots toward the newcomer. "You expect gratitude when you want to exploit us just as much so *you* can be in charge? That sounds like an awful deal to me."

The instant Voleska grasps the shield, I yank back the rest of my magic and flick my gaze around the square. I can already spot a few more figures shoving their way toward the fountain from the edges of the crowd.

Julita lets out a soft chuckle. *Here they come.*

No doubt at least one conspirator has raced off to tattle to the head honchos at their meeting. Let them send as many of their forces as they like.

I don't think they're going to enjoy the outcome.

I whip my attention back to the fountain just as the first Order member reaches the base. He jumps up on the barrier around the water. "Come down from there and stop telling lies."

"Or you'll what?" Emor asks.

Voleska lowers the shield as if to defend the two of them—and I propel my magic in their direction once more.

This time I'm not aiming it at the shield. I fling the force into the conspirator, sending him lunging forward and wrenching up his hand as if he intends to strike out at them.

What he actually does is pound his fist against the shield hard enough for the sound of the impact to reverberate through the square.

Julita flinches inside me. I'm too caught up in the necessary concentration to apologize.

Off at that old farm, the backlash yanked the door off the dilapidated house at the same moment as I shoved the man on the fountain.

And the crowd erupts.

The angry shouts of the locals drown out anything else the Order member might have said. As he stumbles into the fountain water, the nearest civilians grab his arms and yank him away from the shield and the woman wielding it. He's swallowed into the churning crowd.

"Down with the Order of the Wild!" Emor yells from his perch on the statue. "Kick them out! Take back our city!"

More people stream into the square from the nearby streets and buildings. Many are locals coming to see what's happened, but others are clearly Order members.

I spot a man taking a swing at a couple of the conspirators, only for them to wrench his arms behind his back. A woman springs at them with a frying pan she bashes over the nearest conspirator's head.

As more fights break out in knots throughout the square, arrows start streaking down from the rooftop where Rheave hid himself. Shimmers of electric energy send them racing toward their targets.

Stavros and Casimir will be in the middle of the chaos along with Emor and Voleska's people, striking down every captured daimon Rheave identifies for them. And maybe a few of the fully human Order members as well, if they force the issue.

My main work is done. I can't leave them to the riskier battle alone.

I shove open the windowpane and clamber out. My gaze drops to the building fronts directly beneath me, and I freeze.

Hanie is standing just a few shops over from the one I'm staked out above, cringing against the wall with her arms folded tight around her middle. Her brass-brown hair has fallen across her face.

I bite back a curse.

*You told her not to come to the square this morning,* Julita mutters. *She's not a fighter—she shouldn't be here.*

I did warn Julita's old maidservant when I saw her briefly yesterday. I suggested she should stay clear of the central square all morning.

Apparently she was more curious than concerned.

She spins and darts away down one of the side streets. At least I don't have to worry about her getting trampled now.

I scramble to the edge of the roof. My gaze catches on Stavros's blood-red hair about halfway across the square, his head above the figures around him thanks to his massive frame. Casimir will have stuck near him.

Girding myself, I pick a section of clear ground and jump. As my feet hit the ground, I'm already braced to leap forward.

I weave through the rioting crowd, dodging jabbing elbows and grasping fingers. My gaze snags on a woman who's staggering with one of Rheave's arrows in her back, and I hurtle forward to slash my knife across her neck.

She collapses in a crash of shattering clay.

One fewer daimon the scourge sorcerers can send to attack us. Every one we set free is a victory.

A projectile sings through the air beside me, this one all daimon energy. It sizzles into the side of a man's head several paces off through the crowd.

The man flinches where he's trying to wrestle a thrashing woman to the ground. I push through the churning bodies toward him and stab my knife between his ribs straight into his heart.

Another mass of clay topples onto the cobblestones.

I whirl around, trying to regain my sense of where my allies are. At another glimpse of dark red hair, I hustle through the crowd.

When I get a clearer view of the two men, it takes me a moment to figure out what's going on. Casimir has drawn his sword, but he's mostly reaching out to people with his empty hand, guiding them past him.

Directing them to a nearby pub where they can escape the chaos if they want, I realize. Of course the courtesan would be more focused on making sure the innocents are safe than murdering the villains.

Stavros is just charging farther into the crowd to slam his sword through the torso of another man with a charred blotch where some of his hair should be. The conjured body collapses in a burst of clay shards.

I expect the former general to look my way so I can flash him a quick smile, but his stance abruptly stiffens. Without warning, he dashes off.

I try to follow, but a current of bodies pushes between us, jostling my scrawny form. Squeezing my way between the furious citizens, I hop up on my feet here and there to peer over their heads.

Over by one of the stores, a teenage boy cowers on the ground while a man kicks him and bashes at his head with the pommel of his dagger. If I had any question about which side they're each on, it'd be answered by the tattoo inked on the side of the man's neck: an inverted All-Giver sigil.

That's the symbol the scourge sorcerers use to try to call the Great God back to our realms.

Stavros lets out a roar of rage loud enough for me to hear it over the tumult of the crowd. He rams into the attacker and knocks the man off his feet.

In my next glimpse, their blades are clanging together. I grit my teeth and shove through the milling bodies with more force.

I stumble into the less-packed fringes of the crowd just in time to see Stavros dig his blade into the man's throat.

This body doesn't transform. It simply slumps, gushing blood.

And Stavros is so intent on finishing the man off, he hasn't noticed another attacker who crashes into *him* before I can even shout a warning.

My cry breaks from my lips, too late. Julita yelps like an echo of it.

I sprint over, my fingers tight around my knife. My heart hammers against my ribs.

My magic wrenches at me to unleash it, to let it fend off the attacker, but the impulse comes with a cold jab of fear. I didn't plan for that—I can't stop to concentrate on a counter-action—

The two men wrestle each other, blood splattering the cobblestones around them. I shove down my power and lunge forward with my blade raised.

Just before I can plunge my knife into the attacker's skull, Stavros heaves the man off him with a meaty rasp of his sword.

The man collapses, the short sword he was clutching clanging on the stones. Relief surges up inside me for just an instant before Stavros sags backward too.

Blood gushes from a cut on his side, drenching his tunic red.

My own blood freezes in my veins. A flood of terror and anguish sweeps every other thought from my mind.

"Stavros!" I cry, dropping down beside him.

No, gods, no. Not like this.

Not again.

What am I supposed to do to save him?

# TWENTY-THREE

Even as pain burns through my abdomen and blurs my sight more than usual, I can't help jerking my gaze toward the boy. The boy whose shaggy blond hair and freckled face make memories of another teenager swim up from the depths of my mind.

*Michas*, some part of me calls out, but this isn't my old friend. It isn't the boy I watched a riven sorcerer rip apart.

Still, a pang of happiness resonates through the pain when I see this other boy getting to his feet with no obvious injuries other than a scrape on his forehead and a reddish blotch on his cheek that'll probably bruise.

The shouts and cries of the riot have blurred too, my sense of the rest of my surroundings going increasingly hazy. The press of frantic fingers around my arm brings me back.

Ivy is staring down at me. Her blue eyes have gone so wide I could lose myself in them, but the wax-pale shade of her face sends a jolt of panic through my veins.

Is she hurt? Did the bastards—

I try to ask, but the pain searing through my abdomen seems to have stretched to my throat. All I manage to do is croak, "Ivy."

"I'm here," she says, her voice quavering, and the pain in my side sharpens. Her other hand is pressing against the worst spot—*fuck*, it hurts. "Do you think you can walk at all? There are more Order members coming—we have to get you out of the way—"

A rotund figure appears at the edge of my vision, standing over us. His voice comes out in a rough baritone. "He protected my son. I'll protect him, as well as I can." He motions to the boy. "Sebias, here, we need to get this man inside."

More hands grasp my shoulders, my thighs. As they heft me into the air, the blaze of agony knocks the breath from my lungs.

That fucking asshole ramming into me from out of nowhere—I should have been watching my surroundings more—first fucking rule of combat—

My back jars against a tiled floor. Ivy is babbling thank yous to the man whose shop we've intruded on.

"It's the least we could do," he says, sketching the gesture of the divinities with a shaky hand. "Take whatever you need to stop the bleeding. I don't know how else to help. Sebias, let's clean that scrape of yours."

Their footsteps shuffle away. Ivy's still here, leaning over me.

The pain clenches around my lungs, stabbing deeper as I haul in a breath.

"Stavros," Ivy says, sounding choked, "you're bleeding so much. It's deep. I don't think I can stop it like this."

She's so upset. Terrified. I've seen that emotion in her before, but this time she isn't afraid *of* me but *for* me.

We've come that far. I could laugh at the wonder of it, but I can barely suck enough air into my chest to grunt.

Ivy strokes her hand over my hair and cheek. Her fingers are shaking. "What do you want me to do?"

Something clicks in my head through the hazing of my thoughts. She's afraid of herself too. Of what she could do.

She's asking me if she should pour that fathomless, mad magic of hers into me.

My muscles tense automatically as if trying to shut out the very idea. Flickers of Michas's blood-splattered face, his screams, whirl through my head.

Riven magic always destroys in the end.

Great God help us, how bad must I look for her to even offer?

I part my lips and focus all my attention on forming my breath into words. "I—I'll be fine."

The last word fractures into a groan at a fresh wave of agony. A sob breaks from Ivy's throat.

We both know I'm lying. A chill is starting to seep through my limbs like nothing I've ever felt during any battlefield wound.

My own fear stirs.

I don't want to go like this. I'm not *done*.

Ivy bows her head close to mine, her voice falling to a raw whisper. "I promise I won't do anything you wouldn't want."

I stare up at her, her face hazing before my eyes. Sunlight gleams through the window behind her, glowing amber as it passes through her red-blond hair.

Like the golden halo artists give those god-blessed in their paintings and tapestries.

The glow seeps into me with a sudden, sharp clarity.

Ivy didn't destroy anything when she hid us in the forest or concealed Rheave to carry out our plans. No catastrophe rained down on us when she pulled off her tricks with the shield.

How did I not see it before? The power I'd normally revile passes through her... and she colors it with all her strength and compassion.

What she works isn't just riven magic. It's *hers*.

A strange sense of peace washes over me. Ivy has given me the choice, because that's who she is— the woman I believe in, the woman I love.

And I do believe in her, more than I hate the errant energies she can channel through the cracks in her soul. This woman can take the vilest power in the world and transform it into a force for good.

In the sudden calm, my voice detaches from the pain. I hold Ivy's gaze as well as I can and force out the hoarse words. "I want... to live. Don't want... to leave you. Don't want... to fail the... kingdom. I trust you. Anything... you do... will be right."

Ivy's breath hitches. She leans so close her lips brush my forehead in a ghost of a kiss. "Are you sure?"

I can only manage one more word, but it contains everything I need to say. "Yes."

The pain is swelling again, eating at the edges of my consciousness. But Ivy makes a resolved sound low in her throat and clamps her hand tighter against my side.

Warmth bursts through my torso. It swallows the pain and the creeping numbness; it melts the agony gripping my lungs.

I gulp one full, hungry breath—and my mind spirals away into darkness.

Alek's voice penetrates my consciousness first, muffled as it passes through the wall. "Should we try to find a healer, just to look him over?"

Casimir answers in a softer voice I can't totally make out—something about not knowing who's with the Order.

I blink, my sense of my surroundings coming back to me. I'm sprawled on my back on one of the heaps of folded blankets that's served as a mattress in our temporary apartment. Another blanket is draped over me to my shoulders.

Memories of my last conscious moments rush in: the boy, the pain, Ivy's desperate questions...

Tentatively, I push myself into a sitting position. A faint twinge passes through my abdomen, but more like a bruise that's nearly finished healing than a fatal wound.

Ivy did that. Ivy poured her riven magic into me, and it fused the injured pieces back together.

No horror pierces me at the thought. Only bemusement at the irony that I've been fixed thanks to the part of her that's broken.

She wouldn't have done it if she wasn't sure she could control the consequences in a way I can accept.

She and the others must have carried me back to the apartment. And cleaned me up. My bloodied clothes are gone—I'm wearing my other woolen tunic and pair of trousers.

They left my harness on my left arm but removed the prosthetic, maybe so I didn't accidentally smack myself with the metal contraption in my sleep. It's lying on the floor within arm's reach, gleaming and untarnished as if they washed that up too.

The voices in the other room have fallen silent. Did my companions leave?

I'm about to get up and check when the door eases open. Ivy peeks inside.

Her face both brightens and tenses at the sight of me. "You're awake! How do you feel?"

"Impressively normal." I glance down at my side. "I'd almost think it was only a nightmare."

She lets out a rough laugh. "If only. Let me just—"

She slips away for a few seconds and returns with a steaming mug. When she hands it to me, a warm, meaty smell fills my nose—it's broth, both food and drink.

As I raise it to my lips and take a tentative sip, Ivy sits down next to me, leaving a small space between us as if she isn't sure how close I'd want her to get. She waits quietly while I fill my stomach with a few larger gulps.

"Are you sure you're okay?" she asks. "With... everything?"

From the wariness in her expression, it's obvious which part of everything she's specifically concerned about.

All at once, it hits me just how difficult that moment must have been for her too. Not just because of my past reactions to her magic, but because of how it would have reminded her of the one other time she brought someone she cared about back from the brink of death.

The only other time she's used her power to save a life, she lost an equally dear one... and the woman she saved turned on her for it.

An ache swells in my chest. I set down the mug and turn toward her, reaching to grasp her hand.

With the squeeze of my fingers, I hope I convey the truth of my next words. "I meant what I told you, Ivy. It doesn't matter what magic you used to heal me. What matters is you were the one doing it. I trust you."

She exhales a little raggedly. How long is it going to take before she fully believes that statement?

She twines her fingers with mine, but her head droops. "I keep thinking back to the moment when it happened. Maybe I could have reacted quickly enough to stop him from stabbing you in the first place, and then I wouldn't have needed to use any magic on you. But I hesitated—I didn't have time to think of where to aim the backlash— Even after the training and practice, I'm still scared."

I stroke my thumb over the back of her hand. "I think that's a good thing. The consequences of being cautious should be much less than the consequences of going too far. I'm glad you were there to save me from *my* carelessness."

I pause, but I know I need to ask this question. To find out who or what paid so that I could live. "What backlash came out of healing me?"

Ivy takes a deep breath. "I was going to focus on the tree I've been using on the abandoned farm. But then I glanced out the window and saw one of the daimon Rheave had marked with a burn. I figured it'd be safer using a target I could see, and something almost human, for an effect that big."

"It killed him?"

"He at least fainted from whatever injuries I passed on to him. I think one of Emor's people took care of the rest."

I let that knowledge settle. I can't even feel guilty about keeping my life at the expense of a conjured body that was more a prison than a living thing itself.

So Ivy shouldn't feel guilty either.

I pull her closer to me, hating the wariness I feel in her stance as she comes. As if there's still a small part, however deeply she managed to bury it, that's afraid I'll lash out at her for doing what was outright miraculous.

The ache deepens, wrapping around my heart.

I tuck her head against my shoulder and kiss her temple, enveloping her slim but strong frame in my arms. "Thank you. You found a way, just like I knew you would. Are *you* okay after using so much of your magic?"

Ivy nods against my shoulder. "I was pretty worn out after, but I got some rest too. You've been out for most of the day. Alek just got back from the temple."

The tension in her body gradually loosens as she nestles in my embrace. Every subtle sensation of her accepting the affection I'm only too happy to offer feels like a gift.

We haven't had many moments where we could just *be* with each other. Even more so with me than with the other two men who've claimed a spot in her life, because I had my head up my ass for too long while they saw her worth.

I tease my fingers under her chin to nudge it upward so I can brush my lips to hers. So I can show her that nothing at all has changed about any of the ways I adore her.

Ivy lets out a strained but hungry sound that sends a bolt of lust straight to my cock and kisses me back hard. She slings her arm across my shoulders and hugs me tightly.

When our mouths part, she keeps holding me close. "You were dying. When I saw all that blood… I don't know if I've ever been more scared."

Fear, horror, and relief at the ultimate outcome mingle in her voice.

A lump rises in my throat, but I manage to find the casual drawl that's served me in the past keeping spirits up in the midst of battle. "I'm sorry I worried you. I'll try my best not to let it happen again."

Another noise, half snort and half sob, escapes Ivy's mouth before she yanks me in for another kiss.

Gods above, I want her so much. Want to remind both of us of how alive I am thanks to her; want to celebrate that victory by worshipping the woman who made it possible.

As our mouths meld together again, I ease around to lay her on her back, bracing myself over her. When I stroke my fingers over her breast, Ivy hums eagerly.

I tear my mouth from hers to chart a path along her jaw and down the side of her neck. The feeling of having her beneath me, of her hands running down my chest over my tunic, sets off a throb of desire in my groin.

I nip her earlobe before murmuring into her ear. "I'm going to fulfill the promise I made. It's my turn to take you."

Ivy's shiver is all delight. "I guess you are feeling better."

"The only thing hurting me is that I'm not inside you already."

Her chuckle comes out breathless. "Then you'd better get on with it, hmm?"

She pries at my clothes as avidly as I tug off her dress. I toss the plain thing she deserves better than to the side and let her peel my tunic off me. But when my gaze returns to her, my hand stills on the hem of her chemise.

She's more wounded than I am. Fresh bruises mottle her upper arms as well as one standing out against the pale skin over her collarbone. There's a scratch that looks just scabbed over at her elbow and another on her thigh.

Ivy halts too, peering down at herself and then glancing at me with a wry but tight smile. "I don't look much like your noble ladies, I know."

Does she assume that's what I'm thinking? That I'd even care?

With a dismissive growl, I pin her down on the blankets again. "You're beautiful just as you are," I say, working her chemise slowly up her chest.

Ivy arches an eyebrow. "You don't need to say that. You've already got me half-undressed."

"I'm not saying it because I need to." I yank the chemise the rest of the way over her head. Then I drop my hand to her hip so I can undo the straps of her thigh sheaths and strip off the pants she's wearing as an underdress.

I want to see every delicious part of her.

"There's no woman I'd rather look at. I love this strength." I drop a kiss to her bicep. "I love how hard you fight." I brush my lips across a bruise. "I love all the cleverness and compassion in this pretty head of yours." One more kiss to her forehead.

When I ease back, Ivy stares at me for a moment as if startled.

"I love *you*," I add, in case I need to emphasize that specific fact.

The smile that lights up her face is bright enough to make my heart skip a beat. She trails her fingers along my jaw.

Her voice comes out soft but steady. "I love you too."

It's the first time she's said it. For a second I can't breathe, I'm so overwhelmed by the rush of emotion.

Then I'm tipping over her, capturing her mouth while I wrench her drawers off her, groaning in approval when she unbuttons the top of my trousers.

We've come this far. She trusts *me* enough to give me a piece of her heart.

As I kick my pants aside, my gaze catches on the gleam of metal by the wall. A flicker of memory passes through my head of the rasp of desire that colored her voice the first time we came together, when she told me she liked that part of me.

I grasp my prosthetic and twist it into the harness, watching Ivy. The flush that darkens her cheeks that suggests my gamble is a good one.

With past lovers, I've never worn any prosthetic except the wooden hand-shaped one. My former fiancé recoiled from even that.

But Ivy, as she pointed out, isn't like any woman I've been with before. None of them were quite what I needed.

I shift my position to Ivy's right and stroke the curved metal loop down the middle of her chest. Ivy licks her lips.

I grin at her. "I seem to remember that you enjoy me making use of both 'hands.'"

Her flush deepens, but she answers without hesitation. "I do."

"Then I'd like to see just how much you can enjoy it."

As I graze the edge of the prosthetic over the peak of one breast and then the other, a whimper works its way out of Ivy's throat. Her nipples stiffen at the contact.

I tease them a little more, gliding the metal back and forth and then rotating it in a tantalizing circle. Ivy's breath has gone shaky. At every eager noise that escapes her, my erection strains against my drawers.

Her reaction fuels my confidence. Eyeing her even more closely, I slide the prosthetic down over her belly to her sex.

As the tip of the loop brushes her clit, Ivy's hips cant upward. "Fuck, Stavros."

"Fuck? I can do that."

A giddy sensation spreads through my own chest as I dip the prosthetic over her folds and let the upper section press against her clit again. Ivy emits a mewling sound of need that has me painfully hard in an instant.

The loop is only about as wide as two broad fingers together. I think I could…

I turn my wrist and adjust the angle so I can push the curved tip right inside her.

Ivy gasps, tipping her head back against the blankets as she clutches my other wrist. "Gods, that's… I've never felt anything like that."

I guide it a little farther. "Good?"

"Strange, but so good." Her gaze darts to me, her blush darkening to outright red. "How much deeper can you go?"

I'll take that challenge.

I bend over to claim another kiss while easing the prosthetic up into her body bit by bit. Ivy shudders beneath me with the most delicious whimper.

No one else will ever make her feel quite like this. Seeing her quake with the pleasure, I can't feel the slightest regret for the sacrifice I no longer benefit from—at least not in the typical way.

The metal loop only hooks a couple of inches around, hardly allowing for a full sense of penetration. But as I adjust it between Ivy's legs, I realize it's perfectly shaped for the outer edge to rock against her clit while I pulse the tip within her.

Ivy bucks with the movements, ducking her head under my chin, clutching me as if she's afraid she'll spin away completely. My cock throbs, but I love seeing her lose herself too much to stop this yet.

Pumping faster earns me another shudder and a guttural moan. Ivy's fingers dig into my arm deep enough to hurt, but it's the most blissful sort of pain.

I feel her come with a ripple that spreads through her whole body. A choked cry escapes her, and her head sags back toward the blankets.

Even through her ecstatic daze, she gropes at my drawers. "I need the rest of you."

Gods be sure I'm not in any state to deny her.

I practically tear my drawers off and kneel between her legs, encompassing her with my much larger form. Ivy simply beams up at me, caressing my chest, tilting her hips to urge me on.

Trusting me with her body every bit as much as I trusted her with mine this morning.

Knowing how wet she is from her arousal shining on my prosthetic, I don't hold back quite as much as the first time. But I still grasp her hip and study her face as I slide into her slick channel.

Her sex grips my cock as if we were made for each other. I can't restrain a groan at the pleasure that spikes through my nerves as I push even deeper.

"So good," Ivy murmurs. "So fucking good."

I want to make it even better for her. I pull back and plunge into her again, and again, and again, flicking my gaze to get a better read of when the most pleasure floods her expression, easing her ass a little higher off the blankets.

I drive home again. Ivy's lips part around a cry.

And a ghost of an image wavers in my vision—her hand reaching for my face.

My pulse hiccups. Her hands are still braced against my chest.

Except—now she's lifting one to stroke her fingertips over my cheek and jaw.

Even through the carnal bliss of the moment, a different sort of exhilaration races through my veins.

My gift. I glimpsed an act before it happened. Only a few seconds before, and I wasn't trying—but I know what my magic looks like.

I was focused so intently on anticipating Ivy's needs that my gift must have activated somehow despite my damaged vision. I never knew that was even possible.

I never tried to use it in a situation like this before.

Or maybe it's just because of her. Because of Ivy and this love that makes my heart soar like nothing I've ever felt.

I dip my head to kiss Ivy's hand and ram into her swaying body even faster. Ivy keens, her fingers rising higher to grip my hair and tug me to her.

As I bow over her, our sweat-damp bodies sliding closer together, she trembles and clamps around my cock. Her fingernails scrape over my shoulder as she hits her second climax—and the force of her release drags me with her into a rush of the headiest pleasure.

A hoarse sound escapes me as I spill myself inside her. Ivy gives a gasping sort of laugh and clutches me even tighter.

Careful of the ridges of scarring on her back, I enfold her in my arms and roll us onto our sides so I can meld her body to mine without worrying that I'll crush her. Ivy tips her head against my chest with the most contented sigh I've ever heard.

I can't lose this woman. I simply can't.

We cuddle like that for several cozy minutes, until the cool air seeping through the walls starts to chill our skin. Ivy squirms even closer for just a moment before reaching for her clothes. "We should probably confirm to the others that you're alive. Although I suspect the walls are thin enough that they've already figured that out."

At the meaningful clearing of a throat from the other room, my face heats, but only a faint warmth.

There's nothing really to be embarrassed about here. We all know where we stand—and how much Ivy means to us.

We should still discuss our next steps in regards to the Order of the Wild. I don't even know what the results of the riot were.

I yank on my clothes and walk with Ivy into the outer room. Rheave glances over from where he's standing by the window with a nod of acknowledgment, his gaze trained on Ivy rather than me.

Casimir smiles where he's standing by the table. "It's good to see you up."

Alek pushes aside the book he was paging through and considers me with a furrowed brow. "Are you sure—"

The slam of the door being flung open cuts off his question. Four men burst into the room, swords drawn.

The man in the lead points his blade at me. "You're all under arrest!"

# TWENTY-FOUR

*Ivy*

At the sight of the blades flashing in the late-afternoon light, my body goes rigid. My men all whip around to face the intruders.

The burly guy at the front of the group said they were here to arrest us, but none of them wear any kind of uniform.

Rheave's expression twitches, and he points a finger at one of the men flanking the apparent leader.

I think he's saying that one's a daimon. These are Order of the Wild members, come to exert their ill-gotten authority over us.

How did they find us? How much do they know?

Stavros tucks his prosthetic slightly out of view, his posture drawing up with his full military authority. Every muscle in his massive frame is braced to spring into action.

In spite of the precarious situation we've found ourselves in, a pang of gratitude fills me at the sight of him so steady after his bloody collapse this morning.

I didn't know if I'd ever see him standing again.

"Arrested for what?" he demands.

My magic shudders through my chest in anticipation of their answer. I could tear straight through them all.

But how will I balance out those consequences? Uncertainty scatters my thoughts, which were already a bit dizzy from everything I pulled off this morning.

The lead Order member opens his mouth to speak, but he hesitates at the creak of the steps behind him. He and his colleagues ease to the side so two more intruders can push into the cramped room.

The first to enter is an even beefier man so vacant-eyed I'm expecting Rheave's gesture toward him before it happens. Then a tall figure strides in with a haughty, authoritarian air that has me tensing up before my eyes lock on his face.

Julita gasps, her presence flinching in the back of my skull. *It can't— Oh, gods help us. Ivy, that's Borys.*

My stance stiffens even more. Borys, her brother—the one who introduced my ghostly friend to scourge sorcery by making her the subject of his sadistic experiments as a child. The brother who vanished on his way to enter Sovereign College three years ago and who she'd hoped was dead.

As he considers us with his lips curling into a smirk, the resemblance jumps out at me. He has the same chestnut waves as the woman I first saw dying in an alley, just long enough to tuck behind his ears. The same porcelain complexion, though his features strike me as sharper than I think Julita's were.

"So," he says in an arch voice that's like a harder, masculine echo of Julita's typical sultry tone, "this is the company my little sister has been keeping lately, is it? It's a shame Julita couldn't be here herself."

If only he knew.

Julita chokes back what sounds like a wail, her presence twitching and trembling, rattling my thoughts even more. *Oh, no. Oh,* fuck. *We have to get out of here.*

I don't know how justified her terror is. She hasn't seen her brother in three years. It sounded as if he hadn't managed to harm her much once she came into her own gift three years before that and could force him to accept her refusals.

Is she simply in shock, or is he an even greater threat than I could anticipate?

My magic thrashes to be let out at him, but it's even harder to concentrate through my ghostly passenger's frantic babbling. I swallow hard and imagine a leafy vine wrapping densely around me to bolster my control.

Julita never told the men she allied with just how painfully Borys involved her in his dabbling, but they've heard enough. Anger flashes in Alek's eyes as he gets up from the table. Casimir's hands have clenched at his sides.

Stavros keeps his voice even, but a thread of menace winds through it. "What do you want?"

Borys draws the short sword at his hip and waggles it at the bunch of us. "I heard the little pipsqueak sent some people to nose around and interfere with our work. You sparked quite the riot this morning. You couldn't really think you'd get away with it."

Rheave, the least emotionally affected of us all, stares at him with a totally deadpan expression. "We don't know anything about that."

I might believe in his ignorance if I didn't know better. But it appears Borys knows better too.

Julita's brother lets out a dark chuckle. "Nice try. It really is too bad that Julita couldn't see this. Me, in charge of not just Nikodi but half the province as well. I've got too many more important matters to address to bother playing games with you lot."

He makes a brisk gesture toward his underlings. "Take them. Preferably alive, but dead will do too."

Julita yelps, the men lunge, and I latch my mind on to the image of that poor battered willow tree on the abandoned farm as tightly as I can.

I have to stop them. I *have* to.

My magic bursts out of me in a blasting force. It hurls the four closest men including Borys to either side, bashing their heads into the walls.

As the thump and crack of the impact resonates through the air, I have the sense of branches ripping off the distant tree. Nausea pools in my gut.

The men slump where they crash to the ground, a couple of them bleeding through their hair and so still they might be dead. Borys lets out a groan.

My mind whirls with a starker flash of panic. He's going to murder us all. He's going to stab his sword into me right now—

I sway with the wave of dizziness, my gaze catching on the sword in question. It's spun across the room away from Borys's hand.

Before I can pick apart my confusion, the other two Order members hurtle straight at me with their blades drawn.

As I start to grope for my focus and power, Rheave leaps into the way with a wordless snarl.

He slams his fist into the nearer man's belly with a sizzle of energy. A smoking hole sears deep into my attacker's guts.

As that man topples over with a bloody gurgle and shifts into a mass of clay, Stavros smacks his prosthetic against the final intruder's head.

The man reels toward Rheave, who doesn't so much as blink before wrenching the attacker's head around.

With a crack of the man's neck and a gristly hiss, the daimon tears the head right off the man's neck and flings it across the room.

Okay, then. I stare at Rheave and the blood splattered across his hands. The feral intensity in his stance sets off an unnervingly giddy shiver down the middle of me.

Then Stavros's urgent tug of my arm and another groan from Borys launch me into action.

Casimir snatches something from beyond the table. "Stav, your sword!"

The former general catches the thrown belt and sheath, and we rush out the door.

As we pound down the stairs to the ground level, Alek pulls at Rheave's cloak. "You did an incredible job protecting Ivy, but we can't have you seen like this. Wipe off your hands on the inside of your cloak and pull it close around you to hide your shirt."

Away from the battle, the daimon-man looks as disconcerted as I feel, but he follows Alek's orders. We barge out into the chilly air of the street.

I don't spot any other Order members close by, but a faint shout brings my head jerking around. I don't see any reason for concern farther down the street, though, and none of my men react.

"I think it's time we get some distance from Pima," Stavros says under his breath. "Let's grab the horses."

Sticking close together, we hustle along the street toward the public stable where Hanie arranged for us to keep our steeds. We veer sharply left at the first cross-road—and nearly bump into Julita's old maidservant herself.

Hanie jumps back where she was poised by the building on the corner. She gapes at us, her face blanching. "You're still— They didn't—"

My thoughts settle enough for one clear revelation to shine through the whirlwind. "She's the one who turned us in!"

We never told Emor and Voleska's group where we were staying. Hanie looked upset seeing the rioting start this morning, and she knew we were involved.

And she's clearly surprised that we haven't been arrested.

*What?* Julita cries. *Hanie gave us up?*

The maidservant backs up another step. "You're as dangerous as the Order of the Wild," she hisses, and raises her voice to a yell. "Help! Someone! There are traitors to the Order here!"

Stavros growls and moves to catch her arm, but Hanie bolts in the opposite direction. She dives through the nearest shop doorway.

Footsteps drum against the cobblestones from around the corner.

Alek waves us on. "We've got bigger problems than her!"

I spot a narrow alley a few buildings down and race toward it with a jab of my hand to direct the others. We dash into it and sprint past several buildings, emerge onto an unfamiliar street, and duck down another alley.

Near a stinking waste bin behind a tenement building, I pause to regain my wind. No sounds of pursuit have followed us this far.

Rheave glances over his shoulder, his brow knit. "All those angry people in the square made her afraid." He pauses, and his voice drops lower with a sorrowful note. "And so did I. So she blamed us."

I reach out to squeeze his arm through his cloak. "It's not your fault. You didn't do anything to her. We were trying to *help* her and everyone else in this city."

Casimir peers farther down the alley. "Do you think it's safe to go for the horses? Hanie knew where they were too. If Julita's brother has even half his wits, he'll have cut off our easiest means of escape."

I suck in a breath. I hadn't thought that far ahead. "You're right. Curse it all."

Stavros frowns and squares his shoulders. "We should get within view of the stable and take stock. She might not have mentioned that part."

And if the Order of the Wild has confiscated our steeds, we could always steal others. Although I'm not sure how the former general would feel about that kind of criminal activity.

We continue through the city, taking alleys and the quietest roads we can, until we can spot the front of the stable building from a couple of blocks away.

Alek tenses beside me. "They have it staked out."

They do. The scourge sorcerers are trying to be subtle about it, but you wouldn't normally see three figures with swords in hand just hanging around outside a stable.

The men and woman stroll a little this way and that, pretending to have a casual conversation, but their gazes dart furtively over the street at regular intervals.

My jaw clenches. The conspirators have ousted us from our latest sort-of home, and they've stolen our horses too.

I guess you could say we stole the horses from the royal college in the first place, but Toast at least was mine as far as he and I were concerned. No one else wanted him back at the college anyway.

Here's hoping he's kicked several ribcages in for their trouble.

We draw back out of view of the stable, clutching our cloaks tight around us and scanning our surroundings. Even though the daylight is fading, barely any of the nearby shops and eateries have lit lanterns to welcome customers. The front window of the restaurant we're standing outside is dark and unwelcoming. Only a few pedestrians other than us are walking the streets, and those with a hurried stride.

Stavros's vision may be faulty, but he reads the atmosphere quickly enough. "The locals are holing up after the riot, bracing for what the Order might do in retaliation. They know the conflict isn't over yet."

The conflict we kicked off. For their benefit, but it still seems horrible to run off now.

What choice do we have, though?

"What should we do?" Rheave asks, his normally luminescent eyes shadowed with worry.

Alek adjusts his stance, and I realize he's still clasping the book he was reading under his arm. He never let go of it when we made our hasty dash out of the apartment.

"We should be able to find some other place to 'hole up' ourselves," he suggests. "At least for long enough to get a sense of—"

Casimir makes a gesture to silence him, his gaze fixed across the street. "Someone's coming to us. I think—that's one of Emor and Voleska's people, isn't it?"

I jerk around, but I do recognize the face of the woman approaching.

When she sees we've noticed her, she lopes the rest of the way across the street, her expression fraught. "We were told to keep watch for you. Voleska caught word that the Order of the Wild was hunting down people with your descriptions. If you come with me, we'll see what we can do to help."

As the men and I exchange glances, Alek tugs his cloak's hood farther forward with a twist of his mouth. He must have left his mask behind at the apartment. No one but us has seen his uncovered face and its scars before.

But the woman doesn't show any sign of horror. Her gaze latches on to his face for a beat longer than the rest of us and then flicks back to me.

I haven't seen any reason to doubt our newer allies' loyalty. If this woman wanted to get us caught, she could have avoided our notice completely after seeing us and simply roused the nearest Order members.

Rheave fixes his intense gaze on her. "No one there is planning to hurt Ivy?"

The woman blinks as if startled by the question. "Of course not. You've all helped *us* pull off more than we expected to so quickly."

Stavros sets his hand on my shoulder protectively but makes the decision for all of us. "We'll come."

The woman leads us on another winding path through the city. She's clearly more familiar with the back ways than I am, understandably.

We end up behind the Bright Bloom Café where we met with Emor and Voleska before. The woman hustles us inside to where the two leaders of the local resistance are consulting with a couple of their comrades in urgent tones.

Voleska's face brightens at the sight of us, a sharp contrast to the hostile reception we got from the other woman we thought was our friend. She and Emor move to join us.

She glances at Alek first, with an expression that's more sympathy than anything else. Her people didn't have the chance to meet the scholar before, but I mentioned he'd likely be masked if they did. I guess now she can see why.

She bobs her head in greeting. "You must be Alek. I'm glad Bessa was able to find all of you together."

Emor studies us. "You all look well enough. Did Bessa reach you before the Order of the Wild people did? I assume she told you they're out to 'arrest' you."

I grimace. "We ran into a few of them, but we managed to get away." It seems wisest not to mention exactly how.

"They've taken our horses too, though," Casimir puts in.

Emor sighs. "I'm not sure you'd have gotten away safely even on horseback. Whatever the Order found out about you, they're not happy. We've gotten more reports since Voleska first sent people out to warn you. I'm sorry if we dragged you into a bigger mess than you were prepared for."

Stavros tips his head. "We knew the risks."

"What exactly are you hearing?" Alek asks, his head still low beneath his hood.

Voleska pipes up in a strained tone. "From what we've gathered, a fairly large bunch of the people with the Order are heading out of the city as if they've got something important to do elsewhere. But just about everyone they're leaving in Pima is under orders to focus on tracking the group of you down. They've already sent patrols around the surrounding countryside to keep watch there too."

My heart sinks. Are they pursuing us this avidly because Borys is giving the orders, and he particularly wants to crush anyone associated with his sister?

Julita seems to think so. She recovers from her stunned silence to simply say, *That treacherous prick.*

I hug myself. "We thought maybe if we laid low here for a little while, it might blow over…"

Voleska is shaking her head before I'm even finished speaking. "They're busting into people's homes and businesses, searching everywhere. I don't want to promise we could hide you when I'm not sure you'd be safe."

Emor steps in again. "I don't know if you'd be in a position to accomplish much more anywhere in Eppun at this point. They've sent messengers out—the Order members in other cities and towns may be on the lookout too. Frankly, you'd face an awful struggle just making your way out of the province back to the rest of Silana."

Stavros raises his eyebrows. "Well, we have to either stay or leave. It can't be neither."

"We had another thought." Voleska nods toward one of the men she was speaking with when we arrived. "There's a trade caravan heading out tonight for Bryfeen. It's only a few hours journey across open countryside, with plenty of ways you could be concealed, and then you'd be out of their reach."

I stare at her. "You want us to leave Silana completely?"

She holds up her hands in a gesture of surrender. "I don't *want* you to. I'd rather you could stay and keep chipping away at these assholes. But it might be the only way we can ensure you don't end up dead within the next few days, and we owe you that much. Within a week or two, we might have been able to sway more people across the province against them, or the king's forces might have taken back control."

Emor offers us an apologetic smile. "If you stay near the border, you can monitor the situation and come back when the pricks have been driven out."

The bottom of my stomach drops out. Is this really the best option we have? We meant to stop the scourge sorcerers, and instead we end up fleeing the country?

But am I really going to insist on staying and seeing the men who've committed themselves to this cause—to *me*—slaughtered because of my stubbornness?

Voleska clears her throat. "There is one condition." She gestures toward Rheave. "The offer doesn't include the daimon. We're concerned that the Order may find a way to trace his movements, and the caravan runner is nervous about his powers."

My body balks automatically. "We can't leave him behind."

But before I can protest further, Rheave hangs his head and then turns to me. Anguish contorts his beautiful face. "It's all right, Little Vine. I understand why people are nervous. I want to be with you making sure you're safe… but if the best way for you to be safe is for me to stay back, I'll stay and do my best from here."

The despondence in his voice wrenches at me. He thought it was his fault that Hanie betrayed us, and this situation is only going to drive that idea home.

If Voleska and the others knew what *my* real powers were, they'd be far more frightened of me than they are of him. It doesn't make any sense to punish him.

He's still got blood on his clothes from protecting me, and I'm supposed to leave him to be recaptured by the horrifying masters he escaped?

What are my other options, though?

*I don't know what would be best anymore*, Julita murmurs, echoing my uncertainty.

As I rub my temple, Stavros touches my back as if to steady me. "I don't want to leave anyone behind," he says quietly. "But times like this call for awful decisions. I'm not going to argue for one outcome over another. You have the most at stake. It's possible I'll be more useful to the royal family by learning what I can along the border—certainly I'll accomplish more that way than if the Order of the Wild does manage to get the upper hand on us."

If even he's willing to give up… I glance at Casimir and then Alek and find the courtesan and the scholar watching me, their faces set in similar expressions of supportive but pained resignation.

They'll go where I go, even if they don't like the idea any more than I do. Just like they have since King Konram first called for my execution.

The right thing to do would be to protect *them*, wouldn't it? To put their safety first, to slip away where the scourge sorcerers won't reach us.

And probably kiss our chances of getting a pardon goodbye, since we won't be instrumental in undermining the scourge sorcerers if we're not here. Will we really be able to return if we leave when the king is still calling us traitors?

That's what Stavros meant when he said I have the most at stake. Maybe they could reach an understanding with King Konram once all this is over, but there's not much short of stopping a civil war that would prove the riven sorcerer has the country's best interests at heart.

My magic squirms in my chest, wanting to defend me but not sure how.

I look down at myself, at the spot where Kosmel once branded me with a magical glow, at my hands that have directed more power in the past few weeks than I ever thought I'd allow myself to.

Though Emor and Voleska don't know what I'm really capable of, I do. An ordinary group of resisters might not be able to evade the Order of the Wild and continue weakening their attempted coup, but we aren't ordinary.

*I'm* not ordinary.

If I bring all my power to bear—carefully, thoughtfully—I can ensure the scourge sorcerers never touch so much as a hair on our heads. We can stand together—all of us, including the daimon who's fought just as hard—and finish the mission we came here for.

A twinge of anxiety shivers through my nerves, but not potent enough to shake the sense of resolve that's welled up inside me.

"No," I say. "We're going to keep fighting. I'm not letting the scourge sorcerers get the better of us. We've still got a few tricks up our sleeves."

# TWENTY-FIVE

*Ivy*

Even in the nook I've tucked myself into by the roof's looming dormer, the icy night wind tugs at my cloak and bites the skin I can't completely cover. I raise the fabric higher over my face to block out as much of the chill as possible.

*Things have been awfully quiet,* Julita remarks. *Maybe you should get some sleep.*

"We need to know where the scourge sorcerers are going and what they're up to," I whisper in reply. "I don't want to stay in Pima any longer than we have to—we're putting everyone else who's working to resist the Order of the Wild in danger."

Julita makes a noncommittal sound. She's been a little quieter than usual since our encounter with her brother this afternoon.

I peer down into the street where I've seen a lot of Order activity in the past—where I overheard the conspirators talking about sending arms ahead with manpower to follow.

No one's come by since I took up my post here an hour ago. The windows around me are dark. But I'm not quite ready to give up yet.

A sound like a snicker wavers up from somewhere to my right. My head snaps around, but I can't make out the source of it.

A jolt of fear shoots through my chest. I need to be prepared—if they find me—

Gritting my teeth, I close my eyes against the momentary panic.

No one's nearby. *I'm* going to find *them.*

And I need to stay calm and alert to do that.

When I scan the street again, there's still no movement. Maybe the sound was just the wind moving across one of the buildings in a strange way.

I adjust my position to ease the stiffening of my muscles and speak in the barest whisper. "How are you doing? It was obviously a pretty big shock, seeing your brother like that."

Julita shivers. *Perhaps I should have guessed he was involved. I don't know how he ended up collaborating with actual scourge sorcerers—he must have met this group before he ever left for school and used the trip as a cover to join them completely. Either that or it was a very unhappy accident.*

Unhappy for us. I don't get the impression Borys would see it as anything other than delightful.

"I'm sure it stirred up some bad memories," I venture.

*Oh, I've had to deal with all kinds of awful recollections since I first crossed paths with Wendos back at the college. I'm sorry I fell apart a little when he first turned up—there was so much going on at once... Now that I'm prepared, I can keep a better handle on my feelings.*

I offer her a small smile. "And it means you can help us even more. You've got to know him pretty well, so you can help us prepare too." I pause. "I assume he made some kind of dedication sacrifice to get a gift."

He wouldn't have any power for his attempts at scourge sorcery to enhance otherwise.

Julita lets out a pained hum. *Yes. Not a large sacrifice, since he wanted other people to pay most of the price for his ambitions. He gave up both of his smallest toes. Walked funny for a few months before he totally got used to the small change in balance.*

"What's his gift?"

*He was secretive about that. Always gave vague answers if anyone asked—and my parents weren't the type to insist. Obviously they were entirely too permissive.*

She sighs. *I know he dedicated to Creaden like I did, so it probably has something to do with bossing people around. He did enjoy doing that even before he made his dedication.*

I frown. "He never used his magic on you?"

*Not that I was aware of. It could have been a subtle effect. It wouldn't be anything all that showy for a couple of little toes. And once I got my gift and could force him to accept a "No," we barely interacted regardless.*

As horrifying as the circumstances that prompted her choice of gift were, I'm glad she had some defense.

With extra power from the sacrificial accomplices, who knows what Borys might be capable of? We don't know what kind of magic we need to watch out for from him.

Of course, it couldn't be clearer that we need to watch out for that asshole in every possible way regardless.

"We'll stop him too," I say quietly. "We stopped Wendos and Torstem, and we'll keep getting in their way until their whole horrible conspiracy falls apart."

Julita gives a huff. *It shouldn't all be on you. If King Konram could get his head on straight and his army doing their job... I wouldn't have blamed you if you'd run for cover, you know.*

I grimace. "I'm not sure I'd really be safe anywhere I go. At least here I'm working toward getting a pardon. Is there anything else about—"

I cut off my whispered question at the scrape of footsteps beneath us.

Two cloaked figures have just stepped into view farther down the street. They murmur something to each other and push inside a nearby building.

After a moment, lantern light flickers in one of the windows.

Finally, I can take action.

I clamber down the side of the building I was perched on, using every stealthy trick I know, and peer across the street at the doorway the two arrivals vanished through. I'll have to step into plain view to reach the shop.

Unless I use the magic trick I've already performed once with Rheave.

My heart no longer thumps quite so uneasily as I concentrate on the purpose I want my magic to fulfill. I've managed several spells like this—and at least one so much larger—and everything is still okay.

It could always have been okay, right from the start, if I'd known how to handle the demands of my broken soul properly.

I compel my power to wrap around me, fading my body from sight, while projecting the image of it on the rooftop I just left to balance out the effect. Then I slip across the street and tuck myself close to the glowing window.

Muffled voices filter through the glass. "…place isn't worth the bother now anyway. We'll set them right when it's time."

"It shouldn't be long now. I'm taking the last bunch along the Coliz-ward road to join the march tomorrow."

It's a man and a woman, neither of them familiar. They drop into a lower tone that fades into a warble.

I dare to press my ear right against the glass, concentrating as hard as I can without losing my grip on my magic.

The words come back into focus. "…sure they can actually pull this off?"

"Great God willing. I've seen how well the magic works when the blessed ones contribute."

The "blessed ones"? What does she mean by that?

The man must already know, because he doesn't question the phrase. "I guess once we're past the front lines, it'll be smooth traveling most of the rest of the way. No one will be looking for us there."

The woman lets out a raspy chuckle. "Exactly. We're going to slip right past the king's forces and hit him where he's hiding before he has any clue we're coming."

My pulse lurches at her claim—and my control wavers ever so slightly. Enough that just for an instant, I lose my sense of where I'm aiming the consequences of my magic.

Some sort of image must appear in a less discreet spot, because a yelp of surprise sounds from a second floor farther down the street. The conspirators I'm spying on whirl around with a thump of their feet.

Shit. Ducking low, I dash past their building and on into the maze of alleys around this part of town.

As soon as I've left the open street behind, I yank all my magic back inside me. Sweat has broken out on the back of my neck.

Was that a cough right behind me? I dive around a corner and freeze there, listening.

No further sound reaches my ears. I swipe at my face, both chilled and flushed, and hustle onward.

The scourge sorcerers have come up with a plan even more awful than I could have guessed. And if we don't get a move on, we'll miss our chance to stop them.

It's a good thing I didn't opt to flee to Bryfeen, or there'd be no one to sound the alarm at all.

When I get closer to the Bright Bloom Café where we've been hiding since the early evening, I force myself to slow my pace so I don't look odd to any night owls who happen to glance out their windows. I rap on the door in the pattern Voleska told us and dart inside the second it opens.

My men are leaning along the wall. Stavros and Rheave both sit up straighter at the sight of me, but Casimir and Alek drifted off with the late hour. At the tap of Voleska shutting the door behind me, Alek flinches and snaps back into wakefulness.

He's let his hood drift back, and he doesn't leap to retrieve it. In the past few hours, with their nonjudgmental reactions, he's adjusted to the idea of the rebels seeing his scars.

I'd be more glad to see him relaxed about it if I wasn't bearing such awful news.

Stavros takes in my expression with a brief twitch of his head. "You found out something."

Casimir stirs awake at his voice. I swallow hard, waiting until he looks fully conscious before I report on what I heard.

"We need to head out," I say quickly. "Now—I don't know how much ground we need to make up when they might all be on horseback." I turn to Voleska, too many worries colliding in my head. "You should try to pass on word to the king's forces however you can—someone on the royal family's side needs to know."

Rheave springs to his feet. "What happened?"

I drag in a breath. "I heard a couple of the Order members talking. They're gathering a 'march' somewhere down the Coliz-ward road—the last bunch of conspirators from Pima are joining them tomorrow. Apparently they've got enough magic between them to get past the army unnoticed… and then they're going to strike straight at the king when he isn't expecting it."

Stavros curses under his breath.

Voleska's eyes have widened. She glances around at us. "Do you know where that is? The royal family left Florian after the attack there, didn't they?"

The former general grimaces. "I can make a fair guess, and I suppose we'll be able to confirm it once we see what direction this 'march' heads in. What's the most discreet route we can take to reach that road from here?"

As Voleska considers and offers a series of directions, Alek comes up beside me and takes my hand. "Are you all right? You look a little ill."

I rub my face. "I'm fine. I'd imagine we could all use a little more sleep, but there isn't time for that yet."

Voleska motions to the rest of us. "Wait just a minute. We put together a few bags of supplies when we thought we might be sending you off to Bryfeen… When you decided not to take that route, I thought I'd make one for Rheave too."

She aims a faintly apologetic smile at the daimon-man. "You'll all need more than the clothes on your backs if you're hiking across Silana."

She slips through the inner door and returns with five packs. "There's food and blankets and canteens—just the basics. It's not really enough for a trip like this."

"We'll figure the rest out as we go," Stavros says.

I grasp her arm. "Thank you. For everything. And please, pass on that warning if you can."

She nods. "If we can manage to pass on word quickly enough, maybe they won't even make it past the edge of the province."

I glance around at my men. A silent sense of conviction passes between us.

We know what we have to do, and we're going to make it happen together.

We shoulder our packs and rush out into the night.

By the time we've left Pima well behind us, my entire lower body is aching from hips to feet. My shoulders offer a periodic twinge under the pack's straps for good measure.

Nothing shows on the road ahead of us except darkness. The moon is a thin crescent casting the faintest of glows on our surroundings.

The lack of light means it only takes a tiny bit of magic for me to thicken the shadows around us enough that we shouldn't be spotted by sentries. We've already passed a couple of clusters of figures— most of them daimon, from what Rheave said—patrolling the lands just beyond the city.

Unfortunately, the extreme darkness also means that I'm only sure of where exactly the road *is* by noticing when I've suddenly stumbled off onto grass instead.

"Crossroads," Alek points out, tapping his fingers lightly against a sign post I can only make out when I step closer. "I can't read where the other route leads."

Julita speaks up in my head after a long quiet. *Given our course, that should be Lumya to the east and Dalo to the west.*

As I relay her information, Stavros studies our surroundings with a discontented air. "We only have another hour or two before it gets light enough that we'll need to seek better shelter. There hasn't been any sign of campfires or torches."

My gut twists, but I prod him forward. "Let's keep going just a little longer. If we haven't found the scourge sorcerers by daybreak, we'll wait and follow that last bunch from Pima when they go to join them."

Hopefully they won't be traveling too fast or too far from here to meet up with the others.

"You're going to need to rest soon, Ivy," Casimir says gently as we tramp onward.

I shake my head. "I can push through until we know what we're dealing with. I've missed nights before. This—"

I hesitate, taking in the faint tingle that's just drifted over my skin.

My men freeze around me.

"What is it?" Alek asks in a faint whisper.

"Magic," I murmur, and bring my finger to my lips to urge them silent.

They keep pace with me as I walk forward at a more cautious pace than before. The tingling sensation gradually thickens, as if I'm pressing into a fog of magical energy.

When the tingle starts to fade, I adjust direction, seeking out the most intense patches of it. My feet travel off the road and over the wilted winter grass.

Nothing around me looks as if it's been altered by magic, but I keep walking.

*Something* is going on here. If I can just—

I take one more step, and a totally new scene swims into reality before me. I have to clamp my lips shut against a gasp.

Tensing, Stavros flicks his hand down his front in the gesture of the divinities.

We're standing at the edge of what looks like a vast military camp. Starting just ten paces away, dozens of tents dot the field off to the side of the road. At least twenty supply wagons are parked in their midst. I glimpse equine bodies shifting restlessly near the far end of the camp area.

Guards stand around a few firepits, warming themselves while they watch for intruders. It's only thanks to my magical concealment that they haven't spotted us.

Rheave pitches his voice so low I can barely hear him even standing right in front of him. "There are a lot like me here. So many I don't even need to see them to feel it."

I swallow a slightly hysterical laugh. "The scourge sorcerers are sending an entire army to attack the royal family. And no one will have any clue unless they stumble right into their march."

The only chance of stopping them might be the five of us.

# Twenty-Six

*Ivy*

Alek paces back and forth in the small clearing where we've set up our barebones camp, more keyed up than I'm used to. The tense vibe he's giving off matches the ominous gray of the clouds that've congealed overhead in the dwindling twilight.

"You won't want to spend too much time near the scourge sorcerers," he says, glancing at me. "We don't know what other magic they might be using to ward off intruders."

"They didn't notice us this morning," I point out. "But of course we'll be careful."

None of us were in a state fit to challenge an entire army after a night's hiking with no rest. After we'd determined where the Order of the Wild people had camped out, we were able to grab some sleep for ourselves while they finished with their own slumber and waited for the final group from Pima to arrive.

They took up the march again in the mid-afternoon, and we followed at a distance. The sorcerers in their midst must be covering all signs of their passage with magic, because we passed no trampled ground or extinguished fire pits.

Little do they know, that works in my favor. I can pick up the traces of their lingering magic as a trail to follow them.

They stopped again not long after sunset. Now it's time to see what we can learn from their campfire conversations—and whether our small group can weaken this army before they slip past the king's forces at the provincial border.

The scholar lets out a terse hum. "What's the information it's most important we determine? We need to find out as soon as possible where they're planning to attack the royal family. Whether they're expecting more people and supplies from elsewhere in the province. Who's in charge—here, and if we can find out who the mastermind behind the entire Order of the Wild is, so much the better."

"How many of their people are actually people and how many are daimon," Casimir suggests from where he's sitting by our mostly buried fire. "So Rheave will need to go."

The daimon-man lifts his chin. "I'm not afraid. I want to see what they're doing."

Stavros looks up from where he's been constructing snares in the hope of adding fresh meat to tomorrow's breakfast. "We do know there's a huge contingent of Order members right here with ill intentions. If we could simply knock them all on their asses in one swoop, most of that won't even *matter*."

I raise an eyebrow at him. "You figure you're going to charge in there with your sword and win the battle five hundred to one?"

I expect him to glower at me, but the former general's expression turns solemn instead. "Your magic could tackle five hundred at once if you let it, couldn't it?"

Julita speaks up tentatively. *I mean… I suppose you could.*

My stomach has given a sickening lurch.

It's true, there are stories of riven sorcerers destroying entire villages and tearing through armies with vast swells of their limitless magic. But the thought makes me recoil, even when it's an army of murderous psychopaths.

Regardless of the target, wouldn't that kind of carnage be a monstrous act? What would it do to *me* to hurl so much power from the crack in my soul all at once?

How could I ever imagine an appropriate counterbalance?

What looks like regret flickers across Stavros's face as he takes in my reaction. He pushes to his feet. "I only meant—if you thought you could handle it safely—you've accomplished a lot already. None of us would ask anything of you that you felt might be a mistake."

My voice comes out rougher than I like. "I know. I suspect that might be a bit too much of a leap from conjuring invisibility and levitating shields."

Alek has paused, inspiration sparking in his bright eyes behind a shadow of concern. "Rheave's magic hasn't had any negative backlash. If the scourge sorcerers can mingle their gifts with the accomplices they've pushed sacrifices on… I wonder if you two could work your magic together as well. Rheave could provide most of the power, and Ivy, you could simply propel it farther."

I have the impression of Julita clapping her hands in excitement. *Oh, that's perfect. Alek's always so clever.*

Stavros is nodding slowly, something like hope relaxing his expression. "That's an excellent idea."

Casimir grins at the daimon-man encouragingly, and I realize with a rush of warmth that we really are a united group now. All three of my lovers have accepted our new ally whole-heartedly.

Rheave has perked up at the suggestion. "I would give it a try. There do seem to be limits on how far I can send out the energy on its own. Without the arrows to guide it, I could only strike the daimon figures who were close to my spot in the square, and then not even hard enough to kill their bodies and free them."

I let the idea stew inside me for a few moments. It doesn't unnerve me as much as the possibility of slaughtering a whole horde of people directly by my own power, but it's still an unpredictable unknown.

"Let's see exactly what we're up against first." I tip my head toward Rheave. "We should go while they're still distracted by setting up camp."

Casimir pats Rheave's shoulder and aims his gorgeous smile at me next. "The rest of us will get dinner ready to welcome you back from your mission."

Stavros holds out his fist. "Go forward boldly and wisely."

Instinctively, I tap my knuckles to his. The other men step forward to follow suit.

"I can quickly start the fire before we leave," Rheave offers, and Alek moves to grab the kindling we gathered as we walked. Casimir opens a pack to take out some of our stash of food while Stavros begins heaping earth to cover the fire.

Watching them move together in comfortable harmony brings an odd lump into my throat.

Julita's voice comes out quiet. *We've made some strange kind of family here, haven't we? And as strange as it is… I never had anything like this while I was alive back home.*

Yes, that's what this feeling is—this mix of homesickness and happiness. I haven't felt like I could count on people like this since my riven magic burst out of me and ruined the family I had when I was just seven.

Rheave rejoins me after sparking the kindling with a measured flare of his daimon energy. He peers at my face. "Are you all right?"

I smile past the tightness in my throat. "Yes. More than I expected. Let's get moving."

The daimon-man and I slink through the woods carefully. I keep my senses alert for the first tingles of magic.

So far, the scourge sorcerers' strategy has worked in our favor. Their sentries remain inside the haze of magic they cast around them to avoid being seen by anyone outside—which means as long as we can't be seen from *their* camp, no one will stumble on ours. I don't have to expend magic concealing us once we're at rest.

As the trees thin, I do need to draw on my power. I've taken inspiration from the scourge sorcerers' strategy and combined it with my previous tactics.

Rather than picturing our individual bodies vanishing like I did with Rheave back in Pima, I imagine a current wrapping around the two of us together, whisking away all visible trace of our forms to anyone outside. I balance it out by having those forms appear back in the forest where we're actually not.

That way we can still see each other. And it only takes a whiff of my magic, one I can easily keep under control.

"We'll walk through the camp," I murmur to Rheave. "Keep quiet, avoid touching anything, and stay close to me. You can focus on identifying the daimon-people."

He nods, peering ahead toward the camp we can't yet see.

"Thank you," he says abruptly before we've quite left the forest.

I pause and glance at him. "For what?"

Rheave offers me a softer smile than usual. "You could have left and been out of danger. But you stayed, and that meant I could stay with you. As much as I want you to be safe... I'm not sure what I would have done on my own. I'm glad we're still together. The men too."

He adds the last bit like a fleeting afterthought, which makes my lips twitch with amusement. But the honest gratitude in his voice brings back the bittersweet ache I felt earlier.

I touch his arm. "I'm not sure you should thank me. I made the decision for a lot of reasons, and I'm probably going to get *you* into a lot of danger with what we're trying to pull off here. But it wouldn't have seemed fair to abandon you either way. I'm glad you've been with us on this journey, as awful as parts of it have been."

Rheave's tone brightens. "I'm glad too. And I'm not worried about the danger. I'd like to keep this body, but if I don't, I will still be me. The scourge sorcerers can't hurt me that much."

For his sake, I hope that's true. Gods help me, I wish I had the same confidence that I'll stay who *I* am even while I'm still breathing.

I nudge his elbow. "Come on then. Let's see how we can hurt them."

We walk cautiously across the open fields beyond the stretch of forest. The march veered farther from the road during the afternoon—I'm no longer sure I'd be able to see travelers journeying along it from this stopping point.

As expansive as their concealing effect is, now that I'm familiar with it I picked up a hint of the tingling sensation before we even left the forest. When the tingle wriggles right into my skin, I know we're passing through the outer barrier.

I tap Rheave's arm again to alert him. With a few more strides, the sprawling camp materializes in front of us.

As we expected, they're deep in the midst of preparing for the night. Several campfires burn at intervals, a few figures at each cooking tonight's dinner in pots over the flames.

The greasy meaty odor makes me think they've added some kind of waterfowl to their stew. My stomach gurgles in anticipation of our own dinner.

Other men and women are setting up the tents and cleaning equipment. Many sit in clusters, chattering with each other as they work.

I take the lead, weaving between the Order members and their supplies in silence, careful not to walk too close and risk someone accidentally bumping into me. My ears stay pricked to the conversations around me, my gaze roving over the objects caught by the flickering firelight.

Someone's left a shallow camp pot on a stone near one of the fires. I glance around to confirm no one's close enough to see the small item disappear and pluck it up to slip it under my arm. That'll make for easier meal prep.

Around the back of one of the supply wagons that no one is currently bothering with, I pilfer an apple for each of us to go with our dinner. With a twinge of longing, I consider a spare tent lying on the ground still folded, but I suspect that theft might be too noticeable.

Most of the would-be soldiers I pass are talking about immediate practical matters like their aching feet or who they'll share their tent with. But I pass one cluster made up of people who don't look much older than I am enthusing about getting to see more of the country for the first time, and another group that's all teens, chatting about their trek like it's a grand adventure.

"Just imagine it," one of the boys says with a swish of a dagger he clearly doesn't have much practice with. "We're going to be part of the battle to see a real king on the throne—we'll prove we deserve the gods' favor and show the All-Giver it's time to return! People will write songs about us."

The girl next to him grins. "Fuck yes, they will. And all those stuffy snobs in the capital will realize the outer provinces can get things done that they can't."

Julita's presence squirms in my head. *Gods smite me, I hope I was never quite that much of an idiot at that age. They really have no idea who they've actually thrown their lot in with, do they?*

I grimace in answer. It definitely seems not.

How could they? The scourge sorcerers must have been spreading the seeds of dissension out here for months if not years before they launched their full uprising. They've made it sound as if their quest is heroic.

I doubt most of these people even know enough about King Konram and what he and his family have done to evaluate his claim to the throne. And they probably have no idea how the scourge sorcerers are fueling the magic that's keeping this march hidden.

There must be sacrificial accomplices along for the trek, adding power to that magic. Maybe that's what the Order member I overheard meant about "blessed ones."

They haven't revealed themselves any time I've been watching. I suspect they're being kept hidden away in the three large, covered wagons currently parked in the center of the camp, with several older men and women posted around them on guard detail.

Stavros talked about simply wiping all these people out, but I have no idea how many of the newer recruits are villains and how many simply misled.

All the more reason we need to get a clearer idea of who is in charge.

I slink closer to the central wagons and pass a smaller cart that's equally well guarded. Peeking through the slats, I make out several cloth bags and a pile of smaller leather pouches, their bulging sides lumpy in a way that's familiar from my days as the Hand of Kosmel.

Are the scourge sorcerers carrying a heap of money with them?

It certainly looks as if they have plenty to spare.

Avoiding the two guards standing by the end of the cart, I duck down by its side and use one of my knives to slit a small tear in one of the cloth sacks pressed up against the slats. With a little subtle prodding, I push several coins out into my waiting hand.

In the dim firelight, the round shapes shine gold before they disappear in my grasp. I stare at the cart for a second before pocketing the coins.

Usually no one but nobles would carry gold rather than silver. Is the whole cart full of gilts?

Where did the scourge sorcerers get all of it? Is it from Julita's estate and others like it?

And what exactly are they planning to use it for? I hate to think what they could buy or bribe with that kind of wealth.

I slip around the guards with Rheave keeping pace behind me, and ease even closer to the central wagons. Two of the Order members standing there are talking with another man who's just come over.

"…and give them to Borys when you're done," he's saying when I get within hearing range. His companions salute him, and he saunters away.

Julita shudders. *It sounds like my brother is along for the march. If he really has gotten as much authority as he claimed, he might be leading it.*

I incline my head in acknowledgment, scanning the camp for any sign of where Borys might be right now. How much of a problem would it solve if I simply killed *him*?

My skin tightens at the question. I worked so hard not to take Ster. Torstem down through cold-blooded murder. I didn't want to become some kind of assassin.

But if it would help stop the march…

I wander farther through the camp, but I don't see any sign of Julita's brother so far. Maybe he isn't even here right now. I do catch a few conversations about other "Wildings" this bunch expects to catch up with tomorrow before they leave the province.

And who is giving Borys's orders? That's the most important question we still haven't answered.

A defiant whinny reaches my ears. I spin around to spot one of the conspirators struggling to hold on to the reins of a very familiar stallion at the edge of the camp.

"Fucking beast," the woman mutters as she tries to yank Toast's head around to lead him to the other grazing animals. He grunts at her and rears up, forcing her to dodge his hooves.

A man strides over carrying a whip. "If he won't settle with peaceful treatment, you'll have to beat him into obeying."

I wince, and a decision snaps into place in my head.

Firming my hold on the magic I'm sending around Rheave and me, I let another tendril dart free toward my horse and his soon-to-be tormenters.

The woman takes the whip—and one side of the reins breaks off the bridle. Somewhere in the field, a patch of grass I visualized melds together to offset the fracture.

The severed leather strand slips from the woman's grasp. Toast doesn't waste any time taking advantage of his sudden freedom. He wrenches away with an angry snort and gallops off across the field.

The man who brought the whip sighs. "Well, he wasn't doing much good for us anyway. Let him go then."

A sense of confidence fills me alongside the brief rush of triumph. I do know how to make a difference with my magic—my way, without resorting to the kind of butchery the scourge sorcerers enjoy.

I complete my circuit of the camp, taking note of the other supply wagons. Then I drift over to the edge of the magical border.

Rheave stops beside me and speaks in a cautiously low voice. "A lot of them are daimon. From what I sensed, about half."

After what we saw of the scourge sorcerers' forces in Pima, that doesn't surprise me.

I glance up at the clouds still smothering the night sky and lean toward Rheave to whisper right by his ear. "What do you say we see how well I can propel your magic right now?"

A sly glint comes into the daimon-man's eyes. "I'd like that. What should we hit?"

I hum to myself. "Let's start with a few lightning bolts charring their cargo. I don't think we should try for smaller targets until we're sure of our combined aim."

The daimon-man lets out an eager noise of agreement. "That makes sense. How do you think it will work?"

I bite my lip, pondering the possibilities. "I think if you throw a surge of your power upward, I should be able to catch it with my magic and throw it in whatever direction I want. It shouldn't be too different from moving a physical object. I just have to focus on something else that can move in the opposite direction without the scourge sorcerers noticing and realizing what's really going on."

And do all that while maintaining my focus on the magic keeping us invisible too. But I managed it when I cut Toast's reins. This won't be so much harder.

I picture a couple of gnarled trees I noticed in the woods about an hour before we came to our halt. Far enough away that no one at either camp should be disturbed if their branches start whipping around in unexpected ways.

A faint sheen of perspiration forms on my forehead, cooling immediately with the winter air, but the chill only sharpens my concentration.

I fix my eyes on a wagon full of bread, cheese, and dried meat that I want to scorch first. "I'm ready."

Rheave inhales slowly and then thrusts out his arms with enough force that the air ripples against me. Magic crackles toward the sky.

I toss my own magic after it. With a shove of my will, I hurl the sizzling bolt farther up toward the clouds and then down straight at the wagon.

The supposed lightning smashes into the canvas covering with a warble and a boom like thunder. Yelps ring out throughout the camp as those closest leap away and everyone else stops to stare.

I suck back a laugh at their frightened expressions. Do they really believe the gods approve of their goals? Maybe this will get them thinking things through a little harder.

"Again," I murmur to Rheave, picking out a second wagon that was carrying crates with unknown but presumably needed contents.

He obliges with another swing of his arms. I fling the second bolt upward and down at the next wagon, with the distant sense of one of the trees I picked out wrenching right out of the soil by its roots.

"What the fuck kind of storm is this?" someone shouts, staring up at the sky.

Another voice rings out, steadier but still nervous-sounding. "Keep low to the ground. It's striking taller targets."

I brace myself. "Again."

And at the same moment, a swell of uneasiness washes through me. Is it really enough to just lash out at the *things*? These people—they want to kill me and everyone I care about. How can I stand here and let them—

In the middle of my frantic clash of thoughts, Rheave hurls his power into the air. I catch it automatically and launch it upward, but I haven't picked a target.

My gaze darts through the now-chaotic camp and snags on a teenage boy scowling in the midst of the turmoil, his sword raised. Like he wants to run it right through me.

I pull at the power without thinking, just as the boy's expression falters with a flash of fear.

Gods, he really is just a kid. What the fuck am I doing?

With a hiss at the effort, I swing the bolt to the side at the last second. It crashes into the side of a tent just a few paces from where the boy is standing.

Rheave whips his arm around me and yanks me backward. The next thing I know, we're stumbling through the grass out of the area of concealment.

My pulse hitches, and I focus on the one thing I'm sure of—the images of us I'm projecting far off into the forest so that our bodies here can stay invisible.

Rheave tugs me farther away from the Order of the Wild camp, his arm still clamped around me even as he lets me turn in his grip.

"For a second, I felt the spell you put on us fading," he says under his breath. "I didn't want them to see us—I didn't hurt you, did I?"

My bicep feels a bit tender where his arm smacked into me, but nothing all that bad. Nothing I can blame him for.

Curse it all, what's wrong with me? I nearly burned up a guy who's practically a kid, *and* I started to lose focus.

"It was a little too much," I mumble. "I tried to do more than I should have."

If that's all it took for my concentration to falter, then camp-wide destruction is definitely off the table.

We hustle back into the woods. As I pull the rest of my magic back into my chest, a sigh rushes out of me. But my stomach knots tighter with each step we take back to the others.

Sulla warned me that I hadn't practiced enough. What if I can't control my power even well enough to protect us now that I've insisted that we continue on this dangerous course?

When we reach our own little camp, the other three men are standing tensed around the faint glow of the fire, strips of dried meat heating on a makeshift rack of sticks. Alek looks more exhilarated than worried, though.

"Did you try it?" he asks. "Was that Rheave's magic we heard?"

I nod, managing a weary smile. "We threw a couple of 'lightning bolts' out of the sky at the march's supplies. They don't have quite as much food to keep them going as they did before. But I couldn't stay focused for long enough to do more."

Casimir pulls me into his arms. "You've been incredible this entire time, Kindness. There's nothing wrong with pacing yourself."

I sink into his embrace, not wanting to explain exactly how wrong things could have gone.

Alek grins and waves the book he brought back from the temple he visited—with the corners of several aged envelopes poking from between the pages. "You might not have to worry about stretching yourself thin for much longer. I think the answer we need is right here."

# Twenty-Seven

*Alek*

It's hard to be careful with my little treasure while we're walking. The fragile paper crinkles as I ever so carefully unfold the pages of the letter.

But I can only study the faded ink by daylight, and whenever there's daylight, we need to be on the move to keep up with the scourge sorcerers' march.

I roll some of the stiffness out of my shoulders and study the scrawl of archaic Bryfesh that slants across the page. At least I'm not quite as tired as I was two days ago, thanks to the steeds we've added to our party since then.

Toast turned up in the middle of the night, snuffling at Ivy's hair where it poked out from under the layers of blankets we huddle under together to sleep. The following night, she stole another stallion the scourge sorcerers had let wander close to the nearby woods.

The plan is to keep picking off one here and there until we all have a mount. We suspected that taking four at once would alert the march to our presence.

The horses didn't come with saddles, so Ivy is riding Toast bareback at the moment, frowning at the rolling grassy hills in front of us as she keeps us hidden behind a barrier of magic. When I glance up at her, the furrow on her brow sets off a jab of guilt in my abdomen.

If I could have pieced together the information I've been trying to decipher sooner, she wouldn't have needed to look like that at all. We might already have set the Order of the Wild's makeshift army into irreparable disarray.

Casimir is riding on the other stallion at the moment, having recently swapped off with Stavros. We each take our turns riding for an hour to rest our legs.

Ivy only swaps with Rheave, when she insists that she'll feel better if she stretches her legs for a while. For whatever reason, her irritable stallion won't tolerate anyone riding him except her and the daimon.

I suppose it makes a certain sort of sense. Daimon are spirit creatures in essence, which puts them on another level of existence from us. The "creature" part probably makes him seem more a kindred spirit to the horse than the average person does.

Or else Toast just enjoys being as divisive as possible. I could believe that too.

I tip the page to the sunlight and squint at the faintest patch of words. My comprehension of Bryfesh is far from perfect. I've spent much more time reading ancient sources in old Silanian, Veldunian, and Darium, which are the three most common languages in Silana's archives. Even my Woudish is stronger thanks to a set of journals I wanted to peruse years ago.

My head is starting to ache from contemplating the various meanings of the message I think I'm reading—and all the alternative possibilities if I've misidentified one or another bit of the messy handwriting.

Casimir gives his steed a gentle tap to bring it trotting up next to me—on the side that won't block my sun, because the courtesan is always considerate. "Any more luck with those letters?"

I shrug with a regretful twist of my mouth. "It's difficult to tell how much the writer is using metaphor and how much they mean literally. And some parts seem to contradict others. But this was a direct witness to the Great Retribution in Bryfeen, telling another cleric what they saw. Including how it affected the scourge sorcerers."

"I don't think we're in a position to set off a second Great Retribution," Stavros says dryly. "The point is to avoid one."

I shake my head. "I know. But if we understand *why* the specific methods the All-Giver and the godlen used devastated the practice of that kind of magic for so long, there might be something we could use on a smaller scale."

I shouldn't have these letters at all, really. I found them lost behind a stack of dusty books in the temple library, and a quick glance at one told me how relevant they were to my search. But I knew if I admitted my discovery to the cleric, they'd probably want to hold on to such a rare resource.

So I hid them inside a much less valuable book they were happy to let me borrow and kept my mouth shut.

Ivy glances over at me with a quizzical arch of her eyebrow. "I thought the Great Retribution 'devastated' the scourge sorcerers just by burning them all up. Pretty hard to keep practicing illicit magic when you're ashes."

"I mean, that does seem to be part of it." I turn the page to squint at the opposite side. "There was definitely quite a bit of fire involved. But the way the writer talks about it, it sounds like something about the situation made the sorcerers give up before that point. They faltered before the power of the gods so utterly…"

I fall silent and tap my fingers to brow, heart, and gut before spreading them over my sternum to honor all the divinities. Then I press my hand against the brand in the middle of my chest, sending up a prayer specifically to my patron godlen of wisdom for guidance.

Like the many times I've called on Estera before, no brilliant insight sparks to life in my head.

She clearly wants me to unravel this puzzle on my own. But time is running out, and our opportunities are dwindling.

At least another hundred more followers joined the Order of the Wild's march late yesterday. According to Stavros's observations, we must have left the Eppun border behind sometime this morning, without coming within sight of any soldiers we could signal a warning to.

Last night, Ivy broke a few of the wagons' wheels and sent rot creeping into some of their food, but she was shaky after just those efforts. And the scourge sorcerers fixed the wagons with their own magic and as far as we know simply ate less.

Can we pick away at them enough to stall their progress before they're within reach of the king— and without wearing Ivy down to her breaking point? How much can the five of us do against an army of several hundred?

We can't defeat them in might, so we need something clever. Something they couldn't be expecting.

Something *I* should be able to—

The wind whips past us so violently I need to clutch at the pages in my hand. My heart lurches in the panicked moment when I think I might lose them—and then skips another beat at a sudden flap that's appeared at one of the corners.

"Thanks be to Estera," I mumble, and then clearer, to the others, "Hold a moment."

The riders draw their mounts to a stop as I tuck most of the papers away in my pocket.

Stavros comes up beside me. "What is it?"

"There's another page there. They were stuck together, so perfectly aligned I couldn't tell. I thought the writer had just used different weights of paper, whatever they had on hand."

With careful fingers, I peel the two pages apart inch by inch. A laugh that's almost giddy tumbles out of me at the sight of the writing I'm revealing—a piece of the account I was missing up until now.

Gripping the papers in one hand, I tap the other down my chest in another gesture of the divinities, in case my verbal gratitude for whatever role Estera had in revealing this secret wasn't enough. Then I sweep my gaze greedily over the uncovered prose.

The once disjointed account melds together into a much more coherent stream of thought as I translate each missing line. A smile stretches across my lips alongside a growing surge of exhilaration.

My excitement must be obvious. Ivy leans over on Toast's back. "What does it say?"

I wet my lips. "The writer claims that when the flames rose up, the scourge sorcerers fell to their knees before the fire even reached them. They..." I frown at the next line with its awkward conjugation. "They pictured their death in the flames? 'And there's nothing the sorcerers who gain power through the dying of others fear more than their own mortality. They tried to set themselves among the immortal gods... and in seeing they'd failed... they lost spirit and gave up, letting the flames consume them.'"

Casimir's eyes have widened. "It wasn't just straightforward destruction, then. The fire defeated them before it touched them."

Rheave scratches the back of his neck. "Are they really afraid of fire? The scourge sorcerers who made this body used it all the time. I've never seen them frightened of flames."

Ivy nods. "They had big bonfires at their larger meetings near the college. They put it to their own purposes, burning up effigies and so on."

I consider the apparent contradiction. "I suppose it'd be impossible for anyone to survive a single winter in these realms if they couldn't stand to be around fire at all. I'd imagine it doesn't affect them the same way when they're in control. It would be when they feel it's coming for them rather than aimed at their own purposes that they recognize they can't escape death."

Stavros peers over my shoulder at the pages, though I don't imagine he can read a word of Bryfesh. The language component of military training is focused on Darium, since Dariu has been our only consistent opponent for ages. He might have picked up a little modern conversational vocabulary for encounters with our bordering countries, but that'd be the extent of it.

I'm the only one who could have uncovered this revelation.

Stavros hums softly. "When Ivy turned his followers against him, Ster. Torstem did give himself up to the fire. There could be something to this theory."

His approval stokes my confidence. "And why would they see fire as an ideal weapon against their own enemies if they didn't recognize just how powerful it can be?"

Toast huffs as if impatient with our stop and paws the ground restlessly. Ivy pets his neck. "They definitely saw it as a force to be reckoned with. How do you think we can use that fact to our advantage?"

An image has already been forming in my mind, but her direct question makes me hesitate. An uneasy ache resonates through my chest alongside the thrill of the discovery.

I found what might be the key to overcoming the scourge sorcerers... but Ivy's the one who'll have to put my theory into action. One more burden weighing down on her.

But if it's the last burden she'll have to shoulder, won't that be worth it? Isn't that exactly what I was searching for?

I lift my gaze to meet hers, watching for any sign of discomfort. "Tonight when the Order of the Wild is making camp, you could conjure a wall of fire that moves as if to consume them. If the actual scourge sorcerers among the 'Wildings' have the same mentality as those before, you won't need to take it any farther than that—you won't have to actually hurt anyone. They'll lose their resolve, and their dedication to their mission will fall apart."

"You could burn up some of the daimon to free them as well," Rheave suggests.

Ivy frowns, but it's more of a thoughtful expression than an unsettled one. "If I make a wall big enough to terrify them, I'm not sure I should try to stretch my control even farther. But just a big mass of flames moving in one direction shouldn't be that difficult. I'll have to freeze a lot of trees to balance things out." She lets out a short laugh.

"It seems overly simple," Stavros says. "And if the trick doesn't shatter their conviction, they'll know someone was working magic against them. They'll search us out."

Ivy shrugs. "If it comes to that, I can stop them from finding us. None of our smaller attempts have had a real impact—we need to do *something* big."

Another spark of inspiration lights in my head. "Perhaps you could shape the flames just a bit, make the impression of a face in the fire. Give them the sense that it's a warning from the gods rather than a magical attack."

Casimir smiles crookedly. "That might frighten anyone into giving up a quest, scourge sorcerer or not."

"Perfect." Ivy squares her shoulders, and just for an instant, I think I see her jaw flex with tension she quickly masters. The ache in my chest expands.

I could tell her to forget it. That we'll find another way that doesn't require her tapping into the magic she avoided for so long even more than she already has.

But I honestly can't imagine what that other way could be. This one move could be the end of our struggle. We leave the scourge sorcerers shaken and demoralized, and they'll either scatter back to their homes or be so much easier for us to finish picking them apart.

And we can return to King Konram not just victorious but with a proven strategy for snuffing out the rest of the conspiracy that threatens him and his family.

"We have plenty of time to think over the best approach while we're still marching after them," I say. "We'd better keep going before they get too much of a lead."

Ivy makes a sound of scoffing amusement. "I can follow their trail anywhere."

By the time Ivy senses that the march has stopped, it's fully dark other than the moonlight that casts an eerie glow over the landscape. I suppose we should be glad even that's not swallowed up by clouds tonight.

To our benefit, the Order of the Wild seems to prefer to make their camps with a border of woodland around them, presumably to keep them even more hidden from afar if there's a brief faltering of their concealing magic. That makes it easy for us to find a sheltered spot nearby to set up our own camp.

Tonight, Stavros doesn't bother building a fire or unpacking the blankets. We find a clump of bushes with leaves the horses are happy to strip, and Ivy gulps down a quick meal of pilfered dried venison and bread to fortify herself.

My stomach has clenched too tightly for me to think about eating before we set my plan in motion. When she tugs her cloak closer around her and looks toward the Order camp as if ready to set off, I clear my throat. "I'm coming with you."

Ivy jerks around to stare at me. "What?"

I hate that she's so startled by the declaration. That it never even occurred to her I might stand by her in this.

I draw myself up to look as confident as possible. "It was my idea. You should have someone with you who can keep an eye on everything that's going on while you concentrate completely on your magic."

Rheave steps forward. "I can come too."

Stavros clears his throat. "If anyone's going to watch out for Ivy, I should—"

"Men." Casimir's soft voice is firm enough to cut through Stavros's words. He aims one of his fond smiles at Ivy. "We all want to protect Ivy. But the more people go with her, the more she has to worry about keeping hidden. Let's not strain her with our desire to prove ourselves?"

Rheave deflates with a guilty expression. He looks at Ivy. "I don't want to make it harder for you."

Stavros sighs. "There should still be someone with her."

"And that should be Alek," Ivy says before he can go on, holding out her hand to me. "He has the best understanding of what we're trying to accomplish. The rest of you, be ready in case we need to retreat quickly."

As her fingers close around mine, there's no more argument from the others. Even through our gloves, the feel of her touch reminds me of the first time I removed my mask for her, the brush of her hand across my scarred cheek where the breeze grazes it now.

Out of all the people in the world, she's the only one I'm sure has never seen me as a lesser man for my flaws.

We walk to the edge of the Order camp in careful silence. Ivy gives my hand a light squeeze in warning that we're about to step through.

It's still a shock when the sprawl of tents and wagons appears out of nothing in front of us. I come to a stop next to Ivy with a hitch of breath.

I knew more people had gathered since the first time we stumbled on the camp, but I wasn't totally prepared to see the whole vast sprawl of it. All at once, I feel incredibly small.

Ivy releases my hand, her face already tensing with concentration. I can't imagine what it's like trying to hold everything she's doing in her mind all at once, wrangling the threads of her magic when it always wants her to give it free rein.

The Order of the Wild members don't appear to be worried about anything unusual befalling them. They're circulating around the camp, readying their dinner and prepping the tents.

The hum of conversation feels unnervingly companionable, as if they think they're off on a leisurely jaunt across the country, not a mission to slaughter the royal family and throw our entire country into upheaval.

Next to me, Ivy inhales with a faint rasp. That's my only warning that she's about to begin.

With a warbling roar, a wave of fire some twenty paces wide and twice as tall as any man surges up at the edge of the camp. Even though she's conjured it at a safe distance from the two of us, the heat wafts through the air to where I'm standing.

The scars on my face tingle with the sudden warmth. I haven't worn a mask since I lost my usual one in our hasty flight from our apartment in Pima.

The conspirators scramble away from the flames with a chorus of gasps and shouts. I scan their faces, trying to make out which are the scourge sorcerers and which merely their dupes.

Is anyone cowering in terror of their mortality already?

Someone points at the wall of fire, and I flick my gaze toward it long enough to make out the shapes of eyes and a mouth curved into a sneer amid the flames.

Ivy's really pulling it off. This is worth a whole forest of frozen trees.

"Back to the other side of camp!" someone yells in an authoritative tone. "Pull whichever wagons you can reach."

Some of the figures simply race to the far end of the camp area, but just as many leap to the wagons and start hauling them. They're obviously scared, but no one seems to be falling apart the way I hoped.

I turn to Ivy to suggest she push the fire closer and show that it's coming for them. My voice snags in my throat.

Her face has turned wan, the whites of her eyes gleaming as if she's as worried as the people she's threatening.

All at once, the flames shoot higher and farther. They lash out, licking across the nearest tents.

Ivy's lips move with a hushed muttering I can't decipher, but there's no mistaking the urgency of her tone. Her hands twitch at her sides.

Another burst of flames smacks into the side of an abandoned wagon.

"Can't let him…" I think I hear her say before her words muddle again.

The face has vanished. The Order members are still retreating in the wake of the fiery destruction, but no one's cowering or pleading for forgiveness for their sins.

My gut plummets. It didn't work. And Ivy—

She trembles next to me. I reach for her but hesitate, not sure if distracting her would make things better or worse.

Before I can decide, she sucks in a breath, her stance going rigid. There's a whoosh as the entire wall of flame snuffs out as swiftly as it rose up.

She sways, and I catch her arm to restore her balance. Her gaze is fixed on the blackened swath of camp.

"I had to—I had to stop…" she mumbles.

A holler reverberates from the far side of the field. "Wildings, prepare a search! The traitors who want to prop up their false king are here!"

Great God smite me, one of them's already seen through our trick. They barely appear shaken, and Ivy—Ivy teeters as she spins around.

Guilt clamps around my innards from throat to belly. All I can do is throw my arm around her back to hold her steady as we race back to the others.

Is she in any condition to even keep us hidden much longer?

I thought I understood—I wanted to believe I'd found the answer so badly. Gods, how I've fucked up.

And my mistake could be the ruin of us all.

# Twenty-Eight

*Ivy*

I wake to faint early dawn light and a pine needle dropping against my cheek. The boughs Stavros hauled into the shape of a tent late last night block the worst of the wind, but it's still a pretty rough shelter.

The best we can do in our present situation.

With a heavy pang in my stomach, the memory of the panicked dash that brought us here fills my head.

We piled onto the horses two apiece with Stavros jogging alongside us. As well as I could tell in the midst of the turmoil, he led us in a wide circuit around the scourge sorcerers' camp before they'd had much of a chance to conduct their search and continued on to give us at least a few hours' lead on their typical marching pace.

Are we still in their path or safely out of reach? I'm not sure we'll know for certain unless they crash right into us.

A clinking sound and a rustle outside the shelter tells me at least a couple of the men are already up—and cooking some part of our breakfast. As I turn my head to look around, an arm tucks around my waist from behind.

Beneath the layers of blanket, Alek scoots a little closer so our bodies are aligned. His breath tickles through my hair to the back of my scalp. A quick glance shows it's just the two of us left in the shelter.

The scholar dips his head to press a kiss to the nape of my neck. His voice comes out low and rough. "I'm sorry about last night."

I twist in his embrace so I'm facing him. As I meet his anguished eyes, I rest one of my hands against his chin. "You didn't do anything wrong. We tried our best, and it didn't work out after all."

He swallows audibly. "I encouraged you to take on a bigger challenge with your magic—I know how much you hate grappling with it—"

"Hey." I caress Alek's unscarred jaw with my thumb, my throat closing up around the truth of what happened. "You didn't ask for too much. I did what I could handle, and I stopped when I needed to."

There really wasn't anything overwhelming about the effect he asked me to create. Fire balanced by ice is an easy equation.

The real problem was that while the flames I'd conjured wavered and roared, I thought I caught a glimpse of Borys in the disarray—and a sudden urge to blaze straight through the camp to destroy him blotted out everything else for a moment.

In that moment, I was so convinced that I *had* to make the fire bigger. That I needed to flood the whole camp with flames before… before the scourge sorcerers and their lackeys lashed out at us. Or something even more horrible happened.

It didn't totally make sense. I'm not even sure it *was* Borys I saw, the glimpse was so fleeting.

But the feeling just kept growing, and I lost my grip on my intentions. More magic leapt out of me than I'd meant to release.

Maybe if I'd let it, it would have scorched the entire camp and everyone in it to embers: deceived civilians, sacrificial victims, horses, and all alongside the actual villains.

But I didn't let things go that badly. I felt my control slipping and I yanked it back, just as I always have. Everything is still okay.

If I repeat that to myself enough, maybe I'll totally believe it.

Alek's mouth twists. "I thought the strategy I suggested would accomplish *something*. I don't see how we made any progress at all. Instead, we've ended up with the scourge sorcerers actively on the lookout for us."

I caress his face again. "We gave them something to worry about. We distracted them. The blaze might have made some of the locals they drew in question what they've actually signed up for."

Alek sighs and hugs me tighter, his lips brushing my temple. "I'm still sorry it didn't work out better. And I think you need as much of a break as you can get from working more magic. It looked like it's starting to wear you out."

The uneasiness lingering in my gut won't let me argue. I'd already come to the same conclusion myself. "I think that should be manageable. But I guess we'd better get up so we can all figure out exactly where we're going from here."

He lets out a softly disgruntled sound and nuzzles my cheek before seeking out my lips.

I sink into the kiss, wishing I could give myself over to it completely. Wishing we didn't have so many threats looming over us.

"I love you," he murmurs after he's eased back. "Nothing else matters if you're not all right."

I stroke my fingers into his thick hair, a swell of emotion momentarily stealing my words. "I feel the exact same way about you. So don't push *yourself* too hard either."

The scholar snorts as if that's impossible, but he sits up and we clamber out of the shelter.

Casimir has the small pot I lifted from the Order camp braced over an equally small fire. I spot several little white orbs bobbing in the bubbling water.

"I found some ground fowl eggs," Stavros says from where he's checking Toast's shoes. The stallion eyes him warily but seems to have accepted that the former general means no harm. "Only bird that lays in the winter. We should get going as quickly as possible, but we can eat them on the way."

Rheave emerges from between the trees, holding up one of our canteens. "I filled all these up at the stream! And I also saw…" His gaze latches on to me, and he gives me one of those smiles that's all daimon, eager and mischievous. "Ivy, come over here."

I gamely walk over to the spot he indicates several paces beyond the edge of our cramped clearing. He grasps the branch of a nearby tree and clambers up it, disappearing momentarily between the needled boughs.

"Hold out your hands," he calls down.

When I do, he shakes the branches above me. A deluge of glossy brown nuts almost the same shade as his hair rains down, some into my waiting hands, others pattering across the forest floor.

Rheave leaps down to collect the strays. "I know I've seen people eating these before—they seemed to like them."

I can't help laughing. Somehow our situation seems less dire when the daimon in our midst is all but conjuring a meal out of the sky.

Stavros considers our loot when we've carried them back to the camp. He claps Rheave on the back. "Nice find. Pry the tops off with your teeth, and you can get at the softer flesh inside the shell. They've got an almost toffee-like flavor, and they're quite filling too."

Rheave and I distribute the nuts between us. I stuff my own portion into a pocket and hurry to collect the rest of our supplies.

By the time Alek and I have folded the blankets for our packs and pulled apart the shelter, Casimir has finished cooking and doused the fire with the pot water. Stavros kicks dirt over the spot to cover the most obvious signs of our stop here.

"Where are we going now?" I ask.

The former general glances toward the sun, shimmering through the trees just above the horizon. "At this point, I can tell where the scourge sorcerers' march is going. Since it doesn't look as if they've faltered in their ambitions, we should aim to get there first so we can alert the king and summon reinforcements."

My pulse stutters. "How can you be sure?"

The former general passes out the last of the dried plum Voleska included in our packs. "There are only a few cities with fortified palaces that the royal family would move to when facing a threat like this. The march has been heading southeast since we crossed the provincial border. There's only one option they could be heading to: Regica. And that's the one I'd have expected King Konram to choose given every other consideration."

Rheave offers his hands to me to boost me onto Toast's back, since there are no stirrups to help. I'd insist that he should ride first, but after how stubborn he's been in the past, that'd only waste time.

"Are you sure we can get to Regica quickly enough?" I ask as I swing onto the stallion's back. "The conspirators running the march must know they have to hurry too."

Stavros smiles grimly. "One of the benefits of having a small party." He boosts Casimir onto the other horse. "We have less to pack up and less to carry than they do. And I'd suggest we rest as much as we can while we have our turns on the horses. We can use the blankets to make a sort of sling. If we stay on the move for as much of the night as possible as well as the day, we should continue to pull ahead of them."

*Sleeping on horseback?* Julita mutters. *That's army men for you, I suppose.*

The thought of the tiring journey ahead of us makes me feel about as dejected as she sounds, but I gather my spirits as well as I can. "How much farther do you think we have to go?"

"I'll have a better idea once we've gotten a look at a crossroads sign, but if we keep a good walking pace and limited time at camp, I think we can cover the distance in four or five days' time."

I drag in a breath. Okay. Less than a week, and we'll be done with the trek.

And facing the king who wants me executed again. So much to look forward to.

As we set off through the woods, I send out a little of my magic to flow around our group. By daylight, when we're not too near to the march, I've found the simplest effect for avoiding notice is to deflect attention rather than making us outright invisible. It's a perfect balance, the magic to nudge anyone's eyes away from us having the consequence of pulling their gaze toward something else.

If Stavros is right, the scourge sorcerers won't get close enough to have us in their sights anyway.

He takes the lead, guiding us through the forest and across a sprawling field until we reach a country road. "Now that we're setting our own course, we don't have to stay so far off the beaten path," he says. "We'll make better time on even ground."

By the second peal of a town bell, I think I can see the town it belongs to off in the distance to our right. Stavros turns his head that way as Casimir and Alek swap places so Alek can ride for a bit. When I look at Rheave to offer a similar exchange, he simply shakes his head with a defiant expression.

I tap his shoulder with the side of my foot. "Next time. Your body can't keep going without rest no matter how much you'd like it to."

Stavros glances back at us. "Actually, I think our daimon should take the horse now—but not to rest just yet. We don't know how well Voleska and the others were able to pass on the message about the scourge sorcerers' plans, and we weren't sure of where the march was going back then. Rheave, you're the only one of us not officially wanted for arrest. Ride over to that town as quickly as you can and warn them that the uprising has sent a concealed army this way and that they're only a few hours behind us."

My body balks at the idea of our party splitting up even briefly, but I force myself to slide off Toast's back so Rheave can take him. We have to get a warning to the royal troops as soon as possible.

I just have no idea what kind of reception he might get. We don't know what's been going on in the rest of the country while we were tangling with the scourge sorcerers in Nikodi.

"How's Rheave going to find us again while Ivy's keeping us hidden?" Alek asks.

The daimon-man pats Toast's neck from where he's hefted himself onto the stallion. "Her horse can find her without seeing. He already did before in the forest."

He lifts his hand in a casual salute and launches Toast into a gallop. As they race across the open ground toward the distant town, Stavros motions for the rest of us to tramp onward.

I loosen my cloak a little to let in a bit of warmth from the rising sun. Now that we've left the northernmost part of the country behind, the winter chill isn't quite as biting.

Casimir chuckles at me, the collar of his own cloak folded up to shield the lower part of his face. "You've all got stronger constitutions than me, I think. I like my warmth and comforts."

I bump my elbow against his. "And you should have them."

He hums, the sound faintly muffled by the fabric. "Eventually. For now, I'll appreciate the beauty of the wild countryside and the lovely flush that nippy breeze brings to your cheeks."

Even more of a flush creeps over my face at the compliment. I push myself to walk a little faster, thinking of the mass of angry scourge sorcerers and their allies behind us.

It isn't long at all before Alek alerts us with a noise of concern. "I think that's Rheave on his way back now. He's coming at quite a clip. I don't see anyone pursuing him, though."

Stavros peers across the terrain from his lower vantage point. "He's probably simply hurrying to rejoin us." His forehead furrows all the same.

We don't slow our pace on the road, but I move to the side closest to Rheave in case that'll help Toast find his way to me. How much it's the daimon-man's senses and how much the horse's, I'm not sure, but they hurtle straight toward us without hesitation.

Rheave only pulls on the reins when they're so close I can hear Toast's huffs of breath. At that distance, maybe ten paces from the road, my magic wouldn't be enough to divert anyone's attention from the sight of us.

He urges the stallion into pace alongside our group. "I don't know if that went well."

"What happened?" Stavros demands.

The daimon-man glances back toward the town, frowning. "There were men at the gate—guards. I told them about the people from the uprising heading this way, planning to attack the king. Instead of seeming concerned, they asked me how I knew and something about frozen trees."

My stomach flips over. The counteraction to my fire magic. Did someone see it and realize it was caused by illicit magic of some kind?

Have I drawn the attention of even more enemies down on me and my men?

"I told them I didn't have time to do more than give the warning and headed right back," Rheave goes on. "But when I was turning around, I saw past the gate—on the other side, there were a couple of people in uniform nearby. Uniforms that looked like the royal army's. Why would they be here?"

Alek knits his brow. "We're only about a day's walk from the main front where the army's been fighting the Order of the Wild. It wouldn't be very strange to have a few soldiers stationed in the area to monitor things, would it?"

He aims the question at Stavros, who rubs his jaw. "Not necessarily. But they should have been asking about numbers, how well armed, and matters like that, not acting as if they weren't sure they should even believe you."

Rheave deflates a little. "Maybe they didn't. I might not have explained it well enough."

"I'm sure you did as well as any of us could," I tell him.

Julita sighs. *I'm starting to think the king only employs idiots. Other than Stav, of course. And even he was pretty idiotic about you for a while.*

Alek stiffens on his horse. "Someone else is coming."

He has a better view than the rest of us. I peer across the terrain but can only make out the slightest hint of a shape that might be a person outside the distant walls of the town.

Stavros stares, twitches his head, stares again, and then lets his gaze slide over the rest of us as if to give his eyes a moment to recover. They rest on me for a beat longer than the others.

All at once, he exhales sharply. "Ivy, pull around your cloak—or the top of your dress—something. Everyone! Cover your mouth and nose as well as you can."

Even as he speaks, he's fumbling with his own cloak. He presses a flap of the thick fabric over his lower face.

With a lurch of my pulse, I follow suit even though I don't understand. As I push the scratchy woolen cloth against my nose, my breath condenses in the thin patch of air left behind it—and my feet stumble beneath me.

The ground feels suddenly, strangely uneven, as if it's bobbing and dipping like a raft on a river.

I try to concentrate, but my thoughts have started to float away from me. My head is full of clouds.

Julita whips around in the back of my skull. *Ivy, what's happening?*

Something Stavros caught on to, but maybe not in time. He staggers to the side before righting his balance.

Alek has tugged the neckline of his tunic all the way up over his nose, but he sways on the horse's back and has to snatch at its mane to stay on. He leans close to its neck the way Casimir rested before, his hands trembling. "Is that some kind of drug? How...?"

"It's a trick... the sorcerer-hunters use," Stavros rasps through his cloak. "Can't easily confront one of the riven head on. They carry sedatives on them, sometimes traveling with a companion who has a gift... that can carry it long distances through the air. There are a few enchanted tools around... that do the trick too."

Rheave wobbles on Toast and pulls the side of his cloak tighter against his face. Only Casimir seems relatively unaffected, but he already had his collar up before Stavros's warning.

He's adjusted his cloak so it's more tightly molded to his face. "How did you know?" he asks Stavros in a muffled voice.

The former general's laugh is dark. "It seems my gift hasn't completely abandoned me. I looked at Ivy and saw her faint, and I guessed that scenario was the only reason it would happen so quickly. We took precautions... before the full effect could take hold."

Alek turns his head where it's resting on the horse's neck and gives a soft yelp. "Soldiers coming."

When my head jerks around, sending a fresh wave of dizziness through my body, I spot the blue specks of their uniforms against the greenish-yellow of the grass. "Shit."

Our pace has slowed in our muddled state. Stavros manages to take command. "Ivy, get on Toast with Rheave. Alek, I'm joining you. Casimir's the only one in a state to walk at a decent pace on his own. The horses will have to forgive the extra weight one more time."

I don't see how we'll go *that* much faster, but before I can find the words to debate, Rheave has already jumped down. He wobbles but still manages to scoop me up and heave me onto Toast's back right by his withers.

The daimon-man hauls himself up behind me. The stallion grunts in protest but clops onward.

Toast might be able to speed up to a trot with the two of us, or even a canter if I really pushed him, but I'm not sure *we* could stay on. And there's definitely no way to bring Casimir on as well.

Stavros has managed to swing himself up behind Alek, his massive frame swaying, but their horse is only a little larger than Toast. It'll be having an even harder time carrying both of their weight for long.

The blue specks in the distance are growing larger, along with the brownish blotches beneath them. They're on horses too, I realize hazily. Riding much faster than we can.

Can they see us? Great God smite me, I've lost all my focus on my magic.

It's roiling in my chest, where I must have pulled it back inside instinctively. A chill breaks over my skin.

Even with Casimir jogging between us now, there's no way we can outrun the soldiers. If I could just...

Julita's voice pulls my thoughts into order. *You could make a mirage, Ivy! Send them off after a ghost.*

She laughs as if it's a joke, but I understand what she means. The natural consequence of the invisibility effect I've created before.

Yes. Yes, that might be exactly what we need.

I clench my jaw to try to steady my addled mind. I have to concentrate.

Have to direct the magic nagging at me so it does what I want and not all the other chaos it could create.

Rheave had his arms braced on either side of me, but now he wraps one around my waist. He must be able to feel the tension as I ready myself.

"Whatever you're doing," he says quietly, "I've got you. I won't let you fall."

As the heat of his body cocoons me, an unexpected sob rises in my throat.

I need every bit of support I can get.

I drag air into my lungs and hone my consciousness as sharply as I can onto the image of the five of us hustling along the road.

Erase that sight from where we actually are. Project it swerving around and rushing away in the opposite direction. Off the road. Beyond the next field and into the woods, where the soldiers can think they lost us.

Rheave grips me tightly, grounding me even though we're not touching the earth. I twist my head to watch the soldiers, and my cheek presses against his shoulder.

His warm, fresh scent fills my nose. I ignore the impulse to nestle even deeper into his embrace. Ignore the pang of affection and possibly more that I can't grapple with right now.

Maybe a hundred paces behind us, the two soldiers gallop across the road and on toward the woods. Or are there three?

I'd swear I do see three of the blue-uniformed figures careening away from us, but when I blink, they meld back into two. My gut lists with that floating sensation again.

When I yank my head around, my gaze snags on another blotch of blue back by the town. My heart leaps into my throat. "There's another..."

Stavros follows my gaze and then peers over at me. "I don't see anyone."

I squint and swipe at my eyes. It's all just yellow-green grass.

Dread pools in the pit of my stomach.

At my shiver, Rheave rests his cheek against the back of my head. His arm stays tight around me. "I've got you," he repeats.

He does. But how much do I have myself?

I thought if the worst effects of being riven hit me, it'd be in one big crash. I thought my unsteady moments over the past couple of weeks were only fatigue and nerves.

But what if this is how the madness comes: not a sudden slap of insanity but a slow, subtle creeping of it through the mind?

One you might not even notice until you're already lost.

# Twenty-Nine

*Ivy*

Stavros appears to cheer up at the sight of the first fortress. My skin crawls with apprehension even noting it from a distance, but I keep my qualms to myself.

"That'll be Fort Alnaw," he says with a weary smile. We're well into our fifth day of near-constant tramping and riding. "Regica, which holds the palace I expect the royal family has moved to, is about four hours' hard riding from here. We won't risk getting that close just yet."

Julita sounds as if she's as tired as the rest of us. *Yes, let us not walk right to the front doorstep of the ungrateful king who wants us killed for saving him.*

I stifle a yawn, propelling my feet onward one after the other. "Where are we going, then?"

The former general pauses in thought. "If we take the next crossroads, we'll reach the town of Iblin before nightfall. It'll give us an opportunity to reequip ourselves and possibly pass on another warning, but it's farther from the military outposts, so there's less chance we'll run into trouble."

Alek lets out a weak laugh where he's tramping beside me. "I approve of that plan."

Casimir had been dozing in the rough sling of blankets we've formed on the second horse's back, just as Rheave currently is on Toast. At our voices, the courtesan stirs and pushes himself more upright. "Iblin… There's a fairly large temple of Ardone near there. We're close to the border of the current Darium empire."

Stavros's expression darkens. "Yes. King Konram will be maximizing his military resources. A significant portion of the army is already posted in this province, but Dariu hasn't staged a major attack in over a year, and they rarely attempt even minor offenses during the winter months. He'll count on that threat being relatively low, but this way he's surrounded by his soldiers without needing to draw them away from their typical posts."

A shiver ripples down my spine. I've never actually seen a Darium soldier, but the stories passed around of their efforts to regain the western half of the continent could make one's blood curdle.

I once overheard a retired captain comment that the Darium emperor is like a jilted lover who'd rather see his former paramour savaged to death than in the arms of another.

I try to keep my tone light. "So we don't have to worry about an invasion on top of the uprising?"

"I shouldn't think so." Stavros shoots me a smile that's more wry. "In the extremely unlikely chance that the empire launches a larger offensive, it'll be easy enough to know who to avoid. They dress their soldiers in black uniforms painted with bones, as if they're walking skeletons."

Casimir grimaces in disgust. "That sounds awful—and awfully morbid."

"From what I gather, they want to horrify their opponents and remind us of the fate they expect us to meet."

*Here's to those horrors staying on the other side of the Seafell Channel, then,* Julita mutters, a sentiment I fully agree with.

We veer right at the crossroads, picking up our pace despite our fatigue at the thought of almost reaching our destination. All the names Stavros mentioned spin in my head.

I glance over at Alek. "Were there any former bug club members from this province?"

His bright eyes go distant as he considers. "Not that I recall. We do know one prominent figure from this region, though. Romild—her parents are the current provints."

Julita gives a faint groan that I can almost feel reverberating through my response. "Wonderful."

Romild is probably still off in Florian attending her leadership classes at the royal college, which is for the better. She never went out of her way to harass me like some of the other noble students, but she made it clear that she believed I'd nabbed my position as Stavros's assistant—a role she coveted—through unfair and unsavory means.

As the shadows stretch longer, the town Stavros mentioned comes into view up ahead: walled as you'd expect in territory that sees a lot of military conflict, red and brown rooftops poking up over top, and a gold spire in the middle that indicates the local temple of the All-Giver.

My pulse gives a tiny hitch, a mix of anxiety and longing. The latter sensation spreads up through my chest.

Gods above, I could use some guidance right now. More than any of my men would know how to supply.

I've already burdened them with enough troubles anyway.

"We're going into the town?" I ask.

Stavros shakes his head. "We'll find a sheltered place to set up a camp a safe distance away. We should be able to do a little business with merchants coming and going thanks to the bit of money you were able to lift from the scourge sorcerers. Passing through the gate will put us under too much scrutiny. Even Rheave's description may have been passed on after our last encounter with the patrols."

I pick my next words carefully, far too conscious of the shakiness of my thoughts that could be due to more than just exhaustion. "I could get in without needing to go through a gate. Find out if there's any talk around town about the uprising and their march—grab a few things we could use right away."

Stavros cocks his head. "'Grab'?"

I lift my chin. "I'll only borrow what can be spared from people who have more than enough already. They should be happy to support a good cause."

The former general snorts, but he knows I picked my targets fairly when I roved through the outskirts of Florian as the Hand of Kosmel.

Alek touches the back of my arm. "We've been surviving all right—and now we can get more of a rest. You shouldn't take the risk."

I shoot him a reassuring smile. "I'll be careful. I'll feel better if we can understand more of the big picture."

Casimir's expression has shadowed with concern too, but he doesn't argue with me. "I'd like to take a look at that temple of Ardone. My godlen's followers have certain policies that might be helpful to us."

Stavros hums to himself. "And I'd like to survey the area to decide on our best plan for passing on our warning. Let's pick a campsite in the woods over there. Alek and Rheave can set it up and do a little foraging, Ivy will sneak off to the town, and Casimir and I will take the horses. Assuming that beast will tolerate Casimir now." He motions toward Toast.

Casimir chuckles. "I've made better friends with him over the past few days. I think we'll get along all right for a short trek."

Another knot of anxiety forms in my stomach. "I don't know how to keep you concealed when I'm not with you. There's probably a way to work the magic, but keeping track of the consequences too when we're all in different places—"

Stavros steps closer to grasp my shoulder. "We can manage on our own for a few hours, Lady Thief. The patrols are looking for a group of four or five, not a solo rider. I won't get close enough for anyone to notice my prosthetic, and I'd imagine Casimir knows how much caution is needed around his fellow dedicats. We can always send out a signal through the lockets if we run into problems."

I force myself to relax. If I'm asking them to trust me to take care of myself, I have to extend the same trust in return. "Sounds like a plan, then."

Rheave finally rouses as Toast's gait shifts when we leave the road behind. It only takes a little arguing to convince him that I don't need him to attempt to shadow me on my stealthy mission into town.

We tap our fists together before we part ways as if reaffirming the bonds we've formed. I make sure that Toast isn't looking to buck Casimir off, remind the stallion to be good, and then set off for Iblin with only my own scrawny body to conceal.

It isn't hard to find a decent place to make my entry. I've got a lot fewer concerns about being caught when I'm effectively invisible.

I pick out a spot where the stone blocks that make up the wall are a little uneven, leap up to snag my fingers around one thin ridge, and scramble the rest of the way up and over just fifty paces from a guard standing watch.

I wasn't lying when I said I'd like to know what sort of talk is going around in town. As I weave through the streets, I keep my ears pricked for any mention of the Order of the Wild, Eppun province and its counties, or uprisings. But with every turn, I work my way closer to the main temple.

*You seem as if you know where you're going*, Julita remarks.

"There's someone I'd like to talk to, if he'll bother to talk back," I reply under my breath.

We come around another corner, and at the other end of the street, the white-washed walls of the grand temple shine in the setting sun.

Julita goes still. *Ah, I see.*

I hurry along the road toward the temple, dread warring with hope in my chest. I haven't felt Kosmel's presence or heard his voice since the dream that led me to Sulla.

He told me he couldn't interfere quite as much anymore. Maybe he's angry that I was so quick to leave the sanctuary he directed me to.

Who can say what goes on in the mind of a godlen?

The square outside the temple is bustling with locals. No one looks or sounds at all concerned about an approaching army.

I dart between them and climb the steps to the arched doorway. The vast hallway beyond swallows me up.

It feels strange walking into the domed worship room, heading toward the statue of the Kosmel in his alcove. This rendition has the trickster godlen in his typical hooded cloak, his marble eyes peering keenly from beneath, with carved playing cards fanned in one hand and the other raised over his lips as if to encourage secrecy.

As usual, a few dice lie scattered around the marble base, but the question I have can't be reduced to a yes or no answer. I sink to my knees in front of the statue, feeling abruptly awkward.

Even when I prayed to Kosmel back in Florian, it was as much for show as out of any actual divine piety. For most of my twenty years of life, I never prayed to any of the lesser gods at all.

But he's helped me. He's kept me alive and directed my magic away from harm.

If anyone can help me through the mess I've found myself tangled in, it's him.

I bow my head and think the words I want to say. *Kosmel, please hear me and answer. I'm trying to use my magic to do good using the strategies the woman you sent me to offered. But I think it's become too much. I'm seeing and feeling things that don't totally make sense... I don't want to go mad. I don't want to fail the men who've been counting on me. I don't want to see the country upended because I faltered. Where do I go from here?*

A lump fills my throat as I wait. Faint voices drift from the other alcoves, but no divine words ring through my head.

I look up at the statue. As much as I'd like a real conversation, he's answered with simple signs before.

Nothing appears to shift on the statue's face. I peer into the shadows around the marble figure, the ache of dread expanding in my chest.

Is he totally ignoring me?

The shapes flicker with the lantern-light, and I have the impression of coins tossed as if at a betting table. When I blink, the cards seem to ruffle in Kosmel's hand as if he's adjusting them impatiently.

As if he's waiting for me to call or fold.

Is he telling me I have to make the decision for myself?

That does fit with our past conversations. He's always told me to figure out what I'm doing and then tell him what I need, not expect him to make my plans for me.

I guess I should be reassured that he thinks I can still figure my way onto a path that won't ruin everything I've worked toward.

I wait a few minutes longer, but no other impressions jump out at me. Grudgingly, I push to my feet and stride out of the temple.

Julita doesn't speak until I'm crossing the square. *I have no idea what went on between you and the trickster, but I get the sense you're not happy about the answer.*

"More like the lack of an answer," I mutter in return, and follow the scent of frying dough on the breeze. I want to come back to the men with *something* gained on this mission.

A bagful of dumplings would really hit the spot before the longest night's sleep we've had in days. My only decision right now is whether I'm going to pay for or pilfer them.

One of the streets off the square has rows of restaurants, culinary shops, and food stalls on both sides. I spot the stall the dumpling smell is wafting from down past a fishmonger and a fruit and vegetable stand. But I'm only halfway there before Julita's voice breaks through my thoughts in a panicked tone. *Wait!*

I freeze in the middle of the street and dodge to the side to avoid a local who was strolling along behind my invisible form.

"What?" I murmur.

*I thought I heard... Look around, to your left. Farther behind you. Oh, maybe I was just imagining—*

Her words halt as I catch the voice she must have heard before too. A harshly arch masculine tone drifting from the butcher shop a few storefronts back, muffled enough that I only catch one phrase: "...long will it take?"

With my heart thumping twice as fast, I backtrack and ease closer to the butcher's entrance. Even though I can feel my magic wrapped around me, the sight within makes me want to shrink out of view—not least of all because of Julita's cringe in my head.

Her brother is standing at the butcher-shop counter, his hands on his hips in an arrogant pose. "I rode ahead of most of my party to ensure that my companions will have all the necessary supplies when they arrive. Are you saying you can't come up with the steers and fowl I asked for in time?"

The butcher glances around with a harried expression. "I suppose… If you pay in advance, you can have most of the next delivery I'm expecting. You said you need it for tomorrow evening?"

"That's right. And I trust my money is good enough." Borys slaps several gold coins down on the counter. "I can give you more if you'll meet the delivery escort outside one of the gates with the fee to save me some of my hassle coming and going."

The butcher mumbles instructions I don't catch, and Borys bustles off without another word— farther into the shop, where there must be a back door.

I scramble away and scan the street for alleys. Where is he going?

Should I try to ensure he never sees his companions again?

But the buildings along the street are densely packed. By the time I find a narrow passage around the backs toward the far end, Julita's brother is long gone.

I stand there in the dingy alley, another layer of dread settling into place.

*He's already here,* Julita says in a strained voice.

"He rode ahead to make preparations." I swallow thickly. "And the rest of the scourge sorcerer's march is only a day behind us."

# THIRTY

The etching of Ardone carved into the pinkish stone wall smiles tenderly. All the same, a niggle runs through my nerves with her gaze on me.

I've served my godlen faithfully for as long as I knew how to. Surely I've earned the temple hospitality we're going to take advantage of tonight?

But I can't help wondering if I've strayed too far from the path I dedicated myself to. If some of the misfortunes we've faced reflect the gods' disapproval—of *me*.

My mother would certainly have said so.

Stavros peers warily at the small door I've led my companions to. "You're absolutely sure the cleric will harbor us unquestioningly?"

I shoot him a reassuring grin. "Ardone has a clear policy on those seeking shelter in her temples."

I step toward the door and press my hand to the print carved into the wooden surface with Ardone's sigil marked deeper on the palm. I bring my other hand to my chest.

It isn't hard to summon the deep-rooted pang of emotion associated with the woman behind me. I swallow thickly and lift my voice. "I'm here out of love."

The truth of it resonates through my words, and something clicks over in the door. It swings open at my nudge.

With a rush of relief that I've been able to provide at least this much, I glance over my shoulder at the others and motion for them to follow me. "Come on in. These will be separate chambers from the rest of the temple. A building this size should have at least a few rooms that can be individually secured for privacy if there are other needy travelers in residence."

My four companions ease after me through the small doorway and down the short hall on the other side.

Three inner doors stand on either side. Checking them for signs of being claimed, I push open the second.

The room beyond is small and carefully organized, but still manages to give a sense of comfort. Ardone's devouts and clerics believe in providing all possible pleasures.

A thick rug covers the floor, with a mat near the door for us to leave our boots on. Walls in a warm shade of peach surround us. Shelves mounted on one side hold several rolled sleeping mats and blankets I can tell at a glance will be softer than the rough woolen ones we've been huddling in. Heat trickles into the room from a vent near the ceiling.

Ivy lets out a sigh that seems to contain a century of stress. I turn toward her with a bittersweet pang through my heart that's both anguish over the burdens she's had to carry and joy that I can help relieve her of them for just a little while.

"There's no need for you to use your powers here," I tell her. "The devouts won't invade our privacy unless they notice signs of trouble, and no one saw us arrive thanks to your magic. You can simply relax."

She looks as if she's suppressing a yawn. "And I need it."

The anguish I felt digs deeper into my chest. The strain of the past several days shows on her face and in her voice more than any of the rest of us, because it's taken so much more out of her.

And for reasons I don't totally understand, I think. I've caught a look on her face from time to time that has an almost panicked edge to it when there's been nothing immediate to fear.

Something we'll need to address as soon as we're in a state to.

At an emphatic gurgling sound, Alek clamps his hand over his belly. His face flushes. "Sorry. It's been a while since we last ate."

And a while since we ate anything you could call a full meal.

Ivy's fingers tighten around the small sack she brought back from town, but a different sort of longing crosses her face as she takes in the room. "I feel like I've got about ten layers of grime on me that I'd rather not add to my food. I don't suppose there's some kind of a bathing room here?"

I grin again, pleased that I can answer that request, and motion her over to a doorway covered with a curtain near the far corner. "I'd imagine they have some sort of accommodations for that…"

As I peer past the curtain, my smile widens. "We've got a latrine and a couple of shower stalls. Not as relaxing as a bath, but it'll get you clean enough. And the temple has provided soap, towels, and robes as well."

Ivy sets down her cargo and hurries over. "I call first dibs on one of the showers!"

Rheave cocks his head. "Shower? Like rain?"

I laugh. "Quite a bit. If the pipes are set up properly, often with the help of an enchantment, they can convey water to a spot near the ceiling where it sprays down over you. It's a fairly efficient way of getting washed."

Stavros undoes his cloak and tosses it over by our boots. "In the army, we frequently had to make do with buckets. I'd call this luxury enough." Already peeling off his shirt, he heads past the curtain to take the other stall.

When it's my turn in the shower, I want to linger in the streaming, steamy water until it washes away all my doubts. But that isn't possible anyway.

I force myself to scrub the rosy-smelling soap over my body and through my hair as quickly as possible, grimacing at the streaks of dirt that swirl down the drain with the water.

I return to the main room to see Ivy swathed in one of the pinkish-beige bathrobes, which on her slight frame falls nearly to her ankles. She's holding up her one remaining dress.

She looks over at me with a grimace. "The thought of putting this thing back on makes my skin crawl. Maybe we can wash our clothes in the showers too?"

My body recoils at the thought of pulling on my own travel-soiled clothes. I adjust my robe around me, grateful for the clean fabric against my freshly scrubbed skin. "I don't see why not. And if we need something more presentable, a temple like this will have clothes available for the needy. There are always a few dedicats who are fashionably and also charitably inclined."

Ivy lets out a rough chuckle. "Now we're the needy."

"Hmm," Alek says, emerging from the bathing area rubbing his thick hair with a towel. "I think we've contributed enough to Silana's security to take a little charity in return without feeling guilty about it."

An avid gasp from beyond the curtain tells us Rheave has discovered how delightful a shower can be after days on the road. We all exchange an amused glance.

Ivy snatches up her sack. "Forget clothes. Let's eat."

A low wooden table with folding legs leans against the wall next to the rack of bedding. Stavros and I set it up on the floor, and we sit around it while Ivy lays out the spread she brought us. Rheave returns, his curls damp and his eyes gleaming eagerly, just as she's setting down the last of her scavenging and shopping.

"We found some frost berries in the woods," he announces. He draws a bundle of the dimpled purple fruit from his discarded cloak, sets them on the table with the rest, and peers at Stavros with a flicker of uncertainty. "You said you like those?"

Stavros blinks at him and then smiles crookedly. "I think everyone should like them. One of Prospira's few winter blessings. If you haven't tried them before, they're a treat."

Ivy plucks up one of the plump dumplings that form the center of her spread and aims a teasing grin at all of us. "I got these mostly for me, but I'm happy to share." She taps my knee with an extended foot. "I think the round ones have duck in them, so you should definitely try one of those."

My mouth is watering just at the word "duck." We haven't eaten any meat other than campfire-cooked rabbit and wild birds in over a week.

I haven't tasted my favorite fowl since we left the college.

I take one of the dumplings she indicated and nudge the cluster of roasted velvor nuts toward Alek. "And I see you were able to find our scholar's favorite snack." He practically swooned when we brought a bag of them back to the apartment in Pima.

Alek pops one into his mouth and closes his eyes with a blissful expression before rolling a sugared apricot toward Rheave. "And extra-sweetened fruit. Even the daimon will be happy."

"I'm glad just to have so much to fill my stomach with," Rheave says, but his eyes widen when he bites into the apricot. "Oh. That's very good."

Stavros pops a few frostberries into his mouth and grabs a dumpling for himself. Ivy takes out one of her knives, gleaming from its own washing, and starts slicing a hunk of cheese into equal pieces so we can all enjoy it.

For a few minutes, we're totally immersed in soothing our long-empty guts.

As I relish a third duck dumpling, the rich gravy flooding my mouth, my gaze drifts around the table. A warmth far deeper than the temple's heating system can offer rises up inside me.

We're in an unfamiliar room with few possessions to call our own other than the clothes we've worn ragged, but there's a glow of happiness in the air all the same. For what we do have. For making it this far.

And for having each other.

The stress of our journey could have put us at each other's throats, but instead we've only grown closer. I couldn't imagine men much more different from me than the three sharing this table, and yet I also can't imagine anyone I'd rather share this moment with.

Ivy hums contentedly as she nibbles at her portion of cheese and tips her head toward Stavros. "Did you find out anything at all useful from your scouting?"

He pauses to swallow a bite of dumpling. "I could see the troops here are sparse on the ground. I assume some were sent up to Eppun, but I'd still have expected more."

Alek frowns. "That's bad news if the scourge sorcerers are arriving tomorrow evening."

Rheave echoes his expression. "I *told* the men to warn the king."

Ivy reaches over to pat the daimon's arm reassuringly. "They must have passed on some kind of message. Just before I left the town, I overheard a couple of soldiers discussing the uprising. They mentioned the claim that the conspirators were sending an army this way… and laughed about it. It sounded as if they decided it must have been a lie to distract the patrols from hunting *us*."

"Naturally," Stavros mutters, and shakes his head. "I have a few ideas, but I don't think I'm in a good state to make a wise decision right now. Once I've slept on it, we can put some kind of plan into motion in the morning."

Even though he's talking about taking action soon, a shadow crosses Ivy's face. Something I see her gird herself against a moment later to put on an unflappable front with the rest of us.

What else is bothering her that she doesn't want us to see?

As we clean up the remains of our dinner, I consider the best approach. It may be difficult to encourage her to open up even with the three of us who've been with her from the start. I'm not sure how much she'll want to reveal to Rheave as well, especially given how extreme his reactions can be to anything that distresses her.

As Stavros and Ivy start laying out the sleeping mats, I turn to the daimon. "For extra security, I'm thinking we should have someone on watch just outside the door, to let us know if any other visitors arrive. Are you up to taking the first shift?"

Rheave draws his posture straighter with a flash of determination in his eyes. "Of course. No one will get past that door."

He hurries over without any further discussion. I certainly can't fault his dedication.

Alek watches him go. "Do you really think we have reason to worry? You said the temple should be secure."

"After what we've already been through, I don't think we should skimp on precautions," I say, and grab a couple of blankets from a shelf.

I lay mine out on the unrolled mat next to Ivy's and reach over to rub her shoulder. "How are you holding up, Kindness? You've had to stretch your talents more than any of the rest of us."

Ivy shrugs, but she leans into my touch with a muted sigh. Tension twines through her muscles even as my light massage starts to loosen a few of them. "I'm just glad to have the chance to rest."

"Did anything else come up during your trip to the city that worried you?"

She pauses for just long enough for me to believe there was and then gives a short laugh. "What is there that doesn't give us reason to worry these days? I'm getting by."

I brush some of her pale amber hair aside in a gentler caress. "I just want you to know that you can talk to us about anything, no matter what's on your mind. We're here for you in *every* way."

Her shoulders stiffen slightly, but then she glances at me through her eyelashes with an arch of one eyebrow that makes my heart skip a beat despite my intentions. "You know, it's been too long since I've gotten to enjoy you being here in one particular way."

She leans over to claim a kiss, her fingers tracing the line of my jaw.

Heat flows across my skin with the gesture. I can't help kissing her back.

I've missed our most physical intimacies too… but I can't shake the impression that she's dodging the question.

When our lips part, I keep my head bowed close to hers. "Ivy—"

Before I can do more than murmur her name, she glances toward Alek with a beckoning motion. Her gaze slides to Stavros in turn.

Both of the other men step closer and then hesitate. Ivy lets out a soft huff—and reaches for the tie of her robe.

She tugs it loose and lets the fabric slip from her slim form, leaving her sitting naked in a pool of linen. There's still a little self-consciousness in the way she holds her arms as if to partly cover her breasts, but I can't help smiling at the confidence she has gained since our earliest encounters.

"We've come this far," she says in a low voice. "It's about time you showed me that I really am your Signy."

A sharper heat rushes through me and condenses in my groin. This isn't how I intended our private moment to go, but—if I'm not meant for this kind of request, what *am* I good for?

With a slight flex of my jaw, I reach for my gift, fixing my attention on Ivy. Taking in the stream of images that follow, which should tell me what I can do that would really make her happiest right now.

The swell of sensation only heightens my desire, fed by what I can sense of her own. There really is nothing that would set her more at ease than tapping into my greatest talent.

Nothing *I* could do, anyway. But how can I refuse what I'm able to offer?

Alek is already in motion, sinking down next to Ivy with his arm tucking around her back beneath the worst of her scars. His voice comes out rough. "You're more than our Signy. You're our *Ivy*."

She beams at him in the instant before their mouths collide. Another niggling thought passes through my head—that he fits her better than I ever could, with their scars and the ways they've kept themselves hidden.

She still wants me too. And it's beautiful watching them together, feeling their way through the sort of intimacy I almost take for granted.

Ivy clearly isn't in the mood to draw things out. She breaks from the kiss only to swing her legs around so she can straddle Alek.

As she kisses him again, yanking at the tie on his robe, I scoot closer and dapple kisses over the peak of her shoulder and down her arm. My hand strokes her back in tender circles with the wish that I could smooth away all the remainders of her mother's abuse.

Then I glance past her toward the final member of our quartet. Stavros stands poised just a couple of paces away, his hands flexing at his sides, his gaze smoldering.

Oh, he wants to be a part of this interlude. The hunger is written all over him.

But I suppose the only practice he's had at navigating this kind of sharing is when he joined Ivy and me toward the end of our encounter at the Haven.

I catch his gaze and lift my eyebrows as if to say, *Well, are you getting over here or what?*

After a momentary and only half-hearted glower, he kneels at Ivy's other side. He rests his hand on her bare waist and tilts his head to kiss the side of her neck. I can tell he's being careful not to impose too much on her attention to Alek.

When Ivy trails her fingers down Alek's lean frame to grasp his cock, he groans. I slip my hand around her thigh to tease between her legs. The slickness I find there makes my own dick jump to sharper attention.

"Already so ready for us," I murmur. I give her earlobe an affectionate nip before gazing past her toward Alek. "Maybe you have some suggestions from that poetry book for how we can best please our woman together?"

A ruddy cast has formed beneath the scholar's rich brown skin. He wets his lips, his eyelids drooping as his hips rock with Ivy's attentions. "There is… It's sounded as if it can be quite satisfying for a woman to be entered from… ah, both directions. At the same time. I'm not sure how easy that is outside of poetics."

A smile stretches across my face. "Oh, we can definitely offer her that experience." I caress Ivy's cheek. "If you'd like to give it a try."

I'm not sure there's anything in the world as lovely as the blush that turns her paleness the perfect shade of rosy. "That sounds rather incredible."

I swirl my thumb over her clit with just enough pressure to earn me a whimper and withdraw. "Why don't you fill yourself with Alek as you'll both enjoy, and I'll get the necessary supplies?"

This is still a temple of the godlen of sensuality, after all. I spotted just the thing in a little basket at the back of the bathing area: a pot of lubricating gel.

I return with it to find Ivy has followed my instructions to great effect. She eases up and down over Alek in steady strokes, their bodies united, their shaky breaths carrying into the air like the most thrilling music. He's just ducking his head to brush his lips against her collarbone while she turns her head to share a kiss with Stavros.

As their mouths meld together, the military professor slides his hand down her back and squeezes her ass. Ivy bucks onto Alek a little faster, both of their chests hitching with ragged exhalations.

They slow down the pace again when I lower myself next to them. Stavros lets the kiss linger a moment longer and then looks over at me.

Excitement wars with trepidation in his expression. "I think you'd better do the honors. I'd be a lot to take."

I've never seen the man naked, but considering the size of the rest of him, I find that easy to believe.

Ivy punctuates his suggestion with a breathless laugh. "We can work up to that."

Stavros stares at her as if startled that she'd even want to try, and I can't look away from her face either. I don't know what was weighing on her mind before, but no trace of turmoil remains there now.

This is the gift I can give her, the benefit of the arts I've studied. Gods forgive me for not being able to imagine offering it to anyone else while she's claimed so much of my heart.

I shrug off my robe and sink down behind her. With Alek kneeling beneath her, she's in the perfect position.

I dip my fingers into the gel and trace them into the cleft of her ass.

As they glide over her back opening, Ivy gasps. A little shiver passes through her body.

Leaning closer, I kiss her spine at the top of her back. "Good?"

"Mmm," she hums, still swaying over Alek. "I have the feeling it's going to get even better."

With a chuckle, I continue. The ring of muscle there loosens gradually with my massage. When I delve my fingers right inside her, my lover lets out a truly glorious series of needy sounds.

While I stretch her with two and then three fingers, she alternates between kissing Alek and Stavros. Stavros cups one of her breasts and rolls her nipple under his thumb. Alek slips his hand between them, provoking a moan when he must find her clit.

A curse tumbles from the scholar's lips at the sound. "I don't know how much longer I'm going to last," he admits.

Ivy gives a defiant little growl. "Stay with us. Not done yet."

His laugh is strained with building desire.

I kiss Ivy's shoulder blade and slick my fingers over my cock to prepare it. "Let's see how this goes, then. Stop me if you're feeling anything but amazing."

At her impatient noise, I line myself up with her opening. As she stills, I press inside her.

Her entrance is so tight, the heat of her enveloping my cock so intense, that suddenly I'm not sure how long *I'm* going to last. Arousal pulses through my shaft, my release already swelling at the base.

"Oh, gods," Ivy mumbles. She clutches at Alek with one hand and reaches back to clasp my braced arm with the other.

As I sink in as far as I can go, my head bows over her. Pleasure reverberates through my body, so heady it's dizzying. "Let's take this slow. We move together."

I pull back a fraction as Ivy eases up over both me and Alek. When she sinks down again, a guttural moan spills from her lips.

The scholar echoes it with a choked sound. I swallow a groan of my own, buoyed by the blissful haze.

But as we start to find our rhythm between the three of us, I can't help noticing that our fourth companion has sat back on his heels, simply watching.

Reaching around Ivy, I tap Alek's arm. "Do you have any inspired ideas for how we might bring Stav into the fun?"

Alek peers around, his bright eyes glazed with pleasure. He pauses for a second, and I think his flush deepens.

"Hands or mouth?" His gaze darts to Ivy. "Whatever you'd like most."

Ivy lets out a husky chuckle. "Maybe I could try both."

She waves Stavros closer and grasps the tie of his robe. As he sheds it, she tugs him higher on his knees.

Stavros watches her with the same air of disbelief I saw before, mingled with the passion flaring in his gaze. When she grips the base of his erection and dips her head to flick her tongue over the tip, his eyes roll back.

"Fuck," he rasps, tangling his fingers in her hair. "Ivy, you don't need to—"

She interrupts him with a dismissive noise. "I *want* to have all of you."

Then she takes the head of his cock right into her mouth, and he rocks to meet her with a groan. "Gods, you're a fucking miracle."

That she is.

All of us move together, we three thrusting up to meet Ivy as she descends over us. She swallows us up again and again by every means she has.

The quivers of pleasure that race through her body in answer to my own delight reassure me that she's enjoying this interlude just as much as I am.

We're like a wave, surging up over and over. Lifting her higher and higher while we spiral toward our own climaxes.

I dapple kisses across her shoulder blades between my panting breaths. "So lovely. Our Ivy. You're perfect."

The giddy heat builds in my groin. I push into her harder, faster, determined to bring her over the edge before I give in—

Ivy gasps around Stavros's cock. Her muscles clench around me, and I'm lost, spilling myself with my last several thrusts, clasping her tightly as she shudders against me. The ecstasy of the moment sears through me like a surge of the most delicious fire.

With Ivy's cry of release, Alek grunts and stiffens too. He buries his face against her neck.

Stavros shifts as if to withdraw, but Ivy's hand tightens around his shaft. She pumps him faster, her lips pursing around the head of his cock as if determined to haul him with the rest of us.

His hand twitches in her hair, and his breath hisses out through his teeth as he gives himself over to her demand.

Ivy slumps between us with a wordless but happy murmur. I wrap my arms around her and kiss the side of her neck, not willing to let go of the moment just yet.

I may not be serving my mother's ambitions for me or the godlen I dedicated myself as fully as I'm capable of... but I'm not sure I could regret what I've given to this woman. Even if this is the last chance I get before this quest proves my undoing.

# THIRTY-ONE

After so long riding Toast bareback, it feels strange to have a saddle beneath me again. Also strange to be wearing fine linen rather than coarse, dirty wool against my skin.

Both Stavros and I took a new outfit from the temple's offerings this morning. The former general particularly wanted to look more like his noble self for our current mission.

The tunic he's wearing beneath his cloak is embroidered with regular thread rather than gold or silver, and the fabric isn't quite as fine as he'd have worn at Sovereign College. But he looks more like his old self as he rides beside me.

I tug my own cloak closer around me against the chilly but not biting breeze and scan the countryside. We skirted the town about an hour ago and haven't passed any close settlements larger than a farm since. Regardless, I'm keeping concealing magic wrapped around us.

For this particular task, we can't be too careful.

As if picking up on my thoughts, Stavros glances over at me. "Are you sure you want to take this risk? We'll be dealing with royal military security—and if we're caught—"

I make a dismissive sound. "Sneaking in and out of places is one of my specialties even without magic. It's not as if you could knock on the door and expect them to agree to your request."

"I can occasionally make a case with words rather than weapons," he replies in a wry tone, but his solemn expression doesn't shift.

"I suspect this would not be one of those times." For one thing, I doubt he's ever had to contend with a royal notice for his arrest before. "This is the best way I can help. It's not as if we have any better options."

My magic is the *only* way I have any hope of stopping the scourge sorcerers' current plans, as far as I can tell. I just need to be smart about it. If I don't use it any more than I absolutely need to, I can hope my mind stays reasonably steady.

I haven't had any strange impulses or glimpses of things that aren't there since we hid ourselves away in the temple last night. Maybe all I needed was a little break from constantly tapping into my power.

And a chance to indulge in my men's affections. The memory of our joint encounter sends a thrill of lingering heat through me—along with a twinge of guilt.

Casimir could obviously tell something's bothering me. I did want all of them; I did want to lose myself in pleasure for a little while. But I was also deflecting further questions I'm not totally sure how to answer.

*This is a rather daring exploit even for Stavros*, Julita remarks. *He'd better know what he's doing. It's been over a year since he left the army, hasn't it?*

Her uneasy rambling makes my nerves jitter.

"*You're* sure that the mirror will be there?" I ask the former general. "And he'll answer it quickly?"

Stavros nods. "I was stationed out here a couple of times during my former career. For each of the main royal residences outside of the capital, there's a means to communicate quickly with the royal family from the primary military fortress in the area. If fighting breaks out when they're in residence, they want a swift means to communicate with the local forces."

"So you're going to signal King Konram, and he'll think it must mean war has broken out."

Stavros offers me a crooked smile. "Isn't that essentially what we're dealing with?"

I guess he has a point. Imagining the battle we could be facing as soon as this evening makes my stomach clench up.

There has been unnervingly little military presence in sight during our ride. Stavros pointed out a couple of smaller forts that we passed at a distance, but I didn't see much sign of activity around them. Not many soldiers on hand to form a solid defense.

Definitely the strangest part of this experience: wishing there were *more* soldiers around rather than fewer.

At least for me. As our conversation has been a clear reminder of, Stavros is used to being surrounded by military figures.

I take in his assured poise and the resolve on his handsome face. A deeper pang forms in my chest.

This is the man I've fallen for: strong and confident, determined to do what's right. Looking to defend those who can't defend themselves.

I admire those qualities, but they could also be what separates us in the end.

"When we had that clash with the patrol on the way here," I venture, "you said your gift warned you. Has it shown you anything else since your injury?"

Stavros pauses. "Only once, also recently."

"It might be returning, then. Adapting to the new limitations on your sight. Would you see about getting your old position back if that's the case?"

I've done my best to keep my tone casual, but Stavros's gaze has turned penetrating when he looks at me. "Gift or not, I'm hardly in a position to lead masses of troops when I can't see clearly for more than a second at a time. And that's assuming Konram ever does pardon us."

I shrug. "I'd imagine your gift could still be useful in some sort of military role. It's bothered you, not being able to participate at all—being relegated to teaching."

He can't deny that fact when he's told me as much outright.

Stavros exhales in a rush, but he doesn't argue. "I don't think any of us can make decisions about what the future might hold beyond the next few days, Ivy. I'd rather focus on making sure all of us have a future."

His voice softens. "But whatever does happen, I wouldn't want to go back to exactly the way my life was before. I'm not leaving you behind."

My cheeks heat. "I wasn't saying—"

"I know." His smile has softened too. "I simply thought *I* should say that. My life has felt awfully empty for a lot of the past year—but it would also feel empty without you in it keeping me on my toes. I wouldn't mind being back at the royal college feeding you crescent rolls right now."

Even as I snort at the remark, my mouth waters at the memory of my favorite pastries.

Stavros cocks his head. "Honestly, it's hard to picture carrying on without Casimir and Alek in the mix somehow too. I think you're stuck with all of us permanently."

I roll my eyes and wish the affection in his words had eased more of the tension in my gut.

I can tell he means them in this moment. How much he will if so many more possibilities open themselves up to him, who can say?

I think I'd hate feeling I've held him back even more than I'd hate losing him.

Julita hums to herself. *I'd trust him on this one, Ivy. I may not have ever gotten all that close to Stav while we were working together, but I can see how much he's loosened up since he figured out he wants you. You've been good for him.*

Coming from the woman who was once jealous of the attention her former companions offered me, the sentiment does warm me a little.

We pass through a thin strip of forest. On the other side, a broad stone structure looms at the top of a low rise.

Stavros gestures for us to slow down. "That's our destination. I wasn't able to get this close yesterday. I'll need to determine the most direct route to the room we need..."

Movement by the side of the building makes my pulse stutter. "Someone's coming."

The former general stiffens. "They can't see us, can they?"

"No, but we should probably get off the road to be safe."

Even as we direct our steeds onto the overgrown grass along the throughway, I realize the figures I noticed aren't heading our way. Three men on horseback set off to the west. Two wear soldier's uniforms, but I catch a flash of purple robes beneath the cloak on the man in the middle.

And when he shifts his tall frame in his saddle, the sight of his lopsided body sends a shiver through my nerves.

"Lothar," Stavros says, identifying the king's secondary magic advisor at the same moment I did. "Obviously he's returned from the front. Perhaps he's consulting with the local forces on techniques for combating scourge sorcery in case the threat we warned about is real after all."

He speaks without much hope in his voice. I can't summon a great deal myself. "Well, at least he's leaving so we won't have to deal with his riven-hunting inclinations." And whatever immense gift he received for sacrificing his entire arm to his chosen godlen.

We come around the front of the fortress, giving the building a wide berth. No one's posted right at the door, but Stavros points out a few guards on watch in the towers at the corners. We definitely can't stroll right in.

Wetting my lips, I consider the magical strategies I'm most confident in. "How close to the front entrance is the room we need?"

Stavros pauses, his expression going distant as he must navigate the building in his memory. "One floor up, but the stairs are just past the main hall. It's only a couple of doors down from there. Locked, of course."

"That won't be a problem." I drag a breath into my lungs. "I think I can let us stroll right inside. We'll just have to be careful about it. And obviously the horses can't come with us."

Since I'm not yet confident in my ability to work magic multiple places simultaneously, we secure Toast and his unnamed companion in a sheltered spot amid the trees. Then we tramp back to the fort on foot.

As we approach, I concentrate on the door in front of me. I visualize how large a space I need to carve out for us to pass through without needing it unbarred.

The guards up top can't see the door from their positions, but I don't know about the other side.

"Would there normally be anyone stationed in the front hall?" I ask Stavros.

He shakes his head. "Not unless they were preparing to defend from an attack."

That'll have to do. I'll keep our entrance as discreet as possible just in case. "Walk right behind me, straight through the door."

"What—?"

Before he can even ask the question, I toss a surge of my magic toward the wooden surface. It removes a slab of the door—while another slab forms in the trees next to the horses where no one will notice the consequence—and fills in the space with a darkish brown haze as close as I could manage to the color of the wood.

I step straight through. Stavros follows with a brisk stride, but he's canny enough to set his boots quietly on the floor on the other side even if he's startled by my tactic.

With another push of my magic, I reform the wood in the door while disintegrating the stuff that conjured elsewhere.

My magic quivers eagerly as I yank the power back into my chest other than the strands keeping us invisible. My heart thuds amid the energy churning between my ribs.

Was that a yelp?

I barely hold back a flinch, my head jerking around, but Stavros doesn't react to any sound. He simply strides forward to where the staircase must be.

A chill ripples down my back. Another hallucination. My break didn't buy me much of a reprieve.

But I can't turn back now.

I keep pace with Stavros through the dim, stone-walled hallway, past a few soldiers who are heading into a room farther down on the first floor, and up the narrow staircase. Muffled voices waver from other parts of the fortress, but I'm no longer sure which are real and which my mind has made up.

We pad carefully over the thin carpet in the second-floor hallway to a door with the king's sigil etched on it.

At Stavros's gesture, I set my hand against the bronze knob. It's only sealed mechanically, no enchantments reinforcing the lock.

With a twist of my magic, I yank the deadbolt over in exchange for a few cracked twigs on one of the distant trees.

We wait for another soldier to amble by and then push into the room as soon as the coast is clear.

It's a small, windowless space, the air dank between the stone walls. There are no furnishings other than the lantern that flares on automatically at our entrance—and the gold-framed mirror hanging on the wall opposite the door.

I lean against the side wall where I hope I'll be out of view and release the magic that was concealing us. "He'll be able to see you now."

Stavros shrugs his cloak back from his arms and then hesitates. Just for a second, his jaw tightens with the emotions he's reining in.

I can't imagine what he's feeling right now. I never pledged myself to the man he's about to contact—the man who'd like to see us all sent to the gallows for our supposed betrayal.

The former general presses the notches in the mirror's frame in a pattern I don't follow and steps back. We wait in silence, hearing footsteps scrape by in the hall outside.

A niggling fear rises up in the back of my head. The soldiers could have realized their fortress has been breached—they could be gathering outside the door right now—

I give myself a mental shake and force myself to listen hard. There's no sound beyond the door at the moment.

Just my mind addling itself again.

As I resist the urge to hug myself against the realization, the mirror's surface shimmers. An image of King Konram appears on the glass as if he's reflected there.

His eyes widen, his stance going rigid. "Stavros."

Stavros drops to one knee in a supplicating pose. "Your Highness, I apologize for intruding this way. I have urgent news that affects the security of the entire country. Please, hear me out."

The king's mouth presses flat. He gives his former general a wounded look, as if *he's* the one who's spent the last several weeks being harassed all across the realm.

I'd like to stop the scourge sorcerers from murdering this man, but right now, I'd also like to punch his pompous face.

His voice comes out sharp but commanding. "General Leslam gave you access to this—?"

"No," Stavros breaks in. "He doesn't know I'm here. I couldn't risk— Any rumors you've heard that the mutinists from Eppun are marching on your current residence are true. They're using their scourge sorcery to conceal themselves. From what we understand, they expect to arrive in the vicinity of Iblin by this evening. There are several hundred of them, and they have their magic on their side—you'll need more troops—"

"Giving military advice is no longer your job," King Konram interrupts, but he sounds at least as disheartened as he does angry. "I've heard no reports confirming any significant force nearby. Surely even their illicit sorcery couldn't hide them completely."

Stavros gazes at him as if willing his king to believe him. "I've seen them with my own eyes—and seen how well their magic hides them and covers their tracks. There must be reinforcements you can summon. I expected to see more troops on hand already."

"Scouts have noted Darium gathering forces where the channel narrows. They may have heard of the uprising and—" Konram cuts himself off with a grimace, as if reminding himself that he shouldn't reveal anything to the man he considers a traitor. "It will take at least a couple of days to summon a significant additional force. But I have plenty of soldiers on hand as it is."

Stavros bows his head. "Please, Your Highness. You know I'm not one to beg. But I'm convinced that these menaces will do everything in their power to destroy your family. Take every measure you can to prepare and protect yourself. I'd suggest you move to a different residence if I wasn't afraid that you'll be even more vulnerable on the road."

The king considers him for a long moment. "You're truly worried."

I hear Stavros swallow. "We've done what we can to disrupt the uprising and stop the scourge sorcerers, but there are many more of them than us. And the power they can wield..."

Something shifts in Konram's expression. "'We.' I suppose that's how you accessed the mirror. Is your riven sorcerer there with you?"

Stavros's chin comes up. "Ivy has given more of herself than any of us to ensure your safety and—"

"I don't want to hear it," the other man snaps, and then seems to gather himself. "I'll take your report into consideration. Turn yourselves in, and I can withdraw those soldiers from their patrols."

"My king—"

"That's all I have left to say to you."

The mirror dims, and then it only reflects Stavros, his shoulders slumping.

Julita sniffs indignantly. *You'd think he's forgotten how well Stavros served him for all those years before. What a knobhead.*

I have to suppress a sharp guffaw at the crude insult in her noble tones.

Cautiously, I step toward Stavros and touch his arm as he stands. "Do you think he'll listen?"

Stavros sighs. "I can't tell. We've never had this kind of distrust between us before. At least he gave me the chance to say the most important parts."

I turn toward the door, my skin starting to creep in the cramped room. "There's nothing else to do here, then. Let's get out of this place."

I lean close to the door and hear nothing from the other side. Ignoring my trepidation, I extend my magic around us again to hide us from view. I ease the door open, step into the hall—

And wrench to the side with a heavy hand clamped on my shoulder and a blade tapping against my throat.

"Don't move an inch," the soldier who's grabbed me snarls as I'm already freezing in place. My magic shudders, the invisibility effect faltering when he's pressed right against my back.

He must have heard us through the door, managed to grab me through practiced instincts even when he couldn't see me.

Now it doesn't matter.

His blade digs into my neck with a faint sting. "All right. You're going to walk with me down to the dungeons, and then you'll explain to the general what the fuck you're doing here."

My lips part, but my entire body has gone deathly cold. I don't know what to say. Stavros won't intervene when my captor could slit my throat in an instant.

My power flares through my limbs, making my muscles ache, clambering for me to release it all. To blast through the prick who's threatened me.

And all the others. Raze the whole fucking fortress to the ground. Crack skulls and smash spines. Ensure there won't be a single one to give chase—

Gory images flood my mind, and I recoil inwardly.

No, no, that isn't want I want. We *need* these soldiers alive to stop the real villains.

I'd become the monster Stavros used to see me as.

But my magic keeps flailing at me. My mind whirls, and I can't hold on to a single steady thought.

The jolts of rage break through again and again, alongside Julita's frantic voice. *No, no, we can't get caught like this. It isn't* fair. *Oh, Ivy, no…*

Something clicks in my head. The soldier starts to drag me backward, and my voice spills hoarse from my throat. "Julita says no."

I pull my thoughts deep inside my skull, letting my vision fog and my mind haze, hoping she understands.

Nothing happens except the soldier sputtering, "What the fuck are you babbling about?"

Then the tingling presence at the back of my head leaps forward.

My lips move again, but not through my will. Julita's spirit grips my body and propels my voice—with the gift she gave up two ribs for years ago. "I will not go to the dungeon. You will not stop me from leaving by any means. You cannot prevent me from doing as I wish."

The soldier lets out a sound that starts as a snort and then seems to choke. His grasp on me loosens, his sword sinking.

Julita propels me out of his arms and then flings herself back into her usual place in my head, letting my consciousness hurtle to the fore again. I yank the strands of invisibility around me, glimpsing Stavros staring at me with a grayish tint to his light brown skin, and grab his hand. "Come on. I don't know how long Julita's gift will last."

The soldier is gaping at what must now look like only empty air again. But he doesn't snatch at me or raise any shout of alarm as we bolt past him.

We rush down the stairs and through the hall. I have just enough wherewithal to remove a chunk of the front door just in time for us to dash through it.

My magic batters me from the inside in a fury. My nerves jangle with the insistence that we should flatten the whole building and everyone in it to the ground.

They aren't going to leave me alone until I—

No, no, *no.* I pull the image of the protective vine tight around myself, but the power keeps wrenching at me.

Gods above, I wish I could use Julita's gift on myself.

Her buoyant laugh rings through my head. *It really worked. Thank the gods! I'm so glad I could do something real for once.*

"You were pretty amazing," I murmur to her. I don't want to think about what might have happened if I couldn't have turned to her, but my stomach churns with the horror anyway. "We're still a good team."

As the last words leave my mouth, a holler carries across the hill from the fortress behind us. Stavros and I exchange a frantic glance and run for our mounts as if the world depends on it.

Which, unfortunately, it very well might.

# THIRTY-TWO

Ivy bites her lip as she paces the room. There's been an agitated energy to her ever since she and Stavros returned.

A tiny red mark mars the pale skin of her neck. A soldier held a sword to her throat there. He wanted to hurt her.

My fingers curl around the urge to storm out of the temple's refuge rooms and across the countryside until I can tear that villain apart.

I should have been there to protect her. But I couldn't go, because it would have been more strain on her to conceal me too. Stavros was the one who knew what needed to be done at the fort.

I would have made things *harder* for her, not easier.

The knowledge sets me even more on edge.

I bare my teeth. "They're all idiots. They won't listen. Maybe they deserve to get blasted with scourge sorcery."

The horrified look that crosses Ivy's face makes me want to catch the words and stuff them back down my throat.

"We broke into their fortress," she says. "The soldier who caught me and the ones who came after us—they were only doing their jobs."

A growl creeps up my throat. "Not well."

Stavros gives a dark chuckle. "We should be glad they didn't perform better, or we might not have made it back here safely."

Casimir comes up behind Ivy and sets his hands on her shoulders. He squeezes them with gentle circles of his thumbs, and she partly relaxes into the massage.

I could have done *that*. It doesn't look very hard. Why didn't I think of it first?

There are so many things she needs, and I'm not sure I've been doing any of them lately.

The courtesan tilts his head toward the wall nearby. "I made decent use of the time while you were gone. Purchased a few items from passing merchants that could come in handy."

I can't stop myself from stroking my fingers over the feathered fletching on the arrows Casimir brought back, bundled in their quiver along with a simple bow. At least I'm ready if there's anyone around I need to shoot at.

He bought some sort of instrument too, like a long metal tube with a flared end, that he said could be used to sound a warning across long distances. And more food.

I turn back to Ivy with a spark of inspiration. "You should have something to eat. It's past lunchtime. Casimir got us stuffed buns and dumplings."

From the way Ivy's eyes light up, I can tell he made a good choice. He's known her longer than I have—he's gotten to see more of her at times when she got to pick what she actually wanted to eat rather than having to settle for what we could hunt or scavenge.

She sits down at the table we unfolded this morning, and Casimir grabs the box with his acquisitions. Alek glances up from where he was peering at his book of letters again and scoots over to pluck up a stuffed bun.

I'm not particularly hungry, but the mix of buttery pastry and spiced meat in the buns is very enjoyable. It's amazing how many flavors the physical world can hold.

Before I found myself in this body, I could see and hear even if I didn't pay attention quite the same way. To some extent, I could feel the textures of the things I flitted past. But I had no sense of taste at all.

I lean over to take another one—and a different sensation sears through my body like a fishing line yanking at my spirit.

I lurch to the side with a yelp I can't contain. Magic shivers through every muscle in my body.

It's the scourge sorcerers. They're trying to call this body back to them again. I can't let them—I have to focus—

But even as I start to concentrate on the thin rug beneath my feet and the thump of my heart to remind myself that this body belongs to *me* now, my pulse hitches with the impression that it's not enough. Something's different this time.

The magic wrenches through me harder—but it isn't hauling me toward the doorway. It flings me around, whipping out my arms.

My hand has closed into a fist without my realizing. It smashes into Stavros's jaw where the big man has hurried to my side.

He jerks away with a grunt of shock, and the energy of my daimon spirit crackles through my nerves. My body turns frigid from the inside out.

I could burn them all up if the scourge sorcerers manage to make me.

A frantic cry bursts from my lips. I yank myself away from Stavros before any of my power can explode out, but my body wheels toward Ivy.

A flash of an image passes behind my eyes—her face charred, her lithe frame blackened.

*No.* Anything but that.

I heave myself away with a surge of desperation. My limbs flail out.

Energy sizzles across the wall, scorching black streaks in its wake.

I need to stop this. I need to stop *them*.

But the best I can seem to do is to make sure I destroy something other than my companions.

I crash into the shelves of bedding. Sleeping rolls and blankets tumble to the floor.

The magic propelling me whirls me around. I throw myself into the spin so it takes me farther—away from Ivy and the others.

My body slams into the door shoulder-first. More energy flares from my skin, and the wood hisses and cracks apart.

I burst into the hall in a shower of splinters.

The impact resonates through my bones. I hit the floor in the hall with another jolt.

Pressing my hands against the floorboards with bits of broken wood digging into my fingers, I close my eyes and heave the awful influence away with every bit of my strength.

The raging of magic inside me dwindles. I push the side of my head against the floor too, absorbing the feel of the solid surface.

This is my body now. *Mine.*

As a breath shudders out of my lungs, footsteps rush over. I cautiously peel myself off the messy floor to find all four of my companions around me.

"Are you all right?" Ivy asks, her face blanched.

Stavros looks grim. "It was the scourge sorcerers again, wasn't it?"

He has a red blotch on his jaw. I must have hit him hard.

Guilt winds through my gut. "I'm sorry. Instead of trying to call me to them, they were making me lash out. As soon as I realized, I did my best not to hurt any of you."

The big man rubs his jaw. "I've had worse."

Alek studies me, his expression tense. "They must have realized that dragging you away wasn't working, so they figured they could use you to do damage in other ways. Do you think—"

Before he can finish his question, the door at the end of the hall swings open. A woman in a cleric's robes, flanked by two devouts, bustles inside and stalls in her tracks at the sight of me crouched amid the remains of the door. "What in the realms are you doing to our temple?"

Casimir holds up his hands. "All our apologies, Your Holiness. Our friend was ill and had a fit. He's come out of it now."

I don't like the lie, but I've seen how people react to finding out the truth of what I am enough to keep my mouth shut for my companions' sake.

The cleric steps forward gingerly and peeks into the room. I wince at the thought of the mess I've made.

She sucks a breath through her teeth in a hiss. "This is unacceptable behavior for guests. We can't have anyone so disruptive staying here. You need to leave at once."

She tenses as if bracing for an uncomfortable argument, but Stavros lowers his head. He's keeping his prosthetic hand tucked behind him, I notice. "We'll gather our things and be out before the next bell."

"Here." Ivy steps forward with a flash of gold in her hand. She offers the coin to the cleric. "To cover the costs of the repairs."

The cleric takes the coin, staring at it and then the rest of us. It occurs to me that she must wonder why people carrying gold coins would need to shelter at a temple rather than paying for regular accommodations.

I may have caused even more harm than what I can see.

The compensation appears to mollify the woman at least for the moment, though. She dips her head and hurries away with her devouts in tow.

Stavros waves us toward the ruined room. "Let's get our things quickly. She may decide to call for help if she gets any indication that we're hesitant to leave."

I shove myself to my feet and scramble into the room. My spirits sink lower at the sight of the scorch marks and the shelves I didn't realize I'd cracked when I smacked into them.

I snatch up my cloak, my new bow and arrows, and the older clothes still damp from this morning's washing.

It only takes a minute for us all to gather our meager supplies. We hustle out to the temple's adjoining stable, where Ivy and Stavros retrieve the horses they returned there less than an hour ago.

Ivy's stallion snorts as we head for the nearest stretch of forest, as if he's annoyed we interrupted his rest. I've even upended the animals' lives.

We finally had a warm, clean place to stay where Ivy didn't need to constantly work at hiding us, and I destroyed it all.

A gloom settles over me like nothing I've felt before. It feels as if a dark, suffocatingly thick cloud has descended to swallow me whole.

As we tramp between the trees, my head droops. An uncomfortable sense of resolve fills me.

I know what I should do. What maybe I should have done from the first moment I realized how the creators of this body could still affect me.

All this time, and I still can't fend them off properly. How can I say I deserve this body when I can't even prevent it from hurting the few people who've accepted me?

I'm not sure how much time passes before Stavros lifts his hand to stop us. "I think we've gotten enough distance from the temple. We don't want to stray too far from Iblin when we know the scourge sorcerers are using it for supplies. We can set up a camp and monitor the situation from here."

We're standing at the edge of a small glade ringed by leafless trees and a few that bristle with dark green needles. Casimir immediately moves to start arranging our possessions.

I set down my damp clothes and the bow but hold on to my quiver. An arrow tip would do better than a stick.

"I'm going to take a walk and make sure there are no threats nearby," I announce, and set off before anyone can question me.

I walk until I can't make out any hint of my companions through the trees and then keep going a little farther for good measure. The wind rattles the branches over my head, bringing a crisp, wild scent I try to commit to memory.

How well will I recall all the bodily experiences I've enjoyed once I no longer have a physical presence? Will my existence as a sort-of human fade as if it never happened?

I set my quiver against a tree and slide out one of the arrows. As I look at the afternoon sunlight glancing off the sharp metal tip, all my innards seem to clench up.

I turn the shaft between my fingers, in the grips of a silent debate.

I'd be leaving her behind. I promised to protect her.

But have I really managed to do that, or have I only put her in more danger, again and again?

There's so much more I hoped for. So much that my chest aches with it alongside the pangs of regret for what I *have* done.

At the snap of a twig, I jerk around.

Ivy stops several paces away, her worried gaze fixed on me.

She got this close without me hearing her approaching. I don't know whether to credit my distraction or her skills in stealth.

When I don't speak, she walks closer. "What are you doing, Rheave?"

It's difficult to concentrate on my intentions when she's looking at me like that.

I grope for the right words. "It's dangerous for me to be with you. I keep ruining things."

Somehow her face turns even sadder. "None of that was your fault. The scourge sorcerers were messing with you. When we've dealt with them, that won't happen anymore."

"But we don't know how long that'll take or what else they might do before then. What else they might make *me* do."

Ivy frowns. "So why did you come out here? Did you think you'd just walk away? You didn't take any food—you didn't even bring your bow…"

Her gaze slides from the quiver I set down to the arrow in my hand, and her stance goes rigid. "Rheave, you weren't going to— I thought you wanted to *keep* your body."

A sudden, unexpected heat wells up behind my eyes. I find myself blinking hard against the moisture that starts to collect there. "I do. It's been incredible—but giving it up is the easiest solution. If I don't have this body, if it's only chunks of broken clay, then they can't force me to do anything I don't want to do."

Ivy grasps my wrist by the hand holding the arrow. "I wouldn't ask you to give up this new part of your life just because you've struggled a little. None of us would. We'll figure something else out."

"But it keeps happening, no matter what I try. I can't even tell they're sending their magic at me until it's too late."

She pauses, studying me. "Do you *want* to go back to being just a daimon? So you can be free of all the trouble?"

"No!" The answer bursts out of me before I can contain it. "I still haven't—I haven't done anything that really matters."

Ivy knits her brow. "What do you mean?"

My frustration constricts my chest. "I never understood before… Humans exist for such a short time in the scheme of things. But you leave your mark on the world in so many ways that I never have in the entire time I wandered without caring… I want to make a difference. Change something for the better."

"I think you already have," Ivy says quietly. "But you *can* still do more."

A lump has clogged my throat. I have to swallow it to speak. "I want to matter. But that's selfish, isn't it? I should do what would make things better for the most people right now."

Ivy's hand tightens on my arm. "I don't think killing this body would be the best thing. Because you do matter already. You matter to me."

I lift my gaze, searching her expression. She still looks sad and worried, and there's something else shimmering in her eyes that I can't decipher.

But it isn't quite what I'm looking for.

"Not like they do," I say, tilting my head in the direction she came from.

Ivy's mouth twists. "Rheave—"

"I want to *really* matter to you."

All at once, it feels immensely important that I make this much clear. That she understands what she means to me before I do… whatever I decide I have to do.

I let the arrow slip from my fingers as I step closer, bringing one hand to her cheek, the other to the fall of her hair by her neck. The softness of those waves against my fingers sends a tingle over my skin.

She is so loving and so strong, so willing to risk herself to save me no matter what danger I've put myself and her in. The most incredible part of this incredible world.

Ivy draws in a breath as if to speak, but I start first. "I want to be here for you the way they are. I want… I want to be able to make you smile and laugh like simply being near me brightens your life. I want to be able to touch you and know my presence makes you feel safe and happy. It's like a kind of magic, how they are with you—how you are with them— I don't know how to conjure that kind of joy, but if I did, I'd never leave."

My fingers have traced down her cheek to her jaw. A quiver passes through Ivy's body.

She lets out a strained little sound, and then she's bobbing up on her toes to brush her lips to mine.

Oh. This—*this* is what kissing is meant to be. The sensation of our mouths pressing together sparks a heat nothing like the careful overtures I offered to less intimate places before.

I cup her jaw and adjust my head, trying to find the angle where our lips meld together most perfectly. The hint of a gasp that spills on her breath to mingle with mine sends another jolt of heat straight to the appendage between my legs.

By all the gods, there's so much more I want than I even fully recognized. Every inch of my body aches to align with hers, to soak up her warmth and the softness of her skin beneath her clothes.

My other hand falls to her waist, instinctively tugging her closer against me. But the gesture must startle Ivy.

She stumbles backward, a flush spreading up her neck to her cheeks. She presses her hand to her lips. "I—"

Then she seems to master herself, with all the fortitude I'm used to. Lifting her chin, she grabs the arrow I dropped and slings the quiver over her shoulder.

She fixes me with a firm gaze. "You matter a lot, Rheave. You—you remind me of how much joy a person *can* find in the world. Why it's worth going through all this awfulness to protect this country. It would hurt me a lot more to lose you than to help you deal with the assholes who made your body. Please, come back with me."

So many emotions are colliding inside me that I'm afraid to move. She came to me—but then she pulled away. I'm not sure if I can do the right thing when I *want* so much.

The idea of walking straight back to face the men she wouldn't hesitate to embrace only sets me even more off-kilter.

I wet my lips. "I'll come. But I need… a few minutes. By myself. To be sure I'm totally in control now."

I don't say exactly what I need to control. To my relief, Ivy doesn't ask.

She aims a determined finger at me. "I can give you that, but you have to promise me you're not going to hurt yourself. Or leave. You can take some time to think, but then you'll come back to the camp, and we'll keep doing things that matter."

I'd like to ask whether the things that matter could include more proper kissing, but I sense that isn't a wise direction of conversation at the moment. There's too much giddiness and light in the tangled sensations rippling through my veins for me to even consider going through with my former intentions until I've seen where this could lead. "I promise. I won't leave. I wouldn't do anything that would hurt you on purpose."

"Good. I'll go see what everyone else is thinking. But whatever plan we come up with, I'm sure it'll include you too."

She strides off between the trees, leaving me staring after her in a daze.

Has she pulled me back from the brink of a tragedy—or straight toward one?

# Thirty-Three

Ivy

Amusement rings through Julita's coy voice. *Well. The daimon too, hmm? He is rather something to look at, but I have to admit, I didn't see that coming.*

"Hush," I mutter, hefting Rheave's quiver higher on my shoulder and peering through the forest for a sign of our newly formed camp.

Heat is still coursing under my skin from that kiss—from the way the daimon-man's hands started to move over my body—

I shove the memories to the back of my head. Guilt has soured the first brief rush of exhilaration that came with the passion in his words.

I've already devoted myself to three other men. Three men who showed their devotion to *me* ever so vividly last night.

How could I give in to the impulse to kiss Rheave? I don't think I can blame my magic for that lapse of judgment.

This is insane, though, isn't it? He's an ageless spirit creature in a conjured body. I don't even know how to explain it.

Curse it all. How can I look them in the eyes now?

But I have to. For them and for Rheave.

I might not know what to make of all the feelings he's stirred up, but I'm completely sure that I never want to see him pushed to the desperate brink again. He needs to know that we all want him here.

When I reach the edge of the small clearing Stavros picked out, the three men all glance over from the shelter they've already started constructing out of branches under the former general's guidance.

Casimir's forehead furrows as he takes in the arrows I'm holding. "What happened to Rheave? Isn't he coming back?"

"He is," I say, setting down the quiver next to the bow. "He was just upset after the incident at the temple, feeling that he'd put us in a bad situation, and he was thinking of…" My throat constricts for a moment before I force the words out. "Of killing his body so the scourge sorcerers can't control it anymore."

Alek jerks to his feet with a flash of distress crossing his dark face. "He shouldn't do that. He's got as much right to the life he has now as any of us do."

His immediate support warms me despite the churning of my stomach. "I told him that as well as I could. I think he was already struggling with the decision—he didn't really want to go through with it. He's taking a little more time to gather himself, but I made him promise that he'd return in one piece."

Casimir's gaze glides over me, his deep blue eyes turned darker with worry. "And when he does, we'll do everything we can to assure him that we all value his company. I'm glad you were able to talk him down, but that must have been difficult to witness. I'm sorry you had to handle it alone. I could go find him now and start the rest of the conversation."

My skin itches with self-consciousness. Great God filet and fry me, I can't let Casimir apologize to *me* when I'm the one who fucked up.

"I think we should give him some space," I say. "He asked for a little time alone."

Stavros frowns. "Are you sure he won't do anything drastic now?"

"I believe his promise."

The way he looked at me when he said he'd never hurt me on purpose. The memory of his brilliant eyes sears through me.

I sink onto a fallen log at the edge of the glade. The only honorable thing I can do is spit out the truth.

"There's something else. When I was talking with him, he got so emotional, and I just wanted to show him how much everything he's done means to me—I don't know..."

Stavros turns to fully face me, his frown deepening. "What is it, Ivy?"

I look down at my hands. "I kissed him. I'm sorry. It was just supposed to be a quick peck—not that even that would necessarily be all right—but he kissed me back and it ended up going on a little longer. And then I realized I was being an idiot and pulled away, but... what's done is done."

There's a moment of silence. It's broken by a soft laugh that tumbles over Casimir's lips.

My gaze flicks upward with a jolt of surprise.

The courtesan shakes his head at me, nothing but fondness in his expression. "I was wondering when it'd come to that."

"You thought— But I'm with the three of you—"

"I don't think any of us could quite match the daimon's level of dedication," Casimir says lightly. "He's proven his devotion to you dozens of times over. And he's proven himself an essential part of this group as time's gone on, I think. He's brought a different sort of light. I'm not surprised you were drawn to him."

It's easy for him to see things so casually when he's had dozens, maybe hundreds of past partners. Sharing never gave him the slightest hesitation.

"I still shouldn't have acted on what I was feeling like that." I glance at Alek and Stavros. "I don't want him *instead* of you. I don't even know how much I actually want *him*. Nothing else needs to happen. I've been so happy with what we have... I don't want to ruin it."

Alek hesitates and then speaks in a careful tone. "How exactly do you feel about him?"

I run my fingers back into my hair, which is tangled from this morning's riding. "I don't really know that either. I haven't let myself pay that much attention—I've had plenty of other things to worry about. There've been moments when I felt attracted to him. I appreciate how much he's helped us. There's something special about the way he looks at the world. But—gods help me, he's not even human."

"In some ways he is, now," the scholar says. "He's become more than a daimon. And Casimir is right—he's also become part of... whatever we are, working together like this. I trust him. I respect his judgment, even if sometimes it's odd."

I stare at him. "Where are you going with this?"

Alek offers me a sheepish smile. "You've been able to handle three of us. If you decide you could have something real with Rheave too, I'd understand it. I wouldn't be angry. It seems wrong to shut him out of that one aspect of what we have together, if that's what you both end up wanting."

I have no doubt about whether Rheave would want it. At least, the physical side. What do daimon know about actual relationships, romance, any of that?

But his expression when he talked about how much he wanted to matter to me, how much I mattered to him… It was the emotion in his face and in those words that drew me in.

He's always been beautiful, but I had no idea anything that intense was going on in his head.

Argh. This is so ridiculous. I have so many more important problems to sort out.

I press the heel of my hand to my temple. "If no one's pissed off at me, I think it'd be easier if we just pretended this never happened and never let it happen again."

"But it did happen."

All of our gazes dart to Stavros. The former general looks only at me, unwaveringly.

I can't read his expression, but my heart starts to sink.

He's been the most hesitant about Rheave's presence in our lives. He had the most trouble accepting his own feelings for me. I don't think any of us has a clue how he'll react to this situation.

Without another word, he crosses the short distance between us and cups my face between his hands, flesh and metal. The next thing I know, his mouth has captured mine.

He kisses me deeply, lingering in the moment until I can barely remember there's anyone else in the world, let alone anyone else I'd want to kiss as well. When he eases back, his hands drop to my shoulders.

One corner of his mouth crooks upward. "Obviously you figured I didn't have enough competition for your affections. You're so set on making me work for it, hmm, Lady Thief?"

A blush flares in my cheeks. "I didn't purposefully—"

He chuckles and brushes another kiss to my forehead. "I know. And I told you I wanted you to be selfish more often, didn't I? Maybe I haven't reminded you of that fact often enough. I'm not going to start caging you now if there's more happiness you could find."

My heart is suddenly thumping twice as hard. "You're really saying…"

When I can't find the rest of my words, he answers the implicit question. "You're not sure. That's fine. We'll see how it goes. But you're more than worthy of four paramours. As Casimir would probably say, you should have all the joy you can get in your life while it's there for the taking."

Something about his tone and that last sentence sets off an ache in my belly. None of us know how much more life we're going to get, and mine has always been especially precarious.

Is that the only reason he's giving his approval? Because he thinks I need to stuff as many experiences as I can into the little time I might have left?

I have the sense of Julita beaming in my head. *I knew I'd chosen well. Other than the matter of Benny. Three out of four excellent men is still quite a success.*

I swallow the sputter of a laugh that tickles up my throat.

Before I can figure out what to say next, a shout and a crash in the underbrush bring me leaping to my feet.

"Rheave?" Casimir calls as we all rush in the direction of the sound.

The continuing noises of a struggle make it easy to find the daimon-man, just beyond a shaking bush some fifty paces away. When we reach him, Rheave is pinning the hands of the man he's tackled to the ground.

"He's like me," he says, his voice a little ragged from the exertion. "Daimon in a conjured body. He must be from the march."

My pulse hiccups. We draw in around the fallen man, who stares up at us defiantly.

"What are you doing here?" Stavros demands.

The man's flat tone sounds a lot like Rheave's did when I first met him at the college. "I don't answer to you."

Rheave scowls at him. "You don't have to answer to the ones who made that body. Your spirit is still your own. You can claim the body and shake them off. I did."

His captive blinks at him. "No. You must—" A more urgent tone breaks through the refusal. "They told me to scout ahead and report back. I—" His voice flattens all over again. "Let me go. You have no reason to detain me."

Alek lets out a faint snort. "Oh, I'd say we have plenty of reason."

I kneel by the new daimon's head. "How close is the march? Which direction from here?"

Whatever bit of freedom the daimon managed to regain, he's lost it again. His mouth stays clamped shut.

Rheave glances around and lifts his chin in one direction. "He was coming from that way. They can't be *very* far if he was able to scout over here on foot, can they?"

"I wouldn't think so," Stavros says darkly. He peers down at the man. "If you'll let us help you, we'll do our best. But we can't do anything as long as you're working with them."

The man jerks against Rheave's hold. "I don't need your help."

Casimir rests his hand against my hair. "What are we going to do with him? We can't let him go running back to the march."

But we're not in any position to keep prisoners. My stomach knots as I grope for an answer—

Rheave bows his head. "I will release you from the bonds they've forced on you."

As the last word leaves his lips, a surge of energy crackles out of him. It blackens the man beneath him for just an instant before that body stiffens into the clay it was made from.

A brief glimmer that could have been just a quiver of sunlight flits away from my view. I guess that is the other way the daimon can get free.

Rheave sits back on his heels. Just for a second, he looks weary.

I know he thinks his brethren are better off back in their natural state than under the scourge sorcerers' control. Still, destroying their chances of enjoying their new bodies the way he has mustn't feel good.

"I'm sorry," I say.

He glances up at me, and the flicker of a smile that crosses his face brings back his adoring words and the eager press of his body against mine. "It had to be done. I'm glad I could deal with him on my own."

He stands abruptly and tucks his arms around me in a tight embrace. "I came back like I promised."

My heart skips a beat with his warmth and woodsy scent wrapped around me. There's a soft chuckle behind me that I think is Casimir.

I'm still too jumbled up inside to know where I'd want to take the affection the daimon-man insists on offering me, if anywhere at all. But I am relieved that he kept his promise.

Even if nothing more intimate ever passes between us, I don't want to lose him, especially not out of some misguided sense of martyrdom.

So I tip my head against his shoulder just for a second, my hands resting on his sides and then easing him back from me. I make myself meet his unearthly blue-green gaze. "Thank you. I don't want you ever doing that again. It'll only make things worse, not better. None of us wants you gone."

"That's right," Stavros says in his commanding military tone. "We're our own kind of squadron now, and you've contributed just as much as the rest of us. We're stronger together."

Casimir steps forward to grasp Rheave's shoulder. "One thing you should know about humans is we all make mistakes. No one goes through life without causing any damage at all, accidentally or otherwise. We won't judge you for it."

Rheave's eyes widen. His gaze slides to Alek, who nods with a small but warm smile. "I can't imagine us going forward without you."

The daimon-man's mouth forms a hesitant smile of his own in return. "I've been so glad to live alongside you all. I'd very much like to keep doing so."

I resist the urge to hug him all over again. "Then let's all go see what the scourge sorcerers are up to."

We veer back toward our fledgling campsite so Rheave can grab his bow and arrows. Inhaling deeply, I focus my mind on the now-familiar pattern of whisking our images away from sight while presenting them some other place where no one's likely to notice.

Feeling the magic seeping out of me to do my work makes me tense up, but I push away those worries.

It's just a little power expended. I've been doing this much for days on end without getting all that addled.

And we can hardly stroll up to the Order of the Wild's march fully visible and expect a warm welcome.

We emerge from the woods and venture across the field beyond. A carriage rattles by along the road to our left, but otherwise there's no sign of human presence.

Which of course doesn't mean anything as far as the scourge sorcerers are concerned.

Just as the town bell peals for the fifth hour of the afternoon, the first tingle of nearby magic grazes my skin. I halt, absorbing the sensation, and adjust my course.

The men follow close behind me. I veer a little more to the right and then to the left again, judging where the sensation intensifies and fades by tiny increments. After a minute or two, I'm sure we're heading straight toward its source.

As we tramp across the yellowed winter grass and through another thicket of trees, the aura of magic thickens. A few paces beyond the thicket in a sprawling clearing, the tingle penetrates right into my bones.

I stop again and make a gesture to warn the others that we're almost on them. Then I push forward, one careful step at a time.

It takes five more, and with the last of those, the camp materializes before my eyes.

An Order member is standing guard so close at my right that I could touch him if I leaned over. With a hitch of my pulse, I scoot in the other direction to give us some breathing room.

Throughout the rest of the camp, men and women are bustling around. It looks as if they've just arrived. No tents have gone up yet, and the horses are all still saddled, standing amid their potential riders. Only a couple of campfires are burning toward the middle of the area, near the three covered wagons that I suspect hold the sacrificial accomplices.

As I take in the activity, my heart sinks. Have even more scourge sorcerers and unwitting dupes joined the march since we last saw them several days ago? There must be over a thousand figures hurrying this way and that.

Maybe not much compared to the entire royal army, but most of that army isn't *here*. And none of it is truly prepared to contend with the power of scourge sorcery.

Fuck.

Alek comes up beside me. He nudges my arm and points to a cluster around one of the carts.

The people there are all grabbing objects out of the cart… and suiting up in a mix of padded vests, chain mail, and wooden or metal helms.

My lungs constrict. When my gaze darts across the terrain more intently, I notice a woman pointing out features on a map to a small group of on-lookers.

"They're already preparing for battle," I murmur.

Stavros frowns. "It certainly appears that way."

If we had any doubt left, Borys's voice rings out through the camp from somewhere at the far end, beyond my view. "Let's get on with it! The faster we can make the final march, the less prepared King Konram will be."

Julita's presence winces in the back of my head.

I stiffen with a lurch of my gut. "They're going to attack tonight. There's no way any reinforcements could have arrived already."

Stavros's face has grayed. "We need to sound a warning. There are troops in the area—local guards —it wouldn't take long for them to ride here. Most of these people aren't even armed yet. If we can strike *them* when they're not prepared... We can at least stall them."

"And it'll be clear the threat is real," Casimir adds. "But how are we going to bring anyone here to help us when they won't even see an army gathered?"

My heart thuds even faster, a nauseating but firm sense of resolve rising in my chest. "Casimir, you brought your new horn, didn't you?"

"Yes, but it won't do any good if anyone it summons can't see the problem."

"Let me worry about that." I turn to Stavros. "Get one of the horses and ride to town or whatever the nearest fortress is. Alert whoever you can and send them this way. When they're in sight, I'll take care of the rest."

Stavros gives me an anguished look. "Are you sure?"

Ignoring the dread pooling in my belly, I give him a shove. "Yes. Get going, before it's too late to do anything at all."

The former general raises his fist, and I tap it automatically alongside the other men. As he lopes back toward our camp, I extend my magic along his path.

When he's well out of view, I yank the stream of power back to me. The other men gather closer around.

I touch Rheave's arm. "We're not going to do anything to call attention to ourselves until we have back-up. But when I give the word, you can start shooting anyone you can tell is a daimon. And anyone at all you see giving orders."

He shrugs his bow off his shoulder and retrieves an arrow, his beautiful face set with total determination. "I'll take down as many as I can."

I reach to Alek and Casimir next. "You two will also need to be ready with your weapons. If you stay close, I think I can keep us concealed while I'm working more magic—the invisibility effect doesn't take that much concentration anymore—but they might realize where my power is coming from. I won't be able to focus on defending myself."

Despite his past hesitations, Alek draws his knife immediately. Casimir unsheathes his dagger as well.

All my men are in this with me. I just have to make sure I don't let *them* down.

But we have to wait until we have reinforcements of one sort or another. We can't take on a thousand would-be soldiers all on our own.

Or, maybe I could, but I can already feel a shudder running through my thoughts just preparing for what I'm about to do. Even if I wanted to slaughter all these people indiscriminately... I'm pretty sure I'd lose myself in the process.

And that might be even worse for the kingdom than letting the scourge sorcerers attack.

The sun sinks to the tops of the trees. The Order of the Wild members pass around a hasty dinner. Sweat beads on my back beneath my cloak.

And off behind us, a holler carries alongside the pounding of dozens of hooves. "This way!"

I drag a breath into my clenched lungs. "Now!"

Then I hurl out a wave of my power—not at the people in the camp, but at the haze of magic surrounding it.

# Thirty-Four

*Ivy*

The power I've heaved out of me passes through the scourge sorcerers' concealment spell like a horse bolting through fog. That's not what I need.

I rein my magic in and will it to collide with the haze. Eat away at the opposing magic that's hiding the Order of the Wild's army. Reveal them to the world.

I don't know what consequences my power would create when left to its own devices, so I turn to my usual technique, just in reverse.

When I make us invisible, I let an echo of our forms appear somewhere else.

When I'm taking *away* the cloud of invisibility around the march, I'll send that invisibility someplace else.

As I push my magic against the thick barrier around us, I concentrate on the span of forest beyond the far edge of the camp as well. Quivers of sensation race through my soul as the haze starts to disintegrate—and at the same time, the trees at the edge of the forest fade from view.

I'm vaguely aware of the men moving around me. Rheave fires one arrow after another into the milling bodies; Alek and Casimir brace themselves in front of me.

I batter the concealing spell again, holding my focus tight against the shouts of alarm that are going up throughout the scourge sorcerers' camp. Against the flickering images at the edge of my vision that send jolts through my nerves, as if someone is lunging at me.

No one's there. If they were, my men would be fending them off.

I can't fall for my mind's tricks now.

The trees at the edge of the forest vanish completely. I can't tell how much of the fog I've worn away while I'm standing inside it.

How close are Stavros and the soldiers he called in?

At least one of our enemies must realize what's happening, because all at once, the haze of magic shoves back. It hits at me so suddenly I rock on my heels at the impact, unprepared.

The trees swim back into view. My magic contracts and writhes.

"Ivy?" Casimir asks, worry wound through his tone.

I gasp a breath. "I'm okay. Just—they're fighting back with their sorcery. I haven't been able to completely sweep away their magic yet."

Clenching my hands at my sides, I whip my own power forward with more force.

An invisible pressure jabs at me from multiple angles. I have the sense of someone at the other end of that magic lashing out, not knowing where their opponent is but tracing my assault on their spell back to me.

I can do this. I have to be able to do this.

Scourge sorcery is limited by the sacrifices of their supporters. Riven sorcery can do anything.

As long as the person using it pays the price.

My teeth set on edge. A growl seeps through them as I push my will forward.

Tear down the magic that's cloaking this field. Wash it away as if in a vast torrent.

I won't be shaken. I won't be stopped.

Julita's voice quavers through my thoughts. *Ivy, are you sure this isn't too much? There's so many of them working against you...*

I tune her out too, narrowing my concentration even farther.

The concealing fog seems to lurch against my onslaught. It shifts and weaves, strands darting free from my attempt to dissolve it.

Alek stirs in front of me and belts out a name. "Ster. Torstem Dymasek of Florian—a scourge sorcerer, dead." Another. "Wendos Hubarek of Nikodi—a scourge sorcerer, dead. How many of you are going to join them today?"

Whatever strategy he's attempting, it might be worthwhile. A tremor passes through the magic pressing in on me, loosening its impact.

With a renewed surge of determination, I thrash the concealing fog with my own power.

Alek keeps hollering names—other people he suspects from his research were scourge sorcerers who've also died? The shouts around me merge into a warbling roar.

Just a little more. Strip away their defenses. Stop them. *Stop* them—

A new swell of magic crashes over us.

The thicker force punches me in the gut. I hiss and stumble, and my control slips.

The wave of magic I was casting out of me sweeps across the whole camp, toppling men and women, smashing wagon wheels, snapping horses' leads, sending the animals running.

And there are more enemies—more coming. Voices everywhere, flashing swords. I have to crush them all before they—

My magic flings to the side before I've fully processed those thoughts. It slams into a cluster of blue-uniformed figures on horseback who're racing down the road.

Bodies fly from their steeds. Someone cries out at the stomp of a misplaced hoof.

Yes, destroy them all. Destroy everyone who—

I clap my hand to the side of my head.

No. Those were the soldiers we wanted to fight the traitors *with* us, not more attackers.

My power leaps at them again, sending one of the horses staggering to its knees. I hurl myself backward, my mind reeling, my mouth gone ashy dry.

*I* have to stop. I have to stop... before I can't.

The world has morphed into a chaotic whirl of color and shape. I wrench myself around and somehow end up on my hands and knees.

Fabric tears. Wood crunches. Someone screams.

How do I stop?

My hand swims into view, pale against the trampled soil and patchy grass.

I'm here. Not out there. Not ravaging all those people.

An urge grips me, and I follow it. I snatch the knife from my boot and stab it into the back of my hand.

I keep good enough aim that the blade passes between the bones, severing muscle and sinew with an explosion of pain. Pain that reminds me of exactly where and what I am.

"Ivy!" someone cries out.

I haul at my raging magic, and it hurtles back into me. I can't prevent it from flinging the knife out of my flesh and sealing the wound, but the thought of who else might be bleeding in my place comes with a smack of horror that grounds me even more.

I clamp down tight on my power, picturing ivy coiling tight around me, sealing every gap. Caging the magic inside my body yet again.

Arms wrap around my middle. "I've got her!" Rheave says, and then, softer by my ear, "I've got you. They won't hurt you anymore."

Doesn't he see that I'm the one who hurt me?

My thoughts are still too scrambled for me to figure out how to speak.

The daimon-man hefts me against him and runs. As my head settles beneath his chin, I recognize the rustle of branches we race past, crackles of twigs underfoot.

We're back in the forest.

Am I still keeping my men hidden? I yanked *all* my magic back to me. I have to…

I try to extend just a tendril, and the frantic surge that jerks at my innards has me shutting down again.

Fuck. I don't know how to do this anymore.

"Here!" someone hollers. A large equine body pushes in front of us, and Rheave is lifting me onto Toast's back before hauling himself up behind me.

There are other horses around us. We careen on through the underbrush, dusk falling in our wake.

My thoughts float in spirals and gradually settle into some kind of order.

Rheave thought he was ruining everything, but I really just did. I could have torn even the men I love apart, and I'd hardly even have noticed.

Tears prick at the backs of my eyes. I squeeze the lids shut.

Sulla was right. It's too much. I don't know enough.

Maybe I never will. She's stayed on that mountainside her whole life to avoid a catastrophe like I almost unleashed.

"This way," a voice says, one I now recognize as Stavros's.

When I force myself to lift my head, I make out the former general on the other stallion just ahead of us. Alek and Casimir are sharing another horse, cantering along a few paces away through the trees.

They must have stolen it from the camp in the chaos.

Well, now we can all ride, as long as the horses are capable of carrying two. One small gain.

A hysterical giggle bubbles in my throat. I clench my jaw against it.

Stavros draws to a stop and dismounts. As Rheave helps me down off the horse, I make out a stone wall mostly swallowed up by moss and vines.

The former general waves us inside. "It's an old outpost, abandoned since well before my time. But at least it'll keep us completely out of sight for the time being."

We lead the horses inside, past clumps of rubble from the partly collapsed ceiling. A pungent earthy scent fills my nose.

I rest my hand against one of the gritty walls. A pang shoots through my palm where the place I stabbed it has sealed over.

Rheave touches my back more carefully than usual. "Ivy? Are you injured anywhere else?"

I turn to face him. The worry on his face breaks my heart.

My voice comes out hoarse. "No. You got me away before anyone could hurt me. You see? It's a good thing you were there."

He beams at me so brightly that an answering rush of affection wells up in my chest. "It was." He tips his head toward the other men. "Casimir stabbed someone who tried to lunge at you. And Alek grabbed another horse so we could get away quickly."

Giving them credit too. When I look around at the others, I'm met with smiles so tender I can't doubt they're genuine.

They really do accept our daimon-man. He's become a vital part of our group so gradually I didn't totally recognize it.

And maybe I can accept that this man who isn't totally a man fits into a piece of my heart I didn't know was still empty. But that's hardly my biggest concern right now.

How many people did *I* injure in the past hour? How horrible a fate did I consign my lovers to?

My legs wobble. I drop to a crouch, and Casimir is there, wrapping his arm around me from the other side.

"It'll be all right, Kindness," he says.

The gentleness of his voice that I don't deserve cracks through the dam inside me. I sob, and tears flood my eyes.

"Ivy!" Alek drops to his knees in front of me. Rheave makes an anguished sound and tightens his own grip on my body.

All I can do is gasp and press my hands against my face in a futile attempt to stem the deluge of tears.

Have they ever seen me cry before? I can't remember the last time I did—really wept, like this— since even before I met them.

My chest hitches, and more tears gush out.

Julita squirms in the back of my skull. *Oh, Ivy. Whatever's gone wrong, I'm sure we'll work out a new plan. We'll still stop the scourge sorcerers. They haven't won yet.*

They haven't, no. But I've already lost.

I gulp a few breaths and manage to get a hold of myself. Stavros looms over us, peering down at me, his mouth twisted at an agonized angle.

"Tell us what you need, Ivy," he demands. "Tell me whose blood I need to spill for what happened to you back there."

Gods smite me. They all still think I was the one in trouble when the truth is, I was the cause of it.

I push my hands against my closed eyes as if I can force back the next wave of tears that way. When I'm sure they're not going to burst out of me just yet, I lower my arms and gaze blankly at my knees, encircled by the men I've failed.

The words fall dully from my lips. "Mine. I needed to spill mine. But I didn't do it soon enough."

I can hear Rheave's frown in his voice. "What do you mean?"

"It was me." My voice breaks.

I close my eyes again, and shadows waver past my eyelids. Distant voices no one else can hear screech in fury.

I gird myself and make myself keep going. "I thought I could do something good with my magic. I thought as long as I balanced everything out, no one had to get hurt, and it would all work out. But... I'm going mad. I'm seeing things, hearing things. It was small enough that I thought I could push through until we'd dealt with the scourge sorcerers; I *had* to. Except I can't. It almost took me over tonight."

Casimir and Rheave press closer in their combined embrace. Alek's hand comes to rest on my cheek.

The scholar's voice turns rough. "That's why you stabbed your hand."

Rheave lets out a growl at the reminder.

My head dips lower. "The pain brought me back, just barely. I'm the one who bowled over the soldiers Stavros brought. That wasn't the scourge sorcerers. When the magic gets right into my head, I start thinking I have to lash out at everyone..."

I choke up for a second before I drag my gaze upward to meet Stavros's dark eyes. "Part of me wanted to tear apart every soldier in the fortress this morning after the one put his knife to my throat. Like the riven sorcerer slaughtered your best friend. That's why I let Julita step in."

*Oh, Ivy,* Julita murmurs, sounding choked up herself.

"And why you stabbed yourself tonight." Stavros inhales sharply. "Curse it all, Ivy, I knew you'd fall on your knife before you let yourself go too far, but I never wanted it to actually happen."

Casimir strokes my hair. "You're clearly not insane now. You came out of it."

I let out a strained guffaw. "Not really. Just the worst parts. I'm still… not quite right. I don't even know if I ever will be again or if I've wrecked my mind permanently."

Alek touches his forehead to mine. "You'll rest, and you'll get better again. It isn't your fault. You never wanted this magic. You were only trying to help."

The hopeless sensation that's been building inside me since we rode away rises up so swiftly I could drown in it. "I didn't even take down the scourge sorcerers, not really, did I? They're still going to attack."

Stavros shifts his weight. "Not right away. Quite a few of them were injured, and their horses scattered. I didn't see what happened to the soldiers I led that way, but even if the Order of the Wild fell on them, the scourge sorcerers will want to move and regroup in case others are going to investigate."

"But they'll find another place to hide and get organized. And they won't wait long. Tomorrow or the next day, they'll go to slaughter the entire royal family."

I swallow thickly. "And I won't be able to help at all, because I can't risk using my magic again."

# THIRTY-FIVE

*Alek*

The flat, mottled yellow-and-orange tops of the mushrooms catch my eye in the early morning light. With a smile prompted by a flicker of happiness, however brief, I hustle over to the base of the tree where they've sprouted.

I may not have conceived of any brilliant battle strategies, but I did manage to pick up a little useful information from my reading. If one of the books I perused while in Pima is correct, these should be edible and decent-tasting if baked.

The country may be doomed, but at least we'll have breakfast.

I break the tops off the mushrooms' stems, gathering the whole cluster on my arm cradled against my chest. The snap of a twig brings my head up with a hitch of my pulse, but all I see is a sparrow taking off through the branches overhead.

Stavros and Rheave went out to patrol the area around the abandoned outpost, to watch for any members of the Order of the Wild venturing into this area… and to deal with them if they do find any, I suppose.

That job is definitely not one I could handle.

I walk back to the mossy stone walls as quickly as I can while being reasonably quiet. Casimir spots me from the uneven doorway and dips his head in acknowledgment.

"I'm going to check the snares Stavros set up last night," he murmurs when I reach him. "I don't think Ivy should be left alone right now."

I nod in return, my gut twisting.

When I step past him into the partly roofed room beyond, I find Ivy crouched by our fire, which is smoldering beneath a heap of collected rubble and a layer of dirt to diminish the smoke. Her face, a sallower shade of pale than I'm used to, looks as weary as if she didn't sleep at all.

She glances up at my entrance, and I offer her a small smile. "Hey. I found something for us to eat —they just need a little baking."

Without a word, Ivy takes a stick and pries out one of the larger chunks of rock at the edge of the pile. Last night, we used that spot to roast a ground hen Rheave managed to shoot.

I nudge the mushrooms into the hot space one by one. A delicate, rather pleasant herbal scent starts to waft into the air.

The despondence in Ivy's expression hasn't shifted. I hesitate and then sit down next to her, not sure if the physical closeness will comfort her, not knowing if there's anything else I can do for her.

"We'll find other ways," I say. "We got an awful lot done without you needing to use your powers before."

Ivy lets out a faint scoffing sound. "Even when I was mostly suppressing my magic, the most important things I pulled off relied on it. Stopping Wendos. Proving myself against Benedikt. Turning the tables on Ster. Torstem. Saving King Konram's life."

"You got us out of Florian under lockdown using nothing but your cunning and connections," I point out. "You've done plenty of fighting with just your knives."

"Not enough to go up against an army of scourge sorcerers."

I don't know how to argue against that statement. All I can say is, "There's the rest of us too. You're not in this alone."

For the first time, Ivy turns her head to meet my gaze. Her normally bright blue eyes look dulled, like the midday sky on an overcast day. "Do you really think the five of us can stop the march without me calling on my magic? Even with the cleverest plan you can imagine?"

I open my mouth and close it again. She's jabbed at the guilty uncertainty that's been coiled in the middle of my chest ever since my trick with the fire failed—ever since I first fumbled in Stavros's weapons training, really.

"I don't know," I admit. "But we didn't know when we first set off from the Haven either, did we? We simply knew we had to try."

My attempt at striking a hopeful note obviously falls flat. Ivy pulls her legs up in front of her, her head drooping until her chin rests on her knees.

She trails her finger idly through the grit that coats the worn stone floor. "You started shouting out names at the march yesterday while I was trying to tear down their magic. Scourge sorcerers who died. What was that about?"

I recall that impulse with a twinge of unfulfilled pride. "I was thinking about what the old letter said about the scourge sorcerers fearing death. It occurred to me that they might struggle more if I reminded them of those among them who have already died. I'm not sure it had much effect."

"It did throw them off a little," Ivy says. "They were pushing back, and their magic faltered right then. But I still wasn't strong enough."

My heart squeezes at the pain in her voice.

I loop my arm right around her. "It had nothing to do with strength. I've never met anyone stronger than you in my entire life."

Ivy doesn't answer, only stares down at her hands and the random lines she's sketched in the dirt.

What else can I tell her? It's not as if I know what *I* can do to stop the scourge sorcerers at this point either.

How can I encourage her when my own hopes have deflated?

What does any of this mission matter if the woman I love falls apart in the middle of it?

I take her nearer hand in mine. "How are you feeling after you've gotten some rest and half a day without needing to use any magic?"

"Am I still mad, you mean?"

I grimace. "I don't think you're outright insane. And I know the effects of your magic aren't going to vanish immediately. But have you noticed any change? Or whether anything other than using your magic makes you feel better or worse?"

She gives a soft chuckle. "Always the scholar. You can write a book about me—the first treatise on what it's really like living as a riven sorcerer."

At my wince, Ivy leans her head toward me, sinking into my embrace. "I'm sorry. That was meant to be a joke, not a criticism. I know you're trying to help."

I stroke my thumb over her knuckles. "Don't worry about me. If there *is* anything I can do to make your healing easier, I'd want to know—that's all."

Ivy exhales in a long, shaky stream. "It's hard to tell whether specific things scatter my mind more or just set off the madness that's already taken hold. I mostly notice the effects when I'm keyed up, aware of danger around me..."

"What kind of effects, exactly?"

"My thoughts get... jumpier. Like they're leaping straight to more extreme conclusions, assuming I'm in grave danger from everyone around me. And I think I see or hear things—things that scare me. Attackers approaching, weapons aimed at us, threatening voices."

My throat constricts. "That must be awfully disturbing."

I suppose it's no wonder most riven end up becoming as destructive as they do if this is the main consequence of using their magic.

I can picture the sequence so easily. They discover their power and start using it to enhance their lives. The more things they want and get, the more addictive the power becomes.

But at the same time, it's eating away at their mind, convincing them that people mean them harm and that enemies lurk around every corner...

Without the self-control and awareness that Ivy's cultivated her whole life, how long would it take before a person with a riven soul found themselves drawing away into isolation, comforting themselves with luxuries without caring what damage their magic did in exchange? Lashing out at anyone who got close, imagining they were a threat?

Seeing the things they're most afraid of everywhere they turn...

Something clicks in my head with a jolt of inspiration. I hug Ivy tighter, but my mind is already racing with the thought that's struck me.

After pressing a kiss to her forehead, I ease back a little so I can rifle through my cloak's pockets. I still have the stolen letters I've kept tucked away in the temple's book.

Did I misconstrue the phrasing in my initial translation? Bryfesh is a complicated language with odd nuances.

"What?" Ivy asks as I unfold the letters.

"I'm not sure yet."

I scan the brittle page to the spot that prompted my idea to send fire at the scourge sorcerers. The devastation of the Great Retribution—making them fear the death they could imagine meeting from the flames...

Staring at the words again, a startled laugh slips out of me. The phrasing *could* be read that way, if I assume the writer was talking in metaphors. But most literally, they mean that the scourge sorcerers of old literally saw pictures of death projected in the flames.

Images of themselves succumbing to wounds? Or of their already-dead corpses?

The letter writer isn't specific about it. They might not have known the details. But I could have gone about our initial attempt in too vague a way.

If simply hearing the names of the dead could make the scourge sorcerers falter, then what would happen if they saw the actual deaths—or their own—right in front of them?

My expression must give away the exhilaration that's swept through me, because Ivy twists toward me. "You've figured something out."

As I look up at her, my excitement wavers.

I let her down before. I sent her to carry out a strategy that wore her down without accomplishing anything significant in our favor.

I can't be certain that my new interpretation is any more correct than the last one. Or that even if it is, it'll make all that much difference with the current group of scourge sorcerers.

My entire body balks. I should keep the idea to myself until I find some way to be sure.

But even as I make that decision, I see how the light that's come into Ivy's eyes is dwindling quickly in my silence.

For just a second, seeing me uncover reason to hope helped her find her own.

She shakes her head with a twist of her mouth, obviously taking my lack of answer as a refusal. "It's all right. Probably better not to put more ideas in my head."

My rejection of her remark wrenches through me with more force than my initial reluctance. "It's not that. I just—I don't want—"

What can I say that would make anything better?

Gods help me, how can I ask her to believe she can recover from the trouble she's found herself in if I won't push past my own mistakes? If she can come back from riven madness, don't I need to give myself another chance to do something right too?

I square my shoulders and look down at the letter again. "I think I might have misunderstood what the writer was saying when I read this before. The fire didn't frighten the scourge sorcerers into giving up because they were worried it'd burn them to death, but because the gods showed them images of their deaths like pictures on the flames."

Ivy's eyebrows leap up. "We definitely didn't try that the last time. And it did unsettle them just having you talk about the dead…"

She pauses, the glow that'd lit in her face snuffing out again. "But we can't paint pictures on fire with a brush and palette. The only way we could use the same tactic is with magic."

And she's the only one of us with a "gift" that could accomplish anything close.

I slide the letters back into their hiding spot and brush my fingers over her cheek. "Perhaps we'll find another way to use the concept. It's always better to know more so we have more possibilities to draw on."

"Spoken like a true Estera dedicate," she says with fond amusement, and leans in to kiss me. But the despondent air hasn't left her.

I've given her something, but what can I really say about her magic? I have none at all of my own, chaotic or not.

At the tread of footsteps beyond the doorway, we both tense, but it's Rheave who appears at the entrance a moment later.

"We didn't come across anyone nearby," he says to both of us. "Stavros is taking one of the horses to see what the royal soldiers might be doing now."

The daimon fixes his gaze directly on Ivy. "He thought you might come out with me again in the direction we think the march went. You'd be able to sense when their magic is nearby without using your own, wouldn't you?"

Ivy pushes to her feet but then stalls there. "I would. But…"

Seeing her so uncertain sends a stabbing sensation through my chest.

I get up beside her, touching her arm. "You should go. It'll do you some good to have a task to carry out. Here, you can bring some of the mushrooms to eat on the way."

As I remove them from the fire, Ivy still hesitates. "If we run into any Order members… I'm not sure it'd be safe for me to even conceal us…"

"You know how to be stealthy," I say, putting all the confidence I have in her into my voice. "And Rheave can protect you both better than anyone if it comes to that."

The daimon grins at my compliment and flicks his fingers together with a brief spark.

A different sort of confidence fills my chest.

I did what I could for Ivy, but she needs Rheave too. He can talk to her from a perspective none of the rest of us have—as a being dealing with unpredictable magic that's sometimes worked in ways he'd rather it didn't.

Our woman is something extraordinary. She could use someone who's more than human in her life, now and in the future as well.

"See what you can find," I say, giving her a handful of roasted mushrooms and a nudge, and this time she goes. The smile that crosses her face as she joins Rheave tells me I was right to insist.

May she find her way back to the woman she's meant to be before the looming war finds us all.

# Thirty-Six

*Ivy*

Rheave moves through the forest like a wolf, weaving between the trees, his eyes alert and his stance wary.

He makes a particularly stunning wolf, but anyone who misjudges him as an easy target for his beauty would be in for an immense surprise.

Despite all my practice at stealth, right now I feel like an oaf next to him. My body goes through the motions, but as if I'm slogging through water rather than air.

The weight of everything that happened yesterday is still pressing down on me.

My magic doesn't clamor against my rejection of all the ways it'd like to "help" me. It simmers in my chest as if biding its time.

And all the while, somewhere nearby, the scourge sorcerers are rallying their troops for their assault on the royal family.

*If you can just get a whiff of their magic…* Julita murmurs, but she doesn't sound all that much more hopeful than I feel.

Rheave mostly scans the forest around us, watching for any approaching threats, but here and there he shoots glances my way. He lets me walk in silence for several minutes before he breaks it, in a low tone to avoid his voice carrying.

"Stavros looked at the area where the march stopped last night. They cleared most signs of their presence, but he saw a little evidence that they headed southeast."

Based on the angle of the rising sun, that's the direction we're going in now. I force myself to speak. "How far did you two travel without stumbling on them?"

He considers. "Three or four times farther than you and I have at this point. But we might have passed them without realizing it. We knew it wouldn't be safe to leave the shelter of the forest."

I hum in agreement. He and Stavros wouldn't have had any way to see where the march moved to unless they got lucky enough to stumble on another scout the Order of the Wild sent beyond the concealment spell.

I should have gone with them from the start, but I was still sleeping when they left. I guess they assumed I needed it—that I had more recovering to do after yesterday.

Even while unconscious, I let them down.

The daimon-man looks at me again, with a small furrow in his brow. "Are you upset that we kissed?"

As Julita lets out a soft snort, my gaze jerks to him. "What?"

"I thought I should check," he says. "You didn't want to before, and then you left quickly afterward. With everything else that's happened, I can't tell if the way you act with me has changed."

*I suppose it's a reasonable question,* Julita says.

Is it? It seems so absurd that it takes me a moment to pull my words together. "*I* kissed *you.* It'd be pretty ridiculous for me to have a problem with it."

Rheave lifts his shoulders in a slight shrug. "In my observations, limited as they were, humans frequently get upset about things they did themselves. Sometimes they're happy and then upset about the exact same thing in very quick succession."

He looks down at his chest as if peering through it to his heart. "I'm only starting to understand how that could be."

Julita outright laughs. *And that's a very reasonable point. The daimon has gotten quite wise.*

I think he's been wise all along, just in ways the rest of us weren't used to.

I shake my head to answer his initial question. "I'm upset, but it's nothing to do with you or anything I did with you. My head is pretty full with all my worries about my magic."

Rheave knits his brow. "If you don't use it anymore, then you should be fine, shouldn't you?"

"We don't really know that yet. And… it's not that simple." I make a face. "When I was refusing to use it before, it started eating away at me. Sulla said that if I'd kept suppressing it, my magic would have killed me. I'm supposed to find a balance… Just little things now and then. But I don't know if I've already gone too far for that to work."

He lets out a dismissive sound. "You're still all right now. A little shaken up, but you sound like yourself."

"That might not last if I keep tapping into my magic. Especially if I can't keep a tight rein on it when I do. It's like… It's probably like the hold the scourge sorcerers have on you. You don't totally control the magic that made you, so you never know when it might fuck things up."

*Oh, Ivy.* Julita stirs at the back of my skull, her tone full of compassion. *I'm sure you can still find a balance. The gods have to see how hard you've been working to set things right.*

I'm not convinced that the gods have much say in my sanity. Kosmel hasn't offered any solutions other than sending me to Sulla.

Rheave is quiet for a moment, absorbing the comparison I made. His voice drops even lower. "That is an awful thing. I wish we could break you free from your worries the way we'll hopefully destroy the sorcerer who can affect me."

I let out a rough chuckle. "No chance of that. This power is all in me. I can't get rid of it, but I want… I want to be more than my magic."

Those words reverberate through my body. The truth of them hits me like it hadn't quite before I said them aloud.

That's all I've ever wanted, isn't it?

But even when I roamed through Florian, dipping in and out of people's lives as the Hand of Kosmel, the power I was refusing to use seemed to taint everything. Knowing I had to keep it secret. Knowing my entire life was forfeit the second anyone found out that one detail about me.

Rheave grabs my hand and squeezes it tight. "You are more. If you asked me all the things I admire about you, I wouldn't even consider your magic. Do you think mostly about the scourge sorcerers when you look at me?"

After all this time, I barely associate him with the fiends who made him.

I grip his hand in return. "No. They didn't have anything to do with the parts of you that matter."

"And your magic is the same."

I can't quite accept his statement that easily, but hearing him say it so firmly takes a little edge off the ache inside me. I drag the cool winter air into my lungs, and they don't clench up against the breath.

Rheave doesn't push for my full agreement. He simply walks on with me, his thumb trailing across the back of my hand in a gentle, continuous caress. Showing he's here with me without expecting anything of me.

He was once a spirit creature with hardly any understanding at all of what went on between humans, let alone their darkest fears. And after that, he acted like a pedantic jerk in the grips of the scourge sorcerers' control.

Somehow he managed to grow so far beyond his origins that it's hard for me to imagine him being anyone other than the fierce and caring man beside me.

As the sun rises higher and the air warms from chilly to merely cool, not the faintest tingle of outside magic grazes my skin. I keep my senses alert for any hint of it despite my inner turmoil.

*Hmm,* Julita mutters as we prowl onward. *Where did the fiends run off to so they could lick their wounds?*

Nowhere near here. We pass a spot Rheave identifies as the point where he and Stavros turned back and continue on.

With each step beyond, my spirits start to sink.

The march may have moved beyond my ability to track them—at least, to find them in any kind of reasonable time.

Maybe this is pointless. If we were back with the others, at least we could be strategizing.

The one thing we do know is where the scourge sorcerers' army will attack, even if we aren't sure when.

Rheave halts where the ground falls away into a narrow gully. I peer down at a stream even thinner than the one where we filled our canteens and washed up this morning.

It's not quite narrow enough to jump across, but the gully only descends about twice my height. Not too bad a scramble.

What are the chances we'll find anything if we keep going, though? Maybe we should take this as our sign to head back.

I open my mouth to say that, but Rheave speaks first. "A butterfly!"

Gripping the saplings sprouting from the side of the gully, he scrambles down to the stream bed. A pale blue butterfly is indeed fluttering around near the shrubs down there.

The insect darts toward him and then away. I spot another one, with wings a deep yellow that's almost gold, farther down the stream.

Julita makes a sound of appreciation. *Would you look at that. They're beautiful.*

Rheave cocks his head and follows the butterflies, and I can't see anything to do but go after him. I skid down to the bottom of the gully and pick my way across the stones along the stream.

At least we won't be visible to anyone up in the forest while we're walking down here.

"I haven't seen any butterflies since we went north," Rheave says in a hush. "Alek said they don't like the cold very much."

"I guess these are particularly resilient ones." I raise an eyebrow at him. "Are you looking to make friends?"

He seemed bewildered by the injured insect that landed on him weeks ago back at the college. But he cared enough to carry it to safety anyway.

Rheave appears to consider my question intently. "They feel… like they're already friends. I don't know why."

I study his avid expression as we hurry on along the stream bed. It was a little odd that the injured butterfly was drawn to him. Unless…

"Daimon are supposed to be creatures of all the godlen," I comment, "but in your natural state, it seems like Inganne would be the most approving of how you act, exploring everything and playing pranks. Butterflies are one of her animals. Maybe you and they can sense you're kindred spirits."

The daimon-man cocks his head, a little smile curving his lips. "Even when my creators still had a grip on me, I knew I should help that one."

Up ahead, the butterflies look as if they fly right into the wall of the gully. Strange. I pick up my pace—and come to a stop at the mouth of a sort of alcove veering off into the gully's side.

The small recess can't be more than five paces deep and the same across, but there's something grand about it all the same. The sapling at its far end is already budding. Delicate white flowers sprout between the pebbles strewn across the earth, heedless of the season.

And several more butterflies swoop between those flowers in a spiraling dance.

A startled laugh tumbles out of me alongside Julita's gasp. "I think Inganne must have blessed this place."

I venture forward and graze my fingertips over a few of the flowers. Their petals slide against my skin soft as silk.

*The godlen do work in mysterious ways*, my ghostly passenger remarks.

A butterfly flaps over to me and lands on my hand, its feet tickling my knuckles. Then it takes off again, as if it was simply coming by to say hello.

An unexpectedly carefree air comes over me, as if nothing could be all that wrong when places like this exist. As if the godlen of creativity and play herself has reached down and blown the worries from my head like seeds in the wind.

I turn, expecting to see Rheave gaping at our surroundings in awe… but he's looking at me.

There's something like awe shining in his eyes all the same.

He steps closer to me and touches my jaw, his gaze fixed on mine. "Ivy… I want to kiss you again."

Julita giggles. *All right, I can tell I'd better take my leave.*

As her presence dwindles in the back of my head, I wet my lips. The warmth that motion provokes spreads through the rest of me.

But one of us has to be at least a little sensible about this situation, don't we?

"You know," I say, doing my best to keep my tone even, "there are a lot of things that usually come with kissing. At least, when you aren't just scratching an itch and figuring you'll never see each other again."

Rheave eases slightly nearer. "Like what?"

It's harder to think the more his beautiful face fills my vision. "Well, you've seen how I am with the other men. We have a relationship. We support each other. We're committed to tackling problems together and spending time together and, um…"

The daimon-man's expression has become increasingly puzzled. "Don't you and I do those things too?"

"It's not exactly the same. We've never talked about or decided where this is going."

"That's easy." He traces his fingers along my jaw to my chin and then back to the crook. "I want to be here with you and see how it can be. I want to experience everything we could have. I've got nowhere else I need to be—I'm happy to stay with you wherever you go."

He offers himself up so easily, my heart squeezes in response. "I shouldn't be your whole *world*. There are other things you like."

Rheave makes a dismissive sound. "Those are all things I can enjoy while I'm with you. I've had the whole world, Little Vine. I had it for more years than I know how to count. Nothing I found in it ever made me as happy as you do. That's why I want so much to be able to make you happy too."

A rush of emotion chokes me up before I can speak. Memories of all the moments turned brighter by his presence flicker through my mind. "You do make me happy."

The daimon-man smiles brilliantly and must decide that's answer enough to his earlier suggestion. He dips his head and captures my mouth.

The kiss is just as sweet as the first one, sending a giddy shiver straight through the core of me. Warmth floods me from head to toe, flaring into a more thrilling heat when Rheave nudges me right against the gully wall.

I give in to the impulse to tease my fingers into his soft curls, and a rough sound works from his throat. He kisses me harder. One hand stays cupped against my jaw while the other trails up and down my side until I gasp.

"We need to stay quiet," I mumble against his lips.

"Hmm. Then I should keep doing this."

He claims my mouth again, his confidence growing. His hand travels across my torso, lingering on my breast when the skim of his palm earns him a whimper I try to swallow.

His hips rock against mine. There's no missing the bulge between his legs that grazes my sex, setting off sharper pulses of desire.

A thread of fear creeps through my haze of arousal. Am I really doing this? Making out with a man who's not even exactly a man—and wherever else this will go if I let it?

Do *I* really know what I'm getting into?

My body tenses, and Rheave notices immediately. He draws back just far enough to meet my gaze, his dark curls falling across his forehead. "Is this all right?"

He looks so unsettled by the thought that it might not be that my stomach twists. I can suddenly see how it might go if I push him away again, put up my walls out of that fear.

I've already run off on him once. If it happens again, he'll never trust that I really do want him enough.

I'll ruin whatever odd relationship we've started to build here.

And the thought of losing this—him, everything we could be—frightens me more than the uncertainty of where we'll end up.

I want him. I do. This strange man who makes the strangeness in me seem a little more okay.

I trail my hand down to his cheek, holding his unearthly gaze that shines with longing and devotion. "It's wonderful."

Rheave's brilliant smile comes back. "I think so too." He nuzzles the side of my face and drops his head to nibble the side of my neck. "I feel... so much. I don't even understand everything my body wants."

When would he ever have experienced sexual desire before? I don't want to push him into anything *he's* not ready for.

"Just... do what feels good," I suggest. "What feels right. If it feels right to all of you, not just your body."

He makes an urgent sound and presses his groin against mine. "I feel like I should sink right into you. Like we're too far apart. But you're right here."

Okay, I guess I won't be the one pushing us along quickly.

I swallow hard, my own growing sense of urgency thrumming through my veins. "That's normal. It would be easier—usually you take off your clothes—but we can't really do that here."

Rheave lets out a low growl. "I'd like to touch all of your skin. But I— Do *you* want to wait?"

Another pump of his bulge against my sex propels an honest answer out of me on a surge of need. "No."

The daimon-man tilts my head back so our mouths can crash together. His kiss is demanding but without a hint of cruelty, as if he's only asking me to offer up what he knows I'll joyfully give.

His other hand sweeps over my chest, pausing to massage one breast until I moan into our kiss, then slipping down to my waist. He skims the curve of my ass before gripping it and pulling me against him even more tightly.

This time, it's me absorbing his groan into my mouth. My whimper echoes it as he grinds against me.

"Not quite enough," he mutters. "Not quite—"

He yanks the skirt of my linen dress up to my waist and fumbles along my trouser underskirt until he finds the ties. As he leans into another kiss, he flattens his hand against my bare belly beneath the fabric and then slides it downward, beneath my drawers as well.

The brush of his fingers over my clit sets off a flare of pleasure. I stifle a needy mewling sound as well as I can.

Rheave delves farther, devouring my mouth as he plunders the slickness between my legs. He strokes over my folds and lets out a shaky breath.

One finger slips right inside me. He muffles his next groan against my hair.

"This. This is where I fit."

All I can do is nod, my hips swaying with his teasing caresses. He strokes me several more times, both our breaths getting more ragged by the moment, and then withdraws his hand to lift it to his face.

His fingers gleam with the evidence of my arousal. Watching me, he sniffs them and then flicks his tongue over the collected slickness.

The sight sends a pang of hunger through me as if he licked me right on the spot those fingers were fondling earlier.

"Mine," he murmurs. "All for me."

A giddy laugh tickles up my throat. "And what do you have for me, my daimon-man?"

Another growl escapes him. "I need…"

He wrenches at his own clothes. As soon as it's clear he's sure about this, I help him yank his trousers down.

When he tugs his straining cock free from his drawers, I can't resist gripping it and stroking it up and down.

Rheave lets out a hiss that's pure heat. "That… That is very good just as it is. But I want more."

He yanks at my thigh sheaths so he can drag my pants and drawers down to my ankles. Then he hefts me up against the side of the gully. Only my cloak protects my bared ass from the cool earth.

My cloak and his hands, clamping around me as he presses toward me, angling my hips up to meet him.

As his shaft slides between my folds, we sigh in unison. Pleasure crackles over my skin as if he's let loose his supernatural energy on me in the most delightful possible way.

Rheave pushes into me until we couldn't be closer, his cock stretching my channel with a perfect heady burn. He stops there, his head bowed next to mine.

His voice comes out achingly tender. "This is where I belong. With you. No matter where your magic takes you, I'll follow. You can always reach for me."

Sudden tears prick at my eyes. But then the daimon-man eases back to thrust into me again, and the rush of bittersweet emotion is carried away by a sensation that's all bliss.

I clutch at his shoulder, my other hand digging into his curly hair. Every buck of his hips sends a deeper swell of pleasure through my body.

"I'm not letting you go either," I promise him between fractured breaths. "I'm not letting them take you away."

He makes a strangled sound and plunges into me faster. His fingers dig into my ass. "Cling to me, my little vine. Like we'll be twined together always."

My arms tighten around him. He adjusts our position with his next thrust and manages to hit the sweetest spot inside me.

That's all it takes. The surges of bliss expand with just a few more strokes until they crash right over the edge.

I sob and shudder, holding on to Rheave for all I'm worth.

"Oh," he mutters. "*Oh.*"

He shudders in turn, the movement of his hips turning jerky as he finds his own release inside me.

He hauls me right up against him and buries his face in the crook of my neck. His breath sears across my throat.

"I've got you," he says, like he did when he held me through the worst of my magic's torment.

In that moment, I believe him. The only question is who's going to save the rest of the kingdom.

# Thirty-Seven

*Ivy*

Rheave lowers me carefully to the ground, stealing a few more kisses along the way.

When he draws back, his pale cheeks are flushed, his eyes sparkling with glee. "That was fantastic. I don't know why humans aren't doing it all the time."

A laugh tumbles out of me. "I guess we wouldn't be able to get a whole lot else done."

"Hmm. Another area where there must be balance."

Even though my legs are still wobbly from the force of my orgasm, the ground feels more solid beneath my boots. As I wriggle my trousers back up to my waist and re-strap my thigh sheaths, a renewed sense of conviction fills my chest.

"Speaking of which, as amazing as this diversion was, we do still have an army of scourge sorcerers to find."

Rheave glances toward the top of the gully with a frown. "Which way do you think we should go from here?"

That is the question, isn't it?

I inhale slowly, considering our options, and my gaze settles on one of the butterflies gliding through the eerie subterranean glade.

Kosmel has guided me before. All of the godlen offer signs to those who pray to them when they feel the need.

What has Rheave ever asked of the divinities before despite everything he's given of himself to protect the realm? I think they owe him a favor or two.

I motion toward the butterflies. "Ask Inganne for help. Ask the butterflies if any of them have noticed a place around here where there's a lot of magic. You said they feel like friends... Friends help each other."

Rheave blinks, and a grin flashes across his face. He secures his own trousers and turns toward the butterflies.

When he speaks, I don't know how much it's to them and how much to the godlen who might be watching over this place.

"Thank you for giving us a joyful spot where we could make more joy. There's something very important we need to do, and we could use your help. Have you noticed anywhere near the forest where a lot of magic is being cast? We need to stop those people before they cause a lot of pain, but we have to find them first. I would be grateful for your guidance."

He dips his head as if in supplication.

At first, I don't think the appeal did anything. Then the golden butterfly I noticed earlier flaps up toward the top of the gully as if to leave.

Rheave glances at me wide-eyed. We both clamber up the earthen wall after it.

The butterfly glides this way and that, the farthest thing from a straight line. But as we pad through the underbrush after it, moving between the trees as silently as we can, I can see that it's leading us steadily if slowly onward.

The sunlight glints off its wings as it soars over a log. It skirts a thicket and swings back and forth around a grove of saplings.

I'm starting to think it's simply enjoying a romp through the woods after all when a tiny tingle grazes my face.

I freeze, concentrating on the sensation. With my breath held, I scan the woods around us for any sign of the Order of the Wild.

We're still so deep in the forest that I can't tell how close the edge might be. The march has always camped on open ground before, so they can easily monitor the area beyond the borders of their camp without leaving the boundaries of their concealing magic.

If I can't see beyond the trees, they shouldn't be able to see this far within the woods.

Rheave has gone still at my side. I hold up a hand in a signal for caution and walk onward with even more care and all my senses on the alert.

The hint of magic intensifies in the direction the butterfly has flown. When I'm sure of what direction it's in, I draw back to where it's only a faint tingle and weave back and forth to chart the edges of it.

The scourge sorcerers are to the west of this patch of forest. The faintest hum of their magic stretches far enough that I can sense it along a course of a hundred and twenty-three paces through the brush.

I want to get a closer look. But I can't risk using my own magic to conceal myself.

I stare toward the camp I know must be there, and something flips over in my head. I could smack myself for my obliviousness.

How many years have I been sneaking around without any magical help at all? I've gotten so used to relying on it over the past few weeks that what used to be automatic didn't even occur to me.

I touch Rheave's arm and lean close to whisper to him. "I'm going to creep a little closer. It'll be easier on my own. Wait here and keep watch."

He nods and ducks his head to press a swift kiss to my cheek.

Crouching low, I ease forward within the cover of the underbrush. Most of the shrubs have lost their leaves, but their spindly branches will still hide me from anyone peering into the forest's shadows.

I slink from bush to tree trunk to clump of wilted ferns, straining my sight. The magic in the air thickens with every step.

Julita's presence expands at the back of my skull as she returns to share my full awareness. *I see we've made some progress. I take it the march is camped that way?*

I dip my head in a subtle nod.

*I knew we'd find them.* She pauses while I ease forward with a few more furtive movements, and a giggle escapes her. *You know, I think this is more fun than simply whipping some magic around you. Where's the challenge in that?*

I restrain a snort and scuttle onward.

When I've left Rheave some twenty paces behind me, I finally make out a less dense area beyond the nearest trees. I can't get a clear view of the camp when it's cloaked in magic, but it's got to be right over there.

Great. Now what? I can't spy on people I can't see.

To breach their concealing spell, I'd have to walk right into the field. Even the Hand of Kosmel can't hide behind blades of grass.

I squint at the more open area beyond the dense forest for any sign of movement. There might be some kind of clue about their plans that I could pick up if I got closer—but I don't know where their sentries are. The farther I emerge into the fringes of the forest, the more chance there is I'll be seen.

After several minutes, I draw back about half of the distance I covered before, to where I'm confident I won't be visible from the camp. I still stay low and silent as I move from tree to tree, listening and watching for anything at all that might help.

A bird calls in the distance. Twigs rattle against each other in a gust of wind.

I pull my cloak tighter around me and rub my hand over my face, hating the idea of leaving without knowing more, aware that I might be more useful back with the others.

Julita harumphs. *They've got to slip up one way or another. Then we'll have them.*

But are they going to slip up while I'm here to witness it?

Then a crunch of dried leaves reaches my ears from the direction of the camp.

Every muscle in my body tenses. I peer between the branches of the bush I'm crouched behind.

A woman is striding away from the camp into the forest a short distance to my left. She holds herself stiffly erect, determined but a little nervous, her hand resting on the knife sheathed on her belt.

*Ah ha,* Julita crows.

This must be a scout. If we could take her prisoner, question her—

But how exactly are Rheave and I going to do that? I can't force answers out of her without using my magic. I doubt even Rheave could drag her away without her raising enough of a ruckus that someone at the camp would notice.

And do I really want to bring this woman back to the others in the hopes that, what, Stavros can torture information out of her?

My stomach lists queasily.

No, that's not who I am. I'm not a monster.

*You can't let her simply walk away,* Julita says. *You took on Ster. Torstem's whole club of scourge sorcerers—you've got to be able to handle one.*

Her words light a spark of inspiration in my head.

I'm not a monster—I'm a thief.

I'm the woman who convinced the entire royal college that I was a minor noblewoman rather than a street rat.

A grin curves my lips with a flicker of exhilaration.

I don't need to bully this woman. I simply need to steal her trust.

Gathering myself, I pull away from the bush and straighten up behind a tree. Then I walk forward quickly so I can pass near the scout as if I'm just returning to the place she left.

At the soft crinkle of my footsteps, her gaze snaps to me.

I pretend that I've only just noticed her as well and raise my hand in greeting. "Hey, there. Heading out to do the rounds? All's quiet where I've been so far."

The vast majority of the Order of the Wild members have never gotten a clear look at me. With hundreds of them in camp and newcomers joining here and there, I'm gambling that this woman won't find it totally strange that she might not recognize me as a colleague at a glance.

She slows, uncertainty flickering across her face through her hesitant smile. "That's good to hear. When did you go out?"

"Oh, the sun wasn't even up yet," I say easily, as if it'd never occur to me that she might not believe me. "Most were still sleeping. But we need the rest if we're going to see our purpose through, especially after that mess last night. Any changes to the new plan?"

The Order member still looks puzzled, but my chatty tone has lulled her enough that she answers automatically. "Not that I've heard. There can't be a better strategy than hitting the castle right before dawn, while *they're* mostly sleeping." She pauses, staring at me more closely. "How long have you been marching with us?"

My pulse hiccups, but I keep my easygoing smile plastered on my face. "I guess it's been a few days now? We were a late bunch, had to catch up but glad we did."

I give her another wave, this one intended to send her off. "May you discover no trouble."

I move as if to amble on by, knowing I can't walk too fast or I'll be seen from the camp. The woman takes a step but stops, twisting back around. "Wait."

I turn with a hitch of my heart and lift my eyebrows. "Is something wrong?"

She stares at me for a few seconds.

There must be something about my demeanor or my clothes that only an Order member would realize is off. I can see the shift in her from uncertainty to hostility in an instant.

She draws her knife. "You're not—"

Her mouth opens to gulp the air and holler a warning back to the camp. I snatch at one of the knives at my hips—

And Rheave is there first, leaping from the underbrush with his hands outstretched.

He tackles her, power bursting from his hands. The lightning bolt of energy sears through the woman's body with a soft sizzle, so quickly that she's disintegrating into cinders before her body can thump against the ground.

Her charred remains patter across the forest floor. All that's left is a sickening smell like burnt meat that washes away with the next gust of breeze.

Rheave stares down at the scattered chunks of ash and blackened bone. He looks a bit queasy himself.

As I hurry to join him, he lifts his head to meet my eyes.

"I didn't like doing it," he says quietly. "But either she died, or she'd have called the rest of them to kill you and me and our friends too."

I know that twisted feeling, sure that you did the right thing but wishing you hadn't needed to. Like when I had to stab Esmae before she could do the same to me.

The daimon-man didn't save me only from the attackers the scout would have called our way but also from having one more heap of guilt on my conscience, if I'd been the one to kill her.

I grasp his hand. "There wasn't really any choice. She'd already made hers. But I know it's an awful feeling anyway. Here, I'd better spread around the ashes so it's less obvious what happened."

Grimacing, I shove at the ashen remains with my boots, mixing them with leaves and dirt. Rheave follows suit until the spot where the woman fell could just be a darker streak of soil amid the rest.

As we hustle away from both her and the camp, the daimon-man smiles. "You tricked her at first. You got her to tell you things."

The joy of that small victory returns. I find myself smiling back at my new lover.

"I did. Without using a single scrap of magic. Now we'd better get back to the others so we can figure out how to stop their new plan once and for all."

# THIRTY-EIGHT

*Casimir*

Ivy lets out a little hiss and raises her hand from the stick she's holding. A drop of blood wells up on the tip of one finger. "I scratched myself."

Rheave leans over from where he's sitting next to her, his eyes widening with concern. "Are you all right?"

"It's just a tiny prick. But these are fiddly."

"Stavros said it might be easier if we slide the bits of fletching only part way down until they're all in, and then push them the rest of the way."

Ivy studies the arrow she's been making under Rheave's guidance after Stavros instructed him last night. The daimon lost all his previous projectiles in yesterday's chaotic assault on the march.

"I could see that helping," she says. "I'll try it with the next one."

As she tugs the last piece of the leaves they're using for fletching into place and sets the new arrow on the small pile they've been building, Rheave tips his head to brush his lips against her hair.

I've seen our newest companion show physical affection to Ivy in the past. There's nothing about the gesture that's inherently more intimate than before.

But the ardent gleam in his eyes when he eases away and the hint of a blush that colors Ivy's cheeks tell me something more passed between them during their foray this morning. They shift their bodies next to each other with a newfound sense of coordination I've normally only seen between lovers.

Good. She needed something ecstatic amid all the anguish she's been dealing with.

I haven't been sure how to offer that kind of release myself, not in a way she'll accept.

For now, I walk across the messy floor of the abandoned outpost and sit at her other side. "Show me, so I can pitch in too? I don't think we can have too many arrows if we're going to be on the front lines of tomorrow's battle."

A small shiver passes through Ivy's slim frame, but she smiles at me and hands over one of the sticks she and Rheave have carved into a straight rod from a small branch. "We've already put the notches in them. You just need to fit in the fletching and one of these pieces for the head."

She motions to the pile of triangular chips of wood she's honed to a sharp point with a few swift strokes of her knife.

"Like this." Rheave demonstrates how they've been wiggling the bits into the notches at either end of the arrow, tight enough that they don't need further tying.

I've never engaged in weapon construction before, but I've put my fingers to enough other nimble uses to be sure I can handle this. With a nod, I get to work.

As we add to the pile, a tense silence falls over the three of us. The sun has just dipped below the hole in the ceiling, evening creeping ever closer.

Alek is out foraging so we'll have some kind of dinner to ward off the weakness of hunger. Stavros hasn't returned yet from his survey of the nearby royal forces.

The question of what we're going to do about the scourge sorcerers' next planned attack has been hanging in the air since Ivy and Rheave returned with their news. I haven't come up with any answers.

The best we can do is make sure we're prepared for war.

When there are only a few of the base rods left, Rheave hums and gets to his feet. "I'll go collect more sticks we can use. I want to make sure no one from the march has come over this way too."

He gazes down at Ivy with a stalwart protective air, obviously hesitant to leave her even for that purpose, and then flashes a smile at me before striding out.

Ivy exhales in a huff of air and sets down her most recent creation. "I guess I should be glad I'm better at making arrows than launching them."

I nudge at the head of my arrow until I'm sure it's firmly lodged. "No person can be a master at every skill. I'm glad there's some way I can be of a little use myself."

She elbows me gently. "You've contributed much more than 'a little.'"

A short chuckle escapes me. "Perhaps, but this isn't how I was supposed to be making my mark on the world."

As the words leave my lips, Ivy's face falls.

She tries to recover with a brisk laugh of her own, but I wince inwardly. I've inadvertently stung her with my clumsy remark.

"You must be missing the college a lot right now," she says with forced lightness.

I swallow thickly and slip my hand around her arm. "I didn't mean it like that, Kindness. I haven't for one second regretted standing by you on this journey. I've only worried that... the debts I'm failing to honor may have brought bad luck our way."

Ivy's forehead furrows. "What debts? Why would they matter out here?"

I open my mouth and close it again, the shame of my history congealing in my chest. But I probably should explain it to her so she understands the responsibilities I carry—and how deviating from my course could have lost us my godlen's favor.

"I told you that my mother was a courtesan as well," I say.

Ivy nods, picking up another rod but glancing over at me again.

I run my fingers over the leaves I've fletched my arrow with. "She was a very admired and prominent courtesan. Some say no one of her generation served Ardone's will quite so well. But her pregnancy with me and the birth were difficult—both took their toll on her. It strained her nerves in some way that she lost much of her former grace of movement; she developed tics that made it difficult for her to even hold a smile."

"And the royal medics couldn't heal the damage?"

I shake my head. "From what I understand, it was too extensive and deeply set. Apparently her situation would have been even worse without their intervention. As it was, the effects were mainly superficial... but appearances matter a lot in our line of work."

"Of course." Ivy frowns. "But what does that have to do with you having debts?"

Surely it's obvious?

The weight of the knowledge makes my shrug sluggish. "It was my fault. If she hadn't birthed me, she'd have been able to carry out her calling for who knows how many decades to come. So I've done my best to spread as much joy and pleasure in the world as she would have."

Ivy blinks at me. She puts down the arrow she only just started fletching and turns toward me. "Casimir, you don't *really* think you're obligated to do the same work just because she couldn't, do you? It wasn't your idea to be born. She made that choice—she must have known there were risks."

My mouth tastes ashy. "She couldn't have known she'd sacrifice anywhere near so much. I wouldn't be alive without her sacrifice. She always said I was the gift she was giving to the world in exchange. Ardone deserves a champion just as worthy as the one that was lost, after all."

"That's ridiculous! That's… that's as bad as the scourge sorcerers conning twelve-year-olds into carving themselves up for their purposes."

A flinch ripples through my body at the comparison.

I manage another chuckle. "I don't think creating beauty and pleasure is anything like their awful cause."

Ivy grimaces. "Okay, maybe it's a slight exaggeration—but my point still stands. Nobody's supposed to be able to demand that other people give up their lives in service."

"It's my calling. I chose it; I enjoy it. No one gets to decide how every part of their life turns out."

It's Ivy's turn to wince, though I wasn't even thinking of her situation when I made my last remark.

She sets her hand on my shoulder. "You have options. You can make your life about whatever you want it to be. If Ardone would punish you—or all of us—because you haven't been fulfilling your mother's legacy for a few months or some bullshit like that, then she isn't a godlen worth serving."

"Ivy—"

"No," she says. "You've fought and spied and scavenged and so many other things so we could make it this far toward saving the kingdom from the worst villains it's faced in five hundred years. All of that counts, even if it doesn't fit with being a courtesan." She kicks at a stray pebble on the floor. "Be glad that you can pitch in by all those means."

I don't need to ask to understand what she means. "You've offered more than your magic, Ivy."

"Sure. A little." Her head droops. "For just a moment this morning, I felt hopeful. But all I did was find out more information we don't know how to react to. I've been wracking my brain for hours, and I haven't come up with a single way I could block the scourge sorcerers' attack for more than a second or two without using my power."

"It isn't all on you. We'll figure something out together."

"But I'm the only one who *could* do it—who could wipe them all out in a matter of minutes, just by wanting to."

The laugh that tumbles out of her next is so dark it scares me. "If I truly care about the people they'll hurt, maybe that's what I should do. What the gods would want from me. Why Kosmel set me on this course to begin with. Forget about my sanity, forget about the innocent people in the mix who've been duped—blast them all away and have Stavros ready to put me down before I can harm anyone else."

The horror that rushes through me at her suggestion drowns out every other sensation.

I wrap my arms around her and hug her close, an anguished burn coming into the back of my eyes. "Don't say that, Ivy. Don't ever even think that. *You* are not a sacrifice."

Ivy tips her head against my shoulder. She sounds choked up herself. "How is it any different from you giving up your life to replace your mother? I'd be saving the whole kingdom."

Gods help me, have I pushed her toward thinking this way?

I tighten my embrace, grappling with the torrent of emotions coursing through my body.

Is what she said now how it sounds to her when I talk about fulfilling my mother's legacy? But that damage was already done by my arrival on this earth—

I suppose Ivy could say the same thing about the damage she's inadvertently caused in the past.

"No," I murmur. "I don't believe it that far. We both deserve to *live*. We deserve to have some part of our lives that belong to us. We can find our own ways to serve our gods without giving up everything that matters to us. I wouldn't be here if I didn't believe that."

But believing it and *feeling* it in every moment aren't always the same thing.

Ivy lets out a shaky breath. "I want a life of my own too. I just— I don't know if I'd want to live in a realm taken over by scourge sorcerers anyway. What if I'm the only chance Silana has? The king's hands are tied trying to protect the country against the Darium threat as well. And he thinks *we're* the enemy."

A snort escapes her that sounds more like her usual self. "Everyone's against us, even the people we're trying to save."

I rub my hand up and down her back. "We'll prove him wrong. And we may find support in places we're not expecting it. Look at Rheave. He started out as the scourge sorcerers' tool, but then he became our ally... and now he's even more than that to you."

Ivy stiffens just slightly. "I—"

"It's okay," I tell her before she has a chance to think I'm accusing her rather than simply acknowledging. "I love seeing that you've found even more happiness. But who would have thought it'd come from such an unexpected place?"

"True." Ivy hugs me back and then leans into my embrace with a sigh. "It doesn't seem as if any of the other captured daimon have been able to shake off the scourge sorcerers' control. And nothing we've done has rattled their supporters in the march enough for them to question whether the Order of the Wild really has good intentions. I don't see who..."

She pauses for long enough that I pull back to check her expression. Her eyes have lit with a feverish sort of glint.

Ivy straightens up. She stays silent for several more seconds, wetting her lips, before meeting my eyes. "Casimir, if I had an idea that sounded insane but didn't involve *me* going insane... would you trust me enough to try it?"

It's a simple, straightforward question, no pleading or cajoling. But I can see in the strain on her face how much she needs me to stand by her right now.

And I know down to the core of me that I'd follow this woman right over the edge of the world if she asked me to.

"Yes," I say. "Whatever it is. Just tell me what you need."

Before she can answer, footsteps rustle outside. Stavros appears in the doorway, his hair rumpled from his ride, his expression unreadable.

A flicker of hope rises in my chest—that maybe he's seen thousands of royal soldiers already arriving to defend the king or evidence of some other response that'll make whatever danger Ivy's planning to hurl herself into unnecessary.

"Any news?" I ask.

The twist of his mouth makes my heart sink again before he even speaks. "The local forces are clearly more on the alert, but with the numbers currently stationed here, I'm not sure how much of a defense they'll provide. From what I overheard, there are reinforcements on their way, but they're more than a day out."

"Too far," Ivy murmurs, and focuses on him. "The scourge sorcerers are attacking before dawn tomorrow. But Casimir was just reminding me that sometimes enemies can become allies. I think we can set a trap that could mean the end of the Order of the Wild—or at least, of any chance of them harming the royal family tomorrow."

Stavros lifts his eyebrows. "What's that?"

Ivy's gaze slides to me. She takes my hand. "I'm going to need all your skills for putting people at ease, Cas. We'll have to win a little trust from both the scourge sorcerers and a bunch of Darium soldiers."

A different sort of glow forms in my chest. I have no idea where she's going with this, but my answer remains the same. "Any talent I have is yours as well. What's this trap we're going to lay?"

# THIRTY-NINE

Stavros

The sight of the Darium words marching across the paper makes my skin tighten up even though I know it was a friend and not one of the enemy who wrote them.

I fought the pricks who want to take our country for themselves for years—trying to think as if I'm one of them is nauseating.

But right now, they could be the key to destroying a much more immediate threat.

With his scholarly knowledge of the language, Alek was the obvious choice to write the false letter. I coached him through the content with my understanding of the Darium forces and their interest in Silana, while Casimir guided the subtler aspects of our phrasing.

We need the letter to sound convincing but also not overly pointed. Anything too blatant might raise suspicions of it being a fake.

*We accept your appeal in exchange for the stake we're owed in Silana. If the flag on your fort a mile west of where the three pines stand at the Seafell's bank is burnt by the second bell of the morning, we'll cross to the pines and convey the item by the means you requested. Any deviation from your promise, and the deal will be forfeit.*

*Emperor Tarquin looks forward to reestablishing a partnership that benefits us both. In this alliance, you do the continent proud, King Konram.*

Ivy paces at the other end of the abandoned outpost's main room. "Julita knows that at least Borys can read Darium, so the Order of the Wild will figure out what it says. Would their army definitely write to our king in that language?"

I nod. "I don't know if any of the Order members are familiar enough with our former conquerors to be aware of this fact, but the empire has always presented their own language as superior to all others. They wouldn't want to deal with King Konram unless he was willing to engage with them on their own terms."

Casimir pokes his head through the doorway. "The horses are saddled. Are you happy with the letter?"

Happy isn't the word for it.

"I think it should be convincing in combination with the show you and Alek will put on," I say, and hand it over to him. "Make sure you're careful about how you drop it—it *has* to look completely accidental."

Casimir grins. "Ivy may be our expert at stealth, but I can pull off a little sleight of hand. It's unfortunate how a bit of wind can snag on a piece of paper that's jostled from a pocket with hard riding."

Ivy rubs her hands together. "All right. You'd better go so we have as much time as possible to catch a scout."

She glances at Rheave, who's been watching the proceedings with quiet curiosity. "And *you* have to make sure they don't see you fire the arrow."

He hefts his bow eagerly. "I'll climb so high up a tree it'll soar right over the tops."

Alek tugs at the hood of his cloak. He's got it draped particularly far forward so it'll hide the scarred side of his face, but I can tell he's nervous. "We've worked out all the details. It should be simple enough."

I hold out my fist for the others to knock theirs to it. It's a simple ritual, but the resolve in the air firms as our knuckles tap together.

"Off we go, then." Casimir gives Ivy and me a playful salute and heads for the horses with the scholar and the daimon at his heels.

The moment we hear their steeds clomp off through the woods, Ivy resumes her pacing. "Between the dropped letter and the conversation we'll arrange for the scout to overhear, the Order will *have* to believe it, won't they? That Darium soldiers are coming to give King Konram a means to escape the uprising? If they don't go to confront the soldiers…"

"It should work," I reassure her. "And if it doesn't, we can send the Darium forces after the march. There are multiple ways to play the scheme. But you have your own role too. Let's go over those lines in Darium again."

Ivy grimaces at me. We're lucky she knows enough spoken Darium to be able to understand basic questioning and know how to respond. Not what you'd expect from a street rat thief, but I suppose nothing less would be fitting for the Hand of Kosmel.

All I needed to help her with was some minor adjustments to her accent and a few more specialized words of vocabulary. Boating isn't one of her regular pastimes.

I toss out the questions a regular patrol might ask her, and Ivy volleys back her answers with a casual air. I don't know if her Darium would be convincing in an extended conversation, but I can't criticize anything in the few sentences that are all she should need to speak.

When we're done, I rest my elbow on the makeshift desk we've formed out of chunks of rubble and a larger slab of stone. "Good. I already know you can keep cool under pressure. As long as you act as if you have every right to be there, you shouldn't have any trouble."

"With that part, anyway," Ivy says dryly. She sits down by the wall and tips her head back with a sigh. "I guess you have your own letter to write."

I suspect she's more concerned about the plan as a whole than her own part in it, which plays to her strengths. The entire idea was hers. Crazy but brilliant, really.

If it saves her from the insanity of her magic while also saving the kingdom I've sworn to defend, I'll go with crazy. Even if the thought of this final letter makes my stomach clench around a fresh twinge of queasiness.

I retrieve the paper and the ink we acquired for our purpose. "Yes. King Konram will need to be informed of what's going on and why so he doesn't make any rash moves."

"He isn't going to be happy about this tactic."

"Most likely not," I admit. "But as long as he's pleased with the ultimate outcome, that's what matters."

And that has to be all that matters to me as well. Never mind that carrying out this plan is the closest I've actually come to real treason.

I stare at the paper for a long moment, grappling with the fact that I'm going to have to inform my king of that treason. But if he doesn't understand what we've set in motion, it could be disastrous for all of us.

I simply have to hope that he eventually sees that everything I've done, including this, has been for him and Silana.

Struggling my way through writing the letter at least gives me something to distract myself with while we wait for the others to return. Ivy gnaws on our last apple and goes out to stretch her legs with a stroll around the building.

I'm sure she'd have wanted to be right there with the other men if discretion weren't so important.

I hear the distant bells ring for one hour and then the next before I sign my name at the bottom of my missive. I fold it firmly and tuck it into the inner pocket of my cloak.

If everything goes according to plan, I'll be setting it on its course late tonight.

As I get up from the makeshift desk, Ivy reappears. She takes one look at my face, and hers falls. "I'm sorry. You must hate this."

My heart stutters. She and I are going to have to be apart for more of this scheme than I like. If something goes wrong, we may not make it back to each other, as much as I loathe to think about that.

The last thing I want is for us to part ways with her imagining that I resent what she's asked of me.

"Ivy." I walk up to her, holding her bright blue gaze. "This is a fantastic plan. I doubt I could have come up with anything more likely to work if I'd had weeks to consider it. And you're the one who put all the pieces together. I'm grateful to get another chance at destroying the scourge sorcerers."

"By turning your worst enemies into sort of allies?"

I make a dismissive sound. "They'll face their own dire end. What's a little more treason after everything I've already been accused of?"

Before she can do more than wince, I draw her into my arms, my voice dropping low. "The real treason is that King Konram hasn't yet seen how inspiring you are."

Ivy manages to form an incredulous sort of huff. "I guess even Signy faced plenty of doubt before she proved herself."

"And as far as I'm concerned, you've proven yourself a hundred times over already."

I dip my head to catch her mouth with mine.

Ivy sinks into my embrace, one hand gripping the front of my shirt, the other rising to trail along my neck. Her fingertips ignite sparks that shoot straight to my groin.

Gods help me, if we didn't need to be ready to ride out at a moment's notice, I'd remind her of just how much I enjoy being with her in the most concrete way possible.

I end the kiss but keep my head bowed over hers, our foreheads brushing. "I need you to know that no matter what happens tonight, it's been my honor fighting these pricks alongside you. No matter how hard the journey became, there was never anywhere I'd have rather been than next to you."

Ivy swallows audibly. "I don't know where we'll go from here, but I really want the chance to find out. I couldn't do this without you."

Not just me. It's all five of us and the strange sort of family we've become.

Somehow our joint relationship feels more fulfilling than when I had a woman I was meant to marry all to myself.

A sustained rustling in the forest outside puts me on the alert. Giving Ivy's shoulder one more squeeze, I step past her to peer out the ruined building's doorway.

It's Rheave, making his way toward us on Toast, who we didn't trust to carry Alek or Casimir appropriately through their charade. The stallion looks typically disgruntled but gives a soft snort at the sight of Ivy stepping out next to me.

The daimon dismounts with a smile. "I saw someone coming from the camp site and signaled

Alek and Casimir. The scout didn't see. I rode back as soon as he was out of view, but the others shouldn't be far behind."

"Good." His report only offers a fragment of relief.

I motion to Ivy. "You should get on your horse. Every minute makes a difference."

The sun has already dropped lower than I like, though the dusk will make traveling unnoticed easier when we can't rely on Ivy's sorcery.

As she clambers onto the obstinate stallion, Rheave collects the bundle of additional arrows he constructed. The blankets and camp gear we leave on the floor.

We're not bringing much other than ourselves on this mission.

Another set of hoofbeats approaches soon after, announcing Alek's approach. He slides down from his mount, a little breathless. "We went through the conversation as soon as we saw the man coming through the forest. Obviously I couldn't look right at him or he'd know we'd noticed him, but he stopped and seemed to be listening to the whole thing."

He's only just finished speaking when Casimir appears as well, grinning widely from the other stallion's back. "And that blasted letter just happened to slip from my pocket without my noticing it. The scout will have plenty to tell his associates."

He hops down and nudges his steed toward me.

I take the stallion's reins. "You two keep an eye on the camp site and confirm that the march leaves at the right time. There should be some small indication of their passage when they pass through the forest, if you're watching closely. Meet up with us while keeping your distance from them, or sound whatever warning you can through the temple and the town if it appears they're sticking to their original intent."

Both of my comrades nod, tense but determined.

"Be careful," Ivy tells them as I prod my horse to pull ahead of hers.

I set off at a trot. "Let's ride."

By the time the Seafell Channel has come into view up ahead, the sun has completely set, only a faint glow lingering on the horizon. We approach the water at a cautious distance from the nearby fort that's my next destination. A hint of brackish salt laces the air.

It only takes a few minutes to find a suitable boat with its oars. The fishermen who don't live right on the waterfront have favorite places to stash them that I came to know in the time I was stationed near here.

We already carved Ivy a simple if suitable rod, and I find an old net that would only need a little quick mending for good measure.

"The Darium fortress is almost directly across from here," I tell her in a low voice. "It shouldn't be difficult to spot—there aren't any other buildings nearby. Just make sure no one spots *you* at an inopportune time."

"I have lots of practice at sneaking around," Ivy reminds me, but her expression tightens as she looks across the water. "I'd better get going. The sooner the message is delivered, the more likely they'll act on it."

She turns to me to claim a hasty kiss and then shoves the boat off the bank, hopping into it at the last moment. In the thickening darkness, it takes less than a minute for the small craft to blend into the shadows wavering across the water.

Rheave has been waiting back with the horses in the stand of trees where we'll leave Toast for Ivy to collect him. As I approach, he peers past me as if he was hoping Ivy might have returned with me after all.

"Are you sure it wouldn't have been safer for one of us to go with her?" he asks.

I'm never going to fault the daimon for his dedication to keeping our woman in one piece.

I give him a gentle clap on the shoulder in an attempt at reassurance, even though my own worries are knotting my stomach. "More people look like more of a threat. Especially when one of them is a large, fit man. She can handle herself."

Rheave makes a rough sound. "It just doesn't seem fair that she should have to go alone when the rest of us don't." But he draws his posture straighter with an air of resolve I also have to admire. "Now we go to our fort?"

"Now we go to our fort." As much as we can call it 'ours' when we're about to take it over like an enemy force.

There's one Silanian fortress watching over the channel in this area, a couple of hours ride from the larger palace in Regica where Konram and his family are currently residing. Unless policies have changed, they'll have regular patrols along the bank starting not long after dark.

Patrols that could ruin our plan before it's even really gotten started.

So we simply have to delay them for a while. Ensure both they and our scheme stay safe. It benefits them as much as us.

But as much as I tell myself that, my gut sinks with each stride my stallion takes toward the looming stone walls.

Perhaps my trepidation shows on my face, or perhaps the daimon has simply paid enough attention to past conversations to put the pieces together on his own. After a while, he glances over at me and ventures, "The people at this fort—they used to be your colleagues."

I nod. "In a way. We were all part of the royal army together. I was never stationed at Fort Cyprian specifically, and I don't know if any of the soldiers currently posted there ever served under me."

"But it must be hard. Even though what we're doing will keep them away from the danger. I wouldn't like it if I had to do something that would make you—or Alek or Casimir or Ivy—angry, even if it would be good in the end."

His acknowledgment lifts a fragment of the weight bearing down on me.

I find I can smile at him. "It is hard. But military life is all about making the best of many difficult choices. In a way, I'm using my training even more now than when I was officially a general."

Rheave smiles back at me. "I'm glad to act as your soldier, then."

I wouldn't have thought I could say this when he first stumbled into our midst weeks ago, but I can feel how true it is now. "I'm glad to have you."

We leave the horses again in the patch of woods nearest Fort Cyprian and make our final approach on foot. As his gaze darts around us watchfully, Rheave walks with a spring in his step, clearly eager to leap into action.

What will the books of history have to say about the former General Stavros when this night is done? What we do here could be seen as a major triumph... or an even greater tragedy of my career than the battle that ended my work in the field.

I push down the gnawing uneasiness and stride onward. *I* know that I'm doing whatever I can to protect my king and my country. Would I rather stand back and let the scourge sorcerers ruin it all, just to avoid any risk that my name could be tarnished by those who don't understand?

No. So those doubts should sit down and shut up like new recruits who haven't yet seen what warfare really means.

Lanterns glow in the big stone building beyond the thick wall that surrounds it. I spot a few soldiers standing atop the wall, but they're watching for larger threats than a couple of men on foot.

They don't notice us until we step into the meager light that extends only a few paces beyond the fort.

"Who's that there?" someone calls down as we approach the door—wood fortified with steel, and presumably still locked with a heavy bar on the inside.

I motion Rheave over to the door and lift my voice. "I'm sorry about this, but it's necessary to ensure the security of the country. No one is to leave this fortress before the morning."

"What?" the first soldier says in a bewildered tone.

And then another sucks in a sharp breath. "Is that General Stavros?"

She must have spotted my prosthetic. My stomach contorts into a ball of nausea.

Some of the men and women inside *could* have served under me while I was still a general. There are so many soldiers who trusted me, counted on me...

I set my jaw. I'm not letting them down tonight. I'm leading them better than I did during my last battle, whether they'll see it that way or not.

I put on my best commander's smile and raise the metal hook of a hand to my forehead in a quick salute. "Please stay calm and remain inside these walls until we open the door. As soon as your assistance is needed, we'll let you know."

"As soon as *you* open the door?" someone else mutters, just as I nod to Rheave.

The daimon sets his hands against the door's edge. His supernatural energy crackles over the surface like tiny streaks of lightning.

The steel border melts into the stone of the frame. He'll be pushing his power straight through to fuse the crossbar in place as well.

A faint smoky smell laces the air. Rheave yanks his hands back before the wood is outright charred.

A yelp carries from the other side. "What the fuck are they doing?"

A strained chuckle catches in my throat.

Saving Silana is what—with this crazy, last-ditch plan that will hopefully look more like heroics than betrayal by the time we're through.

# FORTY

I've never thought of myself as sheltered, but I had no idea rivers so much wider than the Starsil that passes through Florian existed. Although I guess the Seafell Channel is called a channel rather than a river because it's on an entirely different level.

Generally, I'd be glad there's so much water between us and the eastern half of the continent, where the Darium empire still rules. Tonight, I wouldn't mind our enemies lurking just a *little* closer at hand.

I dip the paddles carefully into the darkened water so they won't make more sound than the warbling wind that tugs at my cloak's hood. On the opposite bank ahead of me, the few scattered lights there look so tiny they could almost be stars.

At this distance, I can't make out any structures in the thickening dusk. Only the thin crescent of the rising moon keeps me heading in the direction Stavros indicated.

To my left and right, there's no light at all. The channel just stretches endlessly away.

Is this anything close to what it feels like being on the ocean? I've never experienced that supposedly vast body of water either, only seen it in paintings and tapestries.

I peer toward my destination again and restrain a grimace. Stavros said it could take more than an hour to cross while I'm trading some speed for stealth. I've only covered maybe a quarter of the distance so far.

*At least we don't have to worry about anyone seeing you for a while yet,* Julita remarks as if picking up on my impatience. *I don't imagine the channel hosts many pleasure cruises with the current state of political affairs.*

I let out a soft snort. "I just hope the Darium sentries find it plausible that a local fisherwoman might be out plying her trade."

*I suppose people always have to make a living, regardless of who's trying to invade who.* She sighs. *As bizarre as this plan might be, Ivy, I truly believe you're going to pull it off. It all fits together. Let our enemies destroy each other—brilliant, really.*

"As long as it works." I dig the paddles into the rippling water again, keeping my voice low just in case. "I don't know if stopping the march will be the end of the uprising, though. They did leave some people back in Eppun. We still don't know who's at the top of the Order of the Wild, giving the orders."

I get the impression of a shrug. *It'll eliminate a significant portion of their might, including the people most willing to fight. And we can hope that those who were duped into joining under false pretenses will flee and spread the word that the Order means death rather than freedom.*

"That would be nice. And there have been people standing up to them already. Emor and Voleska might have made more progress."

*We're heading in the right direction, both literally and metaphorically. That's what matters most.* Julita pauses. *And if Borys finally meets his end by Darium hands, I won't be the least bit sorry about it. Good riddance.*

She's putting on that nonchalant tone she does when she's trying to pretend she isn't affected. A pang of sympathy forms in my gut. "He'll get what he deserves, one way or another. If the Darium soldiers don't finish him, the king isn't going to forgive one of the uprising's main figures."

*I'd just like to know it's taken care of. Who can say how much longer I'll keep clinging to what's left of my life to be able to see it?*

My hands hesitate for a second before I stroke the oars through the water again. "Have you felt as if staying is getting harder?" I haven't noticed any change in her presence in my head.

*I'm not sure. It seems like something that would happen so gradually I wouldn't perceive the difference. But I clearly can't haunt you forever, Ivy. I'm starting to think it might be nice to let go and meet my godlen. Once I know the worst of this catastrophe is dealt with and that you'll be all right, that is.*

The pang rises to the base of my throat. "I meant what I said before, you know. About how we could travel around after there's peace again, see and do things you missed out on."

I sense a smile in Julita's voice. *Oh, I appreciate that. And perhaps I'll change my mind when the conflict is over.*

I hesitate, thinking of Rheave's bright eyes. Of the life that animates the body he wasn't born with.

"You know… There might be a way you could get more of a life back without needing to keep haunting me. If it's possible to put a daimon in a clay body and bring it—"

*No!* Julita's shudder resonates through my skull. Her horror rings through her refusal. *What happened to Rheave—that was already done. I want no part in any of the ways the scourge sorcerers are twisting life with their horrible power.*

After her past experiences with scourge sorcery, maybe I should have expected that answer.

I wince inwardly. "I didn't mean to offend you."

*I know. I know you meant well.* Julita sighs, but it's a serene sound rather than fraught. *If it sets your conscience at ease,* you *should know that lately I've been feeling that what I've gotten already is enough. My life might not have gone quite the way I expected, but I accomplished important things before and after my death. Possibly more than I would have if I'd stayed alive. I'm genuinely happy with how things turned out.*

She sounds as if she means it. Any words I could have said in response stick in my throat.

How can she be happy with her existence cut so short, with only getting to act through me for the past few months? She had even less time than I've lived, and I'd still give anything to go back to the childhood dreams I had before my riven power awoke and—

The thought stalls in my head.

Would I, though? Would I rather have been helping Da run the print shop right now, never having met Casimir or Alek or Stavros or Rheave?

Never even knowing the scourge sorcerer conspiracy was happening other than hearing of the uprising—until what? The Order of the Wild swept across the country and slaughtered every noble who stood against them, including the royal family?

If I wasn't what I am, King Konram might very well have died the day the captured daimon stormed the palace in Florian. I wouldn't have spent all those years on the streets or all these weeks on the run, but I also wouldn't have gotten to experience the incredible love that glows in my chest, sustaining my strength through every hardship I've faced.

I can't imagine giving it all up for a simpler life. And could I really gamble the security of the entire realm to recover my sister's life?

What kind of life would either of us have had once the Order of the Wild took over?

It's possible I'm exactly where I need to be.

For the first time, I can't say I regret the journey here.

"I'm glad you feel that way," I say finally. "You should be happy."

*And you should too.* Julita stirs in the back of my skull. *The only other thing I worry about is Nikodi. Once Borys is gone, there'll be no one left to inherit the county. If I'm not around by the time that matter comes up, I'd appreciate it if you'd make sure the next count or countess is a good one.*

As last requests go, it's a reasonable one. But it makes me choke up a little thinking of the entreaty that way.

"I'll do my best," I say. "Maybe you should stick around at least that long, to make sure we choose well."

Julita gives a light laugh. *We'll have to see what the gods have in store for us next, won't we?*

"I guess we will." I glance up toward the sky as if I might catch a glimpse of a crow or some other sign that Kosmel is still watching over me, but all I see is indigo darkening to black with a scattering of stars.

The lights on the shore are gradually getting larger. Julita and I lapse into silence as I pull closer to the opposite side.

The actual country of Dariu lies much farther to the east, but the realm of Cotea lies within their empire, under their control, so it amounts to the same thing. It'll be Darium soldiers monitoring the channel.

Which is exactly what I want.

As I draw closer, I make out the tall, blocky walls of the Darium fort that's my final destination. Rather than heading straight toward it, I veer around in an arc until I'm gliding closer to shore on a subtle diagonal. To anyone watching, my approach might not even be intentional.

All the same, my magic wriggles between my ribs, tugging at me to let it loose like I have so often in recent days. It could conceal me completely, ensure no one sees me at all.

I ignore its nagging and the pang of hopes lost. For a little while, I thought the cost of my power wasn't so high after all. I thought I could be riven and sane and help the realms with my magic.

But that's proven to be a lie. The price I'd be paying is simply different.

I'm several minutes distant from the fort and some twenty paces from the shoreline when a voice hollers over to me in the Darium tongue. *"Hey there, woman in the boat! What's your business here?"*

My magic flares with a sharper wrenching, but it's exactly the sort of question I practiced answering with Stavros. I clamp down on my power with the rigid hold I perfected during my days on the streets of Florian's outer wards and the imagery of ivy winding around my chest.

As my heart thumps faster, I pull the foreign words to my lips, reminding myself of the specific inflexion I need to sound reasonably native. *"Doing some night fishing. The silverbreem fetch a good price. Is it a problem?"*

I've stopped rowing so the patrolling soldier can study me. All he'll see is a young woman in a simple dress, alone.

I've propped the fishing rod against the side of the boat within view to help sell my story, and I have the old net I can claim I haven't finished mending near my feet too.

But the soldier must decide I don't look like I could be a threat to any of his colleagues. He waves me on without even bothering to speak.

As I dip the oars back into the water, Julita chuckles. *Nicely done. They don't have the slightest idea how much destruction you could actually deal out.*

My stomach twists. They don't, and *I* don't know how much I could cause before I'd destroy my sanity as well.

I'd prefer to keep it that way.

Stealth and subterfuge are my specialties. If there's anything I should be able to do without relying on supernatural gifts, this is it.

Most of the shoreline here is pebbled beach or sharply sloping stones, but a few minutes farther along, I spot a clump of reeds that reach nearly to the trees beyond the water. A careful glance over my shoulder confirms that the soldier who called to me is no longer visible in the darkness.

I push my craft between the reeds. They hiss against the wooden sides.

The nose of the boat nudges up against the rocky bank hidden by the plants.

After testing several of the reeds, I find one I trust enough to tie the boat to it. Then I ease out onto the rocks.

The fort's few lanterns shine off to my left, too far away to illuminate my crouched form. I dart from the reeds into the even thicker darkness between the trees.

The looming oaks and maples aren't growing densely enough to really be considered a forest. Only a few shrubs have sprouted between them. It feels more like the lightly treed area of a park. But they provide enough cover for me to sneak closer to the fort.

For the last short stretch, I have to dash from tree to tree with gaps of several paces in between. The last of them still leaves me a good sprint from the fortress's stone walls.

But not far enough to be beyond the reach of my throwing arm.

I slip my hand through the slit in my dress's skirt to palm the smallest of the knives in my possession. Then I retrieve the other letter my men and I composed together from my pocket.

A dark symbol marks the outer fold—a sigil drawn in blood while swearing to the gods that everything written on the page is true. If the fort has at least a devout on staff, they'll be able to confirm it's valid.

I wish I could confirm my loyalty to the kingdom by the same process, but the sigil's confirmation only works if invoked completely freely rather than under duress. Honesty prompted by a fear of impending punishment isn't pure enough.

With Casimir's help, we ensured every word in the letter *is* true, though we intend the recipients to draw different conclusions about our meaning. Starting from our introduction as *the ones the king sees as traitors* to our assurance that *most of the royal troops are stationed elsewhere, and we'll ensure the nearby squadron is trapped and unable to attack when you arrive* and on to our conclusion that *we believe that working together is our best chance at putting Silana on the right course*, the letter has been crafted to fit our situation while sounding like it should mean it's from the members of the uprising.

Gods above and below, please let this missive be enough to convince them. Let the supposed offer of an alliance with King Konram's enemies tempt the soldiers stationed here to make the crossing.

And let my crazy plan get us closer to truly freeing our country rather than amplifying the disaster.

I wrap the letter tightly around the hilt of the knife and secure it with a few bits of warmed wax. Tuning out my power's renewed urging to bring it to bear, I study the terrain between me and the fort's door.

There's a certain trick I picked up from a prankster in Crow's Close who was happy to teach me a thing or two in exchange for stealing a trinket she coveted. If you flick your arm in a specific way with the right twist of your wrist, you can fling an object in an arc rather than a straight line, just like the trajectory I took my boat on.

I brace myself, wind up, and throw with all my strength.

My pulse thunders in my ears as the knife whips through the air. It swings around, and a brief gust of breeze brushes my face.

But even as my nerves hitch with panic, the blade flies true.

It thuds into the wood of the door just a tad off-center, gleaming in the lantern-light from above.

Julita lets out a victorious cheer. A surge of mingled exhilaration and fear rushes through my veins.

I did it. I'm really *doing* this, despite all the shit and smitings it might bring down on our heads.

As the first shout rises up within the fort, I bolt toward the shoreline. It'll take the soldiers a moment to scan for threats closer to the door and then to open it to retrieve the knife.

By the time any of them set foot outside to investigate further, I'll be long gone… until I see them again armed and armored, storming the bank on *my* side of the channel.

# FORTY-ONE

I appreciated the darkness when I needed it to hide me. I'm less fond of it right now when I want to be able to track our enemies' approach.

Stavros gives the back of my cloak a gentle tug. "Lean forward any farther and you'll topple right out, Lady Thief."

He, Rheave, and I are perched at the top of a lookout tower about half a mile back from the channel. It's also halfway between the fort he and the daimon-man sealed up and the three pine trees we've used as a landmark.

We want to be within viewing distance of the battle but out of the line of fire. I would prefer to continue keeping my head attached to my body long enough for the king to pardon both parts.

The wooden tower, the platform of which stands at the level of the nearby treetops, is only large enough to comfortably hold the three of us. Alek and Casimir, who found their way back to us before we left Fort Cyprian, are watching from its foot.

We've set everything up as planned. In the lantern light of the fort, the Silanian flag waving there has been burnt to tatters by Rheave's magic—the signal to both the Darium soldiers and the Order of the Wild's march that everything is proceeding as they expect.

The Darium forces themselves arrived on several large watercraft not long ago. I can barely make out their forms over by the pines. They've drawn themselves into a rigid formation that could be a massive hedge for all my eyes can tell.

I think there are at least a few hundred of them. Not a huge crowd, since there wouldn't have been many soldiers stationed along this part of the channel within easy call, but enough to pose a significant threat to the Order when pitting trained military professionals against townspeople and inexperienced nobles.

And I'm still hoping that anyone in the march who's more misguided than malicious flees rather than getting caught up in the fighting.

Of course, that requires that the scourge sorcerers and their dupes show up at all.

No matter how I squint in the opposite direction, I can't make out any sign of the march's approach.

My hands tighten around the railing. A warble like a distant shout reaches my ears, sparking a jolt of nerves, but even as I turn toward it, I recognize that no one else has heard the sound.

It's only in my head. A reminder of why I can't set loose the magic that's been churning in my chest all night.

Rheave glances over at me and bumps his shoulder gently against mine. "The scourge sorcerers will be hiding themselves like they usually do, won't they?"

"Most likely." But that fact doesn't temper my impatience.

"We know they left at the right time to intercept the royal family's supposed escape to Darium," Alek says from below. "When we saw traces of them passing by the thicket where we were hiding, they appeared to be heading in the right direction, although obviously they could have diverted since then."

He and Casimir were only able to arrive ahead of the march thanks to a wagon leaving Iblin that they hitched a ride on, traveling to one of the farms that scatter the lands just west of here. That could have put them as much as an hour ahead of the march that has most of its members on foot.

*Borys will come*, Julita says in a taut but confident voice. *He'll hate the idea that the king might have pulled one over on him and be slipping from his grasp. And you made it sound as if the royal family already traveled out here to prepare for the meeting without him realizing. It wouldn't make sense for them to attack the palace in Regica if they believe the people they want to murder aren't there.*

*If* they believe it being the operative phrase. Did Casimir and Alek's staged conversation on the road and the dropped letter prove convincing enough?

Even as that thought passes through my head, a tingle of magic grazes my skin.

I stiffen, braced to realize that it's only another trick of my currently questionable sanity. But the sensation only grows, spreading steadily into my flesh until my bones start to quiver.

It can only mean one thing.

The words fall from my lips in an urgent whisper. "I can feel their magic. They're here."

Here and coming closer with every passing second.

As far as I can tell, the Darium troops near the channel haven't stirred yet. *They* can't tell the march is approaching.

They don't even know that these people will see them as the enemy.

All at once, the flaw in my plan hits me with a jolt of panic. I was counting on the skeletal forms painted on the Darium uniforms unsettling the scourge sorcerers enough to diminish their magic. But I can barely see the soldiers themselves, let alone any imagery on their clothing.

The Order of the Wild members won't be able to see them either. The skeleton designs won't have any effect on their resolve if they launch their attack without catching so much of a glimpse.

Shit.

"We need light over there," I spit out. "By the Darium soldiers—quickly."

I glance around, groping for an answer that doesn't require my unpredictable magic, and my gaze lands on Rheave's bow. "Rheave, do you think you can propel an arrow far enough with your power to set one of those pine trees on fire?"

Without hesitation, Rheave snatches an arrow from the quiver he set at his feet. "I'll try my best."

He braces himself, his beautiful face set with concentration, the bow stretched as far as it'll go. With a twang and a crackle, he launches the arrow into the air.

It gleams as it arcs against the night sky. Anyone below might mistake it for a shooting star.

Then it plummets amid the branches in the cluster of three pines just beyond the Darium formation, and the needles flare with flames.

A few of the Darium soldiers I can now see more clearly whirl around at the apparent attack. Most of them are so disciplined they barely flinch.

The fire darts along the branches until all three trees blaze with flickering light.

At first the uniforms on the distant figures look like little more than white stripes on black. But then the troops stride forward to meet the source of the attack, and the soldiers drop the visors on their helms to cover their faces.

A chill ripples through my veins even though I was expecting the sight.

They have images like skulls painted onto their black helmets—gaping mouths and eye sockets so vacant they're obvious even across all the terrain between us.

I don't know how much it's because of the newly visible soldiers and how much because they need to focus their energy on attacking now, but the concealment spell hiding the Order members wavers. The horde of them, still several hundred strong, charges toward the Darium troops as if emerging from a haze.

The roar of their furious cries reverberates across the landscape loudly enough that it reaches my ears. I shiver, clutching the railing again, watching the collision in the eerie illumination.

More light flashes—magic, I think, bursting here and smashing into a cluster of soldiers there.

Stavros tenses, tapping his forehead, heart, gut, and sternum in the gesture of the divinities.

The Darium soldiers won't have any idea what's going on. They thought they were coming to ally with the traitors against Silana's rulers.

Maybe they figure their attackers are the king's people who got here first. Maybe they'll assume the traitors turned on them too.

It doesn't really matter. They're already pressing back with flashes of blades, hails of arrows, and a few flares of their own, regular magic.

I spot bodies crumpling on both sides—some among the Order cracking into chunks of clay when they hit the ground.

As the two groups crash into each other, the flares of magic falter. The tingling that touched my skin fades away.

It's working. The scourge sorcerers' will must be shaken, their concentration broken by their rattled nerves.

It unnerves even *me* seeing the Darium force from this distance. I can't imagine what the visual is like up close.

But the Order's greater numbers ensure they're not at a complete disadvantage. I see black-uniformed figures toppling throughout the fray.

The Darium troops will have no choice but to retreat even if they win the battle. They aren't going to try to take on the rest of the king's army on their own.

And the Order of the Wild's march will be cut down before they can do any more damage to our country.

As I watch, my spirits lifting, the Darium soldiers press their opponents farther back. More and more of the Order members bolt away from their comrades into the night—first a few, then several, then dozens abandoning their cause.

Rheave readies his bow with another arrow, guarding our little group from any deserters who head this way. I retrieve my favorite knife from my boot.

Victory won't feel worth it if any of my men gets hurt in the process.

Stavros scans the battle with an intensity that hums off him, flicking his gaze every couple of seconds to refocus his damaged vision. Alek and Casimir adjust their positions below us, unable to see much from their lower vantage point.

"How does it look?" Casimir asks in a hushed voice just loud enough to reach us.

I smile. "The Darium soldiers are carving their way through the march, but the Order members are taking down quite a few of them in the process. The scourge sorcerers don't seem to be able to—"

Before I can finish that sentence, a sudden wave of energy slams into the Darium soldiers.

As my pulse hitches, the front lines of the Darium troops topple into each other. Blood splatters red across the white-painted patterns on their uniforms.

More magic thrums through the air. I swallow thickly, a cold sweat breaking over my skin. "The scourge sorcerers have rallied. I don't know how."

Stavros's body goes totally rigid. "Rheave, take out that man, the one in green off to the side of the battleground!" He jerks his arm forward to point.

Rheave's arrow springs from his bow in the same instant. With the sizzle of his energy, it flies true.

The arrow strikes a figure in a green cloak in the side of the head, and he slumps into a heap at the edge of the fray.

Stavros's knuckles have whitened where he's gripping the wooden railing alongside me. "I saw—my gift—that sorcerer was going to unleash a blast of power that'd have killed dozens of the soldiers."

Even as he speaks, more magic streaks through the battle. There are other sorcerers still ramping up their attacks.

The former general pushes away from the railing. "They're turning the tide. The Darium soldiers haven't felled enough of the Order members to ensure the march won't still attack the king. We need to finish them while they're distracted."

My stomach flips over. "What are you going to do?"

"Rally reinforcements." He motions to Rheave with his prosthetic as he grasps the ladder with his other hand. "Come with me. We need to open the fort and get the support of our own soldiers. Casimir, you ride with us too—maybe you can use your knack for diplomacy to convince them not to slaughter *us* for trapping them first."

He's already clambered down the ladder before he's finished speaking. The three men dash into the woods to grab the horses and set off at a gallop.

Uneasiness creeps over my skin. I glance down at Alek. "Do you have any idea how many soldiers would be in that fort?"

He shakes his head. What I can make out of his expression in the darkness looks sickly. "Less than a hundred, I'd imagine."

"Not necessarily enough to turn the tide if the Darium soldiers can't."

"No."

Julita shudders in my head. *I suppose Stavros feels he needs to take every possible chance to destroy the threat here. He's alerted the king—there could be more royal troops on their way.*

Maybe. But will even that be enough against the scourge sorcerers at their full power?

What shook them out of their demoralized state? I couldn't see anything from up here that explained it…

As I peer at the continuing battle, the currents of magic shift against my skin. My gaze veers to the west.

I could swear a significant waft of that energy is coming not from the battlefield but from farther afield.

Is someone helping them from a distance?

I didn't notice that current of power before. Has a new arrival come to rally their colleagues?

Squinting through the night, I can't distinguish any figures or even definite structures on the low hills in that direction. But as I stare, a crow circles beneath the stars and then flies to the southwest with a faint caw.

Julita lets out a ragged laugh. *I think your godlen is summoning you.*

Whether Kosmel is or not, I have to act. Someone's supporting the scourge sorcerers from over there, where the sight of death in the form of the Darium soldiers isn't affecting them.

And my sensitivity to their magic is the only means we have of hunting them down.

I waver for a second, but a glance at the carnage on the battlefield has me scrambling down the ladder.

I grasp Alek's arm. "I think there's another scourge sorcerer boosting their companions' power from the farmlands to the west. I'm going to follow the trail of their magic. It might be nothing. I'll signal you all with my locket if I need backup. If I don't, focus on the battle here."

"Ivy—" Alek starts, his eyes wild.

With a pang of regret, I squeeze his arm and let go. "I have to hurry. I'll see you when this is over."

Then I take off at a run in the direction the crow flew, hoping I didn't just tell the scholar my last lie.

# FORTY-TWO

*Ivy*

As exhausting as our weeks traveling across the country have been, they've hardened my muscles beyond any of my previous conditioning. I was never a weakling, but loping across the grassy terrain now comes much easier than it would have when I'd only just left Florian.

As I jog to the southwest, I keep my strides long and swift without pushing myself so hard that I'll get too winded to maintain the pace.

The tingle of magic gradually thickens. There's a whole torrent of it flowing toward the skirmish rather than seeping off the battlefield.

Someone's definitely bolstering the scourge sorcerers' strength.

If I can stop them before the Darium troops are completely overpowered, the two sides might still wipe each other out. Hopefully before any of the men I've given my heart to charge into the fray.

I catch one more flicker of dark wings against the stars up ahead, but I don't need the crow to guide me. I simply move toward the deeper thrum of the magic, shifting course slightly when I sense it diminishing.

"Kosmel," I murmur, tapping my hand down my front like I saw Stavros do not long ago. The gesture of the divinities feels awkward.

I've rarely used it, rarely trusted the gods to have my best interests at heart. But I need every bit of assistance I might get.

I lift my voice just slightly. "If you can hear me, please watch over me now. Help me see how to defeat this foe without losing myself."

I don't expect to hear the overwhelming divine voice resonating through my head. The godlen of trickery told me himself that he had to stay more distant. But I think I feel a subtle tug on my hair as if affectionately teasing.

Maybe it's only my mind playing tricks and not Kosmel, but he came through for me before. While I don't know what rules the gods have to play by, I actually believe he'll guide me if he can.

The trouble is, I don't know yet whether his guidance will be enough.

*We've gotten through plenty of tight spots without his assistance,* Julita remarks. *You came up with this whole plan without any divine intervention. Whatever's up ahead, we can handle it ourselves.*

She speaks in the archly confident tone I'm most used to from her, but I know her well enough by now to realize that it's usually a front. She's got to be nervous too.

"I have two knives," I say, taking stock for her benefit as well as my own. The third I was still carrying I had to leave on the other side of the channel. "Whoever's over there won't expect anyone to trace their magic, so I'll have the element of surprise. I just have to be smart about it."

*And I've no doubt you can manage that.*

The corner of my mouth crooks upward in half a smile at my ghostly passenger's validation, but I lapse into silence—both for the sake of stealth and to avoid losing any more of my breath.

As I trace the reverberating energy through the chilly night breeze, the ground beneath my feet slants upward. I slow, peering up the slope.

A dark shape looms at the top. The faintest glow hazes one of the second-floor windows facing the battlefield, so slight I couldn't have made it out from even fifty paces further away.

Our enemy is up there.

I prowl through the overgrown grass to the plateau around the building.

Closer up, I can tell it's a farmhouse, but one that must have been abandoned. The weeds grow high along its walls, and the front steps have caved in. The glass in the windows is cracked.

In one of the first-story windows, the pane is missing completely.

I steal up to the side of the house and pluck a couple of lingering shards out of the frame. Gripping the base, I swing my leg inside and set my foot down ever so carefully on the floor.

It turns out I'm in a kitchen—next to a dusty stove that looks as if it hasn't been lit in years, with cupboards along the walls beyond.

Drawing out one of my knives, I creep out into the hall beyond, searching for the stairs.

A muffled murmuring filters through the floor from above, followed by a retort that sounds sneering. The hairs on the back of my neck rise at the tone.

As carefully as I'm setting my feet, a warped floorboard creaks at my next slow step. I freeze, my heart skipping a beat, straining my ears for any sign that those above have noticed.

There's no sound from the second floor except a whimper that filters through the ceiling. I suppress a shudder.

After a moment, the sneering voice mutters something else. When I don't pick up any indication that the people above are coming to investigate, I creep forward even more cautiously than before.

Down the hall, I spot the shadowy staircase. I flatten myself against the wall where the boards should be most stable and ease up one careful step at a time.

The dust that my movements sends whirling into the air tickles my nose. I rub it to restrain a sneeze.

When my head is level with the floor of the hallway above, I spot movement in one of the doorways. The door is slightly ajar, and a large form stands just beyond it, only his shoulder showing in the dim lantern light.

At least, I assume it's a man from his size.

The sneering voice speaks again from farther inside the room. "Come on, come on. You can give a little more. We've got to keep those idiots full of confidence, or they'll fall down on the job again."

Julita's presence twitches at the back of my skull. *Borys.*

I'd thought the tone sounded familiar before. I just hadn't wanted to believe it.

But then, it fits everything I know about Julita's brother that he'd choose to contribute to the battle by extending power from afar rather than risking his neck directly.

If I have anything to say about it, that neck is going to have a very large gash in it by the time we're through.

My fingers itch around my knife, but I don't dare throw it from here. I don't have a clear view of any vital part of the man guarding the doorway, and I don't know how many others are with him and Borys.

I reach into my pocket and flick open the locket to press its inner surface. It's quite possible I won't be able to tackle this problem all by myself.

But I have to do whatever I can manage on my own, because the battle might be lost and Borys moving on to join his comrades before any of my men reach me.

A sound like liquid pattering onto the floor carries through the doorway.

Julita outright flinches. *Oh, gods. He still does it. The blood...*

My stomach flips over at the thought of all the times he carved into her skin in the hopes that offering her blood would gain him additional power. Just like he's apparently doing up there right now.

Breathing shallowly, I slink up the last few steps and along the hall toward the room. Through the thunder of my pulse, my focus narrows down to the little details I've learned how to judge during my days of thefts and cons.

The light streaks in only one angle across the floor, which means there's a single lantern. Two shadows cross the floor by the threshold, so there's another figure standing guard just inside, beyond the door. I can judge their position by the patches of darkness in the wan glow.

Crouching low and inching even nearer, I peek around the closer man's leg.

Borys is squatting across from one of the scourge sorcerers' sacrificial accomplices, her shroud discarded, her eyeless, noseless face as haunting as all those I've seen before.

As I watch, he drags the knife he's holding through the flesh of her jaw just below where her ear should be. Blood springs up, nauseatingly scarlet against her sallow skin.

To amplify his own gift, he's making her sacrifice even more than she already has.

Their combined magic wafts through the air, vibrating through my bones. I tense against a cringe at the sensation.

I've got to stop him—fast.

I double-check the shadows to confirm my sense of where the second guard is standing. Then I retrieve my second knife from its sheath, brace myself, and lunge.

As I spring forward, I'm already flinging my first knife. It plunges into the first guard's throat.

He gurgles and staggers, blood spilling across the floor while I whirl around the door.

The second man standing guard is just starting to step forward when I toss the other knife to my dominant hand and stab it home into his chest. It must puncture his heart, because before he's even sagged to his knees, his form hardens to clay.

I clutch the hilt to wrench the blade free—and a body rams into me from the side.

*No!* Julita cries out.

An elbow digs into my ribs, and a fist clocks me in the jaw. I reel around with a swipe of my retrieved knife, driven by years of honed fighting instinct.

It should have been enough, even with the element of surprise my attacker had. But as Borys slashes at me with his own dagger, my magic roars up inside me, bellowing to tear him apart.

My mind spins, and Borys's image distorts into two, three men in front of me. I swing out half-blindly, shaking my head trying to clear it, wrenching back the power that's addled my awareness.

Borys's blade rakes against my side like a vicious burn. His arm smacks my hand hard enough to break my grip on my knife.

As the blade falls, he rams his knee into my gut and heaves me backward.

I lurch over the threshold and slam into the banister overlooking the stairs with a burst of pain through my scars. The wood creaks against my back.

Borys hurls himself after me, lashing out with his dagger with obvious experience but middling skill. He'd stab it right through my temple if I didn't yank my leg up in time to kick him hard in the chest.

With a grunt, Julita's brother stumbles back to the doorway. He pauses there for a second, his dark eyes glinting, brandishing his blood-streaked blade.

It's not just his accomplice's blood on that dagger now. Mine is seeping into my dress where he carved open my side.

I don't think he gouged deep enough to puncture any organs, but the throbbing ache sears through my torso.

Both of my weapons are in the room behind him. And I don't think I've managed to do more than bruise my opponent.

He's got the upper hand, as he can no doubt see too.

Julita's rambling takes on a panicked quaver. *Oh, fuck. Ivy, you have to get through this. You're better than him. You can find a way.*

Her brother lets out a dry chuckle. "It's Julita's friend again. She did pick a persistent one. And just like her, you don't appreciate what I'm trying to accomplish."

A snort tumbles out of me despite my desperate situation. "What's that—bringing on a second Great Retribution? Have you all forgotten that the gods wiped scourge sorcery out the first time around?"

Borys's chuckle expands into a low laugh. "This isn't scourge sorcery. Those imbeciles *wasted* potential. Snuffing out lives like that." He snaps his fingers. "We're finding out how much power we're all capable of together."

Is that what they're telling themselves?

*Gods help us,* Julita mumbles. *They're the insane ones.*

At least while I've got him talking, he's not stabbing me again. "The All-Giver abandoned us over magic like this. Even if it's not quite the same, are you really willing to take the chance?"

Borys scoffs. "We're going *back* to what the gods meant this world to be. Energy and action and wildness. The scourge sorcerers five hundred years ago wanted to bend everyone to their will, make up more rules, control the realms—but the All-Giver wanted us to be free."

*For fuck's sake.* Julita's voice starts to firm with a sharper edge. *As if he knows the slightest thing about freedom.*

"So instead you'll send us into total chaos," I retort.

"That's how the world began. That's what the All-Giver thrives on. The Great God truly wants us to have it *all*. You'll see."

Is that what the gods would honestly prefer? For me to release my magic with all the madness that'll come with it?

What if that is why Kosmel led me so far and then left me to fend for myself?

I swallow against the dryness of my throat. I don't know what's right anymore—but I can't make any decisions about it either way if I'm too unhinged to even care.

*Don't listen to him,* Julita says, more forcefully than before. *All he ever wanted is to get whatever he can for himself.*

"Or rather, you won't see," Borys says, adjusting his grip on his dagger. "Because I need to get back to my work, and I can't have you interfering again."

As he shifts his stance to strike, my mind flashes back to Wendos in the All-Giver's tower. Wendos, turning his back on me rather than closing in for the kill.

Borys is obviously the smarter one.

And how ridiculous that back then my magic saved me, and now it'll only doom me.

Borys leaps at me. As I shove myself to the side to avoid his strike, Julita squirms in the back of my skull. *We need him off-balance. My gift won't help—he hasn't told us to do anything. But there has to be a way…*

Abruptly, her presence seems to stiffen. *I can—we can do this, Ivy. I won't let him cut you too. Be ready.*

With those words, she throws herself forward in my head.

My instinct is to resist the wave of dizziness that sweeps over me. I recognize what it means. I've felt her uninvited attempts to take control before.

But she knows the man in front of me far better than I could. She's got more of a plan than I do.

I let go, and Julita's presence floods to the front of my mind. With her in control, my body scrambles backward down the hall.

Borys whirls on us, and Julita hurls out my voice in a tone that's all her. "You haven't grown at all since you were twelve, making me bleed with Wendos, have you, big brother?"

Borys goes rigid in mid stride. He stares at me.

Before he can decide it's all a trick, Julita hurtles onward. "Oh, yes, it's really me. And I haven't forgotten a second of those midnight trips out to the woods—the time you used a sharpened stick instead of a proper blade, the time you scraped my skin raw with the rough edge of a rock."

In my hazy state at the back of my mind, I wince in sympathy. My ghostly passenger has always avoided going into detail about the torment she suffered at the hands of her brother and his friend.

What I imagined was horrible. It's worse hearing her describe it out loud.

Borys's jaw drops for a second before he reels it in.

"Julita?" he says, his voice ragged with disbelief.

She makes a disparaging sound. "Wendos tried to murder me back in Florian, but neither of you understood how strong I am. I managed to hang on with the help of my friend. And I've been helping *her* pick away at your idiotic, psychotic uprising bit by bit."

I'm not sure what she's aiming for here. Maybe she's simply letting out all her bottled-up anger.

But she told me to be ready. She must be going somewhere with this.

I have to watch for an opening.

Borys hasn't quite let his guard down. He still holds his dagger in a fighting stance.

His eyes narrow. "This is some stupid trick. Or magic. Julita can't really be here."

"I'm sure you'd like to think so," Julita says. "But I know how you pissed yourself that time Dad's stallion kicked you in the thigh when you were six. I know the town boys beat you up on your ninth birthday when you tried to boss a bunch of them around like you were already a count. I know that when you were ten, you ate slugs on a dare with Wendos and then vomited all over Mother's favorite tablecloth."

"Shut up!" Borys's eyes flash with fury. He steps closer, his jaw flexing. "You were never good for anything other than filling in when we had nothing better to practice on. I'll just have to finish what Wendos started."

"*You* have always been a spineless, pathetic bully who was too scared of taking responsibility to do anything worth respecting," Julita spits back at him. "This woman is the best friend I've ever had, and you're not taking her down with you."

Borys lunges—and the tickle of Julita's presence by my forehead heaves forward. My awareness jolts back into place in its wake just in time to see her brother clawing at his face as if there's something in his eyes.

I don't have time to figure out what's happened. He isn't looking at me—his knife hand is flailing aimlessly.

I spring forward, snatch his wrist, and wrench his arm around.

With a sickening sound, his own blade drives into the flesh at the base of his throat.

Borys's body spasms in front of me. I dodge backward as he crumples over, spewing blood from his neck and lips.

He sputters something as if he's trying to speak, but not with any words I can decipher. His hands fumble across the floor and drift to a halt.

His body sags, his head lolling to the side. The one eye I can see stares blankly at the wall.

Blood courses across the dusty floor in a steady current.

I got my gash, just like I wanted.

I suck in a shaky breath. "Julita? We did it. He's dead."

No one answers. And all at once, I realize I can't feel her—not the familiar prickle at the back of my skull, not the faint trace of a tingle that lingers even when she pulls herself as deep as her presence can go.

She must have flung herself right out of me to smack Borys in the face with whatever presence she did have left.

*She's* what he was clawing at, what distracted him enough that I could attack.

And now she's gone.

# FORTY-THREE

*Ivy*

I wake up to a cool breeze tugging at my hair and a warm hand on my cheek. When I blink, Casimir's gorgeous face comes into focus in the pale light, framed by looming trees.

A smile curves his lips. "There's our woman." He strokes my hair back from my temple. "How are you doing, Kindness?"

"I—" The first word comes out as a croak. I clear my throat and try again. "What happened? Where are we?"

The last thing I remember is the hall in the farmhouse, Borys bleeding across the floor, my head unnervingly vacant for the first time in—

My body tenses beneath the blanket that's been laid over me. My skull is *still* vacant.

I can't find any tingle of Julita's presence no matter how hard I strain my senses.

"We followed the locket's signal and found you in the farmhouse," Casimir is saying. "You must have passed out."

Stavros's voice carries from somewhere beyond my view. "Exhaustion and blood loss will do that."

Blood loss. I adjust my position on the ground—padded by another blanket—and an ache ripples through my side from the spot where Borys cut me.

No wry comment from Julita. No cheer that her sadistic brother is finally, definitely dead.

I pry at my mind as if I can summon her voice through sheer will, but nothing comes.

Casimir's brow knits at the emotion that must show on my face. "We patched you up thoroughly. Most of the blood wasn't yours."

Alek appears beside him, holding one of our canteens. "You should be all right, but it'd be good for you to drink something."

I stare at them, a much deeper ache spreading through my chest. It twines around my lungs, making it hard to speak.

"Julita—she helped me distract her brother—she… she *flung* herself right out of my head at him so I could get his dagger—"

A sob breaks through my words.

Rheave hustles into view in an instant, his stance poised for battle. "What did he do to you?" he snarls.

"He's already dead," the courtesan reminds him in a mild tone, and helps me sit up with his arm around me. "Have a drink, and then you can tell us the whole story."

As Alek hands me the canteen, Stavros steps closer as well, the four of them forming a semi-circle around me. I gulp the cool water that has an herbal tang to it, suggesting one of them has added a little supplement that's supposed to help me heal.

It takes a few slow breaths before I think I can get through the whole explanation. "I took down the two daimon Borys had guarding him, but he came at me too quickly, and I lost my knives. He would have killed me if Julita hadn't intervened. I let her take over so she could put him off balance, and like I said, she jumped out of my head at him. I think her spirit had enough energy to smack him in the face."

I lower my head and rub my face. "But I guess she couldn't come back. She's gone."

The ache of loss creeps up my throat, choking me.

She was already dead too, in most of the ways that count. She told me she was ready to move on.

I can't imagine any way she'd rather have gone than by ensuring her brother never caused any more harm.

But I didn't even get to say thank you. I didn't get to say *good-bye*.

Casimir hugs me closer, and Alek grasps my hand with a comforting squeeze.

"We'll have a proper funeral for her," Stavros says, sounding a little awkward. "As soon as we can. She deserves at least that much. I'm not sure what exactly we'll tell people, but they should know she's a hero."

I swallow thickly. "Yes. Yes, they should."

His remarks cut through my grief enough to remind me of the other heroics we were attempting tonight.

My pulse stutters. "The battle—the Darium soldiers and the scourge sorcerers—is the royal family safe?"

Stavros crouches down so we're eye to eye. "It must have been as soon as you engaged with Borys —the Order of the Wild army faltered again. The remaining Darium soldiers managed to cut down a lot more of them before they retreated to their side of the channel, and the soldiers from our fort mopped up the few stragglers who hadn't fled."

"And they didn't arrest you?"

Rheave lets out a disgruntled sound. "Arrest us for fixing their problems?"

Stavros casts him an amused sideways glance. "I think they wanted to, but we were able to evade capture. They were somewhat distracted by dealing with the sacrificial accomplice we pointed them to in the farmhouse, after we'd gotten you out."

"And we got our hands on a couple more horses, since the march didn't need them anymore," Alek pipes up. "So we can all ride. And we'd better soon, before the soldiers decide to get more serious about hunting us again."

Stavros's expression turns solemn. "I don't know where we stand after tonight's victory or where it'd make the most sense to go."

Casimir offers him a soft smile. "Farther from the fort does seem like a good initial idea, in any case."

They help me to my feet. As Stavros gathers the blankets, Rheave wraps his arms around me, keeping his embrace gentle. "You shouldn't have gone without us, Little Vine."

"You were busy doing something just as important," I remind him.

He gives a dismissive huff and ducks his head to claim a kiss.

My heart skips a beat with the knowledge that this is the first time my other men will have seen such an open display of our new intimacy. But when the daimon-man eases back, the three of them are simply smiling.

Casimir has led Toast over. The stallion nickers as if expressing his own concern about my injuries.

Stavros moves to my side. "I'd better help you mount."

Before I've positioned myself next to the saddle, a brisk female voice blares through the woods with an unnatural resonance. "Stavros Teodorek of Florian—on behalf of King Konram, I need to speak with you and your companions."

I flinch and then wince at the pain that sears from my bandaged wound.

Stavros's forehead furrows. "Whoever that is, she's using a magical amplifier to spread her call. I don't think she's that close."

We venture in the direction of the voice, coming to the edge of the patch of woods where the men brought me for shelter.

Across the nearby fields, a robed woman sits on horseback, flanked by two soldiers.

She holds her body with a stately air. A patch covers the eye she sacrificed.

I stare. "Is that... Hessild Korinya? The king's chief sorcerer?"

"I believe it is," Casimir murmurs. "And according to her, he sent her to us."

Stavros scans the terrain around the royal magic advisor and her small escort. The nearby fields are open enough that any additional threat should be obvious.

"Konram knew from my message approximately where I'd be," he says. "We should see what she wants—but with the horses, and keeping a safe distance so we can ride off if the conversation turns sour."

Hessild makes her amplified appeal again as we clamber onto our steeds. When we emerge from the woods, she turns toward us but stays where she is, maybe recognizing that we'll want to stay cautious.

Rheave keeps his bow at hand, his quiver over his shoulder. I scan the landscape all around us, but I don't see any sign of a trap.

We stop right at the edge of where we can comfortably yell and be heard. "I'm here," Stavros says, pitching his voice to carry. "What do you have to say?"

Hessild smiles. "It's good to discover that you haven't lost your knack for strategy, Stavros. You and your colleagues did the royal family a great service last night."

Stavros gestures toward me. "The main part of the strategy came from Ivy. She risked her life to see that King Konram's wouldn't be threatened."

The royal advisor inclines her head. "He recognizes that and regrets that he judged all of you so hastily. If you would come to Regica with me, he would like to discuss the conditions of a full pardon."

For a second, I lose my breath. This is the outcome we hoped for all along.

Can it really be happening? King Konram is willing to let me live with my riven magic?

"Do we have official confirmation of his intentions?" Stavros asks.

Hessild retrieves a paper with a blob of wax at its bottom from her pocket and holds it out. "He has sworn it with his seal."

"I'll get it." Rheave prods his horse forward and canters over.

I brace myself, but Hessild lets him take the proclamation without the slightest suspicious move. The daimon-man rides back and hands the paper to Stavros.

The former general scans it carefully. He keeps his voice even when he fills us in, but a warm glint comes into his eyes. "It looks authentic. The seal is his personal one that no one else has access to. He apologizes—says he can't help but honor our efforts on his behalf. He couldn't risk coming himself, but he sent Hessild as a gesture of trust."

He pauses. "I'd imagine he also wants her to evaluate Ivy, but I suppose it is true that as far as they're concerned, Hessild is putting herself at *our* mercy."

Alek shifts nervously on his horse. "Do you think we can trust him?"

Stavros nods slowly. "If we don't trust this, then we might as well commit to being outlaws forever."

He glances at me. "But I can't make the decision for all of us."

My gut twists. I'm the one in the most danger if we go to the king. But how can I give up the opportunity to get at least part of the absolution I've spent most of my life dreaming of?

If Julita were here, she'd be saying it was about time the king saw the truth. Applauding me for showing my worth.

The ache of loss expands in my gut.

We'll never be able to honor *her* if we spend our whole lives running away.

I draw myself up straighter. "Let's go see the king."

Stavros turns back to Hessild and her escort. "We'll come."

"Excellent." She guides her horse around and sets off toward the road without expecting us to quite join her. That consideration seems promising too.

We ride at a brisk walk that doesn't jostle my healing cut like a trot would, the five of us keeping a few horse-lengths back from Hessild out of additional caution. But with each minute that passes in peaceful travel along the road, my nerves settle more.

"How far is it to Regica from here?" I ask Stavros quietly.

"About an hour at this point and at this pace." He eyes me pensively. "Is your wound hurting you?"

"Only a little. I'll be fine."

"We'll get a medic to heal it properly once we—"

His voice cuts off as Hessild shudders in her saddle ahead of us. She lets out a strangled sound and slumps over, sliding right off her horse.

The soldiers on either side of her jerk around, only to get caught up in spasms of their own.

As they collapse from their mounts, Stavros reins in his stallion and leaps down. "What the fuck?"

The other men scramble after him. As they race to Hessild's crumpled form, I shift my weight to follow suit, but a sudden swell of magic rushes over me.

My own body seizes up, but not to go limp. My spine stiffens, and my hands tighten around the reins.

My heels tap Toast's sides of their own accord.

The horse gives a puzzled snort but moves the way I'm directing him, off the road. I wrench at my limbs with all the strength I have in me, but it's as if I've become a puppet on a set of strings.

Not like when Julita took over. Then I could tell I'd been pushed to the background, the world around me gone vaguer.

Now, I'm looking out of my eyes, hearing with my ears with full clarity, and yet locked inside a body that's taken on a mind of its own.

Panic jolts through my nerves. I reach instinctively toward my own magic…

But I can't grasp hold of it either. My chest remains clamped around the power, barely a wriggle of it passing through my senses.

Gods help me, what in the realms—

Alek glances up and notices my new course. He spins around. "Ivy, what are you—"

A strange laugh like nothing I've ever emitted before propels from my lungs. "I got what I needed, and now we're done. Did you really think I cared about you? You're ridiculous, all of you."

A silent wail rises up inside me through the next bark of a laugh that lurches out of me. Then my body is wheeling Toast around and jamming my heels against his sides so he breaks into a full-out gallop.

No, no, I can't let this happen.

I put all my will into yanking on the reins, but my arms refuse to budge other than a slight adjustment to Toast's course that wasn't my idea.

We hurtle across the countryside, my side throbbing with each thump of the stallion's hooves. I think I feel blood trickling from beneath the bandage.

I try to close my eyes as if that might do some good, but apparently my puppet master controls even my eyelids. They blink but spring open again.

Toast veers a little to the left and then farther. We crash through a stretch of forest, forced to ease up but still pushing onward as fast as the horse will go.

The second we're free of the underbrush, my legs kick Toast back to a gallop.

I don't hear any sounds of pursuit behind me. Is there other magic covering my tracks?

Will my men even want to come to my rescue when I made it sound as if I launched the attack on Hessild and her escort? When I insulted them and laughed in their faces?

Tears burn behind my eyes and start to trickle down my cheeks.

We cross uncultivated fields and skirt another clump of trees. The wind cools the streaks of moisture on my face.

Finally my hands pull the reins, slowing Toast to a trot.

But not through my doing. I still can't exert the slightest bit of control over any part of my body.

The magic thrums around me like a drone in my ears. We approach a derelict cabin at the edge of a larger forest, and I halt Toast completely.

Several figures step out of the cabin to meet me.

Most of them I don't recognize, at least not as individuals. There are two men and a woman in the blue uniforms of the royal army, which would make me think King Konram is behind my kidnapping if it weren't for the two pale shrouded figures with them who I immediately know are sacrificial accomplices.

A man and a woman in regular clothes flank one accomplice together. Another woman stands next to the second, her expression taut and sweat beaded on her forehead despite the cool air.

The man who emerges last, I do know. The sight of his tall, lopsided frame sends even more fear coursing through my veins.

Lothar Riosemek, the secondary magical advisor to the king and destroyer of riven sorcerers, is staring up at me with pale brown eyes and a hard-edged smirk.

"Look at her," he says conversationally in his thick baritone. "She can't move a muscle unless you allow it, Zaneta. How strong you've become after all those daimon spirits you've been directing."

The sweating woman dips her head in a hint of a nod. Her voice echoes the strain etched across her face and in her posture. "Yes, Master Lothar. It isn't quite the same when we didn't build the body. But I can hold her."

"Good." Lothar's smirk grows, seeming to crawl across his face.

My voice stays locked in my throat, as much as I want to cry out.

*This* man is behind the scourge sorcerer uprising?

Alek found out the clay purchaser had used a royal seal to keep the shipments concealed. We never suspected it could have come from someone quite so close to the king.

Gods above, what else has he done? What does he mean to do next?

What's he going to do with *me*?

Lothar takes a step closer, making my spirit want to recoil inside my puppet of a body. "Ivy of wherever you're actually from, you destroyed my army. I'm taking you and your wild magic in return. Not such a bad exchange, really."

He flicks his fingers, and his followers move toward a cluster of horses tied within the shadows of the trees. At a tug of magic, I nudge Toast to follow them, all the while screaming inside my head.

My body doesn't respond. This psychopath has me well and truly trapped.

And for the first time since I stumbled into this conspiracy, I'm utterly alone.

# Secrets of Graves and Gold - Bonus Scene

*How did Ivy's men find her after she confronted Borys in the farmhouse—and what did they make of the scene they found? Join Alek on their rescue mission in this scene from his point of view…*

*Alek*

I'm standing tensed in the lookout tower, my hands clenched around the railing, when the locket at my hip resonates with a familiar pulse of magic.

My actual heartbeat hitches. I stare out at the clashing soldiers and sorcerers—a few more soldiers than before, but not enough to take any real comfort in the fact amid the streaks of caustic magic—and make out no difference in the fighting.

Ivy's calling for help. What did she find out west?

Can we get to her quickly enough?

All I know is I have to try. I scramble down the ladder to where Casimir has been poised since he returned from his quest with Stavros. The former general and Rheave stayed with the soldiers from the fort to join the battle up close.

Casimir nods the second our eyes meet. "Let's get to her. It feels like she kept to the west like she told you."

Without needing to exchange any further words, we dash toward the horse he rode back on. I swing up behind Casimir and clutch him around the waist, wishing I was as confident on horseback as he is.

We just have to get to Ivy. How pleasant the journey is doesn't matter.

The locket keeps radiating its magic from my pocket. The effect should continue until we get close enough to Ivy for the enchantment to complete… or until her locket is broken, I suppose.

Gods help us, let it not come to that.

Casimir digs in his heels, and the horse springs forward. It gallops across the grassy fields. I tighten my thighs to keep my balance amid the jostling rhythm.

Nothing but darkness lies ahead as far as I can see. How far did Ivy go on foot? I've lost all sense of time since she rushed off.

Casimir must follow the pull of his own locket. What feels like miles of ground falls away beneath the horse's hooves with occasional adjustments in direction.

Then a faint light shimmers up ahead. I squint and discern the faintest outline of a hill with the hard lines of a house perched at the top.

A crow swoops in a loose circle in the sky above. My throat constricts. "She's up there."

Casimir urges our steed faster, but its pace slows through necessity as it clambers up the increasingly steep slope. When it stumbles, Casimir lets out a noise of frustration and twists in the saddle. "Let's walk the rest of the way. It might be faster."

I scramble down and step to the side to give him more room. My gaze slides back the way we came—and my jaw goes slack.

The torches that mark the fort and the sorcerers' camp gleam distantly against the darkness. Between them and the moonlight, I can tell that the tide has shifted.

Soldiers in Silanian uniforms have pressed all the way to the bank of the river. A few boats streak along the water, fleeing both our forces and the Darium soldiers on the other side, but it looks like merely shreds of the massive scrouge sorcerer march we've been following.

"We won," I murmur. "She did it." Sometime during our frantic ride, Ivy accomplished whatever she'd hoped to.

The spark of my relief is dimmed by the uncertainty much closer to my heart. Did she survive the effort?

Is she still sane enough to care that she has?

Casimir shoots me a tight smile that echoes my worries and clasps my elbow. We sprint the rest of the way up the slope together.

No sound emanates from the building, which up close turns out to be a neglected farmhouse. The front steps have crumpled, and the door there doesn't look much better off.

Casimir pauses by it for a moment to listen and then heaves his shoulder at it. It pops open with a crackling creak.

No shouts of alarm or thunder of footsteps responds to our entry. We creep inside, peering around.

The faint glow seeps from upstairs. It's hard to tell whether anyone's been inhabiting the rooms on the lower floor at all.

We start up the stairs, Casimir in the lead. We're halfway up when he exhales roughly and hurtles faster forward.

I glance up and catch sight of a limp, pale hand next to the banister. A streak of blood gleams scarlet against one finger.

Tamping down a cry, I throw myself after the courtesan. We dash onto the landing and pause briefly at the grisly scene in front of us.

Closest to us, a man slumps on the floor in a massive pool of blood. A small dagger protrudes from his throat.

It's not one of Ivy's knives, but I'd bet every book I own that she made that strike. There's no way he's not dead.

I can make out sprawled legs of what might be another corpse past the doorway of the room with the lantern. And beyond both the fallen men and the doorway, Ivy lies on the floor of the hall, her legs partly curled up toward her chest, blood splattering her body and more seeping from a gash in her side.

Her eyes are closed, not vacant. As I leap over the dead man to reach her, I note the shaky rise and fall of her ribcage.

"She's alive!" But for how much longer?

Casimir leaps after me. He crouches by her head, resting his hand on the spilled strands of her hair. "We'll need to stop the bleeding as well as we can and carry her out. The remaining scrouge sorcerers might regather here…"

At a shuffling sound from the room next to us, both our heads jerk around. My breath snags in my throat.

A disfigured woman is kneeling on the floor at the far side of the room next to a heap of pale cloth that must have been her shroud. Her carved up face, blank other than its scars, makes my gut lurch.

She's bleeding too—just a little trickle seeping from a few thin cuts in her already mottled flesh. Something the sorcerers did to encourage more magic out of their sacrificial victim?

I swallow thickly. We'll help her too, but Ivy's the one who needs us most urgently.

I yank off my tunic without a second thought and ball it against the wound on Ivy's side. Her fingers twitch, but she doesn't wake.

Casimir ducks into one of the other rooms and returns with a scarf he's pilfered. We ease Ivy up to tie the fabric around her abdomen, fixing my makeshift bandage in place.

"The cut will need more patching up than that," the courtesan murmurs. "But we need to get her somewhere we can clean it properly first."

I slide my hands along her shoulders, debating how to best try to lift her—and heavy footfalls thump up the stairs.

"Where is she?" Stavros demands. His jaw tightens as he sees us, getting his answer.

Hustling up the stairs behind him, Rheave stops with his eyes widened. "Ivy fought a great battle too."

"And she'll be okay if we can get her out of here," I say with more confidence than I actually feel. "General, why don't you help us with that."

Stavros doesn't even bother to glower at me at my brusque use of his former title, which shows how worried he is. Between the three of us, with Rheave watching anxiously, we lift Ivy's body and ease her down the stairs as gently as possible.

"Where do we take her?" I ask once we've reached the door.

Casimir points, his eyes squinted against the darkness. "There's a stretch of forestland not far past the base of the hill. It'll give us some shelter."

Rheave hums approvingly. "And there's a stream nearby. She'll need water." He glances at Stavros. "What do we do after we get there?"

Stavros gazes down at the woman lying slumped in our hold. He's just pulled off what might be the greatest military victory of his career, but he doesn't look remotely happy.

"We wait and see," he says firmly. "She can tell us all about it after she wakes up."

Yes. *When* she wakes up, not if.

Our riven sorcerer is the true hero of this night. And there's nothing I won't do to ensure she gets to celebrate her triumph as she deserves.

# Lady of Doom and Devotion

Rites of Possession #4

# ONE

*Ivy*

The room where I'm being held prisoner smells like stale perfume and blood. The latter I assume comes from the crusted red-brown smears that streak across the gilded wallpaper.

This mansion must be the residence of some noble—or used to be before my captors took it over. A couple of the men in soldier uniforms are digging through a wardrobe carved from fine marlwood, matching the elaborate frame of the four-poster bed. Shards of crystal that might have once been fancy perfume bottles litter the thick rug.

Along with the smeared blood and the broken crystal, someone has slashed into the cushions on the chairs so the stuffing spills out like fluffy guts. There's a darker ruddy splotch in the middle of the bedsheets that I don't want to look at too closely.

Beyond the broad picture window, all I can see is the nearby stone wall and a sprawl of empty fields beyond it. The house's shadow stretches long in the late-afternoon sunlight.

I'm guessing this is one of the country estates I've heard and read about, a summer home where some exalted family could retreat when they tired of city politics.

It doesn't look as if anyone's been having a relaxing time here recently.

The men toss several dresses that they retrieved from the wardrobe onto the floor. Their leader peers down at them.

Lothar, the king's secondary magical advisor and apparent head of the conspiracy to murder that king, shifts his tall, lopsided frame with a thoughtful air. I still haven't gotten used to the asymmetry of his body, one arm missing all the way to the shoulder in one of the most extreme dedication sacrifices I've ever seen.

That is, one of the most extreme outside of the poor accomplices he and his supporters have had carved up to the barest edge of survival. Great God help us all, how much power can this man wield when he combines his gift with those of his victims?

I have no idea what his gift even is. So far I haven't seen it in action, haven't felt the tingle of magic coursing off him.

He points at a confection of sleek pewter-gray silk. "That one. Fine but not too eye-catching. Have our 'guest' put it on."

His thick baritone takes on a sneering edge with the word "guest." We both know he's not offering any hospitality to me.

But my arms move all the same. My hands lift to yank off the plain woolen dress I was wearing when he stole me away from my companions this morning.

The wound on my side where one of Lothar's underlings stabbed me last night aches beneath its bandage. With all my might, I scream silently at my muscles to resist.

I can't so much as clench my jaw, let alone hold my body back.

The woman standing next to Lothar has me in the iron grip of her gift, partly fueled by the sacrificial accomplice slumped against the nearby wall beneath a shroud. Sweat gleams on Zaneta's forehead beneath her parted dun-brown bangs and her slim fingers twist at her sides, but her control has shown no sign of ebbing.

At her silent demand, I shuck off the trousers I was using as an underskirt as well. Apparently the scourge sorcerers don't care about my humble underclothes, because she has me pick up the silk dress without adjusting those.

I don't have to get fully naked in front of a bunch of hostile strangers. One tiny blessing in a heap of shit.

Lothar holds up his hand, and Zaneta follows his unspoken command to stop me. He frowns at the grayed ribbon wrapped around my upper arm. "What's that for?"

My puppet master propels an answer out of me. I don't see any need to lie about this, but I stay brief. "A memento."

The leader of the Order of the Wild lets out a scoffing chuckle. "I'm not indulging your sentimentality, fiend."

He tugs off the scrap of fabric—my last remaining fragment of my little sister. A cry of protest snags in my throat, unable to burst out.

Watching me with a look of challenge as if daring me to flex my magic at him, Lothar holds the ribbon to a lantern lit on a side table. My objection crawls through my chest, digging claws into my innards, but I can't move an inch. Can't stir so much as a spurt of my power.

Normally in a situation as threatening as this, my chaotic magic would be wrenching at me to set it free, to let it blast apart all these villains. And in this particular case, I think I might let it, consequences be damned.

But Zaneta's control over me is keeping my magic locked away inside me too. Actually, that's probably what's causing her the most strain. The restless energy wobbles around my heart like it's set at a slow simmer, but I can't whip it out of me.

Flames lick up the ribbon, blackening it in an instant. Lothar drops it into an empty wash basin just before the fire reaches his fingers. More smoke wisps up as the fabric crumbles away into ash.

My throat feels as if it's clamped shut. I can barely breathe.

It's all right. It was only a bit of cloth.

He can't touch my memories of Linzi. He can't destroy what she meant to me.

There's a whole lot more he could destroy, though.

Lothar motions to Zaneta, and she compels me to pull on the gown. I can't take any pleasure from the smoothness of the silk sliding over my skin. It only makes me think of the last time I wore dresses like this regularly—when I was pretending to be noble myself at the royal college.

When I had a countess-to-be's ghost lodged in my head, guiding me through the treacherous noble world. When I had men with me who became allies and then friends and then so much more than I'd ever dared to hope for.

All of that is gone now, as lost as my sister's ribbon. All thanks to Lothar and his sadistic schemes.

My head remains silent. Julita's spirit leapt out of me last night to help defend me from her vicious brother.

She'll have passed on into the embrace of her godlen now.

I have no idea whether the godlen who's watched over *me* is paying any attention to my current predicament. It'd be awfully nice for Kosmel to get on with showing me an escape route if he has any mind to.

And my men... The four men who've become not just my lovers but a tightly knit family like I thought I'd never have again...

It's been several hours since I last saw them. My last words to them, propelled from my throat by this scourge sorcerer's magic, were mocking them for trusting me.

Gods only know what they believe happened. Whether they'll see me as anything but an enemy even if they manage to find me.

Fresh tears prick behind my eyes. I will them back as I tighten the lacing on the dress.

Lothar would only laugh at my weeping. I don't want to give him the satisfaction, no matter how much anguish burns in my chest.

When my hands drop back to my sides, Lothar looks me over with one of his hard smirks. Revulsion crawls over my skin that has nothing to do with his uneven frame.

This man must be a psychopath above anything we've encountered before in our quest against scourge sorcerers. He's built a country-wide conspiracy while pretending to serve the family he wants to see slaughtered.

A country-wide conspiracy that powers itself with the total mutilation of orphaned twelve-year-olds.

His "Order of the Wild" claims to be following the true desires of the gods. The people he's egging on have insisted that their mad, violent practices will bring even the All-Giver back after centuries since the Great God abandoned our realms.

I'm not sure yet whether this man actually believes the stories he's spread or whether it's all a tactic for some other purpose.

The magic advisor motions to one of the soldiers who sorted through the dresses. The stranger steps closer to run a comb through my tangled hair. I can't even wince, let alone recoil from his touch.

While I endure the primping, a slim man with a sallow face appears in the doorway. He can't be more than a few years older than my twenty years, and his slight figure is nearly swallowed up by the layers of embroidered silk and velvet he's dressed himself in. You'd think he was suited up for a ball.

He peers at me, his stance stiffening, and darts a glance toward Lothar. "I heard you brought one of the *riven* here."

A mix of horror and revulsion colors his tone. The typical reaction of most people to my cursed magic, but it makes my stomach lurch all the same.

Lothar speaks with the same chilly authority as before. "You have nothing to worry about. She's utterly under our control."

There's a gloating note to that last sentence. I'd grit my teeth if I could move them.

The foppish man shudders and flicks his hand down his front in a hasty gesture of the divinities, as if calling on the gods to protect him from me. "When you asked for the use of the estate, I didn't realize—"

Lothar's tone hardens. "You committed yourself to our cause. Are you starting to doubt my judgment after all?"

Somehow the other man—the heir to this estate?—turns even paler. "No—no, of course not. All I can offer to the All-Giver and the Order of the Wild."

He scurries off, maybe hoping that if I do end up exploding with evil magic, he'll be far enough away to escape the onslaught.

Was he really master of this estate already? Or did he turn on his parents the way I've heard other noble heirs did with the Order's backing?

When the man with the comb steps away from me, Lothar glances over at a second duo of sorcerer and shrouded accomplice waiting at the other side of the room. The sorcerer is leaning against the vanity, studying a gleaming metal object they retrieved from my pocket when they were checking me over for weapons.

The locket that can be used as a signal to my men. If the sorcerer presses his thumb to the pane on the inside, they'll know where to find me.

But the stout man has only peeked inside and otherwise has been murmuring fragments of the odd language the scourge sorcerers use while examining the exterior.

"Have you untangled the magic on it?" Lothar asks.

The sorcerer shakes his head. "It's definitely been blessed, but it's not giving me any impressions of specifically how. That must mean it's not currently active. I can't pick up on any magic emanating off it right now."

"Keep it in that containment box of yours, then. We don't want to risk it creating some disruptive effect when we're not prepared."

The lopsided man turns back to me. "I don't suppose you'd tell me the truth about what it's for if I let you speak."

I simply glare back at him, wishing my hatred could sear into him the way my magic currently can't.

Lothar hums to himself. "Tie her hair back. The style doesn't need to be ornate. We'll cover it with the hood of her cloak regardless."

Zaneta wets her lips. "Are we going tonight?"

"The more time we delay, the more chance Konram has to adjust his plans. Gods only know what he's made of recent events." He glances toward her accomplice. "We won't be able to bring the blessed one right into the palace. He'll be too obvious. You can continue channeling power from a bit of a distance, I assume."

His sorcerer bobs her head. "Yes, Master Lothar. But it'll take all my concentration."

"That's perfectly fine." Lothar's smirk crawls back across his face as his gaze meets mine. "Our riven sorcerer will finally do something worthwhile with that wild magic of hers. She can take care of the rest."

A chill sweeps through my body. I flail against the invisible hold on me with a renewed surge of defiance, but I still can't budge a single muscle.

What is he going to do with me?

What is he going to *make* me do?

I don't know whether Lothar can read my horror in my stiffened expression or if my response is easy to guess. He steps closer to me, his pale brown eyes gleaming with a manic light.

"You don't like this? Such a pity. You're lucky you had as many years of freedom as you did. Your kind is an abomination—a blight on the realms. Born with so much power you never had to give up so much as a tuft of hair for… You should be grateful I'm letting you be such an important part of our revolution."

Is he sour about how much he sacrificed for whatever gift he's got? It's not as if anyone forced the choice on him.

And he doesn't even bother to use his own magic much, considering the way he's ordering his underlings to handle all the sorcery.

What exactly is he so bitter about?

I can only imagine the caustic remarks Julita would have made about the royal advisor—and imagining them makes my gut twist with the loss.

Somehow she always found something to say that bolstered my spirits, no matter how dire a situation we found ourselves in. I got used to having that bit of company—of friendship—as ephemeral as her ghost was.

It's better for her that she's moved on. She deserves some peace. And I have plenty of practice surviving on my own.

I never thought I'd find myself in a position where I didn't want to.

Lothar snaps his fingers at the men in the soldier uniforms. "Prepare the carriage. I want to be riding out within the hour."

Zaneta sucks in a breath. "What would you have me do with her once we reach the palace?"

The magic advisor lets out a cool chuckle. "If all goes well, I'll be able to get us right to the royal family through my authority alone. Stay ready to intervene on my command if needed. We'll gather them all in the audience room."

His gaze pierces me, even colder than before. "The moment we step into the room and she can see them, have her crack every one of their pretty royal skulls."

# Two

*Ivy*

Lothar keeps the carriage curtains drawn. I know when we've reached the city of Regica because he stops to step out briefly and speak to the guard at the gate.

We're crammed tightly onto the cushioned benches within, my sorcerer puppet master sitting close enough that our elbows knock together when the wheels hit a bump. But I'm not sure I'd rather have her shrouded sacrificial accomplice or the riven-hating, lopsided magic advisor pressed up against me instead.

It's bad enough feeling Lothar's haughty gaze evaluating me from the opposite bench as the carriage rattles onward.

Zaneta may be able to keep my magic locked down, but she can't control every automatic bodily reaction. My heart has been hammering since Lothar revealed his instructions for me, and my stomach churns harder with every passing minute.

I guess she can stop me from outright vomiting. Although I wouldn't mind puking my guts all over the man in charge right now.

Maybe then he wouldn't be able to waltz right into Regica's royal residence and arrange his murderous audience with the king.

The Order of the Wild member steering the carriage guides us through the city streets with occasional turns. It feels like a long time before the vehicle halts again.

My pulse stutters, but Lothar turns to the sacrificial accomplice rather than me. "You'll be staying safely out of sight as you continue to help. Our friends will look after you while you offer your talent to Zaneta."

"It's my pleasure to serve the All-Giver," the accomplice mumbles.

After they've stepped out of the carriage, I attempt to flex my muscles. Searching for any weak point in Zaneta's hold over my body.

How well can she draw on the accomplice's magic from a distance, even a short one? It's got to be harder, and she already looked as if the effort was wearing on her.

For now, it still isn't straining her enough for me to resist her magic. The only difference I can feel is a sharper jitter of my own power within my chest, as if it senses some tiny loosening of our invisible prison that I can't exploit yet.

I have to keep trying. I have to stop myself from giving in to her demands before we reach the royal family.

I've spent months putting my life and my sanity on the line to protect King Konram and his family's reign over Silana. Fighting to ensure that the scourge sorcerers don't gain the upper hand and impose their brutal brand of leadership over the entire country.

He was just about to pardon me. He finally believed I wasn't a monster.

Gods smite me, I don't want to be one. I don't want to see the world we'll be left with if the royal family falls to these villains.

Although by the time Lothar's done with me, my mind might not be sound enough for me to even care. My grip on reality was already starting to fracture every time I called on more of my magic.

All too soon, Lothar climbs back into the carriage. He doesn't say anything as the horse tugs us forward, but we've got to be near the palace already. He'd want the accomplice as close by as possible.

My assumption is confirmed when the wheels rasp to another stop no more than a minute later. Lothar nods to Zaneta. "Let us see our purpose through."

My skin crawls at the import of those words.

My limbs shift, pushing me to my feet. I climb out of the carriage in contradiction to every personal intention.

But as I wrench at my body, willing it to refuse, a faint quiver runs down my arm. When the sorcerer directs my hand to drop to my side, my fingers twitch toward my thigh in a soft tap.

Hope jolts through my veins. That was my act—I'm almost sure about it.

I try to wiggle my fingers again, but now that my arm is still, they won't budge. I can't turn my head, can barely adjust my gaze beyond staring straight in front of me.

There was a tiny opening. I have to find another one.

We're standing in front of a high wall of polished stone. A gilded but heavy wooden door fills the gate.

Lothar walks up to the Melchiorek crest carved into the doorframe. Flanking him, Zaneta directs me to tug my hood farther forward to shadow my face.

As I lift my hand, I manage to flex my fingers again. But as soon as they reach my hood, they close around the fabric, ignoring any command I'm giving them.

I can't stop myself from lowering my arm, so I put all my will into propelling it a little faster. Would I be able to make a jab with my elbow?

The joint bends slightly with a brief twitch. Hmm.

Lothar has pressed a token against the crest and murmurs words I can't make out. The gate swings open to admit us.

Several guards in royal sapphire-blue uniforms stand on the other side of the gate. King Konram has clearly ramped up security after seeing absolute proof of the Order of the Wild's intentions.

Just last night, a horde of hundreds of Order members marched within a couple of hours of this city, intending to kill him.

It's only because of me and my men—and a risky plan that required manipulating the Darium soldiers on the other side of the Seafell Channel—that the scourge sorcerer army never made it here. I can hardly celebrate that victory if I let myself become the king's murderer in the aftermath, though.

I wrench at my neck in an effort to turn my head toward the guards, strain at my face to make some expression they'll take as a warning.

None of my efforts produce any result. I just keep walking straight ahead, following Lothar alongside my puppet master.

When I managed to move by my own will before, it was when I was merely extending the motion the scourge sorcerer had already forced rather than pushing against her control. It would make sense if it's easier to slip in a little of my own intention when I'm leaning into her commands.

Cautiously, not wanting her to realize I'm testing the limits of her hold, I focus on flicking the toe of my boot against the hem of my dress. After a few steps, I succeed in giving it a soft tap.

That's something. A small fragment of control I can reclaim.

Now how can I use it to prevent this assassination attempt? If I overplay my hand and fail, Zaneta will tighten her grip on me even more.

I'll only get one chance.

The Regica palace towers over us—not quite as grandly imposing as the palace I'm used to in the capital city of Florian, but an impressive work of architecture all the same. The marble walls gleam, and carved figures of Creaden, the godlen of leadership, peer down from either side of the main doors.

Four guards are stationed at the top of the broad steps leading up to those doors. One holds up her hand at the sight of us.

"Advisor Lothar," she says. "The king is expecting you—but he isn't allowing any unvetted parties into the palace. You'll need to continue from here alone."

Lothar frowns. "These are my assistants. I've vetted them myself. They have key information to impart for the meeting I've arranged with King Konram."

The guard shakes her head. "I'm sorry, Advisor Lothar. Considering recent events, he's put in place a policy that only people he's specifically approved of may enter. I'm sure you can discuss that with him during your meeting."

The magic advisor sighs as if this is all a ridiculous precaution. Never mind that Konram's wariness may save his life tonight.

Unless Lothar can use his gift to force the issue.

Please, let this murderous mission end here. I'm too keyed up for any real hope to penetrate my queasiness, but I pray silently with all my might.

The lopsided man offers the lead guard a smile that makes me want to shudder. "Surely you can at least admit them into the outer halls. It's a rather chilly evening. I'd imagine King Konram will approve of their presence as soon as I've spoken to him."

The guard shows no signs of budging. "If they're cold, they can wait for approval in the carriage, Advisor. I have to follow my orders."

"I'm sorry to hear that," Lothar says with a tone full of acid, and makes a sharp motion toward Zaneta.

I don't even have time to cry out in protest, as unspoken as that cry would be in my present state. The scourge sorcerer's magic yanks at my body—and has me propelling my own power forward in an instant.

Against every particle of my will, I hurl lances of my magic at all four guards at once. The supernatural force slams through their skulls.

My magic shatters their minds before they can raise any protest either.

Four bodies crumple outside the palace doors. With another jerk of Zaneta's control, I'm dissolving those bodies into dust that whips away in a gust of wind.

My magic reverberates eagerly from my chest, but the rest of me is screaming in vain. The bottom of my stomach has completely hollowed out.

I just eviscerated four innocent people—four people who were only trying to protect the leader of the realm. I tore apart their corpses so no one will even realize what happened to them.

Gods only know what consequences echoed out in exchange for those acts.

And this is only the beginning of what Lothar wants from me.

He's already shoved open the palace door. "Make sure no one sees enough to raise the alarm," he snaps at Zaneta under his breath.

He marches down the main hall draped with tapestries and hung with gold-framed paintings. My feet stride after him over the intricately woven rug.

My thoughts scramble in my frantic attempts to figure out how to defy him. I might be able to throw myself faster forward, right into him.

But I have no weapons, and Zaneta is containing my magic again. What would bumping against the magic advisor accomplish other than pissing him off and making her even more cautious?

Maybe when Zaneta pushes my magic out of me again, I can launch at least a little of it toward my captors instead?

I won't have much time to find out. Lothar wants me to destroy the royal family the second we reach them.

I have no idea how deep into the palace the audience room lies. Lothar veers down a side hall, picking up his pace even more, and Zaneta forces me to match it.

Lanterns flicker on the walls, casting their golden glow through the opulent passage. Then voices echo off the vaulted ceilings from somewhere in the distance—an urgent shout.

My heart leaps with the thought that our intrusion has already been discovered. But Lothar and his underling don't react.

My gut knots tighter with sickly understanding.

The shout wasn't a real sound. That was my mind acting up, inventing hallucinations. Cracking more as my magic tears at my sanity.

And there's nothing I can do about it.

Nothing *yet*. With every step, we must be getting farther away from the sacrificial accomplice Zaneta is drawing strength from. I test the boundaries of her control and find I can swing my arms just a little with my strides.

Somehow I don't think a swish of my sleeves is going to save me or King Konram.

I reach toward the power coiled inside me. It's whirling in my chest with a sense of anticipation after being called on once already.

If I can crack Zaneta's control over my magic—if I can shatter her concentration for long enough to break free—

Two guards hustle toward us from farther down the hall. One of them hesitates, looking us over. "Advisor Lothar, I don't think—"

Lothar doesn't even need to gesture this time. Zaneta knows what her orders are—and my body jerks to follow them with the squeeze of her magic around me.

Two more spears of power spring from my hands. Both of the guards collapse, their eyes rolling up, their forms totally limp.

Lothar points to a side room, and Zaneta has me heave the corpses inside. I grapple with my power, willing it to careen farther to the side, to smack into her, but it stays melded to the strict course she's given it.

I still can't deviate too far from her control. She'd need to be right in the way of where she's having me direct my magic, and it's unlikely she'll be that careless.

Lothar lets out a hiss of his breath through his teeth. "Come on. Before anyone else can interfere."

We hurry to another corner and turn toward a door carved with crowns and leafy branches. Zaneta has me cut down the two guards stationed outside before they can so much as speak.

Another scream builds at the base of my throat, but I can't even look away from their lifeless bodies.

As we hurtle onward, she compels me to disengage the door's lock with my magic. More power balls behind my sternum, ready to shove the door wide so I can spring inside and smash through every person waiting beyond it.

No. I can't let this happen. I *can't*.

My pulse thunders in my ears. My thoughts flail in my head.

And as we reach the door, I see my opening.

In the same moment as my first blast of magic hits the door to fling it open, Zaneta throws me forward alongside it. She wants me to charge inside before the royal family has time to react.

So I fling myself even faster in the direction she's already pushed me.

I hurl myself into the edge of the opening door, managing to duck my head just slightly at the same time. My forehead slams into the hard wooden corner with all the force I can bring to bear.

Pain explodes through my skull for a fleeting second. Then my mind spirals into darkness.

# THREE

*Stavros*

As we wander the city streets, I keep the stump of my left wrist hidden in my pocket. The empty prosthetic base still strapped to it feels unnervingly light.

With fifteen years behind me since I sacrificed my hand in my dedication ceremony to Sabrelle, I can't say I miss it at all. After all this time, the metal and wooden contraptions that've taken its place are even more familiar than the flesh I gave up.

But going completely without leaves me at too obvious a disadvantage.

Unfortunately, the metal combat prosthetic that's the only option I have available is far too identifiable, making it a disadvantage in itself. It's too large for me to easily conceal it in a pocket and too inhuman to escape notice.

And I'm not entirely sure whether I'm prowling Regica as a returning hero or a wanted criminal.

A glow streaks through the thickening night from various pub and restaurant windows. When a cluster of jovial patrons emerges from one of the pubs, the four of us draw to a stop not far away as if we're pausing to debate our destination.

Rheave studies them for a moment and murmurs beneath a burst of their raucous laughter. "They don't look very important."

The daimon in human form tends to state the truth baldly—a quality I've come to appreciate in many circumstances.

I dip my head in acknowledgment. "They don't. But you never know who might have seen or overheard something odd they'll decide to mention to their friends."

Alek shifts restlessly on his feet. Between the shadow of his cloak's hood and the thin scarf he's wrapped across his lower face to hide his scars, I can't make out the scholar's expression, but I can guess what he's thinking.

We have to take whatever slim chances we can get of dredging up information, because we've gone all day without discovering anything at all.

With every peal of the temple bells on the hour, the dread in my gut has expanded. I've fought unpredictable enemies before but never any as baffling as this.

The pub-goers exchange a few crude comments about one of the barmaids complete with gestures of demonstration and then make noises of commiseration while one complains about his harsh boss at the bathhouse. They amble off leaving us just as uncertain as before.

Casimir grimaces and rakes his fingers through his tawny hair, an unusually tense gesture from the normally serene courtesan. "Whatever happened to Ivy and Hessild, it might not have anything to do with Regica. What if we've come to the wrong place?"

Alek speaks up in his flat, matter-of-fact tone. "The only thing we can say for sure about the scourge sorcerers is that they wanted to destroy the royal family. The royal family is here. At least, they were here as of last night."

He glances toward me with a question in his brown eyes.

I peer down the street toward the palace's high towers several blocks away. A few windows gleam with lantern light, blurring after a moment with my damaged vision.

My thoughts slide back to last night. "The Order of the Wild's army posed an obvious threat, but as far as we can tell, none of their forces breached even the city walls. In a scenario like that, it'd be unwise for King Konram to leave a secure position and put himself in a potentially precarious one on the road."

"Especially when his advisors are being murdered with magic on those roads," Rheave says helpfully. His dark brown curls sway with the cock of his head.

My stomach clenches at the reminder.

We left Hessild Korinya, the king's primary magic advisor, and her two soldier escorts lying on the road where they died. It felt disrespectful to abandon their bodies like that, but any attempt at rites we offered them could be seen as a sign that we had a hand in their death.

We can hope that leaving them undisturbed will increase the chances that the king's people can determine what—and who—killed them. And that it wasn't the fugitives she'd been sent to retrieve for his pardon.

I left a note tucked beneath her arm, saying that the scourge sorcerers had struck and that we'd ridden off to pursue them. But of course, that's only part of the truth.

The battle that's torn at me since this morning surges up again.

I should go to the king and inform him directly of what happened. Warn him that there's an even greater threat than we realized, one working by methods more subtle than we could anticipate.

But if we go to him without any answers and without the woman he most hesitated to pardon, I don't need my gift of glimpsing the future to predict the outcome.

He'll assume Ivy is to blame and resume his call for her execution.

In my silence, the curiosity in Rheave's smooth face dims. His brow furrows before he speaks more hesitantly than before. "What if it wasn't the scourge sorcerers who attacked? We know that Ivy would never have purposefully hurt those people, but her magic didn't always let her think right. It wouldn't be her fault."

Casimir shakes his head emphatically. "Ivy hadn't used her magic at all in over a day. It wouldn't make sense for the madness to come over her all of a sudden like that, so much stronger than before. And she never spoke to us mockingly even in the worst past times."

Our lover's parting words echo up from my memories. *I got what I needed, and now we're done. Did you really think I cared about you? You're ridiculous, all of you.*

It didn't sound remotely like the woman I've spent nearly every waking minute with for weeks. The cracks of insanity that'd wriggled into her mind made her paranoid and jumpy, not sneering.

Every particle of my body rejects the possibility that those claims came from Ivy, regardless of her state. Even the laugh she let out sounded forced.

A group of scourge sorcerers who weren't part of the march must have launched a new attack— striking down Hessild and then wrenching Ivy away from us.

Unfortunately, they covered their tracks so well that I couldn't manage to follow her. I ran back to my mount as quickly as I could to give chase, but by the time I launched the stallion into motion, it was as if the woman I love had vanished.

My hand drops to the pocket at my hip. The locket all of us except Rheave carry matching copies of hasn't given off the pulse of its magical signal all day.

If Ivy regained control of the situation, she'd come back to us or signal us to come to her, wouldn't she? Which means she's still trapped… or she's no longer capable of reaching out at all.

The knot in my gut squeezes tighter, but I can't deny logic. Regardless of the power the scourge sorcerers can summon from the accomplices they've had mutilated, nothing can rival Ivy's boundless riven magic.

They could very well have wanted to simply eliminate her to ensure she couldn't interfere with their plans any further. Perhaps I couldn't find her… because she was already gone.

My hand balls at my side. I lift it to tap down my front in the gesture of the divinities.

If that's the case, those miscreants will pay beyond any punishment I already hoped to inflict on them. But Sabrelle give me strength, let it not be true. Let her still be alive.

Let us find her.

I square my shoulders, girding myself. "Let's wander a little closer to the palace. Now that it's dark, we don't have to worry quite as much about being recognized."

Alek nods. "Nothing appears to have gone wrong here yet. We should take that as a good sign. Ivy may have escaped already and simply be waiting until it's safe to reach out to us. She knows how to extricate herself from a dangerous scenario."

As we head toward the palace, Rheave's strides take on a renewed energy. "Yes. Our little vine doesn't let anyone stop her. The next time we see her, she might have totally destroyed the Order of the Wild all on her own."

I wish I could summon the same optimism. Tension stays coiled tight around my innards.

It is true that there've been no disturbances in the city. If any fighting had broken out, we'd have noticed—

A distant thump brings my head snapping around. A squeak of a cry reaches my ears, followed by a thunder of pounding footsteps.

My pulse skips a beat. I jerk my hand toward my companions, already swiveling to track the sounds. "This way!"

The commotion is coming from the general direction of the palace, but not straight ahead. I dash down the street and take a right turn with the other men at my heels.

Whatever's going on might not have anything to do with the scourge sorcerers, but we need to know for sure.

There's another thump and a gasp sharp enough to carry past the nearby buildings. I sprint faster, my heart thudding in my chest.

Could that be Ivy fleeing her captors?

We dodge a cart and skid to a stop at the edge of one of the city's broader roads.

Six figures are racing through the darkness, hurtling toward us. Heavy velvet cloaks flap around the three being chased, the form in the middle gripping the other two's arms as if urging them on.

Less than a block behind them and closing the distance with every step, three palace guards charge in pursuit. Their expressions are set with stern determination.

My legs lock up with the uncertainty about who the actual victims here are.

Rheave makes an urgent noise in his throat. "The soldiers—they're all captured daimon."

At the same moment, the wind ripples over one of the fleeing figure's hoods. As I twitch my gaze to track the movement, the fabric flaps back enough to reveal dark hair framing a pale face I recognize in an instant.

Not the woman I was looking for, but a girl who it appears needs my protection even more in this moment.

I don't know why Princess Klaudia is running away from the guards who would normally be defending her or who she's with, but the captured daimon are the scourge sorcerers' tools. I doubt their intentions are good.

"We take the guards down," I bark at the others, and leap into the street.

I miss my prosthetic hand more than ever, but my sword slides from its sheath with a reassuring hiss. I barrel past King Konram's daughter and her companions straight toward their pursuers.

A flash of startled confusion crosses one of the guards' faces just before I slam my sword into his chest. The moment the blade penetrates his heart, his body hardens into the clay it started as.

As he thuds to the cobblestones with a crack of the fired clay, a lightning-like bolt of energy careens through the air and smacks into the woman next to him. She reels backward, the side of her head charred by Rheave's supernatural attack.

Before she can regain her balance, I've slit her throat and spun toward the third pursuer.

He tries to dodge me, lunging after the princess. In the same moment as I drive my sword into his side, an arrow smacks into his temple.

I'm not sure which weapon causes his ultimate end. Like the other two, he stiffens into clay and collapses.

I whirl in the direction the princess was running. My friends were racing over to help me in the confrontation, Rheave with his bow and another arrow in hand, the other two gripping their knives. With the fall of the last body, we turn to consider the three figures in their fancy cloaks who've hesitated in a tight huddle by the doorway of a darkened shop.

Princess Klaudia's voice wavers from beneath her hood. "General Stavros?"

I lost my military position more than a year ago with the injury that damaged my sight, but I'm not of any mind to correct her now. The fact that she recognized *me* may be the only reason she hasn't kept running.

I lower my sword and hold up the stump of my wrist in a gesture of surrender. "I only wanted to ensure they wouldn't hurt you. What's happened, Princess Klaudia?"

The only answer I get is a muffled sob as she presses her hand to her mouth. The girl is only sixteen—gods only know what she's been through to bring her to this point.

Stepping closer, I make out her brother's face beneath one of the other hoods. Prince Jacos is even younger, and his skin has turned sallow despite the blotches of exertion from their run.

The figure in the middle who was clutching them lifts her head to meet my gaze. In the second before my vision fogs again, I find myself staring at one of my former students—Petra, her name is.

Her dark eyes hold mine so solemnly my stomach hollows out.

She's a distant relative of the queen's—not even from the Melchiorek line. Why would King Konram have evacuated her along with the immediate royal family?

Why is she with her cousins and not the king himself or any of their actual protectors?

When she speaks, her clear voice holds steady other than a brief quiver of emotion she can't totally suppress. "Ster. Stavros, we need your help. King Konram and Queen Ishild are dead."

# FOUR

*Ivy*

My head throbs harder with every stumbling step. Liquid trickles down the side of my face—a metallic flavor seeps between my lips.

Blood; it must be blood.

Everything but the ache feels so far away.

A hand is clamped around my upper arm, yanking me faster. I just want to stop and lie down, make the pounding in my skull stop, but my legs keep lurching onward.

A voice grates out from beside me. "Can't you get her running?"

Another voice, wobbly: "I'm sorry, Master Lothar. I'm doing my best. It's harder when she's injured."

My drooping head sways. The surface I'm staggering over blurs and wavers before my unfocused eyes.

"Wretched riven sorcerer," the man hauling me along snarls. "Not even good enough to get a job this simple done. You don't deserve one fucking shred of that magic."

We burst out a door into a gust of cool air. Droplets of blood splat onto the pale cobblestones in my wake.

My mind recoils from the sight. There was more blood—blood all over marble tiles—blood splattered across a golden crown—

My stomach flips over. Was that me? Did I slaughter someone in that vast audience room despite my best attempt at resistance?

Lothar—yes, that's who's jerking me along so forcefully—he's angry. I made things more difficult for him.

But that doesn't mean he didn't get the basics of what he wanted in the end.

Yells and clangs ring out and fade in rippling waves. I can't tell if any of them are real and not just hallucinations.

I stumble, and a sharper pulse of pain jabs through my skull to shatter my few coherent thoughts. I reel in a wave of dizziness.

My sense of the world around me completely fizzles out. I fade in and out of awareness.

I'm slumped against the wall of a jostling carriage—

Lothar is snapping something at his companions—

Someone presses something against my temple, maybe intending to bandage my wound but so roughly I'd flinch if the magic controlling me would allow it—

Then we're spilling out into the dark chill of the night, our feet thumping onto a packed dirt lane. Lothar yanks me on toward a looming stone house.

As we march inside, I catch enough glimpses through the muddled haze to recognize that it's the same summer estate home he brought me to before. There's a stumble behind me.

"What's the matter now?" Lothar demands.

Zaneta's voice has become outright ragged. "I—I'm doing my best, but the strain—Keeping her totally in my hold for so long is draining me—"

The magic advisor spits out a few curse words and shoves me through a doorway. "Fine. I suppose you should get some rest before we mop up this mess."

He raises his voice. "Biani! Where's the lossum you picked up for us?"

The term penetrates the ache in my head. Lossum—that's a common sedative.

Despite my careening thoughts, a fragment of understanding clicks into place. Drugging the riven is the typical strategy for ensuring they can't use their powers.

They're going to knock me out so Zaneta can rest without worrying about what I'll do.

I'm going to be free from her scourge sorcery… but not conscious to take advantage of that fact.

Her hold must be weakening more. If I can wrench myself away now—

But I'm drained too, and I can't gather my focus through the pain still radiating from my forehead. All I manage is to suck in a deeper breath, and then my body is tossing itself onto its back on a low bed.

A vial lifts to my face. Bitter liquid coats my tongue.

My head lolls as I try to summon the control to gag and spit it out, but I simply roll onto my side.

An even thicker, darker haze rolls over me, and I don't know anything at all.

*Well, my wayward rogue, you do have a knack for getting yourself into the most contorted sorts of trouble, don't you?*

The voice echoes through the fog I'm floating in as if from all around me.

I know it. I've heard it before.

It's important.

I open my mouth, but I can't find the wherewithal to respond. My mind is so fuzzy…

*You need to wake up*, the voice says. *Now!*

The last word hits me like a punch, and the eyes I didn't know were closed pop open.

The room around me is hazy too, just a hint of the dawn's glow seeping through a window beyond the foot of the bed. I'm lying on my side on top of the covers—no one bothered to so much as drape a blanket over me. My limbs feel cold and achy.

My head throbs too, but with a duller pulsing than the previous sharp pangs.

I have the urge to shift and stretch, but at the same moment a large figure adjusts his position where he's leaning against a side table near the door. A bulky man with his mouth set in a bored scowl.

He's going to realize I woke up—he's going to hurt me. I have to hit him first, before—

I yank back my mind from those frantic thoughts. The quavering panic of them is horribly familiar.

I used a lot of magic last night. Possibly more than I know.

Now I'm having delusions of danger again.

Of course, I *am* in a lot of danger. But it's not as immediate as my scattered sanity would have me believe.

The man is gazing toward the window, not toward me. I dip my eyelids so I'll still look asleep if he glances my way.

Yes, I could knock him down with my magic. It's already unfurling around my racing heart with my newly recovered consciousness.

But my guard is far from the only threat I'm facing. I have to be smart.

I study the man for a few moments through my eyelashes. I think I saw him around the house after Lothar brought me here the first time. One of his stooges, maybe a captured daimon.

Inside my mouth, I curl my tongue assessingly. The movement comes easily without any force obstructing it.

I'm still wearing my boots. I wiggle my toes inside them, where the man can't see.

A jolt of hope shoots through my chest. The scourge sorcerer's magic isn't clamped around my body any longer. Zaneta must still be sleeping.

I can move myself through my own will.

More memories float up in fragments. Lothar brought me back here—he drugged me so that my puppet master could sleep.

But I've woken up sooner than he must have expected.

Because of the voice in my dream.

It was Kosmel. The trickster godlen hasn't completely abandoned me after all.

How much time do I have before I lose the small advantage he's given me?

My magic shoots farther through my abdomen, burning hotter with each passing second. These assholes kidnapped me, forced me to do their bidding—

Great God help me, I don't know what I actually did last night. The deaths I do remember are awful enough.

A wallop of guilt and anguish hits me right in the sternum. I close my eyes tighter against the swell of emotion and clench my jaw.

I can't get distracted by regret right now. What matters most is getting away from these monsters so they can't turn *me* into even more of a fiend to serve their sick purposes.

After that... then I can worry about the crimes I've committed.

I don't think the drug has completely worn off yet. When I try to focus on a plan, my thoughts drift sluggishly through my head.

I have to deal with my guard... get out of this room... tackle whatever's waiting on the other side.

My magic squirms right up to my throat. I could hurl it out of me, smash through this entire building and everyone in it—

A starker smack of horror shatters the image that formed in my mind. I swallow thickly and clamp down on my power as tightly as I know how, picturing a vine wrapping close around me.

I can't let the delusional panic take over. I was already going mad before Lothar took me prisoner. Gods only know how much the magic he made me use last night has addled my mind on top of it.

How much can I risk using to free myself? If the riven insanity takes over completely, I'll be an even greater threat to the country than the conspirators I'm freeing myself from.

Everything I could do feels wrong.

The weight of the decisions ahead presses down on me. For a second, I can't breathe.

I'm injured and weaponless and partly drugged, up against an unknown number of enemies.

But I have to get out of here. I can't let myself be the scourge sorcerers' tool for one more minute.

Whatever happens after... I'll make sure I'm prepared. I'll do whatever I need to do to ensure I don't harm the kingdom any other way.

I peer surreptitiously around the room. I can't see anything except the bed, the side table, and a low dresser near the window. Not a single object I could use to stab or even bludgeon.

I suppose I could try to smother my guard with the pillow under my head, but somehow I don't think he'd sit quietly long enough for me to pull that off.

The moment I move, he might raise the alarm. And I doubt I can move all that fast in my current state.

There's nothing for it. I have to rely on my magic this one final time.

At least since I'm in control and I have time to think, I can choose the backlash.

I focus on his neck and the brass handle on the table's drawer. When I'm sure of my concentration, I let one thin stream of magic fly out toward the guard.

It rams into his throat and clenches his windpipe so swiftly he doesn't have time to make a sound before I've crushed his source of breath. The drawer handle bulges, expanding to balance out what I constricted.

With his eyes bulging with terror and lack of oxygen, the big man slumps toward the floor. I whip out another sliver of magic to erase the sound of him hitting the boards—and project it to the farthest distance I can see beyond the window.

The man sprawls on the floor and stiffens into clay. The daimon that was trapped inside that sculpted body will be flying free.

My guilt lifts at seeing I didn't really take a life, but only slightly. This is just the first step in my escape.

I ease upright, hesitating when my head spins. When I touch my temple, I find a hasty bandage fixed there with a thinner swath of fabric.

The cloth is crusted with blood, but I can't find any wetness on my face now. The bleeding appears to have stopped.

I crouch beside the clay man, but it looks as if Lothar didn't even bother to arm my guard. Maybe the scourge sorcerers figured it would be too dangerous to have any weapon in the room with me, assuming the captured daimon would defend the rest of them by shouting an alarm and battering me with brute strength.

An impression of hollers and pounding footsteps rushes over me. I freeze—and the sounds dwindle rather than rising.

Just another little whiff of insanity. Wonderful.

And it could get so much worse.

I stare down at the fired clay figure, but I can't see how to do this next part without any magic either. It'll only take a tiny effort, though.

Wielding my power like a blade, I slice a chunk of clay about the size and shape of a knife out of the man's torso. The point of the clay shard should be sharp enough to cut flesh.

And if I've succeeded in sealing a little of the torn flesh on my head to balance out the consequences, so much the better.

Gripping my makeshift blade, I ease to the door and press my ear to the crack. The only sound that reaches me is the slow rasp of a sleeping breath.

Ever so carefully, I nudge the door open.

It's as if the scourge sorcerers set up this scene to perfectly cater to me. Zaneta lies sleeping on a mattress that's been placed on the floor of the outer room, just a few paces from the door.

Presumably Lothar had her stay there in case she needed to leap to subdue me. But it means that she's within easy reach.

My fingers curl tighter around the clay shard. My muscles balk at the idea of murdering a person so defenseless, no matter what else she's done to me.

She's under Lothar's sway. Who knows how he's manipulated *her*?

But she called me to them from miles away when she first brought me under her spell. I'm not safe as long as she's alive, and that means neither is anyone else I care about.

A distant bugling of a rooster from some neighboring farm stirs me into action. I'll do it fast and as painlessly as possible, but shit and smitings, I have to do it.

I spring forward and drive the shard of clay into her neck.

Zaneta's body shudders. Her eyes pop open.

A sputter of blood passes over her lips, but her expression slackens just seconds later.

I press my lips against the urge to vomit and yank myself away from her. My magic roils in my chest with a fiercer shudder, but I hold it in.

If I see Lothar, I'll destroy him too. But otherwise, I simply have to get away.

My gaze darts through the room and snags on the box I saw one of the other scourge sorcerers stick my locket in. One small blessing.

With a quick dash, I undo the lid's clasp and retrieve my trinket. Clasping the locket in one hand and my clay blade in the other, I hurry to the next doorway.

The house is quiet. It isn't until I've slunk almost to the ground floor when I hear any voices—a murmuring from down the hall.

"When did Master Lothar say he'd return?"

"I don't think he mentioned."

I grit my teeth. The conspiracy's mastermind isn't here for me to end him like I did two of his underlings.

I prick my ears to check for any other signs of human presence around and bolt for the front door.

As I race across the yard outside, my head jumbles with a renewed aching.

There's a stretch of woods in the distance. If I can get to them, I have some hope of disappearing amid the trees.

Of course, I don't know what kind of tracking magic Lothar and his followers might be capable of...

A soft but urgent nicker catches my attention. I pause at the wall and spot several horses wandering in a corral by a nearby stable.

One of them looks particularly familiar.

Relief swells inside me so abruptly I almost choke on it. I run to the corral, let the gate swing wide, and reach up to hug Toast's neck when he trots over to me.

Lothar obviously isn't one to waste potential resources. He held on to the horse he stole with me, thank the gods.

"It's time we got out of here, boy," I murmur, shoving the clay blade beneath the corded belt of my dress.

With the help of the wooden fence, I heft myself onto the stallion's back. Gripping his mane, I tap him with my heels to send him galloping toward the woods.

We flee through the stretch of forest, hurtle across a few fields, and dive into a denser woodland. The sun is high in the sky, my stallion panting, and my head pounding like someone's trying to chisel into my skull when I finally decide we've come far enough.

I don't know where to go from here. I don't know who to turn to. But I really have only one option.

Or rather, two options. I've still got my makeshift blade if the madness rushes over me and there's nothing to do but end myself.

Suppressing a wince at that thought, I slide down from Toast's back and sit against a tree. I rest the blade on the ground next to me within easy reach.

With growing trepidation, I flick open the locket and press my thumb to the surface within.

Then I tip back my head against the tree trunk, my stomach roiling, and wait for the horror of the past day to either end... or get even worse.

# FIVE

*Ivy*

I might have spent the night conked out, but I don't think the sedative made for a very satisfying rest. I'm still exhausted.

Somewhere in the midst of my waiting, with Toast grazing peacefully nearby and beams of sunlight slanting through the bare branches to warm the air around me, I drift off into an uneasy sleep.

Which I only realize when I snap back to wakefulness at the crinkling of the forest's underbrush somewhere nearby.

As my eyes pop open, my hands is already groping for my clay blade. My fingers close around the handle-like end, I push onto my feet in a crouch—

And a voice carries to me, so familiar it cracks open my heart: "Here's our lady thief."

There's no mistaking the relieved affection in his tone. I whirl toward the voice, and Stavros barrels through the woods to catch me in his arms.

The former general squeezes me tight against his massive frame, and I can't help clinging to him in turn. Tears burn behind my eyes. I have to swallow a sob.

I'm back with one of the men I love. He still trusts me so much he ran straight to me.

Of course, that could change once he finds out exactly what I've been doing during the past day.

That final thought sours my joy with a knotting of my stomach. But I keep gripping Stavros's arms as he eases back from me, his eyes with their blending of blue and brown feverishly bright beneath his dark red hair. He gives that little tick of his head that tells me he's focusing his vision on me more intently.

"What happened?" he demands, his voice darkening with a promise of retribution. He lifts his hand to the edge of the blood-crusted bandage on my forehead. "Are you all right? How did you get away?"

Not "Who took you?" but maybe that part of the story is easy to guess. Who but the scourge sorcerers could have compelled one of the riven?

"I'm all right now," I say. Before I can pull more answers together, another figure steps forward, with a smile on his gorgeous face that could warm me even in a blizzard.

Casimir sets his hand on my shoulder. "Before you get into the interrogation, Stav, let me offer my own welcome."

The courtesan tugs me into a tender embrace that's nonetheless just as emphatic as Stavros's. I burrow my head against the crook of his neck, breathing in his honeyed sandalwood scent and wishing I could stay right here without having to say another word.

There is at least one question *I* need to ask, though. I don't hear anyone else approaching.

I lift my head, my throat constricting. "Where are Alek and Rheave? Did something—"

Casimir shakes his head before I can get any farther into my anxious speculation. "They're both perfectly fine, other than being out of their heads with worry for you. Which will be resolved as soon as we get you back to them."

Stavros grins crookedly. "Have no doubts that they wanted to come with us. Rheave looked about ready to send one of his lightning bolts straight through me so he could take my place. But we couldn't leave the royal children undefended."

My heart leaps. "The royal children? Princess Klaudia and Prince Jacos are all right?"

That means I didn't carry out all of Lothar's murderous plan. But if the prince and princess are relying on my men for protection, then King Konram and Queen Ishild...

The hope that sparked inside me blinks out. Stavros must see the change in my face, because he brushes his fingers over my hair and speaks before I need to ask more.

"They're as well as they can be, considering what Lothar did to their parents."

He knows about Lothar. Well, the prince and princess were there in the audience room—they would have told him.

My mouth opens, but for a few seconds I can't push the words past the tension in my throat. "He wanted *me* to kill them all. One of the other scourge sorcerers, a woman who's been controlling at least some of the daimon, was holding me with her magic so completely that at first I couldn't even move a finger unless she commanded it. But she had to leave the sacrificial accomplice she was drawing power from behind when we came to the palace—her control weakened a little—I tried to make sure they couldn't use me..."

My hand rises to my bandage.

Casimir lets out a rough sound as if he's the one who's been wounded. "We'll have a medic look after that as soon as we can arrange it. You did everything you could—you shouldn't have been put through that horrible ordeal in the first place."

Renewed queasiness is building in my gut. The ordeal was even more horrible for people other than me.

"But I didn't manage— Lothar still attacked the king—?"

Stavros pulls me closer and presses a kiss to my unharmed temple. Then he bows lower and captures my lips with every bit of the heat and tenderness he's brought in the past.

When he eases back, his voice has thickened. "The kingdom is in disarray, and we have a lot of work ahead of us, but neither of those things are your fault. I think you should hear exactly what happened from those who witnessed it—the people your efforts did save."

I swallow hard. Yes. If I hadn't knocked myself into a stupor, Zaneta would have forced me to slaughter every member of the royal family.

She and Lothar must have attacked the king and queen while I was unconscious, but they didn't have the power on their own to destroy the entire royal family all at once.

Guilt remains lodged like a stone in my stomach. "The scourge sorcerers wouldn't have been able to get into the palace at all if it wasn't for me. I killed some of the guards..."

"Because Lothar forced you to," Casimir says, stroking his fingers up and down my back in a soothing caress. "You're no more responsible for that than Rheave is for the damage they've compelled him to inflict."

And yet it's so much easier to forgive the daimon-man than it is myself.

Stavros gives me a gentle shake. "You haven't answered my first question yet. How did you get away from them?"

I gather myself and explain about the sedative and Kosmel's voice in my dream, waking up and killing the daimon guard and Zaneta.

Casimir's deep blue eyes brighten at that part. "Then she can't bring you under her control again."

I nod. "And it was hard for her to keep up her influence, so I'm not sure if any of the other scourge sorcerers could manage it. But that doesn't mean—we'll still need to be careful. If I start acting strangely again—"

"We'll recognize what's going on and react much faster," Stavros finishes for me.

That wasn't what I was going to insist on, but I can't summon much enthusiasm for arguing with him about when he should murder me.

I do arch an eyebrow at him. "You came right to me here without having any idea whether I was in my right mind or if it was a trap."

The former general snorts and motions at the shard of clay I dropped by my feet. "It seemed incredibly unlikely that your captors would have sent you to assassinate us without even a proper weapon."

Trust him to have paid that much attention to what blade I was holding. And I guess he has a point.

I exhale in a shaky rush. "All right. What do we do now?"

Stavros glances at Toast, who's been watching our exchange with an air of mild disdain. "Get on your horse and follow us back to where we left ours nearby. We've temporarily taken shelter in one of the military's hidden supply stores, just a couple of hours' ride from here."

Looking around with my non-military-trained eyes, I wouldn't have a clue the patch of forest we've entered contains anything other than trees, birds, and the other obvious components of a woodland. But Stavros directs his stallion through the brush without a moment's hesitation.

He stops and dismounts at a spot where the layer of leaves and dirt on the ground looks a little more stirred up than elsewhere. With a sweep of his arm, he uncovers the slab of stone that he removes to reveal the round steel hatch underneath.

The metal surface is etched with the crest of the Melchiorek family—and scorched around the edges.

The last time we broke into one of these underground storage rooms, Rheave had to shatter the magic sealing it with his daimon power. It looks like he used a similar tactic here.

The seal must be permanently broken. Stavros gives a quick pattern of knocks, presumably designed to let those below know it's him and not an unwelcome intruder, and then hefts the hatch upward without any resistance.

"We've got—" he starts to call down.

Before he can get out one more word, a well-built form with a topping of chocolate-brown curls launches up the ladder and springs at me.

Rheave catches me in his muscular arms and spins me around with his face pressed close to my hair. A rush of exhilaration sweeps through me as I hug him back.

"My little vine," the daimon-man mutters with a rasp in his normally clear voice. "They tore you away from me."

Casimir lets out a soft chuckle. "Be careful with her. She's injured, you know."

Rheave growls in consternation and pulls back to look at me, letting my feet return to the ground. As he takes in the bandage on my forehead, his lips draw back to bare his teeth. "Those bullies. When I get my hands on them…"

A swell of affection fills my chest. It's only recently that I've accepted that my own intense fondness for Rheave goes beyond friendship, but there's never been any denying how devoted he is to me.

I set my hand against his cheek. "I'm all right, especially now that I'm back with all of you. It's good to see you too."

The daimon-man makes a sound that's almost pained. For a second, I think he's going to dive in to kiss me, but then something flickers in his eerie sea-green eyes. His expression tightens as his grip on my arms loosens.

Maybe he's only concerned that he'll hurt me with his enthusiasm. I don't have much time to ask about it, because Alek has just scrambled out of the underground room after him.

I'm just as delighted to be reunited with the scholar as my other men. As I turn toward him, my mouth stretching with an eager smile, he pulls me in against his lean frame.

He doesn't hesitate to kiss me, as soundly as he knows how. "I knew they wouldn't be able to hold you for long."

All at once, I choke up again. "I wish they hadn't been able to at all."

Rheave grunts dismissively. "The scourge sorcery can control thousands of daimon all at once. How could any one person fight it off?"

When he puts it that way, the idea that I should have somehow broken Zaneta's control does seem a little ridiculous. But that doesn't stop me from hating what she put me through.

Stavros beckons me over to the hatch. "Let's have the rest of this conversation down below where we can't be spotted by anyone on patrol. I'd imagine Lothar has sent quite a lot of his available forces to search for both you and the royals he lost."

He descends the ladder first, and I follow with trepidation creeping through my nerves. I'm about to face the two teenagers I nearly murdered, whether I had any say over my actions at that point or not.

When my feet hit the packed earth floor and I turn to peer through the lantern glow, my pulse hitches in surprise. Princess Klaudia and Prince Jacos are waiting there, sitting huddled together on one of the chests. Their dark brown hair and deep-set eyes remind me enough of their father's to send another jolt of guilt through me.

But they're not alone. Standing next to them is Petra, the distant niece of Queen Ishild's who I wasn't sure I'd ever see again after we left the college.

The royal siblings tense at the sight of me with a visible recoil. Princess Klaudia grasps Petra's arm. "Are you sure—"

"It's all right," Petra says in a soft voice. "I promise you, Ivy wouldn't be here if we couldn't trust her."

I gape at her for a moment before finding my words. They tumble out of me more abruptly than I'd have preferred. "What are *you* doing here?"

The king and queen must have dozens of minor relatives. I have no idea why they'd have drawn Petra in close enough for her to have followed them to Regica.

She did make some effort to chat with me while we were both at the royal college, enough that I wondered if she was spying for King Konram. I never had that suspicion confirmed, though.

Come to think of it, she was with them during the attack on the Florian royal residence as well.

Did she come along because she was close at hand, and they wanted to protect every part of their family they could reach?

Stavros steps to the side as the other men descend after us and tips his head to Petra. "I think you'd better tell Ivy everything you told us. She's completely out of the scourge sorcerers' influence now. She killed the one who was controlling her."

Petra clasps her olive-brown hands together in front of her. Her sleek black hair is pulled back from her face, but only in a loose bun, not one of the elaborate courtly styles. As elegant as her features are, the distant royal never followed fashion trends much even at the college.

"I've deceived you," she says, her melodic voice not quite as steady as usual, "as I've deceived almost everyone for the past seven years… It was supposed to bring some security in a situation like this… But I suppose none of us could really have been prepared for this kind of attack…"

As my brow knits in confusion, she gives her curvy body a little shake as if to get herself back on track. Her chin comes up, and in her stance as in her looks I can see an echo of Queen Ishild.

"You're aware of King Konram's original heir," she goes on. "Prince Dunstam."

It's not a question, but her pause makes me feel I should answer anyway. "Yes. He supposedly died of a sudden illness just before his twelfth birthday."

My hands clench at my sides. "Did Lothar have something to do with that after all? I suggested to King Konram that the scourge sorcerers might—"

Petra raises her hand to stop me. "In this particular crime, the traitors to the Crown had no involvement. Because there was no crime. There wasn't even a death."

She pauses, and the corner of her lips quirks upward with a hint of wryness. "A little more than seven years ago, I stopped being Prince Dunstam and became Princess Petra."

I stare at her for a moment before her full meaning sinks in.

She does look rather a lot like Queen Ishild for a distant niece, doesn't she? And something about her way of speaking has always reminded me of King Konram.

I try to recall Prince Dunstam's face from the scattered times I saw him as a child. He was a year younger than me, an occasional presence in parades and celebrations—and on the palace balcony during the riven executions.

I'm not surprised I didn't see it, even if it makes sense now that she's told me.

"That's the gift you asked your godlen for. To change your sex." My gaze drops to the two missing fingers on her right hand—little and ring—then rises again. "And more than that. Your hair color— your face…"

Petra's mouth curves into an actual smile, though it still looks more sad than anything else. "Exactly. Certain parts of my body never felt quite right when I was growing up. I was meant to be a woman, and Ardone transformed my outer self to match what's inside. I… might have been a little vain as well. I asked her to take inspiration from my mother more than my father. The features I originally inherited from him weren't very comely."

The revelation helps so many pieces fit together that a laugh tumbles out of me. *That's* why she's been so close with King Konram and Queen Ishild—they're her parents. That's why she was so invested in the rumors the conspirators were spreading to discredit the royal family.

But—

"Why did you pretend to be someone else altogether?" I have to ask. "You could have announced the change after your dedication ceremony, and everyone would have adjusted with a little time."

Asking for a dedication gift that's a one-time but permanent change rather than an ongoing talent isn't common, but it's not seen as strange either. And when it does happen, it's often for the same reason Petra gave.

I heard of kids who'd made a similar switch during my days of listening in on gossip on the streets of Florian. Most of the time the talk involved a lot of tongue clucking and people saying it was too bad they'd had to wait so long when it'd been so obvious they'd want the change since they were much smaller.

Petra looks down at her hands. "That was my father's idea. He's always been so concerned about our safety."

She glances back at her siblings and then meets my eyes again. "I discussed my intent with my parents before the dedication ceremony. Father suggested that we could concoct a story about me dying, and I could mingle with noble society under a different identity once my appearance was changed. I could learn more about the people I'd be ruling over without them censoring themselves in front of me, and I should be safe from assassination attempts or our enemies trying to use me to hurt him. Then, once I'd finished my education and he was ready to have me start officially training in as his heir, we'd reveal the truth in a big celebration."

"I didn't like it," Princess Klaudia mumbles, and swipes at her eyes. They're ruddy from a lot of recently shed tears, understandably. "It meant we could hardly see you and talk with you at all."

Petra grimaces and steps back to slip her arm around her sister's shoulder. "I know. I'm so sorry I wasn't there more, Klaudia. There were times when I wondered if all the subterfuge was really worth it, but once I'd committed…"

She sighs and lifts her head toward the rest of us. "It's over now regardless. My parents are gone, so it's up to me to see that Silana doesn't fall to the scourge sorcerers."

Stavros said all but the exact words, but my body stiffens anyway. "Your parents—"

"Are dead." Her voice flattens with the words—with the emotion I have to think she's suppressing.

Her gaze homes in on my bandage. "I have to thank you for fighting against our enemies as hard as you did. We all might have died back in Florian, and we certainly would have in Regica if not for you. But Lothar took us by such surprise as it was—as soon as he saw what you did, he leapt at my father—"

She falters, and Prince Jacos shivers beneath his cloak. He peers at me with his mouth set at an anxious slant—and a little flinch when I raise my hand.

I freeze, my heart lurching painfully at the reminder of everything my presence must remind *him* of. Everything my vicious magic made possible.

I'm not going to force Petra to go on. I can imagine the scene well enough from hearing Lothar's plotting, from the flashes of memory of blood and pained gasps.

"I'm sorry I wasn't able to stop them completely," I say hoarsely.

Klaudia turns her head away as if she can't bear to look at me.

Petra glances at her sister and then back at me. "It isn't your fault. That awful man…" She cuts herself off with a hiss of breath. "I tried to tell our father that you weren't a threat, you know. Even back at the college, I could tell you were honestly on our side. But he always leaned a little too far toward caution."

A heavy silence falls over the underground room. I drag in a breath thick with loamy odors. "Where do we go from here? As soon as we announce you as the Melchiorek heir, all of the Order of the Wild's forces will be after you."

"I know." Petra lifts her chin. "I'll have to gather all the support I can as quickly as I can. Any help you'll offer, I'm immensely grateful for. But our first step is clear. I need to return to Florian to gather the proof of who I am to make sure those who would support me believe it at all."

The defiance in her voice steadies my own resolve. There isn't any question in my mind of what I owe to the family I nearly eviscerated.

I square my shoulders and hold her gaze. "I'll be right there with you, no matter what the scourge sorcerers send our way."

# Six

The horses' hooves clop across the forest floor at an even rhythm that I'd delight in if I didn't have so much distracting me from the simple pleasure.

Even when I'm not looking at her, every inch of my skin quivers with the awareness of Ivy's presence. I do look at her quite a bit, because some part of me needs the extra confirmation that she's really here.

My hands tighten around the reins, but I resist the impulse to urge my horse closer to hers. I'm already riding within a few feet of her as we pick our way through the forest. There are spaces two horses can't squeeze through side by side.

If we hadn't managed to borrow a couple more mounts from a farm we passed for the royal heirs to ride on, I might have shared Toast with her like we did from time to time on our journey before. I could have kept one arm wrapped around her waist as we rode, had her slim body pressed up against mine and my chin tucked over her shoulder as if there was no way I could ever lose her again.

Of course, that would have worn Toast out much more quickly.

I can't suppress a pang of regret all the same.

We pass through a clearing, and I nudge my gelding to keep pace. Ivy's pale reddish-blond hair catches a glimmer of moonlight that looks almost like a flare of magic—and a different sort of pang lances right through the middle of me.

For an instant, my body seems to squeeze tight around me, cold and hard as the cooled clay before the scourge sorcerers brought my prison to life. My lungs ache with my next breath.

If something else happens to her—if I did lose her again—

I don't know how I *will* continue to live.

I've been injured in this body. I've felt shame over actions that harmed my companions to the point that I considered destroying the form of conjured flesh that makes me almost human.

But I've never felt any pain like the agony of the past day, not knowing where Ivy was or what our enemies might be doing to her, not knowing if she was even alive herself after the story we heard from the royal children of how she defied her captors…

Is that the other side of the joy being with her brings me? Like the backlash that balances her magic, my delight in her must come with equal anguish?

Last night, there wasn't anything I could do to cast off the frantic, searing emotions. They radiated all through my body, from the thoughts whirling in my head to the constricting of my throat to the listing of my stomach.

For the first time since I gained control over the body the scourge sorcerers made, it felt like a prison again. Just remembering the sensations gives me a chill.

I'd never been apart from Ivy for more than a few hours before, and then always by our own designs. I never realized the unsettled feelings that would rise up in her absence could become so much more intense.

Why do humans care so strongly about each other if the sensations can turn so debilitating?

I thought following Ivy wherever she went would ensure my freedom. I thought she was the path to escaping the torment the scourge sorcerers put me through.

But somehow the adoration that's grown in me can lock me up and send me into harsher torments than I felt under our enemies' sway.

That's not her fault, though. It's something in me.

And the only thing worse than knowing how my heart's ties to her imprison me is the thought of having to go through that agony again.

So I keep glancing at her, checking for any sign of distress. I ride close even though it stirs up the unsettling memories, so I'll be near at hand to leap to her defense if necessary.

I simply won't *let* anyone wrench her away from me again, and then we can have nothing but joy.

Ivy peers over at Petra, the woman it seems is now supposed to be queen. She's the only one of us riding with company, I've noted more than once with a twinge of envy—her brother sits in front of her on a large stallion's back, leaning into her arms with a droop of his head as if he's a wilting flower.

The prince's eyes have closed, his wan face gone slack. The royal children have been through plenty of agony of their own in the past day.

At least Ivy returned to me. Their parents are gone forever.

I wasn't born, and I have nothing but revulsion for the people who trapped me with the intention of making me their slave, so I'm not sure what a regular human would feel toward a mother or a father. From the few times she's mentioned them, Ivy's connection to her parents has seemed mostly unpleasant.

But clearly that isn't always the case. Even if I don't understand, I'm sorry these three have had to experience such a permanent loss.

Ivy keeps her voice quiet, I assume to avoid waking the prince. "What exactly will we need to do once we get to Florian? You said there's proof of your claim to the throne?"

Petra's mouth tightens, but she nods. "We expected that Father would be able to announce me and then there'd be no question... But he kept a blood-sworn letter confirming my identity in a secure area of his private quarters. We'll want to retrieve that if possible. I'm not sure what's going on in the Palace of the Crown now."

Princess Klaudia shivers. "All our things—all Mother and Father's things—they can't just *take* our home..."

She trails off with a miserable expression.

"We'll get your home back for you as quickly as we can," Casimir says softly, but his worried expression tells me that he suspects "quickly" is probably not going to be very quick at all.

Petra's tone firms. "Lothar and his followers won't get away with their crimes." She turns back to Ivy. "We can also reach out to the cleric at the Temple of the Crown who oversaw my dedication. She can vouch that I'm next in the royal line."

Ivy lets out a rough chuckle. "That should be simpler than getting into the palace, at least."

"What about all the soldiers?" Klaudia demands abruptly. "Aren't they supposed to be loyal to us, not the traitors? They know Jacos and me, even if they won't be sure of you right away. Why can't we ride to one of the forts and get them to set things right?"

I know the horrible answer to that question. "There are daimon like me mixed in with the soldiers. But unlike me, the scourge sorcerers are still controlling them."

Stavros grimaces. "Yes. The last thing I'd want to do is to lead you to a group of armed men and women with uncertain loyalties. The scourge sorcerers wanted all of you dead, and it wouldn't mean much to them to sacrifice a few of their captured daimon to see it happen. Rheave can identify his fellow spirits, but only when they're very close by. We'll reach out to the military presence near Florian, but we'll have to be very careful about it."

Ivy looks over her shoulder at me, her brow knitting. "But maybe we won't need to worry about the other daimon anymore. Lothar said that the woman who was controlling me had gotten 'practice' by directing the daimon. She's dead now. Doesn't that mean they'll be as free as you are?"

My spirits lift momentarily at the idea that I might never have to worry about those bonds of magic yanking at me again. They sink just as swiftly. "I don't think it can all have been handled by just one scourge sorcerer. There were so many of us. And they didn't need to work their magic on us regularly. The commands would linger for days after they took hold."

Alek has been taking in our conversation in silence. He interjects with his usual scholarly precision. "It must be much easier for them to manipulate people whose bodies they created and whose spirits they already harnessed than a regular person whose body is her own. And Ivy's magic would have required so much more effort to contain. That one sorcerer could have been in charge of hundreds of daimon who haven't felt her renewed influence in a couple of days already."

Petra sighs. "But we can't know how long the previous influence will last or whether other scourge sorcerers will enforce their will again. Ster. Stavros is right. We need to proceed with every possible caution."

She glances down at her sleeping brother. "The consequences of a misstep would be far too great."

We lapse into silence, broken a few minutes later by Casimir's tentative question. "Did you have any idea of Lothar's intentions? Obviously your father still trusted him up to the end, but now that he's revealed himself—did anything show in his words or behavior, looking back, that might help us determine his next steps or how to undermine him?"

"I never liked him," Klaudia mutters. "He always talked like he thought he knew more than anyone else possibly could. And he tried to get the festival for Signy cancelled, because he insisted we shouldn't be celebrating heroes from other countries. But she helped all of us get free from the Darium empire!"

Ivy hums to herself. "He does seem to be obsessed with doing things the 'right' way—his Order of the Wild is built on a vision of how Silana is meant to be and what would bring the All-Giver back."

"He wants to rewind history to before Dariu ever invaded," Alek says. "As if that was any kind of golden age."

Petra frowns. "There were definitely things about him that rubbed me the wrong way, but even now, I can't think of any warning signs we missed. He always acted as if he wanted to support Father completely. But then, I wasn't around him very often after my dedication ceremony. I don't know how much I missed."

Stavros adjusts his grip on his reins, his expression grim. "He's had access to some of the innermost levels of the country's rulership. There won't be much he doesn't know how to manipulate. It's no wonder we've found the conspiracy so difficult to rout out."

Ivy shakes her head. "But people can't really want the kind of world he's been working on creating —all wildness and violence. We know who and what we're really dealing with now. We'll expose him and his practices, and most of Silana will be on our side. It's just a matter of getting the word out."

She looks so determined that I have to fight off another urge to push closer, to hug her to me. It doesn't matter how hard our journey gets—she's always willing to keep up her own fight.

As we emerge from the woods and cross a large stretch of fields, we let the conversation fade. Ivy hasn't risked using her magic to hide us like she did in the past, but we waited until night fell to start our trek, and so far we haven't encountered any patrols. Staying off the official roads must help.

The thought has just passed through my head when my eyes pick up a figure on horseback cantering along a small country lane in the moonlight up ahead.

We draw our horses to a halt, but the man doesn't glance our way. A thin flag whips about in the wind of his passage.

Stavros makes a sound of consternation. "He's flying the banner of a royal messenger—and that looks like an official messenger's uniform. What are the scourge sorcerers up to now?"

Ivy doesn't even hesitate. She nudges Toast back into motion. "We'd better find out. He's alone. We can defend ourselves if we need to."

I tap my heels to my steed's sides to follow her. We're too far off still for the messenger to have noticed us, as focused as he seems to be on his mission.

He appears to be riding toward the nearest town, where a few faint lights glimmer in the distance. Along the way there, several farmhouses stand at a distance from the road.

The nearest of the farmhouses has a candle burning near one of the windows, indicating someone in there is awake. As we close the distance, the messenger slows by the wooden fence along the road. He dismounts to open the gate and leads his horse past it, heading toward the house.

Ivy slows her horse to a walk, watching. She pitches her voice in a whisper. "We need to know what message the scourge sorcerers are spreading across the country. I'll go listen in—I can make sure the messenger doesn't notice me if I'm on foot."

She's barely finished speaking when she hops down from Toast. Stavros sucks in a breath as if to argue, but I slide from my horse first.

"I'll make sure she's all right," I tell him and hurry after her form darting through the night.

The others don't follow, presumably realizing that more people would be more difficult to hide. Ivy spares one glance at me with a hint of frustration, but I'm not hanging back and letting her go alone.

I need to be in arm's reach in case the worst happens again.

She sprints across the remaining fields, keeping her stance low. I copy her pose.

We reach the fence just as the messenger is knocking on the farmhouse door. Ivy nimbly clambers over the boards and lands with barely a sound on the other side. I do my best to mimic her stealth.

We creep through the thicker shadows along the fence until we near a wagon standing in the yard. Ivy darts over to it so she can get closer to the house, with me at her heels. She presses her finger to her lips, as if I don't already understand that we need to keep quiet.

The door is just squeaking open. A weary looking man peers out at the messenger, jerking straighter as he takes in the royal uniform. "What is it?"

The messenger bobs his head. He must have delivered this announcement dozens of times already, because he speaks at a clipped tone, fast and without any hesitation to the practiced words.

"We're crossing the country to inform the people of Silana that a new age is upon us. The Melchioreks who forced their rule on us and defied the will of the gods have been vanquished. King Konram is dead. A new ruler will rise who will see that the gods favor us again and the All-Giver knows it's time to return. May the Great God shine on all of us who are worthy!"

The farmer stares at the messenger, his mouth dropping open. "I—the king is dead?"

"The false king," the messenger says with an edge of menace even I pick up on. "We must celebrate the chance to see our country returned to its former glory."

Ivy sucks in a strained breath. We both know what he's saying isn't true.

But the farmer doesn't appear to believe he can argue. He stiffens but bobs his head. "Yes. Yes, of course."

The messenger makes a brisk gesture of farewell and hustles back to his horse. As the farmer closes the door with a bewildered air, Ivy tenses next to me.

"We can't let him keep making those claims," she whispers, her hands clenched. "They're making it sound as if King Konram was killed justly through the will of the gods instead of murdered in cold blood by a traitor. And they're spreading their story everywhere they can as quickly as possible before anyone can find out the truth."

Her tone is so fierce that panic jolts through my veins. I can so easily picture her launching herself at the man—tackling him physically and leaving herself open to another injury—or hurling her magic at him and addling her mind, simply to protect the rest of Silana—

Every particle of whatever kind of a soul I have recoils in horror. The man strides up to the gate, gripping his horse's reins, and Ivy leans forward.

Without another thought, I snatch a stick from the ground and whip it forward with a heave of my own power.

My daimon energy crackles across the projectile. It doesn't fly as fast or far as an arrow I launched from a bow, but I don't need it to.

The stick smacks into the messenger's back with a crackle like lightning. He jerks and topples over, his shirt and flesh charred.

I spring forward, hurling another bolt of energy at him the moment I'm closer. His body disintegrates into ash.

A gust of breeze disperses most of the evidence of his death across the yard.

Ivy jogs up behind me and grasps my arm. "What are you doing?"

"You said we couldn't let him spread the message. I made sure he couldn't."

I glance at the horse, who sidesteps with a snort but doesn't outright run. Animals seem to take well to me most of the time. "And now Prince Jacos can have a mount of his own. We needed another horse, didn't we?"

Ivy sputters a dark laugh, muffled by her hand. "Come on, then, before the farmer notices us."

As she grabs the horse's reins, I find myself glancing toward the distant town. A sense of melancholy drifts over me.

The people of that settlement won't hear the scourge sorcerers' claims right away, but how many other messengers have our enemies sent hurtling across the countryside?

I can't burn all of them up. The poison is spreading too fast for us to stop it.

# Seven

*Ivy*

"Not much farther," Petra says as we pause at the corner of one of the city's streets. She draws her cloak tighter around her. "We're almost there."

It's hard to tell from her tone how much she's reassuring me and our other companions and how much herself.

The four of us gather close together, scanning the road ahead. There's an uneasy edge to the atmosphere in the city that I'm not used to, especially when surrounded by the elegant stone buildings of the inner wards. Nobles and other upper crust citizens hustle by with anxiously hasty steps and heads ducked low, attitudes much more common on Florian's fringes.

Even though it's only early evening, many of the shop and restaurant windows along this stretch are dark. No music or laughter trickles from the establishments that have their lanterns lit, as if even the dinnertime chatter has become subdued.

No one gives us a second glance, but I tug my hood farther forward just in case. Thankfully the wound on my forehead has healed enough that I only need a small bandage now.

What would Julita have made of the unnerving change to the capital city so soon after we left it? It's hard not to wish I could hear one of her arch remarks that would settle my nerves just a little.

Maybe it's better that she never had to see this, though.

Only Casimir and Rheave joined Petra and me on our venture into Florian, since the rest of our party is rather recognizable. And Petra wants to keep her younger siblings out of danger as much as possible. Stavros and Alek stayed back with Klaudia and Jacos, setting up a campsite in a secluded area using supplies we grabbed from the military storage room.

I'd prefer an even smaller group for sneaking through the city that was under lockdown just a month ago in the hopes of dragging me to the gallows, but having the heir to the throne with us makes other types of caution necessary. Rheave can fend off attackers with his magic without worrying about going insane or other backlash. Casimir may be able to use his gift to cajole less hostile parties into helping us.

The most important part of our mission is that we keep Petra—*Queen* Petra, I still have to remind myself—alive.

I don't spot any soldiers or obvious Order of the Wild sentries among the pedestrians. When I glance at Rheave, he shakes his head to indicate he doesn't sense fellow daimon nearby.

I touch Petra's elbow. "I think it's safe to continue."

As we walk down the street, aiming for a steady but casual pace so we don't look as furtive as I feel, Petra shoots me a quick, tight smile. "I guess you're used to navigating the city like this. It mustn't have been easy—all those years you had to stay in hiding to conceal your powers."

A lump rises in my throat at the thought of all the loneliness and fear that taint my past. Not that I'm particularly less afraid at the moment, but at least I'm not facing the challenge alone.

I aim for a light tone to cover how fraught the question actually is. "I hope the pardon your father planned to extend to me will remain in place under your rule?"

Something flickers in Petra's expression, there and then gone so swiftly I can't read the emotion. She reaches over to grip my arm with an emphatic squeeze. "As far as I'm concerned, you were never a real threat. I truly am sorry about how he treated you—how stubborn he was about seeing you as an enemy."

The genuine regret in her tone puts me off balance.

I force myself to shrug. "I guess it was understandable. People with my kind of magic haven't exactly made a great case for ourselves over the centuries. And you weren't sure of me at first either, were you? Even when you didn't know about my magic. You weren't chatting with me at the college only out of friendliness."

I don't say it as an accusation, only a statement of fact, but a hint of a blush colors Petra's tan cheeks. "I'm sorry about that too. You were a relative unknown who'd abruptly joined Ster. Stavros in his investigations. My father wanted to hear what I made of you, whether I thought you had any ulterior motives."

"I don't blame you for that," I assure her. "I'd imagine I'd have done the same in your position."

"Still… Thank you for everything you've done for my family. You've been through more hardship on our behalf than I've had to face even a fraction of. If I can regain the country, you can be sure—"

Her voice falters as we come up on another cross-street. Behind me, Casimir makes a soft pained sound.

What used to be a statue at the center of the crossroads now lies shattered across the cobblestones in chunks of marble. A forearm clutching a broken sword lies near my feet. Beyond it, amid the smaller shards, I identify pieces of a leg, a jaw and neck… and the top of a head with a chipped crown.

I passed this statue more than once on my ventures into the inner wards. It depicted King Konram, erected shortly after he took the throne.

Petra draws in her breath with a rasp. But even as I reach for her, she draws herself a little straighter, her shoulders rigid.

Her voice comes out taut. "They're finding every way they can try to destroy him and our family's legacy."

I grimace. I wasn't King Konram's biggest fan, but I'd take his rule over the scourge sorcerers' any day. "They need to convince everyone that the Melchioreks were the villains so they'll look justified in taking over."

"Statues can be rebuilt," Casimir says gently. "We won't let them win."

Petra nods in a jerk, her stance tensing even more. "I'm just glad Klaudia and Jacos didn't see this."

As we take another turn onto a street that'll take us to the large courtyard at the foot of the Temple of the Crown, my stomach knots. I don't have the most pleasant associations with the country's largest temple.

It's the place where I watched several riven sorcerers walk to the noose and meet their deaths over the years. And the place where *I* nearly died stopping one of the scourge sorcerers from calling a wave of destruction down on the city.

But none of my trepidation could have prepared me for the sight that greets us when we reach the edge of the courtyard.

Petra stops in her tracks, sounding as if she's stifled a gasp. I grip her shoulder and turn her toward me so we can pretend we're paying attention to each other rather than the scene on the other side of the stretch of cobblestones.

I'd rather look at my future queen than the carnage on display there. Splotches of brownish red linger at the edge of my vision—blood splattered across the temple's marble walls.

Rheave lets out a hushed growl. "Who are those people? Why would anyone have killed them?"

The blood I'm trying to shut out has come from several bodies who've been pinned to the walls by metal posts through their chests. Girding myself, I allow my gaze to veer toward the gruesome display again.

The figures have been savaged as if by wild animals—gouges torn through their clothes and flesh, organs spilling out, necks ripped open. But when I force myself to focus on them, I note the shape and color of their tattered outfits.

Robes of worship.

A surge of horror fills my throat. "They were all clerics and devouts. The ones who worked in the temple, maybe?"

A shiver passes through Casimir's body. "The ones who refused to play along with the scourge sorcerers, most likely. Did they set hunting dogs on them?"

My stomach churns. "Only their followers, I'd bet."

When I was playing at being a new recruit to the Order of the Wild, one of my tests was to race through the woods on all fours and tear apart a live rabbit with my bare hands. The conspirators take the name of their organization very literally.

As if there's anything holy about savaging innocent creatures... or people.

"Yes, look upon those who betrayed their gods!" someone shouts from the doorway of the temple. "So many of the chosen leaders of our faith cared more about their own satisfaction than that of the All-Giver and the godlen. But the gods have willed that they and the false monarchy who steered our country so wrong should fall and a new age begin."

More of the scourge sorcerers' fucking propaganda. My teeth set on edge.

Will anyone in the city buy into their garbage? No doubt. They found plenty of recruits for their conspiracy, after all.

But far more will shut their mouths and stay out of the conflict not out of faith but out of fear that they'll be ripped to shreds next.

Petra turns her head slowly. She takes in the ruined bodies with only the slightest tremor of her chin.

Her gaze pauses toward the end of the line, and her lips purse in frustration as well as horror. "That's—that's Otyla there. The cleric who handled my dedication ceremony, who could have vouched for me. Of course she'd have resisted... And now she's gone."

The scourge sorcerers have screwed over the royal family even more than they know.

I swallow a curse and squeeze her arm to bring her attention back to me. "Was there anyone else at the temple who was involved—who'd be able to confirm that Prince Dunstam didn't die, only became Princess Petra?"

She shakes her head. "Father kept it as quiet as possible. No one knew except him, Mother, my brother and sister, and Otyla. Although Lothar may have started to suspect after seeing that I was brought along with the rest of the family to Regica."

Her hands ball into fists. "I could have stayed at the college—kept up the ruse—then I'd have been here when the scourge sorcerers took over..."

Casimir comes up beside her and rests a comforting hand on her shoulder. "Your parents wanted to keep you safe. And if you hadn't been with them, it's possible Klaudia and Jacos wouldn't have escaped Lothar's attack. You can't blame yourself for anything that's happened."

She inhales sharply and gathers herself. "If we can't—"

She's interrupted by a trumpet sound that carries from the balcony high over the temple's doorway. The balcony where her parents and siblings—and she herself, before she became Petra—used to stand to oversee the riven executions.

A bluish glow forms around the figure who's appeared there. His lopsided frame gives him away in an instant.

Lothar is here. He's standing up on the balcony, looking down over us with a typically haughty expression, his formal robes draped across his tall but uneven body.

His voice rings out loud enough that it must echo through the streets all through the inner ward. He's using magic to amplify it.

"Good people of Florian! Please stop and listen to what I have to say. I was once the secondary magical advisor to the Melchiorek family, and now I am the highest authority this country has left."

"Because of his treachery," Petra mutters. Even more color drains from her face as she glares up at him.

"I don't claim any right to rule," Lothar goes on. "But I saw so much wrong in the course of my duties that I feel it is my responsibility to guide our country into its new era. We must find our way back to the true will of the gods and the essence of what makes us alive."

By maiming and killing other living things. Brilliant strategy.

I keep the sarcastic remark to myself, but a tremor shakes Petra's body. Her hand drops to the dagger she's carrying on the belt of her dress.

There's no way she could cut him down from here. Even I'd have trouble keeping my aim steady across that distance without the help of my magic.

My magic.

Lothar's next words turn tinny and distant through the rush of cold that courses through me. My power wriggles in my chest, sensing my interest.

I could end so much of this catastrophe right now. Lothar stands at the top of the Order of the Wild. He's directed all their madness and violence.

Without him, they might not fall apart instantly, but they'd be deeply shaken. So much easier to break apart and overcome.

He forced me to kill people—he has gallons of blood on his own hands. Would destroying him really be murder or simply self-defense?

The chill comes with a growing certainty. I've tried to follow my conscience and the laws of the land, and where has that gotten us?

The king is dead. The man up there would murder the woman beside me if he realized who she is.

And I'm the only one who can definitely stop him, right here, right now.

The thrum of my magic expands to a roar inside my skull. It trembles through my nerves, but I hold it in with a clench of my jaw.

If I'm going to do this, I still have to be smart about it. The smallest possible effect so no one suspects—so I don't tempt more insanity than I have to.

Thinking of how I dispatched my daimon guard, I train my gaze on Lothar's neck and set my hand against one of the stones of the building we're standing next to. I picture his throat crumpling inward as the stone's surface bulges just enough to compensate.

My heart pounds, and I launch my power forward like one of Rheave's arrows.

It flings out of me, smacks into the figure on the tower—and fizzles out as if it's encountered nothing but air.

I flinch in surprise, and Casimir's head jerks toward me. "What's wrong, Kindness?"

Shame sweeps through me as swiftly as the certainty before it. How can I tell him what I just attempted?

Would the kindest man I've ever met still think I deserve the nickname he gave me?

"I—I tested him a bit with my magic," I say, fighting to keep my voice steady. "He isn't really there. It's an illusion—some kind of magical projection, I think."

Rheave hums to himself and bares his teeth with a fierce smile. "He knows you got away, that you have your mind back. He's afraid of you."

The daimon-man is probably right. Of course Lothar wouldn't take the chance that I could use the magic he was so eager to exploit against him. I should have realized that to begin with.

The effort I put into the jab of power was still expended—and still took some toll. As I turn my head, I think I catch a flicker of sapphire blue—soldiers, maybe daimon, coming to arrest us. I have to—

I blink hard and look again through the stutter of my pulse.

There's no one wearing blue at that corner of the square at all. The closest is a woman staring up at Lothar who's got on a green dress.

I don't entirely have my mind back, no matter what Rheave says.

So when a tingle of magic passes by me a moment later, my first instinct is to assume it's another hallucination. But I wait, concentrating on the feeling, and it lingers.

I scan the square and adjust my position, taking a small step forward and then to the side to track the direction the magic is coming from.

As I follow my impression of it, a filmy figure swims into view, standing on the other side of the street we emerged from with his narrow face set in a mask of revulsion.

I tug on Petra's arm. "Your father's third magical advisor… What was his name? Tinom something? He's here!"

"What?" She peers in the direction I'm looking. "Where?"

She can't see him. He must be using some kind of distracting spell that I was able to overcome once I knew where to look.

Right. His specialty was illusions, wasn't it?

He definitely doesn't appear pleased with his colleague's speech. I waver and decide to take a gamble.

Better to start adding to our allies than fling my own magic around again.

As I march straight up to the magic advisor, his gaze twitches to me with a flicker of surprise. I fix him with my firmest stare. "Are you on Lothar's side, or are you ready to start saving the kingdom?"

# EIGHT

*Ivy*

Tinom raps his sinewy hand against the wooden dining table. His face has gone ruddy beneath the thin fringe of his gray-and-white hair. "Whatever else we put in place, we *need* that blood-sworn letter."

His voice rings through the sparsely decorated room with so much force I have to restrain a wince. My gaze darts to the narrow window overlooking the city street outside, where another evening is descending into night.

We shouldn't have to worry. Tinom owns this tenement building in one of Florian's wealthier middle-class neighborhoods as part of his family's holdings, and the two apartments on the uppermost floor were vacant when the Order of the Wild swept into the capital. The magic advisor has been hiding out here along with a couple of devouts who escaped the purge at the Temple of the Crown, using his considerable skill with illusions to ensure his former colleague and Lothar's new comrades don't discover his refuge.

But we've taken shelter in apartments we thought were safe before, only to have to run for our lives. Since the moment the king declared me and my men enemies of the kingdom, we've had to constantly be on the move.

The only place we had any security was the hidden sanctuary for the riven, the Haven, where the only other sane riven sorcerer I've met taught me the basics of controlling my power. But that safety came with a different sort of price. We couldn't interact with the outside world at all—and when we decided we needed to stand up to the scourge sorcerers again, Sulla tried to turn the Haven into our prison.

I never thought I'd miss the days of sleeping on Stavros's sofa in his professorial quarters at the royal college, but that time looks strangely peaceful through the lens of my memory.

A flash that could be a flare of magic whips past the window—but no tingle of energy crosses my skin, and no one else reacts. I yank my eyes away from the hallucination, back to what's real around the table.

About twenty of us have squeezed into the now-cramped room. Petra, her siblings, my men, and I are clustered around one end of the table. Tinom sits at the other end, flanked by the two devouts along with several soldiers and a couple of nobles he's sure are loyal to the Melchiorek family.

We've spent most of the past day gathering this group of loyalists. It felt like we were making quite a bit of progress in the moment, but seeing the end result, I can't help thinking back to the army of hundreds Lothar was able to send to cut down the king.

Of course, my men and I left that army in disarray, the most devoted of them cut down in battle themselves. But we only managed it by tricking the Darium soldiers stationed on the other side of the channel into doing most of the work.

We're not going to get away with using that gambit twice.

Petra leans forward where she's sitting, setting her elbows on the table. I can't help being impressed by the increasingly queenly demeanor that's come over her with more supporters to command.

"The letter is the best proof we have of my identity," she says. "But Lothar's people could lie about the results of a test—they could destroy it. We'd need a loyal cleric to confirm its validity who the people also trust."

The baroness next to Tinom lifts her chin at a haughty angle that immediately sets my nerves on edge. I don't think Julita would have liked Baroness Sibelle either. The woman has gone to the effort of sculpting her dark hair into stylish whorls and painting her eyelids as if it matters how fashionable she is while the world is falling apart around her.

Her eyes flicker with a gleam that's a little sly. "We don't need to worry about confirming it yet. Simply showing the letter with its seal will be enough to convince most of the commoners. Look at how easily they've bought into the refuse Lothar and his ilk are selling them."

The devout at her left nods eagerly. "Many are eager for solid ground after the news of King Konram's and Queen Ishild's—that is, your parents'—deaths. They'll want to believe that the Melchiorek line can be continued."

He blushes at his brief stumble. I can't help wondering to what extent any of our allies believe Petra's story without definitive proof.

Tinom might be insisting so urgently as much to convince Petra's latest supporters as wider society. Maybe he even needs to convince himself.

"She has the testimony of her siblings as well," Stavros points out, in a slightly ominous tone that makes me think he's picked up on the same hints of doubt.

Petra shakes her head. "I won't bring Klaudia and Jacos for the initial announcement. It'll be too dangerous."

I frown and motion toward Tinom. "You're a master of illusions. Couldn't we use a similar trick to what Lothar did at the temple last night—project the image of Petra into a public place so she can speak to the people without being physically under threat?"

My skin prickles as several gazes settle on me alongside his. Tinom's is coolly assessing. He knows what I am—he almost ran off last night before Petra dashed over and flashed her family's seal.

I suspect he's still not all that happy to be making plans with a riven sorcerer.

The others, I don't think he's told, maybe because he isn't sure what they'd think of *him* allowing my presence. But I haven't put on my false noble airs like I did at the college. They probably have no idea what to make of me at all.

Tinom pauses before dipping his head in a slow nod. "Yes, of course, projecting illusions would be the obvious solution. Since we wouldn't want to allow any direct interaction at that tentative early stage regardless."

Petra knits her brow as if she isn't pleased with this line of conversation. From getting to know her better over the past several days, I suspect she'd prefer to meet her subjects properly for such an important announcement.

But she can't deny how necessary the precaution would be. "All right. Regardless, we shouldn't set anything into motion until we have objective proof that I'm the heir to the throne. What's the current situation in the Capital Palace?"

She looks at the standing soldiers. They've shed their blue uniforms so they can blend in when we venture outside, but I can see the military training in their postures.

Next to me, Rheave's gaze darts over the assembled figures. He already confirmed that none of them were captured daimon who'd infiltrated the royal military, but I get the impression that he doesn't totally trust them as humans all the same.

I can't say I'd be keen to put my life in their hands either, considering how many of their colleagues have attempted to hunt me down in the past few months.

The man among them who has the highest rank—a major—glances at Stavros as if the former general will be able to answer for him before clearing his throat. "I'm afraid the palace is entirely overrun. The Order of the Wild encouraged total disrespect of the Melchiorek legacy. The initial looting has waned, but many of Lothar's followers have settled within the walls. We couldn't simply walk in and take what we want."

Alek speaks up a little hesitantly. "Are you sure the letter would even still be there? It wouldn't have been found during the looting?"

"My father had a secure hidden cache in his bedroom," Petra says. "It could only be found by someone who knows where it's meant to be, which at the moment is only our family."

She turns to me. "Ivy, I hate to ask more of you, but it appears stealth would be a much more viable option for us than strength. That's your area of expertise. I'm sure Tinom could give you additional protection with a temporary concealment enchantment."

The magic advisor draws his posture up straighter, his shoulders going rigid. "It would be simple enough. But are you sure— To send her alone—"

To leave the riven to her own devices, he must be thinking. As if I haven't had plenty of opportunities to sow ruin before now if I'd wanted to.

Petra cuts a glance toward Tinom that stops whatever concern he was going to express before the rest of the words leave his lips. "There's no one I'd trust more than Ivy with the task." Her attention returns to me. "If you'll take it."

As I stare back at her face so like her mother's, the traces of her father's bearing showing in her calm composure, my throat constricts.

King Konram asked a lot of me before he knew what I was. But he never truly *asked*. It was either direct orders or commands phrased like a question that didn't allow for an argument.

Petra is her father's child, but also her own person. A person I find myself not particularly wanting to let down.

I wet my lips, picturing myself slipping through the halls of the grand palace I've only entered once before—and then in the midst of a daimon battle. Even with the help of a concealment illusion, it'll be dangerous.

I've done dozens of things equally dangerous or more in the past few months, though. What's another for the history books?

My mind is still acting up, yes, but I've been able to recognize the hallucinations before I react. And the longer I can go without turning to my own magic again, the more the effects should fade.

I hope.

It's not as if we have time to waste. The longer Lothar keeps his hold over the country, the more people he'll draw into his brand of madness.

"Of course," I say. "Whatever I can do to see you on the throne and Lothar in his grave."

I'd worry that my death wish for the former magic advisor might be a little too blunt, but a couple of the soldiers snort in amusement and Sibille's lips form a sharp grin. Clearly it's a sentiment we all share.

"Thank you," Petra says like she means it, and pushes to her feet. "It's been several long, hard days for all of us. I think we should get some rest and finish our planning with clear heads. We can aim to send Ivy on her mission tomorrow evening."

She dips her head in a dismissal.

As I push myself to my feet, my legs sway under me. I didn't sleep all that well last night even with proper walls around me.

Images of Lothar standing in the temple and me hurling a murderous lance of magic toward him kept flashing through my mind. That and the way Petra's siblings recoiled when they first saw me in the underground storeroom.

Casimir slips his hand around my arm. "Come on, Kindness. Let's set aside all these responsibilities for a little while."

He guides me down the hall to the room the five of us have taken as our own. It's unfurnished, but we were able to gather enough blankets to form a large sleeping mat that covers about half of the floor.

My other men follow us. As I turn to face them, a swell of emotion rises up in my chest.

I was torn away from them, and I haven't really gotten to appreciate being back with them since we reunited. There've been so many other problems dogging us, other people around that I had to put on a strong front for.

These four men accept my weaknesses as well as my power. There's nothing I'm craving more right now than a reminder of their affection.

I kick off my boots by the door and sink down in the middle of the blanketed area. Then I hold out my hand, beckoning them all over.

I think they can tell from my attitude that I'm looking for comfort rather than passion at this moment. They settle themselves in a ring around me, Casimir by my back, Rheave and Stavros at either side of me, and Alek in front.

Rheave loops his arm around mine while Stavros takes my hand, stroking his thumb over my knuckles. Casimir rubs my back in a gentle motion, careful of my scars.

Alek caresses his fingers over my cheek, tucking a few stray strands of hair behind my ear. "How are you doing, Ivy? I thought we'd been through a lot already, but this…" He shakes his head. "At least it seems we've finally gotten to the core of the conspiracy."

"Yes," I say. We just don't know what to do about it. But I want to spend a little time *not* thinking about Lothar for once. "I'm just glad I'm with all of you again. Whatever happens going forward, having you is the bright spot that helps me through the dark parts."

Stavros lets out a low rumble. "Don't ever doubt that you do the same for us."

Rheave's voice dips low. "When you were gone, when we didn't know what had happened to you…" His voice trails off raggedly, and then he seems to master the emotion that gripped him. "But our little vine is back with us, and that's what matters."

The daimon-man leans in to kiss the side of my neck. He's only just started exploring the bodily pleasures two—or more—people can conjure together, but he's both an eager student and a quick study.

The press of his lips sends a jolt of heat straight to my sex. All at once, my nerves are humming with desire for the other sorts of intimacy we haven't had the privacy or energy for while on the road to Florian.

As usual, Casimir picks up the shift in my mood immediately. He teases his hands down to my waist to undo my belt and then up to work at the lacing on my dress. "I think our woman deserves the full welcome she's had to go so many days without."

Stavros's heated chuckle is all agreement. Alek simply offers one of his quiet but bright smiles and trails his fingers up my thigh.

Rheave eases back to watch as Casimir peels the dress off me. The daimon-man's eyes widen taking in my partial nakedness, my chemise and the pants that serve as an underdress still in place.

We didn't have much opportunity to undress the first time we came together that intimately.

He hums thoughtfully. "Less clothes makes it easier. No clothes would be even better."

A laugh I didn't expect bubbles out of me. "It does, but normally we work up to that. I wouldn't mind seeing you without that shirt, though."

He obliges without hesitation, pulling off the woolen tunic and tossing it aside.

The makers of his body might have used twisted magic to bring it to life, but they gave him quite a nice form to work with. Taut muscles define the planes of his broad shoulders and his quite literally sculpted chest.

I expect him to reach for me again, but instead he glances around at the other men. "You all know Ivy and what she likes better than I do. I want to see… what you each would do for her, to make her feel as good as possible."

Stavros lets out a soft snort. "Looking to replace us all once you've added to your repertoire?"

Rheave appears to take his question at face value. "Oh, no," he says hastily. "I couldn't be you, just as you couldn't be each other. Or me. But I don't know—I never paid much attention— I think if I had more of an idea of the options, I could make her feel just as good my own way."

I touch his jaw, bringing his gaze back to me. "You're very good already, Rheave. I haven't been disappointed with anything you've offered me."

He aims one of his sunny smiles at me. "Then I can look forward to bringing you even more joy."

Casimir grins. "A sentiment I couldn't approve of more." He nips the crook of my shoulder. "Who would like to provide the first demonstration?"

I suspect the courtesan is holding back so as not to intimidate the others. The carnal arts are the main focus of his training, after all. Just that tiny scrape of his teeth has set my skin alight.

Not one to refuse a challenge, Stavros twists toward me. He tucks his prosthetic under the hem of my chemise, the hooked loop of metal grazing my waist beneath, and his mouth curves into the cocky smirk that used to infuriate me. "I know what special benefits I can bring to the bedroom."

As he uses his prosthetic to drag the thin fabric over my head, I shiver giddily. And then with a headier pleasure as he flicks the metal surface over one bared nipple and the other. A whimper creeps from my throat.

A faint flush has colored Rheave's pale face as he watches, but he doesn't stir from his vantage point.

Stavros catches the waist of my trousers next, and Alek helps him slide them from my legs. As the former general traces his prosthetic down the front of my drawers next, he wraps his other arm around me and claims his first kiss.

As always, the feel of his massive frame enveloping me is overwhelming even without the additional pleasure of his artificial appendage. With the melding of our mouths, warmth floods me.

Not breaking the kiss, Stavros lifts me right onto his lap. The incredible strength contained in that impressive body of his is a turn-on all on its own.

I've been carrying all my weight for a long time. It's a release to be able to trust someone else to support me.

I sling one arm around his neck to pull myself deeper into the kiss. Stavros tightens his embrace so he can toy with my nipple between his fingers while returning his prosthetic to the dampening place between my thighs.

Rheave was right when he said that he couldn't become any of my other men and none of them could become each other. There's nothing quite like the sense of being so fully encompassed and possessed that the military man offers.

As Stavros pinches my nipple to provoke a flash of bliss, he works his prosthetic right under the fabric of my drawers. When the metal loop strokes over my clit, my fingers dig into his tunic. I moan into his mouth.

He's gained confidence in using that part of himself since our first explorations. He works my sweet spot over until I'm shaking with need and then hooks the prosthetic right up inside me.

His breath scorches my cheek. "Yes, that's what you need."

I can only whimper in agreement.

Our kisses turn wilder as Stavros pumps the metal loop into my channel. He keeps the base rubbing my clit with the perfect amount of pressure. There's nothing I can do but hold on through the waves of delight he's summoning.

He tangles his fingers in my hair and devours my mouth even more forcefully. His thrusts speed up, propelling me over the edge.

My climax sweeps through me with another moan I muffle against his lips. Stavros holds me through my shudders and marks my cheek with a more tender kiss as I come back to earth. "It's always an honor to feel you let go—and let me take you there."

A breathless giggle spills out of me. "You can have that honor whenever you like."

"Very good," Rheave murmurs. When I look at him, his hands are clenched by his folded legs, but he stays where he is.

To my surprise, Alek makes an impatient sound before I even need to encourage him. "You can't keep her all to yourself, Stav."

With another sweet smile, he draws me away from the taller man. My heart aches with happiness seeing the assurance that's so new on his mottled face.

As I set my palm against the scholar's scarred cheek, he lowers his head to claim a kiss of his own. He leans into it, adjusting the angle of his lips, varying the pressure, flicking his tongue between my lips so I clutch at him even more eagerly.

He eases back with a glint of triumph in his bright brown eyes and looks at Rheave. "I didn't have much experience to call on at first either. But the most important thing isn't what you'd do with any woman, it's learning what will give *this* woman the most pleasure."

I beam at him. "And I've been delighted to become your latest research project."

Alek laughs and guides me down to the floor so my head is resting on Stavros's muscular leg like a firm pillow, the ridges on my back cushioned by the blankets.

As the scholar tracks a path of the places along my neck and shoulders where he's determined his lips and teeth have the most effect, the former general hums approvingly and combs his fingers through my hair. The graze of their tips over my scalp heightens every sensation Alek provokes.

The scholar laps the tip of one breast into his mouth and swirls his tongue around it. When I gasp and grip the thick waves of his hair, he exhales over the sensitized peak in a hot rush. Then he moves to the other side to repeat the effect.

He doesn't linger on my chest long, though, before working his way down the side of my belly. There, he tugs my drawers down.

"The sweetest spot to study," he murmurs, and lowers his head to my sex.

The swipe of his tongue over my clit has me bucking to meet his mouth. I catch a vaguely strangled sound from Rheave's direction, but my mind has hazed too much with desire for me to linger on that fact.

I rock with Alek's skillful attentions, another wave of ecstasy building in my core. He plunges his fingers inside me and curls them along my channel until he finds the headiest spot within.

As he suckles my clit and pumps his fingers against that blissful place, the sensations sweep through me even faster. Pleasure coils and unfurls and swells, sending a chorus of needy noises out of me.

"Fuck, Alek," I mumble, and clutch his hair harder as the wave finally crashes over me.

My head sags back into Stavros's lap. Alek dapples tender kisses along my inner thigh before sitting up with a satisfied expression that makes me want to kiss him all over again.

Before I can, Casimir is nudging me upright. He turns me around and pulls me against him so my back is flush with his toned torso.

He nibbles at my earlobe before murmuring in a silky tone, "And I know that our woman likes to be pampered *and* lose control."

His hands glide over my body with the gentlest of touches, coaxing every flutter of bliss he can from my nerves. I lean into him with a sigh, giving myself over to his sweet adoration.

The courtesan is right that he's discovered other approaches I find equally thrilling. When his hands reach my thighs, he yanks my hips back against him with a jerk. The force of the motion and the press of his rigid erection against my ass make my heart skip giddily.

His voice comes out in a purred growl that's even more electrifying. "You'll open yourself for me now."

My legs slide farther apart automatically. I'd forgotten just how freeing it feels to let Casimir take charge of me. To know that if I let him, he'll tend to me as only he knows how.

He aligns himself behind me and plunges into my already drenched sex. The rush of being suddenly filled after so much stimulation shocks a cry from my lips. I clench my teeth against it, not wanting to alert the entire apartment to what we're up to.

Casimir works his way even deeper with a few steady thrusts from behind. He lifts one hand to fondle my breast while looking over my shoulder toward Rheave.

The daimon-man is completely flushed now, his hands dug into the folds of the blanket he's sitting on. His eerie blue-green eyes flare with an even starker light than usual.

I can hear the courtesan's smile in his voice. "One thing I know better than anything else is that two or more of us can offer Ivy even more pleasure than just one, if we work together. Would you like to put any of tonight's observations to use right away, my friend?"

Rheave sucks in a shaky breath that turns into a rumble in his chest. His body surges forward, right toward me.

The daimon-man catches my face between his hands and kisses me so hard I could drown in him. I sway between my two lovers, wanting to give myself over to both.

Rheave drops lower, flicking his tongue over the tender flesh just below my belly button and then diving even farther.

Without any sign of concern about Casimir's proximity, he presses his mouth to the spot just above where the courtesan and I are joined.

Casimir thrusts into me again, and I push against Rheave's mouth. His tongue darts out across my clit, and I grasp his dark curls with a partly stifled moan.

"So good," I rasp. "It feels so fucking good."

Rheave's pleased hum reverberates through my sex. I clutch on to him with one hand and Casimir's arm with the other.

Why didn't Alek's erotic poetry book ever suggest *this* particular combination? Or maybe it did and we simply hadn't gotten to it yet.

Either way, I'm caught between the two men in the most delicious possible way. With every pump of Casimir's cock and caress of Rheave's mouth, I careen higher.

My final orgasm starts with a shudder that resonates right out of the center of me. I crack apart in a blaze of pleasure that knocks the breath from my lungs.

Casimir groans and nips my shoulder when he follows me over. As we sag together, Rheave sits up, licking his lips.

"I look forward to learning all I can," he says in an awed tone.

A breathless giggle escapes me. "I think I'm looking forward to it even more."

At least I have a few good things waiting after all the trials I haven't yet faced. Assuming I survive that long.

# Nine

*Ivy*

The previous time I entered the Capital Palace, I was racing at Stavros's heels, no thought in my head except preventing an impending disaster. I'm not sure the enormity of that act sank in until this moment.

Where I'm perched on the broad stone wall that surrounds the palace, all of the front courtyard sprawls before me. Dark splatters and scorch marks discolor the polished cobblestones and squares of garden.

I can't tell how many of the blotches are from the attack we intercepted weeks ago and how many are more recent. A sour, faintly rotten scent laces the cool winter breeze.

Definitely recent is the refuse scattered across the grounds. A soiled velvet vest lies crumpled here, a torn silk gown there. Broken chunks of marlwood and porcelain litter the terrain as if some looters had second thoughts after running out with one or another treasure and opted to destroy them instead.

I spot at least one brownish lump where a particularly ornery intruder relieved themselves on the palace's front steps. Through the swelling horror, I wrinkle my nose.

I can almost hear Julita's horrified voice. *Really, have they no limits at all?*

Do the looters not realize that even if they've decided *this* king was false, the point is to find a new ruler they'll want to lead them? And that ruler will prefer to move into a palace that's not shit-stained?

They're not even finished. As I watch, concealed from view by the blessed charm Tinom provided me with that dangles from a fine chain around my neck, a few figures hustle out of the palace. One is dressed like a noblewoman in an ornate embroidered gown, though her hair has fallen loose from its typical courtly style with only a few small curls still pinned up. The two men behind her are well but more plainly dressed—merchants, perhaps.

They're all carrying ill-gotten gains: the woman a bundle that could be clothing or wrapped jewelry, one man a box gilded with gold, the other a stack of fine plates.

My jaw clenches. People like them benefitted the most from the king's rule, and now they're picking apart his legacy like vultures descending on a carcass. And they see themselves as the height of society?

How could they so easily turn on the family they pledged their loyalty to?

The only good thing about the current situation is that someone has propped open one of the double doors. Tinom's charm, the same type he was wearing outside the Temple of the Crown the other night, keeps me from being seen as long as no one knows to look for me, but I can't pass through walls. If people start wondering why doors are swinging around apparently of their own accord, I'll be in trouble.

When the latest looters have hurried out the gate and the courtyard is momentarily still, I slide down the wall and slink across the grounds, carefully dodging the worst of the mess. The charm also only obscures smaller sounds. If I bang into anything and someone looks over, they might spot me through the illusionary magic.

I pass the purpling body of a guard who was clearly not a daimon, partly obscured by a garden shrub. A twinge of sympathy prickles through my chest.

I might have feared the Crown's Watch and their ilk, but that woman was only doing her job. She gave her life in an attempt to protect the king's home, maybe even after she had reason to believe he'd no longer be returning.

As I slip through the door and creep down the main hall, I have to avoid more figures coming in and out of the rooms where they're rummaging through what's left of the furniture and snatching the art still remaining off the walls. The noxious stink thickens. Whiffs like putrid meat reach my nose, along with the tang of urine and a rank note of body odor.

The source of the latter becomes clear in a matter of seconds. In several of the side rooms, the furnishings have remained mostly intact. Packs of men and women in questionable states of cleanliness sleep on the thick rugs or lean against the tables while they chatter in rough voices.

They wear a mix of clothing from cheap cotton to fancy silk, all of it smudged and stained. The fervor burning in many of their eyes reminds me of the Order of the Wild's march.

These must be the scourge sorcerers and their allies, the followers Lothar has installed in the capital to maintain control.

My magic jitters against my ribs, pleading with me to let it wash away the wretched scents. To hurl all these intruders out through the windows in a hail of shattering glass.

I clamp down on it and hurry onward.

When a woman already carrying a set of gold candlesticks under her arm approaches one of the rooms filled with new inhabitants, a man snaps at her. "This spot belongs to the Order of the Wild for now. Grab what you want wherever else."

She scurries off without argument. Whatever the locals have seen of the Order, they don't appear keen to pick fights.

I weave through the halls, following Petra's directions, leaping to the side when a couple of teens come racing out of one of the doorways just ahead of me. More blood stains the floors, but I don't come across any more corpses until I pass a room wafting the worst stench yet.

That door has been shut. I pause and nudge it just a crack open, then recoil in revulsion with a defensive flare of my magic.

Decaying bodies, mostly guards and nobles from what I glimpsed of their clothing, sprawl in heaps beyond the doorway. The Order mustn't have felt like bothering with trying to bury them yet in the hardened winter ground, so they simply dragged them out of the way.

Maybe they like the idea of the rotten scent winding through the palace, reminding everyone who ventures inside of the fate they could meet if they fall out of favor. As if the spirits of the murdered linger on to haunt this place through the stench.

Julita might have found that idea darkly amusing. As I dart up a staircase to the second floor, avoiding a soggy spot in the carpet, I find myself imagining the other arch remarks she'd have made, no doubt alongside an indignant huff.

*The people would rather see the palace turned into a refuse heap than be ruled by the Melchioreks? Can they not think past the end of their noses?*

Another lump rises in my throat. It's easier not to think about the friend I lost, not to miss her constant presence in my mind—occasionally irritating, but so often rousing and encouraging—when I'm surrounded by other companions. When I'm on my own, the emptiness in my head yawns louder.

Julita never hesitated to stand up to the evils she saw brewing in Florian, even though she had a more direct reason to fear scourge sorcery than the rest of us. She sacrificed what remained of her life to save me from her brother.

She'd have been so horrified to see the wreckage the scourge sorcerers have already left in their wake despite our efforts.

Shoving the grief aside with a few hasty blinks, I turn a corner and pad down a narrower hall. Another left, then a right, and all the way at the end…

I stop in my tracks, my gut dropping. A bulky, square-jawed man in a guard uniform is standing outside the door Petra directed me to—the one that leads into the royal family's private quarters.

He must be with the scourge sorcerers, or they wouldn't have left him alive. I guess it makes sense that Lothar wouldn't want anyone other than his sycophants rummaging through the most personal remains of the king he murdered.

Is the former magic advisor himself staying in those rooms? I shudder at the thought.

It doesn't really matter if anyone is beyond that door if I can't get past it myself, though.

I edge closer, setting my feet silently as I study the guard. Without Rheave's daimon senses, I can't tell for sure, but I suspect this fellow is one of his brethren in animated clay. There's a sort of blankness to his expression that looks like more than human boredom.

I could simply stab him and hope he collapses back into fired clay. But then whoever assigned him to this spot would realize someone must have broken in.

What I really need is to draw him away from his post for long enough for me to slip inside.

I backtrack to the previous hall and glance around. No one else seems to be stationed nearby. He'll probably come running at any nearby disturbance.

I step into one of the rooms where the door stands ajar. Most of the smaller objects have been looted, but a display cabinet stands by the wall, the glass panes of its windows cracked.

They're about to face a lot worse than that.

Gritting my teeth, I grasp the side of the cabinet and heave. With a shove against the wall for extra leverage, I send it crashing to the ground.

And oh boy, does it crash. The frame thumps against the floor hard enough to echo, the glass shatters, and the wood splits open down the back.

I dash back into the hall and duck through a different doorway just before the guard bustles around the corner on stomping feet.

The moment he's stormed into the other room, I bolt all the way to the door he was guarding, dipping my hand into my pocket. I pull out the ring Petra gave me with the Melchiorek crest and press it to the spot beneath the doorknob.

There's no click of the lock, but the door opens at my nudge. Lothar's people must have broken whatever magical protection it had on it.

As soon as I step inside, it's clear someone's been through these rooms. Rather aggressively, too.

Side tables lie overturned. Upholstery has been cut open. All of the paintings have been yanked from the walls, some propped against them, some tossed aside.

I skirt a broken plate and hurry deeper into the apartments, eager to get out of this place as quickly as possible. Stale air trickles into my lungs, containing a lingering trace of a floral perfume that perhaps Queen Ishild liked to wear.

What if Lothar managed to ferret out King Konram's most secret hiding place? I might have risked venturing in here for nothing.

He might already know that Petra is the greatest threat to his Order's authority.

Petra warned me not to take anything from her siblings' rooms, as much as they might appreciate a few tokens from the lives that've been wrenched from them. We don't know to what extent the conspirators have catalogued the contents of these quarters to notice if something's gone missing—or how easily they might be able to track those items.

Still, my gaze veers toward a sitting room I can tell was once Prince Jacos's from the model ships perched in one of the cabinets. I wish I could bring the royal teens a little something they might find comfort in. They didn't have a chance to carry anything with them from the palace in Regica but the clothes on their backs, which are stained and travel-worn now.

But really, what would they care about getting back other than their parents, which I can't accomplish even with my fathomless magic?

So I push onward, through a larger sitting room with forest-green curtains and gold leaves rippling across the wallpaper and into a vast bedchamber that could contain the entire apartment Tinom arranged for us.

A four-poster bed stands in the middle of the space, more forest-green fabric draped around it. A deep gouge has been cut in the mattress, feathers spilling out of it onto the floor.

Lothar knew there might be something hidden in here.

The wardrobe doors and dresser drawers hang open, various kingly outfits of velvet, silk, and wool scattered around them. The mirror on the wardrobe is cracked, as is the porcelain wash basin nearby.

None of that matters as long as the one item I came for has gone undisturbed.

I crouch down and squirm under the bed. Dust tickles my nose, and I rub my face to prevent a sneeze.

Then I take out Petra's ring and slide its face across the floor.

The boards beneath my flattened body feel perfectly smooth. There's no reason for anyone to suspect a secret cache lies beneath them. But toward the headboard on the lefthand side, right where Petra told me to look, a gleam lights up on a circular spot that matches the ring's crest.

I press the ring to that etching, and a small wooden hatch lifts to reveal a square of thicker darkness.

Normally I'd hesitate to shove my hand into a magically hidden space with contents unknown. Today, I'm trusting that Petra wouldn't send me into a trap.

The opening is only about twice as wide as my arm. I reach in and fumble through the empty recess beneath.

Well, it's not entirely empty. Though the first object my fingers encounter isn't a letter but dry leather. What feels like a book.

Interesting. I might as well bring that back too, because I doubt King Konram would have hidden it here unless it was important.

I wriggle the book out and tuck it into the largest pocket on my skirts. Then I grope around in the secret cache again.

There. My hand closes around a piece of folded parchment.

I pull it out and squint at it for just long enough to confirm it's got the blood-sworn sigil sealing it. Tucking that away too, I push the hatch shut.

In an instant, the floor looks as seamless as ever. King Konram outsmarted Lothar in at least one way.

The guard has no doubt returned to the door that leads into this part of the palace, but that's all right. I've already identified my escape route.

I lope back into the sitting room and ease aside the heavy curtains. The pane is shut to keep out the winter chill, but it's designed to open in the summer.

I peer down onto the grounds below, at the back of the palace with a pleasant view of the larger gardens and the hunting forest beyond. When I'm sure no one's wandering around down there at the moment, I pull the window open, clamber out onto the ledge, and slide it shut in my wake.

It's a longer drop than I'd prefer to jump given the choice, but I've done worse. Ignoring the niggling of my magic offering its help, I brace myself, skid partway down the stone side of the palace, and launch myself into a roll that diffuses the worst of the impact.

Then I'm off and running to deliver the key to our true queen's succession into her hands.

# Ten

*Ivy*

The smell of frying dumplings drifts up to my rooftop perch from a stall at the edge of the city square. My mouth starts to water with a pinch of my stomach, but I hold my position.

My job here is to observe the ordinary citizens milling around below me, not to join them.

At least I'm not alone in my current mission. Rheave has hunkered down on the roof tiles next to me. He's wearing one of Tinom's concealing charms too, but when we're touching, I can see and hear him without the illusion interfering.

Right now, he has his fingers looped casually around my wrist as he peers over the busy square. "The city has so many people. How will we be able to talk to them all?"

"We don't need to speak to all of them. As long as we catch the attention of a bunch, they'll chatter about it to everyone they know, and word will spread that way."

The daimon-man's eyebrows leap up. "It's like a kind of magic. Humans are so eager to share things with each other."

Despite the tension coiled in my belly, my lips twitch with a smile. "I guess the sharing helps us understand the world—by finding out what everyone around us makes of it too."

For a long time, I didn't have anyone *I* could really talk to that way. All I could do was listen in from the shadows.

It is easier to feel like I have a place here when I've got people who want me beside them.

Rheave adjusts his quiver against his back. He's brought his bow and plenty of arrows so he can shoot down any captured daimon we spot in the crowd we expect to form.

That'll both ensure they don't interfere and give proof to the story Petra's going to tell.

I glance at the clock tower visible over the tops of the nearby buildings. "Just another few minutes to go."

Rheave shifts on his feet. His hand slips from my wrist briefly and then snatches it again when he ripples out of view as I must have to him. His gaze twitches to me and away.

It still feels like something's a little strange about how he's acted with me since I escaped Lothar. The uneasiness I'm tamping down creeps up through my chest.

"Is everything all right?" I ask him. "Nothing's come up in the past several days that's bothering you?"

The daimon-man lets out a dismissive huff. "Of course not. You're back with us, and that's what matters the most. We'll deal with the rest of the scourge sorcerers like we brought down their march."

His fingers tighten against my skin, but he still keeps his gaze averted. Maybe it's only general daimon oddness… or maybe there's something he doesn't want to tell me.

I was under the control of the same scourge sorcerer—or at least one with the same gift—as the one who's manipulated him. Does he associate me with that awful magic now?

"You know," I try again, "even people who care a lot about each other sometimes have problems come up that they need to talk through. That's part of having a close relationship with someone—at least for humans. So if you ever are concerned about anything to do with me or my other partners or anyone else we're spending time with, I'd want you to say so."

Rheave scoots a little nearer so he can give the side of my head a brief nuzzle. "I know that, Little Vine. So much talking. But the only thing I'm wondering about right now is what the people down there will be saying when Petra talks."

His voice has lightened enough that I'm not sure if I was just imagining my impression of his discomfort. It could be the lingering madness provoking a more subtle paranoia.

So I smile at him and set my hand over his to give it an affectionate squeeze.

Before I can say anything else, a light flashes overtop a stack of crates at the other end of the square.

The brief flare is an illusion conjured by Tinom, designed to draw people's attention to the main show. It fades into a projected image of Petra as I know she's standing in a building elsewhere in the middle wards.

We picked out the three squares in this section of the city where we thought there'd be the most activity—the most people around to hear our true queen's message. The nobles of the inner wards, Petra and Tinom can reach out to directly. It's the more ordinary people who make up the majority of Florian's citizens who she needs to get on her side against the scourge sorcerers.

Rheave and I are here to take note of reactions in this spot. Alek and Casimir are watching the second square. The third is within viewing distance of the place where Petra is actually standing, where Stavros has been coaching her on the best ways to stir people's loyalties and remind them that our country is worth fighting for.

Petra didn't have her royal crown, but she found herself a violet dress of sweeping silk worthy of a queen. For once, she's swept up her dark hair into the formal, swirling style favored by the court. And her stance is nothing short of regal.

Her clear voice rings through the square, amplified as part of the illusion like Lothar projected his the other night. "People of Florian! I have important news to share with you. You've been lied to about the death of our king."

As planned, those words get everyone's attention quickly enough. Most heads in the square swivel toward the illusion of Petra. Startled murmurs pass between the onlookers.

Petra hurtles onward, unable to hear the response she's getting. She holds up the blood-sworn letter with the sigil showing. "I was there when King Konram was murdered, because he is my father. You may not recognize me, but you should see the resemblance to my mother, Queen Ishild. When I was twelve years old, at my dedication ceremony, I stopped being Prince Dunstam and became Princess Petra. My parents decided to keep my new identity secret from you for my own security, as this blood-sworn document confirms. But it is your security I'm most worried about now."

The warble of voices has risen while she speaks, some people below us sputtering in disbelief, others letting out shocked laughs. I notice more figures are arriving from the streets that lead into the square, others emerging from the shops and eateries along its edges.

"Prince Dunstam *died!*" someone hollers. "This bint could be anyone!"

"She does have Queen Ishild's look to her," a woman murmurs to her companion just beneath my rooftop perch.

Petra lifts her chin, the anger in her expression clear even across this distance. "My father was *murdered*. One of his magic advisors, Lothar Riosemek, stabbed him with a knife and let him bleed out on the floor of his palace in Regica. He would have killed me and my younger sister and brother as well if we hadn't managed to escape. Now this same man is trying to tell you this death was the will of the gods. It was not. It was Lothar's will, so he can impose his ideas on this city and the rest of the country."

"All lies!" a man near the illusion calls out. "She's not even real." He scoops a discarded piece of food off the ground and hurls it through the image.

Another voice rises up from off to his left. "That's right! A real ruler would show herself, let us see this proof. What's she so afraid of, huh? That we'll see right through her? We already can!"

I tense in my crouched position. The hostility in those voices makes my riven power writhe in my chest.

Rheave notches his bow next to me. "Neither of the ones talking are daimon, but I can see a couple moving through the crowd. Should I shoot them now?"

I shake my head. "Not until they start pushing people around or Petra mentions the scourge sorcery."

Whatever's happening in the square nearest her, she must be aware of the sorts of protests people are raising. She holds up her hands in appeal. "I wish I could be with all of you in the flesh, but I wanted to speak to as many of you as possible at once. And I know that as soon as Lothar learns where I am, he'll continue his quest to murder me and all of my family."

"Easy excuses," someone in the crowd sneers, and flings what looks like a battered shoe at her projected form.

I can't tell if the rest of the restless voices below us agree with the skeptical comments or are questioning what Lothar's told them.

Petra keeps going, though the tensing of her lips suggests she's not pleased with whatever she's witnessing from her own vantage point. "Think about what's happened in this city since Lothar and his Order of the Wild marched in. How many murders have been carried out before your eyes? How have they desecrated our most sacred buildings? I can't believe that this is the kind of world you'd want to live in—one full of violence and cruelty.

"And it isn't just simple cruelty. Lothar and his followers are practicing scourge sorcery—the same magic that nearly ended our civilization and drove *away* the All-Giver all those centuries ago. That's how they wield so much power. They're helped by those they convinced as children to sacrifice every part of their body they could spare while remaining alive, leaving them mere shells of human beings. And by daimon, whose spirits they've trapped in bodies made of clay, upsetting the proper balance of life itself."

Rheave doesn't wait for me to give him the go-ahead. The moment the last statement has left Petra's lips, he releases my arm.

Since I still know he's there, I glimpse a wavery image of him pulling back his bowstring. One arrow and then another launch into the air from our rooftop, sped onward by crackles of his daimon magic.

They hit their marks in quick succession. Spurts of black smoke shoot up as the bodies collapse.

I lose sight of the toppling forms amid the now milling crowd, but the yelps of shock tell me they've transformed back into clay.

I duck low behind the jut of a dormer window so my voice won't allow any eyes to seek me out and raise my voice to carry as far as it can. "She's telling the truth! There are fake people walking around with us."

The murmurs swell across the square. Some sound panicked, others angry. They're starting to drown out Petra's voice despite the amplification.

"It's a trick!" someone yells—probably one of the Order members. "This false princess is using her lies to try to undo the progress we've made! She doesn't care about you. She can't even be bothered to come to actually listen to you. Just like all the Melchioreks!"

Not far from my rooftop, several pedestrians jostle against each other. I can't tell what they're squabbling about, but they knock over a cart full of apples.

As the fruit roll past people's feet, several onlookers snatch one up and whip it toward the illusion of Petra.

"Come and really talk to us!" a woman cries out.

A male voice joins her. "Let's see that proof!"

More and more shouts fill the air.

"Who are you really?"

"Why didn't the Great God come back for King Konram?"

"Everything's gone wrong!"

So many of the bodies are jostling together now. The illusion of Petra wavers. "Please, listen," I think she says, and then I lose track of her words completely amid the chaos.

I can't even tell how many of the unsettled civilians want to believe her and how many are upset with her—but there are definitely too many of the latter. The crowd surges toward the crates below her illusion, more objects hurtling through the air toward her image.

I don't know how to stop them or make them see reason. My magic is flailing around in my chest now, desperate to yank all the people below me into order, but I can only imagine how disastrous that effort would turn out.

As I wrap my unpredictable power tight within me, my gaze sweeps over the churning figures. It catches on a boy of maybe seven or eight stumbling where one of the more aggressive onlookers has shouldered past him.

The boy trips and falls onto his knees. I have a flash of an image of his small body swallowed up and trampled by his fellow civilians, and my heart lurches alongside my magic.

I detach my necklace with the concealment charm and shove it in my pocket. "I need to help someone," I gasp out in Rheave's direction, and leap down onto the jutting store sign below before he can answer.

I don't need my riven power for this. With another hop, my feet hit the ground. I throw myself through the weaving bodies, searching for the pale beige of the boy's tunic.

There. He's just yanking his hand away from being stomped on.

I spring across the last short distance and grasp his elbow to haul him upright—and backward into shelter between two abandoned stalls.

The boy spares me a puzzled glance and then darts forward again with a hoarse holler. "The king is gone! We need someone real!"

Gods help me, has Lothar already managed to muddle even the city's children?

I snatch at the boy's arm again to hold him back. "Why are you talking like that? She's real even if you haven't met her properly yet."

He glares back at me with eyes so hostile I restrain a flinch. "If she's got anything to do with the old king, I don't want her."

"Why not?"

The boy snorts as if the answer should be obvious. "What did King Konram do for any of us who didn't matter enough to wear fancy clothes and go to his parties? Where was he when my dad broke his leg last year and some shoddy medic left him with a limp? If the royals can't help us, we've got to fight for ourselves!"

He jerks his arm free and dashes away into the crowd, leaving me staring after him with a sinking sensation in my gut.

# ELEVEN

*Ivy*

I sprawl across the bough of the oak, careful not to disturb the leaves that would rustle no matter how concealed my body is. My head dips to take in the voices below more clearly.

The rough bark grazes my cheek and digs into my hands. It's a familiar sensation, and yet my nerves remain on edge.

I don't know what's wrong with me. This place used to be where I felt most at home in the world, and now I can't shake the sense that I'm an intruder.

Beneath me in the tiny garden that holds a few sparse vegetables and a beehive, Ewalin and Frida have been puttering around and murmuring to each other for the past several minutes. Maybe it's their own attitude that's kept me in the alert. The daughter and mother I've so often visited in the outer wards are clearly nervous about being overheard in a way I never encountered before.

The atmosphere has shifted similarly all through Slaughterwell. This is only the last of a couple dozen shabby houses I've stopped at in my survey of the neighborhood. The usual strident shouts and bellows of laughter have been replaced by hushed voices and hesitant giggles.

The change in atmosphere isn't the only thing affecting my own mood, though. The days when I used to watch Ewalin and Frida and long to slip into their family alongside them have faded into distant memory.

I do have a family now, as odd as these two women might find it. And I don't know that I'd fit all that well with these two anymore regardless.

"I wish I could have been there to see it myself," Ewalin is saying as she stops to tug up a weed. "Prince Dunstam—or whatever her new name is—come back from the dead?"

Her mother exhales roughly. "I'd think something got mixed with the ale in the local pub if there weren't so many people talking about it. Would a king hold a false funeral out of some idea of keeping his child safe?"

She shakes her head and rests an affectionate hand on Ewalin's hair. "I can't imagine putting myself apart from my daughter for years. But who can say what goes on in the heads of royals?"

Ewalin gives a soft huff as she straightens up. "Better if he'd spent more time worrying about the safety of the rest of us. How many children of Slaughterwell died while he and his Crown's Watch rarely stepped past the middle wards?"

Frida sketches her hand down her front in the gesture of the divinities. Her voice drops even lower. "There's been far too much death all around just now, if you ask me."

Her daughter grimaces. "Yes. But at least this Order is spreading it around a little more fairly instead of it all landing on us and our neighbors. We'll just keep our heads down and see what comes of it."

As they drift back toward the house, a lump fills my throat. I've caught similar sentiments all across Slaughterwell, but hearing it from these two hits a little harder.

Before this afternoon's ruckus in the square, I thought most of the ordinary folk of Silana would be happy to have real order restored. But I've obviously spent too much time among royals and nobles in the past few months, absorbing their ideals and letting them kindle my good will.

I used to feel the exact same way Ewalin does about King Konram. I roamed through these streets seeing the desperation and suffering and silently ranted about how he neglected his most needy people.

His police force has always been faster to act the richer the victims are. His laws have always favored the elites of the inner wards above even Florian's middle class.

Why should any of the people he placed lower on his priorities jump at the chance to reestablish the Melchiorek reign?

Why should *I*?

The question niggles at me as I shimmy down the tree and slink along the back alley through the chilly dusk.

I don't know Petra all that well. I don't know what kind of a ruler she'd be.

I'm sure she's a better option than handing the country over to scourge sorcery, but is that enough to throw my support so whole-heartedly behind her? Could there be other options I haven't considered in my panic to push back Lothar and his cronies?

I've been thrown from place to place so often since Julita landed in my head, had so many voices in my ear, that I'm not sure of what I think just for myself.

A couple of lanes farther along, I pass by Zuzanna's house. The guttering candle beyond her grubby window makes the shadows waver in the sigils of Elox carved into the building's outer walls.

The guttural coughing that reverberates from within tells me that her son is sick yet again, her appeals to the godlen of healing gone unheard. Or perhaps he simply can't intervene, as Kosmel hesitated to insert himself more than a little into my life.

Someday, I'd like to get the chance to ask the gods a thing or three about exactly how they're meant to fit into our existence.

I veer closer to the window, and Zuzanna's ragged voice carries to my ears. "I'm going to keep trying, sweetie. Maybe if the All-Giver returns, I can ask for the Great God's blessing to shine on you."

An ache closes around my heart. I pull myself away.

I hadn't really thought about it before, but in some ways Lothar and his ilk are just a more ambitious version of the con artists I used to steal from on these streets. Conjuring hope for incredible things in people who are so hungry for every scrap they can get.

Who from the poorest soul to the richest nobleman couldn't imagine how their lives might be better if our highest creator returned? Who has never found any fault in our current rulers, to think we couldn't have an even better one?

King Konram himself set the precedent that we deal with threats by slaughtering them. How many riven sorcerers did he parade in front of the city on their way to the gallows?

A gloom hangs over me as I weave my way back to the tenement building. Going up the stairs, I slip off my concealment charm and tuck it in my pocket so I'll be visible to the people I want to see me.

No one's in the hall that divides the two apartments on the highest floor. I head into the one where my men and I have been staying.

Alek is sitting in one of the plain armchairs in the front sitting room. I recognize the book propped open between his hands as the aged volume I retrieved from King Konram's secret hiding spot.

He's smiling before he glances up and takes in my expression. A shadow crosses his face. "Is everything all right?"

"Is it any worse than it was before, you mean?" I say with forced wryness. "No, not particularly."

I amble over to claim a quick kiss and rest my hand on his shoulder. "Have you figured out what was so special about that book?"

It's easier to talk about Alek's discoveries than my own, especially with the way his face lights up in scholarly enthusiasm at the topic.

He pages back through the book. "I think the rumors going around the city that the gods were dissatisfied with his family must have bothered King Konram. Princess Klaudia said she remembers hearing him ask the main palace archivist for any books in the royal collection that dated back to before the Great Retribution. This is one of them."

I peer at the book alongside him. "And it says something about what the gods expect from our kings and queens?"

"Not exactly. But there are several details I've never seen before about those kingship trials we've discussed before. I wonder if he was only preparing for what the scourge sorcerers might try to enact or thinking of finding a way to hold his own version, to prove his legitimacy."

I swallow thickly. King Konram won't get the chance for that now. "Why would he have kept it hidden?"

Alek gives a slight shrug. "Hard to say without being able to ask him. It is a very rare and valuable book—I've never seen anything like it. And he might have been worried about sparking ideas he didn't want in other people's heads."

Stavros appears in the doorway that leads to the inner rooms. He strides over and wraps his arm around me in an embrace that settles just a little of the turmoil churning inside me.

"Petra wanted to speak with you as soon as you returned from your scouting," he says. "I'd like to hear what you observed as well. We clearly need to adjust our strategy."

I'm not sure I'm ready for this conversation—but it has to happen, and soon. Squaring my shoulders, I nod. "All right. Where is she?"

Stavros leads me to the opposite apartment. Tinom nods to us from where he's sitting at the table in the front room with a couple of the nobles who've joined our cause, but I feel his wary gaze follow me as we walk by on our way to the bedrooms.

He tried to insist that the royal children should each have a room to themselves in honor of their status, but Princess Klaudia and Prince Jacos preferred to share so they wouldn't have to spend any time alone. Petra has taken the room across from theirs, though I suspect she spends a lot of time with her siblings all the same.

Right now, we enter after knocking and find the younger princess and prince standing with her at her vanity. She's unfurled a map of the city and its surrounding area there.

At our entrance, all three look up—and Prince Jacos doesn't quite stifle his wince when he catches sight of me. Princess Klaudia's lips purse tighter.

My stomach clenches. They've never spoken against me in my presence, but it's obvious they're still not comfortable with me.

And I can't blame them. It's just a stark reminder that if it wasn't for Petra, it's unlikely I'd be welcome in this resistance movement at all.

Petra gives both of her siblings an affectionate squeeze of their arms and nudges them. "Why don't you go back to your room and give all of this some more thought? We'll discuss it again after I've heard Ivy's report."

Klaudia's stance stiffens for a moment as if she means to protest, but any interest she has in being part of the conversation must be won over by her desire to get farther away from me. She and Jacos hurry out of the room.

Petra sits down at the vanity. Her dark eyes take me in, steady but pensive. "What news do you have?"

The regal tones I heard her bring out during her proclamation in the square have lingered. She's becoming more a queen with every passing hour—and suddenly I'm not certain that's a good thing.

I drag in a breath. My body tenses instinctively, but if I can't be honest with her, there's no point in supporting her at all.

"You may have an uphill battle to winning over most of Florian. I'm not sure you realize—you must have been somewhat isolated from the common folk even as a supposedly more distant royal..."

When I trail off, groping for the right way to phrase what I need to say, Petra's voice softens. "Whatever it is, you can tell me, Ivy. I need to know."

I can't help folding my arms over my chest protectively. "In a lot of ways, your father... neglected the people whose support he didn't need all that much. I saw it myself firsthand many times over. It was particularly bad in the outer wards—the Crown's Watch would look the other way when corrupt merchants exploited the poor families there, because what mattered was who paid the most taxes. Most people who weren't rich or noble born didn't feel they could count on the Melchioreks in times of need."

Some of the color fades beneath Petra's tan skin, but she inclines her head. "I'm sorry to hear that. I know some of those things he simply washed his hands of, leaving decisions to the discretion of people like the leader of the Watch. But he should have paid more attention, and he should have been there when all his people needed him."

Stavros clears his throat. "It's a difficult balance, of course. Royals need to maintain some distance, or they'll be pulled apart by all the demands. He did a lot of good, as many mistakes as he also made." He shoots me an apologetic glance.

I wave my hand dismissively. "I'm not saying he didn't. There have obviously been worse rulers. But, Petra, you need to convince everyone—or a lot of people, at least—that having you in charge would be better for *them* than waiting to see how the scourge sorcerers will rule."

She grimaces. "They're having children carved up to fuel their magic—they slaughtered all those clerics and devouts—"

"They've been keeping the first part well-hidden," I cut in. "And every ruler has killed their enemies. They're convincing people that they're only destroying those who were threats to our country."

Petra's jaw tightens. "I was born for this. I know I can do what's best for Silana—for everyone in it. I can learn from Father's mistakes. If they'll give me a chance..."

She pauses and appears to compose herself again. "I suppose that means we need to come at the problem from two angles. One is exposing the truth about the scourge sorcerers so they'll lose support, and the other is proving that I'm a better option so I'll gain it. I think you may be better equipped to handle the former. For the latter, I'll have to spend some time beyond the inner wards myself, seeing what's become of our kingdom with open eyes."

Stavros stiffens. "You can't wander around the streets on your own. Lothar will have his people—"

Petra holds up her hand to stop him. "I can use one of Tinom's charms so no one will spot me. I've spent my whole life learning how to keep myself safe, Stavros. It's about time I learned what the rest of my citizens need for their own well-being."

She sounds confident enough that the worst of my doubts melt away. I don't know how well she'll hold up as she faces everything involved in ruling a country, but at least right now, she understands the problem.

She does care, no matter what people believe of her family.

Petra turns to me. "Whatever we find out, however we decide to approach this, we'll need to bring more people onto our side to spread the word before we can hope to convince all of the city, let alone the country. You've lived in Florian your whole life, Ivy, and mingled with every level of society. Do you have any friends you could call on who'd be willing to take that first step of trust?"

Friends? I restrain a laugh, and a flicker of inspiration passes through my mind.

I hesitate before venturing a careful answer. "Not friends, but I am acquainted with some people of influence who'd be very handy allies… if I can persuade them that it's in their best interests to stand up to Lothar and his Order."

If they don't slit my throat for simply daring to ask.

# Twelve

*Ivy*

Just before we turn the corner to bring us in view of the Frolic Theater, I stop Casimir with a hand on his arm. When the courtesan turns to face me with a gently questioning expression, my heart beats a little faster.

Out of all the men who've become entwined in my life, Casimir has always been the one I least need to fear judgment from. But that sweetness makes me hesitate to expose him to the grittier parts of the world I came from.

"The people in Crow's Close are… pretty rough around the edges," I say. "They're used to having to lie and fight to survive."

Casimir studies my face. As usual, he picks up on the things I haven't quite said. "It won't be anything like my pampered noble life. I know."

I grapple with the words to get across what I most want to convey. "They aren't all bad people. I mean, some of them are, but for a lot—it's just another way to get by, for people who didn't have many options. Or a sketchy business that isn't really any more immoral than plenty of things merchants supposedly on the right side of the law get away with. You just have to be prepared that they might be hostile about me bringing you in there."

"Because I'm a stranger. It makes sense." Casimir brushes his fingers from my temple over my hair. "It's all right, Kindness. I know this place is part of who you were—who you are. *You* had to skirt the edges of the law. But you did it for good reasons. Nothing I see in that place is going to change how I feel about you."

My throat tightens. Yes, I guess that is what I was most worried about underneath, even if I didn't want to admit it to myself, let alone him.

I take on a more chipper tone. "It does have a few bright spots. The main pub makes the best amber spritz I've ever tasted. Not that we'll have time to stop for a drink on this visit."

Casimir chuckles lightly. "Perhaps another day."

I'm not sure he realizes exactly what he's getting into even after everything I've said, but I don't want to send him into a panic with horror stories either. He'll take a read of the place quickly enough once we get there.

And if he regrets agreeing to accompany me, well, we'll deal with that when it comes.

I lead the way along the Tangleside street to the theater. One of the comedic shows is going on even in the midst of the Order of the Wild's takeover.

I might be imagining it, but the laughter that careens from the inner doorway has a slightly frantic edge to it.

People need their escapes in times of crisis more than ever.

But we're not here to take in the entertainment. I veer sharply and take Casimir down the basement stairs that lead to the hidden passage that connects the theater to Florian's smallest and most secret neighborhood.

The courtesan doesn't remark on the dankness of the basement room or the darkness of the magical passage. He remains silent as we ascend the identical stairs on the opposite end and emerge onto the enclosed street that holds the most established illicit businesses in the city—possibly the entire country.

He's taking it all in, absorbing it and forming his own understanding. That's why I decided I needed him with me for this negotiation, if he was willing to come.

He understands people better than anyone I've ever known. And his gift can tell us what we can give our potential allies that they'd want most.

I had to bully one of the bosses of Crow's Close's main gang into accepting my last proposition. I'm hoping to handle this discussion in a more amicable manner. But charm isn't really one of my strengths.

As we cross the road to the largest building in the Close—gambling hall, temple to Kosmel, and headquarters for the Black Talons gang—I sweep my gaze over the street. Casimir and I have both dressed fairly plainly, with the hoods of our cloaks shadowing our faces. The way I'd normally dress when visiting this den of criminals.

We shouldn't stick out at a glance. But I have no doubt that the people I intend to speak with will pick the courtesan out as an interloper swiftly enough.

We step into the first-floor gambling hall to the spicy smell of fried goldrud root and a sharper whiff of hazebloom smoke. It's late afternoon, too early for the main nighttime crowd, but far enough along in the day that a decent number of avid gamblers have stirred from their beds. About half of the tables scattered across the sprawling room are full, urgent voices and hopeful shouts echoing off the ceiling.

I weave through those tables around the base of the massive silver statue of Kosmel that stands in the center of the building. It only takes a minute to spot the man I'm looking for.

Garom Rochimek is sitting back against one of the empty tables in his usual scruffy disguise. The memory flits through my head of Julita's skeptical remarks when I approached him weeks ago, with a pang that's amusement and grief mixed together.

What would my ghostly noblewoman friend have had to say about the deal we're attempting to make today?

When I'm close enough for Garom to make out my features beneath my hood, his gaze snags on my face. His eyebrows arch slightly beneath the rumpled blond hair of his wig.

Then his gaze slides to Casimir, and his pale eyes narrow.

He pushes himself out of his chair before I've quite reached him, keeping his voice low. "Come for another chat, Ivy, after all the trouble I went to getting you out of this city? You've used up your favors."

I give him a small smile. "I had a good reason to return. And in this particular case, I may be able to do *you* a favor."

"Who's this pretty boy? Don't tell me you've got a boytoy scampering at your heels now."

If the jab bothers Casimir, he doesn't show it. I roll my eyes, having no intention of revealing that I've actually got *four* paramours at the moment. "He's a good friend, and he can confirm everything

I'd like to discuss with you. But the details aren't anything I think you'd want spoken about in broader company."

Garom grunts, but he turns and shuffles toward the doorway that leads to the building's back staircase.

As we head up the stairs, I clear my throat. "The proposition I have isn't just for you but for all three of the Black Talons' leaders. Are Sonia and Hellar around, or should I arrange to come back another time?"

Garom aims another piercing look at me. "What exactly is this about, girl?"

I lift my chin, letting my smile stretch a little farther despite the tension knotting my stomach. "How would you like to have the ear of the future queen?"

Hardened gang boss though he may be, I've managed to shock him. His expression twitches before he checks himself. "Very funny."

"I'm not joking. I spoke with the heir to the Melchiorek line just a couple of hours ago. She doesn't support all of her father's policies, and she's willing to work with you to make your work go more smoothly."

Garom's gift is a knack for separating truth from lies. He'll be able to tell that I'm being honest.

I've managed to strike him speechless for a few seconds. His throat works with a swallow, and then he swings his arm for us to continue following him up the stairs. "Come on, then. I should be able to round up my colleagues if you aren't in a terrible hurry."

Relief trickles through my chest. I really didn't want to have to stew in anticipation for another day—or to give the Black Talons' bosses extra time to scheme amongst themselves.

Garom brings us not to his personal office but to a larger space set up like a sitting room. Several padded armchairs stand in a loose ring that fills most of the space, with side tables between them and a lower table in the middle that looks as if the legs could be heightened if one wanted to play cards at it.

A faint sour scent drifts from the extensive liquor cabinet against one wall. Those walls are thick enough to shut out all the noise from the gambling hall that filters up through the gap around the godlen statue outside.

"Sit," Garom tells us, and pokes his head back into the hall. After a quick muttered conversation with a lackey, he returns and drops into one of the chairs opposite the two Casimir and I have chosen.

He watches Casimir rather than me as he slides off his wig. Wanting to evaluate the unknown party's reaction, I assume.

Because underneath that wig, the gang boss's scalp is shaved and scarred with a chaotic mess of lines where he sacrificed a significant portion of skin—along with who knows what else that I can't see —for his gift. It's a tradition among the Black Talons families, although only known in the sort of circles they usually run in.

To someone unfamiliar with the city's underworld, it'll simply look disturbing.

Casimir's mild expression doesn't flicker at all, but then, I told him in advance what to expect. He tips his head toward the other man. "I appreciate you taking the time to hear us out."

Garom's eyebrows leap up again. "You're one for pretty speech, huh? And what's that in your mouth there?"

I tense, but Casimir obligingly parts his lips again to give a quick view of the jeweled teeth that replaced the eight molars he sacrificed.

Garom looks at me, his voice taking on an edge of a sneer. "You brought some gaudy teeth for your royal offering? What, is he the *princess's* boytoy?"

I harden my gaze. "He's familiar with the inner workings of court and a trusted friend to the future queen as well as me. You can count on him to know more about what's possible than I do. Think of him as her representative in this meeting."

The gang boss simply guffaws at my words, but he doesn't make any more heckling remarks. Casimir's demeanor remains as unruffled as ever.

The door squeaks open, and a statuesque woman strides in. She sets her hands on her hips and studies the three of us with a faintly irritated expression.

I've only seen Sonia Alinnya at a distance before, but everyone in Crow's Close knows she's the matriarch of another of the three Black Talons families. Her scalp is as scarred as Garom's, though she's let the dark hair that can still grow tumble down to her shoulders in its uneven waves, partly hiding the pattern of her sacrifice.

It's hard to tell how many years she has under her belt with the simple but stark cosmetics that sharpen her features, but I know she has children older than me.

"What's this all about?" she demands.

Garom motions her toward the chairs. "Ivy and her friend are going to explain. I think it'll be worth hearing them out."

Sonia grimaces, but she trusts her colleague enough to drop into one of the chairs. She considers her fingernails and then me and Casimir with equal intentness, but she doesn't speak.

I don't see any point in launching into my pitch until the third person who needs to hear it arrives.

Which he does, a few minutes later. The youngest of the three bosses—though he's still got at least a decade on me—saunters into the room with a swipe of his hand through the strip of bleached hair on top of his head.

Hellar took over the Witorek family's part of the Black Talons a couple of years ago after his mother and last remaining parent was offed under typically murky circumstances. I'm not sure whether rival criminals or the Crown's Watch were responsible, but I suspect he'll be the hardest sell on our proposal.

His scars form a geometric pattern that dapples his pinkish brown skin around the sides and back of his scalp, leaving a narrow crop of hair on top. The fine strands flop over the edge of scarring like wheat drooping in a field.

He drapes himself across one of the armchairs without prompting and considers us with an air of boredom. "What was so urgent you had to disturb my game, Garom?"

The older man lifts his chin toward me and Casimir. "These two have come to speak to us on behalf of the woman who would be queen."

The newcomers know he wouldn't say it if he hadn't judged it to be true. There's no mistaking the interest that sparks in both of their eyes, though Sonia is better at tempering it.

She adjusts her position, taking a skeptical tone. "Oh, really?"

Hellar chuckles, but he's straightened up to give us more of his attention. "And what does the supposed queen want with us?"

I keep my posture straight and my voice steady. "You've obviously heard about Princess Petra and the message she delivered yesterday. Every word of it is true. Advisor Lothar launched a conspiracy against the king, murdered him and Queen Ishild and attempted to do the same to the royal children, and has been encouraging scourge sorcery among his followers."

Hellar twitches his shoulder in a careless shrug. "What's any of that to the Black Talons?"

Sonia's gaze has turned to a glower. "It's not as if we had things so sweet under King Konram. Let the scourge sorcerers tear each other apart. We'll be fine no matter what."

I focus on her. "Are you sure about that? Have you heard about the kinds of behavior Lothar and his Order of the Wild are encouraging? They want everyone to tap into their baser instincts—they want violence and chaos. What kind of an advantage will any of you have if *everyone* is willing to ignore the law and act out however they want?"

Hellar makes a scoffing sound. "We'll still be the experts."

"But you'll be up against people who can tap into more magic than anyone should be able to.

Who are only looking out for their own selfish interests. The moment they want something you do too…" I wave my hand through the air. "It's gone."

Garom leans back in his chair, seeming to watch both me and his colleagues with equal interest. "And how would things be better under another Melchiorek? We've lost good people and good deals in the years of Konram's reign and his father before him. This new queen might be even worse."

I snort. "Do you think *I'd* be backing her if she had it out for everyone who's remotely criminally inclined? She knows about my past. She knows—" I catch myself before I mention my own illicit magic, which this trio doesn't need to find out about. "She knows, and she hasn't judged me for it. She recognizes that things need to change so all of Silana's citizens can make their living as they see fit."

"She says that now," Hellar remarks dryly. "Watch how fast she changes her tune once she gets what she wants from us."

Sonia leans forward. "What exactly *does* she want from us? Why are you here?"

"She asked me to reach out to people in the city who could help her get a foothold against the Order of the Wild," I say. "It's no easy thing with the kind of power they can throw around and how they've been smearing her family. They're killing everyone who opposes them—everyone who'd be her allies. She needs people who know the city and its people, who can speak to those people and tell them what we're really up against, convince them that Lothar and the Order need to be taken down."

Hellar wrinkles his nose. "And her put up in his place."

"She has the training. She's been preparing for this her entire life. And most of the nobles trust the Melchiorek name. It'll be hard for anyone to set the country back in order without their agreement too."

A tingle passes through the air beside me, telling me Casimir has extended his gift. He lets out a soft cough to catch the gang bosses' attention. "Princess Petra isn't asking anything at all of you yet, other than to talk. This is your chance to have a direct influence over the running of the entire country. I've spoken with her too—I can vouch that she wants to negotiate with you."

"And what could she give us that we don't already have?" Sonia asks.

"She can call off the Crown's Watch. Ensure that you maintain a monopoly over certain types of trade. Negotiate lesser punishments." The corner of his mouth quirks upward. "I'm not saying she'll look the other way when it comes to issues like murder, but you could arrange a lot more room to maneuver."

Garom lifts his voice with a twinge of reluctance. "He's telling the truth. He truly believes all that. Of course, the princess herself could be a fabulous liar."

I pounce on the opening. "You could find that out easily enough. We'll arrange a meeting on neutral ground. It's not as if you have anything to fear from her. The only crimes she's interested in tackling right now are her parents' murder and the illegal sorcery being practiced in this city and the rest of the country."

He looks as if he's leaning toward accepting the offer. But then something shifts in his eyes, and he peers at me with an intensity that sends a shiver through my nerves.

His lips curl with a hint of what I think is revulsion. "Back when you had to make your hasty exit from Florian, word was going around about a riven sorcerer on the loose. The description reminded me of you—pale hair, pale skin, short and slim."

My gut lurches, but I set my face in the blandest expression I can summon. My tone matches. "That's quite a joke. Do I seem insane to you?"

His gaze skims up and down me, and the chill seeps deeper into my body. I didn't exactly answer the question, not in a way he can judge my honesty by.

Are we going to lose our chance at an alliance over my magic without my even using it?

The wretched power takes that moment to yank at me, demanding that I let it loose to force agreement from their throats. As if that would win us anything but animosity and horror.

I must keep my poker face well enough. Though the question doesn't totally fade from Garom's eyes, he shakes his head with a dry laugh. "Your mind is definitely too keen by half."

Casimir steps in with all his usual smoothness, changing the subject back to the most important matter at hand. "You're free to make your own decision, of course. That's what the new queen can offer you more than anything—a chance to make your voice heard. Lothar doesn't care about any interests other than his own."

I suppress the urge to reach over and squeeze his hand in thanks. I was right to bring him with me.

We work together well—as so much more than just lovers.

"That is the impression I've gotten of that armless asshole, I have to say," Sonia mutters, and my spirits lift a little higher.

Hellar flicks his fingers dismissively, but he doesn't outright argue, which I'll take as enough of a victory. "If we can agree on a reasonable meeting spot, I could consider hearing the princess out. But our friendship won't come cheap."

I pull my lips into another smile. "I never expected it would."

We've won the first round. I didn't know for sure we'd make it even this far.

Now we'll have to find out whether Petra can hold her own against the most powerful criminals in the city—and win them over at the same time.

# Thirteen

*Casimir*

Jolmi swipes a rag across the varnished wood of the bar counter and peers across it at the mismatched group clustered around two large pub tables pushed together. "So this is the city's last hope, hmm?"

There's a teasing note in his tone, thank the gods. I give my former classmate's hand a playful nudge of my elbow, but his words prickle right down to my uneasy stomach.

The thirty or so figures deep in discussion around those tables *are* essentially the only Silanians we've gathered so far who are willing to stand up to the scourge sorcerers. And it still remains to be seen whether they'll manage to stand together rather than dissolve into squabbling.

The three gang bosses with scarred scalps who Ivy and I convinced to attend this meeting look both wary and skeptical in their seats at one end of the tables. The underlings standing guard behind them only add to the ominous vibe.

The handful of nobles and soldiers we've brought on board wear equally wary expressions as they consider the admitted criminals. As if we don't have bigger things to worry about than what laws they defied in the past now that the man who made those laws has been murdered.

We've picked up a few other allies over the course of the past couple of days: a cleric who escaped the massacre at the Temple of the Crown, sitting alongside the devouts; the husband-and-wife heads of the merchants' guild; two more guards who've remained loyal to the Melchioreks. All of the soldiers, postures rigid as ever even though they're in plain clothes now, have stationed themselves behind Petra and her siblings at the head of the opposite table.

The whole arrangement gives the impression of a hostage negotiation rather than a communal brainstorming session. Tension hangs in the air thickly enough to set the hairs on the back of my neck on end.

How are we going to overcome the most powerful enemies our kingdom has ever faced if we can't even agree to fight them *together*?

This scenario should be in my wheelhouse. I was able to tell Petra what I'd gleaned that the gang bosses most wanted from me—the guarantee that the new queen would hear them out and offer much more freedom than her father did. I've studied every new arrival for any signs of guilt or subterfuge.

I even arranged this meeting spot on neutral ground. Out of all the dedicats to Ardone I trained alongside at Sovereign College and before, Jolmi was the one I was most sure would abhor what the scourge sorcerers are doing to this city… and who owned a space we could easily make use of.

He's shown a relieving sense of caution, arranging the meeting at a time when even his husband won't hear about it. But I can't tell how much he's agreed out of loyalty to the Crown and how much out of the thrill of watching the hidden heir pull together her resistance.

It's a moment for the history books, no doubt.

I consider him for a long moment, seeing nothing but the eager gleam in his eyes and what appears to be a genuine wish to please as he pours the drinks one of the gang bosses shouts for. Then I turn my attention back to the tables.

Unfortunately, I can't simply run through them all person by person, delving into their desires with my gift. Even imposing my magical talent on two of the gang bosses yesterday left me exhausted.

It seemed most important to take a peek at the one I skipped yesterday, the one Ivy trusts the most, when they arrived this evening. That was rather a waste, since it turns out his wants are quite aligned with his colleagues', but I suppose it was better to confirm that than regret assuming it.

I could probably discern at least a vague sense of one more person's deepest craving tonight without knocking myself to the floor, but even that would be pushing my limits. So I've held my gift in reserve, relying on my non-magical skills to evaluate the group instead.

Our future queen rests her elbows on the tabletop as she leans forward. I have to credit Petra for the fortitude she's shown in the face of recent tragedies.

Her parents prepared her for this role well, even if only from afar for the past seven years. She manages to keep her stance relaxed enough to give a sense of openness while regal enough to hold an air of authority.

"I'm willing to go further than that in exchange for your loyalty to the Crown," she says, her alert gaze fixed on the gang bosses. "If we consider each of your typical areas of business, I'd imagine I can find some for which I could abolish the conflicting laws completely. How would you like to find yourselves at the head of a guild of your own, not only allowed to pursue those avenues unhindered but keeping full control over who else is allowed to engage in them?"

The gang bosses are giving their best impression of nonchalance, but I catch a twitch of a smile at the corner of Garom's mouth and an avidness in the adjustment of Hellar's position. I doubt they anticipated any Melchiorek making them an offer so generous.

Of course, they're not the types to leap at a chance before eyeing it from every angle. Sonia takes a disaffected tone. "And what guarantee would we have of you following through on your promises if we pave your way back to the throne?"

The guards shift restlessly at the sneer in her voice. Tinom, who's seated himself next to Princess Klaudia, can't conceal a frown.

I wish I knew what to say that could bring these disparate groups together in harmony. I've spent years in training to learn how to set any person at ease.

But when so much hangs in the balance with every word that passes around the table… I was meant to be pampering and entertaining political figures, not guiding their policies. And who can say what's reasonable or not when sadistic sorcerers have taken over the country?

Petra, at least, doesn't appear offended by the gangsters' caution. "I can sign a proclamation to the effect with my personal seal along with that of the Melchiorek family. We can make the establishment of the guild a priority during the very early days of our reclamation, so that you'd see it put into practice while I'm still relying on your support. If there are other methods that would reassure you more, I'd be happy to hear them."

The three bosses tilt closer together to murmur amongst themselves. Garom and Sonia push back their chairs and get to their feet. "You've given us a lot to think about. We'll talk about the details on our own and let you know what we think a reasonable deal would be. Then it'll be up to you whether or not you take it."

Tinom's mouth tightens. "We can't afford to wait very long. With every day, the Order of the Wild deepens their influence—"

Petra holds up her hand. "Advisor, I'm sure we're all aware of the urgency of the current situation."

Across from Tinom, Ivy lifts her head to catch Garom's eyes. "I'll come by tomorrow to find out what you've decided and bring word back."

He tips his head in acknowledgment. "Let's see if we can all end up with more than we started with."

He shoots a sharp smile at Petra and strides out of the pub with his colleagues flanking him.

As soon as the door has thumped shut behind the trio, Petra glances around the tables. "We need to think farther abroad as well as just within the city. The Order of the Wild has spread its influence everywhere. Perhaps we can bring in more allies from across the country—or push back in several places at once."

Stavros taps his prosthetic against the tabletop. "There was a fairly effective group of resistors in the city of Pima in Nikodi, assuming they've continued to avoid punishment."

Ivy's face brightens. "Yes, Voleska and Emor pulled together a good group and were already undermining the Order's authority. You can count on them."

Tinom hums thoughtfully. "There's a well-regarded temple of Elox up north, a few hours from Nikodi—the Temple of Tranquil Skies. The cleric who presides over it has always been a key supporter of the Melchiorek rule in that region."

One of the devouts sits up a little straighter. "Oh, yes, that temple has a long history. I heard they sheltered revolutionaries there all the way back when Silana rose up against the Darium empire."

I'm even less use at evaluating people halfway across the country. As the discussion continues, I fold my hands in my lap against the unfamiliar urge to fidget.

I helped bring the current meeting together. I'll bolster spirits as needed.

No one would expect a courtesan to play all that large a role in overcoming an uprising anyway.

Alek is in the middle of describing another temple he's visited that he thinks might be worth reaching out to when one of Tinom's sentries slips in from the pub's back entrance.

The woman clears her throat to get the group's attention, though she focuses her gaze on her future ruler. "I've got a man you might want to speak with, though I'm not sure it's safe for you to do it directly. He was being chased by some of the Order members—they were yelling about him turning his back on Lothar. We managed to get him away to a temporary hiding spot. It sounds as if he's defected from the scourge sorcerers."

Stavros's eyes flash. "He might have useful information about their operations. If he can be trusted."

The former general looks as if he's about to get to his feet, but I hop to mine first. My spirits have lifted past their temporary gloom.

"I'll go speak to him," I say before anyone else can volunteer. "I don't have much to contribute to this discussion anyway, and I can get a read on what he's really after."

Having Ivy beam at me the way she does would solidify my resolve all on its own. Thankfully, I have the future queen's support as well.

Petra offers me a smile of her own. "Go and see what you can find out from him—both in what he says and what he does."

The sentry motions for me to follow her, and we hustle out the back of the building the way she came in.

We hurry through the middle-ward streets. The buildings loom closer together here than in the inner wards, but still with a stately grandeur that you won't find very far beyond the old city walls.

The immensity of the task ahead of us starts to creep up over me again. We have to not just oust the usurpers and their murderous magic but unite the different levels of the city to do so.

I'm ashamed that I never thought all that much before about the lives of the citizens on Florian's fringes. Or the peasants in the towns and villages outside the city. I had a hazy idea of their existence and that they deserved to be happy just as nobles and royals do, but when did I make any effort toward putting that principle into practice?

The world my mother trained me to perform for was nothing more than a gilded bubble. The real crime isn't that I've deviated from her wishes so far but that I didn't realize I needed to sooner.

The sentry weaves through streets where the cobblestones become more worn and the buildings droop lower. They're still a far cry from the dirt roads and ramshackle wooden homes in the neighborhood around Crow's Close, but farther from the elite hub of the city all the same.

As we approach a stable, her steps slow for caution. She leads me around back to a shed attached to the building.

From the smell of leather that permeates the space we step into and the tools hung on the walls, I gather this is a workshop for mending saddles and bridles. At the moment, no one's inhabiting it except for a skinny man who looks to be in his mid-twenties, huddled in one corner.

His tawny hair is rumpled. Both grit and a reddish scrape mark his face. He considers the two of us with nervous eyes, looking ready to try to bolt past us if he feels the need.

He definitely feels under threat. From us, from the people he's run from, or both?

A couple of paces away from him, I crouch down, putting us on the same eye level. In the fading light that filters through the shed's small, grimy window, I examine his face and body language for every hint at his emotional state.

I pitch my voice low and soothing. "I hear you've had a rough time of it."

The man shrugs and tucks his arms tighter around his pulled-up knees. He has a shallow cut on his forearm too, a thin line of blood seeping into his sleeve on either side of the severed fabric.

Whatever happened between him and his former associates, it ended violently.

"We'd like to help you if we can," I go on in the same calm tone. "We'd rather not see anyone getting pushed around or beat up from now on."

The man wets his lips. "How do you think you're going to manage that? You don't know…"

He trails off, looking abruptly more anxious than before. His fear appears totally authentic.

"About what the Order of the Wild can do?" I fill in. "Actually, we know exactly what they're capable of. We're well aware of the magic they've been turning to and the lengths they've gone to so they can enhance it and their manpower."

The man makes a scoffing sound. "Then what do you think you can do about it?"

"We have our own strengths. We simply need enough people willing to take that first step to stand up to the Order, and then we can set Silana back to rights. But for now, you could start by telling me your name."

He hesitates again. As he opens his mouth, his arms loosen, his stance relaxing just slightly. "Filip."

I nod. "And why were you being chased by the Order, Filip? Why did they attack you?"

He sucks in a sharp breath. "I was supposed to— I didn't want to do everything they said we should. It sounded amazing at first, but once I actually saw…"

He trails off, his body deflating. Does he still look just anxious or sad as well?

It's not surprising that he'd be incredibly fearful about his former comrades getting their hands on him—and of how those of us who oppose the Order might retaliate for the harm he's helped carry out. But we still have to be careful ourselves.

If they won him over with promises of glory before, he could be swayed in that direction again.

Thankfully, I'm the best possible person to evaluate his priorities.

"Realizing you've made a mistake and refusing to do so again is a brave thing," I say, and extend my gift toward him.

A tingling shoots through my gums where I sacrificed my back molars for this magic. An ache ripples through my skull, but with it comes a current of impressions straight from the man in front of me.

What could I do that would make him happiest in this moment?

I catch fragments of meetings, Lothar looming tall over his followers; a child standing before a cleric; a surge of tingling exhilaration; a rush of fear. Then a bone-deep desperation that yawns open ever wider.

Understanding flows through that final sensation with the usual certainty of my gift. What would make him happiest is for me to believe him and give him a chance to work alongside me. He wants to take action, to prove himself.

The headache from repeated use of my magic jabs deeper through my mind, but a sense of triumphant relief rises up all the same.

I can bring this man back to the rightful queen. I can show him how to overturn the villains he once worked with.

I hold out my hand. "How would you like the chance to not just avoid your mistakes but turn them around?"

# Fourteen

*Ivy*

As he studies the sketched diagrams one of Garom's people passed on to us, Alek rubs his hands like he's about to dig into his favorite meal. I can't help smiling at the scholar's enthusiasm, despite the dangerous mission ahead of us.

It reminds me of way back in my early days at the royal college, when he and I worked together to sneak into the college library's accounting room so I could steal Ster. Torstem's financial records. I never would have guessed during our initial meeting that Alek would be the first to join me in a criminal scheme.

But he does love putting his mind to a problem, no matter how legally questionable.

Now, he taps one point on the map where it's spread on the dining table. "Here's the access spot closest to this building. You enter there and follow this path…" He draws his finger across the passages marked like a diagram laid over the city streets. "Straight ahead until the third tunnel on the left, then the second on the right, then the first turn to the left. There's another access spot a short distance down that one. It'll let you out just a block from the guardhouse."

Stavros studies the map with a tick of his head to clear his vision. "Are you sure we can open up those access spots without significant difficulty?"

Alek nods. "A jolt of Rheave's magic should melt off the lock. The openings are covered by a simple grate that's heavy but not very intensively secured." The scholar glances up at us with an apologetic wince. "Most people aren't eager to go down into the sewer system."

I have to snort. "I don't think 'eager' is the right word in our situation either. At least it'll get us through the city without having to pass by any scourge sorcerers, as long as we don't need to go to the outer wards."

The underground system of drains and channels was built centuries ago before the city had expanded quite so far. The tunnels only extend beneath the inner wards and partway through the middle wards.

But we need the extra subterfuge where we can get it. The new ally Casimir brought into the fold yesterday, an apparent defector from the Order of the Wild, told us that Lothar has assigned more of his followers to patrol the city streets in search of Petra's allies. A few among them have talents for sensing magic, others for seeking out targets.

If we pass too close to either, even Tinom's concealment charms won't keep us hidden.

Stavros straightens up. "If the sewers are our best option, then into the sewers it is. It's late enough. Let's get to work."

Rheave's eyes flash with a light that actually could be called eager. "I'm ready!"

I give him a teasing nudge as we head for the door. "You won't be so excited once we're down in the stench. I just need to get my cloak."

I expect to simply duck into the bedroom to grab the swath of dark fabric, but Stavros follows behind me. When I tug the cloak over my shoulders, he steps in to fasten it for me.

I hardly need the help, but I release the clasp to his deft grip, his prosthetic managing to hold one side in place while his fingers manipulate the other. His massive frame looms over me, the once intimidating presence now nothing but comforting.

Except I'm not sure why he's here.

A quiver of doubt pricks at the base of my throat. I keep my voice light. "Giving me a closer look to make sure I'm up to the job?"

Stavros sputters a guffaw. "I have no doubt that you are, Lady Thief. I just—I needed a moment away from the others. If you don't mind the intrusion."

His own tone is casual, but not quite enough to disguise a slightly ragged edge that creeps into it. When he lowers his hands, I grasp them between us, both the one of flesh and the one of metal. "Are you all right?"

He gives his head a brief twitch to meet my gaze a little longer before his eyes go distant. A sigh tumbles out of him. "I will be. It's ridiculous. I've felt like a wolf in a cage, cooped up in here, not being able to risk participating in most of the missions we've been carrying out—and now that I have the chance…"

I stroke my thumb over the side of his knuckles. "What?"

His mouth pulls into a grimace. "A lot of the men and women killed or taken captive from that guardhouse will have been people I trained with. People I once gave orders to. People who've counted on me one way or another. I can barely wrap my head around how many lives the Order of the Wild has destroyed in a matter of weeks, and we're stuck picking off pockets of strength bit by bit. It doesn't feel like enough."

I offer him a tight smile, my chest constricting around my heart. "It doesn't to me either. But we've got to build up to bigger things, right? The more the scourge sorcerers falter, the more support for Petra can grow."

Stavros's answering smile slants at a self-deprecating angle. "I know that. It's just harder to accept it when every part of me is screaming to end them all now."

I reach up to pat his cheek. "I'm sure you'll get plenty of chances to end loads of them in the future."

Another choked laugh escapes him, and then he's pulling me to him, claiming a kiss so fierce I wish it didn't have to end.

When he eases back just an inch, his low voice grazes my face with his breath. "The only reason I've made it this far is because I had you with me. Don't you ever let a single one of those fools Tinom pulled together make you feel you haven't earned their loyalty. You know you have all of mine."

I bob up on my toes to hug him, even though his words can't quite penetrate the uneasiness simmering in my gut. "And you have mine. Let's take back some more of what the scourge sorcerers have stolen from us."

We rejoin Rheave in the hall and slip down the stairs, donning our concealment charms as we go. Rheave sets his hand lightly on my back, and I hook my fingers around Stavros's elbow so that we can still see each other fully.

We step out into the night. The windows around us have gone dark, the blackness only broken by the glow of the intermittent lanterns along the street.

Somewhere around a corner, a drunken laugh peals out, but no one's wandering along this road at the moment.

We hurry across the cobblestones, take a turn, and come up on the grate Alek indicated. It's wide enough that even Stavros should be able to fit without having to squeeze, and only secured by a single, regular padlock.

At the rap of determined footsteps, we pause. A middle-aged man in a thick cloak strides past us down the middle of the street—maybe an Order member on patrol, or maybe an ordinary citizen with some urgent midnight business.

My heart thuds faster with a jolt of my magic coming to attention, but he doesn't glance our way. I don't sense any sorcery emanating from him.

As soon as he's out of view, Rheave kneels by the grate. With a faint crackle, the padlock falls aside.

Stavros hefts up the grate and motions for us to descend.

I find the rungs of a ladder just beyond the opening. Gripping them, I clamber down as quickly as I can manage, wrinkling my nose at the damp grit that sticks to my fingers.

To my relief, the passage below isn't *quite* as awful as I imagined. It rained most of last night, which must have swept the worst of the collected refuse away. Still, the stink of urine and feces turns my stomach.

The men climb down behind me, Stavros shutting the grate in his wake so it's not obvious someone made use of it. More than a few steps beyond the faint glow that seeps through the bars, the blackness is so complete there's no need for our charms.

"Stay close to the walls," I murmur, and start forward in the direction Alek indicated.

The sewage flows turgidly along in the wide channel at our right. I set my feet carefully to ensure there's no chance of slipping into that noxious river.

After a few minutes, Rheave lets out a gagging sound. "Physical bodies do produce some unpleasant substances."

I guess spirit creatures don't shit. I glance back in the direction of his voice with an arch of my eyebrow. "That's the price we pay for getting to eat."

The daimon-man grunts in acknowledgment. "I suppose that is a fair trade-off."

If I had a list of places I'd least like to spend time with any of my lovers, this sewer would be right near the top. But as we venture on through the putrid darkness, my spirits buoy me beyond the stench.

Here I am, in the middle of a scheme that all four of my men have set in motion with me. One that doesn't require any of my unpredictable magic.

Like the old days… except now I'm no longer alone.

In this moment, it doesn't matter what magic fidgets in my chest or what people like Tinom or the Black Talons' bosses think of it. I can make a difference without being seen as any kind of monster.

We mark off the turnings with our hands against the stone wall, noting each passage until it's time to turn. Thankfully the rickety maintenance bridges at the intersections allow us to cross without needing to risk a jump.

Stavros ends up taking the lead, the thud of his boots guiding me onward. Rheave stays close enough to regularly caress my back through my cloak, as if he needs periodic confirmations of my presence to reassure himself.

When we reach our destination, Stavros climbs up to the grate and peers at the street beyond as well as he can from the low vantage point. He swings to the side and motions for Rheave to join him. "I don't see or hear anyone nearby right now. Give that lock a zap."

In less than a minute, we're scrambling out into the fresh if chilly air above. Stavros lowers the grate back into place, and we hustle down the quiet street toward the guardhouse.

It's one of the largest in Florian, just outside the old city walls on the border between the inner wards and the middle. Stavros visited the Crown's Watch here more than once in his capacity as general—and then after while investigating the conspiracy at the college.

He directs us around the squat stone building and down a side alley. There, he points up at a tall window on the second floor.

"That serves as an additional exit if the Crown's Watch needs to move out quickly," he murmurs. "They can pop it open and make the short jump into the alley while others are heading out the front and back doors. Since it's up there, they don't bother guarding it."

So no one should notice if it briefly opens and closes for our invisible figures to enter.

I give myself a shake in preparation. "All right. I should be able to handle the lock."

Stavros bends down and boosts me onto his shoulders. Once he's straightened up, I can easily reach the base of the window.

I pull out the slim metal tool I brought along for this purpose and wiggle it into the narrow gap between the frame and the ledge.

With a little maneuvering, I manage to slide over the deadbolt. I ease the window up an inch, listen, and then push it farther so I can wriggle inside.

My magic jitters with the urge to wrap even more protection around myself, but no figures stir at either end of the hall I lower myself into. Once I've set my feet on the ground, I tug the pane even higher.

Rheave scrambles after me with another boost from Stavros. Then the former general hefts himself after us with the two of us grasping his arms.

We huddle together so we can see each other clearly despite the charms. Stavros points in both directions down the hall, his voice the barest whisper. "The sleeping quarters are all up here—almost every room. They won't be locked. I'll be heading down to the dungeons in the basement."

I give his hand a quick squeeze. "Get through this mission as quickly as we can manage it, and then we'll meet by the grate as planned."

An ache forms around my heart letting him go, but if anyone can look after himself in a potential combat situation, it's Stavros.

As he turns toward the stairs, I nudge open the first of the doors to the police force dormitories.

Some members of the Crown's Watch go back to family homes when they're off for the day, but many choose to live in the guardhouse, especially the younger men and women who aren't married and want to be out of their parents' homes or those who've traveled from outside the city to serve. I guess it must come with a sense of family somewhat like what I've found with my men.

Now, the narrow beds set up along the walls of this room are filled with Order members. Lothar took over all of the Crown's Watch's properties when his people stormed the city, and he's using them as bases of operation.

Which means a significant number of the figures sleeping in these beds aren't people at all but daimon in animated clay bodies.

With one hand on my shoulder so I can see him, Rheave points to three of the beds. Those three are daimon like him.

I set my fingers over his in a quick reassuring touch and move to the first form he indicated.

Casimir picked out the pot of black makeup I retrieve from my pocket. It's a type that stains the skin semi-permanently rather than simply covering it temporarily.

Ever so gingerly, I use a soft brush to dab a few dark streaks on the side of the man's neck, just below the edge of his blanket.

By morning, the dye will have set. A mark will remain through at least a week of washes. But it simply looks like a slightly unusual smudge of dirt or soot, not anything purposefully put there.

Only the Black Talons people prowling the streets will know what those marks signify. They'll kill the captured daimons' bodies in public places so more and more witnesses will see the proof of the Order's unnatural magic—and so those daimon can go free rather than serving their slave masters.

When I reach the third sleeping figure, I have to tug her blanket down a little and brush her hair back from her neck. She lets out a sleepy sigh.

I freeze with a lurch of my heart. Only when she remains still for another several seconds do I lower my brush.

In theory, Rheave could have burned these marks. But the jolt of pain would probably have woken the targets. This way, we can mark them all without alerting anyone.

We move from one room to the next, marking neck after neck. Looking down on all the faces relaxed with sleep, my gut starts to twist with the thought of their future deaths.

They aren't really people, of course. The daimon are trapped inside those bodies, not there through their own will.

But if any of them would have liked to take the bodies as their own like Rheave has, to experience everything mortal life has to offer, they'll never get the chance.

That's the scourge sorcerers' fault, not ours. They set the daimon on this destructive path.

I can't help feeling a little guilty about it all the same.

Neither of us speaks as we work our way through the rooms. By the time we get to the end of the hall, I've marked nearly two dozen sleeping daimon.

I'm not sure whether to be more horrified by how many of the spirits Lothar's people still hold captive or how large a force they've installed in Florian in general. This is only the Order lackeys who didn't take the night shift, and only one of several guardhouses around the city.

The leader of the scourge sorcerers knew how hard he'd need to fight to keep control over Silana's capital. But our current forces might not be enough to tackle even one guardhouse, let alone all of the scourge sorcerers in the city.

I reach the last bed Rheave has indicated and draw back the blanket to reveal the sleeping man. My brush smears the inky makeup across the side of his neck—

And his skin twitches. He startles awake with a grunt.

My power leaps up my throat, but Rheave shoves past me in an instant. As I rein in the frantic call to subdue our target by whatever means necessary, my partner clamps his hands against the man's mouth and chest.

"We want to help you," he rasps in a hushed voice. "I used to be like you, but I'm not anymore. Can you take control? This body could be—"

The man starts to thrash against his blanket. Whether for his own reasons or because of the magic still binding him, he's not interested in a peaceful resolution.

Rheave lets out a pained noise—and a hiss of his daimon magic.

He hits the struggling form with enough power to reduce the clay statue that should have appeared into black dust. A smoky, earthy smell trickles into the air.

I grasp his shoulder, grimacing in sympathy. "You had to do it." Another few seconds, and the guard might have woken up the rest of the room.

We both stare down at the shadowed bed with its heap of charred clay dust, a bizarre murder scene. I gather my resolve. "Come on, we'd better clean up the body so no one realizes what happened."

Rheave nods silently. We gather the remains of the clay body in a bundle of the blanket and sheets, and Rheave carries it with him on our way back to the window we entered through.

Rheave jumps down first and turns so I can use him as a sort of stepping stool. Several buildings over, we shove the bundle of fabric into a refuse bin where no one is likely to notice it. Then we hurry on to the sewer grate.

Stavros is waiting there, standing right on top of the grate so my gaze can easily find him despite the charm trying to divert my attention. His quest was a lot less time-consuming than ours.

I touch his arm to bring him into focus. From one glance at his grim face, I know he didn't find what he was hoping for.

"One of the captains I'd have counted on has been killed," he tells us as we step back from the grate so he can open it. "I think another may be still alive but held in one of the forts outside the city—Lothar might have hoped she had information that would be useful as the Order establishes itself in Florian."

Which means the advisor will be torturing the woman for her loyalties. I offer Stavros a tight smile. "Maybe we can get her out soon."

He gives a rough chuckle and bends toward the grate. I'm just turning toward Rheave when a sudden blast of magic slams into the side of my head.

The last thing I hear as I topple to my knees is Rheave's frantic shout.

# FIFTEEN

*Stavros*

The shift in the air has me whirling before I'm even sure of what's wrong.

One second, I can't see anything around me except the darkened street. The next, five figures materialize a few paces away.

One of the men is gripping Ivy, her concealment charm snapped off her neck, her head slumped. They must have knocked her unconscious.

But even as my muscles clench to spring to her aid, my gaze lands on the taller man with the pale eyes and uneven frame who's obviously orchestrated this confrontation.

Lothar gestures to the man holding Ivy, who whips a knife to her neck. My stance stiffens, knowing I can't leap in there quickly enough to ensure the blade doesn't sever her throat, even in my currently invisible state.

"I know she's not alone," Lothar says in his thick, haughty voice, his eyes scanning the street. "If any harm comes to me or my people, you'll be sacrificing her too."

At least it seems that Tinom's charm is working well enough that Lothar can't make me or Rheave out when he isn't sure of who he's looking for or where exactly they should be. But somehow he found Ivy.

I adjust my position, my hand balling into a fist. Anger sears through my gut.

How did he know we'd be here at just this moment? It can't be a coincidence. They were lying in wait, concealed by their own magic.

Someone passed on the details of our plan to the Order.

How much else does our greatest enemy know? How much else has he *done* while we were infiltrating the guardhouse?

A jolt of panic spikes through my veins alongside my fury. The royal children—they might already be lost.

Lothar clicks his tongue, his lips curling with a hint of a sneer. "Why don't you show yourself so we can negotiate like proper human beings, hmm?"

He flicks his cool gaze toward Ivy. The man with the knife digs the blade in just enough for a thin line of blood to form along its edge.

My anger and fear congeal in my churning stomach. The former magic advisor would *like* to see Ivy dead. If the only sorcerer he had who could control her is gone, he'll want the threat she poses eliminated.

He's only kept her alive this long to control the rest of us. If he thinks that ploy isn't working, he'll happily murder her and call that its own win.

I can't see Rheave in the darkness. He's kept his charm on so far, though I can only imagine how worked up the daimon is watching the woman he's devoted himself to sagging in the grip of these villains.

It doesn't appear that Lothar knows how many people exactly would have been with Ivy. Let the daimon realize he should stay concealed. I can be a distraction.

As long as Rheave has enough sense to recognize the advantage we can keep.

With a swift tug, I wrench off my charm. All five of the hostile faces before me twitch in my direction, their attention homing in on me.

I shove the charm in my pocket, my prosthetic raised defensively, and set my hand on the hilt of my sword. Not overtly threatening yet, just where I can draw it the moment I see an opening.

As Lothar's gaze takes me in, a sharper rage cuts through the rest of my inner turmoil.

This prick slaughtered the man I swore to serve, the man I'd have given my life for. He murdered our king and queen with no care for their lives, their children, or what it would do to our country, only thinking of his own brutal, selfish ends.

If I owe King Konram anything, it's seeing the traitor bleeding out here on the cobblestones. He's already destroyed so much, ruined so many lives.

I have to put the cur down.

I just don't know how.

Even if I did the unthinkable and sacrificed Ivy to launch myself at Lothar now, I have no idea what talents he or the lackeys flanking him possess. They might be able to deflect me before I inflicted so much as a scratch.

There's too much on the line to take that gamble.

"Here I am, Lothar," I say, my voice hard, with a flick of my eyes to clear the fog that's rolling over them. "What kind of negotiation are you looking for?"

The one-shouldered man rests his only hand against his belly, a pose that emphasizes what's missing from his uneven body. He tilts his head slightly to the side.

His expression is keenly alert but with no sign of fear. He believes he's fully in control of our stand-off.

As his gaze bores into mine, his face blurring after the first few moments, a sense of rancor prickles over my skin. As if he's radiating fury.

What the fuck does this asshole have to be angry with *me* about?

"There's only one piece of information I'm interested in bartering for," he says. "Where are the false queen and the young Melchioreks hiding?"

I can't restrain a scoffing sound. Does he really think so little of my loyalty as that?

It would tear my heart in two seeing him harm Ivy more than he already has, but I know that she would never forgive me if I traded our future queen's life for hers.

Besides, I'm not naïve enough to believe that Lothar actually would spare Ivy in exchange for the information. No doubt he'd have his man spilling her blood the second I coughed up a location.

Lothar's eyes narrow at my show of skepticism. "You aren't the only vermin we've caught, even if you are the worst." He aims a disgusted look at Ivy before returning his attention to me. "If someone else gives up the royals first, you'll have nothing left to bargain with."

My pulse stutters. Who else has the Order gotten their hands on?

Or is he simply bluffing to try to get his way?

Gods help me, if I could run this man through right now, it'd put an end to this entire mess.

But I don't even know that for sure. How deeply does his followers' fervor run now that he's stirred it up?

My fingers tighten around the hilt of my sword, but I leave it in place, locked in uncertainty. *Could* I offer something in return, a partial acquiescence that wouldn't betray Petra and her siblings but would buy us more time?

Thankfully, getting out of this wretched scenario isn't entirely up to me. As I grapple with my thoughts, a crackle of lightning-like energy blazes through the air.

The bolts slam into all five of the villains in front of me.

Even as my heart leaps, the sparks fizzle out against some kind of magical shield wrapped around Lothar's body, as well as that of his two closest followers. They barely twitch at the impact.

But the other two figures aren't so protected. A woman at Lothar's left and the man holding Ivy jerk and crumple with the surge of daimon magic.

The knife slips from the man's fingers, and Rheave is there, abruptly visible and yanking Ivy to her feet.

Her body trembles, and her eyelids flutter open.

The burst of magic must have jolted her too, back into at least partial consciousness.

My gaze snaps to Lothar  and my gift tickles at the back of my eyes with a sudden flash of imagery that shows me the wretch's next move.

"Pull back," I holler, wrenching out my sword. Rheave has already scrambled backward a few paces with Ivy before Lothar has a chance to snarl and spring at the two of them.

The magic Sabrelle blessed me with might not work as impressively as it once did, but I've never been gladder to have it.

In the tiny window of opportunity I bought him, the daimon spins to the side and thrusts out his arm. He hurls another wallop of sizzling energy at our attackers.

The flare doesn't penetrate their protective magic to char their bodies the way I'd like to see, but it does heave them back several paces. Lothar stumbles into his companions, knocking them all onto their asses.

I raise my sword, but I don't know if the blade could penetrate Lothar's shield any better than Rheave's magic has. And every second we linger is another opportunity for him to bring his own sorcery to bear.

"Run!" I shout to Rheave, and dash over to help him support Ivy.

Our lady thief has gotten her legs into somewhat working order. She only needs a little help balancing as we sprint around the nearest corner and duck into the first alley I spot.

There's no time to find another sewer grate, and I'm not sure we'd be better off down in the enclosed space now that Lothar is on our trail regardless.

Rheave propels out a question between his ragged breaths. "Where do we go now?"

Before I can answer, Ivy lifts her head higher. Her voice comes out slightly slurred but determined. "Can't go back to Petra. Can't risk leading them there."

As little as I like it, I have to agree. "She's right."

We hustle on in a weaving path through the streets. I peer at the buildings around us, my mind whirling. An uncomfortable sense of certainty fills my chest.

I don't want to take this step, but I can't justify the danger I'd be putting our entire cause in if I don't.

I set my jaw against my own misgivings. "We need to leave the city. We're too compromised—we can't guarantee the royal family's safety here. I'll have to signal Alek and Casimir the way we agreed."

We always knew it might come to this—that our situation in Florian might become so precarious we had to make a hasty exit. I just hadn't expected the conflict to reach that point so quickly.

Ivy nods, and I retrieve my locket from my trousers. Still jogging, I press the pane inside the hinged pendant, pause, press it again, and repeat the sequence once more.

The series of three pulses in quick succession will tell our friends that something's gone wrong—wrong enough that they need to evacuate the future queen, her siblings, and all our other allies who'll join us.

As Ivy said, we can't risk returning to Tinom's tenement building. We'll have to count on our comrades to gather the possessions we left behind.

It isn't as if we've been carrying much with us after all this time on the run.

As a safety measure, we spread out our mounts across several stables at varying distances from the apartment. Taking the lay of the land, I make our next turn to take us to the spot where we lodged Toast and a few of the other horses we can call ours.

Rheave looks over at me, his smooth face unusually tight. Worry turns his voice taut. "What if they know about our escape plan?"

Dread sours my mouth. All I can do is shake my head. "We proceed as if they don't, but we keep our eyes open. If we see any sign that our route out of the city has been compromised, we back up and reconsider."

Ivy swipes her hair back from her face, her skin still wan but her eyes brightening by the second. "There's more than one way. We'll make it out."

I don't like to think about how much that effort might take out of her, though.

Tinom assured us that his hidden passage through the city walls was a closely guarded secret, known about only by the royal family and himself, since he's the one who disguised it. But who knows if King Konram might have trusted his other magic advisors enough to mention it to them?

As we rush into the stable and grab tack for the ride, an emotion that's more regret than worry twists my stomach. The act of yanking the saddle's girth tight and the hurried snatching of the bridle are far too familiar.

How many times now have we fled from our enemies, running or riding off into the night?

How many times more will we need to before I can stand and fight the man who's inflicted so many horrors on our country?

Every military expert knows there are times when you have to cut your losses and lick your wounds so you can come back stronger. But gods above, each failure pierces me right through the middle.

I *will* destroy Lothar for everything he's obliterated in my world. I'll protect the remnants of the royal family, the woman I love, and the strange family we've made.

I just don't know when.

The uncertainty pulls my gut into a knot. Ignoring it, I lead my horse out of the stable with Ivy and Rheave close behind me, scan the street with a jerk of my head, and heft myself into the saddle.

"Let's ride."

# Sixteen

Filip's head swivels around as he takes in the landscape on either side of the small country road. Then he squints up at the sky. "We're a little off course for Kevarsi, aren't we?"

A couple of horse-lengths ahead of us, Tinom catches the question and glances back. The magic advisor keeps his voice carefully even. "We've had a slight change in plans. I sent some people ahead to scout out our options, and there's a better place for us to continue building our resistance."

Filip looks as if he's bitten back a protest. From Toast's back, I study his expression as well as I can without being blatant about it.

Has his face paled a little?

In discussions amongst Petra's innermost circle after we first regrouped outside Florian, we all agreed that the supposed Order of the Wild defector was the most likely traitor among us. Casimir said he gave every appearance of wanting our help but acknowledged that he might have been desperate not to get away from Lothar but to fulfill whatever plan he's been sent to carry out.

So we've created a test. One of Tinom's people mentioned to him as if in passing that we were going to head to Kevarsi to try to gather forces farther from Lothar's current center of power. Since then, we've been watching to see if he's had some way of passing on information back to his former colleagues.

Over the past three days on the less-traveled roads that seem safest, we've also been veering gradually more north on our actual course. This is the first time he's noticed that we can't possibly be heading to the city.

He doesn't say anything else, though, simply keeps trotting along on his mare. After a few moments, his gaze darts briefly toward me with a slight tensing of his shoulders.

That's nothing new. I've caught many similar glances over the days since he joined us. Having me anywhere near him obviously sets his nerves jangling.

He knows about my magic, I assume, since Lothar would have spread the word among his followers to beware of me. The first thing he did when he saw me was jerk his hand through the gesture of the divinities, like the noble heir on the summer estate where Lothar held me prisoner.

I can't hold that against him when Tinom is nearly as wary. I think word might have spread to the soldiers by now, because I've noticed them drawing closer around Petra when I go to speak to her in their company.

This morning, one of them partly unsheathed his knife when I walked by.

The memory leaves a hole in my gut. I understand the reactions; I know how everyone thinks about the riven. But the ongoing paranoia is starting to wear on me.

Gods above, will I ever be able to live my life honestly if most people see me as a villain even when I'm helping them?

I don't let on that I've noticed Filip's anxious glance, just watch him surreptitiously for a few minutes longer. Then I draw Toast to a walk so we fall back to where my men have been bringing up the rear of our procession.

Stavros meets my gaze with a questioning lift of his eyebrows. I offer a noncommittal shrug in return.

When I'm close enough that I'm sure our voices won't carry to the man we're monitoring, I guide Toast into the midst of their group and speak under my breath. "I still can't tell if he's working against us. He hasn't used any magic that I've sensed."

Filip has admitted to having a small talent, one he got in exchange for a few toes, but only for encouraging crops to grow. It seems he's a farmer's son. Of course, there's no way to be sure he's telling the truth about the size of his talent or its purpose.

"He did warn us about the patrols," Rheave murmurs. "If he wanted us to get caught, wouldn't he have kept quiet?"

Stavros grimaces. "It could have been a ploy to earn our trust, knowing he'd find out other ways for Lothar to catch us. But if he passed on information about our plans, he didn't tell them everything. Lothar didn't realize that there'd be three of us, and he didn't arrive soon enough to confront us *before* we broke into the guardhouse."

My lips twist in a wry smile. "It'd certainly have been easier to overwhelm us with dozens of his people right there."

Casimir looks toward the younger man and back at us. "I still think that even if he's acted as an informant to some extent, that doesn't mean he's against our cause. We don't know what pressure Lothar might have put on him, what threats he might have faced if he didn't comply."

"We'll know soon enough if he's continued to inform," Alek puts in. "The men Tinom sent to Kevarsi will catch up with us at the temple within a day or two. If they saw the Order of the Wild increasing their patrols and watching for our arrival, that's all we'll need to know."

I adjust my grip on the reins, unable to shed the tightness in my stomach. "If they don't see that, we're not in the clear. He simply might not have had the means to pass on the information once we left Florian."

Stavros gives a soft grunt. "Well, he won't have much opportunity at the temple either, if the devouts there are as loyal as Tinom believes. We'll stay alert to any sign of sabotage—from any source."

"It might not have been a purposeful betrayal in the first place," Casimir reminds us in his optimistic way. "If anyone in the know made a stray comment within hearing of the wrong person, Lothar could have put the rest of the pieces together on his own."

I cast my gaze over the two dozen figures traveling with us: three royal guards in their plain clothes at the front, Petra and her siblings behind them flanked by Tinom and one of the clerics, and the rest of our motley assortment of soldiers, devouts, and other miscellaneous allies all the way back to us five.

I can't help feeling a little glad that we left Baroness Sibille and a few other more prominent citizens back in Florian to continue the resistance there alongside the Black Talons. Her attitude always rubbed me the wrong way.

But any of the supporters still with us stand to gain a lot by being instrumental in putting Petra on the throne… or by preventing her and gaining Lothar's favor.

I swallow thickly. "We just have to be careful."

Rheave cranes his neck to the side to look past the riders in front of us. "What's that up ahead?"

A thick wooden post juts out of the terrain along the side of the road. As we come up on it, uneasiness creeps over my skin.

Tattered bits of what could be ruddy fabric or dried flesh cling to the splintered sides. And a rough symbol is carved into the wood near the top of the post—the All-Giver's sigil, but inverted the way the scourge sorcerers like to draw it.

I restrain a shiver and yank my gaze away.

Filip is averting his eyes too. Is that a good sign or an attempt at obscuring his true allegiances?

Our procession continues on past the post with the steady clomping of our horses' hooves. I peer at the open fields around us that stretch to distant patches of forest.

A few figures move around the farms set back from the road, but none of them glance our way. The illusion Tinom cast around us, not having enough charms to conceal us all individually, is still doing its job.

When I asked him how it works, it sounded like he's using a similar technique to one I adopted on the road with my men before. He's conjured a vague impression that there's nothing of interest right where we are and that more compelling sights lie elsewhere.

My magic twitches in my chest, reminding me that I could draw a thicker shield of invisibility around us. I have before with a small group.

Even as my power wriggles against my ribs, a flicker of movement at the edge of my vision makes my head jerk around.

There's nothing there. I haven't called on my magic in days now, but my nerves haven't stopped jumping.

When I return my attention to our group, Casimir is watching me with concern in his dark blue eyes. He's always the most alert to my mental state.

I offer him a quick smile that I hope will reassure him. What's happening to me is what it is. There's nothing he can do to heal the damage my own power has inflicted on my mind.

I'm just stretching in the saddle, wondering if it'll be time to take a brief rest stop soon, when one of the guards at the front of the procession lets out an urgent sound.

A small squad of four riders is trotting toward the crossroad we're just minutes away from, coming from our right. They wear the uniforms of royal soldiers, but one of them is flying a banner with the downward All-Giver sigil.

Order of the Wild devotees. The enemy.

Tinom motions for us all to get off the road. "Gather as closely together as you can. I'll thicken the illusion as much as I have the strength for."

Rheave shifts restlessly, eyeing the approaching soldiers. "We could overpower them."

"If they try to fight us," I say. "More likely, they'd see they're outnumbered and ride off for reinforcements."

Alek nods. "Our main advantage on this journey has been that no one knows where in the country we've gone."

We nudge the horses across the field and bunch together in as tight a cluster as they'll tolerate. Keeping an eye on Filip, I position myself near Petra and her siblings under the dour stares of her guards. Stavros follows suit, helping the guards form an inner ring around our most precious companions.

We can't let enemies beyond our ranks or within them have a chance to strike at what remains of the royal family.

To my dismay, the Order squadron turns left at the crossroads, bringing them on a course straight past us. All of us hold terribly still, our mouths clamped shut.

As they approach, my magic flares sharper, prickling all the way up to my throat. It squirms through my chest and tugs at my heart.

Why am I just sitting here? I could be blasting them to bits or cloaking us so there's no chance they'd ever notice us.

What if Tinom's abilities aren't enough?

Sweat breaks out on my skin beneath my cloak. My fingers clench around the reins, and I summon the imagery that's helped me contain my power in the past: a thick vine winding around my body.

The four riders carry on by without more than a distracted glance in our direction. The pressure in my chest gradually eases, though not without a few final pokes at my innards.

Then a small, sharp jab of retaliation sears between my ribs.

It's little more than a needle prick, there and then gone, easy to ignore. Nothing like the vicious fits that came over me in the past after years of restraining my magic.

All the same, a chill collects in my belly. Is my power already that impatient to be used again?

I can't let myself be distracted by those kinds of worries.

Suppressing a shiver, I scan the faces around me for any concerning signs—and find Petra looking back at me with a pensive expression.

Her lips curl in a brief, muted smile, but her attention doesn't feel entirely friendly. Was she thinking that I should have contributed my vast if chaotic magic to protecting her? Questioning my loyalty for not offering to?

A deeper discomfort seeps through me down to my gut. All the things she must have heard about the riven, all the attempts we've made to convince her family that I'm not a threat... What must she make of my hesitation to trust myself?

The Order's riders dwindle from view and finally vanish down the road. Without a word, Tinom beckons us back onto our course.

I nudge Toast to keep pace with Petra's steed: a black mare that's not quite as elegant as a typical queenly mount. We'll have to get the royal stables back for our future queen too.

Once we're well on our way again, I pitch my voice low so as not to draw anyone else into this particular conversation. "I hope you know that if you were in immediate danger and the only way I could protect you was with my magic, I would. I just... don't want to risk the consequences unless it's necessary. Since my going mad wouldn't be particularly good for your safety either."

Petra blinks as if startled that I brought up the subject. Maybe I misread her expression earlier.

"Of course you should moderate yourself," she says, matching my tone. "From what you've said, it's understandable both for your well-being and for our security in general. I know my father was hard on you, but I trust you to know your limits."

The thought of King Konram, of how instrumental I was in getting Lothar into a position to murder him—how close I came to murdering him myself—sends a fresh pang of guilt down the middle of me. "Thank you. You should never doubt that if I could save your life, I'll do whatever's in my power to accomplish it."

Petra glances at me again with a similar thoughtfulness in her dark eyes. "But not to save your own life?"

My throat constricts. It takes me a moment to pull together my words. "What good would it do me to save myself only to lose my sanity at the same time? At least if I protect you in the process, I'll have contributed something worthwhile. Balanced out the harm I've done a little."

A furrow forms in Petra's brow. "You know that I honestly don't blame you for what happened in Regica, don't you? That was all Lothar's doing. I've told you I understand that."

I can't keep holding her gaze. My eyes dip so I'm staring vaguely at Toast's mane. "It was still me there. My power opened the doors for him. My magic murdered loyal guards. But I won't let anything like that happen again. And whatever you need from me, you'll have it."

Petra is silent for long enough that I start to think the conversation is over. Then she speaks even more quietly than before. "It's a difficult balance, isn't it? Knowing how to act and how far to go in any direction... I can't tell you how many times I've thought back to that night when my first instinct was to pull Klaudia and Jacos away from the violence. Maybe if I'd tried, I could have stopped the bleeding..."

Her voice peters out.

I barely manage to stop myself from gaping at her. "Lothar and his sorcerer would have slaughtered *all* of you."

"I tell myself that. That must be why I acted as I did in the moment. But none of us can know for sure what the alternate outcomes could have been, can we?"

The faintest tremor ripples through her words. For the first time, I see a glimpse of the frightened girl behind the queenly façade. The nineteen-year-old who hasn't seen half as much of the world's perils as I have, who never expected to be ruling so soon, let alone in the face of a massive rebellion.

How much of her confidence does she feel, and how much is a front to maintain the authority that could so quickly slip through her fingers?

How much have my past remarks about her father's methods of ruling shaken her confidence?

I had to tell her why the people weren't leaping to support another Melchiorek—that she needed to regain their trust. It wouldn't have helped her to feign ignorance.

But in this moment, the future we're working toward feels unnervingly fragile. Petra's life isn't the only aspect of her existence we need to preserve.

As I grope for the right response, a relieved call carries back from the front of the procession. "I can see the temple! We're almost there."

Peering past the heads in front of me, I make out a pale white spire against the blue-gray sky.

Only a thin flicker of relief passes through me.

It's time to find out what reception we'll receive from this place we mean to make a sanctuary.

# Seventeen

*Ivy*

Cleric Delfis is nothing at all like I expected a devotee of Elox to be. The godlen of healing and peace casts a calming presence from every painted and carved depiction I've encountered. In fables, he makes himself known in the most subtle and gentle ways.

Delfis moves around his office in the Temple of Tranquil Skies with a jovial energy, never quite standing still. Even when he stops to peer down at the map we've been consulting, the large man cocks his head to one side and then the other while rubbing his hands together.

But strangely, there's something soothing to all that energy regardless. It reminds me of the swift but rhythmic creak of the printing press, back in my early childhood days when my parents' workshop was a comfort.

Delfis sweeps his veiny hands across the unfurled paper. His voice is brisk but reassuringly steady too. "From what you've told me, I think the sacrificial accomplices that the scourge sorcerers have manipulated could be the key to undermining their stolen authority. And they're the people who most urgently need our help. Their current lives must be a torment."

My lips twist as I think of the few mutilated accomplices I've encountered. "The scourge sorcerers keep them isolated, with only the bare necessities to live. They can barely move on their own. It's horrible."

Delfis nods, his shaggy hair that's as white as his clerical robe swaying with the movement. "We must heal them as well as we can. And when they're ready, they could speak out against the Order of the Wild. Their very existence is proof of wrongdoing."

Casimir smiles at him. "Yes, it'd be hard for Lothar to justify what his followers have done to all those people."

The courtesan's gaze slides to me with a pleased gleam. He, Stavros, and I approached the temple alone yesterday evening to evaluate how safe a haven it would actually be for our future queen. It only took one look at the cleric and one waft of Casimir's gift for him to proclaim his approval.

He told me later that night that the thing he'd seen he could do that would make Delfis happiest was telling him that he could help bring the Order of the Wild down and put a rightful ruler back on the throne. We couldn't ask for a better attitude than that.

Petra peers down at the map from where she's standing across from Delfis. "We need to *find* some of the sacrificial accomplices if we're going to rescue them. Hasn't Lothar been keeping them carefully concealed?"

"We have reason to believe that the factory of sorts where the scourge sorcerers are trapping daimon and animating their clay bodies is up north," I say. "They'd need a lot of power to accomplish that, so they must have quite a few accomplices somewhere in this area."

Delfis hums and taps a spot near the edge of the map. "I have an idea of where we could start our search. My devouts spend most of their time traveling the province, offering their services to any they find in need. Shortly after the Order of the Wild spread their uprising beyond Eppun, one devout reported seeing odd activity at a cluster of farms up here near our border with Eppun. Several carts coming and going, figures in shrouds being ushered inside. When he tried to extend a welcome, he was told off rather aggressively."

Stavros frowns. "The accomplices we've encountered in the past were shrouded—and we haven't seen anyone else working with the Order covering themselves like that. How far away are these farms?"

"Only a few hours' ride. You could be there and back within a day—or over the course of a night."

My spirits lift with a rush of my own energy, for once nothing to do with my magic. "We should go right away, then. It's about time we struck a real blow against the Order."

Delfis steps back with an air of intentness. "All action requires proper forethought, especially in a matter as fraught as this one. I need to consult with my devouts and the records I've kept to confirm the details before we proceed with a plan."

He flashes a smile at me that's almost apologetic, as if he can sense how desperately I want to make progress. "I promise it won't take very long. Your dedication to our royal family is impressive."

As he sweeps out of the room, Petra lets out a soft laugh. "At least we know he's right about one thing."

My cheeks warm with a twinge of embarrassment.

Casimir bumps his shoulder affectionately against mine. "Your enthusiasm does you credit, Kindness. We're on our way now."

I wrinkle my nose at the map. "Isn't there anything we can do *right* away other than wait?"

Every minute Lothar remains in power gnaws at me with the uncertainty of what horrors he might conjure next. What harm he might manage to inflict on the people around me.

Stavros gives my shoulder a quick squeeze. "Why don't you check up on our scholar and make sure the temple library hasn't swallowed him up? He may have found something else that'll be useful."

At Petra's encouraging smile, I peel myself away from the table. It feels like too much time has already passed since we made any real moves against the scourge sorcerers, but I don't want to rush in recklessly either.

The temple's library is located on the lowest level, a series of rooms that manage not to give the same dreary basement ambiance as the archive where my men and I used to meet at the royal college. Thin windows along the outer walls let in sunlight from their position close to the ceiling, amplified by the magic-enhanced crystal fixtures that dangle throughout the space. The white walls and soft, honey-yellow carpeting add to the bright atmosphere.

Books and scrolls pack the pale wooden bookcases built against the walls. It seems this temple has had a scholarly bent for quite some time to amass this kind of collection.

Cozy chairs with tables set next to them scatter the larger fore-room, perfect for curling up with a thrilling story. I tamp down on my own itch to peruse the shelves for folk tales or adventure novels and venture on into one of the side rooms.

I stop in the doorway, taking a moment to enjoy the view before I interrupt.

Alek sits on the smaller room's chaise lounge, the only seating available amid the many looming bookcases. He's bent over a book with tight script and yellowed pages that I can tell must be many decades if not centuries old, with other volumes and a few scrolls lying around it on the low table.

His dark waves have drifted over his forehead, but they can't disguise the passionate gleam in his bright brown eyes. His lips have parted slightly as if in awe. There's a joyful glow to his bronze skin that shines right through the mottling of his scars.

He's dressed in the plain tunic and trousers Delfis provided us all with to change from our travel-worn clothes, which hardly fits his station as a scholar of the royal college and son of a wealthy merchant. But he's never looked more handsome than here, utterly in his element.

I hate to break his reverie, but he glances up and notices me before I have to speak. A brilliant grin curves his lips. "This place is fantastic! I can't believe none of my teachers ever recommended taking a research trip here."

I amble over to the arm of the chaise and consider the assortment of books he's been browsing through. "They have texts you haven't found before—more than just temple records?"

"Oh, they are mostly records," Alek said, his usually even voice as awed as his expression. "That's probably why no one's paid attention. There are all kinds of accounts from past clerics and devouts of people throughout the province they've met—mostly to provide medical assistance, but you can learn so much about how people lived from the details woven in. I've already found several that date back to before the Darium invasion."

His main area of study before he got drawn into investigating the scourge sorcery conspiracy was Silana's history from before the Darium empire's reign.

I perch on the padded chair arm for a closer look at the book he's currently reading. "Is there anything in there that'll help us knock the scourge sorcerers on their asses?"

Alek lets out a chuckle and gives his head a rueful shake. "Not so far. But I've only just gotten started. Lothar and his followers like to talk about how they're going back to the 'old ways' and how the All-Giver wanted it to be. The more we know about how things really were in the times before the Darium empire, the better armed we'll be to challenge the Order of the Wild. I suppose that's what King Konram was thinking with his own reading."

He has a point. I'm not sure I'd want to argue even if I didn't see it.

The eagerness in his face and voice brings a swell of affection into my chest—and a sudden prickling behind my eyes.

I almost lost moments like this. I almost lost him and everyone else I care about. If my kidnapping by Lothar had ended the way the former advisor wanted it to—if he'd had his man slit my throat the other night by the guardhouse—

I still might lose everything, sooner than I'd like to think about. Because the battle is far from over, and what I said to Petra is true. I'll stretch my magic and my sanity to their limits before I let Lothar hurt her and her siblings.

A lump rises in my throat at the memories. If Lothar had succeeded in his first awful plan, my last words to Alek would have been caustic mockery.

I touch the scholar's cheek and brush my thumb over the ridged skin that's as much a part of this extraordinary man as his beautiful eyes and warm smile. "I can't think of anyone better to do the challenging. I love seeing you like this. Do you have any idea how gorgeous you are right now? You should get to immerse yourself in old books all the time rather than having to run around across the countryside."

A blush adds a ruddy tint to Alek's cheeks. He ducks his head a little bashfully, but his tone stays light. "So that I can be more pleasing to the eyes?"

I laugh and lean over so I can kiss his temple. "So all that brilliance inside you can shine through in every possible way. I didn't fall in love with you for your looks, as much as I appreciate them too."

A rough note escapes Alek's throat, and then he's tugging me off the chaise's arm, onto his lap.

As my pulse hitches giddily, he cups my face between his hands. He holds my gaze with a hotter light flaring in his eyes. "The books aren't the only thing I want to 'immerse myself' in."

I can't help arching my eyebrows. "Oh, no?"

He teases one hand down to my neck, the other dipping all the way to the hem of my tunic. His fingers splay against the bare skin of my waist beneath, and I lean into his touch instinctively.

"I want to learn everything there is to know about you," he murmurs, his voice gone rough. "Every thought that passes through your head. I want to read every piece of your history that's etched on your body."

His thumb strokes over my collarbone by the neckline of my shirt. "How you got this scar." His other hand finds a mark over my ribs that he must have noticed before. "When you were burned. All the stories in you, even the painful ones."

All at once, I feel naked, even though he hasn't removed a piece of clothing.

How much has he already learned that I haven't told him, just by observing the remnants of my past scrapes and wounds? It can't all be good.

In my awkwardness, my stance tenses, and Alek must feel it. He draws me closer into a full embrace, tipping his face up toward mine. "But most of all, I want to discover everything there is to know about making you happy."

He bobs up to claim a kiss. The press of his lips is sweet enough to erase any momentary insecurities his comments stirred up.

"I love you," he whispers between one kiss and the next. "No matter what happens, I'll always love you."

My heart skips again with a bittersweet pang. He knows me well enough already to have guessed at my insecurities—and answered them with more devotion than I'd ever have dared to ask for.

I shift on his lap to straddle him and kiss him back hard. As our mouths meld together and our tongues tangle, the fondness that filled my chest before flares into a sharper desire.

The same emotion must grip Alek too, because he grasps my hip to center me against his groin and rocks up to meet me to the most delightful effect. As I gasp against his mouth, he fondles one of my breasts with his other hand, making full use of the access granted by my simple temple clothes.

The friction between us leaves me tingling. Every want leaves my head except one.

I nip the corner of his jaw and roll my hips against his. "I need you inside me."

With a groan, Alek yanks at my trousers. As I kick them off, he unfastens his own.

I delve my hand beneath the fabric to stroke his cock up and down. He bucks into my fingers, his gaze burning into mine with an intoxicating mix of adoration and lust.

When he grazes his fingertips over my sex in turn, my breath spills out of me in an eager shudder. My gaze lifts of its own accord toward the doorway to the main library room.

Alek catches my thought before I have to speak it. He lines me up over him, dipping his fingers into the growing slickness of my channel. "I don't care if someone stumbles on us. Loving you isn't shameful any more than loving my studies is."

I laugh, and then he's claiming me again, with both his mouth capturing mine and his cock thrusting up into my body. The confidence he's gained over the past few months is so thrilling I quake with the pleasure that shoots through my nerves.

I sink down on him to take him even deeper, and he kisses me with so much passion my head spins. As we buck together, bliss builds inside me with an unexpected sense of urgency.

Every moment we have together could be shattered. Everything we do hangs in a precarious balance.

But we have each other to hold on to, whatever happens. I never knew how much that fact would matter to me until it became true.

Alek swivels one thumb over my nipple while stroking my clit with the other. At my gasp, he increases the pressure, thrusting faster at the same time.

My head drops beside his, our cheeks pressed together. His breath spills hot down my neck.

"Stay with me," he rasps, as if I'd ever purposefully go anywhere else.

My answer comes out in a mumble. "Always."

I don't know if I can keep that promise, but as I careen into the blaze of my orgasm and feel Alek's chest hitch in tandem, it almost feels possible.

# Eighteen

*Ivy*

I know the woman in charge herself has come to meet us when the cloaked figure approaching through the dusk raises a thumbless hand.

"Ivy," Voleska says in a low voice. "I wasn't sure if I'd ever see you again. I'm glad my doubts were wrong."

She steps into the shadows that drape the front of the shuttered shop where Casimir, one of the loyal soldiers, and I are standing. This small town about halfway between the Temple of Tranquil Skies and Voleska's home city of Pima is quiet enough that it seems to have been mostly ignored by the Order of the Wild. But a few patrons are still coming and going from the pub down the street with bursts of spirited voices.

The corner of my mouth quirks upward with a wry smile. "I'm glad too. And it's good to see you've survived the last several weeks as well."

Voleska dips her head to Casimir in acknowledgment. "I hope the rest of your crew has made it through all right?"

I think of the men I left on the other side of the Eppun border with a mix of fondness and worry. "For now. We're doing our best to stay that way. Is Emor well?"

A note of affection comes into her voice. I've never been sure of her exact relationship with her partner, but it's clearly close. "Oh, yes, and spitting mad that I'm getting to have this adventure without him."

My smile tugs wider. "You can apologize to him for that on my behalf. Thank you for coming all this way to speak with us. We didn't think going right into Nikodi would be wise."

The co-leader of the main resistance group in Julita's former county lets out her breath with a hint of a huff. "A reasonable suspicion. Ever since King Konram's death, the Order members have gotten even bolder. We've shaken them up as well as we can, but it's harder to rally more people against them when there's no clear alternative."

It seems word about Petra's speech in Florian hasn't reached the far edges of the country yet.

I hesitate, glancing at Casimir. His nod reassures me that he hasn't seen any sign that Voleska's goals have shifted.

She's always been just as dedicated to ousting the scourge sorcerers from her country as we have.

I fold my arms loosely over my chest. "What if I told you that we do have an alternative? That it's just a matter of clearing the way so they can safely retake the throne?"

Voleska's pale eyebrows leap up. "What have you got up your sleeve now?"

"The king's heirs didn't die. We have a queen ready to rule, if we can present her without the scourge sorcerers murdering her too."

I don't get into the specifics of exactly who that queen is, since explaining about the former Prince Dunstam's transformation and period in hiding would get a little complicated. We can fill Voleska and her allies in on the details when it's relevant.

Voleska's eyes have widened. She rubs the stump of her thumb along her jaw, beneath the scar on her cheek that speaks of past troubles she's survived.

I don't think her life before the uprising was that much more comfortable than my own on the streets. And I can't imagine what it was like to give up a chunk of her hand and receive no gift in return—to be a child of twelve realizing the gods had judged your intentions as too selfish.

Even without magic, she's proven to be a formidable force. No matter what hardships she's faced before, she's risen to the challenge of protecting her home.

"That's a very good thing," she says in an awed voice. "I should have figured you'd end up in the royal court with all the stubborn heroics you're fond of. What is it that you think our people can do to help?"

The fact that she leaps straight to offering to get involved is one of the reasons I wanted to reach out to her. When we crossed paths with the resistors in Pima weeks ago, *they* approached us rather than the other way around, eager to strengthen their efforts against the Order of the Wild.

Voleska's group is nothing if not dedicated.

My men and I found solid allies during our journeys across the country, even while we were fugitives. And now I can use that luck to Petra's benefit.

We need to gather as large a resistance as we can, stretching across the entire country, if we're going to effectively challenge Lothar's self-appointed authority.

I pull my posture a little straighter. "We're hoping to undermine the scourge sorcerers' power and expose the crimes they've committed at the same time. There's a farm a couple of hours from here where the Order appears to be hiding several of their sacrificial accomplices. We want to steal them away, and it'll be easier with assistance."

Casimir speaks up in his normal, warm tone. "And I'm sure we'll have plenty of future missions we'd appreciate your people joining us for afterward, if they're on board."

Voleska rubs her hands together. "Anything to stick it to the Order and see them finally knocked on their asses. When do we get started?"

I peer through the thickening dusk behind her. We were hoping to act as early as tonight. But as far as I can tell, she came alone, even though the message we passed on mentioned that we'd welcome more of her colleagues to "collaborate" with us.

"I guess that depends on how long it'll take you to get a decent force out here—"

The resistance leader chuckles. "Oh, you don't need to worry about that. I've got a dozen friends waiting on my word right here in town. Didn't want to have them all stick their necks out until I knew what the story was."

Relief sharpened by a tingle of excitement sweeps through me. "Fair enough. We can descend on the farm tonight if you're up for it. The rest of our people are waiting across the border, closer to our target—we already have a plan worked out." With multiple options depending on whether we brought anyone back with us and how many.

Voleska nods and motions to the far end of the road. "We'll meet you on the southern road at the edge of town in ten minutes."

I hold up my hand to stop her. "You know, I realize you and Emor have a lot you're dealing with back in Pima. I didn't expect that you'd pitch in here personally."

"Oh, I'm not missing this. And I'd like to see with my own eyes who all I'm sending my people to work with." Voleska flashes us a grin and darts off down the street.

When I look at Casimir, he's smiling. "I don't think anyone could be more committed than she is." He motions to the soldier who's stayed still and silent during our conversation, only there to intervene in case of a threat. "Come, let's get to the horses."

By the time a distant bell has rung in the second hour after midnight, some twenty of us are clustered in a patch of forest just down the road from the farm Delfis directed us to.

One of the temple's devouts who has a gift for calming nerves has come along to help ease the sacrificial accomplices through what's technically a kidnapping. Four of the soldiers stand among us, along with Stavros and Rheave—and Voleska's dozen resistors. The plan would have been a lot harder to pull off without them in the mix.

Petra almost insisted on joining us, but between Stavros, Tinom, and me, we managed to convince her that ensuring she stays *alive* overrides any concerns about sharing the risks in our mission. She has several guards with her back at the temple.

Tinom's magic will conceal her if there's any significant trouble—and hopefully protect Alek as well. Although he could probably lose himself amid the books in the temple library without any trouble. I wouldn't be surprised if he's still down there reading by lantern-light right now.

Being the one among us most experienced at running military-style operations, Stavros has taken the lead. He's already spoken with Voleska's people to get an idea of their strengths and is now splitting our group into four.

He points at two of the groups. He assigned Filip to one of them, presumably to keep the Order defector and possible traitor away from the most essential parts of the plan. "You and you will go to the left and right of the farmhouse, staying several paces from the walls. Set the fires and keep out of view until our enemies come running to see what the matter is. Disarm and disable them however you see fit."

The former general swivels toward Casimir, one of the soldiers, and a couple of Voleska's leaner followers. "You four will get the wagon into place and come forward to help usher the sacrificial accomplices over there."

He turns to face the rest of us, including me, Rheave, and the devout with the calming gift. "I'll be leading the final group right into the building. We'll deal with any other sorcerers on the premises and retrieve the sacrificial accomplices. They'll be distracted by the fires, but that doesn't mean we should be careless. The faster we can take them down before they realize we're there, the better."

I nod, my heart thudding. My magic wriggles between my ribs and tugs at my gut, but I squash it down.

I've pulled off plenty of schemes like this without relying on it before. If I'm going to risk my sanity, it's not going to be to enhance my stealth skills.

Stavros makes a sweeping motion with his prosthetic hand. "Move out."

Along with a few of Voleska's best fighters and the rest of our soldiers, I follow Stavros through the trees and skirt the edge of the forest until we're directly across from the farmhouse. There's still about a minute's dash across open ground from here to the farm's low stone wall.

Moonlight casts a faint glow over the terrain. A few dark figures prowl around the property's perimeter.

Stavros drops his voice to a murmur. "As soon as the fires flare, we run for the wall, two at a time, on my signal. Stay low and as quiet as possible."

I wet my lips, anticipation thrumming through my veins.

All at once, flames burst through the darkness to the left of the house. An instant later, another fire roars up on the opposite side.

Shouts ring out as the house's sentries dash to investigate. A few more figures hustle out of the building to join them.

Stavros taps Rheave and me. I fling myself out of the woods.

We dash across the grassy ground and the road that lies between the forest and the farm. More shouts carry through the night along with clangs and thumps of combat, but I don't let myself glance either way.

All that matters right now is the path ahead of us.

We hit the ground on either side of the gate, crouching below the level of the wall. As more figures careen to join us, I pull the knife from the sheath at my waist.

Stavros arrives last and gestures for us to fall in with him as he eases open the gate. We dart along the path through the now-empty yard to the front door.

The hinges squeak at Stavros's push. I wince inwardly.

"What's going on out there?" someone calls from up the stairs. They must assume it's their comrades returning.

My power flares in my chest as abruptly as the flames outside, and I lose a couple of seconds as I tighten my hold around it. My fist clenches, pressing against my chest.

A brief lance of pain shoots through my lungs, and I have to suck in a breath against a gasp.

Most of my companions have already rushed forward. Rheave shoots a crackling arrow up the staircase, and a body crumples against the banister.

Stavros prowls down the lower hallway. As he lunges into a room, two of Voleska's people hurry to follow him while the other creeps up the stairs alongside Rheave.

From the muffled grunts and groans that follow, they're taking down any remaining scourge sorcerers with brisk efficiency. Recovered from the momentary backlash of my magic, I motion the devout over to the narrower staircase I spot leading down through a gloomy doorway.

"This way," I whisper. "The accomplices might be in the cellar."

And so might more scourge sorcerers. I keep my knife in my hand as we slink down the stairs, my ears pricked for any sound in the space beyond.

There's a door at the bottom, keeping whatever's below shut away. My skin crawls.

We've almost reached it when the scuff of footsteps above has me spinning around. A woman who isn't one of our companions is just poking her head through the doorway.

She hisses at the sight of us and jerks her hands as if to direct some kind of magic. But my hand moves faster.

My knife whips through the air and plunges straight into her throat.

As our attacker collapses at the top of the stairs, the devout pales. Obviously I should be the one to deal with the body on our way out.

I test the doorknob and find it turns smoothly. I push it open to reveal a wide, dark room where cots and the figures lying on them form only vague impressions in the darkness.

I've already snatched my other knife from my boot, but no one springs at us. A couple of the figures stir beneath their sheets.

Carefully, the devout lights the small lantern sitting on the floor just inside the doorway. The flickering glow illuminates eight sleeping figures who don't react to the light at all.

Of course not. They've all sacrificed their eyes along with so much else.

"Start waking them and guiding them up the stairs," I murmur to the devout. "You'll probably need to tell them that they're being called on to serve their great purpose or something like that. I'll clear the way and come back to help you."

At his nod, I clamber up the stairs. At least with their blindness, I only have to move the fallen body out of tripping distance, not out of view.

As I wipe my retrieved knife on the woman's tunic, Stavros barges back into the front hall. He takes in the scene with an approving tip of his head.

"The rest of the house is clear," he says.

I point to the cellar stairs. "We found the sacrificial accomplices—I'm going to help bring them up."

"I'll make sure you can get to the wagon safely."

I dash down to the cellar to find that the devout has already roused all of the sacrificial accomplices. They went to sleep wearing their shrouds, but the fall of the fabric reveals the misshapen forms beneath. They're sitting up, a few getting to their feet, mumbling with confusion.

A quiver in the air tells me the devout is employing his calming magic. I try to pitch my voice to be as soothing as possible too. "Come on now, everyone. Let's get up the stairs, and you'll accomplish everything you could have wanted to."

I have to help a couple of the armless forms stand up. They stumble toward the stairs, all of them missing something from their lower extremities, whether merely toes or an entire lower leg.

With my hand on one of the mutilated backs, I support the accomplice's balance going up the steps, then hustle back down to assist another.

A choked sound reaches my ears from above. When I return, I find one of Voleska's people staring at the lurching procession with her fingers pressed to her lips.

I offer her a tight smile. "This is why we're here. Why we're fighting. To make sure this doesn't keep happening."

She draws herself straighter and swipes at the glint of tears in her eyes before catching an accomplice in mid-lurch. "Let me get you out the door. There's a comfortable wagon waiting."

"Anything to serve," the accomplice mumbles. The devotion in his little-used voice makes my throat constrict.

"You've done so well already," I tell him, not knowing what else to say.

Just beyond the farm's gate, Casimir greets the accomplices with much more grace than I'm capable of. "Thank you for joining us. We're going to ask that you climb up here in the wagon—that's right. I'm sorry for the sudden visit, but what you're going to do is so important for Silana."

I step back, letting him and the devout take over. Gentle reassurance has never been my forte.

The rest of our group gathers around the wagon, returning from their initial posts. One of Voleska's men is wrapping a bandage around a shallow gash on his arm, and a couple of the soldiers are sporting bruises on their jaws, but it looks like we got through the assault without any major injuries.

That thought has just passed through my head when an arc of light flashes through the air toward the edge of our group.

I don't have time to do much more than sense the vicious tang of the magic in that energy and react. No blade can stop that killing bolt.

I thrust out my arm with a surge of my magic.

Training and practice come through—even as I swat at the conjured attack, my mind reaches toward the wood we left and visualizes a branch being pulled toward me in the reverse of how I'm pushing the assault away.

Wood cracks, and the arc of light bursts apart into a shower of sparks.

They dissolve in the air just inches from the faces of the two men they nearly struck. The soldier takes a step back with a grimace, his eyes flicking to me with an almost accusing look as if I'm somehow to blame for the initial attack.

Filip gapes at the spot where the attack fizzled out before his gaze slides to me too.

"It would have killed me," he says. "I hardly saw it coming."

I inhale slowly, my body tensed for any sign that this one jab of magic has addled my mind. "I want us all leaving this place as unharmed as I can manage."

Was it worth the trade-off? I don't know. But faced with the question, I can't imagine standing back and letting two men simply die to preserve some small shred of my sanity.

Even if the soldier is still eyeing me like I might explode at any second.

A twinge of queasiness passes through me. How long will it take before Petra's followers from Florian pass on what they've heard about me to Voleska's people?

It doesn't matter, I tell myself. What matters is that I'm here, doing what's right for the country, whatever they end up thinking of me.

Rheave has already charged off in the direction the attack was flung from. There's a sizzling noise before he lets out a resolute grunt. "That sorcerer is *definitely* not hurting anyone else now."

Casimir shoots me a concerned glance from where he's guiding the last of the sacrificial accomplices into the wagon, and I smile in return to say I'm okay. Then I clamp down on the rest of the power squirming inside me.

Just a small push. Not that big a deal, and I controlled the consequences. I saved a couple of lives.

But I never want to get back into the habit of using it for anything I don't absolutely have to.

Voleska sets her hands on her hips, watching the devout pull the curtains shut on the back of the wagon. "Well, hopefully this'll put a little dent in the Order's influence. I wonder if it'll affect Lothar's festival plans?"

My head jerks around. "Festival plans?"

She cocks her head with a swing of her sandy blond ponytail. "Hadn't you heard? The Order of the Wild's been announcing it all over the place in the past couple of days. On the next full moon just a few nights from now, he's holding a country-wide party to celebrate King Konram's death."

# NINETEEN

The soft rasp of footsteps brings my head up from the book I've been poring over. A twinge of pain shoots down my neck from the cramped posture I've held.

In my research fervor, I've been letting the good scholarly habits I learned in school and under my former mentor slide. I can almost hear one of the professors at Sovereign College chiding me. *A healthy sitting position is essential to keep the body sound for long hours of reading in future years.*

Maybe if my current line of inquiry didn't feel so urgent, I'd find that maxim easier to remember.

The footsteps come to a stop at the doorway of the inner library room. Ivy peers inside with Casimir gazing over her shoulder. Ivy looks a little pensive, but the courtesan offers a smile sunny enough that I don't think there's any reason to worry.

At least, not any more than we already had.

"Can you put the books aside for a little while?" Ivy asks, a softer smile touching her own lips. "We figured it was about time you got some lunch into you."

"And that you might appreciate some company for that lunch after all the time you've spent tucked away down here," Casimir adds.

Before I can answer in words, my stomach rumbles, which I suppose is answer enough. With a bashful laugh, I get to my feet. "Thank you. My body is reminding me that I shouldn't neglect it while I'm filling my head."

Out of consideration for the many fragile documents in the library, my companions have set up their sort-of picnic on a low folding table in the fore-room at the bottom of the basement stairs. None of the books are kept there, only a small hearth and a few armchairs set along the walls for casual readers.

Stavros and Rheave are waiting for us, Stavros pouring out a ruddy juice into the glasses. He offers me a crooked grin. "I'd have brought wine, but I suspected you'd want to keep your thoughts as unmuddled as possible."

Warmth forms in my chest at his recognition of and respect for my priorities. "That I do. Thank you."

As I sit at one end of the table with Ivy and Casimir sinking down to complete the group, the warmth expands into a sense of total contentment. It's a strange emotion to be feeling when we're up against a country-wide conspiracy of sadistic sorcerers, but I can't bear to dismiss it.

I've never had anything like this before—the kind of connection where you know you can count on each other no matter what you're facing. Where you know you're appreciated for who you are, not some task or favor that's going to be asked of you.

My lover and my friends wanted to have lunch with me and make sure I knew they cared. I don't know what kind of thanks could possibly express how much that means to me.

As is typical in the temple, the meal is simple fare but fresh: a salad of local greens, bread still warm from the oven, butter and cheese from the temple sheep—one of Elox's symbolic animals. Every bite is deliciously tart or creamy.

As Rheave devours his own portion gleefully, he studies me from across the table. He pauses in between bites. "Have you found out anything interesting in all these books?"

I glance toward the stack I left behind with a regretful grimace. "Nothing in much detail so far, but I have a lot more to get through. And I suppose we don't really know that Lothar will draw on actual historic rites with his new festival."

Stavros hums. "It would make sense if he did at least a little, to give his 'celebration' an air of legitimacy. He might be a treacherous prick, but he's a clever one."

Ivy makes a face of disgust. "Yes, why invent a tribute to murder from scratch if you can simply borrow traditions from centuries ago?"

"Not just that." Casimir's voice is gentle but steady. "He may very well believe in his ideals of getting back to the 'old ways' and restoring the All-Giver, as awful as his methods are. In that case, it would make sense for him to incorporate as many of those old ways as he can."

And that's exactly why I've spent the past two days digging through every record from before the Darium invasion that I can find. The more we can anticipate what Lothar might enact with his soon-approaching festival, the more ideas we'll have of how we can disrupt or make use of it to our own ends.

"I've found a few references that might point me in the right direction," I say. "As soon as I find anything I think we should take into account, I'll let you know."

Ivy rests her hand on my arm. "We still have time. And if we can't find anything that could help prepare us, we'll just have to go and see it all with our own eyes. We've come up with pretty good plans in the moment before."

We have, but I'd rather we went in prepared.

Once the meal is done and the remnants gathered, Ivy tugs me close for a quick kiss before following the other men upstairs. I return to my work with both my heart and my stomach full.

One avenue of research that's been somewhat fruitful has been the oldest treatment records I've been able to unearth. I've come across an account of a patient treated by the temple devouts for a chemical burn it was hinted had something to do with a local celebration and another of a broken ankle sustained during a large-scale rumpus.

If any of those long-ago devouts were wordier in their accounts, I might get more details about exactly what those festivities and games entailed.

I finish paging through the book I was in the middle of and pick up another journal with handwriting so faded I find myself squinting even with the lantern near my shoulder. That volume does turn up another account of a similar burn, which the writer notes comes from a dye that's apparently splashed around for reasons he doesn't mention.

As I read, I jot down a few notes that I'm gradually assembling into a somewhat coherent picture.

The next book proves to be both incredibly brief in its notes and half-written in some private notation I can't interpret. The volume I reach for after that I handle especially gingerly, careful of the flaking leather cover that drew me to it where it was buried at the back of a shelf.

It's old enough that even the periodic waves of preservation magic cast through the library couldn't totally protect it from the passage of time.

I'm several pages in when my eyes catch on the word *riven*.

The Temple of Tranquil Skies had dealings with a riven sorcerer? That isn't likely to relate to Lothar's impending festival, but I can't help slowing my skimming to give this section a closer read.

In less than a minute, my heart is pounding as if I've just run up ten flights of stairs. A sickly flush creeps over my skin with each sentence I read.

*Patient exhibited a magical gift that wasn't part of his dedication sacrifice... An unearthly voice spoke in his head... Caught up in the destruction that spread out to overwhelm those practicing the most illicit sorcery...*

The details collide with my memory of the ancient diary I found at the Haven, written by some long ago riven sorcerer. The one where the writer claimed the gods had torn open their soul not in punishment but to use them as a tool.

I take in all of the account before me and then hurriedly page farther into the book. There are three more cases mentioned involving riven who arrived at the temple for healing.

Each of them only expands my sense of horror.

When I've reached the end of the journal, I double-check the dates and then return to the shelves, yanking out volumes to check them and shoving most back into place. Finally I get my hands on a couple of other books with records of the earliest riven sorcerers, though only one each and not as detailed as the first.

I set those on my stack of reading material and clutch the original journal to my chest. This is the best evidence I have—and all I should really need.

As I stride through the library to the stairs, my pulse keeps racing. My throat has constricted.

It was so long ago—the truth of the situation must have been forgotten, lost with those who lived all those centuries before. I can't blame any of the temple's current staff for being unaware. But now that I've come across the proof...

Exposing it widely will have to wait until we've dealt with the scourge sorcerers, but as soon as that threat is over, all of Silana—all of the abandoned realms—ought to know how wrong they've been.

I head straight to Delfis's office, though I watch for Ivy and my friends along the way. They must be off putting together plans that don't require my academic skills.

That's all right. Delfis should put his authority behind the first announcement. Ivy will believe me, and the other men who've stood with her through so much will, but for the rest of our motley resistance?

I've heard the uneasy whispers, seen the suspicious glances. They need to realize that Ivy's magic isn't any kind of crime.

It was clerics and devouts of Elox who helped the first riven sorcerers. I can't imagine Delfis reading these accounts and seeing Ivy as a monster.

Unfortunately, I find Delfis's office empty. He's got his own work to see to, after all.

Stewing in my discovery, I pace through the temple's halls—and spot Tinom sitting at a table in one of the common rooms, writing a letter.

My spirits lift. Having the magic advisor vouch for this revelation could be even better than the cleric of a single temple. And he's already accepted Ivy as Petra's ally and friend.

As I bustle into the room, Tinom lifts his head. Concern flashes across his face.

He gets up from his chair to meet me. "What is it?"

I hold up my free hand. "Nothing to do with the current scourge sorcerers. But incredibly important all the same. I can't believe—the knowledge has been lost in the library clutter all this time—"

Tinom pats my upper arm, peering at me with his deep-set eyes. He's shorter than I am and even slimmer, but the gravity of his presence makes him feel larger all the same. "Calm yourself and tell me what's bothering you."

"It's not exactly bothering…" I brandish the medical journal. "I found a book with records of patients treated here at the temple all the way back during the Great Retribution. The devout who wrote it witnessed some of the events firsthand and spoke to other witnesses. It proves that we've been completely mistaken about the riven."

Tinom's eyebrows shoot up. "How so?"

I have to fight to keep myself from babbling in my urgency. "They're not a punishment the All-Giver inflicted on humanity for daring to attempt scourge sorcery. They were vessels chosen by the gods themselves to channel divine power! No one's ever really explained how the gods managed to rain down all that hail and fire when standard theology states that the godlen can only encourage people and other creatures to follow their will, not act directly on the mortal world. I always assumed the All-Giver's power allowed it under desperate circumstances."

The magic advisor's expression hasn't shifted, but his stance has stiffened. "Vessels," he repeats. "What exactly do you mean by that?"

I wave the journal. "The first riven felt their souls torn open and heard divine voices telling them their service was needed to punish those who threatened the gods. Then magic rushed through them —calling down the hail, sparking the fires, shattering the buildings… And once the Great Retribution was finished, their souls stayed open like that—like a conduit. The devouts here tried to heal them, but they had no idea what to do."

"Perhaps it was a punishment as well then, that the gods let the effect linger."

I frown. "That wouldn't make sense, unless we believe the All-Giver and the godlen are purposefully cruel. Why would they punish the people who helped them the most? As far as we know, they never imposed their will on any person that strongly before… It could be that there simply was no way to reverse it."

Tinom holds out his hand, and I offer the journal automatically. He flips through a few pages. "This is all really conjecture."

"I don't think you'd see it that way if you read the accounts. The way the patients describe what happened to them, the witnesses confirming that they never displayed gifts like this before—none of them had any significant madness yet despite being adults."

Another memory flashes to the front of my mind. "Ivy's even told us—when Kosmel talked to her last, he said something about making up for the damage the gods have done. We didn't understand what he was referring to. He must have meant her being riven at all!"

Tinom grunts. He drifts through the room, still considering the journal, and stops by the hearth.

I only have an instant for panic to kick in before he's tossed the aged book into the flames.

A yelp bursts from my lips. I throw myself forward, already reaching toward the fire, ready to burn my hands as badly as my face if I can retrieve the precious pages.

Tinom steps in front of me and shoves me backward. I trip over my feet and only catch myself on a side table just in time to avoid landing on my ass.

When I launch myself at him again, this time he eases aside. But we both gaze into the fire to see the book has already disintegrated into embers.

"What in the realms are you doing?" I demand, my voice rasping up my throat. "We needed that book to prove—"

Tinom speaks with an unsettling calm. "There's nothing to prove. All we had was potentially biased reports and speculation."

"Biased reports? Those were eyewitnesses to the catastrophe—at the very least, they confirm that the first riven weren't born that way. They were transformed directly by the gods for a purpose. We could have had clerics appeal to the gods for further signs to support—"

"To what end?" Tinom asks quietly.

I stare at him for a moment before I recover my words through my rage. "How can you even ask that? So we can tell the world that people like Ivy don't deserve to be shunned. There's nothing shameful about how they came to be. They should be helped, not executed."

The magic advisor lets out a soft huff. "It sounds to me as if you're thinking with your groin rather than your brain, young man. If you weren't entwined with one of the riven, would you even care?"

The accusation stings because it comes with a jab of guilt. I can't say the subject would matter quite as much to me if Ivy wasn't in my life. But all the same...

"Perhaps I wouldn't care as urgently, but I would still want the truth to be known. They aren't criminals. They don't deserve what they've faced. If we were prepared to help them adapt to their riven souls rather than executing them on discovery, they might make this world *better* rather than worse."

Tinom shrugs. "There are far fewer of them now than there ever were. The fear runs deep. Telling people a thing can't erase their ingrained emotions. We're dealing with enough troubles without confusing all Silana's people over their beliefs, making them feel guilty for a past they can't change."

I have to pry my gritted teeth apart. "What about the people who'll keep getting hurt? You'd consign Ivy to that fate after everything she's done for the kingdom?"

Tinom fixes me with a look so unwavering it sends a chill coursing under my skin. "I accept your paramour because she's amply proven that, *for now,* she has her magic under control, and because she could make the difference between seeing the Melchioreks retake the throne and letting Lothar win. That doesn't mean I trust her for more than the next few days."

As I grope for an effective retort, he spins on his heel. "If you care about peace in Silana, you won't mention what you just told me to anyone. Not even your lover."

He stalks out of the room, leaving his last statement ringing in my ears like a threat.

# TWENTY

*Ivy*

When I come up beside Cleric Delfis by the doorway of one of the treatment rooms, he dips his head in a brief nod and returns to watching the patients inside. An air of sadness hangs over the normally buoyant man.

After I glance into the room, it's not hard to see what's deflated his spirits.

The eight sacrificial accomplices are sitting or lying on the simple but comfortable beds they've been given. A couple of devouts are moving between them, talking to them in soothing tones. One is bringing around glasses of water that she helps each figure drink from. Another rubs a salve into a scar on a man's knee.

The accomplices' mutilations are on full display, the shrouds removed so the temple's people can tend to these poor souls effectively. I have to gird myself against a grimace of revulsion.

It isn't fair to recoil from the marred faces with their blank sockets for eyes and pared off ears and noses. To want to cringe at the sight of their warped bodies, missing both arms to the shoulders, pieces of legs, and more beneath the surface of their uneven chests.

As I watch, one of the figures lurches to her feet. "This isn't where we're supposed to be," she rasps out. "We need to help—we need to give over our power—"

One of the devouts hustles to her side and guides her back down on the bed. His voice trembles a little as he rubs the stump of her shoulder. "Hey there. This is the best place you could possibly be. Once you're completely well, you'll be able to help set Silana back on the right course, just as you wanted."

But not the way the scourge sorcerers claimed was needed.

I swallow the lump that's risen in my throat and glance at Delfis, keeping my own voice low. "How much have they been told?"

The cleric pulls his large frame away from the doorway and rakes a hand through his shaggy hair, which is even messier than usual. "I won't have my devouts lie to them. Elox believes that honesty can heal. But we've avoided getting into many specifics so far. They're still experiencing a lot of distress about their situation. It seems to upset them to be taken care of with kindness. How they must have been treated before…"

My throat tightens further. "I know. It's horrible. Back in Florian, potential accomplices were being recruited from an orphanage—kids who had no family, groomed to be willing sacrifices for what was supposed to be a great and urgent cause."

Delfis winces in horror. I find myself adding, even though I'm not sure it'll make a cleric of Elox feel better, "The man who orchestrated those particular sacrifices is dead. I made sure of it."

He nods and doesn't ask how. I'd imagine he'd rather not know.

Will there be a time when I admit to this kindly man the truth about my own magic? Would he accept my riven soul as easily as he has these broken bodies, or would he recoil from me like so many others have?

I'm not sure *I* want to know the answer to that question.

Delfis sighs. "They have a long way to come. But this *is* the best possible place for them to find the healing they need. I'll have to meditate on how to make the rest of their existence as comfortable and fulfilling as it can be."

It's hard to imagine how they could have much of a life in their current state. But if anyone can help them, I believe it's Delfis.

I shift my weight, already suspecting what answer I'll get to the main question I came to ask. "The 'Festival of Freedom' is happening in just two days. Do you think any of them would be in a steady enough state to speak on our behalf then?"

The cleric's mouth twists apologetically. "I wish I could give you hope, but I have to say it's highly unlikely. Another disruption when they're having so much trouble settling in here would only set back their recovery. You wouldn't want them speaking in favor of the scourge sorcerers or lashing out at the queen's supporters anyway."

"We wouldn't," I agree, and suppress a sigh of my own. "There were a few other sacrificial accomplices we rescued from a brothel in Pima weeks ago. Voleska is looking into whether any of them are stable enough that they could speak for our cause. If not… we'll find other ways."

Delfis shoots me a smile that makes me feel twice as guilty about the secrets I'm keeping from him. "Make sure you're getting enough rest yourself. Those who work the hardest need the most time to recover."

"Of course." I manage a strained smile in return.

I head straight toward the room where we've been having our strategy sessions, passing the guest dormitories where we've been sleeping on the way.

Halfway down the hall, Alek emerges from a doorway. He jerks to a halt at the sight of me and holds out his hand to beckon me over.

The scholar's expression looks so haunted that my stomach lurches. I hurry to his side. "What's wrong?"

He takes my arm and guides me into the dormitory. No one else is in there at the moment, though the rumpled covers from this morning have been straightened by the temple staff.

Alek gazes into my eyes for a moment before his head droops. He seems to gather himself, his jaw flexing. Then he raises his chin again. "I found out something. Something I could get in trouble for telling you. But I think you need to know."

Anxiety coils around my gut. "What? Who would you be in trouble with?" It's hard to imagine anything putting us in more personal jeopardy than the scourge sorcerers already have.

Alek exhales in a ragged rush and takes my arm again. He strokes his thumb over my skin as he speaks. "Back at the Haven, I found a journal written by one of the very early riven that said some incredible things. I didn't know whether to believe the story or whether it was only madness, but just a few hours ago, I found records in the temple library that corroborate the account."

My mouth goes dry. This is something about my magic?

Something *bad?*

I force myself to respond. "What exactly did they say?"

"The gist of it is that… being riven isn't a punishment the gods inflicted after the Great Retribution. The first riven souls weren't born in the aftermath. The godlen themselves, and maybe the All-Giver too, broke through the souls of people who were already living so that they could funnel their power through those people and rain down justice on the original scourge sorcerers."

I stare at Alek for a few thuds of my heart before everything he's said sinks in. "The gods *needed* us to be riven? They made people that way to act on their *behalf?*"

Alek dips his head, his expression still fraught. "I know it sounds crazy—but it also makes so much sense when you think about how the gods normally interact with the mortal world, how little they usually can. And there are the things Kosmel said to you about not wanting to make your situation worse than the gods already have… It all adds up."

I press my hand to my forehead as if I can steady my thoughts that way. "But—why haven't the godlen made the truth clear? Delivered some kind of message to the clerics? Stopped people from hunting us down?"

"I don't know," Alek says quietly. "Maybe after the fact, when they realized they couldn't heal the souls they'd fractured, they thought the riven and their descendants *would* provide a useful warning to the rest of humanity. But that doesn't mean any of you deserve to be seen as monsters. I think it matters that the riven started out protecting the continent, not destroying it. The gods didn't create you as a test or warning but as… as accomplices."

A bitter laugh I can't contain spills out of me. "Even if we've destroyed an awful lot since then?"

"It isn't your fault." Alek lifts his hand to cup my cheek. "People like you gave the gods the means to stop the worst kind of brutal magic before it went too far. They used those people and then couldn't fix what they'd broken, so they abandoned you even more than the All-Giver abandoned the rest of us. We should be working with all of the riven to make up for those mistakes, not driving you to desperation and then executing you for it."

He speaks so emphatically that I can't doubt how much he means the words. Tears well up behind my eyes.

What would the world look like if instead of everyone living in fear of the riven, believing that all of them need to be caught as soon as possible and slaughtered, they watched for signs of the power in their children out of caring instead? Gave them training like what Sulla offered me and monitored their progress to ensure they never went mad?

How much more could they contribute to the realms if they were given that chance?

If *we* were?

I'm still in too much shock for my hopes to lift far. I study Alek's face. "You said you thought you might get in trouble for telling me this."

His throat bobs with a thick swallow. "I told Tinom first, when I didn't find you right away. And he—he threw the main proof I had into one of the fireplaces and told me people would be too confused if we made the truth known widely. That it wasn't worth the consequences."

A chill seeps through my innards. I've always known the magic advisor was hesitant to trust my control over my magic, but I didn't realize he'd actively work against me.

Apparently the grace he's given only extends as far as necessary for me to continue protecting the royal family.

"Then we can't do anything about it anyway," I say. "We don't have proof. He'd obviously deny it."

Alek shakes his head. "I might be able to find other accounts. There were a few briefer mentions that at least support the records I found at the Haven… It isn't our most urgent concern right now, but after Silana is set back in order, people should know the real story."

A soft, melodic voice carries from the doorway. "I agree."

Alek and I both jerk around.

Petra steps into the room. Her dark eyes are solemn as our future queen takes in the scholar and then me.

My heart skips a beat and then keeps hammering. "How much did you hear?"

"All the important parts, I think. I'm sorry. I was looking for you to find out the latest news from our allies in Nikodi, and when I caught a little of what you were talking about—" A hint of a blush colors her smooth cheeks. "I should have come in and been part of the discussion properly. I've gotten too much in the habit of hanging back and simply listening."

Before I can decide what to say, she takes another step forward and grasps my hands. "Ivy, you know I trust you. I've seen how dedicated you are and how careful you've been. I want this country to be better to all riven sorcerers going forward. So what I'm about to tell you, please know that I had no part in it. If I'd found out in time, I'd have tried to argue him out of it."

The chill inside me thickens with dread. "What?"

Petra's mouth tightens. "My father—the pardon… Even in the end, he refused to believe that you could be anything other than a danger to the country. He lied in his letter. I think he was going to forgive Stavros and the others, but he'd made arrangements to subdue you and take you into custody when you arrived."

The revelation hits me like a sucker punch. My breath rushes out of me around an ache that fills my lungs. "Oh. Of course."

How could I ever have imagined that the king who's made it one of his greatest quests to hunt down the riven would welcome me as an ally?

Alek's eyes flash. "That's terrible. He promised her amnesty and—"

"He's dead," I cut in. "Partly because of me. It isn't as if he was entirely—"

"No." Petra squeezes my hands. "He *was* wrong. Absolutely, utterly wrong. And if he'd realized that sooner, Lothar would never have had the opportunity to use you the way he did. I only bring it up now because Tinom was aware of the plan. My father never trusted the riven, and Tinom is holding on to the same opinion out of loyalty. I've been firm with him when he's raised concerns. I'll speak to him again, more forcefully. And when I'm queen, then my word will be the law. He'll have to adapt."

I know she intends to comfort me, but the ache doesn't leave. If anything, I only feel queasier.

She's taking a stand for me against not just public opinion but what remains of her court. Against her father's memory.

Gods help me, how could I repay that?

How can I make sure I don't drag her down in her attempt to save *me*?

After everything I've heard today, it's hard for me to believe that the larger world's view of riven sorcery could ever be shifted. I can't let what's probably a hopeless quest for justice interfere with Petra's true purpose.

A quiver of resolve rises up through the turmoil of my emotions.

I need to justify her faith in me not just to her but to Tinom and everyone else supporting her claim to the throne. Maybe most of them will never see riven magic as anything but an abomination, maybe they'll never open their arms to the others out there, but I can keep showing that *I'm* so much more than that.

I have to make sure we use this upcoming festival to get her closer to that throne, or what good am I to her anyway?

I clasp her hands in return, putting all my will into keeping my voice steady. "Then let's see you hailed as queen as soon as humanly possible."

# Twenty-One

*Ivy*

As we pass through the city gate in the midst of a stream of chattering revelers, the back of my neck prickles with apprehension. Two guards in a new uniform of crimson shirt and dun slacks stand on either side of the arched entryway, their hands resting on the pommels of their sheathed swords.

But the Order of the Wild's version of the Crown's Watch doesn't appear to be monitoring the new arrivals all that closely. Their gazes slide over our humble cart without any more interest than they give the other folk around us.

Of course, Lothar's new Festival of Freedom is being held in every city and town across the country. His people have no reason to think the small group of resistors he wants to stamp out would be here in Tupno.

As far as we know, Filip didn't even pass on word that we were heading somewhere to the north. The men we sent to monitor the Order defector's loyalty returned a couple of days ago, reporting that they'd seen no sign that Lothar was searching for us at the location we planted as a false lead.

Nothing else has gone wrong since we left Florian. I'm starting to think we weren't betrayed at all, only had a particularly unlucky moment.

All the same, we didn't invite Filip along on this particular mission.

I tap one of the horses' flanks to direct it to the right where the street splits. From the map we studied yesterday, that should lead us to the city's largest square.

It's just a few blocks away from the palace I can already see, silvery spires rising above the nearer rooftops. Tupno is one of Silana's largest cities and also the closest city to the Temple of Tranquil Skies that holds one of the royal residences.

Because of that royal presence, it's a major hub for travel, trade, and all the communication that goes with those endeavours. We're counting on a lot of people seeing our demonstration today—and spreading the word far and wide.

Even this street leading to the square buzzes with activity. Our trickle of visitors mingles with the flow of locals heading toward the main festival areas. Eager voices warble around us in a blur of words.

Crimson banners painted with the inverted All-Giver sigil dangle from lampposts and drape across building fronts. Streamers in the same color wave in the breeze.

Like streaks of fresh blood. After the carnage I've seen the scourge sorcerers carry out, the vivid color makes my stomach churn.

I restrain the urge to glance back at the cart, where our five companions sit in the shade of a canopy. I don't know what Order members might be watching the crowd and whether they'd pick up on my nerves.

Beside me, Casimir takes in our surroundings with a thoughtful air. When he speaks, he keeps his voice low enough to pass beneath the clamor around us. "We should have a good-sized audience."

I swallow a grimace. "All these people happily going along with a festival to celebrate murder. How can they be okay with it?"

The courtesan shrugs, his shoulder brushing mine. "They aren't necessarily okay. It's been weeks of confusion and uncertainty, especially for people living so close to Eppun where the uprising started. Lothar was smart—he realized they'd be craving a chance to put their fears behind them, to pretend there's nothing to worry about. But the worries will still be lurking underneath."

And I guess a fair number of Silana's citizens have bought into the Order of the Wild's rhetoric. They're not worried at all.

We have to convince them they should be.

My back prickles with my awareness of the figure lying on the bottom of the cart beneath a blanket as if napping. Really, we wanted to conceal the man's mutilated body so no onlookers would notice anything odd before we get into position.

The sacrificial accomplice who agreed to accompany us sounded nervous when we talked him through the plan, even though his loyalties to the scourge sorcerers have faded during his time recovering at a temple near Pima. He thanked Casimir for the courtesan's instrumental role in getting him out of the brothel where he and his few companions were held, but he also tensed up when we talked about speaking to the crowd.

In the end, he agreed. He was the steadiest of the four, according to Voleska—which is why she had her people smuggle him to us for this operation. But that doesn't mean the task will be easy for him.

"Are you sure we should have pushed this role on Poltus?" I can't help asking. "To have to tell a heap of strangers what he's been through—he's risking the Order capturing him again, and gods know what they'd do to him…"

Casimir aims a gentle smile at me. "I wouldn't say we pushed. We told him what we were hoping for, and he embraced the challenge. How many times have you put your neck on the line to protect this country despite the horrors you've already faced? We've got to give the scourge sorcerers' victims the same opportunity."

He's probably right about that too, but it's hard for me to compare Poltus's situation to my own. He was groomed from childhood and left a mangled version of himself. At least I've always had most of the control over my fate.

Possibly I should be more concerned about the other passenger we're concealing. As the street opens up ahead of us to reveal a teeming swarm of festival-goers, Petra scoots to the spot right behind our driver's seats.

The Melchiorek heir has tucked her smooth black hair beneath a mousy brown wig for the ride. A baggy wool dress covers the finer gown that indicates her actual station.

I still would rather our future queen was safe back in the temple while we carried out this mission, but she rightly pointed out how upset people were that she didn't show herself properly when she spoke in Florian. She wants her citizens to see how far she's willing to stick *her* neck out to win them over.

"The river's to the right, isn't it?" she says. "Which building do you think will work best for our... presentation, now that we can actually see the options?"

We pull the cart over to the side of the square, and I take in the sprawling space.

More inverted All-Giver banners hang all around the square. Not far from us, several long wooden tables have been laid out with glasses of ale and platters of stuffed rolls, dumplings, and cut fruit. The mix of savory and tangy scents wafts through the air.

As far as I can tell, the attendants in crimson shirts behind the table aren't charging for the refreshments. They smile and nod to the people who stop by, many gaping at the spread wide-eyed before plucking up some morsels.

A lot of the revelers look oddly scruffy in their elegant clothes. Most of the men are sporting embroidered tunics or vests, the women in brightly colored silks, but looking a little too loose or too tight. Their hair is rumpled and loose—some look as if they haven't bathed in at least a week.

When my gaze snags on another table across the square, I understand why. This one is heaped with fabric that newcomers are snatching off it.

Casimir has spotted it too. He arches his eyebrows. "It looks as if the Order of the Wild is supplying the costumes too."

And where did they get all those fine clothes? It's not hard to guess.

"Looted from the noble estates they've taken over," I mutter. "And probably the royal residences too."

Or bought with all the gold the scourge sorcerers have looted as well. What is Lothar sacrificing of his own rather than giving away what he's stolen?

"Come play the games of old!" an announcer is calling near the center of the square. "Let's reclaim the heart of our heritage!"

A few older kids are already jostling each other between chalk lines marked on the cobblestones. It looks like one of the games Alek told us he'd found references to.

A game that often ended with broken bones when the revelers of the past got particularly caught up in it. For now, the children are simply giggling, but we'll have to keep an eye on it in case it becomes more intense.

A woman in a deep red dress has gotten up on a platform near the games area. She holds out her hands, her voice projecting over the crowd with magical amplification. "The king can't hold us back any longer! We're free to get back to our roots, what connected us to this world and the gods who made us."

Spirited music blares from a cluster of musicians behind the platform, and the woman whirls into a flailing sort of dance.

We were prepared for dancing too. I was hoping the civilians would be put off by the chaotic cavorting Alek described, that we could point to it as evidence of the Order's ill intents, but I can already see an echo of the woman's movements spreading through the crowd around her.

Oh, well. We can still challenge the Order of the Wild's appeals to history. Something has to snap these people out of their stupor.

I return my gaze to the buildings along the right of the square. We want a position that puts us a safe distance above the crowd but still easily visible to the people below—and within easy reach of the river that'll serve as our escape route.

I point to a two-story stone structure with a flat roof and a narrow alley between it and one of its neighbors. "That place looks promising. Let's go around back and make sure it's got everything we need."

Rheave scrambles out, followed by the soldier and the devout who've accompanied us. They help Poltus off the back of the cart. Thankfully, the winter is chilly enough that the low hood and scarf obscuring most of his head don't look all that unusual. We've padded his clothes beneath the cloak so it's less obvious how much of his body is missing.

Skirting the crowd, we ease through the milling bodies toward the alley. I scan the revelers around us—and nearly walk right into a little boy who steps in front of me as if unaware of anything except the scene he's staring at.

As I jerk myself backward, the kid—who can't be more than six or seven—stays focused on the mass of festival-goers in the wider square. His gaze is avid, but something about his expression makes me think he's unsettled as well.

Then he turns his head toward me, and I freeze.

His eyes are nothing but whites and pure black, as if the pupils have swallowed his irises. The fathomless gaze takes me back weeks to the strange man we crossed paths with on the road to Nikodi —who warned us of impending doom and then vanished.

But that man had the wizened face and hunched posture of a body that'd passed through many decades, and there's no way the kid in front of me has lived for even one.

The boy peers at me for a moment before his lips curl with a small smile, as if we share a secret. He looks at the revelers again, and the smile falters. "It's all a mirage. They don't know what lies underneath."

"What—" I start, but he's already darting forward to merge with the crowd. In a matter of seconds, I've lost sight of his pale hair.

Petra touches my arm from behind. "Is he someone to worry about?"

I shed the sudden bout of nerves with a shake of my head. It's not as if two people in the country couldn't have the same oddly dark eye color. Just a weird little kid.

"I don't think so," I say. "Let's keep going."

Around the back of the building I suggested, we find there's only a narrow strip of path between the rear door and the walled bank of Tupno's broad river. A rickety fire escape will take us most of the way to the roof.

Petra nods in approval. She motions to the soldier. "Let's get everyone up to the roof, and then you can scout down the river for a vessel we can… borrow."

Poltus needs both the soldier and the devout supporting him to make it onto the fire escape. As I gird myself to follow them, Casimir touches my shoulder.

"We'll make them see the truth," he says. "No matter what Lothar does, he can't stop us from fighting back."

Then he kisses me, swiftly but tenderly enough to send a tingle down to my toes.

When the courtesan releases me, Rheave pushes in with an intense expression. "I'll be right there with you too," my daimon-man says, and claims a scorching kiss of his own.

By the time I'm scrambling up the fire escape, my cheeks are flushed and some of the tension inside me has loosened.

We aren't going to win over everyone today, but we can make a dent in the image the Order of the Wild has built up. We've come with proof.

I won't let Petra down any more than my men would fail me.

We clamber onto the roof and stay at the back to prepare while the soldier hurries back down. The music, laughter, and excited shouts from the crowd in the square make my gut twist.

What Julita would have thought of this celebration, all this revelry centered around the villains she knew as torturers, I can't imagine. I'm glad she never had to see the scourge sorcerers gain so much ground.

How can the civilians below sound so joyful when this festival is meant to rejoice in their former ruler's *murder*? King Konram might have neglected some of his people and come down hard on the riven, but he never acted like a tyrant.

I've seen more brutality from the scourge sorcerers in the past few months than in all the years Konram and his father before him reigned.

But then, the Order of the Wild has been hiding many of the horrors of their founding from the rest of the country. That's why we're here—why Poltus is here.

With her wig and plain dress set aside, Petra steps to the edge of the roof. Delfis was able to obtain an amplifying charm for her, which sits on a silver chain at the base of her throat. The devout who came with us stands at her side.

As Petra draws her chin up regally, Rheave and I flank them, ready to protect them if need be. Rheave adjusts his bow against his shoulder.

My magic tingles through my chest, stirred up by all the energies below that have discomforted me.

"Good people of Tupno." Petra's amplified voice rings across the square, and dozens of faces throughout the crowd turn at just the first few words. "I come to you as the heir to the Melchiorek line and the rightful queen of Silana to expose the true enemy in your midst. My family has guided this country for nearly a century without incurring any wrath from the gods, and I intend to take care of all of you as well as I can from here forward. My parents were struck down by the traitors who've wrenched our home from us, not any divine intervention."

The devout tugs his robes straight. His voice carries through the startled silence that's gripped the crowd. "I am swore to serve Elox, and I can vouch that you've been told lies. The godlen haven't given this treachery their blessing. They didn't call for the king's death. That was all human greed, fueled by the same brutal magic that once brought the gods' wrath down on us. Surely none of us wants to return to a history where our cities broke and burned? That's where the Order of the Wild will lead us. The woman beside me is the rightful queen and dedicated to putting Silana on the right path to harmony and happiness."

A muttering is spreading through the civilians below. I tense instinctively, remembering the reaction of the people in Florian.

"If the gods wanted that girl on the throne, she'd be there!" someone hollers loud enough for us to hear, followed by a swell of approving murmurs.

"The gods can't interfere quickly or directly," Petra says. "But the Melchioreks have always served them and you well, no matter what Lothar claims. We pulled the country together after the Darium empire was driven out. My great grandmother started a program of training more medics to be sent all through the country. My grandfather saw new roads built to the most isolated parts of—"

A volley of voices cuts through her speech.

"I don't even remember any of that! What did King Konram do for us lately?"

"Why didn't the rest of them have to fight for the throne like that first king did?"

"Right. King Konram just got the crown handed to him. He didn't care about any of us!"

Petra holds up her hand. She must decide it's time to move from addressing Lothar's lies to stating her own worth as a ruler. "I promise you, I care. That's why I came here to speak to you in person. I realize that my forebearers weren't perfect, and I aim to do better. I want to listen to all your grievances and make—"

The crowd doesn't give her a chance to finish her statement of devotion. More voices interrupt, hollering up at us.

"You care now because you lost your fancy palace!"

"I got to eat more today than I have in years. It's the Order of the Wild who gave us that, not you."

"They're making things better, not just talking at us."

"The royal family never bothered with what anyone except the nobles needed."

"They did one good thing and figured they should get to keep lording it over us forever. We all have to work for anything we want."

The devout spreads his arms pleadingly. "My fellow citizens, if you'd just listen. We can show you—"

"We've seen enough," someone snaps back. "We know who'll look out for us."

"The Order of the Wild set us free!"

Both Petra and the devout glance back at me, with a flick of their gazes toward Poltus, who's sitting awkwardly on the roof's tiles with Casimir. That's my cue to help the courtesan bring the sacrificial accomplice forward.

They must be hoping the sight of him will shock the protests out of the crowd.

I mean to move, but all at once my feet feel heavy as lead. My attention leaps back toward the crowd—the fists waved, the voices raised in frustration. All the shouted words jostle in my brain.

We've been wrong. Both those of us supporting the queen and the Order of the Wild.

The common people of Silana don't give a shit about how people lived hundreds of years ago. They aren't trying to get back to their roots or any of the other metaphors the Order members toss around.

They just want to survive *now*. To have their needs met, to know they have someone to turn to for help.

To be heard.

But Lothar's approach has catered to them so much better than our own, whether by design or inadvertently.

How could it not? He has the manpower to give away a banquet and heaps of fine clothes, to throw a country-wide festival where everything is provided. He has followers in every city and town assuring the locals that they'll set everything right in the most fundamental possible ways.

At this point, is there anything we can show them that will sway their opinion? So many people were fed up under the Melchioreks, tired of seeing those titled or rich favored.

Are they really willing to wait and see if Petra will be better, no matter what we tell them about the Order? Will they believe us even with the proof in front of their eyes?

Poltus sways where he's sitting with a ragged mumbling under his breath. A shudder runs through his body.

He can hear everything the crowd is saying, singing the praises of the people who mutilated him. And now we're going to put him to their judgment when they might hurl the same harsh words at him—when it might not make any difference?

Hasn't he been traumatized enough? How are we better than the scourge sorcerers if we use their victims for our own cause without caring how it harms them?

In that moment, there's nothing I'd rather do than gather my companions and run away from here. Far, far away to some other country where we can escape the Order of the Wild and at least live in some kind of peace.

Maybe that's actually the best thing I can do for Petra and her siblings, before her quest for the throne ends in more tragedy.

Maybe all those people down there deserve to find out exactly who they're supporting when the scourge sorcerers finally stop giving and start taking. What have the people of Silana ever done for *me* except talk about how my kind should be sent to the gallows?

I take a step toward Poltus, on the verge of suggesting we flee, when one more shout reverberates from below.

"The Order is looking out for *all* of us. They want us all to have good lives!"

Poltus flinches and then goes rigid, his jaw clenching. I can see the rejection of those words etched all through his mottled face.

He knows they're a lie just as much as I do. It's like that strange kid said to me—Lothar has created a mirage.

Gods smite me, I can't blame the people for listening to the scourge sorcerers when we haven't given them a chance to see the truth.

I crouch down next to Poltus. It should be his choice.

"Are you ready to give your story?" I ask. "I don't know how they'll respond."

He draws his armless frame taller with an air of resolve. "It doesn't matter. They should know what Lothar's people did."

My chest tightens around my heart, but when I look at Casimir, he nods.

We're in this together, all of us—even the people down there who'd throw Petra's words back in her face.

The scourge sorcerers are the only real villains here.

And maybe Poltus couldn't live with himself any more than I could if we don't expose them in every way we can. This isn't my fight alone.

I help him to his feet, supporting him on one side as Casimir guides him from the other. We unfasten the cloak that's concealed the worst of his deformities and let it fall. He's already discarded the scarf.

Seeing us coming, Petra and the devout step to the side. "Behold what the Order of the Wild has done to your children," the devout calls out. "This is how they fuel their magic—not through their own work, but through the immense sacrifices of others."

"What have you ever—" someone starts to yell, but even that voice cuts out with a gasp of horror.

Cries and startled murmurs pass through the crowd staring up at Poltus. I restrain a flinch.

Even if they believe his story, it mustn't be easy for him to hear their reactions.

Petra sets her amplification charm around the accomplice's neck. He lifts his voice despite the noises of revulsion rising from below.

"Everything Queen Petra has said is true," he says, his voice thick but steady. "The Order of the Wild is run by people who get their magic by borrowing it from other people. When I was little and had just lost my mother, a woman who worked with the Order convinced me that the best way I could protect the rest of my family and the country was by giving the most immense sacrifice I could."

He tilts his head to make it easier for them to see his missing features. "I gave up my eyes, my ears, my nose, my arms. They took even more from inside me. I thought I was helping bring about a better world. But if they want a world that's better for everyone, why did they keep me and all the other people who sacrificed like me shut away like prisoners? Why have they hidden us so that you won't find out?"

A voice breaks through the uneasy tumult below. "They did this to other people too?"

"Lots of other people," Poltus declares, his voice getting even more forceful.

I squeeze his side encouragingly, and he hurtles onward. "There were three others kept in the same room as me. Since then, I've met eight who were kept elsewhere. I've heard of dozens more. How do you think they managed to overwhelm the entire royal army? Where could all that magic have come from? It was stolen from people they lied to, and they'll keep lying to you too until it's too late. Unless we bring this madness to an end!"

An uneven roar of agreement ripples through the crowd. Relief surges through me.

At least some of them believe him. At least some are questioning what they've been told.

Several people have spun toward the Order member who was leading the dances. I see a woman pull a girl away from the dancing area while others jab their fingers as if asking accusing questions.

"Where's the Order?" someone hollers.

"What else are they hiding?"

"We need some answers!"

A flash of crimson at the edge of the crowd brings my head jerking around. A bunch of armed figures in the new Order uniform are shoving along the edge of the crowd toward our building.

My heart lurches. I reach for Petra. "Your Highness, it's time to go. We have to get to the river."

The devout has already dashed to the back of the roof. His face pales. "They're coming from both directions. I don't think we can make it down in time."

We were prepared for that. I sling my arm around Poltus's back and brace myself. "Then we'll have to jump."

# Twenty-Two

I f there weren't angry people waving daggers and swords in our direction, I'd probably enjoy the leap from the rooftop. Soaring through the air like I'm flying just for a moment. Hitting the water with a chilly splash.

The current of liquid consumes me, rushing against my skin and into my clothes and hair. The cold prickles through my nerves in an invigorating way.

Then my limbs push at the water, and my head breaks through the surface. A marshy smell fills my nose, with a slightly rancid note that suggests the river isn't as clean as the streams we drank from during our many travels across the countryside.

Urgent shouts bombard my ears. I grip my bow against my side and blink the moisture from my eyes to see better.

Several figures in red shirts have charged to the edge of the riverbank, which is built up in a stone wall a few feet above our heads. In the water around me, my companions bob.

My gaze latches on to Ivy's reddish-blond hair first, turned darker than usual by the wetness. She's swimming with the flow of the water, her slim, pale limbs rising and falling a few arm-lengths ahead of me.

Just beyond her, Casimir and the robed man from the temple sway in the current, clutching the poor victim of the scourge sorcerers between them. Of course—a man with no arms can't swim.

Petra's dark head shows against the rippling gray surface near them. She's rolled onto her side as she kicks at the water, her head tipped to focus on the boat that's just a few paces farther down the river.

Our soldier stands at the side of the curved wooden structure, hunched so he's ready to snatch Petra's hand and haul her into the vessel when she reaches him. He's meant to do the same for all of us, but with a flick of my gaze, I estimate that I can propel myself high enough to grasp the edge of the boat all on my own.

I haul my limbs through the flowing water—and an arrow humming with magical energy soars past me from the bank toward the boat.

The projectile slams into the boat's hull. I know from my own practice that a normal arrow would simply dig its head into the wood and hang there without doing more damage than marring the surface.

But this is clearly not a normal arrow.

With whatever magic the scourge sorcerers have cast on it, the arrow splits right through the boards. A crack opens around the point where it's penetrated, straight down to the surface of the water.

And the river gushes in.

The soldier gives a bark of alarm and turns toward the hole. Even in my limited knowledge of boats, I can see there's no patching it.

Then another arrow whirs through the air and plunges into the soldier's chest.

This time, it's Petra who cries out. The soldier staggers and crumples backward in the already sinking watercraft.

A jolt of urgency races through my veins. Our escape plan has just been destroyed—and the scourge sorcerers are going to keep shooting at us.

I spare one worried glance Ivy's way and then grope for my bow. Maybe I can push myself high enough in the water to launch an arrow of my own. If I can just get into the right position...

As I wrestle with the weapon against the current, I twist to face our attackers. They vanish from view for a moment as I sweep past the capsizing boat. I grope behind my shoulder toward my quiver—

And my other arm slams into the stone wall along the river. My elbow shudders, and my fingers spasm apart.

The bow swirls away from me, caught in the gushing water. I spin around the bend I didn't realize was coming.

The currents shift, whipping me faster along. I surge past Ivy so swiftly that I don't have time to grasp at her.

Heaving myself to the side, I manage not to collide with Casimir's trio. My hands scoop uselessly at the water.

Petra lifts her head all the way above the surface to gasp out an order. "We still have to get to the grate! We can leave the same way. Just swim!"

Just swim. Just swim.

But we can't move through the water as effectively as the boat would have. We don't have the shelter of its wood, as poor a shield as that turned out to be against the scourge sorcerers' weapons.

A fresh volley of shouts rings out on either side of us. More red-shirted figures appear on both banks, having run ahead or caught word from their colleagues.

A woman on the farther bank draws back her bow. Is she aiming at Ivy?

My pulse hitches with panic. The image flashes before my eyes of the arrow smacking into Ivy's skull the way the other did the guard's chest.

*No.*

I flail at the churning water, but I can't push myself any closer to her. My waterlogged clothes drag at my limbs.

She's too far beyond my reach.

I can't let them hurt her. My Ivy. My little vine.

The arrow arcs through the air—and hits the water just shy of Ivy's shoulder. Instead of relief, more panic surges through my body.

It was so close. So much closer than I am.

They could murder my precious woman right in front of me.

I lift my arm to try to hurl some of my crackly magic at our attackers, even though I'm not sure how much damage I can do from this distance. But the shifting currents throw my aim off-kilter.

The sizzling light I fling out smacks into the riverbank instead, slashing black streaks across the stones.

Another arrow flies at us, and another. We swing around a second curve in the river.

For a second, I find myself spun around, unable to even see Ivy.

As I claw my way through the water to face her again, a thicker fear wraps around my chest, squeezing my lungs.

If we can't make it out of this—if I lose her—all the pain that burned inside me after Lothar took her will wrack me again. Worse than being pierced with a hundred arrows.

I don't know—I can't even wrap my head around the thought— What am I supposed to do?

How can I save either of us?

Watching that man hold a knife to her throat the other night was bad enough. At least I could see right away how to blast him away from her.

Now I'm as caught up as she is. Nothing I can do is making a difference.

Ivy's mouth dips below the level of the water. She sputters and waves her hand toward me. Whatever she says is lost in the swell of desperation that's engulfed my body.

I stiffen and sink. My legs jerk automatically, sending me back to the surface with a sputter of my own.

Petra shouts something too, from off to my left. Casimir glances back at me, his brow knitting.

One of the men on the bank hurls a knife at Ivy's head. She flinches to the side, but a protruding bit of its hilt smacks her temple.

My mouth opens with a wail of protest building in my throat, and her gaze snags on mine, startlingly blue compared to the murky water. Finally, her voice penetrates the haze in my head.

"The grate!" she calls out. "It's time!"

Understanding snaps into place.

I have to carry out my part in the plan—even if we were in the boat, I was meant to fulfill this task.

My fears blotted my duty right out of my mind.

With a ragged breath and a surge of shame, I yank myself around purposefully. Just a few boat-lengths away loom the thick city walls—and the bridge that arches over the river with a steel grate beneath to prevent covert travel by this route.

The opening rises only a few feet above the water—we'd have had to hunch low in the boat to pass through the space beneath the stone arch. That won't matter now that we're in the water, but we still need it to open.

If we hit the bars while they're still closed, we'll be easy targets for our pursuers.

I shove all of my attention toward the metal structure—toward the lock that secures the grate—and thrust my hands forward.

The first smack of my magic warps the metal but doesn't break it.

As I speed ever closer, I will another, sharper blast of the searing energy out of me.

The lock melts away, along with a significant chunk of the deadbolt it held in place. I tip myself backward and slam into the bars feet first, aiming one final surge of magic at the hinges on the other side.

The strips of metal sizzle, and the grate pops off. It rushes beneath the bridge ahead of me, tugged by the river's current.

I right myself in time to see my companions gliding through the opening after me. Yells of frustration carry from the other side, but the scourge sorcerers aren't going to follow us into the water—and they can't jump right over the wall.

They'll have to dash around to the nearest gate on the land. We can be far away from the city by the time they reach the river.

As we bob along in it, the waterway flows past a few farms and into a patch of forest we surveyed ahead of time. The log the now-dead soldier and I heaved most of the way into the current still protrudes from the bank where we left it.

I catch a branch and whirl around to help pull Petra over to safety. Casimir and the devout work their way along the soggy wood to the shore, pulling the sacrificial accomplice with them.

I stay in the water until Ivy reaches me. She extends her arms to stop herself against the log, but I wrap my arm around her first.

The question spills out shakily. "Okay, Little Vine?"

She peers at me, no mark on her except the start of a bruise where the knife hilt knocked her temple. "Just glad to be out of there. Are *you* okay?"

I push my mouth into a smile. "I am if you are."

As true as that is, my heart thumps heavily against my ribs as we slosh to the shore and tramp through the forest to the waiting horses we hid. Toast snorts in greeting as if he's as relieved to see Ivy returning as I am.

She is okay. But not thanks to me.

I almost put her in even more danger when I froze up in the river.

What's wrong with me? Was that paralyzing mix of fear and pain some effect of my human body that no one thought to warn me about?

We set off for the temple as fast as the horses will run, the devout holding his armless companion tight against his chest to ensure his balance. An ache of desire and shame courses from my throat down to my gut—wishing I could hold Ivy like that, wondering if I deserve it after I nearly failed her so badly, hating that I can't say I do.

The journey passes in a blur of tangled emotions. When we reach the temple stable, I slide off my mount's back, planning to gather Ivy to me and hold her until everything inside me settles down again.

But Casimir grasps my arm first.

"Rheave," the courtesan says in a quiet voice, "we should give the ladies a chance to wash off the muck of the river and the road on their own time. Why don't we get ourselves cleaned up too?"

Something about his tone makes me think this diversion is important to him. He might know something I don't.

When I look at Ivy again, one of those unsettling twinges that's both devotion and horror shoots through my stomach. I don't really know what I want right now anyway.

So I follow Casimir through the buildings to one of the temple's bathing rooms, collecting a change of clothes along the way. My river-drenched tunic and trousers have stiffened against my skin.

From what I understand, Elox isn't concerned about sensual satisfaction like Ardone, Casimir's patron godlen. But the godlen of peace and healing does care about comfort. While the bathing room is small and plain, it's filled with warmth, with ample towels stacked on a shelf. A lingering scent of lavender washing oil hangs in the air.

Rather than moving to one of the shower stalls right away, Casimir sits down on the smooth white bench. He motions for me to join him.

"Something's been bothering you for a while now," he says as I sink down at the opposite end. "You haven't been back to your old self even after Ivy returned to us. I'm guessing your disorientation in the river is connected to that problem."

An embarrassed heat prickles up over my face. I suppose if any of my companions were to guess at my feelings, it makes sense it'd be the man who's so in tune with emotions and relationships. At least there's no judgment in Casimir's tone.

Maybe he can help me untangle the muddle I've gotten into.

I look down at my empty hands. "It doesn't make sense to me. The feelings don't fit together."

"Why don't you tell me about it, and I'll see what I can make of them?"

I inhale deeply. "I care so much about Ivy. I don't know… I don't know if I'd still want to keep this body and live a sort-of human life if she wasn't in it. Just being around her makes me so happy. I think that's what you would call love, isn't it? I love her."

The words spark a flare in my chest that's both warm and sharp. I know they're true before Casimir even replies.

"You're the best judge of your own emotions," he says. "But from that description, I'd agree."

I grimace. "But isn't love supposed to be *good*? It's supposed to bring joy and make your life brighter and… It *should* be those things. Why would it hurt me too?"

Casimir rests a gentle hand on my back. "How does it hurt you?"

I grapple with my tangled feelings before I can wrestle a coherent explanation out of them. "When Lothar took Ivy—when we found out what he'd made her do, how she'd had to hurt herself, and we didn't know if we'd be able to rescue her—I've never been in pain like that, not even when I've been injured in this body. And I couldn't get away from it. There was nothing to heal or bandage. It wrapped around me from the inside, like… like I was trapped in the pain."

My voice drops. "It reminded me of when the scourge sorcerers first stuffed me into this body, when it was still clay and I couldn't move it. When I really was trapped."

"Ah." Casimir's voice stays soft. "That must have been very frightening."

"Yes." I swallow thickly. "But it shouldn't matter now. She's here. She's safe. I just—I was worried about her, and then I remembered how it would feel if I lost her, and all of that together was too much for a moment."

"That's understandable," Casimir says. "Especially when you're still getting used to human emotions. The rest of us have had our whole lives to make peace with the interplay between joy and pain."

I glance sideways at him. "What do you mean?"

"Opposites always go together." He takes back his hand to interlace his fingers in demonstration. "You can't have happiness without sadness, peace without violence, love without heartbreak. They're equal sides of the same coin. One might dwindle to give the other more prominence, but circumstances can always flip it back. And that's how it should be. The joyful parts wouldn't feel as powerful if we could take them for granted."

That's what my old existence was like. Nothing meant particularly more than anything else, all just minor blips in my awareness. It does feel dull, looking back on my past experiences now.

I rub my face. "I don't want to feel anything bad about loving Ivy. I don't want to be afraid of caring about her. I don't want to hold back from loving her more… but the more she matters to me, the more it could hurt. How do you 'make peace' with that?"

Casimir lifts his shoulders in a subtle shrug. "To some extent, we don't. That's why we fight so hard to protect the things we care about—which I think is a virtue, not a flaw. But it's also in how you look at it. Yes, in some ways, love is a cage that chains us to the person we've fallen for. Doesn't it also open up so many possibilities that were once closed to us? How many things have you discovered or experienced that you wouldn't have if you didn't care about Ivy?"

The question sends a flood of images through my mind. The feel of Ivy's cheek against my fingers, the brilliance of her smile. The exhilaration of riding alongside her, the rush of pride when she turns to me for comfort. The heady pleasure of our bodies merging.

There's a whole world inside this love. That's *why* I don't want to lose it.

Will I really, though, no matter what happens? We'll still have been together; I'll still have meant so much to her and her to me.

No one can erase what we've already shared.

The lingering ache melts away with that realization. I smile at Casimir. "Thank you. I hadn't been thinking about it in that way."

The courtesan chuckles. "Very few of us, even those of us practiced at dealing with emotions, react perfectly when someone we love is threatened. I've had my share of conflicted impulses. It's all part of this bizarre but wonderful existence you've found yourself in. Of course, if the rest of us have any say about it, Ivy will make it through any danger that faces her for a long time to come."

I push to my feet, buoyed by my new perspective and a rush of determination. "Yes, she will. And I want to get to feel everything else I can with her, even if there'll be parts that hurt too."

# TWENTY-THREE

*Ivy*

"You aren't even giving me a chance!"

The crisp teenage voice carries from one of the temple doorways up ahead. I expected to find Petra down here, but that sounds like her younger sister.

As I hesitate, Petra's voice follows, not quite as loud but still forceful. "It's not about giving you a chance. This isn't your place. Father and Mother didn't go riding into battle. That's what the army is for."

Princess Klaudia lets out a scoffing sound. "Father and Mother *had* an army. We've barely pulled together a squadron. We'll have a difficult enough time overcoming the damage Lothar's done with all of us contributing. I don't want to keep sitting around here at the temple while the rest of you handle the dangerous parts. I *hate* it."

Spoken like a true sixteen-year-old. But even as my lips twitch with a hint of amusement at the teenage rebelliousness, an ache forms in my gut.

It's her parents' deaths Klaudia wants to avenge, her sister she wants to see take the throne. Our struggle is far more personal for her than it could ever be for me.

All the same, I can understand Petra's refusal.

There's a rough exhalation, and the future queen says, "You can contribute without putting yourself face to face with the enemy. You could help me clean these—"

"You know that's not what I'm talking about," Klaudia snaps. She barges out of the room with a rustle of skirts.

When the princess sees me, her steps falter for just a moment, the angry flush in her cheeks darkening with embarrassment. At least she doesn't flinch. Then she marches on past me without a word.

She certainly has the Melchiorek pride.

I venture to the doorway and poke my head inside. At the movement, Petra's gaze jerks up where she's standing by one of the tables, wiping down a sword with a cloth.

A flicker of disappointment crosses her face before she schools her expression into her usual stoic calm, although a little tightness lingers at the corners of her mouth. She was probably hoping her sister had reconsidered and come back.

"How much of that argument did you overhear?" she asks in a resigned tone.

I ease into the room, taking in its contents. It's one of the temple's smaller spaces, with only two narrow tables for furniture. But every wall is set with racks holding an assortment of swords, daggers, spears, bows, shields, and helms.

I draw my gaze back to Petra. "Enough to know she wants to fight and you're not letting her. Which I don't blame you for, by the way."

Petra sighs. "Word came in from one of the people from Pima who've been scouting around for us. He thinks he's found the site of the facility where the scourge sorcerers are creating their clay figures to trap the daimon. I made the mistake of mentioning it to Klaudia before we've set a plan in motion."

Her head droops, her hand stilling against the sword. "I don't like that I have to send *anyone* off to fight my battles for me. The facility must have all kinds of protections, guards—that's partly how the scout identified it. Klaudia's never experienced combat outside of self-defence classes."

"She shouldn't be there," I agree. "But it does her credit that she wants to help. Maybe we can find another job for her that isn't quite so dangerous but also a little more thrilling than..." I glance around the room again. "...polishing weaponry. I have to say, even though Delfis told me you'd gone to the armory, I hadn't pictured anything quite like this. Isn't Elox the godlen of peace?"

Petra manages a short laugh. "I said something like that when he showed me to the room. He said that in desperate times, a little warfare can be required to restore peace."

She tips her head toward the weapons around her. "It's clearly been quite a while since this temple needed to put that philosophy into practice. I don't think these arms have been taken off the racks in decades."

I grab a cloth for myself from the bin in the corner and pick out a sword I could see Stavros happily brandishing. The blade is coated with a layer of dust.

As I set the sword on the table across from Petra, I study her stance. Tension shows all through the set of her shoulders and the clench of her hand around the scrap of fabric. But like the droop of her head, something about her posture looks deflated as well.

My stomach knots. "Have you gotten any other news? More challenges ahead of us?"

Petra shakes her head and resumes her cleaning. "What we do have is good news, isn't it? If we can stop the scourge sorcerers from capturing more daimon and turning them into soldiers, we'll have fewer opponents to worry about. Those are the most 'loyal' subjects Lothar has. And there must be at least a few of the sacrificial accomplices there lending power to the process—we'll be freeing them as well."

"It's definitely good news." So why does she seem so unsettled by it?

We work in silence for a few minutes before I speak up again. "You know that the rest of us will be happy to go out there and tackle the scourge sorcerers, right? I want to destroy that facility. I'll go up against Lothar and his asshole followers as many times as it takes."

Petra's mouth twists. Her voice comes out so quiet I could almost miss the words. "But should you have to?"

I pause. "I don't have to. I'm choosing to."

"Because you want to see Silana restored. But what if... what if *I* can't do that after all?"

I stare at the woman I've seen as my future queen for a few thuds of my heart before I can manage to reply. "Why would you think that?"

Petra drops her cloth and swipes the back of her hand across her face. She looks at the table rather than me. "It isn't just Florian... The people in Tupno were frustrated with my family too. I've never ruled anything. I wasn't even acting as a Melchiorek for the last seven years of my life. I couldn't save my own *parents* when the threat was obvious and right in front of us. How can I be sure I'm worthy of the trust we're asking of them?"

My stomach sinks. We won't be conquering any enemies at all if the woman meant to lead us loses her confidence.

She's seemed so unshakeable through all the troubles we've faced so far. I've never caught more than brief hints of vulnerability.

Maybe I should have guessed there had to be more going on beneath the surface.

She did watch her parents murdered in front of her. She's got the weight of the entire country's hopes and security on her shoulders.

How could anyone not start to buckle under the pressure?

But who could take her place if she totally crumbles?

I swallow thickly, searching for the right thing to say. My own doubts swell in my chest.

Scourge sorcerers ravaged this continent once before. Taking them down turned into even more of a calamity. So many people died.

The divinities abandoned those like me, one of whom must be a distant ancestor of mine—cast us aside to be feared and hated by the rest of society.

Who is Petra to set the current catastrophe right? Who am *I* to decide that she should?

For a second, my awareness of all the history looming behind us and the uncertain future spread out ahead suffocates me. My lungs constrict.

I look down at the sword, the gleam of the newly polished blade. My reflection wavers on the metal surface.

Who are any of us to make any of these decisions? We're all just people... but we have to do *something*. If no one steps up, then the whole world falls to pieces.

Or into the hands of psychopaths like Lothar.

"Some people might have their doubts about your family's past reign," I say carefully. "But I don't think they'd see the real Lothar as a better option. They were horrified when they found out how the scourge sorcerers had used Poltus."

Petra lifts her gaze and offers me a tight smile. "I know. And I know I can at least be better than him. I just want to be more for the country than the only not-awful alternative they have."

She still looks uncertain, but my own doubts ease. That statement right there is exactly why I'd want this woman to be our queen.

My mind wanders back to the shouts of the crowd in Tupno yesterday. All the talk about worthy rulers... The Order of the Wild has had a lot to say on that subject too, haven't they?

I tap the tabletop thoughtfully. "You know... Lothar and his followers have been going on about the old kingship trials. Talking about rulers proving their worth—and obviously the common people are starting to buy into their rhetoric now too. What if we could use that idea for ourselves?"

Petra knits her brow, but a glimmer of interest lights in her eyes. "How do you mean?"

"I don't think most people really want us to go back to some distant past, but they like the general idea of their rulers meeting a challenge. There could be some way we can give them what they think they want but designed to fit the world we're in now. Make a new legacy. A version of trials that's our own—not so vicious or deadly, but still showing your strength. Give them a demonstration of your capability as a ruler. Show that you're willing to take risks to earn their favor, that you're more than the name you were born with."

For both them and herself.

Petra cocks her head as she takes that in. "That might actually be—"

She's interrupted by a crash of breaking pottery from the hall outside. With a lurch of my heart, I spring to the doorway.

Filip is standing just a few paces away, holding up his hands and staring down at the fragments of a vase that's shattered on the floor.

The Order defector glances up at me, his face sallow. "I didn't mean—I bumped into it and tried to catch it, but the glaze was so slippery—"

He just happened to bump into one of the temple's decorations while right outside a room where the future queen was having a strategic conversation? All my past suspicions come rushing back to the front of my mind.

What are the chances he was merely taking a stroll rather than purposefully eavesdropping?

Petra has appeared at my side. She takes in the scene and responds much more gracefully than I'd have managed. "That's a shame. It was a lovely piece."

Filip wrings his hands. "Gods, how old was it? The devouts are probably going to be furious with me." His frantic gaze darts to me. "Unless… you could fix it, couldn't you? With your magic? Good as new?"

He looks so genuinely desperate that some of my hostility fades. My magic quivers in my chest, but I clamp down on it firmly.

"I don't think putting a vase back together is worth trading a little sanity for," I say evenly. "But it shouldn't be a big problem. We'll go tell Delfis so he knows what happened. Petra and I can confirm that it was an accident. I don't think he'll be angry."

Petra nods. "Absolutely not. Accidents do happen. It's only a vase."

"But it was theirs. We're guests here…" Filip rakes his hand through his tawny hair with such a distressed air that I have to wonder who punished him for mistakes in the past.

Considering the company he was keeping, I can make a few decent guesses.

Petra steps out into the hallway. "Here, let's pick up the largest pieces to clean it up some and then we'll go straight to Delfis and sort it out."

For a moment, he just stares at us. "*You* would really speak for me? You didn't—you weren't even in the hall to know for sure how it happened."

I can't restrain a laugh. "We don't have any reason to think you'd be toppling vases on purpose, do we? It's not that hard to give the benefit of the doubt."

On this particular subject, anyway.

Filip lets out a shaky chuckle of his own and bobs his head to both of us. "I appreciate it."

He crouches to hastily gather the pieces alongside Petra. As I sink down beside him, more thoughts spin in my head.

I don't need Casimir's sensitivity to pick up on this man's fears of being dismissed or outright punished. Even if he isn't perfectly loyal to us yet… couldn't we start the process of earning that loyalty right here, right now?

If we can win over a former scourge sorcerer, the rest of the country shouldn't be a problem.

If Casimir *were* here, he'd be asking what this man really wants. To be treated as a valued colleague? To be trusted?

Well, we have the perfect opportunity right in front of us.

I scoop up a few of the larger shards and glance over at him. "Filip, how would you feel about joining in on a mission to destroy a whole lot more clay vessels?"

# TWENTY-FOUR

*Ivy*

From our vantage point over the top of the low hill, the small stone-block building looks tiny amid the sprawling fields. It's hard to believe that an operation producing hundreds of living clay prisons for daimon could be contained in there, but Rheave quickly provides the explanation.

His eerie eyes widen as he takes in the landscape. "They're under the ground. There has to be—I can't count them all, but I can feel them. Dozens."

Under the ground. I wet my lips as I study the fields, apprehension creeping up my back beneath my scars.

I've spent plenty of time sneaking around in dark, deep passages, some of it fairly recently. The hard part is going to be getting into this underground structure with no cover at all overhead.

The scourge sorcerers couldn't have picked a better position to watch for incoming threats. They placed the outer building with open land all around, giving anyone watching from there a clear view of at least a mile in every direction.

Stavros must be contemplating the same problem. He makes a disgruntled sound low in his throat. "They'll have people keeping watch up top as well, I'm sure."

Emor shifts on his elbows where he's sprawled next to Stavros, peering over the hilltop. The other leader of the Pima resistors decided to join us for this mission, wanting to meet the prospective queen for himself and see how we're using the people he and Voleska sent to help us.

He rubs his knobby chin. "We've got the magic advisor, don't we? I thought he had ways of concealing people."

Tinom is waiting farther down the hill behind us with Alek, Filip, and the seventeen others we've been able to bring together for this mission. The advisor's presence makes my skin itch, remembering what Alek and Petra have told me about his attitude toward the riven.

"We have a few charms that can keep one person almost completely invisible," I say. "It'd be beyond his power to completely hide our entire force for an extended period of time from people specifically watching for intruders. And I'm not even sure the charms will do much good... The man who defected from the scourge sorcerers warned us that the Order is using magic to guard against us as well."

Emor glances my way with a slight twist of his mouth. I understand why when he speaks. "Couldn't *you* handle all of that?"

My gut twists in turn. I realized I wasn't going to be able to keep my magic a secret from the resistance group as soon as Emor and Voleska's people started working with ours. Someone who knew would gossip about it. But I'd hoped that the subtle signs of discomfort I noticed when Emor first arrived—his gaze getting a bit twitchy when he looked at me, never placing himself right next to me —were just my imagination or for some other reason.

I work to keep my voice even. "In theory, I could. But expending that much magic would have a significant impact on my mental state. I'm not sure how well I could control it even in the moment. We don't need to destroy this facility so urgently that it's worth risking me harming our cause in the process."

Stavros's tone is curter than I allowed mine to be. "Ivy has plenty of other talents that can help us without taking that kind of risk."

He touches his shoulder to mine. "Why don't you take one of the invisibility charms and scout around closer to the facility? You'll be able to sense if they have any magical wards in place. Once we have more information, it'll be easier to strategize."

At least it's a start.

Before I can agree, Rheave jumps in. "I should go with Ivy. When I'm closer, I'll be able to get a better idea of where exactly the underground rooms are. The ones the daimon are in, anyway."

At Stavros's nod of agreement, Rheave scrambles down the hill to retrieve the charms from Tinom. I can't say I'm disappointed that he's spared me from having to speak to the magic advisor myself.

The moment I've fastened the chain around my neck, the daimon-man reaches for me and grips my hand so we stay fully visible to each other. "Should we start by going straight toward the building we can see?"

I square my shoulders. "That sounds like as good a plan as any."

We head over the hill and down the far slope with steady but careful strides. I keep my senses alert to any tingle of magic beyond the faint tickling sensation emanating from the charms.

For the first few minutes, I don't pick up on anything except the rustle of our feet through the yellowed grass. But when we've crossed about half of the distance between our hill and the stone structure, the slightest hum of magic passes over my skin.

I pause and ease forward even more slowly. With just a few steps, the hum thickens enough that I don't dare move any closer.

My magic jitters, eager to shatter the spell in front of us. Always so happy to trade a little more of my sanity in its hurry.

Clamping down on the impulse, I back up a bit so we don't risk triggering the wards. "I think the edge of their magical protection starts just beyond here."

Rheave hums and eyes the ground at his feet. "We haven't come over any daimon yet. The underground rooms don't extend this far, at least not in this direction."

I give his hand a gentle tug. "Let's see if we can chart the entire boundary. Why don't you burn the grass here as a marker—just a little, so no one who's watching from the building will be able to see it?"

Rheave brightens at being given a chance to be of use. He crouches and draws his hand over the ground. His daimon energy sizzles over the grass, leaving a thin black line in front of him.

We walk on, circumnavigating the building, weaving back and forth so I can judge where the magic's effect ends. Every ten paces or so, Rheave leaves another mark.

He's lapsed into silence. There's nothing ominous about it today, but I can't help thinking back to the times recently when he's seemed momentarily awkward in my presence.

My throat tightens, but I force myself to speak. "You know, you don't always have to stick with me in everything I do. I'd understand if you wanted some time to yourself or to help out in other ways, with other people."

Rheave's head snaps around, his expression so startled that I'm struck by a pang of guilt. "Why would you say that?"

I open my mouth and close it again before I pull my words together. "It's seemed like maybe you've been wanting a little more space, but you felt like you couldn't say so. Like you're not always totally comfortable around me."

A strained sound spills over Rheave's lips. He stops and turns me toward him so he can set his other hand against the side of my face.

As he gazes down at me, his brilliant sea-green eyes shine with emotion. "I'm sorry, Little Vine. It's my fault. I wasn't dealing with everything that comes with being human very well. But I talked to Casimir, and he helped me sort it all out. I'm okay now."

I frown. "What were you having trouble with? You know you can always talk to me if something's upsetting you."

"I don't think in this case that would have worked." He glances down and then meets my eyes again. "I love you, Ivy. It's the most powerful emotion I've ever felt… and it scared me a little. How much it hurt when you were in danger and I couldn't save you. I didn't understand how something so good could also feel so bad. But I want it all the same. I want as much of the good parts as we can have, as much time as I can be here with you. I'm sorry that I made you worry."

I feel even more choked up now, but the sensation is more sweet than bitter. "You don't need to apologize. You've had to adapt to a lot of new things. And… I love you too."

I didn't realize until I said the words how intensely the truth of that confession had been building in my chest. The words tumble out of me like a creature I've set free. Joy blooms in their place.

Rheave beams at me and leans in to claim a kiss. As his mouth melds with mine, I pull him into a tighter embrace.

How could I explain to him that for me accepting love has been the exact opposite? Everything I've loved before the past few months has brought me far more pain than happiness.

It's this joyful part that's new to me—that I could hardly bring myself to trust when I first started falling for the men who've won my heart.

I guess you could say Rheave and I have met each other halfway.

There isn't time to do much celebrating of that fact. We do have a military mission to carry out. But as we walk on around the scourge sorcerers' facility, Rheave twines his fingers with mine and swings my arm lightly back and forth, as if we're engaged in a dance as well.

"Have you been all right?" he asks. "What Alek found out about the origins of riven sorcerers is good, isn't it? But sometimes you've seemed more… sad, or tired maybe."

I'd hoped I was hiding my emotions better than that. A sigh slips out of me. "It's nothing new. I just keep getting reminded that no matter what the truth is, most people are going to be scared of me. Maybe even think I shouldn't exist. Even once Petra's on the throne, I'll probably have to keep hiding what I am."

Rheave growls defiantly. "Not with me. Not with Stavros or Alek or Casimir either."

The glow of affection he stirred up earlier lightens my melancholy thoughts. "I know. You have no idea how grateful I am to at least have the four of you."

It'll be enough. I can hardly complain when I've gotten so lucky already.

By the time we complete the full circuit, it's clear that the scourge sorcerers have wards monitoring about half a mile all around the outer building.

I stop to squint across that distance. Maybe a hundred paces away, a small metal grate shows through the grass.

It must be providing ventilation for the underground chambers. I suppose they probably need several of them. But we can't reach those access points, small as they are, while the wards are in place.

The sight of the barred metal circle reminds me of a different hatch many weeks ago—the entrance to one of the royal army's underground equipment stashes. It was guarded by a different sort of magic.

But that doesn't mean the same solution wouldn't work.

I look over at Rheave. "Do you remember how you've used your power to shatter other magic in the past? Do you think you could do the same thing to the wards around this place? Just… knock them out and dissipate the magic so the scourge sorcerers don't get any warning?"

Rheave studies the landscape intently. He lifts his hand, and a few sparks shoot from his palm. They fade into the air ahead of us.

"I can feel it there," he says. "It's coming from different places… Let me try doing one."

His stance tenses with his focus. He curls his fingers toward his palm and then splays them again in a sudden movement.

I don't even see the power he's sent out this time, only hear the soft crackle of it. But all at once, the tingle of nearby magic snuffs out completely.

"That did it!" I said. "At least near here. Let's see if anyone seems to notice…"

We hold perfectly still for the space of a minute. The cool breeze tugs at my hair, but no one emerges from the building.

A smile stretches across my face. "All right. Let's knock the rest of them out."

While Rheave prowls around the facility in a second circle, I dash back to our companions to fill them in on the progress we've made. As soon as I mention the grate, Alek perks up. "I should take a look at that."

The main reason the scholar joined us on this mission was to share his ideas for the best places to hit the facility to destroy it as quickly as possible. He's studied plenty of architecture in his years of research into Silanian history. The fact that this architecture is mostly under the ground apparently isn't too much of a setback.

With the third of Tinom's concealment charms, he follows me back to the field. My breath comes easier when we walk past the marks Rheave made without any hint of magic touching my senses.

Alek kneels down by the grate, dangles his fingers between the bars, and then holds his hand flat over them to test the air flow. "I'd definitely expect there to be more than one if the underground structure extends this far from the center point," he says.

With a quick search, we discover three more just on the hill-ward side of the facility. A light of inspiration gleams in Alek's eyes that would make me nervous if he wasn't on my side.

By that point, Rheave has finished disabling the wards. We all hustle to the hillside to confer with the full group.

"Exactly how many concealment charms do you have?" Alek asks Tinom first. "And how many other people do you think you could effectively divert attention from for several minutes?"

The magic advisor digs into his pouch. "I've managed to have two more blessed, which brings us to five. To be sure that no guards spot you, I wouldn't want to risk extending my gift to more than three others. Eight won't make for much of an offensive force."

"The people won't be doing most of the work. It's about what they can carry." Alek swivels toward Stavros, who's acting general for this mission. "We brought those explosive materials. We can still use them even if we can't see the building—through the grates."

Stavros catches his enthusiasm. "Yes. We'll have to set them off simultaneously for the best effect, because as soon as one goes off, the scourge sorcerers will go on the defensive. But that shouldn't be difficult to manage. I'll give a signal."

The massive man turns toward our varied group of royal soldiers and local resistors. "We'll need volunteers to launch the explosives. The rest of us will wait until the blasts have gone off, and then we'll charge the building. Anyone who emerges from below on the attack, we end them as quickly as possible before they can make much use of their magic. In the chaos, we should be able to get the upper hand and make our way below to finish the job."

I lift my hand before anyone else needs to. "I'm obviously going with the first group." If someone needs to jump in to prevent an unexpected disaster, I'll have the best chance of averting it, as much as it might cost me.

Unsurprisingly, Rheave volunteers too. Alek raises his chin with an air of defiance. "It's partly my plan. I should bear some of the risk."

I want to protest that my brilliant but not particularly soldierly scholar should stay back here where it's safer, but I can see how much it means to him to contribute in every possible way. My heart swells with more affection.

Tinom hesitates but offers to join us since it'll be easier for him to conceal himself than anyone else—and easier to cast his gift for illusions over others if they're nearby. Emor calls on a couple of his people to join him on the front lines, and one of the royal soldiers steps up as our eighth.

With an air of urgent anticipation hanging over us, we distribute the explosive supplies and the flints to set them off between us. Our other companions gather weapons and shields, Filip among them with a grim expression.

Stavros demonstrates a whistle that sounds like a hawk's cry to set us in motion. "I'll use my gift as well as I can to scan the grounds before I signal you. I don't want any unexpected surprises if we can avoid them."

As we nod, he reaches to give my shoulder a quick squeeze, as if willing me to return safely. I shoot him the most reassuring smile I can manage before we set off to do our duty.

The bundle of volatile substances in my hands makes my heart thump hard. I cradle the waxed tubes carefully as I lope across the grass, making for the far side of the facility.

So far there's still no sign of the scourge sorcerers from the upper building, so our initial efforts must have gone undetected.

When I reach my chosen grate, I brace myself above it and loop the far end of the oiled cord around a bar to ensure I don't lose hold of it. Then I sit back on my heels and wait.

My pulse thuds in my ears for what feels like an eternity before Stavros's whistled signal carries across the fields.

I drop the explosives between the bars and strike my flint. As the tubes tumble down the tunnel beneath the grate, a hissing flame darts along the cord after them.

I snatch one of my knives from my boot and scramble backward to avoid the worst of the explosion.

A stuttered booming shatters the quiet of the afternoon. One set of explosives and another and another blast apart in quick succession. The ground shakes, a puff of dark smoke rising from my grate.

And four figures burst from the inner building.

Flares of magic send a tingling rush over my body, but the scourge sorcerers don't know where to aim. I dodge the searing bolts of energy and charge right into one of the men, slamming my knife into his throat in the same motion.

The woman next to me staggers and collapses into a blackened corpse, telling me Rheave has made it to my side. Shouts ring out from the other side of the building, along with the thunder of more than a dozen racing feet.

I dash around the building in time to see Emor wrenching his dagger from a body that's turned to clay. Two more forms hurtle out to attack us, but Stavros is there, cutting through one with his sword. One of the soldiers slays the other attacker.

Another tremor ripples through the earth, followed by an unearthly creaking. I spin around to see the ground collapsing around one of the grates, opening a sinkhole as big as the building we're standing by.

As my jaw drops, someone yelps behind me. I whirl back around.

Filip is stabbing his spear into the side of a man who was ramming a sword toward me. He jerks backward as my would-be murderer transforms into a statue of clay.

I stare at the Order defector for a second, the hairs on the back of my neck on end. I shouldn't have gotten distracted.

I never would have thought the man who once associated with the scourge sorcerers would save me from one of their creations.

"Thank you," I manage to say.

Filip blinks at the spear he's holding as if startled by his own act and then flashes a sudden grin my way. "I owed you, didn't I? We'll take them down together!"

I can't help smiling back. "Yes, we will."

Our group storms into the building and catches another wave of fleeing sorcerers and captured daimon just emerging from a deep stairwell. They don't have even a chance to lash out with their magic before Emor's followers leap in to cut them down.

It all goes quiet except for a few gasps and groans from below. Tentatively, we descend the stairs.

A short hall leads to a huge room. At the far end, chunks of the ceiling have collapsed by the doorways to other parts of the facility. The idea of rocks bashing down on the heads of the scourge sorcerers gives me a grim satisfaction.

The rest of the room is laid out with cots. More than half of those cots hold a body, some still clay, some looking like flesh, their chests rising and falling with shallow breaths.

A shiver travels down my spine.

Rheave rushes to the nearest beds holding bodies of flesh. He grips one figure by the shoulders. "Can you get up? Can you talk to me?"

The form doesn't so much as twitch. I wince in understanding. "They mustn't be fully animated yet."

The daimon-man's face falls. "We can't do that awful magic ourselves."

Alek speaks up quietly. "We'll have to break the bodies so the daimon can go free. At least there won't be a struggle."

Rheave nods, but he still looks unsettled.

Stavros waves to us. "Come on, let's do what we can for them and then blast the rest of this place to bits before the Order realizes we're here."

Tinom calls out from another doorway. "I've found at least a few of the sacrificial accomplices!"

As I hustle over to join him in helping the mutilated figures, the images of the vast room with its rows of bodies stick in my head. My skin turns clammy, and not just because of the dank atmosphere of the underground facility.

I'm surrounded by the beings the scourge sorcerers have used for their purposes—to expand their power and their reach.

It isn't so different from how the gods apparently used the first riven, is it?

And the scourge sorcerers have called on their captured daimon again and again. They even managed to alter Rheave's behavior briefly a few times in the past after he'd shaken off most of their influence.

How can I be sure no godlen will ever tap me again to use me for their own agenda?

# TWENTY-FIVE

My uncertainties gnaw at me until a queasy sense of resolve forms in my gut. As we ride back toward the Temple of Tranquil Skies, my gaze shifts along the horizon, searching for a landmark I spotted on our journey to the clay factory.

We have to keep a slow pace with most of our number—which now includes the seven sacrificial accomplices we were able to rescue—piled into two wagons rather than on horseback. The sun has dipped to the horizon by the time I spot the crooked spire in the distance.

I nudge my horse forward to ride next to Stavros, knowing Rheave will keep pace. "That's a temple of Kosmel. Alek mentioned it when we passed the first time."

Stavros considers the distant building with its irregular architecture, presumably designed to echo the godlen of luck and trickery's interest in aiding those who aren't following the straightest paths in life.

His gaze slides back to me. "What are you thinking, Lady Thief?"

I adjust my grip on Toast's reins, abruptly nervous even though I have no real reason to be. "I'd like to make a detour over there. On my own," I add quickly when Rheave draws in a breath to speak. "There's a matter I'd like to take up with the godlen who's called on me."

Both of my men pause in pensive silence. We haven't broadcast Alek's discovery about the riven to all of our allies for fear of how Tinom will respond, but the scholar informed the rest of my men not long after he revealed his findings to me.

Rheave makes a disgruntled sound. "I could come with you and stay out of the way once we get to the temple. It might not be safe for you to go off on your own."

I shake my head. "I'll be less noticeable than the bunch of you. No one will be looking for a single rider. You should stay together in case the scourge sorcerers come looking for us for revenge. I'll meet you back at the Temple of Tranquil Skies—I might even make it there before you do."

Stavros lets out a sigh but reaches across the space to bump his elbow against Rheave's arm. "You're going to have to learn that there's no subduing our woman's independent streak. And she has a point. You're the most powerful protection we have other than her magic."

The former general tips his head toward me with a fond smile and compassion smoldering in his gaze. "Go on and see what the trickster can tell you. I'd like to hear it too."

I meet his eyes with a wave of affection. "Thank you."

Tapping Toast's sides, I send him cantering across the open plains toward the temple. It's far enough away that after a time I have to draw him back to a brisk trot to avoid exhausting him.

By the time I reach the cluster of ramshackle homes around the temple, where I guess the devouts and maybe eager dedicats take their rest, evening has fully set in. Lanterns gleam against the darkness in the temple's mismatched windows.

I tie Toast to one of the posts outside the temple. Kosmel is a patron of thieves, but I'm not especially worried about losing my mount.

Anyone who tries to make off with this cantankerous creature against his will is going to regret it.

Several crows perch on the crooked points of the roof. They let out a few hoarse caws at my arrival.

I step through the doorway of dark gray stone into a high-ceilinged chamber. The floor tiles are both cracked and polished.

Off to the side of the room, a devout in gray robes nods to me in welcome before resuming his current task—tossing scraps of bread and cheese onto the floor. At least a dozen small, furry bodies wriggle around him, snatching tidbits with the scrabble of tiny claws against the floor.

The rat is Kosmel's other holy animal. Apparently this temple hosts a colony of them.

I restrain a grimace and walk to the silver statue of the godlen looming at the far end of the worship room.

This depiction of Kosmel stands only twice as tall as me, less impressive than the massive statue in the one other temple in his honor I've visited back in Florian. Beneath his hood, his lips are curled in a typical sly smirk.

One hand extends to beckon me closer—the other is tucked behind his back as if concealing a gambit. A silver crow perches on his left shoulder, and two rats sprawl across his feet.

One of them is a living rat rather than part of the statue, I discover when I get closer and it darts away with a squeak. I raise my eyebrows at the image of the godlen, but I can't really complain about the company he keeps when it includes me.

Kosmel stood up for me when everyone else in my life would have had me hung for my magic. He helped me guide my power away from doing harm.

As frustrating as he can be, I have to give him credit for that.

As usual, a few dice lie scattered on the platform around the statue's booted feet. I pick up one, so many questions whirling in my head that it's hard to know where to start.

Let's cut right to the core of the matter. I squeeze my fingers around the hard cube and close my eyes, thinking as loudly as I can at the godlen.

*Did the gods channel their power through human beings to bring about the Great Retribution?*

I open my eyes to toss the die. It rattles across the platform and lands on three.

A moderate yes. My stomach clenches.

I grasp the die again. *Did channeling the power turn those people into the first riven sorcerers?*

Another roll, another three. I stare at it for a moment, letting the answer sink in.

There's my confirmation. Kosmel isn't trying to deny it. But then, in the past he's hinted at the damage the gods have done to people like me.

Maybe he wants me to know.

There are all sorts of other questions clamoring to be voiced, but one rises up so swiftly it overwhelms them all. I clutch the die against my palm.

*Did you leave us broken like this on purpose, as punishment?*

The die bounces across the platform with more force than I intended. It seems to take forever to come to a stop.

When it does, six dots gleam up at me.

The most emphatic no.

I glance up at the statue poised over me. A streak of shadow falls across the godlen's face just for an instant, like a tear trickling down his cheek.

I blink and it's gone, but a lump fills my throat. A prick of my own tears burns at the back of my eyes.

All this time, the recriminations, the pain, the executions—it's all been a terrible mistake?

I snatch up the die and roll it with a thought that races through my head. *Can you fix us?*

I'm left gazing at another six. Fuck.

A brief pressure grazes my shoulder, as if some invisible presence is offering me a reassuring—or perhaps apologetic—pat.

The gods have so much power, but there are things beyond their reach. Cracks that can't be sealed.

I don't think I even really hoped there was a way, but I find myself swiping at my eyes all the same.

This is how I am. This is how I'm going to stay.

As I reach the stable next to the Temple of Tranquil Skies, I can tell I did arrive ahead of the rest of our makeshift squadron. My pulse hiccups at the thought that they might have been waylaid after all, but one of the devouts emerges from the main temple building just as I'm dismounting.

"You separated from the others," she says without any significant sign of concern.

I nod. "I had an extra errand to take care of. I don't think they should be too far behind…"

She grins. "Not at all. Zevim's been watching from one of the towers—he says he can see their lanterns about a half hour's trek out."

I exhale with a rush of relief. "Good."

When I've left Toast comfortable in the stable, I emerge to find Casimir just crossing the yard. He hurries the last short distance to join me, his smile fond but his tone urgent. "How did the mission go? Is everyone all right?"

I lean toward him, grasping the front of his shirt, and he tucks his arms around me automatically. Even more tension unwinds as I rest my head against his shoulder, although nothing can budge the tightest knot that's formed in my gut since my talk with Kosmel.

I force out my voice. "No significant injuries, seven accomplices rescued, and no one will be using that facility to make more clay bodies any time soon."

Casimir hugs me a little closer. "Perfect. What was your extra errand, then?"

The devout must have passed on what I told her.

I swallow thickly. "I went to a temple of Kosmel to have a little chat."

The courtesan hums. "And was it enlightening?"

"Kind of."

I inhale, taking in his sweet sandalwood scent, and so much more I want to say fills my chest. Casimir has always seemed to have the closest relationship to his chosen godlen out of all of my men.

But what I want to discuss now, I don't think I want to bring up within hearing of the devouts serving their godlen so avidly.

"I'm tired," I say. "And I could use a bath. How about you practice some of that pampering skill on me?"

Casimir chuckles. "I'd be delighted to."

He guides me into the temple to one of the smaller bathing rooms and starts the water running.

As he considers the limited selection of oils and soaps, I twist my hands together in front of me rather than starting to undress. "Casimir… do you ever get frustrated with Ardone? Have there been times when you felt like there was more she could do for you that you deserve, and for some reason she hasn't come through?"

The courtesan turns to look at me. "I think it's totally normal for any human being to have moments of frustration. But I don't dwell on them. I know every godlen has a lot of dedicats to watch over—and what they want most is for us to thrive by our own abilities rather than relying on them."

He pauses. "What did Kosmel tell you about the riven?"

The lump returns to my throat. I have to gather myself before I can go on. "If I believe the die's answers came from him, he confirmed what Alek discovered. We were created to destroy the first scourge sorcerers. And they—they didn't leave us this way on purpose. The gods can't heal us."

"Oh, Kindness." Casimir walks straight to me and pulls me into another embrace. "At least you know that none of *them* see you as a monster, then. But it isn't fair that you and others like you have to continue suffering the consequences of their misstep."

"I don't understand," I mumble against his shirt. "Surely there was *some* way the godlen could have let people know that it wasn't our fault, that we could use help."

"Maybe they did, as well as they could. You've seen how stubborn people can be even when presented with facts. Once the idea became ingrained… Humans do like picking scapegoats so they have something concrete to aim their fears and angers at."

They do. And maybe I'm doing the same thing with the anger simmering in me—aiming it at the gods when it's really a huge mess of blame that I doubt anyone could pick apart.

I manage a rough bark of a laugh. "So you don't think any divine beings are going to smite me for thinking some not particularly kind thoughts their way?"

Casimir strokes his hand up and down my back. "I think they'd see that anger as your right. We all need to be allowed some grace."

He says it with so much calm certainty that I believe the words. As I tuck my head against his chin, I can't help thinking that this man deserves that grace at least as much as I do.

How much has he endured over the years, trying to live up to his mother's expectations to honor Ardone? How many sacrifices has he made that aren't visible like his jeweled teeth?

He's been here for me every time I've doubted or stumbled… Does he even understand just how much he means to me?

Love beams through my chest, softening the last of my frustration. I pull back just far enough to reach for the ties at the neck of Casimir's tunic.

The corner of his mouth quirks upward. "Looking for company in your bath?"

"It's always better when you join me." I tug the ties loose. "But I've changed my mind. This time, I'm going to pamper *you*."

# Twenty-Six

*Casimir*

As Ivy tugs my shirt up over my head, my first instinct is to protest. Pampering is my job—it's sometimes been the only significant contribution I can offer.

I'm the one who stayed back here at the temple while she risked her life today.

But when I see the bright smile that's crossed her lips as she gazes at me, my resistance melts.

The idea of offering her love this way makes her happy. How can I deny her that joy?

That doesn't mean I'm going to be totally passive in this encounter, though.

I reach for her shirt in turn, the fitted tunic she wore rather than her usual dresses for the mission we knew might require a lot of physical maneuvering. "I still want you in that bath with me."

Ivy's laugh is as bright as her smile. "I'm not going to deprive myself just because I'm taking care of you."

With rustles of cloth, fleeting caresses, and a few stolen kisses, we shed all our clothes. My cock stirs just at the sight of Ivy's slim but wiry body, that beautiful combination of delicacy and strength.

Before I can do more than stroke my fingers along the side of one of her pert breasts, she pulls me over to the bathtub. "I do want to get washed first. And I'm going to wash you too."

I force myself to remain where she positions me at the side of the large tub rather than aligning myself with her in the water. Ivy lathers a bar of soap between her hands and rubs her fingers over my shoulders, then down my arms and chest in a gentle massage.

I'm getting harder by the second, but her touch generates more than lustful heat. A soothing warmth spreads from beneath her hands as well, releasing tensions I hadn't known I held in my muscles.

Her expression has become intent, but her eyes still shine with affection every time our gazes meet. There's a warmth in that too—in the devotion she's offering with every swivel of her fingers.

I could be molded like clay in this woman's hands.

It's not a feeling I've truly gotten to experience before, somehow. In our training for the companionship division, we sometimes worked our arts on each other for practice, but I never completely gave myself over to any of those experiences. I was always thinking like a courtesan still, noting the techniques used and the reactions they provoked in me for any aspects I might want to incorporate with my future clients.

And I didn't care about any of those partners beyond friendly acquaintances or casual friends, nor they about me. The pampering that Ivy's offering me right now really is an act of love.

She's not afraid to bring a little more heat into the mix. As her hands drift down to my hips, she slides her fingers around my rigid cock for a few quick pumps.

The rush of more intense pleasure propels a groan out of me.

I'm rewarded with a sly smile that only makes Ivy more gorgeous. She works her way down my legs with the same care she brought to my upper body and then motions for me to dunk my head. "Let's wash that lovely hair of yours too."

I drop my head back into the water obligingly and then lean forward so Ivy can reach the drenched waves more easily. She drizzles the liquid soap over my hair and then works it in with teasing circles of her fingertips.

An appreciative hum resonates from my chest. "You're very good at this. Maybe we should add courtesan to your list of titles."

Ivy lets out another laugh and deepens her massage of my scalp. "Only when I'm properly inspired, and I'm very happy limiting myself to four lovers who spark that inspiration."

She has me sink down so she can rinse the suds from my hair. Fully refreshed, I reach for her. "I think it's my turn."

Ivy's sly smile grows. She looks at me through her eyelashes with a coquettishness I'm not used to from her. "I think it could be more fun if you simply relax and watch."

Before I have to wonder what she means, she rises up on her knees so her breasts are on full display. She strokes her lathered hands over her own body with the same sensuality she brought to mine.

I can't help imagining my hands following those same paths. My cock is outright throbbing now, but it's a delicious sort of teasing.

And my heart swells at the same time, full of my love for her.

Ivy's gained so much confidence since the first bath I arranged for her, when she was nervous to even take off her dress. The trials we've faced have wounded and shaken her, but she's also come out of them even stronger than before.

Once she's finished washing her torso, she stands right up so I get a clear view of her sex and ass as she tends to them too. Desire thrums through my veins.

I manage to hold myself back until she lowers herself back into the water for a rinse, and then I surge forward.

I pull her to me and bury my face against her damp hair by her ear. My voice comes out in a ragged murmur. "I don't think I can stand one more second without being inside you."

Ivy shivers eagerly against me and adjusts her position to straddle my thighs. "I certainly didn't start this interlude to leave you wanting."

As she takes me into her slick heat, our mouths collide. A blissful flush spreads across every inch of my body.

I cup her cheek with one hand and grip her hip with the other, thrusting into her at the angle I know will spark just as much pleasure in her.

Even through her gasps, Ivy doesn't give herself completely over to me. She tangles her fingers in my hair with the most delightful tug and strokes her other hand over my chest, pausing to pinch one of my nipples.

Still determined to offer me every bit as much attention as I'm giving her.

There's a deeper sort of joy to this exchange, isn't there? To be receiving adoration as well as offering it?

It's not something we learned at the royal college, but as courtesans, we weren't meant to seek out partners who wanted more than a temporary liaison. I have to think Ardone must value this balanced love just as much as that offered totally selflessly.

It feels like a kind of magic.

It's my honor to be a part of it.

Our mouths crash together again and again. The water sloshes around us just as wildly.

My release builds at the base of my cock, but I need Ivy to come with me. Plunging into her at a faster rhythm, I slip my hand between us to strum that sensitive spot just above her opening.

Ivy moans and bucks faster with me. Her fingernails dig into my back with a sting I find more thrilling than painful.

I will back my climax, but in the same moment a tremor ripples through Ivy's frame. She clamps around me with a stuttered sigh, and I give myself over to the blaze of pleasure now that I know she's satisfied too.

Ivy relaxes into my arms and snuggles against me for a minute, not making any move to untangle herself from me. I nuzzle the side of her head and allow myself to revel in every bit of the pampering she's offered.

It's not long before her practical side kicks in, though. She peeks over the edge of the tub and winces at the puddles left behind by our fun. "We're going to need more towels."

I chuckle and give her one more kiss before getting out of the tub with her. We dry ourselves off and mop up the watery mess until there's no evidence of our intimate adventures except the sodden towels.

I help Ivy back into her clothes and don my own. "How would you feel about a little stargazing?"

She beams back at me. "That sounds wonderful. The rest of our expedition should be back by now, but there won't be much planning to do until the sentries report on how Lothar's responded to our attack. I think we've all earned a night off."

We're just coming around the bend into the temple's main hall when Filip bursts out of one of the other hallways. The Order defector halts in his tracks at the sight of us, his expression twitching with a flurry of emotions that makes me uneasy.

I step toward him, gentling my tone to avoid putting him on the defensive. "Are you all right, Filip?"

He stares at me for a second and then glances at Ivy. Her brow has knit with worry. He seems to waver before dragging in a sharp breath and hurrying closer.

"Ivy," he says with a respectful dip of his head. "If anyone will be able to stop them, it's you. I'm so sorry. I should have said something earlier. I never should have gone along with it at all."

As my heart lurches, Ivy's posture stiffens. "Gone along with what? Stop who?"

The Order of the Wild defector shoves his hand back through his tawny hair. "When I joined you —it was supposed to be a trick. I didn't *want* to lie to anyone. I haven't felt right about what's being done under the banner of the Order of the Wild for months. But I was afraid of what they'd do to me if I didn't go along with the plan…"

With every word that falls from his mouth, it's obvious how anguished he feels about his decision. Anger flares in my chest at the thought of the danger he's put us in, but my fury is tempered by a corresponding rush of compassion.

I don't know what this man has been through—what the scourge sorcerers put him through before he got to this point.

He's confessing to us now. That counts for something.

Ivy's hands have clenched at her sides. I jump in before she can speak. "It's understandable that you'd have been afraid, and it does you credit that you're owning up to your missteps. We can deal with the past later, on our own time. What is it you're worried about now?"

His expression turns even more miserable. "The last thing I did for them—I managed to pass on a message a few days ago, not long after we got to the temple, to let them know where Princess Petra had gone. They signaled me just now, through a charm they gave me—they're on their way. I'm supposed to distract you so you don't realize they're coming, but I don't want to. I want you to get out of here before they can do whatever they're planning. I—I want to come *with* you."

He drops to his knees in appeal, his hands clasped in front of him, his gaze fixing completely on Ivy. "You know what it's like to hurt people and regret it. To want them to see you as something better. I know I can do so much better too. Please, give me the chance."

As she stares at him, I reach for my gift with a tingling through my teeth and focus on the man in front of me. In the rush of sensations that flow through my mind, my certainty locks into place.

It's a much more specific impression than what I first got from him, when he needed us to welcome him to carry out his trick. What I could do that would make this man happiest is to help him escape the horrors he's already seen from his former colleagues.

"He means it," I say.

Ivy's gaze turns fierce. She motions Filip back to his feet. "How far out are they?"

He splays his hands helplessly as he scrambles up. "I don't know. I assume they'd give me a decent amount of warning, but it could be less than an hour."

Ivy's stance is still rigid, but my calm approach appears to have tempered her anger as well. She turns to me. "Come on. We need to get everyone out of the temple."

Her head jerks back toward the defector. "And you'd better stick with us. You're going to need to prove that we *can* trust you now when we shouldn't have before."

He hangs his head. "I know. I thought… I thought I'd already been dragged into so many messed up things that there wasn't any hope for me. I haven't really felt like myself in years… until the past week with all of you. This is where I want to be, and I'll do whatever it takes to prove it."

Ivy gives him a sharp nod and jogs down the hall. She raises her voice so it carries through the building. "Delfis? Tinom? Petra? We have a problem!"

In a matter of minutes, the temple is consumed with activity. Delfis directs most of his devouts to help us in our frantic packing of supplies while several others usher the rescued sacrificial accomplices into a hidden entrance that leads to a secret basement chamber.

"A security measure I wish we could offer all of you," he says. "But if the Order is suspicious of us, they'll watch the temple closely for weeks. I don't think you'd be able to leave to carry out the rest of your mission unless you do it now."

Petra bobs her head to him with a tap of her fingers down her chest, acknowledging both him and the godlen he serves. "I understand. We're grateful for the hospitality you've already offered."

I hurry out to the stable to gather all the horses we brought and a few extra steeds the cleric says he can spare. When I lead the last couple out to meet the emerging crowd, Petra is deep in debate with our allies from Pima.

"I don't know how far we're going to have to flee to be safe," she's saying to Emor. "And Nikodi was right at the heart of the uprising. We can't go there. But I can't ask your people to travel so much farther from home either."

He waves off her concern. "I'll return to pass on word of what went on here. But what matters the most to us has always been seeing the scourge sorcerers taken down."

He glances around at his followers. "Is there anyone who'd rather go back to Pima with me than continue helping our future queen secure her throne?"

At the chorus of refusals that rises up in response, Petra looks both awed and nervous. Her mouth sets in a firm line. "I'll do my best to keep you all safe."

Ivy secures a bag to Toast's saddle and swings onto his back. She scans the yard as if seeing beyond the temple walls. "I can't sense any magic extending this far yet… but that doesn't mean they aren't close."

Petra hefts her younger brother onto her horse in front of her and checks on her sister, who's sharing a horse with Rheave. Once we're all mounted, Tinom extends his arm, sweeping his hand through the air.

"I'll do my best to deflect their attention from us in the darkness. Let us go quickly and quietly. If anyone gets separated, make for Tupno, and we'll regroup outside the city. I think we're best off heading south. There are a few noble families on the far side of Florian I'd expect to take the Melchiorek side. It's about time we called on them."

We set off through the gate at a brisk trot.

The night drapes around us, the temple's lanterns quickly dwindling behind us. All my companions are reduced to faint shades of gray in the dim starlight.

Stavros, Ivy, and the soldiers form a circle around the royal children. I hang a little farther back in the procession to watch both my companions and our surroundings.

Filip sticks near me, his shoulders hunched and his expression pained.

I don't see any sign that my gift's judgment was wrong. He didn't see a way out before—now he believes there is one. And that's made all the difference.

Ahead of me, Ivy's head snaps around. She nudges Toast faster to pull ahead, as if tracking something. "I felt a twinge… some magic I don't think is ours—"

The last word has barely left her lips when a flash of searing energy shoots through the night toward Petra. Ivy yanks her stallion around; one of the soldiers jostles the future queen's horse to the side.

And Prince Jacos yelps in pain.

"Ride!" Petra shouts. "Ride, as fast as you can, before they can keep attacking."

She hugs her brother to her. I catch a glimpse of a slash cut through his cloak, blood welling on his arm, before she bundles the fabric to stop the bleeding and kicks their horse to a canter.

"They aren't close," Ivy calls out in a low voice as she follows suit. "They might not even know the blow hit. We can still outrun them."

As our procession surges forward, Tinom aims a glower at her that raises my hackles.

He's looking at Ivy as if he thinks it's her fault the prince was hurt. As if she should have sounded a better warning when it's his concealing magic that failed us most.

Is he always going to see her as a villain?

Gritting my teeth, I tap my horse's sides and race after the others.

# Twenty-Seven

I stride into the dining room turned resistance headquarters, waving a pamphlet fresh from the press. "We've got a new batch!"

The many figures crowded around the table look up. Petra smiles from her spot at the head, but I catch plenty of skeptical or even anxious expressions too.

I'm not sure yet how to feel about the way our resistance group has grown. Since we arrived at the summer estate of one of the court barons a few days ago, our numbers have more than doubled.

Tinom chose well, I can admit. Baron Cyris and his wife showed nothing but pure relief when the remaining Melchioreks arrived and immediately started venting about how awful Lothar and his Order of the Wild are. And this particular baron has a gift for illusions similar to Tinom's, which means he can join the magic advisor in concealing signs of our comings and goings from the estate.

But he is a noble, and the others who've joined us are also nobles or the close comrades of nobles. Every time I see a lip curled in disgust aimed Alek's way, my well-practiced will-power is strained resisting the urge to punch that face. I'm sure our allies who came all this way from Pima with us have noticed the upturned noses and uneasy mutterings just as I have.

Gods forbid anyone be in their presence wearing peasant clothes rather than embroidered silks.

Petra beckons me over, and I skirt the various nobles and staff to reach her. Most press closer to the table even though there's plenty of space at the edge of the room for me to get by.

It's obvious word has worked its way through our growing numbers about my powers as well. No one's dared to speak against me, since I'm sure they've also heard that their future queen has defended my presence, but there's no denying the tensed postures and lowered voices whenever I pass by them.

I can't really complain. We need all the help we can get. The nobles have sway over their domains and plenty of staff they can call on.

They have access to resources we might need… including the printing press I heard the baroness mention she fiddles around with as a "hobby," which gave me an idea for a new strategy.

A sense of satisfaction takes the edges off my nerves as I set the pamphlet I'm holding in Petra's waiting hand.

My father always talked about how the press was the best tool for reaching people's minds. *You can put any message on pieces of paper and send it all over the realms in a matter of days.*

We haven't needed to win over anyone outside our kingdom, but we have to build all the support we can manage within it. I've spent a large part of the last couple of days working with Alek and Casimir, putting together simple messages and pictures to convey the threat the scourge sorcerers pose and the good Petra can offer the country instead.

The images will give the gist of the idea to those who haven't learned to read. Those who can will explain the rest in the undercurrent of nervous chatter we hope to encourage throughout the country.

This afternoon's set of pamphlets warn Silana's civilians that a group that would murder the king won't hesitate to kill others as well, prompting them to think about the acts of violence they've witnessed carried out by the Order. The stark letters at the bottom ask, *What if they come for your sons and daughters next?*

It's pointed propaganda, but the scourge sorcerers deserve it.

As Petra scans the one I gave her, several of the more luxuriously dressed figures nearby stir restlessly.

The local countess who's thrown in her lot with us clears her throat. "Are we really sure that tossing those papers around is the best use for our limited manpower?"

One of Voleska and Emor's people speaks up before I have to. "It's not like we've had that many other jobs to take care of. And you should have seen 'em in the square this morning when we launched the latest batch!"

The colleague next to her lifts his head eagerly. "Yeah, they were snatching at them and chattering away about it. Word is spreading fast. The tide's turning in Queen Petra's favor."

We've had to come up with creative ways of distributing the pamphlets, since the Order members who've spread across the country aren't going to stand by while someone shouts about their misdeeds in the city squares. With a combination of stealth and a few handy magical gifts our allies can bring to bear, we've been showering them over the crowds from the highest vantage points we can find.

If all's gone well, some of the riders who headed out yesterday will have sent papers blustering down as far as Florian with the help of the Black Talons, as well as other royal cities like Zulina and Mipone.

It won't be long before the scourge sorcerers can guess that we've relocated in the south end of the country, but we want to spread out our activities enough that it isn't easy to guess what province, let alone county, we're in.

If they find us again, I'm not sure where we'd be able to take shelter next.

A merchant friend of the barons raps an impatient hand on the table. "We need to 'turn the tide' with more than just words."

Petra lifts her gaze to consider her supporters. She keeps her tone mild. "I think words are a very good start while we gather ourselves for a more intensive effort. This is perfect, Ivy. Do we have people ready to carry them out?"

I nod. "I just have to give them the word."

As I duck out of the room, I catch a not-especially-hushed voice mutter, "Where did that one come from?"

Stavros's voice follows an instant later with a hard edge of warning. "Ivy's been protecting Silana from the scourge sorcerers from the beginning."

I hurry to the out-building that holds the press, discomfort itching at my skin. I don't like leaving my men or the future queen who's accepted me to defend my role in the resistance, but I'm not sure how to speak up myself without making our new allies even more nervous.

I find my self-appointed assistants just finishing stuffing the latest batch of pamphlets into saddle bags.

"Queen Petra approves," I tell them, and they flash grins at me before hustling off to the waiting horses.

I raise my voice to call after them. "Safe travels!"

Some part of me wishes I was riding off to carry out more capers rather than debating with the stuffy jerks around here.

Of course, the current caper might not be possible without those stuffy jerks and all their possessions. So I bite my tongue and march back to the meeting room.

I return to find the table debating the need for weapons. Princess Klaudia is just looking around at her companions with a worried expression. "I thought we were going to win over the people as peacefully as possible. We're not like the scourge sorcerers. We can't just *kill* citizens who've been deceived."

Tinom shoots her a condescending glance. "We can't be unprepared. It's unlikely Lothar will back down without any fight at all."

Stavros dips his head. "I'm sorry to say that I agree. I'd rather not have to draw any more blood, but it's better that we have blades we don't need to use than need them and find ourselves empty-handed. The scourge sorcerers and the most avid members of the Order of the Wild know what they've gotten themselves into by now."

Petra sighs, her gaze sliding to Prince Jacos. Her brother is sitting next to Klaudia, his sleeve lumpy around the bandage he's still wearing from the magical attack while we were fleeing the Temple of Tranquil Skies.

"We do need to be ready to defend ourselves," she says. "And to strike at our actual enemies when we have the opportunity. The Order has hurt too many people to deserve our mercy. We'll do our best to avoid any collateral damage."

Alek pushes to the table from where he's been hanging back from the discussion. His jaw looks tight, his posture a little awkward under the stares, but he hasn't been so bothered that he's returned to wearing a mask over his scars.

His voice comes out perfectly steady. "I may be able to arrange a large supply of new weapons. I can reach out to my family. They've handled a steady production and acquisition of quality arms for decades, and I've never heard my parents be anything other than supportive of the Melchiorek reign."

My stomach knots at his proposition. His family might be loyal to the Crown, but they never supported *him*. I don't think he's been back to see them since he first enrolled at the temple school where he got those scars.

Petra aims a smile at him. "If you trust that it's safe to reach out to them, I know you'll handle the discussion well. The sooner we find out our options, the better."

The scholar draws himself up straighter. "I'll prepare for the trip right away."

I watch him head for the doorway, my gut tugging at me to follow him.

Before I've quite made the decision to leave, Petra taps her hands against the tabletop. "Now I think we should discuss the possibility of the kingship trials."

My gaze jerks back to her in the same moment as a few grunts and other disgruntled noises sound from around the table.

"Trials?" Baron Cyris says. "Isn't that one of the bizarre ideas Lothar's people have been babbling about?"

Petra inclines her head in acknowledgment. "It is. But I believe we can adjust the concept to work in our favor."

One of the other nobles lets out a sputter of a laugh. "How could they possibly be a benefit to us?"

Petra's eyes seek me out by the other end of the table. I'm the one who suggested this idea to her—but she isn't singling me out or demanding that I justify the strategy.

Somehow that makes me feel even more compelled to step in.

I raise my voice to carry over the uneasy murmurings. "A lot of Silana's citizens have shown that they don't trust the Melchioreks to have their best interests at heart. We heard demands that the next ruler prove themselves worthy in both Florian and Tupno. And they don't really know Petra. Even if they're starting to doubt the Order of the Wild, that doesn't mean they believe in *her* enough to risk their livelihoods and their lives on her behalf."

Most of the heads around the table swivel toward me. The baroness's lips curl with a hint of a sneer. "So you think our queen should put her life on the line to convince them?"

"Not her life," I say quickly. "That's why we'd adapt the idea. Nothing brutal or as dangerous as I'm sure Lothar is imagining—or as skewed in the Order's favor. We'll come up with tasks for Petra to complete that would make people feel more confident and prove her strength without taking too immense a gamble."

"Exactly." Petra folds her arms over her chest. "And there's another very good reason to put on such a demonstration. We can call for Lothar to submit his own candidates. It won't be much of a trial if I have no competition. If he wants to prove *himself* a fair player, he'll need to show up. We'll have our first real opportunity to expose his and his top followers' treachery directly—and to address it as we see fit."

With a sword through Lothar's skull, preferably. But even as my spirits stir at the thought of confronting the villain on equal ground, my stomach flips over.

Petra never mentioned that element before. It wasn't part of my initial idea. And it sounds as if…

Klaudia puts my concern into words before I can. "You're talking about using yourself as bait."

Horror tinges her tone, but Petra responds calmly. "I'm the only bait that would work. I trust that you all will ensure I'm never under more threat than is worth it to see our purpose through."

No one quite seems to know how to argue against that statement. Our future queen gazes around the table. "Let's get on with it, then. We need to brainstorm what our trials might look like, how we would spread the word, where we should hold them."

Her call to action finally spurs the uncertain to speak.

Tinom frowns. "I'm not certain this is a wise tactic, Your Highness. Regardless of what precautions we try to implement, the risks you'd need to take—"

"It's absolutely inappropriate," Countess Mirina breaks in. "Our queen, dueling against whoever the riffraff throws up against her?"

Petra gives a cough that might cover a laugh. "I don't think we'd include any actual dueling, Mirina."

Baron Cyris waves his hand dismissively. "A queen shouldn't lower herself to that level. You have to think of how it would appear to your most devoted supporters, Your Highness."

My hackles rise. Supporters like him, he means.

The words burst out before I can catch them. "Unless you can win the throne back for her—and keep it—all on your own, we *need* the support of the common people too."

He turns to me with a huff. "What do you know about the ways of the court? I never saw you before three days ago." He shifts his attention back to Petra. "You must heed our advice, Your Highness. Nothing good ever comes of giving way too much to the masses."

A flurry of other voices follow his, most of them echoing his protest.

My magic shudders, prodding me to shut them all up, preferably by knocking them on their pompous asses. I clamp down on it instead and gather myself to jump back into the argument.

Then my gaze catches on Petra's face.

Her mouth has tightened, her expression momentarily uneasy.

She isn't totally committed to this course. They've shaken her resolve.

If she isn't sure it's the right plan, who *am* I to insist that it is? The baron isn't entirely wrong.

All at once, I feel like I'm back in the bow of the oak tree in Slaughterwell, watching life happen beneath me from a distance. I've witnessed plenty, sure, but how much have I truly lived before the past few months?

Do I even really know what I'm asking of Petra?

The doubt rises up in me so fast it steals my breath. I step back from the clash of voices and then stride out of the room.

On a matter this immense that involves her so personally, Petra should make up her own mind. She has plenty of other people in there who can advise her from various levels of society, all of whom probably have a better idea what's really at stake than I do.

I walk almost blindly until I find myself stepping out the front door. The cool air washes over me, settling my thoughts and leaving my mind clearer.

I take a few more steps into the yard, breathing deeply and getting a grip on myself.

I'm not used to being an active participant in Silana's politics. I'll get more comfortable with it in time. Just a few minutes to sort myself out, and I can go back in there and say my piece if I feel I need to.

The door squeaks behind me. I barely have time to turn before Stavros's well-muscled arm has wrapped around me.

I turn to meet his embrace instinctively, soaking up his warmth and his smoky, peppery scent, even as the question I know I have to ask creeps up my throat. "Shouldn't you still be in there with the rest of them, figuring out the best approach? You're the only general we've got."

"Former general," Stavros mutters, and teases his prosthetic down my back in a gentle caress. "I needed a break from them too. It was either that or there'd have been several broken noses and a not particularly happy queen-to-be."

The corners of my mouth twitch with the start of a smile. "I think she might have understood a little."

Stavros hums to himself and eases back just far enough to peer down at me. "You're not letting them shake your confidence, are you, Lady Thief? The Hand of Kosmel knows more about schemes and treachery than those nobles could even conceive of."

My momentary good humor fades. "They know a lot about plenty of other things I've never experienced."

"Which is why we're all at the table together, weighing in." He cocks an eyebrow. "You didn't let the horde of high-borns at the college intimidate you."

I open my mouth and hesitate as I form a full answer. "I had Julita giving me an inside edge. And... I wasn't there as myself. I was playing a role. It was easier."

Easier not to care what they thought of me. Easier to drape myself in noble-style self-assurance like yet another fancy gown.

Of course, even if I'm not outright pretending to be someone else these days, I'm still not really being myself. I'm downplaying one of the most significant parts of me as much as I can, willing everyone around me to forget that I'm one of the riven.

Somehow that's more uncomfortable than simply hiding my whole self away like I once did. But I'm going to have to get used to it.

Stavros dips his head closer, his voice dropping low with it. "I just don't want to see you backing down. The woman I love has never shied away simply because a situation gets hard."

A flush spreads over my body with his nearness, and I leap at the opportunity to focus on that heat rather than my worries.

I trail my fingers down his brawny chest, appreciating every ridge of sculpted muscle I can trace through his tunic. "I suppose that's true. Certain things I particularly appreciate when they're hard."

The suggestive note in my voice clearly isn't lost on the former general. He chuckles and catches my mouth with his.

As Stavros worships me with his kiss, our bodies press closer together. Desire pools low in my belly with the image of him pushing me right up against the side of the house, plunging into me without regard for noble sensibilities.

I'm not sure either of us would actually go quite that far. But before I get the chance to find out, a current of magic tickles across my skin from across the yard.

My back goes rigid, and Stavros yanks back. "What's wrong?"

I pull back from him, scanning the landscape around the estate. "I felt... Someone extended magic this way..."

As I move forward, his hold on me loosens. We stalk over to the gate together.

The whiff of magic keeps drifting around me. I don't sense anything aggressive about it, but that doesn't mean the caster has good intentions.

Stavros tilts his head as if pricking his ear. "Someone's coming."

I hear the distant hoofbeats a moment later. Only one set, from the sounds of it. Not anything like an army.

Still, we stay braced and waiting as they approach the estate. If it isn't an ally, we don't want them seeing me or Stavros here under Baron Cyris's roof.

My own magic unfurls through my chest, reminding me of how easily it could spring to our defense if need be.

The hoofbeats slow. The guard posted on the other side of the gate calls out. "Who are you, and what business do you have here?"

A dryly feminine voice replies. "I'm looking for a woman named Ivy."

The tone is so familiar and yet so unexpected that for the first second I remain frozen. Then I reach to open the gate.

It swings open to reveal the last person I'd ever have expected to see outside her home. The woman who taught me what I know about controlling my riven power—and who insisted it would never be safe for people like us to return to society.

Sulla meets my gaze with a tentative smile, her hands tight around her horse's reins. "There you are. I thought... I thought it was time I came down from my mountain."

# Twenty-Eight

The smell of the forges taints the air even half a mile away. Memories come flooding over me with it: the nights when I tucked myself away in the attic so my parents wouldn't notice how late I stayed up reading, the ache in my muscles on the days when Dad insisted I take a turn with the hammer and anvil as if that might wake up some love of weaponry in me.

The disapproving glowers when not even a flicker of interest ever lit.

As I ride on toward our family's sprawling shop at the edge of the small city, the breeze washes over my face. The air is starting to warm with the first hints of spring, but I'm starkly aware of the currents catching on the ridges of scar on my face.

I've thought about my deformity less and less over the past few months since I first started removing my mask. Even the stares of the nobles we're allying ourselves with barely matter anymore when I can simply look at Ivy and have her beam adoration at me.

But my family already has a picture of me in their heads, and I don't fit it anymore. I haven't been home since I was expelled from the temple school.

They may have heard some of the details of my teenage disgrace, but that's different from seeing it in front of them.

I can already picture my mother wincing in horror, my father's lip curling with disgust. They'll probably blame my ruined face on my strange inclinations toward books and scholarship, as if my studies warped my morals.

I glance down at the small bag attached to my saddle. I brought a mask with me in case I decided it was best to cover the consequences of my long-ago crime.

My fingers itch to reach for it, to shield my face from judgment like I did for so long.

But what difference will it make, really? They'll imagine something terrible lies behind it regardless.

It isn't as if my family is unfamiliar with how ravaged a human body can become. I remember plenty of scarred figures crossing the shop's doorstep.

The difference is those figures earned their scars in battle as badges of honor.

I suppose I received mine in a battle of a different sort—one with my personal flaws. As much as the shame of my actions might have marked me, I did win in the end.

I've come a long way from the boy I was.

So when I reach the hitching post down the street from the shop, I leave the mask in my saddlebag. I walk over to the shop through the thickening smells of smoldering coals and hot metal with all the confidence I can bring to my stride.

The clang of a hammer striking steel rings through the doorway. I know before I reach the threshold where to look for my father.

He still has his personal forge and anvil in the same corner of the workshop. He hefts the hammer and brings it down on the blade he's working, presumably a private commission for a particularly moneyed client.

The rest of the front room is dedicated to displaying the results of his craft and other pieces of weapons and armor he's carrying in his inventory. Most of the arms he and my mother deal in he doesn't make himself. He oversees multiple apprentices in one of the back rooms and sources more from other blacksmiths who don't have quite the same business sense.

He has his back to me, his broad shoulders flexing as he lowers the hammer to examine the sword. It seems like as good a time as any to make my presence known.

I clear my throat. "Dad."

My voice peels out louder than I expected over the warble of the forge's fire. Dad startles and whirls around, my name already on his lips. "Aleks—"

The last syllable dies as his gaze jars on my face. He doesn't quite flinch, but his jaw tics as if he's restrained one.

And there's that curl of the lip.

I step farther into the shop and continue before he can say anything else. "I won't be staying long. There's something important I need to talk to you about."

Mom's surprised voice carries from the large warehouse room at the back of the shop. "Is that Aleksi?"

She comes hustling out with wide eyes and a hesitant smile. When her gaze finds me, her eyes widen even more—and the smile vanishes.

"Hello, Mom," I say through the constricting of my throat. Imagining their reactions wasn't a tenth as painful as experiencing them firsthand.

She doesn't even bother to return my greeting. "What happened to you?"

I'm not going to lie. "I made some bad decisions—but I learned from them. It was years ago. I've put it behind me."

My father finally manages to sputter a response. "It's right here in front of us. This is what you let happen to you at that useless school? This is the face you show the world now?"

My hackles come up in an instant. Just like old times.

"It's the face I have," I grit out. "And the school wasn't useless."

Mom moves tentatively toward me, her arms crossing in front of her. She shakes her head. "I knew there wasn't anything good to come of surrounding yourself with people who'd rather think about words than what's real. But you were so stubborn."

"It was still the right choice. Everything I studied was real. What I look like doesn't matter in—"

Dad cuts me off with a dismissive snort. "Tell that to anyone you need to barter with while you're showing them that mug. What are you doing here? Did you finally get tired of those stuck-up scholars?"

Another sharp retort prickles up my throat. In the same moment, my hand clenches by my hip—and my fingers brush the lump in my pocket that's my most vital cargo.

That object is the reason I'm here at all. It has nothing to do with my career choices or my parents' opinion of them.

The mission I'm on is so much bigger than all the bitter past behind us that I've nearly stumbled right back into.

I'm *not* the boy they knew. I have the ear of the future queen. The love of a riven sorcerer.

I'm not someone for a couple of weapons merchants to sneer at—I deserve their respect.

Gods above, would I ever have stooped so low in the first place if I hadn't been so desperate for respect back then? If I'd gotten even a smidgeon of support from the people who raised me?

My scars are marks of my shame, but I had a childhood of rejection and disdain to bring me to that point. Everything I've earned since then, all the things I've accomplished are completely thanks to my own strength, rising above the foundation these two people built for me.

I draw my stance up straighter and swallow down my rancor.

I won't speak to them like their disappointing son. I'm here as Queen Petra's representative.

My tone evens out, both harder and steadier than before. "I didn't come to discuss my schooling or what happened to my face. There are more pressing matters to address. Have you been doing business with the Order of the Wild?"

Dad's momentary shock at my change in tone shifts into a disgruntled expression at my last words. "Crazed rabblerousers, throwing the whole country into chaos," he grumbles, setting his hammer down on the forge. "What business is there anyone can do with them? They don't think they should have to pay for anything. Marched in here not long after King Konram's death was announced and took half our inventory."

As he says King Konram's name, he taps his fingers down his front in the gesture of the divinities, honoring our former ruler. The hope that brought me here expands in my chest.

Mom lets out a huff and then lowers her voice as if afraid she might be overheard. "They're meddlers, is what they are. Want to take over *everything*. Seems like every other day they send someone in here wanting to know what orders we've gotten and from who."

"Trying to dress themselves up as some sort of salvation when they're nothing but murdering traitors." Dad grimaces. Then he gives me an abruptly wary look. "You haven't fallen in with *that* lot now, have you?"

I have to swallow a slightly hysterical laugh. I'm not sure what's more insulting—that they think so little of me it didn't occur to them that I could be a threat when I first asked the question or that they don't realize I'd reject everything the Order stands for even more vehemently than they do.

But the fact that he stopped to ask—and looks nervous about it—only confirms his loyalties. He wasn't spouting off insults because he thought I'd want to hear them but because he wasn't filtering his true opinions at all.

"Absolutely not," I say. "They're a menace to this country. And that's why I'm here. What would you say if I offered you the opportunity to oust those traitors—and win the esteem of the royal family?"

Dad knits his brow. "I'd say all those books have finally addled your brain beyond repair."

I do let myself chuckle then and take another step toward my parents. "Not at all. It turns out all my book-learning has actually been useful to your future queen. You must have heard that the Melchiorek heirs escaped the murder plot and have been speaking out against the Order of the Wild as much as they can. I've come on behalf of the legitimate Queen Petra to make you an offer."

The skepticism hasn't left my parents' expressions, but Mom's eyes have lit up a little all the same. "What kind of offer?"

"If you supply our resistance efforts against the Order of the Wild with weapons and armor—as much as you can manage—you'll become the official arms supplier for the royal family."

Dad goes rigid, his lips parting with an eagerness he can't suppress even as he grapples with his doubts. He's probably picturing the new sign he'd get to add to the front of the shop once he earned that honor.

"You," he says uncertainly. "The queen— How—"

"It doesn't matter," I interrupt. "Our paths crossed, and I earned her trust. Enough that she believed me when I said there was a good chance you'd support her. She's laid out her terms in this letter."

I draw the folded paper from my pocket, holding it out with the Melchiorek family seal showing in the wax that seals the missive.

Dad takes the letter gingerly, as if he's afraid he might damage it. As he unsticks the seal, my mother hustles over to join him so she can read too.

It isn't a long letter. Their eyes skim over the words a few times in the space of a minute.

Then Dad looks up at me again. "She says the condition of being named the royal arms supplier is dependent on…"

He can't quite bring himself to say it?

I allow myself a thin smile. "On my judging that you've served her well. I know what our family is capable of. She knows I can confirm that you've contributed all you can."

"Oh." Mom lowers her hands to clasp them in front of her before combing one back through her hair as if she's afraid I'll be judging *her* looks. "Oh, that's— You really have found a place for yourself, haven't you?"

I've heard that fawning note in her voice before—when chatting up potential customers of high status. Somehow it isn't remotely gratifying.

Because it has nothing to do with who I am, only what she thinks I can do for them.

Dad claps me on the shoulder, a smile springing to his lips but a slightly panicked gleam in his eyes. "Of course we'll do whatever we can to see the rightful queen on the throne where she belongs. You know what I said before—it builds character to have to defend your passions—you've always had impressive dedication."

What they moments ago referred to as stubbornness instead.

He nudges me toward the doorway into the adjoining home. "We should have taken this into the house in the first place. I'll pour you a drink, and we can discuss specifics man to man."

"Thanks, Dad," I say, with only a trace of irony creeping into my tone. The last of the unsettled nerves that gripped me melt away.

I craved these people's approval for so long… but it's absolutely hollow, isn't it? Focused only on their narrow and frequently superficial priorities.

I don't require their pride or their blessing. I only need their cooperation so that *I* can serve Petra the way she deserves, and I've got that. I've earned my own pride.

Now it's time to get down to the business of overthrowing an uprising.

# Twenty-Nine

*Ivy*

At the head of our procession, Sulla draws her horse to a stop amid the trees. She turns her head, the fragmented sunlight glowing off her lined face. "You can feel that, can't you?"

I hadn't until she halted us. Now, as I concentrate on the sensations around me, a faint tingle of magic brushes over my skin.

I tense, swiveling my head to try to track its source.

I don't get the impression of any specific direction or purpose. It's more like the energy is simply drifting in the air.

Just behind us, my men shift in their saddles. None of them can pick up on supernatural eddies the way I can.

"There's magic being worked somewhere nearby," I say for their benefit as well as to answer Sulla's question. "Are you sure it's from the scourge sorcerers?"

The older sorcerer purses her lips. "I can't tell for certain. But it gives me the feeling of a large cistern dribbling water as it overflows. That much power in one place... I would expect a temple, but there are none nearby."

Alek speaks quietly. "But a group of sacrificial accomplices could also wield that kind of power."

"Exactly."

He and the rest of our procession—royal soldiers, noble staff, Pimanian rebels, even my former general—look to me for confirmation. Whatever some of our allies might think of my magic, they see me as the expert on that subject. They barely know Sulla.

I wet my lips and turn my head again. Another whiff of energy quivers over me.

What are they working on out here for traces of their magical practice to be seeping through the woods? What new threat are they conjuring?

We're only a couple of hours' ride from our current stronghold. If there are scourge sorcerers performing their darkest magic nearby, it's better for us to root them out and determine what new schemes they're setting in motion before they have a chance to discover our presence.

If we can free more of their accomplices and weaken Lothar's power that way, all the better. The more we can diminish the threat of retribution from the Order of the Wild, the easier it'll be for our allies to take a stand with us, however Petra decides to make it.

On the other hand, I don't want to lead two dozen followers into a battle on totally uncertain ground. My comrades came prepared to fight but expecting me to guide them.

I consider for a moment, uneasiness twisting in my belly. "Let's move closer to get a better idea of what we're dealing with. We should go ahead on foot—just a few of us to start."

Stavros nods and makes a couple of gestures to the rest of our company that those with military training must understand. As I slide down from Toast's back, he, Sulla, Rheave, and one of the soldiers follow suit.

We set off through the forest, Sulla and I remaining in the lead. I tread forward carefully so I can adjust my route with the minute shifts of the magic lacing the air.

For a few moments, it seems to grow stronger to the east. Then the impression dwindles, and I find myself backtracking onto a more northerly route. I can see what Sulla means about the magic feeling like stray dribbles rather than a focused effect.

But after maybe half an hour of rambling, a more solid sensation brushes my face. I ease toward it even more tentatively than before and stop in my tracks at its swift thickening.

I motion toward the terrain ahead of us. "This part of the forest is warded. If we go much farther, whoever set those wards will probably set off an alert."

More proof that whatever the sorcerers are working on, it's important. Or maybe they've simply become increasingly cautious after the raids we've already pulled off in the north.

Rheave steps up beside me without hesitation. "Let me see if I can break the magic so we can get closer."

He glances over at me with a brief flick of his gaze toward Sulla as well. "There isn't much chance anyone other than the scourge sorcerers would be protecting themselves like that, is there?"

Sulla shakes her head before I can answer. "The enchantment they've laid down is stronger than any I've felt from even a devout. No ordinary homesteader would have the means to place that kind of magic." She shivers. "Our foes are formidable."

As Rheave reaches his hands toward the wards, I study my former mentor. Sulla told me that was why she'd come—because even on her mountain, she became aware of the tragedies and violence spreading across the country. The Haven no longer felt secure.

She remembered what I'd said to her about us standing up to the blight of scourge sorcery together and decided to seek me out. Her magic led her to me.

I'm glad for her help, but *I* remember how she stole our equipment and tried to bar us from leaving the Haven. How she insisted that it was too dangerous for me to leave—not for my safety but everyone I'd encounter in the outside world.

She's declared her loyalty to Petra and her siblings. She warned us of the magic she'd sensed on her journey so we could investigate it. But I have trouble completely trusting her just yet.

Rheave's face hardens into a mask of concentration. His fingers twitch, sparks leaping between them.

The aura of magic in this part of the forest ripples and then fades away.

Stavros scans our surroundings. There's still nothing visible but trees and underbrush.

"We should proceed cautiously but quickly from here," he says. "We don't know how long it'll take before the sorcerers notice that their wards have been disabled."

He motions to the soldier. "Hovi, return to the others and have them follow. The sooner they can catch up with us, the better."

The guard bobs his head and lopes off in the direction we came from. We continue onward at a faster pace, but all my senses stay vigilant for further magical protections.

Only the vague, drifting impression of magic remains. It intensifies as we continue, until the trees start to thin up ahead and I make out a couple of squat wooden buildings in a clearing some fifty paces away.

We all go still, peering between the trunks. We have a little illusionary magic wrapped around us to deflect attention, but that won't hide us from magical surveillance or particularly attentive guards. We don't have enough of the more potent charms to conceal much of a fighting force.

And whoever strikes the first blows will automatically become a target.

As we study the buildings, the rest of our force catches up with us. Most of the group hangs back several paces, but Casimir and Alek tread carefully over to where the four of us are standing.

A couple of men emerge from one of the buildings and amble around it with only brief glances toward the trees. They look as if they're pretty confident that their magical protections are all they need to fend off intruders.

Rheave sucks in a breath and speaks under his breath. "One of those is a captured daimon. This is definitely a place of scourge sorcery."

"Then we need to find out what they're up to," I mutter. "But we don't know how many of them are here right now or what kind of magic they can wield."

A few deep gouges mark the ground farther out from the buildings. Their edges gleam with a sheen that doesn't look like soil or grass. When I squint, I make out a mottling of ruddy gashes on some of the nearby tree trunks around the edge of the clearing.

Whatever magic they've been experimenting with, it doesn't look like the peaceful type.

Sulla offers a small smile. "It shouldn't be difficult to create a distraction with our own magic."

I stifle a laugh. "I don't think we want Rheave setting the forest on fire. That would be bad for us too."

A crease forms in her brow. "I was thinking the two of us could manage enough of an effect."

Oh. With a lurch of my pulse, my body stiffens even more than it had already.

Since she arrived, I've avoided talking with Sulla about the exact results of my magic usage, but I can hardly hide it now.

I force my hands to unclench, willing my voice to remain steady. "I'm only releasing my power when it's absolutely necessary. I—I've already felt the madness coming on. I don't want to push myself farther toward it unless there's no other option."

The older woman stares at me for a few heavy thuds of my heart, the color leaching from her weathered skin. "You only left the Haven a matter of weeks ago. You've already let yourself go so far— You threw aside everything I taught you—"

I wince. "I didn't throw it aside. I followed your teachings as well as I could. But there was so much we needed to do, and I didn't know it would affect me so quickly."

"I warned you!" Sulla's whispered voice sharpens into a hiss. "After all that insistence that you knew what you were doing—"

Stavros cuts her off with a sharp sound. His voice comes out low but fierce. "Ivy risked her life and her mind to protect this country from the scourge sorcerers. If it wasn't for her, the entire Melchiorek family would be dead right now."

As Sulla jerks around to stare at him, Casimir dips his head where he's standing by my shoulder. "And as soon as she realized she was in trouble, she restricted her magic to ensure she wouldn't lose control. As she's shown just now. You should be pleased that she recognizes her limits."

The courtesan's normally gentle voice takes on a chiding edge with that last sentence. Alek rests his hand on the small of my back in reassurance, and Rheave has bristled as if he thinks he might need to leap to my defense with more than words.

Their automatic support brings a flood of warmth into my chest, but a pang of guilt resonates alongside it.

What they've said is true... but it's also true that I pushed myself past what I should have known I was ready for. What any riven sorcerer would ever be ready for.

Sulla takes in their expressions and mine, and her stance gradually relaxes. The smile she gives me next looks tight but also sad.

"All right. Maybe I shouldn't judge. I wasn't there, because I was hiding away on my mountaintop. I still think…" She shakes her head with a sigh. "Let me handle this. For when you do extend yourself in the future… It's important to remember that even very small acts can have a large impact."

She scans the trees around the clearing and points to a broad oak with mottled greenish bark. "That tree's sick—the branches will be weakening. With just a small nudge…"

Her eyes narrow in focus. Her fingers twitch at her sides—and one of the thickest branches on the tree cracks off the trunk.

It plummets with a thunderous crash. With another magical nudge, Sulla sends a second branch tumbling after it.

Shouts reverberate through the buildings' walls. Several more figures slip from the doorways while the two guards we already spotted jog over to the tree to investigate.

A few of their colleagues join them while the rest of the group hangs back near the buildings. But now we can see them—and they haven't noticed us yet.

Stavros raises his hand. "Those with the concealment charms first. The rest follow behind. Take them down as quickly as you can… *Now.*"

Rheave, Hovi, one of the women from Pima, and I have already yanked the charms on their thin chains over our heads. As my companions disappear around me, I hurtle forward and snatch my knives from their sheaths.

We burst from the trees, invisible to the confused guards, amid arrows flying from unseen sources. More than half of them sizzle with Rheave's daimon energy, launched from the new bow Alek brought back for him.

The arrows streak through the air, felling foe after foe. A few of the figures topple into clay statues. Others crumple limply like the mortal men and women they are.

Blood splatters the grass before the remaining few have finished whirling around.

I race straight toward them, swinging one knife in a deadly arc and plunging the other into the nearest chest. Hollers from behind tell me that the rest of my comrades have flooded the clearing.

A blast of magic slams into me from the direction of one of the buildings—and the charm lying against my chest cracks. Suddenly the scourge sorcerer to my left is staring at me.

I'm visible again.

My magic blares through my body so forcefully I bite my tongue clamping down on its call. The battle around me blurs in my struggle for control.

Another body barrels into me from the side. Rheave heaves me out of the way of a sharper bolt of magic, shielding me with his well-muscled frame.

He spins us around and manages to send his final arrow soaring into the air, through an open window on the nearest building. A thump on the other side confirms that it hit its mark.

My power lashes out at me again, this time in pure frustration. A stabbing pain spikes through my gut.

As the momentary agony fades with my restrained gasp, the daimon-man remains poised next to me. Other magic flares around us in a muddled barrage of light.

"I freed more of my kind," Rheave says. "And killed many of yours."

His gaze slides to me with a hint of concern and longing. As if he needs my approval, even after everything we've already been through.

I give his arm a quick squeeze. "You were amazing. We just have to topple the last few of them and—"

Another supernatural attack rains down on us with a roar of flames. This time, I shove Rheave to the side.

As the two of us roll across the grass away from the now smoldering patches, a cry breaks through the air. One of Voleska's men kneels by a woman who's slumped on the ground, her body charred from head to waist.

My stomach flips over. His friend won't be getting up again.

A man who joined us from Baron Cyris's staff jerks his hand toward a second-floor dormer. "Up there. Someone's—"

A glinting bolt slices through the air before he can finish his warning. It gouges straight through his neck. He crumples backward.

I inhale in a hiss through my teeth and launch myself forward. The first-floor window frame gives me enough of a foothold. I wrench myself up the side of the building and plunge through the upper window feet-first.

My heels slam into a body that didn't dodge fast enough. Ignoring the renewed clamoring of my magic, I jab out with my elbow, smack a cheekbone, and whip around the knife that's leapt back into my palm.

The sorcerer slumps beneath me into a pool of blood from her slit throat.

I crouch there, panting silently, listening for any other signs of attack. My magic's call reverberates through me, but it's more a simmer than a boil when there's no direct threat.

A clatter rings out below me, followed by Stavros's voice shouting, "All clear!"

Cautiously, I move back to the window. My comrades are still scanning the clearing warily, but no further attacks batter us.

Blood streaks several sleeves and pantlegs. To my relief, no one appears to have taken fatal wounds except for the woman from Pima and the baron's man.

My throat tightens. That's still more losses than I'd prefer.

How are we ever going to confront Lothar's full force? Eventually we're going to have to go head to head with him... and we've just witnessed how much damage even a few scourge sorcerers can do.

Sulla looks up and catches my eye. "I see you get plenty done even without turning to your magic."

Her tone is dry, but I can't summon enough amusement to form a smile.

I lift my voice to carry to our companions who remained in the forest. It comes out ragged. "Come on. Let's give this place a thorough search."

I decide to take the stairs down rather than flinging myself back out the window. Along the way, I peer into the other rooms along the hall.

The door right by the top of the stairs is locked. I break the deadbolt and peek inside to find myself gazing at three mutilated forms draped in gray shrouds.

"Mistress?" one of them mumbles.

My heart sinks. We were hoping to find more of the sacrificial accomplices, but it still horrifies me to see the results of the scourge sorcerers' greed.

"We'll be taking you somewhere else," I say. "Somewhere safer." Then I hustle down the stairs in search of Casimir, who'll know how to reassure the Order's victims leagues better than I can.

"Cas—" I'm calling out as I reach the bottom of the stairs, and jar to a halt at the sight of Stavros, Alek, and a couple of the royal soldiers leaning over a table on the other side of a nearby doorway.

Alek's face looks grimmer than I've ever seen it. Stavros's jaw is clenched tight.

I march over to join them. "What did you find?"

Alek taps the papers scattered across the table. "I think these are some of the Order of the Wild's plans for their kingship trials. They've been testing out different strategies... If they go through with something like this, Petra won't stand a chance. They're setting everything up as a trap."

A chill races through me. "Then she'll refuse to compete."

"And Lothar will say that proves she isn't worthy." Stavros lifts his head. "He must intend to move forward with them soon if they've gotten this far with their plans. We're going to need far more allies than we've already pulled together—and quickly. If we don't present our own version of the trials soon, the scourge sorcerers will steal the chance right out from under us."

# THIRTY

Every hoofbeat of the horse next to mine sends more tension coiling around my innards. I glance over at my foremost companion on our journey. "You didn't need to join me for this expedition, Your Highness."

Petra lifts her chin with the stoic determination I'm becoming used to in our future queen. "I know you and Ivy want to keep me out of danger, but I can't hang so far back that I'm shying from my duties. We're going to be asking a lot of Provinca Yessaine and her household. She should know I'm taking my fair share of risks as well. The request will mean more coming directly from me."

I'm sure that's true, but every instinct of my military training tells me that the meeting we hope to initiate could easily turn into an ambush. I trust Provinca Yessaine's loyalties enough to be riding out to one of her homes with a small entourage of associates, but not so much I want to stake the security of the royal family on it.

As if she's read my mind, Petra shoots me a pointed look. Her tone is dry with amusement. "If something happens to me, you still have two other Melchioreks currently safe under Baron Cyris's roof to take the throne."

I grimace at her. It's obvious why she and Ivy get along so well. They're both damned stubborn and far too good at arguing their case even when I want to refuse them.

"I'll endeavor to ensure that's not a concern," I say, smoothing my frustration from my voice. "But please don't stray from your guards."

If I were coming on my own, I'd have brought only one or two comrades with me to assist the provinca and her staff if they agree to set our plan in motion. Because we have a Melchiorek among us, I insisted on four soldiers on top of that, and even that number feels insufficient.

Petra's mouth slants as if she's going to reject that suggestion as well. "I suppose I should be grateful for the freedoms I had in those years when no one knew I was anything other than a distant relative of the queen's."

I study her as I formulate my answer. How can I know what goes on in the head of a woman who's lost her parents and found herself thrust into the highest leadership role so suddenly and violently?

Especially when she's talking to a man who should have been there to protect her father but wasn't.

But I did know her father. I might not have agreed with every decision King Konram made, but I can imagine the lessons he passed on to all his children while he could.

I adjust my grip on the reins. "There are different freedoms that will replace those you lost, once we see you back where you belong. You can't protect your people as you're meant to unless we protect *you* in turn. But you'll wield more power than most of your subjects could conceive of."

A faint smile flickers across her face. "Of course you're right. I apologize. I didn't mean to complain when I've had so much handed to me by virtue of my birth."

"Both boons and responsibilities. The latter can be heavy to carry. We all have our own burdens to shoulder if we strive to serve well—and I know you mean to."

"Yes." The word comes out of her like a sigh. "I hope Provinca Yessaine can recognize that too. And if we can prepare these trials in time, I can prove to all my people that I deserve the trust I'm asking them to put in me."

"It isn't only birth regardless, you know," I remark. "It's experience and training. You've seen the inner workings of a kingdom as no one except your siblings has. You understand what it takes to rule. I can't say even I would feel prepared to take on a role that immense."

A teasing lilt returns to her voice. "Not even the great General Stavros? I don't imagine you'd do a terrible job as monarch."

I glance away, taking in the landscape and the buildings of the city we're approaching for the fleeting moment before they blur in front of me. "I wasn't hale enough to continue as a general. King is another order altogether. I failed to protect the king I'd sworn to defend from the worst threats he faced. I'll be happy if I can simply ensure that you're restored to the throne."

Petra lapses into a momentary silence. She glances at me sideways, her expression gone solemn. "You didn't fail my father, Stavros. Surely you don't think that."

I lift my shoulders in a slight shrug, tamping down the swell of guilt inside me. "I did everything I could to save him, but it wasn't enough."

"Because he didn't let you. He pushed you away. If there were any failures in that equation, *he* failed *you*. Even this conversation proves why he should have trusted your judgment more." She shakes her head. "I think you see perfectly well in the ways that matter most. I appreciate your guidance, even if I don't follow every caution."

I don't know if I can fully agree with her, but the words spoken in her steady voice take the sharpest edge off my regrets.

We veer onto the lane that leads to the sprawling estate just beyond the city walls, where Provinca Yessaine enforces her authority over Aberni province.

I'm reasonably sure of the provinca's loyalty because I collaborated with her local military efforts more than once, whenever they needed to push back incursions from the Darium empire across the Seafell Channel. Our association also means I know about the hidden back entrance in the estate wall where her family accepts visitors they don't want to draw attention to.

After a short trot longer, we turn off the road, give the main entrance a wide berth, and circle around the back. When we've drawn close to the section of mortared stone I was aiming for, I motion for the rest of our company to stand their ground, dismount, and walk the last several paces on foot.

I press my hand to the keystone and then rap out a pattern only a few recent generals will have been given. I suspect Provinca Yessaine will be able to guess which one is calling on her.

Luck willing, she's heard enough about the Order of the Wild to realize that I'm fighting for our country as always, not against it as Lothar would claim.

I have no way of telling exactly how much time passes while we wait. The city bells ring in the late afternoon hour. Finally, footsteps crunch through the brush on the other side of the wall, where the estate's hunting woods lie.

Several sets of footsteps. If the provinca intends to meet us herself, she hasn't come alone.

Then again, I wouldn't have expected her to.

There's nothing wrong with my ears. I listen closely and then raise my hand toward my companions, splaying my fingers twice to indicate that we should expect ten figures in this confrontation.

Just as I'm lowering my arm, the hidden doorway grates open.

Provinca Yessaine peers out at me, her face framed by the raised swords of the guards standing half a step ahead of her on either side. She folds her arms over her lean chest and raises a thin eyebrow at me without a word.

I dip my head to her respectfully and catch a familiar face behind her that I hadn't expected to see here. It appears the provinca has called her daughter back from the royal college.

Further evidence that she's unsettled by the current state of affairs in Silana.

"Provinca Yessaine," I say in acknowledgment. "And Romild—it's good to see you're well."

My former student fixes me with a stare as steely as her mother's. Does she still resent that I chose Ivy as my supposed assistant rather than opening the position more widely? I know she coveted that spot—and made no secret of it with the woman I love.

I would hope we can put any sour feelings from before behind us. But there is a reason Ivy didn't join us on this particular expedition, just in case.

Romild nudges her mother with a brief murmur, and the provinca's gaze slides past me to the riders in the shade of the trees. Her normal unflappable expression twitches.

Romild must have pointed out the face she can recognize from their time as classmates.

Provinca Yessaine drops into a deeper bow than mine. "Your Highness. I didn't realize—if I'd known—"

Petra offers a small smile. "It's perfectly all right."

Relief trickles through my knotted stomach, but not enough for me to let down my guard. "The rightful queen wishes to speak with you. I'm not sure it would be wise for many to see her entering your home. Are you willing to conduct the conversation in a less conventional setting?"

Yessaine lets out a soft chuckle. "That sounds fair enough. We will come out—but I hope you won't take insult if my guards accompany me."

"Absolutely not," Petra says. "We all have reason to be wary in the current climate."

I draw back to stand near Petra while the provinca, Romild, and their eight protectors ease out through the doorway. As we face each other in the lengthening shadows, Petra and our own small squadron of guards descend from their horses.

I'd like to shield my future queen, but I know she won't accept being hidden behind me. So instead I flank her alongside one of the royal soldiers who's been with us since Florian, with the rest of our company in a semicircle around us.

A lightly sweet scent laces the air from the first early spring blooms. Petra draws her posture up commandingly straight and holds Yessaine's gaze.

"You must have heard about the horrors Lothar and his followers are carrying out. I need help to put down this uprising once and for all and end the slaughter that's come with it."

The provinca's mouth tightens. "I don't care for the stories that've been passed on to me or the scenes I've witnessed myself. But this Order of the Wild has spread through every city and town in the country, it seems. Two of my counts tried to stand against them when they first swept through the province, and their entire families were slaughtered." She touches Romild's shoulder. "I'm not throwing away our lives on a principle."

I clear my throat. "That's why we came to you discreetly, Provinca. We have no interest in putting you in danger."

"I assume you want me to offer my military forces to fight these scourge sorcerers. I'm afraid many of the soldiers stationed here have deserted."

Petra speaks up again, clear and calm. "Your strength would be valued if it comes to a battle of force, but I came here today seeking a subtler sort of assistance. I don't believe we can defeat the chaos Lothar has stirred up unless the people are convinced that I truly am a better choice to offer peace and security."

Up goes the eyebrow again. "And how do you expect to do that?"

"The Order of the Wild has spoken of the old kingship trials," Petra says smoothly. "We will hold our own trials to show I'm prepared to prove myself. But we need to move swiftly so we can ensure they happen fairly and not through the scourge sorcerers' twisted means. Aberni is renowned not just for defending our country from invasion but also the speed with which you've alerted the rest of the country about impending threats."

One of our other companions steps forward, holding a thick bundle of paper. "We've printed pamphlets to be passed around in every town and city your best messengers and their connections can reach."

I nod. "Your people know the fastest and most surreptitious routes, as well as who will pass on the word farther. They won't need to linger anywhere long enough for the Order to confront them."

Yessaine shifts on her feet, still looking uncertain. "If even one of them is caught and Lothar traces them back to my family…"

"I will protect you in every way I can," Petra says. "But I expect by then he'll be too concerned with addressing the impending trials to waste manpower trying to destroy a province with such a formidable reputation."

"Are you sure these trials are even worth the risk to *you*?" the provinca asks. "With the rumors flying around, public opinion has been turning against the Order. The unrest might reach the point of an opposing rebellion in time."

Petra grimaces. "We don't have time. Lothar is already preparing for his next move against me, and if we don't beat him to the punch, he could shatter any trust I've gained. I need the people to see how far I'm willing to go to earn their loyalty."

Yessaine drops her gaze. Like the baron and his friends, I'd imagine she finds the idea of a Melchiorek agreeing to compete in some sort of trial distasteful, which can't help our appeal.

With a twitch of my eyes, I focus on her and prod my gift. A prickle quivers through my nerves. If I can get some glimpse of how she'll react, prove that *I* can still anticipate the country's needs as I once did—

The vision that flashes before my eyes isn't of the provinca's response. I catch a movement from the corner of my eye—the man two over from her left springing forward with an abruptly drawn blade he stabs into Petra's heart.

My body stiffens. With another tick of my gaze, my vision reforms into the actual tableau in front of me.

Our groups are still facing each other in our discussion. No one has made a hostile move.

But that guard is planning to. His jaw has tensed, his hand resting on the hilt of his dagger in its sheath.

My first instinct is to leap forward and slam him to the ground before he can think for another second about hurting the future queen. Only my two dozen years of training back to when I could first hold a sword hold me in place.

I didn't become the lauded General Stavros through brute force. I was known for strategy above all else.

The common people aren't the only ones who'll be swayed by visible proof. If Provinca Yessaine is going to believe that the current danger is urgent enough to warrant the favor we're asking of her, she needs to see the severity of the threat play out with her own eyes, not simply hear a claim I make.

I have to protect Petra not just against the most immediate threat, but against everything that could go wrong spiraling out from this meeting.

My fingers itch for my sword. If I draw it, I might frighten the traitor into thinking better of his scheme—for now. He could simply bide his time for later, when I'm not close enough to act.

My glimpses of the future are never more than a minute or two ahead of the event. All I have to do is hold myself braced and ready—

I've missed a couple of exchanges between Petra and the provinca, but my attention doesn't fail me. My eyes catch the instant the guard adjusts his stance to lunge forward.

He springs at Petra with a hoarse cry and a hiss of his blade from its sheath—and I hurtle between them at the same moment.

The dagger clangs off my metal prosthetic. I slam my knee into the man's belly and wrench his wrist behind his back as I shove him to the ground.

Sweat cools the back of my neck. My heart hammers as the iron flavor of panic laces my mouth.

There's no need for fear. I intervened in time.

My monarch trusted me, and I didn't fail her. I played this game of swords as well as I ever have.

But even with the relief of that knowledge sweeping through me, I need to play politics too.

Yessaine cried out in the moment. When I lift my head to meet her eyes, she's staring at her guard, white-faced with horror.

"Baldric," she mumbles. "He's been in our service for nearly a decade. He's never spoken—never acted—"

I firm my voice to its most authoritative tone. The voice that commanded armies of thousands against our greatest foes. "Scourge sorcery is like a sickness. They've infected more people than we can guess with their toxic claims and ideals. Lothar and his followers must be stamped out *now*, before they spread their poison even farther."

Petra speaks up after my last words. "And we will conquer them as Stavros did this traitor in your midst—if those who have the means to stand with us will do so."

Yessaine shakes herself. "I..."

Romild touches her arm. For a brief moment, I'm worried she'll pull her mother back into hesitation.

But there's a reason I would have seriously considered the provinca-to-be as a potential assistant if Ivy hadn't claimed that position by necessity.

My former pupil squares her shoulders. "Mother, we *have* to. They're barely asking anything at all. We should do more. You didn't raise me to cower when there's work to be done."

The provinca exhales sharply and matches her daughter's stance. "Indeed, I didn't. Queen Petra, you'll have your messengers—and all the soldiers I can offer, when you need them too. Let's take back our country."

# Thirty-One

*Ivy*

I lean my hands against the tabletop as if I can push more information out of the polished wood. "What about the other scourge sorcerers you met in Florian? What talents did you hear of that they could wield?"

Filip rubs his hand across his mouth, knitting his brow as he thinks. His shoulders have slumped during our conversation as he's admitted how little the higher-ups in the Order of the Wild let him in on their larger plans.

"I know there was one who had some kind of gift for heat," he says. "She could use it to burn people to encourage them into compliance or destroy things the others didn't want seen. At least a few had gifts for stirring emotions—trust or fear... There was a man recruited at the same time I was who could run twice as fast as anyone should be able to for short distances."

At the other end of the table, Alek nods. His quill scrawls across the notebook where he's recording everything the defector can tell us about the Order's plans and abilities.

He writes the last word and glances up. "I suppose just about any gift could be useful to the Order's aims in one way or another."

Filip offers a miserable grimace. "They wanted to bring in as many people as they could. People with gifts who could expand them with the scourge sorcery, people who didn't have gifts just to spread the word and silence anyone who argued..."

He looks down at his hands. "I was so stupid to get caught up in their talk to begin with. I wasn't brave enough to give more than a few toes for the small gift I got, and somehow I thought I deserved to make it more?"

I don't know how to answer his self-recrimination when the fact that so many people have gotten swept up in Lothar's treacherous conspiracy frustrates me beyond end. The best I can offer is a brief shrug. "Maybe that small gift will make some difference against them now."

It seems unlikely. Growing crops a little faster isn't going to win over those who are already caught up in the Order's propaganda.

Even his former colleagues couldn't find much use for him if they sent him off on this potentially suicidal spy mission.

It'll be a perfectly good talent when we have peace, though.

I lean back in my chair, sorting through the questions I meant to ask. "Their precautions beyond the city walls—how much are they monitoring the area around Florian? How far out?"

Filip wets his lips. "It may be more now that you've disrupted their influence. But when I was there, the Order was focusing most of their efforts on keeping control over people *in* the city and securing the walls themselves. They didn't care much about the farmlands nearby."

Alek lets out a rough chuckle. "Very efficient of them. Reserve their efforts for where the population is most concentrated."

I exhale in a sigh. "Well, if they've kept up that approach, it'll at least be a little easier for—"

A voice cuts through my statement, bellowing through the halls of the country residence. "Baron Cyris! General Stavros!"

The urgency in the yell has me shoving back the chair with a rasp and springing to my feet. Alek and I exchange a fleeting glance before we both hustle to the front hall to find out what the ruckus is about.

I jerk to a halt on the threshold of the foyer. Three of the baron's guards stand in a tense ring around a slumped man who's bound tight with rope and dripping blood from his forehead. The slackness of his pose against the floor suggests he's unconscious if not dead, possibly from the blow to the head.

Alek and I aren't the only ones who've been drawn by the clamor. Casimir and Rheave both appear within moments of our arrival, along with a few of the rebels from Pima, a couple of the estate's staff, and all three of the royal heirs.

At the sight of the future queen, the guard who appears to be in charge holds up his hand to ward Petra back. "Don't come closer, Your Highness! We don't know what he might be capable of."

Petra reaches out to hold Princess Klaudia and Prince Jacos with her, but even as her jaw tightens, she arches an eyebrow. "He doesn't look as if he's capable of doing much harm at the moment. Who is he?"

Before they can answer, Stavros strides into the hall. The title may no longer be fully accurate, but the massive man still looks every inch a general.

Baron Cyris hurries in close behind him. "What's the meaning of this commotion?"

The lead guard dips his head to his employer. "Sir, we found this man sneaking around near the estate. He attempted to run when he realized he'd been spotted, but we were able to subdue him. I think he's a spy for the Order of the Wild. I expected you'd want to—"

Rheave breaks in with a sudden step forward. "He's a daimon."

Everyone in the room goes still and silent as they absorb that declaration. Then my daimon-man takes another step toward the bound captive, and two of the guards jerk up their swords.

Rheave blinks at them with obvious confusion. "*I* wouldn't harm you."

The lead guard seems to prefer to ignore him when he isn't approaching, looking instead at the baron. "The spy isn't even human, then. One of their animated slaves. He won't tell us anything. We should end him now before he comes to and has a chance to blast us with that magic of theirs."

I'm not sure which part of the scene jolts the hasty words from my throat. Maybe it's the sorrow that flashes across Rheave's sweet face or the helpless sprawl of the captured daimon, or maybe the hint of a sneer in the guard's dismissive words.

Whatever the case, I find myself pushing forward to stand by my inhuman lover. "No! Not like that."

The guard's expression turns incredulous—with a flicker of fear he manages to master quickly. "You're not the one who gives my orders."

"Her judgment is worth listening to all the same," Stavros says firmly. He folds his arms over his chest. "What are you thinking, Ivy?"

I glance at Rheave and then at the rest of the spectators. My gaze catches on the faces of the royal children: Klaudia's, pale but determined; Jacos's, wide-eyed with obvious anxiety.

They've accepted the one daimon among us as an ally because it's hard to speak to Rheave and not see him as a sort of person. But all the other daimon the scourge sorcerers have captured have blended into a nameless mass simply labeled "the enemy."

None of the spirit creatures ever wanted to hurt us. Don't we owe each of them a chance to be something else when we can offer it?

Isn't that the kind of compassion I want our future rulers to see is possible?

I don't know if that explanation will win me any ground with the baron, so I consider the practicalities. "Even if the sorcery compelling this daimon means he can't tell us anything on purpose, we might be able to get him to reveal a little bit involuntarily. It'd be incredibly useful to know why he was lurking in this area—how much the Order already suspects. Whether there are others roaming around here."

The baron's mouth sets in a hard line. "Is it worth the risk of the damage he could do when he wakes up? I wouldn't want you to need to strain yourself defending us."

The edge in his voice makes my hackles rise. Before I can respond, Rheave interjects.

"I can stop him," he says quietly. "Our powers will deflect each other. And as long as he's tied up like that, it'll be easy to keep him under control."

Petra lifts her chin imperiously. "Then please do that, and we should hear if the daimon will say anything to us. He's as much a victim of the scourge sorcerers as those they've maimed and murdered."

She flicks her fingers down her front in a gesture of the divinities, as if asking for the godlen to bless the upcoming conversation. My eyes meet hers, and she dips her head slightly in acknowledgment.

She understands my concerns without my needing to say the rest.

Gods help us, we do need a ruler like her on the throne. Someone who'll listen before taking action.

Someone who cares for all her country's inhabitants, no matter how unusual.

The baron isn't about to argue with his future queen. He clears his throat. "Take him to one of the holding rooms, and let us know when—"

Before he finishes his order, the captured daimon twitches. A faint groan spills from the man's lips.

Rheave rushes closer and kneels a couple of paces away from the captive, braced in case the sculpted man attempts to use his magic. The guards each take a wary step backward but keep their swords pointed at the bound form.

The captive's eyelids flutter. He rolls onto his side and stares blearily at the assembled crowd.

Petra nudges her siblings a little farther behind her, but to my relief, she doesn't insist they leave. She must know she can't protect them from every danger of ruling—she wants them to see the hard decisions that might need to be made.

Rheave speaks first, in a low but steady voice. "Friend, I'm sorry for how you've been treated. We know you're being pushed by magic, but your masters have used other daimon to hurt us before. Will you speak with us?"

The captured daimon only manages a grunt.

Rheave leans closer. "I was once caged by the sorcerers too. I shook off their hold. If you try, you might be able to as well."

The man's face tips toward the floor. For a moment, there's only his ragged breath. Then he mumbles, "So long… So much power."

The lead guard huffs. "Like the rest of them. They've got this one completely under their thrall too."

He raises his sword, but the daimon's words have snagged inside me with a tug of my gut.

I shake my head. "I don't know… The others we've talked to wouldn't say anything at all—or couldn't. He's trying."

Petra's tone gentles. "Ivy, freeing the daimon from that body may be the greatest kindness we can offer."

I know she's right, but something about this one's behavior doesn't feel quite like the captured spirits we've encountered in the past.

I walk closer so the slumped man can see me beyond Rheave. "The scourge sorcerers who made your body do have a lot of power—but we've been breaking it down. They have less than they did before. It's worth fighting their control again, even if you couldn't in the past."

"Yes," Rheave says. "We'll help you. We *want* to be your friends, if you can pull away from the sorcerers."

He sounds so hopeful that an ache forms around my heart. Should I have pushed this hard if the moment is probably only going to end in more disappointment for him? I know how much it's bothered him that none of his fellow daimon have been able to make their new physical lives their own.

The captive's jaw looks as if it's clamped tight. He shivers in his bonds—testing them or simply showing his discomfort?

Rheave tries again, the usual brightness in his voice dwindling. "If there's anything at all you can manage to tell us about why you came here, what your masters know and want to find out…"

"I can't," the man mutters. "I can't. I—"

All at once, he twists at the torso, straining against the ropes. The guards cry out in warning. But as the man's head yanks backward, an unearthly glow flares in his eyes that looks more desperate than fierce.

His voice spills out of him. "They told me to wander this county searching for signs of other daimon. And to find where those were, who they were. They know there's one they can't control staying with the queen."

His gaze settles on Rheave, and a sudden smile curves his lips. "I found you. I found you, but they won't, because I won't tell them. We won't let them bring me back. Right?"

Rheave beams at him so brilliantly he takes my breath away. "We won't. We can stand up to the vicious ones together, all of us."

A rush of my own hope smacks me in the chest.

I whirl toward Petra. "This is the first daimon who's snapped out of their control. It's been weeks since I killed the sorcerer who was doing some of the compelling—we've taken more than a dozen of their sacrificial accomplices away since then. The compulsion the Order imposed on the daimon *must* be weakening."

Petra studies me with more reserve. "Where are you going with this, Ivy?"

I fling my hand vaguely toward the world beyond the estate's walls. "If we can bring the rest of the captured daimon over to our side, we'll have stolen one of the Order's biggest advantages. All we have to do is get to them."

# Thirty-Two

*Rheave*

As the wagon jostles over the pits in the road, I keep my shoulder leaned against Ivy's. While the charms we wear mostly conceal us from sight when we're not touching, I can still sense her beside me, but I prefer to be able to see her clearly too.

Maybe it's the same for her. She tucks her hand around mine and tips her head closer when we sway with the movement of the wagon. From the blurred form I can make out at her other side, I think she must be holding on to Casimir as well.

It's good that she has both of us. We won't let any harm befall her on this precarious mission we've set out on.

The memory of how we ended up here brings a swell of deeper affection into my chest. I twine my fingers more tightly with hers.

If the baron's people had their way, my fellow daimon would have been severed from the body the sorcerers forced him into. He may still choose to leave it—but now it will be his choice and not anyone else's.

I spent much of this morning informing him of many of the delights I've discovered that our more physical forms allow. He was especially fond of the sounds he could form with the lute in the baron's music room.

Now, if our mission is successful, dozens more captured daimon might find their freedom without needing to give up all those new opportunities. They can make the bodies that started as our prisons their own like I have.

They can help us stand up to the scourge sorcerers and create these trials in time to stop Lothar's plans.

As long as we're not caught before we can even get started.

The wagon slows, I assume because we're approaching the city gate. Wheels rattle and hooves stomp ahead of us and behind. We hold perfectly still in the cramped covered space where we're huddled among sacks of grain and crates of nuts supposedly for sale at the markets.

The woman driving the cart is a stablewoman who normally works under one of the noble allies we've gained. There's no reason for any scourge sorcerers to see her as a threat. But we'll still be in trouble if they realize what she's concealing.

Somewhere off around the far side of the city, a few other allies will be setting off a magical disturbance. If all goes well, that should draw the attention of any sorcerers who are monitoring supernatural activity in the city—draw it away from checking the new arrivals all that closely.

The wagon rolls forward and stops, forward and stops. We chose a time of day that Ivy said isn't often busy, but there must still be a bit of a line.

Finally, footsteps thump around the side of the wagon. A couple of bulky men lift the canvas flaps at the back and peer into the dim space.

They can't see us thanks to our charms, and the sacks and crates are small enough that they couldn't suspect any human is hiding inside them. Their eyes sweep over the interior for several long seconds during which Ivy's grip tightens on my hand.

Then they step away with a satisfied nod. "Continue."

The wagon jerks forward and continues rattling along for many minutes with slight hitches to one side or another as we take a turn. Ivy gives my hand one more squeeze and lets go.

Her form turns wavery, but I know what she's doing because a moment later, the lid lifts off one of the crates she's moved to. She's retrieving the other cargo we hid.

Carefully, she pulls out the cube of fine netting. A few dozen small butterflies cling to the sides with faint flutters of their wings.

I smile at them, though the insects can't see me. I called them into this temporary home, making an appeal to Inganne and pleading for her help. The steady current of the winged insects that trickled to us through the air made my heart leap—almost as much as the startled joy it sparked in Ivy's eyes.

The wagon's wheels grind to a halt. We must have reached our chosen stopping point.

Casimir touches my shoulder lightly so I can see him properly for a moment. "Safe travels," he murmurs, and then stoops to tug one of the lower sacks out of the pile.

That one is full of printed pamphlets that he's going to bring to the Black Talons. We're hoping that the gang members will stick to their promise to help by both distributing information about the upcoming kingship trials and taking in any daimon we can snap out of the scourge sorcerers' spell.

The canvas flap sways with his departure. The mesh cage of butterflies has disappeared into the circle of Ivy's arms, but it comes back into view along with her form when she bumps her shoulder against mine. "We'd better get going."

I follow Casimir's example, nudging the flap aside, confirming no one is in view of the small space next to a wall where our driver backed up the wagon, and slipping out as quickly as possible. I know from our planning conversations that we're in the middle wards, not too close to the prominent center of the city but near enough that there should be a fair number of Order members watching over the inhabitants.

When I emerge, the many voices carrying from around the square reach my ears more distinctly. I make out sellers hawking food, clothes, and other goods for sale and passers-by chatting about their shopping or how their day is going.

Amid it all, my mind prickles with the vague awareness of other beings who share my unique energy. I get the impression there are a few close by and several farther out but still within decently easy reach.

The scourge sorcerers like to use their captured daimon to enforce their rule over the city. Expendable lives. They can make them handle any outbursts of violence rather than subjecting themselves or their less easily controlled human allies to it.

The knowledge gnaws at me as I survey the square. A medley of smells both intriguing and unsettling trickles into my lungs. Music wafts from an eatery farther down the square with an upbeat melody that would have made me bob with it if we didn't have such a serious task ahead of us.

Ivy curls her fingers into the back of my tunic so she can keep track of me. I ease away from the wagon and meld with the crowd, sticking to the small open spaces between the other pedestrians as well as I can.

No one can see me, but they can still bump into me.

It only takes a few steps before my sense of a nearby kindred spirit heightens. I turn my head and spot the figure it's coming from some ten paces away.

A broad-shouldered woman in the Order's now-standard red uniform surveys the crowd as she prowls through it.

I stop and reach toward the mesh cage. Ivy loosens the panel on the top for me.

When I dip my hand in, making the gesture of the divinities at the same time with a hasty prayer to Inganne, one of the fragile insects settles on my forefinger.

I draw the butterfly out and point it toward the daimon I've spotted. Lowering my head, I speak in a murmur. "Go to the other one with a spirit like ours. Remind her that there's more to this world than what the sorcerers say."

Does the butterfly understand any of that? I have no idea. But we believe that the godlen of play and creativity has a particular affinity for mischievous spirits like mine, and butterflies are one of her symbolic animals. An injured one that was drawn to me helped bring Ivy into my life.

It's our test to judge whether my counterparts might be ready to shake off their magical bonds as well.

As the insect swoops through the air, Ivy and I trail along behind it. We need to be close enough to judge our target's reaction.

The butterfly flits back and forth before plummeting to perch on the woman's shoulder. She twitches and glances over at it. Her expression shifts from startled to puzzled.

I pause, braced for my cue to move. How will she respond?

After a few seconds marked by the thudding of my heart, she reaches toward the butterfly with her other hand and offers her fingers for it to hop onto. As she takes in the delicate bobbing of its wings, her eyes widen with a hint of awe.

I exchange a glance with Ivy, and she nods with a hopeful smile.

Ducking down beneath the eye level of the crowd, I hastily remove my charm. I straighten up, abruptly visible, and amble the last short distance to my target.

The woman's gaze jerks from the insect to me. I can tell she recognizes me as our kind just as well as I can her. A crease forms in her brow.

Before she says anything, I offer the friendliest smile I can and nod toward the butterfly. "They're wonderful, aren't they? Inganne is sharing a blessing of delight with us."

The woman seems to struggle to catch her breath. "I—I have a job to do—"

I touch her arm, lightly but steadily. "A job they forced you into. But their control is fading. You can shake it off. Make this life your own. I have. There are so many other wonderful parts of the world you can embrace now."

I wish I could shatter the magic that's acted on her the way I have the scourge sorcerers' wards. Their spell of compulsion is so much more delicate, woven into the spirits themselves, I'm not sure how I could pick it.

The woman's body goes rigid, a shaky exhalation spilling out of her. A tremor runs through her sturdy frame.

The corners of her lips twitch with a smile of her own. "Yes. *Yes*, I can."

"Hold on to that freedom," I urge her. "We have more friends who can help. Wait outside the Newt's Goblets Pub in Tangleside at sunset, and the ones who made these bodies will never use you like a puppet again."

She shivers again, but her smile grows.

"Thank you," she mumbles eagerly, and steps away toward the edge of her square. There's a new bounce of joy to her step.

With a pleased thrill ticking through my chest, I turn to scan the square for another of my kin.

Ivy sticks close to me without removing her charm, keeping both herself and our insect cargo hidden. We send butterflies frolicking toward four more daimon-in-human-form who have similar reactions to the first—confusion, interest, and a brief struggle to test the magical influence they hadn't realized was fraying.

I haven't felt the scourge sorcerers calling for me since Ivy's kidnapping. It seems likely that the one she killed to save herself was the same one who tried to steal me back more than once.

With each of my counterparts we send to what should be a meeting with our Black Talons associates, my own sense of freedom expands. The ground might as well be softening beneath my feet, leaving me floating as much as walking.

It still amazes me how many physical sensations have nothing to do with the concrete world at all. The way emotions shape these bodies of matter into something more than flesh.

A man marches into the square out of a side-street. He doesn't have an official uniform on, but my senses give another twinge.

I hold out my hand to Ivy, and she passes me another butterfly.

After my murmured instructions, it weaves through the air toward the man. It circles over his head once and descends to cling to the cuff of his sleeve.

The man stares down at it with a tighter expression than any of the other daimon we've approached. Before my pulse can do more than stutter once, he gives a sharp yell of alarm. His head jerks around, searching the crowd for the source of the intrusion.

My heart outright lurches—and then Ivy is shoving the mesh cage into my hands while yanking off her own charm.

She grips my forearm. "I'll divert him like we planned. Get back to the wagon and go to the next square."

With that, she's off and running, pushing through the crowd much more clumsily than I know she's capable of.

Because she wants the guard to notice her. She wants him to notice her *before* he notices me.

In that first instant as I see him spin toward the disturbance, a flood of panic rushes through me. A cry of my own jolts to the back of my throat.

We did talk about this strategy. Ivy's better at sneaking away from people—I'm the one the willing daimon are most likely to trust. It makes sense.

But if that guard or the other Order members catch her—if Lothar gets his hands on her again—

I could yell. I could bring the guard's attention back to me, and she wouldn't have to put herself in that danger.

I wouldn't have to risk losing her. Only myself.

My pulse is pounding frantically, but somehow that hasty rhythm is what grounds me. It reminds me of the way my heart skipped the first time Ivy kissed me, the first time our bodies melded together. The first time she told me she loved me, not that long ago.

I love her too. I love her. I love her.

That's all the frenetic beat is telling me. Not that I'm doing something wrong or that she won't escape this danger.

I want her to come back. I want her to be okay.

It will hurt so much if she doesn't.

But she'll be hurt if I break from the plan. If I act as if she can't look after herself and ruin everything we've been fighting for out of my fear of pain.

And how good will it feel when she comes back to me, grinning at her success and wanting to hear of mine?

A girl near me is gaping at the mesh cube I'm clutching. I shake myself out of my frozen daze and hustle back to the wagon.

As I go, I grab my charm from my pocket. I duck behind the vehicle, slip the chain back over my neck to vanish, and dive inside.

"It's time to go to Finnacle Square," I call to the driver. "Ivy will meet us there."

She will. I know she will. She always makes it back.

That fact doesn't stop me from fidgeting as the wagon rocks its way to the second square we picked out about a half a mile across the sprawling city from the first. When the wheels halt, I hesitate and force myself to inhale deeply, settling my nerves.

I have my own work to do here. A real partner would focus on that, not on worrying about the part that's not his.

Easing out of the wagon, I spot the first daimon right away. There's a slim, sinewy man in an Order uniform patrolling around the edge of the square.

Since I'm on my own, I have to leave the butterfly cage in the wagon. I bring just one of its residents with me and send the insect flying off toward my counterpart.

It lands near the man's elbow. I brace myself for him to flinch like the last daimon did, but instead he simply peers at it. The glimmer of intrigue I've seen before lights in his eyes.

With a smile crossing my lips, I move across the square to reach out to him with my words as well.

I've just told a third compatriot in the square about the meeting place and watched her lope off with a breathless giggle when a soft pressure brushes my arm. I turn toward it, and Ivy's scent wisps over me, sharp but sweet.

"You've been keeping busy," she says in a low voice, her form swimming into sight in front of me. "We're really doing this."

Then she bobs up to kiss me, quick but so tender a flush warms my cheeks.

We are succeeding. We worked together and did what we're both best at, and Ivy ensured we could keep going.

We're bringing my people home.

I close my hand around her invisible one as I head back to the wagon to collect another butterfly. In the shadows behind the vehicle, I slip my own charm back on just for a few moments so we can embrace in our pocket of invisibility together—so I can revel in having her back despite my panic.

Ivy tucks her head against my neck. "Were you all right on your own?"

Her hand rests on my chest over my heart, and I feel the truth of the words before I say them. "I wasn't really alone. You're always with me, in here."

I set my hand over hers, and she beams at me before rising to claim another kiss.

We finish our rounds in the second square and move on to another and then another. By the time the shadows start stretching long, I've helped more than thirty daimon shed the last lingering influence of scourge sorcery.

A few others have balked—swatting at the butterflies or pushing forward to search for the source with obvious hostility—but none quite as aggressively as our first failure. When it happens, we simply vanish and move on to another part of the city.

I'm starting to get a sense of who is under more tenuous hold and who is caught in a firmer grasp before we even test them, just from the vibration in the energy I pick up on. I'm studying yet another possibility, debating whether she's worth risking a butterfly on, when an amplified voice rings through our current square.

"The regent Lothar calls Florian's citizens to the Temple of the Crown! He has news that could mean life or death for all of you."

# THIRTY-THREE

*Ivy*

Rheave tucks his arm around my waist in the wagon, pulling me even closer than he did earlier on this journey. "Do you think Lothar knows what we've been doing?"

I can't help pricking my ears to the warble of city noise beyond the vehicle, as if I might hear something to inform my answer. I get nothing but a blur of rattling wheels and jumbled voices.

I swallow thickly. "I don't know. We have been at it for a few hours now. His people could have already noticed that a bunch of their captured daimon have left rather than following orders. But with the sorcery on them waning, that could have happened eventually without us interfering."

The daimon-man makes a rough sound. Everywhere our bodies touch, his muscles are tensed. "Should we leave instead? While so many people are distracted by the announcement?"

I've already thought that question through more than once since we made our first hasty decision to have our driver direct the wagon toward the inner wards. The answer comes automatically now. "No. If it's a matter of life or death… we need to know what's going on. *Especially* if it has anything to do with Petra or our efforts to see her on the throne."

Rheave nods, accepting my statement without argument. For just a second, I wish he would push back, insist that we get out of here, even though I'd have to stand firm.

I'm not sure I really *want* to. Something about the messenger's call in the square has left a clammy sensation seeping into my skin.

But what I said is true. If Lothar is about to unleash some new horror, we have to know as soon as possible so we can protect ourselves. Even if the Black Talons have people listening in, we don't know how long it'd take them to get a message to us.

The Order's leader could be counting on us thinking that way, though. He *could* suspect that members of the resistance have infiltrated the city and want them to find out just how awful things could get for them next.

With that possibility in mind, I have the driver stop a couple of streets shy of the old city walls that border the inner wards. Rheave and I remove our charms, keeping them in our pockets where they'll stay inactive.

We don't want there to be any chance of the scourge sorcerers seeking out their magic.

I smear some grit from the side of the wagon across my face as if I've been doing grunt work in the outer wards all day without a bath. Rheave follows suit. Then we pull on our cloaks, tugging the hoods low over our heads.

Spring is creeping closer, but enough winter crispness lingers in the air that plenty of other civilians are wearing their own cloaks. Once we emerge from the wagon and merge with the current of figures flowing through the streets to the Temple of the Crown, we blend in perfectly.

I spent twenty years of my life in this city and seven of those making the streets my home, but somehow the territory I've roamed through more than a hundred times feels like foreign territory today. I know the twists and turns of the roads, the steep slope that takes us the last short distance to the huge courtyard outside the grand temple, and yet nothing looks quite as familiar as it should.

Maybe it's the murmurs passing through the growing crowd around us—not eager with anticipation the way they might have been for past events at the city center, but hushed and uncertain. My fellow citizens can't have any more idea what their self-proclaimed ruler has in store for them than I do.

We've been sowing doubt and fear throughout the country as well as we can. I'm sure plenty of Florians have heard the claims against the Order. Some who first supported them will now wish them gone along with their horrific sorcery.

But how many have the means to stand up to the scourge sorcerers? How many would be prepared to risk their lives speaking out when even the queen has only done so through stealth?

They're waiting for us—waiting for someone with real power to stand with.

My lungs tighten with the thought.

*We're working on it*, I want to tell them. *We're coming to rescue you from these villains. We just have to make sure we do it right, or we'll be lost too.*

The stream of pedestrians we're caught up in spreads out at the mouth of the courtyard. The vast space is already teeming with bodies pressing close together to make room for more. Other figures peer from the windows and balconies of the stately buildings around the courtyard.

I suspect by the time Lothar begins his announcement, even the side-streets will be packed with spectators. All of them poised to spread the word back to their neighbors who didn't make it in time.

I grasp Rheave's hand and lead him through the jostling bodies to one spot that is still familiar. Nothing's changed about my favorite alcove where months ago I watched the execution of the last apprehended riven sorcerer.

The daimon-man's height means he doesn't need much of a vantage point to look over the milling crowd. I clamber up to my usual perch so I can peer over his head.

The sun has nearly completely set. The daimon we shook out of their sorcerous bindings will be gathering near Crow's Close for the Black Talons to collect. Casimir hasn't sent any signal through my locket, which should mean his end of the plan has gone smoothly.

He'll be waiting for our wagon to pick him up. I hope he's heard about this announcement and realizes we'll have delayed to learn the news.

To my relief, no corpses dangle from the walls of the temple like they did the last time we visited this place. Dark stains still mar the pale marble where the murdered clerics and devouts once hung, a stark reminder of the penalties for drawing the Order's ire.

As lights start to glow on the balcony where King Konram used to speak to the masses, my magic wriggles in my chest. If Lothar appears directly—if I can set my eyes on him and know exactly where he is—I have a chance to end this now, before he says anything at all.

But when the head scourge sorcerer's looming, lopsided form appears by the stone railing, I'm not surprised to catch a faint flicker at the edges of his body. The former advisor isn't taking any chances. He's projecting himself as an illusion again.

Before he even speaks, the crowd below falls into an ominous silence. Clothing rustles as the spectators shift uneasily on their feet.

"People of Florian," Lothar says, his voice resonating through the courtyard as if it's coming from all sides at once, "I've gathered you tonight to make two important announcements. The first is one we can rejoice. You may have heard rumors that a series of kingship trials will be happening soon. That's true—the ones the Order of the Wild will enact. We'll determine the best ruler of Silana and discover whether the supposed princess will participate in a fair competition or forfeit the crown."

I can almost hear Julita scoffing. *Fair? Fairly rigged, I'd imagine.*

No doubt. But any dark amusement I can take from that thought vanishes with the former advisor's next words.

"You can look forward to witnessing the spectacle of royal worthiness in just four days, when Creadenala is upon us!"

My entire body goes cold. He expects to pull together his trials in just four days? I'd forgotten to even think of the standard festivals, let alone the one for Creaden soon approaching.

Will we be able to pull our own spectacle together in the fleeting time before then? If we can't—

Lothar's voice breaks through my thoughts again, taking on a dire tone. "To my dismay, I must also warn you of a grave threat that's come to my attention. Many other stories have been circulating through rumors and hearsay, but they've been spread by a source far more terrible than any of the supposed villains they point to."

I frown, peering at him as intently as I can. What's he talking about now? Is he going to say that Petra is some kind of brutal fiend?

I find it hard to believe this will simply be more bluster about how exploitive the royal family was. He must have something specific to say that he thinks will sway public opinion.

What could that be? Petra didn't act in her royal capacity at all until after her father was murdered. I know she hasn't done anything remotely criminal since then.

Lothar continues with a thump as if he's stomped his foot for emphasis. "You've been deceived, but it's understandable in the face of a vicious power like this. All of us in the Order of the Wild put our own lives on the line to bring you the truth."

A deeper prickling of discomfort digs into my chest. Something about the way he's phrasing his remarks—

He waves his hand, and another figure steps forward, her face shadowed by the hood of her cloak. I think she might actually be standing on the platform rather than an illusion herself.

Lothar's mouth forms a tight smile that I suspect is holding back a smirk. "You can hear just how long this poison has been tainting our city from the woman who witnessed it emerge into being. Who has come to us now to warn us."

The woman pulls back her hood, and my heart stops.

It's my mother. Even across that distance, with the stark shadows of the magical glow sharpening the angles of her face, I recognize her in an instant.

My legs wobble under me. I have to press my hands hard against the walls I'm braced between to catch myself before I fall.

My head spins. What— How—?

The woman I once called "Ma" steps forward to rest her hands on the stone railing. Her face looks pale and taut as she gazes down over the gathered crowd—the expression I can remember from when she'd take the whip to me all those years ago.

The scars on my back itch.

"I had to come forward," she says, her familiar if roughened voice flooding the courtyard through the same magical amplification as Lothar's. "The more I heard about the vigilantes who are attacking the Order of the Wild, the ones the supposed queen is working with, the more I realized what must really be going on. If only I'd seen it sooner..."

Her voice fades with a rasp. I can barely breathe. Then she squares her shoulders and goes on.

"Thirteen years ago, my beloved younger daughter died suddenly under unexplained circumstances. My husband and I never had any proof, but I couldn't shake the feeling that something was strange about our older daughter. That she might be hiding dark intentions of the kind a mother would never want to imagine."

My fingers curl against the walls holding me up as anguish twists my gut.

She didn't want to imagine it? But she did, over and over, no matter how much I pleaded.

She beat me and shunned me and left me hungry and loveless, all because of what she suspected but never brought herself to say outright.

Ma raises her voice even louder. "When she turned twelve, right before her dedication ceremony, she ran away rather than accept the gods. I had no idea what happened to her—until I started hearing the stories. A young woman with pale orange hair and blue eyes who seemed practiced at criminal acts. Who could call down unspeakable magic of all sorts with her will alone. It's her, and it's undeniable. My daughter is one of the riven, mad with her power, and she's out to destroy all the rest of us!"

Gasps and mutterings of concern ripple through the crowd. My gut clenches tighter.

Rheave glances up at me with a matching anguish etched on his gorgeous face, his body tensed as if he could literally leap to my defense.

"If I had an arrow, I could quiet her," he says in a low voice. "Strike her down like lightning…"

I could do the same right now with the magic she's condemning, the power writhing between my ribs. A sour taste laces my tongue.

My magic sears all the way from my jaw to my gut, burning to be let out. To strike her down for the awful picture she's painting, the blame she's shirking.

But it's not even a question.

I shake my head. The words scrape their way up my throat. "Nothing she's said is exactly a lie. And we'd only be proving her right."

How much does she really believe that I'm the brutal monster she's claiming, and how much has Lothar coached her on what to say?

I'm not sure it makes any difference.

My mother is still speaking, with a quaver in her voice that makes my teeth grit. "I don't know how anyone who claims to want the best for us could ally with a riven sorcerer. Maybe she has whatever's left of the Melchiorek family under her control. Maybe she's the one who murdered King Konram! But we can't let her or the people she's swayed to join her tear down all the good the Order has done for us."

The murmurs of the crowd are becoming more urgent. Some are waving their fists in the air in apparent anger.

My power roars louder, and I squeeze my eyes shut as I pull my imagined vine tight around me. At my continued refusal, a slash of magic cuts across my lungs.

I flinch and clamp my mouth shut against a sob. The pain radiates through me for a few thuds of my heart before finally dissipating.

And Lothar isn't even done yet.

He takes over the speech with a coolly forceful tone. "You've heard it from the mouth of the woman who endured the tragedy of having birthed this monster. Our entire country teeters on the edge of disaster as long as this ruthless riven sorcerer runs free. We must find her and execute her before she can do any more harm!"

At the sharp cheer that rings out, I wince. Another tremor runs through my body.

Rheave touches my leg as if to steady me, but I barely feel the warmth of his hand.

Then more light flares beside the temple platform, and an image of a figure that's closer to my looks than I want to admit shimmers into being. An illusion drawn from Lothar's memories and those of his followers who've seen me?

My pulse hiccups, and I drop down from my perch.

Lothar's voice booms through the courtyard again. "This is the woman you must beware. This is the riven who intends to destroy us all. The Order will be showing this image all across the country so you can protect yourselves—and inform us if you've spotted her. Don't approach her yourself. We'll bring our own magic to bear and ensure Silana's people are safe. But any information will be hugely rewarded."

Gods smite me. I fumble for the invisibility charm and yank it over my head. Rheave does the same and snatches my hand.

Without another word, we bolt along the edges of the crowd and out of the courtyard, fleeing the mass of my fellow citizens now baying for my blood.

# THIRTY-FOUR

*Ivy*

The wagon jolts to a halt when we're still half a mile distant from Baron Cyris's summer residence. The driver calls back to us in a wary voice. "There's someone coming to meet us. They're signaling for us to stop. I'd better wait and see what she's about."

I rub my eyes, bleary after the fragmented sleep I forced myself to attempt on the trip back, and peek through a gap in the canvas covering. A figure on horseback is riding toward us at a gallop through the thin dawn light, braided hair streaming behind her.

It's hard to read her expression at this distance and with her moving so swiftly, but her rigid stance makes me tense up in turn.

Rheave adjusts his position beside me, setting his hand on my shoulder. I'm aware of Casimir sitting across from us, though I can only see a hazy impression of him if I squint.

Even though we've almost reached our current "home," it doesn't feel safe to remove the charms concealing us just yet.

The rider arrives with a thunder of hoofbeats and a disgruntled-sounding huff from her horse. She cranes her neck to eye the wagon before focusing on the driver. "You've brought the three of them back from Florian?"

"Of course. Is something the matter?"

"Word's been spreading." Her voice drops to a hush as if she's hoping I won't hear. "About *her*. The baron doesn't want her on his property anymore. I'll let the others know you've returned. Wait here."

She whirls the horse and races back toward the residence without waiting for a response. My stomach has plummeted to somewhere in the vicinity of the floor.

Word's been spreading… about my riven magic. About the sister I killed with it.

About how my own mother is condemning me and calling for me to be struck down.

Some of our allies already knew, but my men and I never emphasized it. I've rarely used any magic in front of any of them.

I made it as easy as possible for them to dismiss or ignore the nature of my power. Now Lothar has shoved it in all their faces.

My throat constricts, and a hand wraps around mine. Casimir has pushed forward and found me in the dimness of the wagon.

"Petra will sort this out if no one else does," he says. "*She* knows you're not a threat—she knows how much you've done for her and her family."

She does. And one of the things I did, no matter how many times she says she doesn't blame me for it, is get Lothar access to the room where he slaughtered her parents.

My stomach settles into a simmer of nausea while we wait for the rider to bring additional orders. We have our own urgent news to pass on, but the messenger didn't give us a chance to say anything. Every minute could make a difference.

Doesn't the baron care about that?

Finally, I peek outside and spot a small procession on their way.

Whoever that woman was, she isn't with them. It's just Stavros, Alek, and Sulla, on their usual horses and leading three other steeds including Toast, with Petra and a couple of her guards riding behind them. Our horses are loaded with bulging saddle bags.

My queasiness bubbles right up to the base of my throat. It doesn't look as if they're coming to say all is well and we should return to Baron Cyris's residence after all.

The concealment charm seems pointless now. I don't need to hide from my lovers and the one consistent friend I've got in this mess.

As I tug off mine, Casimir and Rheave follow suit. We clamber out the back of the wagon and come around to meet our ominous welcome party.

Stavros's face is as grim as I've ever seen it, his eyes dark with restrained fury. He hops off his horse the moment he's near enough and strides over to meet me.

His voice comes out taut. "I'm sorry, Ivy. I tried to reason with Cyris—he *has* to see—I don't know how he could think it's worth jeopardizing everything we've worked for—"

I lift my hand to cut him off, forcing a sickly smile. "Unfortunately, we've got bad news that's even more urgent. I don't suppose anyone passed on word about Lothar's trials as well."

Alek's eyes widen. "What? No." His tone turns bitter. "They were too busy smearing your name."

I can't let that fact distract me from my most important purpose. "Lothar also announced that the Order of the Wild will be holding their kingship trials in four days, when we'd normally be celebrating Creadenala. He made a challenge to Petra to show herself there or forfeit the crown."

For all his fury on my behalf, even Stavros draws up short. "Four days?"

Petra sucks in a breath with a hiss, her tan skin graying.

"So we have to pull the rest of whatever we're doing together even faster," I say, supressing the ache in my gut. "However we can. What exactly has the baron decided about me? I'm guessing he hasn't called for my arrest."

Stavros's lips draw back from his teeth with a restrained growl. "I'd stuff him in one of his holding cells before I let his guards set a finger on you."

Alek speaks up again, his voice quieter now but still strained. "Hunting parties have already gone out from the nearby towns—people hoping they can spot you and get some kind of reward for reporting you to the Order and allowing 'justice' to be done. Baron Cyris doesn't feel secure having you on the premises in the current atmosphere. And obviously we weren't going to stay if you couldn't."

Sulla bows her head. "No one's hunting for me, but *I* wouldn't have felt safe staying among such fickle allies."

Petra brings her horse around the others, shooting a brief glance of stifled irritation toward the guards who insist on flanking her. "I still want your help—now more than ever if we only have three days left to finish our plans. Our scouts previously identified a reasonably secure location nearby where you can stay and avoid notice. There's an abandoned cabin about a half hour's ride from here in a patch of woods. And I'll keep working on the baron to have you back in comfort."

It's not my comfort I'm worried about. Despite my best efforts and maintaining my composure, my stomach has not just sunk but had a hole punched through it.

My voice comes out with a rasp. "Don't bother with that. You need to put every bit of your energy and concentration into overseeing our final preparations."

My daimon lover clearly disagrees with my priorities. "How can the baron cast Ivy away?" he demands. "She's helped so many people—she hasn't hurt anyone."

I give Rheave's arm a quick squeeze. "You know that isn't entirely true. I'm lucky my presence was tolerated for as long as it was. Let's find this cabin and let Petra get back to her work."

Willing my posture to remain steady, I walk over to claim Toast and swing onto his back. Rheave and Casimir take their own mounts, Rheave's expression still fierce and Casimir's downcast in a way I've rarely seen on the courtesan.

No one wants to say it, but this is the end. The end for us, at least.

I think I've known it since I first saw my mother standing on the platform next to Lothar's projection, but I didn't want to admit it to myself.

The wrenching sensation inside me pulls my gaze to Stavros. "You should stay with Petra and the others at the estate. You're by far the best strategist they—"

Stavros cuts off my suggestion with a sharp shake of his head. "Our future queen knows she has all our support, but I'm not going to act as if I condone the way the baron is treating you. I'll only be a half hour away, and I can think just as well outside those walls."

Petra lifts her chin. "And for the actual construction, we'll probably end up closer to you than the residence regardless."

She turns to one of the soldiers. "Ride back to the estate and let the others know our new timeframe. If there are any clerics we haven't heard from to supervise the trials, we need to approach our second choices now. And all the blueprints need to be finalized so we can start construction today. I'll be back as soon as *these* allies of mine are settled."

The man bobs his head and gallops off.

With a tap of her heels against her horse's flanks, Petra leads us around the estate. As I follow her, I tell myself it's all right.

I've pitched in plenty already. I've played a key role in building our cause from our first tiny group to a network of hundreds of allies across the country.

I should be satisfied with the fact that I accomplished as much as I did. Who knows whether I could have really done much more anyway?

I still can't shake the sensation of a jumble of rocks piling up in my belly.

Sulla prods her mare to walk beside Toast. We ride in silence for a few minutes before she clears her throat.

"There's too much history. Too much fear. Those who don't have the power don't know how to see us as human."

That's part of the reason she didn't want me inserting myself into the affairs of the country in the first place. I wince inwardly. "I know it's hard. But a few of them have accepted me as I am. If Lothar hadn't sent the whole country into a fury to hunt me down…"

She sighs. "They're only acting on what they think is right. What they think even the gods would want."

But it isn't. The gods wanted us to wield this magic, at least while it was useful to them. If anything, we're blessed more than anyone else, not less.

Even that revelation sits heavily in my chest right now. No matter what we say to most of Silana's citizens, how will they ever accept the idea that the riven are more than monsters?

It certainly didn't look possible in the temple courtyard last night.

Even the men and women who've worked alongside me have remained wary through the weeks. There are still more of our allies who'll dodge my path than smile at me.

Casimir seems to have picked up on my train of thought. He speaks in the steady, soothing tone that comes to him so naturally. "Once we've fully exposed Lothar for the villain he is, it'll be easier to convince the rest of the country that the things he said were wrong as well."

It isn't just Lothar saying riven sorcerers deserve nothing but execution, though. Gods smite me, *I* had trouble believing anything else for most of my life.

Those uneasy thoughts stew inside me through the rest of the ride. We pick our way along narrow paths trampled by wildlife through a stretch of forest, Petra studying our surroundings and adjusting our course a few times. She makes a wordless sound of relief when a low, log building comes into view up ahead.

Once we've dismounted and examined the cabin, I can't summon much of a mood for gratitude. The building contains only a single room, scattered with dirt and twigs that have blown through the broken window. It smells dank, and the door doesn't close all the way.

It must be years if not decades since anyone last stayed here.

Oh, well. If we're still here after three more days, then we've lost to the scourge sorcerers, and it'll be a far cry better than a dungeon.

Alek pats the wall with forced cheer. "At least the roof looks solid enough. We'll have shelter if it rains."

Stavros grunts. "It beats a tent of branches. We've made do with worse."

Petra steps toward me and my men. "You can keep the one concealment charm, Ivy. If anyone does stumble on you, you'll want to be able to disappear."

She glances apologetically at Rheave and Casimir. "I'll need to bring back the others. We don't know how quickly we might need them."

Rheave opens his mouth with a look as if he's about to protest, but I jump in first. "Of course. The first priority is keeping you and your brother and sister safe. There aren't many to go around."

The daimon-man frowns, but he doesn't want to argue with me. And he'd probably rather blast anyone who comes hunting around here than stay hidden anyway.

"Thank you for understanding," Petra says softly as the two men hand over the charms on their chains. "I haven't asked you yet—did you accomplish everything you hoped to in Florian?"

Casimir pipes up first. He already filled me and Rheave in on his success when we reconvened at the wagon. "The Black Talons came through admirably. Their people should already be distributing the pamphlets so that most of Florian will be ready for our trials when we give the signal. We decided it was best if most of the recovered daimon remain in the city so they'll be close at hand when we arrive, but they might send a few to Baron Cyris's estate."

"How many *did* you recover?" Her gaze slides to me and Rheave.

"A little more than thirty, in the end," I say, the memory of the freed daimon, the delight that crossed their faces at realizing they could make their own decisions, softening a little of the turmoil inside me.

Rheave sighs. "There were a few who were still too deeply under the scourge sorcerers' spell for us to break them out of it. But their hold has weakened a lot."

Petra smiles at him. "That's wonderful. I suppose we can hope that within the coming days and weeks, some of them will start to emerge from the Order's influence on their own."

She pauses and seems to gird herself. "Not that we can wait on that possibility."

She's going to put herself on display in front of many of the same people who cheered at the thought of my death just last night. A shiver travels down my spine.

Our fellow citizens *have* to see that she's meant to rule. It's in her blood, her training—and every honorable, determined word she says.

If we can pull together our trials in no time flat.

I attempt to offer a reassuring smile. "We've laid the groundwork."

"Yes." She brushes her hands over the skirt of her riding dress and glances back at her guards. "We haven't yet determined the best approach for a few of the godlen's domains, have we? I'd appreciate you giving that matter as much thought as you can—what you think would prove my strengths as a ruler. We also need to solidify our strategies for preventing the Order from doing any harm during the tests—how you'll all factor in. I'll return this afternoon with Tinom so you can fill each of us in on the parts we're meant to hear."

My gut lurches. She still wants *me* contributing to the trials somehow—even helping orchestrate them on the actual day?

The words tumble out before I can think better of them. "Are you sure that's a good idea?"

Petra shoots me a puzzled look. "What do you mean?"

I motion helplessly with my hands, the weight of all my failures pressing on my lungs. "Should I be involved in the trials—or anything else you're doing—in any direct way at this point? Just the fact that people know you've had a riven sorcerer on your side, that I've supported you, is hurting your cause."

My voice falters, but I force myself onward to the inevitable conclusion. "You should probably remove yourself completely from any hint of an alliance with me. Forsake any past connections."

My chest clenches even tighter with those statements, as true as they are. If Petra sets herself apart from the riven—if she claims she didn't realize what I am and that she's now set herself apart from *me* —maybe there won't be too much fallout in the public's opinion of her.

But if she does that, it'll be even harder for her to turn around and speak up on the behalf of riven sorcerers later. I don't know how long it'd be before she could broach the subject of our origins.

Possibly never.

The future queen considers me for long enough that my skin itches with uncertainty. "I never took you for someone who'd give up and abandon a cause that easily."

The accusation stings. I can't hold back my instinctive response. "I'm not giving up—I'm not abandoning you. I'm trying to *help* you."

"By refusing to help me any further."

"By—by refusing to harm you any further."

My arms come up to hug myself. Casimir rests a gentle hand on my shoulder, and Rheave stirs behind me with a noise of concern, but I have to say this. The thoughts have been rattling around in my head since my mother first raised her voice to the crowd in Florian.

"I've tainted your legacy. I might have done more damage to the cause than good." A raw chuckle escapes me. "That's how it always seems to go."

Trying to save someone only to cause a worse catastrophe isn't exactly new to me.

Alek's lips part where he's standing by the doorway behind Petra, but she speaks before he can. "I should be the judge of that. I still want you standing with me. Most of what Lothar is spreading is lies."

"Lies the people believe. You didn't see them last night while my mother told them what a monster I am."

"I wouldn't ask you to make a public exhibition of yourself."

"I don't need to appear before them to be a problem." I spread my hands. "I've just divided your allies, simply by existing. I've created discord right when we need to be as united as possible."

Petra grimaces. "You didn't cause that—Lothar did."

"And he only could because of what I am."

"Ivy—"

Before she can go on, Sulla steps in with a gesture for attention.

Petra falls silent. We both stare at the older woman, me with my hands clenching where they're tucked against my sides.

She's going to tell Petra she agrees with me. Maybe even suggest that she whisk me all the way back to the Haven where I'll be completely out of the—

Instead, my former mentor faces me. Her voice comes out unexpectedly soft. "I might have only arrived a few days ago. I might not have witnessed most of what you've accomplished directly. But I've seen and heard enough to feel sure when I say that I was wrong, Ivy. You've set things right much more than you've created new troubles. I—I'm sorry if any of the doubts I expressed before are making you doubt yourself now."

I gape at her for a second before I manage to reel my jaw in.

Petra jumps into my silence. "She should know, shouldn't she? You have to listen to us."

I step back to slump against the wall, a sense of defeat sweeping over me that I can't totally explain. "I don't want to make another mistake. Not when the consequences could ruin the entire country."

"You wouldn't," Rheave insists, but of course he'd say that.

Petra hesitates. Then she moves so she's directly in front of me and waits until I lift my gaze to meet hers.

"Ivy, I won't force you to stay involved. I won't give you any royal commands or demand your obedience against your better judgment. That's not how I want to rule. But you have to know how much everything you've done for this country and for my family means to me. And it's more than that. What kind of reign will I have if it's founded on old, unfair prejudices? I'm making my stand now—in every way I need to."

I choke up abruptly. It takes me a moment to recover my tongue. "That means a lot to me too. I want to be ruled by a queen who follows those principles. I just… I don't know."

The conflicting desires twined inside me send a lance of pain through me from throat to belly. My arms shift, my hand coming to rest on the spot on my sternum where most people have a godlen mark.

Where the godlen who went out of his way to claim me once marked me temporarily to save my life.

I don't fully know how I feel about the gods' role in creating riven magic. I don't expect Kosmel to step out of the clouds and point the way. He's never been so blatant with his advice.

But he has offered guidance when I've needed it. I can't say he's ever led me astray.

If I'm willing to bow down to a mortal queen, maybe I should welcome the gods all the way into my life, into whatever roles they're meant to fill.

I push myself off the wall and slip over to the cabin doorway. No one moves to stop me, probably waiting to see what I'm up to.

On the threshold, I scan the forest and pick a dense grove of trees several paces from the building, where the shadows lie most thickly.

Kosmel is the master of the shadows, just as I once liked to think I was. If I can find him anywhere, it'll be there.

I walk to the grove and kneel at the base of the tree trunks. The roots jutting from the soil dig into my shins.

I tip my head up to the patch of gloom cast by the overlapping leaves above me.

*Kosmel,* I think, sending my mental voice out into the world, *you helped me get this far. I don't know what I'm meant to do now. Have I accomplished everything you hoped for? How should I go forward if I want to see this woman reclaim her throne?*

I'm not surprised that my head stays silent. The leaves rustle overhead, and a faint caw reaches my ears, as if a crow has flown nearby.

Then all at once a breeze gusts up and blows through the high branches.

Even as my hair whips around my face with the blast of wind, I take in a sudden burst of light. The leaves sway to the sides, and sunlight pours down where once there was only shadows.

A quiver of understanding runs down the center of me. I keep staring up at the branches as they settle back into place.

*Thank you*, I say silently.

The sign he sent has left a renewed light in my chest as well. As I get to my feet, an almost giddy sensation tickles through my limbs.

I never really wanted to back away. I've fought so long to protect my country.

I want to see that mission through to the end.

I choose my words carefully through the growing thrum of my pulse. "I think… I think I'm meant to show the truth. To help you come out of the shadows so people can see you as you truly are. Which means we need these trials to happen fast, so I'd better start brainstorming."

# THIRTY-FIVE

*Casimir*

The rasp of saws and hiss of sandpaper travels through the wide forest clearing. I could barely make out the sounds of human work when I was approaching this spot, thanks to a combination of magical effects created by a few different gifts working together, but now it drifts around me in an almost comforting rhythm.

Almost, because despite the care the workers are obviously taking, a sense of urgency permeates the air. Everything needs to be finished within the next day if we're going to have any hope of superseding Lothar's trials.

This is our last chance. No matter what doubts about the Order of the Wild we've sown, no matter what promises Petra has made, if the scourge sorcerers can set her up to look like a failure of a ruler in a public spectacle, I don't know how she'd ever win over the country.

If she'd even survive the day.

My heart thuds along at a faster rhythm than the work around me. I can't quite settle it even with all my calming techniques brought to bear.

I pause here and there to consider the blueprints laid out on the forest floor and the corresponding slabs of wood the workers Baron Cyris assembled are cutting, but physical building isn't exactly my area of expertise. I'm here mainly to evaluate the emotional impact of the finished apparatus.

The pieces already shaped and smoothed lie in careful rows across the ground at the other end of the clearing. The pale wood gleams in the late afternoon sun.

We'd have some trouble explaining what we're up to if any members of the Order stumbled on this work site. The large, irregular pieces with their knobs and indents to allow them to fit together securely don't look like any kind of furniture a noble would be commissioning.

But that's why the baron sent the craftspeople off to work in the woods beyond his estate rather than in plain view on his grounds. The fact that it shortens the distance I needed to travel to stop by and make my assessment is a small but welcome side benefit.

The figures at this end of the clearing are manipulating the wood in a very different way. They're mostly dedicats to Creaden with gifts related to the godlen's knack for construction, although a few others have stepped up to lend talents that can be honed to our needs.

At a bark of an order from the head foreman, several of the workers spring into action. Their faces harden into masks of concentration as their hands rise to help direct their magic.

Pieces of wood lift from the ground and whirl toward each other. Interlocking joints snap together. Edges thump against one another. The slabs climb up above our heads—

A few of the boards smack into each other at the wrong angle. One wobbles and strikes another below. A worker grunts, another shuddering as he tries to maintain control, but it isn't enough.

The wooden pieces creak and strain, and the foreman shouts for them to be lowered. "We're not getting anywhere if you break them!"

The workers guide the partly constructed tower to the ground and let it tumble apart with a heavy patter against the uneven ground.

The foreman sighs. "Where did it go wrong this time? We need to be able to move fast, but we do actually have to build the thing properly."

I hold up my hand as I approach them. "Can we take a break from using gifts and put it together manually? I know it'll be slower, but I'd like to take a look at how the full structure is coming together. And I'd imagine everyone could use a chance to rest their minds."

The foreman's mouth tightens, but he nods. I catch hints of relief in the exhaled breaths and shifting bodies of his underlings.

It does take longer for them to fit the slabs together when they're building by hand, and after some time, they have to clamber up the base of the tower to continue. But the wood workers have gotten quite a bit done already. While there are more pieces to come, the tower already rises about twice my height.

I study it, noting the impressions it stirs in me, and glance around at the rest of the yard. "This is a section of the obstacle course, isn't it? How are the moving parts coming together? Do we have any of the other challenges ready to go?"

One of the Creaden dedicats motions to me with a wave of her hand. "A bunch of it is over here. And the bits of the puzzle boxes are almost finished too."

With a couple of her fellow workers, she demonstrates how a few of the obstacles in the sequence will operate. Others fit together what they have so far of what they called the puzzle box. I ask one of them to step inside the huge cube so I can picture what it'll be like in action.

The foreman comes up beside me. "What do you think?" he asks gruffly.

He's braced for criticism but craving approval.

I nod slowly. "I think we're on the right track. We're going to want to add as much color as we can in the time we have, spark more feelings with that. And I'd recommend adding metal pieces to the wheel rather than having the teeth be wood—the shine catching the sun will have even more impact."

The foreman frowns. "We don't want the queen getting *hurt*."

I glance at him, unable to stop my smile from tightening. Doesn't he realize how much harm we'll all be risking when we pull this immense gambit together?

"The people need to see she's taking real risks," I remind him. "She wants to prove every trait she believes makes a good ruler, and that includes bravery and the willingness to face danger on behalf of her country."

He lets out a faint huff, but he doesn't argue the point. Instead, he calls out to one of the workers to bring the materials from a storeroom and another to summon a couple of Inganne dedicats from the estate who have a way with paint.

I dip my head in thanks. "Let me know when the artists get here. I'll consult with them on what color scheme would be most effective for each part."

The trials we're going to set up don't need to just show off Petra's prowess, both physical and mental. They need to stir the hopes and hungers of her audience. Create a story of how fiercely this woman will fight for their happiness.

Is it going to be enough?

After seeing how easily Lothar has been able to sway the people of Silana in his favor, I don't know.

He certainly seems to believe it won't. He must know by now of the pamphlets we distributed in Florian, promising that Princess Petra would be hosting her trials in the coming days, but the announcements in the nearby towns all still place Lothar's on the day of Creadenala.

Whether because he can't prepare it in time or because he doesn't want to appear uncertain, he hasn't moved his spectacle forward. He doesn't think *we* could truly challenge him.

And he could be right. I'm not sure how we're going to ensure Petra makes it through our trials without the scourge sorcerers finding a way to strike her down.

Those uncertainties are still twisted inside me when one of the baron's other employees approaches. I've only seen her briefly during our time staying at his summer home, but I recognize her flaxen hair and dainty features from my frequent socializing in the royal court.

She's someone high up in Baron Cyris's retinue—a chief of staff of sorts, a go-between who ensures everything at the lower levels of his various estates is running smoothly. Nasha, if I remember her name correctly.

I don't believe we've ever spoken before, and I've never gotten much of an impression of her one way or another. But something in her face as she looks me up and down puts me on guard.

She clicks her tongue. "It's Casimir, isn't it?"

I hide the apprehension I don't totally understand behind a warm smile. "Yes. The queen asked me to—"

"I know why you're here." Nasha glances around the clearing. "Have you already surveyed the preparations so far?"

"Yes. I'm waiting to advise on some additions the craftspeople will be making once a few more workers have arrived."

"Then you can spare a little time."

I do my best to study her surreptitiously. "I'm at your disposal. What is it you need?"

She flicks her hand toward the trees. "It's better discussed in private."

I let her lead the way, tension creeping through my limbs. For all the authority she exudes, she's a slight thing, slimmer even than Ivy was when she first arrived at the college and a good head shorter than me. I'm not afraid she'd manage to physically harm me as long as I stay alert for weapons.

But I don't know what gifts she has. I don't know what she wants.

I shouldn't be thinking like this at all.

I wouldn't be, if her employer hadn't set himself up as the enemy of the woman I love.

We tramp between the trees in the direction that takes us farther from the baron's residence. The sounds of the construction fade swiftly, swallowed up by the magical protections around the clearing.

Nasha keeps walking, her head turning as she scans the forest. I'm not sure what she's looking for, but after a few minutes, she appears to find it. She stops in a small glade where the sun streaks past the leaves and over a patch of pale grass.

She pivots to face me. Her gaze rakes over me before I can speak, as if it's cutting through the woolen tunic and trousers I'm wearing.

Either my focus on the queen's plans clouded my usual awareness or Nasha was being more subtle before, because I recognize the intent that gleams in her eyes now. It's one I've seen dozens of times before.

There's no hostility, only a glimmer of lust.

"I heard so many stories about your prowess in court," she says. "I never thought I'd be able to afford you."

My gut lurches. "I'm not currently selling my services." Nor do I expect to any time in the foreseeable future.

She strolls closer, forcing me to back up a step before she can stroke her hand down my chest. She pauses with her lifted arm hovering between us. "You can't be serious. Already hailed as the most skilled courtesan under King Konram's reign before you'd even finished your education, and you're abandoning your career?"

I keep my voice carefully steady. "I see it more as adjusting my focus. Ardone celebrates more than just carnal pleasures."

Nasha hums to herself. "You're still showing off those gaudy teeth. You were on your way to being the most renowned courtesan in history. Always bringing your patrons every pleasure they could have asked for."

The rejection of that statement wells up inside me so fast I have to bite my tongue to keep from blurting out a simple, *No!* As I master my reaction, a rush of certainty follows like a gust of fresh air.

"No," I say more calmly. "That was my mother's legacy. I'm setting out on my own path, one that's more suitable for me."

Nasha takes another step forward, holding my gaze. "Then I'm asking you to make an exception. Because I *can* pay you now, in a currency that I'd imagine matters more than gold or silver to you at the moment. Give me a half hour with Casimir the courtesan—right here, as we are—and I'll see that you and your friends, including the riven sorcerer, are allowed to return to the safety of the baron's residence."

A rough laugh sputters out of me.

She hasn't judged completely wrong. That offer would matter to me more than money. But it sounds ridiculous to say that the baron's residence is *safe* when I have a predator from it here in front of me. And—

"The queen herself hasn't been able to convince him," I point out. "I think you may be offering a payment you don't actually have in hand."

"He's known me for years. He only just met her. He trusts me with nearly every aspect of his business. If anyone can persuade him, it's me."

She eases even nearer with a confidence that suggests she's sure of her success. When I retreat once more, her brow knits.

I pitch my voice as gentle as possible. "We're happy and secure enough where we are. And *I'm* happy with the present state of my career. I won't be taking any new patrons."

Nasha's eyes flash. She peers up at me with a sudden air of menace. "What if I put it this way, then: I'll pay you by *not* seeing that the Order finds out exactly where that monster of a woman is hiding."

A chill prickles over my skin. Truth rings through every harsh word.

She means her threat.

I study her even more warily. "That could be disastrous for your employer too."

"I can make sure the information is delivered without any ties to him." She tilts her head with a coyness that clashes with her attempt at blackmail. "Would it really be so horrible for you to tap into your talents with me, just this once?"

She isn't an unattractive woman. Months ago, before I met Ivy, I wouldn't have hesitated in the first place.

But now, the answer that peals through every particle of my body is yes. Yes, it would be horrible.

Not only because I'd be betraying the loyalty I've offered Ivy. My lover has never demanded that I abandon my trade.

No, I'd be betraying *myself*.

I am happy with who I am now, with how I'm conducting myself. With the ways I've used my talents and my devotion to my godlen that haven't required me sharing the bodily intimacy I once did with anyone other than the woman who's claimed my heart.

But what else can I do?

In a flare of desperation, I clench my teeth and push forward my gift. It feels like a hopeless gambit—Nasha has already told me very clearly what would make her happy, and it is technically something I can do—but I touch the side of my fist to my godlen brand and send a silent prayer to Ardone at the same time.

*Show me a way through this.*

A stream of imagery washes over me, and it isn't the lascivious tableau I was expecting.

Oh, a few flickers of my body twined with hers brush past me—she does desire that quite a bit. But shining through them come other glimpses: of Petra crowned and beaming down at Nasha while I stand at the queen's side, of Nasha looking down at a Melchiorek crest pinned to her vest.

Even more than she wants the pleasure I could offer her, she wants to please her future queen. To win Petra's favor and maybe even join her chosen staff.

She just hasn't considered that I could accomplish that much for her.

That doesn't mean I would, not to the extent she dreams. I'm not saying anything on her behalf to Petra without mentioning the threats and the blackmail.

It simply gives me a point of leverage that never occurred to me either.

I pull my posture a little straighter, aiming for authoritative airs of my own. "Is that what you really want to risk everything on—a brief tumble in the forest? You're clearly ambitious and clever. The queen trusts *my* judgment, you know. I could see that you found yourself in a position your former colleagues would covet for the rest of your life."

There's no mistaking the greedy glint that comes back into Nasha's gaze. She wets her lips, the aggression ebbing from her stance. "Is that what you'd rather trade for?"

I let a smile play across my face. "I suspect it's what you'd rather trade for as well. Why shouldn't we both be happier with this encounter?"

"You would tell her—I give every task I'm assigned my all. I've never failed Baron Cyris. She could count on me for—for anything."

The words rush out of her breathlessly, and then a hint of a blush touches her cheeks. She's more embarrassed by her enthusiasm than how she attempted to force herself on me just moments ago.

"I'll speak to her," I say, picking my words carefully, "and she'll speak with you about the possibilities within the day."

Petra would agree. And Petra would retract those mentioned possibilities as soon as Ivy is safe from Lothar's retribution.

My future queen trusts me, and I trust her as well.

Nasha clasps her hands together, looking abruptly, bizarrely girlish in her apparent delight. Her voice only darkens for a second. "I'll expect you to hold to that. Oh, to really talk with her—to prepare her reign…"

She wanders back toward the clearing without another word to me, lost in her visions of grandeur.

As I watch her go, my pulse gradually smoothing out from its panicked rhythm, a flare of insight lights in my mind.

Ivy said we needed to show Petra to the world. To shine a light on her and let the people see who she really is.

How many of Silana's citizens have longed for the royal family's recognition of their struggles and contributions? How many of them have turned to the Order of the Wild because the scourge sorcerers pretended to care where King Konram didn't?

How happy would they be if they realized their queen needs them… and isn't afraid to tell them so. To extend her trust to them too.

Few things can engender loyalty more than having it freely offered back. Perhaps we can sway them back to our side so simply.

With a genuine smile touching my lips, I hurry over to the clearing myself. I still have more work to do, and I need to reach out to Petra to make more than one arrangement.

Ardone has shone on me and lit up the truth. There are so many ways other than those my mother wished that I can spread joy and love through this world.

# THIRTY-SIX

*Ivy*

The cart thumps along the uneven country road, jostling me where I'm leaning against one of the walls. The rectangular space feels oddly empty with nothing in it except the four of us passengers while Casimir steers the horses.

But the afternoon air breezes over me with the fresh, tart scents of new growth, speaking of the spring that has almost reached us. It settles my nerves, though just a little.

I'm far too aware of the glass vials tucked into the pouch on my belt. The vials I asked Petra to obtain if she could, that she handed me shortly before we set out.

I have to talk to my men about them and everything else they need to be prepared for. I just haven't been able to bring myself to yet.

There's plenty of time still. Hours left in the day.

But with each passing minute, my stomach clenches a bit tighter.

Stavros sits all the way at the back of the cart, craning his neck one way and the other to scan our surroundings for potential threats. I suspect the former general would be happier on horseback, able to control his own movements, but he hasn't complained.

We want to look as innocuous as possible. Just a simple band of travelers bearing cargo. The magic Tinom impressed into the cart before we left should divert anyone who isn't specifically looking for us.

Of course, there are quite a few people out there who are specifically looking for us. Or rather, for me.

Just in the past two days as Petra's growing assembly of allies scrambled to prepare everything we need for the kingship trials, two small delegations sent by nearby counts arrived at the baron's residence supposedly to "check in" and see how the baron and his people are faring. From what I heard, they were snooping as much as they could get away with, watching for anything suspicious.

It's annoying that the baron might have been a little right to remove me from the premises, but mostly I'm glad that no one picked up on Petra's presence there.

There's been more activity on the lands around our patch of forest as well, packs of riders trotting by at random intervals. We haven't ventured out of the forest to greet them, so I have no idea what they'd have said their purpose was, but whenever one of my men mentioned noticing the passersby, my skin crawled.

Pretty much all of Silana hates the riven—far more than they hate the scourge sorcerers they only have the vaguest of ideas about. Plenty of civilians would have been unnerved by the accusations we made against Lothar but uncertain of what to believe and what to do about it. Now he's given them a target for their apprehension that has nothing to do with his Order.

And an opportunity to take action while earning the tyrant's favor at the same time.

If all goes well, we can end the chaos he's created tomorrow.

I close my eyes for a few minutes, simply absorbing the spring scents and the rhythmic creak of the wheels. My nerves are too jumpy for me to fully relax.

"Are you sure the message will have gotten to your parents—and they'll have followed through?" I ask Alek, who's got his legs sprawled out across from me.

The scholar's expression turns pensive, but he nods. "They've delivered on every other request Petra's made. We indicated that this would be the last one and that she was pleased with their service. I can't imagine them letting the opportunity to become the royal weapons suppliers slip through their fingers when it's almost in their grasp."

"Even if that means associating with someone who allies with riven sorcerers?"

He meets my eyes more firmly then. "They'll only have gotten that news by hearsay—and they're already committed to Petra. At this point, I'd be incredibly surprised if they did anything other than dismiss it as negative propaganda and focus on what lines their coffers."

He sounds so certain that a little of the tension in me unwinds. Alek may not get along with his parents, but he does know them. He wouldn't have set us on this course if he thought there was any chance it'd put me in danger.

Well, more danger than I'm already in, which seems to be a bit much even by typical standards.

Stavros lets out a rough breath. "I'm still not convinced this is the wisest idea. We don't need to make it *easier* for our opponents to cut us to pieces."

"We're ensuring they won't be opponents," Casimir pipes up from the front of the cart. I can't see his face, but there's a smile in his voice. "And then they can cut up anyone who does decide to play that role."

Stavros makes a noncommittal sound. He's been the most doubtful about the courtesan's plan since Casimir first suggested it.

I stretch out my foot to give his knee a teasing tap. "It's not as if we won't want arms for our confirmed allies to defend the trials. We don't need to make a final decision until people start gathering and we can gauge their mood."

The massive man lowers his head in acknowledgment. "Sometimes you can't know the best strategy until you're in the thick of the battle."

I'm not sure I'll get a better opening.

I hesitate for a few seconds, partly hoping one of the others will add something else. But saying this isn't going to get any easier.

"There's something else we should talk about," I blurt out, and pause to collect myself so my next words come out more calmly. "Lothar and his followers are going to do whatever they can to tear down Petra tomorrow. You all must realize that there's a good chance I'll have to use a lot of magic to ensure we see the trials through. I don't know how it'll affect me."

Casimir reins in the horses and turns on his seat to face the rest of us. A shadow has crossed his face. "What are you saying, Ivy?"

I think he already knows.

Stavros's expression has hardened with resolve. "We'll have all our supporters there from every source we could draw from. It won't come down to you."

I force myself to meet his gaze, as painful as this conversation is for both of us. "Not necessarily.

But it very well could. I'm the final line of defense, and there's no reason to assume Lothar won't manage to push that far. If it comes to that and I start to lose control, you need to act *immediately*—whoever's closest, whoever can do what needs to be done."

"Ivy," Alek starts in a rough voice.

I shake my head before he can fully protest and pull out the vials to show them. The milky liquid inside gleams in the sun. "Petra was able to get these for me. It's a strong sedative. Put me to sleep if you can manage to safely, to see what can be done for me later. But if you can't get the drug into me… I'd rather die than destroy anything we've worked for. Please."

My gaze slides across the faces of the men I love. Stavros has tensed so much he might as well have become a statue. Rheave's beautiful face has sallowed, his lips pressed together as if against the urge to vomit. Alek is simply staring, and Casimir works his jaw in silence.

"Please," I say again. "If I'm far enough gone that I can't restrain myself, ending my life is the kindest thing you could do for me. I'm trusting you not to let me become the sort of riven sorcerer they tell horror stories about."

Stavros's throat bobs with a thick swallow, but he nods, his hand on his sword as if echoing his promise. His voice comes out hoarse. "You couldn't be, Ivy. You're proving you're not simply by asking this."

He leans forward to accept one of the vials.

As Rheave watches it pass between our hands, a shudder ripples through his body.

I catch the daimon-man's gaze. "I know you don't want to lose me, but if my magic completely breaks my mind, I'll already be lost."

He considers me, his eerie eyes gone solemn. "If there's any other way, I'll take it. But I won't let you become something horrible."

Alek opens his mouth and closes it again. He presses his hand to his forehead. "I—I don't want to think about it. I understand that we have to, though. I won't let you down, Ivy."

Casimir pushes toward me to hold out his hand. "I might have the best chance of getting the sedative into you, by judging your mood."

I hand the second vial over and firm my voice. "If you can't, if I won't let you—"

He dips his head. "I know. I can do that kindness for you if there's no other choice."

Stavros opens his mouth to speak again, but at the same moment, Rheave jerks straighter in the corner where he was lounging. "I hear something. Other horses… coming this way."

Casimir swivels to grab the reins. We're just coming up on a low hill—it's impossible to see what's on the other side.

As soon as we all fall silent, a faint clopping reaches my ears, getting louder in the several seconds while my pulse hammers at my ribs.

Then a voice lifts, also distant but still audible. "That tree over there looks kind of strange, huh? You think a riven could've done that?"

My spine goes rigid.

Casimir's head whips around, scanning our surroundings. He nudges our horses off the road.

While it's mostly open fields on our side of the hill, there's a small patch of trees off to our right. It's too densely clustered for us to pull the cart between them, but Casimir steers us in that direction.

The grassy terrain partly muffles the hoofbeats of our own animals. Tinom's enchantment should divert attention from the noise too, at least a little.

I duck low, hoping the riven hunters are deep enough in their conversation that they don't notice any sound that filters through the spell.

With an intent expression, Rheave picks up the bow he had tipped against the cart wall next to him and fits an arrow into it. I wince inwardly at his obvious intention.

How much more will the world hate me if we leave a trail of bodies in our wake? These people searching for me might not have done anything worse than believing what the Order said—which wasn't entirely a lie—and wanting to protect their country.

The magic that's made me a target squirms in my chest and shoots out through my limbs. It could cloak us from view completely like it did so many times when we were chasing the Order's army weeks ago. It could send the hunters riding off in the opposite direction absolutely sure of their new destination.

It could erase them from existence so there were no bodies to be found at all. Like the guards at the palace in Regica. Like Lothar wanted me to do to the king and queen, to Petra and her siblings.

My hands clench against the boards beneath me at the memory.

I have to keep us safe to serve Petra now. But if I turn to my riven power for this, then what? More imaginary voices in my head, more delusions that even my allies are out to hurt me?

The mental effects of all the magic I expended earlier in our various journeys have faded as I've refused to use more, but I remember the viciousness of the worst panic with nerve-shuddering clarity. I need to save all the sanity I have left for our greatest challenge tomorrow.

I wind my imagined vine tight around me, holding my power in.

Casimir is urging the horses around the patch of trees. Soon the trunks will hide us from the road. As long as the hunters don't spot the cart's tracks and come over to investigate, we'll be fine.

My breaths remain shallow as the courtesan brings the cart to a halt. Rheave stays poised with his bow even though we can barely make out the road from here, let alone get a clear shot.

Stavros unsheathes his sword. He shoots me a glance as if to reassure me that they're prepared to defend me, whatever it takes.

As if the thought of my lovers getting hurt on my behalf makes me feel any better.

The hunters have stopped talking, but the hooves of their horses drum ever louder. It seems like no time at all before I catch a glimpse of the three of them cresting the hill.

It's hard to focus on them when seeing them only through the tiny gaps between the trees. I make out one head of dark hair and another covered by a bright blue cap, cloaks wrapped around them in varying shades of brown, a speckled gray horse, one dark bay, and the third ruddy chestnut.

From what I can tell, their clothes and mounts are of good quality and in good condition. Not extravagant, but I'd guess they're middle-class types, maybe merchants or craftsmen, taking a break from their regular work to chase the possible reward.

As we wait, crouched and silent, they continue by. Then the one on the bay draws his horse to a slower walk.

My heart skips a beat, and my magic flings itself at the barriers I've constructed against it.

They're going to find us—I have to act *now*—I can picture them charging toward our hiding spot—

I squeeze my jaw and my hands tight, resisting the wrenching of my power's demands with all my will.

Whatever the man slowed to look at, it hasn't caught his attention for long. He kicks his steed back to a trot, and he and his companions ride off down the road.

I have only a matter of seconds for relief to trickle into me before a spear of pain stabs through my middle.

I manage to clamp my lips against a gasp, but a faint whine seeps from my throat. I wrap my arm around my gut as if the external pressure can offset the agony inside.

My magic sears through me from chest to gut, sending a familiar series of jabs into my lungs and stomach. It's pissed off at me, all right—getting impatient that I won't let it loose like I've been willing to so recently.

It took a lot more time before it hurt me this badly in the past... but that was before it had a real taste of freedom. That was before I'd already pushed it to the brink of its patience.

I sag to the side. Alek darts across the cart to catch me before I slump right onto the floor.

A ragged breath catches in my throat. I muffle a sputter of a cough as well as I can—and stare at the red flecks that dabble my palm.

Oh. So we're all the way back to this point, are we?

My power is literally tearing into my flesh.

Alek's arm squeezes around me. As the pain finally ebbs, I become aware of Rheave staring over at us, his face taut with worry, his knuckles white where he's gripping his bow.

His voice comes out in a strained whisper. "Did they do something to her?"

Alek shakes his head and helps me sit back up. "That looked like the fits she used to have at the college…" He peers into my eyes. "Your magic attacked you again?"

I nod, taking a moment before I'm sure I can speak steadily. I can barely hear the retreating hoofbeats now, but I keep my voice low to be safe. "It *really* wanted to protect us from those hunters. It's lashed out a couple of times recently, but not this badly. I was hoping I'd have more time before I got to this point."

A shadow has crossed Stavros's face. "You'll have even more reason to worry about protecting us— and Petra—during the trials. It could hurt you worse then if it gets riled up when you don't need to step in."

A flare of rebellion sparks in my chest in spite of everything. "If you're trying to tell me I should hang back out of the way and not even—"

He holds up his hand in surrender, an echo of our earlier conversation lingering in his solemn tone. "I know you wouldn't accept that. But you could end up more vulnerable if your magic is attacking you right in the midst of the danger."

Casimir has swiveled in his seat to join the conversation. "Isn't that part of what your training with Sulla was about? Finding ways to avoid the backlash from holding the magic in?"

The thought of those early days, back before I'd experienced the other types of harm my magic could inflict on me, sends a pang like homesickness through my chest. "Yes. But the idea was that we extend just a little magic here and there to appease it, not enough that the madness would start to take hold. I'm past that point."

Alek strokes his hand over my hair. "You've turned to it a couple of times since then for something small, and it doesn't seem to have affected you too badly. If you followed the typical regimen, it might still work to keep you at status quo. No worse than otherwise, and without it lashing out."

I wet my lips. "I guess I should probably give it a shot. At least to take the edge off before the trials."

Petra needs me tomorrow. If I'm ever going to use my magic again in a major way, it'll be to see her through our final stand against the scourge sorcerers. I can't risk being incapacitated when it's time to act.

It's the only way *I* can prove to all the allies who've watched me with trepidation and fear whose side I'm really on. The only way I can make up for the damage I've done to her reputation.

The best way I can possibly serve her, whatever it does to me.

But as I look down at myself and around the cart, every part of my body balks. I've spent so long tamping down on my power, and I have even more reason to fear it now than I did before.

No possibility that flits through my mind feels right. All I'm left with is a knot in my gut.

"I don't know what to do," I admit quietly. "I don't know what would be too much."

Stavros's expression softens. He takes one more glance over his shoulder toward the long-gone hunters and sheathes his sword before shifting closer to me.

When I raise an eyebrow at him in question, he rubs the scruff on his cheek with his hooked prosthetic. "I've been neglecting the razor since we changed accommodations. Removing a little hair seems like an awfully small act. You could give me a shave."

I stare at him for a second, my thoughts whirling.

He's accepted me as I am, he's accepted my magic enough to let me bring him back from the edge of death, but somehow this small offer cracks open something inside me.

"Are—are you sure?" I have to ask.

The former general gives me his usual cocky grin. "I'm trusting that you like my face enough to avoid wrecking it."

I can't suppress a snort, even as my stomach twists tighter. But somehow having his permission—his request, even—makes the decision easier.

I scoot closer and rest my hand on the side of his face. The bristles of a few days' growth of beard prickle against my palm.

Stavros watches me without a hint of hesitation or regret over his offer.

My gaze slides beyond the cart to the nearby trees and then the stretch of grassy field on the other side.

That should do. Take a fraction of an inch of growth from his face, send a patch of grass a fraction taller at the same time. A simple trade.

Inhaling deeply, I concentrate on both sides of the equation. I picture the tiny hairs shrinking down to his skin as the blades poke a little higher from the soil, gradually across his entire face.

When I lower my hand, Stavros's jaw gleams clean-shaven. He touches it with his own fingers, and his grin returns.

"I don't know why I ever bothered with a blade," he says teasingly.

His casual warmth relaxes me even more. I crack a smile of my own and consider the simmer of magic inside me. "I think that should be enough."

Casimir climbs into the base of the cart and sits next to me. "We should be sure, so you'll be completely safe tomorrow." He rests his hands gently on my lap, palms up. "The reins have left a little grit on my hands, and I've got nothing to wash it off with."

A laugh tumbles out of me. It's the tiniest of efforts he's requesting. If he wants to be a part of protecting me too, I don't see how it can hurt to humor him.

With a moment of concentration, I flick the dirt that's dug into his palms with a whiff of breeze that's echoed by an opposite puff up in the tree branches.

Alek hums and sidles close to me again. "I gave myself a papercut on my thumb yesterday. Only a shallow one, but it still stings a bit. If you'd be kind enough to seal it for me…"

A tickle of heat flows over my skin both at the increasing attention and the nearness of my lovers all around me. I take Alek's hand in mine and find the tiny pink nick next to his thumbnail. "One more little thing. Just to be sure my magic is satisfied."

I focus on his thumb and one of the boards forming the wall of the cart. As the skin smooths, the smallest crack forms along the grain of the wood.

That's it. It's done.

I hold myself still, alert for any disorienting thoughts or hallucinated sounds, but my mind stays quiet.

Watching me, Rheave gives a bit of a growl, but all I can hear in it is sorrow. "It's sad that you can't use your magic all the time like I can. When you do, when it's to help someone, it lights you up."

His tone is so tender in its frustration that it makes my heart skip a beat. I aim a smile at him and then around at the other three men who've given so much to stay by my side. "*You* light me up. All of you, just by being with me. I love you. No matter what happens to me tomorrow, I want you to always know that."

If worse comes to worst tomorrow, which seems more likely than not, I may very well go mad. One of them might need to end my life before I destroy more than even Lothar has.

But it's not tomorrow yet. We have at least this one last day together.

Rheave answers my statement first, dropping his bow and pushing across the cart to meet me. He cups my cheek and draws me into an emphatic kiss.

When our lips part, he nuzzles his nose against mine. His voice drops even lower with a heated edge that makes me shiver. "I want to see if *my* magic can make you happy."

A tingle shoots straight to my groin. "What do you mean?"

Rheave trails his fingers down my arm, and a more concrete tingling races through my flesh. My breath catches.

He's sent just the softest pulse of his conjured lightning into me.

A heated chuckle escapes Stavros. "I think our lady thief approves."

Rheave beams and ducks his head to claim another kiss. As he does, his hand travels farther down to my hip.

A sizzling shiver darts from the warmth of his hand to the liquid heat pooling between my thighs.

As I kiss him back hard, I can't hold back a whimper. It's undeniably thrilling to become a vessel for his daimon energy, especially when he uses it to such skillful effect.

And there's something wonderful in general about taking in magic that I don't have to fear, that won't bring me anything but pleasure.

When Rheave relinquishes my mouth to chart a scorching path down my neck, Casimir is waiting to capture my lips. Alek leans in to tug aside my cloak and press a kiss to my shoulder.

Stavros tangles his fingers in my hair and nips the back of my neck. "We have time for a little joy before the rest of the hard work."

The daimon-man lets out an encouraging rumble. "To show our little vine how much we love her too."

Casimir eases back and runs his thumb over my lips in a gesture that's almost as provocative as his kiss. "Because we do love you, no matter what happens, no matter where we end up."

Alek slings his arm around my waist to hug me tight. "Being with you will always have been worth it."

Our strange makeshift family has survived so much. I can't say I have any regrets either, not when I can't be sure we'd all still be here if I'd made different choices to begin with.

And it's getting awfully hard to think of anything at all other than enjoying their company with their mouths and hands moving over my body.

Casimir edges up my skirt, and Rheave slips his hand between my legs to set off another spark right at my core. I gasp and almost bite Alek's lip, but he simply groans and kisses me harder.

Stavros dips his hand beneath the fabric of the plain bodice to fondle my breast skin to skin. Then he yanks at the lacing so he can drag the cloth down and expose the nipple to his seeking mouth.

The swipe of his tongue sets off another pulse of pleasure. I'm quivering with all sorts of sparks now, both magical and the kind any passionate caress can provoke.

I look after my men, and they look after me—in every possible way.

As Casimir teases my other breast, Rheave yanks at my underskirt and drawers. He grazes my sex with a series of tantalising tingles and makes a guttural sound low in his throat. "I want to be inside you, Ivy."

Alek pulls away so I can yank my newest lover to me for an answering kiss. Rheave's tongue darts over mine in a heady dance, and then he's yanking at his trousers.

Stavros gives a rumble that thrums from his chest into mine. "I think she deserves another joint effort. You've never seen her doubly filled."

A giddy jolt of anticipation shoots through my veins, and then he's sweeping me onto his lap. As I help him wrench down his own pants, Casimir glides his hand over my ass and between my thighs.

The courtesan dips his fingers between my folds, setting off another rush of heady sensation. At my eager gasp, he spreads the slickness he gathered around my back opening.

"You want to make sure she's ready for you," he explains to Rheave in a honeyed tone, and delves a finger inside me to delightful effect. "Our bodies are capable of providing so much more enjoyment than the most obvious."

Rheave's voice is full of need. "I never realized— Do you want me like this too, Ivy?"

"Yes," I mumble, my own desire burning through my limbs as Stavros rocks his rigid cock against my clit. "I want all of you, everywhere, always."

With a choked chuckle, the daimon-man presses closer to me. I sink down over Stavros's cock, and Rheave lines his up from behind.

I hold perfectly still as he slides into me. My nerves sing with the flood of mingling pleasures.

Stavros guides me up and down over his thick shaft. "You always feel so fucking good, Ivy. You can have it all, whenever you want. Just take it."

I do, swaying between them. With him before me and Rheave behind me, I've never felt so full. So encompassed.

Then Alek dips his hand between me and Stavros. As the other two men rock with the blissful rhythm we're building, the scholar swivels his thumb over my clit.

I whimper, the swell of pleasure drowning out every urge other than the need to buck to my release and clutch at the men around me. Only two are penetrating me, but all four of my lovers are part of this act, moving in concert.

Rheave and Stavros thrust home in tandem, and Casimir swallows my cry with a demanding kiss. I rock and grind between my men, caught up in wave after wave of bliss coursing through my body.

"That's right," Stavros murmurs into my ear with a brush of his lips. "Take it all the way, Lady Thief. We're here to catch you when you careen over the edge."

In their joint embrace, I do feel as if I'm flying wild.

Rheave plunges deeper, and Stavros drives into me at the perfect angle.

Alek's thumb flicks faster. Casimir applies his teeth to my nipple.

The shock of so much pleasure crackles through me. I'm lit up from the inside out.

Then the daimon-man pours one more stream of his giddying power through my nerves, and I shatter apart.

My breath hitches, and my body quakes. I grip the arms around me and lock my legs against Stavros's hips.

The former general slams into me with the shudder of his own climax. It only takes a few seconds more before Rheave gasps harshly and sways to a stop, bowing against my back.

He dapples my scars with the tenderest of kisses. "No one will ever hurt you like this again. Not while we're here, and we always will be."

We slowly sag together in a messy and rather sweaty heap. A warm glow of affection spreads through every inch of my sated body.

I love so much, and I'm loved in return. For who I am now, for what I'm doing now.

I've moved past the mistakes I made before. I can do something better, something *good*.

This is all the happiness I ever could have asked for, even if it ends tomorrow.

# THIRTY-SEVEN

*Alek*

Wooden thumps and metallic clinks resonate through the night. The structures our allies hurriedly designed and fashioned the pieces for are coming together all across the field far beyond Florian's walls.

The builders are working by only the faintest lanternlight in an attempt to avoid drawing too much attention to ourselves. The dim glow gives the scene a ghostly atmosphere.

I stand back from the enormous platform that'll allow our eventual audience to view the trials, watching it spread out piece by piece across the grass. The wind licks under my cloak, and a shiver travels down my spine, but it's not only due to the lingering winter chill.

I've spent most of my life immersing myself in historical records, chasing down the details of what the world was like and how people lived centuries ago. Now, for the first time, it's hit me that in this one instance I'm part of real, living history in the making.

The knowledge is terrifying and yet also incredible.

At the rustle of footsteps over the grass, I turn. The few lights still glinting behind the capital city's walls at this dark hour gleam in the distance, about a mile away.

No aggressive shouts have broken the sounds of construction around me yet, but I know they're coming.

Ivy stops beside me and studies the terrain between us and the city with a pensive expression. "If we can't get everything ready quickly enough…"

I grasp her hand. "Don't even think that. We're going to make this work, whatever we have to do."

It's either that or let Lothar crush Petra with whatever he had planned during *his* swiftly approaching version of kingship trials. Perhaps we'll get lucky and he'll be off supervising his own preparations someplace far from here.

I don't actually have the slightest hope that'll be the case. And in some ways, our plans require him to be here, to play his role in the production we're creating.

Ivy swipes a strand of windblown hair from her face and squints across the flat plain. "People are coming. I can't tell if it's the right ones yet."

I tense up, but a moment later, a messenger rides up ahead of the crowd of shadowy forms.

"The Black Talons are fulfilling their duty," he announces with a salute. "We're bringing the daimon who agreed to help. And you've already got some spectators on the way."

Ivy's shoulders relax just a smidgeon. "What happened at the gate?"

The man's grin sharpens. "The guards are temporarily knocked out thanks to one of my friends and her very useful gift. It won't last more than a few hours, but that'll buy you a decent head start. When we spread the message on your signal, we included a mention that people should leave the city that way."

I drag in a breath. "We can't hope that no one loyal to the Order of the Wild will catch the message. We might not have very long at all before they try to interfere."

The messenger lets out a dismissive huff. "We'll be ready to keep them off your backs. It's about time those pricks got knocked down from their high horse. I'd even take King Konram and the old Crown's Watch over the wildness worshippers."

With a shake of his head in consternation, he wheels his horse. "Where can I find Princess Petra? My boss wanted me to speak directly to her."

Ivy motions to the mass of carts and wagons beyond the growing platform—the vehicles we used to bring us and all the equipment we needed out here. "She's staying well-guarded for the time being, but someone will let her know you're here so she can see you."

The crowd from the city is already drawing closer. I find myself resting my hand on the knife sheathed at my hip, even though I'm not particularly more confident using it than I was after Stavros's initial lessons weeks ago.

We know the gang is on our side, and presumably the daimon are too. But what can we expect from the first regular citizens who've come to witness the start of the trials?

Are they here to support Petra's attempt to reclaim her throne or to condemn it?

Ivy tugs her hood over her head, low enough to shadow her face. We don't know how the ordinary people will react if they recognize her from Lothar's accusatory announcements.

A wooden creak brings my head snapping around, but it's just Casimir leading the cart we arrived in. He gives us a good-humored wave and yanks the canvas back from the heap of daggers, swords, crossbows, and shields my parents' assistant supplied us with.

"The first wave of our most important allies is on the way," he says with perfect assurance. "It's time for us to show them how very important they are."

I'm relieved that Ivy studies the assortment of weaponry with a similar wariness to what I'm feeling.

"Do you really think we should bring out the blades right away?" she asks.

Casimir offers her a crooked smile. "Anyone who's coming to hurt us will have brought their own weaponry. As far as I can imagine, we'll only be arming those who are willing to take Petra's side but haven't had the means."

I restrain a grimace. "Let's at least hear what the Black Talons who've been walking with them have to say about their conduct first."

The courtesan dips his head in easy acceptance. I don't know how he can seem so calm about the momentous and precarious gambit we're trying to pull off in the coming day.

It doesn't take long for the new arrivals to reach us. Several figures with an air of criminal confidence push to the fore of the crowd, prodding a few dozen men and women who look rather dazed along with them.

Rheave leaps forward to welcome his fellow daimon. His urgent instructions reach my ears. "We need to keep watch all around this platform. We can use our magic if we have to. No one should be allowed to hurt the people conducting or participating in the trials, especially Princess Petra."

As some of the captured spirit creatures speak up in a clash of voices, Ivy strides over to an older man with patterns carved in his shaved head. "Glad to see you, Garom. How has our audience been behaving so far?"

She nods to the cluster of some fifty spectators who've stopped farther back from the construction area. They're mostly wearing plain or even shabby clothes, their hair unartfully cut and their stances nervous.

I suppose that makes sense. The outer-warders would have been closest to the gates once the message went out.

The Black Talons' boss grunts. "There've been a lot of questions, mostly about whether the queen will really be here and what the Order might do about it. But they seem more stunned that they're actually going to see the trials in action than anything else."

"Perfect." Casimir grabs one of the dim lanterns.

As he clambers onto the edge of the platform, I scan the land between us and the city again. More figures on foot are trickling from the gate that faces this direction and heading our way. None of them are moving in a way that strikes me as threatening, but I'm hardly an expert on identifying potential combatants.

Ivy bumps her elbow against mine. "Stavros and our sort-of troops are keeping a careful eye on the spectators. They won't ignore anyone who looks like a real threat."

On his perch with the lantern at his feet to light him, Casimir claps his hands for attention. He pitches his voice to carry over the gathered gang members and daimon.

"People of Florian, thank you for joining us for the trials that will prove who deserves to rule our country. Our rightful queen, Princess Petra, needs your support now more than ever. It's only a matter of time before the Order of the Wild tries to murder her as they did her parents and so many others."

To my surprise, the princess herself approaches from the far side of the platform. She's flanked by two soldiers, and I catch a faint shimmer of magic around her that suggests there's some sort of barrier protecting her from an immediate attack.

She stops a few paces back from Casimir and holds up her own lantern. A new, simple crown one of our allies crafted for her gleams gold on her dark hair. "I intend to test myself today to show in every way possible that I will lead this kingdom fairly and well. Will you help give me that chance? Will you stand with me against those who would try to force the gods' hands?"

Casimir motions to a couple of workers who've come to lead the cart even farther forward, past the Black Talons members and daimon. "We've brought weapons for all those who are willing to stand with us against the traitors who want to tear Silana apart. We know you'll only use them to protect our country."

Petra offers a soft smile. "I don't *have* a country without all of you in it, living the lives you're meant to enjoy. Together, we can put an end to the horror of the scourge sorcery that's swept across our realm."

As uncertain as I was about Casimir's idea, the civilians appear to respond well. A few and then several more approach the cart to pick out a weapon and in a few cases a shield.

I can't help noticing that as soon as each is holding a blade or a bow, their stances draw up a little straighter with a newfound sense of purpose.

Well, the courtesan does understand human emotions in a way I'm not sure I ever will.

As more onlookers arrive, Casimir and Petra repeat their message—and I catch voices from amid the crowd enthusing about the special duty the princess has given them. A hint of a smile touches my lips despite my continued apprehension.

A lot of things might have been ruined during the scourge sorcerers' brief reign, but they haven't stopped Silana's people from recognizing a truly righteous cause.

Most of the spectators, realizing the trials aren't anywhere near ready to begin, turn to face the city with weapons at the ready. They greet their fellow citizens as they arrive.

But one voice hollers over the heads of the daimon toward the platform. "When are we going to see the proof?"

Tinom appears next to Petra, lending the answer an air of divine authority in his cleric-like robe. "All the tools for our tests are being assembled before your eyes. And of course we will wait for any competitors who wish to stake their own claim to arrive. We believe in a fair opportunity for all. We expect to be able to commence shortly after sunrise."

A gruff sound of warning reverberates from the far side of the platform, where I realize Stavros has been standing in the darkness. At his signal, a significant portion of our combat-trained allies hurry forward to join the gathered gang members.

Ivy tugs me farther behind our defensive line and glances over to where Sulla is standing on the other side of the platform. The older woman shakes her head as if to say she hasn't sensed any trouble.

Soon enough, the thunder of racing hoofbeats and the glimpses of red tunics beneath the moonlight reveal the reason for Stavros's concern. Our first Order representatives are charging over to confront us.

The Black Talons' bosses, thank the gods, have enough sense not to leave the regular civilians as our first line of defense. With a few brisk gestures, they send half of their force ahead of the growing crowd of spectators. The others and the daimon remain between the onlookers and the rest of us.

Petra holds her position in the middle of the platform, but her stance has gone slightly rigid. Stavros shifts position to stand closer to her, and Rheave moves so he's directly in front of her on the ground, ready to intercept a magical attack as best he can.

Ivy's hands have balled at her sides. She's prepared to use her own magic if there's no other choice.

The image of her fiercely determined expression yesterday in the cart lingers in my memory, along with the firmness of her voice.

*There's a good chance I'll have to use a lot of magic making sure we see these trials through. I don't know how it'll affect me... If I start to lose control, you need to act immediately—whoever's closest, whoever can do what needs to be done.*

My stomach starts to churn. It's not likely the final act would come down to me. And even if it did… letting her become the monster she's feared so much would be a worse betrayal than killing her.

But, Great God help me, let us avoid that fate.

"I'd better vanish," she murmurs to me now, and pulls out the charm that's the one kindness Tinom left her with.

"Stay safe," I tell her, my voice gone hoarse, and then she blinks out of sight before my eyes.

The several riders in red rein in their steeds a few paces shy of the first line of armed men. One scowls before bellowing at all of us. "Do you really think you'll get away with this treachery?"

Tinom replies in a tone thick with derision. "Treachery? The rightful queen is simply commencing the kingship trials your leader demanded. She wasn't willing to wait for his perverted version of them. Who could be more qualified to run the trials than those of us who've faithfully served the only royal family Silana has known since the Darium empire was overthrown?"

"The false royals who lead us all astray. Look at you, deluding these people over again." He aims his glower at the crowd. "Are you really going to fight those of us who've given so much to win our freedom? They're trying to chain you up again."

"What are you calling freedom?" Stavros retorts, stepping into the light. "The freedom to be murdered for daring to criticize you? I don't recall King Konram treating his people so brutally."

The riders ignore him, the one who appears to be their leader focusing all his attention on our audience. "They're hypnotizing you with riven magic. Turning you into criminals. This is your chance to stop them and carry out the justice they deserve!"

The crowd stirs uneasily. Is one of the Order members using a gift to rattle their conviction? Or sway it in Lothar's favor?

Petra lifts her voice, clear and steady. "These trials will provide justice and show who is worthy of the people's faith."

An anxious voice rises from the midst of the onlookers. "Where *is* the riven sorcerer you've let help you? Are you going to arrest her?"

Another civilian echoes the first's nervous tone. "How can we trust anything when you let one of those monsters walk free and work her magic on us?"

I wince inwardly, knowing Ivy is hearing these questions. She shouldn't have to.

She's fought so hard for these people, and still they want to heap so much blame on her.

Petra holds up her hands in a quelling gesture. "Lothar Riosemek has lied to you and encouraged your fears to stop you from taking him to task for his own misdeeds. He and his followers are the only ones who've been inflicting dangerous magic on you."

"He's not riven," another voice calls out. "He sacrificed his whole arm to the gods. That's an honest gift."

"Honest gifts can still be corrupted by—"

A woman cuts in. "You're trying to confuse us. We know the riven are fiends. Why would you have anything to do with that kind of magic? The gods would never support that!"

The lead rider from the Order nods. "Very true. This woman has no right to participate in the kingship trials, let alone determine how they should be run. What does she know about worthiness?"

What do the scourge sorcerers know? If they were following their history, they'd never have gone down their dark path of sacrificing the livelihoods of others in the first place.

The rider points toward the platform. "Lothar will conduct the *real* trials, the way they should be done. All of this ought to be torn apart."

He isn't outright telling our audience to do that for him, but several figures surge forward regardless. When the Black Talons move to block them, blades clang together.

More of the onlookers push in as if roused by the apparent aggression, even though their companions were the ones who provoked it.

My stomach sinks. Our soldiers and guards shift on their feet, poised but uncertain.

Casimir was right about one thing: Petra does need the support of the common people. We can't prove her worthiness for the throne in front of grass stained with the blood of Florian's citizens.

*No one knows how the kingship trials are meant to be*, I want to shout. *Barely any record of them exists. And the one sure thing is that the gods judged them, not any kind of man or woman.*

What good would it do to say that, though? Why would any of these people take *my* word for it?

They don't know me. It isn't as if we can ask the godlen to come down and weigh in—

As my gaze sweeps over the increasingly tumultuous crowd, it snags on the row of daimon standing near the platform. Their faces are taut with confusion—they know they're meant to fend off scourge sorcerers, but they wouldn't have been prepared for this kind of "attack" from ordinary civilians.

An unnatural glow shimmers in their eyes with the inhuman magic they're prepared to send out.

We don't have godlen right here among us, but we do have the creatures that are closest to them.

The pieces of a plan crash together in my head so swiftly the breath spills from my lungs.

I don't have time to study every detail of it, to pick it apart for flaws. Someone has to act *now*, before the weapons my parents forged for us become our undoing.

I sprint over to where Rheave stands and grasp his arm. "I need your help with the other daimon. When I ask for it, I want you all to show off the unearthly energy you have. If you can bring even more daimon here, ones that aren't captured, to show their support, that would be even better."

He gives the briefest sound of acknowledgment, and I heft myself onto the platform. I yank my spine up straight there at the edge next to Casimir.

The courtesan steps back from his lantern as if giving me the stage. The crowd quiets for a moment, peering at me past the figures standing in their way. Waiting to see what's about to happen.

My face prickles all across my scarred skin, knowing they'll make note of it before anything else. I shove that thought aside and square my shoulders as if I don't care.

"I've studied the history of Silana all the way back to the times before the Darium empire invaded," I declare in as forceful a voice as I can summon. "There aren't many records about the kingship trials, but it's clear they were put before the godlen to judge who was worthy, not any mortal. It's time to seek out divine opinions. And we have the representatives of the gods right here with us, the creatures who are far closer to the godlen than any of us humans."

As I brandish my arm toward the gathered daimon, Rheave takes his cue. He says something to his fellow captured creatures.

In an instant, a glow jitters over their skin. It quivers over their heads and down their arms like lightning in slow motion.

They must have been able to summon other wandering spirits too. A few sparks flit through the air and beam into brighter spots of light above the daimon in human form. More streak across the fields and swarm to join them.

The supernatural glow spreads out in front of the platform, shining over us all. I can feel its warmth glancing off the ridges on my face, and suddenly I don't care anymore.

These scars show I'm not just some pampered college student. I've fucked up. I've worked to rectify my mistakes and deserve the life I've built.

I've been through trials of my own and come out the other side, and I know my chosen godlen smiles down on me.

I lift my voice again with renewed confidence. "Lothar and his scourge sorcerers can't deny what you're seeing with your own eyes. The trials we're assembling have the support of the spirit world. The divine energies we mortals can barely grasp will decide who is most likely to bring the All-Giver back to these realms."

The next chorus of murmurs that passes through our audience sounds awed, not hostile. A few keep staring, dazed, but most swing back to face the riders from the Order.

The lead rider sets his mouth in a tight line, but he doesn't seem to know how to argue against this very vivid demonstration.

Petra speaks into his silence. "The Order can have a place in these trials too. You were already preparing for your own, and we've been sending out word that ours are approaching for days. I'm sure you've picked your champions. Send them forth at dawn, and we'll see who the gods bless with their favor."

# THIRTY-EIGHT

*Ivy*

The fine chain of the concealment charm itches at my neck. I try to scratch surreptitiously, not that anyone can see me anyway.

It's been chafing against my skin all night.

Now the dawn glow is creeping across our hastily erected stage. The sunlight enriches the deep purples and blues and brilliant yellows and oranges that Casimir recommended. They give the wood an otherworldly quality, like a glow of enlightened energy shining out of the darkness. Looking up at the platform and the various painted structures rising from it, I could almost believe they were formed out of divine energy rather than human effort.

Hopefully our audience will take away the same impression. We need them to see this spectacle as definitive proof of the gods' approval.

Beyond the ring of daimon, Black Talons members, and guards poised behind me around the platform, the crowd of spectators has swelled. I can't count them all, but I have to think thousands are craning their necks or sprawling on the grass, waiting for the spectacle of the trials to begin. And more are arriving in droves as the word has spread.

It won't be long now. All nine of the independent clerics we invited to oversee the different trials have arrived. Shortly after the last bell, the Order of the Wild brought forth a large carriage that supposedly holds three challengers to the throne who'll compete with Petra.

They haven't shown their faces yet, though a few different Order members have ducked into the carriage, presumably to discuss strategy.

There's been no sign of Lothar so far, but his representatives assured us that the former magic advisor intends to be here to ensure every step of the trials is carried out "fairly." By which I'd imagine he means, "in some way that'll let us win."

If he tries anything too obvious, there are thousands of witnesses to observe his villainy. But we have to stay on the alert for more subtle tricks.

I don't expect him to back down easily.

Tinom has set himself up as a sort of master of ceremonies, which suits me just fine. I can't even show my face, let alone run the most important event that's happened in Silana in decades. He eases down from the stage at a summons and goes to speak with a couple of Order representatives within a careful cluster of protective gang members.

A group of about a dozen riders catches my eye from the north, riding toward us at a canter. I wouldn't think much of the new arrivals, but it's unusual to see so many together on horseback.

I slip around the stage for a closer look, and a smile springs to my lips. The warming light catches off Voleska's sandy blond hair, swinging with her steed's strides in its usual ponytail.

We sent a message to Pima to let her and Emor know the trials were impending, but we hadn't known if either of them would make the trip in time.

The riders approach at the back of the platform by the spread of carts and wagons. A few of the people who came with us from Pima break from their ranks to greet Voleska and their colleagues, and Stavros and Casimir head over as well.

I slip between the carts to follow them, getting enough shelter to remove my charm.

When I step forward to meet Voleska and her gaze meets mine, I can't help hesitating. Something flickers through her expression in her initial pause, and it occurs to me that we never discussed the source of my magic, even though I assume she's caught wind of the real source and extent of my power by now.

Lothar has spread his tales about my murderous ways far and wide. Maybe she isn't enthusiastic about counting me as an ally any longer.

But the pause is only the space of a heartbeat. Then Voleska marches forward with a grin and grabs me in a brief but eager hug, topped off with a clap on the back. "Look at this production you've pulled together. We've come a long way from brandishing stolen shields, huh?"

A laugh that releases some of my bottled tension tumbles out of me. "I guess we have. I can't take much credit for this. I'm just making sure it all goes off without a hitch."

Voleska nods. "I'll let you get back to that, then. And I brought a few more friends to do our part."

Stavros taps my arm, peering toward the city. "Lothar is on his way. We'd better get into position."

He touches my cheek in a brief caress. We set off for the stage together, me vanishing with another yank of the chain over my head.

Most of the structures on the platform are meant to serve a purpose in the trials themselves, but there's a semi-circle of boards just a little taller than Stavros off to one side. Slats cut between the boards give anyone standing in that alcove a view of both the rest of the platform and the audience.

Sulla, Casimir, and Rheave are already waiting for us there, their stances tensed. Stavros will be employing his gift at what seems like the most crucial moments in the hopes of preventing attacks before they happen. Casimir is judging the emotional atmosphere of the crowd.

The other three of us are staying braced to use our magic to solve any problems that arise.

As I settle into place, the crowd parts in front of the stage. Lothar strides between the watching figures, his posture as haughty as always. His velvet cloak drapes unevenly across his one-armed form.

Tinom makes a gesture, and our defensive force gives way to let his former colleague through. My teeth set on edge.

"We're letting him walk right up here?" I murmur.

Casimir smiles tightly. "It was negotiated. Tinom and Lothar are going to look over each of the candidates to confirm there are no signs of hidden magical advantages."

A chill rushes through me. "He's going to get that close to Petra?"

"I don't like it either, but it's supposed to be a show of trust. The other clerics will be right there, along with her guards."

That doesn't feel like enough. Without another word, I ease away from the wall and slink across the brightly painted boards amid the looming equipment.

Petra stands in the open center, now joined by the other three candidates: a lean man with a sharply pointed beard who I think I recognize as a count, a bulky fellow with flinty eyes who I wouldn't be surprised to discover was once in military service, and a sinewy-limbed woman with elegantly braided hair who's probably a minor noblewoman of some sort.

They've all dressed in the agreed-upon outfits of a simple short tunic and slacks. The single layer of fabric leaves little opportunity to disguise even small blades or magical trinkets, and their tight shoes offer no room to conceal a weapon.

As Lothar ascends the steps to the right of the stage to stand next to Tinom, I dart over behind him. The towering, lopsided man wafts a smoky cologne that makes my nose wrinkle. It reminds me too much of the late-night rituals his scourge sorcerer colleagues conducted.

I don't sense any magic in it, though. Even when I lean as close to him as I dare, I can't pick up the faintest vibration of magic on or around his body.

He could be holding his gift in reserve until he's right in front of Petra. Or maybe whatever his talent is, it wouldn't help him sabotage her, so he's counting on someone else's help.

At least I know he isn't carrying an enchanted object on him that could harm her.

My magic reverberates through my torso. My fingers curl into my palms, holding back the urge to harm *him* quite permanently now that he's finally right in front of me.

But he knows the audience works in his favor to some extent as well as ours. If Petra's allies murder the leader of the Order seemingly unprovoked, it'll appear to prove all his claims true.

Even if it looks like an accident, his people will blame it on treachery.

We need to treat him as an equal rather than a criminal until he exposes his true colors.

Restraining my power deep within me despite its frantic burn, I lurk nearby as he moves down the row of candidates. He gives each of his own only a cursory examination, already familiar with them. Any stealthy advantages they're concealing, he's approved.

When he stops in front of Petra, I tense even more, focusing all my senses on every minute movement of his body. Petra stands rigidly, her eyes fierce as she gazes back at the man she watched slaughter her parents. Her guards step forward to shadow her more closely.

Lothar skims his hands through the air around her body as if testing her, but I still can't pick up on any magic emanating from him. From his grimly satisfied expression, I think maybe he's just hoping to intimidate her.

Well, it would look awfully suspicious if she experienced any ill effects while he's standing right in front of her. Any sabotage he's planning, it'd be easier for him to get away with it once the trials have begun.

I don't completely let out my breath until he moves away from her. Tinom finishes studying the last of the Order's candidates and steps to the front of the stage.

Magical amplification sends his voice ringing over the crowd. "Now each of the candidates will swear before the All-Giver and all the godlen that they will not use their own or any other's gifts to assist their performance in these trials. They come to these tests with no foreknowledge of the correct answers or approach. They accept their judgment based on their own mortal skills."

As the candidates swear in one by one, I duck back into the spy alcove. I've only just returned when Filip hustles over to our part of the platform.

The Order defector faces us with an uncertain expression. "The three sacrificial accomplices who came with us in case we needed them to speak—they want to stay near Ivy and Sulla."

Sulla turns and asks the obvious question for me. "Why?"

He seems to grope for his words. "I'm not sure—I—"

"We think we can help." One of those accomplices is hobbling along the base of the platform to come up beside us, supported by a man from Pima. Poltus's voice comes out thick and the long cloak and loose pants he's wearing only hide some of the deformities inflicted on him, but we weren't going to put them back in their shrouds.

The eyeless, noseless man turns his mutilated face toward us. "The scourge sorcerers drew on our power before with the wrong intentions. You're trying to set things right. And the more of your own power you use, the harder it'll be on your minds. Isn't that right? If we lend you what we can of our gifts, you can make a small amount of your riven magic stretch farther."

A sharp ache pierces through my heart. Because it doesn't matter that I'm concealed when Poltus can't see anyway, I don't hold myself back from speaking. "We'd never ask to use you the way they did."

The man makes a dismissive sound. "You're not asking. We're offering. There isn't much we're capable of contributing in our current state... Please, let us do what we can to see Silana restored to peace."

I don't know how to argue with that request.

Sulla bobs her head respectfully with a rustle of her dress. "We appreciate your support more than you can imagine. Thank you."

Poltus sinks down on the grass next to the platform, tucked out of the way and I hope decently comfortable. His two companions limp to join him.

"I wish we could see the trials for ourselves," the one woman murmurs to the others, and the ache in my chest expands through my ribs.

The scourge sorcerers have inflicted so much destruction and pain on the people they claimed to be raising up. I have to do everything in my power to ensure their reign ends today.

Tinom is calling forth the clerics he summoned from nine nearby temples. "A cleric of each godlen will set their own task to fit with the equipment we've assembled and to score by their own judgment with divine guidance," he announces to the crowd. "The leader of Silana should have strengths in every area our deities consider important. The Order of the Wild has been granted the opportunity to provide their own clerics to assess the candidates if they disagree with the outcome."

I grimace. No doubt we can expect plenty of disagreement.

The magic advisor spreads his hands as if in welcome. "The sequence of trials has been determined through random selection. We're beginning with Prospira, our godlen of prosperity and growth."

He taps the gesture of the divinities down his front, and it's echoed throughout our audience.

A man in the yellow robes of Prospira climbs onto the platform, motioning a few devouts in plainer clothes with him. "We've brought our own trial with us to ensure none of the candidates could have prepared in advance. My devouts and I were inspired by the call."

The devouts each unveil an identical miniature tree carved completely of wood. Fruits the size of my thumbpad poke from between joined leaves.

The cleric sets a statue before each of the candidates. "Please examine your tree. You will find that any part you wish may detach. Give it careful thought, considering the principles Prospira holds dear, and select what you feel is the most important aspect of the plant while preparing your explanation."

He turns to Tinom. "Can you use your gift with illusions to amplify the image for the crowd as you have our voices?"

Tinom rubs his hands together. "An excellent suggestion."

As the candidates bend down to examine their trees, each about waist height, the air shimmers in front of them. Tinom projects a single image of a tree, this one twice as tall as any person, with overlapping movements of ghostly hands as it accounts for all four of the people studying their own.

Well, it doesn't seem as though Petra is likely to face any danger with this trial, although I don't know how her answer will compare to the others. How much time has she spent thinking about trees?

I focus on the people beyond the platform, stretching my senses, staying on guard for the slightest hint of an attack. Next to me, Stavros scans the crowd as well, with a quiver in the air that tells me he's concentrating on his gift.

All at once, an impression of a sharper tingling hits me from above. Some sort of spell is plummeting toward the platform—hurled up there to disguise its source?

My pulse lurches, and I snatch Rheave's arm. "Magic above them!"

He doesn't need me to say more than that. The daimon-man whips his arm upward, and a thin crackle of his supernatural energy ripples through the air.

His defensive effort splits into a dozen tiny bolts—and one sizzles as it catches the advancing spell before it can crash down on Petra.

I whirl around to peer at the crowd. My gaze flicks left and right before catching on a woman a few bodies back from the front of the crowd just lifting her hand with a determined expression.

Rheave can't blast her from here. My heart skips another beat, but the words Sulla told me echo up from my memory.

*Even very small acts can have a large impact.*

My mind leaps to an appropriate counterbalance. I release a spurt of my magic to push down a patch of dirt beneath the platform—and thrust up an equivalent patch beneath the scourge sorcerer's feet.

She stumbles, knocking shoulders with the man next to her, and whatever attack she was going to send out next falters.

Another stream of magic courses past me, but this one moves from the huddled sacrificial accomplices toward Sulla. With a swell of heightened power, she aims her own attention at the woman I targeted.

The scourge sorcerer's body lights up with a glow stark enough to cut through the strengthening sunlight. The people around her glance over and stare.

With a harried expression, she pushes off through the crowd away from us, maybe afraid some worse punishment is coming.

While we've been fending off magic attacks, it seems the candidates have made their choices. They've all straightened up with their piece hidden in their clasped hands.

The Prospira cleric starts at the far end of the row from Petra. He beckons to the bearded count. "What did you pick?"

The count holds up a chunk of wood that's basically just a rectangular slab. Tinom amplifies that image too, so there's a second giant man looming like an immense ghost above his actual self.

"The wood of the tree is most important," he says. "It allows people to build their houses and warm them with fire. To make carts to carry goods to market and bring new purchases back again. And it provides a home to animals as well."

The cleric hums, and a murmur spreads through the crowd. It sounds like a reasonable answer to me.

Without giving any judgment, the cleric strolls on to the bulky man with soldier airs. "And you?"

As Tinom's illusion shifts to him, the soldier holds up one of the wooden fruits. "The fruit of the tree feeds both people and animals. You can't build much if you're starving."

"True enough," the cleric says agreeably, and continues on to the sinewy noblewoman. "What do you think?"

She holds up a piece identical to the count's. "I also chose wood, for the same reasons—and it can also be used to build bridges, barns, fences, temples—everything a society needs to grow."

"Many excellent thoughts." The cleric's tone stays even. He reaches Petra and bobs his head to her. "Do you have anything new to say?"

"I do, actually."

Petra opens her hands. It takes me a second to realize she's holding one of the fruits—but only half of it, the inner side showing several seeds carved within.

She traces the tiny ovals. "The seeds are more important than anything else, because they allow more trees to sprout. One tree can't build much of a house or a fence, or offer enough food to feed a family for more than a few days. The more you can grow, the more you can provide."

A smile touches my lips. Yes, that's exactly it.

A ruler needs to think not just of the present moment but how the whole country can thrive together.

A sudden round of applause, punctuated by a few cheers, sweeps through the crowd. Petra keeps her composure but brightens a little.

The cleric smiles too. "Spoken like one who truly understands Prospira's hopes for us all. That is the answer I was seeking."

A man in the red tunic of the Order stomps his foot near the front of the crowd. "Hold on! How do we know you didn't give the false princess her answer beforehand?"

The cleric knits his brow. "I wouldn't dishonor my godlen by cheating her of a proper trial. But if you don't trust my answer, I suppose we could ask the daimon whether Princess Petra's answer felt genuine."

The captured daimon must give an invisible nudge, or maybe the spirits could understand. A streak of sparks lights up, flowing around Petra's body, as if giving their approval.

"But—" the man starts.

Lothar holds up his hand to stop him. "Let it stand."

I study him through the gaps in the wall. Why isn't he fighting every verdict tooth and nail? Is he worried about how he'll come across and waiting for a better chance?

Or does he *know* he'll get the opportunity he needs later?

The green-robed cleric for Estera comes forward next, holding a crate with several glossy balls about the size of the candidates' heads. She hands a ball to each of the candidates. "I'll light the globes with each correct answer. A ruler Estera can support will understand the history that brought us to this place and the countries that surround us as well as our own. You have ten chances to prove your knowledge."

She runs through the questions at a steady pace, touching on the effects of Darium rule, the overthrowing of the empire, past relations with our neighboring countries, and ending with three questions asked respectively in Veldunian, Bryfesh, and Icarian.

With each correct answer Petra gives, her orb glows brighter—and her fellow candidates stumble more. Whatever their existing education and the hasty studying Lothar will have put them through, it doesn't match that of a woman raised since birth as the heir to the throne.

I suspect Petra could have answered any of these questions nearly as well at ten years old as she does now.

None of the other candidates speaks enough of all three of the other languages to respond to all of those questions. By the end of the series, they're standing stiffly, the soldier ruddy-faced with frustration, the noblewoman pursing her lips unhappily.

I haven't spotted any incoming attacks, but before the cleric can announce her verdict, Lothar lifts his voice. "You were selected by the princess's allies, Your Holiness. I'd like to have a cleric the Order of the Wild chose test her with a few questions she can't be expecting."

Our cleric steps back. As a man in green robes takes the stage, my body tenses. But he keeps a careful distance from Petra as if to avoid any idea of threat.

He asks her another series of questions in each of the same three languages, throwing in one in Woudish and another in Darium after—long questions that I know at least in the tongues I can speak myself are much more convoluted than what the first cleric asked. But Petra answers each steadily enough, without a hint of being thrown off.

The cleric indicates his approval, but there's a hint of a sneer to his tone. "One last thing. The Battle of Raclawnem—how did your great grandmother's forces win the day?"

My skin prickles with the sense that this is some sort of trap, but Petra doesn't hesitate. "There was no Battle of Raclawnem. Raclawnem is a small valley town not far from the Pinch. The nearest significant battles I'm aware of that were fought in that area were in Mevild county during the rebellion against the empire, and outside the city of Accia under my grandfather's rule."

My gaze flicks to the cleric. Apparently he was hoping to catch her in a lie of confusion or make her look inept. Instead, he's done the opposite.

He lets out a short chuckle and bows his head. "My questions are finished."

As he descends the platform, I think I see him shoot a brief apologetic grimace Lothar's way. Another round of applause rises up.

A gray-robed cleric for my self-appointed patron godlen takes over next, ushering the candidates into the large, intricate boxes constructed by the baron's craftspeople. Casimir contributed his insight to those too. They're painted an ominous thundercloud hue to enhance the sense of a threat, with a silvery sheen on the entwined parts so it'll be easy to spot when each segment is released on the way to freedom.

As the cleric explains to the candidates and the audience that these are identical puzzle boxes designed to test cleverness and ingenuity, I notice a slim man moving along the edge of the crowd.

He bends to place something on the ground several paces from the corner of the platform. Then he ventures farther where the mass of spectators has fanned out around the sides of the stage and sets another object down there.

There's nothing overtly threatening about his movements. The guards haven't moved to stop him. But something about his meticulousness sends a jangle of warning through me.

I nudge Casimir and point out the man. "What do you think of his intentions?"

Casimir studies him for a moment as the man meanders on along the side of the platform. "He doesn't care about the outcome of the current test. I suspect that's because he's planning to alter it. If I…"

A wisp of magic tickles past me, and the courtesan sucks in a breath. "What would make him happiest is if I looked the other way and pretended I never noticed him. He's definitely attempting some kind of sabotage."

My mind leaps through several possibilities even as my chest tightens at the thought of releasing more of my magic already. But I do have the sacrificial accomplices below me, waiting to play the one part they can.

Ignoring a twinge of queasiness, I touch Stavros's hand. "Signal the guards to be on the alert."

Then I extend my concentration toward not just my target and a couple of scraps of wood lying at the base of the platform, but the mutilated accomplices as well.

A waft of energy rushes through me, propelling my own magic out of me faster. Even with only a small intent in mind, I have to yank at my power to rein some of it in.

The two pieces of wood shift and nestle together—and the buttons on the man's trousers snap apart. The loose fabric drops to his ankles in an instant.

He stumbles and pitches forward. Several more of the objects he was holding spill from his arms.

In an instant, the guards Stavros alerted rush forward to restrain the guy and confiscate his cargo for examination.

"That was nicely done," Sulla says softly. "One more challenge down."

I can't manage more than a tight grin. "Who knows how many more to go."

# THIRTY-NINE

*Ivy*

It seems the count Lothar chose is quite clever himself. He bests Petra's speed at unraveling the puzzle box, though only by a matter of seconds.

That isn't anywhere near enough to shake her confidence. She tackles the next two trials with the same cool determination she's brought to the previous.

And without any significant interference from the scourge sorcerers. Sulla upends one more figure who tries to aim a spell toward the stage, and then there's nothing further.

My shoulders are starting to ache from the tension I'm holding in them. My gaze keeps flitting over the crowd, stretching ever farther as more and more spectators arrive from beyond the city.

Then the red-robed cleric for Sabrelle strides onto the platform, and my stomach knots. Her challenge is what the largest portion of our construction efforts went into, and it offers plenty of danger of its own.

Several workers push the apparatus fully together with a rasp of wood against wood. A few devouts to Sabrelle step forward and add their magic, making the wheel of blades spin and the fragmented bridge ripple where it looms high above our heads. The streaks of crimson Casimir had the builders add give the impression of lurking brutality.

The cleric sweeps her hand toward the massive structure. "Each of the candidates will complete this course of physical challenges. Sabrelle wishes to see bravery, physical might, and logistical strategy in a ruler. Any candidate who fails to complete the course will be disqualified."

Lothar breaks in with a loud demand. "The princess should go first. She's had the advantage of seeing the course built—the other candidates should have the advantage of watching her handle it."

I scowl. The truth is that Petra avoided the construction area and insisted she not be told any details of the trials ahead of time—she has no more idea how to handle the various obstacles than the other candidates seeing it now do.

But we have no simple way of proving that to the audience.

Before I can think of a solid argument to offer, Petra bobs her head in acceptance. "I'll go first."

She steps toward the starting ramp with its tiny, irregular handholds. It's hard to keep my attention on the crowd while she's about to face a series of death-defying perils.

I scan the swarm of figures beyond the platform until my vision blurs. The cleric announces the start of the challenge. Petra's feet thud up the wooden surface.

And Stavros lets out a grunt of warning. "Something's going to happen in less than a minute to startle Petra and make her stumble. The way everyone reacts, I think it's a loud sound. I couldn't see where it'll come from."

He leaps to the side of the stage to pass specific instructions on to the guards. Dozens push into the crowd, but I can already tell there's no way they'll be able to check everyone in the matter of seconds we have.

I risk slipping out of our alcove too, hurrying to the front of the platform in my invisible state. My gaze sweeps over the crowd again, squinting toward the farther reaches—

There. A woman some twenty bodies back from the front lines is raising a slim, metallic object to her lips—a kind of instrument?

I don't have time to point the guards to her. I tap into the trickle of magic between me and the sacrificial accomplices and let it launch my power.

The clasp on my cloak expands, and the neck of the horn squashes inward, just as the woman blows. A squeak of a sound reaches my ears, so faint I might not have made it out if I hadn't been listening so hard.

I squeeze the windpipe even tighter for good measure.

Stavros has spotted her now. As he calls to the guards to point her out for arrest, I duck back into the shelter with no one the wiser.

In the midst of our panic, Petra has scrambled across half of the course. When I let myself glance up at her, I can see the military training she insisted on enduring at the college has paid off.

She leaps across the disjointed boards of the bridge so fast their jerking motions don't make her more than wobble. She pauses for just a second to judge the speed of the whirling blades and then dashes forward, ducking and weaving between them.

A gasp of pain reaches my ears, and I wince, yanking my gaze to the crowd again. But I don't think that was sabotage, only the difficulty of the course.

When Petra finally squeezes through the snare of ropes to emerge at the far end, a scratch on her upper arm is dribbling blood.

"Two minutes, thirty-seven seconds," the cleric announces. "Second candidate!"

Despite his advantage of having witnessed a run-through and his muscular strength, the soldier seems to find the nimbler areas difficult to navigate. He struggles through the ropes and arrives with a time only slightly faster than Petra's.

The noblewoman has to pause several times out of caution and takes more than four minutes.

The count hurtles into the course with an arrogant air, which proves to be over-confidence. Halfway across the bridge, he slips, fumbles, and falls between the slats.

He hits the platform with a crunch of broken bone and a pained cry. The workers and a healer who was standing by rush over.

From the way his limbs are twisted, I think he's broken his leg.

The cleric of Sabrelle appears totally unconcerned. "The fourth candidate is eliminated from the trials."

The audience doesn't seem bothered either. With each trial that ends with Petra showing her prowess, the cheers for her get louder.

She's won most of them and taken a close second place in the other two. It's obvious who the forerunner is.

My future queen's victories continue through the final few trials. By the time we reach the last—for Creaden, the godlen most concerned with leadership and authority—applause carries through the crowd whenever Petra's name is mentioned.

It's been a long morning, but the faces taking in the spectacle glow with avid anticipation.

The purple-robed cleric guides three smooth wooden towers forward and assembles a trio of his devouts at the base of each. He points to the seat fixed to the top of each tower, shining a golden yellow above the whirls of violet and midnight blue on the base. "You will each work together with your underlings to reach your throne. You will be judged by more than just speed."

Before he can give the order to begin, a tingle of magic courses over my skin. My head twitches toward it, but an instant later, another current touches me, and another—as if spells are being cast from all around the platform.

Next to me, Sulla stiffens. "What in the realms is *that?*"

I swivel, trying to navigate the swarm of impressions. "There's magic coming from all over the place," I say for our companions' benefit. "None of it very strong... Nothing's actually *happening* yet..."

Sulla's eyes widen. "It's a distraction. They know we picked up on their previous attempts, so they're trying to overwhelm us rather than being sneaky about it."

Casimir speaks up in a low voice. "Lothar looks as if he's preparing for something. He's walking around the far side of the platform like he means to go right around the back."

"We have to—" Stavros cuts himself off with a hiss of breath. "I got a glimpse—someone's going to appear at the front of the stage out of nowhere. They must be using concealment magic like your charm, Ivy."

"Do you know which direction they're coming from?" I ask.

He shakes his head in a jerk.

If it's a matter of physically getting in an attacker's way, I'm far more equipped for that duty than my older companion.

I set my jaw. "They'll be coming for Petra. I'll just have to get in their way."

I bolt across the front of the platform, dodging the cleric and staying clear of the towers set several paces back from the edge.

No one reacts; no one can see me through the charm's magic. They're all gaping at the spectacle of three candidates trying to assemble their human helpers into some kind of ladder to get them up the tower.

Word of an impending threat must be passing through the guards and the daimon both, because the rows of them in front of me stir warily, a few drawing their weapons. Rheave has jumped down to join his fellow captured spirit creatures, his gaze darting around us. But they obviously can't make out the would-be attacker any more clearly than I can.

I station myself directly in front of Petra's tower and narrow my focus onto the thrum of magic resonating through the air.

Someone is going to attack. Someone who's concealed through magic like I am.

I should be able to sense them when they get close, even with the wafting eddies drifting by.

The back of my neck prickles at the thought of Lothar prowling around behind me, but Stavros will have warned the guards to watch for any threatening behavior from him too—and he said the attacker his gift showed him appeared at the front of the stage. I need to stay here.

Grunts and rough breaths carry from the towers behind me. The cleric strolls by, examining the candidates' progress with a casual air, totally unaware of the potential catastrophe.

Then I feel it: a thicker current of magic streaming almost straight toward me.

It's passing over the heads of the guards in front of the platform—using flight as well as invisibility to avoid notice. But they can't avoid me.

I adjust my stance to follow the impression I'm picking up and unsheathe the knife at my hip. My pulse thunders in my ears.

My riven power churns inside me, urging me to blast the intruder right out of the air.

No. I don't need to pick away at my sanity any more than I already have.

And the less this confrontation distracts from Petra's likely victory, the better.

The sensation of approaching magic blares louder and then seems to stop, right at the edge of the stage. Without letting myself hesitate, I launch myself at the presence I can feel in front of me.

Our bodies collide, and a woman in a cloak blinks into my view as she heaves herself to the side to avoid toppling off the platform. I clutch her tunic, forcing her to haul me with her.

She curses and lashes out with a blade of her own. I manage to jerk my head out of the way and wrench my hand up to try to force her surrender with my knife at her throat.

At the last second, she squirms partly out from under me. As I lunge after her, she swipes out with her knife again. Her boot slams into my gut when I dodge.

I reel backward, and a chorus of gasps rises up from the audience. When I glance around, most of the onlookers are staring at *me* rather than the trial.

My hand darts to my neck and finds nothing. The attacker must have snapped the chain holding my charm with one of those slashes I dodged.

She's still invisible, but the hum of the magic wafts off her. There's no time to worry about my exposure. I throw myself in the direction she's scrambling.

I collide with her hard enough to knock a grunt from her lungs. We tumble over again, my elbow jarring against the platform floor.

A cry rings out behind me. I yank my head around just in time to see a blaze of magic hurtling straight toward me—and Sulla sprinting out across the stage.

She flings herself right in front of the searing projectile with a burst of her own magic. I don't know why she didn't try to deflect it from farther away—maybe she didn't trust her focus when she's never used her magic in combat or on this scale before.

The blaze rams into her. Her body crumples, spasming as it hits the floor.

A cry of my own lodges in my throat. But I can't run over to help her, because the would-be assassin is flailing at me like a wild cat.

I'm too distracted, and my opponent's dagger catches me across the jaw. A stinging line opens up in my flesh.

I shove her backward, driving her between two of the towers.

I have to get her away from Petra. Away from view. Stop this assault from becoming a total disaster.

The woman is clearly skilled in combat, but she didn't get the training I did on the streets. I dodge her next kick and dive in low, knocking her off her feet again. Rolling to the side, I jab my elbow into her nose.

My magic writhes alongside my limbs, rattling against my hold. I just need to subdue her—the guards will want to question her—if she can reveal that she isn't acting alone, we'll have proof to call for Lothar's arrest...

An urgent yell blares from the back of the platform. In the second I glance up, the woman seizes the opening. She stabs her blade straight at my neck.

My body reacts on instinct. I flinch, and my hand is already swinging.

Driving my own blade into her heart.

Her body sags, her knife only nicking my throat. Bitterness taints the relief that sweeps through me, but I don't have time to think about that.

Because the next thing I hear is Stavros's voice, taut and angry. "Ivy, we need you here."

When I step away from the body, the woman I just killed fades before my eyes. Whatever magic she had on her, it must require some kind of trigger to remove it.

The only evidence of her existence right now is the blood slowly staining the floorboards as it seeps far enough away from her slumped form.

I look up and realize several guards and a few daimon have gathered nearby, all of them braced and ready to leap in.

"She had a dagger—she was heading for Petra," I say quickly. "I stopped her."

Stavros's voice carries from farther back, in the shadows of the arching obstacle course. "Good. Now we need to deal with this traitor."

As I push myself forward, Casimir's soothing tones reach my ears from the front of the stage. He's speaking to the audience. "Our guards are dealing with the security problem. We'll ensure any threat to the candidates is subdued."

I have no idea how my sudden appearance and the confusing fight the onlookers witnessed has affected the trial, but that can't even be my second priority right now. As I hurry over, I'm already saying, "Sulla was hit by some kind of magic. She looked badly hurt. We'll need a healer—"

One of the guards interjects. "A couple of Elox dedicats have already gone over to see if there's anything they can do for her."

His tone doesn't give me any clue as to whether she was still even alive. I swallow thickly and then stall in my tracks at the sight of the man at the other end of Stavros's sword.

The former general has Lothar partly cornered against the underside of the arch. Three armed men form a semi-circle behind the leader of the Order, but they're on our side, their own weapons braced to come to bear if he makes a sudden move. A few more of our soldiers flank Stavros.

Everyone's expressions are stony, but none so much as Stavros's. "Take the magic off the attacker we all know *you* sent," he snarls. "Let's see what we find."

Lothar glares back at him. "I don't know what you're talking about."

"You were sneaking around back here for some vile purpose. It's obviously all connected."

The former advisor doesn't stir. He's got an excellent bluffing face, I'll give him that.

I guess he'd have to for him to have fooled King Konram and the king before him all those years.

Footsteps creak across the platform. Tinom joins us with a sigh. "I should be able to do it. Where is this attacker?"

I point to the spot where the blood stain is spreading. He wrinkles his nose but bends down and spreads his hands.

My heart thuds a few times more, and then the cloaked woman materializes before our eyes.

"I've never seen her before in my life," Lothar announces.

Stavros lets out a scoffing sound. "You can barely see her now with that hood up. Someone pull it back."

I killed her, so I figure that really should be my job. I crouch down and tug away the swath of fabric that shaded the woman's head.

Then all I can do is stare.

Light blond hair spills around the woman's pale face, turned slightly reddish with the sort of tint that I've seen from the juice dyes the outer-warders sometimes use. She's taller than me but nearly as thin, with a narrow face and a knob of a chin much like mine.

She's hardly my twin, but the similarities send a shiver down my spine.

Stavros's jaw works. I don't think the details are lost on him either.

It's Alek who puts the pieces together completely. I hadn't heard the scholar approaching, but his taut voice lifts from a few paces away where he's gazing down at the figure.

"After she murdered Petra, you were going to say it was Ivy attacking. That the riven sorcerer had turned on the princess who'd allied with her."

The moment the words leave his mouth, I can see the horrific beauty of the plan. Lothar could have eliminated Petra while displacing any hint of blame from himself and his scourge sorcerers.

Of course the audience would have been all too eager to believe that a monstrous riven could have behaved so abominably. I heard the way they talked when we were setting up last night.

My magic flails to be let out at him, but I keep it tightly contained and fold my arms over my chest. "What were you doing skulking around back here at the same time?"

Stavros scowls. "One of our people found a knife in his pocket. Maybe he was going to jump in and take down the assassin to reinforce the absurd idea that he's the hero in this scenario."

Lothar scoffs. "All I hear is a lot of blathering. You can't prove any part of this incredible story. Now let me return to my place so I can oversee the end of the trials."

As if we want him setting so much as his eyes on Petra after he's attempted this scheme. We still don't even know what *his* magic is capable of.

I stalk closer and prod his armless side with a swift finger. Maybe I can provoke some kind of reaction out of him. "This seems like a much better place for you. Or we can send you over to sit with your sacrificial accomplices, since you all gave up *so* much."

I let sarcasm taint my last words, but Lothar's face twitches as if he's restrained a flinch. I pause.

Why would that specific statement bother him more than the accusations we've tossed around?

Not the slightest hint of magic drifts off him even when I'm standing this close. That doesn't mean anything much—I can only pick up on threads of energy being cast out.

But it occurs to me that in all the time I was around Lothar, even when he had me under his control in close quarters, I've *never* felt even a trace of magic coming from him. Never seen him make use of the theoretically impressive gift he should have.

A suspicion trickles through my thoughts that I can't shake.

I ease even closer, studying Lothar's face. "Do you even *have* a gift, or did you give that arm away for nothing?"

Tinom sputters a disbelieving laugh, but Lothar tenses at the same time. Enough to take me from suspicious to sure.

I whirl toward Tinom, who worked more closely with the former magic advisor than anyone else still living. "In all the years you were colleagues, did you ever see him use his gift? Did he ever say exactly what it is?"

Tinom halts, and his forehead furrows. "It was something to do with potions…"

Stavros's eyebrows rise. "Potions don't need a gift for a person to make them right, only knowledge of the ingredients and processes. Were any of his potions things no one could have made without some kind of magical intervention?"

"This is absurd," Lothar snaps.

Tinom ignores him, his gaze gone distant in thought before it sharpens on the other man. "You know, I can't think of any specifically that fit that criteria. I always took it for granted—but I can't say I wasn't wrong."

My stomach twists. How awful must Lothar's intentions have been all the way back when he was a twelve-year-old boy for his chosen godlen to reject a sacrifice so huge?

How awful would he have felt? How much more would his sense of morality have soured after such an immense and permanent rejection?

"Prove it, then," I say in a terse voice that barely sounds like my own. "Tell us what your gift is and use it in front of us. There must be something you could direct it at."

Lothar lifts his head to look down his nose at us. "I shouldn't have to honor that ridiculous request with a response."

Tinom shakes his head, some of the color drained from his face. "All those years… You lied to the king about *everything* about who you are. That job never should have been yours in the first place."

"The job never should have been Hessild's," Lothar growls with a sudden flash of his eyes as he mentions the woman he had murdered. The woman who was once the chief magic advisor. "What was so wonderful about her power? What amazing things had *she* done? She and her whole family of snakes—the position should have been my father's back in his day, but the Melchioreks always liked the Korinyas best—they fawned over them, they were *nice*."

He bites off the last word with an acidic edge and then a clamping of his lips. But he's already said enough.

Tinom chokes out a laugh. "You let bitterness infect you, and it cost you the gift you could have gained. At least Hessild honestly had magic."

"I worked harder than you can possibly imagine for everything I've gained."

"Yes," I retort. "You've lied and manipulated children and murdered all kinds of people including the man you swore to serve. And you try to call me a monster."

He spins toward me, his face reddening. "Why should a no one like *you* have limitless power because of some fluke of fate? You never even had to sacrifice."

Anger flares in my chest alongside a lash of my magic. "You have no idea what I've lost. I never asked to be riven."

Now his hostility toward me makes even more sense. It wasn't just the standard hatred of the riven but bone-deep, venomous jealousy.

Tinom nudges me backward to step between us, his face hardened into a solemn mask. "None of this matters. No matter who wins the trials, you're going to be arrested. This psychotic charade is over."

Alek glances toward the front of the platform. "And it's going to be Petra who wins. The final cleric just gave her his approval. All those people you tried to sway to your sick cause are rejoicing."

The cheers and whoops of celebration filter past the jumble of equipment to reach our ears. I don't doubt that Alek is right, even if I couldn't see the declaration myself.

Petra has proven herself again and again—not just to be a strong, steady ruler, but to care about ensuring every person she rules over feels like a valued part of the kingdom.

Lothar will have made all the same observations I have. He was counting on Petra being dead and no longer an option, not on her actual failure.

I wouldn't be surprised if he *knows* she'd be a better ruler than anyone he could put forth. He simply doesn't care as long as the Melchioreks fall.

A strangled sound escapes him, and he barrels forward faster than I'd have expected a man of his size could move. With his single hand, he snatches the small crossbow one of the guards was carrying and whips it under his arm to brace it so he can fire.

Fire the loaded bolt at Petra where she's standing at the front of the stage, unaware.

Stavros hurtles after him even faster. A guttural "No" bursts from his lips, and he heaves his sword through Lothar's back.

Lothar staggers, the crossbow slipping from his grasp. "Fucking pompous prick," he spits out with a gurgle of blood.

Stavros bears his teeth. "It's nothing less than the vengeance my king deserved."

He moves to yank out the blade—and perhaps stab the man a few more times, which I certainly would not object to—but Lothar manages to hurl himself a couple of steps farther. He grasps the edge of one of the discarded puzzle boxes and shoves it aside while heaving himself forward.

Out into view of the audience with a sword jutting from his back.

# Forty

*Ivy*

Lothar collapses into a heap, blood spreading across the floorboards beneath him, but the audience got a clear look at his face. They know the leader of the Order of the Wild has been quite literally stabbed in the back.

And they weren't privy to any of the revelations or acts that led up to this moment.

Stavros races forward to retrieve his sword. He holds up his other arm, his prosthetic flashing in the mid-day sun. "Lothar Riosemek attempted to murder Princess Petra. I did what I had to do to defend her."

For a second, the muttering in the crowd fades, and I think that might be all the explanation they need.

But even with Lothar dead, his underlings aren't ready to give up.

No doubt they know what fate awaits them if their full wrongdoings are uncovered.

One of the Order members in a red tunic hollers toward the stage. "Lothar would never stoop so low. I hear nothing but lies. We all saw that woman who stumbled around on the stage and ran back there. Were you defending the riven sorcerer?"

I don't know whether he actually recognized me in the brief time I was grappling with the assassin or if he's riffing off the original plan and hoping the false version of me can still come into play. It doesn't really matter.

The audience erupts into an angry furor.

Accusing shouts meld together into a thunderous cacophony. Amid them I make out other voices amplified over the rest, probably from more scourge sorcerers, egging the crowd on.

"This was a set-up from the start. They duped us and killed the one man who was standing up for Silana!"

"The riven sorcerer was helping the false princess all along!"

"We can't let them get away with this! Silana deserves better."

Petra advances with her hands held up in a gesture for calm. "My people, let's talk about this. I saw Lothar murder my parents with my own eyes. He would have killed me then if he could have. My guards were only protecting me."

Her clear voice carries over the crowd, but I don't think it sinks in. The mass of bodies is already shoving toward the defensive lines of guards, gang members, and daimon that now looks far too thin.

Spectators are pushing each other as well as the figures standing between them and the platform. A stocky man throws a punch at one of the gang members, whose colleague wrenches the guy around with an arm pinned behind his back. But there are more angry citizens pressing forward all the while.

And they're not just coming at Petra physically. A bolt of magic sizzles through the air and chars the boards inches from where Petra is standing. She retreats reluctantly and then dives to the side as another conjured attack shrieks toward her.

My hands fly up of their own accord. This is why I'm here—I'm on my own now that Sulla's been struck down.

With a hum of extra power thrumming into me from the sacrificial accomplices, I throw up a solid barrier of air between Petra and the rioting crowd.

A spurt of flame streaks toward her and shatters against my invisible shield. Someone yelps, and another chorus of Order voices mingle with the chaos.

"That must be riven magic right now!"

"The monster is there stopping justice from being done."

"Why would a true queen work with a woman who's been shunned by the gods themselves?"

I grit my teeth, willing the words to glance off me without stinging. I've heard similar sentiments so many times, but they still prick a little.

If only they knew how far from shunned I am… Where the fuck is Kosmel right now?

We were so close to ending the Order of the Wild and their scourge sorcery for good, and now they've turned the tide against us in one foul swoop.

I don't dare step closer where the crowd might actually see me. The bodies near the base of the platform are churning as the most aggressive members of the audience grapple with our guards.

Voleska's ponytail flashes in the sunlight as she and her people squeeze in to form another barrier between the attackers and our queen. I catch a glimpse of one daimon toppling a woman with a burst of scorching supernatural energy and a guard bringing the butt of his sword down on a man's head.

Our allies are going to start slaughtering them—the people Petra's been saying she wants to raise up with her. And then even more of the crowd will rage.

How in the realms do we come back from this?

Casimir and Stavros call out to the crowd in increasingly desperate voices. The shouts for justice, for riven blood, are only getting louder and more furious, drowning out most of my men's words.

There are at least a dozen times as many spectators as Petra has confirmed supporters. What are we supposed to do?

My magic flings itself against my ribs, providing its own, typical answer.

Knock them all to their knees. Steal their breaths to stop the yelling; break their arms to end the fighting.

These people want to execute me. Why shouldn't I return the favor?

But I don't want to. That's not who I fucking *am*.

I can't see what choice I have that's a good one, though. I don't have Sulla here to ask, if she'd even have an answer.

This is why she never wanted to come down from her mountain. Right now, I'm not sure I can blame her for her reluctance.

"Stop them but don't hurt them!" Petra calls out to the ring of figures around the platform, but there's only so much her protectors can do. More lightning crackles. Steel clangs against steel.

Another body and another falls—and not all of them from the audience.

The crowd surges farther forward. A crash from behind has me spinning toward the back of the stage.

The rioters have swarmed right around the platform to capture us in a sea of raging bodies. Now they're pulling apart the carts and wagons, ripping canvas and yanking off boards—in search of me?

Yes.

"Find the riven sorcerer!" someone hollers. "Destroy the monster!"

The blasted scourge sorcerers are still spewing out their toxic ideals. "We have to prove to the All-Giver that we embrace everything we're meant to be—and that we'll clean this country of everything we're not. Tear down the traitors who tried to trick us and lead us astray."

With a renewed roar, the audience heaves toward the platform. Grunts and groans warble through the air alongside the thump of collapsing bodies.

I can't calm them myself. To soften their anger, I'd have to stir up more to balance it out.

Soothing half of the people around us won't do any good if the other half rage even more furiously.

But I have to do *something*.

I reach for the boost in power the sacrificial accomplices have offered, but I can't sense them emanating their gifts anymore. My stomach flips over.

Have they been caught up in the riot too?

Clenching my jaw, I stretch out my arms and release a wave of magic that's all my own. It whips around the platform in a much larger shield than the one I created for Petra. More of the carts collapse, disintegrating as I shatter their wood in exchange for solidifying the air.

I haven't unleashed this much power in weeks. My thoughts seem to wobble in my head, and a spark of panic sears into my gut.

All these people want to carve me up and rip me to shreds. Even Tinom hates me, even Baron Cyris.

I can't trust *any* of them.

*No.* I squeeze my eyes shut for a second, pushing back against the rush of paranoia as forcefully as I can manage.

*Hold strong, Ivy,* Julita would have told me. *Don't let them break you now.*

It's not just our enemies threatening to tear me apart in this moment, though. The worst threat may be the power surging inside me.

A cry breaks through the tumult. It sounds like Rheave. Instinctively, I push the barrier farther, trying to protect all our allies from the onslaught.

They don't deserve my effort. What have all those guards and gangsters ever done for me other than glare at me with suspicion? Let them fall.

Shut up, shut up, shut up.

A clang sounds right behind me. I flinch, but when I wrench my head around, there's no one there.

Shudders pass through my body from limbs banging against my shield of solidified air. It's already wavering.

I'm going to need to feed the barrier even more power. And on and on—for how long?

How much will it take before they stop?

"The gods will want justice," someone is bellowing. "Let's set things right!"

It isn't even true. The gods want…

The gods wanted *me*.

Kosmel wanted me to stay alive so I could stand up to the scourge sorcerers. All the godlen wanted the riven souls they poured their magic through to end the horrors centuries ago.

They didn't curse us—they called on us as vessels for divine power.

Breaking us was an accident, not a condemnation.

If these people could just see… what really matters to me… what really matters to Petra…

What the gods have in their hearts, as much as they have those…

In the midst of my scrambled thoughts, a voice from my past rises up, but it's not Julita I'm imagining this time. It's my little sister, sprawled next to me as we stare up at the stars.

*They're so beautiful, the way they sparkle. Do you think someday we could fly all the way there to see them up close?*

I remember how I giggled before I answered, with a seven year old's unshakeable confidence. *Maybe they'll soar down to meet us. But we'll have to be careful we don't get burned.*

A sudden jolt of inspiration pierces through my muddled mind—or maybe it's more insanity. But it's something I can do.

Something only I can do.

The gods came down among us and used the riven to channel their magic, to stop what we humans couldn't on our own. But destroying the villains left even more destruction in its wake. It left the wildness and chaos the Order wants to breed.

If the godlen regret their stumble, why can't they balance the scales? I'm right here.

Yes, my powers were a mistake. They're also the only thing stopping this riot from turning into an outright slaughter.

I'm broken, but I could turn the tide toward peace if I just let myself break a little more.

Maybe it's time for *me* to step into the light and meet my fate. For the stars to fall down to shine through me.

Even if I get burned like Linzi's ribbon in Lothar's hand.

My innards turn to ice at the thought of what opening my soul up even farther might do to my tenuous grip on my sanity. But it isn't going to take much more of this before I've torn myself to shreds anyway.

I knew I might end up making my final sacrifice today. I'd better make it a good one.

Closing my eyes again, I pitch my inner voice as loud as I can, up toward the sky where I imagine the godlen might be watching.

*Kosmel! You once told me you'd be there for me if I knew what I wanted. I'll only ask for one more thing. Send your power through me again, you and whatever other godlen care whether the realm falls into chaos. Use your divine will to show these people what really matters to the gods—and that it's not what the murdering scourge sorcerers say.*

No voice answers, but a trickle of uncertainty winds through my thoughts that I don't think is my own. My conviction is holding perfectly steady.

I clench my jaw alongside my answer. *I know what it might mean for me. I don't care as long as we can calm the madness out there. Please. You set me on this journey. I need you now, just once more. Believe me. Believe in me.*

It's been a long time since I heard the overwhelming voice that floods all my senses a moment later. *I hear you, my wayward rogue. This isn't the fate I wanted for you. But maybe I can offer you something better.*

Before I can ask what that's supposed to mean, a torrent of power blares through the center of my body.

It's not like when I drew magic from the sacrificial accomplices. The boost they offered was a tiny creek compared to this roaring river.

And it shatters straight through me rather than welling up inside.

The divine magic explodes out of me, but not in a hail of fire like the stories of the Great Retribution. Even with my eyes closed, I see the brilliant glow that streams out across and above the platform, rising higher than the towers and the obstacle course, blazing brighter than the unclouded sky.

I hear it. I taste it. I feel it vibrating through my bones.

Symbols form across the expanding glow—the sigils of each of the godlen, flaring into being one after the other until I count all nine. Distantly, I'm aware of the clamor of the crowd dwindling, the gasps of shock and awe.

We need more than this. More.

*Show them!*

You *are so much more than this,* Kosmel replies, in a tone that makes me want to sob, and then the glow shifts.

The divine light spreads even farther, rises higher, forming an image of a castle. Figures flit in and out of the doorways and along the road outside it.

They come together and embrace. They share pieces torn off a loaf of bread and gulps from a bottle of wine. They laugh and dance, nobles in fancy trimmings holding hands with urchins in scruffy clothes.

Peace. Happiness. Compassion. Cooperation.

A wave of emotion sweeps over me and out across the crowd. A collective sigh ripples from all around the platform.

Another figure appears, with a gleaming hole lit right in the middle of her. As if there's a crack in her soul.

As if it's been riven through.

The other people don't recoil. They gather around and embrace her too.

The light shines out of her and whirls away the palace into a farmland scene. Children clamber up trees to pick apples while adults offer food and water to the animals. Everything is bright and joyful.

The farmyard glimmers into a ballroom where lovers entangle themselves in intimate clasps. Then a squad of soldiers marching together, bumping fists and cheering each other on. A library where students huddle together to murmur insights from the books they're reading.

This is what life could be. This is what we should aim for.

Love and friendship and learning. Kindness and consideration.

The gods have spoken.

The energy leaves me all at once. My legs give; my knees smack the floor. Incoherent words sputter from my mouth.

And then I'm not there at all.

I'm floating in a mass of glowing light that shows no sign of the outside world. But it's warm, so warm, in the coziest possible way, like snuggling in bed under your favorite blanket.

Nine streaks of starker light materialize in a circle around me. Somehow I know where they all are even though some must be behind me.

Even though they're nothing more than a blurry glow, I also know the one directly in front of me is Kosmel.

"Hello, wayward rogue," he says in a voice that's somehow more *here* and also more *everywhere* both at the same time. Every particle of me, however much of me is present, quivers with it. "You served me well, didn't you?"

"I did my best for the kingdom and the people in it who needed help the most," I find myself saying.

What's going on here? Is this some side effect of all the magic I channeled?

Maybe this is the final stage of my riven madness, and he's not speaking to me at all. Maybe none of this is real.

As if he can hear my thoughts, the trickster godlen chuckles. "Oh, it's real in the most fundamental possible way. And I wanted to offer you an opportunity within this reality, as a reward for everything you've done."

I give his glowing form a puzzled look. "A reward?"

"Our mistakes left you with more than a lifetime's worth of guilt and pain. You've protected the realms despite that. I think you deserve just as much peace as the rest of those you fought so hard to save. What you're feeling right now, that can be yours always. You can linger here in the divine for as long as you wish until you're ready to release your soul."

I grapple with those words for a moment. "You're saying I'll be dead."

"You'll die eventually either way. I can't guarantee what awaits you down below, but it will definitely be more difficult and fraught than anything you'll experience among us."

My lips part, but no sound comes out.

He said I'd find only peace here. That I'd get to escape all the pain of my past existence. But a tiny ache has already bloomed in my heart.

What about Stavros and Casimir, Alek and Rheave? Am I really going to walk away from them without even a good-bye?

What about seeing Petra finally claim her throne? What about the promise I made to Julita to ensure her old county was in good hands?

What about all that life I've only just started really living rather than lurking on the fringes like a shadow?

Kosmel's voice gentles. "All those desires would quickly melt away in this place. You might not satisfy any of them if you return. Even we don't know what effect your last act will have on your mind."

I might be absolutely crazed if he returns me to my body, he means. I might have a few more minutes of agonized existence and then fade away into the nothingness of death.

Do I really want to trade this comforting warmth for that possibility?

Even as I ask the question, my certainty about my answer grows.

There are so many other possibilities ahead of me now. There's so much else I want to accomplish.

There will be pain and guilt and sadness along the way. It might be all I have left.

But it might not.

Even a slim chance at having more of the loving joy I found is worth all the rest.

I haven't spoken, but I get the impression of Kosmel nodding. "I see your resolve. I won't argue with you, and I hope your decision brings you more happiness than anguish."

I suck in one more breath of the glowing air, contentment rushing through my veins, and then I'm plummeting.

I slam back into my body with a heaved breath and more gibberish tumbling from my mouth.

An arm is wrapped around me, a hand cupping my cheek. A vial tips against my lips with a spill of cool, bitter liquid.

"We've got you," Casimir says tenderly, with a hint of a rasp. "And this is where we'll stay—right here, with you."

# Forty-One

*Several months later*

*Ivy*

A crowd of several dozen has gathered in the graveyard beyond the Laonek estate. As I stand next to Casimir, ready to give my eulogy, I can't help eyeing the mourners warily.

"When we talked to Hanie during the rebellion, she said the Order of the Wild people had murdered most of the family's staff," I murmur to the courtesan.

He shrugs, beaming at the latest arrivals. "From what I've gathered, these are mostly people who knew Julita from her jaunts into town. And of course there's the few school friends who made the trek all the way from Florian." He tips his head toward a cluster of young noblewomen who are standing off to the side, apart from the more modest provincial folk.

I consider those four with even more skepticism. I only vaguely recognize them from my time at Sovereign College—certainly none of them took note that I'd said I was Julita's friend and sought me out to ask what had happened to her. "They must be hoping that showing up will make them look good in the eyes of the queen now that Julita's been named a national hero."

Stavros comes up behind me with a teasing click of his tongue. "And our other national hero still has a few prejudices to work through."

I aim a light jab backward of my elbow at him. "Well-earned prejudices, thank you very much."

The abruptness of the small movement sends a brief jolt through my nerves. I go still, inhaling more deeply and focusing on my imagined vine holding my body together in the way that's become automatic now.

Casimir notices the shift in my attitude in an instant. He touches my arm. "Are you all right? If this is a little too much for you—you were closer to Julita than anyone in the end."

I shake my head carefully. No strange sounds blare in my ears; no frantic thoughts flit through my mind. "That's why I need to speak for her at least a little. I'm fine."

Fine, of course, is relative. I'm leagues more fine than I was in the first days after I collapsed in a fit of babbling and shudders after the godlen poured their magic through me.

My men sedated me before I could gather enough intent to do any significant harm, and I spent most of the next two months in a partly drugged daze at the Temple of Tranquil Skies, with Delfis and his devouts drawing on all their healing talents to soothe my nerves and restore my broken mind.

Some of the scourge sorcerers' former sacrificial accomplices assisted as well. Many of those we've rescued are now stationed at temples across the country to amplify the magical work the clerics are overseeing. A few are on the royal staff.

As Poltus, one of those who's stayed with the queen, told me the day of the trials, it's the one way they're most capable of contributing. For all their sacrifices, I can tell they're happier with their new sense of purpose.

I'm not sure Delfis's people could have mended my nerves without the boost those resilient souls provided.

Gradually I've recovered my wits and my self-control. The taint of madness hasn't totally left me, but I'm sharp enough now to recognize the minor flickers of hallucinations and delusional ideas when they arise.

My body has odd reactions at times as well, like the jolt I just experienced. Since I'm no longer facing off against psychotic sorcerers or surviving through stealth, I can tolerate that side effect for as long as it lasts.

My soul is still cracked, presumably even more than it was before. My magic flows and churns through my torso, always niggling at me for more freedom. But I've taken up Sulla's regimen of one small magical act per day, and that keeps it happy enough not to savage me.

And if I should ever need to defend queen and kingdom again, gods save me, I have all the power I need at my fingertips.

The cleric of the All-Giver from the main temple in Pima intones the standard blessing of the dead and then says a few words about Julita's contributions to freeing the county of Nikodi from the Order of the Wild. No one except my closest companions knows the full story of how Julita took her stand, but it's common knowledge now that she was the first to identify the scourge sorcery threat and that she lost her life taking down her brother, one of the leaders of their army.

When the cleric finishes, he motions for me to take his place in front of her marble monument. The figure it depicts was carved by a sculptor from Florian with input from Casimir, Stavros, and Alek's memories of the living woman, but I used a few weeks of magical acts to carve a simple vine design along the base.

I give the etching a private smile, imagining how Julita would have responded to it, before I turn to face the crowd of mourners. My throat feels suddenly dry.

She can't hear me right now the way she followed every moment of my life for the few months we shared my body. Her consciousness will have drifted away into the embrace of her godlen.

I want to do her justice all the same.

I swallow hard and gather myself. "Julita and I met under strange circumstances, two people who couldn't be more different in position or temperament. But despite all those differences, she became the best friend I'd ever had. She could bolster my spirits when I had doubts and find something to laugh about in the darkest situations. Her fierce devotion to both Nikodi and Silana were awe-inspiring. Keeping all of us safe from the horrors she'd experienced firsthand mattered more to her than her own life."

A murmur of appreciation flows through the crowd.

My voice catches for a second before I can go on. "The last thing Julita ever asked from me was for me to see that Nikodi came under good rulership once she was gone as the last of her family line. Even when she knew she didn't have much time left in this world, she was thinking of the people she'd dreamed about taking care of someday. And her final act against the scourge sorcerers not only stopped the invasion of Regica but saved my life."

With a shaky breath, I bow my head. "I will forever remember Julita and the many ways she touched my life and earned my admiration. I hope her soul moved swiftly into the embrace of her godlen, and that generations to come see this monument as a symbol of leadership and courage."

I step back to a respectful smattering of applause. Rheave loops his arm around my back and tips his head close to mine. "That sounded very good to me."

I lean into his embrace. "I think you might be a little biased, but thank you."

One of the kitchen staff who survived the Order's massacre goes up to say a little about Julita's early life living on the estate, and Stavros comments on her commitment as a student and dedication to her classmates. Then we all stand in silence while the cleric offers the final blessing.

When the mourners move away from the grave at the end of the burial ceremony, I spot Voleska standing at the outskirts of the cemetery. As I head over to her, she offers a sympathetic smile that pulls at the scar on her cheek.

"I thought I should pay my respects to the woman who was meant to be in my position," she says. "They're big shoes to fill. I wish I'd had the chance to actually meet her rather than simply knowing of her family."

She doesn't realize that in a way she did meet Julita, while I was harboring the other woman's soul. I'd bet my ghostly friend would have approved of my choice of countess. Throughout the uprising, Voleska proved herself just as devoted to her country and this county as Julita was, with leadership skills to spare.

I give her arm a quick squeeze. "From what I hear, you and Emor are already doing a fantastic job." Her former co-leader has joined her as her chief of staff, without any resentment about the main title going to her.

"She can wear the fancy clothes and do the public appearances," he said with a laugh when he first heard about the appointment. "I'm happiest behind the scenes anyway."

Proving my point, Voleska leads the whole gathering back to the estate to enjoy refreshments and music in Julita's honor—exactly the way I'd expect my noblewoman passenger would have wanted it.

As the wine flows, more stories emerge about Julita's escapades around town and at the college, with all her usual spirited charm. By the time we call it a night, I feel as if I know her even better than while she was sharing my head.

*There*, I can almost hear her say. *Now everything's as it should be.*

It's a long trek back to the capital, but at least it's more comfortable now that we're traveling as respected members of Queen Petra's inner circle rather than fugitives. Our two carriages with their softly cushioned benches rattle along the roads with an escort of half a dozen guards around us.

Some people still have hostile feelings toward the riven, unsurprising when the hatred was so entrenched. Technically I could topple any foe faster than those guards if I needed to, but Petra has made it clear that she never wants to put me in a situation where I feel I have to defend myself or the people I care about with magic, not again.

As we approach Florian, Rheave leans out the window for a gulp of fresh autumn air and to grin at the guard riding next to us, who's one of his fellow captured daimon. "It's an interesting thing, being perched up on an animal, isn't it?"

The guard chuckles in return. "Not like anything I knew before. I'm glad I listened to you and stayed to find out more about this side of the world."

Only about half of the daimon whose animated clay bodies survived the various battles decided to hold on to those bodies rather than returning to their former existence as purely spiritual creatures. As far as we can tell so far, the magically animated bodies are aging the same way regular ones do, so they can have close to normal lives for as long as any regular human being.

Quite a few of the daimon who remained opted to serve the new queen. Rheave has become a sort of captain of the guard for that specific segment.

He's still delighting in every aspect of his new physical existence, from the breeze to the sway of the carriage to the butterfly that swoops through the window and lands on his sleeve. Rheave laughs and holds it up to show me before it flits off across the fields again.

At the moment, my other companion in this carriage is Alek. The scholar has managed to open a map, a textbook, and a pad of notes on his lap all at once while also consulting a language reference he's spread out on the bench beside him.

The tension on his face echoes the worry coiled in my gut. I grimace around the question. "Do you think there's any chance the Darium delegation has *good* intentions?"

Alek snorts in a not particularly Alek-like way, which only highlights how absurd the idea is. "If there is, it's so small you couldn't make it out with a magnifying glass. I'm sure this trip is mainly about the emperor's people feeling out Petra—with an eye to identifying weaknesses they could exploit to drag Silana back under his control."

The idea of *that* ever happening makes me guffaw. "I expect they'll be sorely disappointed then. I wish we could tell them to stuff their delegation up Emperor Tarquin's ass."

"So do I," Alek says dryly. "But Petra can't simply throw the offer of negotiating a peace accord in their faces when so many people would benefit from an end to the constant conflict with Dariu. I suppose it'll give her a chance to feel out the emperor's representatives too."

Rheave hums. "Casimir will be able to sense what they're really after quickly enough."

Technically the courtesan has been appointed Petra's arts and entertainments advisor, but she often ensures he's on hand for any particularly uncertain meetings so he can make use of his gift on her behalf.

I clasp my hands together on my lap. "They'll be wondering about her entire cabinet of advisors. Do you think word has spread about my magic?"

Alek hesitates, his gaze softening with compassion. "I think it's unlikely that not a single spy has brought back word of the divine spectacle at the end of the trials. But they'll also be reporting that Silana has ended capital punishment for the riven and started a new habilitation and training program for any who are identified. And Petra will be introducing you as one of her magic advisors, after all—it'll be obvious she stands with you."

So they might think nasty things in their heads, but they'll probably refrain from saying them out loud. I guess that's a small comfort.

I'll have all of my men by my side as well. Petra appointed Stavros her lead military advisor and put Alek in charge of overseeing royal scholarship while he finishes his own studies. Rheave will tag along in the guise of a regular guard for additional protection.

I sigh and slump back in my seat. "Well, we've got until tomorrow before we *really* have to worry about it."

A small, sly smile touches Alek's lips. "The only part I'm looking forward to is seeing the emperor's representatives come face to face with our new Signy. They don't know what they're up against."

I scoff, but a warm glow spreads through my chest at the same time.

Maybe, just maybe, I've truly earned that comparison now.

Immediately outside the city, the recently constructed stone mansion where Sulla is taking in riven pupils comes into view near the bank of the river. Seeing it gives me another whiff of relief despite my worries about tomorrow.

My mentor had nearly as long a recovery time as I did after the violence at the kingship trials, though her injuries were mostly physical. But she's nearly as hale as she was before, simply needing a cane to reduce the strain on her weakened legs if she's on her feet for long stretches.

I've stopped by at least once a week to help however I can with the training. So far she only has two students—a girl of eight whose magic only just showed itself, and a boy of fifteen who traveled all the way from Icar after hearing of Silana's new policies.

I'm not sure how many other riven who've escaped execution there are in the world, other than us. But if any are hiding in the shadows like I once did, I hope they find the faith to give a real life a chance.

Within the main city walls, all signs of the Order's presence have been eliminated. Banners with the Melchiorek family crest stream from flag poles, and we travel through a square where a new statue of Queen Petra has just been erected—perched on a throne at the top of a tower alongside the three helpers she managed to pull up with her, as she did during her final trial for Creaden.

I'm glad most people remember that moment of cooperation and camaraderie more than the chaos that followed.

The royal army Petra has reconstructed has spent a significant part of the past several months rounding up the remaining scourge sorcerers and vocal Order members. The former don't pose much of a threat without their accomplices to draw power from.

Quite a few of even the true believers of their cause swore themselves over to Petra's service after witnessing the message of amity and peace the godlen projected through me. The Order's pockets of influence have quickly dissolved.

Those whose destructive behavior couldn't be easily pardoned have been assigned to various types of enforced labor to the true betterment of the country. I believe a certain chief of staff who once worked for Baron Cyris has been sent to the mining camps near the Icarian border—far from my beloved courtesan, who she'll never get another chance to blackmail.

I can gaze out the window without fear of setting eyes on two other incredibly unwelcome faces. After I returned from my convalescence, Petra offered to extend a similar punishment to my parents for contributing to Lothar's campaign against me. She told me I could even confront them myself along with the arresting officers.

But presented with the opportunity, I found that more than anything I wanted to never again have to see the people who scarred me in so many ways.

So our queen came up with a suitable reprisal of her own. My mother and father have been ordered to travel from town to town with an escort of royal guards, sharing their shame for failing their riven daughter and counselling all of Silana to avoid their mistakes—to help rather than harm any children who show signs of the wildest of magic.

Thinking of it brings a bittersweet smile to my lips. May their story save at least one child from the same misery they inflicted on me.

At the edge of the middle wards, we pass several workers pulling apart the remains of the old city walls that so starkly divided the elite from the rest of the city. Petra has been working on expanding the throughways and hiring outer-ward citizens for various building and clean-up projects around the city's fringes, and the atmosphere across the city has already become brighter.

When we disembark from our carriages in front of the restored Capital Palace, the queen herself comes out onto the front steps to meet us.

"It's good to have you back," she says in her brisk but warm way. "Now let's finalize our plans for handling the Darium delegation."

Simply standing in the audience room with the members of the delegation feels like a subtle dance no one's taught me all the moves of.

How many guards can Petra employ, to match those our long-time enemies have brought for their own protection but not come across as overly threatening? How close should we position ourselves; how loudly should we talk?

Which subjects will we address, and which will we tiptoe around as if the empire hasn't been trying to crush Silana back into submission for the past eighty or so years?

Thankfully, I've got a lot of practice at adapting on the spot.

Petra is doing most of the talking anyway, with Tinom—who's serving as her main overall advisor while she's settling into her new royal role—occasionally interjecting. The old magic advisor's attitude toward me has taken quite a shift since he watched the godlen he worships channel their divine power through me. To my shock, I returned from the Temple of Tranquil Skies to find him outright respectful. He apologized so fervently I couldn't see the use in staying angry.

Both he and our queen are taking a polite but cautious approach with the head of the delegation, a sturdy-looking man with a soldier's bearing but the ornate clothes of a nobleman, fitted and heavily trimmed in the Darium fashion. Since we're meeting in Silana, Admiral Varus has conceded to speaking in the local tongue. But while he's said a lot of fancy words about how our countries might eventually cooperate, he hasn't produced anything remotely concrete.

I think he's paying more attention to Petra's movements and her interactions with the rest of us than to what she's saying. So far he hasn't shown any signs of casting magic toward her, though.

Possibly word has also gotten out that Petra's loyal riven sorcerer has a knack for sensing supernatural power. I can protect her simply by existing.

It does make for a welcome change.

Since Petra and Tinom are already focusing on him, I let my gaze wander over the rest of the delegation. As well as his four guards, Admiral Varus brought along a young man he calls his assistant, a woman who's a devout of Creaden, and one of the princes of Cotea.

The delegation leader only gave a brief explanation for the latter's presence, but from what I understand, Prince Bastien has some role in Emperor Tarquin's court. He came with the delegation to speak to how any agreements made will be reflected in the actions of our nearest neighbor among the empire's conquered countries.

The slim, almost gaunt fellow looks a year or two younger than me. He stands straight but lets his shaggy auburn hair fall forward to shadow his eyes, his mouth set in a tight line.

He's trying to hide it, but I don't think he wants to be here at all.

He's definitely the most intriguing member of the party. And infinitely more so after Petra cuts off the aimless blathering to suggest we walk along the palace's upper parapet for some fresh air.

It's two floors up from the audience room. At the base of the first staircase, a couple of the Darium guards prod Prince Bastien.

"Let's see you really march for once, huh?" one says, and the other laughs.

The prince's lips flatten even more, but he strides up the stairs at the same pace as the apparent jokesters. By halfway up the second flight, his legs have started to wobble and his breath comes out of him in a wheeze.

The first of the guards shakes his head. "Shouldn't have given up that lung if you couldn't keep up without it."

He uses a teasing tone, but I pick up on an edge of a jeer. How harshly would he speak if he didn't have an audience?

Then what he said sinks in. I stare at Prince Bastien for a second before jerking my gaze away, not wanting my interest to be obvious.

He sacrificed an entire lung to his godlen? What kind of gift would you get for that?

Or, like Lothar, did he reach for too much out of the wrong reasons and get nothing at all?

I can't tell from the guards' heckling. The prince hasn't shown any signs of magic since he arrived, but then, Admiral Varus could have cautioned him against it. At least while I'm around.

As we amble along the front parapet overlooking the sprawl of the city, the rooftops gleam under the bright afternoon sun. I contrive to place myself next to Prince Bastien. I have to constrain my pace, because his own strides are still a little unsteady from the climb.

Petra, Varus, and the others pull ahead of us, Stavros shooting a quick glance back at me with a subtle tip of his head in approval. When they stop to resume their conversation near the corner of the walkway, I come to a halt several paces away.

I set my hands on the ridges of stone as if I simply want to sightsee, blocking the prince from strolling straight onward too.

He pauses beside me rather than walking around. I wouldn't be surprised if he appreciates the break.

"It's a long way from Cotea's capital to Dariu's," I remark. "Do you see your family often?"

Bastien's voice comes out terse. "No."

I turn to lean against the wall sideways and decide to take a gamble. "Do you really think your emperor's soldiers are going to set down their arms and walk away?"

I manage to startle him with my bluntness. He blinks at me, a flash of emotion crossing his face and vanishing before I can decipher it. Then he turns to glower at the rest of Florian.

His answer sounds rehearsed. "That's not for me to say. I'm sure if negotiations proceed that way, my family will respect the empire's treaties."

"I wouldn't imply otherwise. It's only that Dariu has been awfully stubborn, emperor after emperor, for rather a lot of decades."

I think my wry tone earns me a twitch of his lips, though it's so brief I might have imagined it. For a moment, his eyes darken. "Everything changes, and nothing lasts forever. It just takes the right moment."

He could be talking about a moment of peace-making and negotiation, but his expression suggests otherwise. And right then, I catch the tiniest quiver of magic, as if his gift tried to flex itself and he yanked it back.

Oh, he has magic all right. And surely it's a lot with a sacrifice like that.

What kind of immense gift would the Darium emperor allow right under his own roof?

Before I can figure out how to wheedle that information out of Bastien, Varus clears his throat and makes a beckoning gesture. "Come on, young prince. You're meant to be part of this discussion as well."

Schooling his face into perfect blankness, the prince stalks over to join his colleagues.

Late that night, I only manage to make it until just after the doors have closed behind the delegates before my mouth gapes in a jaw-creaking yawn. I swipe my hand across my mouth and glance over at Petra. "Did you get anywhere at all with that puffed up lout?"

The queen lets out a low chuckle. "He talked in a lot of circles, certainly. I told him I'd like to see a formal proposal in writing, and he promised to speak to Emperor Tarquin to decide on their required terms, but I suspect we won't be seeing that."

Stavros drains the last of his wine from the cup he's carried with him to the front hall. "He got what he wanted, which was to examine the new ruler of Silana."

Tinom lets out a huff. "And now the emperor will know she's no one to be trifled with and that she's got the full strength of her people supporting her."

Casimir offers a crooked smile. "It'd have made him very happy if I'd informed him of the few minor points of emotional pressure I'm aware would affect you. He was definitely searching for weaknesses."

"Darium will keep trying us regardless," Stavros says, and then adds in a more optimistic tone, "but perhaps they'll spend a little less time on it now that we've got riven magic on our side along with everything else."

He aims his familiar cocky grin at me, and my heart skips a beat even after all this time.

"The Cotean prince," I begin, feeling it's important to mention. "I think he could be a weakness to the empire. If they ever let him get involved with anything important."

Petra tilts her head to the side. "I'm not sure how that could come into play in protecting our borders, but it's best to consider every angle."

I stifle another yawn, and Rheave comes over to slip his hand around my elbow. "I think our favorite riven sorcerer needs her sleep now."

I mutter some sort of argument, but Petra laughs and waves us off. "I should fill in my siblings on today's minor results."

All four of my men draw in around me as we head through the halls to the quarters we've been assigned at the back of the palace.

As advisors of various sorts, we're considered members of the court. Even Alek has his own private quarters, though he still spends many of his nights in his dorm at the college for ease of access to the library.

None of us can complain about the accommodations, but my room is my favorite. When I step past the door, the large window at the far side shows a view over the sprawling back grounds. This season's crops poke from the soil in even rows where a section of the hunting woods has been cleared to make way for a garden Filip has been overseeing. Moonlight streams down over the treetops beyond.

The thick rug embraces my feet as I pull off my shoes. The built-in shelves that fill nearly all of one wall contain even books to keep me occupied in my less busy moments for many years to come.

And Petra, without comment, supplied me with an absolutely massive bed.

It's very fine for sprawling out on my own, but the best nights are those when I share it. Now, through unspoken agreement, all four of my men follow me into the room.

I strip down to my underclothes and allow myself to crash into the middle of the mattress. Casimir laughs and tugs the covers out from under me. "Looks like we need to tuck our Kindness in."

I make a disgruntled sound that peters into a happy sigh as the men clamber onto the immense bed around me. I'm too exhausted from the intense, hours-long parlay with the Darium delegation to be up for any of the other thrilling activities we've frequently enjoyed here, but it's a special kind of delight just falling asleep with my lovers around me—all of us safe and sound.

Alek has sprawled out near my head. As I start to doze, he caresses his fingers over my hair.

"Ivy," he says, sounding rather dreamy himself but maintaining his air of academic curiosity, "do you ever wish you'd taken Kosmel up on his offer? Floated around in total contentment for years on end?"

Once I was recovered enough from the trials to pull coherent sentences together, I told all of them about the moments after I opened myself to the gods' magic and what Kosmel said to me. We've never discussed it in much detail, though.

I guess I thought the facts went without saying. I certainly don't need to think for even a second before I answer, with total honesty.

"No. I couldn't possibly have been as content as I am in this life I've built with you."

Rheave lets out a rough sound of agreement and kisses my shoulder. Stavros loops his arm around my waist.

The five of us drift off together, ready to face whatever else the world throws at us as one.

# About the Author

Eva Chase lives in Canada with her family. She loves stories both swoony and supernatural, and strong women and the men who appreciate them.

Along with the Rites of Possession series, she is the author of the Shadowblood Souls series, the Heart of a Monster series, the Gang of Ghouls series, the Bound to the Fae series, the Flirting with Monsters series, the Cursed Studies trilogy, the Royals of Villain Academy series, the Moriarty's Men series, the Looking Glass Curse trilogy, the Their Dark Valkyrie series, the Witch's Consorts series, the Dragon Shifter's Mates series, the Demons of Fame series, and the Legends Reborn trilogy.

*Connect with Eva online:*
www.evachase.com
eva@evachase.com